MORE PRAISE FOR
BELVA PLAIN

Her special power is to create worlds in which we live . . . characters who reach out to embrace us . . . sagas in which we discover a heritage that magically becomes our own.

EVERGREEN

"Anna will find a place in your heart and stay there long after the last paragraph is read."

Pittsburgh Press

"A grand, sweeping panorama of immigrants and America . . . richly written, finely detailed . . . vivid and memorable."

New York Daily News

RANDOM WINDS

"Wonderful. A convincing, sweeping novel. A real page-turner."

Philadelphia Inquirer

"Triumphant!"

Los Angeles Herald Examiner

EDEN BURNING

"Sweeps the reader through a complicated web of passion, politics, and history. . . . Love itself dies and is rekindled."

Booklist

"Captures and holds the reader's interest."

Cleveland Press

BELVA PLAIN

THREE COMPLETE NOVELS

BELVA PLAIN

THREE COMPLETE NOVELS

EVERGREEN

RANDOM WINDS

EDEN BURNING

WINGS BOOKS

New York • Avenel, New Jersey

This 1994 edition is published by Wings Books,
distributed by Outlet Book Company, Inc., a Random House Company,
40 Engelhard Avenue, Avenel, New Jersey 07001,
by arrangement with Delacorte Press, an imprint of Dell Publishing, a division of
Bantam Doubleday Dell Publishing Group, Inc.

Random House
New York · Toronto · London · Sydney · Auckland

Printed and bound in the United States of America

Library of Congress Cataloging-in-Publication Data

Plain, Belva.
[Novels.   Selections]
Three complete novels / Belva Plain.
p.   cm.
Contents: Evergreen — Random winds — Eden burning.
ISBN 0-517-10066-5
1. Immigrants—United States—Fiction.   2. Family—United States—Fiction.
3. Domestic fiction, American.   I. Title.   II. Title: 3 complete novels.
PS3566.L254A6   1994
813'.54—dc20   93-32354
                                                    CIP

8   7   6   5   4   3   2   1

CONTENTS

EVERGREEN

To my husband,
companion of a lifetime

One generation passeth away, and another generation cometh: but the earth abideth forever.

ECCLESIASTES

CONTENTS

BOOK ONE

RUGGED ROADS

1

In the beginning there was a warm room with a table, a black iron stove and old red-flowered wallpaper. The child lay on a cot feeling the good heat while the mother moved peacefully from the table to the stove. When the mother sang her small voice quavered over the lulling nonsense-words; the song was meant to be gay but the child felt sadness in it.

"Don't sing," she commanded and the mother stopped. She was amused.

"Imagine," she told her husband, "Anna doesn't like my voice! She made me stop singing today!"

The father laughed and picked Anna up. He had a sandy beard and dim blue eyes. He was slow and tender, especially when he touched the mother; the child was comforted when he put his arms around the mother.

"Kiss Mama!" she said.

They laughed again and the child understood that they were laughing at her and that they loved her.

For a long time the days and the years were all the same. In the house the mother moved between the stove and the table. The father hammered boots and cut leather for harness in his front-room shop. On the big bed in the room back of the kitchen the mother brought new babies to birth; one year there were twin boys, red-haired like Anna and Papa.

On Friday nights there was a linen cloth on the table; there was sugar in the tea, and white bread. Papa brought beggars home from the synagogue; the beggars were dirty and had a nasty smell. They were given the best food in the house, the plum jam and the breast of chicken. The room was shadowed; the white light of the candles burned through Mama's hands as they moved in blessing and flickered on the pearls in her ears. There was a lovely and lofty mystery in her words and on her face.

It seemed to the child that the world had always been and would always be like this. She could not imagine any other way for people to live. The road through the village was dusty in the summer, muddy and icy in the winter; it stretched to the river where there was a bridge and went on for miles, it was said, to other villages like this one. The houses were strung along the road or clustered around the wooden synagogue, the market and the school. All of the people who lived here knew you and called you by name.

The ones who did not know you—the Others—lived on the far side of the little river where the church steeple rose over the trees. Beyond there cattle grazed, and farther still you could see the wind make tunnels through the growing wheat. The milkman came every day from that direction, two heavy wooden buckets swinging from his yoke. People seldom went there. There was no reason to go unless you were a peddler or a milkman, although sometimes you did go with Mama to buy vegetables or extra eggs.

The days were measured and ordered by the father's morning, afternoon and evening prayers; by the brothers in their black coats and visored caps going to and coming from school. The weeks ran from Friday night to Friday night. The year ran from winter to winter, when silent snow fell and voices rang like chimes in the silence. The snow turned to rain, drenching the lilacs in the yard, strewing petals over the mud. Then before the return of the cold came the short, hot summer.

Anna sits on the step in the breathless night, watching the stars. Of what can they be made? Some say they are fire. Some say the earth is fire like them, and that if you could stand far off and look at the earth it would glitter like the stars. But how can that be?

Papa does not know; he does not care about such things. If it is not in the Bible he is not interested in it. Mama sighs and says that she does not know either. Surely it would be wonderful if a woman could be educated and learn about things like that. A rabbi's wife in a far-off district runs a school for girls. There, very likely one could learn about the stars and how to speak other languages and much else besides. But it would be very expensive to go to such a school. And anyway, what would one do with that kind of knowledge in this village, this life?

"Although, of course," Mama says, "everything need not be *useful*. Some things are beautiful for themselves alone." Her eyes look into the distance and the dark. "Maybe it will be different after a while, who knows?"

Anna does not really care. The stars glow and spark. The air is like silk. Clouds foam up from the horizon and a little chill comes skimming on the wind. Across the road someone closes the shutters for the night with a *clack!* and *click!* She rises and goes back into the house.

Sometimes she listens to scraps of talk, the parents' evening murmur that repeats itself often enough to form a pattern. They talk about America. Anna has seen a map and knows that, if you were to travel for days, after a time you would come to the end of the land called Europe, which is where they live. And then there would be water, an ocean wider than the land over which you have come. You would sail for days across that water in a ship. It is both exciting and disturbing.

Of course, there are many people in the village whose relatives have gone to America. Mama has a second cousin in New York, Cousin Ruth, who has been there since before Anna was born. Tales arrive by mail: in America everyone is alike and it is wonderful because there is no difference between rich and poor. It is a place where there is equality and justice; every man is the same as every other. Also, America is a place where it is possible to become very rich and wear gold bracelets and have silver forks and spoons.

Papa and Mama have been talking for a long time about going, but there has always been some reason they cannot leave. First, there was Grandmother who had suffered a stroke. The people in America would not have let her in, and of course the family could not just have gone away and left her. Then Grandmother died, but Eli and Dan, the twins, were born. After them came Rachel. Then Celia. And Papa had to save more money. They would have to wait another year or two.

So they would never go, Anna knew. America was only something that they talked about in their bed at night, the way they talked about household things and their neighbors, about money and the children. They would stay here always. One day, a long, long time from now, Anna would be grown, a bride like Pretty Leah whose father had the chicken farm just past the bridge, led under the canopy to the dance of violins, with a white gauze veil over her face. Then she would be a mother, lying in the bed like Mama with a new baby. But still it would be the same life; Papa and Mama would be here, looking no different from the way they looked now.

Yes, and the sheltering house would be here, too. And Rachel stirring in the bed. The old dog jingling his chain in the yard. The blown curtain; summer nights of pine and hay and Mama's bush of yellow roses at the gate. Rustle of night-birds, trill of frogs: I am alive, I am here, I am going to sleep.

{2}

Whenever Anna told or thought about the story of Pretty Leah she fell into the cadence and language of the twelve-year-old child she had been when it happened.

"Mama sent me to the farm to buy some eggs. Pretty Leah and I stood in the courtyard counting the eggs. Then I wanted to go into the barn to look at a newborn calf, and I was there when the men came, three of them on plow horses, cantering into the yard.

"I think Pretty Leah thought they wanted to buy some eggs because I saw her smile and look up at them. They jumped off the horses and one of them took her shoulders. They were laughing, but they were angry, too, I think; I didn't know what they were, really, but Pretty Leah screamed and I ran up the ladder into the loft and hid.

"They dragged her inside and shut the barn door. Her screams, oh, her screams! They were drunk and saying dirty words in Polish; their eyes were all puckered in their flat cheeks. They pulled her skirt up over her face. Oh, they will smother her, I thought; *I mustn't look,* and still I could not look away from the things they did.

"Like the bull and the cow, that time when Mama and I were out walking and Mama said, *Don't look* and I asked, *Why mustn't I?* And she answered, *Because you are too young to understand. It will frighten you.*

"But the bull and the cow had not frightened me at all. It seemed a simple thing, what they had done. Not like this awful thing. Pretty Leah twisted and kicked; her screams under the skirt had turned to weeping and pleading, soft, soft, like a baby animal. Two of the men pinned her arms and the third lay on top of her. Then they changed places until all three had lain on her. After a while she stopped moving and crying. I thought, *My God, they have killed her!*

"When the men left they flung the barn door wide. I could hear the hens clucking in the yard. The light came in and fell on Pretty Leah with the skirt over her face, her naked legs spread wide, blood sticky on her thighs. After a long time I came down the ladder. I was afraid to touch her but I made myself draw her skirt down. She was breathing; she had only fainted. There was a cut on her chin; her black hair had come unbraided. When she wakes up she will wish she were dead, I thought.

"Then I went outside and vomited in the grass. I picked up the basket of eggs and went home."

That was the way she remembered it, all the years of her life, the way she would often think of a man with a woman, although she would not want to think of them like that.

In the evening after the dishes had been put away Mama said, "Come, Anna, we'll sit outside on the steps and talk awhile."

But it was dark blue dusk. There were shadows and movement of Things behind the trees, and someone was walking in the distance, rapping on the road, the fast steps coming closer.

"I don't want to go outside," Anna said.

"Very well, then, I will ask Papa and the children to sit in the yard and we can talk by ourselves."

The mother lay down on the bed beside the daughter and took her hand; the mother's hand was hot and rough.

"Listen to me," she said softly. "I would give anything if you hadn't seen what you saw today. Such an ugly, ugly, evil thing!" She was trembling. The long quivering shook her body, shook her voice. "The world can be so frightful and human beings worse than beasts. Still, you must remember, Anna, that most people are good. You must try to put this out of your mind as soon as you can."

"Will nobody punish those men?"

"In the first place, nobody could prove who did it. Nobody saw it."

"I saw it. And I remember the faces. Especially the short thick one. He wears a red shirt and sometimes he goes into Krohn's Inn to get drunk."

The mother sat up. "Listen to me, Anna, do you hear? You are never, never to mention that to anybody, to anybody at all, do you understand? Terrible things would happen to you! To Papa, to me, to all of us! You must never, never—!"

The child was frightened. "I understand. But then, there is nothing that can be done about people like that?"

"Nothing."

"Then how can we know it won't happen again? Even to you, Mama?"

The mother was silent. And Anna pressed, "How can we know?"

"I suppose we can't."

"Then they can always do what they want to do. Kill us, even."

"That, too. You're old enough now to know."

The child began to cry. The mother held her. After a while the father came in. He stood at the door. His face was crumpled and creased.

"I've made up my mind. Year after year we put it off. But this year, by spring, we'll manage it somehow! We'll sell the furniture, your earrings, your mother's silver candlesticks. We have got to get to America!"

"There are seven of us."

"And if there were seventeen we would still have to manage it. This is no place to live! I want to lay my head down once without fear before I die."

So all the time, in this home of theirs, they had been afraid. Mama so calmly and skillfully arranging things, Papa humming and smiling while his strong arms hammered and cut. The child thought wonderingly: I didn't know, I never knew.

*   *   *

THE WINTER OF 1906 was strangely warm. Snow fell briefly and lay puddled in
soggy gray slush. A damp wind blew; people perspired in their heavy coats,
sneezed, shivered, ran fevers. Late in February the rain began, racing in long,
even lines down the dark sky. The village street turned to sucking mud; the little
river that curved at the bottom of the rise rushed over its banks and flooded all
the yards along its length.

The sickness started down there at the river. In the middle of March a baby
and a grandfather died in one house. On the other side of the river, where the
peasants lived, a whole family died. Each day brought more sickness and some
deaths. Sickness traveled north and south; people on farms five miles away
brought their dead to be buried in the churchyard. It was like the black rot that
spreads some years in the potato fields, creeping down the rows. And there was
no place to go, nothing that anyone knew how to do but wait.

Some said it was because the floods had brought filth into the drinking water.
The village priest said it was because people had sinned. Hour after hour the
church bells rang for funerals and masses of intercession, making a grave, bronze
clamor in the rain. Whenever the rain stopped the processions formed: the priest,
the altar boys holding candles, carrying banners and a bone relic in a glass box.
Men lifted a statue of the Virgin on a swaying platform; women cried.

In Anna's house the shutters were closed. "If this sickness doesn't stop soon,"
the father said, "they will start blaming us."

The mother spoke sadly. "I don't know which is worse, fear of the cholera or
of them."

"In America," Anna said, "there is no cholera and nobody is afraid of anybody
else."

"And by summer we'll be there," Papa said.

Perhaps at last they really would have gone that year. Who knows?

The father and the mother died at the end of March after an illness of just two
days. Celia and Rachel died with them. Anna and the twins never fell sick at all.

They lived, the spindly red-haired girl and the ten-year-old boys, followed the
four pine coffins to the cemetery, shook in the whipping wind while the prayers
were chanted, saw the first clod of earth strike the wood. Hurry, hurry, it is so
cold, Anna thought. And then she thought, I shall forget them. Close your eyes:
Think of their faces, remember the sound of their voices calling your name.

They stood in the kitchen of what had been their home. Someone had aired
and disinfected the house. Someone else had brought soup. The little room was
crowded with neighbors in dark wraps and shawls.

"So, what's to be done with these children?"

"No family! People without relatives shouldn't marry each other!"

"That's true."

"Well then, the community will have to provide!"

And who is the "community"? Why, the richest man, naturally, from whom all
charity is expected and to whom all respect is given. He steps forward now,
Meyer Krohn, innkeeper, dry goods merchant, money-lender. He is a tall, pock-

marked man in peasant boots and cap. His gray beard is rough, his voice is rough, but it speaks with authority.

"So who'll take them? What about you, Avrom? You, Yossel? You have room enough!"

"Meyer, you know I give what I can. I'll gladly take one of them, but not three."

Meyer Krohn frowns; the furrows in his forehead are deep enough to bury the tip of a fingernail. He roars.

"We don't separate families! Now, who here will take in these three orphans? I ask you, who?"

Nobody speaks. Anna's legs are weak; the bones melt.

"Ah," Meyer says, "I know what you're thinking! You're thinking: *Meyer's rich, let him do it!*" He thrusts his enormous arms out. "What am I, Rothschild, that I have to support half the community? 'Meyer, the school needs a new stove; So-and-so broke his leg and his family is starving'—is there no end to what is expected of me?"

Coughing and shuffling. Eli has been told that he must be a man now. He is trying not to cry.

"All right," says Meyer Krohn. "All right." He sighs. "My children are grown and gone. The house is big enough, God knows. There's a room for the boys and Anna can share a bed with the servant-girl." His voice lowers quietly. "What do you say, Anna? And you, Eli? Which one of you is Eli and what's the other one's name? I always forget." He puts his arms around the little shoulders of the boys. "Come along home," he says.

Oh, he is decent, he is kind! But Anna walks naked; everyone is looking at her growing breasts, the secrets of her body. Her clothes have been stripped off. She has been shamed, she has been outraged. Like Pretty Leah.

THE KROHNS LIVE prosperously. Their house has two stories and wooden floors. There is carpet in the front room. Aunt Rosa owns a fur cape. A servant does the cleaning while Aunt Rosa measures cloth and waits on customers in the store. Sometimes she helps in the tavern; sometimes Uncle Meyer helps in the store.

Anna works wherever she is needed, and she is always needed everywhere. She is often tired out. But she has grown tall like her mother, with bright, healthy hair. The Krohns have fed her well.

"How old are you?" Uncle Meyer asks one day. They are rewinding cloth on the heavy bolts and lifting them back onto the shelves.

"Sixteen."

"How the years fly! You've turned out well in my house. A nice girl, a worker. It's time we found a husband for you."

Anna does not answer, but this does not bother Uncle Meyer. He has a way of talking without noticing whether anyone answers or not.

"I really ought to have done something about you before this. But I never seem to have time. People think: he's a rich man, Meyer Krohn, what has he got to worry about? My God, when I lie down at night I can't sleep, my head spins, a hundred things at once—"

He is always complaining, there is always an undertone of resentment even in the best humors. But Anna knows that is because he's afraid. Growing up in a stranger's house you learn to watch for moods, to anticipate and analyze, to look at the outside and see what is inside. Yes, Uncle Meyer is afraid, even more than Papa was, because he is important and conspicuous in the village. When a new commissioner of police is sent to the district it is Meyer who goes to him for favors that may possibly buy the safety of the community. Also, he has his personal bribes, gifts to the peasants so the store will not be looted and wrecked during the holiday rampage. The same friendly fellow who comes with his cajoling smile to ask for credit—and who, of course, receives it—can just as easily return to boot you down the stairs or set his wicked dogs upon you.

"Yes, and there are your bothers to think about. What's to become of them? Let's see, how old are they now?"

"Fourteen."

"Hm. Fourteen, already. What's to be done with them? How are they to support themselves?" He thinks aloud. "Rosa has an uncle in Vienna. He went there years ago, perhaps we've mentioned him? He sells furs. As a matter of fact, his son will be coming through here this spring to buy fox skins. It's an idea."

He LOOKS LIKE a fox himself, Anna thought. The young man from Vienna was thin and lively; his reddish eyes snapped; his city suit fitted like skin and he talked so much and so fast that even Uncle Meyer was subdued. Eli and Dan were fascinated.

". . . and the Opera House has marble stairs and gilded carving on the walls. It's so enormous that you could fit thirty houses, one whole side of your village, into it."

"Bah," Uncle Meyer could not resist. "Who hasn't seen big buildings? I've been in Warsaw; I've seen buildings in my time."

"Warsaw? You compare that with Vienna? I'm talking about a cultured country! Where Jews write plays and teach in the university, where they don't have pogroms whenever the drunken peasants feel like having a little fun!"

"You mean," Dan asks, "that Jews in Vienna are exactly like everybody else?"

"Well, naturally they don't attend balls at Franz Josef's palace, but neither do other people. They have grand houses, though, and carriages, and they own big shops with porcelains and Oriental rugs and fashions—you should see where I work, we've just doubled the place. Why, if you work hard and use your brains, you can see your family rising for generations to come and no limit!"

The foxy young man has planted thoughts that sprout like seeds.

"I may go to Paris in the spring," he says carelessly. "Did I tell you that?"

"You didn't tell us," Dan says.

"Yes, well, we sell furs to some concerns there and the boss wants to discuss matters. And naturally, you can get new styles in Paris, new ideas for the retail end. The boss has promised to take me along."

The cat scratches vigorously; the water bubbles for tea and the questions hang in the air.

"I shan't be coming back here again. We're making new contacts for furs. In Lithuania."

"So in other words," Uncle Meyer says, "if you're going to take these boys back with you it will have to be right now."

"That's about it."

Dan turns to Anna and she sees his eagerness, his pleading. She thinks: It's true, here there is nothing. Uncle Meyer can't do anything for them. What will they become? Porters with ropes around their waists dragging bundles through the streets of Lublin? Or learn a fine trade in Vienna and wear the look of prosperity and ease?

Good-by, Eli. Good-by, Dan. Little snub-noses, little dirty faces. I am the only person who can tell you apart. Eli has the mole on the side of his nose; Dan has a chipped front tooth.

"I'll send for you from America," Anna tells them. "I'll get there and I'll earn money enough to send for you. America will be better."

"No, we'll earn it and we'll send for you. There are two of us and we are men. You can come back from America. If you go."

People don't come back from America.

THEY HAD BEEN gone a few weeks when Aunt Rosa said, "Anna, I have something to tell you. Uncle Meyer has found a nice young man."

"But I'm going to America."

"Nonsense. All the way across the world alone, at sixteen?"

"I'm not afraid," Anna said untruthfully. Maybe, after all—? At least, the village was home. At least, its threats were familiar ones. And yet—America. For some reason she always saw it lying at the end of the voyage like a tropical island rising out of the sea, a silver-green lure. Of course, she knew it was not like that, but that was the way she saw it.

"I shall miss you," Aunt Rosa said shyly. "You've become like a daughter to me. My own I never see since they married and moved away." And coaxing, "Just look the young man over one time. You may change your mind."

He came to dinner on Friday, a gentle person from another village, earning his way as a peddler of tobacco, thread and sundries to the farms. He had pimples, garlic breath and a kind, mournful smile. He was disgusting. Anna was ashamed of herself for being disgusted by a decent, honest human being.

Her thoughts ran back to Pretty Leah, those men, what they had done. But this young man was no drunkard, no brute; it would not be like that! Disgusting, all the same.

"Really, Anna," Aunt Rosa said, "you have to look at the facts. You're a poor girl without money or family! What do you expect, a scholar? Or a merchant prince? Ah," she sighed, "these foolish unplanned marriages! It's the next generation that suffers and pays! Your father was a good-looking man, he had a trade; and if he had married a girl with some family and substance he could have built up a business and left something for his children!"

"My parents loved each other! You don't know how happy they were!"

"Yes, of course, I'm not speaking against them! Your mother was a charming woman, a religious woman; I knew her well. It's only that—well, here you are, you see! However, it could be worse. Thank God you're pretty, otherwise you'd have to marry an old widower and raise his children for him. At least this man is young and he'll be kind to you. You don't think we didn't inquire? We wouldn't turn a girl over to a man who would mistreat her."

"Aunt Rosa, I can't . . ."

Aunt Rosa clasped her hands together. Her face puckered into wrinkles. "Oh, but Uncle Meyer will be angry! After all that he's done for you! Anna, Anna, what do you want?"

What did she want? To see the world beyond this village, to be free, to hear music, to wear a new pink dress. To have her own place and not have to say thank you for everything. Thank you for this corner under your roof which keeps me out of the wet. Thank you for the food; I would like a second portion but I am ashamed to ask for it. Thank you for this thick, warm, ugly, brown shawl which you no longer wear and have given to me. Thank you.

She owned four silver candlesticks, a pair from each grandmother. Keep two, the ones with the feel of Mama's hands upon them. Sell the others for the price of one passage to America. And go.

A<small>T THE TOP</small> of the rise the wagon stopped to let the horses rest. Below lay the village, held in the curve of the river. There, the little wooden dome of the synagogue. There, the market: jostling and churning at the stalls; flurry and squawk of crated fowl. Round and round, the busy lives in the order of their days.

"Well, come," the driver said. "We've a long way."

The wagon creaked along the road above the river. There, the last huddle of houses, the board fences and a glimpse of lilacs. In another month Mama's yellow roses would flower like a celebration.

Then the road turned and led downhill across level fields, dark earth steaming and wet new greenery swimming in spring light. The village was gone, erased in the moment of turning. The hill blocked out the past. The road led forward.

Dust, flies and dirty inns. The border: guards, papers, sharp questions. Will they perhaps not let us through? Then Germany: neat railroad stations with candy and fruit for sale. Be careful not to spend too much of the little treasure in the knotted cloth wrapped up with the silver candlesticks.

The immigrant-aid people come to expedite the journey to Hamburg. They are German Jews wearing fine suits, ties and white shirts. They bring food, sign documents, rearrange the boxes, bags and feather beds. They are generous and kindly. They are also impatient to get the strangers onto the ship and out of Germany.

The Atlantic is a ten-day barrier between worlds. It is the lonely mourning of horns in dark gray fog. It is wind and the heaving sea, the breaking and cracking of the ship. It is retching out of an empty stomach, lying in a top berth with all strength drained and hands too weak to hold on. There is a noisy turbulence of voices: laughing, arguing, complaining in Yiddish, German, Polish, Lithuanian, Hungarian. And thefts, the poor stealing from the poor. (A woman lost her gold crucifix. Don't let the bundle with the candlesticks out of sight.) A child is born; the mother wails. An old man dies; the widow wails.

Suddenly it is over. There is a wide, calm river. From the deck one sees houses and trees. The trees draw closer; the wind turns up the silver undersides of the leaves. The air is tart and brisk, like witch hazel. Gulls flow over the ship, circle, climb and slide down the sky.

America.

❊{3}❊

The house on Hester Street was five stories tall. Cousin Ruth lived on the top floor with her husband, Solly Levinson, their four children and six boarders. Anna would be the seventh.

"You don't have room for me," she said in dismay. "You're kind to offer but I'd be crowding you—"

Ruth pushed the hair back from her sweating forehead. "So where do you think you'll find a place where you won't be crowding somebody? Better for you to stay here where at least you're a relative. And to tell you the truth, it's not all kindness on my part, we can use the money. We have to pay twelve dollars a month for this place, not counting gas for the light and coal in the winter for the stove. We'll charge you fifty cents a week. Fair enough?"

The smells! The stench surged from the street door and up the four flights: cooking grease; onions; an overflowing toilet in the hall; the sickening steam of pressing irons; a noxious drenching of tobacco from the front apartment where the cigar-makers lived. Anna's stomach contracted. Yet how could she refuse? And if she refused, where could she go?

Ruth coaxed. Her anxious, pretty eyes lay in two circles of dark blue shadow. "When we're through with the sewing at night Solly and I put up the cot for ourselves in the kitchen. We put the machines in the corner and get out the mattresses. The women have the best room to themselves, the room with the windows. And the men sleep in the rear by the air shaft. It's not so bad, really. Can you sew?"

"Just mending. And I can make a plain skirt. I never had time to learn because I worked in the store."

"Well, it doesn't matter. Solly can take you to the factory tomorrow, he has to bring the finished work back."

In a corner stood a pile of black bags stuffed with coats and pants. Two sallow, curly-haired children lay sleeping on top of the pile.

"You can help Solly carry the bags, you'll meet the boss and they can show you how to stitch pants in no time. A good finisher gets thirty cents a day, you know."

Anna set her bundles down and unfastened her shawl. The dark red braids fell free.

22

"They didn't tell me how pretty you are! A child, a baby—" Ruth put out her hands. Her arms were black to the elbow with the stain of the pants fabric. "Anna, I'll look out for you, you won't be alone. It's maybe not what you dreamed it would be but it's a start. And you'll get used to it."

THE NOISE WAS the worst. The smells and the crowding could somehow be endured. But Anna had sensitive hearing and the noise attacked her like brutal fists. On the street below the old-clothes man chanted through his nose: "Coats, fifty cents, coats, fifty cents!" Wagons rumbled. The "L" ground into the station with the squeal of metal on metal. And always until midnight the sewing machines whined. Would they ever sleep, ever slacken the struggle?

Sometimes on breathless nights Anna and Ruth went out to sit on the stoop. It was impossible to sleep indoors and they were afraid to join the others on the fire escape since a woman from across the street had rolled off in her sleep and smashed to the street. The sky was a cloudy pink from the glow of factories that smoked all night; you could scarcely see the stars. At home on summer nights they had been so clear, winking and pulsing above the trees.

"You're so quiet," Ruth said. "Are you worried about anything? About your brothers?"

"I miss them. But they're all right, they're doing well. They have a nice room in their boss's house and Vienna is beautiful, they say."

"It's not beautiful here, God knows."

"That's true."

"But one has a future here. I still believe that."

"I believe it, too. I wouldn't have come if I hadn't believed that."

"You know," Ruth said, "you know, I've been thinking there isn't any reason for you to work as hard as you're doing. At your age you ought to have some life. You ought to be meeting men. It's my fault, I've done nothing for you, after four months. I'll ask Solly to look around for you, for a dancing class. There are lots and lots of good dancing classes."

"If I'm going to take the time off I'd rather go to night school. Working here like this I've had no chance to learn English."

"That's not a bad idea, either. If you could learn enough to be a typist you could find a husband more easily, a better class of man. Typists don't earn much, just three dollars a week, but the work has prestige. Only," Ruth's voice grew doubtful, "I really think you have to be American born. Still, it's worth trying."

"I'm not so interested in finding a husband. I just want to learn something."

"You're like your mother, I remember her well." Ruth sighed. "I, too, would like to learn. But with all the children to feed, and now another—" She sighed again, resting her hand on the swelling beneath her apron.

Only ten years ago Ruth had been the age Anna was now. Was this what marriage made you, so tired, so resigned? But Mama hadn't been like that. Or could she have been? What could Anna when she was twelve years old have really known about her mother?

Ruth said, lowering her voice, "One doesn't want to complain. But it's hard to

get ahead. Though some people do, I don't know how they do it. There's a knack
to making money. My poor Solly hasn't got it."

A shifting light moved in the window. Someone inside had got up to light the
oil lamp and a yellow flare fell over the steps.

"There was a girl who came from home with me—Hannah Vogel, your mother
knew her. She married a fellow she met on the boat. He didn't have a cent when
he came, but he was smart. Somehow he made a connection and moved to
Chicago. Opened a haberdashery there. I hear he owns a chain of stores now—"
Ruth's voice brightened. "My Solly's got very friendly with the factory manager.
You never know, changes are always being made; he might decide to open his
own place and take Solly in with him."

Anna thought of Solly in the corner, bent over his machine. A thin man with
the timid pointed face of a mouse. Poor hopeful Ruth. Poor tired Solly. They
would never get out of here.

People who had come from Europe twenty years before them still lived on
these streets. The old men were thin, with dark, beautiful eyes; they seemed more
fragile, somehow, than the old men Anna remembered from home, leading their
wagons of secondhand clothes, chickens, hats, fish and eyeglasses. Their old
wives were fat, potato-shaped and potato-colored, their hanging white flesh untouched by the sun.

Where were the pink dresses, the freedom and the music?

Still, there were many marvels. The streets were almost as bright at night as
by day, not like home where you stumbled down the road holding the lantern
high. In a vacant store down the street there was a machine, a nickelodeon,
where you could look in and see a picture that moved: Indians attacking a train, a
beautiful woman named Irene Castle and a tall man swooping and gliding in a
dance.

Anna walked, taking no particular direction, just walking and looking. Under
the Second Avenue elevated the women sat at the horseradish machines, weeping
their smarting tears. She avoided the tramps who slept over the baker's ovens in
the yard. She went past the synagogues in the tenements on Bayard Street. She
walked five, ten blocks and more, until the people on the streets looked different
and spoke in languages that she did not understand. On Italian streets the children swarmed more quickly than on Hester Street. A man sold pink and yellow
sweet ices from a little cart. An organ grinder wearing a bandana and earrings
made melancholy music in the bright morning; on his shoulder sat an eager, tiny
monkey in a red jacket. She watched; she listened to the melody of Italian speech.
It was like singing.

Then the Irish streets. The saloons with harps and shamrocks on the signs
above the doors. The beautiful women in their ragged dresses and the curving
sweetness on their faces.

And Mott Street, where the strange-eyed peddlers sold watermelon seed and
sugar cane. Through half-open cellar doors you saw Chinese men playing fan-tan.
Their pigtails came below their knees. You never saw Chinese women or children.
Why was that? How could that be?

Worlds. Every few blocks another world. From what strange places had all these different people come? Villages in China, in Ireland—how different could they be from home? Had these people felt fears like ours? Are they perhaps like me after all?

❧{ 4 }❧

Her name was Miss Mary Thorne. Thin and precise in her dark serge skirt and starched shirtwaist, she stood at the front of the classroom with the map of the United States on one side and the portraits of Washington and Lincoln on the other. She looks like them, her face is American, Anna thought. Americans are always tall and slender, with long faces.

Evening school was held in a room that must have housed ten-year-olds by day. One's knees didn't fit under the desks; one had to sit twisted sideways. The ceiling bulb glared harshly and the heat from the sizzling radiators made people yawn. They shifted restlessly. But Anna hardly moved. She watched. She listened. Miss Mary Thorne was pouring knowledge like a good drink out of a pitcher.

Toward the end of the winter she was called to the desk after class. "You've done amazingly well, Anna. It's hard to believe you never studied English before. I'm going to promote you to my intermediate group."

"Thank you, miss," Anna said. Proud and embarrassed, she stood looking at Miss Thorne, not knowing quite how to leave the room with grace.

The teacher looked back at her. People were often intimidated by Miss Thorne: she had a stern face most of the time, but not now. Her eyes, magnified behind the unrimmed glasses that clung to the bridge of her nose, were soft.

"Do you think about what you want to do with your life, Anna? I ask because it seems to me you are different from so many others. I see so many. . . . Every so often someone sits in this classroom who is different from the rest."

"I don't know what there is for me to do," Anna said slowly. "I suppose what I really want is just to know things. I feel that I don't know anything, and I want to know everything."

Miss Thorne smiled. "Everything? That's a large order."

"Of course, I didn't mean that. But you see, the way it is, sometimes I feel there is a screen between me and the world. I want to pull it away to see more clearly. I don't know anything about the past, or the way the world is now, except for these few streets and the village that I came from."

"Did you study anything there in the village?"

"There was a woman teacher who came to the houses for the girls. We learned numbers and writing and reading. In Yiddish."

"Not Hebrew? Oh no, that's only for the boys, isn't it? The sacred language."

"Yes, only for the boys."

"Well, it's not like that here, as you know. A girl can study whatever the boys do."

"I know. That's a good thing."

"Yes. Well." Miss Thorne stood up and went briskly to a shelf of books behind the desk. "The secret to it all is reading, Anna. Nothing else. I'll tell you something: if you read and read and read you don't even have to go to school, you can educate yourself! Only don't tell anybody I said so! First, you must read the newspaper every day, the *Times* or the *Herald.* Don't read the *Journal,* it's cheap and sensational. Then I'm going to make up a list of books for you, long enough to take years to get through. You'll be reading it long after I don't see you anymore. Now, tonight I'm going to start you with this, you must learn about your new country from the beginning. It's a book about Indians, a wonderful poem called *Hiawatha,* by one of our best poets, Mr. Henry Wadsworth Longfellow. When you have finished it, bring it back and tell me what you thought about it. And then I will give you another."

OVER THE FIREPLACE there was a round mirror in a gilded frame. Everything looked queer in it: she could see herself holding the flowered teacup on the embroidered napkin, see the little table with the teapot and the cake plate and Miss Thorne on the other side of the table. All of these were squat, condensed and flattened out. Even Miss Thorne looked wide and flat.

"That's a bull's-eye mirror," Miss Thorne said, following Anna's gaze. "I don't see much point in having it myself. But then, it's not my house."

"Not?"

"No, my nephew's. He and his wife have only the one child and it's a large house, so when I came down from Boston they invited me to live here with them and it has been very nice for me indeed."

"And were you a teacher when you lived in Boston?" Anna asked shyly.

"Yes, I've been a teacher ever since I left school myself. I came to New York to be the assistant headmistress at a private school for girls. That's what I do all day, you see. Then at night I teach English to newcomers like you."

"And what do you teach the girls in the daytime, since they already know how to speak English?"

"I teach them Latin and ancient Greek."

"Oh. But why—excuse me, I ask too many questions."

"Not at all. How will you find out if you don't ask? Tell me what you wanted to know."

"Well, I want to know what Latin is. And ancient Greek."

"A long time ago, two thousand years ago and more, there were powerful countries in Europe where those languages were spoken. The languages aren't spoken anymore; we say they're 'dead,' but the laws, the ideas those people left to us, are very much alive. And it's also true that the languages are the great-great-grandparents of English. Do you understand what I'm saying?"

Anna nodded. "I understand. Those girls in your school are so fortunate, learning all these things, I think."

"I wish they all thought so. Or had your eagerness, Anna. That's why I like to teach in your school, at night. Because so many of you want to learn—I feel I'm doing something really important."

Now that she had been invited here to tea Anna felt bolder. It was different from the classroom, with the elevated platform where the teacher sat above everybody else.

"Do people speak differently, is that why you speak differently, because you're from Boston?"

"What do you mean, differently?"

"I notice that some words are different. The way you say 'park,' for instance? That's not the way some other Americans say it."

"Extraordinary, your ear! Yes, it's true, we have a different accent there. In the South, in the Midwest, there are all sorts of accents."

"I see. And will you answer something else, please?"

"If I can."

"Please, I've never had tea in a cup like this. What must I do with the spoon after I've stirred the tea?"

"You just lay the spoon on the saucer, Anna."

"That was probably a foolish question. I might have figured it out for myself. Except that I should like to do things right, the American way."

"It wasn't a foolish question. Only, let me tell you something. Wherever you go, and I hope you'll go far, don't ever be nervous about manners. Manners are mostly common sense, being tidy about things and considerate of other people. I don't think you'll have the slightest trouble about either of those, Anna."

"Then, may I have another piece of cake, please? It's very good cake."

"Of course. And when you've finished I want to give you the list of reading that I've made out for you. I finally got around to it. That's one of the reasons I asked you to come today, because we can talk better than at school."

The list was pages long, written in a neat script that looked like Miss Thorne herself. Anna scanned it.

Hawthorne: *The House of the Seven Gables*
Hardy: *The Return of the Native*
Dickens: *David Copperfield, Bleak House*
Thackeray: *Vanity Fair*
Henry James: *The Bostonians, Washington Square*

"Washington Square? That's where we are now, the same?" Anna cried.

"The very same. Henry James lived not far from here before he went to live in England. My family, my father's people, knew him well. My mother's family came from Boston."

"Really American," Anna murmured.

"No more than you. We just arrived sooner. You can be as American as anyone, never think otherwise. That's what this country is all about, Anna."

Anna said, suddenly troubled, "I only wish, I wish I had more time to read all these books. It takes me so long."

"You'll find the time. You can get a lot done just on Sundays alone."

"Sundays I work." And as Miss Thorne looked puzzled, she explained, "I took the afternoon off today because you invited me and I was so honored, I wanted so much to come. But I'm really supposed to be working."

"I see. Sewing, where you live at home."

Anna nodded.

"Tell me, then, is there any place where you can read by yourself? I suppose not."

"Alone? Oh, no! Only on the front stoop when the weather is warm, and it's noisy enough there. But in cold weather, there's no place. It's so hard even to write to my brothers. With everybody talking I can't think of what I want to say."

"A pity, a pity. And so many empty rooms in this house alone. If only one could do what one wants to do. One thing, though: my niece is about your size, and I'm going to ask her whether she has a good warm coat to give away. It would be better—shall we say, more American?—than your shawl. Also, I have duplicate copies of a few of the books on this list and I'm going to give them to you to keep, so you can start to build a library of your own. I'll get the things to you, since it's hard for you to take time to come here."

Anna put the shawl around her shoulders and they went out into the hall. On the other side a door was ajar; a room was filled with books from ceiling to floor; a little boy was practicing at a huge dark piano.

"You don't mind the offer of the coat, Anna?"

"Mind? Oh, no, I'm glad, I want a coat!"

"Someday you'll be one of the people who gives, I'm sure you will."

"I shall be happy to give if that day ever comes, Miss Thorne."

"It will. And when it does I hope we shall still know each other. Then I'll remind you of what I said."

I don't believe we shall know each other, almost surely not. But just as surely, I will remember Miss Mary Thorne. Yes, I will, always.

❧{ 5 }❧

"You must be Anna," the young man said.

He stood above her as she sat reading on the steps: *This is the forest primeval. The murmuring pines and the hemlocks—*

Unwillingly she returned to the street, stilled on the Sabbath afternoon, the old men in their long black coats walking on quiet feet, and now this new voice prodding softly.

"May I?"

"Of course. Sit." She moved over, observing him without seeming to. Medium, he was. Medium height and age; medium brown suit, eyes and hair; medium features in a neatly fashioned face.

"I'm Joseph. Joseph Friedman, Solly's cousin."

The American, so called because he had been born in New York. The house painter from uptown. And of course Ruth had arranged this. The same as Aunt Rosa! They can't rest until they've got a man for you. He can be ugly, stupid, anything, as long as he's a man. Not that this one is ugly, but I wanted to read and I'm not thinking about men right now anyway.

"Ruth asked me to come down here to meet you. To tell you the truth, I almost didn't come. They've tried to hitch me up to every girl who ever got off a boat; I was getting tired of it. But I can tell straight away I'm glad I came this time."

Anna stared at him, weighing his astonishing words. But there was no conceit in his face, only the direct and simple return of her look.

"I'm so embarrassed," she said. "I knew nothing about it. Ruth shouldn't have—"

"Please! I know you had nothing to do with it. Shall we take a walk?"

"All right," she said.

He pulled her arm through his. He had clean hands, clean fingernails, a fresh collar. She respected that, at any rate. It is no easy thing to be clean when you are poor, in spite of what people say.

They began to see each other every Saturday. In the afternoon heat they walked the shady side of the street. They could walk for two or three blocks without speaking. Joseph was a quiet man, Anna saw, except when a mood came on him

30

and then one could hardly stop him. Still, he was interesting, he had a vivid way of describing things.

"Here's Ludlow Street, there's the house where I was born. We lived here while my father had the tailor shop. After his sight failed—he couldn't even see the needle anymore—we moved where we are now, my mother and I. Or where my mother is now, I should say. Two rooms behind the grocery store. What a life! Open six days a week until midnight. Bread, pickles, crackers and soda. My mother made salad in back of the store. Such a little woman, such a patient smile. When I remember being a child, I remember that smile. And what the hell was there to smile about? It didn't make any sense."

"Perhaps she was happy about her children, in spite of everything else."

"Child. Just me. They were both over forty when I was born."

"And your father? What was he like?"

"My father had high blood pressure. Everything upset him. He was probably already worn out by the time they got to America. But why don't you stop me? Here I am, chewing your ear off!"

"I like to hear about people. Tell me more."

"There isn't any more to tell. You live here. You know what it's like to live on these streets, just walking around, because there's no place to be comfortable inside. We were poor, and that's the whole story."

"Even poorer than we were in Poland, I should think."

"Well, I don't know how poor you were, but I can remember making supper sometimes out of bread and pickles—before we had our own store, that is. Not all the time, of course, but often enough."

"Still, I think," Anna said thoughtfully, "it hasn't hurt you. I think you're a very optimistic person after all."

"I am. Because I have faith, you see."

"Faith in yourself?"

"Yes, that too. But what I meant was faith in God."

"Are you so religious?"

He nodded seriously. "Yes, yes, I believe. I believe there is a reason for everything that happens, even though we don't see it. And I believe we must accept everything that happens, whether good or bad, on trust. And that we, we as individuals, must do our best, do what God intended. I don't give a damn for all the philosophy you hear them spouting in the coffee houses where the loafers sit around and solve the world's problems. They were all solved years ago on Mt. Sinai. That's what I believe."

"Then why is there still so much trouble in the world?"

"Very simple. Because people don't do what's right. Very simple. You're not an atheist, Anna, I hope?"

"Oh, no, of course I'm not! I just don't know much about religion. I don't really understand it."

"Well, naturally, women don't have to. But I can tell what you are all the same. Honest and kind and good. And very smart. I admire you for educating yourself with all these books."

"You don't read, ever?"

"I don't have time. I'm up before five, and when you've been craning your head back on a scaffold with a paintbrush all day you're too tired at night to improve yourself. Although, to be truthful, I never was a student. Except in arithmetic. I had a good head for figures. At one time I even thought I might become an accountant."

"Why didn't you, then?"

"I had to go to work," he said shortly. "Tell you what, there's a place over on West Broadway that's pretty good, we could have supper there. Soup, stew and pie for thirteen cents. Not bad, with a schooner of beer thrown in. Will you go with me?"

"Yes, but I don't drink beer. You can have mine, too."

Ruth said: "One good thing about this country is you don't have to have money to get married. It's not like the other side. Of course, some people still go to marriage brokers, but modern people don't. You like each other, you get married. You both work." And when Anna did not answer, she said: "Tell me about you and Joe."

"Joseph. Nobody ever calls him Joe."

"And why not?"

"I don't know. But Joseph seems to fit him. It's more dignified."

"All right, then, Joseph. Tell me about you and him."

"There's nothing to tell."

"Nothing!"

"Well, I like him. But there's no—" Anna looked for a word. "Fire. There's no fire."

Ruth threw her hands up. Her eyes and brows moved upward. "So why do you go with him?"

"He's a friend. It's lonesome without a friend."

Ruth looked at her. I might as well have spoken in Chinese, Anna thought.

"You know how many people around here have never even been north of Fourteenth Street?" Joseph had asked Anna.

"I'm one of them."

"Wait, then, I'm going to show you something."

The slippery cane seats were cool and the spring breeze ran along with the trolley car as it gathered speed up Lexington Avenue. The bell clanged with authority. When the car stopped at the corners one could see on the side streets row after row of narrow houses, all brownstone, with high steps and tubbed evergreens at the front doors. Hester Street was a thousand miles away.

"We'll get out at Murray Hill and go over to Fifth," Joseph said.

They walked through the quiet streets from sun to shade, from shade to sun. Now and then a carriage passed; the horses had glossy hair and braided tails.

"Going for a ride in Central Park," Joseph explained. Anna was surprised that he knew so much about this part of the city.

A motorcar stopped in front of one of the houses. The lady in the back seat wore a wide hat tied with a veil. The driver, in uniform and leather boots, walked around and helped her out of the car. She had two small fawn-colored dogs, one under each arm. Then the house door was opened from inside and a young woman came down the steps. Her dress was narrowly striped in blue and white; her little apron was edged with lace and her cap matched it. She took the two dogs and followed the lady up the steps.

"There! What do you think of that?" Joseph asked.

"Oh, it's nice here!" Anna said. "I never imagined anything like this."

"This is nothing. Wait till you see Fifth Avenue. That's something to see!"

The sunshine glowed. The trees in the park across the avenue at Fifty-ninth Street glowed green and gold.

"That's the Plaza Hotel," Joseph said. "And on this side, this is the famous Hotel Netherland."

A young man wearing a straw hat ("That's called a 'boater,' " Joseph said) came out under the awning. The girl with him wore a bunch of violets on her coat, a beautiful coat, pale as the inside of a peach. They crossed the avenue walking swiftly, going somewhere. Anna and Joseph ambled along behind them, going nowhere in particular. When the policeman's whistle blew, the traffic started up and they were stopped on the concrete island where General Sherman, larger then life, reined in his horse.

"Some statue, hey?" Joseph said.

Anna read the inscription. "That's the Union general who burned all the houses when he marched through Georgia during the Civil War."

Joseph was astonished. "I never heard about him! I know about the Civil War, of course, but how do you know so much?"

"History. I've a book of American history," Anna said with pride.

Joseph shook his head. "You're something, Anna, you really are."

Beyond General Sherman stood a great house of red brick and white stone, with iron gates. "The Vanderbilt mansion, that is. Or one of them, I should say."

"That's not a hotel?"

"It's a house. A family lives in there."

She thought he was joking. "One family? It's not possible! There must be a hundred rooms."

"I'm telling you the truth."

"But how can they be so rich?"

"This particular family made it in railroads. All up and down this avenue I could show you dozens of houses like this. Fortunes made in oil, steel, copper, and some just from owning land. You know where you live downtown? A lot of those tenements are owned by people who live here. When people like us pay rent it goes to these people here."

She thought of the crumbling house on Hester Street. "Do you think that's right?"

"Probably not. Or maybe it is, I don't know. If they're smart enough to get it, maybe they're entitled to it. Anyway, that's how the world is, and until a better world is made I'll adapt to this one."

Anna was silent. And Joseph went on, his voice rising with excitement, "I'm going to live like this someday, Anna. Oh, not in a palace like these, but uptown in one of those nice places on the side streets. I'm going to do it, mark my words."

"You are? But how?"

"Work. Buy land. Land is the key to wealth, you know, as long as you own it free and clear. Its value may go down for a time but it always rises again. This country is growing, and if you can hold on to land you're bound to be rich."

"How do you get the money to start?"

"Ah, that's the question! I'm trying to save enough for a small house of flats, but it's hard." He said stubbornly, "I'll do it, though. I'll live like this one day if I have to break my back."

The fierceness that she saw in him disturbed Anna. He hadn't shown it like that before. All of a sudden he seemed too angry and too large, although he was not a large man at all. His voice was too loud. She thought windows would open and people lean out to look, although no one did.

She said quietly, "You think too much about money."

"You think so? I'll tell you something, Anna. Without money the world spits on you. You're nothing. You die like my father in a dirty little shop. Or rot away like Ruth and Solly. You want to rot away like that?"

"No, of course not." One shuddered to think of it. But still it couldn't all be as he said. "The great writers, the artists, they had no money. And the world honors them. You make everything too cruel, too ugly."

Joseph turned her face up to his. His eyes were suddenly soft. "You look about fifteen years old, Anna," he said gently.

THE IDEA CAME to her on a stifling night, when the smell of frying hung in the airless rooms. The hair at the back of her neck was wet with sweat; she longed for a bath in cool water. But there was no place, no privacy. Other women walked in while you were meagerly sponging off. Some of these women disgusted her; they weren't clean. And one poor creature cried and whimpered into her pillow all night. Ruth's five-year-old was sick and restless. It was impossible to sleep.

She thought of the maid coming down the steps of the house with the tubbed evergreens. On the ship crossing the Atlantic, some of the peasant girls had talked of the jobs that waited for them in America, jobs in neat, clean houses like the ones uptown. In such a house she would sleep quietly, and have a place to keep a shelf of the books which Miss Thorne had given her, maybe even save money and buy some more for herself at second hand. After all, there would be no rent to pay and no food to buy. One could live decently, one could walk on those fine streets. She lay awake, thinking and thinking, and at last made up her mind.

"Ruth says I'm crazy to go to work as a servant," she told Joseph, a few days later.

"Why so? It's honest work. Please yourself, Anna, not other people," he told her.

This, then, was how they looked inside, these houses behind the long windows where the shades, demurely pulled, were like downcast eyelids in a quiet face. Velvet carpets; your footsteps made no sound. Pictures in gilded frames. Fresh roses, cream and pink, although it was September. And stairs, turning up and up again. Anna followed Mrs. Werner.

"We're a small family. My daughter is married and living in Cleveland. So there are just Mr. Werner and I and our son, Mr. Paul. This is his room." She opened a door and Anna saw books on crowded shelves, riding boots in a corner and over the mantel a large blue banner: *For God, for Country and for Yale.*

"They're all Yale men in our family. Mr. Paul won't be home from Europe till next week but I'd like to have the room dusted every day all the same. Now, on the top floor is your room." They mounted the stairs again; more dark railings and no carpet on this flight. "This front room we use for the seamstress. She comes for two or three weeks every spring and fall to do my clothes. Back here is Cook's room and yours is next to it."

The two rooms were identical: a neat bed, a dresser, a straight wooden chair. Cook's room had an enormous wooden crucifix above the bed. Unbelievable. Rooms like this, all for one person. With electric lights. Even a bathtub for the maids, a high white bathtub on claw feet.

"Do you think you would like the position?"

"Oh, I would, I would."

"Very well. The wages will be fifteen dollars a month. Ordinarily I pay twenty, but you have no experience, you'll need to be taught. Have you any questions?"

"No."

"Anna, it is proper to say, 'No, Mrs. Werner.' "

"No, Mrs. Werner."

"Do you want to start today?"

"Oh, yes! Yes, Mrs. Werner."

"Then you may go back and get your things. It's eleven o'clock now—let me see—I shan't be needing the car until two. Quinn can drive you down."

"In a machine?"

"Yes. It's a miserable trip in the trolley carrying heavy parcels."

"I haven't got very much. Just my clothes and my candlesticks."

"Oh?"

"They were my mother's. They're very valuable."

"Well, bring them, then, of course." There was a touch of amusement, not unkind, at the corners of the lady's mouth.

The cleanness of it. First the bath, the high tub filled with hot, hot water. Anna almost fell asleep in it. Then the fresh clean bed all to herself; she could turn, she could spread her arms and legs to the very edge.

Her mind went back over the day. The ride in that car, all closed in; it was like a little room, lined in pale sand-colored cloth as smooth as silk. A rug of dark gray fur with a big W sewn on it. Quinn the chauffeur sat outside without a roof. He didn't talk to me. I think he didn't like going down to Hester Street with all those people staring at the car. There was hardly room for it because of the pushcarts. Then the children started climbing on the car and Quinn got angry. But he did help me with my boxes.

I wish Joseph had been there to see that car. Ruth said again that I was crazy to give up my freedom to be a servant, but I can't see what freedom she has. And if I stayed there, I'd only get like her. Still, I shall miss her.

"How is it that you are called Mrs. while I am called by my name?" Anna inquired of the cook in the morning.

"The cook is always called Mrs.," replied Mrs. Monaghan. "You're the first Jewish housemaid we ever had here, you know that? Even though the family's Jewish."

Anna was astonished. "The Werners are Jewish?"

"Of course they are, and grand people, too. I've been here seven years now. My sister-in-law told me I was making a mistake to work for Jews but I've never regretted it. A lady and a gentleman, and no doubt about it."

"I'm glad to hear that," Anna said stiffly.

"And did you sleep well, I hope? Your first night in a place, it's hard to sleep."

The coal fire, which had been banked all night, flared up. Something with a smoky pleasant smell was frying in a pan.

"What's that?" Anna asked.

"That? Why, bacon, of course. What's the matter?"

"But you said these are Jewish people! How can they eat bacon?"

"I'm sure I don't know. Ask them. Mister has bacon and eggs every morning. She only has a cup of tea, toast and marmalade in her room. I'll show you how to fix her tray, and you're to take it up at a quarter past eight. You'll have to step lively, there's no time to waste in the morning."

"I can't eat bacon," Anna said, the acid of nausea in her mouth.

"Well, don't eat it!" Then Mrs. Monaghan's face brightened. "Oh, it's your religion, ain't it? You're not allowed to."

"No," Anna said.

"And why would that be?" Mrs. Monaghan asked, flipping the bacon.

"I don't know. It's not allowed. It's bad."

Mrs. Monaghan nodded sympathetically. "Now, the butcher boy will be ringing in the areaway to take the order for dinner. The family will be having duckling and, seeing that it's Friday, I'll be having fish."

"Why must you have fish because it's Friday?"

"Well, our Lord died on a Friday, you know."

Anna wanted to ask about the connection between fish and the death of the Lord. But the bell sounded in the pantry and Mrs. Monaghan scurried.

"Heavens, she's early this morning! Here, reach me a cup and saucer, the blue and white china. And put the *New York Times* on the tray! Oh, for pity sake, that's the iceman ringing! Answer, will you? Tell him fifty pounds, there's a good girl—"

It wasn't hard to learn the life and ways of the house. Open the door and take the lady's coat, the gentleman's hat and stick. Serve from the left and remove from the right; don't chip the china or the crystal. Water the flowers; don't spill a drop on the tables, it turns the wood white. Bring in the tea things at five o'clock: remember Miss Thorne? Mrs. Werner and her friends come in from shopping; the chill air enters on their furs; their perfume smells like sugar. Learn how to use the telephone; you crank it on the wall, you give the number to central and put your mouth close to it when you talk. Be sure to write all messages accurately on the pad.

And when you are all finished in the evening, you may go up to your room, your own private room, with the row of books standing on the dresser. You can lie in bed and read, finish *The Cloister and the Hearth*—what a wonderful story! . . . and even have an orange or a bunch of grapes.

"Might as well eat them," Mrs. Monaghan says, "before they go bad."

"Yes," Mrs. Monaghan says, resting her elbows on the kitchen table, "rich people is queer, all right. The Mister's folks has got a place in the Adirondack Mountains, a big homely house made out of logs, like those pictures of Lincoln's cabin, only big. You look out the windows and all you can see is the lake and trees, not a living soul for miles. Gives you the positive creeps, I wouldn't pay a penny for it. Takes you all night to get there from here. You go up in a sleeper. Though I must say, that part of it is kind of an adventure.

"They was awfully good to my nephew Jimmy! After he broke his leg they took him and his sister Agnes up there with us for the whole summer. Jimmy and Mr. Paul is the same age, you know. They had a great time. When they was kids, I'm talking about. Jimmy works in a garage now and Mr. Paul's in the family bank. Did you know they own a bank? Big place, Quinn says. On Wall Street or somewheres.

"You'll like Mr. Paul, he's that nice and easy to like. They say he's smart, but he's that plain, you'd never know it. Except he keeps buying books all the time. There'll be no more room in the house for them soon, I'm thinking."

It is a treasury of books. Anna always takes her time doing his room. There are antique books on yellowed paper, in tiny print. There are volumes of vivid art: columned marble archways, palaces; mothers and children; women naked under casual scarves; even pictures of the cross and the hanging man (the peaceful expression while the blood oozes from the hands and feet!). Anna turns those pages quickly.

What kind of man is he who owns all these?

He arrives home early in September, taking the front steps two at a time, followed by Quinn and a pile of cases labeled: Lusitania, First Class.

It comes to Anna, standing in the front hall with the family, that she must, without thinking, have expected him to resemble his parents, to move neatly in small spaces as they do, to measure his speech neatly.

He moves, instead, like someone striding fields, too loose a person for narrow halls. His bright blue eyes (surprising eyes in a dark face!) look as if they have just finished laughing. He has brought presents for everyone and insists now on giving them out immediately.

"Perfume?" says Mrs. Monaghan. "And where would I be wearing perfume, an old woman like me?"

"To church, Mrs. Monaghan," Mr. Paul says firmly. The blue eyes twinkle: *Funny old soul, isn't she?* "There's no sin in bringing the smell of flowers to your prayers. Doesn't the Virgin herself wear flowers?"

"Oh, the glib tongue of him!"

"And a bottle for Agnes; she hasn't entered the convent yet, has she?"

"Not yet, and I don't think she will, although it'll break her father's and mother's heart if she don't."

"Oh, I hope not, Mrs. Monaghan." The laughter leaves his face. He says seriously, "Agnes must do what she must with her own life. That's her right and she oughtn't feel guilty about it."

Anna lies in bed that night unable to sleep. She thinks she hears her heart pounding. Whichever way she lies, on either side or on her back, she feels her heart. It seems to her suddenly that the world is full of sharp and beautiful excitement, that it will pass by. She is missing it all, she will work and die, having missed it all.

"Well, what did you think of Mr. Paul?" Mrs. Monaghan asks.

❦ 7 ❧

The vine grows imperceptibly during the night. In the morning it looks the same as it did the evening before. And then there comes a morning when one sees that it has grown halfway up the tree; how did that happen? It must have been growing all the while, because here it is, thick and strong, clinging so tenaciously that one can barely tear it away.

It is so ridiculous, so shameful to be thinking about Paul Werner all the time! How did it happen? She doesn't know a thing about him and she has no business knowing! He walks in one day, a stranger who scarcely knows that she exists, and he takes possession of her mind. Absurd!

In the morning, straightening his room after he and his father have gone to the office in their dark suits and hard, round hats, she has to hang his dressing gown in the closet and arrange his brushes on the bureau. Her hands tremble. It troubles her so to touch these things, to smell them (hair tonic, shaving lotion, pipe tobacco?). Often she hears his voice from the floor below. Knocking at the door of the upstairs study, he calls: "Father? Father?" Then afterward in her mind's ear the voice repeats, exact in tone and timbre: "Father? Father?" And all day long she hears it, while she is dusting the procelains, even while she is talking to Mrs. Monaghan at lunch.

Mrs. Monaghan likes to gossip about the family. They have, after all, been almost her entire world for so long. She tells about the cousins from Paris who came visiting. She tells about the daughter's wedding at the Plaza. "You should have seen the presents! It took a van to carry them out to Cleveland. We gave the bridesmaids' dinner here at home; twelve girls, and every one of them got a gold bracelet from the bride. The ice cream came from Sherry's, molded in wedding bells and hearts, oh, it was lovely!"

Mrs. Monaghan would be only too pleased to talk about Paul Werner. Anna could easily guide the conversation that way, but she is too ashamed, not because of the old woman, but because of herself.

When she looked in the mirror her face went hot with embarrassment. The house was full of mirrors. Ten times a day she met herself in apron and cap: a becoming cap, really, a lace coronet on her dark red hair which was now piled high because of course she could hardly wear braids anymore! Sometimes it seemed to Anna that she was a very pretty girl, and sometimes she thought she looked stupid in the cap and apron. Stupid like the organ grinder's pathetic monkey in his cap. She felt anger inside. Why should he look at anybody like her? Why should he? He hardly ever did look at her, except at breakfast and dinner, and he was often out for dinner. She wondered about the places where he must go and the girls who would be there, girls in taffeta and feathered hats like the occasional daughters who came calling with their mothers in the afternoon. At breakfast he only smiled, "Good morning, Anna," which he would have done if she had been Mrs. Monaghan. *Well, what did you expect, Anna, foolish Anna?* Mr. Werner always had some extra remark, some little pleasantry about the weather, all that cold stagnant winter, gray with snow: "Better put earmuffs on if you go out today, Anna, or you'll freeze your ears off."

But the son never said anything.

Whenever she had to talk to him it seemed he must know her thoughts, that they must be visible in her face. The saying of her few words, the delivery of a message (Mr. So-and-So called and will call again at nine o'clock) were made to seem so much more important than they could really have been. Then his answer would sound in her head: (Mr. So-and-So, you said? He will call back at nine?)

Why should one human being be drawn to another this way? Why?

"You aren't yourself," Joseph observed after some minutes' silence. They were having supper in the kitchen on Mrs. Monaghan's Sunday out. Mrs. Werner, having met Joseph once in the basement hall, had remarked that he was "a very nice young man," and that Anna was welcome to ask him to stay to dinner. "What's bothering you? Aren't you happy here?"

"To tell the truth, I don't like it so much."

"But you said the work was easy!"

"Oh, it's easy enough."

"What then?"

"I don't know, exactly."

"You're awfully secretive, Anna." Joseph's eyes were troubled.

She felt a wave of guilt because of her thoughts. He couldn't know what she was thinking: dull, he's gray and dull, no color in him.

"You're so good," she said. "You're so good. But don't worry about me, I'm all right."

"I think I know what it is," he said, brightening. "You're worried about your brothers. You miss them. That's it, isn't it?"

"I miss them, of course I do. But they're very well. Dan writes that he and Eli will be going to Paris with their boss the next time he goes."

Joseph shrugged. "Fine. But I can't understand why they would want to stay in Europe when they could come here."

Anna said, "I heard Mr. Paul telling somebody on the telephone that if he could be born again he would either choose France or northern Italy. He says Lake Como is the most beautiful place in the world."

"Bunk! Why doesn't he move there, then? The U.S.A. can get along without him, I'm sure."

"You don't have to be nasty about it!"

"I didn't mean to be. But talk like that makes me angry. People should be proud of this country and appreciate it. Especially a fellow like him, living in a house like this."

"He didn't mean anything, I'm sure." She spoke eagerly; she could almost hear the eagerness in her own voice. "But I suppose when you've always lived like this you take it for granted. You don't see how wonderful it is."

"Yes, after your family's put a fortune into your lap you can afford to take it for granted."

"Joseph, you're envious, that's all."

"Of course I am!" He leaned forward in the chair, all tense and tightly wound. "I'll tell you something. I hope the day will come when my children will be able to take these things for granted. Only I hope they won't do it. I hope they'll have a little feeling for the father and the country that gave it all to them. Other than that, I don't care what they do, raise chickens, for all I care." He sighed. "Ah, when you have money you can do anything. Money is class and class is money, even in America. Because human nature is the same everywhere, and that's the truth."

"I suppose it is," she answered, not caring to hear his philosophy.

"Anna, are you really all right?"

"Yes," she said impatiently, "I told you I was."

"Would you tell me if anything were wrong? If you were sick or anything?"

"I would tell you, I promise." She stood up, went to the stove and took the kettle down for tea.

Last night in her room, while reading, she had come upon a word she did not know. She had looked it up in the dictionary. Obsession: persistent feeling which a person cannot escape. She thought now, pouring Joseph's tea, handing the plate of buns, clearing the table, moving dreamlike across the room, *Obsessed. I am obsessed.*

Anna was still working in his room when Paul Werner came home unexpectedly one Saturday before noon.

"I'm sorry," she said. "I'll hurry, I didn't know."

"That's all right! You didn't know I was coming back early," he said considerately. "Oh! You're interested in paintings?"

She had left one of the enormous books opened on the desk. "Excuse me! I only—"

"No, don't close it! What were you looking at? Monet?"

"This," she faltered. A walled and fruited garden. A woman in a summer dress. Sunlight without heat: cool, fragrant and cool.

"Ah yes, that's a marvel, isn't it? One of my favorites, too. Tell me, do you look at these often?"

Might as well tell the truth, come what may. And he was young, not stern like his mother; he would not be very angry.

"I look at that one especially. Every day."

"You do!" he said. "And why that one?"

"It makes me happy to look at it. To think that there is such a place."

"That's as good a reason as any. Would you like to borrow the book, Anna? Take it to your room for a while? You're welcome to take it, or any book you like."

"Oh, thank you," she said, "oh, thank you very much." Her hands had begun to tremble. She was sure he could see the trembling and she clasped them behind her back.

"Don't thank me. Libraries are meant to be used. Here, take it now."

"I haven't finished sweeping the floor. Do you want me to finish?"

"Go ahead, I don't mind. I've a letter to write."

He sat down at the desk. She ran the carpet sweeper over the floor. Downstairs in the yard next door men were beating carpets hung over clotheslines. *Thwack! Thwack!* they went, frightening the sparrows, raising spurts of dust in the chill sunny air.

"How is your young man?"

She looked up, startled.

"I said, how is your young man?"

"My what?"

"Your young man. My mother told me you have one. Is he a secret? Have I said something I shouldn't have said?"

"Oh, no! It's just that—he's only a friend. It would be too lonesome without any friends at all."

"I should think it would." He put the pen down. "Do you see him often?"

"Only on Sundays. On my day off he has to work."

"And which is your day off?"

He hadn't even noticed when she wasn't there. "I go out on Wednesdays."

"And where do you go when you go out?"

"Sometimes I visit my cousin downtown. Sometimes I walk in the park or go to the museum."

"You do! What museum do you go to?"

"The Natural History. Or the art museum. I like that the best."

"What do you like there?"

"It's so big, I haven't seen it all yet. But I liked the Egyptian things. . . . And last week I found Cleopatra's Needle out behind the building. I had missed it before."

He shook his head. "I'm thinking, Anna, how strange it is that here we've been living under the same roof for all these months and we've never talked until today!"

"Not so strange, when you think about it."

"You mean, because it's my parents' house and you just work in it."

She nodded.

"Isn't that artificial, though? Isn't that stupid? But thank goodness that sort of thing is changing. People make friends where they find them nowadays, not just in the same little group that their families grew up with. Much better that way, isn't it?"

"Oh, yes, much better!"

"Tell me something about yourself, Anna."

"I don't know what you want to hear."

"What your parents did, what your home was like, what made you leave it."

"But I can't now. I have to go downstairs, I have work."

"Next Saturday morning, then. Or whenever else we can find the time. Will you?"

THEY FOUND THE time, odd minutes of it, on Saturday mornings, or in the hallway after dinner—he standing in the doorway of his room, she standing by the staircase, whenever she happened to be going up or down on some errand or other. She told him about her village. He told her about their Adirondack camp. She told him about her father. He told her about Yale. She thought of their talk as a game, a ball going back and forth over a net. She was as breathless as though it had been a game. She sang as she went about the house, and had to catch herself. She laughed a lot and was aware of it.

One day halfway through spring, he said: "Tell your friend not to come next Sunday. I want to take you to tea."

"But I don't see how we can! I don't think—"

"What don't you think? I want to talk to you, to sit down and have a proper talk!"

She hesitated and felt a creeping fear.

"Nobody needs to know, if that's what you're worried about. Although there's nothing to hide! I'm not asking you to do anything to be ashamed of."

They sat on gilded chairs with a screen of palms at their backs. A waiter brought cakes on a little cart. Violins waltzed.

"You look really beautiful, Anna, especially in that hat."

He had insisted on buying the hat for her. When she had protested he had bought it anyway, a magnificent straw hat crowned with red silk poppies and wheat.

"I can't take it," she had said. "It wouldn't be right."

"Oh, damn the proprieties, how idiotic they are! Here am I, a man with plenty of money to spend, and here are you, a girl who needs a spring hat and hasn't got enough money for a nice one. Why shouldn't I make myself happy by giving it to you?"

"You make it sound so simple," Anna had said.

"It is simple. Take it and wear it to tea."

So here she sat, the greenhorn Anna, in this vast perfumed room, watching the people come and go, all the tall, easy, graceful people who belonged here.

"I've been thinking a lot about you, Anna. You're so young and already you've done so much with your life."

"What have I done? Nothing, it seems to me."

"But you have! You've taken your life into your own hands, coming across the world by yourself, learning a new language to get along in—"

"I've never thought about it like that."

"While I have only been acted upon. You see what I mean? I was born in the house where I live now; I was sent to school, then put into my father's, actually my grandfather's, business. It's all been done for me. I don't really know anything at all about what the world is like."

"That's what I think about myself!" Anna laughed.

"You are absolutely lovely when you laugh. I go all over the city, and do you know, I never see girls as lovely as you?"

"Why, right here this minute there are such beautiful girls! Look over there at that one with the yellow dress, and that one, coming through the door—"

"Not like you. You're different from them all. There's wonder in your face. You're alive. Most of these people wear a mask. They're tired of everything."

Tired of everything? How could that be? You would need to live a hundred years to see everything you wanted to see, and then that wouldn't be enough.

The orchestra struck up a charming, spritely dance. "How I love the sound of violins!" she cried.

"You've never been at the opera, have you, Anna?"

"No, never."

"My mother has a ticket for the matinee tomorrow, but we're all going to my great-aunt Julia's funeral. I'm going to ask her to give it to you."

THE MUSIC QUESTIONS and insists. It asks *Where?* and answers *Here!* Asks *When?* and answers *Now!*

She leans forward in her seat. Two large ladies in the row ahead have dared to whisper. She taps one on the shoulder, mighty in her outrage.

"Will you be quiet, madam?"

Ashamed, they stop talking and she leans back again. The music swells and rises. The angelic voice of Isolde soars above it. All grief, all longing, all joy are in that radiant song. Tristan replies: the shimmering voices twine and fuse into one.

It is all here: the girl-child's ignorant dream of love and the passion of the woman. It is all here: flowers, sunlight, stars, rapture and death.

I know, I know, she thinks.

She does not move. Her hands are clasped.

It ends. The storm rests and the tension breaks. The final chords sound quietly and die.

Her eyes are wet; she cannot find her handkerchief. The tears fall on her collar. The great curtain falls and the marvelous beings who have pretended to be Tristan and Isolde come before it, bowing and smiling. Applause clatters, people stand to clap. In the rear young men are calling: "Bravo! Bravo!" People are twisting into their coat sleeves. And Anna sits there, unwilling to return from the Breton coast and the summer sea, from dying Tristan, the clasping arms—

The lady in the next seat is curious. "You liked it?"

"I—pardon?"

"I asked whether you liked it?"

"It was—it was heaven! I never imagined there could be—"

"Yes, it was a very fine performance." The lady agrees, nodding pleasantly, and steps out into the aisle.

IN THE EVENING Mr. and Mrs. Werner paid a condolence call and Mrs. Monaghan went to the basement to iron her Sunday shirtwaist. Anna climbed the stairs to her room. When she came to the landing at the floor below it seemed entirely natural that he should be waiting for her there.

She clung to him. The wall at her back, which was all that held up her weak legs, was warm and firm. The man was warm and firm, but soft, too; his mouth, wandering over her neck and face, was soft. Finding her mouth it fitted there with a long, long sigh.

Her eyes shut; things spun in a luminous dark.

He broke away. "You're so lovely, Anna! I can't tell you how beautiful you are."

She was dazed, re-entering the light. Gently, he guided her to the last flight of stairs. She thought, between fright and glory, that he was going upstairs with her.

"We must—you must go upstairs," he said gently, and went to his room.

She stood for a long time looking at herself in the mirror. She raised her nightgown. Statues in the museum had breasts like hers. At Cousin Ruth's she had seen women undressed; some had enormous, shapeless mounds; some sagged into long, flattened tubes; others had almost no breasts at all. She took the pins out of her hair, letting it slant across her forehead and fall over her shoulders. The hair felt warm on her bare shoulders. Music sounded in her head, a lovely flow, Isolde's song. He would not have kissed her like that if he did not love her. Now surely a great change had come into her life. A greater change was coming. Now surely.

From the yards below where the clotheslines ran from fence to fence came a wild, lonely cry, the wail of a lost child. Anna started. But then she thought, *It's only cats* and turning out the light, smiled into the darkness and fell asleep.

❧{8}❧

In the morning Mrs. Monaghan said, "Company tonight, you know. My niece Agnes will be coming to help. Just a family dinner, the madam says, but sounds fancy to me. Turtle soup, lobster mousse, lamb. She wants you to go up with her now to set the table."

The dining room glittered with crystal, lace and silver. Silver platters and candelabra. Silver bowls for the chocolates and the roses.

"Some of these pieces are almost two hundred years old," Mrs. Werner explained. "This coffeepot belonged to my great-great-grandmother Mendoza. See, here's the M."

"They brought all this from Europe?"

"No, this is American silver. My people came here from Portugal a hundred years before this was made."

"So different from me," Anna said.

"Not really, Anna. Just an accidental turn of history, that's all. People are the same everywhere." Mrs. Werner's rare smile softened her cool face.

There's something about her that's like Mama, Anna thought. I never noticed it before. Something dependable and strong. I would like to put my arms around her. It would be good to have a mother again. I wonder whether she knows anything?

Mrs. Werner was handsome in dark red silk. She had wonderful white shoulders for an old woman, over forty. The guests at the table looked like a family: parents, a grandmother and two sisters about Anna's age. They had fair, freckled skin; their prominent, arched noses made their faces proud.

"I'd much rather go to Europe," one of the sisters said. She wore blue lawn and her long pearl earrings moved like little tassels.

"Still, a month in the White Mountains is so lovely, don't you think?" the grandmother remarked. "I always come back utterly exhausted from Europe."

Anna moved around the table, passing and repassing the silver platters, pouring ice water out of the silver pitcher. Be careful not to spill. That's Valenciennes lace on the grandmother's collar. Mrs. Monaghan told me about Valenciennes. I'm glad he's not looking at me. Shall I see him later?

Talk circled the table with Anna. Flashes of it sparked in her ears.

46

"The Kaiser is a madman, I don't care what they say—"

"I hear they've sold their place in Rumson—"

"This outrageous income tax, Wilson's a radical—"

"—bought the most magnificent brocade at Milgrim's."

"Ask Mrs. Monaghan and Agnes to come in, will you please, Anna?" Mr. Werner whispered.

She was not sure she had understood and he repeated it. "Then bring the champagne," he added.

He poured three extra glasses and handed them to Agnes, Mrs. Monaghan and Anna. Then he raised his own glass, and everyone waited.

"I don't know how to tell you how happy we are. So I'll just ask everyone to drink to the joy of this wonderful day in all our lives. To the future of our son Paul and to Marian, who will soon be our daughter."

The wine goblets touched, making chimes. Mr. Werner got up and kissed the cheeks of the girl in pale blue. The girl said something, very sweetly, very calmly, and made the others laugh. The laughter popped like champagne corks.

Mrs. Werner said, "Now I can confess that this is what we've been hoping for ever since you two were children."

Someone else said, "What a wonderful thing for our two families!"

And Mrs. Monaghan said, "The saints bless us, another wedding in this house!"

Only *he* had said nothing. He must have said something, though, something she hadn't heard. But it was all swimming, blurred and faint and far away—

Back in the pantry, Mrs. Monaghan whispered, "Anna! Go pass the cake for second helpings!"

Anna leaned against the cupboard. "The cake?"

"The walnut cake on the sideboard! What on earth is wrong with you?"

"I don't know. I'm going to be sick."

"Jesus, Mary and Joseph, but you do look green! Don't upchuck in my kitchen! Agnes, here, take her apron and go back to the dining room. That's the girl! And you, Anna, get upstairs, I'll look to you later. What have you gone and done to yourself? Of all times!"

"You're feeling better this morning, Anna?" Mrs. Werner was troubled. "Mrs. Monaghan told me you wanted to leave. I couldn't believe it."

Anna struggled up in bed. "I know it isn't right to leave you so suddenly, but I don't feel well."

"You must let us call the doctor!"

"No, no, I can go to my cousin's house downtown. They'll get a doctor."

Mrs. Werner coughed lightly. The cough meant: *This is nonsense because both of us know what's the matter with you.* Or possibly it meant: *I can't imagine what's come over you but I am obligated to find out.*

"Is there anything you want to tell me, Anna?"

"Nothing. I'll be all right. It's nothing." No tears. No tears. *He kissed my mouth. He told me I was beautiful. And so I am, much more than she.*

"Well, then, I don't understand." Mrs. Werner's hands clasped the bed rail.

Her diamonds went *prink! twink!* "Won't you talk to me, trust me? After all, I'm old enough to be your mother."

"But you're not my mother," Anna said. *An accidental turn of history, was it? People are the same, are they?*

"Well, I can't stop you if you've made up your mind. So when you're ready I'll have Quinn take you in the car." At the door Mrs. Werner paused. "If you ever want to come back, Anna, you'll be welcome. Or if there's anything we can do for you, call us, won't you?"

"Thank you, Mrs. Werner. But I won't come back."

On a damp night a few weeks later Joseph and Anna sat on the front stoop talking. The sun was down. In the last light boys played a final game of stickball on the street. One by one their mothers called them in with long, shrill cries: Benn-ie, Loo-ey! Peddlers led their tired nags back to the stables on Delancey Street, the shaggy heads sunk, the shaggy hooves trudging. The life of the street ebbed away.

They talked about this and that, fell silent and talked again. After a while Joseph told Anna that he loved her. He asked her whether she would marry him. And she answered that she would.

❧{9}❧

He worshiped her. His eyes and his hands moved over her body and worshiped her. In the new brass double bed which he had bought he raised himself on his elbow and studied her.

"Pink and white," he said. He twisted a length of her hair around his wrist, her slippery, living hair. He laughed and shook his head in wonder. "Perfect. Even your voice and the way you pronounce 'th.' Perfect."

"I'll never speak English without a foreign accent. A greenhorn, I am."

"And you've read more, you're more clever than anybody I know."

"Just a greenhorn, Joseph," she insisted.

"If you'd had a chance at an education, half a chance, you could have been something, a teacher, even a doctor or a lawyer. You could."

Sighing, she stretched out her hand, the one with the wide gold band on which he had had engraved "J to A, May 16, 1913." "I'm a wife," she said aloud.

"How do you feel about it?"

She did not answer at once. He followed her gaze through the door to the yellow-painted kitchen and the clean, new linoleum on the parlor floor. Everything was clean in the home he had prepared for her. Unfortunately, the rooms were level with the street so that the shades had to be drawn all day. When you raised the shades you could see feet passing on the street, at eye level. You could crane out to see the Hudson and the Palisades, and feel the fresh river wind. At night the bedroom was a closed private world, the bed a ship on a dark quiet sea.

"How do you feel about it?" he repeated. This time she turned to him and laid her hands lightly over his. "I feel peaceful," she said.

She stretched and yawned, covering her mouth. Ten chimes struck delicately from the clock on Joseph's dresser.

"Pompous, silly thing," Anna cried.

"What, the clock? I don't know what you've got against that beautiful clock. You just don't like the people who gave it to us."

One day, a few months after their marriage, a delivery man had brought a package from Tiffany.

"He looked puzzled," Anna said. "I don't suppose he's ever delivered in this neighborhood before."

It was a gilded French mantel clock. Joseph had placed it carefully on the

49

kitchen table and wound it. Through the glass sides they had watched its exquisite rotating gears and wheels.

"I knew the Werners were going to give us a present," he had said. "I wasn't to
tell you, but they sent their chauffeur down to Ruth's to ask about your health
and she told him we were married. Aren't you pleased? You don't seem pleased."

"I'm not," she had answered.

"I can't understand," he remarked now, "why you resent those people so. It's
not like you, you're always so kind."

"I'm sorry. Yes, it was good of them to do. But it's too rich for this house.
We've no place to put it, even."

"True. But we'll have a better place someday. Good enough for this and your
silver candlesticks, too."

"Joseph, don't strain so much, don't work so hard. I'm satisfied the way we are
now."

"Satisfied with a basement flat on Washington Heights?"

"It's the best place I've ever lived in."

"What about the Werner house?"

"I don't really *live* there. It wasn't mine."

"Well, it ought to be. That's the way I want you to live. You will live like that,
too. You'll see, Anna."

"It's after ten," she chided him softly. "And you have to be up by five."

Anna's breathing whispered in the dark. She moved her legs and the sheet rustled.
Footsteps hurried, clacking on the sidewalk only a few feet from his head. The
little clock went *ting!* eleven times. There was no sleep in him, only a rush of
thoughts, sharp and clear, one after the other, clear as etching on glass.

He worried. It seemed to him that as far back as he could recall he had always
known worry. His parents worried. All the people in the houses on Ludlow
Street, all the way over to the East River, worried. They worried about today and
tomorrow. They even worried about yesterday. They were never able to let yesterday die.

Naturally, he had never seen the Old Country, yet he knew it well. It was a
landscape of his life as surely as the street and the five-story tenements, the
crowds and the pushcarts. He knew the Polish village, his grandfather's horse, the
frozen walls of snow, the sliding mud, the bathhouse, the cantor who came from
Lublin for the holidays, the herring and potatoes on the table, his mother's baby
sister who died in childbirth, his grandmother's cousin who went to Johannesburg and made a fortune in diamonds. He knew all these, as well as the terror of
hooves on the road and the whistle of whips, the heavy breathing in the silence
behind closed shutters, the rush of flames when a torch is put to a roof and the
sigh of ashes settling in the morning breeze.

The burning of Uncle Simon's house had been the act that decided his parents. They were a strange couple, still without children, so without reason for
living, no? (What else is there to live for but to have children and push them up,
healthy and learned, to a region higher than your own? That's what it's all about,
isn't it?) But they had none, and his mother grew old before her time. Not fat and

old from birthing and nurturing, but dry-old, pinched-old, empty-old. She had a stall in the market, and was known for her charity. His father was a tailor with round shoulders and red eyelids. He sighed as he worked, unaware that he was sighing. When he put his machine away he went to the synagogue. When he had said his prayers he went home. Tailor shop, synagogue and home, the triangle of his days. Why should such a pair bother to go to America? For what?

Then came the burning and something galvanized the husband.

"Your father came in," his mother said. "The village was quiet. They had burned five houses, not ours, but it was an awful thing to see your neighbors, the women crying and the men just standing there, looking. So your father came in and he said, 'We are going to America, Katie.' Just like that he said it, and no more than that."

"Did you want to come? Were you scared?" Joseph used to ask.

"It was all so fast, I didn't have time to think. We got our tickets, I said good-by to my sisters, and we were at Castle Garden."

"And then what happened, Ma?"

"What happened?" Her eyebrows went up, rising in a semicircle under her stiff and fading wig. "As you see, we opened a tailor shop. We ate, we lived. The only difference was that here everybody was all jumbled up, without grass, without trees." For an instant there was slight regret in her voice. "Also no pogroms, no killing and burning."

"And that was all?" Joseph used to press, waiting for the next part, the important part.

His mother played along. "Of course all! What else should there be?"

"I mean, nothing else happened to you after you came here?"

His mother would frown a moment, pretending to be puzzled. "Oh, yes, of course, one other thing! We were here two years—a little more, actually—when you were born."

Joseph would stifle a smile of pleasure. When he was very young, at seven or eight, he liked to hear this part. Later, whenever the subject of his birth arose, he would frown and wince inside, would change the subject or leave the room. There was something ridiculous in such old people having their first, totally unexpected child. He was the only one of his friends who had parents like his; more like grandparents, they seemed. The other boys had thin agile fathers and mothers, who moved about the streets quickly, yelling and running after their children.

His father, heavy and slow-moving, sat all day behind the sewing machine. When he stood up he was stiff, he moved awkwardly, grunting and shuffling to the back rooms where they ate and slept, and to the toilet in the yard. On Saturday he shuffled to the synagogue, came home and ate, lay down again on the cot in the kitchen and slept the afternoon away.

"Shh!" Ma would admonish when Joseph banged the door, "Your father's asleep!" And her warning finger would go to her lips.

At night Pa would move from the cot to the bed where he slept with Ma. Where they would—? No, not decent to think about that. You couldn't imagine him doing— He was so quiet. Except now and then when he fell into a terrible rage, always over some trivial thing. His face would flame, the cords stand out on his temples and in his neck. Ma said that someday he would kill himself like that, which was exactly what happened. Much later, of course.

The house smelled of sleep, of dullness and poverty. There was no *life* in it, no future. You felt that what had already been done there was all that ever would be done. Joseph spent as few hours there as he could.

"What, going out again?" Pa would ask, shaking his head. "You're always out."

"A boy needs companions, Max." His mother defended him. "And as long as we know he's in good company— He only goes to play at the Baumgartens' or over to your own cousin Solly."

Solly Levinson was a second or third cousin of Pa's, only five years older than Joseph. Joseph could remember him in that first brief year after his arrival in this country at the age of twelve, that first and only year when he went to school, before he began to work in the garment trade. He had learned English astonishingly quickly; he was bright and timid, or perhaps only gentle and hesitant. Strange how he metamorphosed after five children and fifteen years of working on pants! As different from what he had been as the caterpillar is from the butterfly. Strange and sad and wrong, Joseph thought, remembering Solly teaching him to dive in the East River, Solly playing stickball, wiry and fast. He had come from a very rural place in Europe, had swum in rivers, had known how to move and run. Such a brightness in him! And now all quenched.

Anyway, Joseph had liked to go to Solly's. The rest of the time he lived on the street.

His father complained. The streets were dangerous, full of bad influences. He heard his parents talking, often in his presence, more often from behind the drawn curtain that separated his cot in the kitchen from their bed in the back room.

"Bad influences," his father said again. Gloom and foreboding. Joseph knew he was talking about the boys who had gone socialist and worse, the boys who stood in knots on the sidewalk, lounging on the synagogue steps to taunt the worshipers, even smoking on the Sabbath, while the old men with their derby hats and beards looked the other way.

"Joseph is a good boy," his mother said. "You don't have to worry about him, Max."

"Show me a mother who doesn't say her son is a good boy."

"Max! What does he ever do that's bad? Be sensible!"

"True, true." Silence. And then he would hear, how many times had he not heard? "I wish we could do more for him."

Now Joseph understood, but even then when he was a child he had begun to understand, to pick up truths about his parents and the life around him. He knew that his father, like most of the fathers, was ashamed of doing even worse for his family in America than he had done in Europe. He was ashamed of not speaking the language, so that when the gas man came to ask a question about the meter, an eight-year-old son had to interpret. Ashamed of the meager food on the table toward the end of the month when the money was being scrimped together for the rent. Ashamed of the noise, the jumbled living in the midst of crowds and other people's scandals. The Mandels upstairs, the terrible screaming fights and Mr. Mandel leaving, disappearing "uptown," Mrs. Mandel's bitter weeping and scolding. Why should a decent family be subjected to the indecencies of others? Yet there was no escape from it.

The father was ashamed too of the dirt. He hated it. From him Joseph knew he had inherited his extreme love of cleanliness and order. For a man to love those things in a place where there was little cleanliness and no order!

They used to go to the baths together once a week, Pa and Joseph. In a way the child dreaded it, the smell of the steam and the press of naked men. How ugly old bodies were! And yet, in another way, it was the only time they ever talked together, really talked, there in the steam and later on the five blocks' walk home.

Sometimes he was subjected to homilies: "Do right, Joseph. Every man knows what right is and he knows too when he has done something dishonest or unjust. He may tell others and himself that he doesn't know, but he does know. Do right and life will reward you."

"But sometimes wicked people are rewarded too, aren't they, Pa?"

"Not really. It may seem so on the surface, but not really."

"What about the Czar? How cruel he is, and yet he lives in a palace!"

"Ah, but he hasn't lived his life out yet!"

Joseph considered that doubtfully. His father said with firmness, "When you do wrong, you pay. Maybe not right away, but you always pay." And then he said, "Would you like a banana? I've a penny here, and you can buy two at the corner. One for your mother."

"What about you, Pa?"

"I don't like bananas," his father lied.

When Joseph was ten Pa's sight went bad. First he had to hold the paper very far away. Then after a while he wasn't able to read it at all. Joseph's mother had never learned to read. In the Old Country it wasn't essential for a girl to learn, although some did, of course. So Joseph had to read the paper in the evening, because his father wanted to know what was going on in the world. But it was difficult; Joseph didn't read Yiddish very well and he knew his father wasn't satisfied.

For a while Pa had struggled on in the tailoring shop, hunching lower and lower in the yellow flame from the gaslight, for even at noon the daylight was shut out by the fire escapes outside the window. When it was evident that he could work no more they had closed the shop and his mother became the unacknowledged breadwinner.

The store was the square "front room," with the counter running across the back and the large brown icebox standing at one side. In the two rear rooms separated by a dark green cloth curtain, they lived, their arrangements the same as they had been in the tailor shop two blocks away. The kitchen table was covered with oilcloth once blue, now a spoiled gray. Here they ate and here his mother made the potato salad and the coleslaw that went into the brown refrigerator in the store along with the soda bottles and the milk. Bread was stacked on the counter; coffee, sugar and spices stood on the shelves; crackers and candy were in boxes and barrels on the floor, along with the pickles floating in their scummy brine. A bell jangled when the door was opened. In the summer you didn't hear the bell because the screen door's spring was broken. His father never knew how to fix anything, so the door hung open. Curving bands of yellow flypaper hung from the ceiling fixture, and huge black flies collected on it, disgusting flies, black and wet when they were squashed, bred in the horsedroppings on the street. . . . Strange that his father, who was so fastidious, didn't seem to mind them, Joseph thought, until he realized that the old man didn't see them.

From six o'clock in the morning until ten at night his mother stood behind the counter. Not that they were so busy; it was just that one never knew when someone might come in to buy. Sometimes the jangling bell would ring past ten at night.

"Oh, Mrs. Friedman, I saw the light, I hope it's not too late. We're out of coffee."

For the neighborhood it was a convenience, a place where one could go at odd hours to pick up something one had forgotten, after the markets had closed and the pushcarts were covered with tarpaulins and guarded for the night. A small convenience. A small living.

"Max Friedman," read the sign above the door. It should have read, "Katie Friedman." Even at the age of ten Joseph was able to understand the tragedy in that.

H E HAD A snapshot of himself sitting in front of the store, the first picture taken of him since his infant portrait when he lay naked on the photographer's fur rug. He was twelve years old, in knickers and cap, high shoes and long black stockings.

"How solemn you were!" Anna said when she saw it. "You look as though you had the weight of the world on your shoulders."

Not the weight of the world, but a great one, nevertheless. For that was the year when he went from childhood to adult knowledge in one night. Well, make it two or three nights, at the most.

Wolf Harris came into the store one day where Joseph was helping after school. He was some very remote relative of Solly's on the other side of Solly's family. He was eighteen and aptly named. His nose was thin; his large mouth was always drawn back in a scornful smile.

"Want to make some money, kid? Mr. Doyle wants a kid to run messages for him."

"Doyle?" Pa had come from his chair next to the stove. "Why should Mr. Doyle need my son?"

"Because. He needs a boy he can trust to deliver stuff on time, not to lose things. He'll give him a dollar and a half a week to come in after school every day."

A dollar and a half! But Doyle was rich, Doyle was from Tammany Hall. He was Power, Government, Authority. Nobody knew exactly what he did, but they did know you could go to him for anything. He had no prejudice. Astonishing America, where the government didn't care whether you were Chinese, Hungarian or Jewish! If you needed money for a funeral or a ton of coal or somebody in the family was in trouble, you could ask Doyle and he would take care of it. All you had to do in return was to mark the square he told you to mark on election day.

Pa went inside and Joseph heard his parents talking for a minute or two. Then Pa came back.

"Tell Mr. Doyle," he said to Wolf, "that my son will be happy to work for him and we thank him, his mother and I."

Doyle had a dignified office near Tammany Hall on Fourteenth Street. Every day after school Joseph went over through the front room where a row of girls sat at their typing machines and down the corridor to the back where he knocked and was admitted. Doyle was bald and ruddy. He had a stickpin in his tie and a ring on his finger which Wolf said was a real sapphire, "worth a fortune." He liked to joke. He would offer Joseph a cigar or pretend to hand him a coin: "Go down to Tooey's Bar and get yourself a beer." And then he would always give a treat, an apple or a chocolate bar, before sending him on his errands.

Doyle owned a lot of property. He owned two houses on the street where Joseph lived, as a matter of fact. Sometimes Joseph had to deliver papers to plumbers or tinsmiths and others having to do with Doyle's houses. Sometimes he had to take envelopes to saloons, or pick up papers there that felt thick, as though there might be money inside. He learned to go right in at the front door and ask for the proprietor, who was usually behind the bar, behind the bar with the glittering bottles and the painting of a naked lady. The first time he saw a painting like that his eyes almost popped out. The men at the bar saw what he was looking at and thought it was very funny. They told jokes that he didn't understand, and he felt uncomfortable. But it was worth it. A dollar and a half! Just for walking around the city carrying envelopes!

One day Mr. Doyle asked to see his handwriting. He got a sheet of paper and said, "Now, write something, anything, I don't care what."

When Joseph had written very neatly, *Joseph Friedman, Ludlow Street, New York, United States of America, Western Hemisphere, World, Universe,* Doyle took the paper away and said, "Very nice, very nice . . . how are you on arithmetic?"

"It's my best subject."

"Is it, now! Well, what do you know! How would you like to do a bit of writing and arithmetic for me? Would you like that, you think?"

And as Joseph looked puzzled, he said, "Here, I'll show you. See these two ledgers? Brand new, nothing written in them? I'll show you what I want. I want you to copy down in these from the lists that I'll give you. See here, a list like this, with names and doll—numbers, never mind what it's for, you don't need to go into all that. . . . Just copy all the names in this ledger with these numbers, see? And then put the same names in the other ledger with these other numbers, see? Think you can do it?"

"Oh, sure, sir, I can do it. That's easy."

"It's important to be accurate, you understand. Take your time. I don't want any mistakes."

"Oh, no, sir, I won't make any mistakes."

"Good. So that's what you'll be doing from now on. You'll work at the desk all by yourself in that little room next to mine, and nobody'll bother you. When you're finished you'll hand the ledgers back to me. And Joseph, one other thing. You're a good religious boy, aren't you? I mean, you go to synagogue regularly, don't tell lies?"

"No, sir, I mean yes, sir, and I don't tell lies."

"You know God punishes you when you do wrong."

"That's what Pa says."

"Of course. Then I can depend on you to keep your word. Never to talk about what you write in the books. Never to mention the books to anybody at all. It's just between you and me. Government business, you understand."

Doyle was very pleased with him. Wolf told him so. And one day when Doyle was in the neighborhood he came into the store and talked to his parents.

"Your son's a very smart boy. Dependable, too. A lot of kids, you can't count on them. They say they'll come to work, then they go play ball or loaf around and forget."

"Joseph's a good boy," Pa said.

"What do you plan to do with him? What's he going to be?"

His father shrugged. "I don't know. He's young yet. He should stay in school, maybe go to college. But we have no money."

"He'd make a topnotch accountant. And there's always money around for a smart boy like him. When the time comes, I'll see that he gets a chance. He could go to N.Y.U. Just tell him to stick with me."

"Could be only nice talk," his mother remarked that evening. "To make the parents feel good, telling them what a fine boy they have."

But Wolf said otherwise. "He thinks a lot of you, he means it. He wants you to study accounting. He can do it, too. He can get anything done, lay his hands on money whenever he needs it."

Joseph was curious about what Wolf did for Doyle. There were always so many people around Doyle, you could never figure out what they all did. Some were connected with the police and fire departments, others had to do with building inspections or the courts, with Doyle's real estate or with elections, a maze of businesses and interests. Wolf lived with an older brother; he always wore good clothes and had cash in his pocket. But you would never ask Wolf about anything personal. There was a distance between him and you. It was hard to say why; there was just something that put you at a distance.

Joseph had a best friend, Benjie Baumgarten. They walked to school together and back, went to the synagogue on the Sabbath and sat together and confided everything in one another. Benjie was curious about Wolf and Doyle.

"What do you do for him?" he pressed.

"Run errands. And write records."

"What sort of errands? And what do you write?"

"It's confidential. Business," Joseph said importantly.

"Oh, you dumb ass! Sure, private business with the Governor, I'll bet. Or the President, maybe."

"No, really." Benjie was envious, of course. Joseph could afford to be tolerant, lofty. "I'd tell you if I could, but I promised. You wouldn't want me to break a promise to you, would you?"

"No . . ."

They were crouched on the cellar stairs in number eleven, an abandoned building down the street from Joseph's house. The house had been condemned and the tenants had all moved out, except for some tramps, who, everybody knew, slept in the basement to get out of the cold.

Benjie had brought a plug of chewing tobacco which they were trying for the first time. This was a good place to avoid being seen.

"The sign says keep out—penalty of the law," Benjie said. "What'll happen if the owner catches us?"

"Nothing. Mr. Doyle is the owner, if you want to know. Well, a part-owner anyway. He wouldn't mind." Joseph felt important.

So they were hiding under the stairs, feeling faintly nauseated and neither one willing to admit it to the other, when the door in the yard creaked open and a wedge of late afternoon light appeared. Wolf Harris came in, carrying a can.

They drew back, making no sound. The can was filled with some liquid, which Wolf poured out as he moved around among the empty boxes, piled newspapers and broken baby carriages. When he had emptied the can he went softly out and closed the door. The fumes of kerosene rose up the staircase.

"Now why do you suppose he did that?" Benjie whispered. "I'm going out to ask him."

"You shut up!"

"Why should I!"

"Because. Wolf told me never to talk to him unless he talked to me first. Not to speak to him on the street, especially when he was with somebody else."

"That's funny. I wonder why?"

"I never asked him."

"You scared of him?"

"Yeah, a little."

"He's got a fierce temper, Wolf has. Once I saw him beat up a guy and break his nose. The blood came like water out of a pump."

"You never told me!"

"Well, it happened!"

"I believe you."

"Why do you work for Doyle?"

"What's Doyle got to do with what we're talking about?"

"Nothing. I just wondered."

"Because we need the money, stupid!" He wasn't going to mention anything about the accountancy course. Benjie might get the idea and horn in on it. Friend or no friend.

"Wolf scares me," Benjie said irrelevantly.

"Oh, shut up, will you!"

Joseph felt suddenly uneasy. The tobacco juice puckered his mouth. "I'm going home," he said.

The fire sirens woke him during the night, they and the noise of the crowd in the street. He and his parents got up and went outside. Number eleven down the block was blazing. Smoke, blown by the wind from the East River, stretched in ribbons across the sky. Flames exploded like rockets inside the tenement. Their light went surging from the first floor to the second, to the third. On the third floor faces appeared at the windows; arms moved in anguish.

"Tramps!" Ma cried. "My God, the house is full of tramps and they can't get out!"

Of course. In the winter, most people puttied the windows shut to keep out the cold.

"Oh, my God," Pa said.

The fire burned all night. Its flames warmed the night air all down the street. The water from the fire hoses froze on the sidewalks. The fire horses neighed at the flames and stamped their huge feet. Toward morning the fire burned out. The interior of the building had been hollowed; the blackened stone front was a jagged ruin. There were seven known dead. The crowds came silently to stare.

Joseph was very quiet. All day at school he turned things over in his mind: to tell Pa first and then Mr. Doyle? Or to go straight to Doyle? He wanted to talk it over with Benjie but Benjie had not come to school that morning.

On the way home at three o'clock Benjie hailed him. "I went over to see your boss this morning, Joseph."

"You went to see Mr. Doyle?"

"I told him I knew who set the fire. I told him about Wolf and the kerosene."

"Did you tell him I was with you?" Joseph demanded.

"Oh," Benjie said, "I'm sorry. I didn't. I guess I wanted to take all the credit myself."

Well, he had no one to blame but himself. Why hadn't he thought of staying out of school today and running over to Mr. Doyle's? Then Wolf would be arrested and Joseph would have been the hero instead of Benjie. Slow, like Pa. Old-fashioned. Let everybody get ahead of me. I don't think fast.

"I can't understand the whole thing," Benjie puzzled. "I thought Wolf and Mr. Doyle were thick. So why would Wolf want to burn the man's house down? Can you figure it out?"

"Oh, hell," Joseph said, brushing past Benjie.

He was still puzzling things over at breakfast the next morning, sore and silent, angry at Benjie and most of all at himself, when Mrs. Baumgarten appeared at the curtain to their kitchen.

"I'm sorry to bother you but I thought you might know where Benjie is? He didn't come home last night."

"I saw him yesterday after school," Joseph said.

Mrs. Baumgarten began to cry. "What can have happened to him?"

Joseph's mother spoke comfort. "He's probably staying with a friend, that's all, and didn't tell you."

"Where? What friend? Why would he do that?"

"Don't worry, nothing's happened to him, I'm sure."

But something had happened. Benjie's body was pulled out of the river on the following Saturday afternoon. The police came to the synagogue looking for someone to come and identify it. Joseph's father shouted to him not to go but he pretended not to hear and went along with the crowd. Afterward he was sorry he had gone. They had killed Benjie with an ice pick and fish had eaten away a part of his face.

Joseph walked back home. People pulled at him with questions, whispering as people do. But he couldn't talk, just walked on past the burnt-out tenement. It was said that the insurance had already been collected. All of a sudden the boy, just twelve years old that summer, saw and understood the whole thing. He went into his parents' store, pushed open the curtain and sat down on the cot next to the stove. All of a sudden he was old; it seemed to him that he had just learned all there was to know about life. That people will do anything, that people will kill for money.

He began to cry. His father and mother came over and sat one on each side of him. They put their arms around his shoulders and sat there with him, not speaking. They thought he was crying for his friend, and of course he was, but also he was crying for much more, for his father's innocence and his own lost innocence, for everything that was dirtied and ruined in the world . . .

He never spoke to Wolf again, making sure that Wolf would never see him. Wolf wasn't around too much on this street, anyhow. It was said that he owned a fancy suit and went to dinner at Rectors with millionaires and Diamond Jim Brady. Another world.

He never saw Doyle again, either, except once to go and tell him, trembling inwardly, that his mother was in need of help at the store and he couldn't work for him anymore. For a long time he wondered, and in a way still did wonder, how you could reconcile the kindness of Doyle, the undoubted kindness (just for votes? just for power and votes?) with all these other things. . . . That would be what some might call the gray area. Well, he didn't believe it; to him nothing was gray. It was black or it was white. You make it too simple, a man said once years later over beer, a learned Russian man who wrote for a newspaper: things are never that simple. Perhaps not, but Joseph preferred simplicity. He was at ease with it. Black or white. Good or bad. That's why religion was a comfort. It gave you the rules of the game, the signposts on the road. You knew where to go. You couldn't go wrong.

For two years his father kept asking him why he wouldn't go back to work for Mr. Doyle when there was such good opportunity in it for him. But he could not, he would not, explain. Perhaps if his father had had more time he would eventually have got the truth out of him. Perhaps. But he didn't have more time. He dropped dead a few months later after a silly argument with the milkman who had left the milk to sour in the sun. *Worked himself into a rage over a few bottles of milk,* his mother said afterward, shaking her head, mourning. But Joseph knew it had not been the milk that had caused his father to stand there, shaking his helpless fists until the cords stood out on his temples, turning his blind eyes toward the flaring, angry light; knew that it might just as well have been a nail or a penny or a scrap of dust that turned on Pa's bitter rage because the world was not what he wanted it to be, what it could be and what it never had been for him. Joseph understood all that. He was not quite fifteen years old.

* * *

"Your father wanted you to go to college," Ma said.

They were on the roof where he was helping her hang up the wash. In four directions the tenement roofs stretched like a prairie, a network of clotheslines, chimney pots and iron cornices. Beyond to the east were the river, factory chimneys and the flung arch of the Brooklyn Bridge. Farther north and out of sight were Fifth Avenue, mansions, banks and churches. He had been there once and never forgotten them. They too were New York. The real New York.

"I'm not a scholar, Ma," he said.

She pressed hopefully. She was always pressing him, not too hard but ceaselessly. Join the debating club, make a name. There's a city-wide contest, you might win. Mrs. Siegel's son goes to law school at night. You're a smart boy, what are you going to do, stay in the grocery store? Is that what we came to America for?

He wanted to say, *You certainly didn't come for my benefit, you didn't know you were going to have me. . . .* But instead he said, "Even if I wanted to we haven't got the money. We need what I make."

Right after high school he had got a job with a painting contractor. Now, after two years, he was quite skilled and, through working in the tenements alongside other trades, he had picked up some knowledge of carpentry and plumbing as well.

"You could go at night. And I manage in the store. We could manage."

"Ma, I don't want to be a lawyer."

"But Mrs. Siegel's son—"

"Yes, and the Riesners' two sons are doctors and Moe Myerson teaches high school. . . . But I'm not Siegel, I'm not Myerson or Riesner. I'm Joseph Friedman."

His mother started to pick up the clothes basket. He took it from her. She was so old, so much older since Pa died, as if it was an effort to live. His heart ached and he was sorry that he had spoken sharply.

"So tell me, what does Joseph Friedman want to be?"

"Joseph Friedman wants to make money and take care of his mother so she won't have to keep a grocery store."

She smiled. It was a small smile, faintly sad. "It's not easy to make money without a profession."

"That's where you're wrong." He spoke eagerly. "My boss, Mr. Block, started as an ordinary painter and now look at him! He gets the work from all the banks that own property on the lower East Side. Well, a lot of them anyway. His family lives uptown on Riverside Drive. And he did it all simply by working hard and planning and he's still a pretty young man."

"So that's what you want to do? Be a contractor?"

"Ma, I know you'd be terribly proud for me to be a doctor or a lawyer or something and the fact is I have a lot of respect for men like that. It's just not me, that's all. Tell you what, I'll make money and my sons will be doctors and you can be proud of them."

"I won't live to see your sons."

"Please, Ma!"

"I'm sorry. It's just that there's more to life than money. A man wants to be proud of what he does, to use the mind God gave him. Then, if he makes money, that's wonderful too, of course one needs money, but—"

Round and round. One needs money, one wants to pretend it isn't important, one tries to get it while all the time pretending that one isn't trying to get it. I have no time for that, my children will afford that luxury. I'll see that they can afford it.

"I have a chance to work uptown," he said carefully. He had waited a week before getting up the courage to tell her. "Mr. Block has made connections uptown. On Washington Heights. There's a man named Malone who works for him and they want to start a crew uptown. I'd have to live up there."

She did not look at him. He knew that she had always expected this moment of separation and had prepared herself, no doubt, for a long time past. She said quietly, "You want to go?"

"Yes. Well, I mean, I don't *want* to leave you, but it's a good chance. He's offered me fifteen dollars a week, believe it or not. . . . Well, I give him a day's work and more besides and he knows it."

"I'm sure you do."

"I'd come back down and see you every week and send you half of what I make. I want to see you get out of that store."

"I don't mind that store. What else would I do with my time?"

"You don't mind my going, then?"

"No, no, go and be well. Only one thing . . . Joseph?"

"Yes, Ma?"

"You won't lose your faith, going uptown? Living up there mostly with Gentiles, I suppose?"

"There are plenty of Jews, too, and I'd rent a room with a Jewish family, of course. But a man's faith is inside him, he takes it wherever he goes. You needn't worry about that."

She took his free hand between hers. "No. I know I don't have to worry about that."

SHE WAS STILL in the store. He sent her money every week, brought more whenever he came to see her, but he saw no signs that she used any of it. She wore the cheap cotton dresses sold from the pushcarts and to the synagogue she wore the same black dress she had worn when he was a small boy. He suspected that she saved everything he gave her and would someday, at her death, return it all to him. A vast lonely sadness filled him when he thought about her. She was sixty-three and looked much older. More than once he had urged her to sell the store and move uptown to the Heights. But she would not. She had made one great move in her lifetime, across the ocean, had put down a few tentative roots on Ludlow Street and that was enough.

The only thing she seemed to want was for him to be married. One day a year or so after he had moved uptown he had come back to see her and found a visitor sitting at the table in the kitchen, a bearded middle-aged man in a creased black suit. A briefcase lay on the table.

"My son Joseph," his mother said. "Reb Jeselson."

A matchmaker. A flash of anger went through Joseph. He stood rigidly, without acknowledgment.

"Your mother tells me you want to get married."

"I do?"

"Reb Jeselson came by, we happened to meet and we got talking," his mother interposed. There was alarm in her eyes. "And I happened to mention that I had a son, it just came about quite accidentally and he asked, Well, does he know any nice girls, would he like to meet any? And I said, I suppose he knows some girls, of course he must, but I suppose he might want to meet some more, so if you happen to know any nice girls. . . . After all, a man can never know too many!" she said with gaiety, as if they were joking at a party.

Reb Jeselson removed a folder from the briefcase, spreading half a dozen photos on the table.

"Of course we shall have to talk, you and I. You'll tell me what you have in mind. For instance, do you want an American-born girl or one from the Old Country? I'm sure you want a religious girl, I know something about your background," he murmured. "No, not that one, she's a very fine young woman," removing one of the photographs, "only the problem is she's so tall, taller than most young men. You wouldn't want to look up to a wife, now, would you? Let me see, now here's a girl from a wonderful family—"

"I'm really not interested," Joseph said firmly. And, softening at his mother's look of dismay, "Some other time. I didn't expect you today. I wasn't prepared—"

Reb Jeselson waved him aside. "No obligation. None at all. I only want an idea of what's on your mind. Then we'll make another appointment at your convenience, no hurry—"

"But you see," Joseph said desperately, "you see, I already have a girl. So I'm really not interested at all, thanks just the same."

Reb Jeselson turned reproachfully to Joseph's mother. "You didn't tell me! And I went to all this trouble!"

"I didn't know!" she cried. "Joseph, you didn't tell me. Why didn't you tell me?"

"I didn't know until just now myself," he said.

They both stared at him as though he had gone crazy, as though he were an idiot or a fool.

ANNA. ANNA, WHITE-AND-PINK. A flower on a tall stem in a garden. He had never seen a real garden, yet in some way he knew what it would be like. Fragrant and cool and moist. He hadn't thought he was ready to be married yet; actually he had planned to wait until he was older, thirty perhaps, and well on his way before he encumbered himself. But now it seemed that he was ready, after all. Almost from the first time he had seen her sitting on the steps, reading some learned book in English, and she not a year off the boat!

Her voice, her little feet in kid boots, her sweet-smelling hair, her pretty laugh. The funny, serious way she talked about things. A girl from a village in Poland, and she knew about painters in Paris and writers in England and musicians in

Germany! How did she keep it all in that proud, bright head! Oh, Pa would have
been pleased with her! He smiled. Pa wouldn't have had the faintest idea what
she was talking about, he would have known less than I, and that's little enough.
But he would have known quality when he saw it.

Again she stirred in the bed beside him and murmured something in her
sleep. He wondered what she might be dreaming, and hoped it was no pain or
sorrow. He knew so little about her. Lying there in the dark, he thought how
separate they were after all: is it always so? Oh, surely not! Surely if she needed
him as he did her they would come together. . . . He knew that her need, her
love, were not like his. But they had been married so short a time, only a few
months. He could be patient. They would have a child and that itself would draw
them nearer. Yes, they would have a child: perhaps one was already on the way?
In the powerful surge and release when they came together surely there was the
creation of a child? Such feelings must result in something; wasn't that what life
was all about?

His body began to grow light under the covers. His mind began to blur. He
thought: now, now I'm falling asleep. Keen thought lost its edge; his mind began
to float in a lustrous mist, a wash of shifting shapes and color, red ovoids,
lavender spirals, columns of cream and silver rising like smoke. Then a curtain
fell, dark foliage of dreams, and through the dusky green a spray of gilded dots,
confetti dots. No, coins they were, golden coins, and when he reached out his
hand they fell through his fingers and into his palm: not hard, not metal at all,
but soft like rain, a soft, protecting rain to wash over Anna and his mother and
his father. No, no, he thought, it is too late for my father and soon will be too late
for my mother. But for Anna, over Anna, the warm and lovely golden rain must
fall.

By midnight he was asleep.

❖{10}❖

They stood modestly back to back in the women's bathhouse until their bathing suits were on, black taffeta skirts, black stockings, slippers and straw bonnet tied under the chin so the breeze couldn't blow it away. Anna had never worn a bathing suit before; her legs, except for the stockings, were uncovered to the knees and she felt ashamed to go out in public like that. But she would not have admitted it to Ruth, who had been often at the beach and was very sure of herself.

"See, I told you the suit would look fine!" Ruth said. "You don't show at all, and the baby due so soon! As for me, I always look like an elephant when I'm expecting. Come, we'll find a good spot before the crowds arrive, that's the best thing about getting here early," she went on, as they lifted their feet through the heavy sand.

Solly and Joseph had already spread the blankets. Harry and Irving, big boys of nine and ten, knobby like their father in maroon striped suits, were already in the water. The little girls had shovels and pails.

"Ah, there you are!" Joseph cried. His expression, that no one else would have noticed, told Anna that she looked very fine. In these few months they had already got a kind of secret "married" language; she had thought it would take longer for a man and woman to do that.

"Now I can really see the ocean!" she said. "It was different when we crossed over, so dark and angry, it seemed."

Here the sea was mild and lovely, the surf breaking in rows of ruffled white and sighing softly out again.

"We'll be going in for a while," Solly announced.

"Let me go too!" Anna cried.

Joseph frowned. "No, no. God forbid that you should fall! Next year I'll bring you, I promise I will."

The blankets had been spread next to a breakwater. Ruth propped herself against a rock and put the lunch basket in its shade. "Wait till you see the fireworks tonight. It's a pity there aren't more holidays! Decoration Day we come but it's usually too cold to go in the water then. Look at those boys of mine, look at them splashing! They'll get water in their ears! Maybe I'll just duck in, too, for a minute."

Anna lay back. The baby moved in her, thumping weakly against her spread palms. Her body was languid from its warm burden and the warm sun. What would he be like, this child? She was so impatient to see his face. What would he be *like*? Would he live with them happily, would he love them? Sometimes, no matter what you did for them, children did not love their parents. Would he be like anyone they had known, or perhaps like someone long dead whose name they had never even heard?

Oh, but this was a wanted baby, as much by the father as the mother! Joseph took such pride in her swelling body, the skin stretched tightly, blue-white as milk. He worried and fretted. "You don't have to be cleaning and cooking all day. A couple of eggs for supper will be enough for me. You don't get enough rest, you're always running and doing something." Then, a moment later, he would admonish, "Be sure to get out and take a long walk tomorrow, it's very important to have exercise. That way you'll have an easier time, Dr. Arndt says." She had been astonished. "You spoke to the doctor?" "Well, I wanted to hear for myself that you were all right, so I stopped in."

Yes, Joseph would always take care of things. She thought of him as a builder and planner, moderate and careful; he had come to their marriage with confidence; he would build it carefully, stone on stone, to rise and last. In him there was no betrayal. He meant what he said and he said what he meant. In him there was only trust. Lying beside him at night, she felt his sturdiness, the safety of sleeping there, the tenderness.

And tenderness was all she wanted. The other, the force that drove him as though he would plunge in and become part of her, she did not need. She knew that he was feeling something very powerful, but she felt nothing of it herself. It was only the loving warmth that mattered. She supposed, anyway, that women never really liked anything more than that; the rest was only to satisfy a husband and to have children. Not, of course, that she had ever discussed the subject with anyone. Perhaps, if she had had a sister? But then the sister wouldn't have known any more about it than she did.

Once, when she had been stitching trousers at Ruth's, Anna had overheard two of the women whispering something about being so tired at night, and how no matter how hard they worked men were never too tired. Still, it was good to know that your husband wanted you. The things he whispered at night—it was embarrassing to remember them. But men were made that way, so it must be a good thing, it must be right.

"You look like your mother, Anna," Ruth said. Anna opened her eyes. Ruth was standing over her, drying herself with a towel.

"Do I?"

"I never saw her very often, but certain things about her come to my mind. She was different from other people."

"How different?"

"She didn't talk about the things women in the villages talked about. I always thought she ought to have lived in Warsaw or maybe Vilna, where the schools are. She would have fitted there. Although she never complained, not that I remember, anyway."

"You don't remember anything more?"

"No, I was only a child myself, after all, when I left home."

And I remember standing in the windy burial ground thinking that I must try to hold on to their faces and voices before they should slip away. And now they have really slipped away. And there isn't a human being on this side of the ocean who knows anything about my life up to four years ago. It is a severance, the major part of my life cut off, except in the privacy of my own mind.

"It's too bad when a family is split like that. You've no one close here for your children to know, except for Joseph's mother, of course."

"She's sixty-four," Anna said.

"Is she? I would have thought even more, she seems so old," Ruth remarked.

"She's had a hard life. We wanted to bring her today, she's never been at the beach. In all these years, imagine! But she wouldn't come."

"What will you do when she gets too old or sick to keep the store?" Ruth was curious. "Do you suppose Joseph will want her to live with you?"

"I don't know. We've never talked about it," Anna said, suddenly troubled. That gloomy, sour-smelling old woman in the house! Then came a wave of shame and pity. Poor thing, poor thing! To be old in another woman's house, a strange young woman who didn't want you!

"If that ever happens and Joseph wants her, why, we'll have to do it, that's all," she said quietly.

"You're a kind girl, Anna. I'm glad for both your sakes that I sent Joseph down to talk to you that day."

"I've never thanked you," Anna said, with embarrassment.

"Pshaw! I wasn't looking for thanks! But *he* thanked me, he was quite mad about you from the very first time. He thought you didn't like him, that's why he was afraid for so long to talk about marriage. You know," she explained, "he thought you were in love with somebody else, but I told him you weren't. If it had been anyone but Joseph I would have let him go on thinking so, because generally it's a good idea to keep men guessing. But Joseph is different, he's so—" Ruth sought the word—"honest. Yes, that's it, he's so honest."

"That's true," Anna said. "He is." And she sat quite still while Ruth talked on, only half hearing, feeling, in the pouring sunshine, how good it was to be like this. Down at the water's edge Joseph was throwing a ball to the boys. He looked like a boy himself, fast and happy. She could hear his voice ring. She hadn't known he knew how to play. This was the way a man ought to be, the way he ought to live. Perhaps this was what God intended for man when He put him on the earth, to be free, to run in the bright air with all the other living things.

But no, how was that possible? Who was to pay for it? Always it came back to that. This outing today, the carfare, the food, they had to be paid for. "In the sweat of thy brow shalt thou earn thy bread," Joseph always said. He liked to quote from the Bible. It seemed that he could find an explanation for everything in the Bible.

After a while the men came back and sat down. "Feeling all right, Anna?" Joseph asked.

"Just wonderful!"

"Tell me if you get tired."

"Tired! I'm tired of doing nothing!" She took her crocheting, a long rectangle of white lace, out of her basket.

"Solly, look!" Ruth cried. "It's gorgeous! What are you making?"

Anna felt suddenly shy. "A cover for the baby carriage. It will go over a sateen lining, pink or blue, as soon as we know."

Ruth shook her head admiringly. "You know how to do things, Anna! You're so clever, between baking and handwork—"

"Tell her," Joseph interrupted, "about the carriage," and went on to tell about it himself. "We bought it last week on Broadway. White wicker, with a top that rolls back for sun or shade, whichever you want."

"Oh," Ruth said, "the first baby is wonderful. You've plenty of time for it— Vera and June, stop throwing sand at Cecile! You ought to be ashamed of yourselves!"

"Bet you don't know what sand is," Harry said importantly.

"Sand? Why, it's what's on the beach," his mother answered.

"Hah! It's rocks, ground fine, after millions and millions of years. I knew you didn't know!"

Anna picked up a handful. The fine, dry stuff poured between her fingers, sharp, twinkling particles on her skin. Yes, it was like pieces of rock, the shining splinters in rock.

"So, you are getting an education from my son," Solly observed, and in a lower voice confided to Anna and Joseph, "They tell me he's number one in his class. He wants to know everything and he never forgets. You tell him something once, he never forgets," he repeated with pride. Then, falling sober and silent, "I wish I could get ahead! I mean really get enough together so I could start a little business of my own." He swung around, addressing Joseph alone. "Some people do it, I don't know how. My boss started the way I am, but I never seem to get ahead."

"Five children," Joseph said gently. "That takes some doing."

"Yes, yes, God bless them, it does. And I want to do so much for them all!" And he sat a moment, looking out to sea, as though an answer were waiting for him there. Then he jumped up.

"This air gives you an appetite! How about feeding the hungry army, Ruth?"

"Wait, wait, I'm coming!" Ruth admonished, unwrapping the paper bags, and delving in the basket, withdrew one after the other a corned beef, a salami, pickles, sour tomatoes, coleslaw, hardboiled eggs and two long loaves of dark bread.

"And watermelon for dessert," she finished. "Leave that in the shade till we're ready for it."

"Cookies," Anna said, producing a neat box tied with ribbon. "I baked yesterday, two kinds."

"And an orange for each of you children," Ruth added. "Here, boys, don't grab. Vera, keep your feet off the blanket, you'll get sand in the food."

Joseph always said Ruth talked too much, Anna remembered with amusement.

"Here, Solly, don't eat so fast! That husband of mine, he'll choke himself someday, God forbid, and the boys are the same. Now Cecile, on the other hand, I have to open her mouth and stick the food in, a bird eats more! Joseph, help yourself, there's plenty. And make your wife eat, she shouldn't forget she's eating for two!"

Anna met Joseph's eyes and suppressed a smile. Again, their private language: "Don't get me wrong, I like Ruth, she's the salt of the earth. But if I had to live with her, I'd go crazy. Her tongue never stops: gabble, gabble, gabble."

Solly rubbed his stomach. "A real feast," he sighed, and remembering his duties as a host, "You're enjoying yourself, Anna?"

"Oh, I am, I am! Think, here we are on the very edge of the continent! If you looked straight ahead across the ocean, all those thousands of miles, you'd see—"

"Poland," Ruth interjected. "And I'd just as soon not see Poland again, if you don't mind."

"Not Poland," Anna corrected. "Portugal. And behind it Spain. I'd like to go there someday. Miss Thorne was in Spain, her father was a United States consul there. She says it's beautiful."

"Not me! I never want to see any part of Europe again." Solly shook his head. "Especially now, with the way things are. They look very bad if you ask me."

"What do you mean?" Joseph asked.

"There'll be war," Solly answered seriously.

"You always think the worst!" Ruth cried. "Why do you have to say such things?"

"Because it's true. As soon as I read last week that a Serb had shot the Archduke Ferdinand in Sarajevo, I said, 'There'll be war, you mark my words.' "

"Who was he, this archduke?" Anna asked.

"The Austrian archduke, heir to the throne. So that means Austria will declare war on Serbia, and then Russia will come in with Serbia. Germany will have to help Austria; France will come in with Russia. And there you have it."

Joseph took another slice of watermelon. "Well," he said practically, "all that's across the ocean. It won't bother us here."

Anna sat with her head down, fear running through her like water.

And Ruth said with sudden insight, "Anna is thinking of her brothers. They'd have to fight for Austria."

"What's the point of this gloomy talk of things we don't even know about?" Joseph demanded. "Nobody can tell what's going to happen. I'll wager it will all blow over, anyway. Nobody wants war, and here we are spoiling a beautiful day with worry over something that will probably never happen."

"You're right," Solly apologized. "You're absolutely right, Joseph. Who wants to waste a day like this? Let's go back for a swim."

THE SUN WAS low and red in the west. "That means it'll be a hot day tomorrow," Joseph predicted, coming toward the women.

"The days I can stand but it's the nights that are awful," Solly said. "Sleeping on the fire escapes, it's torture."

They gathered up the blanket and their baskets. "The girls will come with me," Ruth directed. "Harry and Irving, you go to the bathhouse with your father and change. We'll all meet at the entrance in front."

Across the boardwalk lay Surf Avenue and the roving crowds, the life of the evening. The sky was darkly streaked, gray against coal gray, smudged with a remnant of rose. The lights of the Scenic Railway arched and soared; the Ferris wheel hung like a spider web; in all the booths, lights winked and twinkled. Far ahead, band music blared and faded with the veering wind; near at hand the merry-go-round jangled. Anna was enthralled.

"I don't know where to go first!" she cried. "Where shall we start? Will there be time to see it all?"

"We'll do our best!" Joseph said. "Want to start with the Streets of Cairo? I went last year and you can walk right through a real Egyptian street, the real thing. They've got donkeys, you can ride on a camel—no, I forgot, you can't do that, but you can watch and next year when we come again you'll ride a camel."

She felt, and knew she was feeling, a child's delight, perhaps even more than the children did, who began to be tired. So much to see and hear all at once! Such bright colors, and all the music was like colors! Spinning and wheeling, like one of those little machines—what did you call it?—a kaleidoscope, where you put in some simple thing, a piece of cloth or a couple of pins, and when you turned it endless, unfurling patterns came, a dazzle in the eyes.

Then it was dark and time for the fireworks to begin. Too bad there wouldn't be time for the side shows! But Anna had seen pictures of a calf with two heads and a dreadful bearded woman; she was glad not to go. Luckily they found seats for the fireworks, which were absolutely splendid: rockets of red, white and blue; stars that rushed into the night sky, each one higher than the one before, showered back upon the earth in a spray of gold. Last, the sound of cannon fire, shuddering and crashing until the final boom that almost shook you out of your seat. And silence. And the band striking up "The Star-Spangled Banner" while everyone rose in his place. Anna was proud that she was one of those who knew all the words: "—and the rockets' red glare, the bombs bursting in air—"

It was over. Ended and over, the wonderful, wonderful day. The crowd shoved slowly toward the trolley, the Coney Island Avenue line. Solly knew the quickest way to get there ahead of the rush. Otherwise they would never have got seats. As it was, the boys had to stand leaning on Joseph and Solly, each of whom held one of the sleeping girls. Ruth held the littlest one, and Anna took the baskets. People were standing all long the aisle, even hanging on the outside of the car. The conductors could hardly pass through the crowds; they were hot and sweaty and you couldn't blame them if they were cross. They'd spent the whole day riding back and forth on the cars while all these others had been on the beach. It grew hotter and hotter as they rode through Brooklyn toward the bridge. The breeze died, and what little there was of it was moist. The babble of talk and laughter died, too. People are tired after the long day, Anna thought. Also, they are thinking about tomorrow. It almost takes the pleasure out of the day, this ride and the surging heat again and thinking about tomorrow. Almost, but not quite.

After they parted with the Levinsons and changed to the Broadway car it was not so crowded, not so bad.

"We're lucky we caught the last car," Joseph said. "It will be midnight before we get home. Did you have a good time?"

"Oh, I loved it!" she said.

"Put your head on my shoulder. I'll wake you when we come to our stop."

She didn't sleep. The bell jangled and the motorman sped up Broadway in the dark, the trolley swaying with the speed. She could feel the heat of Joseph's skin through his shirt. "He'll be burned," she thought. They had forgotten the cocoa butter, left it home on the dresser. Perhaps it would not be too late if she put it on him when they got home. He had such fair skin.

My friend, she thought. My one friend in all the world. Now I really know what it is to be married. Not *fairy tales,* she thought scornfully. No girl should know so little about life as I did: when I have a daughter I will not allow her to be so stupid, so unworldly. *Tristan and Isolde.* Fairy tales.

And yet, yet . . . all that soft sparkle, the soaring and the singing, the longing, the touch, the ache and the sweetness, all of those, not true? I'm nineteen now, I ought to know. Why do I still wonder about it?

Joseph bent down and kissed her hair. "We're home," he whispered.

He helped her down the trolley's high step. The wind came blowing from the Hudson when they turned the corner. Their shoes went slap and click on the sidewalk, the man's heel flat, the woman's needle-high, slap and click through the sleeping street.

❦{11}❧

The boy Maurice was born in his parents' brass bed on July 29, 1914. He weighed seven pounds, and had a head of thick, light hair.

"Three hours' labor for a first baby!" Dr. Arndt exclaimed. "Do you know how lucky you are? At this rate, you ought to have six more!"

Outside a newsboy cried alarm. "Extra! Extra!"

"What is it?" Anna asked, and Joseph went outside to see. He came back with the *New York Tribune*.

" 'Austria declares war,' " he read. " 'Rushes vast army into Serbia; Russia masses eighty thousand men on border.' Solly was right. The war has come."

The doctor grumbled, "More crazy slaughter, and for what?"

Anna said, "Eli and Dan will be in it." There came a flash of old, old memory: Mama in her bed, the twin boys lying with her, some woman standing there, a neighbor or midwife. She seized the baby.

"Nothing will happen to this little boy. I'll never let anything happen to this little boy!"

"No, of course not," the doctor said gently.

THE YEARS OF the war were marked off in Anna's mind by the growth of her son. She would remember that the *Lusitania* had been sunk on the day he took his first step holding on to her two fingers, and he only ten months old! When the Russian army drove the Austrians back to the freezing mountains of Carpathia—she trembled, shedding tears for Dan and Eli—that also was the time Maury said his first words. By the time the United States entered the war—the poster with the bloody hand: *The Hun, his mark. Blot it out with Liberty Bonds*—by that time he was almost three, genial, alert, delightful.

She studied the face she had so longed to see, the features emerging from the formless round. The nose was straight. The eyes were almond-shaped and darkly blue. There was a cleft in the chin. Whom are you like, my son? Yourself alone, like no one in the world before you or to come.

She felt profoundly that he had made a great change in her. She no longer thought of herself as a girl. A long age had passed since the time before his coming. He had enlarged her, so that she had new feeling for the blind man passing in the street and the young men dying in Europe. And yet, in an entirely

71

...e way, he had made everything but himself so unimportant that she didn't ...what happened anywhere, as long as he was safe.

During the night she often heard Joseph get out of bed to go in to the crib, ...nd she knew that he was listening for the baby's breathing. No child had ever been more loved than this one! No child was ever more carefully fed and bathed, dressed and played with, than this one.

"Maybe he'll be a doctor," Joseph said.

"A lawyer would be fine, too."

They were able to laugh at their own foolish pride. Yet they meant what they said.

She read to Maury, long before he could possibly have understood the words. But somewhere she had heard that infants can absorb the sound and feel of words even though they do not understand them. So she read peaceful things, poems of Stevenson and Eugene Field.

"Sleep, little pigeon, and fold your wings—little blue pigeon with velvet eyes."

In front of the apartment house the mothers sat with their carriages and strollers, observing, criticizing, counseling each other.

"You need another baby," they told Anna. "You're spoiling this one. It's not good for him or you."

Of course she wanted more children. And certainly Joseph wanted a large family. But none came. Yet really there was no great need to hurry. These years with Maury, only a few hundred days out of a long life, were too perfect to be wished away. All day long, after Joseph had gone to work before light, until he came home after dark, they had each other, Anna and Maury.

Oh, little Maury, little boy!

Darkness still covered the earth and the street lamps still burned near their bedroom window. It was not quite five o'clock. In another minute Anna would rise and make Joseph's breakfast. It was hard to get out of bed these winter mornings. The water stopped running in the bathroom; he had finished his shower. Now he would hang the towels back on the rack and wipe the tub, leaving it without spot.

His clothes for the morning were ready on the chair. He did everything with such care and method. His books of appointments and bills owed and money due him were all in order, so that he was always prepared, always on time, and no moment was wasted.

He came from the bathroom now and stood at Anna's mirror to brush his hair, making an exact center part. The clean overalls that she had washed were in their paper bag by the door with his painter's cap. He always wore a suit on the way to work. It was not, she knew, that he was ashamed of his work; he took pride in his labor and skill. It was just that he saw this work as a way station on the road to another life. He saw himself, she understood, as a man who went to work wearing a collar and tie.

It seemed to Anna, and had from the beginning, that he was a clear and simple person to understand. Yet lately she had been concerned. He was so quiet. He had always been quiet, true. But now he had almost nothing to say. Often he fell asleep in his chair after supper, and she would have to wake him to get him to bed. Of course, he was on his feet all day. . . .

The silence, of itself, did not bother her, for evening was her only time to read in peace. It was the reason, if any, behind the silence that troubled her.

At breakfast he said, "I read your brothers' letters last night. I woke up around one o'clock; I couldn't sleep, for some reason."

"It's so good to be hearing from them again." Their letters since the end of the war had been cheerful enough. Dan had emerged unhurt from four years of fighting. Eli had shrapnel in his arm and would never bend the elbow again, but he had been given a medal for valor and his firm had promoted him, the three men ahead of him having been killed.

"If you aren't killed you can make a good thing out of a war," Anna said now, "outrageous as it is."

"It would seem so," Joseph answered bitterly. "You have only to look at what the war did for Solly."

Who would have thought that Solly, of all people, would have prospered so? His boss had made a fortune turning out fatigue pants for the army and Solly had gone into the new factory, first as an assistant and then as supervisor. They had moved uptown to five nice rooms on Broadway at Ninety-eighth Street, much nicer rooms than Joseph's and Anna's.

"I'm glad for them," Anna said and meant it. "With all those children, they needed some luck. Ruth told me confidentially that Solly and one of the other men may go in business for themselves. Solly's saved a few thousand dollars, you know."

"All you need is luck."

"You're not envious of Solly?"

"Of course I am! He's a decent fellow—you know what I've always thought of him—but, my God, he's no brain, is he? He's a humdrum plodder and now he's way ahead of me. Haven't I got a right to be envious?"

"We're doing fine, Joseph," Anna tried to coax him.

"Fine!" He slapped the table. "I'm twenty-eight years old, thirty before you know it, and I'm exactly nowhere. Living in a dump!"

"It's not a dump! Nice people live here, good solid people!"

"Sure! Department store clerks, bus drivers, postmen. Poor wage slaves living from hand to mouth. Like me." He stood up and began to pace the kitchen. "And when I get older and can't work ten or twelve hours a day anymore, what then? With prices rising while you're looking at them? We'll have even less than we have now, that's what then."

That part was true. Since the war everything was becoming more and more expensive. True too that they were not advancing.

"Anna, I'm scared. I look into the future and for the first time I'm scared," he said.

There were small veins at his temples. One of them jumped when he talked. She hadn't noticed that before. His hands were spotted with paint. They looked like the spotted hands of an old man. She thought, He looks older than twenty-eight. And she, too, was suddenly afraid.

*   *   *

ONE DAY JOSEPH came home and began to talk in a bright, excited voice. "You know what Malone the plumber told me today? He knows an apartment house near here that you can buy for almost nothing. The owner lost a pile in some business and on top of that both his kids have asthma. One of them almost died with it in the winter. So he's got to move west and he wants to sell the house fast." He walked up and down the room, as was his habit when he was tense. "Malone and another guy want me to go in with them. I need two thousand cash. Where can I get two thousand cash?"

He left the food on his plate. He picked up the newspaper and let it fall.

"Your magazine is on the table," Anna said.

He always read the *Saturday Evening Post;* it was all he ever read, except for the evening paper. He had no time for the morning paper.

Now he leafed through the magazine and put it aside. She saw that he was entirely intent on his idea. But nothing will come of it, she thought pityingly, and began to mend Maury's overalls. The silence needed to be broken but she didn't know how to do it.

Presently Joseph said, "Anna, I've thought of something."

"Yes?"

"You know, when you were at the Werners', they were very good to you. Maybe, if you asked, maybe they'd lend us some money."

"Oh, no, I'm sure not!"

"Why? I would pay interest. They might just be willing to do it, rich people like them. I've heard of such things before."

She felt weak with dread. What was he asking of her?

"It can't hurt to try, can it?"

"Joseph, please, I'll do anything for you, only don't ask me to do that."

"But I'm not asking you to do anything wrong! Are you too proud to ask for a loan, is that it?"

"Joseph, you're shouting, you'll scare Maury."

They went to bed. She felt his anger and it frightened her. He was so seldom angry. "Joseph, don't make me," she whispered, and moved to touch him, but he drew away and pretended to be asleep.

In the morning he began again. "Damn it to hell, I could do so much with that money! I know I could! Malone and I could fix that place up, raise the rents, then sell it. Don't you see, this is the start I've been waiting for and it may never happen again!"

He will wear me down, Anna thought.

"I'd go myself, but I don't know the people. They'd listen to you."

And on the third day she gave in. "Enough, for God's sake! I'll call Mrs. Werner on the telephone tomorrow."

SHE CLIMBED THE steps of the Seventy-first Street house on Saturday morning. It was a warm day for March, but not warm enough to cause the sweat on the back of her neck. *That woman,* Anna thought. "How well you look, Anna," she will say.

"And so you have a son, how lovely!" She will write out the check (will she, possibly?). And hand it to me with her little smile and all her dignity.

The bell tinkled through the house. A moment later Paul Werner opened the door. He was wearing his topcoat and he had a package in his hand.

"Why, Anna," he said. "Why, Anna."

"I have an appointment with your mother."

"But Mother's in Long Branch for the week. The whole family's there."

"She told me to come at ten o'clock."

"She did? Let's go look on her desk. She might have left a message there." And as Anna waited at the foot of the stairs, "Come up, Anna."

The morning room was the same. The flowered chaise and the embroidery basket were still there. There was a new photograph on the desk, a large professional portrait of a baby. His baby?

He rummaged through papers. "I don't see anything. Wait, here's her calendar. It's next Saturday, Anna; you're a week ahead of time."

My God, she thought, I look like a fool. And Joseph needs the money by Wednesday.

"It's too bad. They're down at Cousin Blanche's farm for the week. There's a big house party and Mrs. Monaghan and Daisy went, too. Daisy has your old place, Anna."

She had forgotten his dark, rich voice. Like the deepest notes of a cello, it was.

"Is there anything I can do, Anna? What were you going to see Mother about?"

"I was going to ask whether she would lend us some money."

"Oh? Are you in trouble? Sit down, tell me about it."

"But I'm keeping you. You have your coat on."

"Then I'll take it off. I only stopped in to pick up a package and then I'll catch the afternoon train to the shore."

Her voice murmured, telling Joseph's short story. The house was very still. The house was a fortress, safe and solid against the world's attacks, cushioned with soft things: silk curtains, carpets, pillows.

She did not look at his face. With eyes turned down, she saw only the long legs, one crossed over the other, and the fine, burnished leather of the shoes. These strong, lean legs would ride, play tennis, never grow old. Joseph already had varicose veins. From standing so much, the doctor said.

"I didn't want to ask you," she cried suddenly, almost angrily. "I didn't see any reason why you should lend two thousand dollars to a man you don't even know."

He smiled. How could eyes be so bright? Nobody else had such eyes, deep and vivid. "You're right. There isn't any reason. Except that I want to do it."

"You want to?"

"Yes. You have a lot of spirit and courage. I want to do it for you."

He drew a checkbook out of his pocket and took up a pen. Such easy power, commanding life, your own and other people's!

"What is your husband's name?"

"Joseph. Joseph Friedman."

"Two thousand dollars. When you get home have him sign this. It's an I.O.U.

You can mail it to me. No, mail it here in care of my mother. I'm sure she would have done this for you herself."

"I don't know what to say!"

"Don't say anything."

"My husband will be so grateful. I don't think he really expected—it was just a last hope. Because we don't know anybody else, you see."

"I understand."

"He's really such a good man. The most honest, good man, believe me." Why did she chatter like this? "But then that's silly of me to say, isn't it? What woman would tell you that her husband was dishonest?"

He laughed. "Not many, I imagine. But really, I hope this will accomplish what you hope."

Anna had unbuttoned the jacket of her suit. She saw now that his glance had gone to the front of her shirtwaist, to the row of spiral ruffling that lay between her breasts. She ought now to stand up, repeat her thanks, and go to the door. But she did not move.

"Tell me, Anna," he said. "Tell me about your little boy."

"He's four years old."

"Does he look like you?"

"I don't know."

"Red hair?"

"No, blond. But probably it will be darker when he grows up."

"You're even more beautiful than you used to be. Do you know that?"

"Am I?"

Her hands were limp in her lap. When he came to kneel on the floor beside her chair and turned her mouth to his, she had no strength at all.

There were nine pearl buttons on the shirtwaist. Then the petticoats: first the taffeta, then the muslin with the blue insertion. And the corset cover. And the chemise.

His voice came from far away, as if from another room. It echoed, a voice within a voice. Her eyes closed; her arms were too heavy to move. She was lifted to the flowered chaise.

"You're cold, my dear," he said tenderly, and reached for a quilted throw to cover them both. They lay in a bliss of warmth. His lips were pressed into her neck; she felt, and heard, his rising, falling breath. She thought: This is a dream.

She opened her eyes. The room was dim with a pearly northern light so pink and pale that it seemed like evening light, like evening calm.

Soft, soft. She closed her eyes. His fingers were moving through her hair, loosening the combs and pins. When the freed hair slipped over her shoulders he pulled it back from her temples.

"Lovely," she heard him say. "Oh, lovely."

Slowly he moved, not like an eager man in a hurry for his own quick release and then sleep, but slowly, flowing over her skin, beating in her blood, murmuring in her ears.

Never, never before.

A tide came sweeping. It rose and receded a little, then rose again, higher. For an instant something called in Anna's head. She thought she had whispered—perhaps she really had whispered "Please"—but his mouth came down over hers, crushing the word. The tide came swelling, wave after rolling wave. And then nothing, nothing in the world, could have stopped the rushing of that tide.

SHE WAS JERKED awake. Below in the street a hand organ ground and jangled. "Santa Lucia-a-a," it sobbed, and stopped. Silence followed. Anna's heart began to pound. How long had she been lying here?

She heard footsteps below. He had got up and left her to sleep. Her clothes had been picked from the floor and decently folded on a chair.

Slowly she put them on. The room was freezing cold. She trembled. She picked up the scattered hairpins and the combs. Her hands shook, doing her hair. One side of her face was red, roughened by—

She felt weak and sat down on the edge of the chaise, then jumped up and stood there looking at it. *Not good enough for a marriage bed, only for this,* ran through her mind. It looked so naked there, humiliated, a lady's sofa meant for an afternoon nap, or a book and a box of chocolates. And they had—

But it wasn't his fault. You're always proud of being honest; then be honest and fair. He married another girl? That has nothing to do with today.

Wretched confusion. Oh, wretched.

Paul was at the foot of the stairs when she came down. She passed him and ran to the door.

"Wait!" he cried, seeing her face. "Anna, you're not angry at me?"

"Angry? No." Only terrified.

"Anna, I want to tell you—you are the most enchanting woman I've ever known. And also I want to say, in case you think—well, I want to say that I respect you more than any woman I've ever known."

"Respect me? Now?"

"Yes, yes! Do you think, because of this—? It was marvelous, you know it was, marvelous and natural. Remember that."

"Natural!" she cried. Her voice cracked. "I have a child, a husband—"

He tried to take her hands, but she pulled away. Her mouth quivered; tears, forced down, burned the backs of her eyes.

"But you've done them no harm," Paul said gently.

"Oh, God!" she cried.

"Don't, don't feel like that. It's not a thing to cry over. Anna, listen, I've thought about you ever since you left here. I wanted you so. But when you lived in this house you were a girl, a child, and I wouldn't have touched you then."

This must be unreal. The thing that had happened upstairs only a little while ago could not have happened.

"And you wanted me," Paul said, very low. "I know you did. Is that something to be ashamed of, Anna dear, is it?"

Shame. Me. I. Anna Friedman, wife of Joseph, mother of Maury, I did this. On the fourteenth day of March, at noon, I did this.

Nausea lumped and gagged in her throat. "I have to go! I have to get out!" she cried, fumbling with the latch.

"I can't let you leave this way! Here, sit down a minute, let's talk. Please, I'm sorry, please——"

But she was blind, was deaf with her terror.

"No! No! Let me out!" The latch gave. The door flew open. She pushed him aside and fled down the steps.

The street was an ordinary New York street in the spring. A cluster of boys played marbles at the curb. A wagon approached, the peddler calling out his wares and prices: asparagus, rhubarb, potted tulips. But she had to run; something was at her back, as in the dark hall of an empty house. She had to run, away and away. Or else home.

She ran home.

Joseph was out with Maury. No doubt they had gone to the river to see the warships that were anchored there. Little boats went scurrying back and forth between the ships and the shore. You could see the sailors on the decks.

She went into the bathroom and ripped off all her clothes. She ran the water scalding hot in the chipped old tub. *Shame.* I wanted to be lifted and folded, I wanted to *feel.* It's true that I did. I can't blame him. He wouldn't have done it if he hadn't known that I wouldn't stop him.

Her skin began to sting. *Filthy.* She took a bath brush and scrubbed hard up and down. The soft pale skin on her forearms began to bleed. I could drown in here. I could slide down with my face under the water and they would think I had fainted.

The front door opened and Joseph came in with Maury.

"Anna?" he called outside the bathroom door.

She came out pulling a robe around her. "I got a check. It's on the bureau. You can call Mr. Malone."

"They gave it to you," he said wonderingly, as if he hadn't understood. Then he looked as though he were going to cry and he shouted, "You got it! You really did! Oh, Anna, this will make all the difference in the world! You'll see, you'll see." He began to question her rapidly, excitedly. "How did you ask her? What did she say? Did she want to know anything about me?"

"She wasn't there. It was the son who gave it."

"Anna, was it very hard? Yes, it must have been hard for you to ask. But what kind, what decent people! To trust us! You know, now I can tell you the truth, I really didn't think they would do it! But it was the only way I knew."

"Yes. Kind people."

He looked at her. "Is there something the matter? You don't seem——"

"My stomach. I had a sandwich downtown. The butter tasted bad, I think."

"Poor girl! Then go lie down, I'll feed Maury and keep him away from you."

When he had closed the bedroom door she went back into the bathroom and took another bath. Filthy, I am filthy.

Am I going to lose my mind?

At breakfast a few days later Joseph watched Anna closely. He was puzzled. "I thought you would be so pleased now that I've bought the house."

"But I am pleased. Very."

He reached under the table for her hand. "Is it—I've been thinking—this is hard to say, but is it because I haven't come near you at night? I know it is a couple of weeks now, but you see, when a man is worried he doesn't feel like it. I mean to say, it had nothing to do with you."

She grew hot. The palms of her hands were wet. *Oh, my God.*

"Have I embarrassed you? But we shouldn't feel embarrassment with each other. These things are natural, aren't they?"

"You don't seem as happy this time," Dr. Arndt remarked.

"I don't feel as well this time."

"Each pregnancy is different. Carry a sweet cracker with you in your purse and don't wait too long between meals. In another two months it'll be over."

Wise and fatherly Dr. Arndt.

Joseph bought a brand-new Model T Ford for three hundred sixty dollars. "I need to get around," he explained. "Malone and I are going to fix up this house and turn it over fast. We're going in for real estate in a big way, I tell you! I have a lot of confidence in Malone. He's honest and he's smart. The two of us are going places."

"I'm glad."

"Have you noticed how things come in bunches? Bad or good. We got the house and we're having another baby. Things are really looking up!"

"I know."

"I'll be able to start paying back next September. I figure I'll be able to give Mr. Werner a thousand dollars. I really ought to go and thank him personally, don't you think? For a total stranger to do what he did!"

"People like them are too busy," Anna said faintly. "A note would be better."

"You think so? Well, perhaps you're right. Do you still feel sick today, Anna?"

"Yes. The nausea—it's dreadful."

"Maybe we ought to get another doctor."

"No, it will pass soon."

If only I had someone to talk to. If I had my mother. But would I tell such a thing to my mother? God forbid. The rabbi, whose wife goes daily down the street with the rest of the women, pushing the carriages to the dairy and the butcher? Dr. Arndt, who will come to deliver my child while Joseph waits in the other room? Impossible.

Ruth came up to visit one day. They walked over toward the river behind Maury on his little tricycle. Ruth prattled down the list of her children. Harry had skipped a year, still at the top of his class. Irving had a business head; no doubt he'd go in with his father. The girls were such a joy; what a difference it made living and going to school uptown! But Cecile was overweight; she had such an appetite for sweets—

The air was heavy. Anna could hardly breathe.

"Why, you can hardly walk!" Ruth cried, becoming aware.

"I'm all right. Ruth, you've seen a lot of things, I want to tell you something terribly sad. There's a girl up here, the women are talking about her, she had—well, she had an affair, you understand. I feel so sorry for her; you see, she's married and she thinks—she knows her husband isn't the father of the child. Can you imagine such a terrible thing?"

"You feel sorry for her? I'd call her a whore!"

"Yes, of course, it's awful! But still, you know, one can feel sorry for such people. . . . The poor girl, she made a mistake, one mistake, and now—I don't know what to tell her."

"What to tell her! My advice is, stay away from her. Friends like that you don't need."

"Of course. But what's to become of her?"

"Why worry your head over such a person? She made her bed, let her lie in it. Right?"

"I guess you're right," Anna said.

The new life grew and fluttered awake. Anna thought, I need to love it, I need to long for the sight of its face. But she did neither. Poor thing, poor thing, this creature feeding in her, not wanted in her. At night she lay awake. Joseph's hand loosened on hers; he liked to hold her hand as they lay together falling asleep. If only she could have turned to him and cried out for help.

If only she could tell the truth! Sometimes the truth came rising to her lips so that she tightened them in fear of its escape. The words had a taste. They had a shape and color: bloody red in the darkness. She could hear their sound as they would fall into the quiet room.

Terror plucked at her skin like something alive, and ran over her body, raising the little hairs on her arms.

Joseph said, "I wonder how Maury's going to take it? Maury, would you like to have a baby brother or sister?"

He planned aloud. "I hear there's going to be a vacancy on the corner, five rooms on the second floor. Time we graduated from this dump! And then in a couple of years," he said, "maybe we'll even move to West End Avenue! Might as well aim high, right?" He threw Maury over his shoulder. "How'd you like to live on West End Avenue, son? Think you'd like that?"

My God, he doesn't see that I am strangling.

She got out a book of poetry. The contents were listed under Consolation: Courage: Suffering. She read from Henley's *Invictus* (what pompous nonsense!) to Kipling and Shakespeare. There was no consolation. You had to find your own courage. She put the book away.

One Saturday afternoon she said, "I'm going to look for a hat. You can take Maury for a while, can't you?"

"Of course. But it's going to rain."

"I'll take an umbrella." She had to get out. Last night she had dreamed about a long, curved, evil knife. Someone was coming toward her raising the knife. But who would want to kill her? She ought to do it herself.

The traffic rolled on Broadway through the rain. If I walked in front of the trolley, just stepped quickly in front as it came down the hill, it would all be over. But then—Maury. My little boy. Oh, my little boy.

She struggled in the wind. Her heart began to pound. The seven-months-old burden pressed down in her enormous belly. No strength. No strength at all. If I fall, I'll scream, scream it all out here on the street and everyone will know. I'm losing my mind.

The wind drove the greasy rain into her face and soaked behind her collar; wet wool clung to her neck. The wind rose and the rain came raging. The day grew dark. People shouted, jostling for shelter in doorways, anywhere. There was a flight of shallow steps: a post office or a school? There were people scurrying up the steps. Anna followed, into a place that was dry and still.

It was a church. For the first time in her life she had entered a church.

On three sides there were statues and pictures. The vivid young man with bright yellow hair, his body twisted on the cross. A pale blue plaster woman: that must be Mary, the one they call God's mother. Anna shut her eyes. I didn't buy a hat and Joseph will wonder why I spent a whole afternoon just walking around in the rain.

Someone began to practice on the organ, starting, stopping and starting again. The music rose like smoke, circling behind the gilded altar into the corners. She sat down and rested her forehead on the back of the seat and cried.

Dear God, listen to me, if the temple were open I would go in there. No, I wouldn't, I'd be afraid someone would see me. Dear God, I don't even know whether I believe in you. I wish I were like Joseph because he believes, he really does. But listen to me anyway, and tell me what I'm to do. I'm twenty-four years old. I have so many years to live through and how am I to get through them?

Someone asked, "Are you in trouble, daughter?"

She looked up at the young priest, in his long black robe with the metal chain around his waist. She had never been this close to a priest. At home when you saw one coming down the road you went the other way.

"I'm not a Catholic," she said. "I only came in out of the rain."

"I don't mind. If you want to sit here you're welcome. But perhaps you wanted to talk?"

A human being, a good face. And she would never see him again.

"I am in such trouble that I want to die," Anna said.

"Everyone feels that way at some time in his life." The priest sat down.

How to begin? "My husband trusts me," she whispered. *That's a stupid way to start.* "He tells me I'm the only person in the world he can absolutely trust."

The priest waited.

"He says he knows I would never lie to him. Never—"

"And you have lied to him?"

"More than that. Oh, more than that!" She could not look at him. Not at the statue or the pictures, either. Down at the floor, at her own hands in her lap. "How can I tell you? You will think that I am—you will not want to hear, you've never heard—"

"I've heard everything."

Not this. I can't say it, no, I can't. But I can't keep it all alone inside, either. Not any longer.

"Has it to do with the child you're expecting? Is that what you're trying to say?"

She didn't answer.

"It's not his child? Is that it?"

"No," she whispered. "Oh, my God, I would be better off dead!"

"That's not for you to say. Only God knows whether you would be better off and He will decide, you may be sure."

"But do I deserve to live?"

"Everything that lives deserves to live. And certainly this child deserves it."

"I would feel better if I could pay, if I were punished."

"And you think you won't be? Every day of your life."

The organ, which had stopped for a time, began again. The quiet music curled like smoke, like mist.

"I've looked for the courage to tell the truth to Joseph. I've prayed for the courage, but it doesn't come."

"Why must you tell him?"

"To be honest, to feel clean again."

"At the price of his peace?"

"Do you think it would be?"

"You think about it for a minute."

But no thoughts came, nothing coherent except the face of her little boy. He was sitting on the kitchen floor eating an apple.

"Is it, perhaps, that you love this other man?"

"No. No, it's my husband I love." An easy answer. True, and yet. . . . Peace and life and goodness; Maury, child of my heart; all these, weighed against that short exaltation, that rapture.

She cried out, "And so I have to go on like this!"

"If you were blind or crippled you would. People do." The priest sighed. "Human beings have so much courage, I marvel at how much."

"I've used up all my courage."

"You'll find it again. And thank God for giving it back to you." His voice was even, without reproach or sympathy.

"I hope so."

"And after a while things will be easier for you."

"I hope so."

Perhaps he does know something. He hears and sees so many things. Surely this must have happened before to somebody else?

The priest stood up. "Do you feel any better?"

"A little," she answered truthfully. Some of the weight had been relieved, as though she had taken it from herself and put it on him.

"Can you go home now?"

"I think I can. I'll try. I want to thank you," she whispered.

He raised his hand. His heavy skirt swept down the aisle.

THE BIRTH WAS hard. A neighbor took Maury and Ruth came to help.

"Odd that this baby took so long," she said. "The second is always easier."

Joseph studied the tiny girl in the bed with Anna. "Poor little thing! She looks worn out, too."

Anna sat up in alarm. "Why, is there anything wrong with her?"

"No, no. Dr. Arndt said she's perfect. I only meant, she's thin and that makes her look frail."

She was not pretty, the way Maury had been. She had sparse black hair and a monkey face. She looked anxious. But that was absurd.

"To think you two haven't got a name ready for her!" Ruth said.

"I left it to Anna," Joseph explained. "Maury was named after my father, so now it's her turn."

"My mother's name was Ida," Anna said.

"Something beginning with an 'I,' then," Ruth mused. "You don't want Ida, do you? It's so old-fashioned."

I'm so tired, Anna thought. What difference does a name make?

"Isabel," Ruth suggested. "Or, I know, Iris! That's a lovely name. There's been a serial in the paper about an English countess, Lady Iris Ashburton."

"Iris," Anna said. "And now if you'll put her in the basket, I think I could go to sleep."

SHORTLY AFTER THE new year she wheeled the carriage homeward from the grocer's. Maury trudged along holding her free hand. Halfway up the street a man in a priest's dark suit came abreast of them and stopped.

"Boy or girl?" he asked.

Heat surged into Anna's face. It had been dark in that place, but he remembered.

"A girl. Iris."

"Well. God bless you, Iris," he said, and walked on quickly.

God bless us all. The infant's lips moved hungrily. "I want lunch," Maury said.

"We're almost home. I'll feed you."

And care for you both with all my strength. Where had it come from, this new strength? Like water in a river that had gone dry. Power flowed into her arms and legs, pushed her up the hill. I'm gritting my teeth; I must stop gritting my teeth. I am getting better, though. God bless us all.

❧{12}❧

The city stretched and spread. Its long legs touched the edges of Brooklyn and Queens, and leaped the bridges past the Bronx to the borders of Westchester. The city raised long arms into the sky. All along Fifth Avenue the wrecker's ball, making way for new towers, crushed the Renaissance mansions of the million-aires. Those that were not crushed were turned into museums or offices for philanthropic agencies.

Hammers rang, steel on steel. Huge cranes, delicate as a dinosaur's head, moved over the street. Ten thousand rivets were driven between morning and night, ten thousand steel woodpeckers in a steel forest. Laborers climbed the great skeletons, forty stories above the ground, sixty stories, eighty. Up and up. Everything was rising, the towers, the stock market and the fortunes of men.

These were the years of Harding and of "normalcy," although they were not normal at all: such times had never been seen before and would not be seen again until after the next great war, a quarter of a century away.

Those who in 1918 had counted their assets in hundreds of dollars could in a few years' time, if they were canny, hard working and lucky, count them in tens of thousands or more. The building business exploded like a rocket. Houses were sold before they were finished. Land values doubled and tripled and doubled again. If you were smart enough to keep ahead of the forward movement you could turn a tract of empty acres on Long Island into a tidy community of two-family houses or six-story apartment buildings, into a lasting income or a splendid profit.

Not that it was easy. The telling is a great deal easier than the doing. Starting from nothing, one had to work eighteen hours a day to get a foothold. One had to keep on at eighteen hours a day if one were not to lose the foothold. Because, once it was lost, how would a man ever manage to get another?

A painter and a plumber began together with one small, heavily mortgaged apartment building on Washington Heights. They put themselves into it, all of themselves, their strength and every dollar beyond what they needed to buy the food on their families' tables. They bought new stoves and bathroom fixtures. They scraped the floors; they repaired, they renewed from bottom to top. They painted every apartment and every hallway. They polished the brasswork and puttied the windows. They even bought two potted evergreens to stand beside the door.

There was no building on the block, or for many blocks, that looked like theirs when they were finished.

The tenants were astonished; it was years since the place had been so clean. A sign was put up outside: *No Vacancies.*

And then they raised the rents.

One morning a broker called. He had an investor, interested in well-kept, fully rented property needing no repairs. So they sold the house, having owned it not quite one year. Their profit was twenty percent.

They went to the bank that held their mortgage, to the real estate department. "See what we can do," they said. "Now give us a mortgage on another building and we'll do the same."

By the end of the year 1920 they owned two houses on Washington Heights. Neither of them had had a new pair of shoes or an evening out since they began. They were plowing every penny back into property. They bought three vacant lots in Brooklyn. Then luck, pure luck, came into the picture, because the syndicate that owned the property adjoining needed their lots to put up a hotel. They named their price and the syndicate paid: it had no choice.

Now they met an electrical contractor and a firm of masons, father and sons: could they not pool their trades and do some building of their own? The mason knew a lawyer who had clients with cash to invest. They bought more lots and built a row of two-family houses: it is wise to start small. They had to rise at four in the morning to get to the job in Brooklyn on time.

The houses were sold before they were completed. A dentist down the block approached them with a proposition: would they be interested in a piece of Long Island land? He would like to go in with them. They could have the land for a song. Well, not quite a song exactly, but the price was right enough. More confident now, they built a whole tract of two-family houses, seventy-five houses and a row of stores.

Cautious, patient, tenacious plan and labor. Brick on brick, stone on stone. Buy, build, sell, hold, pyramid and grow. Very slowly, so very slowly at first. Then faster and bolder. A loft in the garment district. A garage on Second Avenue. Big syndicates, big mortgages. Growing profits and a growing reputation. That is how it was done.

And, of course, the times were right.

The times were right for lawyers or brokers, for textile merchants, manufacturing furriers or wholesale jewelers. Immigrants and the sons of immigrants moved northward from the tenements to the simple, respectable reaches of the Bronx and Washington Heights. Most never went any farther than simple respectability. Others, the more clever and the luckier, kept moving with improving fortunes. As the great fortress apartment houses rose along West End Avenue, with their elevators and doormen in uniform, these families came down from the Bronx and Washington Heights to fill them. They came with brand-new Oriental rugs and silver, the acquisitions of an astounding, quick prosperity; brought, too, their vigor and a driving ambition.

*   *   *

THE BUILDING ON West End Avenue was sixteen stories tall, with two apartments to a floor. Joseph and Anna leased the one with the river view, nine spacious rooms and a large square entrance hall on the eleventh floor. Standing in the center of the hall one could look into the living room where the sky filled the tall windows, into the paneled library where Anna's books in their boxes were still packed, into the splendid dining room with the long table, ten tapestried chairs and a Chinese screen concealing the door to the kitchen.

"Beautiful," Ruth said admiringly. "And to think you put it all together so quickly! How did you do it?"

"I would have liked to take more time," Anna said. "I'm not sure I like everything as much as I should. However, it's done."

"Not like everything! Anna, it's gorgeous."

"Joseph wanted it to be finished right away. You know how neat he is! He can't stand living in a mess. He says he lived in one long enough! So he asked Mrs. Marks—that's his lawyer's wife—to show me where to shop, and here we are."

"Well, it's gorgeous," Ruth repeated firmly. "Even a baby grand!"

"A surprise from Joseph."

"Well, a home should have a piano, even if nobody plays. It looks so nice, don't you think?"

"Iris will learn to play. Maury too, if he wants, but you know how Maury is. He won't do anything unless he wants to. Iris will learn, if only to please her father."

"Little old lady," Ruth said. "Little four-year-old lady."

"Let me show you her room."

Iris' room was pink and white and rose. There were shelves for her books, a little white bed with a canopy, a doll house on a table in one corner.

"Oh, the doll house!" Ruth cried.

"Yes, it was Joseph's present for her birthday. She's really too young for it, but he buys her everything he sees."

"Men are always like that with their daughters. June is getting as fresh as her spoiled friends. I don't allow her to get away with it but Solly can't say no to anything."

"And this is Maury's room. I let him help me fix it up. He's a big boy, after all, and so excited about moving here," Anna said fondly, inspecting again the plaids, the trains spread on the floor, the banner on the wall between the windows: *For God, for Country and for Yale.*

"What's that for?" Ruth asked.

"Oh, I thought it was nice. Besides, I would like him to go to Yale."

"My sons are at N.Y.U. and we find it good enough."

"Of course, of course," Anna said quickly. "What's the difference?" And wondering how to avoid the appearance of parading their success, she said timidly, "Joseph's lawyer, Mr. Marks, suggested a good school for Maury. It's where his own children go."

"A private school?"

"Well, you know, I would never have thought of it, but Joseph meets these men, builders and architects, and he comes home with such ideas! . . . What can you do? It's his money, after all, and he can spend it as he wants."

"Private school," Ruth repeated.

"Yes, and Iris will start kindergarten there in the fall. It's more convenient to have them both at the same place, naturally." Anna heard herself apologizing, and was annoyed with herself. What was there to apologize about? If Ruth was a little green-eyed, well, it was only natural.

"And you have a radio! We haven't got one yet. What do you think of it?"

"I don't get much of a chance at it, between Joseph and Maury. They take turns with the earphones. But it is a miracle, really."

"I read that next year they'll be putting out a model where you don't need earphones, so the whole family can listen at once. You'll have one, I'm sure, Joseph seems to buy everything in sight."

"Ruth, do you ever think of where we lived downtown and ask yourself how this happened? I often think, I don't deserve all this."

"How it happened? We worked like slaves, Solly and I, and we both deserve whatever we've got. Not," Ruth added, "that we have anywhere near what you have, but we're doing all right. Solly's got a clever partner, and there's a future."

"Sometimes it doesn't seem real to me," Anna said slowly.

"It's real enough. You'll find out when you try to keep this big place clean, I can tell you! I should think you'll be needing a cleaning woman once a week at least."

"I already have two girls, Joseph called an agency. They're coming tomorrow."

"Two girls? How many days?"

"Well, there are two rooms on the other side of the kitchen. So they'll be living in. Very nice girls," Anna said hurriedly into Ruth's silence. "Two Irish sisters. Ellen and Margaret."

"And to think you were once a maid yourself!" Ruth said.

If she wants to make me angry, she won't succeed, Anna thought.

"Yes, to think," she answered calmly, "that I came to this country with a cloth bundle and two candlesticks! Which reminds me, I'd better unpack them before somebody steps on them."

And reaching into a box, as yet unpacked, by the diningroom door, she took out the candlesticks, heavy ornate silver, very old. She blew the dust off; she set them lovingly on the table.

These, too, had seen so many places before this place! She stood there studying them, then looked around the room at the English china and the French crystal, at all the costly, fragile, glossy things that now were hers. And somewhere, under the excitement, lay a certainty that was grieving, guilty and afraid. A quiet certainty that this could not, would not, last.

❊{13}❊

Her parents don't know she is awake. They think she has finished her homework—she is in the fourth grade and they still don't get very much of it—and has gone to bed. They don't know what a hard time she often has falling asleep. Sometimes she gets out of bed and stands at the window. Her room is on the corner; at oblique angles she can see both westward over the river to the lights on the Palisades, and eastward down West End Avenue where fewer and fewer cars pass as the night grows later. She thinks about nothing in particular, just wishes it were already Friday so there would be no school for two whole days; hopes for rain on Saturday so she can read at home and her mother won't make her go out for fresh air; hopes that on Sunday it will not rain so that she and Papa can have their morning walk around the reservoir.

Their Sunday walk is her special time. Mama sleeps later on Sundays and Maury does too, unless he has plans to go skating or somewhere with his friends. Papa never sleeps late.

"Years of habit," he says, "of getting up at five. Now I stretch it and get up at six."

By half past eight they are in the park. On the other side of the reservoir rises the jagged line of buildings on Fifth Avenue. The wind blows, crimping the water. Joggers pass panting in their gray sweat shirts, passing them sometimes twice in their round, although Papa and Iris walk briskly.

"I love being with my girl," Papa always says.

Iris loves to be with him. Often she thinks how nice it would be if Mama and Maury went away. (Died? Is that what she means?) Then there would only be Papa and herself at the dinner table, Papa and herself to sit and talk in the library in the evening. She is guilty about these thoughts. Bad, bad thoughts, they are.

Across the corridor now the light shines out under Maury's door. He studies late, but he has to; he is learning Latin and algebra, he has to keep up his marks to get into Yale. Iris has good report cards too, but it is not as important for her. A girl—a woman—Papa explains, doesn't have to *do* anything with her education. It's a fine thing, of course, for her to learn and improve her mind, because then she will be a better wife and mother, a better person. But she doesn't actually have to *do* anything, the way boys do. Once Mama said someday it might be different, and women would go to work and do all the things men did. But Papa said that was absolutely ridiculous and he'd like to see any wife of his go to work as long as he was able to support her!

She is wide awake. It's chilly; she puts on her robe, and in bare feet—she likes the rough feel of the carpet on her soles—goes padding down the corridor to stand in the corner where it joins the front hall. From where her parents sit in the library they cannot see her. But she can hear them, and their voices comfort her, especially when she is worried about something. (Often she worries about the math teacher, an impatient angry woman. Math is the only subject in which Iris does not do very well and she is afraid to go to school because of it.)

Sometimes her parents don't talk at all. Mama is always studying something. Shakespeare or a course at the Museum of Art. Papa often works on rolls of blue paper spread on the table between the windows. He makes a short remark about them. Mama tells him she has taken a subscription to the Philharmonic on Friday afternoons with Mrs. Davison. Papa says that's fine, he knows how she enjoys it and he's sorry he doesn't, but he might just as well be truthful about it.

Other times they talk about interesting things. Mrs. Malone has had a miscarriage and Mama says it's too bad but, after all, seven children ought to be enough. She learns that Mama is to have a mink coat; Papa wants her to and they can get a good buy from the furrier on the floor below Solly's place. She learns that Maury will get a new bicycle for his birthday. Maury is always surprised that Iris knows everything before he does.

She is a little afraid of being found out, but not much. Papa wouldn't be angry. He is never angry at her. Mama would not be exactly angry, either, but she would get up and say quite firmly, "Little girls belong in bed. And nice people don't listen to other people's conversations. Come, Iris." And Mama would make her go back to bed. That is the difference between Papa and Mama.

Tonight she becomes aware that they are talking about her. She draws in her breath and hears her own heartbeat.

"I wish she would go to camp in Maine. It would do her good, out in the woods with other children."

"Joseph, she would hate it!"

"Maury seems to get so much out of it. He can't wait to go back every summer."

"Maury is Maury and everything's easy for him. Iris would be miserable."

It's true. All that she has ever heard about camp tells her that she would be. The very thought of living in a cabin at the mercy of five other girls, so far from home, from her room where she can be safe, is terrifying.

Last year she had a friend. Amy was a small, quiet girl like herself. They used to "sleep over" at each other's houses on weekends. They wrote poetry together. They were best friends. Then in the summer Amy went away to camp, while Iris went with her parents to the rented house at Long Beach. The first day of school she was so glad to see Amy again.

"I wrote some more poems over the summer," she told her.

And Amy answered, scornfully and very loudly so that other people could hear: "Who cares? I'm too old for that stuff anymore."

And Iris, shocked and wounded, saw that Amy had changed, had gone over to the "others." Now she passed Iris in the halls pretending not to see her. Now she and Marcy were best friends. Marcy has long braids that the boys pull. When boys are around, Amy and Marcy always laugh very loud so that the boys come up to them and ask, "What's funny?" The boys are so stupid, they can't see that these girls are doing this on purpose so they will notice them.

"Strange," Papa says, "two children, and so different! The same home, the same parents, and so different!"

Yes, true. Maury is on student council and the lower school basketball team. Next year he will be on the varsity that plays against the city's other big private schools. People are always surprised that Iris is his sister, although grownups are too polite to show it. But kids in school often don't believe it.

"You are *not* Maury Friedman's sister!" they say, and once a girl in her class walked up to Maury after a basketball game and asked, "Are you really her brother? She says you are."

"Sure," Maury said, surprised. "Sure I am."

"Maury is like my brothers," Mama declares. "Especially Eli. He reminds me so much of him."

On her dressing table she keeps enlarged snapshots of her family in Europe. Uncle Dan has a chubby wife surrounded by children. Uncle Eli and his wife stand on skis in front of a mountain house with icicles on the eaves. Their little girl is on skis, too. Her name is Liesel. She is Iris' age and she has long unreal blond hair. Liesel and her parents look like sunshine. Iris' head is full of thoughts like that, comparing people with things. Ellen and Margaret are ears of corn, tall and narrow, with large yellow teeth.

Do other people have such thoughts? she wonders. Is there anybody else in the world like me?

Her parents' voices fall away. She leans forward to hear.

"He's supposed to be a first-class pediatrician. I thought he was very thorough."

"And? What did he say?"

"Nothing, really. There's nothing wrong with her. Peaked looking, but basically healthy, outside of being somewhat nervous. But we've known all that."

"She's so sensitive!" Papa says. "Do you know what she asked me when we took our walk last Sunday? She said, 'Papa, do you ever look at your arm and think about how it was made out of people who died hundreds of years ago and wonder whether they would like you if they could know you?' Imagine, a child of nine saying a thing like that!"

"Yes, she's a thoughtful child. An unusual child."

"You know, I often remember when she was only a few weeks old and I used to go in to look at her in the crib. She touched me, Anna, in a way that Maury never did. He was so strong and hungry and healthy. But she! . . . I used to go to the door and come back to look at her again, and I remember thinking that she isn't going to find life easy."

Her mother doesn't speak, or if she does, Iris doesn't hear her.

Then Papa says, "She's my whole heart, Anna! But how I wish she looked like you! It wouldn't matter that she was timid. People would flock to her anyway."

"Ruth said the other day that Iris is the kind of plain girl who will improve with age, and I think she's right."

"Would you really call her so plain, Anna?"

"It's hard to judge your own child. But I wouldn't say she was pretty."

Not pretty. *Not pretty.* You might as well say: *You have a terrible disease. You'll never walk again.* You might as well say: *You have one month to live, you're going to die.* And so that's the way it is. That's what people think of me.

Now suddenly Papa says, "Anna! Mrs. Werner died! It's here in the paper. Survived by husband Horace, son Paul, daughter Evelyn Jonas in Cleveland."

"I didn't know."

"You really should read the obituaries. She was just sixty. I wonder what she had."

"I've no idea," Mama says.

Werner. Iris never forgets names, rarely forgets anything. Those are the people they met downtown when they went to buy her spring coat last week. And the lady *told* Mama she was sick! Why is Mama telling a lie?

They were coming out of Best's that day when the lady stopped them on the sidewalk. "Excuse me, but you are Anna, aren't you?"

"Yes, I'm Anna," Mama answered. "How are you, Mrs. Werner?"

"Paul, you remember Anna, of course?" the lady said.

The man—he was very tall and looked like the lady, so you could see he was her son—just bowed a little and answered, "Of course." But he didn't say a word to Mama.

The lady was really nice. She told Mama, "You were always pretty, but you've become even more so."

Funny red spots came out on Mama's face. She certainly wasn't very polite to those people. She always tells me to say thank you for a compliment and she didn't say a word.

Then Mrs. Werner asked, "Is this your daughter?"

"My daughter, Iris," Mama said.

So Iris had to shake hands and say, "How do you do?" The lady smiled at her, but the man just looked at her very hard and didn't smile.

Then the lady said softly, "I see you've had great good fortune, Anna."

Mama didn't say very much, only, "Yes, I have," which was unusual because Mama always talked so long whenever they met one of her friends.

The lady had beautiful gray hair, almost silver, and a fur coat like Mama's. But her eyes were very dark, and the skin below them was dark. She looked sick.

"We've moved from the house, you know, on account of the stairs. All of a sudden my heart's gone bad. But you, you look marvelous! You haven't got one bit older."

"Oh, yes," Mama said, "years older."

"Well, you don't look it. Do come and see us sometime, Anna. We're at Seventy-eighth and Fifth. And my son lives just two blocks down, which makes it very nice."

When they walked away Mama said, not really talking to Iris, but to herself, "Fifth Avenue! Naturally, the West Side wouldn't be fine enough anymore!"

Iris remembers all of this perfectly.

"The funeral is Wednesday at eleven," Papa says now. "I'll try to go with you if I can make it. Otherwise you'll have to go alone."

"I'm not going at all," Mama says calmly.

Iris hears the newspaper rattle. "Not going? You can't mean it!"

"Certainly I do. I haven't seen the woman in years. I meant nothing to her in life, so why should I go to see her in death?"

"Why do people go to funerals at all? Because it's only decent to pay one's respects! I'm amazed at you!"

Mama makes no answer and Papa says, "Besides, they were very nice to us, in case you've forgotten. There's such a thing as gratitude."

A touch of anger comes into Mama's voice. "Gratitude? You take a loan at a bank, you pay it back with interest, and you're supposed to be grateful to the bank?"

"This wasn't a bank. Anna, I don't understand you!"

"Where is it written that you have to understand everything?"

This is not like Mama, who is always saying things like: The man is head of the house, remember that when you get married. Or: Marriage isn't fifty-fifty; the woman must go most of the way to keep the peace of the home.

The door of Maury's room bangs open and he plunges down the hall. "You little sneak!" he cries, and thumps Iris on the back with his fist.

Her parents come running. "What is it? What are you doing?"

"This sneaky kid's been standing here eavesdropping! If you ever do that to me, Iris, I'll punch the breath out of you, you damn pest."

"Maury, that's no language," Papa says. "Come in here, Iris. What's going on? Were you really standing there listening to us?"

"I didn't mean to listen. I was going to the kitchen for an apple."

"Like heck she was!" Maury says.

Mama shakes her head at Maury. "Please, Maury, go back to your homework and let us handle this. I want to know what you heard, Iris."

She wants to cry out: "I heard you say that I'm not pretty, and Cousin Ruth said I'll be better when I'm older. It's none of her business and I hate her and I hate you!" But she is too proud to say it.

Her mother's forehead is worried. Meanly, craftily, Iris takes pleasure in what she is about to do. "I heard you tell Papa you didn't see that lady, but you did see her!"

"What are you talking about?" Papa asks.

"Mrs. Werner," Iris tells him. "We saw her last week downtown with her son."

"Is that true, Anna?"

Mama sighs. "Yes, we ran into them on Fifth Avenue. I didn't think it worth mentioning."

"But you thought it worth hiding just now, for what reason I can't imagine."

"Joseph!" Mama says. "This is hardly the place—" And Iris knows she means: *Not in front of the child.*

"Very well, then," Papa says. "Iris, your mother will give you some hot milk in your room and then I want you to go to sleep."

"I want you to give it to me, Papa!" Iris protests.

Her father holds the glass while she sips the milk. "Feeling better now? Something's upset you, so can you tell me what it is?"

Her eyes fill. She whispers, "I haven't any friends. I'm not popular."

He says indignantly, "If all those kids are too stupid to see your worth, that's their loss! You're the smartest one of the lot! You're my little queen and when you grow up you'll run rings around them all, you'll show them!"

"I'm not pretty," she says.

"Who says you're not? I'd like to hear anyone tell me you're not!"

"Marcy has thick braids with ribbons on the ends."

"So what? I don't even like braids! Your kind of hair is much nicer."

"Papa, it isn't!"

"Honey, I think it is. Tell you what," he says, taking the empty glass, "Next week's your Thanksgiving vacation. How would you like to go to a movie with me? We can go to my office in the morning, and we'll even have time before the movie to buy you a new dress. Mama's having a dinner party and I'd like to show you off to all the people in a brand-new dress. Then we'll see who's pretty!"

"I'd like to go to your office and the movie. But not to the party."

"All right, we won't talk about it now." He bends to kiss her. "Are you sleepy now? Will you go right to sleep if I turn off the light?"

She nods and he turns out the light. But she isn't sleepy. She lies in the dark and her thoughts rush.

Lots of times during school vacations, Papa takes them to his office. Papa is proud of Maury in his navy blue suit and cap, of Iris in her good coat that has a beaver collar, of the braces on their teeth. He takes them into the private room where he has a great mahogany desk, just like Mr. Malone's across the hall.

Mr. Malone is fat and tells jokes. He keeps a box of chocolates in a drawer. The Malones are like family; when Mama had her appendix out Mrs. Malone came to the hospital every day. They live in an apartment quite nearby, except that theirs has more rooms because they have so many children. These children are all big and healthy looking; Iris feels weak and sallow in their company, as though they could see the shoulder blades under her dress, like the frail wings of birds when you pull the feathers back. The Malones like Maury, as everyone does. He goes all over their apartment, looking at stamp collections and baseball cards, eating cake in the pantry. Iris sits with the grownups until Mrs. Malone calls the daughter who is nearest Iris' age. "Mavis," she says nicely, "why don't you take Iris into your room and show her the doll house?" And Iris goes, knowing that Mavis doesn't want her, knowing she ought to say something lively and unable to think of anything to say at all.

Mama goes on talking in the Malones' living room. She can always talk to people, to Mrs. Malone's sister who is a nun, to Ellen and Margaret at home, to a cranky saleswoman in a shop. People always smile at her. Papa says her voice is like a bell; it is one of the first things he ever noticed about her. "Most women yap and shrill like busy little dogs," he says.

Yes, he loves Mama, it's plain to see. He's always talking about how smart she is and what a wonderful cook, much better than Margaret who gets paid for doing it. He boasts about her beautiful red hair and was upset for three days after Mama had it cut off.

Yes, he loves Mama; he talks about her too much. "Listen to your mother, Iris," he says, "your mother knows what's right!"

But tonight he is angry at Mama. They are quarreling inside. She hears them now, in their bedroom. Good, good. I'm glad he's angry at her.

"It's mighty queer," Papa says. "I don't know who it is that you've got it in for, the mother or the son? You get all stiffened up whenever those people are mentioned."

"I do not!" Mama screams. Iris has never heard her shriek like that.

"Yes, you do! It makes me wonder sometimes what the devil went on in that house to make you react like this? Can't even mention a chance meeting, won't go to the woman's funeral. I can't make head or tail of it—"

The door slams. There is more loud talking that Iris cannot distinguish; then the door is opened again and she hears Papa say, "Very well, I suppose it's just false pride. You've risen in the world and don't like to be reminded—"

"Will you leave me alone!" Mama cries.

Then there is silence.

A long time later the door to Iris' room is opened. A wedge of light comes in and widens. Her mother walks over and stands by the bed.

"Iris?"

She does not answer.

"Iris, you're awake. I can tell by your breathing."

"What do you want?"

Her mother sits down on the bed and takes Iris' hand, which lies in hers, not moving. "I wanted to come in and hold your hand before you fell asleep."

Her face is partly turned away, but Iris sees that her eyes are funny; they look swollen. "Have you been crying, Mama?"

"No."

"Yes, you have. Was it because I told about that lady and that man?"

"What lady and what man?"

Pretending again! "You know!" Iris says crossly. "The lady who died."

"No," says Mama, looking away.

Then something rises in Iris, something she has never felt before. It is a kind of softness, feeling sorry for Mama.

"I did it on purpose," she says. "I wanted to make Papa angry at you."

"I know."

"Aren't you angry at me?"

"No. We all have feelings sometimes of not liking people, or wanting to hurt them."

She wants to say, I'm sorry I can't love you as much as Papa. She says instead, "Papa wants to buy me a new dress for your party, but I don't want to come in and meet all the people."

He always calls her in when they have company. She has to stand alone in the doorway while all the people, the ladies in their perfume and bracelets, sit in a row around the room, their faces turned to Iris as she stands there being looked at.

"I don't want to," she repeats. "Do I have to?"

"No," Mama says. "You don't."

"Do you promise? No matter what Papa says?"

"I promise."

"Because I hate it! I hate it!"

"I understand," Mama says.

She sighs with relief. "I feel sleepy now," she says.

"Do you? That's good." Her mother goes out and closes the door very softly.

SHE COULD NOT then have known what she knew much later: that her father in his blind love lied to her, maybe not even realizing that he did. He lied when he called her a queen, for she had been no queen then and never would be. He lied when he talked of the great things she would do and the people she would "show." She would be embarrassed to remember how foolish his loving words had been.

But Mama gave no false hopes. Mama was often ill at ease with Iris, that was plain to see. For this Iris was often to feel great anger, to feel that she could really hate her mother. And at the same time she knew that they were and always would be as closely attached as the fingers to the hand and the hand to the arm. How could she have understood such things when she was nine years old? It was only after passing through a great deal of life that she would understand.

Yet perhaps in a way, though surely she could not have expressed it when she was just nine, perhaps in a way she did understand it, even then.

⚜{14}⚜

Nothing was done by any of the family in that house, or outside of it, that his father didn't know about. Maury felt sometimes as though his presence was everywhere, even when he wasn't at home. Some of his friends didn't like their fathers; one or two really hated them. Some of them felt that their fathers weren't interested in them. That was not true of Maury and Pa. He was interested in everything about Maury: his friends or his teeth or his manners. He taught him how to tie a tie. He showed him how to shake hands: "A man gives a firm handshake, as if he means it," he said.

Pa took Maury to his barber because he didn't like the way the old one cut his hair. They played checkers and Pa had promised to teach him to play pinochle, although Ma didn't approve. But Maury knew he would teach him anyway. Sometimes they wrestled on the living-room floor—his mother didn't approve of that either—and although Maury was almost as tall as Pa, Pa always won. His muscles were like iron. "That's from years of labor," he said, and now he kept up with exercises every morning. Once Maury saw him pick up a heavy man who had fallen in the street and carry him to the sidewalk all by himself.

But Maury wished Pa wasn't so interested in him. Sometimes he wished Pa would just let him alone. Iris, that stupid whining kid, could talk him out of anything. Not Maury; Maury had to "toe the mark." That was one of his expressions. Another was "measure up," an expression that Maury hated.

This morning Maury was angry, mad-angry, because he had to go with Pa to visit his grandmother. She was in an old-age home.

"Aw, gee," he said, "do I have to go? A bunch of us were going to the rink this morning."

"Of course you have to go," his mother said. "You haven't seen your grandmother in months, and she's asked for you." She handed Maury his tie and jacket and got his good camel-hair coat out of the closet. She was all rushed and anxious. "Hurry, hurry, your father's already got his coat on. You know he can't stand being kept waiting!"

Maury strained into his sleeve. "Washington's Birthday, and I have to waste it! When do I get a whole day off to go skating?"

He knew that, if it were up to her, she'd let him go. She did look sympathetic for a moment, but then she said cheerfully, "Go, go. It won't be so bad," and pushed him to the front door where his father was ready to leave.

She remembered something. "Wait, wait, Joseph," and thrust a flowered tin box into Maury's hands. "I baked cookies for your grandmother. I'm sure they don't get such wonderful food in that place."

She kissed his father. She was tall, her face was on a level with his father's. In the morning she wore loose robes, blue or yellow or pale green like the insides of bonbons. Her clothes smelled sweet like candy. His father was all dark, except for the white shining board of his collar. He wore dark suits, sometimes a blue that was almost black, sometimes a gray that was almost black, a hard round derby hat and black shoes.

It was cold this morning; they felt it even in the elevator shaft as they went down to the street floor, and then the wind blasted and slammed them across the sidewalk to where the chauffeur held the door of the car.

"We're going up to the home, Tim," Pa said.

"Yes sir, Mr. Friedman." Tim always touched his cap and asked whether it was cold enough today. Then he went around to the front of the car and swung into the driver's seat.

The home where Maury's grandmother lived was on the fringes of the Bronx. Once it had been open country but now it was empty lots, with scatterings of new brick row houses and stores. It looked unfinished. Maury didn't know anybody who lived here and he only came here to visit his grandmother, which was not very often. It had been a year since he had seen her last, just before his Bar Mitzvah, when his father was so upset because she wasn't able to come and "see this day."

"The car runs like a charm," Pa said. He lit a cigar. He always had half a dozen rich black ones in the inner pocket of his jacket; he and his friends liked to exchange them. They urged their brands on one another, blowing out a blue-gray haze of smoke, not unpleasant, although some women objected to it violently. But Pa seemed proud that his wife like the fragrance, although Maury knew that even if his mother didn't like it she wouldn't say so.

His father struck another match, fumbling with the soggy end of the cigar, took it from his mouth to study it, replaced it and puffed again.

"Ah," he said and repeated, "the car runs like a charm."

The car was new. They had owned cars as long as Maury could remember, but this was the first car meant to be driven by a chauffeur. It had a sliding glass panel between the back of his neck and where the passengers sat. Maury's father was still not used to it, was perhaps still uncomfortable with the chauffeur. There had been some talk about it at the dinner table.

"I drive a lot," he had explained, but it sounded like an apology. "We've got jobs all over the city now and out on the Island. It's too hard to have to worry about parking. Besides, this way I can go over papers and save time while I'm being driven."

Where he himself was concerned, Pa always had to have a practical reason for anything he spent. He would buy the most expensive things for his family, toys or furniture or fur coats for Maury's mother, but with himself he was frugal.

He unfolded the *New York Times* and handed the first section to Maury. "I already read it at breakfast," he said. "Read it thoroughly; it can be a big help with your school work."

Pa was so concerned with what Maury did at school. He never had time to go to teacher conferences; Maury's mother did that, but in the evening Pa wanted to know everything that had been said. And he read the report cards very carefully when they came twice a year. He was always pleased.

He would slap Maury on the back. "Very good, son, very fine," he would say. "That's as it should be."

Maury wondered what would happen if the reports were not "as they should be." He knew his father wouldn't punish or scold too hard, the way some fathers did. But he also knew what his father expected.

The home was an old stone mansion, with wings and additions, lawns and a portico over the door. The inside was a net of corridors and cubicles, the corridors clogged with wheelchairs and tin trays of dirty dishes standing outside the rooms. And such a smell! A smell of disinfectant, frying grease and urine. Maury hated it. All the old, old people pushing walkers, and the young nurses, brisk and rapid, rushing in and out of rooms where through half-open doors you could see more old people lying in the beds, their gray hair mussed on the pillows. Maury hated it.

"Your grandmother is seventy-eight," Pa said now. Her room was at the end of the hall and she lived in it alone. Most of the people lived two in a room.

"Danny has a great-grandmother. She's ninety-two."

"That's very rare. And she had an easy life, that woman, never worked a day or worried a minute. Mama, hello, how are you?"

The grandmother was sitting with four other old men and women in an alcove outside of her room. If his father hadn't spoken to her, Maury would have gone right past without recognizing her. All the old women looked alike in their sweaters and printed dresses, either black or lavender. Those who weren't blobby were shriveled. Maury's grandmother was shriveled.

"Aren't you going to say something to your grandma?"

Maury said hello to her and kissed her. He knew he was expected to. He didn't want to kiss her. His stomach went queasy at the touch; she had a sort of milky film over her eyes that were turned up to him and the spittle was collected thickly at the corners of her mouth. She disgusted him.

Pa drew up a pair of straight wooden chairs. "Give your grandma the cookies," he said, and then corrected himself. "No, put them in her room, she can eat later." He leaned toward her. "Well, Mama," he said again.

The old woman stared at him and wrinkled her forehead. Her eyes were empty.

"It's Joseph, Mama," Pa said. "Joseph, your son. And I've brought Maury to see you."

Was she deaf, or what? Didn't she know her own son? Maury stared uncomfortably.

Then suddenly she began to talk. She leaned forward and took Pa's hand. She cried and laughed. Pa answered her in Yiddish, and Maury understood none of it.

The fat old woman on Maury's other side touched his arm and tapped the side of her head. "She don't talk sense," she whispered loudly. "Don't pay attention," she said in English. "Her mind goes sometimes. She talks foolish."

Pa heard and frowned. But the old woman was not to be discouraged. "You're too thin," she told Maury.

The old man in the circle stared at Maury and said, "He ain't too thin!"

"What do you know? You got any children?" the old woman argued. "I got four children, three grandchildren, what do you know?"

"I got nieces and nephews, anyway. You got to have children? You got eyes in your head, that's enough!"

"I say he's too thin."

"Maury, why don't you take a little walk around and see the place?" his father suggested.

"There's nothing to see," Maury told him.

The old man asked, "That's your grandma?"

Maury nodded.

"Why you don't talk to her, then?"

Maury flushed. "She doesn't speak English."

Now she was talking volubly to his father, laughing or crying or some of both, perhaps. She was telling a long story, making complaints or requests. Did they make any sense or not? Maury couldn't tell; his father just listened. Now and then he would nod or shake his head.

Then the grandmother looked at Maury and said something and his father answered. Maury looked away.

The old man said suddenly, "Your father's an important person. I'm eighty-eight and I know an important person when I see one. You can be anything you want," he told Maury. "A boy like you."

Maury looked down at the floor. The old man was wetting his pants. The stain was spreading on his trousers and sliding down the leg. It was starting to soak the tops of his shoes.

Jesus, let me get out of this loony-bin.

A nurse came hurrying and took the old man by the arm. "Oh, my. Oh, my, we have to go to the bathroom, don't we?"

His grandmother began to cry again.

"Maury," Pa said, very firmly this time, "Maury, wait outside. I won't be long. Or take a walk and look around."

"Why don't you go see the beautiful recreation room your father gave us?" the nurse suggested. "Turn right at the end of the corridor, you'll see it there."

It was boiling hot on account of the old people; he'd heard they were always cold. He took off his overcoat and stood in the doorway of the new room. It was large and light, with a bright blue linoleum floor and imitation leather chairs. Some old people were playing cards. There was a new upright piano in one corner and a woman was playing on it, the same chords over and over: "My Old Kentucky Home." A brown radio stood on a table in another corner next to a machine that gave out Cokes and candy bars. There was even a platform with curtains drawn back and fastened to the wall so it could be used as a stage. An

old man got up onto it now and shuffled, doing a cakewalk. Maury felt embarrassed for him. Then on the wall beside the double doors he saw the bronze
plaque: *This room furnished through the gift of Joseph and Anna Friedman,* it said.

His father gave a lot to charity. The mail was always full of requests from the
blind and from hospitals and the Jewish poor. He used to see him writing out
checks at his desk. Once Mr. Malone even sent some priests. Maury had opened
the door and been surprised to see these two men in their turned-around collars.
Pa took them into his den and after a while they came out smiling and saying
thank you. "We shall remember you in our masses," they said when they left.

Maury remembered feeling a certain pride in that. People respected his father.
Wherever they went people listened to him as if they wanted to please him.
Sometimes Maury went with him to the construction sites and followed him
through the din and bustle of unloading trucks and cranes, cement mixers and
men running wheelbarrows full of bricks. They climbed through all the confusion
of boards and pipes and tubing and rolls of wire, through the damp, dank smell
that is the smell of new building. His father asked questions and pointed out
something that had been done wrong or not done at all. He knew what all these
things were for. Then they went outside to the little wooden house at the curb
marked Rental Office, and there Pa went over books and talked on the telephone.
He unrolled plans, white ink on blue paper, and talked courteously to people
who came in to inquire. They went back on the sidewalk. Men in hard hats came
over and his father introduced him: "My son Maury," he said, and the men shook
hands and looked at him respectfully as if he weren't just thirteen years old. And
he knew that the respect was because of his father.

A nurse came up behind him. "What do you think of the room?" she asked
Maury.

"It's very nice."

"Your father's been good to us. He's a very generous, kind man," she said.

Pa beckoned from the end of the hall. Maury was relieved and pretended to be
surprised. "Are we leaving already?"

"Yes, your grandmother isn't feeling well. I don't want to tire her."

"Do you want me to go and say good-by to her?" He hoped not, but knew that
he ought at least to ask.

"No, thanks, it won't matter," Pa said. "She's gone to her room."

They stopped at a desk near the elevator where a nurse sat in front of telephones and charts.

"That matter we talked about," Pa said. "I don't want it to happen again.
There's no excuse for allowing her to fall out of bed."

"We'll do our best, Mr. Friedman, of course. But you know, she is failing fast
and—"

"That makes no difference," his father said firmly. "I don't want it to happen
again."

"Yes, Mr. Friedman, of course." She smiled brightly, artificially. "This is your
son, isn't he? What a handsome boy! He looks like an Englishman."

"Yes. He's a good boy," Pa said, still not smiling.

She arched her lips at Maury. "I have the most gorgeous little niece. I'll have to introduce you in a couple of years—"

The elevator door opened and closed on her words. "Idiotic woman!" Pa said.

But Maury was annoyed at something else. Here he had given up his holiday because his grandmother wanted to see him and she hadn't even known him! That ruined, old, old—*thing*! Impossible to think of her as part of himself or of his father or anybody at all.

Back in the car Pa took a sheaf of papers out of a briefcase. "Excuse me, Maury, I want to go over these for a minute. I just thought of something."

Maury knew it was the new apartment-hotel, the largest job his father had undertaken yet. Last week the brick was up to the third floor; above that the red steel framework made a design of squares, forty-two stories of squares against the sky.

"The newest thing in apartment-hotel living," Pa said now, pausing over the papers. "The newest thing in the city. Did you know we're half rented already, with completion date not till next fall?"

He reached into his pocket for a cigar and matches and took a few puffs of enjoyment. "You know, sometimes I don't even believe all this has happened. Sometimes I wake up in the morning and I see the light coming through the curtains and for a second I don't know where I am. Isn't that queer? I'm not sure it's all real. Can you understand that? No, how could you? You've never known anything different, thank God, and I'll see to it that you never do."

He would, too, no doubt of that. He could do anything he wanted to do.

"Only in America," he said now. "Think of it! The sons of immigrants. Malone from the bogs of Ireland. And in ten years we've put our mark on the city. Whenever I see our green and white 'M and F' I think of that. But we give good value, we've rightfully earned whatever we get. I can truthfully say we have never cheated the public, our work is solid as the pyramids and that's more than a great many men in our line can say."

He went back to his papers and Maury started the second section of the *New York Times* for lack of anything else to do. It wasn't very interesting. But then, neither was looking out the window. They passed a clock in front of a bank. It said half past twelve and he thought, There's still plenty of time.

"Pa," he said, "is it all right to drop me off at the rink? I could borrow somebody's skates."

His father looked at him and right away Maury knew the answer would be no. "You've missed religious school for two weeks running because of your cold," he said. "You must be way behind."

A memory like an elephant. You would think that a man who had buildings going up all over the city would have no time for stuff like that. "I can make it up tomorrow. I'll get up early before school."

"You know you won't. No, you'll stay home this afternoon and prepare your work."

If he'd only leave him alone with this religious stuff! Most of the boys at his school didn't have all this religion to fuss about. Their families had given it up as narrow and unmodern. Pa's attitude was so stern, so solemn and boring. Now, with his mother, he didn't mind it as much. She made a pretty ritual out of it, the way she blessed the candles on Friday nights, and her silver candlesticks that she had brought from Europe. It was almost like poetry.

On Saturday mornings he hated to get up and go to the synagogue.

"Let him sleep," Ma would urge. "He studied late last night. I saw the light under the door."

"No," Pa said. "There is a right way and a wrong way, Anna."

"There won't be time for his breakfast. Let him miss it this once, Joseph."

"Then let him go without breakfast."

Pa always talked like that. He was angry when people were late and wouldn't wait more than ten minutes for anyone. He was angry when people broke rules. One of Ma's friends was going to Reno for a divorce and they were talking about it at the dinner table. Pa said, "There's no excuse for her, Anna. People know very well what's right, so let them do it and that's that."

"You sound so hard, Joseph," Ma said. "Isn't there any forgiveness in you?"

"There's a right way and a wrong way, Anna," Pa replied, just as he did on Saturday mornings: "Maury is to get up and go with us. No excuses."

He always went; he knew he had to go and no doubt it would have been easier to get up on time and go without protest. But he never did. Somehow, the battle had to be gone through first. He didn't know why it was like that between his father and himself.

And riding home now in the car, Maury thought: He runs everything and everybody. It seemed to him, in some vague way, that his father would loom over him for the rest of his life. Would there ever be a time when he would be able to say what he wanted to say to his father? And get his own way and be rid of this— this *battle* with someone who was always more powerful than he?

He was sullen the rest of the way home and up into his room. The last thing he heard before closing the door and sitting down to his work was his father's voice, not angry, but very firm and positive: "And, Anna, I don't want the lamb to be underdone the way it was last time. Tell Margaret."

JUST BEFORE DINNER his father called him into his den. On the table before him lay a cardboard box filled with pictures, snapshots and photographs.

"Here, son, I want to show you this. I got these out to put them in order."

Mounted on thick cardboard was an old, old photo of a girl, standing against a wall. Her skirt covered her shoes and her dress had big sleeves that went out from the shoulders like balloons. She had two thick long braids, and even in those queer clothes you could see she was very pretty. In the lower right-hand corner was some foreign name, the photographer's name, and the word "Lublin." That was a city in Poland, he knew that much.

"Who is it?" he asked.

"My mother," Pa said. "Your grandmother, before she was married."

Maury looked again. She had one hand on her hip in a pose almost impudent, and she was laughing; perhaps the photographer had just said something funny.

"I was always told she was a beautiful young woman," his father said. "And you can see she was."

That—that they had seen today—*that* had been *this*?

He had a flash of amazed vision, a frozen moment, in which for the first time he seemed to see everything there was to see and know everything there was to know. There was a phrase, a line from a poem or something read in English class, something about "long corridors of time." And he thought: This is what happens.

Suddenly, without intending to, he bent over and kissed his father, something he had been embarrassed to do since he was a little boy.

{15}

The *Berengaria* sailed for Southampton at noon with pennants snapping and music spangling the river wind. Engines rumbled and shook; the ship backed out into the Hudson, turned and moved out past the Statue of Liberty and past the place where Castle Garden used to be, the place where Anna had touched land in America. She hadn't been as excited then as she was now, and wasn't that strange?

Below in the stateroom the empty champagne bottles from their bon voyage party had not yet been removed. The dressers were crowded with gifts: three pyramids of fruit, enough for ten people; boxes of chocolates and cookies; a pile of novels; flowers; a ribbon-tied package from Solly and Ruth.

Anna opened it and took out a leather-bound, gilt-edged diary. "My Trip to Europe" was embossed on the cover.

Joseph smiled. "Ruth knows you're a scribbler, doesn't she?"

"I shall write in it every day," Anna said firmly. "I don't want to forget a minute of this."

> June 4th
>
> To go so far away, to the other side of the world! I still can't believe this is happening.
>
> All of a sudden one evening last March Joseph said, "I want to do something grand for our anniversary this year. I want to go to Europe. We can afford it."
>
> It struck me funny that when we are poor in Europe we think only about getting to America so we can get rich enough to go back to Europe.
>
> "Not Paris," Joseph said. "You didn't come from Paris, you know."
>
> So I shall actually be seeing Paris, the Louvre, the Tuileries, the Cours La Reine where Marie Antoinette came riding in from Versailles! I think of the city as an enormous crystal chandelier, all fountains, lights and sparkle.
>
> But mostly I shall be thankful to see my brothers in Vienna. I wonder whether we will even recognize each other?
>
> A whole crowd came to see us off, friends and business people and of course the Malones. Malone and Mary are going to Ireland for about six weeks after we get home in September. They want to see where their

ancestors came from. Joseph said he surely wasn't going to go back to Russia to see where *his* came from!

Malone is so hearty, I think that would be the best description of him. He gives the impression of never being worried. I asked Mary whether that was true and she said she thought it was. It must be very easy and relaxed to live with a man like that. He brings humor into every situation. We were watching people arrive up the gangplank and Malone kept joking: "There's Lord Throttlebottom!" (A long man like a string bean with mustaches that went out of style thirty years ago.) "And there's Lady Luella Pursemouth!" He's not unkind, though, just funny.

After they called "All ashore that's going ashore!" we went up on deck. Maury and Iris looked so small standing with Ruth and Solly far below. I would have taken the children to Europe with us, but Joseph wants a vacation without children. We've never had one, not even one day! I can't get over Joseph's being willing to take a vacation at all, he who has worked six days a week and sometimes even seven for as long as I've known him. But I shall miss the children.

Ruth put her arm around Iris and I knew she was giving me a message not to worry. I do worry some: Iris is only ten, and so shy, so wan. My heart sinks, thinking of her, although I know Ruth will take care of her.

Dear Ruth! You were the first person to greet me when I came to America. I remember how you got up from the sewing machine in that dreadful little room. How far we have come since then, you and I and all of us!

Our stateroom is at the top of the ship, the Veranda Deck. I walked out just now; there is still daylight in the sky, although the ocean is black. There is no land in sight. We are really at sea. There's nothing, nothing at all, but sky and sea.

June 5th

Joseph was really angry at me this morning. I'm not used to anger from him, except rarely and then over trivial things. We were reading on deck when suddenly he almost shouted at me: "Where's your ring?" (meaning the diamond that he gave me last month for our anniversary). And when I told him it was downstairs in my drawer with my clothes he was furious. He says I am to wear that ring all the time, every minute. I said I didn't think it was appropriate to wear such a large diamond with a sweater and skirt but he said he didn't give a damn, that the ring was very valuable and I should understand that it had to be guarded at all times. He sent me downstairs to get it and on the way I was terrified that perhaps someone had stolen it. It must have cost a fortune! but, thank God, there it was, safe among my stockings.

The thing is, I never really wanted it. Things like that truly don't mean that much to me, although Joseph cannot understand that. He thinks all women are absolutely mad about diamonds. I suppose most of them are. I know all my friends were so impressed when they saw it. I do believe that is the real reason Joseph wants me to wear it all the time, why he wanted me to take it on this trip in the first place.

June 7th

At our table I learn that there is a world of ships, and that this voyage, which is such an adventure for us, is a way of living for others. These people all cross the Atlantic as casually as we take the Fifth Avenue bus. One couple from outside Philadelphia, people about our age, are traveling with three children and a nursemaid who take their meals in their suite. They come to Europe every year, renting a house in England, Switzerland or France. Joseph was surprised, he didn't think they looked all that wealthy, but he doesn't realize that their simplicity is very expensive. They don't talk very much and when they do they have more to say to the old lady than to us. The old lady is the widow of a New York banker; she travels all over the world, it seems, with her daughter. The daughter is in her late twenties. She looks lonely and bored. I feel sorry for her.

I listen to the conversations of this traveling fraternity. They know the names of all the captains and pursers on the great ships. They talk about whom they met on this or that voyage and what cocktail parties they were invited to. One night all these people were asked to the captain's table and Joseph and I had the table to ourselves. The hierarchy of the ship! I suppose we were put here because there were two seats left over; certainly we don't belong here. Joseph is more quiet than ever and I know that he feels out of place. Naturally, I am just as out of place but it doesn't bother me; I find it interesting. I watch the spectacle, the procession descending the stairs to dinner: sagging women in brocade and diamonds, tired-looking men, honeymoon couples. Turning heads, energetic smiles, the chirp of greeting: "How *are* you? I haven't *seen* you in ages!"

I watch the food, the great fish carved in ice, the vegetables like a Dutch still life, the spun-sugar baskets, the little iced cakes arranged like a bouquet. What labor and art to cook like that! I look at the nice, fresh faces of the boys who wait on us. They seem so cheerful and respectful as they pull your chair out: "Good evening, madame, have you had a nice afternoon?" I wonder what they really think about all of us.

After dinner last night we went up to dance, and I was saying all this to Joseph. He was a little annoyed. "Can't you ever just enjoy yourself, without all these serious thoughts?" he asked. I told him I was enjoying myself and I couldn't help my thoughts. "Don't you want me to tell you anything anymore?" I answered. And then he said, "Oh, come on, you can tell me anything you want, you know you can." So then he was very good-humored, and we danced until after midnight. The music was splendid and Joseph dances very well. Really we ought to do it more often! It clears the head. One feels so light and easy, not thinking about anything at all. He's right, I *ponder* too much.

June 8th

It rained today and the wind bends you double as you round the corner of the deck. Everyone is inside. Joseph has found a couple of kindred souls and they are playing cards. Some have gone down to the movie. But I don't want to miss a minute of the sea. I went up alone on deck and stood in the blowing spray. How fierce the North Atlantic is, even in the summer! One has a sense of danger, something elemental, although of course on this great modern liner I am only fooling myself about elemental dangers!

The day after tomorrow, when we wake up, they tell us we shall see Ireland. How will the Malones feel when they see it for the first time?

June 11

I think I must know all the streets in London. The first morning we went out for a walk. Our hotel is on Park Lane. We had planned to see the changing of the guard at Buckingham Palace, and Joseph wanted to see Hyde Park Corner where the radicals come and rant. When I told him to turn left he looked at me in amazement and said: "Are you sure you haven't been here before?" And I said that I had been, in dozens of books, Dickens and Thackeray and all the books on the list Miss Thorne once gave me. That was eighteen years ago and I only finished the list last year. Of course I did read things in between besides all my courses in art and music history.

I wonder about Miss Mary Thorne. I suppose she must be retired now, back in Boston probably, making tea in a little room with shelves and shelves of books. How could she or I have guessed the things that would happen all these years?

June 13th

Joseph has a business appointment with some British investors who are interested in New York real estate. I was sorry that business had to interfere with sightseeing, but he didn't mind at all. I think he really welcomed the interference. So I took the boat ride to Kew Gardens by myself. *Have you been to Kew in lilac time?*

I sat next to a very nice man on the boat, an American from New Hampshire. He teaches history at some famous school; I've forgotten the name. His wife died six months ago. He said they had been planning this trip abroad for quite a while and she had made him promise to go anyway after her death. She had said it would be good for him, that he mustn't sit at home and mourn. What a wonderful, unselfish, large-minded woman!

He asked me where I came from. He thought, because of my accent, I suppose, that I might be French and seemed surprised when I told him the truth.

We got talking about England. He'd been hiking in the Lake District, Wordsworth country, and I said I was sorry we wouldn't be going there. I think I should love a vacation like that, walking through the villages, seeing how people really live, instead of just staying in large hotels where you only see other tourists. He agreed with me. We had a very nice conversation, and by the time we got to Kew, it was only natural to walk around together. It's a marvelous place! What a pity Joseph missed it! Maybe he would have enjoyed it after all, in spite of his saying he wouldn't.

The man's name was Jeffers. They had no children, which is too bad, since now he has nothing left of his wife at all. I told him about my children when he inquired, mostly about Maury, how he planned to go to Yale and was interested in literature. He mentioned some professors there who are especially fine and famous. All in all, it was a very pleasant time and we found ourselves talking as though we had known each other a long while. I seldom, or perhaps never, meet men who like to talk to women. I was thinking how warm it was, how consoling, although that's really not the right word; perhaps cheerful would be more accurate.

On the way back, when we were almost at the end of the trip, Mr. Jeffers said he'd had an unexpectedly wonderful afternoon.

"I shall be so sorry not to see you again," he said. He looked straight at me when he said it, and I saw something very serious and regretful in his face. He was not being a "smart aleck"; goodness knows I've seen enough of that to recognize it. He really meant it, and so I said, "I'm sorry too, and I hope you'll be very happy again, someday." And I really meant it. I think we had only begun to talk. There would have been so much more for us to say to each other if—a hundred ifs.

Joseph was waiting on the embankment. He first asked how I had enjoyed the trip and then he wanted to know who the man was.

"You seemed to be having quite a conversation," he said. "I was watching you while the boat drew in."

"Oh, yes," I said, "he's an American, a schoolteacher. He gave me some very good advice about Maury."

"You talked about Maury the whole time?"

"I didn't spend the whole time talking to the man, Joseph!"

"Don't you know that I'm jealous?" he said.

But he has no reason to be and never will. I am absolutely, I am completely, to be trusted. And I will stake my life on that.

                                                              June 26th
We are on the train, crossing the border into Austria. In a matter of hours I shall see Dan and Eli! Joseph is almost as excited as I am about it. He feels for me and for our long separation. "Families shouldn't be torn apart like that," he says, and he is right. But what can you do?

The scenery here reminds me of *The Student Prince*, which we saw a couple of years ago. First the fortress on the peak above Salzburg. Then an hour or more of lakes like big blue tears spilled on the earth. And a monastery, gloomy, powerful and secretive; "Melk," it says in the guidebook. Now woods, the Wienerwald no doubt, the Vienna Woods. And in a few minutes more, the station where they will be waiting.

Joseph is watching me. "Don't you ever get tired of scribbling?" he asks, and takes my hand and smiles. He knows I am like jelly inside, and strokes it to calm me. I put this book away.

June 26th, later

My brother Eli is called Eduard now. We were met on the platform by him and Tessa. I confess I would not have known him! Nineteen years, after all! But his hair is still red. We cried, both of us, and Joseph was very moved seeing us, but I think Tessa was embarrassed in front of their chauffeur. However, she was very sweet, kissed me and welcomed us. She is not an especially pretty woman but thin and graceful. One wants to look at her, although Joseph doesn't agree. I think he disliked her at once, which is unusual for Joseph, who rarely says much about people.

Eli-Eduard wanted us to stay at their house and was distressed when we told him we had a reservation at Sacher's Hotel. But Joseph says no, we are staying two weeks and that is too long a time to stay in anyone's house. We can see them every day, without getting in the way of their family. That too is like Joseph, very considerate. Or is it independent?

June 26th, later

We are back at the hotel to dress for dinner. Eduard will send the car for us. But first we went out to his house in the eighth district. It is rather far from the center of the city, almost a suburb, with large houses and grounds. They call them villas but, by American standards, I would call them miniature palaces! Eduard's has gold plaster cherubs on the ceilings. I tried not to crane my head up all the time while Tessa was serving coffee and cake. We sat for a while in the garden, a lovely spot with high trees all around, making a private outdoor room, bright with mauve and scarlet flowers. I really ought to learn the names of flowers. I am completely ignorant of anything except a rose or a daisy! Oh, I forgot to say, all the rooms are heated in winter by huge stoves that look like high boxes made of porcelain tiles, with beautiful designs on them. Joseph was amused. On the way back he said, "To think of heating with a stove in the twentieth century! How far behind us Europe is!"

The children came in to meet us, a handsome little boy and two blond girls. Liesel is just Iris' age. She played the piano very well, I thought, although I am no judge. What lovely manners the children have!

June 27th

Now that I have spent a day with Eduard I can clearly see the outline of the boy who parted from me: the same very charming smile, the prominent jaw, the eyes that crinkle. And yet he looks like an Austrian gentleman. I see that he cares about his clothes, or else it is Tessa who cares for him.

But I am saddened about Dan. He doesn't look like his brother anymore, and they are identical twins! He is quite round-shouldered and his smile is almost apologetic. His wife Dena is rather pretty, although too plump. She doesn't care about her figure; she took two helpings of whipped cream. Anyway, she's nice and I liked her at once. I felt easy with her, as I did not with Tessa.

I can see that Tessa does not think much of Dena or Dan; it is obvious that they live in different worlds. Dena helps Dan in his fur shop, though it must be very hard on her. They have six children, and she whispered to me after dinner that she expects again!

I wish I could have had more children. I could have them still; perhaps it isn't too late? I am only thirty-five. Joseph is terribly disappointed that we have only two, I know, although he never says a word. I suppose he thinks it would be a reproach, or perhaps that there's no use discussing things that can't be helped. He is supremely practical and doesn't waste words, as surely I ought to have learned by now.

It was rather an awkward evening. It is apparent to me that my brothers do not get together very often, although no one said so. But what really amazed me was that there should be a language problem between them! An entirely manufactured one, to be sure. Dan and Dena speak Yiddish at home. Dena is a poor girl with no education and she has lived among people like herself ever since coming to Vienna. Tessa naturally speaks no Yiddish, only German and French, as she took pains to let us know. However, Yiddish and German are really so closely related that, with a little effort, they would all be able to understand each other. Joseph swears that they do, that Tessa only pretends not to. He had very little difficulty understanding Tessa's German, he said. I think she is an *unbending* woman. I wonder whether Eduard can be happy?

July 1st

We have been so busy seeing the sights here that I haven't had time to write. We have seen all the museums and the Hofburg, the great palace where the last Emperor lived up to a few years ago. Also the Spanish Riding School, a most glittering hall. Such courtly ceremony, such marvelous white horses, a true spectacle! Joseph enjoyed it, I'm sure, but he did remark to me later that such stuff is at best childish and at worst wrong, in that it perpetuates a useless way of life, catering to people who do not work. Of course, to Joseph that is the worst damnation of all, not to work. I did not think we would get him in to hear the Boys' Choir in the chapel but to my surprise he went, and had to admit that the chapel is gorgeous in the original sense of the word: it glitters.

Oh, and we saw the Burgtheatre and the lovely Burggarten. Eduard has been so eager to show us everything and, since he has his own business, he can take all the free time he wants. We went to Schönbrunn and I was enthralled to think that this is where Maria Theresa lived, and in France at Versailles we shall see where her daughter lived and died. I want to reread Stefan Zweig's *Marie Antoinette* when I get home. Now that I have seen all this she will seem much more alive to me. I am making so many good resolutions!

July 2d

Eduard has been so wonderful. I told him I am almost sorry to have had this time with him because now it will be so very hard to part. It's funny how different he is when Tessa is not with us. And yet I'm sure he loves her; he looks at her with such pride.

This afternoon we were invited to Dan's house and Eduard said he would take us there. (It is Sunday and all the church bells are ringing, there must be thousands of them. That's another thing I shall remember about Europe, that sweet clamor that makes a vibration up the spine. Joseph doesn't like the noise, he says, but I think it is simply that he doesn't like churches.)

Anyway, we drove to Dan's. He lives on a poor street where the stores are all open, in spite of it being Sunday. It is like the lower East Side. They sell dress goods, men's suiting and other dry goods, wholesale and retail. The men sit in the doorways and coax you to come in and buy. Yes, it is like the lower East Side except more quiet and orderly, without pushcarts. But the people live upstairs above the shops in the same way.

Dan's flat is dark and crowded. The furniture looks too big for the rooms. It must be a struggle for Dena to keep house there with all those children and her father, who lives with them. He is a little old, old man in a long black coat and side curls. He looks more like her grandfather.

Eduard stayed for more than an hour. Dena brought out coffee and cake. They seem to exist on coffee and cake in Vienna but I must say it is delicious, and so rich . . . (Eduard took us to Demel's for pastry yesterday and it was superb). We got to talking, the three of us, about the things we remembered of home. It was very warm and good, not sad as I might have expected it to be. Joseph and Dena sat listening and seemed so happy for us. Joseph said he liked to enjoy my relationship with my brothers because he was an only child. Dena has three sisters but they all live in Germany and she hasn't seen them in years.

"But it's not far!" I said, and then was sorry I had said such a stupid thing because Dan explained, "It's very expensive to travel, Anna." And Dena added, "It's not easy for us here, but in Germany it's even worse. Many people there are starving."

"Business is booming in America," Joseph said. "Anybody can get ahead there. Have you ever thought of coming, Dan?"

Dan said he hadn't thought of it; he was doing all right and this was home by now. He didn't want to move and wander again. And then he added almost mischievously, "I notice you don't invite my brother."

Joseph looked flustered for a moment, but Eduard said, very simply, "No, I've been lucky."

He was so different in that house, speaking in Yiddish to Dena's father, telling jokes. And finally, when he said that he hated to leave but had to, we knew that he meant it.

Dan was different in his own house, too. We had a good supper, a bowl of rich soup, and chicken with dumplings on a platter in the center of the table.

"You can talk and be yourself without all those wooden statues standing around the way they do in Eduard's house," Dan remarked. There wasn't any envy in the way he said it, but I didn't tell him that we had maids at home too, although our Ellen and Margaret are hardly as stiff and formal as the people at Eduard's.

I asked Dan how Eduard had met his wife.

"Die Gräfin, the Countess?" he replied, and Dena scolded him: "Dan, that's not nice!"

"Well," Dan said, "I call her that, anyway. Oh, she's not really bad, just different. How he met her? He became a hero during the war, you know, and there was a party at someone's house—rich people were always giving parties—and that's how they met. I know her father wasn't so pleased at the beginning, but after a while he came to think the world of Eduard and he took him into the family businesses. They have so many connections, textiles, banking, government. So that's the story."

After supper it was still light and I helped Dena clear away while Dan and Joseph went for a walk. Dan said that since Joseph was in the construction business he wanted to show him something. They were gone more than an hour and were in great good humor when they came in. They had visited a schoolhouse from the seventeenth century with walls three feet thick, still in use.

We get along so well together. It is really a sad thing that we must live as strangers! When we left Dena hugged me and said those very words: "It is a sad thing that we must live apart like strangers."

July 4th

Today is the Fourth of July. It seems queer not to be at the beach, going out on the porch to see the fireworks exploding over the water. Iris will be watching at Ruth's this year. She always gets so excited. I remember the first fireworks I ever saw, that Fourth when we went to Coney Island just before Maury was born. I feel far from America, far from my home.

July 6th

I must say Tessa has been very gracious to me. This afternoon she took me shopping and we must have gone in and out of every shop on the Graben and Kärtnerstrasse. I bought a petit-point bag for myself, some gifts and a wonderful porcelain tea service. I told Tessa that, considering what it cost, I should have to wash it myself. I wouldn't trust anyone with it.

"Ah yes," she said, "I can understand that. Of course, I don't have to worry like that because I have Trudl, who came with me from my parents' house when I got married. She takes care of things as though they were her own."

It must be nice to be as confident as Tessa is. I don't think she means to sound arrogant. I think it is we who misinterpret. Are we perhaps envious of her confidence? Anyway, I'm glad I brought the good clothes Joseph wanted me to bring. The women here are really elegant.

I bought a gold wristwatch for Joseph. It cost much less than it would at home, but still it was plenty. I've saved a good bit out of the household money; it is the only way I could get something really fine for Joseph, since he will never buy anything for himself. I shall not show it to him until we are on the ship, or he will make me take it back.

Tessa came in with me for coffee at Sacher's. Joseph was waiting when we walked in with the packages. He looked pleased that I had bought things.

"Wait till she gets to Paris," he told Tessa.

Tessa said that since we hadn't been there before we would undoubtedly enjoy it, but as for herself, it bored her. Her parents used to take her every year for shopping and every year her mother had said it was the last time, because the workmanship in Vienna was far superior.

Joseph was amused, I saw, but he made no comment, for which I was thankful.

July 9th

Eduard and Tessa gave a big party for us tonight. It was splendid and I understood why Dena and Dan had declined to come. I'm sure Dena would not have had anything to wear. There were all sorts of people there, musicians and government people and even a couple whose name began with "von," which meant, Joseph said, that they didn't work because somebody else worked for them, or stole for them, a few hundred years ago! Nevertheless, it was very exciting for me. When have I ever, when will I ever, see such an evening again?

After dinner we went into one of the drawing rooms where rows of gilded chairs had been set up. There was a string quartet and a piano. Most of the pieces they played were Mozart. I don't know much about it but I've tried to learn. It's funny, when you first hear Mozart it seems rather dry and twangy. One has to grow used to it. After a while it becomes very beautiful, clear and sprightly. I could tell that Joseph didn't like it, though. The only music he likes even a little bit is Tchaikovsky's, which one of the teachers in my music course likened to an emotional bath. But what's the matter with taking an emotional bath if it makes you feel good?

After the concert everyone went out into the garden and Eduard—how much he reminds me of Maury!—introduced a man who bent over and kissed my hand. When Eduard left us the man, a very good-looking man who spoke beautiful English, asked me what I had seen of Vienna. So I told him we had driven through the Vienna Woods that afternoon.

"Ah, then you know the story of Marie Vetsera and the Crown Prince?"

I knew vaguely that they had had a love affair, but I hadn't known that he was married, she was pregnant, and he had shot them both to death.

"Well, what do you think of the romantic story?" he asked, when he had finished.

I told him it was not as romantic as I had thought, that it was rather more sordid.

"You Americans are so innocent, so moralistic!" he said. "It would be fun to take an innocent woman like you and teach her a few things."

Well, I have met with that sort of thing before! The words and the accent may be different but the question in the eyes is the same: "Do you—? Will you—?" And I know just how to turn blank eyes which say, "I don't and I won't." Thank God that I know how.

I don't know whether to be flattered or insulted at such times. Perhaps a little of both.

July 12th

Tonight was our last night. We invited everyone to dinner at the hotel. Joseph ordered a grand dinner with the famous Sacher torte for dessert. He told the wine steward to bring the best wines, using his own judgment since, "I'm an American and I don't know the first thing about wines." That is something I always admire about Joseph, his utter honesty and absence of sham.

The dinner was gay, and sorrowful too. My heart was very full. We are leaving early in the morning for Paris and we told them not to take us to the train, but to say good-by right here. It would be easier for us all. So we left with many promises to visit back and forth, which I doubt will be kept. Little Dan . . . little Eli . . . when they had left and we went upstairs, I lay down on the bed. Joseph came over and lay beside me, and took my hand. After a while he told me that he had asked Dan whether there was anything he could do for him and Dan had said that there wasn't. But Joseph had put some money in a bank account for him anyway and he wouldn't get the notice of it until after we had left. I cried with gratitude for this kindness to my brother, this kindness of my husband's.

July 22d

We have been in Paris almost a week and I have been too tired, too busy, too exhilarated to write a word until today. We have seen the great sights of this city, my "crystal chandelier." Today we went up the Eiffel Tower, having saved it to the last.

From the top you can see blocks of white stone buildings, squares and streets thick with summer trees. The awnings are all of a dark burnt orange. I told Joseph that I wanted to stand and look so I would remember it forever.

"We have an appointment at three o'clock," he said, and was so mysterious about it. But when I pressed it turned out not to be an appointment; it was just that he had made up his mind to take me to a courturier for some clothes. I told him they were far too expensive and really I didn't need any. Nobody we know wears Paris clothes. But he insisted, and so we went. I think he learned about the place from a fashion magazine which someone had left in the lobby.

Anyway, I now own a fine navy suit which I shall get a lot of wear out of and a pale pink evening dress which is the most beautiful thing I have ever owned. When I move it floats, and when I stand still it stands in folds like the stone folds on a statue.

Joseph said he thought that red-haired women should never wear pink. The vendeuse, a rather haughty person in black, said, "On the contrary, red is very subtle for her. Madame is very striking. But, *vous permettez, madame?* Not so many bracelets. And never, never costume jewelry with real." I knew it, Joseph always insists that I wear too much jewelry.

"It is like a room with too much furniture, too much jewelry," she said.

Speaking of furniture, I should so much like to get rid of all that fancy stuff when we get home. Now that I have seen real French furniture I realize that ours is an overblown, expensive imitation. I wonder whether Joseph would let me get rid of it.

On the way back to the hotel I thanked him for the clothes, which really cost far too much, and he said, "You can wear the pink when Solly's boy gets married next winter. You'll stand out from all the others in their fringe and beads!"

The wedding is to be at a hall in Brooklyn. She's a sweet girl, I met her one afternoon at Ruth's. The dress will be quite out of place there, but I know Joseph wants to show it off.

July 23d

I stand and listen to people speaking French in the stores and on the street. It's such a pert, crisp language, elegant as rustling taffeta. I wish I could speak it. Another one of my many wishes!

August 4th

We are back from our tour of the château country. I have no time to describe it, and no words, except to say that it is a dream of enchantment. They have rushed my dresses through these past two weeks, and Joseph has made an appointment for a portrait of me. He got the name of the artist from an American man whom we met at one of the hotels. It seems that "everyone" is having his portrait done by this particular artist. I am to wear the pink dress. I feel silly but Joseph is so enthusiastic about the idea that I can't say no. The picture is to be framed and completed after our departure and will be sent to us.

August 11th

The artist has finished the preliminaries of the portrait. The face is finished, the rest just outlined, but enough so that I can see what it will be like. Anyone can tell it's me; it's a good likeness. But the very idea of myself being painted for posterity in that dress seems so ridiculous! My mind goes back to Me stitching pants at Ruth's, Me rolling cloth and dusting the counters at Uncle Meyer's. Me going for eggs across the river to Pretty Leah's—although I don't want to think about *that*.

August 12th

Tomorrow we take the boat train. Europe, good-by!

August 14th

The voyage home is different. There is a touch of sadness in it. I know it will be a long time before we can come back, if we ever do. And still I am in a hurry to get home. Maury has been growing so fast this past year, I wonder whether he is much taller? And even though Ruth has written that Iris is fine, I wonder whether she really has been. Ruth might have wanted not to worry us or spoil our vacation. Or else Iris might appear to be fine and happy; she has that way of concealing things, while inside she may be miserable. I feel sometimes that I know my daughter so well, and then at other times that I don't know her at all. Maury is easy to understand, I think. Or do I delude myself? Joseph says I worry about them both too much.

August 15th

We have better people at our table going back, or should I say people who are more like ourselves, easier to get along with? One of the women, a Mrs. Quinn, reminds me of Mary Malone. She has the same fine white skin and those lovely round Irish eyes. Her husband is in the auto supply business. He and Joseph were talking about a piece of property for him. Later and as always I said to Joseph: "Don't you ever leave business behind? You'll be home soon enough."

August 16th

At the table next to ours there is the strangest couple. The women at our table keep watching them. He is an old, old man, finely dressed and slender, with white, well-groomed hair. But his skin is dry as paper; he must be eighty. And with him is a young girl, who looks like nineteen, although she is probably older. She has the light bones of a swallow. One would think she might be the granddaughter, traveling with him. But no, they are married!

After dinner we saw them again at the entertainment. They were listening to the singer, a young man who sang a romantic song in Spanish or perhaps Italian. It was quite beautiful, passionate music, probably filched from Schubert. I kept looking at that young girl and wondering what she might be feeling while the young man sang.

I mentioned it to Joseph and he said, "She's a whore, what do you think! Some women will do anything for money."

But I think there must be more to it than that. One needs to know the circumstances that make people do what they do. Joseph says I am too soft and always make excuses for people. I think he makes things too simple

August 18th

One more day and we shall be in New York. I am standing at the prow facing into the wind. It is cold and so clean on the skin. Then I go to the stern and watch the wake fanning in a "V," flat silver ripples in the green. Tomorrow I know, as we draw near land, the gulls will come to follow the ship as they did on the way over. I am told they are waiting for the garbage to be thrown out. I had preferred the poetic idea that they came to welcome us in. Oh, well, an incurable romantic, I!

I woke this morning to the thought that we are only one day away from our children. I can't wait. I could get out and push the ship. Then something else came flooding. I realized that all the time we were away I had forgotten, or not thought of—is it possible?—the thing that otherwise is with me every day. Even when I am not consciously aware of it, I know that it is there. Like someone standing behind a curtain, waiting. Now it has come back again, behind the curtain. The presence, waiting.

On the Day of Atonement you ask God to forgive you for sins against Him. Sins against men can be forgiven only by the person who has been sinned against. But here is my dilemma: how can a person forgive another for a sin against him that he doesn't even know about? Yet to tell him would be another sin because it would bring such useless suffering. And anyway, if this particular person did know, this particular person would never forgive. Never, never, never.

My head aches. That man, the priest of another religion, was right when he said: "Do you think you will not pay, every day of your life?"

August 19th

We have just come through the Narrows. Our luggage is on Main Deck and I have run down to check the stateroom to make sure we have left nothing behind. Joseph is standing at the rail because he doesn't want to miss the Statue of Liberty. When I was up there with him just now he put his arm around me and asked me whether I was glad to be home and whether it had been as good a time as I had hoped for. The answer to both is yes, and I said so. "Life has been very good to us," he said, and it is true. I don't deserve the goodness it has given me.

❖{16}❖

In the first week of September, 1929, New York roused from its summer siesta. The balmy, gilded streets were crammed with back-to-school and back-to-the-city shoppers. Fifth Avenue windows drew crowds of ladies to see the latest news from Paris: waistlines had risen from the hip and skirts were definitely dropping to the middle of the calf. The color of the year was *bois-de-rose* and brocade would be favored for theatregoing. Theatre-ticket brokers were rushed, the musical spectaculars being sold out months ahead. The rattle of riveting was heard on the avenues and the towers rose in set-backs and terraces, glittering with glass in the new style of Le Corbusier. The stock market, which was the cause and also the effect of these things, stood at its all-time peak.

On the third of September a single share of Montgomery Ward, bought for one hundred thirty-two dollars in the previous year, was worth four hundred sixty-six dollars. Radio Corporation of America, bought at ninety-four and a half, sold at five hundred five. Many individuals owned thousands of shares like these. One could buy them, after all, for only ten percent down and owe the broker for the rest.

On the fourth of September a little dip occurred, not worth noticing. On September fifth the *New York Times* index reported a drop of ten points, still not worth noticing, although Roger Babson, the financial writer, said that the ride was over and a depression was on the way. But he was some sort of nutty alarmist; everybody knew that nothing went straight up without a break; there were bound to be small, inconsequential dips from time to time before the rise resumed.

But early in the week of October twenty-first the slide had gone too far and brokers began to send out margin calls. When the money was not forthcoming—and how could it be?—the dumping began. And on Thursday, October twenty-fourth, the structure of the market cracked like a rotten nut. Millions of shares were pitched into a screaming chaos on the floor of the exchange, while outside on this Black Thursday, at the corner of Broad and Wall, the crowds stood stunned and curious, talking in quiet voices. They couldn't believe it. Surely something would happen to retrieve it? Something?

For five days it went like that until full panic struck on the twenty-ninth of the month and the slide hit bottom, like a stone crashing to the pit of a well. On one of those days alone General Electric, one of the soundest stocks in the country,

118

lost forty-eight points. There was a still lower level to be reached, although people didn't know that then. They didn't know that by 1932 United States Steel would be down to twenty-one and General Motors to seven.

But if they had known it wouldn't have made any difference. They were already ruined.

Within the next few months the towers stopped rising, and it became apparent that their stone had rested on the foundation of Wall Street's paper. The riveting was stilled, that confident *rat-tat-tat,* that proclamation to the future. Children born in the city that year would finish high school without once hearing the sound.

EVERYTHING SEEMED TO be standing still, waiting for Joseph. In his nightly dreams and waking visions he saw a cluster of white faces all turned up to him, questioning and waiting.

It began with poor Malone, the week of October twenty-first. He hadn't known that Malone had put everything into stocks. He himself had never owned many; he believed in land. What he had owned he had sold before leaving for Europe, on the theory that nobody can look after a man's affairs as well as he can himself.

When the broker telephoned, Malone was still spending the fall in Ireland. He needed at least a hundred thousand dollars, or he would have to sell him out.

"Give me until the day after tomorrow," Joseph pleaded. "I'll reach him somehow." And he wondered where Malone would find cash like that.

He tried to transatlantic telephone and after hours got a tinny voice, fading in and out, from a hotel in Wexford: Mr. and Mrs. Malone had rented a car to go visiting relatives out in the country.

No, they had left no address and no, they wouldn't be coming back. The ship wasn't due to sail for another week and by the time he could reach them there it would be too late.

He went to bed haunted by his friend's disaster.

In the morning he was awakened by the telephone. Solly excused himself for calling so early, but he hadn't slept all night and he was calling Joseph only as a very last resort: would Joseph get him forty-five thousand dollars today?

Well, that was an awful lot of money.

Yes, he knew it was, but the bottom had dropped out of his stocks and he'd had a margin call for eleven this morning.

My God, what a terrible thing.

Yes, it was terrible. That was all he had in the world except for his life insurance.

Joseph had thought by the way they lived that Solly would have had more than that, which just went to show, you never could tell.

But this was only temporary, Solly assured him; he had a hunch the market would rebound in a month or two. So if Joseph could just tide him over, as soon as the stocks went up again Solly would sell and pay him back.

That was a lot of money, Joseph said again, not knowing what else to say, not knowing how else to tell him that he wouldn't risk money like that on Solly's

hunch, or that if he had been going to take any risk it would have been for
Malone.

Solly would gladly pay interest, if that's what Joseph wanted.

No, that wasn't what he wanted; he certainly didn't want to make money out
of someone he knew and loved as much as Solly. It was just that he couldn't
afford to endanger his own family. He hoped Solly could understand that. He
really wished so much that he could come to his rescue. Was Solly sure he had
tried everything: the banks, the professional money lenders? . . . Joseph's voice
trailed weakly.

Yes, Solly had tried everything and Joseph was his last hope. Was this really
his final word?

Yes it was, and he was so sorry. Solly would never know how sorry.

That was the last time they spoke together. By five o'clock that afternoon Solly
was dead.

On the way home from the office Tim happened to pass through the street
where Solly lived and found it blocked by police cars and crowds. He leaned out
and asked a bystander what was wrong.

"A man jumped out of the window," she reported, and Joseph knew, he
simply knew, that it was Solly.

When he got home he went to the telephone. A strange voice answered at
Solly's house, a neighbor perhaps.

"Has anything—is everything all right?" he asked, the question not seeming
odd at all.

"No," the woman said, muffled and crying. "Oh, my God, Solly has killed
himself! . . ."

He put the receiver softly back, and sat for a while alone, and summoned
Anna. For the next few days they were occupied with Ruth. She was so calm it
was as if she had died too. People kept coming in, hesitating, with shock in their
faces. What should they say to her? They didn't know what to say. So they put
their arms around her, pressing their cheeks to her face, and then went into the
dining room where neighbors had put out a coffee urn and platters of food, fruit
and cold cuts and cakes, because the living must go on eating and living.

Every few minutes someone said, "I don't think she even realizes it yet," and
another answered, "Next week, next month, she will really know what's happened."

In the meantime Ruth sat in the living room on Solly's chair. The fat white
mourning candle burned in its holder on the piano which was newly draped with
the Spanish shawl that Joseph and Anna had brought from Europe only a few
weeks before. It was black silk with flowers and fringe, a gaudy thing that Ruth
had wanted so badly. Now she stretched out her hand, thin and transparent
against the candle flame.

"Empty, empty," she said, and was silent.

He kept starting awake. He knew he had been dreaming but in the instant of
waking the dream fled, and he could only remember that he had been standing or
climbing or kneeling on the fourteenth floor and down, straight down, were the
tops of cars, crawling like beetles. There was a wind in his face. No, it was not his

face, it was Solly's. Was it Solly or Joseph hanging there and in the ultimate instant, frantic with terror, pulling back? Too late, too late, all hold was loosed. Was it Solly or Joseph? The street rushed up, tilting, screaming— Who, Solly or Joseph? Then a hand on his shoulder, Anna's hand.

"Hush, hush. You were dreaming. Joseph, Joseph, it's all right."

And he worried about Malone. The man was whipped. He sat in his office with his telephone turned off. He must have lost twenty-five pounds of jolly fat; the skin hung on his neck in folds.

Once Joseph came in and found him staring out of the window. When he turned, Joseph saw that he had been crying, and would have left the room, but Malone said, "Why didn't I know that what goes up has to come down? Tell me, why didn't I know?"

"You've plenty of company," was all Joseph could think of to say.

He worried about the building that was near completion, but Malone was in no condition to talk about it. So he called his lawyer and learned that their bank might not be able to make the final payment on the construction loan. Three large banks had already failed and the way people were lining up to withdraw their deposits, even a bank in sound shape could be made to fail. What if this one failed; how would they finish the job?

He decided to have a talk with his man at the bank tomorrow morning. Do it in person, not on the telephone, and handle it carefully; you didn't just walk in and tell people there were rumors they might be going under.

When he arrived at the bank at ten o'clock the next day there was a crowd on the sidewalk. Old women, men in business suits, men in overalls were shuffling and bustling at the doors. The doors were shut.

What was to be done? Nine stories and penthouse on the stylish upper East Side, a gem of a little job, half of it rented. A hundred thousand dollars would finish it. There was nothing else to do but to use his own funds. After all, it was only lending it to himself, he reasoned. But in doing so he had almost depleted his capital.

He came home, somber and thoughtful, to hear another tale of woe.

"It's Ruth," Anna said. "We thought she had Solly's insurance, at least. But it seems she signed some papers, signed it over when he borrowed money for the stocks. And now they tell her it isn't hers! And Joseph, she hasn't a cent, she's over in that apartment without a cent!"

He thought, he thought with pounding head, "I wish people would leave me alone!"—and remembered Solly teaching him to play ball, and Ruth coming to Anna when their children had been born and there had been no one else to help, and the summer just past when Iris had stayed with them and been so warmly cared for.

"Find out what she needs," he said. "They were good to us, Anna. I don't forget."

THAT WINTER THERE were heavy snows. The city advertised for men to shovel and long lines formed before morning light. Some of the men who came were middle-aged; they wore hand-tailored suits and velvet-collared overcoats. All over the city there were lines: bread lines, soup lines. Joseph passed them while riding in his car; once he saw the face of a man he knew and looked quickly away so that the man would not know he had been seen.

The speed with which disaster had spread was unbelievable. Sitting in his good, solid car behind Tim, on his way home to where it was still warm and there was plenty of food, he could reassure himself that he was not like those poor devils in the lines. And yet, and still, speaking of devils, the small devil fear was there all right, perched inside his head and waiting. Waiting for what?

The new building, the little gem, was not renting. The penthouse had finally been leased for half what they had expected to get. The chain store which had taken a ninety-nine-year lease on Madison Avenue had gone bankrupt. The lofts in the fur district were partly vacant; the swinging racks heavy with furs were gone. The two prime apartment houses on Central Park West were emptying out, but the interest and taxes and maintenance went on. He had been using up his personal funds to keep them going. Malone had nothing to contribute. How long could this last, this slump or whatever it was? How long could he go on?

Advertisements were appearing, offering a five-year lease on an apartment for one year's rent in advance, offering free decoration, free remodeling, anything. Only come in and sign up.

And no new work in sight.

At night he lay awake and held a dialogue with himself.

Air, he said indignantly. They say it was all bubbles and air. But I go past the houses, fifteen stories high, with the doormen in maroon uniforms standing under the awnings, and I know the insides of those houses the way a doctor knows a body. I know the miles of brass pipe, the hardwood floors, the imported tile in the lobby. And you tell me that's all air?

Built on promises, that's what they mean.

Promises? Oh, you mean mortgages, promises to pay. But these buildings cost millions; what man, or group of men, would be able to construct them without borrowing?

That's true.

We always pay back, don't we? And have enough left to live very well, besides.

You pay back as long as somebody else pays you.

The rents, you mean?

Of course.

Of course.

But what when people no longer pay the rent?

They'll pay the rent. They can't find better places to live.

But when they lose their jobs, what will they do?

I don't know. You think it will be that bad?

It is that bad already.

Silence.

There are ten million unemployed.

Silence.

You'll have to dispossess a lot of them.

You mean, put them and their furniture out on the street?

That's what it means to dispossess.

I can't do that. I wouldn't sleep if I had to do that to people.

Well, then, you'll lose your properties, you'll lose everything.

And if I put them out, what then?

You'll lose everything anyway.

Yᴇᴛ ʜᴇ ᴅɪᴅɴ'ᴛ panic. Month after month he trimmed and cut back and managed. Malone and he moved from their lavish office and gave up most of the staff. He sold the car, but kept Tim on as an office boy in spite of not needing one, for Tim had two babies to bring up. The maids were dismissed and Iris changed to public school. She hadn't been very happy anyway with that bunch of snobs, Joseph told himself, knowing it for a rationalization. And he pawned Anna's diamond ring to meet a mortgage payment on a building which he later lost. It was one of the bitterest moments of his life when she drew it from her finger and handed it to him. She urged him to sell it but he fiercely refused. He would get that ring back for her one day if he had to burst his heart to do it.

In the end he saved one building, a small apartment house on Washington Heights, where they had begun, and it was that which fed them during the famine years.

❦{17}❦

"A man called on the telephone for you today," Iris informed Anna at the supper table. "I forgot to tell you."

"Well, who was he?"

"He didn't leave his name. I thought it was the dry cleaner, you said you expected him to call about Papa's suit. But it wasn't."

"Iris!" Anna said. "Do please get to the point."

"I am! It was Mr. Werner and he said he was calling about the picture he'd sent."

"I thought you said he didn't leave his name," Maury scoffed.

"That was the first time he called. The second time he told who he was!"

"Cheer up, folks! This kid will learn how to take a message one of these years," Maury said.

Anna laid down her fork, then picked it up again and took a mouthful of carrots.

"Werner? Picture?" Joseph repeated.

"Yes, he said he'd sent Mama a picture and he hadn't heard from her, so he wondered whether it had got lost or something."

"Oh," Anna said, "I meant to answer. I just haven't got around to it. He did send a picture when his father died. He wrote that they broke up the apartment, and he—Paul Werner—and his sister were going over the things and he—they—came upon this picture and they thought it looked like me, but it doesn't at all, it's a silly-looking thing, but they—he—sent it and I really forgot all about it, that's why I didn't even think to mention it—" She got up and began clearing the plates away. "Coffee or tea tonight, Joseph?"

"Let's see the picture, Ma," Maury called into the kitchen.

"Yes, let's see it, Anna," Joseph said when she came back.

"You really want to? I've stuck it somewhere, I'll have to go rummaging all around—"

"I'd like to see it," Joseph repeated.

She is acting very queer about it, Iris thought.

Anna propped the picture on a table in the living room. It was a crayon drawing of a woman. There was a small gold label on the carved gold frame. Iris bent to read it. *Woman with Red Hair*, it said, with the name of the artist below it.

The woman was seated. Her body was a sweeping curve: the bent head with its washerwoman's knot of dusky red hair, the long, slender neck, the naked shoulders, the suggestion of breast, the arm lying on the lap, the hand fading into shadow. Iris bent closer. There was a piece of knitting on the lap; the ball of yarn had fallen to the floor.

It gave Iris a fine, pleased feeling. She looked back at the artist's name. "Mallard. I've seen his work. It was in the museum when our class went with the art teacher. He must be famous!"

"Don't get excited," Anna said coldly. "It's only a crayon sketch. Not worth any fortune, you can be sure."

What a crass thing for Mama to say! Not like her at all. And that sharp tone!

Joseph tilted his head to the side. He looked doubtful. "It must be valuable. They wouldn't put such an expensive frame on it otherwise, would they?"

Anna's mouth twitched. Iris saw it.

"I'm trying to see the resemblance," Joseph said. "It certainly isn't at all like the one we had done of you in Paris."

"It certainly isn't. This one is art," Maury said.

That annoyed Joseph. "Ahhh—what do you know about art?"

Iris was amused. She put her arm around her father's shoulder. "Papa dear, it's you who don't know about art."

"Maybe not," Joseph grumbled, "but I know what I like. This doesn't look like your mother. I can't see how those people can think it does."

"A picture isn't a photograph," Iris explained earnestly. "A good picture suggests. That's what the art teacher said. It shows character, makes you *feel* the person."

"Poppycock!" Joseph snorted. "It either looks like a person or it doesn't."

"As a matter of fact," Maury declared, "this does look a good deal like Ma."

"What!" Anna cried suddenly. "With that pointed nose and a long neck like a goose?"

"It has your spirit," Maury argued. "I'm surprised at you, Ma. You're the one who knows all about art in this family and you can't understand what we mean?"

"Oh, don't bother me with the thing!" Anna cried in an unnatural voice.

Iris felt sudden pity for her mother. She didn't know why, and she hoped Maury wouldn't answer back.

Her father remonstrated, "I don't know why you're getting so worked up, Anna. I know you hate to be reminded of the Werners, but—"

Anna stared at him. "Nothing of the sort. Are you still harping on the fact that I worked for them and I'm supposed to be ashamed of it? Don't talk like a fool. I've never been ashamed of working with my two hands."

Joseph looked at her steadily.

"What is it, then? Why are you so angry?"

"I'm not angry. I don't like it. Do I have to like it? I didn't ask for it, but here it is, causing dissension in the house. It's ridiculous. It's absurd!"

Joseph threw up his hands. "All right! Nobody's asking you to like it. I'll take it to the office. It's not as bad as all that. You won't have to look at it, then."

"It will look really handsome hanging between the map of Manhattan and your certificate from the Board of Realtors. Just what you need!"

Now that's odd, Iris thought. Papa switching sides like that. First he doesn't like it, next he offers to hang it in his office.

Joseph sighed. "All right. Do what you want with the thing. It's really not important, is it?"

"That's just what I meant all along," Anna said. "It's not important."

Iris was brushing her teeth that night when her mother came into the bathroom.

"Iris, tell me, what did Mr. Werner say?"

"I did tell you."

"Was that all he said?"

"Well, after I said you weren't home, he asked me whether I was the girl with the big eyes. He said he remembered meeting me with you on Fifth Avenue."

"Anything else?"

"I guess not. Oh, he said something more about my eyes. He said he hadn't forgotten me. That my face was half eyes. I thought that was kind of a silly thing to say, wasn't it?"

"Very silly," Anna agreed.

Something different has happened, Iris thought when she was alone. But I'm glad they're not quarreling. She lay awake, listening for sounds of anger from her parents' room, but there were none. Not like that night which she could still remember, although it had been four to five years ago, after they had met Mr. Werner and his mother, and Papa had been so terribly upset.

So much had changed since then. They'd been rich and now they were poor. She knew; she heard the whispering about bills and knew they didn't want to talk in front of her and Maury. She'd heard them say it was a shame to worry the children.

Yes, there was trouble enough now, and so she was glad things were quiet tonight. Not that her parents quarreled very often. Some of the girls at school talked about their fathers and mothers fighting all the time. One of the girl's parents were even getting divorced, which must be awful. It scared you to think about a thing like that.

She had a fleeting thought before falling asleep: she wished that Mr. Werner would stay away, wouldn't call up again.

THE PICTURE DISAPPEARED. Iris saw a flat parcel, wrapped in brown paper, at the back of the top shelf in the hall closet, and guessed that was probably it.

A few days later a letter lay on the desk in the living room with an envelope beside it, a letter left open as if Mama had wanted it to be read. So Iris did. It was very short.

"Dear Mr. Werner," she read. "My husband and I thank you for the picture. We were sorry to learn that your father died. Sincerely, Anna Friedman."

What a queer, curt note! Written on cheap white paper in a sloppy scrawl, with a blot on the page! Not at all like the pretty notes Mama wrote to her friends with black ink on crocus-yellow paper, in her pointed European script like the marks of birds' feet.

Queer!

It HAD TAKEN almost a week for her to feel normal again. My God, Anna thought, he must have gone out of his mind to call our house. And to talk to Iris! That night at the dinner table when the child had told of the call, it was a wonder she hadn't gone faint with the shock.

A wonder, too, that Joseph had taken it so easily. That argument over Mrs. Werner's funeral—she would never forget his jealous rage. For that was what it had been, although he would never have admitted it was. This time he had merely asked a few questions and then accepted, or seemed to accept, her explanation that the gift was a gracious gesture from Paul Werner *and his sister*.

But Joseph was changed from what he had been five years ago. He had lost the firmness with which he had ruled the house when things were going so well. Sad to see. He reminded her in a way of the wistful, poor young man she had first known.

She was thinking all this one afternoon on her way home from neighborhood errands, thinking too that the apartment was growing shabby, and how it didn't take long for misfortune to make itself visible when, half a block away from home, someone called her name. Turning, she saw Paul Werner standing there, tipping his hat.

"I got your note," he said.

She could hardly speak. For an instant her heart seemed to pause and then it began to shake in her chest. "Why are you doing this?" she cried. "Why did you send that picture? And now you've come here and if anyone sees you—"

"Don't be frightened, Anna! I telephoned openly and left my name. There's no subterfuge, no reason for anyone to be suspicious."

As she walked he kept pace with her. She had turned down the side street toward the river, away from the apartment house. Iris would be coming home from school any minute and Iris had watched her so warily the other night—

"Please go!" she pleaded. "Please go, Paul!"

But he persisted. "Your letter was so unlike you, Anna! I surely didn't mean to offend when I sent the Mallard. It was simply that I hadn't seen it in years— Father had stuck it away somewhere—and when I came upon it I was thunder-struck by the resemblance. And I wanted you to have it."

They reached Riverside Drive. Cars streamed by, glittering in the lemon-colored light. The air wavered, its radiance trembling before Anna's dizzy eyes. She stood there beside the river of cars, clutching a bag of groceries, frozen as if the curb were a precipice and the avenue an abyss.

Paul took a strong hold of her arm. "We have to talk. Cross over. We'll find a bench under the trees."

Her legs moved. This could not possibly be happening! One minute walking home from the market on a bright, windy afternoon of early spring; the next minute sitting on a bench with this man whom she had thought never to see again! How could it be happening?

"Anna, I had to come," he said. "You've never been out of my mind. Never. Can you understand that?"

She was afraid to look at him. "I can," she whispered.

"I think of you sometimes in the middle of a conference, or when I'm driving the car or reading a newspaper—suddenly, there you are. I wake up and remember you, even when I had been dreaming of something entirely apart from you. But—there you are. And when I saw that painting, the memory of you became so vivid that I had to do something about it."

Her breath had begun to calm. She turned her face to his. "It's a beautiful thing and I felt so—so *stirred*. But it's crazy of you to be here, all the same. Don't you know it is, Paul?"

"Anna, I had to. That's all there is to be said."

He took her hand, his fingers twining in hers. In spite of the thickness of glove leather she could feel the force, the heat, the life of his flesh.

"Don't," she murmured.

But neither of them withdrew and the entwined hands lay on the bench between them. The world went by: children rolling on their skates and bicycles; dogs pulling at their leashes; young women pushing baby carriages. All of these were oblivious to the man and woman on the bench.

After a while Paul said, "Tell me how you are."

She felt a great weight, she felt entranced. "No, I find it hard to talk. You tell me."

"Well," he began obediently, "I've just come back from Europe for the firm. From Germany. Things are going bad there and they're going to get worse with this Hitler fellow. I've been trying to rescue some investments for our clients before it's too late."

There were chords in his voice that Anna would have recognized if she had heard them among strangers on the other side of the world. From her room at the top of that house the music of his voice had carried up the stair well while she had lain in her bed, listening for it—

Now, because he saw that she was unable to speak, he tried to find something more to say. "Other than that—well, I've been collecting art and I go to a sculpture class. I'm not very good at it, but it's a challenge. And I've kept up with Father's charities. He was a great benefactor, an efficient manager, and it's hard to fill his shoes. But I'm trying."

She heard a smile in his voice and turned back from where she had been gazing at the river. Those large, hooded eyes under heavy, rounded lids—brilliant eyes, like dark jewels—his mother had had the same, as well as the high arched nose. And Iris had them.

"You're staring at me, Anna!"

"Am I? I didn't mean to."

"I don't mind if you do. Look at me some more."

Flushing, she looked back at the river. Her heart began to race again; she could hardly breathe.

"Perhaps you want to know more about me? I—we have no children. Never will have. Marian had an operation a couple of years ago."

"I'm sorry," Anna responded automatically.

"So am I. So is she. But we shan't adopt. And she keeps busy with her charities, too. She's very generous with her strength and time, not just with money." He stopped again, then said, "So that's my life. Now will you tell me about yours?"

She drew a deep breath and began. "An ordinary life. Like women everywhere. Keeping the house and children. Coping with bad times."

"Have they hit you very badly?"

"We've lost almost everything," Anna said simply.

"Do you need money? Can I help you?"

She shook her head. "No, no, we manage. And anyway, you don't think I could take it from you, do you?"

And, suddenly overcome by a wave of chill reality, she withdrew her hand, clasping her own two hands together in her lap.

"I suppose you couldn't," Paul said bleakly. There was a long silence. Then he cried out, "I should have married you, Anna! Would you have married me?"

"Oh," she said, "you know I would have, the way I felt then! But what's the use of talking about it now?"

A little boat sped down the river. A cloud darkened the spring green on the Palisades. Anna saw them through a curtain of tears. How different everything might have been! You take one path and it leads you here and you become this kind of woman; another path leads you there, and you become another kind of woman. The same body but another life, and therefore another woman. She thought she had forgotten—well, almost forgotten—how it might have been. Goodness knew she had tried to forget.

She turned on him almost fiercely. "Why didn't you marry me? You see, I'm not proud anymore. I don't want to be proud. So I ask you, why didn't you?"

Paul's eyes looked straight into hers and through them. "I was a boy then," he said at last, "not yet a man. While you already had the spirit of a woman. I didn't have courage enough to marry someone I—wouldn't be expected to marry." His voice grew rough. "Can you understand that and not despise me for it? Can you?"

Something sprang alive in Anna, a singing, a flowering, a tenderness of joy and vindication. "Oh," she said, "I was so terribly hurt that I wanted to die! And after that, so angry. So bitter and angry. . . . But I could never 'despise' you, never."

And she thought, Perhaps, after all, I should tell him now? Hasn't he a right and a duty to know that my daughter belongs to him?

Paul said abruptly, "I haven't told you everything. There's something else."

"What is it?"

"Do you remember the time we met on fifth Avenue a few years ago? I keep thinking of the way you stood with your hand on your little girl's shoulder. I don't know why that moved me so, but it did. And the child's face haunts me. You'll think I've gone mad, but I had—and have had—a revelation that she was mine. My child. And I haven't been able to get it out of my head."

It did not surprise Anna that he had come upon the truth. That rare, discerning mind, those far-seeing, through-seeing eyes—not much eluded them! No, it did not surprise her. Her lips parted to speak, but he interrupted.

"It's true, then, isn't it?"

"It's true."

"I'm not stunned. I'm not shocked. It's as though I'd always known it." He lit a cigarette with an effort at calm control; but she saw that his hands were shaking. "And Joseph?" he asked after a moment.

Anna shook her head. "Only I know."

There was a long, long silence, while the pungent smoke drifted. Paul's eyes closed and he did not move. After a while he opened his eyes and spoke again. "How you must have suffered, Anna!"

"I was so guilty, I thought I wasn't fit to live," she replied, very low. "But then my strength came back, thank God. I suppose human beings can endure much more than they think they can."

"You've had to endure too much! Losing your parents, poverty in a strange country and then this! Why didn't you tell me, Anna?"

She looked at him ruefully.

"All right, I shouldn't have asked that. I know you couldn't have. But will you let me do something for her, at least? I could open a trust account so that she would never be in want."

"No, no! That's not possible! You know it's not! The best thing you can do is to stay away from her. Can't you see that?"

Paul sighed. "Tell me, please, what she's like."

Anna considered how best to sum up a complex, aloof and sensitive little girl.

"Iris is very intelligent, very perceptive. She knows music and books; she has your feeling for art, I think."

He smiled faintly. "Go on, please."

It became easier to speak. Her words, hesitant at first, began to flow. She was, after all, a mother talking about her child. And this listener wanted to hear. So she told about food and school and amusing remarks, searching her own mind for words that might make Iris live in Paul's mind.

"And does she love you very much? I hope so. It's not every child who has a mother like you."

"We have no great problems, she and I. But she's more attached to Joseph. He adores her, she's the heart of his heart. But then, that's the way it is between fathers and daughters," Anna concluded, immediately sorry to have been so tactless.

But Paul quietly agreed. "That's true."

"I'm not really good with her!" Anna cried suddenly. "Not what I ought to be, Paul! I'm good *to* her; I love her just as much as I love Maury. It's just that I'm not at ease with her. It's—different," she faltered.

"Of course. It would be."

"When I look at her I try to think of her as having been born—" she was about to say, "as Joseph's and mine," but said instead, "differently. And most of the time I can do it. I've put you away at the back of the past, you see. And now today the past is here, and whenever I look at Iris I shall think—" She was unable to finish.

Paul took her hand back, stroking it gently.

Then Anna said, "I wonder how much she feels of all this, poor Iris. She *must* feel something!"

Neither of them knew what to add to that.

Presently he said, "I've not been fair. I've not asked you to tell about Maury."

"You're only being kind. You can't really be interested in Maury."

"Yes, I can. He belongs to you, he's a part of you. Tell me."

"Maury is the son everyone wants, the son you think of when you imagine having a boy. Everyone loves him, he—" Anna stopped. "I can't, Paul. I'm brimming over. There's been—too much—this afternoon."

"I know. I feel that way myself, Anna dearest."

And taking the hand between both of his he removed her glove, raised the hand and kissed it, the palm, the fingers, the pulse that fluttered and jumped in her wrist.

They became aware of stir and movement in the park. Mothers began calling to their children and gathering scattered toys. The afternoon was coming to its end.

Paul put Anna's hand down and stood up, startling her. He walked a few paces away with his back to her, facing the river. He seemed so solitary there in his velvet-collared coat, a stranger among the pigeons and the children playing hopscotch on the walk. This tall, powerful man who could command almost anything he might want, this man was also vulnerable through her. He was separate from her and yet bound to her for as long as either of them might live, or as long as Iris lived or whatever children Iris might have, or—

He came back and sat down. "Listen to me, Anna. Life is short. Just yesterday we were twenty, and where's the time gone? Let's take what we can, you and I."

"What do you mean?"

"I want to marry you now. I want to take our little girl and give you both what you ought to have. I want to stop waking up at night wondering how you are. I want to wake up and have you next to me."

"As simply as that?" There was faint bitterness in her tone; she could hear it. "And what about Maury? And Joseph? What about the small fact that you already have a wife?"

"It wouldn't destroy Marian if I were to ask for a divorce. Trust me, Anna. I am not a destroyer. I don't hurt people if I can help it."

"Hurt? Do you realize what it would do to Joseph if he knew I was sitting here with you now? He's a devout, believing, strait-laced man. A puritan, Paul! This would be past his forgiveness. Divorce? He would be ruined!" Anna's voice rose. "I sit with him in the evening, I look across the room at this man who married me when—when you wouldn't have me, who takes care of me, who gave me every material thing when he had it, and gives me loving kindness now when he has nothing else to give. Sometimes I can't bear the thought of what I've already done to him."

"Everything has to be paid for," Paul said gently. "I understand what you're saying and I understand that it would be very, very hard in many ways. Still, you have to weigh all that against your own life, what you want to do with your own life. And I know—*know*, Anna!—that you want to come to me."

The blood poured into her cheeks. "Yes, yes I do! I can't deny that I do!"

"Well, then, you see?"

"But also, we've been through so much, Joseph and I!" She seemed to be musing, recollecting, almost as if she were alone, letting her thoughts run. "Struggling uphill, then sliding almost all the way back down again. And he works so hard! I think sometimes it will kill him. And he never wants anything, never takes anything for himself. It was all for us, for me and the children."

"For my child," Paul said.

Anna sighed, a long quivering breath like a sob. "So how can I, Paul? Can I put a knife into a man like him, can I? And besides, I love him! Do you know what I mean when I say that I love him?"

He didn't answer.

"But you do see, Paul, you do see the way it is?"

He cried out, "I'm so sorry for us all! Oh, my God, how sorry I am!"

Anna began to cry.

"Ah, don't," he whispered then, and took out a handkerchief. "Here, you mustn't go home with red eyes. Then you'd really have some explanations to make!" He began gently to dry her eyes. "Anna, Anna, what are we to do?"

"I don't know. I only know I can't marry you."

"You think so now. But things change. I'll wait. It will look different to you after a while."

Anna shook her head. "We shouldn't see each other anymore. You know that."

"And you know that's impossible. Neither of us could stand it."

"I told you before, people can stand a whole lot more than they think they can."

"Perhaps so. But why should we torture ourselves to prove we can? I want to see you again, Anna, and I'm going to. Surely I have a right at least to hear about Iris now and then?"

"All right," she said softly. "I'll figure out some way. I can't think right now. But I will."

She took a mirror from her purse, anxiously examining her face.

"You look fine. Can't tell a thing. Except that you're still an entrancing woman, even in that coat." He flushed. "I didn't mean there was anything wrong with your coat. I only meant—well, it doesn't do for you what black velvet and a pair of diamond earrings would do."

She laughed and he said, "That's better. I love to hear you laugh. It's a long time since I first heard that laugh."

"I'd better go back, Paul. It's awfully late."

"Go ahead, Anna darling. But I'll telephone in the morning around ten. Will that be all right?"

"Yes. At ten."

"You'll have had time by then to decide how we can meet again."

* * *

"You stored the picture away," Joseph said that night when they were in bed.

"Yes. Since neither of us liked it."

"I wonder why that fellow sent it to you?"

"Rich people like to give things, that's all. It makes them feel powerful."

"But he hardly knows you. It's not as if you were someone in his circle."

She didn't answer and he did not press her. Poor Joseph! He was skirting the subject, wanting to ask more and yet afraid to. These past years had been too much for him, had beaten down some of that first strong assurance. He had been ladling out the ocean with a cup since the Depression began and he was tired. Soft pity moved Anna and she spoke lightly, wanting to soothe and ease his mind.

"What it comes down to is simply that I was a pretty little maid in that house and people are kind to pretty little maids. You're surely not jealous?"

"Well, I could be, but since you explain it that way, I won't be."

"Please. Let's not have any repetition of that business when I met them on the street that time."

"I was awfully angry, wasn't I?"

"You were. And without reason."

He was silent.

"Joseph? Please. No tempers now. I just—can't take it."

"Why? Am I so fierce?"

"You can be."

"I won't be. Anna, dear, forget it. Forget the damned picture. It's not worth talking about. Let's go to sleep." He sighed and, drawing her to him, lay his head in the curve of her shoulder.

He sighed again. "Ah, what peace! No matter how cold and tough it is outside I have this refuge! For a few hours here at night I can forget debts and new business and the office rent. Just think of basic things, of you and me. That's what it's all about, Anna, the way it all began. Just you and me and the beautiful little boy and girl we've made together."

She swallowed hard. There was such a lump in her throat, such a lump of pain.

"And I have to fight for all of you, my people. Ah, well, maybe with this new man, this Roosevelt coming in, things will be better. I hope so," Joseph murmured.

When he had fallen asleep Anna turned over. Such trust, such loyalty and trust! It was an armor that he wore without knowing that he had it on. You couldn't wound a man who wore such armor. A line of poetry trailed through her head, something Maury had memorized for his Latin class, something like "virtue defends him." Tears trailed down her temples toward her ears. Alone I am, entirely alone. For who else can get inside my head, my heart, and feel what I feel? All my confusion, tension, terror? I stand before the great dark future and I can't know what is waiting there for me.

It grew cold. Fear chilled. She crept toward the solid bulwark of Joseph's back, feeling for comfort in its warmth. Then came a fleeting recall of Paul's words: "I want to wake up and find you next to me." A feverish wave of heat dispelled the chill; she trembled with desire, shame, fear, and then grew cold again.

The clock's hands glimmered on the night table. With wide-open eyes Anna lay, watching the hands move steadily forward through the night.

THE TELEPHONE RANG at ten o'clock. It rang once only; she had been waiting beside it.

"I didn't sleep all night, Paul," she told him.

"Neither did I. Have you decided when and where?"

"Paul, I can't see you now. I don't say never, only not now."

"I was afraid of this."

"It's I who am afraid. Guilty and afraid. I haven't got the strength to cope. Please understand, and don't be angry."

"I don't think I could ever be really angry at you. But I am miserably disappointed."

"It's so hard! So very, very hard!"

"You're sure it's not you who're making it harder?"

"I don't think so. I did try to explain to you yesterday how it is."

"Yes, you did. And I understood. But I'm not going to let you cut the cord between us, Anna. Not ever."

"I'm not asking you to. If you let me know where you are I'll send you a postcard every now and then, a harmless postcard that anyone might read. Only you will know that it is about Iris and me."

"Tell me again: I think you said a moment ago that you didn't mean 'never'; you only meant 'not right now.' Isn't that what you said?"

"Yes, yes."

"Then I'll be patient. And I'll always let you know where I am. With a postcard, too. Do you have women friends who travel?"

"Oh, yes. Pick any name. It won't matter."

"I'll do that."

"Paul? Will you hang up now?"

"In a moment. Just remember this: when you have changed your mind about meeting again or about marriage, or if you ever need me for anything, send me three or four words and I'll come to you. And you will change your mind, you know."

"I'm going to hang up now," she said softly.

"All right. Hang up. But don't say the word 'good-by.'"

BOOK TWO

RANDOM WINDS

❊{18}❊

Maury was the only one of the family who made no changes; they had kept him in the school because it would help him, they believed, to get into Yale. Besides, it was more important for a boy. Joseph knew Maury would get as good an education at City College; some of the best brains in the nation had come from there. But somehow it had always been taken for granted, he didn't remember how or why, but just as far back as he could think it had been assumed that Maury would go to Yale. It had been a kind of promise and he couldn't diminish himself in the eyes of his family by breaking it. However much they might deny the diminution, and they would, Joseph would feel that it was.

And so the acceptance had come from Yale and the family was gathered around the table to celebrate. The Malones, who had "known Maury before he was born," were invited, too. Besides, Joseph had some other news for them.

Anna removed her apron before sitting down and hung it on the doorknob. The only elegance that remained from the past came from her silver candlesticks and the flowers she had put out, a handful of inexpensive daffodils from the market. She had cooked all the things the family loved best. There were stuffed fish in its own silky, quivering jelly; a pot roast in dark gravy; potato pancakes crisp as celery; baked carrots sweet with prunes; hot, puffy rolls; a tart, cool salad and apple strudel running with cinnamon juice, crunched with nuts, wrapped in its rich brittle crust.

Joseph leaned back and sighed with repletion. He looked around the room at the people he loved and it came to him that things could have been a great deal worse.

After the young people had left the table, the others lingered. "Now," Joseph said, "I have something to tell you. I went to see the president of the bank last week. I'd been thinking and thinking of something for us to do. We can't just coast along until prosperity appears around that corner they sing about. So I told him, I said, 'Listen, Mr. Fairbanks, you owe us something. We only got back fifty cents on the dollar from our accounts and I'm not complaining—not too much, anyway. But I think you owe us a chance to make a living. We're going into the management business—' "

"We are?" Malone interrupted.

Joseph put up his hand. "Let me finish. I said, 'I want your properties to manage. We know how to take care of buildings, my partner and I. Goodness knows, we've built enough of them.' And he said he'd think it over."

"He won't do it," Malone said glumly. "They've been using the same people for years. Why should they give the business to us?"

Joseph smiled. "I don't know why they should, but they did. He called me this afternoon, and we're to go in on Monday morning for instructions."

Malone stared. He opened his mouth and shut it and opened it again with a whoop. "Well, I'll be damned! If this isn't a smart man, a real man, my idea of a man, if you want to know! And the best friend I ever had in the world, or hope to have. I want to propose a toast to him, and then to us!" He stood up and flourished his empty glass.

Joseph pushed the bottle in front of him, ignoring the signal of Anna's small frown: *he's had enough.* If the man wanted to drink this was surely no time to stop him; it was the first time in a couple of years that he had laughed.

"I want to tell you a story about our trip abroad," Malone said. "Our one and only trip abroad, cursed be the day! For if I'd been home—ah, well, that's another story. Anyway, we went to visit the family in Wexford. So here we were, pulled into this hick burg; God, the toilet all the way down the hall, and cold, cold, I've never felt such cold! So I said to my cousin, little old wiry guy with a wool hat, 'Fitz,' I said, 'look here, the wife and I want to invite the family to dinner tonight. I'll order up a big feast and you go out now and do the invitin', ask all the relatives, okay?' So he says sure he will, and Mary and I go in and order steaks and pies and all the liquor you can drink. Then we go to dress up, the relatives from America showin' off, you know, and we go downstairs and there they are waiting for us. Would you believe it, I guess you wouldn't, but I'll swear to you there were fifty-four of them there. Fifty-four! It's a good thing I had plenty of traveler's checks because they ate enough for a hundred and fifty-four."

He sat back laughing at the memory of it, then suddenly sobered, the tears of laughter turning to real tears, and he wiped his eyes.

"Oh, what a fool I was, what a fool! On top of the world, and look at me now; look what I've done."

"Well," Joseph said, "consider it this way. If you had sold a month before the bust you'd be a millionaire now and everybody would be saying how smart you are."

"Yes, and if my aunt had balls she'd be my uncle."

"Malone!" cried his wife, shocked and mortified.

"Let him be," Joseph said. "There are no children here and I'm sure we've all heard the word before."

Anna was laughing. She looks so young, he thought. With all the troubles she looks so bright and young. What would I ever do without her? She had put the apron back on to clear the table and at that moment stood beside her portrait, which hung in its carved and gilded frame between the windows. He had an instant's vision of their years together, all the way back to the stoop on Hester Street where he had proposed, and his real life had begun.

* * *

Sʜᴇ ʜᴀᴅ ʙᴇᴇɴ painted like royalty, seated for all time in a highbacked chair, with one hand, the one with the diamond, resting on the arm; the other was curled, fingers up, in her lap. Her skirt, a fountain of pink silk pale as the inside of a shell, spread to the floor. And on her face, Anna thought long afterward, although she had not seen it at first, on the slight upward curve of her smiling mouth, the artist had placed a look of surprise.

❈⟨19⟩❈

The Bar Harbor Express made a nice click and clatter rolling through the night. They were an hour and a half out of New York; the berths were made up and the observation car where Maury sat was emptying. The man across from him, a neat man in a summer suit, about his father's age, finished the newspaper and smiled over at Maury.

"Going up to your family's place for the vacation?"

"No, visiting friends about fifteen miles down the coast."

"Well, as one Yale man to another, have a good stay."

"Thanks. How did you know?"

"The emblem on your racket cover. I saw you get on at Grand Central. I was a tennis player, too."

"It's a great game," Maury said politely.

"That it is. I still play every morning I can." He stood up, nodding a pleasant good night. "Enjoy yourself, son. These are the best years of your life."

"Yes, sir," Maury said.

He sat on awhile, watching the speckle of small-town lights as Connecticut went by. The best years of your life. The language was full of clichés like that, and middle-aged people were especially apt to use them. But still there was a good deal of truth in some of them.

He had gone up to Yale with a mix of feelings. (He supposed this was the meaning of adulthood, the discovery that nothing is simple.) First, there had been satisfaction. His parents, his mother primarily, had in their innocence taken for granted that their bright boy would be accepted. His headmaster had assured him that if any boy in the school was going to make it, Maury would. So he had been really pleased about not having disappointed anyone. But also he'd had a very small feeling of guilt because it was a financial strain upon the family, and hence a strong sense of pressure to do very, very well.

"You're one lucky boy, Maury," his father's friends would tell him when the men were talking in his parents' house. "Yale, in times like these! You've got a good father."

And they would sigh, these tense, worried men, and look at him. He knew they were seeing him in his fortunate youth, as though he had gone to inhabit another world.

And it was another world. The seasons moved in neat progression, from golden fall to commencement—stately music under ancient trees—and back to fall. Four whole years of that, a gift of time. Oh, if he could stay there, stay there! . . . Wouldn't that be something? Sometimes, late at night when he had put his books away, he would sit at the window and just let himself feel the peace. How old it was, how tranquil in the white winter nights! Solid and rooted. Trees like these, buildings like these, had nothing to worry about. No one would ever tear them down or burrow underneath them for a subway.

It crossed his mind that lately his thoughts didn't fit the image people had of him, or that he had of himself. The image was of a boy to whom everything was easy, sports, learning, life. Well, learning was easy enough; not, he saw honestly, because he had any tremendous thirst for it, but only because his memory was superb. His memory served just as well for the store of jokes that gathered laughter in the center of a group, the laughter which made him a "great guy" or a "sunny personality," expressions which depended upon the age of the person who was talking about him. This new quietness of his which was almost, but not quite, melancholy—this he didn't like to think about. He guessed that it too was merely a part of growing older.

Anyway, there was no melancholy in him tonight. He got up and made his way back to the sleeping car. By morning light he'd be in Maine. He could almost smell tart pines and briny water, remembered from the years at camp; he could feel the cheer of being with Chris again.

It was the most unlikely friendship, one would have thought. Chris was a "preppie," whose great-great-grandfather had grafted the pride of Yale into the family's bones. His mother's family, he explained, always went to Harvard; his grandfather had been a trustee there. It made for an odd situation, he would say with mock gravity, at the Harvard-Yale game every year.

He belonged to all the good clubs. His family had a summer home. His father sailed in the Bermuda races. Yes, it was an unlikely friendship indeed. And it never would have come about if Chris hadn't torn a ligament one icy night, crossing the quadrangle on his way home from a date, and if Maury hadn't happened to be stargazing at the window.

"There wasn't a soul out that night; I'd have frozen to death on the ground if Maury hadn't seen me." Chris liked to tell it that way, and it was probably quite true.

They talked frankly about their different backgrounds. Chris wanted to know about Maury's family and asked questions about his religion. He had never really known a Jew before.

"Of course there've been Jewish fellows in all my classes," he said. "But you know how it is, you just don't mix. Funny, you and I would have gone all the way through without knowing each other if it hadn't been for my accident. I wonder what the *real* reason is, why we don't mix?"

Maury didn't know, either. These artificial differences! Who the hell cared who your grandparents were or where they had come from? They got along so well; he and Chris laughed at the same things, wrestled and punched in the locker room after swimming and were perfectly matched at tennis, which they discovered as soon as the courts were ready in the spring. Tennis was what they both liked almost more than anything. "A couple of tennis bums," they called themselves. They liked to bicycle into the country on Sunday afternoons, with a stop for beer, now that repeal had come. Sometimes they studied together, although Chris and his friends weren't so great at that. A solid B would do them, or even an occasional C. Why break your head? Such easy optimism was calming to Maury, although he never was able to bring himself to apply it to himself.

His roommate, Eddy Holtz, was puzzled. He frowned, shaking his head, and his heavy black curly hair wobbled like a cap.

"What are you doing with that crowd, Maury? You don't fit. Why are you doing it?"

"What do you mean, I don't fit? They like me, we're friends."

"They don't like you well enough to take you into their clubs."

"That's not Chris's fault. He thinks that sort of thing is stupid. But prejudices die hard, although they all do eventually. And meanwhile, we've a lot in common."

"Something disturbs me. It's as if to them you were an exotic pet, a new kind of dog that nobody else in the neighborhood has."

"Thanks, thanks a lot!"

"I'm sorry, maybe that was a bad way to put it. What I mean is, there's a barrier. There's bound to be, and you know it, Maury. You can't ever be sure you won't say something they'll disapprove of and then—"

Eddy reminded him of his father, the part of his father that had always disturbed him. He was so apprehensive, plodding and somber, poring over his books to get into med school. There wasn't a laugh in him. And he told him so.

"You sound just like my father."

"Maybe your father and I know something you don't know."

That sort of talk from a person his own age infuriated Maury. "You people are paranoid!" he cried.

And Eddy had sighed. Always that sigh of weary, knowing gloom. There wasn't a trace of that around Chris, none of that tension. Chris was vigorous, cheerful, healthy.

"I'm sick of being constricted," Maury had burst out. "Shut into your fears, your narrow choices. There's a whole free wide world out there, Eddy! I'll leave you to the burdens of being Jewish, since you're afraid to get rid of them."

"Shit," Eddy said. "You're burdened and you're constricted as much as I am. And you've no way out. My advice is: get used to it."

As soon as they were able to change rooms they did so. They had been best friends, he and Eddy Holtz, and they never exactly became enemies. They still waved a greeting in passing, but neither would go so far as to cross the street for anything more than that.

Maury settled the suitcase and stowed the five-pound box of candy for Chris's mother in a safe place. Ma had bought the candy and laid out his clothes, whitened his shoes, sent his white flannel trousers to the tailor for pressing and even bought him a couple of new ties.

He smiled now, remembering his mother. "You're not taking those old slacks? They're faded, Maury!"

"I know. We're going fishing. And anyway, these people don't dress up."

"Better listen to your mother," his father had warned. "Rich people with a summer house like that are bound to dress. You don't want to look like a beggar."

Maury had tried to explain, feeling as he spoke a surge of enthusiasm. "They're not rich, Pa, not in the way you think of it. Chris doesn't care what he wears. His sweaters have holes in them. He and all his friends are simple. They don't struggle. You'd be surprised."

"Maybe I wouldn't be surprised," his father said. His eyebrows rippled. "They don't struggle, you tell me. They can afford to be simple. If I go downtown with a hole in my overcoat, they'll say Friedman's broke and they'll have nothing to do with me. People like us have to dress right."

From the moment he was met the next morning at the station he was glad he had used his own judgment. Chris, his brothers and their friend Donald were in an old station wagon loaded with sacks of dog food. Their clothes were as old as the car and their sneakers were tattered.

At dinner, though, they dressed, and then he was glad his mother had taken care of his white flannels, he thought with amusement.

The house was low, with brown-weathered ells and wings. From the row of wicker chairs on the front veranda one looked out over lawns and water to the pine hills on the other side of the cove. After dinner they all went out to watch the stars come up.

"As you can see, we're not famous for our night life here," Chris remarked.

"No apologies in paradise," Maury answered.

"This is my fifty-seventh summer in this house," old Mr. Guthrie remarked abruptly.

"Sir?" Chris asked.

That was something Maury had never heard. At home you asked: What did you say? when you hadn't understood.

"I said, 'This is my fifty-seventh summer in this house,'" the grandfather repeated.

"I thought that's what you said."

The old man, erect in the fan-backed wicker chair, tapped Maury's knee with his cane. "Young man, would you like me to tell you about how this house came to be built?"

"Yes, sir, I would."

"It was in 1875 and I was twenty-five years old, just out of law school. I had been married a year and my wife was expecting our first child. Her people had been seafaring folk here on the coast and, although she was contented enough in Boston during the winter months, she hankered after her home place in the summer. So when I came into a little unexpected legacy from my grandmother I decided to build a house near my wife's family village. We had to travel by boat then, you know, from Boston to Bar Harbor; then overland by buckboard for the luggage and buggy for ourselves. It took five hours on a single-track dirt road all the way. I'm eighty-two years old next Thursday."

"Do you like being eighty-two, Gramp?" asked Tommy. He was eleven, the youngest of Chris's brothers.

Everybody laughed and the old man answered, "Can't say that I'm delighted with it. But since the alternative is to have died young I'll say, yes, I like it well enough."

In the gauzy light Maury's eyes moved around the semicircle. What an agreeable, variegated family! First the grandfather's baby brother Ray, a lively tennis player at the age of seventy-one. Then Uncle Ray's daughter with her husband and two vigorous children, who had come in their camper from a nature tour of the national parks. And Chris's Uncle Wendell with his wife; both close to sixty, he estimated, but, like all the rest of the family, thin and flat of stomach and taut of skin.

"Uncle Wendell's a departure from the family pattern," Chris had explained. "Didn't give a damn for banking or law or business. Teaches classics at St. Bart's, when he's not on a dig in Greece or someplace."

"I wonder how James is doing," Chris's mother remarked now.

Someone answered, "As usual. He insisted that Polly and Agatha come for the Fourth, which is like his usual considerate self."

Chris explained to Maury, "My Uncle James is crippled from polio and he doesn't always feel like traveling, though he comes sometimes. But it's a long trip. They live over in New York State. Brewerstown."

"How horrible!"

"Yes, it is. He was a prominent lawyer, representing American banks in France, when this happened to him about twelve years ago. So he came back home and runs a small practice to keep busy. But the whole thing just turned their lives upside down, as you can imagine."

"Aggie's great, you'll like her," Tommy said now. "She goes to Wellesley. Last year when she came for Gramp's birthday we went to the fair and we rode on the Ferris wheel. She plays a great game of tennis, too."

Mr. Guthrie laughed. "Tommy's enthusiastic about girls because he's never had a sister. A girl is a real novelty around our house, I can tell you." He stood up. "Well, I don't know about all of you, but I'm turning in. Who's for tennis early in the morning, and I mean early?"

"Maury?" Chris asked. "I thought we could pack a lunch and sail down the coast tomorrow. But we could get a set of doubles in first, if you're willing."

"Any time you say."

"Six o'clock. Game?"

"Game!"

He was so pleasantly tired, yet he didn't fall asleep for quite a while. He lay in bed listening to the night, to low thunder from a little storm passing in the hills and to rising wind. He was enchanted. This graceful, peaceful family, this simple ease. Oh, this is where I want to be, where I fit, where I belong. . . .

*   *   *

He supposed you wouldn't call her beautiful, and yet he didn't want to look away from her. She was small and moved lightly. He thought of birds and fawns, of quick, alert, soft things. She was tan; her skin, her hair, even her eyes were golden brown. Cat's eyes. If there had been such a name for a girl, he would have thought she ought to be called September.

They lay on the float together on her second day. Everyone had gone sailing, but Agatha had not wanted to go. "Don't go sailing," she had said to Maury, "keep me company for a swim. No, of course I don't mean that. Do whatever you want," she'd said.

And he had answered, "I want to keep you company."

So they lay, while the sun burned and the wind cooled. And Agatha spoke into a drowsy silence.

"Maury, do you mind if I ask you something?"

"Ask away."

"Are you poor?"

He sat up on one elbow. "What a question! What makes you ask that, of all things?"

"I'm sorry if it sounded horrible. But most of Chris's friends are so awfully rich, and I wondered whether, well, whether the reason you seemed kind of quiet was that maybe you were poor. Because we're the poor ones in our family, so I sort of know how it feels."

Poor, Maury thought, remembering the tenements from which his parents had come, where people still lived and eked out their days . . . poor, he thought grimly.

"No," he said quietly, "not really. My father manages all right, considering the times."

"Well, then, I suppose it must be because you're Jewish."

He was astounded. He didn't know what to say to this girl.

"Chris told me you were."

"Is that such an interesting subject?"

"I think it is. I don't know many Jews, just one or two girls in my dorm. But Dad talks about them so much that it's made me curious."

"There's nothing to be curious about. They're only people like everyone else. Some saints and some sinners."

"My father hates them. He blames them for all the troubles since the world began. It's a kind of hobby with him, like Uncle Wendell's digs in Greece."

A kind of hobby! He swallowed and changed the subject. "That must be an interesting life, your uncle's."

"Oh, yes, you ought to get him talking sometime. He's got more stories to tell! He's from the bookish branch of the family. Not like this house."

Maury had observed that the house was filled with plants and needlework, all the cozy comforts, but no books. Nothing to read except an old set of the *Britannica* and the *National Geographic* magazine.

"I'll bet Chris seldom gets over a C, does he?" Agatha remarked.

"Well, now, I really can't—"

She laughed. "Don't worry about being disloyal! It's no secret and his parents don't care."

"Don't care? I can't imagine that."

"Why? Do your parents care so much?"

"I should think they do." He thought of the last semester in high school, when he had got his first grade below an A minus. It had been a B minus in chemistry; he hated science. And his father had said mildly enough, "Maury, I saw your report card. What's the B minus doing on it?"

"They never pushed me," he said now, "not the way some parents do. It's a kind of silent pressure. You know they want you to do well. They expect you to take advantage of all the good opportunities and somehow, if you don't do well, you feel as though you had hurt them."

"I've always heard that Jews set so much store by education."

There it was again. You could hardly touch on any subject without having that creep in. The Difference.

"Have I said something to upset you?"

He turned to her quickly. "I want to know, are you like your father?"

"I? How do you mean?"

"About Jews, I mean?"

She laughed. "Of course I'm not! How can you ask? I don't believe in that stuff! Nobody else in the family does. Why, Uncle Wendell is the most liberal, broad-minded man—"

"And your mother?"

Aggie waited a moment. She said slowly, "Mother is—well, it's hard to know what Mother would be if it weren't for my father. But she's been especially influenced by him since he's been home all the time. I really think a lot of his thinking is because of his sickness. When you don't move around in the world, you narrow down, you don't see any new people, and you get—well, fanatic. Goodness," she said ruefully, "he doesn't even like Catholics, especially the Irish! And maybe Mother has got a touch of that. Yes, I would say she had."

"She doesn't know about me?"

"I'm sure it hasn't been mentioned." Agatha frowned. "Maury?"

"Yes?"

"Perhaps it would be better not to mention it to Mother."

Ah, the hell with them all! The hell with her frosty, pinch-faced mother and the whole damned lot!

"Maury?"

"Yes?"

"I don't want you to think, I mean, it's a dirty bird that soils its own nest and all that sort of thing. . . . My father is really a very wonderful, kind man in spite of that. He's suffered horribly and I really love him very much. I wouldn't want you to think I came from some sort of abnormal, awful family where the people all hate each other."

Why should she care what he thought about her and her family?

She looked into his face. She had the most appealing, sweet, sweet smile. He smiled back. Her smile broke into a laugh, not the silly artificial laugh of a girl who wants to show how gay she can be, but a bright laugh, honest and true.

"Hey, you know you people have been stewing in the sun for two hours?" Chris called over the water.

They scrambled up and dove in, racing to the shore.

She put an idea into his head. Maybe Chris hadn't told his parents, had only mentioned it to Agatha? He didn't want to ask, to seem to be making a big thing out of it. In a way he hoped that Chris had told his family, because if he had not and it were later to come out that Maury *was*, why, then it would appear that he had come under false pretenses.

At dinner that evening something had been said that made Maury think they did know. In talking about a banker whom he had met in London, Chris's father mentioned that the man possessed a famous collection of paintings and that he was a man of great culture, as so many Jews were. So Maury thought probably they knew, or else why would he have said that? Or maybe it was the other way around?

Very distressing, a nuisance really. Of course, the name ought to tell them something. Still, it sounded German. Or did it? What a nuisance! Not that there was anything to be ashamed of. Surely he was not ashamed of his people who had given the world so much, and been so unjustly treated by the world. Certainly he was not ashamed. But what, then? Well, he was ill at ease, wondering what they might be thinking, since undoubtedly so many of them did think. Or perhaps didn't think, merely just felt something? Funny, he hadn't been this way, really hadn't been this way on the campus with Chris and the other fellows. He'd felt equal, genuinely comfortable and good.

But in the presence of these polished elders it was, for some reason, different. For the first time since his arrival he felt that it was. The dinners here were so different from home. He looked at the cool table, sparsely set, the thin-sliced roast beef on the platter. No wonder they were all so lean! He could have eaten more, but Mrs. Guthrie paid no attention to anyone's plate. At home Ma would have been urging, insisting that everyone take more, and sometimes when they refused she would put it on their plates herself. Here there were formal manners. At home there were discussions, often emotional ones, about business, about politics, about Iris' math teacher who seemed to torment the poor child.

Yes, it was different. He felt angry that it should be. Angry at whom? At himself? Or at life that had made him what he was?

By the Fourth of July, for some reason, his mood had lifted and floated away. When he woke in the morning to the sound of firecrackers booming in the hills, he felt good again and normal. They had played two sets of tennis, had a big breakfast, then gone swimming; and now at noon they stood on the main street, really the only street, of the village watching the parade go by under the elms.

People had come in farm trucks and on foot; there were even a couple of wagons drawn up in front of the post office. There were groups of summer people like the Guthrie group, scouts in uniform and volunteer firemen with equipment. Some of the farm families had brought lunch and sat now on the grass near the bandstand, with their dogs and children running loose. Maury was delighted. It was an old engraving, a print by Currier and Ives. It was real America.

One band after the other came swinging down the road: the firemen, the high-school band, the American Legion and a grade-school group with their teacher, singing "Yankee Doodle." And at the last, in an open car, driven slowly so that everyone might see, came three old men bowing and waving their blue caps, the last veterans of the Civil War.

"The one in the middle," old Mr. Guthrie said, "that's Frank Burroughs, some sort of relative by marriage of my late wife's, I never did figure out the relationship."

"He must be awfully old," Maury whispered.

"Not much older than I am," Mr. Guthrie replied.

The flag went past; hats that were not already off were swept off. A band played "The Battle Hymn of the Republic" and, hesitantly, somebody began to sing. Then others joined and Maury's heart was stirred here among these people in their home, on this old street under the leaves, with the thump of the brasses, the triumphant drums, the regimental flags and the voices. He heard his own voice, firm and joyous and proud: "Mine eyes have seen the glory—" and stopped, struck with embarrassment as Chris turned and smiled.

"Go on, sing!" the grandfather said. "Sing out! I like to see a young man with enthusiasm. And you've a nice voice, too."

So he sang out with the rest until the parade had passed and vanished to disband in back of the school, and people started home.

"Who wants to walk back with me?" Agatha asked.

There was a general groan. "It's two miles, for Pete's sake."

"I know. But it's a beautiful walk, by the short cut, not the road. Who'll come?" she waited.

"I will," Maury said.

They entered a lane, a dirt track that led off the road through pasture and brush. It was early afternoon and very still. Even the cattle had lain down, chewing with solemn faces in the shade.

Presently Agatha asked him, "Why did you have tears in your eyes at the parade?"

He was so humiliated that he was furious. How could she be so candid? And he answered stupidly, "Did I?"

"Why are you ashamed?"

"You make me feel foolish."

"Why? I was touched myself. And I was curious to know why you were."

"Well, I suppose because for a while there I felt so much a part of it. I felt what it must be to have roots in a place like this, to say, 'this is my place.' And when an old man marches with the Civil War veterans he's someone of your own blood. I was just very much moved by all that, and wondering what it must be like."

"What it must be like? You don't know?"

He opened his mouth to explain and closed it. How could she possibly understand the whole complex, forlorn, confusing business?

Then he began, "You see, we—my people—we're all fragmented. Not whole, not of a piece, like you. My mother, for instance, came from Poland. Her brothers live in Austria; they fought on the other side in the war. Now they don't even speak the same language to each other. One of them has a wife whose father's people live in France, and my father has relatives in Johannesburg; I don't even know what language they speak!" And he repeated, "We're all fragmented, don't you see? All scattered."

"But I should think that would be very interesting! Old American families like mine, who've been in one place for centuries, they're like a little enclave into which nothing fresh or new ever enters. I sometimes think, especially since I've gone away to college, that we're even rather boring, we're so predictable."

"No," Maury said, patiently, "you're basic, you're strong." And he was suddenly compelled to go on. "Sometimes I think: What are we, where do we belong? What country is ours, really ours, where we have always been and will always be? I feel so light, so without grounding, that it seems as if I—all of us— my family and our friends, all the people I know, could be blown away like leaves and it wouldn't matter. Nobody would even notice."

"That sounds so sad!"

"I'm sorry, I didn't mean to be depressing."

"It's my fault, I asked you. Here, here's our short cut, up the hill. Let's run! There's the most gorgeous view at the top, you've never seen anything like it."

He never had. The hill fell away beneath them in loops and folds, and rose again all silvery-gold in the sun and green-black in the running shadows of the clouds. The land was cut by the bay and its crooked coves. Islands lay scattered in the water and beyond rose other hills, as far as they could see.

Agatha spoke deliberately in a warm and lovely tone,

> *"All I could see from where I stood*
> *Was three long mountains and a wood."*

Maury smiled and answered,

> *"I turned and looked another way,*
> *And saw three islands in a bay."*

They stood still, looking at one another. Agatha said, "I thought when I first saw you that you were like Chris and most of his friends, with nothing on your mind, sort of."

"I don't know what I'm like, really."

Something so moved him that he turned away. There were some tall plants in a clump, taller than he. "What are those things, with the little white flowers?"

"Oh, those? Just meadow rue. It's a weed."

"And this stuff, that's so fragrant?"

"Another common plant. It's yarrow."

He looked up. She was still standing there, with such an expression on her face— He said, "I don't really care what they're called, you know."

"I didn't believe you did."

And then they were standing together, their flesh joined from mouth to knee, with a hundred pulses beating, beating through layers of cotton cloth.

"When do you have to leave, Agatha?"

"Tomorrow morning. And you?"

"The day after. You know that we'll have to see each other again."

"I know."

"When? How?"

"In September. You'll come to Boston, or I could go to New Haven. Either way."

"Something's happened that's crazy. I'm in love."

"It is crazy, isn't it? Because I am, too."

He was certain he must look different, that people must surely notice it. But nobody did and it was better so. Even Chris had no suspicion and Maury, with a certain premonitory caution, was glad to keep it that way.

He heard her voice in his head. Sometimes, driving the car, her face rose up in front of the windshield, to dazzle him. He thought about her naked body, tried to imagine it, and grew weak.

They met in Boston in September. Once she came to New Haven and he rode the train back with her. They walked and walked and lingered over drawn-out meals in restaurants. Their feet ached in the museums. On the sidewalks, as the weeks moved toward winter, it was clammy cold and the wind seeped through their clothes. There was never any place to go.

One time she produced a key. "This is for my friend Daisy's apartment. They're away skiing in Vermont."

"No," he said, "no, we can't."

"Why? I trust Daisy. And we've never been alone. I should just like to sit someplace together, quiet and alone."

He was trembling. "I couldn't just sit alone in a room with you, don't you know that?"

"Well, then. I'd do anything you want to make you happy. I want so much to make you happy."

"But it wouldn't make us happy afterward. Aggie darling, I want to start right, to do everything right. We've so much against us, I don't want to add more."

She dropped the key into her purse and snapped it shut.

"You're not—you don't think I don't *want* to, Aggie?" he cried.

"It's just," she said bitterly, "that I wonder whether we ever will be alone in a room together."

"Of course we will. You mustn't have thoughts like that."

"You haven't mentioned anything about me at home?" she asked.

"No. Have you?"

"My God, no! I've told you about my father. Oh," she said, "we even got in a fight last time I was home. He was talking about how the Jews are in back of Roosevelt; of course he thinks Roosevelt is the arch villain of all time and our descendants are going to have to pay for what he's doing to the country.

"And I said what you told me your father had said about Roosevelt, that people are starting to get a few dollars in their pockets and that probably he is really saving the American system . . . I thought my father would have a stroke! He asked me what kind of crazy, radical professors we had at college, and then Mother signaled to me not to say any more, because he gets so excited. So that's the way things are in my house."

"We'll think of something, some way," Maury said confidently. A man was supposed to have confidence in his powers. But he didn't feel very much.

THE TELEPHONE WAS a life line and a misery at the same time. Agatha took his calls in a cubicle at the end of a corridor in her dormitory. For all the clattering, slamming and talking she was barely able to hear him. He had to repeat in a shouting whisper: *"I love you, I miss you so,"* feeling foolish, frustrated and sad. And then silence while time raced, with nothing to say, or rather, so much to say and no way to begin. Then the three minutes were up.

Thanksgiving vacation had to be endured. He went with his father to the apartments on Washington Heights to collect the rents and check repairs. He stood on the sidewalk and watched the lift vans being unloaded as the refugees began to arrive from Germany; stood while heavy ornate furniture from some villa in Berlin-Charlottenburg was lifted out, furniture too big and dark for the flat over the delicatessen or the laundry. His father stood there too, talking to the new arrivals in a mixture of German and Yiddish. His face was grave and he sighed. Always that sigh: What's to happen? What's to become of us? It was depressing.

Then home to Iris at the dinner table, giving her earnest daily rehash of the *New York Times,* pushing the untidy hair behind her ears. "You can't oversimplify, Pa. This thing that is happening in Germany has its roots in the Versailles Treaty and the economic collapse—"

Poor Iris! Would any man ever rejoice in her as I rejoice in Agatha?

He recalled the dinner table at Chris's house. Everything was so *emotional* here. But perhaps that was unfair? Perhaps the emotion was in him, too?

At Thanksgiving dinner there were some new faces.

"Mr. and Mrs. Nathanson," Pa said. "He's our new accountant and a very bright guy. His daughter's coming too," he added casually.

Just as casually, the daughter was seated next to Maury. But he had to give them credit. They had too much respect to foist just anyone upon him. She was a nice, a really nice girl. She went to Radcliffe and she was very smart, but she didn't try to impress him with it. He liked her pale gray wool dress and her shiny thick black hair. He even liked her nails, dark red ovals, perfectly manicured. Aggie had short nails like a little boy's; he suspected that she bit them. But he could have been locked in a room with this girl, or any other girl, and it wouldn't have meant a thing.

"What are you planning to do after Yale?" the girl asked.

Everyone at the table had caught her question. He hadn't planned to answer as he did, hadn't even been sure of what he wanted. It was just an idea that had been growing, perhaps because of Chris's own plans or Chris's fine old grandfather.

"I want to go to law school," Maury said.

His father's mouth fell open. He almost chuckled. "Maury! You never said a word!"

"Well, I wasn't certain."

"By golly, this is great news! You know," he confided to the table, "when he was a baby his mother and I used to talk, we'd talk about him being a doctor or a lawyer. Well, you know how it is."

The Nathansons smiled. They knew how it was.

"So what's it to be? Harvard or Yale?"

Maury answered modestly, "I'll have to see who'll take me."

"Well, well, I'll have to do some hustling, but I'll do it. For Maury I'll move the earth if I have to," his father said.

"When the building business comes back," Mr. Nathanson observed, "it'll be a good thing to have your own son handle the legal end. You'll have it made. And you too, Maury. It'll be a good thing for you, too."

That was not at all what he had in mind, but he didn't say so. What he had in mind, as the idea took form and grew, was a good American life in some old town, or some small city. He saw himself sitting behind a roll-top desk with maple trees outside the window. He felt an atmosphere clean and quiet and austere. Like Lincoln in Springfield. Yes, that's how it would be. Like Lincoln in Springfield.

A few days later his mother remarked, "A nice girl, that Natalie, don't you think so?"

"Oh, very," he agreed. His mother was waiting for more but he did not give it.

Then a few weeks later while they were talking on the telephone, his mother said, "I spoke to Mrs. Nathanson today. She happened to remark, I don't know how it came about, you never called Natalie."

"No."

A pause. "You didn't like her?"

"I liked her."

"I don't want to interfere. A young man wants his privacy, I've never interfered, have I, Maury?"

"No, you haven't." And that was true.

"So forgive me this once. . . . Have you got another girl, is that it?"

"Well, it's too early to say. I'll tell you, Ma, I promise, whenever there's anything to tell."

"I'm sure you will. Whatever you do will be fine with us, Maury, you know that. As long as she's a Jewish girl. Not that it's necessary to say that to you. We trust you, Maury."

CHRISTMAS VACATION WAS no better. Agatha came to New York for a Christmas party. He met her in the lobby of the Hotel Commodore. Feeling fiercely jealous, ineffectual and stricken of manhood, he listened to her assurances that Peter So-and-So and Douglas So-and-So meant nothing to her at all, that they were only party escorts, that nobody meant anything to her at all (Oh, God, Maury, do I have to tell you?). And he knew that was the sacred truth and died of his jealousy anyway: hands that would touch her while they danced; ears that would listen to her voice; eyes that would look at her freely, publicly, with no apology. . . .

By March and spring recess he was close to desperation. "Pa, I'd like to have a car for a day or two," he said. "I'd like to run up and visit a fellow near Albany."

He drove north on the Albany Post Road, then crossed the river at West Point. It grew colder. The little villages were still shut into the silence of winter and there was snow on the slopes. He stopped for lunch in a place that smelled of hot grease. When the door opened cold air came in with the noisy men who pushed to the counter, bantering mock-sexy innuendoes with the middle-aged waitress. He had a desolate, hopeless feeling. He thought of turning around and going back, but he did not. Instead he filled the tank at the next gas station and drove. The farms grew larger and farther apart. There were miles of woods; of old, unpainted houses and shaggy cattle penned in barnyards. Toward evening he drove into Brewerstown.

He thought he had driven into the eighteenth century. He felt an absolute surge of delight and recognition. My time, my place! But of course that was absurd; it was only in pictures that Maury could have known this place. Yet he knew it perfectly. He knew the wide, wide streets and the elms that would form a dark green aisle in leaf. He knew the white church with the graveyard on one side, the parish house on the other. And all the white fences, the brick walks, the fanlights, the driveways lined with rhododendrons. It took half a century to grow rhododendrons that size.

The town was shut down for the night, except for a drugstore on the main street. Maury went to the telephone book and marked down the address and the telephone number. The store was empty except for the man behind the counter.

"Is Lake Road far from here?" Maury asked.

"Depends where you want to go on Lake Road. It goes five, six miles around the lake, then joins up with the highway. Who you lookin' for?"

Maury shook his head. "Oh, I don't plan to visit tonight. I'll call first."

He dropped a nickel into the slot and gave the number to the operator.

"The line is busy," she said.

He wondered whether he would have the courage to try again. The man behind the counter looked at him curiously while he waited.

"You're not from these parts?"

"New York City."

"Ayeh. Been in New York once. Didn't like it."

"Well. Can't blame you. This is a beautiful town."

"Ayeh. My folks came here when they was just Indians around."

Maury put the nickel in again. This time someone answered. "Is Agatha at home, please?"

"Miss Agatha?" He was relieved to know it was a maid. "Who shall I say is calling?"

"Just a friend. A friend from New York."

When she came to the phone he whispered, "Aggie, I'm here in town."

"Oh, my God, why?"

"Because I was going out of my mind without seeing you."

"But what am I going to say? What am I going to do?"

Suddenly he was decisive. "Say you need something at the drugstore. Anything. I'll be waiting down the block in a tan Maxwell. How long will you be?"

"Fifteen minutes."

"That's just about as long as I can hold out," he said.

They drove about two miles out of town and stopped the car. When they put their arms around each other it was like the healing of a wound.

"I have to know," Maury said, "what's going to become of us."

She began to cry. "Don't, don't," he murmured. "Ever since that Christmas dance in the city I've been thinking the world is full of enemies, people who want to take you away from me . . ."

"Nobody can do that," she said fiercely.

"Then will you marry me? In June, after I graduate? Will you, Agatha?"

"Yes, yes, I will."

"No matter what?"

"No matter what."

At least he knew now where they were going. He hadn't the faintest idea how they were going to get there, how he would manage law school and this marriage, but he had her promise. It sustained him, through the spring session, through the finals, through commencement.

His mother had a habit of drinking a late cup of coffee in the kitchen before going to bed. He sat there with her on the night after commencement. He had known all day that there was something she wanted to say, he knew her so well.

"Maury," she began now, "you have a girl, haven't you? And she isn't Jewish."

He felt a giggle, an absurd shocked giggle and quelled it. "How did you guess?"

"What other reason could there be for you to be so secretive?"

He didn't answer.

"That's where you went when you borrowed Pa's car last spring, isn't it?"

He nodded.

"What are you going to do?"

"Marry her, Ma."

"You know, of course, what trouble this is going to make?"

"I know. And I'm sorry."

His mother stirred her coffee. The spoon made a pleasant, comforting sound against the cup. She began to speak softly. "My mind is so often divided. I can see two sides of everything, as though I were holding a ball between my hands. I think: Maury, you're right. If you really love another human being—if it's real, and God knows there is so little real love and it's made up of so many things that even at my age I don't understand it, so I suppose I should use the word 'want' rather than 'love' . . . if you really want to be with a person, why shouldn't you be? Life is short enough; why suffer and sacrifice? One is born with a label, one could just as easily have been born something else. You see what I mean, Maury?"

"I see. But what is the other side?"

"The other side," she said quietly, "is that you *were* born what you are, nothing can change it and your father is right. So that side says to me: Tell Maury to listen to his father."

"You know what he's going to say? You've discussed it with him?"

"Of course I haven't! And of course I know what he's going to say, just as you know it." She swallowed her coffee.

What a beautiful face! he thought. She has a lovely, serious, gentle face, my mother . . .

"He'll say," she went on, "and he'll be right—he'll say that you come from a proud, ancient people. You may not always think so when you look around at the children of the eastern ghettos. We're not educated; we're often noisy; we don't have the finest manners; where could we learn them? But we're only one very small part of the history of our people."

"I know. I understand."

"Sometimes I've wondered," she said, "I've wondered whether perhaps, since you've been in a different world at college, whether you might have been ashamed of me, only a little? A foreign-born mother with an accent. Has that bothered you?"

"No, Ma, no," he said, and felt a touch like pain. She was so assured, with her tall carriage, and good clothes or what remained of them, her books and her courses. He thought: Has this been inside her all the time? We don't know anything about anybody, after all.

And it seemed to him as he sat in the cold, white kitchen among the looming white boxes, the tall rectangular bulk of the refrigerator and the lower bulk of the stove, with the chilling glare of the ceiling light in his eyes, that it was an operating room and he was helpless, pinned down, fastened and exposed like a patient on the table.

"Ma, I can't, I can't."

"Can't leave her?"

He could hardly speak. For a grown man to weep! The thing in his throat was a lump of tears. "Can't leave her," he repeated thickly, and closed his eyes.

She was silent. He did not look at her, but he felt a stir of warmth in the air behind him and knew that she was standing very close, not touching. Then she did touch him, her hand stroking his hair.

"Maury, Maury, I'm sorry. Living can be so terribly hard."

"Now, you wanted to talk to me, Maury?" Pa asked.

They were in his den among his familiar things: cigar smoke, the mahogany humidor and all the photographs of Ma and his children and his own parents, the father in a derby hat with the tiny wife next to him, wearing a plumed hat and an 1880s dress. The globe stood in front of the window. It was Iris' present. She always gave presents like that, a globe or books or antique maps.

"I suppose Ma has mentioned what I want to talk about," Maury said.

"She has. But you must know there is really nothing to talk about," his father said gently. "Not that I refuse to talk. I'm willing to listen."

Maury began. "What else is there to say but that I love Agatha? I love her so—"

"I'm sorry. Sorry to see your pain."

"It needn't be pain. It could be so simple."

"It's never simple."

"It was for you and Ma, wasn't it?"

"It's never simple, I tell you. And your mother was a Jewish girl."

"Pa, tell me, you're a practical, rational man. Is it so strange for me to be in love with Agatha? She's such a lovely person. You would really like her. She's so intelligent and happy and kindhearted."

"I believe you. I don't think you would care about anyone who wasn't all of those things. Still, to marry her—it's impossible."

"How can you feel that way and still be such friends with Mr. Malone?"

"Why not? Malone and I understand each other, that's why we're friends. He's a good Catholic and he expects his children to marry Catholics. And I respect him for it."

"But why? Really why? You still haven't explained. I'll grant that it's easier not to marry out, but—"

Joseph stood up. "Come," he said, spinning the globe. "There, that's Palestine. That's where it started. We came from there. There we gave the world the Ten Commandments, and if everybody would obey them there would be no trouble. There we gave the Christian world its God. And from there we were burned out and dispossessed and driven here—" his finger made a long sweep across Africa, up into Spain. "And here—" a sweep of the palm across Europe, eastward into Poland and Russia. "And then here, across the Atlantic, and everywhere else you can think of. Africa, Australia—"

"Yes, yes," Maury said impatiently, "I've had a bit of education. I know our history."

"You know, but you only read the words, you didn't feel them. Maury, all this history, this wandering, has been written in *blood*. And it is still being written today, right now, while you and I stand here. Tonight in Germany our people are being tortured for no reason at all and the world does nothing, it doesn't care. Oh," he said passionately, "how we have suffered, this People of the Book, this proud, strong people who have enriched the world! My son, we need every soul we can hold on to. There are so few of us and we need each other. How can you turn your back on your people? How can you?"

He was moved, and angered that he was moved. His father had never been so eloquent. It was not like him, silent man that he was, not gifted with words. Tears had even come into his eyes as he spoke. He has no right to do this to me, Maury thought, and he knew he was losing the battle, knew he had already lost it.

He made one more try. "Pa, I wouldn't turn my back. I wouldn't change. Did you think I would convert? I'll stay what I am and Agatha will stay what she is."

"And your children? What will they be? I'll tell you: nothing! And you ask me, you come in casually and ask me to accept, as if it were only a small thing, that I should live to see my grandson, son of my son, a nothing? Why don't you come in and ask for my right arm? Why don't you?"

"Pa, will you at last meet Agatha? Let me bring her here. Then you can talk to her and—"

"No, no, I tell you. There's no sense in it!"

"Then you're no different from her people. You're just as much of a bigot."

"What? No difference between the murderers and the murdered? You must be crazy! So her people are against it too, are they?"

"Of course! What did you think?"

"So you see, you see how impossible it is? Oh, Maury, listen to me, I want to reach your heart and your mind. Believe me, there is nothing a human being can't get over. You don't think so now, but take it on faith, please do. Parents lose children, husbands and wives die and hearts break, but they go on living. And eventually the break heals.

"Believe me now, you'll suffer for a couple of months, I know you will. But then it'll be over and you'll meet a fine girl of your own kind, and she'll meet another man, this Agatha. It'll be better for her, too."

Something burst in Maury. "I don't want to hear that! Don't dare tell me that!"

"Maurice, don't raise your voice to me. I'm trying to help you, but this sort of thing won't do any good."

He went to the door. He wanted to break something, throw the lamp to the floor, smash things. God damn world! God damn life! "What will you do if we get married anyway?" he asked.

His father's face looked sick. It looked green. "Maurice," he said very low, "I hope you won't do that. I hope for your mother's sake, for mine and for us all that you won't do that. I beg you, I warn you, don't bring the unthinkable to pass."

Aᴳᴀᴛʜᴀ ᴡᴀs ᴛᴇᴀʀꜰᴜʟ on the telephone. "I talked to my parents, Maury. Or at least I tried to. They were absolutely horrified, I thought my father had lost his mind, he went into such a tirade. He said he thought I must be insane! I can't begin to tell you the things he said!"

"I can imagine," Maury said grimly.

"He went on about our family, our ancestors, and what they stood for and what America stands for, and the church, and all our friends. And he said that if —if I did this I'd be no daughter of his. First my mother cried and then she got furious at me because Daddy turned absolutely white and she thought he was going to have a heart attack. She made me get out of the room. Oh, Maury, how terrible to be married this way, to walk out of your home like this!"

He thought for a moment. "Do you suppose if I spoke to Chris he could talk to them?"

"Oh, Maury, I don't know. Try it!"

"He's coming to New York for the weekend. I'll go see him at his hotel."

"Oʜ, ʏᴇs," Cʜʀɪs said, "my parents spoke very well of you. 'A very attractive young man,' my mother said. I remember her words."

"Well, then, if they thought well of me, maybe they or you would talk to Aggie's parents? It would help a lot, I think."

"I don't really think it would," Chris said gently.

"You don't? Aggie thought it would."

"Aggie knows better. She's grasping at straws."

Maury put his head in his hands. He thought he had spoken so persuasively.

Chris went to the window and looked out for a minute, as if he were making up his mind about something. Then he turned back to the room. "Listen, I have a proposition. Your nerves are pretty bad, one can see that with half an eye. Why don't you just chuck everything and sail to England with me next week? If money's a problem I can lend you some. We'll go tramping through England and you'll be born again. What do you say?"

"You don't understand. You say you want to help me. Then why don't you give me the help I want? Tell me, Chris. Be honest with me."

"You mean that?"

"I mean it."

"Because I don't approve of the marriage. If I had known about you and Aggie I wouldn't have let things get this far."

"Why, Chris, why?"

"Come on, Maury, you're not that naive. Because you are what you are, that's why."

"And in what way am I so different from you?"

"I don't think you are, but the world thinks so. And you'd be asking Aggie to be the world's victim along with you."

"She doesn't care."

"She thinks she doesn't care. Clubs and friends, many of her friends—she'd have to give them all up. Her children would be rejected by people and in places where she's been welcomed."

"She doesn't give a damn, I tell you!"

"She gives more than a damn about her parents! Aggie is very close to them, especially her father. Ever since he had polio she's been his right hand. I remember when she was a little kid, no more than eight or nine, and she used to help him learn to walk again. It would have broken your heart."

"And this doesn't break your heart?"

Chris looked at him, not speaking. Maury opened the door. "*My friend. My good friend,* Chris. Well, you can go to hell!"

THEY WERE MARRIED at city hall on a blazing day in July. "You could fry an egg on the sidewalk today," the clerk said as he stamped their certificate.

In their stifling room at the hotel a fan stirred the air at ten-second intervals. Through the open window came the sound of a record playing "Pagliacci" over and over. They sent downstairs for a meal of overcooked steak and soggy potatoes. It was the most beautiful room, the most sumptuous dinner, the most marvelous music they had ever known.

Aggie took a bottle of wine from her suitcase. "I brought some wine for our wedding toast. Look at the label. Nothing but the best!"

"I don't know a thing about wines. We never had any in our house."

"I got used to it, living in France. You drink it there instead of water."

"Don't people get drunk?"

"Just a pleasant haze. Your health!" she said.

"And yours, Mrs. Friedman."

So they drank to each other, pulled the shade and went back to bed, although it was only three in the afternoon.

In the morning, after he was sure that his father had left for work, he telephoned his mother.

"Maury," she said, "oh, how I want to see you! But I can't. Your father has forbidden me." And she cried, "Dear heaven, if only you hadn't done this! It's like a morgue here since yesterday. Iris and I, we can scarcely breathe. And your father looks ten years older."

He was not angry at her. "Good-by, Ma," he said softly, and hung the receiver up.

Between them they had a little more than four hundred dollars.

"If we're very careful," Maury said, "we can make this last a couple of months. But I'll have a job long before then." He felt very strong, very confident.

"I'll get something too. I can always teach French as a substitute until there's a permanent opening."

"Meanwhile, we'll find the cheapest decent apartment we can until we decide where we want to go permanently."

Cheerfully, purposefully, they bought newspapers, took subways, and finally found a furnished apartment on the top floor of a two-family house in Queens. The owner was Mr. George Andreapoulis, a polite young Greek-American who had just graduated from law school into the Depression. On a trip to Greece he had gotten a bride, Elena, a strong girl with a white smile and hairy arms.

The apartment was newly furnished in yellow maple. There were clean curtains and an ugly imitation Oriental rug.

"I should get fifty a month for it," said Mr. Andreapoulis, "but the times are so bad that, frankly, I'll be willing to take forty."

Maury stood looking out of the kitchen window to the small concrete-and-cinder yard, the endless lots without trees, just dry waving grass as far as the distant billboards on the highway. Bleak, even in the glittering sunlight. If the world were flat this would be the place where you dropped off into the void. Still, it was immaculate, the landlord was respectable and friendly and they wouldn't be here long anyway.

"My wife speaks no English," said Mr. Andreapoulis. "We're newlyweds, too. Maybe you will help her to learn English, Mrs. Friedman? And she will teach you to cook, she's a wonderful cook." He looked suddenly flustered. "Excuse me, how stupid, I only meant that so many American young ladies don't learn cooking— although probably you're a fine cook already."

Agatha laughed. "No, I can't boil water as the saying goes. I'm ready to be taught. Until I get a job, that is."

So it was settled. They made two trips on the subway with their suitcases, a heavy box of books, and their one purchase, a superheterodyne radio which Maury bought for thirty-five dollars. They placed it on the table in the living room next to the lamp.

There was a certain amount of guilt over its purchase, but in the end it turned out to have been a good investment. People needed some recreation, and the movies cost seventy cents for the two of them. For nothing at all, the radio brought the Philharmonic on Sunday afternoons, and a good dance band almost any time. They could dance on the kitchen floor to Glen Gray's Casa Loma Orchestra or to Paul Whiteman at the Biltmore. They could Begin the Beguine, Fly Down to Rio, or turn off the lights and Dance in the Dark, alone together in their private world. Dazed and entranced, they moved like one body across the room to where, still not separating from her, he switched off the sound, and then in the sudden fall of silence they moved again like one body to the bed.

⚜{20}⚜

They walked up Riverside Drive and turned toward West End Avenue at Iris' street. It was a warm evening for April and people were out, fathers of families walking their dogs and young people singing "When a Broadway Baby Says Goodnight," shoving at one another and laughing boisterously. They were on their way to a party. Iris and Fred were coming back from one.

"Sorry to break it up so early," Fred said when they reached the building where Iris lived. "I shouldn't have left so much homework for Sunday night. My fault," he said apologetically.

"That's all right," she told him. "I've got work too," which was not the case.

They stood a moment. It was awkward; should she ask him upstairs for a few minutes, after all? She didn't really want to and she knew he didn't want to come.

"Thanks for inviting me," he said. "It was a great party. I didn't know you and Enid were friends."

"We're not. It's just that our mothers work on the same charity committee and it happened through them." It occurred to her as she said the word 'charity' that it really was odd for her mother to be doing charity when there was never an extra dollar at home. But then, Ma always said, we must be very thankful, there are so many people far worse off than we are.

"Well, it was a great party," Fred said again. He started to move away. "Don't forget, newspaper meeting after school tomorrow."

"I won't forget," she answered. She went inside and took the elevator upstairs.

Her mother was reading in the living room. She had a look of surprise. "So soon? And where's Fred?"

"It broke up early. And he had homework."

"My goodness, it's only nine-thirty. He could have had something to eat. I put the cocoa pot out and some cake."

"We had too much to eat, we were stuffed."

"So you had a good time, then," her mother said. "Don't bother your father, he's doing the income tax. I guess I'll go read in bed, it's more comfortable."

Iris went to her room and took her dress off. It was emerald green, the color of wet leaves. Her mother bought it when Fred first took an interest in her. That was when they started to work on the school paper together. Her mother said she ought to pay more attention to her clothes now that she was fifteen.

Fred was a serious boy. When he filled out he would be a fine-looking man in spite of his glasses. Right now he was very tall and skinny, but he had a nice face. And he was one of the smartest boys in school.

They had been having such good discussions all winter, working in the editorial room, and sometimes walking home in the late afternoons. He was interested in politics and they had great arguments, although mostly they agreed on things.

"I respect your mind," he told her. "You reason things out. You think for yourself."

They felt, although they did not say so, rather superior to most of the other kids. They filled their lives, they didn't waste time. Fred did a lot of reading too, and they talked about what they read.

She knew he liked her, and this was one of the happiest things that had ever happened to her. It was like having something new to look forward to every day.

A week ago he had invited her to a wedding. One of his cousins was getting married and he had been told to bring a girl. It was to be a big formal wedding, and everyone would wear evening clothes. Iris had never been at any wedding at all, and she was excited about that and about having been asked by Fred.

Her mother said, "Well, we shall have to get you something very nice to wear." She had an idea. She went to a box on the top shelf of her closet and took out a dress. It was pink silk and Iris recognized the dress in the portrait of her mother, her Paris dress.

"We can take it to a dressmaker and have it altered for you," her mother said. "Look," and she pulled the skirt out into a fan, "ten yards of material, and such material! We can make a magnificent dress for you. And shoes dyed to match. What do you think?"

It was truly beautiful. Iris wondered, though, what the other girls would be wearing and wondered how she could find out.

Now she hung up the green wool dress. At this party tonight there was a girl who kept looking at Iris' dress. She was one of those girls who look good with an old sweater tied around their shoulders, the sort of girl who is born that way and cannot be made. This girl gave Iris' dress a long, slow look, so that she sank lower into her chair and knew that her dress must be awful, must be all wrong. (Years later she was to meet this same girl at someone's house and the girl was to tell her: You had a dress once, emerald green, the most beautiful color; I never forgot it. But of course Iris could not know that now.)

It had really been a dreadful, miserable party. She was sorry she had invited Fred, but Enid had told her to bring a boy. All those friends of Enid's were the kind of people Fred didn't like: shallow and showoffy, speaking in wisecracks which you were supposed to answer with more wisecracks. It had been very tiring. Fred and Iris had exchanged looks and she had known he was thinking the same. She telegraphed her regret, and Fred brought her a plate of food. "The food's good anyway," he said, and went back for more. He had an enormous appetite.

Iris had watched the girls. It had been almost like a show, to see them giggling and giving the boys that arch look, the sideward and upward sliding of the eyes. Boys were so stupid they didn't see how affected it was. Except for Fred, who would see and understand. It was remarkable how his mind and Iris' worked on the same track.

"My goodness," Enid had said, "you look as if you'd lost your best friend! Aren't you having a good time?" She had smiled, but it was a cold smile.

Iris had been mortified in front of Fred. "Of course, I'm having a very good time," she had answered stiffly.

Perhaps she really ought to smile more. Cousin Ruth had told her once that she had an unusually nice smile. In fact, what Cousin Ruth had really said was: "A light seems to turn on in your face when you smile." After that Iris had gone home and practiced in front of the bathroom mirror. It was true. Her lips did draw back sweetly and her teeth were very bright. When the smile withdrew her face fell back into severity, although she didn't feel severe. She must remember to smile, but not too much, or she'd look like a nut.

Enid and some of the boys had taken up the rugs in the hall and put the phonograph on. Everyone got up to dance. Fred held his arm out. Iris loved to dance. She must have got that from her mother; her father danced well but he didn't love it all that much. She remembered the day she came home and found her mother all alone, dancing in the living room. Mama hadn't heard Iris come in and there she had been, whirling around in a waltz, with "The Blue Danube" playing on the phonograph. It was an Edison, with thick records; you had to wind it up when the record was only half over. Iris had been so embarrassed for her mother, but Mama hadn't been at all. She had only stopped and said, "Do you know, if I could be reincarnated for a few days, I would like to be a countess or a princess in Vienna and go whirling in a marvelous white lace dress, waltzing under the crystal chandeliers. But only for a day or two. It must have been a very silly, useless life."

"I wish they would put on a waltz," Iris had said to Fred.

"They won't," he had answered, and laughed and put his cheek on hers. She had felt very excited, being that close to him. It had started to be a good time, Iris thought now.

She went to the bathroom and ran the water for a bath, although she had taken one before getting dressed this evening and was certainly quite clean. But she wanted to lie in the warm water and think. There was great comfort in warm water.

If that girl hadn't arrived it might have been lovely, after all. The minute she walked in everything had changed. She was one of those lively girls who make everyone look at them. They don't even have to be pretty.

"This is Alice," Enid had said. "She's just moved here from Altoona. We went to camp together."

"Alice from Altoona," Alice had said and everybody laughed, although it wasn't funny. Right away everybody was interested in her. They all wanted to know: When did you move? Where are you going to school? This your first time in New York?

She had taken all the attention as though she expected it. No doubt she had always had it. Iris had watched her, thinking again: It is like a play, only now the leading lady has come in; the others were just bit players up to now. Iris had observed what she did, what was different about her. She saw that Alice didn't talk too much. When she did say something, it counted; usually it was something to make people laugh. Or else it was a compliment, not too thick, just a comment almost casual, something to make the other person feel important. It looked so easy, the way she did it, never overdoing it, but Iris knew it really wasn't.

She had told Enid's mother that the apartment was just beautiful and she'd love to have her own mother see it. (Her mother would be invited.) She had let everyone know that her brother was a sophomore at Columbia. (The girls would ask her to all their parties.) She had told every boy there that he was a simply marvelous dancer. "I couldn't help noticing," she said. (Immediately, they all wanted to dance with her.)

"You're so *tall*!" she had said to Fred, as though, Iris thought disgustedly, he were some sort of giant that she had never seen before.

But Fred had been pleased and asked her to dance. They did the Peabody; Alice knew some variations. "We know a thing or two in Altoona," she said and did a whirl. Her skirt swirled high till it showed the lace on her panties. Fred picked her up the way they do at the ballet and everybody stepped back into a circle to watch the performance of Fred and Alice. Fred was delighted and exhilarated.

Iris had tried to look as if it were really fun to stand there and admire. When Enid had changed the record, Fred had gone right on dancing with Alice. Soon everyone was back on the floor except Iris. Then a boy came and invited her; she was so relieved until she found out that he was Enid's little brother. He was almost thirteen. His hand was sweaty on the back of her dress and he didn't really dance, just walked around the floor. He kept on and on as the record changed; perhaps he would have liked to get rid of her and didn't know how? She would have liked to get rid of him and didn't know how. After a while she told him she wanted to sit down.

Fred had seen her sitting and had come over. No doubt he remembered his duty as her escort. Besides, someone had cut in and taken Alice away from him.

"You know," Iris reminded him then, "it's Sunday and don't you think we ought to get going home soon?"

She had been surprised when he agreed. He said he still had homework to do. She had thought that now probably he would want to stay to the very last. But he had agreed.

Now she ran more hot water. Her mother always warned her not to fall asleep in the tub, but it was such a soothing place to think. Perhaps Maury would know what I do wrong? Everything Fred always said he didn't like is what that girl did. Perhaps Maury would know. So often she wished she could ask him about what she always thought of as his golden charm, but he would be so embarrassed. Once, when she was perhaps eleven, she had peeked through the crack of his door and seen him sitting at the window for minutes and minutes. And finally she had gone in and asked him, "Are you unhappy about something?" And he had been so cross. "Damn pesky little kid!" he had yelled at her. But then later that night, she remembered, he had come to her room and said he was sorry, and asked her whether she had wanted anything. He could be so tender, Maury could, but he didn't like to show that side to people.

I feel so sorry he has left us this way. I suppose he couldn't help falling in love with Agatha. Anyway, religion never meant very much to him. I used to see on his face that he wasn't feeling anything when we went to services. Not the way Pa or I do. (I never could tell about my mother; I know she loves the music.) But I truly love it, I love the old, old words and the ancient people. I think of a long caravan of people, trailing back in time, I think of all the people in all the rows as if they are a part of me and I them. Afterward, when they get up and go out, they will be strangers again, not caring an instant's worth about Iris Friedman, but while we are there and the mournful, plaintive music sweeps over us it draws us all together and we are one. When I was very little, I used to think that God was like Pa, or Pa was like God and could do anything, could make anything happen. Now I know he can't. . . . He couldn't do anything about Maury. He is so sad about Maury; I know he is, because he doesn't talk about him anymore. When Pa isn't home my mother talks about Maury. She talks so much about when he was a baby. She never says: When you were a baby, Iris.

The water began to grow cool. She climbed out of the tub and put her nightgown on. The telephone rang in the hall. Her mother answered and called her.

"For you," she said.

Iris looked at the clock. It was almost eleven. She picked up the phone and Fred said, "Iris? I'm awfully sorry to call this late, but I just found out something and I wanted to tell you—"

"Yes?" she waited.

"It's about the wedding," he said. "I'm so embarrassed. But it seems that I or somebody made a mistake and I'm not supposed to bring a girl, after all. I feel lousy about it, but—well, I know you'll understand."

"Sure." She spoke brightly. "Sure, I understand."

He talked a minute or two longer, something about the paper, but she wasn't really listening. She was thinking: Why don't I tell him not to bother to lie? I know perfectly well he intends to take Alice. He probably went back to the party after he left me. Why don't I?

When she hung up her mother came out of her bedroom. "My goodness," she said, smiling, "couldn't he even wait until he sees you tomorrow in school?"

"It was about the wedding. He made a mistake. He's not supposed to bring a girl, after all."

"Oh," her mother said slowly, "I see." She looked troubled for a minute, and searched Iris' face, which was guarded and proud. Then she said, "Oh well, there'll be other weddings. You'll make the best of it."

Mama didn't mean to be indifferent, not at all. That was the way she treated herself. "Short of a catastrophe, you will never admit when anything has gone wrong," Pa always complained, and yet he was really grateful for his wife's placid optimism, which Iris often found so exasperating. Didn't anything ever upset her? When Iris asked her that one time she didn't answer at once, and then she said, "If it does, I keep it to myself. Your father has enough to worry him already."

She went back to her room, brushed her teeth and got into bed. It was funny, but she didn't feel as bad about this as she would have expected. Perhaps, in a way, it was a relief not to have to go. Not to have to think about what impression you were making, or to worry about girls like Alice. Anyway, Fred was only a boy. Someday there would be a man, a real man, who would have eyes only for her.

I'm sure my mother thinks now that I'm crushed because of this—for she knows as well as I do that Fred lied. She used to think I was unhappy when we were at the beach years ago and there was a crowd of kids out on the lawn, while I was in the hammock reading. I remember the summer I read *Ivanhoe* and *The Last Days of Pompeii,* all those fat, wonderful books, the stories and tragedies that are so sad but never real enough to break your heart, just enough to make the sweet tears rise. I used to lay the book down and let them rise and I was very happy.

When I get to college I want to major in English literature. I've been in love with the sound and cadence, the charm and fragrance of words, as long as I can remember, probably ever since Mama first read stories aloud when I was three years old. Maybe younger than that. You can feel words, the way fingers feel velvet. Once I made a list of words that are especially beautiful. Sapphire. Tintinnabulation. Grass. Angelica. I wish my name was Angelica. I must make it a duty to learn five new words every day.

She wanted so much to write. The problem was that she had nothing to write about. Once she had writen a piece about a lonely girl away at camp, and the teacher had said it was lyrical, but that was the only time. She guessed she didn't have any special talent, although perhaps after she had really lived she might find something to say.

At school there was a girl, only Iris' own age, who left to study at a conservatory; she had already played with an orchestra. How marvelous it must be to have such a way of expressing what is in you! It seemed to Iris that something was alive inside of her that wanted to get out and couldn't. There was a rising in her chest, so beautiful and dazzling that people would stop and look with surprised faces if they could know about it.

It's true, Iris thought, the person who lives inside me and the person that other people see are not at all the same.

⚜{21}⚜

In the autumn of 1935 there seemed to be no place for a well-spoken, fine-appearing graduate of Yale who had majored in philosophy and was willing to do anything at all. Nor was there a place for an attractive Wellesley girl of excellent family who had studied fine arts in Europe and spoke French better than many of the natives of France. She couldn't even fill a job as a lunch-room waitress because there were fifty applicants for every such job and they had all had experience. He couldn't get a job as a porter because in the first place he didn't look like a porter and in the second place everyone was laying off, not hiring. There was no sense in it.

Every night at midnight Maury went out for the early-morning editions of the papers, read the help-wanted pages, then took the subway at five o'clock, walked from store to loft to factory, rode from the Bronx to Brooklyn and back and came home with nothing.

By October they had to believe that there were no jobs. They had seventy dollars left. And one day Maury didn't bother to buy the newspaper; it would be wasting a nickel. That was the day when, for the first time, they knew panic.

Agatha asked timidly, "Don't you know anybody? I mean, you've always lived in New York—"

How to explain? He had lost touch with all his childhood friends. He couldn't call up now and beg a favor. Besides, most of their fathers were doctors or lawyers who couldn't do anything for him, or else they were in business and had their own troubles.

The only possibility was Eddy Holtz. To be sure, they had drifted coolly apart. Yet there was something about Eddy that would make it possible for Maury to swallow his pride, and he recognized what a tribute that was to some quality in Eddy. Eddy was at Columbia Physicians and Surgeons. His painful grind had paid off and Maury thought wistfully that he would always hang on and get where he wanted to go. His father owned three or four shoe stores, a small chain, in Brooklyn. Perhaps he just might—

"I'll ask my father," Eddy said. "I'll see what I can do. You're happy, Maury?"

"Yes, yes, except for the job situation. You'd heard I was married?"

"Chris Guthrie's cousin, isn't she?"

"Yes, and our families don't—we don't have anything to do with them. That's why I thought of you. I may not always have agreed with you, Eddy, but I knew you wouldn't forget the time when we were friends."

"I haven't helped you yet. But I will try."

THE STORE WAS two blocks from the subway station, which was good. He didn't have far to walk. It was a long, narrow store wedged between a Woolworth's and a Kiddy Klothes shop. One entire window was a display of children's shoes. There were two other salesmen, Resnick and Santorello, men who had been there fifteen years. They earned forty dollars a week. Maury was to get twenty, taking the place of an older man who had dropped dead the week before.

"Boss saves money with Binder gone," the other men told him. "He was here longer than we were; he got forty-five dollars."

What worried Maury was that there really wasn't enough work for three men. Sometimes no more than half a dozen people came in during the hours before three o'clock: mothers with toddlers, a man buying work shoes, young girls buying cheap patent-leather pumps for dancing, an old woman with shoes cracked and split, who counted out her money for the new pair in dollar bills, the last dollar in coins from her change purse. After three, when school was out, there was a flurry and scurry of children crying and fighting over the hobbyhorse. He learned to handle them with dispatch and patience so that, coming with the rest of the family on another day, the mothers often asked for and waited for him. It saddened him that these shabby people could clothe and shoe their children only by neglecting themselves.

During the long mornings he stood at the windows and found that he had acquired Resnick's and Santorello's irritating habit of jingling the change in their pockets out of restless boredom. He watched the dull, ambling traffic, the bus discharging at the corner and two or three people coming out of the subway in midmorning: going where? An ambulance came for someone in a store across the street; that was an event of note. He would have liked to bring a book from the library. He could at least have used the time to take himself away from that dreary street, away from 1935 to a brighter place and a more vital time of man. But to do so would be to turn his back upon the other two men, and he knew it would not only be unwise to incur their dislike by seeming different, but in some way unkind. He didn't participate fully in their conversations, except when they talked baseball, which they often did. Mostly they talked about money and family and these came down to the same thing, making one word, money-family. How to pay for the wife's hysterectomy, what to do about the father-in-law who was unemployed. They would probably have to take him and his wife in with them, which meant that their oldest boy would then have to sleep on the sofa, and then where would the daughter entertain her boy friend? She was keeping company with a nice fellow who had a good job with Consolidated Edison, and it would be a helluva thing if she lost her boy friend because of that old bastard, who had never done a thing for them when he had it! But after all, Santorello said, he's my wife's father and she cries her eyes out, it's hell to go home at night and listen to her. And Resnick nodded, understanding and wise; his dark hooded eyes, somber, cynical and resigned, reminded Maury so much of Pa that he sometimes couldn't look into Resnick's face. Resnick nodded and sighed: family, family, my brother owes me a hundred and fifty dollars, I know I ought to make him pay, he could take a loan someplace, he keeps promising, we've always been like *that*— with two fingers raised, pressed side by side—I hate to make trouble between us, but, gee, a hundred and fifty dollars.

At least, Maury thought, feeling such pity for them, for me this is temporary. These times can't go on much longer. For me at least, there's something else. But for these two who are, after all, not really any different from me except that I've read some books that they haven't read, is this all there is? Bending over feet and tying string on a shoe box until the end?

Too much time to think. Melancholy. Must stop. Be thankful I have Aggie at home, not their nagging, miserable women. And we are getting along. Two weeks' wages go for rent. That leaves forty dollars or thereabouts for the rest of the month. Eight a week for food, that's thirty-two, with eight over for carfare, gas and electric. Can manage, as long as the clothes hold out and we have no medical bills. Anyway, George Andreapoulis said something about needing some typing done. He can't afford a secretary in that two-bit office. Aggie could do it for him; she knows how to type pretty well. Only, George would have to provide the typewriter because I gave mine to Iris and Aggie left hers at home, which means it's lost to us. Unless—his head whirled and it occurred to him that he'd never spent so much energy on so many details—unless Iris could prevail upon their parents to buy another for her and return his to him? . . .

He had come home one afternoon a month or so ago and found his sister sitting at the table with Aggie. She'd come directly from school, wearing a plaid skirt and sweater and the string of pearls, probably the good ones that she'd had since she was a baby, and the saddle shoes that all the girls wore. She had her books in a heap on the floor next to her chair. She'd risen to kiss him.

"I've surprised you, Maury?"

"And how! Gee, I'm glad! You girls introduced yourselves to each other?"

"I just got here a few minutes ago," Iris had said. "I got lost. I've never been in Queens before."

"How'd you know where to find us?"

"From the post office. I figured you must have arranged to have your mail forwarded."

"I ought to have remembered how smart you are."

She had flushed; the pink had made her austere face look tender.

"Did you—did you tell anyone you were coming?"

"I told Ma, and she cried a little. She didn't say anything but I knew she was glad."

"But that's all you told." He couldn't, wouldn't say the words: Pa, father.

"Well, I didn't want to be sneaky, so I said this morning that I'd be late because I was coming here. I said it loud enough so Pa could hear it from the hall. I wouldn't do anything sneaky," she had repeated with pride.

Something had welled up in Maury. She was a *person*. Either she had changed or he had. He'd never really looked at her before, just known she was there like a sofa or chair that has been standing in a room as long as you can recall, and that sometimes gets in the way when you stumble over it in the dark. But she was a *person*.

"I love you, Iris," he said then, simply.

Aggie, with the tact that was part of her charm, had made a bustle with the tea, saying cheerfully, "Iris is right where we were five years ago. Puzzling over college catalogues."

"Not really," Iris had said, "there's no choice for me. I'm going to Hunter. Not that I mind. I'm looking forward to it."

"What's Hunter?" Aggie had wanted to know.

Maury had explained, feeling a wave of guilt, though it wasn't his fault that they'd kept him in private school and sent him to Yale, "Hunter's a free college of the city of New York. You have to be very bright to go there, have to have top grades."

"Oh. And after that, Iris? Have you thought what you wanted to do? I hope you have, then you won't be in the position I'm in."

"I'm going to teach," Iris had said. "That is, I will if I can find work. At least I'll be prepared."

She'd stirred the tea. There'd been something quite calm and collected in the way she sat. She's come out of childhood, Maury had thought, and as he was looking at the top of her dark, bent head, suddenly she had raised it and asked, "Don't you want to know how things are at home? Is it that you just don't want to ask me?"

He had been astonished at her perception. "Well, then, tell me," he'd said.

So he learned that Pa and Malone were building up more management work. They were making ends meet, although just barely. Ma was busy in the same ways. Ruth and two of the girls had been staying with them for a few weeks in between moves. June was married and the others had parttime jobs working for June's father-in-law.

"But most of their support comes from Pa," she had finished, and Maury could supply what she had left unsaid: try to remember how good Pa is, try to understand him, don't hate him too much.

But Iris was always the one who loved Pa the most.

And then Maury had walked with her to the subway entrance because it was growing dark and had seen her descend the stairs and, turning, call back to him: "I'll come again," and take a few steps and then, turning once more, call, "I like your wife, Maury. I like her very much," and hurry down the steps, her books piled in one elbow. He had stood there until she was out of sight with a hurt in his throat, such a softness of pity or loss or goodness knew what. A whole mush of feeling, he'd thought angrily, blinking his eyes, and turned back home.

Well, that's how it is, and while you can't expect life to be entirely clear and uncomplicated, surely for some people, somewhere in the world, it must be so sometimes. But not for us in this damned place, this damned time. I want so much for Agatha, he thought; she ought to be surrounded by flowers. He counted the buses at the corner; that made two within the last five minutes and sometimes you had to wait half an hour for the next one. Ridiculous, he thought, and was thinking that when the door opened and three skirmishing boys came in with a weary mother.

"Mister! We need three pair of sneakers."

ONE DAY A few months later they received an invitation to the wedding of a girl who had been at college with Aggie. Maury saw it lying open on her bureau: Fifth Avenue Presbyterian Church, reception immediately following at the River Club.

"Hey," he said, "this ought to be fun! You'll see all your friends."

She was slicing bread, and didn't look up.

"Is anything the matter?"

"No. But we're not going to the wedding."

He thought instantly: She has no dress. That's why. "Aggie, we'll get a dress," he said gently.

"We can't afford one."

"You could get a nice dress for fifteen dollars, maybe even twelve."

"No, I said."

Lately he had noticed a sharp protest in her voice. Nerves, and why not? he thought, and said no more.

The next day he said gaily, "I saw a dress in Siegel's window that looks like you. It's white with blue flowers and sort of a cape thing. Go on down tomorrow and look at it."

"I don't want to go to the wedding," she said.

"But why don't you want to?"

"I don't know." She was knitting. The needles twisted in and out and she did not raise her eyes.

He felt rejection and anger. "Don't shut me out! What's this mystery? Are you ashamed of me?"

She raised her eyes. "What a disgusting thing to say! You owe me an apology for that!"

"All right, I apologize. But talk to me, give me the reason."

"You won't understand. It's just that it would be so artificial. One afternoon and all over. We'll never get together, we're in different worlds. Why start something you can't continue?"

"So I have taken you away from everything, after all."

"Oh," she cried. She jumped up and put her arms around him. "Maury, I didn't mean it that way. Do you think I really *care* about Louise and Foster? It's just all so complicated. Sometime when we're settled in a permanent place I'll be more in the mood and we'll have lots of friends."

Holding her there in the center of the little room, he was for the first time not close to her at all.

On the day of the wedding he came home feeling especially tender; he thought she must be thinking of her friend, coming down the aisle in the lace and flowers that Aggie hadn't had. He opened the door—and saw at once, to his utter disbelief, that she was drunk.

"I'm celebrating Louise's wedding," she announced, "all by myself."

He was completely bewildered, angry and scared. He had had very little expe-

rience with this sort of thing but, remembering black coffee, went into the
kitchen to prepare some for her and made her drink it.

He saw, through her attempts to make a joke of it, that she was ashamed. "I'm
really sorry," she said. "I took a bit too much on an empty stomach, I should have
known better."

He said carefully, "What puzzles me is why you took any at all, sitting here by
yourself."

"But that's just it," she said. "That's why I did. It's so depressing here. The
stillness rings in my ears. Stuck all day in this dreary hole—"

"Can't you read, go for a walk, find something else to do?"

"Maury, be reasonable, I can't read till I go blind, can I? Do you ever stop to
think what my life is like? I do a little typing for George, run the dust cloth over
these few sticks and that's my day."

"I'm sorry, Aggie, I didn't realize it was that bad."

"Well, think about it! I take a walk, I don't know a soul, they're all pushing
baby carriages and we've nothing in common, anyway. Oh, I forgot, I do know
one soul, Elena. I can always take her to the market for her English lesson. This is
a radish, say rad-ish, cucumber—"

"How is it that Elena gets along? She's thousands of miles away from home
and can't even speak the language."

"Come on, Maury! Elena's got a whole loving family here, real family plus
dozens of friends in the Greek church. Her parents adore George. She's as loved
and sheltered as anyone can be. . . ."

He understood what she meant and was silent. Somehow they would have to
find a fuller life than this. But he didn't have any idea how. Tense and restless in
bed he twisted from side to side, until suddenly he felt her turning to him, felt
her arms and her mouth, and everything, all tension, fear and worry ebbed and
drowned.

He was drifting into the softest sleep when suddenly he heard her whisper:
"Maury, Maury, I forgot to put the thing in. Do you suppose—"

"Oh, for God's sake," he said, awakened and alarmed. "Oh, for God's sake,
that's all we need."

"I'm sorry, it was stupid of me. I won't let it happen again."

But he was cautious now. On the next night he suddenly drew back. "Have
you got the thing in?"

She sat up. "What kind of a way is that to talk? My, you're romantic, what I
would call an ardent lover!"

"What the devil do you mean? Haven't I got a right to ask?"

She began to cry. He switched on the light.

"Turn the light off! Why do you always have to have that glare on?"

"Don't I do anything right? I'm not a lover, I turn the light on—I ought to just
shoot myself and be done with it. Hell, I'm going into the kitchen and read the
paper."

"Maury, don't! Come back to bed. I'm sorry, I'm awfully touchy, I know."

He was instantly softened. She was a child sitting there in bed, with her wavy
cap of hair, the ruffled white cotton nightdress, the wet eyes.

"Oh, Aggie, I'm touchy too. It's not your fault, I only meant we can't afford to have a baby. And I'm scared. Maybe I shouldn't tell you that. A woman ought to be able to lean on her husband."

"Tell me, tell me, darling."

"I'm afraid I'm going to lose the job. Santorello said today he heard they may close this store. There's not enough business."

"Maybe Eddy's father will give you a job in another store."

"No, I wouldn't even ask. He's got men who've been with him ten years and more. He couldn't fire one of them and take me."

Toward dawn he woke with the sensation of being alone in the bed, and he got up. There was a light in the kitchen. Agatha was sitting there, just sitting at the kitchen table looking at nothing, her face sunk in sadness. There were a bottle of wine and a glass on the table.

"Aggie, it's five o'clock in the morning! What the hell are you doing?"

"I couldn't sleep, I was afraid my twisting and turning would wake you, so I got up."

"I'm talking about the wine."

"I've told you, it relaxes me. I thought it would make me sleep. Don't act as though I were drunk or something."

"It's a bad habit, Aggie. I don't like it. You shouldn't depend on it to solve your problems. Anyway, it's expensive."

"I used the fifteen dollars that you wanted me to spend on a dress and I bought a couple of bottles. Don't be angry, Maury."

The job lasted another month. On the Friday when he got his final pay he dragged home. He went quietly up the stairs hoping that George Andreapoulis wouldn't hear him and come out with an evening greeting. On this night he was in no mood for old-world courtesy.

He opened the door. Tell her now, get it over with and then sit down and puzzle out what we can do. Pray heaven that Andreapoulis has a lot of typing these next few weeks.

Agatha was sitting on the sofa, with her hands clasped in her lap. She looked like a little girl in dancing class, waiting to be asked to dance. "Maury, I'm pregnant," she said.

Everything happened to them against a background of heat. When I am old, Maury thought, and I remember New York and all our troubles, I'll remember the subway grinding and the sour smell of hot metal. I'll remember the signs that read *No Jobs* and damp sheets and Agatha lying on top of them with her belly swelling. And the public library where I spent the days after noon rather than go home: if you didn't find a job early in the day there was no use looking any further that day; you might as well go to the library.

"Summer is the worst time to be looking for a job," said George Andreapoulis sympathetically.

"The winter will be worse. I'll need an overcoat this year and new galoshes. My luck, the snow will be knee-high this year."

"Maybe," George said doubtfully, "one of my clients will have a job . . . I'll keep an eye open. I drew up a will for the man who has the delicatessen over on the avenue. He's doing pretty well and maybe he'll take on a man in the fall."

One morning in September, Agatha said, hesitating, "I don't know how you would feel about this; promise you won't be angry?"

"I won't be angry."

"Well, then, I was thinking; you know my father has a cousin, I've mentioned him, I always called him Uncle Jed. He's really just the husband of my father's cousin, and she's dead now, but I'm sure he hasn't forgotten me. He never had children and he was so fond of me. I remember he always sent the most beautiful dolls for Christmas and when I was sixteen he gave me my first pearls."

"Yes, yes." He stifled his impatience with her prattling. They ought to be so happy now. No worries. Damn world to spoil what should be so beautiful. His child and Agatha's child, his child growing in her, its little fingernails and eyelashes. So beautiful.

". . . vice-president in charge of trusts at the Barlow-Manhattan Bank. I didn't want to involve him because I didn't want Daddy to hear about it, but that's false pride and now I don't care. Would you go to see him?"

He was silent. Crawl before those people? Beg?

"I'd call him first, of course. Maury?"

For her. For the baby, the soft thing growing in her. When it comes out it will be pink, naked and soft; I'll have to warm it, feed it, fight for it.

"Call him in the morning. I'll go," he said. "Did you get polish for my black shoes?"

THE DOOR SWUNG inward from Madison Avenue to a lobby with murals of Peter Stuyvesant, of Indians on the trail, the Treasury, George Washington taking the oath of office, hansom cabs on Fifth Avenue, children rolling hoops in Central Park. No pushcarts, no tenements.

He walked tall and easily across the moss-green carpet. A Yale graduate, as well educated, as presentable and worthy as anyone; what was he afraid of?

Jedediah Spencer, it said on the door. Funny! That old Hebrew name had dignity when you saw it in brass on a mahogany door. Nobody he knew would ever think of giving a child a name like that nowadays.

Everything was dark brown, the wood, the leather and Mr. Spencer's suit.

"So you are Agatha's husband. . . . How do you do?"

"How do you do, sir?"

"Agatha telephoned to say that you were on your way. I'm sorry she didn't call sooner. She could have saved you the trip."

"Sir?"

"We have no openings in the bank."

"Sir, we weren't thinking of that. We thought—Agatha thought—that in your position, knowing so many people in so many businesses, perhaps you could recommend me somewhere."

"I make it a policy never to ask personal favors of our clients."

Mr. Spencer opened a drawer and took out a pen. His hand was hidden by a large photograph in a silver frame, and Maury did not see what he was writing until a paper was handed to him. It was a check for a thousand dollars.

"You can cash it at a window in the lobby," Mr. Spencer said. He looked at his watch. "Naturally I don't want Agatha to be in want. Perhaps it will tide you over until you can straighten yourself out."

Maury looked up. In the cool, correct face he read intense dislike. "Straighten yourself out." It's not I who need straightening out, he thought. It's the world. And he laid the check back on the desk. "Thank you very much. I don't want it," he said, turned on his heel and walked out.

His hands were sweating and his heart pounded. He felt a terrible shame. It was like one of those dreams in which you are walking on a grand avenue when suddenly you look down and find that you have gone out in your underwear. After the shame came nausea.

There was a drugstore on the corner. He had had only coffee for breakfast, and he knew the nausea was from hunger. He wondered whether he could afford a sandwich and an ice cream soda, a thick, rich soda, with cream on top.

He sat down at a table, too weak to sit at the counter stool, even though a table meant another dime for a tip. The cool bastard, he thought. He didn't even have the kindness or decency to say he would try to help, even if he didn't mean it. He had so much contempt for me that he didn't even bother to pretend. . . .

A man came in and took the other seat. Maury became aware that the man was looking at him steadily. Then the man said, "I think I know you. Saw you at a wedding in Brooklyn a couple of years ago."

"Yes?" Maury was cautious.

"Yeah. Solly Levinson—may he rest in peace—his boy Harry got married. You're Joe Friedman's boy, aren't you?"

"Yes. I don't—"

"Name's Wolf Harris. I knew your old man when he was a kid. I wouldn't be high-class enough for him now, though."

Maury was silent. A strange encounter. And since the man had so frankly been staring at him, he returned the stare, seeing a keen, immaculate face perhaps fifty years old, a face like thousands of others on the streets of the city except for the fierce, intelligent eyes. His clothes were dark and expensive; his watch and cuff links were gold; the shoe that was exposed in the aisle was handmade.

"I wouldn't have made that crack about your old man if I didn't happen to know he kicked you out."

At another time, when Maury was younger and not as battered, when he had more pride—or more false pride, if you wanted to call it that—he would not have allowed such an intrusion. But as it was, he said only, "I know two things about you. You have a remarkable memory and a good information service."

The man laughed. "Information, no. Just an accident. I met Solly's daughter on the street, you know the fat kid who talks too much?"

"I know. Cecile."

"So she told me about you. Not that I give a damn or wanted to hear. But my memory, that's something else again. A memory I've got, never forget a fact. Never. That you can't take away from me. What's funny?"

"I was thinking, I don't believe anybody could take anything away from you."

Wolf stared a second and laughed. "You're damn right! You're okay. You're not so dumb yourself!"

"Thanks."

The waitress came with pad and pencil to take the orders.

"Gimme a double cheeseburger, French fries, onions on the side, a malted and a couple of Danish."

Maury said, "I'll have a tuna sandwich on toast."

"To drink?" The girl was impatient.

"Nothing. Just the sandwich."

"Come on! That'd feed a canary. Give him the same as me, miss. That's right. On me."

Maury flushed. Was it so visible, then, the hunger? No, it was the suit. The collar of his shirt was worn, and perhaps he had seen Maury's shoes when he walked in.

"Place is a dump. But it's quick and I've got to see a man at Forty-fifth and Madison at one."

There was a silence. Maury had nothing to say. Then Mr. Harris leaned forward. "Well? What's new? What are you doing these days?"

He felt—he felt like such a child, timid and obedient. Why couldn't he just say, I don't want to talk about my business. I'm not in the mood to talk at all. Why? Because he had nothing and was nobody. And that's what happened to you when you had nothing and were nobody.

"The news is that my wife is expecting a baby. And what I'm doing, unfortunately, is nothing."

"Unemployed, eh?"

"I had a job in a shoe store but they closed the store."

"What can you do besides sell shoes?"

Bitterness rose in Maury. He could taste its heat. "To tell you the truth, nothing. Four years at Yale and the result—nothing."

"I quit school at the seventh grade," the man said, with slight amusement.

"And?" Maury raised his eyes to meet the other's sharp, bright regard.

"And I'm in a position to offer you a job, if you want to take it."

"I'll take it," Maury said.

"You don't know what it is."

"Whether I can do it, you mean? If I don't know how, I'll learn."

"Can you drive a car?"

"Of course. But I haven't got a car."

"No problem. I'll buy you one."

"And what do I do with it?"

"You drive around, Flatbush section, drive around to some addresses I'll give you, pick up some papers every morning and take them to an apartment."

"That's all?"

"That's all. You haven't asked me about the pay."

"Whatever it is, it's more than I'm earning now."

"You're really beat, kid, aren't you?" The tone was surprisingly gentle. "Well, put your head up. I'm offering you seventy-five dollars a week."

"Just for driving around and delivering papers?"

"And for keeping your mouth shut. You understand?"

"I think I do. I'll ask you the rest when we're out on the sidewalk."

"You've got the idea. Eat. And if you're still hungry after all that, speak up. I like people who speak up. At the right time, that is."

He had been starved, not just because of this morning, but hungry for weeks. He never ate quite enough of real food, just crackers and canned soup, saving the milk, the oranges and the lamb chops for Aggie. He felt the good warmth deep inside now: the meat, the cheese, the rich malted milk. *Policy.* That's what it must be, of course. *Numbers.* Well, it didn't hurt anybody, did it? Nobody suffered or died because of it. The rich gamble for thousands in casinos and that's all right; why can't the poor try their luck with pennies? So I'm rationalizing, and I know I am. But the refrigerator will be filled; we'll buy things for the baby and some winter clothes for Aggie. I won't have to avoid Andreapoulis when the rent is due.

They went out to the sidewalk. Madison Avenue was friendly. Two vivid young office girls went by laughing and glanced at Maury. A man went into a haberdashery store. The window was full of good shirts and nice foulard ties. The world was friendly.

"What a piece of luck that I happened to sit down at your table, Mr. Harris," Maury said.

"The name's Wolf. And here, this is my number, where you'll call me tomorrow morning. Come in and I'll lay it all out for you. No use talking more now. You know what it's all about."

"I know," Maury said. "And you can rely on me absolutely. I want you to know that."

"If I didn't know that I wouldn't talk to you in the first place. I size men up in two seconds flat. What are you going to tell your wife?"

"That I collect rents. She wouldn't understand."

"I figured as much. High-class, is she?"

"Sort of."

"Yeah, well. Call me tomorrow then. At ten-thirty. No earlier. No later. And here's a twenty for expenses in the meantime. Wait, here's another. Buy yourself a pair of shoes."

"I don't need twenty for shoes. I can get a pair for six dollars."

"Twenty. I don't like cheap shoes."

THERE WAS AN autumn chill in the air and Maury brought the baby in. He pulled the perambulator up the steps and parked it in the hall by the stairs; the Andreapoulises were nice about things like that. Anyway it was a kind of ornament, that carriage. It was the finest English pram, navy blue leather and chrome, the kind you saw on Park Avenue pushed by a nursemaid in a dark blue coat and veil. They'd sent it from the office when Eric was born. No doubt that meant Wolf Harris had ordered it, the way he did everything, so lavishly, so meticulously: funeral flowers and a basket of fruit when Scorzio's mother died; presents for

weddings and First Communions and Bar Mitzvahs. He had an astounding memory.

Maury lifted the sleeping baby. The warm, fragrant head flopped on his shoulder. He carried him upstairs and laid him, still asleep in his crib. He looked at his
watch. A half hour before the next bottle. He slipped a finger under the diaper.
Wet. Well, better not to disturb his sleep for that; he'd only be wet again in
another fifteen minutes. He smiled, feeling expert and competent. On afternoons
when he came home early, and they were frequent because his hours were so
easy, he was glad to let Aggie go out. This whole summer in the months since
Eric's birth he'd sat with a book on the front step while Eric slept. Some of the
women in the neighborhood, especially the foreign-born, nudged each other as
they passed. They thought it was funny for a man to be doing that. To hell with
them.

Aggie would be home soon. He'd given her a nice check with which to go out
and buy clothes. She had already bought a suit the color of cranberries, and
looked delightful in it, as slender as she had been before the baby. There was
nothing like it, the feeling a man had when he commanded: Go out and buy
yourself something, buy what you want. A man felt like, he felt like—a man!

They'd given him a raise. He was making ninety dollars now plus the expenses
of the car.

"Get a black coupe," Wolf Harris had instructed him that first morning. "Keep
it inconspicuous. Be careful not to get a ticket, no parking tickets, nothing. And
when you're out, watch through the rear-view mirror. Keep your eyes on it all the
time. If you have any idea you're being followed, drive slowly, don't arouse any
suspicion. Stop at the first bar you see, and get out slowly; go into the men's
room and empty your pockets into the toilet. Then when you come out, slowly,
you understand, go on up to the bar and have a beer, like any guy minding his
own business, and then out to the car again, clean. Everything clear?"

Quite clear. He'd bought a black Graham-Paige and had no trouble so far. It
was nice; they'd even taken the baby out to Jones Beach in the car. He didn't feel
like a conspirator. He didn't even feel he was doing anything *really* wrong even
though it was against the law; that part he hated. But as for the actual *thing* itself,
it didn't seem so terrible. They weren't hurting anybody. It was the law that made
it evil.

They had the "offices" in various apartment houses, which were changed every
few months; they were now on the second one since he had started working.
They kept their books and took their calls in the kitchen of a very modest
apartment. The woman looked even younger than Aggie, if possible. She had two
babies. It all seemed so innocent, sitting there tallying the books, while the little
girls had their lunch!

And the men he worked with were no more criminal types than Maury was.
Scorzio, with his "dese" and "dose," and Feldman, too, were just like the men
who had worked in the shoe store, family men like them except that these weren't
worried sick about money. These sent their children to summer camp and talked
about their piano lessons. Windy, called that for somewhat indelicate reasons,
although tough in manner, was so decent, so generous. The day Maury had had

the flu he'd driven him home and couldn't have been more considerate. Bruchman the accountant, there was a brain! Quick as an adding machine; if it hadn't been for the Depression he wouldn't be doing what he was doing, that's sure. Tom Spalding, the detective who stopped by every week for his hundred— there was a nice open face, looked like Thomas Jefferson. No harm in him, except the need of money. He had four children, one in dental school; how could he have managed otherwise?

Talk about money! The amount that went through their hands was staggering. And this was only one small group. Total it all up and you had a few million dollars a week! And this was only one of Harris' enterprises, not even the main one. They said he was gradually relinquishing this to other hands; he didn't need it anymore. Since repeal he'd gone legitimate. He owned distilleries in Canada, a network of liquor-importing firms here and with all that cash had branched out into choice real estate all over the country. Fascinating, a study in itself, the ramifications, both financial and human, of all this. The man behind it, a bigger boss than Harris, Scorzio confided one day in whispered awe, was actually Jim Lanahan, father of the Senator. He and Harris had made theirs during Prohibition, and now Lanahan was worth tens of millions. Harris was nothing by comparison; he only counted his in millions, Scorzio said, grinning.

"But Harris is a prince, never forget that. He likes you, he does for you. Nothing is too much."

Maury wanted to know whether they ever saw Harris. He himself hadn't seen him since the day he was hired.

"Only about once a year. Around Christmas, he gives a party. Has a place way out on the Island, big place with a stone wall around it like Central Park. You'll be invited next time."

Naturally Aggie wanted to know whom he worked for and what he did. Collect rents for a big real estate outfit, he said, and then, not wanting to lie entirely, feeling somehow cleaner if there were some truth in his story, gave the name of Wolf Harris, which meant nothing to her, of course. From time to time he mentioned the names of some of the men in the office, names which also could mean nothing to her.

She pressed him to make some friends for them where he worked. "I don't see why you can't invite some of the men and their wives one evening," she insisted. "We don't see a soul except George and Elena, and there's no way of making friends in this neighborhood. We've no other contacts possible except your office."

"They're not your type," he said lamely.

"Can't I meet them and judge for myself? At least I could talk to the women about their babies, couldn't I?"

Of course she was dissatisfied. It was unrealistic of him to think that the baby could be enough. A woman needed more than that, especially a woman with all the life that was in Aggie, the life that had drawn him to her the first time he had seen her. What they needed, he knew, was to belong somewhere, to be a part of something, to have roots. He hadn't used that word for a long time, not since he had seen the rootedness of Aggie's home town and envied it. A place where you walked down the street and people knew your name! Friends telephoning and coming to the door! Well, someday, surely: it was what he aimed for. He grieved over the pain she must feel at her loss of it. Her mother's letter hadn't helped, either. Son of a bitch!

Apparently Aggie had written to her parents when Eric was born, although she hadn't told him. But, going through bills on the desk, he had seen the answering letter and read it through. "You and your little boy are welcome"—or something like that. "But your father will not receive your husband. I myself would reconsider, but I can't press the issue with Dad in his state of health. His heart is absolutely broken, he looks like a sick man. Everything he stood for is gone, his only child is gone." And then something about how nothing was forever and if a mistake had been made it was better to correct it than to live with it, so if Aggie should ever change her mind about what she had done—And then the conclusion: "Be assured again that we love you still, and you may come home with the baby and be so welcome."

He was outraged. "Be assured—!"

"Excuse me," he'd told Agatha, "for reading the letter. It wasn't honorable, but I couldn't help it."

"I don't mind," she'd said. "I would have told you anyway," and had begun to cry. If he had had her stupid mother and bastard father there in the room he would have killed them in cold blood.

The baby stirred and broke into a cry, a bleat like a lamb's. Little soul! Round mouth open, hits himself in the face with his own fist, slams his heels against the sheet. Furious, aren't you, because you're hungry? Swiftly, pleased with his own swiftness, Maury unpinned the diaper. Wonderful little body, the firm thighs not seven inches long, joined by the marvelous tiny convoluted rose of maleness! Little man. Homunculus. He fastened the diaper firmly, settled the boy in the crook of his left arm, inserted the bottle, not too warm, just right.

The baby sucked and bubbled. He doesn't know anything but warmth of hands, warmth of voices. May he never know anything else! No, that's impossible. The gray eyes, light as opals, studied his father. One hand went up and curled around the father's finger with surprising strength. My son. I promise myself to remember this, no matter what else happens, how far he goes away from me, and he will, I promise to remember this day in October, with the sun on the floor and his hand around my finger.

He heard Agatha at the door and didn't move, wanting her to see them like that.

"I want to talk to you," she said, and at her harsh tone he turned. She was standing in the doorway, wearing the cranberry suit, holding a hat box, a shoe box and a newspaper.

"You lied to me," she said. "You don't collect rents. You're a racketeer. You collect policy slips. Here, it's in the paper."

"What's in the paper? What are you talking about?"

She held the front page for him to see. The police had raided an apartment rented by Mrs. Marie Schuetz and arrested a man named Peter Scorzio. A large operation had been uncovered, he read, with an estimated take of one hundred fifty thousand dollars a week.

"I doubt there can be two men named Peter Scorzio," Aggie said.

The baby had finished, Maury moved him over his shoulder to burp him. He didn't say anything.

"So the food we eat, the clothes I have on, everything that touches Eric, comes from this *dirt*!" Her anger was cold and controlled. "Why did you lie to me, Maury? Why did you do such a thing?"

He began to tremble, not only because of her, but also because if he had stayed late today, they would have caught him too. Somebody must have slipped up, perhaps a new cop in the district.

"I was ashamed. I knew what you would think. So I took the easy way of lying and I shouldn't have."

"What are you going to do now?"

"What can I do?"

"You can march over there in the morning and tell them you aren't coming back. Or no, you can call him up now, whoever runs the gang," she said scornfully, "and tell him you're not coming back. That's what you can do!"

"Then what? You think I haven't tried to see whether there was anything else? Yes, I found a job, one job, at the A & P for twenty-two dollars a week!"

"Well, take it!"

"Can we live on that? Milk for the baby, the pediatrician—can we? And now we've become used to more—"

"Do you think it was worth it? Oh, I should have guessed there was something odd! A boss sending gifts like that when Eric was born, and a wristwatch for me at Christmas. How naïve I am! Do you know what? I feel dirty in these clothes, I could take this watch and throw it into the garbage pail!"

He let her talk; he couldn't think of anything to say. She began to cry. "But most of all, most of all, Maury, what might have happened to you! Suppose it had been you instead of that Scorzio! To spend years of your life in jail, a man like you, people like us, ruined, ruined—"

"He won't spend years of his life, not even a night. He'll be out on bail, he probably is already. And in a few weeks the charge will be dropped for lack of evidence."

She stared. "You mean, somebody will be paid off—a judge, or somebody."

"Exactly. That's the way it works."

"You think that's right?"

"Of course I don't think it's right. If I could change it I would, and as soon as I can get away from it I will. But in the meantime—"

"You're going back?"

"In the meantime I'm going back."

The telephone rang. He handed her the baby. "That'll be for me, telling me the new address for tomorrow."

HE NEVER KNEW what he would find when he got home. Agatha might be on the floor with Eric and a pile of blocks. Now that Eric was walking, the floor was always strewn with his toys, making a disorder which pleased Maury, a natural, cheerful disorder. The sound of their two voices, the child's and the mother's, would ring into the hall before he got the door open. And there would be the fragrance of cooking, something spicy and foreign; he thought with amusement, Aggie has turned out to be a pretty good Greek cook. He might open the door on all that.

Or else he might open it on a dark kitchen, a dim living room and Eric crying in the playpen with his diapers soaked. Agatha would be asleep on top of the bedspread. He never knew.

He bought a book on alcoholism. It took him four days to muster courage enough to buy it. When he had unwrapped the book and placed it on the seat of his car he knew he had made the final admission to himself.

Above all, the book advised, don't lose your temper; it will accomplish nothing. More easily said than done! Yet he was being quite patient, he thought. Not that she was ever offensive, maudlin or nasty; she just merely began to feel hazy and fell asleep. But it was sick; he knew so little about it but he knew that much, and that people used alcohol to relieve their anxieties. Apparently his wife's anxieties were too much for her.

"Elena asked me today what kind of job you had," she reported once. "I'm sure they suspect something. Even if there were women around here for me to make friends with I'd be afraid and ashamed."

Such heavy guilt he had, remembering the place where she had been born, the white houses, the old, old calm and dignity. And now this. And all his fault.

While the key was still in the lock one evening he heard the delightful sound of crowing, and knew that the boy was in his high chair, spraying a mush of pureed carrots or spinach on his bib. He threw his coat on a chair and hurried into the kitchen. His sister Iris was feeding Eric.

He stared. "Where's Aggie?"

"Nothing's wrong! She was lying down when I got here. Had a little headache, that's all. So I told her to stay there and I'd feed Eric."

"Don't lie to me, Iris! Don't cover up for her! She's been drinking again and you know it."

"There," Iris said, "all through! Let Auntie Iris wipe your mouth, and we'll have some peaches."

"Damn it," Maury said. He beat his fists on his thighs. "Damn it to hell and back again."

"Don't do that now. Get it out of your system later, Maury. You're scaring Eric."

The child had turned his head away from the spoon to stare at Maury. He walked out of the room. He went to the bathroom. He walked to the living room window and looked out at nothing. He opened the bedroom door; it was dusk and he could not see Aggie's face. She was huddled on the bed asleep, her knees drawn almost to her chin. Fetal position, he thought disgustedly, and walked closer. Her hand with the wedding ring lay open on the pillow. Something made him touch it to see whether she would stir, but she did not. He was furious, pitying and grieving. He wished he could make sense of all the things he was feeling.

He went back into the kitchen. Iris had put the baby into the playpen, where, now that his stomach was full, he would be content for half an hour, at least.

"There's nothing in the refrigerator except a roasting chicken. I guess Aggie intended it for supper. But it's already half past five."

"Make some scrambled eggs. I'm not hungry. I hope you aren't." He sounded gruff. He hadn't meant to.

"I'll make a jelly omelet," Iris said.

"Anything."

They ate silently. Suddenly Maury realized how ungracious, how self-absorbed he was being. "You've just finished mid-terms, haven't you? How did you do?" he inquired.

"I did well," she answered quietly. "And you don't have to be sociable, Maury. I know you have a lot of trouble."

He didn't answer.

"Aggie told me what you do for a living."

"She had no right to!"

"Don't be angry with her. She told me months ago. A person has to talk to somebody, you know."

"Well, am I doing anything so terrible?" he burst out.

"She's not used to things like that."

"And I am used to them?"

"Of course not. Except that you seem able to stand it. You feel you have to. But she's made differently and she can't face it. That's why she takes a drink, don't you see?"

"She doesn't help herself that way. She doesn't help us."

"I'm sure she knows that, and it makes her feel worse."

"Do you always understand so much about people?"

She looked up quickly. "Are you being sarcastic?"

"Iris! For God's sake! I meant you understand so much, and you're only seventeen."

"That's funny. Most of the time I think I don't understand very much at all."

He put his head in his hands. "I wish I could find a decent job but there isn't anything. I've tried, believe me I have."

"I believe you."

"Tell me, do they know at home what I do?"

"They found out. Not through me! Through Cousin Ruth. You know she has relatives who keep up with Wolf Harris. It seems all some people do is talk about other people."

"Did they have anything to say about it? The truth."

"Ma didn't. She waited for Pa the way she always does. And he said it was a disgrace, a scandal."

"Then can he get me anything better?"

"You never asked him to."

"Would you, if you were in my place?"

"Don't make me take sides."

"Why doesn't he call me? Answer that!"

"He's older, Maury. He is the father, after all," Iris said quietly.

Agatha was still asleep when Iris left. He ran the water for Eric's bath and wondered how she was with the child while he was away. She could be so delightful! She loved to sing, and often he had heard her singing while taking her own bath or working in the kitchen. He hoped she wasn't silent all day. Since Eric had been born he'd been reading the child-care articles in the newspaper and learned that babies can sense moods and read expressions. He hoped the boy was getting a good start.

Eric was sleepy after the bath and Maury lifted him up and held him. The child was a comfort to him; wasn't that odd? This tiny sleepy thing to comfort him? His mind darted, darted. He laid Eric down and went to their closed bedroom door. Seven o'clock. She ought to have something to eat. His hand was still on the knob, half unwilling to turn it. He had an odd flash of recall: long before they were married they'd had a conversation, about being behind a closed door together, and he thought how strange it was that once they would have almost died as a price for one hour alone together, behind a closed door.

She was just waking up. "What time is it?" She sat up, startled, frightened, apologetic. He sat down on the edge of the bed and took her hand.

"Aggie, I am, I really am going to try to find some other job," he said.

THEY GAVE HIM a new stop. Timmy's place, they said: be there around eleven for the pick-up. It was a summer day, one of those days when the sky is lofty blue as porcelain, and anywhere else but here the air would smell of grass.

He drove out New Lots Avenue and turned left. The landscape was familiar: the ragged, unkempt edge of the city, with a few rows of attached houses among empty lots and some one-storied buildings with small stores. Taxpayers, they were called, which meant that they just about paid for themselves and no more; you kept them until times were better, then tore them down and built something that would show a real profit. Until ties were better.

He stopped in front of Timmy's. It was a candy store on a neglected street. You couldn't do much business here unless there was a school somewhere in the neighborhood, he thought idly. Then it would be busy after three o'clock and on warm nights when the kids would congregate. He went inside. A couple of fellows, a short one and a tall one, were at the magazine stand. They didn't look like cops but he glanced at them to be sure, raising his eyebrows at Timmy for a signal.

"Come in," Timmy said and they went in back, so the men must be all right, not cops. Timmy had expected him, of course.

"I'm Maury, expect you'll be seeing more of me," he said by way of affability and took what Timmy handed him and put it in his pockets. On the way out, just to be sure, but also out of friendliness, he bought a pack of Luckies, then went outside and started down the block to where he had prudently parked his car.

A car had drawn up behind his. If it's cops, he thought, I'll just keep walking steadily. He heard running steps behind him and, turning, saw the two men from the candy store. He stepped aside but they slammed into him where he stood and knocked him to the ground. Somebody in the car opened the door and he was dragged in yelling and kicking. There was nobody on the street, which was empty as a cemetery. Not cops, he thought, but who—? And then he was on his back on the floor and the men were holding him down. The car roared away.

"What are you doing to me? For Christ's sake, lemme go, what do you want, I'll give it to you—"

"He'll give it to you, Shorty, you hear that?" the big one said.

The car filled with laughter and he couldn't tell whether there were one or two in the front seat. Shorty brought his fist down on Maury's nose. The pain was dazzling.

"Who are you?" he cried. "What do you want? Just tell me. Please. I'll do what you want, only don't—" The tall one had slid half off the seat, digging his knee under Maury's ribs.

"You tell us," the big one said. His knee ground deeper. "You tell us what you were doing in Timmy's place. We know what you were doing, we just wanna hear you tell it."

"If you know, then you know I was picking up for Scorzio . . . Jesus Christ!" Maury screamed. Shorty brought his fist down and when Maury twisted away in time to save his eye, it caught the cheekbone and the side of his bleeding nose. "Ask Scorzio. Call him. He'll tell you—"

"You're a friend of Scorzio's? Ain't that nice?"

"Call him, ask him!"

Someone in the front seat called back, "Christ, is this fruit for real? Where the hell do they pick up a fruit like this?"

"Bull, you tell him," Shorty said, mincing his words. "This is my friend Bull, this gentleman. His real name's Bullshit but we call him Bull. He'll tell you all about it."

Bull's knee dug deeper. I'm fainting, Maury thought, fainting or dying.

"Look dearie," Bull said, "you got yourself into a helluva lot of trouble just now and Scorzio can't help you out of it. You and Scorzio just happened to cross over the line into our territory. Now, Scorzio may think it's his, but he's thinking all wrong because it ain't his, it's ours, and you goddamn son of a bitch better keep the hell out of it." He caught Maury's ears, and pounded his head against the floor of the car.

"I didn't know—" Maury was crying, weeping, screaming. "So help me God, I didn't know, so help me, I wouldn't have—"

"Shut the friggin' bastard up," someone said. "Toss him the hell out, we're through with him."

The car lurched and swung and slowed. They were opening the door; it fell wide; they were shoving him, lifting him, kicking him; he heard his own screeching terror, and grabbed crazily, blindly at the door beyond his reach, then at the running board, then at the air.

It WAS DARK and there was a distant humming as of bees or traffic on a highway. He struggled to discern it, raised his head and felt a pain so sharp that he thought a knife had been thrust into his ear. He screamed and suddenly everything flashed light; he was in a room; there was a fluorescent bulb on the ceiling and someone was standing over him; there were low voices. Then one by one things floated into reality. These were nurses and he was on a bed. It had been their voices, humming and buzzing.

"Mr. Friedman," one said, "you're feeling better."

The other voice inquired: "Do you know where you are?"

He frowned, not comprehending, and then came a white rush of clarity and he understood that they were trying to see whether his mind had been affected. He would have laughed, only his mouth hurt, and he said, mumbling, "Ospil? Os-pil?"

"Yes, you're in St. Mary's Hospital. You've been here two days. You fell out of a car. You remember that?"

"Yesh." Remember. Panic, crimson blinding before the eyes. They're killing me. Wet his trousers. Pinned down. Pinned. Screaming, witch voices. Witch screams. Theirs? His? And the opening door, rush of speed, air. Remember.

He shook, gasping.

"There," the nurse said. "There. You'll sleep. Don't talk. I know you under-stand me. I just want to tell you before you sleep that you're going to be all right. You've had a bad concussion and a cut on the forehead that will heal nicely. Your collarbone is broken, and two fingers. You're lucky to've come out like that. Your wife's been here with your neighbors. We sent her home, and she's all right, too. So don't worry about anything."

Flat calm voice of authority. A mother's voice. He went to sleep.

Later on, a man's voice. Smooth, cool, also authority. "I'm Detective Collier. The doctor says I can have five minutes with you. Can you tell me what hap-pened?"

Alert now, thinking clearly. The fuzz of drugs mostly gone, so the pain is sharp. Face all sore, wonder what it looks like? Careful how you answer.

"They pushed me out of the car." Feign sluggishness. He won't know the fuzziness is gone.

"We know that. Who were they?"

"Two men. Grabbed. Pulled me in. Then pushed me out."

"Yes." Very patient. "Do you know the men, ever see them before?"

"Never."

"Think, now. Is there anything you remember about them, the way they looked or a foreign accent, or anything? Did you hear them call each other by any names? Think carefully."

Anything I remember? Never forget. Ugly gnarled fellow, left eye wandering toward the shoulder, tall muscular guy like a Western movie, green tie, tie staring at me, he leaning over, pounding my face. Bull, name of Bull. Short for Bullshit, Shorty said, laughing.

"Take your time. I know it's hard for you."

Oh, I'd like to see them hang, I'd stand there laughing. But they know who I am, Agatha alone in the house. He shuddered. "Can't think. Sorry, I want to, but—"

"Did you happen to hear the name Bull? Have you heard that before?"

"Bull? Bull? Nope, nope."

The voice, not as patient now. "I hope you're not trying to conceal anything, Mr. Friedman. It's hard to believe you don't remember anything, not one word, that was said from the time you got into that car. What were you doing when they pulled you into the car?"

"I was on the sidewalk."

"Yes, yes, of course. What were you doing in the neighborhood, what was your business there?"

"Bought a newspaper in the candy store."

"Yes. Well, what do you do for a living? You weren't working that time of the morning?"

"I don't have a steady job. Laid off."

"Unemployed?"

"Yes, unemployed."

"We were at your house to see your wife. You live quite well. Drive a nice car."

What would Agatha have said? He felt strings winding, netting him, and wasn't able to think strongly.

Then another voice, "Sorry, Officer, it's more than five minutes. This man's been badly hurt and you can see he's not fit to answer any more questions."

"I could get at the heart of this in less than a minute, Doc, if only he'd cooperate."

"Cooperate? Officer, take a look at him! He doesn't even understand what's going on! You'll have to go, I'm sorry." Firm. Firm. "You can try again tomorrow. There ought to be improvement by then, I hope."

"Look, I'll go easy. Just another minute."

"No, now. You'll have to go now."

Much later, the doctor's voice, tough Brooklyn snarl. "I don't like cops."

"That why you helped me this morning? You knew I understood everything."

"Yeah. I knew. Lie back, I'm supposed to look under this bandage."

Light fingers, almost fluttering. "Am I hurting you? I'll try not to. We don't want any infection under here. Spoil your handsome mug."

Small thrill of pain, tingles down to the belly.

"Sorry, had to be done."

"It's all right." Wincing, looked into narrowed eyes, black brows like caterpillars, intern, about my age, no, has to be three years older. "Why'd you help me this morning?"

"I'm always for the underdog . . . and today you were it. In my experience cops are always against the underdog."

He's all mixed up. Sometimes the cops *are* the underdog. He's mixed up, but no matter, this isn't the place for philosophy or sociology. "Tell me the truth, Doctor, am I going to be all right?"

"It'll take a couple of weeks. Take it easy, let the collarbone heal and get over the shock."

"Just a couple of weeks, you're sure? I've a family to support, I've gotta get working." All panicky again thinking about it. Feeling the responsibility. Like lifting a ton.

"How many children?"

"One boy. God, I couldn't afford any more, not now."

The doctor stood back from the bed, far enough for Maury to see the whole of him. The stethoscope hung from the pocket of his long white coat. Interns were proud, liked to display that first stethoscope. You could see the pride in him. Also fatigue. Also intelligence, very, very much intelligence.

"And your wife? How is she?"

"She's all right. The nurse said she was coming back today."

"A very lovely girl. And frail."

"Is there something wrong? What did you see?"

"Don't be alarmed, I shouldn't have said that. I only meant I could see she's delicate, can't stand up under too much. So I know what you mean by responsibility. Am I right?"

Maury sighed. "You're very perceptive, Doctor."

"That's what they tell me."

HIS HEAD THROBBED with every step. He had been home for three days and the doctor had said he ought to walk a little. He went to the end of the block. There was a grassy space between the houses and he sat down on a stone. His forehead had begun to itch under the bandage, and that meant it was healing. A big gash, they had said, but it will heal fast because you're young. Thank goodness, he'd saved his eyes from those vicious animals. Animals? Animals didn't do things like that to each other. It was a warm day, but he still felt cold. He had even worn a thin sweater. Nervous shock. It would take time to get over it. He was surprised Agatha was doing as well as she was. She had been so scared about him that she hadn't even asked what he was going to do.

When Bruchman had come to the house she had gone into the bedroom with Eric, but she had overheard their conversation. Bruchman had begun by explaining that somebody—he didn't say who—had made an awful mistake, hadn't clarified the new districts, and so Maury had mistakenly been sent into an area that wasn't theirs. But that had been corrected now. Also, the detective who had questioned Maury in the hospital had been taken care of and nobody would be asking him any more questions. By the way, Maury had handled that very nicely. As a matter of fact, as soon as he got on his feet, they would be wanting him in the office, and no more running around the way he had been doing.

"No, thanks," Maury had said.

If it was a matter of money, surely he knew that money was never a problem. He could earn double what he'd been getting. Hadn't they paid for his private room in the hospital and come right out here to make sure his wife had money while he was gone? No, it wasn't a matter of money, and indeed Maury appreciated everything, but quite simply he wanted to be through. No hard feelings, he just wanted to be through. He lied to make it easier. He might even be moving away from New York.

Bruchman had tried some more, had even been quite insistent, but then finally, seeing that it was no use, had gone out after shaking hands and wishing Maury good luck.

Agatha had opened the bedroom door and come out crying. The tears were running down her face, but her face was shining and she had clung to him. "Oh, if anything had happened to you, I don't know what I would have done, how I would have borne it!"

"I'll take care of you," Maury had said, "I swear I will." And she had replied, "I know you will, Maury, I know."

But how he would, he had no idea. How? Where? He got up and walked slowly back to the house, remembering the want ads and the patient lines at five in the morning, a hundred men for every job, the lines and lines from the Bronx to Brooklyn and Queens and back again.

How? Where?

He turned the corner, his head still throbbing, and climbed the stairs. Agatha heard him and opened the door. Then behind her in the living room he saw his mother, and sitting on the sofa, holding the little boy, his father.

"Ma?" he said wonderingly.

"Who else?" Her voice was bright and trembling. "And you don't have to talk. We know it all. Thank God, thank God, you're alive."

❦{22}❧

He stood in the dusty office waiting for the girl to make out his paycheck. The room had a linoleum floor and there was a zigzag tear in one of the window shades. He thought of the big office on Broadway: three floors, rows of desks, mahogany, rugs, like a bank.

Pa hung up the telephone. "I read your mind, Maury. It used to be different."

"At least, you're in business."

"True, true. We're keeping our heads above water." His father lit a cigar, not a Havana of old, but black and pungent nevertheless.

"The cheap ones smell better to me than the ones you used to get from Dunhill's."

"That's because you don't know anything about cigars. I've still got the humidor and the day will come, mark my words, when I fill it with Dunhill's again."

"I hope so, Pa."

"I know so. I have confidence in this country. We'll pull out of this. In the meantime, I'm sorry I can't do more. Fifty dollars a week isn't much to pay. But it's the best I can do."

"I'm lucky to have a job at all."

"Ah, but it's a disgrace that you, with all your education, should be walking around tenement houses collecting rents. I could get sick thinking about it."

"Don't think about it, then. As you say, we're keeping our heads above water. That's more than a lot of people are doing. Well, I'll start home. Don't forget, we expect you at seven."

"You could wait and ride in our car. Why take the subway?"

"Thanks, but I want to get back to see Eric and give Aggie a hand."

"I hope she's not going to too much trouble over dinner. We're not company, after all."

"Aggie likes to cook. Don't worry about that."

"Your mother's bringing her strudel, enough for an army. You know your mother."

"Aggie'll be pleased. Well, I'll see you."

"Maury, wait. Are things all right at home? You're happy?"

He could actually feel his face closing up, the muscles growing stiff. "Why, yes, of course. Why not?"

Now his father's face closed. "Good, good. I only asked."

The subway lurched and roared. Games. Playing games with each other. Pa knew he knew they were aware. Iris was loyal, but surely it had been discussed anyway. Well, he was not going to talk about it. Not now, not yet. Maybe sometime it might spill out of him. He couldn't swear that it wouldn't, but he wasn't ready yet to expose the secret places.

Maybe after they moved, his mind said, and the other half said: That won't make any difference and you know it won't. They still had almost a year to go on their lease. His father had mentioned an apartment in one of the buildings he managed; you could get three good-sized rooms, really four counting the kitchen, for forty-five dollars a month. It was on the Heights, though, which these days was jokingly—some joke—called the Fourth Reich because it had filled up with refugees from Germany. You hardly heard English on the streets.

He couldn't imagine Agatha up there. It occurred to him now that whenever he was somber or serious he thought of her as Agatha, but when everything was going along happily he thought of her as Aggie. Well, he couldn't imagine Agatha sitting in the park and wheeling the stroller up there on Washington Heights. She would be a total outsider as she was where they lived now. Come to think of it, she would be an outsider almost anyplace in New York City except on Park or Fifth or the streets in between. He thought wryly, We are hardly ready for that.

The subway swung around a curve, his body sagging with it. He was tired. His work didn't warrant such tiredness. This was a tiredness of the spirit, of frustration. She wouldn't admit that she drank. He could come in and see it in her eyes, smell it on her breath, and she would only insist stubbornly that he was imagining things. She would go over to the attack, leaving him on the defensive. He begrudged her an afternoon nap, she said; he was suspicious, a monomaniac. For a while he had measured the bottles and sought out the places where she hid the cheap wine she bought a bottle at a time, a small one so that it could be quickly consumed and spirited away in the garbage. He had done all that, but had got nowhere and finally stopped because it was a futile proceeding, without point.

He reasoned with her . . . "You said your nerves were bad because of the work I was doing and I could understand that. But now I'm working respectably for my father, and you've nothing to be afraid of. Why are your nerves bad now?" To which she countered with entire reasonableness, "If a person could tell you why his nerves were bad they wouldn't be bad, would they?" So there they were, round and round. Nowhere.

But he knew what it was. He was sure he knew. She was sorry she had married him. She might not know it herself, but she was. She loved me when she married me, oh, God, she loved me! And she loves me still, but it's wrong for her, all the same. Of course she won't leave me, and I won't leave her. I couldn't leave her. Not I, son of my parents and all their parents before them. A man doesn't leave his wife and child. But I couldn't do it, anyway. I wouldn't want to live without you, Aggie. Only, why aren't you the way you were? Why?

Round and round.

The subway doors were jammed. All the gray-faced city people in their dark clothes were carrying packages in red and green wrappings. He had forgotten it

was Christmas on the day after tomorrow. Now Santa Claus came in and hung on
the strap, across from two little boys with scared, awed faces.

"What's he doing on the subway?" one whispered, and Santa turned, clearing
his throat.

"Just giving the reindeer a bit of a rest," he said, and people smiled approv-
ingly and winked and patted the boys' caps.

Most people don't want much, Maury thought. When you come down to it
they just want a place where they don't have to be afraid of what's coming, and
they want somebody to love them.

So much for philosophy, he thought, and was glad to get out into the damp
night air, and walked the few blocks to his house looking forward to Eric, who
was always so totally, so unreservedly overjoyed to see him, thinking of Eric's row
of teeth and his thickening hair, his feet in red galoshes, his pealing laugh.

The first thing that he saw when he opened the door was the tree. It was a
bushy one, sharply fragrant and as tall as Aggie. She had a carton of glass ornaments and tinsel and had begun to decorate the tree. She hadn't told him a word
about it.

"You haven't forgotten that my parents are coming?"

"Of course I haven't! Can't you smell the turkey? It's almost done."

"But the tree," he said. "The tree."

"What about it?"

"Perhaps it's my fault," he said. "I didn't know you were going to get one. I
ought to have told you . . . we don't have Christmas trees."

"We don't? Who's we?"

"Why, my father and mother, I mean. They don't have a Christmas tree."

"Well, of course I know that! But what has that got to do with us?"

This was not a question of too much wine. She hadn't had any, he saw at
once. This was another question.

"I should think," he said carefully, "that it had something to do with us."

"I don't see how."

"Well, it's not that I personally have any objection. You can have all the trees
you want as far as I'm concerned. But it would be an awful shock to my father,
Aggie, and after all the grief we've had in this family I just don't want any more."

"Your father can do what he wants in his own house. But I don't see why Eric
should be deprived, do you?"

"Eric hasn't the least idea what this is about," Maury said patiently.

"All right, but what about me? A tree is one of my loveliest memories of
home."

"I shouldn't think you'd have too many lovely memories of home." He regretted the words as soon as he had said them. Hitting below the belt, that was.

"If you're referring to my parents' prejudice, I can only answer that yours get A
in that department, too."

"Okay. I don't want to argue about it. But please, Agatha, I beg you, take the
tree down. Don't slap my father in the face with that the minute he opens the
door. We've come this far, must we spoil it? Please."

She answered him gently and stubbornly, "Maury, I truly don't want to make

things harder, but this is our home and if your father really wants to accept me—
us—isn't it better not to sham?"

"Aggie, the man is going on fifty and he's had a tough struggle. Do we need to upset him?"

"That sounds like a Jewish mother, having a heart attack every time one of her children displeases her."

"I don't care for that kind of remark, Agatha," he said stiffly.

"Oh, come on, don't get all huffy about it, as if I were an anti-Semite! Jokes about Jewish mothers are part of the language, for heaven's sake! Besides, they *are* possessive! And you always say Gentiles drink too much, don't you?"

"No, I don't say Gentiles do. I say *you* do."

She ignored him and, reaching up, tied a red satin ball on a branch.

"What the hell am I going to say to him when he comes in? You don't know what this means to Pa. Listen, Agatha, in the towns where his parents grew up, where my mother grew up, Christmas was the time that the Cossacks and all the local rowdies used to come riding in with dogs and whips to rape and burn and—"

"There are no Cossacks here and it's time you people stopped living in the past. This is America. Besides, you yourself said your father lives in the past. Behind medieval walls, I think you said."

Maury flushed. "Probably I did. But then your parents are so modern, so broad, so kindly! And at least my father is here!"

"What did it take to bring him here? You had to be almost killed before anything could penetrate that heart of his!"

"At least he's here," Maury repeated.

"Maybe mine would be here too if I had let him know the truth! Perhaps I should have told him my husband is running numbers and some thugs have beaten him up, so please come, I need you!" The chiming clock on the radio struck half past six.

"Agatha, they'll be here any minute. Take it down now, and I promise I'll help you put it up again tonight after they've left. I swear I will," he said, unfastening a silver ball.

"Don't touch that! Listen, is this our house or isn't it? You resent any suggestion that you should hide your heritage; why should I hide mine? How would you like it if we went to visit my parents and I asked you to—"

"That's an academic question. You know damn well they don't want to see me in their house. And do you know something? I don't want to see those bastards either."

"Do you have to be so vulgar?"

"Sure, I'm a kike. Kikes are vulgar, don't you know that?"

From the room across the hall came Eric's sudden wail.

"See what you've done? He'll remember this, Maury. Children remember these things." She began to cry. "It was going to be so lovely and you've ruined it! I hate your voice when you yell like that! You look mean! You ought to see yourself."

"All right, all right. Stop crying, will you? Keep the blasted tree and I'll explain it—"

"I don't want the tree. Take it away." A glass ball fell to the floor and broke into chips of glitter. "All the joy's gone out of it. I'm going in to Eric."

SHE RESTED HER head on his shoulder. "Was it awful, Maury? Was the evening all spoiled?"

"No, no, they had a good time. They were just glad to be here."

"Because I wouldn't want your parents to hate me."

"They don't hate you, Aggie. They like you, honestly." He stroked her trembling back, feeling the great sadness in her. How gay she had been—

"Such a hard world," she said. "How is one to bear such a hard world, tell me?"

"It's not hard all the time. And it's the only world we have."

"Do you think I've been drinking, Maury?"

"I know you haven't."

"Then give me a brandy now. I'm awfully cold."

"Hot tea will warm you. I'll make some."

"It's not the same. It won't relax me. Please, I *need* it tonight."

"No. Let go, I'll make tea for both of us."

"Then never mind. Just stay here."

"Aggie, darling, everything's all right. You are. We are."

"But I'm afraid, I'm so afraid. Oh, my God, Maury, what's happening to us?"

❧{23}❧

The evening that they would remember began in the kitchen, now the heart of the house. When Joseph came home from work he went straight there; this night he had brought Maury. Iris had gone downtown shopping with Agatha because winter coats were on sale, and later they were all to have dinner.

Anna stirred a pudding on the stove. How many years it had been since Maury and Joseph had consulted together! Report cards, camp, religious school, all those things that had been of topmost importance then, were nothing compared to this.

"When did you really know?" Joseph asked.

"There's no date to put a finger on," Maury answered. "I can't say: On such and such a date I was sure of it. For a long time I knew she liked to take a little something to help her over a bad spot—"

"Bad spot!" Anna cried out. "A lot she knows about bad spots! What troubles has she ever seen in her life?"

"Very few, until she married me, Ma. But she's had plenty since then."

"No one forced her to marry you!"

Joseph stood up. "You're talking wildly, Anna. Anger won't solve this. You hear me?" he asked, taking hold of her arm.

His fingers hurt her flesh. He was right, of course. But his calm tolerance amazed her and had, throughout all the secret discussions between Iris and themselves, up till the time that Maury—she wasn't sure just how—had brought everything into the open.

"How often does it happen?" Anna wanted to know. "Iris said—"

Joseph put his hand up. "Leave him alone, Anna. We don't need to go over the details again. I know them already."

"You and Maury have talked?"

"We've talked," Joseph said shortly.

How invariably, when there was a crisis, people began to snap at each other! "I see," she replied. "And what did you say when you talked, do you mind telling me?"

Neither of them answered. The pudding foamed over on the stove with the smell of burning sugar and Anna dabbed at it angrily. "Oh, what is the matter with that girl? The shame of it, the shame!"

"Not shame," Joseph corrected. "Sickness. Don't you understand she can't help it?"

"A rotten sickness!"

"All sickness is rotten, Anna."

"Well, if it's such a sickness, let her go to a doctor!"

"She won't go."

"Send one to her, for God's sake. What are you waiting for?"

"That's already been done."

"Already been done! And what happened?"

"She ran down the back stairs. She wouldn't see the doctor."

Maury got up. His chair scraped abruptly and Anna turned from the stained mess on the stove. A line of sickly flesh stretched across his forehead. It would probably remain, a permanent reminder. He looked so much older than twenty-four! Why should just he have all this pain, why should just his life be so hard? He had been so bright and quick, always busy coming and going, carrying his books and tennis racket; the house had been noisy with his friends; they had struggled so to see him through college. Even Ruth's children, in spite of what they had been through, even they were enjoying some youth, while my son, only my son, is burdened like this— The anger swelled in Anna's throat.

Joseph sighed. "You took her away from her people, Maury, she went with you willingly. For better or worse. So now it's worse and we'll have to find a way to make it better."

Maury looked up. "How?"

"Yes, how?" Anna repeated.

"I don't know." Joseph frowned. "But I've been thinking, Maury, why not take Agatha and the baby to Florida for a few weeks? I'll pay, I can swing it. A few weeks on the beach, just getting away, can work wonders. Sunshine heals, you know."

"Sunshine heals alcoholism?" Maury asked gently.

"Well, but the time away together in a beautiful place—it helps the spirit. Who knows?"

"It's awfully good of you, Pa. I want you to know I appreciate it. I really appreciate it."

"Then you'll go?"

"I'll talk about it with Aggie."

Anna thought of something. "When you speak to her about the drinking, what does she say?"

"She doesn't admit it. But it's well known that people seldom do."

The swinging door from the dining room whirled open. "You're talking about *me*?" Agatha cried. "Maury, you're talking to them about *me*?"

"We were only—" he began.

"Don't lie! I heard every word. You didn't know we had come home—" She beat with her fists on his chest. "Apologize! Admit that you lied about me?"

Maury caught her hands. "I'm sorry, perhaps I shouldn't have discussed this even with my parents. But I won't say it's not true, because both of us know that it is."

"I don't understand—" Agatha turned to Joseph and Anna. "He's got this—this puritan obsession about having a drink! Just because he doesn't like it, he thinks that every time a person has one or two he's drunk. Or if I lie down for a few minutes it can't be because I'm tired. Oh, no! It must be because I've been drinking!"

Joseph and Anna were silent. Such a child, Anna thought with pity and dislike, a child standing there in her jumper and blouse, with her tear-smudged, angry face. She wasn't even pretty; what had he seen in her? When I think of the girls he could have married, such beautiful girls! And then, pity again. The man-woman thing! How helpless we are, like netted birds, when we are caught by desire! I, surely I, know all about that—

"We'll never get anywhere, Aggie, if we're not honest with each other," Maury said. "If you would only admit you have a problem, we could help you."

"A problem? I? Or maybe I do have one and you're it!"

"Why? Because I find where you hide the bottle behind the stove?"

"What's happening?" Iris interrupted. "I was on the phone when I heard such a racket! I had to hang up!"

"Iris," Joseph said, "we're having a discussion here. Will you leave us for a few minutes?"

"I want her to stay!" Agatha cried. "She's the only one here I can talk to. Did you know they're accusing me of being a drunkard? Tell them, Iris, have you ever seen me drunk? Tell them!"

"Leave Iris out of this," Joseph said sternly. "Now listen, Agatha, listen calmly. I want you to come into my den and we'll sit down together and talk."

"Why don't we have dinner first?" As though she were standing outside herself, Anna heard her own words, offering food again. So often it seemed to be the only thing she knew how to do. "I've a beautiful roast and it's all ready."

"No," Agatha said. "I'm going home! I can't stay here, can't sit down at your table!"

Iris blocked the front door. "Aggie, I don't know what started all this, but listen to me, stay a little. Anyway, it's pouring, you can't even see to drive the car, wait a little."

But Agatha's coat was flung on, she was out of the door, and Maury was in the outer hall arguing at the elevator door, "I'm not going to let you drive. If you insist on leaving at least I'll do the driving."

"If I want to drive that car I will," they heard her say, and then the elevator door opened, and closed, and they heard its smooth sigh as it descended to the street.

Anna put the food on the table and the three of them sat hardly touching it, hardly speaking, except that once Anna said, "Never once, in all the years in this house—" but did not finish. Iris helped her clear the kitchen and Joseph sat in the living room with the evening paper, not reading it. The wind from the river rattled the windows. Down on the deserted street the rain blew whirlpools in the puddled light of the street lamp on the corner.

Later, when after a long, long time they were able to speak or to recall the particular sound and feel and texture of that February night, they saw it as a play in two parts, a prelude and an ending, with no middle.

It was almost half past eight when the doorbell rang. When she saw the two policemen in their wet, black rubber capes, Iris was sure she knew.

"Mr. Friedman?" one said.

Joseph rose from his chair and came toward them, walking so slowly, Iris thought impatiently: Hurry up, do hurry up!

"Come in," Joseph said.

"There's been—I have to tell you," one began. He stopped. The other one, older, so he must have done this sort of thing before, took over. "There's been an accident," he said softly.

"Yes?" Joseph waited. The question waited, repeating itself in the dull light of the foyer. "Yes?"

"Your son. On the boulevard in Queens. Can we sit down somewhere?"

Quarreling, Iris thought, fighting in the tight little car.

The policeman had such an odd expression. He swallowed as if there were a knob in the back of his throat. "They were—a witness said—the car was speeding very fast. It passed them, too fast in the rain, and it missed a curve."

"You're telling me that he's dead," Joseph said, making a statement or asking a question. And this, too, hung in the air repeating itself: that he's dead, he's dead.

The policeman didn't answer right away. He took Joseph's arm and sat him like a doll in the stiff carved chair in the foyer.

"They didn't feel anything," he said, very softly. "Neither one of them. It was over so quick."

The younger man stood there, turning his wet cap between his hands. "No, no one felt anything," he said again, as if this confirmation, this assurance, were a gift and a mercy.

"They couldn't tell who was driving," the first one said. He turned to Iris. "Young lady, is there any whiskey in the house? And may we call someone? Someone in the family, or a doctor?"

In the background near the door to the inner rooms, and yet sounding far away, came a stabbing scream. Again and again it ripped the air, over and over. It was Anna.

"They were such a nice quiet couple," said Mr. Andreapoulis. He sat with Joseph and Anna in his little parlor. Through the open door to the kitchen they could see his wife rolling some dough on a table. "They never said anything, but we knew from the start there was something sad about them. No one ever came to see them. They used to go for long walks together. We felt sorry for them, my wife and I."

Neither of them had ever mentioned their families, not until after the little boy was born. Then one evening they had come downstairs looking very serious and said that they supposed now they ought to have a will, and would he draw it up for them? Not that they had anything much to leave, but there ought to be some plan for the care of the child in case something were to happen to them both. Mr. Andreapoulis had concurred in that. They had been uncertain and uneasy, but finally they had decided that, in the event of their deaths, the little boy should go to live with his mother's parents as guardians. He had asked them whether they had discussed this with her parents, and they said that they hadn't, but that it would be all right; her parents lived in the country and had plenty of room. Then they had begun to laugh, out of a kind of embarrassment which Andreapoulis had understood. A will is such a formal and pompous document for young people to be writing. People their age don't die and leave a baby behind. It was all academic and therefore foolish, in their thinking.

So that was how it had come about. They had left the will with him and he supposed that, given their attitude, they had forgotten about it. As a matter of fact, he had forgotten about it himself until the night of the accident.

"And so," Joseph said, "there's nothing that can be done to change it."

"Well, as I've told you, anyone has a right to contest a will. But you certainly couldn't show undue influence in this case, could you? These people didn't even know about it." Mr. Andreapoulis' hooded eyes were mournful. "And they really want the child, you see. Although any court would give you visitation rights, of course."

"In their house?"

"It would have to be, wouldn't it?"

"Like visiting in a jail," Joseph muttered.

"Well, do you want to fight it? I don't hold out much hope, but you never know."

"Courts and lawyers. A dirty business. Excuse me, nothing personal, only—"

"I know what you meant. It's all right."

"A dirty business," Joseph said again. His eyes filled.

The young man looked away. He waited.

Joseph stood up. "We'll think it over," he said, "and let you know. Come, Anna."

Oɴ ᴛʜᴇ ᴡᴀʟʟ behind the doctor's desk hung an arrangement of diplomas, forming an impressive frame for his head. The bookshelves on the side nearest Joseph and Anna were filled with texts, the doctor's own and many more. *The Psychology of the Adolescent,* Anna read, and *The Psychology of the Pre-School Child.*

"Yes, I would say this baby has suffered trauma enough," the doctor said. "Of course I know what I've told you is not what you were hoping to hear."

Anna wiped her eyes. "No, I believe it's right. I can see that it makes sense. Splitting the time would be no good for him even if the court were to allow it, which the lawyer says they very likely wouldn't, anyway."

"That's mature thinking. Courageous, too, Mrs. Friedman."

"And yet I don't know!" she cried out bitterly. "If the will had read the other way I wouldn't have treated those people the way they're treating us!"

"But I would," Joseph said. "I would have done exactly what they're doing. And that's the truth."

"Which proves," Dr. Briggs remarked, "why the child ought to be spared exposure to such hostility. He's had enough confusion and shock in his little life already. The kindest thing, if you really love him, and I see that you do, would be to bow out and leave him alone. Let these other grandparents rear him and give him stability. He's not a prize to be fought over."

"Not even to visit," Anna said.

"I wouldn't, if I were you, in these circumstances that you've described. How would he cope with so much hatred? And why should he be forced to take sides? When the boy is older he'll want to see you. Teen-agers are very concerned with identity. Then that will be another situation entirely."

"Teen-agers!" Anna cried.

"It's a long time to wait, I know," the doctor said.

AT HOME ANNA mourned, "If we hadn't known him, it wouldn't hurt like this. He was starting to call my name, did you know that? He called me Nana the last time I saw him."

I never knew I loved Maury so much when he was alive, Iris thought. But when I remember Eric, his little face, his little hands, I know how I loved my brother. And now that they have taken Eric away, it's like losing my brother twice over.

❈{24}❈

After the first blinding pain of loss came long, desolate nights and days. Why? Why? And no answer. Nothing anymore. Never. It was too much effort to eat, too exhausting to dress or go down to the market, a burden to answer the telephone.

Then one morning there came to Anna a stirring of desire to feel again. And she took out a sheaf of letters, tied together, that had arrived from Europe during the terrible time when Maury had been struck down. Voices called out of the dark: her brothers' (Eli and Dan, snub-nosed, freckled boys in their mother's kitchen and suddenly, in Vienna, as old as their father had been when he died); Liesel's (Eli's fair, silvery little girl); the unknown voice of Theo, the little girl's husband.

1.

Vienna, March 7, 1938

Dearest Uncle Joseph and Aunt Anna,

Now that I am actually sitting down to write you a letter I feel ashamed and must begin by apologizing for not having written before, except for the note in which I thanked you for the beautiful wedding gift that you sent to Theo and me. I suppose my only excuse for not having written in all these years, and not a very good one, is that Papa writes to you, and it seemed that he was really writing for all of us. Anyway, here I am, your lazy niece Liesel, sitting in the library, looking out at the melting snow and the little garden room where we had afternoon coffee when you were here. Was it really nine years ago? I was such a baby then, staring at the relatives from America! And here I am, married; our boy Friedrich, Fritzl, we call him, is thirteen months old, just starting to take a few steps, and now *we* are going to America! I can't believe it.

For that is what I want to write to you about. Theo left for Paris by train this very morning. He will take a ship from Le Havre, arriving in New York on the nineteenth. He has your telephone number, so don't be surprised when you get a call! He spent three years at Cambridge and speaks English beautifully, not like me. (That's why I'm writing this in German; because I remember that you were able to understand it very well.) I know you will like each other so much.

The reason Theo is making the trip is to make plans for our immigration. As you know, he is a doctor, and has almost finished his work at the clinic here, studying plastic surgery. I saw the work he did on a child with a burned arm; he is so talented and loves his work! He needs to find out how you go about getting a license to practice in the U.S. and perhaps he might find a doctor who needs a young assistant. . . . It is all quite unsettled, as you can imagine. So I thought that maybe among your many friends you might know a doctor who could advise him. Also, we shall be needing an apartment. Theo wants to sign for one and have everything ready; then he will come back and get Fritzl and me, and arrange to have all our furniture shipped. Perhaps you could tell him where to look for an apartment.

I have such very mixed feelings about all this, I must admit. Theo is absolutely certain that the Nazis are going to occupy Austria within the next year or so. He has been saying it since before we were married, even when we first met. He is very interested in politics and sounds too convincing; he is determined to save us by emigrating. My parents and all Mama's relatives and Theo's own parents, too, think his ideas are pure nonsense. They refuse to leave and they are heartbroken that we are going. For a while Papa was really angry at Theo because he is taking the first grandchild and their daughter away, but now that the actual time is drawing near, he is too crushed to be angry.

As for me, I shall miss my parents, my young brother and sister, most terribly. And Vienna. Theo's father and Papa had arranged to buy a lovely small villa for us near Grinzing. Up to now we have been living in a very nice apartment only a short walk from the Ringstrasse. I shall miss it all so much. . . . And I forgot to mention I was invited to start next season playing with a small orchestra here. At last I felt I was really getting somewhere with the piano. It will be hard to start all over in New York.

But I realize, if it should turn out that Theo is right about the Nazis, our lives here would be in danger because of being Jewish. It's strange, because I have never felt Jewish. I have always felt Austrian—Viennese, to be exact. Forgive me if I offend you, since I remember Papa said you are still quite religious. But then, I am sure you will understand; to be religious or not is entirely personal, is it not? And one does whatever makes one happy.

Speaking of religious people, you may not know that Uncle Dan has already left. He and his whole family went last month to Mexico. He tried to go to the United States but it was impossible because of having been born in Poland; the quota is filled for years ahead. Of course Papa thinks Uncle Dan is quite stupid—they never seemed to get along very well, did they? Anyway, I hope they will succeed there, better than they did here.

This has turned out to be a very long letter, longer than I intended.

Now I hear Fritzl up from his nap. We all thought he was going to have red hair like Papa and you, Aunt Anna, but his hair has turned quite blond, almost white.

I hope you are all very well, and I thank you so much for whatever help you can give to Théo. He doesn't need any money, only advice.

With hearty greetings,
your loving niece,
Liesel Stern

2.

Vienna, March 9th, 1938

Dear Sister and Brother-in-law,

Your letter came here this morning, and I am sick with sorrow. To lose your son, your dear son! Destroyed in a pointless accident! Not even in a war, fighting for his country! That would be painful enough, but at least there is some reason in it, and hence some consolation. But this! I am sick for you, heartsick, and so is Tessa, so are we all. (I understand that Liesel wrote to you only a day or two ago, not knowing.) If only I could do something for you, dear Anna, dear Joseph.

It seems that all of a sudden the world has gone mad with sorrow. Not that I compare my burden with yours, of course not, but we here are bent down with the grief of parting. . . . As you have learned by now, my son-in-law, a fine young man of excellent family, has got a wild idea into his head about going to America. Please do not think I am prejudiced against America. When you went, Anna, from where we lived, it was understandable. But to leave Austria, because some fanatic across the border makes threats—it's absurd. Even if the Germans were to take Austria, and believe me, it would not be so easy, even then it would not mean the end of the world! Possibly some of the extremists here would deprive some Jews of their jobs; there's nothing new about that. We've always had that sort of thing in Europe, sometimes a little more, then again, a little less. It's nothing that one can't live through. And anyway, I tried to tell Theo, his own parents tried to tell him, with our family connections we are the last people to be bothered.

Tessa's people have lived in Austria for so many centuries that nobody knows when they first came. Her father is a top-level official in the Finance Ministry. Her grandfather's sister married a Catholic and converted; one of their grandsons just became a bishop! So much for Tessa. I can't boast of any such connections of my own, unfortunately, but I have made my modest success. Also, as you know, I fought in the war and wear the Emperor's Medal of Valor. Really, I can't see any reason for this hysterical behavior. Ah, well, the young are often unreasonable, and so it is.

Forgive me for talking about all this when your hearts are so full. Please, take care of yourselves and your daughter Iris and the surviving grandchild. Know that we are thinking of you. We are with you, praying that you will find the strength to endure this terrible thing, and go on.

Ever your brother,
Eduard

3.

Paris, March 15, 1938

Dear Aunt and Uncle,

I write in haste to explain my failure to arrive in New York. By now you must be wondering why I wasn't on the ship, or perhaps you have understood from the news why I wasn't.

The day before I was to sail Austria was occupied. I have been trying to get through by telephone to my house, to Liesel's parents or to mine. But the lines are dead. I must assume that they have all left Vienna for the country. Perhaps they have gone to Tessa's people's mountain house near Graz. At any rate, I am taking a train tomorrow for Vienna, where they must have left some message. I will write as soon as I know something.

Respectfully,
Theodor Stern

4.

Paris, March 20, 1938

Dear Aunt and Uncle,

I write again in great haste because I can imagine how anxious you are. I am almost out of my mind. I can't find out anything. It has been a nightmare. I tried to get back to Austria, but they told me in France here that if I tried I would be arrested on the train. I didn't want to believe it, but then the papers here in Paris began to print names and incidents involving people who had tried to rush back to their families just as I was trying to do. And it's true, they were all seized and imprisoned. So, obviously, that would not have done anyone any good. But I have some contacts here that will surely be of help. I shall keep you informed.

Respectfully,
Theodor Stern

5.

Paris, March 26, 1938

Dear Aunt and Uncle,

Still nothing. The earth has opened up and swallowed all the people I love. But that's not possible. I can't believe it. I won't. I am working day and night. I shall write immediately whenever I learn anything.

Respectfully,
Theodor Stern

6.

Paris, April 3, 1938

Dear Aunt and Uncle,

Thank God! They are alive! They are in the detention camp Dachau where prominent people in government, journalism and so forth have been taken for interrogation. I am told that the purpose is to weed out subversives . . . so then we have nothing to fear; certainly our families have hardly been subversive! So it should be over for them very soon. I have people working in the highest circles and shall be getting them out to France to join me here.

The way I found out all this you can't imagine. I mentioned my father's business contacts here in Paris. But I recalled also that one of my friends from Cambridge, a German fellow, was now attached to their embassy here. So I got in touch with him, and through him, plus the International Red Cross, I managed to get some important telephone calls through.

Oh, if they had only listened to me! True, I did not know it was coming so soon. I thought we had another year's leeway, or I would have made Liesel and the baby go with me right now. But there is no use in such thoughts.

My German friend assures me that they will be released in a short time. I have put a large sum of money at his disposal and that can't help but hasten things, the world being what it is. Meanwhile, I am making arrangements with the Cuban visa office to have Liesel's parents go to Cuba, where they can wait in peace and comfort for my father-in-law's turn to be reached on the Polish quota for the United States.

I shall write to you again, probably by next week, as soon as I hear more.

Respectfully,
Theodor Stern

7.

Marigny-sur-Oise, August 14, 1938

Dear Monsieur and Madame Friedman,

You don't know me, but I am a friend of the family of Dr. Theodor Stern, and so I believe indirectly of your family's, too. Dr. Stern has been living with my wife and me for the last three months. We had been acquainted with his father many years ago. Last April we met him again in Paris, where we tried to be of some service to him with regard to his wife, child and parents . . . but, tragically, we were able to do nothing.

I understand that when you last heard about your relatives they were in the concentration camp Dachau. Dr. Stern had moved heaven and earth to obtain their release, but it is heartbreaking to say that he was unsuccessful. All of them, the entire family, has gone to its death, some there and some in other camps to which they, and many thousands with them, had been transferred. The only detail we know is that the baby died of pneumonia a few days after their arrest. As for the others, one doesn't want the details.

Dr. Stern was taken very ill at the news. I personally had been concerned about him even earlier, as he had had no rest, hardly slept, was unable to eat, ran around Paris like a madman calling upon every source of possible help. When the news came he collapsed, quite understandably. It was then that we took him to our country house, a quiet place, where we obtained an excellent doctor, and have tried to do the best for him.

He seems somewhat recovered now. He eats a little and is calm, but very quiet. He asked me to write this letter for him, and I thought it was a good suggestion, rather than have him put all this into writing, freshening it all in his mind again, as it were.

Yesterday he told us that he had decided to go to England where he spent such happy years at the university. He plans to offer his services to the British army and be ready for the war which he is certain will come soon. I am to tell you that he will write to you again, since he feels you are a link with the wife he lost.

> Be assured of my very kind regards,
> Jacques-Louis Villaret

8.

Mexico City, August 23, 1938

Dear Joseph and Anna,

It is a long time since I have written to you, and you must be wondering what happened to us. So I write to tell you, and hope that you will let our brother Eduard and his family know where we are. Give them our address and please send me theirs. I suppose they must have left Vienna, but as Eduard has always had so much influence in high places I am sure they are all right, and thank God for that.

As for us, well, it has been quite a change, as you can imagine. We would have preferred coming to the United States, not only for the sake of the country itself, but because it would have been good to live near you. Family is everything; what else can you count on in this world? I would so like to be with you, to break bread together every Friday night, but it can't be helped.

Still we are doing all right for a beginning and we can't complain, especially when we read about what is happening in Europe. It doesn't bear thinking about, and I could wet this page with my tears if I were to go on thinking about it.

Mexico City is very grand. The mansions along the avenues are more grand than anything in Vienna! We arrived last February having left in great haste and it was very odd to be in such a springlike place at that time of the year! We have rented a quite decent little house, built around a small courtyard, the way they build houses here. Dena has planted flowers. Everything grows in this sunshine. And the old man—I forgot to tell you the old man is with us, ninety-three years old, and still keen in the head—the old man sits outside moving from the sun to the shade, and he actually enjoys it here, I think. At first he didn't want to come, you know, but of course we wouldn't leave him behind, so we forced him and he stood the voyage very well. You would be surprised.

I have got a job as a furrier with a fine firm. The fur business is good, in spite of the mild climate. There are many rich people here and they are very fashionable. Tillie, our younger daughter-in-law, is a first-class seamstress and has also got a good position with a dressmaking establishment, copying Paris models. Saul is a watchmaker and he has a job too, while Leo is still looking, but I am sure he will find something. Our younger ones, all five of them, have started school and have learned Spanish so well in these few months that we take them with us for shopping or business. For Dena and me it is much harder to learn a new language. After all, we are over forty, and this is the second time in our lives that we have come as immigrants and strangers to a new country and a new language. But we shall manage. Even the old man has learned a few words. You would laugh to hear him!

Our plans are to save as much as we can and then in a few years my sons-in-law—and by that time my sons will also be old enough—we shall open some sort of import-export business together. I think it will be much easier to get ahead here than it was in Vienna. There seems to be room for newcomers here as there wasn't over there. Anyway, thanks be to God, we are at peace here. We rest easily at night, all of us together, and what else matters when you come down to it?

We hope you are all well, and now that you know where we are let us hear from you often.

Your loving brother,
Daniel

P.S. I had no idea North America was so big. I was about to say come and visit us, when I looked at a map and saw that New York is thousands of miles from Mexico City. Still, perhaps you will come anyway?

❈{25}❈

On a blowy, bleak morning early in November the telephone rang. When Anna answered it, she heard an unmistakable voice.

"Anna? I'm here. I got off the ship last night."

"Paul?" she questioned in disbelief.

"Right after your card arrived I caught the *Queen Mary* over. I don't know what I can do for you, or whether anyone can do anything. But I had to come."

Ah, yes! A month or more ago, on a very hard day and in one of those hours that come long after a great grief, and are worse to live through than the first hour was, in such an hour, driven after long silence by some unexplained impulse, she had sent a card to Paul. "Maury is dead," she had written, and nothing more: no signature, no date, only a cry from the heart. She had mailed it to London and afterward been sorry that she had.

"Anna? Are you there?"

"I'm here. I can't believe you've come all this way—"

"Well, I have. And I'm taking no chances this time with broken appointments. I'm downstairs across the avenue with a car. So put your coat on and come."

Trembling and agitated, she ran a comb through her hair, found a purse and hat and gloves. All these years! Three or four times a year their brief messages had gone back and forth: "Iris graduated third in the class"; "Leaving for Zurich on business, back in six weeks." She had grown used to thinking that this was all the contact they would ever have. Now here he was.

He was waiting beside the car. When he took her cold hands in his, it was without greeting, without a word. How thin he had grown! Thin and grave, Anna thought as she stood there, letting him search her with his eyes. When they were in the little car together she repeated, "I can't believe you've come all this way."

"Can you tell me what happened, Anna? Do you want to talk about it?"

Very simply, she told him. "It was an accident in a car. His wife was killed, too. Last March."

"Last March? Why have you waited so long to tell me?"

She made a little gesture of resignation.

Paul mourned, "I know what Maury meant to you."

"He left a little boy, two years old. But we don't see him."

"Why not?"

"There's been a sort of feud. His other grandparents have him."

Paul said softly, "It's a good thing you're very, very strong."

"I? I feel so weak, you can't imagine."

"You're one of the strongest people I've ever known!"

He put the car into gear and it began to roll down the avenue.

"Let's ride around a little. Do you want to tell me any more? Or would you rather not?"

"There isn't any more to tell. That's it, the whole of it."

"Yes, it speaks for itself."

"But it is good to see you, Paul. It's been six years since that day in Riverside Park."

"Seven in the spring," he corrected. "It was the third of April."

The car turned eastward through Central Park, emerging on Fifth Avenue where General Sherman still rode his proud horse to victory. The first time she had seen that statue she had been a greenhorn, fresh from Miss Mary Thorne's class. The city had sparkled like diamond dust, city of a million secrets: secrets between the covers of books and behind the doors of great stone houses. A rich city it had been, rich with music and flowers; the world itself had opened before young eyes like a great curled, closed flower.

"We went to the Plaza for tea," Anna said, thinking aloud.

"Yes, and you didn't want to accept the hat I had bought for you." He smiled.

"I wonder whether it's a good thing or not that we can't look ahead to see what's going to happen."

"A bad thing," Paul answered promptly. "If we could see we'd do a lot differently."

"Not if what is to be is ordained anyway."

"Ah, metaphysics! You know, it seems forever since I've been in New York! London is a magnificent old lady, but New York is a young girl preparing for a dance. Look there, Anna! To ride down Fifth Avenue! Isn't it splendid?"

She knew he was trying to coax her into a lighter mood, but she answered anyway, "Only when you've got nothing on your mind and something in your pocket, I think."

"How are things in that area?"

"Better, although we're being terribly frugal. Joseph is putting every cent he can find into land. When the Depression ends prices will soar, he says."

"He's right. They will. Tell me, do you have to be home at any special time today?"

"I have the whole day. Joseph's not coming home to dinner and Iris is going to study at a friend's house."

"Then you can spend the day with me. I want to hear about Iris. I want to talk about everything. Do you like the seashore in the winter?"

"I've never seen it then."

"Ah, it's beautiful! Just gulls and silence! Even the noise of the ocean is another kind of silence, I always think."

He turned the car toward the tunnel. "We'll drive to the Island. I've a little place there, which has been rented out the last few years. But it's vacant this time of year, of course. We'll walk on the beach and it will do you good."

The highway was almost empty. They sped easily through villages and past sere fields.

"You wanted to hear about Iris. She's a fine student, doing very well at Hunter."

"What about boys? Is she enjoying life?"

"Not really. She's so timid, so self-conscious. She thinks she isn't pretty."

"And isn't she?"

"I've a picture here in my wallet. You can decide for yourself."

Paul drew to the side of the road. For a few minutes he studied the photograph. While he was doing that Anna studied him, his keen profile, his somber eyes. What feelings must be stirring in him now at sight of this young woman who belonged to him and whom he did not know?

At last he spoke. "No, she isn't pretty, is she? But she has a distinctive face. I've seen the same face on young Roman noblewomen whom people call beautiful only because they're aristocrats and haughty."

"Iris is far from haughty. It would be better for her if she could be, just a trifle." Aristocrats. Joseph used to call her his queen when she was a child. Anna sighed.

"She looks more like my mother than anyone," Paul continued.

"Yes, but your mother had style and confidence. I haven't given them to Iris."

"Maybe confidence is something that can't be given, Anna."

"I think it can. But—I've never been at ease with her. I told you that once."

"What does—he think?"

"Ah, Joseph thinks the sun rises and sets in Iris! He can't see that there's anything lacking at all. If ever a man adored a daughter—" She stopped abruptly.

Paul started the car again and they drove on through wider fields and more scattered villages into a calm countryside.

"I wish I could see her," he said. "A part of myself is alive, walking through the world with thoughts and feelings perhaps like my own—and I don't know her." And when Anna made no comment he went on, "When you walked away, that day I learned the truth about her, I sat there on the bench until dark. I had no strength at all. I remember trying to sort my feelings out, what I was supposed to feel and what I actually did feel."

"And have you sorted them out?"

"No, not even now. What can a man feel about a—a biological accident? Can I love her, when I've only seen her once for five minutes?" he asked bitterly. "And still, when I think what a miracle it is that she is made out of you and me, I do love her. . . . Oh, Anna! I've dreamed so of a message from you! 'I've changed my mind,' it will say. But it never comes."

"Please," Anna whispered.

He glanced at her. "All right, no more. You've had enough to think about. I want this to be a day without problems for you, and no pressure."

They stopped on the single street of a tidy village: saltbox houses under maples, a white board church and belfry, bow-front shop windows displaying books, tweeds and imported foods.

"Pleasant, isn't it?" Paul remarked. "An artificial enclave in a sooty world, very privileged, very unreal. And, to be honest, I enjoy it. At least, for a couple of months in the summer, I do."

There were few cars or people on the street. Obviously the village was three-quarters asleep and would not wake up again until Memorial Day.

"Come, we'll get ourselves something to eat before we go out to the place."

The food shop shone like a jeweler's. Paul took a wicker hamper, filled it with quick decisiveness and carried it to the counter.

"You've enough there for six people!" Anna protested, for he had bought cold meats and cheese, crackers, cake, fruit, tinned artichokes, a little jar of caviar, a bottle of wine and a long French bread.

"You'll eat. My guess is that you haven't been eating very well."

"That's true," she admitted. "I haven't been hungry."

"This air will make you hungry, I promise."

From the end of the street a blacktop road led past comfortable houses and, between clumps of woods, quick glimpses of the slate-colored sea. Then came a dirt lane; brittle, brown mulleins and milkweed stalks stood tall on either side of it. The car bumped along for a quarter of a mile before Paul stopped.

"Here we are," he said.

A little house of weathered boards shone silver in the vast light from the ocean that crashed only a few yards from its front door. A low fence, to which still clung dead sticks of last summer's roses, kept the wild marsh grass from intruding on the yard.

"How lovely!" Anna cried. "It must be very, very old!"

"No, although this part of the island was settled in the seventeenth century and there are some genuine survivors left. But this is just a skillful copy."

"Oh, lovely," Anna repeated.

It was spare and simple, with rag rugs on a polished floor, a cavernous, blackened fireplace, country furniture and not too much of it. Dried flowers stood in a brass bucket on the mantel.

Paul ran a finger over the mantel. "Clean," he announced. "I've got a tiptop caretaker. Wait, I'll get more heat up in a minute." He flipped the thermostat switch and a low rumble rose immediately from the cellar.

"We're well equipped. It can be chilly out here in late August. Come, let's go walking till the house warms up. You'll want to wrap the scarf around your head because the wind's fierce on the beach."

The tide was coming in. It raced up the hard sand to its appointed mark and raced out again. It boomed and thundered at the breakwater, where clouds and mists of spray obscured the view that elsewhere lay clear to the gray horizon. Every few minutes a listless sun slid behind the clouds and as quickly slid back. The wind tore savagely at Anna's scarf. It drowned their voices so that they had to shout at one another to be heard, and so they walked together without speaking. A tern plummeted into the sea for a fish, its forked tail tipping toward the sky as its head went under water. Herring gulls cried their wild cries. In the marsh at the end of the beach, wood ducks, black ducks and pintails quacked and scuttled as Anna and Paul drew near.

There was no one in sight. At the far end of the marsh Paul stretched his arm toward the point where, past acres of sedge, a rambling wooden structure faced the sea.

"The inn," he shouted. "Great seafood! One of the best vacation hotels in the world!"

Joseph would scorn a place like that—old, ramshackle and remote. Why did she always think of what Joseph would think? Even now?

Back at the cottage they rubbed their hands in the welcome warmth. "But we need a fire for extra," Paul said.

In a few minutes he had got one started. From newspaper to kindling wood to a great cedar log the flame spread, fluttering, swaying, stretching its filaments of orange, of scarlet and white-gold. Anna watched while Paul fanned and poked.

"I'm entranced," she said slowly. "I feel as if I'd traveled a thousand miles since this morning!"

Paul rose from his knees and straightened up. "This place suits you, Anna. Or, better yet, I see you in some Elizabethan country house, coming down the steps to the garden." He made a sweeping, intentionally romantic gesture. "Or else in a white Spanish villa with a red-tiled floor and a fountain in the courtyard. I don't see you in an apartment house on New York's West Side."

"Nevertheless," she said quietly, "that's where I live."

"Well, you oughtn't to! When I first knew you I used to think, 'There's a woman for whom beautiful things were meant to be, diamonds and—' "

"I had a diamond, a huge one. I never wanted it. Joseph had to pawn it. I told him to sell it but he wouldn't; he plans to get it back with the first money he can spare, he says. I don't know why it should matter so much to him that I wear a diamond," she mused.

"But I do know," Paul said harshly. He frowned. Then his voice turned gentle. "Let's move the little table nearer the fire and have some lunch."

"You see," he exclaimed a while later, when Anna had emptied her plate, "the air did give you an appetite!" She admitted that it had and he added, "You've lost a lot of weight, haven't you?"

"I guess so. I haven't really been paying attention. But you're thinner, too."

"I'm working very hard," he answered briefly.

He lit a cigarette, making much of the small ritual and prolonging it. Anna sensed that his thoughts had for the moment left the room where they were. Then he shook his head, as though he were trying to rid himself of some troubling reflection, and spoke again.

"About Iris—you must see that she learns something practical, not just humanities, some Latin, some madrigals and a course in nineteenth-century drama."

"You sound almost scornful!"

"Not at all. Those are all fascinating subjects. But one must also be prepared to earn a livelihood in the world."

"Joseph will take care of her," Anna replied defensively.

"That's not what I mean. There's also the question of self-respect. It's bad to have to take from others all your life, especially if you think as little of yourself to begin with as you say Iris does."

Anna hadn't thought of it that way. One expected a girl to get married; every girl, any girl. Moreover, it struck her that she hadn't given very much thought to Iris anyway during these past few years of Maury's troubles and death.

"I do see," she said now. "Yes, you're right. Well, she's taking some education courses, so she will be able to teach."

"Ah, well, that's all right, then."

She was not accustomed to having a man take charge like this, analyzing and planning. Joseph had never—yes, yes, she corrected herself, for Maury he had! Maury's homework, Maury's religious school—she recalled the battles over the latter—and Maury's law school which he hadn't entered, all had been part of his father's ambition for him. But for Iris there had been nothing of the sort, nothing but a cherishing, blind, protective love.

Paul had risen to clear the things away. When Anna moved to help, he waved her back. "No, today you're my guest. Sit there."

But she stood up to walk restlessly about the room, and stopped before a dusky antique mirror between the windows. Something in her own posture now reminded her of the woman in that painting which Paul had sent: the same thin face; the head top-heavy with dark red hair, its wind-blown wisps loose on the long neck; the quietude which could be read either as tranquillity or melancholy, as one chose.

When Paul was ready they sat down on the rug before the fire. They glanced at each other and then quickly looked away, as strangers do who have just been introduced and are then left alone together.

Anna searched for a way to break the sudden silence between them.

"And are you going to stay, now that you're home?"

"No, I shall be in London until the war comes, and it's going to come soon, you can count on that. Then I'll have to get out."

She was puzzled. "But your business, your bank is here."

"I'm not on bank business there."

She understood that she was to ask no more and waited. He poked at the fire, unnecessarily, for a fountain of sparks gushed up. Some fell on the rug. He beat them out, then looked at Anna.

"Oh, why shouldn't I tell you? It's this: I have been making trips into Germany to rescue some of our people from the concentration camps and prisons. First we raise funds, and then we make contacts. For money, you see, these Nazi thugs will do anything. The trouble is, there isn't enough money to save more than a very few here and there, the lucky ones whom we happen to hear about."

"That's what you meant when you said you were working hard?"

"Yes. I'll tell you something: it tears the heart out of you. When you know that what you're doing is only a drop in the bucket, and when you see some of the survivors—I met a man at the French border who had been released. One eye was gone and every tooth in his mouth had been knocked out. A professor of bacteriology he was, or had been. What's left of him will never be fit to do his work again."

Anna considered. "You yourself go into Germany? But that's dreadfully dangerous, isn't it?"

"I won't say it isn't. I'm an American citizen and that's a great protection, but also I'm a Jew, so one never knows. People can disappear there swiftly and secretly. The American embassy wouldn't be able to prove a thing."

"Where will it all end, in heaven's name?"

"Perhaps heaven knows. I surely don't. But we have to try. We're also working in Palestine. The British are trying to keep us out but it will be the only haven for many and so there's a giant's work to be done there, too. Only that—I'm sorry—that I cannot talk about."

"I have a very general idea of what may be going on. I know that Joseph sent a check last week, money he couldn't spare, but he sent it anyway. . . . Paul, don't get killed there."

He smiled. "I shall certainly try not to. But someone has to do the dangerous jobs, and a man like myself who has no family to care for, has plenty of money and is young enough to have the energy—such a man has an obligation," he concluded simply.

Anna's eyes filled with tears and she turned her head away. But he had seen. "Anna, what is it?"

"You'll think, you'll think I have nothing but troubles! It's almost unreal, the things that have happened in my family . . ."

"Tell me, what is it?"

"My brother in Vienna. He and his wife and children, all of them died in Dachau." She put her head in her hands.

Paul stroked her hair. "You've had too much. My God, it isn't fair."

The hollow of his shoulder was so firm, the wool rough on her cheek as she murmured, "Like sleepwalkers we are, walking the edge of a cliff. I've been so frightened since we lost Maury. I keep thinking, although I try so much to be reasonable, still I keep thinking: What terrible thing is going to happen next?"

"It's all thrown dice, my darling Anna. The odds are that you've had everything thrown at once, and after this there'll be no more."

Turning her face, he kissed away a few tears on her lashes, kissed her wet cheeks, found her mouth and held to it.

It was warmth and balm; his strength was comfort and ease. With a little cry, she clasped him closer and the grieving soreness ebbed from her chest. After a while she lay back in the firelight as, with quick and gentle purpose, he drew off her dress. For a moment she was aware of her own hand stretched toward the blaze, its fingers curled, translucent in the brightness. She saw his luminous eyes before closing her own. Then she was not aware of anything at all but hunger and demanding need, a clamor for pure assuagement and a wish to prolong the marvel forever. . . .

A long, sweet time later came a fine calm while his arms still held her and, finally, the soft flow of sleep.

Paul sat on the floor beside her, anxiously scanning her face. "I was afraid you would be conscience-stricken again."

She blinked. "No, strangely enough."

"Then what were you thinking of before you opened your eyes?"

"I just woke up."

"You've been awake for a minute or two. Your eyelids were moving."

So sharp he was! You could never hide anything from this man. "All right. I was remembering how I used to think of that other time, and wonder whether it had really been like that or whether I had only been imagining it."

"And had you?"

"No. It really was—is—like that."

He laughed. "Good! Good!"

The sight of his triumphant pleasure brought a smile to Anna's lips, and then a laugh. It was the first time she had laughed in months. Yet the sorrow was still there, she knew, and it would surge again when this hour was past and gone.

As if he were able to read her mind, Paul said, "I want to tell you a story I once heard. There was a woman whose child had died, in some especially tragic way. When they came home from the hospital, or maybe it was the funeral, the husband wanted to make love to her. And she was outraged, so he felt terribly guilty and they couldn't understand each other at all. What do you think about that?"

"Oh," Anna said, "he wanted comfort, he needed love! And she didn't see that? Because when you're all alone, when you're dying inside, loving like this brings you back from the grave. It is the most alive thing you can do. Yes, yes, I do understand."

"I think you understand everything," Paul told her.

When they were dressed they came back to the fire. The log was burning down, and the afternoon outside was darkening. Paul turned the radio on.

"Tell me," he began, "if you can be like this when you and I are together, how can you be happy with anyone but me? I'm not speaking of these last tragic months. I'm excluding those."

Anna considered and answered slowly. "What is being 'happy'? I have peace, warmth and order. I am busy, I am loved."

"I know I said in the car that I wanted no grave talk today and that I wouldn't press you for anything but—marry me, Anna."

She shook her head. "I'm tied, Paul. Don't you see? I think of Maury and one day, perhaps, his little boy—"

He interrupted. "You can't live for what is gone or for a hope that may never come true! And don't you owe yourself anything *now*?"

"I do owe myself something, that's just it. I couldn't cut myself away from my family and live."

"But how can you weigh anything—anything at all—against this afternoon? You don't think I'm *fond* of Marian? But I am! She's a fine person and I would do anything to keep her from harm. Yet we could part as friends, with decent feelings. Knowing that she was well and would never lack care, I could put her out of my mind. And she would do the same with me."

"But I—I should be thinking of Joseph every day of my life!"

Paul sighed. It was a grieving sound from deep inside. "I hope he knows what he has."

"He does. He loves me. He believes in me."

The fire crackled as it burned out; music sang tenderly from the radio. And Anna cried out in pain, "Paul, tell me, how is it possible to care so much for two different men in such different ways? Is there something wrong with me?"

"You've just said it yourself. 'In such different ways,' you said. Here, put your head back on my shoulder."

So they sat until the light left the sky. The fire was a sprinkling of sparks in ash. The music, having risen to a passionate finale, came to a stop.

"I'm going back tomorrow," Paul said quietly.

She sat up straight. "Not tomorrow? But why?"

"The *Mary* returns at midnight. I only came to see you, Anna. I have to get back."

"All this way to see me? That was the only reason?"

"Reason? It wasn't a thing I reasoned out. It was something I had to do." And, standing up, he gave her his hands to pull her to her feet. "Come, Anna, my Anna. It's time to go."

Today was mine, she thought, alone in the silent apartment, for neither Joseph nor Iris had yet come home. It was for me. I know I am rationalizing, finding a pardon for what I have been taught is wrong. And inasmuch as deceit is always wrong, it was wrong. But we are flesh, and it was inevitable. We are acted upon far more than we act.

The door will close with a hollow thud when Joseph comes in. He is coughing again. Very likely he will have the flu for the third time this year; he strains himself; he works far too hard; I tell him to stop it and I don't want him to strive; it was good to have things but there's nothing I want at the price that he is willing to pay. Yet I can't stop him.

Iris is earnest, prolix and troubled. There's nothing I can do to make her what young girls are supposed to be: genial and rosy with dreams. Yes, I was such a young girl, rosy with dreams, but perhaps I was foolish. Anyway, I can't change Iris.

Things happen. Things are. I am I, torn in two directions. Shall I ever see Paul again? I believe that I shall, but I can't really know. Tomorrow night he will set out across the ocean, into a thousand dangers. He will wait, he says, for the message that I have changed my mind. It will not come, Paul. It will not come.

But I shall not forget today. The other time I scrubbed myself in the bathtub; now I cherish the feel of your flesh on mine. I was young that other time and the world was either black to me or it was white: a simple view, with nothing in between. Now I know it is not like that, although Joseph always says it is. Perhaps Joseph is right? But if he is, I can't help that either. Today was mine.

I have hurt no one. I shall hurt no one.

"Oh Maury! Iris, Joseph—" she said aloud.

The front door opened with a key and Iris let herself in. "You're still reading? Is Papa home yet?"

As always, she asked for Papa.

"No, he'll be late tonight." Anna got up and crossed the room. "Iris," she said, pushing the girl's hair back and kissing her forehead.

"Mama, what is it? Is anything wrong?"

"No, no. It's only that you mean so very much to me, my darling."

Iris was startled, perhaps embarrassed. "Well, but I'm all right, Mama."

"Nothing must ever happen to you. Nothing, do you hear?"

"But nothing will! Go to bed, Mama! Take a book and you'll fall asleep reading. Go on, do."

Sleep. Yes, sleep, if it comes, if it wants to come. One cannot command that, either. Sleep comes and peace comes with it, if it wants to. The thoughts roll in, pour in: Iris, Joseph, Maury. And Eric. And Paul. They surge, they beat, they crowd like waves of the vast ocean and peace doesn't want to come.

❧{26}❧

One day the mood stirred again—her "cleaning fits," Joseph called them—and ever since the mood had come over her Anna began to work on closets and shelves, rooting in drawers that had been untouched for the last few years.

The lower drawer of the desk in the hall was stuffed with papers: postcards from friends in Florida, receipted bills, letters, wedding invitations. One was from a name she didn't even recognize, out of the years when people gave lavish entertainment to other people whom they hardly knew. Throw those out. Here was a pile of letters from Dan in Mexico: most of the people were Indians, he wrote; their monuments were marvelous, they still spoke their ancient languages. It would be a wonderful thing to see all that, to see Dan again, but they couldn't possibly afford it. Here were letters from Iris, the summer they had gone to Europe: "Dear Daddy and Mommy, When are you coming home?" Here was the wedding announcement from Eli in Vienna: "Elisabeth Theresa to Dr. Theodor Stern"; the pointed Gothic letters were like the peaked and medieval roofs of middle Europe. And these letters, this paper on which their hands had rested, was all that remained, the only trace of people swallowed up? She ran her fingers over the engraving—and put the card back into the drawer. Here next was a letter from Maury at Yale; shall she open it, shall she read it? No, some other day perhaps, and she put it too back into the drawer, knowing that there would never be another day when it would be easier to sift through any of these things.

After Maury had died, in that long wet spring of dirty snow when it seemed the sun would never come to comfort, that spring when the letters from Vienna had arrived—she remembered them lying white on the diningroom table where they were first opened, a summons to doom, a cry of horror, an accusation so terrible that it seemed the pages must burn the hand—all that spring she had walked and walked, back and forth, and ended always in what had been Maury's room. There she had gone into every corner looking for something that would tell her why. She had found one sneaker, a high school text of *Julius Caesar* with Maury's name in a flourish of bright green ink and a doodle of a fat man smoking a pipe, his teacher perhaps. The crumpled banner, *For God, for Country and for Yale,* had been there too, along with a Red Cross swimming card award for one hundred yards' back crawl or trudgen crawl; what was a trudgen crawl? She had found all these, but no answer, and had longed for work, hard work, carrying bricks or stones, something to break her nails, to tear her skin and to exhaust her.

They didn't talk about Maury anymore. On his birthday Joseph didn't say a word. Perhaps he didn't remember; he wasn't very good at remembering dates, but perhaps he did; with Joseph you could never tell. For a long time after Maury died it had seemed that Joseph was strengthened by his faith and Anna had wished she might feel whatever it was that made him able to say, and actually appear to mean, that we must praise God even in our suffering. "That's what the Kaddish is," he said, "a prayer of praise to God, and that's why we use it in time of death." And he tried to explain, seriously and at length, how we must pray that someday it will be given us to know why we suffer. "Surely there is a reason for it, as there is for everything," he said, and if she had not known him to be a man without hypocrisy and a totally honest person she would have scoffed.

Joseph believed in sin and retribution. But what was Maury's sin to deserve such punishment? Or the sin of the child who had lost his parents? Yes, she thought, if I believed in retribution I would have lost my mind by now. Because then all of it would be my punishment, for what I did.

She had read too much about primitive religion, too much Freud and his search for the father figure—or, to be exact, too many articles about them—not to have diluted her earliest faith. So now she could not truthfully say of herself: *I am a believing person,* nor yet, *I don't believe at all.* She was, rather, a person who wanted to believe and often did, but that was a very different thing from what Joseph was.

Yet how much had he hidden, did he perhaps still hide, from her? She remembered a night, weeks or months after it happened, when, lying in bed, she had stared at the white oblong of sky through the window; they were so high up there was not even the comfort of trees, and she remembered the trees of her childhood in the attic room where you looked out upon warm, dusty leaves, and in the windy seasons twigs scratched on the windowpanes. Here in this city you were in limbo, hung between earth and the cold enormous sky. Strange how she noticed such things after Maury's death; she had not thought of them before, but when you had sleepless hours the tags and remnants that slipped in and out of your head were astonishing. Lying there like that, she had felt something in the wide bed, then knew that what she had felt was a shaking cry and, putting out her hand, touched Joseph's face wet with tears. She had said nothing and only held him, and made no sound. Nor had he.

They never spoke of it afterward. Nor did Anna tell of her recurrent dream, always the same dream. She was walking into a room, known or unknown; there was a window, with a large wing chair at an angle so that she could see the crossed legs of a man sitting in it, but not his face. She came nearer, and when the man turned she could see he was very young. He began to rise in greeting and she saw that he was Maury. "Hello, Mother," he said. The same dream over and over.

The gilded clock chimed in the bedroom; it still stood on Joseph's dresser. How perverse that, of all the gifts and gadgets which had come to them in their prosperous years, it should be just that clock which appealed to him the most!

Not that its presence bothered Anna anymore; with or without it, she knew what she knew and felt the weight which had been placed upon her. She felt a stinging behind her eyes, and watched in the mirror as a swollen tear, slick as glycerine, filled one eye and slid over. How ugly we are when we weep! The grimace of sorrow, the spotted red skin stretched over the animal skull! And when we see how ugly we are the tears come faster.

The house was so still. Iris would be home soon; she must have been delayed after school. She had gone to work two years ago at her first job, teaching fourth grade. Jobs were easy to find because all the young men were in the army. Iris was a fine teacher; she would do anything well, for she had Joseph's commitment to hard work. It was good for her to be earning her own money and to clothe herself, not that she cared very much about clothes. Too bad that in just these years of her youth the men were all gone! If only she were a little older or even a few years younger, for surely the war would be over soon. But she was just in the middle years, twenty-three, and there were so few men left at home. There was one odd small fellow who taught in her school, a reject of the army and, not to be unkind, of much else besides. He was the only man who had ever called Iris more than two or three times. Friends gave names of men stationed in the area; Ruth's daughters invited her to meet men, but they rarely called back. Ruth's daughters! With all they had gone through, none of them as bright as Iris, and not all that much better looking, either, all of them were married. Often Anna met them at their mother's, wearing the harried look of overworked motherhood, which is a mask for their satisfaction and their pride. But whatever it was that they had and Iris lacked, she wasn't suddenly going to acquire it now.

Who will care for her? Who will love her? She's not all that lovable. Sometimes I want to put my hand out to her but she will only shrink from my touch. She always does. There is no enmity between us, never a word, now that she is a woman; still, I know, as one knows such things, that she doesn't want me to touch her. Ruth says she is jealous of me; I wish Ruth hadn't said it. Sometimes Ruth says things that are too intimate and I am not prepared for them. Yet perhaps it is true; can it be true?

Jealous of me. And Anna put her hands to her heated face.

Days go by sometimes when I don't think of it and then suddenly it strikes me. Like the times when Joseph says, so lovingly, "I think she looks like me, don't you think so, Anna? She certainly isn't like you." No, and not like Joseph, either. Those eyes, the nose, the long chin— He and his mother, all over again. Only without their poise and pride, poor little soul! Almost as if she knew she was born wrong. My fault. My fault.

If I had these thoughts every day I think I'd go mad. But time, as they always say, is merciful and so it has been. One finds a way to favor a wound, to spare a crippled leg. Just once in a while comes a misstep and a cruel thrust.

Last week at the picture gallery (Joseph doesn't really like exhibits, but he goes to please me, and besides, they're one of the few recreations that don't cost anything), I said, unthinkingly, "Goodness! I've seen that one lots of times before!" And Joseph said, "You couldn't have. It says this is the first time it's ever been on loan." And then I knew. The walled and fruited garden, trees spread flat against the wall, a woman in a white dress, reading. ("Take it to your room, Anna, books are meant to be used.") A book on a table, in a room in a house that I can't forget.

Four years it is since I saw him. There's been no word; no more cards go between us, since the only one he wants is one that will offer him what I can't give. So it is better this way.

The key turned in the front door. "Ma?" Iris called.

"In here, in my room," Anna called back cheerfully. It wasn't good for the girl to see that she was in a "mood." And she took an armful of clothes on hangers and laid them on the bed.

"What are you doing?" Iris stood tall and anxious in the doorway.

The dark brown dress with the white collar made her neck look elongated. The dress was stern and clerical.

"Cleaning out closets. Look at these, they must be fourteen years old, above the knees! And here they are back again. If you keep things long enough they'll be new again," Anna said, prattling, feeling a need in Iris to be met with unemotional, trivial words. The world is good, it's not all that frightening and everything is manageable, such prattle said.

"Where's Pa?"

"He'll be late. He and Malone went to Long Island to look at some more property. Their potato farms."

"He works too hard. He's not that young anymore," Iris said darkly.

"It's what he wants to do."

"I won't be having dinner. Carol's invited me to her house."

"Oh, nice. Is it a party?"

"No. We're just going to the movies together."

"Oh, nice." That was the second time she had said that and it sounded stupid. "Are you going to change?"

"No. What's wrong with this dress?"

"Nothing. I just asked."

"Then I'll be going. I think I'll walk, I want some air. What are you smiling at?"

"Was I? I was just thinking, you do have a lovely voice. It's a pleasure to hear you talk."

"You're funny," Iris said. "Your daughter's twenty-three years old and you're just noticing her voice." But she was pleased.

Really, her face was attractive when she was pleased about something. It was a fine, intelligent, gentle face. Yet something to which other human beings are drawn was missing. There are children in the kindergarten who stand aside while the others fight and play. Why? What is missing? Whatever it is, one learns early that it isn't there. Wanting it, trying and wanting so much, one develops a timid posture, smiles too eagerly, talks too much out of a fear that silence is boring and dull. It *is* boring and dull.

Oh, my children, my fairy-tale children who were never born, grouped around me, their mother, smiling in some eternal sunshine! I can't do anything for you, Iris; I couldn't for Maury, or for Eric, either.

A gust of wind struck like a stone against the window and Anna got up to draw the curtains shut. The pane was cold as ice. You could almost feel the cold upon the river and the streets below. She thought: It's colder where Eric is. I should hate it; I like to be warm. But perhaps he will grow up loving it. In a flash she saw him in sweaters and knitted caps, on a sled or on skis. She saw all of that, but not his face, which she did not know.

"Please don't send any more gifts," they had written. "It will soon be too hard to explain."

"I don't give a damn," Joseph said.

He wouldn't know now what love went with the yellow wagon and the stuffed cat, but later, when he was grown, he would remember these things for the joy they had given and, by then, he would know who had sent them. When he was old enough to read they would send books and the giving of books would tell him something about them, what sort of people they were.

"I have to stop this," Anna said aloud. "It's been going on all day, a wasted, useless day. I have no right to waste a day. There is nothing I can change."

She went into the bathroom and brushed her hair. Thank goodness it was still dark red. People said she looked years younger than her age. Anyway, the forties weren't old these days. Her hair made an oval frame about her face. She wondered how different her life might have been without her beautiful hair; perhaps no one would have noticed her! The speculation made her smile, appealing to some fortunate dash of irony or humor which was, she knew, the only thing that saved her from her own romanticism.

Then she went into the kitchen and made a cup of tea and some toast with jelly. She sat there stirring the sugar in the cup; the click of the spoon was a homely, reassuring sound in the silence. Tomorrow was Red Cross day again. Perhaps a troopship would be sailing. They never knew until the last minute, when they were summoned to the docks to stand while the young men filed past toward the gangplank, pausing for their cup of coffee and their doughnut. The last time it had been the *Queen Mary* going out, stripped and darkened for her race across the Atlantic. She remembered that young man on the dock; when Anna handed the cups she rarely looked at their faces, and this was partly out of haste but also because she didn't want to look at them, knowing where they were going. This time, though, she had looked up and been so startled to see Maury's face, even the separation between the two front teeth, and the eyebrows rising in an inverted "V" to give the face a faintly wistful gaze. She had held the cup an instant in the air between them, and then he had taken it. "Thank you, ma'am," he'd said in flat Texas speech, and turned away.

Enough! She got up and emptied the rest of the tea into the sink, took an apple and a book, went into the living room and turned on all the lamps. She was sitting there with the apple core and the book in hand when Joseph came home with Malone.

"Let me fix you a drink," Joseph said to Malone.

"Just a quick one. Mary's waiting up for me." He sat down heavily and as quickly jumped up. "I've got Joseph's chair."

"Goodness, no. Sit wherever you want."

A good man. Going quite gray, looking much older than Joseph, although he wasn't that much older.

"You seem especially thoughtful, Anna."

"Do I? I was remembering the first time I saw you, up on the Heights. Joseph brought you in, carrying your plumber's tools. You were going into business together."

"I remember the day."

"And the war was just ended. It felt more like a war then, I was thinking, with all the songs and parades. This time it seems like just suffering and getting it over with. We've learned more, I guess."

Malone said, "My boys are in places I never heard of. I looked some up on the map, took me ten minutes to find them."

I know that my son is dead and I've learned to live with the knowledge; I've had to. But Malone is tortured every day: are my sons still alive this morning and will they be alive by tonight? "How's Mary?"

Malone shrugged. "Worried, as everyone is. One thing's good, though: Mavis is taking her vows in June. That's something Mary prayed for, and thank God it's one thing that's come true."

"I'm happy for her," Anna said truthfully. Mary Malone had been praying that one of her daughters would enter a convent and at least one son become a priest. So half of her prayer had been answered, and for that Anna was glad, although for the life of her she would never understand it.

Joseph came back with the drink. "You know what I was thinking on the ride home? I was reminded of when we started out together, Malone. We had nothing but energy and hope, and it's not a hell of a lot different now."

Malone sighed. "Except we've learned a few things in between." He raised the glass. "This drink's to us! If we don't make it this time—"

Anna asked, "What do you mean?"

"Didn't he tell you? We bought the land, three hundred acres of potato farms."

"I always thought you were joking about the potato farms."

"No joke," Joseph explained. "There's no building going on now, but after the war there'll be ten years or more to make up for. You remember, when the Bronx River Parkway opened in 1925, how they started building houses, how the towns spread out? It'll be the same after the war, only more so, because the population's bigger. And the prices will soar. That's why we're taking every penny—and I mean penny—we can lay our hands on. . . . After this I've got my eye on a farm in Westchester. I want you to go out with me on Friday, Malone." His words snapped briskly, his alert eyes snapped and he looked six feet tall. "Listen to me," he went on, "there's going to be a whole new way of life. People are going to move out of the cities. There'll be a big demand for low apartment buildings with green space between them. There'll be a need for shops. People won't want to go into the city to the stores, so we'll bring the stores to them. I predict that every one of the major New York department stores will have suburban branches within ten years after the war."

"You talk as if the war were going to be over tomorrow," Anna said. "We've got a long way to go yet, it seems to me."

"True. But I want to be ready. We'll have something for your boys to do when they come home," Joseph said, turning to Malone with a smile.

The men stood up and went to the door. "Give my love to Mary. I'll let you know what time Friday."

Anna put out the lights and they went to the bedroom. "The salt of the earth," Joseph said.

"There's something sad about him, I always think."

"Sad? I don't know. Of course he's got a lot on his mind and always has. It's no cinch to raise seven children."

"I suppose not."

"Still," Joseph said, drawing off his shoes, "still, I wouldn't have minded having that many. I think I could have managed."

"You would have. Sometimes I believe you could manage anything."

"You mean that? That's the nicest thing you could have told me. A man likes to think his wife has faith in him. And I'll confess, Anna. Lately I feel young again! I feel I'm going to accomplish big things, to put us on top of the world."

She had a vague, floating sensation, hard to define. It was almost a fear, a fear of challenge, of conflict and tension. She thought of the breathless rush of their first ascent, how hard he had worked, and all of it came to nothing. She wanted to say, We've had enough of that, let us live quietly in a small way, with no more large undertakings, no more feelers put out into a cutthroat world. And she said, not knowing how else to express all of that, "Joseph, we don't need to be on top of the world. There's nothing the matter with the way we are right now."

"Come on! Nothing the matter? We've lived this meager existence for almost thirteen years! We haven't been any farther than Asbury Park! I want to move out and up. Some day, not too far off, I want to own a house with ground around it. I've got a head full of plans for us."

"A house? Now, at our age? It's not as if we had a family to rear. What would we do with a house?"

"Live in it! And what do you mean by 'our age'? Look at yourself! You're a young woman still."

"Are you really serious about the house?"

"Not now, not yet, but as soon as I can."

"Iris wouldn't want to leave the city."

"Iris will come, and if she doesn't, she has her own life to live. Anyway, she'll probably be married in a few years."

"I don't think so. I worry about her so much; I don't always tell you."

"I know how you worry. But you can't be all mother forever."

"You're a fine one to talk! You don't worry?"

He laughed ruefully. "You're right. We're a pair of worriers. I suppose we're no different from other parents. No, I'll correct that. Everybody isn't like us and maybe they're right, and we're wrong. People owe something to themselves, not just to their children."

From her dressing table she could see him in the mirror. He had laid the newspaper down and was sitting up in bed, watching her.

"I like your new hair style," he said.

Since the war began people had started to wear their hair high over the forehead in a pompadour, then flowing softly over the ears. Her mother had worn it that way. More and more Anna saw her mother in herself, or, at least, what she thought she remembered of her mother.

"I didn't think you'd notice," she said.

"Do I neglect you so much, Anna? I don't mean to."

She laid the brush down, a monogrammed silver brush from a long-ago birthday. "You don't neglect me."

"I don't want to," Joseph said seriously. "You're the heart of my life, though I don't say it well."

She looked away, down at the pattern of the carpet: three whorls of rose against beige, a spiral, a moss-green leaf, three whorls of rose.

"I'm very glad," she answered, "since you are the heart of mine."

"Am I? I hope so. Because I know I wasn't when we were married."

"You shouldn't say that!"

"Why not? It's true," he said gently. "It doesn't matter now, but don't deny it. Everything must be open and honest between us, always."

"I was a very young, very ignorant girl who didn't know a thing about life! Nothing at all, don't you understand?" Tears prickled and she wiped them roughly away. "Don't you understand?" she repeated.

"Now that we're talking about it, I'm not sure I do understand everything. I've felt—I feel—there are things I still don't know about you."

Fear that was almost panic washed through Anna. "Why? What can you possibly not know?"

He hesitated. "Well, as long as we're talking, I'll tell you. Do you know when I was really beside myself?"

"I can't imagine," she lied.

"It was the time when Paul Werner sent you that picture, the one that was supposed to look like you. I tried not to let you see it but I was pretty frantic inside."

"But that was—that was years ago! And I thought we had talked it all out and settled it then!"

"I know we did, and I suppose it's foolish of me to let it stay in my head. But I can't seem to help it."

"It's a pity to make yourself miserable for nothing," Anna said softly.

"You're absolutely right. But tell me just once again, and don't be angry: did you love him? I won't ask whether he was in love with you, because it's obvious that he was, and besides, I don't mind that. I only want to know whether you loved him. Did you? Anna?"

She took a deep breath. "I never loved him." (I went through agonies of longing, and often I still do. But that's not the same, is it? *Is it?*)

I wonder what it would be like for me now if I were married to Paul. Would I feel that he needed me the way Joseph does? Does perfection—and it was perfection—would it, can it, last?

Joseph was smiling. "I believe what you tell me, Anna."

"You won't bring it up again? It's really finished and over?"

"Finished and over."

She thought, if only I could feel sure of that, Joseph! What I would give not to have hurt you! You've become so dear to me, you couldn't know. And it's strange, because we are such different people. We don't even like or want the same things most of the time. Yet if it were necessary, I would die for you.

So, is that love? Love is only a word, after all, like any other word. If you repeat it a few times you take the life out of it. Tree. Table. Stone. Love.

"Anna, darling, put out the light and come to bed."

Her bathrobe dropped to the chair with a swish of silk. The wind struck again, shivering the windowpane. Feeling her way in the dark across the room, her thoughts flew as they had been flying all that day.

We are driven by random winds, blown and crushed under passing wheels, or lifted to a garden in the sun. And for no reason at all, that anyone can see.

BOOK THREE

MEADOWS

❖{27}❖

Gramp had a blue Chrysler with a top that could be rolled down in fine
weather, and usually was, even on such a cold, bright April day as this. He was a
believer in fresh air as a medicament for everything. The car had been specially
fitted for his almost powerless legs; the clutch worked by hand when the gears
were shifted. They kept the car back of the house in what for past generations had
been the barn and stables. When Gramp went out on his crutches, he reminded
Eric of a crab, the way his legs jerked, the way he veered to swing himself up onto
the front seat. When he was seated there with his cap on and his pipe in his
mouth he looked like anybody else; you couldn't tell he was crippled. Maybe
that's why he liked to go driving so much.

"Okay, young fella," he said, "be sure the door's closed; put the button down."
He reached to fit the key into the ignition and suddenly stopped. From the clump
of trees between the barn and the lake came a sweet whistle: *"Pee-wee! Pee-wee!"*

Gramp put his finger to his lips. "Shsshsh . . . know what that is? That's a
wood pee-wee. Close cousin to the eastern phoebe."

"What does it look like?"

"Gray, like the phoebe, except for two white bars on the wings."

"Pee-wee! Pee-wee!"

"Could I see it if I got out now?"

"You probably could if you went in under the trees there verrr-y quietly and
sat down and didn't move, not even a finger. I wonder whether you could learn
to use my binoculars? I don't know why not. Maybe tomorrow I'll show you how.
They're on the second shelf of my cabinet in the library, next to my bird books."

The car slid into gear and down the driveway, turned through the gate posts
and on down the road past his friend Teddy's. Next came Dr. Shane's big yellow
house, then the Timminses' and the Whitelys' who kept saddle horses on their
long fields. The car slid into the main street of Brewerstown.

"We need gas," Gramp said. "Reach me the ration book in the glove compartment, Eric, please."

The gas station man was stooping under a car. When he saw them he straightened up, wiping black, oily hands on a rag.

"Afternoon, Mr. Martin. Fill her up?"

"If you please, Jerry. I'm being extravagant today. It's Eric's birthday and we're going for a ride."

"Is that a fact? Happy birthday! You must be nine, or is it ten?"

"Seven," Eric said, very pleased.

"Seven! You're mighty big for seven!"

"Tell me, what do you hear from Jerry junior?" Gramp inquired.

"He'll be finished with basic training at Fort Jackson next week. I guess he'll be going over soon after that."

Gramp didn't answer. There was no sound but the whir of the pump; then it shut off, and they waited while Gramp handed over the ration book and some bills. Jerry tore out the stamps and handed the book back soberly.

"Well, good luck," Gramp said softly. "Remember me to Jerry junior. Tell him I expect him back. We all do, soon."

"Thanks. I will."

Gramp started the car again and they rolled down Main Street to the lake road.

"Where we going, Gramp?"

"I'm doing a will for Oscar Thorgerson. You know the big farm on the other side of Peconic? I thought I'd run over with some notes to see how he likes them. Then I can draw it up officially. It'll save him a trip in ploughing time and it gives you and me an excuse for an outing." He smiled down sidewise at Eric.

The road ran beside a strip of groves and summer cottages, still boarded up. There were glimpses of the lake between the trees. Then the road curved away from the lake, mounted a ridge of hills and straightened, dividing a wide valley with farms and fields on either side. The wind made a rushing noise like a waterfall in Eric's ears. A man was ploughing an enormous field; ahead of him it was dry tan with stubble of last year's corn; behind him it was dark and wet like melting chocolate. The great horses trudged steadily uphill.

"It's been years since I've seen horses pulling a plough," Gramp said.

"Why? How else can you do it?"

"With tractors. But now there's a war on and no gas, so the horses are out again. Say, look at that!"

A flock of birds soared and slid and whirled across the sky.

"Swallows," Gramp said. "Oh, birding has been one of the great pleasures of my life! I've sighted birds that people wait years to see. And when we lived in France I had to learn a whole new vocabulary, not just the names, but new kinds of birds that we don't have here. I remember the first time I heard and then saw a nightingale. It was a delight, a pure delight."

"Say something in French, please, Gramp."

"*Je te souhaite une bonne anniversaire.*"

"What does that mean?"

"I wish you a happy birthday."

"It sounds pretty."

"French is a beautiful language. It's like music."

"Can you say anything you want to say in French?"

"Oh, yes. Although I'm not as proficient as I was when we lived there. You need to use a language or it slips away from you."

"I'd like to go to France. Are the trees and houses and everything the same as they are here?"

"Well, yes, and then again, no. I mean, trees are trees and houses are houses, aren't they? But there are differences. Someday you'll go and see."

"Will you go with me?"

"I'm afraid not, Eric. It would be too hard for me to travel with these crutches."

"Then I won't go either. I'll stay with you."

His grandfather took one hand off the wheel and covered Eric's hand with it. "You'll go and see things. I want you to. And I'll wait for you to come back. I'll be here waiting." He withdrew his hand. "I was going to surprise you, but I can't keep a secret. Gran and I have a surprise for your birthday. It's a present that you can't have until the middle of the summer. Around the Fourth of July, I should think. Oh, don't look disappointed! We've got other things for you that you'll get at your birthday dinner tonight. But this big present that you have to wait for— can you guess what it is?"

Eric frowned. "No, I can't. What is it?"

"Something you've been wanting very much. Something you've been asking for."

A smile started somewhere in the back of Eric's throat and then bubbled up to his eyes and lips. "A dog? A puppy? Is it, Gramp, a dog? Really?"

"Yes siree, a dog. And I mean a dog of dogs. A prince. A great big Labrador retriever like Dr. Shane's."

Eric bounced on the seat. "Oh, where is it? Where are you going to buy it? Can I see it now?"

"That's one of the reasons I took you along. Mr. Thorgerson's lady dog is going to have puppies any day now. The reason you have to wait is that it'll be too tiny and young to take away from its mother for a while. But as soon as it can eat by itself out of a dish we'll come and get it."

"Oh, Gramp, oh, Gramp, I want a boy dog! I want to name him George."

"That's settled then. George."

A long lane led off the road between fences. The house was attached to the barn, making an "L" with the barns and sheds. Chickens scratched under the wet and scattered straw. Gramp stopped the car. A moment later Mr. Thorgerson, in rubber boots up to his hips, came around the corner.

"Seen you coming up the lane. Been fixing my pump and got myself soaked," he said. "How you, Mr. Martin? How you, young man?"

"Fine, thank you, Mr. Thorgerson."

"I've brought these papers for you to look over," Gramp said. "You and your wife can think about them for a few days, and then if you're sure this is what you want, then give me a call. I'll have it drawn up properly and you can sign."

"Good enough. Let me go into the house and wipe my hands 'fore I dirty them up." He leaned over and whispered something in Gramp's ear.

"Is that so?" Gramp looked pleased. "Well, I'll tell you, I wasn't able to keep the secret. I told Eric on the way over so he knows all about it. What do you think, Eric! Lady had her puppies this morning, and if you'll be very quiet and not disturb her Mr. Thorgerson will take you in and let you look."

The mother lay with her puppies on a soft pile of blankets in a corner of the kitchen. Stretched in a panel of sunshine they made a black fur tangle like a rug. The puppies, not much larger than mice, Eric thought, mewed and wriggled one over the other.

"They're just starting to get hungry," Mrs. Thorgerson whispered. She stood looking over Eric's shoulder. "She's going to be a good mother, she's so gentle. I've been working here in the kitchen all morning and she never minds a bit when I step near."

"She knows you won't hurt her puppies," Eric said wisely.

"Which one do you want?" Mr. Thorgerson asked.

"I can't tell. They all look alike."

"He's right, Oscar. You'll have to come back in a couple of weeks when they're a little older and then you'll pick the one you want."

I'll put out my hand, Eric thought, that's what I'll do. And the one that crawls toward it, if he's a boy, is the one I'll take because I'll know he likes me. And I'll bring him home and he'll sleep in a basket in my room, maybe even on my bed. And we'll be friends and I'll be so good to him. Maybe that one?

They all laughed. One of the puppies, all tiny, wet, blind things, but this one a bit stronger than the rest perhaps, rolled over and, with a piping squeal, shouldered another one out of its place at the mother's nipple.

"Would you like a jelly doughnut?" Mrs. Thorgerson asked.

"Yes, please, I mean thank you, I would."

"They're still warm. . . . Does your grandmother allow you to?"

"Oh, yes! Sometimes I go to Tom's Bakery in town after school. But Gran says they're greasy. She doesn't like me to have them, only if they're homemade."

"Well, these are certainly homemade," Mrs. Thorgerson said. "Here, sit down and have a glass of milk while Mr. Thorgerson goes outside and talks to your grandfather."

The kitchen smelled pleasantly of sugar and hot baking. There were plants on the windowsill next to the table where he was given his milk and two doughnuts on a white plate. It was nice to eat in the kitchen, handy to the icebox and the stove, more comfortable than their dining room at home, where you had to be careful not to spill anything on the carpet or on the shiny wood table. You had to keep everything on the place mat with its lace border and the mat was so small. But at home only Mrs. Mather, the housekeeper, ate in the kitchen.

Mrs. Thorgerson stood looking down at him. "Was that good?"

"Very good, thank you." It was good, but still he liked the ones at Tom's Bakery better, to tell the truth. Only he didn't tell the truth, of course.

"It's a long time since my boys were home to eat at this table," Mrs. Thorgerson said, sighing a little.

They went out to the car. Mr. Thorgerson was leaning against the fence talking to Gramp. "He'll ruin the country. Something for nothing, these loafers want. Mark my words, this young fellow here will pay for it. All the generations that come after us will be left with the bills."

"Roosevelt again!" his wife said. "You raise your blood pressure, harping on that man. I swear you do, every time."

"Me too, then, Mrs. Thorgerson," Gramp said. "Any man who's worked hard and knows the value of a dollar can't help but feel disgusted with things. Time he got out anyway, war or no war, before he ruins the country. We've had ten years of him and that's ten years too many. Let me see, is that jelly on your face? Here's a handkerchief." He took a white handkerchief from his breast pocket. He was so clean, Gramp was, even a little jelly bothered him.

"He had jelly doughnuts," Mrs. Thorgerson said.

"Well, that was nice, wasn't it, Eric? Doughnuts and a new puppy. What a day!"

"Gramp," Eric asked, when they were out on the road, "what did you mean when you said Roosevelt was going to sroon the country?"

"Sroon?" Gramp looked puzzled. "You mean ruin! That means to spoil."

"Oh. Why is he going to?"

"Well, that's a bit hard for you to understand. It's just that we don't agree with the way he manages things. We think another man would do a better job."

"What other man?"

"Almost any other man, I should say."

"Do you hate him? I think Mr. Thorgerson hates him. He was awfully angry."

"Not hate. We have to respect him because he is the President. But we think he desecrates the office. Do you understand? Desecrating is like—well, it's like having no respect, wearing your hat or laughing out loud in church. Something like that. Do you see what I mean?"

Eric nodded, and thought of the familiar face in the newspaper, with the cigarette tilted upward out of the side of the mouth.

Gramp said seriously, "It's a wonderful thing to be an American, Eric. It's a kind of sacred trust, do you know what I am trying to say? It's having something you love very much that was given to you by your family and you must take the best care of it so that you can hand it over to your children unspoiled.

"Ours is a very old family, Eric. Our people came here when the English king still owned this land, when Indians camped here. This road that we're on was one of their trails to what now is called Canada. They came here when it was all forest, hundreds and hundreds of miles of trees." He swept an arm out. "All you could see here was dark trees. And they cut the trees and cleared fields, built cabins, planted crops. It was hard, hard work, much harder and more dangerous than anything you can think of that anybody does today."

"Did the Indians kill any of them? With tomahawks?"

"I'm sure they did. There's plenty in the history books about that. There were forts all through this state. Fort Stanwyx, Fort Niagara. Forts are where the people went for safety when the Indians attacked."

"But there aren't any Indians now."

"No, that was a long time ago. After a while everything was calm here and people made beautiful big farms like Mr. Thorgerson's. Our own family were all farming people, except here and there a son went into some profession. I had an ancestor, let me see now, he would be your great-great—no, your great-great-granduncle, he was one of the engineers who worked on the Erie Canal. I remember hearing from my grandfather about that uncle. He was present on the day, November 4, 1825, when Governor De Witt Clinton poured a keg of Lake Erie water into the Atlantic Ocean. The canal joined the waters of the lake with the ocean, you see. A great piece of work, that was. And we had soldiers, of course; we've had men in all the country's wars. And schoolteachers and lawyers."

"That's what you are! A lawyer!" Eric cried triumphantly.

"Yes, I'm a lawyer and I've always been proud of my profession. But I never forget that my origins were in the soil, on the land, the basis of everything. My origins and your grandmother's too. Her family is as old as mine."

Eric remembered something. "Is that her father in the picture? The one over the mantel in her room?"

"No, no, child, that's her grandfather. Your great-great-grandfather. He fought in the Civil War." Abruptly, Gramp swung the car around. "We're only a couple of miles from Cyprus. I want to show you something there."

The car rode lightly along a level stretch of road between apple orchards, faintly white. "Cyprus is the county seat. That's where the courthouse is and the Civil War monument. They've a statue there put up to honor the men from this area who fought in the Civil War. And they've written on it the names of the ones who were killed in the war. You'll see that man's name there."

"Whose name?"

"The man in the picture in your grandmother's room," Gramp said patiently.

The courthouse stood back on a stretch of lawn. A walk with rows of stiff red flowers, tulips, Eric knew, ran to the front where a kind of porch was held up by plump white wooden columns. On one side of the lawn stood a tall flagpole. The flag made a snapping noise in the wind. On the other side, in the center of a concrete circle, was a statue of a crouching soldier wearing a kind of square cap; he was pointing a gun, and the pedestal on which he was placed had names cut in the stone on all four sides.

"Walk over there," Gramp said. "The names go by the alphabet. You can find the 'Bs,' can't you? Then look for a long name, it's almost at the top of the 'Bs.' Bellingham. Go look. It's too hard for me to get out of the car."

Eric walked over, found the "Bs" without any trouble and was proud that he could read the names. The first one was Banks. Then came Bean. That was funny, because you could also spell it without the "A." Some of the kids in his class got mixed up by things like that, but letters never bothered him. They were easy. Here it was: Bellingham. He stood there a minute looking at it, and at the way the shadow of the soldier's stone arm fell right in the middle of the Belling—. Then came a comma, and another name: Luke. He knew that it was like his prayer that Gran said: "Matthew, Mark, Luke and John, bless the bed that I lie on."

He ran back to the car. "I found it! I found it! It says Luke Bellingham, right near the top."

"Good. I knew you could. Be sure to put the lock down, that's it. Yes, that was your Gran's grandfather," he said, as they turned around the square back to the road they had come on. "He was at the second Battle of Bull Run, Antietam and many more. That's when Abraham Lincoln was the President."

"Did he deserate like Roosevelt? Lincoln, I mean?"

Gramp laughed. "Desecrate? I should say not! He was one of the greatest men in the world, Eric. When you are a little older I shall tell you about him, and give you some books about him. Anyway, now you've seen the name of your ancestor cut in stone. Gran's name was Bellingham, you know, before she married me."

"And your name is Martin."

"That's right."

Eric considered a minute. There was a question he had on his tongue. Then he asked it. "Why isn't my name Martin, too? Why is my name Freeman?"

"Because. Because people take their father's names."

"Why do they?"

"Because that's the law. That's the way it is."

"Who makes the laws?"

"A lot of men are chosen to think up the laws for us. They sit and talk about things and then vote to decide. They're called the legislature."

But he didn't really want to know about that. "Did the legislature decide what my name had to be?" he persisted. Something nagged at him. He didn't know exactly why he felt that something was a secret.

"Not just your name. Everybody's."

Eric thought there was a change in Gramp's voice. Was he cross about anything? But no, he looked at Eric and smiled and said with his teeth locked around the stem of his pipe, "I'm going to put some music on the radio. There's a program that goes on at four."

Piano music was plucked out of the air. They were riding along on the smooth road and above their heads the leaves were starting to come out, unraveling small sheaves of yellowish-green. Piano music tinkled through the leaves.

Freeman. His father's name was Maurice Freeman. He had asked Gran once, "Was my father French, Gran?"

"No, he wasn't French." And her mouth closed in the straight line it made whenever he asked for something he knew he wasn't going to get, like permission to sleep overnight in the woods, or a third piece of pie. *No, you may not.* Her mouth would shut in a straight line like a dresser drawer closing tightly into its frame. *Snap. Click.*

"I thought the name sounded French. Because of Gramp's friend in France that he always tells about. His name was Maurice, too."

"He wasn't French."

"What was he, then?"

"Why, American, of course. American."

"Oh. Can I see a picture of him?"

"You could if I had one."

"Why haven't you got one?"

"I don't know why I haven't. I just haven't, that's all. Oh, Eric, now I have to go back and count my stitches again, you've got me so mixed up." She was always knitting sweaters for him like the navy blue one he was wearing today. He didn't like her sweaters. They itched. The back of his neck itched now, thinking of it.

He had been very stubborn that day. "If you haven't got a picture, tell me what he looked like."

"I don't remember what he looked like. I only saw him once."

He had been about to ask, "Why?" But he opened his mouth and closed it again. In some way he knew that she would not have an answer for him. There was a blankness there, an end, like being closed in someplace and trying to get out, or being shut out and trying to get in. You might try and try but there was no way. He felt that with no particular emotion, only a kind of puzzlement.

Now his mother was different. Pictures of her were everywhere, photographs in silver frames on desks and dressers, and a painting over the piano, wearing a short white dress and a ribbon bow on her head. She was in leather albums, snapped on the deck of an ocean liner with a life preserver in back: *S. S. Leviathan,* it said. "That was the year we went to live in France," his grandparents told him, bending over into the lamp light on the library table, turning the pages, going too slowly and boring him with things he didn't care about. "That's the place we took in Provence one summer. See, those are olive trees, and there in the background, see those terraces? That's how they grow grapes. Your mother acquired a Provençal accent that summer; she already spoke French like a native, anyway."

He liked the picture of her as a baby, maybe two years old, sitting on the front step with a big white collie. There above her head was the brass knocker with the head of a lion. He went outside and, when nobody was looking, sat down in the same spot under the knocker and rubbed his palms over the stone step, this very step where she had sat, his mother; and felt that maybe some of her was still there on the stone; and felt not sad, not regretful, but only curious.

He could barely remember when he had first known that his position and his life were not like the other children's whom he knew. Somebody, Gran? Gramp? Mrs. Mather, the housekeeper? Somebody had told him his parents were dead. He was an Orphan. That was wrong, though. In fairy tales like *The Little Match Girl* and *Cinderella* an Orphan was a sad person. An Orphan was hungry and had to sleep in doorways. How did you sleep in doorways? Where did you stretch your legs and wouldn't people trip over you, going in and out?

But he, Eric, had a house and a big room in it with a fireplace and a bed with a quilt that had animals printed on it, and a shelf of books, and a cupboard where he kept his Erector set and Lincoln Logs and his big dump truck and hook-and-ladder. And he had plenty to eat. They were always making him eat when he wasn't hungry. *You must finish that good hot cereal before you go to school.* So how could he be an Orphan?

Because of the Accident, that was why. Something had happened in a car far away, in New York City. The car got smashed and after that he didn't have any father and mother. He had come here to live with Gran and Gramp. After the Accident. He saw it like that, in big letters. Like the letters on the monument: Luke Bellingham.

"Well, here we are," Gramp said, switching off the radio. "Hand me my crutches from the back seat, will you please, Eric?"

His grandmother came out of the house to help Gramp in. "Why, I was worried about you, it's almost five o'clock and Teddy's here waiting for you."

"Oh, we had a fine time. Eric saw his new puppy that got born this morning, and we had a beautiful drive. I see you're all dressed up."

She had on a white silk blouse and her gold-and-pearl brooch. "Of course, it's Eric's birthday."

"Look what you've got!" Teddy shouted as soon as they came into the hall. "Look what you've got!"

An enormous carton lay on its side and half in, half out, was a bright red perfect car. It was big enough to sit in and pedal. It had headlights and a brass horn and bucket seats like a racing car.

Eric's heart stopped. "For me. You bought this for me."

"I didn't, silly!" Teddy said. "My present's still wrapped up in the dining room with your others."

"It's from Macy's in New York," Gran said. She turned to Gramp. "I thought it was those folding chairs you ordered, so I opened it."

"Couldn't you have—?"

"Teddy was with me. We opened it together and then it was too late."

"I see," Gramp said. "Well, you'll enjoy the car, I'm sure. Better go up and wash your hands and change. We'll be having dinner soon."

"I'll go home and put on my suit," Teddy said. "My mother says I have to wear my good suit because it's Eric's birthday."

"Yes, of course. Be back at six, Teddy," Gran said.

Eric shook his head. "I can't believe it."

"What can't you believe?" his grandmother asked.

"The puppy George and this car, all in one day."

"Ah, but you haven't seen everything yet!" Gran said gaily. "Go on up, dear, will you?"

His suit and clean underwear had been laid out on the bed. His Sunday shoes stood under the bed. He was so happy, so excited! The dog, the red car with the headlights from Macy in New York! He didn't know Macy but it surely was nice of him to send a present like that. *"Wheeeeeee,"* he said and turned a somersault on the rug near the bathroom, and then another and another, four of them before he reached the farther wall with a thump. He wondered where he would keep the car. In the garage, perhaps? He wanted to find out right now.

His grandparents' adjoining rooms were at the end of the hall. He could barely hear them talking. It was a very quiet house. "Don't ever call from one room to another," his grandmother always said. "If it's important enough to tell me, it's important enough for you to walk where I am."

He went down the hall. They were talking quietly in Gramp's room. Suddenly his grandmother's voice grew louder and he heard her say, "But I couldn't secrete it! How could I when Teddy was there? He would have told Eric. I'm sorry, James. It couldn't be helped."

"I thought they had agreed that it was for the child's own good that there be no contact. It's too confusing, too unsettling! They agreed, didn't they? So why don't they keep their agreement?"

"Well, they have kept it, really. I suppose they feel that a gift isn't—oh, I don't know, they must feel some need to give something."

"Awfully ostentatious! It must have cost a hundred dollars."

"I'm sure it must. Well, I'll write an acknowledgment and let it go at that. But I do feel a little sorry for them, James."

"I have one concern, and that's for Eric," his grandfather said firmly.

"Well, of course."

There was a rustling, as of someone rising from a chair. Eric scurried back to his room.

Why were they annoyed with Macy for sending the car? That was funny. Such a beautiful car! Better than anything Teddy had. And that was good, because sometimes Teddy made him angry. "Don't you feel awful not having any father and mother?" he would say. Well, he didn't feel awful at all. He had everything he wanted, Gramp and Gran gave him everything he wanted and they loved him. And he didn't feel awful at all! He stuck out his tongue at an imaginary Teddy. You haven't got a car like this, Teddy! And you haven't got a dog like George, either!

But it was a funny thing about Macy. He remembered last winter he'd got a pair of skates from him and it wasn't even Christmas. Gramp had said something to Gran. He'd thought then that they weren't pleased about the skates, but afterward he'd forgotten about it. Anyway, he had the skates and now he had the car and it didn't matter really. Only, it was funny.

THERE WERE STEAK, fried onions and biscuits and all his favorite things. Teddy had given him a kite. Gran and Gramp had bought a sailboat that came up to his waist; he could sail it on the lake. Mrs. Mather had made a chocolate cake with white icing and seven candles. No, eight, because there had to be one to grow on. First she turned off the lights in the dining room. Then she brought it in with the candles flaring and everyone singing "Happy Birthday." Eric blew out the candles and cut the first slice.

"What did you wish?" Teddy wanted to know, but Gran said, "If you tell it won't come true," so he wouldn't tell. He really didn't know what he wished; there was nothing he wanted except that he knew he wanted it always to be now. Just the way everything was now.

"You must thank Mrs. Mather for the beautiful cake," Gran said. "Go into the kitchen after dinner and thank her."

So he went in to thank her and she bent down and kissed him. "Bless your heart," she said.

Then he and Teddy rode the red car. They took turns up and down the hall, while Gran and Gramp went to listen to Gabriel Heatter with the war news on the radio, the way they did every night. Every time Eric passed the door they looked up and smiled at him, his grandmother from the chair by the window where she sat with her shawl around her, for the house was chilly and they were saving heat. "A good citizen should," his grandfather said. He himself sat upright, intent on the news, in his own wing chair that smelled of leather-dressing, a clean sharp smell that was like Gramp's shaving lotion; his own smell that he always used, in the chair where he always sat.

Presently it was time for bed. Teddy's father came for him from across the road. And Eric went up to bed. Gran kissed him and folded the sheet around his shoulders.

"It was a lovely birthday, wasn't it?" she said, and turned out the light.

He lay there all warm and sort of floating away. It wasn't entirely dark yet. He could partly see the late spring evening past the window, and partly imagine the familiar landscape: the yard and the lawn, the hemlock grove, the thickets where you could be an Indian and the lake beyond. Peepers set up a sharp, sweet call, one note over and over. A bird, thinking perhaps that it was morning, whistled once and was still. Tomorrow he would find the phoebe and ride in the car, and sail the boat. He would have to get string, a terribly long, long string for the boat. Then he would eat up what was left of the birthday cake. Seven. Today I was seven. Sev—

The peepers throbbed.

❖{28}❖

Joseph and his reflection traveled down Madison Avenue together, going back to the office. Whenever he looked away from the afternoon press of taxis and buses, whenever a glass door swung open or a flame of opalescent sunlight struck a window, he saw a vigorous man in a gray suit walking fast, swinging his arms. He hadn't realized how high his arms swung.

He was in good shape. Didn't look his age. In the morning, after waking automatically at six, he did his calisthenics. He watched his diet, although not stringently: he didn't run to fat. Anna was envious; she would go for days on cottage cheese and salads to keep thin. A little weight wouldn't hurt her, he always said, and was told that his tastes were old-fashioned. Well, at fifty-five, why shouldn't they be?

Still, that wasn't old these days. It was hard to think that his father had been only two years older when he died, worn away, shuffling and bereft of will. That was the main thing, will. You got old when you lost it.

He ought to be, and he was, thankful down to the marrow that he hadn't lost his. He'd been able to build again from the ruins, or at least to make a promising start. It wasn't given to everyone to have a second chance. Poor Solly. Ruth was living now in three rooms that Joseph had let her have in that very first apartment house on the Heights, the one for which Anna had borrowed the money. That house, he admitted with amusement, was a foolish kind of talisman to him. He didn't suppose he'd ever sell it. Anyway, Ruth was living there. She paid a small rent. He would have given it to her for nothing, but she wouldn't accept that and he admired her refusal. He would have done the same if the circumstances had been reversed. God forbid.

Waiting at Fifty-sixth Street for the light to change, he was shocked into a reminder of sadness by a window that still displayed the black-bordered photograph of Roosevelt, dead two weeks. It was a personal grief, the death of this President. A solemn grief: the funeral train from Georgia, the slow march down Pennsylvania Avenue, the horse with stirrups reversed. Symbolism of the fallen warrior. A brave man. He felt he would miss that man, his fine confident voice on the radio.

Yet there were people who had hated him . . . and not the very rich alone, those who thought of him as a traitor to his class! Joseph knew a workman who

240

had lost twin sons in the war; he blamed Roosevelt, said we should never have gotten into the war. But that was nonsense; frantic, bitter, ranting. Understandable, but ranting all the same. Malone had lost a son-in-law, Irene's husband, killed at Iwo Jima, and now Irene had come back home with her two babies . . . not an easy thing for the Malones, what with teen-agers of their own still at home, but they never complained.

Irene's boy looked like Eric, or what they could remember of Eric when he was two. Joseph felt his mouth twist. Always that small involuntary twisting when certain things came to mind.

Don't think of them, then. Don't think of what can't be helped.

The light changed and the crowd poured across the street. Crowds looked different today from the ones you used to see in midtown New York. For one thing, they were larger. The city was so crowded that you couldn't get into a restaurant, couldn't get a hotel room. He'd had an architect come in from Pittsburgh last week and they'd had to put him up at home. People were jamming the shops; people who'd never had anything before the war were coming in to the fancy stores with cash to buy furs and pianos and diamond watches, never even asking the price of anything!

For me too, Joseph thought, and in a very limited way, it's been like the twenties all over. The land they had scrimped for during the late thirties—when Anna said they were crazy to go into real estate again—had doubled and tripled. They'd built three hundred houses for the workers at the Great Gulf Aviation plant on Long Island, just rolled them out in rows on the old potato fields and sold every one in eight weeks' time.

Then they had moved on and done it again.

Yes, like the twenties, except for a steadier caution. He'd never again feel as confident—and ignorant—as he had back then. He knew now what can happen.

Knew also what a terrible thing it is that there is so much wealth to be made out of human blood.

Still, that was the way of things. Now his desk and his head were full of plans again for undertakings they would start as soon as the war was over. They said it was only a matter of months. . . . Suburban shopping centers, he reflected; he ought to get to some of the big stores before anybody else did.

They had a good office now. Maroon carpet. Nice prints. Dignified, but not lavish. Anna would see to that. He smiled. She was always restraining him, Anna was, and she was probably right. Not that they could have afforded anything too rich anyway, the rent was so high. They were in a very good building, a prestigious address near Grand Central. Convenient for commuting, too, now that they'd got the house.

Let's see. Three months to the closing and a couple more to fix it up. They ought to be in by the end of September.

Anna hadn't wanted a house, but then, Anna never wanted very much of anything. She had her friends and her Friday afternoon concerts again, now that they had a few dollars to spare for things like that. She had her women's committees for half a dozen charities. And when she wasn't doing any of these, she read.

But he had been wanting a house for a long time. When the Malones bought a place in Larchmont a year ago he'd made up his mind. They had spent every fall and winter Sunday driving around Westchester. He reflected how perverse it is that when you haven't got a cent all you see are things you wish you could have; now that he had a good down payment and could afford something decent, they couldn't seem to find it. Maybe because they didn't really know what they were looking for? And then two weeks ago on one of those warm, windy days of April, they'd come upon this house and Anna had gone crazy over it.

He couldn't understand her. It was a big old place, probably in its eightieth year, with twelve—he'd counted in dismay and disbelief—twelve gables and three chimneys. It had a spiral staircase, a turret, six carved marble fireplaces, even in the bedrooms, and a porch fringed with wooden lace. Name of heaven! Even the young man from the real estate agency had looked doubtful. Not a very good salesman. Brand-new and inexperienced, to wear his doubts on his face!

"What style do you call this?" Joseph had demanded of him.

"Well, sir, they tell me it's an authentic type, Gothic Victorian. I'd have called it gingerbread, myself. This was the Lovejoy family home," he had explained. "One of the oldest families in the area." And, irrelevantly, "I'm not from here, I'm from Buffalo. But I'm told they once owned a couple of hundred acres. The last one of the Lovejoys has a house over there, over the rise; you can't see it unless you go upstairs and look out over the trees. He wants to sell this old place off with two acres."

Anna spoke for the first time as they climbed the stairs. "It's like something in a book. Feel the banister," she said.

The dark old wood was worn as sleek as silk; they'd had the best materials in those days. But all these angles, nooks and crannies!

"Look here!" Anna cried. "This round room in the turret! This could be the most wonderful office for you, Joseph. You could spread your maps and—come, look at the view!"

On the lawn below, the hyacinths—or so Anna said they were—had come into bloom, rising out of a bed of last year's wet leaves. "A south terrace! It would catch the sun way into the winter, Joseph. You could wrap up in a steamer rug, the way we did on the ship, remember, and read—"

He noted that the cement was crumbling and the bricks were rotted away.

". . . up there on the hillside, those are apple trees. When they bloom it will be all white. Imagine opening your eyes and seeing that, the very first thing in the morning!"

He followed her downstairs. The agent and Iris, who had come along this day, followed him. The kitchen was in sorry shape. There was an old black monster of a stove. The icebox was in the entry, an enormous brown, scarred relic. The cabinets were so high that a woman would need a ladder to reach them. But the cabinets would all have to be ripped out, anyway. Hell, the whole kitchen would have to be ripped out.

"See," Anna cried. "They've a separate room with its own sink: I do believe it's meant for a place to arrange flowers! Yes, it is! Here are some old vases left on the shelf. Imagine having a separate room for flowers!"

She was talking like a not-too-bright child instead of a woman fifty years old. He'd never seen her like this before.

"Any house can have a separate sink for flowers, Anna," he said irritably.

"Any house can, but none of them do," she answered.

"It's got a thousand things wrong with it," he burst out. Ordinarily he would have had more tact in front of the agent; he'd been harassed often enough himself in this business to know how it felt. And, wanting some support, some confirmation, he turned to Iris. "What do you think?" Certainly Iris would be more practical, more cool in judgment than her mother was.

"You know," Iris said, "it does have a lot of charm, in spite of its faults."

"Charm, charm. What kind of talk is that? You're not talking about a woman!"

"All right, if you want another word, it has *character*."

"Character! Oh, for God's sake! Now can you possibly tell me what you mean by that?"

Iris had been patient. "It's original. As if the people who built it had done a good deal of thinking about what they wanted, so that it pleased *them*. It had meaning for *them*. It wasn't just a house stamped out by the hundreds to sell in a particular price range but to please nobody in particular."

"Hmpp," Joseph said. He had never been able to win an argument with his daughter. Never wanted to, was more the truth.

Anna cried, "Oh, Joseph, I love it!"

The young man waited without comment. Inexperienced as he might be, he was clever enough to know when he was winning and not to spoil it.

Joseph walked off by himself. He walked around examining the outside, the shaggy shrubbery, and the garage where horses had been stabled. He went down into the cellar. The coal furnace hovered in the corner like a gorilla. The vastness and the darkness reminded him of a dungeon in one of those castles through which Anna had dragged him when they were in France. He climbed back upstairs into the light with relief.

The bathrooms would all have to be torn out and replaced. With these high ceilings it would take a lot of oil to heat the place. You could bet it wasn't insulated either. Heaven only knew what condition the plumbing was in! Probably corroded, and every time you ran the bath water or flushed a toilet the pipes would groan and shudder through the house.

But she loved it.

She never asked for things, he thought for the hundredth time. Never spent any real money except on books; her few extra dollars went to Brentano's. Sometimes on Fifty-seventh Street she would bring him to a halt in front of a gallery window and say, not complaining, just musing, "Now, if I were rich that's what I'd have," and she'd point to some picture of a child or a meadow. "If it costs anything within reason I'll get it for you," he'd tell her. And she'd smile and say, "That's a Boudin," or some such foreign name, French probably, since she loved anything French—"It's at least twenty-five thousand," she'd say.

She loved this house.

The roof was slate and in good condition. That at least would last forever. The house was probably cool in the summer too; the walls were a foot thick. They didn't build that way anymore, that was certain! Nice piece of land for the money too. Someday you could even sell that stretch up the hill where the orchard was and turn a fine profit. Land here was bound to soar, it was so near New York. Actually, it was worth the price for the land alone.

"Well, I'll think it over," he told the agent. "I'll call you in a couple of days."

"Very good," the young man said, adding predictably, "There's another couple very much interested. I think I really ought to tell you, not that I'm rushing you into a decision or anything. But they'll be making up their minds this week."

Naturally. Anna shouldn't have let him see her enthusiasm. A very poor way to do business.

"Well, I'll let you know," he'd repeated, and gone home and lain long awake thinking.

It did have a kind of elegance, something solid and real that belonged to another age. In a very small yet undeniable way it reminded him of those great stone houses on Fifth Avenue where he'd used to walk and gape and marvel at the beginning of the century. It would, he thought, it would make a setting for Iris. It was the kind of place that you saw in magazines, where old, distinguished families gave their daughters' weddings. Inherited wealth likes to be a little dowdy, out of fashion. He laughed at himself. Distinguished families! Inherited wealth! Still, perhaps it would do something for Iris, enhance her, put an aura about her that a West End Avenue apartment couldn't give?

His thoughts embarrassed him. They hurt him, too. As if his daughter were an item on sale! Yet, a girl needed to be married; who would take care of her through life, and when her father was gone?

There was something about Iris, his lovely, lovely girl. He'd tried to talk about her to Anna, but for some reason, Anna was never able to talk about Iris without such visible pain that he would drop the subject. She could talk more easily about Maury! He wished sometimes that he himself could speak openly to Iris but he couldn't do that, either. He couldn't ask: "What are you like when you're out with fellows? Do you smile, do you laugh a little?" Hah! Out with fellows! There was less and less of that every year. She was getting older: twenty-six. And the men were mostly away. He tried. That young widower he'd brought to dinner last winter. His wife had died of pneumonia. Might he not be looking for a fine, steady wife to mother his baby? But nothing had come of it.

So, maybe the house would make a difference.

He'd gone back three times to look at it that week, wavering toward the thought that he had really wanted something newer and more impressive, and back again to the fact that Anna loved it. In the end he had signed the contract of sale. It was like putting his name to a written blessing. Words like "dear home" and "peace" floated through his unashamedly sentimental head while he wrote his name.

He turned into his building and, waiting for the elevator, sought his name on the directory: Friedman-Malone, Real Estate and Construction. He put his shoulders back. Look forward.

"There've been a couple of calls," Miss Donnelly said. "I've put the messages on your desk. None of them urgent except one. A Mr. Lovejoy wants to see you this afternoon."

"I'm seeing the accountant at four. What Lovejoy? The man who owns the house? What does he want?"

"I've no idea. I told him you had a four o'clock appointment, but he said he'd come over at half past. He'd wait for you to see him at your convenience."

A GRAY-HAIRED, QUIET-VOICED, Brooks Brothers type. "I don't want to waste your time or my own, Mr. Friedman. We're both busy men. So I'll get to the point. I've come to ask you to withdraw your offer for the house."

"I don't understand."

"The agent made an unpardonable error. He was supposed to have given preference to another couple, very dear old friends of ours, as a matter of fact . . . He actually sold it right out from under them."

"I still don't understand. I gave my check and your agent signed the contract of sale."

"I've been in Caracas, just docked this noon and went home, but as soon as I learned what had happened I came right back to the city. I'd given the agent a power of attorney to sell the house, with the understanding that if my friends should decide they wanted it, it was to go to them, you see."

"Apparently they didn't want it, or he wouldn't have sold it to me, would he?"

"He was an inexperienced young fellow, substituting for his uncle who was in the hospital. I'm afraid he's been severely reprimanded for the mistake. I'm truly sorry."

Maybe this was an omen, a sign that the house was wrong for them. They could go out looking again, now that the weather was fine, and come up with something much more to his liking.

"I'm prepared to return your check with two thousand dollars' profit to you," Mr. Lovejoy said.

Joseph picked up his pen and tapped it on the blotter. Why should the man be so eager? There was something odd here. It was like feeling a presence in a dark room: you can't see it or hear it but you know something is there.

He fenced. "My wife likes the house."

"Ah, yes. These other people—the wife went to boarding school with my wife and it would mean a very great deal to them both if they could be neighbors."

Mr. Lovejoy leaned forward a little. There was a certain *pressure* in his voice and his eyes were anxious. His forehead was gathered into a small lump over each eye. For a moment Joseph had some fleeting thought of a criminal conspiracy: Mafia, perhaps, who needed the house? But that was absurd. This man was of a definite class, in banking, brokerage or shipping. Something like that. His dress, his face, his accent, all belonged in that category.

"You know how women are . . . old family friendship, going back for three or four generations . . . it would mean a very great deal to us, I assure you, if you'd withdraw. And I'm certain this very same agent could find you another house which you'd like as well or better. After all," he smiled deprecatingly, "the house is awfully old and quite run-down too, as you no doubt saw."

"Oh, I saw," Joseph said. "It's run-down, all right. But as I told you, my wife loves it." The man was pushing him, ever so delicately, but pushing all the same, and he didn't like it.

Mr. Lovejoy sighed. "Perhaps there are a few things you haven't considered. I mean, you don't really know the area very well . . . you're strangers to the town, aren't you?"

"We're strangers."

"Ah, yes. Well, then, you see, we're a very old community, very close knit. We even have an association on our side of town: the Stone Spring Association, you may have heard of it? It's a kind of improvement group and social club of people with mutual concerns: our gardens and tennis courts, maintenance of the road-side shade trees, protection of our general interests in the town. Things of that sort."

"Go on," Joseph said.

"You know how it is, when people have lived together most of their lives, their attachments are formed. It's very difficult for a newcomer to move in. Difficult for them and for the newcomer. . . . Just human nature, after all, isn't it?"

A flash bulb flared and went out in Joseph's head, illuminating everything.

"I see," he said. "I see what you've been trying to tell me. No Jews!"

A flush spread up from Mr. Lovejoy's collar; it was the pink of rare roast beef. "I wouldn't put it that way exactly, Mr. Friedman. We're not bigoted people. We don't hate anyone. But people *are* always more comfortable with their own kind."

It was a statement, but it had been presented like a question, as if the man expected Joseph to answer. He didn't answer.

"A good many people of your faith are buying over toward the Sound. They're even building a handsome new synagogue, I'm told. Actually, it's better over there, much breezier in the summer . . ."

"Usurping the better part of town, are they?"

Mr. Lovejoy ignored that. "The agent should have told you all this, as a service to you. He really did a very poor job."

"I wouldn't say so. I didn't ask him to do anything but show me the house, which he did, and take my money, which he did. As simple as that."

Mr. Lovejoy shook his head. "Not simple. There's a great deal more to buying a home than four walls. There's a whole neighborhood to be taken into consider-ation. All kinds of social events. People give parties—I should think you wouldn't want to live someplace and be left out."

The man is absolutely right. But to retreat now? It's unthinkable. For myself I don't give a damn. Whether he wants me there or he doesn't, it's all the same to me. I could do a lot better than that old heap of a house. In fact, some people will think I'm out of my mind to buy it, and me in the building business. . . . That stuff about people wanting to stay with their own kind: fine, I'm the first to say so myself. Except that it should be by choice, not by being told you must.

He said, "We don't expect you to invite us to your parties and we don't expect to invite you. We only want to live in the house. And that's what we intend to do."

"That's all you have to say?"

"All."

"I could take this to court, you know. It would be a long, complicated legal tangle and would cost us both a good deal of money and time."

He was thinking: She's never had anything except for those first few hectic years before the crash. A trip to Europe. A diamond ring which I had to pawn and only got back now. (I knew she didn't even want the ring, but I want her to have it; it's for me.) And a fur coat which she wore for fifteen years. He could see her creamy face above the rusty old fur which she had kept on wearing because they couldn't afford a new cloth coat. If she knew about this business today she wouldn't want the house. She'd make me back down. So she'll never know. I'll never let her know.

"Mr. Friedman, I don't want to wrangle this out in court. I'm too busy, and I'm sure you are too."

Yes, and it's too ugly to be brought out in the open, Joseph thought, still not speaking. He was very, very tired and angry with himself for being hurt. What, after all, was new or surprising about this conversation? He ought to have known better.

Mr. Lovejoy, too, was struggling with anger. His voice rose ever so slightly. "If you're not satisfied with two thousand we can talk it over."

Joseph looked up from his vision of faces: first Anna's, then Iris', even Maury's and lastly, strangely, Eric's: a face he could only imagine, which had been taken from him by just such a man, very likely, as this one: this thin man, gaunt almost, wearing the ascetic expression of some figure in an engraved historical tableau, wearing that and a blue silk foulard tie.

"I'm not to be bought off," he said softly. "I want the house."

Mr. Lovejoy rose and loomed above the desk. Joseph looked up at him. He was the tallest man he had ever seen.

"Is that your final word, then, Mr. Friedman?"

"It is."

Mr. Lovejoy walked to the door and turned back. "You ought to know," he said, "that in all my dealings with your people, all my life, I have found them baffling, difficult and stubborn. You're no exception."

"And for two thousand years in our dealings with your people we have found you the same, and worse." *I shall go home and tell Anna that the tension between us could have been cut with a knife. No, of course not; I shan't tell Anna anything at all.*

Mr. Lovejoy's hand was on the doorknob. Such cold eyes he had, gray as the North Atlantic in the winter: deep, deep, cold and gray. He bowed slightly, then turned and went out, shutting the door without sound behind him, as a gentleman should.

Joseph was still at his desk when Miss Donnelly came in with her hat on.

"Is it all right for me to go home, Mr. Friedman? It's after five."

"Yes, yes, go ahead."

"Is there anything the matter? I thought perhaps—"

He waved his hand. "Nothing. Nothing at all. I was just thinking."

Anna's eyes. When she didn't know he was watching her, he could catch a look in them, as if she were seeing things other people didn't see. Mourning eyes, and wondering; eyes that could lighten so quickly into laughter. Quality, his father used to say. You can always tell quality. And this man says he doesn't want her living on his street. His fury mounted.

I'm going to have that house if it's the last thing I do.

PAINTERS AND MASONS were still working when, in early September, they moved in so that Iris could start the school year. She had been fortunate to get a position as a fourth-grade teacher in what they later learned was the best school in the area. It was not what she had wanted. She wanted, she said, to teach poorer children whose need was greater. If she could have had her way she would have liked to teach on the lower East Side, or even Harlem.

Joseph groaned. "It's taken most of my life to get away to a place where there was no chance of being pulled back down there. I could take all the bathrooms out of this house so you'd get the feel of Ludlow Street, if you want."

He was the first to admit that his humor wasn't humorous, although Anna laughed. But Iris looked exasperated, and Anna's laugh turned to a sigh.

Oh, Iris was so earnest! She had no real joy in anything, just seemed to stand apart, watching and making her skeptical, acerbic comments. She thought the neighborhood too polished, too self-consciously expensive, and the children she taught reflected the houses they lived in. She disapproved of the things Anna was having done to the house.

"I liked it the way it was," she said, as the kitchen took new form with stainless steel, white porcelain and dark red tile.

"You can't mean that!"

"Naturally I don't mean the dirt. But what you're making is like something in a magazine."

"That's what I'm taking it from. A magazine," Anna said firmly.

It was the first time in her life that she could really have what she wanted. The costly pseudo-French furniture which they had been living with all these years had been Joseph's choice. The odd thing was that when at last she had gotten rid of it and the second-hand men had carried it out of sight with its gilded curlicues, painted flowers and bulbous legs (as if it had rheumatoid arthritis, Anna had used to think) she had felt a pang. They had gone through so much living with these tables and chairs! And when they took the sideboard which Maury had once gouged with his toy hammer she had turned away. (Only the little white bed from Iris' childhood room had gone with them and was wrapped now in the attic of this house, although Iris didn't know it. She would have understood what Anna was still hoping for.)

Joseph had told her to buy what she wanted, and she was doing so, spending far less than he would have spent. She'd furnished the dining room at an estate auction in the neighborhood, with a long, plain pine table and an enormous Welsh dresser. . . . These high rooms needed massive pieces and massive pieces were old; they didn't make them anymore for the cramped spaces of this century. There were flowers all over this house: clustered on the carpet in the library, scattered in blue and white bouquets on the walls of an airy bedroom. Geraniums in wooden tubs stood at the front door.

It was beginning to take on the look she had striven for, the look of a family which had lived long in one place and slowly collected its possessions through the years. (Hadn't she lived once in a house like that? *This silver has been in my family since before the Revolution,* Paul's mother said.) A false impression? Of course! But so much of life is bound to be false. . . . And middle-class? Oh-so-genteel, so understated, so English-countryside! Such a house for Joseph and Anna, once of Ludlow Street! And why not? If they liked it, and were comfortable with it? And she had done it well. If it didn't look like this when the original owners lived in it, then it ought to have.

The one concession to Joseph, who was far too busy these days to care about anything else, was the hanging of her portrait over the mantel in the living room. No, two concessions: the other was the gilded clock, which was to go under the portrait.

"I just don't like meeting myself every time I walk into that room," Anna objected, to no avail. About the clock she said nothing.

She unpacked the silver candlesticks, clutching them in her fists for a moment, feeling them before putting them on the dining-room table. The places they had seen before this one! The shelf on Washington Heights, because there had been no dining room table there, wrapped in a blanket for the ocean crossing. She could remember her mother saying the blessing over them, but where were they kept during the week? She thought and thought, straining herself to remember, and could not. And before that they had stood in the houses of a grandmother and an unknown great-grandmother. Her own mother had died before Anna had thought to ask about those other women, or had even cared about knowing. So now she would never know.

When everything else was in place, Anna unpacked her books. She took long afternoons arranging them on the shelves in sections according to the subject: art, biography, poetry, fiction. Under those headings, she arranged them again in alphabetical order according to author.

Here Iris gave approval. "You really have the makings of a library. I'd no idea we had so many."

"Half of them have been stacked away in barrels and boxes all these years."

Iris looked at her, Anna thought, with curiosity. "You're really happy, aren't you, Ma?"

"Yes, very." (It's a thing you learn and cultivate, this "happiness." You count what you have and are grateful for it. And if that sounds pompous, I can't help it.) And, not wanting to ask, yet not able to refrain from asking, "I hope you are too, a little, Iris?" The question came out almost like a plea.

"I'm all right. I'm better off than nine-tenths of the rest of the world."

Quite true. But it was not the answer Anna had wanted.

If only she would make more friends! There had been two or three young women who taught at her school in New York whom she saw regularly. They used to go to theatre and lunch together on weekends. But now even these few were lost to her unless she wanted to go into the city every week. Mostly now she stayed at home playing the piano, reading or correcting papers. No life for a person of twenty-seven.

She didn't stop and talk to people. She'd nod and go walking on; Anna had seen her do it often enough. But you needed to make an effort; people didn't just drop down the chimney and seek you out! On the Broadway block where Anna had done her shopping for all those years she had known everybody; generations of roller-skating kids, the shoe repair man, the butcher. Hadn't the butcher had a nephew just out of Columbia Law School, and asked for Iris' telephone number to give to him? But when Anna had mentioned it Iris had been furious.

She had tried, since moving here, to get her out to some of her own activities. There was a very active group of women at the temple sisterhood, some of them even younger than Iris. But, naturally, they were all married. There were the League of Women Voters and the Hospital Guild, which was right now raising funds for a new wing. Anna liked that sort of thing, had done it often enough in the city. People said she had a talent for making these fund raisers a success, for getting the people to come and finding speakers who could hold their attention. It wasn't hard; you just put a smile on your face, let people know you were available to work and you could be busy every day. It was almost a challenge to move into a new community and see how quickly you could make a place for yourself!

"You must have won the popularity contest," Iris remarked one afternoon when, on arriving home from school, she found a ladies' meeting just breaking up. The way she said it, and she had said it before, was odd: in part it was an accusation, in part a question.

Anna had tried the simple answer often enough: *When you're friendly to people they're friendly to you.* But it had produced no results, except perhaps irritation on Iris' part. And anyway, it sounded like some scout maxim or else one of those pious declarations that used to be embroidered on samplers or printed and hung over the boss's desk in an office. So she fell back on lame humor.

"My red hair, no doubt." And kept it at that.

If it hadn't been for all these friends or acquaintances, whatever you wanted to call them, the house would have been unbearably empty. Empty rooms were the hazard of middle age. After the birds have flown the nest, et cetera. And if there had never been a nestful at all?

Mary Malone was distressed about her son Mickey, who'd been in Hawaii during the war and had gone back there to live. But she still had the rest of them nearby, not to speak of the grandchildren already born and yet to come! While I, while we—

More than once Anna had thought of getting into the car with Joseph, driving up to that town and knocking at the door: "We've come to see our grandson," they'd say. And then what? No, it couldn't be done in the face of those people's refusal. The child would be the one to suffer. It couldn't be done. Someday, when he is older, people said, someday he'll want to see you. Yes, after all the lovely years of his childhood were past, he might, perhaps, come to them. A stranger, come out of curiosity or God knows why else.

On days like that Anna would need to be active, to work with her hands. She would go down into the kitchen and help Celeste with the cooking. Celeste had represented herself as a "good plain cook," but had turned out to be more plain than good. Anna was just as glad that the cooking hadn't been taken out of her own hands. . . .

She hadn't wanted anyone living in the house in the first place. With three adults, two of them gone all day, they could have done very well with a woman to come in once or twice a week to clean.

But Joseph had been firm about it. "This enormous house? No, you're to get someone and without delay. I insist," he'd said.

And so Celeste had come to them. She was a large, dark brown woman whose presence was marked by a loud voice that laughed whenever it wasn't singing sorrowful hymns. She had come north from Georgia for no reason that she ever disclosed, leaving behind her a vague family: children? Husband? She never told them and, after one unsuccessful attempt, they never asked her.

She was to live in their house as long as they did and know them perhaps better than they knew themselves.

DURING THEIR SECOND autumn, before full dark, Joseph came driving home from the railroad station and was startled by something at the side of the road not far from his house. He backed the car up to look again.

It was a small dog, lying in tall grass. He leaned out of the car. The dog raised its head an inch or two and fell back. Its chest and one of its legs were soaked in blood.

He'd never been very useful around blood or pain and he knew it. Maybe he ought to leave the dog and telephone the police when he got home. But in the meantime some other car might come along and kill it or just mangle it some more. He shuddered and looked again. It was a little white dog with a sheep's face, the Lovejoys' dog. He knew nothing about dogs and really didn't like them. But he remembered this one because when they had seen it on the Lovejoys' lawn Anna had exclaimed over the sheep. Then Iris had looked in a book—leave it to Iris to look things up—and told them it was a dog, a Bedlington terrier.

Would it bite if he were to pick it up? He couldn't leave it there like that. It raised its head again, or tried to, and he heard its whimper. No, he couldn't leave it there like that. He got out of the car. There was no cloth, nothing to lay it on. He took his coat off. If the spots didn't come out it couldn't be helped. The dog whimpered again when he picked it up, feeling clumsy and sick with pity for it.

He drove up the hill and turned into the double driveway of the Lovejoy house. A maid answered the bell, and in the hallway behind her he heard a woman's voice.

"Who is it, Carrie?"

"It's Tippy, Mrs. Lovejoy. He's been hurt."

"I found him on the side of the road," Joseph said. "I'm Friedman, your neighbor."

Mrs. Lovejoy gave a little scream. "Oh, my God!"

Joseph held out his arms and she took the little bundle of dog and coat. "Carrie, tell Bob to get the car and call Dr. Chase, tell him we're on our way." She whirled back to Joseph. "How did this happen?"

"I don't know," he said, and, suddenly understanding, added, "I didn't do it. I found him on the road."

She turned away. He saw that she didn't believe him. "My coat, please. May I have my coat?"

And when it was dropped upon the floor he picked up his bloodied coat and let himself out the door.

At dinner, having said nothing about the incident to Anna, he heard himself asking her quite suddenly, "Tell me, do you ever think this house is too far from your friends?"

She looked surprised. "Well, everyone does seem to live twenty minutes or so away, but I don't really mind. What makes you ask?"

"Just wondering. We've been here awhile and I wondered whether you liked it as much as you thought you would. We can always sell and get another place."

"Oh, but I love it here! You must know I do."

Yes, true. The way she stands in the doorway after we've been out, and walks around touching things. At night when it's warm she sits on the steps, watching the stars. She used to do that when she was a child in Poland, she says.

The doorbell rang and after a moment Celeste came in. "There's a gentleman to see you in the hall."

Just inside the door was Mr. Lovejoy. He stood somewhat uncertainly.

"I came over to thank you. My wife was terribly upset about the dog. She realized afterward that she hadn't thanked you."

"No, she hadn't. But that's all right."

"He had cut himself on a broken bottle. The vet said he would have bled to death in a short while if you hadn't picked him up."

"I don't like to see anything suffer. Not animals or human beings, either."

Anna had come into the hall. "What's this all about, Joseph? You didn't tell me!"

"There was nothing to tell," he answered shortly.

"Your husband was very kind. The dog means a lot to us, like one of the family."

"Then I'm glad he could help," Anna said. "Won't you come in for a minute?"

"Thank you, I'd better be getting back. You've made some changes in the house," he added, addressing Anna. "I'd hardly recognize it."

"Anytime you want to see it you're welcome."

"Thank you again." Mr. Lovejoy bowed and the door closed behind him.

"Well! You weren't very gracious to that man, Joseph. I've never seen you so rude."

"What did you want me to do? Kiss him?"

"Joseph! I don't know what's got into you! Such a nice man, too."

"What was nice about him? What could you tell in half a minute? Sometimes, Anna, you talk like a child!"

"And you talk like a nasty, insulting crank! I don't mind, but I should think you'd want to be nice to the neighbors. We might get to be friends, for all you know."

"Sure! They're waiting for us!"

"Well, we're friends with the Wilmots down the street, aren't we?"

"Okay, okay, have it your way." He patted her on the back.

Friends? Hardly. But something human had come through, all the same. He stood a moment looking through the door down the length of the living room where the fire sparked under the mantel and Anna's portrait hung above it. No, he wouldn't sell, wouldn't leave this house. It was his house. It was—home.

⊰{29}⊱

At the last minute her parents remembered that they had been invited out to dinner and Iris would have to be hostess alone to Theo Stern. It was a clumsy trick. They might have thought of something more clever.

As if it would make any difference! It was just one more humiliation and this one worse than most, because Theo was so un-ordinary and would see right through it. They were always praising his brilliance, so how could they think he would be stupid enough not to know what they were doing?

She was afraid. What to say to him during the long meal and the longer evening, knowing he would be wishing himself away and back in New York? He came to their house to see Joseph and Anna, not her. She had really never been alone with him, unless one could count four or five polite invitations to theatre by way of repaying her parents' hospitality. And one time at the beach with two of the Malone sons and their wives.

Celeste was coming upstairs, humming. Did she know she was constantly singing, or was it by now an unconscious habit? Iris came out of her room.

"Celeste, there'll only be two at dinner."

"Your ma told me. What I wanted to know was, shall I make a pie? There's time enough."

"Good heavens, anything. I don't care. This dinner tonight is the last thing I wanted."

Celeste looked sly. Sly and merry. "You shouldn't oughta say that. He's a real nice man, Dr. Stern. I taken a liking to him the first time I opened the door and him standing there asking if this was the Friedman house. I knowed right away I liked him."

"I like him, too. That's no reason why I have to entertain him, is it?"

"He likes you, I see that."

"Of course he does! He likes all of us. You, too."

"Then I'm going to make the pie. And biscuits with the chicken. He ate four biscuits last time we had them."

Even Celeste was captivated by his Viennese charm! But it wasn't fair to be sardonic about that: there was so much else beneath the courtesy and wit, including one's awareness of what the world—the Nazi fury—had done to Theo Stern.

He had tracked them down last year upon arriving in New York. The last they had heard before then was a letter written from England just after the United States had entered the war. Mama's eyes had run with fresh tears, reading all over again about the Uncle Eli family, all destroyed: the old people and the young, Theo Stern's wife Liesel and their baby—all annihilated. Horrible, horrible! Like one of those ghoulish fairy tales in which ogres devour children and people are thrown into furnaces. But this had really happened. You looked at Theo and, remembering, were so *moved*—you wanted to put your hand on his, you wanted to say I know, I know. Except that you didn't know: how could you, unless you had been there?

He never spoke of himself directly. His story had been drawn out of him in short sentences, answers to questions tactfully and obliquely put.

He'd had friends in England, made in the years he'd spent at Cambridge, and these had taken him in, had given him a base from which to reconstruct himself. When he enlisted in the British army it was not as a doctor. He had wanted to fight, to be used in a less passive way than healing wounds. He had wanted, he said, to work "vengefully," and that's how they had put him to use. As a child Theo had lived four years in France while his father opened a branch of his business there. Because of that he spoke colloquial French, slang and all. So he had been enlisted to work with the underground, and had been parachuted into France, complete with a French identity. He was supposed to have been born in a provincial town, son of a teacher; to have gone to school and church there and prepared for the university; all this was in case of capture by the Nazi occupying forces. He had seen, Iris reflected, seen in the flesh all the things that made you shudder and turn away when you saw mere bits of them in the newsreels. Theo had lived through them.

Once her father had risen and put his arm around Theo. He had been deeply affected, and Theo had been too. For that instant, standing there, they had seemed to the others in the room like a father and a son. As if, Iris thought, as if my brother Maury had come home.

She moved quickly, choosing her dress and shoes, then ran the water in the bathtub. She had never gotten over the need to ease herself in hot water and her mother had never ceased to warn her that she might one day fall asleep in it and drown.

She sank into the burning heat and lay her head back. She would have liked to stay in this deep comfort, then get into bed and read the evening away.

Papa was making a—a project out of Theo! He'd talked him into opening an office here in the suburbs rather than New York, had even helped him find office space.

"If you really want the Grosvenor Avenue building I can help you, I know the owner. I might be able to get a good deal for you on the rent," he'd suggested.

And if Theo was short of money for equipment, which came high, why, Joseph would be glad to advance him some. No, Theo wasn't short. Money was no problem. But he would never forget the offer; they were being as good to him as family. Well, they *were* family! He felt that way toward them. They were all he had.

Iris' flesh prickled with embarrassment. Papa came on so *strong!* Yet, if Theo minded, he didn't show it.

He was a good-looking man, too thin now and older looking than his age. His features were what is called "strong." He had attentive eyes that searched you when you spoke to him: Iris had had to turn her own away sometimes. Women would be attracted to him. Probably he would get anyone he wanted badly enough. He would want, she guessed, someone like the one he'd had before. "A beauty," her mother said. "She had a brightness like my brother Eli." And like Maury, because Maury was like Eli.

Men. What do men want? Beauty like that, naturally, if they can get it. But not only that, and not always. The mothers of the children she taught came in all shapes and sorts, with every kind and degree of tenderness, intelligence and manner. Yet must they not all have had something in common to have been chosen? What? What?

If you talk too much, that's not good. If you're too quiet, that's not good. You lie in bed at night thinking about it and trying not to. You are surrounded by sex, the man-woman thing. The movies, the embraces that will end in bed, even though they don't show it. But you know that's what it's all about. Always. Even the women's magazines with their preachy articles and stories. Educated women should have more children, they tell you. Motherhood and wifehood are the most rewarding careers. Decorate the house, drive the station wagon, work on the school board, campaign in community politics and make your town a better place for your children to live in. Charities are obligatory (making the world a better place for other people's children to live in). But it all starts with the bed. Man-woman. Sex.

I feel sometimes—I feel so *cheap.* As if, when people look at me, they must know what I want and can't have, will probably never have. My mother tries to be so tactful. She talks to her friends and sometimes even to me, so seriously, so respectfully, about my "career," as if she wasn't at the same time putting out her feelers for every stray man who passes. Papa brings a widower to dinner, thinking he must be needing a mother for his children. Not me, Iris, for what I am. No, a mother for his children.

Why don't I give up? Give up in my mind, I mean. One more birthday after the next, and I'll be thirty. It's time to settle for what I have. A job with tenure in another year, so if I want to I can plan to go on teaching for the next forty years in the pleasant brick school with the old trees and the nice lady teachers. Papa says I'll never have to worry about money. I'll have a nice home full of good books. I'll listen to good music in the evenings and maybe take a trip to Europe now and then with a group of teachers.

That's living?

"What's that plant I smell?" Theo asked. "It's a little like perfume and a little like burnt sugar."

"It's phlox. My mother planted a bed of it under this window."

She turned on the outdoor light, picking the phlox out of darkness. The cream and lavender domes were bent with the weight of the rain. The trees dripped in a forest stillness.

"My mother's become a country woman. Those are raspberries by the hedge. We had them for breakfast."

Theo said quietly, "It seems centuries since I knew people who were able to plant something and wait peacefully for it to grow."

No answer seemed to be called for. He went on, "Do you really know how wonderful this home of yours is?"

"Oh, yes. Most of the years of my growing up were depression years. We've only been living like this a very short time."

"I didn't mean the house. I meant the family. You have wonderful parents. Warm people. Gentle people. I have a feeling they seldom argue with each other. Am I right?"

"I think because my mother anticipates whatever my father wants. Not only that, of course. But that's part of it."

"A European woman!"

"She was born in Europe. I don't know how European she still is."

"But American women are different, aren't they?"

"It's a land of variety here . . . who can say what 'American' is?"

"Tell me, are you like your mother or your father?"

Those attentive eyes! As if her answer were really important. As if it were even possible.

I don't really know, she thought, what my parents are "like," let alone myself. No, that's wrong. Papa is relatively simple. But my mother has hidden places. I think Papa knows she has, too, and can't puzzle them out. He teases her about being mysterious, yet he means it, it's more than teasing. It's true that they love one another; one *feels* their devotion; also, though, one feels a tension. Sometimes I have odd thoughts: Could Mama really be keeping some great secret from us both? I remember that man, Paul Werner, as if in some way, I don't know how, he were involved with us. With her. Then I'm so ashamed of my thought. Mama, so *moral* and honorable and—how can I think such things? Yet I do think them.

She blinked herself back into the present. Theo was waiting for a reply, and so she said lightly, "It's hard to see yourself, isn't it? But—well, I like books; that's the main way I'm like my mother. And I'm sort of, more than sort of, religious. Like my father."

"Religious! You must know, that's something quite new to me. We never thought about it at home. Nor in the house of my father-in-law, Eduard. Oh, you called him Eli, didn't you? I forgot for the moment. Your Uncle Eli."

"You think it's ridiculous?"

"No, no, of course not!"

"Tell the truth. I won't mind."

"All right then, I'll tell you. I find it rather charming, rather picturesque. Perhaps I'm even a little sorry that I have no feeling for it myself."

"But you must have. Not the form, perhaps. And forms change, anyway. Like Papa being Orthodox and now he goes to Reform; at first he was shocked by the thought, but now he likes it tremendously. So what I mean is," she said earnestly, "it's not the form but what you feel that counts. And I'm sure you must feel the truth of all the things we believe in!"

"Such as?"

"Well, you've seen better than I have what a nation without religion, that's to say without morals, can do."

"Yes, I suppose that's true. I just never thought to connect religion with those events."

"I guess when you're in the midst of—what you were in, you can't do much thinking. You just want to live through it," she said gently.

"You don't even care much about living through it. One of the feelings I had, as a matter of fact, was guilt that I *was* alive."

"I understand."

"And then when it's over and the world begins moving again, you start to feel angry. All that ugliness and waste of years! When you might have been—growing raspberries!"

"I hope you don't still feel it was a waste . . . what you did, I mean."

"No, I have a better perspective on it since I've been in America. All war is criminal waste, but in a purely personal sense I didn't waste the years. I spent myself with profit. I fought back."

He got up and walked to the end of the room, pulled a book from a shelf and replaced it. "So now, so now I just want to live. I want to work and listen to music, and to the devil with politics and getting ahead! I just want *real* things. Like looking at a woman with marvelous eyes and a lovely blue dress. That is a lovely dress, Iris. It's the color of your name."

"The New Look," she said shyly. "My mother bought it."

"Your mother buys your clothes?"

"Oh, no! This was a present. She knew I wouldn't buy it, I only shop when I have to. I'm not interested in clothes."

"So? What are you interested in?"

What she had to say was so stilted, formal and dreary. Yet she knew nothing else to say. "I always thought I'd like to write. I tried short stories, but I got too many rejections and I've given up. I play piano too, but not well enough to do anything much with it. So I'll say I'm interested in teaching, because it's what I do best."

"And you're happy."

"Oh, I like it. They tell me I'm good at it and I feel that I am. Except that these children don't really *need* me. They're so well cared for already; they have everything, and what I do for them is—" She was talking too much, and she finished abruptly, "I guess I really want to do something more important, only I don't know what."

"I am imagining you as a child," Theo said irrelevantly, "a very solemn little girl."

"I'm sure I was." Still am. Solemn.

"Tell me about your childhood."

"There's nothing much to tell. It was very quiet. I read a lot. It was almost a Victorian life in the twentieth century."

Why was she talking so much? This man drew the words from her.

"I sometimes think I should have been a Victorian. In the early part of the century, before the factories and billboards, when the world was still green and lovely."

"It's the factories that have made this beautiful house possible, you know. A hundred and twenty-five years ago you would have been living in a hovel, or a Polish ghetto more than likely."

"That's what my father says. And of course you're right. I'm just given to silly talk, sometimes."

"It's not silly to reveal yourself. Goodness knows I've just been doing it."

Theo lay his head against the back of the chair. She shouldn't have reminded him of Europe and the war. The rain began again, splashing on the heavy leafage at the window, and the room was quiet.

Presently he stood up and went to the piano. "I'll play something jolly. Have you ever heard this?"

He played a teasing little waltz, played it with a sparkle, and swung around on the bench. "I'll bet you can't guess the title of that."

"I'll bet I can. It's Satie. He wrote three of them, called 'His Waist,' 'His Pince Nez,' 'His Legs.'"

They burst out laughing, and then Theo's laugh broke off. He stared at her.

"You're the most extraordinary girl!"

"I'm not. I happen to have a crazy kind of memory, that's all."

He stood up and came to where she was sitting. He took her hands and pulled her lightly to her feet. "Iris, I'm going to say it right out while I have the courage. Why shouldn't we be married? Can you think of a good reason why we shouldn't be?"

She wasn't certain she had heard. She stared at him.

"Because I think we go so well together. I don't know about you, but I haven't been happy like this for so long."

Was it, could it be, some sort of cruel wit, some kind of mockery that passed for a game in sophisticated circles? Still she didn't answer.

"I'm clumsy. I should have done something before this to prepare you. I'm sorry."

He was looking into her face, forcing her eyes to his, which were troubled and soft. She saw it was not a game. It was true.

She began to cry.

He put her cheek to his and kissed her forehead. "I don't know what that means," he said. "Does it mean yes or no?"

"I think—I think it means yes," she whispered and felt her tears wet on his cheek.

"Iris, my dear, I want you to be sure. Tell me you are."

"I am sure. Yes, yes, I am."

He pulled out his handkerchief and dried her eyes. "We'll be very, very happy. I promise we will."

She nodded, laughed, and her tears kept pouring.

Theo, understand why I am crying: because I so hoped this might happen and knew it couldn't; because of being almost thirty years old; because of the narrow bed in which I sleep alone. And now you are here.

Iris has done something wonderful. There is a murmur of flattering laughter all through the house. Celeste carries in the packages of gifts, the silver and the crystal in their tissue-paper wraps. Her mother works at her desk and on the telephone over the menus, the invitations, the bridal veil. (It is an embarrassment to be dressed like a teen-age bride at an age when other women are taking their children to kindergarten.) At least, her mother will keep things fairly simple, although not as simple as Iris wants. Papa would have her come riding in on a white elephant, its howdah embroidered in brilliants. He is so happy, engrossed with his plans for Theo's new office. The blueprints are spread on the big desk in the round room; Theo and Papa confer over them after dinner. Papa is ecstatic because she is marrying a doctor. A doctor from Vienna! And now there will be a son in the house again, vigorous and bright and full of hope, as Maury was once. Our Maury, so long ago. Poor Papa! Poor good Papa!

It is almost as if Theo were a trophy she has won. She is ashamed of the joy in the house. She is ashamed of herself for begrudging them their joy. Her heart beats faster almost all the time now.

Sometimes she thinks she is dreaming the whole thing.

They lay on the sand. It was a perfect, silken Florida afternoon.

She had thought, when they were alone in that first room together, that she would fail. She had read so much, had bought and hidden marriage manuals and Havelock Ellis. It seemed there was so much to know about what, after all, had been done long before books were written!

Her mother had asked, while looking at the floor, "Is there anything you want to know?" And had been relieved when Iris had told her there wasn't.

It had seemed from the reading that there were so many ways in which you could please or displease, succeed or not; and if she failed, if she did not satisfy, what then?

But she had not failed. It was the marvelous delight, the most total merging of spirit and flesh that could have been imagined, and she had certainly imagined it enough! To have waited so long! That was the only pity, to have waited so long!

Theo said lazily, "You look pleased."

"I am. Pleased and proud. Smug and proud."

"Proud?"

"To be your wife."

"You're a darling, Iris. And puzzling, in a very nice way."

"What way?"

"I'd thought, you see, you gave the impression that you might be hesitant or timid in bed."

"And I'm not?"

He laughed. "You know very well you're not! I'm a very, very lucky man!"

He took her hand and they turned over to burn their backs.

"This day is too perfect to know what to do with it," Iris said.

"It seems to me you know quite well what to do with it. And with the nights too," he answered.

"When I was a little girl," she began.

"You still are a little girl."

"No, but really, listen, I want to tell you. I was about seven and there was a doll that I had been wanting. It had a pink velvet coat with white fur, and long, dark curls. I remember it exactly; it was the incarnation of doll. Do you know what I mean? And I had been wanting it so long. Then on the morning of my birthday, when I found it sitting on my chair, I had such a queer feeling, not disappointment, but a kind of ebbing away. . . . It was so perfect! I didn't want a speck of dirt to touch it, and still I knew that it would, that with each second some of its perfection was passing away."

"Such sorrowful thoughts on a day like this!" Theo protested.

But she persisted. She wanted him to understand. "I'm not sorrowful. It's so wonderful that I want to keep it, remember it always. Theo, someday years from now we'll look out on a soggy winter street and we'll talk about how we lay here in the sun predicting how we'll be looking out on a soggy winter street—"

"You're thinking about years from now and I'm thinking about tonight. I'm hoping they serve that fish soup again. It's the best I ever ate."

"Theo, darling, tell me again, tell me you love me."

"I love you, Iris. I do love you."

She raised her arm toward the sky. Her skin was turning reddish gold.

"What are you looking at? Your ring? I wish you hadn't insisted on a plain band. Let me at least buy a diamond one for evening."

"No."

"Is it because you think I can't afford it? I can."

"It's not that. It's just that I'm never going to take this one off."

"Never?"

"Never. I know it sounds superstitious or something, but this is the one I wore when we were married and now it's like another part of myself."

"That's primitive."

"Maybe. All I know is, something happened to me when you put that ring on my finger. And I know that if the ring ever comes off all of my life will come loose and I shall be left floating, without an anchor."

"All right, then, no diamonds."

The clouds moved slowly; the sun poured on their joined hands.

"I'm falling asleep," Theo said.

Iris closed her eyes. Sparks whirled through her lids, a catherine wheel of ruby, mauve and peacock blue. So beautiful! Life, and the vibrating earth! I want to have it all, see it all, be everywhere at once. I want to hear all the music ever written and never die. Let Theo never die, just stay like this in the sunlight, forever and forever and forever.

❧{30}❧

Cousin Chris stowed the oars, letting the boat dance of its own will. There was something different about him today and it disturbed Eric. Usually when Chris came it was so jolly. He didn't visit very often; he had a wife and children and a job, although you wouldn't think it to look at him. He seemed too athletic and quick, just too young for all that sort of thing. Still, he had been Eric's mother's favorite cousin, so he couldn't really be that young. They'd used to have great adventures at Chris's house in Maine when she was a girl. Like the time they'd got caught in a fog on the bay—

But Chris had no stories for Eric now. He bent forward, his sober face looming large, while behind his head, far at the end of the lake, the hotel buildings and the golf course lay spread like a toy village on green felt.

"So I told your grandmother. We had a long talk last night—"

"I heard you downstairs," Eric said.

"You heard what we said?"

"No, just your voices. But I knew it was something serious. I thought probably you were talking about me."

"Yes. Well." Chris had anxious, troubled eyes. He began speaking fast, as if he wanted to get all this over with. "You're thirteen, almost grown-up. I told your grandmother you're old enough to handle the truth. Women never think you are, but—"

"The truth about Gran?"

"To begin with, yes."

"You don't have to tell me. I know it's cancer." This was the first time he'd said the word out loud. People always whispered it or said C.A. or else just *looked*. He didn't know why he didn't feel more, saying this awful thing. Was there something wrong with him, that he didn't feel more?

"How long have you known?"

"Since last winter. That time she was in the hospital, people stopped talking when I came in the room. So I guessed that's what it must be."

"I see," Chris said.

"Is she afraid?"

"She hasn't said she was. But I should think so, wouldn't you?"

Chris waited a moment. "What she's really worried about is you. And that's why I want to talk to you. She asked me to. She thought it would be easier for both of you if I did the talking."

"She needn't worry. I'll take care of her. I was very good with Gramp, and you know how crippled he was."

"I know you were. But this is different."

"How different?"

Cousin Chris didn't answer right away. Instead, he took the oars and the boat sprang ahead. They had to bend their shoulders under a fall of willow leafage, and in this hidden cove at water's edge he put the oars down again. The boat lay still.

"How is it different?" Eric repeated.

Chris took his wristwatch off. It was an extraordinary watch. He'd bought it overseas when he was in the air force during the war, and he'd shown it to Eric yesterday. It could tell the date and it had an alarm. You could read the dial in the dark; it was a wonderful watch. Now Chris examined it, shook it a little, held it to his ear, frowned and slowly strapped it on again.

"Something wrong with your watch?"

"No, I just wanted to check it." Suddenly the words came rushing out. "Eric, the difference is, your Gran is going to die. I didn't know any other way to tell you but like this."

"But Jerry—he's a boy in my class—his father had cancer a long time ago when we were in third grade, and he's fine!"

"It doesn't always work that way."

"I'm going to ask Dr. Shane!"

"Do, if it'll help you any. But he'll tell you the same thing, Eric." Had he been asking himself a minute ago why he felt nothing inside? Now, suddenly, there was a tightening, a pounding in his chest and his head. He thought he tasted something hot under his tongue, hot like blood.

"I don't believe it! It isn't true!" he shouted.

"I know how you feel. It was the same for me when my grandfather Guthrie died."

Beyond the screen of leaves a motorboat shot by, rocking the quiet water. Billy Noyes and his father in their Chris-Craft, probably. They were always racketing around together in that boat, Billy and his father.

"I know how you feel," Chris said again.

Neither of them spoke for a minute or two. Then another bleak thought formed itself into words.

"I'm thinking of how empty the house will be with just George and Mrs. Mather and me in it."

"Well, that's what I was coming to next," Chris said. He felt for the pack of cigarettes which was sticking out of his shirt pocket in plain sight, but he seemed to have trouble getting hold of it. Then he had to fumble in another pocket for a match, and after that had more trouble lighting it.

"The thing is," he said at last, "the thing is, you won't be able to stay here. I mean, Mrs. Mather isn't family, so she couldn't be responsible for you, could she? You need to live with someone in your own family, you see."

"Would I go to live with you?"

"Well, no. Not that I wouldn't like it a lot, but as it works out—" He paused. Oh, if he would just say it all quickly! "As it is, well, Gran has had this on her mind for a long time, and she's talked about it with me and my parents and Uncle Wendell, even with Dr. Shane and Father Duncan. And they all think, they really all think that the only right home for you in the circumstances is with your father's people."

Chris's voice made a final descent to a period, as at the end of a speech or a piece of music. Eric saw that he was watching him closely. He had a kind of narrow expression that said: "Well, now, that part's done with and what's to come next?" Eric himself had a habit of observing faces closely: the masters at school to see whether they were only satisfied with your answer or really liked it, all grownups to see whether they were telling you the whole truth or keeping something back. He saw now that Chris was telling him the whole truth.

"I didn't know my father had anyone!"

"Oh, yes," Chris said carefully. "He had parents and a younger sister."

"Alive?" Eric's voice rose, and squeaked, as it often did recently.

"Yes. Living in New York City. Or, I should say, nearby."

"But why, but why? Why has everybody lied to me up till now?"

"I wouldn't say it was lying, exactly. They never told you that your father's parents were dead, did they?"

"No, but they were always saying: 'You're all we have, Eric, and we're all you have.' So I thought—"

"Well, that was a way of putting it. Not a lie, just not talking about it. There's a difference, isn't there?"

He was so shocked, so absolutely stunned. He had no feeling as to whether this was a good thing or bad.

Chris went on, "They planned to explain it all when you were older, probably would have done so before now if your grandfather had lived. Then you could have met these other grandparents." He went on confidently, more rapidly, "Yes, that was definitely their intention."

"But why was it a secret for so long?"

Chris paused. "You know how it is, Eric. People don't always agree about things. To put it quite simply, they didn't like each other. There was a lot of hard feeling when you were taken to live with your mother's parents instead of your father's."

"You mean, they wanted me, too?"

"Oh, yes, they did, very much. After all, they loved their son and you're their son's child."

"But what was everybody angry at everybody about?"

"I hate to say this, Eric, although I'm sure you've learned a few things about this imperfect world by now . . . it was a matter of religion."

"Were they—were they Catholic, then? Was that it?"

"Not Catholic. Jewish."

Jewish! But that was—that was the *craziest* thing! How could that be?

Jewish! Like David Lewin at school. He couldn't think of anyone else he knew who was. He remembered when David had first come to the Academy in fifth grade. Everybody liked him except one boy, Bryce Henderson. No, two boys. Phil Sharp also. They'd said nasty things to David about being Jewish and David had punched Bryce and made his nose bleed. Then the headmaster had called David in and asked him why he'd done it and David wouldn't tell, because everybody knew the headmaster was always talking about bigotry and prejudice. "That's something we tried to wipe out in this war we've just finished," he would say. So David didn't tell on them and took his demerit, which was really swell of him and afterward most of the guys said it was.

Yes, he was a nice enough guy, David. Once he and Jack Mackenzie had been invited to David's house, near where his parents had the clothing store in Cyprus. It was some kind of holiday with a big dinner and wine. The father drank his out of a silver cup and everybody sang. It was neat, yet queer and foreign, too. Eric had invited David back to his house once, but that was all. There hadn't been any reason why they should become special friends, although probably David would have liked to.

And my father was like David! Hard to *believe!* His heart was really drumming now. He didn't *like* it. It was too odd, too strange. Different. Like David.

"I suppose they really should have told you before." Chris was almost talking to himself, thinking out loud. "At least, I always thought they should. We all thought so. . . . But they did what they believed best, goodness knows, they did."

"Did you know my father?"

"I certainly did. He was a very great person. He was one of my best friends at Yale."

"He was?" Eric felt a smile break out on his lips, a silly smile close to laughter; and close to crying, too. And he felt excitement, the way you do at a mystery movie when you're so scared of what may be coming next, and you laugh because you're scared. . . . "Have you—I never even knew what he looked like."

"Have I got a picture? I'm sure I've got snapshots of us playing tennis. I'll look when I get home and send them to you. I'll do it the minute I get home."

"Tell me in the meantime what he looked like."

"Well, something like you, as a matter of fact. I think you're going to be tall like him. He had light hair, too, and thick eyebrows like yours." Cousin Chris leaned forward with his chin in his hands and the boat rocked. "Funny, we were both going to be lawyers . . . we were both so certain of the future. And he's not here, and I'm in the oil business. Life is changes and surprises, Eric, as you're finding out right this minute. We never know what's around the next corner."

He had a sudden awareness of the planet whirling in empty space around the sun, with nothing to hold it up but its own speed. What if it were to slacken and fall? Fall where? A terror came over him. There was nothing to hold to, nothing firm, not even the ground under your feet.

"When am I supposed to go?" he cried in panic.

"When the semester's over at the end of this month."

"I don't want to go to live with them! I don't even know them! How can I go live in their house?"

Chris swallowed. He had a huge Adam's apple and it moved under the skin of his neck as if it would pop out. Eric had watched it at dinner last night. "Listen, Eric," he said, "I know it's a helluva hard thing, I wouldn't want to be in your shoes, and I'm going to level with you about that. You know I wouldn't fool you, would I?"

"I guess you wouldn't."

"You know I wouldn't. So listen to me. These have got to be good people. They couldn't have had a son as kind and good as your father if they weren't. They're going to love you; they love you already! It isn't their fault that you don't know them. And they're as close to you really as Gran and Gramp, don't forget."

I don't want to go, I don't want to go. . . .

He thought of something. "What about George? I can't go without George!"

"I'm sure you can take him."

The dog, hearing his name, pricked his ears and looked from one face to the other as if asking a question. Then he laid his enormous paw on Eric's knee.

"Why can't I live with you, Chris? I wouldn't be any trouble, I really wouldn't."

"I know you wouldn't. But you see Eric, Fran and I are going to Venezuela for the company, it might be for four or five years. And we have three children already."

"I could help with the children."

Something rippled across Chris's face. Eric thought he looked as if something hurt. "Eric, I wish I could. But Fran is expecting another baby, and she can't—she doesn't feel she can take on any more responsibility. You see what I mean? Do you, Eric?"

He didn't see, and he didn't, wouldn't, answer.

"I know it's hard for you to understand. My brothers are bachelors, my parents travel all the time now that Dad's retired, Uncle Wendell's past eighty. But you do have another place where you'll have a home and an education and—Eric, you'll see, you'll be happy there! I'll write to you, all the time, and you'll answer and tell me what you're doing and how happy you are, you'll see you will. Eric? You do understand, don't you, that it's not because we don't *want* you? Eric?"

He knew that if he were to answer his voice would come out in that high silly squeak again. There was a pain in his throat, and he didn't want to bawl like a little kid. He hadn't cried in years.

Suddenly he was bawling like a little kid, sobbing, his breath in gasps. He couldn't believe the sounds he was making. He was so frightened and ashamed of himself, and alone, cold and alone. And, hiding, he put his hands over his face.

For a while Chris didn't say anything. Then he began to talk in that way he had which was so quiet, as if he were almost talking to himself again and didn't care whether you were listening or not.

"I cried when my friend was shot down over Germany. Yes, I remember how I cried. I saw the plane go down, a long flame like a red pencil across the sky. . . . For a long time I had nightmares and woke up crying. I saw a lot of grown men cry in those years. Yes, yes."

The boat bobbed. George left his seat and went to lie down on the bottom, his nose resting on Eric's shoe. After a few minutes Eric felt a handkerchief being thrust into his hand. He wiped his nose and eyes and looked up. Chris was turned away from him, still not looking at him. Then Chris bent to the oars and began to row, parting the lime-colored curtain. They came out into sun and water so bright that it made you blink. They moved slowly toward home.

"Cousin Chris? Do I have to go right away? Couldn't I just stay here till the end of the summer, and then leave in time for school in the fall?"

Chris looked at him for a moment. Then he said gently, "That wouldn't be a very good plan," and Eric understood that he was saying, *Gran may not live until the end of the summer.*

"So then," Eric began, "are you going to tell them?" He didn't know what he was supposed to call them. He couldn't say "Mr." and "Mrs.," could he? But he certainly couldn't say "Gran" or "Gramp," either. "Are you going to call them up and tell them that—" He couldn't finish.

"That's already been done. As a matter of fact, they're on their way here now to see you."

"Today? This afternoon?"

"Yes, it's much too sudden for you, I know. I was supposed to get here last week to talk to you, but I had to go to Galveston instead and that's why it's all being done at the last minute. I'm sorry."

"I just wish I'd had more time to think about it before they came."

"Maybe in a way this is easier. Not to have so much time to think about it, I mean."

George climbed back up on the seat, his great head almost on a level with Eric's. The dog leaned heavily, closer, as if he knew. Eric was sure George knew when to give comfort. He thought of the time he had been scolded, his worst and only real, furious scolding, the time when he was ten and he had started the car up and taken it out the driveway. And then there was the time, not long after that, when Gramp had had his heart attack and died out on the porch after dinner. He remembered going up to his room, and sitting there all that evening with his arm around George just like this. There was something between himself and George that he'd never felt with anybody else.

The boat drew up at the dock with a soft bump and Chris tied the rope.

"Gran will be wanting to talk to you, Eric." They walked up through the hemlock grove toward the house. "You know, she's been far more worried about you than about her sickness. You'll make it easier for her to go back to the hospital and—you'll make everything easier for her if she knows you're all right. Remember it's hard for her, too. Not only for you."

He knew he would find her at her desk in the upstairs sitting room. She was mostly there lately, paying bills and going over papers, those stiff long crackly sheets that come from lawyers' offices. Trusts and wills and deeds, he heard her say, when she talked on the telephone.

He waited in the doorway. "Gran?" he called. Sometimes she didn't hear people coming up the stairs. "Gran?"

She swung round in the chair and he saw at once that she had been crying. It was the first time in his life that he had seen her tears. Even when Gramp died, she had said very quietly with a still, sad face, "He went without suffering, in his own home, at the end of a happy day. We must remember that and not cry."

But now she was crying. She stood up and put her head on his shoulder. He was as tall as she. And he was consoling her the way Chris had been trying to console him in the boat only a few minutes ago.

"I'll be all right, Gran, I promise I will." *Remember, it's hard for her too,* Chris had said. "Just take care of yourself, Gran. Don't be afraid for me."

She straightened up. "Oh, my dear, how wrong of me! As if there were anything for you to be afraid of! You'll have a good home, you'll be cared for! I'm not crying about that, it's just that—"

And he understood that they were being uprooted, torn away and apart. It was all without warning, like the night that the storm had destroyed the great elm in front of the house, the tree that had soared above their roof for almost seventy-five years, Gramp had said. In a few minutes of rage the storm had torn it out of the earth and it had fallen, with its great roots ripped, the clotted wet earth dripping from them. He remembered wondering whether trees could possibly feel pain.

"Sit down," Gran said. She wiped her eyes and wiped her glasses, straightening her face into the one he knew. Her face never changed very much. Even when she was happy it was kind of firm and plain. When she was cross—and she could get quite cross sometimes—he'd even hated her face. But not now. All he could think of now was that this face was soon going to disappear.

"Surely there must be a lot of questions you want to ask me? Things Cousin Chris didn't explain?"

"He explained, but I still don't understand it."

"No, of course not. How could you absorb all these changes in just a few minutes? I wish so much that there were more time."

"Tell me, why didn't they come to see me before? Why was everything such a secret?"

"We agreed, we all agreed, it would have been too confusing for a young child. You were only a baby. . . . This way, you had no doubts about where you belonged. It was really healthier for you. Yes, it must have been right, because you've always been so happy. . . . Still," she said thoughtfully, "still, I always did feel sorry in many ways. Mr. and Mrs. Friedman—by the way, Eric, we've been spelling your name differently, because we wanted to make it easier, more English. But they say 'Friedman. I, E, D.' That's the German way." When Eric didn't comment, she added, "I know it must be awful for you to find out that even your name isn't spelled the way you thought it was." He was silent.

"You'll make a new life, Eric. You'll see so many things in the city! You remember what a fine time we had that weekend last year when we went to the theatre and the planetarium and—"

He didn't want to talk about things like that. "Why did everybody hate everybody else so much? Why did it matter so terribly that they had another religion?"

But while he asked the questions he knew the reason, really. It was because—because Jews were odd people, not like the ordinary, everyday people you knew.

They were different. He didn't know why, but they were. And he was one of them! Was he, or wasn't he? Yet, if he was, he didn't feel any change in himself.

Gran sighed. "The hatred, if you want to call it that, well, whatever it was, it wasn't all on our side. Believe me. Of course, Gramp did have very definite ideas, I can't say I agreed with them all. Sometimes they were extreme, but he was a very proud American and in a sense I can see what he meant by keeping your own ways, among your own people. . . . 'Let them go their way and I'll go mine,' he always said."

"But if he—disliked them so—how is it he never talked about them to me?"

"I suppose he felt he'd be talking about you, or a part of you, wouldn't he? And he loved you so!" She stopped. Her eyes had a remembering look, as though she were seeing things that had happened long ago, and hearing voices. "Yet I always felt," she went on, "that I would have done it differently, if it had been left to me. Not that I'm finding fault with your grandfather. He did what he thought was best for you. Perhaps he was right; dividing a child between two worlds is wicked and harmful. . . ."

Eric thought of something. "Did you ever see them? My father's parents?"

"Only once, when your own parents died. Oh," Gran said, "they're nice people, Eric! Gentle people, I thought. They'll talk to you about all this, I'm sure, when you get to know them. I've been speaking to them on the telephone these past few weeks and—"

Chris knocked at the door. "May I join you, or is this private?"

"Not private. Eric and I were only finishing what you began. I think—I hope he understands things a little."

"Aunt Polly? Perhaps you ought to go and lie down for a bit," Chris urged.

"Yes, I think I might. For fifteen minutes or so." She stood up and Eric saw that she tottered and had to take hold of the back of the chair. Her face was an awful yellowed gray; there were sweat stains under her arms. She was so fastidious. He'd never seen her sweat before.

He looked past her to the window. When the wind moved the leaves you could see the flat silver shimmer of the lake. He would be leaving that, too. It was like shedding one skin and growing another. This house, these trees, these faces would all be here, except for Gran's face! They would be here, and he not here. He would be someplace else, where he had never been before.

"Gran! Have you asked them—I mean, I have to take George. I can't go without George, you know."

"I'm sure that will be all right," Gran said. She looked at Chris and smiled. At the door she remembered something. "Eric, don't forget who you are. We've tried to teach you and I know you've learned good ways. You won't forget them?"

"I won't forget," he said. "And now I think I want to go out." And, seeing the question on their faces, added, "Not far. I won't be long."

He had a vaguely formed idea of talking to Dr. Shane, but when he passed the yellow house and saw that there were no cars in the garage he was in a way relieved. As Chris had told him, the doctor would only repeat what he now knew. He retraced his steps to his friend Teddy's, but Teddy had gone to the dentist and again he was relieved. He felt that he had to talk to somebody, had to tell somebody, like Chicken Little in the ridiculous childhood tale, running out to report that the sky had fallen. And yet he didn't really want to talk to anybody at all.

The Whitelys' horses were grazing near the road. He went over and stood by the rail fence, waiting until they saw him. He wondered whether they really knew him, or were only smelling the sugar in his pockets. Their soft noses snuffled into his palm. The brown and white pony, Lafayette, had a habit of shoving into the hollow of Eric's shoulder. He thought, I'd like to get on him and ride through empty woods; I'd just like to shed everything, feel empty of everything but motion, not think about Gran or school or whether I'll make senior basketball (I never will now, not in that school, anyway: somewhere else, perhaps; but where?). Not to think of anything at all. Animals understand. Dogs and horses. I'd rather be with them than with people sometimes. Gramp had promised him a horse of his own when he got to be twelve, but Gramp was dead by that time and Gran said that, what with tuition at the Academy and all, she just couldn't afford to maintain a horse. But the Whitelys were really nice; they let him ride Lafayette anytime.

"No more sugar," he said aloud, giving the last, and then walked on down the road, not knowing where he was going, with George plodding slowly behind. Now and then their feet cracked last year's fallen twigs.

At the top of a small rise the road branched off. Half a mile beyond you could see where one branch ran into the state highway. This was as far as he had been allowed to walk when he was a little boy. He remembered how, when he was so young that he had hardly been out of Brewerstown, he had stood there looking at the blacktop road with the white dividing line, wondering where it went after it rounded the curve and fell out of sight, who lived there, what *happened* there, where he couldn't see. He smiled to himself. Such a *child!* He hadn't known anything at all, still didn't, for that matter. He hadn't been anywhere except to Maine, to Niagara Falls with Teddy's family and last year to New York City with Gran. He wondered whether any of that curiosity, that surging excitement, would come back again, that feeling that there must be "something down the road." It didn't come back. There was only a great, looming dark. School and Teddy and all his friends, the scout troop, his boat and his room and Lafayette, all to be wiped out, to disappear, as when you wipe the eraser over the blackboard.

He turned around and started back. He was ashamed; he oughtn't to be thinking about himself, when Gran was going to lose everything. He oughtn't to be thinking about what would be coming next for him when for Gran there would be nothing coming next. Or probably there wouldn't. He hoped he was wrong about that, hoped she would really meet Gramp again, as she was certain she would. (Was she really, truly certain? Or did she only say so for his sake, and perhaps for her own as well?) Anyway, one thing he could hope for her, that she wouldn't have too much pain.

Ahead of him he recognized Father Duncan's car turning into the Busbys' driveway. He would be making his weekly visit to the old lady, who had broken her hip. He started to cross over, not wanting to be caught up in greeting or conversation, but Father Duncan hailed him and he was caught after all.

"So everything has been straightened out, has it, Eric? I talked to your grandmother on the telephone a while ago."

It seemed that everyone except himself had known about what was to happen to him. His future had been disposed of the way you sell a horse or a dog, except that he would never sell a horse or a dog, never send it away from its home.

"Yes, Father. All settled," he said.

Father Duncan had a keen gaze, a way of putting his head on one side as if he were estimating your size and weight. "If there are things that puzzle you, that trouble you, Eric, come and talk to me. Tomorrow or anytime. Will you?"

"There isn't anything," Eric said. Or rather so much that he didn't want to talk about it. It was like looking for the needle in the haystack; you'd never find it, so why even try?

"Let me just say one thing quickly, Eric. Your other grandparents—they're of a different faith. You must respect it. I know I don't have to tell you that. Respect it, but hold on to your own. You can. It's perfectly possible for you to live there happily and love them as I know they love you, and still keep your faith. You understand?"

"Yes, Father."

"You remember Christ said to his disciples, 'And lo, I am with you always, even unto the end of the world.' If you remember that He is with you, times when you may feel lonely, missing people, it will help enormously."

"I know," Eric answered, feeling nothing.

"Well, I'll be going in to Mrs. Busby," Father Duncan said.

Dr. Shane's car was still out. Lafayette was still grazing near the fence. Nearing home, Eric saw the car in the driveway. It was a long dark car. Even from here he could tell it was a Cadillac.

He slowed his walk. Jeepers, he thought, and hoped they wouldn't get all sloppy, maybe cry and hug him and kiss him and all that crap. He went sweaty with embarrassment and fear.

Gran was standing with some other people on the front steps. She was looking up and down the road, looking for him. Then she saw him.

"Eric!" she called.

His heart began to knock, actually knock inside him. He was so scared he hoped he wouldn't do something awful like crying again or throwing up. He had a crazy flash of memory, something about Gramp and Indians and battles and brave ancestors. He knew it was ludicrous, that it had nothing to do with the present situation. Still, Gramp would have expected him to put his head up.

They were all turned now, looking toward him. There was a man in a dark city suit. There was a tall lady in a bright dress, looking too young to be a grandmother. His grandmother. He had a crazy sense of unreality: maybe I am dreaming all this? The lady had red hair, and that surprised him. He hadn't expected red hair, although he didn't know just what he had expected.

They were coming down the steps. He straightened, and with one hand resting on George's collar, walked toward them slowly across the grass.

❖{31}❖

Anna lifted the warm dough from the bowl as carefully as if it were alive and placed it on the porcelain table, then floured it and took up the rolling pin. A fine, soothing calm washed over her, as always when she had the kitchen to herself. She moved without haste, handling the familiar pans and spoons.

Eric came in from the yard. "What are you making?" he asked.

"Strudel. Do you know what that is?"

He shook his head.

"It's a kind of pie, only much better, I think. I've already made on batch this morning for your Aunt Iris' house. It's in the pantry. Go take a piece and tell me how you like it."

When the dough had been rolled flat she brushed it with salted butter and began to pull it carefully, so as not to tear it, stretching it as thin as tissue paper until it hung over the edge of the table. Eric watched silently. He had cut a small piece and stood there, eating.

"Is that all you took? Don't you like it?"

He nodded.

"Well, then, take more! Go take a big piece. A tall boy like you, you've two hollow legs to fill up." She smiled and he smiled back, returning measure for measure. She wondered whether her own smile had been as urgent. Probably it had been.

"Don't you want milk? Something to wash it down with?"

He went to the refrigerator and poured a glass. She saw that he had been thirsty. Cutting the strudel dough, mixing the filling, she watched him without letting it seem that she was doing so.

After four months of living together she was not yet accustomed to the sight of this stranger who was of her flesh. She kept noticing new features: a mole on the cheek, a scar on the elbow. He would have distinction when he was grown, she thought. His hair, now sun-streaked, was exceptionally thick and rich. The aquiline nose, found usually on darker, Mediterranean faces, gave his a kind of elegance. His eyes were guarded by the arc of heavy lids; when he lifted them abruptly you were surprised by a gaze of charming candor.

She wondered whether, in that other life, he had ever been talkative. When boys came over after school now, pushing noisily into the house on these bright

272

fall afternoons, she saw that Eric always stood a little apart, a little quietly. It was not that he was rejected or ignored; it was just that he seemed to be not quite *of* them. She suspected that it was his height and good looks which were passing him successfully through the cruel gamut of adolescence. Thoughtfulness at that time of life, she reflected, remembering Iris, was not a social asset, especially when it was accompanied by private school manners. Eric's homeroom teacher here in the public school had told him not to address teachers as "sir," an instruction which had confounded Eric; he still forgot sometimes and used the form when speaking to adults.

But he had brought assets with him, too. He was a top basketball player and the years of living at the lake had made him a sturdy swimmer. Iris, concerned as always with "psychology," had gone to the school before it opened and spoken to his advisor about Eric. She had followed up again only last week and been told how well he had adjusted. Extraordinarily well, Iris reported, considering the bewilderment anyone would feel after such an upheaval.

The courage it must have taken! On the ride back, that first ride from Brewerstown, if that man Chris, the cousin, hadn't come along—and stayed for two days to help "settle in"—it would have been unthinkable for them all. As it was, the boy had spoken hardly a word on the entire ride. What was there to say? Joseph had been so tense that he hadn't talked, either. So Anna and Chris had spent a couple of hours making conversation about Mexico, where he had just spent six months. He had described Mexico City from one end to the other. He knew the area where her brother Dan lived; the houses there were very fine, he said. Then he had talked about Maury. She had forgotten that Chris was the young man whom Maury had so admired and visited in Maine. He'd talked of how bright Maury had been and of how they had met when Chris had had an accident. And Anna had thought: A stranger falls on the ice on a winter's night, and half a dozen lives are changed. A new life exists because of it. How does one begin to understand it all?

But Eric was doing well. Thank God, he was doing remarkably well. Everyone said he was.

She opened her mouth to say something, wanting to make a connection, such as: Eric, I love you; I'm still not over the marvel of your being here; Eric, it's like having your father back again—

But she had done that once. It had been during his first month, when suddenly she had been moved to tears, tears so jubilant and so painful that she had not been able to hold them back. She had seized his hands and kissed him. And he had pulled away with such an expression (of alarm? distaste? embarrassment?) that she hadn't done anything like it again.

She said calmly, talking half to herself and half to him, "Now we put in the apples, some raisins, some almonds, and I always like to add currants. Most people don't, but it gives a nice tart flavor, don't you think?" she went on, turning the long, fat roll over and over on the table before cutting it into three sections and putting it in the oven.

Eric nodded again.

This time she had to say what was on her mind. "You never call me anything, or your grandfather, either. Of course you can't call us 'Gran' or 'Gramp.' But I do think we need to have names. Won't you decide on something?"

"I don't know what to choose," Eric said.

"When you were a tiny boy, just starting to talk, you called me 'Nana.' "

"I did? I don't remember."

"Naturally you don't. But would you like to call me that? And your grandfather could just be 'Grandpa,' couldn't he?"

"All right. I'll start now, Nana."

"Eric? Is it very hard for you here? What I mean is—oh, I've put it clumsily, of course it's all been hard for you—but what I meant was, because it's *here*. Is it too different? That's what I meant."

"No, no. It's very nice here. I like the school and my room and everything. Honestly."

"I realize that we're probably very different in ways that we mightn't even be aware of. It's not simple. But if you'll just remember that we love you it will be simpler. Can you understand me?"

"I do understand."

"Well, then, enough of that! What are you planning to do with this nice Saturday?"

"I've got a pile of math to get out of the way. I thought I'd go sit outside to do it."

Every chance he got he went outdoors. Perhaps he felt confined in the house? This town, this house and yard, must seem so small after all that free space.

"I told you Cousin Ruth is coming to spend a few days, didn't I? Grandpa's gone into the city to call for her. Maybe if you're finished with your work by the time they get here he'll take you out to buy the football helmet and things you need."

"That'd be neat."

She watched him spread out his books and then started upstairs to change out of her work clothes, thinking with a pleasant thankfulness of him and Joseph going out in the afternoon. Joseph had taken charge of fitting Eric out for school and that was good; the boy needed a man; he'd been too long with an old woman, and a sick one, at that. Joseph and he had had lunch and gone to a couple of baseball games during the summer; it seemed as if they were really coming together. A pity that Joseph couldn't spend more time with him! But he was always so busy.

They had joined a small beach club for Eric's benefit. People here sent their children to camp and, except for the two Wilmot boys down the street whose parents couldn't afford to send them, there had been no one around all summer. But Iris, because Anna had never learned to drive, had dropped off the Wilmots and Eric at the beach every day, which was generous of her, busy as she was with her two babies.

Such darling little boys! Just eleven months apart and Stevie was walking now. Their coming had made such a difference in Iris. But not only their coming: first Theo's coming, and the house, and the perquisites that go with the title "Mrs."! If she were a Sicilian peasant, Anna reflected, Iris would have a dozen children gladly. She was at her best when she was pregnant. All the tension went out of her face. Even her voice was pitched more softly, more confidently. She had grown enormous each time, but she hadn't made the usual attempts to minimize her size. In fact, she had flaunted it, especially in front of childless women or women with only one child who weren't able to have any more.

She'll not stop at two. It isn't kind of me, but I envy her fruitfulness.

Not kind of me, either, that I feel such pride in showing Iris off to Ruth. Not that Joseph won't have been doing it before they reach here, if only to save himself from her babble. "That woman talks my ear off," he'd grumbled again before leaving this morning.

But I do feel pride! All those years of having people feel sorry for Iris! Especially Ruth, with her three daughters married young. Now Iris has what she wanted; she's had so little. (The innocents, born into trouble, Iris—and Eric, too.)

Ruth will be amazed at Iris' new house. Joseph had built it for them; it was nothing that either he or Anna would have wanted, but it was what Iris wanted and Theo apparently had no objections to it. A kind of glass box it was, glass and dark, stained wood, standing in a grove. A startling house, airy and light, but quite plain, almost severe. Still, it had been written about in an architects' magazine, and people did slow their cars down to stare at it when they went by.

One thing, surely: Iris would never, nor would her children, have to stand in shame in front of an Uncle Meyer waiting for somebody to offer kind charity and a roof. Nor would Eric.

She glanced outside. He had moved to the top of the wall. His books were open beside him and he was sitting quietly, looking toward the orchard, with his arm around the dog George. Curious, she watched. What was he thinking? Certainly he was not demonstrative or revealing, as Maury had been. Maury had worn his heart on his sleeve. He must be like his mother.

He had been remarkable at his grandmother's funeral, hadn't cried at all. Of course, her death had been expected, but it had been shocking, all the same. Death always is. It had been in Eric's second month with them that the call had come and a dry, old voice (Uncle Wendell, he'd said) had told them that Mrs. Martin had passed away. So Joseph and Anna had driven back to Brewerstown with Eric, purposely avoiding the street where he had lived, but he had been asleep on the back seat anyway.

"Such calm!" Joseph remarked later. "That part of him certainly isn't like our family." Anna had acknowledged that he was referring especially to her, who cried so quickly and easily.

But Eric had sat quietly through the funeral service, shaken hands with the minister and dozens of townspeople, then got back in the car with them and fallen asleep again all the way back, a good six hours' drive.

"He's got courage, that kid has!" Joseph said. "He can take what comes. That's what you call grit."

But it was a hard time, all the same.

Hard for me too, Anna thought with abrupt irritation. I didn't realize I could get so tired. I thought I was younger than I am. People assume I can do everything: help Iris with the babies, rear a teen-age boy and start to worry about

college and all the other complications— With equal abruptness came the prickle
of hot shame. Self-pity! Of all the disgusting qualities a human being can have!

She heard the car come up the drive and, a moment later, Ruth's and Joseph's
voices in the hall.

"Where's Eric?" Joseph inquired of Celeste.

"He and the dog walked down the road a few minutes ago, Mr. Friedman.
Went down toward the Wilmot house."

"Oh, well, you'll see him later," Joseph told Ruth. He carried her suitcase
upstairs to the guest room and set it down. "Well, I'll leave you girls to yourselves
and look at the paper till Eric gets back." Beneath the courtesy Anna could read
his impatience and knew that he had been drowned on the ride by torrents and
floods of words.

"So how are you?" Ruth asked, and went on without waiting for an answer,
"Country life agrees with you!" (She called this coming to the country!) "You look
better every time I see you, Anna, in spite of your troubles."

"I have no troubles!" Anna objected. As if, she thought wryly, by denying
them they will cease to be.

"Good, then, good, that's more than I can say. I don't know what I'd do if
Joseph didn't let me have the apartment so cheap. He's a prince, Anna. You know
the old saying, a mother can provide for five children and five children can't
provide for one mother. Not that I'm complaining. After all, they have their own
children, things aren't so hot for any of them, and you can't take blood from a
stone, right? So what's this room? This isn't Eric's room?"

"Yes, it's Eric's room. We bought all new furniture, light and cheerful, as soon
as we knew he was coming."

They had had to return the desk because he had brought his own. It was a
completely incongruous drawing room piece, ponderous in its dark Chippendale
dignity. But they hadn't dared tell him so. Apparently it meant a great deal to
him. On it he had placed photographs of his mother and grandparents. Hanging
above it was a portrait in oil, very old, of a man with mutton-chop whiskers and a
string tie.

"That's my great-grandfather Bellingham," Eric had told them when they inquired. "No, my great-great-grandfather. He was a sort of hero in the Civil War.
Have you any portraits on your side?" he'd asked Joseph, who seemed to have
thought for an instant that the boy might be joking. But of course he had not
been.

"They didn't have portrait painters where I came from," Joseph had answered
gently.

Beside the desk Eric had hung a shelf of books, all about birds, Anna saw, the
identification and classification of birds. But when she had made comment he
had said no, he wasn't especially interested in birds. She had wondered, but
asked no more. Celeste reported that Eric wanted the desk because his grandmother had always worked at it. Probably there was some similar memory attached to the bird books.

"I felt so sorry for him when you brought him here last June," Ruth remarked
now.

"I know."

Nevertheless, he had been cared for most lovingly. That was plain to see, Anna thought with some jealousy. And then: how sad it all was! How hard for that woman, after so many aloof, proud years, to have to appeal at the end to Joseph and Anna, after all!

"What courage it must take to face one's own death like that," she had told Joseph.

"We all face our own death, don't we?"

"Not like that. Not to have to say, 'By August I shan't be here; now what shall I do about this, that and the other?' As if you were preparing to move to a new house."

Ruth interrupted her thoughts. "As usual, Joseph hasn't spared anything, has he?"

Anna smiled. No, he hadn't. He had filled the shelves and closets with books and clothes, cameras, ice skates and tennis rackets. There were a radio and a record player. He had even wanted to buy a television for Eric, although they already had one downstairs and most people didn't own any yet. But Anna had said a firm no to that. Too much was too much and besides, a boy ought to do his homework in his room and read, not watch television. Iris agreed and the subject was dropped. Often it annoyed Anna that Joseph would take advice so readily from Iris, but when *she* said the same thing he might choose not to hear it.

Eric's photograph album was open on the bed.

"This is where he lived?" Ruth never bothered to hide her curiosity.

"Yes. Look through it. Eric won't mind."

It was a record of his years in Brewerstown, the pictures carefully dated.

"You had a good time with that car we sent, didn't you?" Anna had remarked of a picture that showed Eric, aged seven or eight, sitting in a huge toy car.

"You sent it?"

"You didn't know? We sent you many, many things. Your rocking horse and roller skates and your two-wheeler." Then she had stopped, hearing herself boastful and bragging. But she hadn't meant to sound that way.

Joseph joined the two women briefly at lunch.

"My son Irving tells me he sees your signs all over Long Island," Ruth told him. "They tell me you're one of the biggest builders in the East. Well, I knew you when! That's right, isn't it, Joseph?"

"You knew me when," he agreed quietly, and Anna knew he was amused.

Ah, the sin of pride again! I'm full of it, she thought. But she was proud, proud of Joseph in the dignity of his achievement. She was aware that a rivalry existed between herself and Ruth, different from the ordinary rivalries that existed among all women, whether they are willing to admit it or not. Theirs came because they had known each other so long; they had started out at the same place and edged on parallel tracks through life.

Ruth was discussing the refugees in her neighborhood. "So hoity toity, talking German! They only came here ten or fifteen years ago. I've been in the country almost fifty years."

The Daughters of the American Revolution versus the Society of Mayflower Descendants, Anna thought, amused again.

Lunch over, they went out on the terrace. It was mild for October, the sun just hot enough to be a comfort on the flesh. A flock of crows flew clattering above the trees, and pointed south.

"This brick needs doing again," Joseph observed. "He did a lousy job. Where the dickens did Eric go, anyway? We were going to buy his football stuff."

Anna saw that he was bored and restless. "He'll be back soon. In the meantime, I've made strudel for Iris and Theo. Why don't you run it over and see the babies?"

"Good idea," Joseph said, sounding relieved, and disappeared into the house.

"So Iris is doing well? Joseph drove me past her house on the way up. I can't say I like the style but it must have cost a fortune."

Ruth's tart remarks had no more power to wound, poor thing. Anna responded calmly, "Yes, everything has turned out very well for Iris."

"She certainly wasted no time in starting a family! Of course, at her age, one can't afford to wait too long. Still, I must say, I was right, Anna. I'm the one who always told you she was going to improve in middle age and you must admit I was right."

She wanted to say, "Iris is thirty-one, which is hardly middle-aged," but caught herself and said instead, "I made pot roast for tonight with the recipe you gave me when I was first married. It's still the best way."

"Why do you work so hard over cooking when you have Celeste?"

"I just enjoy it. I send a lot of things over to Iris. Theo likes my cooking."

"You cook when you're worried," Ruth said sagely. "I know you a long time, don't forget. You cook, and I sew. I make dresses for my granddaughters, which they probably never wear."

Anna was silent, and Ruth went on, "Why don't you take a trip? You never do any traveling. If I had your money, believe me, you wouldn't see me for dust. Why don't you visit your brother in Mexico City? You haven't seen him in years."

"Twenty years. But we couldn't go now and leave Eric."

"I suppose not. Tell me, how are you going to bring him up? His religion, I mean. What's he to be?"

Anna sighed. "To tell you the truth, I don't know. Joseph and I hadn't thought of it, I'll admit, but it was Iris who said he might want to go to church. So Joseph said, all right, he would take him. And Iris said, 'You'll go in with him, of course.' Well, we had thought of bringing him there and calling for him. But going inside? No. Iris said, 'How can you let a child that age walk in alone?' So we took him to that big Episcopal church in town. It was so strange, wondering what any of our friends would think if they should see us, and wondering what the people in the church might be thinking, those who might know us." Anna paused to recollect. A splendid organ, singing, and Eric's clear voice. Great decorum, a *high* atmosphere.

"And so?" Ruth prodded.

"It was a very pretty service, Joseph said. I almost laughed. If it hadn't been so serious and so confusing, I would have. Can you imagine, *Joseph* in a church?

'Will it kill us?' he asked me. 'As long as the boy believes in something,' he said. But after the first five or six times Eric wouldn't go anymore. And do you know, Joseph was upset about it?"

"Why didn't he want to go?"

"He said he didn't believe in it anymore. We tried to talk to him, but he wouldn't go back."

"Maybe he wants to go to temple, do you think?"

"We took him there once. And Joseph asked him if he might like to learn something about our faith, but he said no, he didn't care about that either. So that's where it stands."

Ruth sighed. "Well, you've got plenty of problems, Anna. I don't envy you."

Joseph was just coming in. "Problems? What problems? We haven't got any. Eric's a great kid, if you're talking about him. He's got guts and he's one of the brightest boys I've ever—"

"Was he at Iris'?" Anna interrupted.

"No, they haven't seen him today."

"I wonder where he went? It's almost dinner time."

An hour and a half later Celeste came to the door. "Shall I wait dinner? Eric's not home yet, is he?"

"No. I mean, no, he's not home yet. Do you want to wait dinner, Joseph?"

"Might as well eat. I'm going to have a talk with him when he does come in. Funny, he's so well-mannered, so considerate. He never did this before."

"There's always a first time. And he's only thirteen." Her voice pleaded, but pleading was entirely unnecessary, she knew. For if anyone were ever going to "have a talk" with Eric about anything, it would not be Joseph. He was that soft with the boy.

Celeste served the dinner. Ruth was the only one who ate. Anna began her usual struggle against the sense of doom, the dark half of herself which she had been trying all her life to submerge. Why am I so distressed because a boy is late for dinner? It must happen in thousands of households every night of the year.

"He's been gone since morning," Joseph interrupted one of Ruth's monologues.

"Then why don't you call some of his friends, if you're so worried?"

"Who's worried? Why, are you?"

"No," Anna lied. "But go call the Arnold boy, he's the captain of the basketball team. Maybe Eric's visiting there."

From across the hall they could hear the murmur of Joseph's voice at the telephone. Apparently, he was making one call after the other. Celeste brought in the dessert, which Anna didn't touch. She strained to hear Joseph and couldn't. Even Ruth fell silent.

Joseph came back. "Well, nobody's seen him. But there are seventy-five boys in his class. I can't very well call all of them," he said brightly.

And a minute or two later, "I wonder whether he could be avoiding dinner with me? I hurt his feelings about the dog, I think."

"No, no, of course not! And he got his way about it, didn't he? Joseph didn't

want to let the dog into the living room," she explained to Ruth, "on account of
the light carpet."

"I should think not," Ruth agreed. "Carpet like that costs a fortune."

"Joseph is neater than I am," Anna admitted. "Besides, I feel sorry for the dog.
He hates being left alone."

"My wife and her animals! I'm liable to find a stray horse in the house some
night, too," Joseph said. He got up and went out again, adding, "I just thought of
another call I could make."

"The real reason," Anna whispered, "why he gave in about the dog was that
Eric said his other grandmother never even minded that he slept on the bed with
him."

"On the bed! Is that quite clean?" Ruth asked doubtfully.

Anna shrugged. "What's the difference? So now George is allowed everywhere,
as long as Eric promises to wipe his paws first before he comes in from outside."

Joseph came back. "That kid!" he said, and turning to Ruth, "You know, he's
so well liked, there's no telling what friend's house he might be at. Probably
playing chess, forgetting the time. He's quite a chess player for his age; it's a
scientific game, you know that, of course. An intellectual game. We've got a very
brilliant boy on our hands," he concluded.

"Of course, of course, Joseph. I told Anna, anyone can see that."

"So," Joseph said, "I'm going upstairs to look over some papers I brought
home, and you girls can entertain each other. Let me know when he comes in.
I'm going to give him a piece of my mind. But not too big a piece." He winked at
Ruth. "Sure you girls can get along without me?"

The joviality was entirely unlike him, and it worried Anna. "You go on up and
do your work," she said, "and don't be upset, Joseph."

"Will you stop talking about being upset? For heaven's sake, it's eight o'clock,
and a thirteen-year-old boy is a little late. Honestly, Anna, sometimes you—" He
shook his head, took his briefcase and trudged up the stairs.

"Shall I turn the television on?" Anna asked.

"No, it hurts my eyes. The children got me one for my birthday and would
you believe it, I hardly ever look at it? I've got a magazine here, the last install-
ment of my serial."

Anna took *The Conquest of Mexico* from the shelf. Joseph had promised a visit
to Mexico time and time again. When Eric had been with them a little longer, she
was determined to visit Dan. Perhaps during this winter's vacation; they might
even take Eric with them! It would be a fine experience for the boy.

The book was hard going. She forced herself to concentrate, almost to memorize, as if she were going to take an examination on it. Her chair was turned
deliberately away from the clock. It struck nine. Or had she counted wrong? Had
it actually struck ten? She refused to turn around and look. Her mouth was dry.
She was unexpectedly frightened.

"It's getting cold outside," Ruth remarked. "Listen."

"Those branches need to be cut," Anna answered, forcing a level tone. "They
always knock against the window in the least wind."

She got up and went to the front door. A gust of chilling damp rushed into the hall. On the front lawn the tops of the trees tossed violently against a white sky. At eye level the darkness was absolute. There were no street lights in this section of town; that was one of its rural charms. But tonight the darkness was grim. The wind rushed like ocean tides. She closed the door.

Joseph was just coming down the stairs. "It's ten-thirty," he said.

"Perhaps you ought to call the police," Ruth suggested.

Joseph flashed her a furious look. "What? The police? Why? Ridiculous! What was he wearing, Anna?"

She frowned, trying to recall the morning, which seemed to have been ages ago. "A plaid shirt, I think. It's hard to remember."

"The radio said the temperature has fallen twenty degrees since six o'clock," Joseph said.

Anna was silent. She went back to her book, read one sentence four times without understanding it and laid the book down. In the kitchen, she could tell by the sounds, Joseph was making tea. She heard the kettle whistle, heard the cabinet door click as he took out a cup and saucer. Ruth sat quietly, she who could never sit more than two minutes without chattering.

It began to rain. There were no preliminaries, no first patterings. The squall simply came raging out of the sky and beat at the windows.

Joseph walked in, carrying his tea. "It's raining," he said, raising his voice above the drumming.

"I know." They looked at each other.

"This time I'll really let that kid have it!" Joseph shouted. "You know, it's not being fair to a child to let him get away with things. A child needs to know limits," he said, as if he were imparting some discovery or lecturing a class. "Yes, a child is happier when he knows what's permitted and what isn't. No doubt he's sitting somewhere with one of his friends, having a good time, not giving a thought to us, how we're—"

The doorbell rang. Their hearts lurched in their chests. It kept on ringing as if someone were leaning against it.

"My God!" Joseph cried, running to answer.

He ripped the door open to the vicious weather, to the bobbing arcs of a pair of flashlights in the hands of two state troopers who stood behind Eric and the huge, wet dog.

They stepped inside. "Is this your boy?"

Ruth screeched, "God above, where have you been? You've frightened your Grandpa and Nana to death, you ought to be—"

"Not now, lady." The trooper turned to Joseph. "You're the grandfather? We found the boy on the highway, trying to hitch a ride. He was heading for Boston, but he thought he was going northwest. Someplace in upstate New York . . . where was it, kid?"

"Brewerstown," Eric said. "It's where I live. I wanted to go back."

He stood there shivering and suddenly very small. The borrowed Windbreaker enfolded him like a cape and hung almost to his knees.

"I don't understand," Joseph said. "You were running away?"

Eric kept his eyes on the floor.

"Seems so," the trooper said. "It's a good thing we came along. He got a lift, he and the dog, with some guy who was—you understand," he said, glancing at Anna and Ruth, "excuse me—some sort of queer. Luckily he was able to get out of the car when it stopped at a light. I guess maybe the dog protected him, too."

The veins pulsed on Joseph's forehead. "Why did you do it, Eric? You've got to answer me. We've been good to you, haven't we, Eric? Why did you do this to us?"

Eric raised his eyes. "Because I hate it here," he said.

Joseph and Anna looked from one to the other, then at Eric, and back to each other.

"Kids!" the trooper said. "Don't pay too much attention, Mr. Friedman. He needs a good old-fashioned hiding and he'll shape up. They usually do. Only not tonight, I wouldn't. He's tired out and scared to death." He turned to Eric with rough kindness. "You're some lucky boy, living in a house like this. I wish I could have grown up in it! And you had a narrow escape. You could be in plenty of trouble by now, and don't you forget it."

He replaced his cap. There was a flurry of thanks, then offers of repayment and refusal.

"A drink? A cup of coffee, at least?"

"No, thank you, Mrs. Just take care of the boy here. And you, mind your grandfather from now on, hear?"

The door closed, thudding into silence. Where Eric stood, in cotton trousers and thin shirt, a smudge of wet spread on the floor.

"Eric, tell me," Anna whispered, "tell me what's wrong?"

"I hate it here! It's a mean, ugly place. I hate this house! You had no right to take me away from my home, and I'm going back. I'm not going to stay. I'll run away again. You can't keep me—"

"What kind of crazy talk is this?" Joseph cried. *"This* is your home. You know there's no place else, no one but us to take care of you. You ought to be glad that—"

"Joseph! Hush!" Anna commanded. "Eric, listen to me. We can talk about all that tomorrow. But tonight it's late and you can't go anywhere in weather like this. There's nobody out tonight."

He swayed and grasped the back of a chair. "Come, come upstairs and then in the morning we can decide what to do," Anna coaxed, urging him toward the stairs.

He was so weary that he had to pull himself up by the banister.

"I'll heat a can of soup," Ruth whispered.

Joseph followed them and started into Eric's room.

"No," Eric said, "I don't want anybody. Leave me alone, all of you. I hate you all."

The door slammed in their faces. They stood in the hall.

"I don't understand it," Joseph said again. He twisted his hands together. "He's been so cheerful, so agreeable. We were going to buy football gear today. I don't understand—"

Last week Anna had noticed that Eric trembled, or so she thought, but when she had mentioned it, Joseph had said it was nonsense. She didn't remind him now.

Ruth came up with a cup of soup and joined them in the hall at the closed, defiant door.

"I don't know what to do," Anna whispered.

"This is ridiculous," Joseph said. "Three adults intimidated by a naughty boy. I'm going in."

He pushed the door open. Eric lay on the bed in his underwear, his face half hidden. His wet shirt and pants were on the floor. In the weak smudged light from the desk lamp they could see that he was weeping.

Joseph laid a hand on his shoulder. "Now, why should you be crying? A big boy like you, basketball champ, football player?"

"Joseph, get out," Anna said fiercely. Talking to the boy as if he were a back-sliding three-year-old who had soiled his pants! He forgets how *he* cried, how we held each other when this child's father—

"What did you say?"

" 'Get out' is what I said."

"What are you talking about? Here's Ruth with hot soup, we only want to help—"

"You'll help by leaving him alone. Yes, there's one thing you can do. Hand me a quilt from the linen closet; there's a heavy blue one on the top shelf. And then go," she said, turning upon him a look which seemed to amaze him.

When she had covered Eric and shut the door she came and sat down on the bed.

"Now cry," she commanded. "God knows you've had reason enough. Cry it out. As loud as you want."

She had a glimpse of an anguished face; then the head went down to hide in the quilt, the body thrashed, shaking the bed. The sound of grief, deadened at first by the muffling quiet, rose into gasping cries, tearing the air, tearing the heart.

What can he think of a world in which his family always dies? Twice now, his home has been destroyed. Is he afraid that we too will die, Joseph and I? And then where will he go? Ought we to talk to him about that? Some other time, of course, not now?

A baby, Anna thought. Because he's tall and smart and speaks well we think he can cope with anything. It's hard enough for us to cope, old as we are. One foot stuck out of the muddle of quilt, one arm thrust over the head. Thin childish arm, large dangling hand of a man. Voice that veered from a squeal to a growl. And the first fuzz on the cheeks, so cherished, so anxiously examined in the mirror every morning. Maury used to take a hand mirror to the light at the window.

"Yes, cry," she repeated. "You've had enough to cry about."

On the opposite wall the haughty, elegant face of Bellingham looked at them from above the desk, surrounded by the books and photographs, the relics of the shrine that Eric had made. Yes, a shrine, built for the same reasons men have always made shrines.

Long minutes later (how many? Five? Fifteen?), the heap of quilting moved and struggled. A wet face emerged and was laid upon Anna's shoulder. Her arms went out and she raised the cheek to her own. And they sat there, rocking slightly, while the weeping died away into a long, shaking sigh. Then a quick sob, another sigh, long sighs and quivers and, finally, ease.

"Ah, yes, ah, yes," she said.

"I'm not asleep," Eric whispered. "Did you think I was?"

"No."

"Where is Grandpa? I want to tell him something."

"Grandpa, if I know him, is walking up and down the hall outside this room with his hands behind his back, the way he always does when he's terribly upset. Shall I call him?"

"Yes."

"Joseph?" she called.

The door opened instantly. "You want me?"

"Eric wants you."

Eric's head went back under the protection of the quilt. "I only wanted to tell you I don't hate you," he whispered, without looking up. "I don't hate it here."

"We know you don't," Joseph said. "We know." He cleared his throat. He coughed.

"George is hungry," Eric said.

Joseph cleared his throat again. "I fed him. He was very hungry. And thirsty, too. He's asleep now in the living room."

"I feel sleepy too, I think."

"Yes, yes," Anna said. "Lie down, I'll cover you properly."

"Doesn't he need something to eat?" Joseph asked.

"No, better for him to sleep now. In the morning he can have a big breakfast."

"Here, let me fix the quilt," Joseph said.

She stood a moment, watching his clumsy arrangement of it, feeling his need to do something, some little thing, anything.

Oh, for Joseph's sake, for mine, oh, not to lose this boy, too! Was it our fault? Can one ever say, "If this hadn't been, then that wouldn't have been"? But if it was our fault, let us hope not to repeat it—

So much to learn about this child, so little time left before he would be a man. And always, always, the secret places never to be entered. On those ancient maps that Iris collected there was a lonely boundary with a legend: *Terra incognita.* Unexplored land.

West of Gibraltar, Anna thought, where the world ended. They went out softly and as softly closed the door.

❈{32}❈

Vision blurred in the shimmering light; the sky, the sea and the sand merged in a white glare; figures were seen as red or blue dots in a painting by a Pointillist. But sound was distinct. It carried from far down the beach; swimmers' voices were heard on shore; they had the clarity of voices heard across snow.

The little boys were laughing in shallow water. Or rather, Jimmy was laughing while Eric held him, teaching him to swim, although he was only two and a half. Steve screamed and resisted.

Anna said, "It's strange that it's the older one who's scared."

"Jimmy's a tough little guy." Joseph chuckled. He admired toughness.

Iris was silent. She laid her book face down on her enormous belly, which formed a shelf; she was pregnant again, only five months, but she looked almost ready to deliver. She was thoughtful. People were beginning to think Jimmy was the elder boy. He was almost as tall as Steve and when they were seated Jimmy looked bigger and sturdier. Only this morning, when they had all arrived at the beach, Mrs. Malone had walked over to greet them and made the mistake. Iris read so much about the psychology of children but the books didn't really tell you what to do. In each special situation you had to use your own judgment.

Steve screamed again and Eric released him. He sat down in two inches of water.

"Don't you think—?" Iris began, but Theo, who had been walking on the beach with a colleague, came up behind her.

"You don't have to worry with Eric there. He knows what to do."

Theo had great regard for Eric. They all had. He was so dependable for his years, Eric was.

Now Eric carried Steve to the semicircle where they were all sitting. Jimmy trudged alongside. His walk was still a baby waddle.

"You don't have to," Eric soothed. "We won't swim anymore if you don't want to!"

"What's the matter? Why is he scared?" Joseph wanted to know. "Shouldn't you make him go back and learn that there's nothing to be scared of?"

"He can't learn all stiffened up like that, Grandpa. You'd just make him hate it. He's only three and a half, anyway."

"Yes, only three and a half," Anna repeated. "We forget because he's so smart."

Steve had astounded them this past week by picking out some words in the newspaper. He had remembered the "c" for "cat" in a picture book, the "a" for "apple" and the "t" for "tree." He had recognized the word "cat," and after that two or three more words, amazing the family.

Steve dove for his mother's lap. He burrowed, but there was no place to sit, so he butted his head hard against her.

"No, no," Iris said, holding him away. "You'll hurt Mommy, you'll hurt the baby in her tummy."

Joseph shook his head disapprovingly and muttered, "What next? You think he understands that? Much easier to tell him it's the stork and be done with it."

Privately, Anna agreed, but, after all, it was Theo's and Iris' business. "Come here, come to Nana," she said. "Look what I have for you."

She was sheltered under a beach umbrella to keep her thin skin from peeling. She had a beach chair and a bag. The supplies that came out of this bag were seemingly endless: tissues, sun lotion, handkerchiefs, Band-Aids, a bag of home-made spice cookies, a novel for herself and picture books for the children. People always laughed affectionately at Anna's organization and took advantage of it.

"Here, sit down, Nana will read you a story," she told Steve.

He crawled on her lap, dripping wet sand. If he couldn't have his mother's lap, Nana's would be a good substitute. He was still shaking from his fright in the water, although he trusted Eric, knew Eric wouldn't hurt him. But he was scared anyway. And Jimmy was splashing water in his eyes. Jimmy hurt. Mommy was always saying, "Don't be so rough with Jimmy, he's still a baby." But Jimmy *hit.* He threw his pail at me.

He leaned his head against Nana's softness. She read *The Little Engine That Could.* Every day, somebody read it to him. It was his favorite book and he knew where all the words were supposed to come, beneath every picture.

Nana pulled two cookies out of the bag. "One for you," she said. "And one for Jimmy. Come and get yours, Jimmy."

Jimmy took his and walked to some people sitting near them on the sand. He stood and stared, holding his cookie.

"Oh, isn't he darling!" a woman cried. "Look, Bill, isn't that the cutest ever? What's your name, sonny?"

"Not sonny. Jimmy," he said.

"Well, hello, Jimmy. Bill, look at those eyes!"

Theo scrambled up to fetch Jimmy and apologized.

"He isn't bothering us . . . he's just a very sociable fellow."

"That he is." Theo smiled proudly, agreeing.

Jimmy came over and stood listening to Nana. He never listened very long. Nana said it was because he was too little to understand very much of the story. He still hadn't eaten his cookie, although Steve had finished his. He always walked around carrying his food as if he didn't want it and sometimes he would even drop it on the floor, but if Steve should pick it up and eat it he would howl. Seeing him standing with that uneaten cookie made Steve want another one.

"I want another cookie," he said, but his mother heard and said no, he wouldn't eat any dinner and one is enough. At Nana's house, he knew, he would have gotten another, but now Nana said, "Your mommy said no."

Jimmy's cookie was almost touching Steve's arm. He couldn't take his eyes away from it.

"Why don't you eat the cookie, Jimmy?" Nana asked.

Jimmy didn't answer. He laid it on the sand and picked up his shovel. Steve reached out and took the cookie. Jimmy howled and hit Steve with the shovel.

"No, no!" Nana cried.

Steve slid out of Nana's lap and shoved Jimmy. He fell and hit his head on the umbrella pole. He screamed.

His father jumped up and grabbed Jimmy to examine his head. There was nothing wrong with it, but Jimmy kept crying. His father yelled at Steve, "If you hit Jimmy again you're going to be sorry!"

"He hit me with the shovel!"

"That's true," Nana said.

"I don't care, he's the older one and he's got to learn."

"I want my cookie," Jimmy sobbed.

"Did Steve take his cookie?" Mommy wanted to know.

"I think," Nana said, "I think he thought Jimmy didn't want it anymore."

Joseph groaned in mock despair. "Good God! You need King Solomon to settle this."

"Sibling rivalry," Iris explained. "A pain in the neck and perfectly normal."

Eric had just swum in from the float. "Come on, I'll build you a sand castle," he told the boys and drew them to the water's edge. "I'll build you a great big one, big as you are. I'll show you a shell I found. I'll put it to your ear and you can listen to it."

"Have you seen his shell collection?" Joseph asked. "Tell him to show it to you when you come next Friday, Theo. He's got a cabinet full in his room, all classified and labeled. Very methodical."

"He built the cabinet himself," Anna interposed. "You know, he's got golden hands. He can fix anything. Last week I wanted to call the plumber for the kitchen sink but Eric figured out what was wrong with it for me."

"You think he's content here, Theo?" Joseph asked anxiously.

"Yes, yes, he's come a long way in two years. You can see it for yourself, can't you?"

Joseph nodded happily. "Sure, but I wanted to hear somebody else tell me."

The beach was given over to the young. They dove off the dock and raced to the floats where they could be seen, when you shaded your eyes and squinted in the lowering sun, prone and spread-eagled, rocking and tilting on the water. They paraded along the strip of sand at the water's edge and gathered at the shed where ice cream was sold. The group of boys and girls formed and reformed in a ritual of watchful laughter and calculated ease, a ritual as carefully rehearsed and learned as fencing or ballet.

Three girls with new breasts and not one blemish sauntered casually toward Eric. Their perfect skin reminded Anna of a fresh white dress, just lifted out of tissue paper and not yet worn; it would never look quite like that again.

Eric said something to the girls and they saw him turn in their direction. Iris called to him and he walked over.

"Go along with your friends," she said. "You didn't come to baby-sit. And thanks for amusing the boys.

"Good!" she exclaimed when Eric had gone down the beach with the girls.

"What's good?" asked Joseph, who had roused from a half nap.

"That he didn't ask permission. He just went and didn't say where he was going." And when no one answered, Iris declared, "He's fifteen, you know. It's time."

"Yes, you're right," Anna said. Iris had the true gift of understanding. She had established something easy and trustful between herself and Eric. He dropped in often after school to visit; he was at home with Iris and Theo. That was as it should be. All the adults in his life had been too old, like Joseph and herself.

"Eric's so patient with the boys," Iris remarked. "He really loves them, you know?"

Anna observed, "Because he's been an only child, I suppose."

No, Theo thought, not so. Because, like me, he's been an orphan of the storm and he's grateful for the warmth. Grateful, that's what we are, he and I.

THE SUN STRUCK with a penetrating sweetness; at the same time a breeze moved over his flesh. It was so good drowsing here, good to do nothing, to think of nothing. He lay back on the blanket. Theo liked beach life. Having grown up in Austria, he had never had any, yet now that it was available he didn't have much time for it.

But that was all right; he surely wasn't about to complain that his practice had grown so large! Sometimes he couldn't believe the changes in his life during these few years since he had emerged from disguise and taken part in the liberation of Paris. A friendless stranger only a few years ago, and now so—so established! A fine, gentle wife. Two and a half children. A beautiful house. He smiled inwardly. He really didn't admire the house; it was too modern, too austere with its abstract paintings and bare floors. So Spartan. The food was Spartan too, for Iris was no cook and didn't even know how to train a maid to cook. But all of that was unimportant, and plain food was better for you anyway. Besides, Anna kept sending things over to them, or inviting them. At her house one dined richly on sauces, wines and whipped-cream cakes. Afterward one relaxed on flowered chairs; Anna would bring out fruit and chocolates; Joseph would pour brandy. They were lavish givers and enjoyers of good things, his parents-in-law. They reminded him of Vienna. He closed his eyes . . .

And started up, his heart drumming, bruising itself against his ribs. Had he cried out in the agony of the dream? But no, no one was looking toward him. He shut his eyes again. It had been a few years now since this terror had last come over him, half waking, half sleeping. An explosion in slow motion, it was, like a movie montage: fragments of peaked Nazi caps and smart boots; his own garden wall; a tiled corner of his roof; the rose-carved bed where he slept with Liesel; the fuzzy head of their newborn baby; his father's hands, pleading and chained;

Liesel's eyes, screaming; all rose roaring into the fiery air, splintered and crackled and broke, then settled into ash.

It is said that time is merciful and that is true. The first mad anguish fades to heavy sorrow and, after a long while, into a soft weakness of tears that can be blinked away before anyone sees. But not always.

In an old gesture he reached to twist the wedding band on his fourth finger, a habit of his when he was agitated. Then he remembered that in this marriage he wore no ring.

This marriage, this new life. He had been thinking before he drowsed that Anna and Joseph reminded him in some ways of Vienna. Of course they were not at all like Vienna in many other ways, or at least not like the Vienna he had known. He remembered his parents' somewhat formal, somewhat rigid bearing, the modulated voices at the table, with never any argumentation, no bickering, friendly or otherwise. *That* part was surely not like the Friedmans', where everybody talked at once, with such eagerness to be heard! When they had more than a few guests the confusion was dizzying. He smiled to himself. His heart had slowed to its normal beat. Calm and reality returned. This was *now* and he was *here*. These were his people. Such good people, such *home* people!

On Sunday mornings Joseph got up as early as on every other day and brought fresh lox and bagels to their door. On Friday nights when Iris and Theo arrived for dinner there was a package with two toys for them to take home to Steve and Jimmy. No use protesting that the old man was spoiling the boys. It was his pleasure, and he wouldn't have listened to the protest anyway.

Usually Theo went home after the dinner while Iris went with her parents to the synagogue. But now and then of late he had gone with them too, surprising himself by doing so, for he had hardly been half a dozen times in a synagogue during his entire life. He found it boring and meaningless, but it pleased Iris so much that he went, and pleased his in-laws too. Joseph especially was so proud, so bursting-proud, to be seen walking in with his son-in-law, the doctor.

He felt a true fondness for Joseph. You would have to be callous to return nothing to a man who so evidently loved you, even though you knew you were in part a substitute for his dead son. No matter. A kind, kind man, Joseph was. He liked to call himself a simple man; it was a favorite expression of his. And actually he was. His pleasures were simple, not counting his work, which was probably his greatest pleasure. Other than that, he liked to eat the food his wife prepared, to be honored among the prominent for his charities and to play pinochle with old friends who were simple, too. One of them still drove a taxi; he always arrived at the house in his yellow taxi.

Theo liked to think of his children growing up in this uncomplicated family. A warmth spread in his chest, thinking of it. The security, the safety! This broad peaceful country, this orderly town where his children slept in their clean beds. It was a miracle and there could be no other word for it. Out of the dregs and chaos of his own life, all this. This house, this family, these people. His.

A ripple of rising wind fell chill upon his shoulders. The sun was low in the sky. In small reluctant groups of threes and fours people were gathering their towels and bags and walking toward the parking lot.

He got up and helped his wife to her feet. She plodded heavily through the sand, holding Steve and Jimmy by the hand. The little boys were sleepy; they curled up on the front seat between Theo and Iris, their legs interlaced with one another's, for once not squirming or fighting. The grandparents sat in the back.

"A lovely day," Anna sighed.

Quiet settled over the beach. Even the gulls were gone (where had they gone?) except for one who stood at the end of the dock, a dark, still shape against the light. The sun blazed its last fire, balanced on the rim of the sea, bleeding pink into the clouds.

"It'll be a hot one tomorrow," Joseph predicted, shaking his head.

Tomorrow and tomorrow and tomorrow. Separate from the other unnamed billions who walk the earth, each of these little groups of three or five or twelve, brought together by the shuffle of chance, then welded by blood, sees in itself the whole of earth, or all that matters of it. What happens to one of the three or five or twelve will happen to them all. Whatever grief or triumph may touch *any* one will touch *every* one, as they are carried forward into the unknowable under the brilliant, terrifying sun which nourishes all.

❈{33}❈

In the beginning it was primeval forest, ash and hemlock, maple, elm and oak. Then came the settlers to level the woods, plant corn and graze cattle. Trees were planted again for summer shade. During long years, two hundred or more, the farms were given by father to son and the land flourished.

Toward the end of the last century came men of wealth from the cities, gentlemen farmers assembling their estates among the working farms, building their country mansions behind walls and wrought-iron gates. Still the trees flourished, for these men liked to play at rural living. On their terraces they sat and watched their fine blue-ribbon herds; their burnished horses hung their heads over the post-and-rail fences that kept them away from the gardens and the specimen shrubs.

After the Second World War the developers arrived, answering the pressure of population from the cities. Now, for a second time, the trees came down, not selectively, a few here where needed, a few there, but drastically and ruthlessly, in a total leveling. An oak stood tall against the sky, its leaves at the crest still tossing in the summer wind, while the saw screeched at its base. It stood, leaned very slightly for an instant, then plunged in a wide arc to the ground and lay there shuddering, prone on the earth out of which its first soft, timid finger had emerged a century and a half before.

So the trees came down; the meadows were divided and sub-divided and the bulldozers ripped the earth. Acre after acre, row after row of identical houses like checkers on a board lay flat in the glare of the sun. The streets were given the aristocratic English names of poets and admirals. The houses were sold as "manors" or "estates," in spite of the fact that very often one could reach out of a window and shake the hand of a neighbor leaning out of his.

Like a stain on a tablecloth the tracts spread over the countryside, covering the land. Then came the shopping malls, the crisscross highways; great transit systems in which roads looped and turned back upon themselves to handle the enormous flow of cars, so that the traveler who wanted to go west had first to turn east, find an overpass and swing back in the opposite direction.

Growing, growing, spreading, with no end in sight.

❊{34}❊

Eric sat on the steps of the sales bungalow, waiting for his grandfather. To the left stretched long rows of completed houses, all alike under the gray March sky. To the right, frames were going up; hammers racketed; dust rose in spurts of reddish cloud when a truck dumped a load of bricks; cement mixers rumbled. Enormous pipes, wide enough for two men to crawl through, lay among coils of glittery copper wire. A truck ground up a small incline. Another dropped a load of sheetrock. Confusion out of which, to be fair about it, would come order.

Soon he would be starting the fourth year in his "new family," so he had been on these visits to the building sites many times by now. He didn't really mind, as long as he wasn't asked to go too often. Today they had combined the trip with shopping for shoes and a raincoat. Grandpa said that was a man's business, not a grandmother's.

He didn't really need a new raincoat. Gran would have looked at his old one and said, "It'll do for another year," just as Gran used to say, "You already have enough sweaters, you don't need another one." Or, "You've really had enough to eat, Eric," a statement that would be unthinkable in the Friedman house.

Here, food was urged upon you, more than you could swallow sometimes. Here, something was always being bought for you. "You like the sweater? It's nice, I'll get it for you." Giving was a way of loving, not as a substitute for time or caring but only because, Eric realized, they never seemed to find enough ways. If Chris and the family had had any worries about how he would be loved—and he had no reason to think so—they needn't have had them. He was bathed, surrounded and enveloped with it.

Chris wrote to him regularly. The other Guthries wrote from wherever they happened to be. Cards were mailed on 'round-the-world cruises. Greetings and small presents came from the house that the elder Guthries had rented in the south of Portugal. Chris wrote really long letters with descriptions of Venezuela and snapshots of the children sent, Eric knew, to stave off any loneliness Chris thought he might be feeling. Eric tried to respond in kind. I've made the basketball team, playing forward. I got a new bike for my birthday. Everybody is good to me. I've got lots of friends. I'm in a new scout troop.

The truth was more complex than these flat facts. It was so very different, this household. For one thing, it was so busy. The sense of a busyness almost hectic

292

came from his grandfather. Take today: it was supposed to be his free day. But as always there was some emergency which he absolutely had to attend to, even today, with Passover starting at sundown. He was always rushing somewhere. Eric had been surprised to learn that his grandparents had only lived seven years in town; they were as involved as if they had been there all their lives. His grandmother was on the hospital board and so many other charitable boards that he couldn't remember them all. Grandpa had built a chapel for the new temple and turned over his half of the profits as a gift. (Grandpa wouldn't have told him, but Aunt Iris had; she was so proud of him.) Last week a policeman had been run over chasing a suspect and the town had taken up a collection for his widow and children; Grandpa was the head of the committee. There was talk of his being appointed to a state commission to study public housing. No, he was not the kind of man with whom a boy could spend long afternoons in the woods with book and binoculars, hunting for birds. He wouldn't have been interested, even if he had had the time.

Perhaps, though, that wasn't fair? When you thought of his life and where he had come from? Once in New York they had driven past the house on Ludlow Street where he had grown up and past the house on Hester Street where Nana had come as an immigrant. He'd been shocked at the narrow, crowded streets and the mean houses. He'd never seen such places except vaguely in pictures. . . . What could you learn of forests and birds living in places like those?

Last fall before school opened Grandpa had had to go to Boston on business, and Nana had suggested they travel north through New England for a few days. It was surprising, but Grandpa had agreed. They had gone all the way up to Mt. Monadnock in New Hampshire, staying in old wooden hotels with sunflowers in the yard and stacks of pancakes to start the chilly mornings. They'd walked around the white little towns and Nana had gone into antique shops and bought knickknacks of old glass.

"Keeps a woman happy, buying toys," Grandpa had said, and winked at Eric.

They had walked down a road, Grandpa and Eric, and stopped on a bridge over a stream where a couple of boys were fishing.

"Know anything about fishing?" Grandpa had asked and when Eric said yes, he'd often used to fish for trout outside of Brewerstown, he'd looked out over the sloping fields where the corn stubble was dry, and then to the hills, to the far blue ranges overlapping one another; he had looked and looked and finally said, "There's so much I've never seen, Eric."

So perhaps it wasn't right to say he wouldn't be interested.

On the way south it was Nana who had made a suggestion, as if she had been reading Eric's mind. "Maybe we could go back through New York State and Eric could see Brewerstown again."

It wasn't that he'd been afraid to ask. By this time he knew he could ask them for anything and they would give it or do it. The reason was that he hadn't wanted them to think he was homesick or not happy with them. They were so dreadfully sensitive about him! Once he had overheard his grandmother talking to that old lady Ruth who came to visit.

"Eric has grown even closer to our hearts than Maury was at that age," she had said. "Joseph used to be strict with Maury, remember? But Eric can do anything he wants." And she had sighed. "I don't suppose he can have any idea of what he means to us."

They would have been surprised to learn that he did have, that he observed far more than they knew. He saw, for instance, that when Grandpa was working especially hard and long he could be quite cross with Nana. Small things irritated him, a purse or a pair of gloves left lying on a chair, or being kept waiting for five minutes. And Nana didn't answer him back. But he was never cross with Eric, never once, although Nana sometimes was, but not very often, either.

They were soft with him because they were afraid he wouldn't love them, he knew that clearly. There had been times when he'd been so sorry for himself, especially during the first year; no kid he'd ever known had been in his position. In a way he still sometimes felt a little sorry for himself. But most times he was more sorry for the two old people, he didn't know just why.

So they had stopped in Brewerstown. Driving down the main street toward the house he'd had a sick feeling and slumped in the car, hoping nobody he knew would see him. He'd remembered the day he left the house almost three years before. Gran had gone back to the hospital where she was to die. They had carried her out, all shrunken and dark yellow, with a strange unpleasant odor not like Gran, who had always smelled of lemon soap. When he had gone down the front walk for the last time he had been thinking that the house would be lonesome for them. On the way out he had stopped to stake an enormous peony head that otherwise would have drooped in the dust along the front walk; Gran was so particular about her peonies. He'd tried in those last minutes to memorize everything: the hawthorne tree, a real hawthorne from England, with wicked needles; the mulberry bush where he used to make a shady cave for himself and George when they were both very young. It had seemed to him that all of these were aware that he was going away. He'd gone down the path between Grandpa and Nana, strangers then, had got into their car and all the way down the road, until the house was out of sight, had not allowed himself to look back, had just stared straight ahead.

So now they had come up before the house again and, astonishingly, it looked the same. There was a doll carriage on the front walk. A baby carriage with a mosquito netting stood on the porch. They had sat in the car observing a croquet set on the side lawn and wash blowing on the line near the garage. The house was alive, as if Eric had never lived in it and left it. . . .

"Would you like to go in?" Nana had asked. "I'm sure the people wouldn't mind—"

"No," he'd said firmly. "No." They had understood and started the car and driven away.

Wanting to say something, Eric had pointed out the horses in the Whitelys' field. "That's Lafayette, the brown and white one. I used to ride him almost every day."

"You never said you could ride! Why didn't you tell us? I'll buy you a horse," Grandpa had exclaimed. "There's a good stable not fifteen minutes away from our house!"

"No," he'd refused. "No, thanks. I don't have the time now, with school and basketball practice and everything."

But that wasn't the truth. The joy of riding, the free wind, the horse-companion—all that belonged to the other life. He mustn't mix them up. It had been confusing enough. He must keep the lives separate. That other was finished and closed. Forget it.

The door swung open now and Mr. Malone came out. He sat down with Eric on the step.

"Your grandfather will be through in a couple of minutes." He wiped his forehead. "This is some big job, let me tell you. Think you'd like to run this business?"

"I don't know, sir," Eric answered politely.

"Silly question, wasn't it? How could you know? But you will! My boys have taken over magnificently. And your grandfather will be in seventh heaven the day you hang your hat in our office." He lowered his voice. "You know, Eric, he's a different man since you came. Not that there was anything wrong before, but now it's as if he'd shed years. I can tell. I've known him long enough. You know how long I've known him?"

"No, sir."

"It was in 1912. Let's see, that's thirty-nine years. We've seen a lot of life together. Did he ever tell you how I was wiped out in the stock market in '29 and how he took care of me?"

"No, sir."

"Well, of course, he wouldn't. But I'll never forget! He fed me and my whole family until I was able to pull myself together again. Yes," Mr. Malone said, "old times. Old times. Seeing you here reminds me of when your father used to come to visit the job in the city. He was younger than you are. You don't mind my mentioning your father?"

"No, sir."

" 'Sir.' I like the way you say 'sir,' although I wouldn't object if you didn't. But it shows you've been well brought up. Kids these days don't say it. Except the parochial school kids. *They* have manners. They have to, or Sister would rap their knuckles for them."

Strange how many different kinds of people there were around here, Eric reflected. Mr. Malone was so Catholic! And one of the engineers was Chinese; after you got used to his odd face you could see it was really handsome.

"Your grandfather had better put a move on." Mr. Malone looked at his watch. "If he wants to be home in time for the Seder."

Imagine Mr. Malone reminding his grandfather of the Seder!

Grandpa came out and they got into the car. "Some project, hah?" he said, as they bumped their way around bulldozers and cranes. "Three million dollars' worth! Don't get me wrong, we don't make that out of it." He laughed. "Not by a couple of long shots, we don't. What I meant was, we have to get that much together from the banks and syndicates to get the thing started. A thousand hours of headache, I can tell you that. But it's a great challenge, Eric, a thrill to drive past when it's all finished, and see the cars in the driveways, curtains in the windows, kids playing on the sidewalks. To think that you—we—conceived it in our heads and saw it through. Think you'd like it?" he asked, as Mr. Malone had done.

"There's an awful lot you have to know," Eric said.

"Ah, but you'd take to it like a duck to water, you would. We sold nineteen houses last weekend alone. What do you think of that?"

"Gosh," Eric said.

"Say, it's your birthday next week, isn't it? I don't suppose you'll tell me what you want. You never do."

Actually it seemed to him that he already had everything. But then, as the car turned a curve and they passed a pair of gates set in stone pillars, he suddenly did think of something he would like.

"You know what I would like, Grandpa? If it isn't too expensive, I think it would be great if you'd join the Lochmuir Club. Then I'd have a place for tennis anytime I wanted. Even in the winter."

"The Lochmuir Club? What do you know about that?"

"It's really nice. I was there, remember, last year when those friends of Chris's were visiting relatives in town? And Chris asked them to look me up? They took me out to dinner there."

"I didn't know that's where you had gone."

"Some of the kids at school belong. They've got squash courts and an indoor pool. The swimming pro there trained for the Olympics, too."

"Sounds very fine," Grandpa said slowly.

"So you think we could join, do you?"

"No," Grandpa said, "we couldn't."

"Is it too expensive? Is that why?" Although, if that was the reason, it would be the first time his grandfather had ever denied anything because of it.

His grandfather took his eyes off the road for a moment. "That isn't the reason. Don't you know what the reason is?"

"No."

"Think, Eric."

It dawned upon him, and a warm flush prickled his neck. "Is it because you're—"

"Don't be afraid to say it. Because we're Jewish and we are not admitted to that club. Not as members. Not as guests in the dining room. You never knew about that?"

"Well, I've read things here and there, but I guess I've never thought about it very much."

"No, you haven't had to, have you?" His grandfather's mouth looked grim.

They rode for a few minutes in silence. Then Eric said, "Those people said they were coming back east this summer and they'd call me again. I'll tell them I can't go."

"You don't have to do that. You can go."

"I don't think I want to."

"Well, it's up to you." Another silence. Then his grandfather turned with a smile, a manufactured smile? Eric wondered. "Well, here we are, in plenty of time to change for your grandmother's big dinner. You remember, of course, that we dress for Seder, Eric."

"I remember," Eric said.

THE TABLE WAS set with a lace cloth and the silver candlesticks which always flanked the bowl of flowers in the center. Tonight were added the holiday objects which Eric would be seeing for the third time, not counting the dinner, long ago, at the house of that boy David, the dinner which then had seemed so queer and foreign, but which now seemed very natural. It was a festival of freedom, as Grandpa had thoroughly explained. He recognized the matzoh under its embroidered cover, the plate of horseradish, symbol of the bitterness of slavery, and the green parsley that celebrated the first fresh growth of spring. He knew that the silver goblet, already filled with wine, had been prepared for the prophet Elijah who was to announce the coming of the Messiah, and it was there "just in case he might be coming tonight," Grandpa would say with a wink.

There were twelve places at the table this year, places for friends who had no family to go to, and a place for a young man at Grandpa's office who had just tragically lost his wife. Two of the places were for Steve and Jimmy, old enough this year to be present for the first time.

Everyone was dressed up; the clothes looked new and the women had just come from the beauty parlor. Everyone babbled. Aunt Iris was worried about the baby, Laura, who had been left at home. She was worried that the little boys wouldn't behave. "So what's the difference?" someone said, "it's family!" Grandpa picked the boys up and squeezed them. It was Jimmy who would ask the four questions, Eric knew, because he was the youngest male at the table. Yes, by this time Eric knew exactly what would happen, the order of the evening. " 'Seder' means 'order,' " Grandpa had told him. He knew that the food would be delicious. Nana had been working in the kitchen over soup, fish and chicken; there would be cake and strawberries and macaroons for dessert. But it would be a long time until dessert, a long time even before they had the first mouthful of food, and Eric was prepared to be restless.

Grandpa took his place in the armchair and waited for Nana to bless the candles. His eyes were shining. This was one of the greatest hours of the year for him. His eyes rested in turn on everybody up and down the table. Then he turned back to the illustrated Haggadah which lay open beside his plate. He lifted his cup and said the blessing over the wine. The men at the table—except for Eric and Uncle Theo-joined him in the old words that they must first have heard when they were the ages of Steve and Jimmy, who were sitting surprisingly still, with big, round eyes.

"Now, what does Passover mean? It commemorates the night when the Angel of Death spared the homes of our forefathers in Egypt and we were led out of slavery."

Eric watched and listened. It was all bright and beautiful, like poetry. But it would be artificial for him to learn this ritual. It was not his. Aunt Iris told him once (they had had many talks together; she was frank and honest to talk to) that his father hadn't really liked being Jewish.

"He wanted to be more American," she had said. "But I never saw any conflict. We have a four-thousand-year-old tradition and it's a part of the American tradition, woven into it. The Puritans were Old Testament people, you know."

"It's strange," Eric had observed, "that he and you lived in the same house and this means so much to you. Why do you suppose—"

"I don't know," she had answered.

And Eric had told her, "I don't especially want to be Jewish either. I don't *not* want to be; it's just that I don't care one way or the other. Can you understand?"

And she had said, "You don't have to be. You have a choice either way. Or no way, although I don't think that's so good."

Then he had cautioned, "Aunt Iris, don't tell Grandpa or Nana, please."

"No, I certainly won't," she had promised.

He had added, "I feel guilty about it, do you know? To have thoughts like those and keep them hidden?"

And she had told him not to feel guilty, that guilt was a crippling thing, that you could get sick because of it. "All young people keep things hidden from their elders. It's quite normal, Eric."

He always found it so easy to talk to her. "And you? Did you keep anything hidden?"

She had looked at him steadily. "For years I suffered because I knew they thought I was a homely girl whom nobody would ever want."

"I don't think you're homely," he had told her. "You don't look like most other people. I think you're even sort of pretty. Doesn't Uncle Theo think you are?"

And she had laughed and said, "I guess he must. If he doesn't he's cheated himself."

When she laughed, which wasn't often, Aunt Iris really did look pretty, Eric thought. And she was smart. Sometimes when he had to do a history project or something and didn't know how to go about it, she'd give him ideas. She could make things so direct and clear.

They were both smart, she and Uncle Theo; their kids would learn a lot from them. Uncle Theo's name had been in the paper last month in an article about some doctors in New York who were reconstructing the faces of Japanese war victims. "An international gesture," the paper said. He had a plastic surgery service at the hospital here where they'd built a new wing—Grandpa had made a big donation for the wing; there'd been a dinner and speeches and Grandpa's name had been in the paper too.

Now Eric was starved. They were still going through the ritual, eating the matzoh, "symbol of the bread of affliction," Grandpa said.

Jimmy was prompted. He had been rehearsed by his mother all week, and he spoke up in a pure chirp, asking the first of the four questions: "Why is this night different from all other nights?"

Aunt Iris reached around Jimmy's chair and took Uncle Theo's hand. She was really crazy about Uncle Theo. Once, when Eric had been at their house and they hadn't known he was coming through the door, he'd seen her run up to Uncle Theo and throw her arms around him and kiss him so—so *violently*. It had made Eric feel all strange, embarrassed and strange.

Now everyone started to sing. The song was in Hebrew. Naturally Eric had no idea what it was about, but it sounded merry. Nana had a thin, sweet voice, not loud, but you could hear it clearly alongside all the other voices.

She liked to sing. Often when she worked in the kitchen he heard her singing as far away as his room upstairs.

"My mother used to sing in the kitchen," she'd say, and he'd try to imagine what it must be like to remember your mother singing.

Once he asked her, "What was my mother like?" and waited, almost holding his breath. What would she answer? He had an idea, although no one ever told him so, that she hadn't liked his mother.

She hesitated, as if she were trying to recollect, and then she told him, "Your mother was a gentle girl. She was quite small and graceful. She was intelligent and quick-witted. She loved you and your father very, very much."

Nana had been making buns that day, pouring the yellow batter into the pans, and she said, "These were your father's favorites. He could eat a half a dozen at a time."

She spoke almost shyly. Eric had already learned that she never mentioned his father in Grandpa's presence. He had felt bold enough to ask her why that was so.

"Gran used to talk about my mother. Why doesn't Grandpa like to talk about my father?"

"Because it hurts him too much," Nana answered.

"Doesn't it hurt you?"

"Yes, but people are different," she said quietly.

He still sensed something heavy and unsolved in the air, and thought he knew it was because his grandfather was sorry about something he must have said or done. He was grateful for the little things that Nana told him at unexpected times.

"Your father used to say your eyes were like opals," she had told him once, and he had felt a smile creep about his mouth. She had a way, with these remarks, of making his parents, especially his father, seem real. Up to now they had been cut-outs, silhouettes; even his mother, who was talked about so much in the Brewerstown time, always seemed like a doll to him, too sweet to be true. His first knowledge of his father, coming to him through Chris, had been no knowledge at all. What is it to say, Your father was a great guy, a great student? He got much better grades than I ever did? He played a great game of tennis, too?

That was only a caricature of the manly man at Yale. *Who was he?* It helped more to learn from Nana that he liked buns.

Still, it wasn't enough. Eric began to understand that it never would be enough, that his quest for knowledge of his father and mother would be a journey without end, a passage through rooms and doors, each one leading, after he opened it, to another room with another door. Doors going nowhere. Or else not opening at all.

Grandpa spoke now in a grave, impressive tone. *"Ani ma' amin:* I believe. I believe in the coming of the Messiah, and though he tarry, yet will I believe."

(Christ said, "Lo, I am with you always, even unto the end of the world." The Egyptians put food and clothing in their tombs to be ready for the next life. They, too, were sure they were right.)

For the moment the ceremony came to a halt. The fish was being served. With enormous appetite and relief Eric took up his fork.

THAT ACHE IN the throat and behind the eyes was what Iris called her "brimming" feeling. It was not so much that the cup of joy would overflow; it was rather that the cup would break from the pressure. How could life sustain so much?

The little boys in their twin suits were staring at Papa in his carved armchair. To a child, Iris thought, remembering how it had been when she was the age of her sons, that tall, dark chair stands like a throne on another level. The voice that issues from the throne is transformed, not Papa's everyday voice at all. It is kind but serious and, if anyone dares to interrupt while that voice is speaking, he is immediately, sternly silenced.

She smiled now at her boys, shaping silently with her lips, "Good boys." They looked awestruck; they looked almost as if they understood what their grandfather had said, although that was impossible. Yet it was true that they would never forget all this.

Eric looked remote except when he was eating. Even then he was only concentrating on the food. She doubted that he even heard what was being said. Suddenly Iris remembered sitting in the kitchen with Maury and Aggie when Eric was born. They were talking about him and one of them said, "Let him be free, he can choose what he wants to be when he grows up." Iris had made no comment. She had been a schoolgirl; what could she have known? But when they asked her, "What do you think?" she had told them: "A child should know who he is." And Maury had answered, "A good and decent human being, that's who. Isn't that enough? Does a person need a label, like a can of soup?"

They had seen it so simply but she remembered having thought even then that they were wrong. It wasn't that simple.

Papa was laughing with Mr. Brenner at the other end of the table. Probably it was a joke that he considered risqué. Yes, they were saying something behind their hands and Papa was glancing at the women to make sure they didn't hear. Papa's idea of a risqué joke was something that would bore the average boy in junior high today. Papa must be the last of the Victorians. Not the hypocritical Victorians (Iris had read enough about the period to know the subtleties of it), but one of that high-minded breed who lived what they believed and believed what they lived.

That steady optimism, that certainty that anything can be straightened out; what would we all do without it? Only once did it fail him, when Maury died. And even so he managed. I don't know what we shall do when Papa is gone. Sometimes I feel that he holds us all in his strong hands.

"Iris, Mrs. Brenner is talking to you," Mama chided.

"What? Excuse me. I'm daydreaming. It's all that wine," she apologized.

"That's all right," Mrs. Brenner said. "I only said something about your mother's new crystal bowl. I love Lalique, don't you? And your mother says she's bought one just like it for you."

"You didn't tell me," Iris protested. She didn't want the bowl. It didn't fit in their house. Mama persisted in bringing presents of her own taste, which was too fussy and flowery for Iris.

"I forgot to tell you," Mama said. "I meant to give it to you today."

Iris caught Theo's look and his message. He sometimes told her she was sharp with Mama. She supposed she might be when Mama annoyed her, yet she knew she had no right to be. Why was it often so difficult for her and her mother to say the simplest things to each other?

"Thank you, Mama, it's handsome," Theo said now. "You're always too good to us."

"Yes, thank you, Mama," Iris said. "It's beautiful."

Mama smiled as if it were she who had been given the present.

THE WINE STIRRED in Anna's head, too, along with the rising heat of the room and the spice of carnations. Her thoughts rushed from the strawberries, which weren't as good as they should have been, to what Joseph was saying about how free we were here in this glorious America, and how we mustn't forget those places in the world where men were still in chains.

He spoke well. His ideas were organized and clear. A man like him, unread, with so little education! He had been called upon to talk fairly often of late, at the county real estate board, at the Community Chest dinner last month. She was always so proud to see him on the platform, honored and tall. He really wasn't tall, but he looked it, and she always felt herself sitting taller as she watched him.

Hard to think he was the man who went to work carrying his painter's brushes and overalls! Yet he hadn't changed. He was still plain and direct. He had no airs like some who pretended they'd never been down on the East Side, that they'd never heard of Ludlow Street and couldn't understand Yiddish.

Of course, he did have a quicker temper than he used to have. He got irritable over trivial things. Yet he was so quick to say he was sorry; one mustn't forget that. He worked too hard and too long, but try and stop him.

"I have a tiger by the tail," he said. "I can't stop."

Anna wanted him to have his portrait painted. He insisted that was too highfalutin for him. She reminded him that he hadn't thought it was highfalutin for her to be painted years ago in Paris.

"Women are different," he told her.

But Anna wanted it. She knew just where she wanted to hang it, over the mantel in the dining room, a fine portrait of him wearing a dark suit like a nineteenth-century diplomat. She'd have to talk to Eric. If Eric asked Joseph to do it, he'd do it. He'd do anything for Eric. So would we all.

She glanced down the table. Iris was leaning over to talk to Eric. She knew that Eric and Iris often had long talks, especially about Agatha and Maury. It had worried her one day that Iris might let slip some things about his parents that Eric shouldn't know.

"I haven't said a thing," Iris had assured her. "But now that you bring it up, why shouldn't he, at least someday, know the whole truth? Isn't that what growing up is about, to face the truth?"

And Anna had answered, "Only when it will make a difference, when you need to know. Some truths can destroy, and then it's kinder to lie." Secrets. So many secrets around this table. And still everything holds together. Please God that it always will.

She remembered now that Iris had looked at her with surprise.

"Delicious, Anna," Joseph said. And he proclaimed to the guests with pride, "No prepared or ready-made food in our house. My wife makes everything herself."

At the far end of the table Anna was serving the little boys. The ring sparkled on her busy hands. Her sleeves fell back from her white wrists. He thought: We should have had a big family like Malone's; she was meant to have one.

This was not the evening for regrets, yet emotions ran in currents and cross-currents. Under the joy he regretted. If only his achievements of the seven years since the war had come sooner! So many years of their lives had been drably wasted in keeping alive. (As with most of mankind.) Well, he had put away enough in tax exempts now so that none of them would ever have to be afraid, especially if anything should happen to him. He had seen to that. God forbid that there should be a repetition of the thirties. The economists all said there wouldn't be; too many safeguards had been built into the system. But who knew?

If only Eric had come earlier, he thought, watching the boy accept a second helping. Nothing shy about his appetite! He wondered what Eric really felt about this ceremony, whether it moved him at all with any sense of family, if nothing more. Even a sense of history? Probably not. It was all too recent and too sudden. He had been thirteen already when he came to them. It had been hard enough to make Maury see it as he should. And Maury had been nurtured in their house.

No matter. Just let the boy be healthy. Let him be happy and never mind anything else. I never thought I'd hear myself saying that. He seems happy. He's smart in school, talks like a professor sometimes! And the boys like him. He's an athlete and that opens doors, always did, even in my day when they admired the guy who was fast at stickball, dodging the pushcarts. He's good with his hands, too. Anna mentioned something in his hearing about a bird house and didn't he go and build one for her? With a front porch and a chimney?

Yes, Joseph thought, there's so much to be glad about. He felt a surge, a bursting in his throat. He was afraid his eyes would tear in another minute. They often did when he was moved and it was embarrassing. He filled the cup of wine again.

"Let us say the third grace," he said, and suddenly thought he heard his father's voice issuing from his own mouth. "Praised be He of whose plenty we have partaken and through whose goodness we have lived."

BOOK FOUR

THUNDER

❊{35}❊

The new Home for Convalescents opened with fanfare, flourish and publicity in the papers. The architects, so it was said, had been inspired; they were young men with radical ideas about "the human dimension," the use of light, curved space and greenery. The builders had done an admirable work of carrying out the design without cost overruns; quality had been adhered to; in short, there was a panegyric of compliments.

Joseph and Malone were photographed and interviewed. Joseph was shown bending over a spread of blueprints. He was asked about his personal history. "This modest man," one reporter wrote, "spoke with gratitude of the good fortune that has come his way. It was learned that he began his rise with the purchase of a small apartment building on Washington Heights in 1919. He had to borrow two thousand dollars to do it." He went on to say that the building's official opening was to be celebrated with a dinner, at which the architects and builders would be honored along with the many benefactors of the Home.

ANNA HAD ALWAYS been of the opinion that clairvoyance, ESP and all that sort of thing were absolute nonsense. And yet she knew, she had a feeling—absurd!—that Paul Werner would be at the dinner.

So, shortly after they had finished the main course, when she saw him walking across the enormous dining room to the table where Malone was sitting with his family, she was actually not surprised. She watched as Malone rose to shake hands, observed the introductions and Paul's easy little bow, heard in her mind's ear the throb of his voice, although he was too far away to be heard, and knew that in a few moments he would come to their table.

What shall I say? What will he say? Will my face flush? It gets so hot and red, and people will see. Surely too, they'll hear my drumming heart.

Paul came directly to Joseph and held out his hand.

"Paul Werner," he said. "I came to congratulate you and Mr. Malone on this magnificent building. I've just had the tour."

For an instant Joseph was startled. Then he stood and answered with dignity, "Thank you. You're very kind." He turned to the others. "This is the man who first gave me my start. He—"

"Please," Paul interrupted. "That's not important. What you've done, you've done by your own efforts."

"You know my wife, Anna," Joseph said. "And this is our daughter, Iris. And our son-in-law, Theo Stern. Doctor Theodore Stern."

He hadn't looked at Anna; what should she do when he did turn to her?

Joseph drew up a chair. "Come join us, Mr. Werner."

Paul sat down. Anna felt a lightness in her head. She mustn't be sick here, she mustn't.

"Are you alone?" Joseph inquired. "Perhaps your—"

"My wife wasn't able to come. Actually," Paul explained, "this evening is in the line of business for me. I'm on the board of the Parsons Trust, you see, and since we contribute to the Home it's my duty to see how some of our money's being spent." He smiled. "And I shall be happy to report that it seems to be spent very well. What I like, you know, is that here you've got the functionalism of the Bauhaus style but you've eliminated the bareness."

One of the other men at the table addressed him. "As an architect I must say I'm gratified; that was our purpose exactly: the surface decoration to take away that spare factory look. Are you an architect, Mr. Werner?"

"No, only a banker. But I dabble. Perhaps I'm a frustrated architect."

How carefully he manages to turn in the other direction, Anna thought. How could he have done such a daring thing as this? She met Iris' gaze and smiled back weakly. Why was Iris staring at her? But perhaps she wasn't really. Suddenly conscious of playing nervously with her pearls, Anna put her hands in her lap. Then she was conscious of the pearls themselves, three fine, matched strands. Paul would see that Joseph treated her well. Vulgar thought! She flushed.

Paul saw her distress and felt contrition. This was a rotten thing to do to her. (I knew she would be here and I wanted to see her. And everyone has a right to be selfish once in a while. Lord, she's beautiful! There was a time when a woman in her fifties was old. But Anna looks as if she'd never had a day's worry or done a day's work.)

"My wife is quite a fund raiser herself," Joseph was saying. "She's head of the hospital drive in our town, and head of their opera benefit in the spring too. Why, those women raised a small fortune this year! I wish I could get paid help in the office to work as hard as they do for nothing."

Paul addressed Iris. "And are you one of those hard-working ladies, too?"

"I'm afraid not. We have three children and they don't leave me much time for anything else," Iris said, thinking, Mama is acting funny. She has two red spots on her cheeks. What's the matter with her?

"But my wife used to teach school," Theo put in with pride. "She has an outstanding talent for it. They keep calling her to come back."

"Perhaps when the children grow older—" Iris began.

"Nonsense!" Joseph interrupted. "You've enough to do raising your family."

"What did you teach?" Paul asked.

He is sounding her out, Anna thought. He wants to know her, poor Paul. Surely people must see how alike they are! Fear dried her mouth and her palms were wet.

"I taught sixth grade, a gifted class. I would rather have taught at a slum school in the city, but Papa didn't approve." She smiled to Joseph.

"Listen," Joseph said, "I've come up from the slums too recently to want to be reminded. Maybe that's selfish. But a person who doesn't come from there can't know how a man feels when he's reminded. I wouldn't allow it, not while she was under my roof. Have a cigar?" And he offered a handful around the table, stopping at Paul.

"No, thank you. Cigarettes are my vice." Paul's long fingers unclasped the cigarette case.

I'm not ashamed to say where I come from, Joseph thought defensively. Not like some these days. Anyway, this man knows. And he sees where I am now, too. Hell, I know it's small potatoes to be proud. But I'm only human, and he'd feel the same in my position. Anybody would.

"Did my partner happen to tell you what we've got on the fire in Florida?" he inquired of Paul.

"He mentioned something very briefly."

"Well, it's a huge thing, the biggest we've done yet. Condominiums, and single-family homes, all tied in with a first-class shopping center, a golf course, a marina—you name it. There's our architect, right there across the table."

The young architect, eager to be heard, said to Paul, "As a frustrated architect, Mr. Werner, you must be familiar with the Scandinavian new towns. We're trying to reproduce some of their self-sufficiency; streets without automobile traffic, that sort of thing."

"Now that's really innovative," Paul said.

And they launched into a conversation illustrated by drawings on the backs of the menus and little structures built of forks.

Anna watched Paul's hands. She tried not to look at them but she was drawn back, under the pretense of interest in the subject, to his hands. They were strong and supple. Joseph had strong hands, too, but they were blunt and different. Different.

Joseph wasn't interested in the conversation. Theories were not for him. Give him the design and he would carry it out. Instead he observed Anna, who was listening so carefully. Anna knew and cared about things like that. She was so lovely in that dress, all iridescent gray and rose. Changeable taffeta, she'd said it was, tonight while they were dressing. "Do you like the rustle?" she'd asked, and flounced across the room, making the skirt swish. Wonder what that fellow thinks of her now? The scared girl going up the steps of their fine house. And now this. Only in America.

". . . the refreshing simplicity of Danish design," someone concluded.

Anna saw that Paul was trying to extricate himself from the conversation. "And have you ever been in Denmark?" he inquired of Iris.

"I've never been in Europe," she replied.

"Ah, haven't you? You must try to go soon. There's nothing like seeing it with young eyes. And young legs," he added.

"Theo isn't happy about seeing Europe again," Iris said quietly.

"I keep promising Anna a trip," Joseph interjected. "She's dying to go back. Only, I get so darned busy, I keep putting it off."

Paul returned to Iris and Anna understood that he was trying to draw her out. He simply wanted to hear her talk. He wasn't aware that one had to know Iris a long time before she would talk. She wondered what had gone through his mind at first sight of Iris, grown-up. She wondered whether Joseph was puzzled over Paul's staying so long at their table.

"No, I never want to see Europe again," Theo said. "I lost my family there."

"I understand," Paul answered. He paused for a moment. "Then perhaps you ought to see Israel. It is, after all, the remedy for the sickness that attacked in Europe."

"Have you been there yet?" Theo asked.

Words took shape in Anna's mouth: *Why, he was one of the movers who created Israel!* Startled, she thought: What if I had blurted that out loud?

"Many, many times," Paul told Theo. "Both before the state was founded and since then too." He smiled. "I recommend a visit, especially to you."

"When the children are older," Iris said, "perhaps we'll go then. My father has done a lot too, not on the scene, but raising funds. We all feel very involved."

"I'm glad to hear that," Paul responded.

He said to himself, She's prettier than I expected. It must be the marriage that's turned the trick. She's certainly poised, and speaks so well! And those enormous, brilliant eyes! Anna hasn't said a word. I shouldn't have shocked her like this. She's a good actress, though; you wouldn't think there was a thing going on. Come to think of it, I'm a pretty fine actor myself; my heart's in my mouth, but nobody knows it. Except Anna. She knows it.

"Why aren't you young people dancing?" Joseph asked. "Go ahead, don't mind us!"

Iris stood up with Theo. That man and Mama, she was thinking. That man. Doesn't Papa see anything?

A moment later Malone came over. "Mr. Hicks would like to see us both," he told Joseph. "He's in the office."

When Joseph had excused himself and all the others at the table had got up to dance, Anna and Paul were left alone.

Then for the first time he looked at her. "Fifteen years, Anna," he said at last.

"Oh, Paul, you should at least have warned me—"

"I know. It was thoughtless. But forgive me. A man's entitled to one lapse."

She didn't reply. The heat in her neck was suffocating.

"When I read about this in the paper I knew you would be here. I hoped she might be here, too."

"What do you think of her?"

"She's lovely, and different. Complicated, also, with a lot held back. And I have a feeling she's curious about me."

"What do you mean?" Anna asked quickly.

Paul hesitated. "Nothing precise. It's just a feeling I have about her feeling."

"She's made a fine marriage. It's been good for her."

"I knew. I saw the announcement."

"It's a marriage your mother would have approved. Socially, I mean."

"That's hitting below the belt, isn't it, Anna?"

"Perhaps it is." Yes, it was. But she couldn't resist. "Theo comes from a very distinguished family in Vienna—or they were, before they were wiped out. Distinguished and rich. He was educated at Cambridge and—"

"Fine. I'm sufficiently impressed. What kind of a man is he?"

"A wonderful, good man. And they're happy together."

"So you're not worried anymore."

"Well, I do feel that Iris is on her feet, and that's probably added a few years to my life!"

"And there are three children."

"Yes, two boys, very bright, especially the elder one, Steve. He's a bit of a problem, he's so advanced. The girl, Laura, is an angel, a healthy, good-hearted child." Anna stopped. Paul's face had simply closed, that subtle, tense, patrician face. And she knew that her recital, although he had asked for it, had touched a deep, wounded place.

"Go on," he said.

"Go on?"

"Yes. Tell me everything that has happened. Fill in the fifteen years."

She could have wept for him. "Well," she resumed, "well, one beautiful thing did happen. Eric came back to us five years ago. He's going on eighteen now."

"Eric?"

"Maury's son."

"I'm glad for you, Anna. And for Joseph. You know," Paul said ruefully, "one has to like Joseph. I have very jumbled feelings tonight."

"Mine are pretty mixed up, too." Anna's lips quivered suddenly.

Paul looked away. "Anna, dearest, I'm upsetting you. It isn't fair to do this to you here."

"No."

He looked out over the dancers, changing the subject. "Who's that Iris is dancing with?" For Iris and Theo had switched partners.

"One of the Malone sons."

"He's a handsome specimen."

"All the Malones are 'specimens.' One more healthy and handsome than the next."

"You'd have liked a lot of children, wouldn't you?"

"Oh," she said softly.

"You deserved to have them. It doesn't seem like too much for a woman to ask."

"Who is to say what's too much, Paul?"

He made no answer. For just an instant she had the strangest sensation of unreality: it was impossible that they should be sitting here together! She knew nothing about him, after all these intervening years, and yet he was Paul; she knew him well and dearly. Now suddenly she needed to know everything, to fill in, as he had said, the fifteen years.

"What are you seeing in the air, Anna? You're a thousand miles away."

"No, I'm right here, thinking about you. I'm trying to imagine your life and I can't see beyond offices, ships and airplanes: you rushing here, going there. That's all I see and I want more."

"Well, but that's pretty much the way it is. I go wherever I want. Last year I needed a vacation, so I went to Morocco and through the Atlas Mountains. It was fascinating."

"That's still not telling me anything about *you.*"

"Oh," he said somberly, "I've just been dodging, haven't I? All right, then. Here it is." Roughly he stabbed the fresh cigarette into the ashtray. "My wife and I . . . there's nothing particularly wrong between us and nothing particularly right, either. Her family's in Palm Beach. She spends most of her time there. I hate the place, so I'm rarely there. I work and I like my work. I have women wherever I go and whenever I need them. But they don't mean anything." He looked up. "I can't get you out of my mind, Anna."

"It hurts. It hurts me that you're unhappy," she said softly.

He lit another cigarette, cleared his throat as if it were tight, and went on, "I suppose I could be philosophical and ask you back, as you've often asked me, What is 'happiness' anyway? And whatever it is, why do we think we're entitled to it? All that sort of talk, in which, incidentally, there's a good deal of sense. The fact is, Anna, I really don't know. I'm confused. I'm guilty and I'm angry, although I don't know at whom. At the fates, perhaps? Or at myself? I should think that after all these years I could forget you—"

"I know," she murmured.

"Do you remember our last time? At the beach house?"

"I remember. We were still young and—"

"But you're young now. You always will be." He leaned forward. "Do you know a crazy thing? I still have hopes that someday, in some way, you and I—"

"Please," Anna interrupted with alarm. "Don't look at me like that. Iris is watching."

Paul leaned back and Anna poured another cup of coffee, which she did not want. But it was something to do with her trembling hands.

"I wish," she began to say, when the music stopped short.

Theo and Iris came back to the table. Then Joseph returned with Malone. There were a few pleasantries. Paul walked away. It was over.

"MY GOODNESS, MAMA," Iris remarked curiously, while they were riding home, "you looked so serious, you and Mr. Werner! I couldn't help seeing you. What on earth were you talking about?"

The partial truth came easily. "I'm sorry to say I was telling him about Maury and Eric. And I'm afraid I may have gotten somewhat emotional."

"That's understandable, God knows," Joseph said. He sighed heavily, then brightened. "He seems to be a nice enough chap, that Werner. To tell the truth, I always pictured him as kind of a snob, but he isn't, is he?"

"I don't think so," Anna said.

"Funny how he and I met, after all these years."

"Yes, very."

It was late when they reached home. Joseph went to the refrigerator. "I'm going to make myself a sandwich. Food's always lousy at those affairs. Want one, Anna?"

"No, thanks." She went outside to the terrace. The night was cool and fresh. It smelled of wet earth. There were millions and millions of stars in a clear, limpid sky. Beautiful, so beautiful! And such a sadness at the heart of it! That marvelous order which held the stars where they were and moved them so predictably, while human life was just—just confusion!

All chance. Where you were born, when, and to whom. Whom you met and married. All chance.

"What are you doing, standing out there?" Joseph called. "You'll catch a cold!"

"Just looking at the sky," Anna said, coming indoors.

"You and your stars! You should have been an astronomer. Come up to bed."

"So," he said, sitting on the edge of the bed while he took off his shoes, "so I met the great financier."

She ought really to show a normal interest. "Is he truly a great financier?"

"Well, it's a small private banking house, no Morgan, but a power, all the same. Very well run. And what do you think? He told Malone they'd be glad to consider an application from us to underwrite our Florida project. Eight million dollars' worth!"

"That much?"

"Of course! What did you think? It's one of the biggest projects on the East Coast!"

Anna looked up. His eyes were shining. "You know, Anna, I couldn't help thinking of that first loan, with us coming, hat in hand, for two thousand dollars. And today that same man is eager to do business with me in the millions! It's kind of unbelievable, isn't it?"

"Yes. Yes, it is."

"Werner must have been thinking of it, too. But of course he wouldn't mention it. He's a gentleman, no question."

"And are you going to deal with Werner's bank?"

"No, Malone told him we're practically signed up elsewhere. But I got kind of a kick out of it, all the same."

The shoes dropped to the floor with a bang. "Imagine, three, maybe four generations in the business! Boy, that's the way to do it! Pick the right grandfather, that's all you need, hey? We didn't do it right, did we, Anna? Still," Joseph went on gaily, "I'm steaming ahead under my own power! Yes, I believe our grandchildren will be able to say they picked the right grandfather."

In sudden panic, Anna ran to him. She put her arms out, held to him tightly. Ah, love me! Don't let me do anything crazy that will ruin us all! Even if I should ever want to, don't let me!

He kissed her. "You looked beautiful tonight, Anna. I was so proud of you, you can't know how proud! Why, what's the matter? You're not crying?"

"Not really. Only a few tears. Because everything is just the way I want it to be, with Eric here and Iris' babies only ten minutes away. And I'm so afraid it won't stay like this."

"But you've always been an optimist! What's got into you?" And Joseph laughed. He shrugged and spread his hands out to the universe, in a gesture left over from childhood. "Everything is so good, and she worries, she cries! No wonder a man can never understand a woman!"

ANNA WENT TO the lobby during the last intermission. The opera house was filled with women, for the ladies' hospital guild had taken a huge block of seats and sold them all. Pleased with success, she walked down the corridor to the water fountain.

"Anna," someone said.

Even before she looked around, she knew who it was. He was standing against the wall as if he had been afraid to startle her by coming forward. "Don't be angry with me, will you?"

"I'm not angry! But I am scared. Paul, you shouldn't have."

"It's the only possible way I could think of to see you. We couldn't really talk at that dinner."

"We can't really talk here."

"Afterward, then. Let's go somewhere afterward."

"I can't. I have to go home, Paul."

"Well, when?"

"I'm afraid," Anna said. "If I see you again, something will happen."

"Maybe. I don't think so."

She stared at him. His gravity reminded her of Iris in that lonely time before Theo came. She put her hand on his arm and they stood there, barely touching, just looking, looking—

"If I believed in reincarnation, Anna, I would say that in some past century I had had you and lost you, and that I've been searching for you ever since."

A woman, coming from the fountain, gave them a frank stare, having perhaps caught their last words or sensed, as it is possible to do, the dense emotion that lay between them.

If I had had to see him every day all this time, Anna was thinking, who knows what might have happened? For all my strong belief in permanence and stable trust? Twenty times one would refuse to go away with a man, yet perhaps the twenty-first time, one wouldn't refuse. And in sudden terror she thought: Can any human being be that sure of his will? Chemistry! Only a modern term for the enchantment, the pull between the sexes, the lure against all prudence, all—

Chemistry!

Paul's expression was very tender. "You still glow. That brightness you had when you were a young girl—it's never been put out, has it? In spite of every-thing."

She felt a small, cutting pain. "I've been so torn, for so long. I wish I could feel whole!"

The bell sounded for the last act. People began moving back inside, brushing against them as they stood by the wall.

Paul grasped her arm. "I understand what you mean. I won't tear your family's life apart. Nor hurt Joseph. Or my daughter. Do you think I would hurt Iris? Trust me. But we must see each other again."

"I'll have lunch with you."

"Tell me what time and—"

Two large ladies in "afternoon" dresses and droopy furs bore down on Anna, one of them shrilling gaily, "We've been hunting for you everywhere! Hurry, the curtain's going up in a minute!" And she was led back between them into a chattering group of friends, without a chance for another word.

Paul stood an instant looking wildly after her, as if he would pursue her. Then, with a small despairing shrug, he gave up and walked rapidly away.

THE DEPARTING CROWD pushed Anna outward through the main door. As had been arranged, Joseph was waiting.

"Come. The car's around the corner. How was it?"

"Marvelous. I always love *Aïda,* anyway."

The car turned northward, heading out of the city. In the west the somber winter sky had been torn open, and in the empty space between the clouds lay a lake of lavender, pearl and green.

"A beautiful sunset," Anna said. "The days are getting longer."

"So they are."

Joseph was very quiet. This must have been one of his difficult days. It was just as well; she wouldn't have to make conversation. If only sleeping dogs were allowed to lie! She had been feeling, for the last year or two, a welcome lightening of care—the natural result of Iris' good fortune—and in consequence she had been able to go for more than a week sometimes without even thinking of certain things. And now the sleeping dogs had been awakened.

Her body was drawn into a tangle of hot, trembling nerves. She pushed her coat back over her shoulders.

"What's the matter? Heat wave in February?"

"It's this dress. It's meant for a winter in Lapland, not New York," Anna complained.

He said no more, except to ask, a short while later when she lay her head back on the seat, whether she was not feeling well.

"I have a headache," she answered. "I think I'll just close my eyes."

They were almost home when Joseph spoke again. "You had a big crowd, did you? All women, I suppose?"

"Almost all. Just a couple of older men, like Hazel Berber's husband. But then, he's practically retired."

"I suppose you saw a lot of people you hadn't seen in a long time."

"Well, naturally, at an event like this." Something in Joseph's voice alarmed her. She sat up, pretending to fuss with her coat, and glanced at him. But he was looking straight ahead with a quite ordinary expression.

In their room she began to change into a cooler dress. The heat was still overwhelming. Then she heard Joseph coming up the stairs, striking each step with force, warning her of confrontation. He entered the room and firmly shut the door.

"Well, Anna! I waited all the way home. I gave you every chance to tell me and you didn't."

Best face it armed with innocence. "What can you be talking about?"

"You're a very good actress, but it won't work. Because, you see, I was there. I got there early, before the final act, and I saw the whole thing!"

"Would you mind telling me what you're talking about? What whole thing?"

"Come on, Anna, come on! I wasn't born yesterday. You were talking to that man for fifteen minutes."

"Oh!" she cried in a high, clear voice. "You mean Paul Werner! Yes, I ran into him at the water fountain. What's wrong with that?"

"You didn't just 'run into' him, you had fifteen minutes of very serious conversation, so don't try to tell me—"

Go over now, go over to the attack. It's the best defense. "What did you do? Carry a stop watch? And why didn't you come up and talk, the way any husband would instead of standing there spying?"

"Any husband in my place would be damned curious to know what his wife was doing! He came on purpose to see you, Anna! He knew you were going to be there because—I recall it now—I said you would be."

"Did you mention it on purpose to trap me?"

"Damn you, Anna, for a dirty thought like that!"

"And what about your dirty thoughts?"

"Don't try to put me on the defensive, because you can't do it. He came to see you and you lied to me. Those are the bare facts. You can't make anything else out of them."

"I did not lie to you! I just didn't think of mentioning it."

"Why didn't you?"

"Because I—" She heard herself stammering and began again. "Because it was of no importance to me. It was trivial. Do I give you a list every night of the people I happened to run into during the day?"

"Happened to run into!" Joseph mocked. "It's so usual for you to run into Paul Werner, isn't it? Like the milkman or the mailman! Do you think I'm an ass? But on second thought," he said slowly, "on second thought, maybe you do see him. Maybe it isn't so unusual."

"What a monstrous thing to say! Have you gone completely out of your mind?"

"No, I'm not out of my mind. I'm thinking very clearly. And I want to know why he came and what you were talking about. I'm waiting," Joseph said.

She had seen tempers often enough, explosions over the children when they were little or over household trivia, but never a cold fury like this. She drew her thoughts together. Everything was at stake, everything. "We talked about—let's see, the opera, of course, and the new tenor. Then he asked the usual polite questions about the family, things like that. Nothing, really, when you come down to it."

Joseph whipped the evening paper through the air and snapped it against the back of a chair. "No, that won't do! He grasped your arm. You pulled away. I saw your face when you went inside and I saw his. You can't tell me you were talking about the new tenor! What did he want, Anna? You will have to tell: what did he want?"

She bent her head. It whirled, as though she were going to faint. "I feel ill," she murmured.

"Then sit down. Lie down. But you can't get out of it that way."

She sat down, holding her head. Celeste had turned up the radio in the kitchen; a blare of revival music sounded up the stairs before it was cut off. A horn blew in the yard across the road. The stillness inside the room rang in her ears. He was still standing there waiting. She didn't know whether one minute had passed or five. She raised her head.

"Well?" Joseph said.

She wanted to cry out: Mercy! Leave me alone, I can't stand any more. But she was silent.

"Well?" he repeated.

And then she saw it was no use. She wet her lips, and sighed, and spoke.

"He asked me to have lunch with him. The reason I didn't tell you was that I knew you would be very angry. And I knew you had business dealings with him. I thought it could end in dreadful unpleasantness, so I thought it better to handle it myself." She stopped, trembling.

"And how did you handle it?"

"How do you suppose? I refused. I told him never to ask me again."

She looked directly into Joseph's eyes, and he into hers for a minute or more. Then he turned away.

"The bastard," he said quietly. "The fine gentlemanly bastard. Goes behind a man's back to make—arrangements—with his wife."

He walked the length of the room. He raised the window shades to look out into darkness and, after a little while, turned back to Anna.

"He's in love with you, isn't he?"

"Why? Because he asked me to go to lunch?"

"You can't be that stupid! Or shall I be tactful and call it naïveté? A woman of your age! What in the name of heaven do you think he wanted?"

"The fact is he asked me to lunch and that's all."

"The city's full of women, a lot younger than you, for a man to take to lunch and for whatever comes afterward. There's got to be more to this story."

"Perhaps it's just—one of the things some men do. I mean, he saw me at that dinner and I suppose he—liked me. Don't men do things like that?"

"A cheap philanderer! Another man's wife! You haven't seen him since that time?"

"No."

Joseph passed his hand over his forehead; he was sweating. "It's funny, you know, I never mentioned it, but at that dinner, I thought I saw him looking at you. I thought I felt something. But then I told myself not to act the fool. I put it out of my mind. I told myself it was nothing."

"But you see," Anna said softly, "it really was nothing very much. Another man on the make. I suppose he found me—interesting. Because of having known me so long ago."

How ugly this cajolery, this deceit! Even the slander of Paul was so ugly. But there was no choice. She had to defend herself, and not herself alone. They were all bound up in what was being said and believed, here in this room.

Below, in the kitchen wing, a door slammed and there were voices. Eric would be coming in from basketball practice, too hungry to wait for dinner. What disaster for him if this couldn't be straightened out!

We are all so interwoven. There is no way ever to isolate the evil, the sickness. Everyone is touched by its cold coils: Joseph and I and Eric and Iris, with her children. And Paul. Yes, Paul. We cause each other so much suffering without wanting to.

"Anna, tell me. I have to know. I've asked you this before and you've always denied it, but I'm going to ask it again: Were you in love with each other, years ago?"

"Never. No, never."

"And there was never anything between you?"

Her fists were clenched at her sides. She relaxed them and breathed deeply. "No, never."

"Will you swear it?"

"Joseph, isn't it enough that I've answered you?"

"Maybe it's foolish of me, but I would feel great relief if you would swear it. By the health of Eric, and Iris and her children. Then I would know it was true."

She was in a corner. She had actually retreated to the corner of the room and it seemed now that the corners were narrowing their angle, curving to trap her between the walls.

"No, I won't do that. I won't swear by their lives."

"Why won't you? If I ask you to?"

"It's insulting to ask me to do that, as if you didn't take my word."

"I don't mean to insult you. It's just that—"

"And for another, I feel superstitious about it."

"Why? Afraid that something would happen to them? It wouldn't as long as you were telling the truth."

"No, Joseph."

"Swear without that, then. Say, I *swear* I never had anything to do with Paul Werner that my husband couldn't know about."

Now, from some corner of Anna's soul, fierce strength emerged, born out of terror. She went over again to the attack.

"Now it's I who'll be angry, Joseph! Why do you want to humiliate me? What kind of a marriage is it in which people don't trust one another?"

"I want to believe you," Joseph said, retreating before her anger.

"Then believe me!"

There were tears in his eyes. "Anna, I couldn't bear it if—The world is a shifting place; you never know where you stand in it. There has to be one person who never changes. If I lost that, I tell you—you know the things I've been through, and I've kept on going—but if I thought that you—" He swallowed. "I wouldn't care to open my eyes on another day. So help me God."

"You haven't lost it. You won't lose it," she said, gently now.

"I know I'm lucky to have you. A woman like you could have had any man she wanted."

Pity. Pity. The tension broke in her and she began to cry.

"Anna, don't. It's all right. I'm over it. I understand what happened now."

He never could bear to see anyone cry. Iris had known that when she was a little girl. *Papa will give you anything if you just stop crying.*

"That damned bastard," Joseph muttered. "To put you in a position like that! He'd better not come around here."

"He won't."

Someone knocked at the door. "It's me, Eric. Celeste says dinner's ready."

"We'll be right down," Joseph called back.

"I'm not hungry," Anna said. "You go eat with Eric."

"No, no! I don't want the boy to think there's been anything wrong. Wash your eyes. Nobody'll notice."

Faces are for concealment, Anna thought, powdering her pink eyelids. They speak of "frank" faces; who looks more candid than I do? She bent to the mirror; yes, an innocent face, still young. A lovely face: a fraction of an inch here, another there, and the combination could hold such power over men! Because Paul loved her, he pursued her. Because Joseph adored her, he believed her. And also because, she reflected with pity and tenderness, Joseph was a very simple man. He believed the best of almost everyone, in spite of his bluster. Paul would never have let her get away that easily if the situation had been reversed. That subtle mind would have seen behind and through her.

Tomorrow she would have to tell Paul how things were. And the long silence between them would have to begin again. It would have to be that way.

Then, if she could but speak to Joseph, loose the whole load of lies and be free of them forever! Yes, and she would be free of everything else besides, free in the ruins of all and everyone she loved! Never. No, never. Live and carry the load alone. So help me God, as Joseph had just said.

So help me God.

❊{36}❊

Iris runs among enormous, ancient trees. She turns, seeks, walks back and turns again. There is no end to these woods. No one has ever seen such trees before. The trunks rise like cathedral towers, yet their dark, soft tops sway like plumes against the rim of the sky. She knows where she is: these are the Muir Woods, north of San Francisco. She has never been there, but she knows; knows, too, that she is dreaming.

She runs faster. She mustn't stop. Race, hurry, for Steve is lost. He is somewhere among these endless trees. How did it happen? How can it be that nobody had seen him? Can a child, can anyone just disappear like this? She tries to strangle her tears; when panic stuns one can't think, and she must be calm, be sharp, to get back her little boy. Have you seen him? she implores, for these are not tree trunks, after all; these are people, tall, silent people who won't answer. Surely somebody must have seen him? she pleads. A little boy like him?

Mama! she cries, to a woman with a face like her mother's; but the mouth is stern and no answer comes from it.

Papa! she cries, help me, oh, help me, Papa! He bends to her, he puts out his arms. But his face is Paul Werner's face, sorrowful, pitying. He speaks; she cannot understand what he is saying. She strains to hear, but he melts away into fog. She cries: Papa! Father! She thinks, I am losing my mind.

She is frantic. There is a pain in her chest, it runs up into her throat, the pain is colored bright red. Is it possible to suffer like this and live? Somewhere her child is looking for her, crying for her; he can't be far. But she has looked everywhere, running, running through shadow and striped shafts of light, and he isn't here. Such loss she feels, such anguish. How will she live with such loss and anguish?

There are shadows on the ceiling and the beam of the hall light cuts across them, falling on her eyes as she turns her head toward Theo's shoulder. She wonders whether she may have cried out during her dream, her nightmare. But no; Theo sleeps lightly and he hasn't stirred. Whatever can have caused this? Safe here in her bed with her children asleep down the hall: what reason can there be for such internal strife?

It's so cold; the winter air seeps into the house on nights like this. She doesn't want to get up, but she has to. She creeps down the hall to Steve's room, careful not to bump into anything in the dark, for he, too, sleeps lightly. She steps on his stuffed cat. He always goes to bed embracing it, but sometime before he falls asleep he throws it out of bed. He is a rounded hump under the blankets, lying on his stomach with his head pushed against the headboard. So soft, so small. Even the sound of his breathing, the breath of his life is so small.

On silent feet she goes back to her room. Theo has turned and in his sleep reaches out, his arm flung over her as she lies back into the warmth. She remembers that she didn't go to look at Jimmy or Laura just now. But she knows that they are all right. Her cheeks are cold and sticky with the tears of her dream.

❖⟨37⟩❖

They came out of Carnegie Hall into a crushing wind and fought it toward the parking lot. Theo turned his face up into the cold. It felt bright as light, as clear and soaring as Verdi's *Requiem,* which they had just heard, and which now and forever after would sing to him of a particular death.

A cluster of people waited at the corner to hail taxis or to cross. Thrusting through them, he glanced at a face; it vanished and then it turned and reappeared. He saw it clearly, hesitated for a second and was sure—

"Franz! Franz Brenner!"

"Theo! *Mein Gott!* I heard you lived in New York, I couldn't find you—"

"What are you doing here?" And remembering Iris, "This is Franz Brenner, one of the finest lawyers in Vienna! We grew up together. Iris, my wife."

Franz laughed. "Theo is too generous. And I'm too old to have grown up with him."

"But we can't stand here! Come, we'll get something to eat."

In the light of the Russian Tea Room they searched each other's faces.

"Theo, you look well! You must be happy, you haven't changed."

"And you—"

"Don't tell me I haven't."

Franz had gone almost completely white. There was a deep crease on one cheek, a fold of flesh like a wound, which twitched when he spoke.

"What are you doing here?" Theo asked again.

"I'm here on business. Knit goods. But I live in Israel."

"No law?"

Franz shrugged. "Israel is crammed with German and Austrian law degrees. They don't mean much there. But tell me—"

"Order something, order a supper," Theo interrupted. "We need time to talk! Or, listen, I have a better idea!" He felt the rise of his own excitement. "You'll drive home with us. We live only an hour away. You can spend a day or two."

"*Ich kann nicht, ich fahre morgen ab.* Excuse me, Mrs. Stern, I'm not used to English yet. I studied years ago at the university, but I forget and start to speak German. What I mean is, I have to fly back tomorrow morning." He leaned across the table. "So tell me what you do, Theo! You have children?"

"Two boys and a girl. And you?"

"No children. I lost Marianna. . . . But I married again, a widow with grown daughters. I have a pretty good job. The living is hard there; still, it's home to us now. But you know, I heard—a grapevine, do you say? I heard you were in New York. But there was nothing in the New York telephone book. Did you know it was worth a fortune in Europe in those days, a New York phone book? You might find the name of a relative in it—a third cousin of your grandfather, maybe—or any name of any stranger who would send you, out of human pity, the papers that would save you from the fire in Europe."

"I only lived in the city a year. I had a room here when I first came, in '46."

"Ach, so! Well, Liesel learned that you—"

"What did you say?"

"I said that Liesel had learned—"

Theo sat up. "God almighty, what did you say? What Liesel are you talking about?"

Franz was astonished. "Why, Liesel your wife, of course," he murmured.

"Franz, Liesel is dead."

"I know, I know that."

"She died in Dachau with all our family. It's not decent to speak of her! Don't you know any better? We never mention her name!"

Franz's face was still. His steady eyes didn't blink. He said: "She didn't die in Dachau. I thought you knew. I thought the committee, the people in Tel Aviv, had informed you."

"Damn you, Franz! Damn you! Will you talk, or shall I shake it out of you?"

"Theo! Theo!" Iris laid her hand on his arm. A man at the next table turned quickly and looked as quickly away.

"I don't know now where to begin," Franz pleaded. "Dear heaven, I—"

Something went wild in Theo. "Begin at the beginning. Or you'll never get on that plane tomorrow. What do you know?" And as Franz glanced toward Iris, "She can hear it! Damn you, I want to *know!*"

Franz looked down at the saltcellar. "I met Liesel in the winter of '46 in Italy. I had tried to get to Palestine but the British had turned us back. So I was preparing to try again, waiting for an old tub willing to run the blockade. There were a few hundred of us, some who'd lived through the camps, some who'd hidden out with false papers."

"She—had false papers?" He was charged electrically. He thought his head would explode; he thought he was dreaming; he thought he was going to be sick.

"No, no false papers."

"What then?"

Franz raised his eyes. "Theo, she's dead. That I know, I was there. What's the use of all this? Let it rest as it is."

Theo trembled. "I have to know. Or you won't get on that plane, I tell you!"

Franz sighed. He took a deep breath, like a child beginning a recitation before the class.

"Well, then. They came. It was the very first week after the *Anschluss*. The Germans came to the house for the family. It was strange, they thought their influence would help them, but it was just the opposite. Other people, those who were not so important, many of them had time to get away.

"So they came. It was early in the morning, cold and raining. The baby was sick with a fever. She begged them not to take him out into the weather. And they told her she could leave the baby behind if she wished: 'You can take him or leave him here alone in the house. It's your choice,' they said.

"As they were leaving, one of the soldiers knocked a painting off the wall. His superior was angry: 'Don't wreck things! It's a first-class house and we'll be needing it!' So they knew they wouldn't be coming back.

"They rode with two men in S.S. uniform. The baby screamed all the way. He had not yet had his bottle that morning."

Iris caught her breath. She began to cry.

"Stop it!" Theo said furiously.

"After a few days the baby developed pneumonia and died. Then for a while the others were together in the camp, before they were separated, sent to Poland. Ah, Theo, you know all this! You know how it happened! The whole world knows, even the ones who don't want to know."

"Go on!" Theo said.

Franz's gaze went back to the saltcellar. "The old people, they went quickly to the ovens. The young and strong were put to work. So she—there was a work-shop where they made belts and gloves, leather things for the army. She worked there a long time . . ." He swallowed, resumed in an even drone, "Then, some long time after, I don't know how long, it might have been a year or perhaps two, yes, it could even have been longer—I don't remember exactly—"

"Never mind *when*. Just say *what*. Go on!"

"Well, then, you see, one day some officers, some higher-ups from the Ge-stapo, came in. They were looking for, you know how it is, they were looking for girls. Pretty girls, blondes who looked Aryan. For the headquarters father front." Franz was silent a moment. Then he looked up, afraid. "They took them away and stamped their arms: 'For Officers Only.' "

Theo started fiercely, scraping his chair. A glass of water overturned and spilled across the table.

"Please, Theo, you don't have to listen anymore," Iris whispered. "Mr. Bren-ner, Franz, there's no sense in this, it's enough."

Theo sat down. "Franz, don't make me pull it out of you. I want all of it, every word you can remember. And Iris, shut up."

"She told me, she said that the person who saved her sanity had been a prostitute, and this girl—she came from Berlin—this girl said to the others, 'Listen, they're not touching *you*, not *you*, you understand? It's only flesh, skin. If you were made to clean filth with your base hands, you wouldn't despise your hands afterward, would you? You wouldn't cut them off. So this is the same, these are filth, swine, shit.' Excuse me," Franz said to Iris.

So she closed off her mind and lived waiting, waiting for the Germans to lose the war. . . .

"The doctors came regularly to examine them for diseases. Cold, hard men they were. She—Liesel—was astonished that doctors could be such. She had thought always of doctors as different. She had been, so she said, so ignorant of the world, had known so little about human beings.

"One day a man came in who recognized her, a lawyer, Dietrich, from Vienna."

"I knew him, he was a bastard. One of the first to jump on the bandwagon."

"He recognized her because he used to play in a string quartet that met in somebody's house. Her parents', I believe."

"My parents'. It was my father's Tuesday night music group and she—came in sometimes to play the piano."

"Well, he remembered her. And shortly afterward she was put back in the factory. Because of him, of course. She thought it was an act of mercy. She was still innocent, even after all that. Of course it was because the war was ending and a lot of these torturers were suddenly becoming 'humane.' They hoped that some wretched survivor might put in a good word for them when the judgments were handed down.

"Anyway, we met in Italy. She didn't know me at first; I had lost sixty pounds. . . . For a minute I didn't know her either . . . she had got old. One would have thought she was well over thirty—but somehow she was still—still lovely. Even those monsters couldn't destroy all of that. . . .

"We waited for weeks in Genoa. They kept coming, the walking corpses with skin sores and shaven heads who had crawled across Europe, out of hiding, out of the camps, and now were fleeing from the Russians. . . . All they wanted was to get out of Europe and never see it again. The group with which I spent my days was waiting like me to get to Palestine. We spent the few pennies which we got from the Joint in cheap cafés. You could sit forever, as one did—does still, I suppose, in Europe?—over a glass of wine or a cup of coffee. We sat in the sun and tasted the feeling of not being terrified, the feeling of being alive. And we talked about the future.

"Some of us persuaded Liesel to go with us. We thought you were dead, you see. There were so many rumors in those days. At all the places where people like ourselves were gathered, whenever a newcomer arrived there would be questions and comparing of notes. People carried lists, with dates, names and addresses: have you seen, or heard, of So-and-so? A man came who had heard from someone who had been in one of the camps where French Jews were sent that you had been rounded up in Paris, and that you were dead. Later somebody else confirmed it; he was certain he had seen you among the contingent that went right after the fall of France.

"There was no reason not to believe it. After all, everyone else was dead, her parents, brothers, child; why not her husband also?

"God above, the bravery I've seen! The patience, the will!" Franz stopped. He stared at the wall. And began again:

"Then, I remember, a terrible thing happened. . . . There was a doctor in the group that was waiting for the ship, an older man who had suffered like the rest of us and, like the rest of us, was overwhelmed at the absolute miracle of having survived. He was very steady, very firm and kind, talking to people who weren't doing so well emotionally, encouraging them with so much hope and wisdom—

he was a rod and a staff. And suddenly one day while we were sitting there—I remember I was eating a pasta; I couldn't ever get enough to eat at that time—all of a sudden this strong man jumped up from the chair and ran across the square. There were some *carabinieri* standing, chatting with a shopkeeper, and the doctor grabbed one of their guns and started screaming, simply went berserk there in the sunshine on the square. They wrestled for the gun, and the doctor was shot, shot and killed. Lying there on the ground, our kind, wise doctor.

"After that, there was a change in Liesel, as if—I think she actually did put it into these words—as if it was a delusion to think you could ever straighten out such lives as ours, to go back again to normal living; that it was simply too difficult, too hard to believe in hope.

"Anyway, the boat came. It was a miserable old tub, scarcely seaworthy, but that was the least of our worries. The real one was the British blockade. We had to sail at night without lights. On deck we whispered.

"So we crept across the Mediterranean toward Palestine. The ship was crowded and filthy. People were seasick. Children were bored and crying and so many of the adults hadn't strength enough to be patient. Still they tried. And everyone was so afraid, so tense. We watched and strained for the sight of ships, the nearer we got.

"One day during one of our interminable talks, a man mentioned an encounter he'd had with a German-Jewish refugee, a soldier in the American army. This man had a letter with a list of names from a certain Dr. Weissinger who had gone to America from Vienna in 1934. The list was of others from Vienna who were in New York, and Theodor Stern was on it. You see, in those times, it was important to write everything down, to bring people together, to know who might still be alive. You must know Dr. Weissinger, Theo?"

"He died a few years ago. Yes, he was one of the smart ones. He came here at the beginning when nobody believed how it would turn out." Theo's voice was unfamiliar to his own ears. It was a false, artificial voice. The true one would have howled and cursed and beaten the air.

"This man had copied the soldier's list. And we saw your name, with the address where you had lived in Vienna, although none for New York. Still there could be no doubt.

"I told Liesel that as soon as we got to Haifa we could write, that it would be simple to find you. I myself could have traced you after she died. I don't know why I didn't. Perhaps because someone told me the authorities had informed you. Yet a lethargy comes over a person when there's so much confusion and up-rooting. One doesn't know where to begin. And then one has to start making some kind of a living.

"We talked a great deal together, she and I. We sat on the deck until late at night. It was so hot and noisy below."

"Tell me everything she said." He thought he couldn't bear to hear any more. Yet he knew that if he didn't hear it all, afterward he would not be able to bear that, either.

"It's hard to remember. One speaks of so many things in the course of days. And still, one doesn't really say very much, does one? She did say several times, she said: 'I hardly remember Theo. I remember things we did: the day we walked down *Mariahilferstrasse* and bought the wedding rings. Theo wanted to buy them right away and I asked whether he wasn't going to speak to Papa. He said of course, he was, but since we knew Papa was going to say yes, we might as well buy them now. I remember that,' and she laughed. 'But I can't remember his face,' she said.

"Oh, and she talked sometimes about skiing. She said she remembered especially a day in the Dolomites, how you skied all day and then played duets for everyone in the evening after dinner at the hotel. Things like that she remembered. And she said, 'We were so young; how could we ever have been so young?'

"That's how she talked. Often she would be silent for a long time. And I was too; I had my thoughts. We all did. It was a ship burdened with thoughts. Strange, all those heavy thoughts, on those marvelous, mild nights with the air like warm water on the skin.

"Except that last night. It began to rain, and the ship wallowed through a slow, heavy swell. A lot of people were sick, more than usual. We went up on the covered deck, she and I. The rain blew on us in a mist.

" 'It's so clean up here,' she said. 'And I'm so filthy, Franz.'

"I remember protesting, saying the things one would say, and her arguing, 'Why would anyone want to touch me again?' and I arguing back as one would.

"And she said, 'I wonder how many people have just slipped over the side of a moving ship at night?'

" 'What a morbid thing to wonder about!' I told her. I was alarmed.

"She said that it wasn't really, that it would be a pure way to die, going down into clean water . . . she used the word 'clean' so often . . . she said it would be like coming into a room waiting for your comfort, the covers turned down on the bed and the lamps low.

"I wasn't sure what to think. After what we had endured such talk was common enough. We were all given to it at times. It was a pattern from which, as our hopes rose, we gradually emerged. Still, I wanted to be cautious. I urged her to come below because it was late. 'No,' she said, 'it's stifling and dirty down there. At least up here in the air it's clean and free.' I said I would stay with her, then, and she protested, but I stayed."

Franz raised his eyes. "Only, I fell asleep. Theo, I fell asleep. And when I woke up, she was gone. And that's all there is."

Beneath the shirts in the middle drawer he had laid the double photographs of his parents, still in the leather traveling folder that he had taken to Paris so long ago on his way to America. What impulse had, at the final moment, caused him to put them in the suitcase? If he had not done so, there would now be no record of their faces, except in the minds of those who had known them, and for as long as those minds survived.

Iris was still downstairs. They had driven home in silence; she had not even tried any words of comfort, and he was grateful for that, because there could be none. . . . He supposed, as he opened the folder, that she must have seen these when putting his clothes away. But she had never remarked on them and for that, too, he was grateful.

The photos of his parents had been taken in that time when youth turns gracefully into the pride of early middle age. His father wore the officer's elegant uniform of the First World War, and with it the appropriately stern expression. His mother was dressed in the limp silk of the era, her overskirt edged with lace, her pearls waist-length. She was slender and stood tall. Young girls of her time were taught to stand that way, she always said. Had she walked straight and slender to the freight car, the van, or whatever vehicle had taken her to her death?

He studied them. For some time now he had been able to look at them. Then he slid his mother's picture out of the case, removed what he had hidden beneath it, what he had not been able to look at, all these years.

She gazed up at him: smiling or not smiling? It was hard to tell about the mouth, which turned up naturally at the corners. But the eyes smiled. They seemed, unless he imagined it, unless it was just the way the flesh happened to be molded, they seemed to hold mirth even when she had been quite serious or even angry. They were hazel eyes: cat-colored, he had used to tell her. The little boy was on her lap, holding a felt polka-dotted ball. He remembered the ball. He had bought it one afternoon on the Graben. Fritzl had rolled it under the sofa and they'd had to move the sofa to get at it. One leg was tucked out of sight; the other dangled from his mother's lap. There was—Theo bent closer—yes, you could see a dimple in the round knee.

Liesel, darling Liesel, what did you ever do to anyone? And I thought you had died quickly. My God, how did you manage to live so long?

The bedroom door opened and the light from the hall filled the opening. Iris' steps had made no sound. She came beside him and for a long minute examined the photograph. He saw fear in her face, as if she knew that something had changed and would change. He was sorry for her: wasn't that crazy? To be sorry for Iris, who was alive?

"I swore at poor Franz," he said.

"It's all right. He understood," she answered quietly.

Then he began to weep. She put his head on her shoulder and stood there holding him, and was very gentle, and did not speak.

❧ 38 ❧

Theo had been mourning for more than half a year. It was too much for Iris to endure. He was distorted and crippled with grief and she felt all the pain of his crippling.

That first night when they had left Franz Brenner on the sidewalk at Fifty-seventh Street she had offered to drive the car home, but Theo had walked to the driver's side. She could still see his mouth, set like a gash or a scar upon his face; she could remember her own awful fear, not so much that they would have an accident, the way he drove, but that this night had done something to him that was irrevocable. And why shouldn't it have done so?

The family gathered, encircling Theo. Papa had come to their house the next day and silently put his arms around him. Mama had cried—of course, she never restrained her tears—cried all over again for her brother and his family.

"Oh, that lovely child!" she said when they were alone. "I can see her now in the garden of Eli's house. She had a velvet band around her hair, like Alice in Wonderland." And she whispered in recollected horror, "I saw a girl raped in Poland."

"You never told me!" Papa exclaimed.

"One wants to bury a memory like that," she answered.

Eric was stunned. Of course he had known about the atrocities of the Nazis, but somehow, he admitted, they had always sounded a little exaggerated. Somehow.

Theo went back to the office on the second day. All that first day or two Iris feared for him. She couldn't have said specifically what she was afraid of, but she feared. She kept telephoning his office on pretexts, not asking to speak to him, but just to find out from the secretary in some oblique way whether everything was normal there.

At night she felt him lying awake. She heard him swallow a sob. But after that first night he wanted no comfort.

"I have a cough," he said clumsily, and this foolish deception touched her almost more than anything.

With the children he became exceptionally gentle. His voice was tender even when he said the most ordinary things at table. "Steve, are you sure you washed your hands? Jimmy, you have to finish your milk before you may have dessert."

Once she found him sitting with Laura on his lap and his arms around the two boys as if he were guarding them all. There was such an expression on his face! Something so resolute, fierce and sad! When she spoke to him he started; she had to repeat her words and she saw him blink, shaking his head to bring himself back to the room from wherever he had been.

Every evening now, although not in Iris' presence, but when she was having her bath, she heard the drawer being opened and after long minutes shut again; she knew he had been looking at the photograph of Liesel and their child. Sometimes, coming down the hall and entering their bedroom unexpectedly, she could tell by his swift movement that he had just taken it out again. One day, for some reason, the action evoked in her not shock and pity, but irritation: "He'll wear out the paper, handling it so much." Immediately she was ashamed of herself and wished with utmost penitence, truly wished, that it were possible for her physically to lift his anguish and take it on herself.

She was deeply alarmed. How long could a human being carry such a heavy load? With all that he had to do at the office and the hospital? With a wife and three children, and now this other thing clouding his mind?

And she raged against the rotten world that had savaged such good and gentle people.

At what actual moment her sorrow began to turn toward resentment Iris could not have said. Was it in the third or fourth month, or the fifth, that she knew she could no longer stifle or deny the resentment? Perhaps it was the morning when one of Theo's secretaries telephoned. Somehow, Iris had no idea how, the people at the office had learned the story.

"We've just heard what happened to the doctor's wife," the woman said. "It's not believable in the twentieth century! We're all so terribly sorry, and we want you to know that we're trying to make things as easy as possible at the office for the doctor."

Iris had thanked her with proper gratitude and hung up. *What happened to his wife.* Horrible, horrible and true. But now I'm his wife and I'm here. How long will this grieving go on? Everybody tiptoeing around Theo—my parents, Eric, those few of our friends who have been told. An atmosphere of mourning, a house of mourning.

He had developed the habit of staying up late. Very well, she could understand his sleeplessness. She had tried staying up with him but her eyes had fallen shut and he had told her to go to bed, that he'd come up soon.

One night she had peered downstairs to see what he was doing. He was sitting in a chair staring at nothing, just sitting. Then she saw him get up and go to the piano. He began to play, very softly, so as not to awaken anyone.

Night after night she heard him playing. The sound of it drifted up the stairwell; mostly Chopin nocturnes, nostalgic music of summer gardens, of love and stars.

One night she raised herself on her elbow and looked at the radium dial of the clock: one-thirty. For two hours she had been lying there alone while her husband was lost in the music of another time and place, with another woman.

When he came upstairs and found her still awake, he moved toward her. She felt that he expected from her as always an eager, quick response. But her desire struggled with humiliation. All the times of their lives when she had been so absolutely uninhibited, so free in expression of her passion for him, had he perhaps not been thinking of *her*, not wanting *her* at all? Had he been thinking of—

She did not want him to touch her. Don't come to me with this face of mourning, she wanted to scream at him; she screamed it silently, even while she put her arms around him. You've shut me out. *Me, me,* don't you understand? Keep away until you can be what you were again. But can you ever be?

She knew this sort of emotion was dangerous. If she didn't bring it to a stop soon, it would go out of control. But how to stop it? In the eye of the hurricane lies a lonely hollow where nothing moves, where panic lies still. The darkness rustles and morning is an eternity away. After such nights, there were hollows under her eyes. Her face was sallow at best; the hollows gave her a look of tragedy. People ought to look pink and cheerful in the morning, and the awareness that she did not depressed her. That, and Theo's haunted face. There was a tired silence now at the breakfast table, filled by the crackle of the newspaper.

Little by little, inch by inch, a wall is built.

Then one afternoon he came in and told her they had joined the country club. She was astonished. They had both agreed that club life wasn't something they would enjoy enough to warrant the expense. It was true that Theo was a good tennis player, but he had been satisfied with the public courts in town. Iris was clumsy at sports and wouldn't have used any of the facilities at the club. Some of their friends belonged, but most of them did not. Many of their closest friends were Europeans, random doctors and others in the musical groups who played in quartets at each other's houses. So she was astonished.

"I want to get out among people who aren't so serious," Theo said. "People who like to dance and laugh."

Well, she loved to dance! What did he mean? For a moment she felt that he was accusing her. She felt a rush of quick anger which subsided as quickly. He was only trying to escape his thoughts by changing his routine! She who prided herself on her "understanding" ought to understand that much, oughtn't she? Poor man! Rightly or wrongly he thought that crowds, new faces and "jollity" would bring forgetfulness and ease.

Yet there was something else behind his jollity: Anger? Bitterness? Defiance? Something has eluded us, Iris thought; slid out of our hands.

She remembered thinking, a long time ago when she had first known Theo, that he was a man who could have any women he set his mind to wanting. At the club, all through this past summer, he had gathered women to him without effort: young girls and women much older than Iris. He would stand at the bar holding a long drink—he drank very little, one tall glass sufficing for an hour or more—and the women would be drawn to his knowing eyes, his barely promised admiration. Then, of course, there was his accent, the faintly foreign, faintly British accent. He really did nothing she could blame him for. She felt sometimes like slapping him, all the same.

Once at home again his sadness came surging back. It was never expressed in words—for Theo had caused the subject to be closed—but in tone and gesture and above all in silence. The sadness was a presence, like a tiny draft from a forgotten window that has been left open a crack: just enough to chill the air. His friends at the club would not have recognized him if they had seen in his home.

He had become two people.

If she could have talked to somebody about what was happening in their house! But it was too intimate: She had never been able to be intimate. Iris knew herself and knew she had too much pride—false pride?—to disclose anything as close to the bone as this. Perhaps in absolute extremity she could talk to Papa. He was the only one. Yet she couldn't talk to him about this, wouldn't let him know that his daughter's life was troubled or less than perfect. He needed to believe that it was perfect. Papa wore blinders. He had a picture in his head of the ideal family of tradition. That's the way it's supposed to be; therefore it must be. There's no other possibility.

She stood in the center of the bedroom trying to make up her mind what to do with the morning. It was Saturday and Theo had gone to the club for tennis. Downstairs on the lawn she heard the creak of the swings; Nellie was outside with the children. Really she ought to go downstairs and be with them, letting Nellie do her work indoors. She ought to take Laura shopping, for all her clothes were too short. And Steve was a worry: surely he was much too solitary? Thrusting up the hill alone after school, with his shoulders hunched and head down, whereas Jimmy tore along with a crowd of friends? But she had no energy to deal with these things; she felt so great a lassitude. It was hard to make a decision to move.

The telephone rang.

"Why don't you and Theo come over for lunch? I just thought of it," Mama asked.

"Theo's having lunch at the club. Besides, you just got back from Mexico! Do you have to start entertaining already?"

"Having you at lunch isn't entertaining. And Eric's coming down from Dartmouth. He phoned last night that he'll be here by noon. So come, and Theo can drop in after lunch. Bring the children, too."

"No, they're playing nicely. Nellie can watch them. I'll come alone."

She had so little patience with the children lately. She seemed to have lost her strength for nurturing and comforting; she wanted those things for herself. Thought of the luncheon table in her parents' house brought now a total recall of childhood when, after a bad day at school, she had fled to the warmth of home. She needed her parents—her father—and was terribly ashamed of having the need.

There was an autumn melancholy in the burning sun as she drove through the town. It felt hotter than summer, yet yellow leaves were falling, floating down in windless air. The main street was crowded with station wagons. These were loaded with dogs and children, and adorned with the stickers of prestigious colleges: Harvard, Smith, Bryn Mawr. On the sidewalk in front of the bank women sat behind rickety tables selling raffle tickets for cerebral palsy, mental health, Our Lady of Sorrows and B'nai Brith. All these things were now unimportant.

She passed the school where next year she would move up to the presidency of the P.T.A.; then the temple, and Papa's handsome wing outlined in autumn flowers, marigolds and zinnias, burnt yellow and dark red. Unimportant.

"I can't go to temple anymore," Theo had said last week.

Iris had stopped in the center of the room. She didn't mind so much that he didn't want to go. He hadn't come with them in the last few months anyway. If only he had said it differently! There had been argument in his tone, a throwing down of the gauntlet. And she had picked it up.

"No? Why can't you?"

"I wonder that you need to ask me. Can you really expect me to sit there listening to all that talk about God? God, who allowed Dachau to exist?"

"It's not for us to judge what God allows. There are reasons for things that are beyond our understanding."

"Bosh! Rubbish! I only see that your God destroys. I'm more merciful than he is: I spend my days rebuilding."

"One might say it's God's work that makes you want to rebuild."

"Come, come, you're too educated to believe that! Your parents I can understand, but not you! Mount Sinai and the Torah given to Moses, carved on stone! You know better than that. You don't really believe those legends!"

"Don't I? Then why do you think I go to services every week?"

"You go because it's a lifelong habit. Nice people are supposed to go. And besides, the music is beautiful. You take an emotional bath in it."

"I could be furious but I won't be. Theo, more to the point, when are you going to get over all this? I don't mean to be unfeeling, heaven knows, but after all, Liesel isn't the only human being who died cruelly. Look at my brother, don't you think that my parents—"

"I don't want to talk about Liesel," he'd said coldly.

"I was only trying to help you."

"There is no help. 'We are born, we suffer and we die.' I forget who said that, but it's the truest thing that anybody ever said."

"I don't know about that. It sounds more profound than it really is, once you think about it. And it's awfully, awfully bitter."

"Iris, there's no point in this conversation. I'm sorry I started it. Go to your temple, if it makes you happy. It isn't even kind of me to take it away from you when it makes you so happy."

"You couldn't take it away from me. But thank you anyway."

At what point, Iris thought now, reliving that particular conversation, at what point, on what day, had they begun to talk to each other like that? With irony and coldness, like debaters sparring cautiously? Whence this distance, this semi-courteous enmity?

Her heart beat heavily all the time. Driving the car through the quiet streets, turning into the driveway of her parents' house, she was aware of its slow, steady thudding and of the chill in her flesh. It was a sensation she remembered from school when you entered the room where finals were being held: the same chill and thudding as the unknown loomed.

At the front door she arranged her face into a standard welcoming smile. "Hello, hello, Papa! Mama, you look marvelous! Eric, how are you?"

The house smelled of furniture polish and fresh air; the table in the dining room was set with pink linen mats; Mama's hair was perfect. She was aware of her own hair, which she hadn't bothered with in a week, and tucked the untidy strands behind her ears.

"Too bad you didn't bring the children," Papa said. "We'll have to run over later this afternoon, after Laura's nap. Has she grown any, my doll?"

"I can't tell, Papa, I see her every day." Papa's doll, red-haired, lucky Laura who had skipped a generation and looked like Mama.

"So," Mama sighed, when they were at the table. "So I got my wish, I saw Dan and I'm satisfied. It's a fascinating country. They took us all over."

"Did you see the Pyramid of the Sun at Teotihuacán?"

"Of course, of course! I'm glad I read *The Conquest of Mexico*. Otherwise it would have been a heap of stones, an engineering feat and nothing more. But this way it really meant something. I could see it all in my mind, the way it had been when Cortez came. Such brutes!" Mama exclaimed.

Iris half heard. Dan. Dena. Their children and grandchildren. Stone house with a wrought-iron fence. Shop in the Zona Rosa. Wholesale operation with seventy employees.

"And Dan said your mother looked beautiful, she had hardly aged at all," Papa finished. "Yes," he said, "I made a good choice, I did. You do as well as I did, Eric, and you'll have it made. Oh, I had plenty of girls, but none of them ever worth more than ten minutes of my time until I met this one."

Iris drank the coffee with downcast eyes. *Her* husband couldn't say that about *her*.

"Theo in better spirits?" Papa inquired. He shook his head. "What he's been through!"

"I imagine," Mama said, "the club does him good. Tennis and all the exercise. It's therapeutic."

"I must say," Papa observed, "it was a surprise to me when you joined a country club." He shook his head again. "There's a very fast crowd up there. Do a lot of drinking."

"Oh, nonsense," Anna contradicted. "You pick and choose wherever you go! We've loads of friends who belong and they're hardly what you'd call fast."

"All the same," Papa insisted, "there's a lot of hanky-panky going on. I shouldn't have thought the atmosphere would appeal to Theo."

"He plays tennis, takes a swim and comes home," Iris said briefly.

"You don't enjoy the club, do you?" Papa asked now. For some reason he seemed determined to pursue the subject.

"I don't mind it one way or the other," she replied.

"A whorehouse. Pardon me for the expression. Morals like alley cats."

Eric laughed and Mama raised her eyebrows. "My goodness, Joseph! Those are strong words!"

"Maybe they are. I had lunch a while ago with a crowd of men who belong. Some of them my age, one even older. I think I and two others were the only ones there who were living with their first wives. I got dizzy listening to them: three sets of children; stepchildren; one guy married to a girl younger than his own daughter; another shacked up with some other man's wife. Crazy! Crazy!"

"So, Grandpa? What can be done about it?" Eric asked.

"I don't know. Tell you one thing, though, we're too easy on that sort of thing. There won't be any whole families left, at this rate. You know what the Bible says you do with an adulteress? Take her out and stone her, that's what!"

"Surely, Joseph," Mama said very quietly, "you don't believe in that?"

"Of course not. That was speaking figuratively. But I'll tell you one thing you don't do; you don't invite her to your house to sit at your table and meet your wife. People like that should be dead to the community! All these divorces and shenanigans," he grumbled.

"You sound like Mary Malone!" Mama said. "Like a good, old-fashioned Catholic!"

"The Malones and I are very close together on most things. You ought to know that by now. Hi, here's Theo!"

Theo stood in the door of the dining room carrying his racket, with his tennis sweater tied around his shoulders. He had such easy grace as he stood there; Iris wondered how many other women saw it too. He took a seat at the table.

"We were talking about the club," Papa told him.

"I know. I heard you as I was coming in."

"Yes. Well, our people are becoming assimilated, aren't they? All the dirt of modern civilization clinging to their skirts as they pass through."

Theo laughed. "They seem to be enjoying it."

"Oh, they enjoy it well enough! But they'll pay for it, you can be sure. Some fellow wrote an article in the magazine section last week about Rome, all the filth masquerading as pleasure. They paid too, in the end."

Theo stirred uncomfortably. He always said that his father-in-law had just one flaw: he moralized like an Old Testament prophet. He turned to his mother-in-law.

"How was your trip? What did you think of Mexico City?"

Anna began to go into raptures over the Reforma as compared with Fifth Avenue, the Champs-Elysées and the Graben. Then Theo joined in with word-pictures of Vienna, which for years he hadn't mentioned or wanted anyone else to mention, Iris thought angrily. Why, Vienna had been wiped off the map, as far as he was concerned! And now he was talking to Mama about the Prater and Grinzing; Mama was joining in as though she were an expert on the city, after having spent two weeks there a quarter of a century ago . . . Theo was laughing. It was almost like flirting, what he was doing, and he was doing it, she knew, only to irritate her.

He rose abruptly. "I'm going to go home and shower. By the way," he said, addressing Iris directly for the first time since he had come in, "I made a reservation for dinner with some people at the club tonight. Seven-thirty."

"All right," she said and became aware of her mother's eyes, examining her.

She dropped her own eyes, feeling a blush prickle on her neck. Mama was too sharp; she saw too much.

She stood with the cold glass in her hand. There seemed to be no place to set it down. She was squeezed into a corner talking to an elderly lady, a Mrs. Reiss, who knew her mother. Always she seemed to end up talking to old people! Yet, she had to admit, it was more comfortable and easier to talk to them. But now her mouth ached from having smiled for the last hour, and she wished they would serve dinner so she could sit down and stop talking.

Gusts of perfume, smoke and whiskey poured on her as people squeezed by. She couldn't move, couldn't wriggle out of the corner where she was pinned against a topply vase of roses on a table at the small of her back.

"—seven hundreds in the Boards, he's always been an outstanding student, but the competition is murderous, you never—"

"—offered them a hundred twenty-five thousand for the house without the adjoining lot and really I would consider it a mediocre neighborhood. Ray says—"

"—everybody admits the course at Shadyvale is far superior, if you want to put up with the class of people they're taking in. We're quite comfortable here at Rolling Hill."

"I see they've got those little water chestnut things," Mrs. Reiss remarked, raising her voice above the noise. "Shall we get some?"

"No, thanks," Iris said.

"Well, I think I'll just go try to find some. Will you excuse me?"

Even an old lady like that is bored with me. I've the personality of a clam. No poise. When Theo married me I began to have it. I know I did, because I never thought about it anymore and when you don't think about it, that means you have it. I just *knew* I was somebody when we were married, and now I don't know, I've lost it again.

She found Theo in the middle of a jovial group, almost all of them new to her. She had hoped they might be sitting with Jack and Lee, their neighbors, or with Dr. and Mrs. Jasper, good, solid people with whom there would be things to talk about. These were all new people, his tennis friends probably, and she saw at once that they had sized her up and found her wanting.

They went in to dinner. She felt a frenetic activity in the room. Everyone seemed—she sought a word—feverish; yes, that was it; their alert eyes looked past and beyond to the next table; the people at the next table are always more important. *How can I get myself invited to sit with them next time?* That's what they're thinking. *How can I get to meet the So-and-so's?* Not that there's anything wrong about wanting to know people and be liked. But they're so *intent* on it, using all their energies, like a runner sweating to the finish line. And then, the crafty cruelties that go with this sort of climbing! The flattery and snubs!

Only Theo doesn't need to climb; he's already there. He lures and captivates without even trying. He ought not to have a dull wife like me. He ought to have an equal.

He ought to have a wife like Liesel.

Theo leaned toward her. "You're a thousand miles away," he said.

"I? I'm just watching everyone, enjoying the scene." Her lips were dry. Why can't I say I'm uncomfortable and I want to go home? "Who's that, that woman in red? I seem to know, but I can't place her."

"Oh, that's Billie Stark. She's a great tennis player. We played doubles today and I really had a workout."

Oh, Lord, another of those vivacious types! The agitated red bird comes swooping in our direction. One heard her approach from the far end of the dining room, her little animated squeals and whoops and shrieking mirth. Her mouth stretches from an ellipse for a smile to a circle for astonishment. *No, you can't mean it!* Eyes blinking, popping, batting, scrunched in a nest of fine dry wrinkles, or stretched in ingénue affectation. Tossing hair, flung arms, pelvic twists. Never quiet, never still for more than a second or two. Exhausting to watch her gyrations. No peace where such people are.

Lady in red, Billie Stark, why the hell don't you shut up or go away?

"Of course I remember you, you're Billie Stark. How are you?" Iris said, holding out her hand.

Why don't I like anybody; why do I feel they don't like me? I used to have compassion, used to try to understand people. Maury always said I understood so well. At least, I used to try. I know I've helped Eric.

Somebody asked Billie Stark to dance. Then everyone got up to dance.

"Aren't you having a good time?" Theo asked, as they circled the room. "You're so quiet."

"All right," she said. It was on the tip of her tongue; she tried to hold the question back but could not. "You like that woman, Billie Stark?"

"Well, she's lively. She certainly knows how to enjoy herself."

Was that meant for me, I wonder? I could enjoy life too, if you were—

"Don't you feel well, Iris? Are you coming down with something?"

He knew perfectly well she wasn't. "I'm well. But I feel like a stranger here. I don't belong with the Billie Starks. And I'm trying to figure out what makes you think you do. *Do* you belong? Which is you, Theo who plays in Ben's quartet on Thursdays, or this one?" There was pleading in her voice. She could hear it.

"Which am I? Must I be either one or the other? Can't I go wherever I choose whenever I want to?"

"But one has to fit somewhere, to *be* something."

The music beat and stabbed. It was absurd to be jiggling there in the middle of the floor, feeling the way she did.

"You read too much junk popular psychology," Theo said with annoyance.

She allowed herself to be annoyed in return. "Do you know what I really think of your new friends? They're full of crap. Racing around outsmarting and outdoing each other. They have to see your Dun & Bradstreet report before they decide whether it's worth their while to say hello to you."

Theo didn't answer. She knew he didn't entirely disagree with her. He had made similar comments often enough himself. But they drove home without speaking. He turned the radio on and they listened to the news as if it were the most important thing in their lives.

She knew that, while she was having her bath, he would go to the drawer in his dresser and take out the picture. Tonight she got quietly out of the bathtub and put on her robe. By opening the door very quickly, she was able to catch him holding the photograph up to the light. She caught a familiar glimpse of the Madonna pose, the long hair curving, the child on the lap, before he put it back in the drawer.

They stood there looking at each other. "You should never have married me, Theo," Iris said at last.

"What are you saying?"

"You don't love me. You never have. You're still in love with her."

"She's dead."

"Yes, and if she had lived you'd have been happier than you are with me."

"At least she wouldn't have nagged me!"

"There, you see? Well, it's too bad, isn't it? Perhaps I should accommodate you by dying. Except that that still wouldn't bring *her* back, would it?"

He slapped his fist into the palm of his hand, making a loud crack in the room. "Of all the stupid, childish—Iris, how long is this going to go on? I shouldn't have said that about nagging, I really didn't mean it. But I don't know why you're so insecure. You value yourself so little! It's pathetic."

"Maybe I am insecure. If you think I am, why don't you help me?"

"Tell me how. If I can, I will."

She knew she was burning bridges and yet she couldn't refrain.

"Tell me that if you had known she was alive you would still have chosen me. Tell me you love me more than you ever loved her."

"I can't say that. Don't you know that every love is different? She was a person, you're a different person. That's not to say that either one was better or worse than the other."

"That's an evasion, Theo."

"It's the best I can do," he said gently enough.

"All right, then. Answer the other half of my question. If you had known she was alive would you have left me and gone to her? Surely you can answer that."

"Oh, my God," Theo cried. "Why do you want to torture me?"

She knew she was beating him like a helpless dog on a leash. Once on the street she had seen a man doing just that and had been sickened by it. But she couldn't stop.

"I ask you, Theo, because I have to know. Don't you see it's a matter of how I am to live, to exist?"

"But this is brutal! I simply cannot, I cannot answer these pointless questions."

"So we get back to what I said in the beginning. You never wanted to marry me, really."

"Why did I do it, then?"

"Because you knew my father half expected you to—"

"Iris, if I hadn't wanted to, ten fathers couldn't have made me."

"—and because you were lonely and worn out and came to rest in my family. And yes, because, after all, I'm intelligent enough for you, and have your tastes, or had. Your cultured European friends can come to our house and I know how to talk to them. But that's not love."

Theo considered a moment. Then he asked, "What do you mean by love? Can you define it?"

"Semantics! Of course I can't. Nobody can, but everybody knows what he means when he uses the word."

"Exactly. Everyone knows what 'he' means. So it's a different thing for everyone."

"Oh, this calm, philosophical trickery! Putting me on the defensive! When all the time you know what I'm talking about."

"Very well, let's define it then, let's try. Would you say that being unselfish, thinking of the other person's welfare and good, is a part of love?"

"Yes, and one could do that for one's aged grandfather."

"Iris, you're twisting my meaning. You're making unnecessary grief for yourself. If I only knew what you want!"

Her lips began to quiver. She put her hand to her mouth to hide it. "I want . . . I want . . . something like Romeo and Juliet. I want to be loved exclusively. Do you understand?"

"Iris. Again I have to say—that's childish, my dear."

"Childish? All the world is enthralled with it! It's the most intense, deep, marvelous thing that can happen to a human being. It's what the world's art and music and poetry are all about. And you call it childish!"

Theo sighed. "Maybe I used the wrong word again. Not childish. *Unreal.* You're talking about emotional peaks, high moments. How long do you think they can last? That's why I say *unreal.*"

"I'm not stupid. I know life isn't a poem or an operatic drama. But still I would just like to experience some of those 'high moments,' as you call them."

"And you don't think you have?"

"No. I've been sharing you with a dead woman. And now with a lot of cold and silly featherheads as well."

"Iris, I'm sorry for you. Sorry for us both. Did the photograph bring all this on tonight? All right, I won't look at it anymore. Time would have brought that to a stop anyway," he said bitterly. "But if that won't satisfy you— It seems there's something in you that doesn't want to be satisfied, that wants to suffer."

"Ah, so now we are going in for psychoanalysis!"

"You don't have to be an analyst to see things. You *want* to be hurt, otherwise you would listen to my reasoning."

"Reason has nothing to do with it. This is something I feel. And you can't reason yourself out of something you feel. Or else you would reason yourself out of remembering Liesel, wouldn't you?"

Theo passed his hand over his forehead. "Can we continue this in the morning? It's past midnight and I'm exhausted."

"As you wish," she answered.

They lay down in the wide bed. Her heart began to pound. Her hands were clenched and her arms held straight at her sides. She wondered whether sleep would come to relieve her. And she knew by the sound of Theo's breathing that he was not sleeping, either.

After a while she felt his hand upon her, sliding over her shoulder, touching it softly in a gesture meant to comfort. Then his hand went to her breast.

"No," she said. "I can't. I don't feel anything. It's gone."

"What do you mean, gone? Gone for always?"

"Yes. It's dead. It died in me." She began to weep. Cold tears slid down her temples into her hair. She made no sound, but she knew he was aware. He put his hand out again, trying to reach her hand, but she drew away. Then she heard him turn, heard the swishing of the sheets, and knew that he had turned his back to move as far apart as he could.

Early in the morning, after a night with only an hour or two of sleep, Theo got up and went downstairs. He had no trouble finding the number he wanted in the New York City telephone book. He paused a moment.

A week or two ago, coming out of his dentist's office—he went to a dentist in the city—he'd had to wait at the threshold for the slackening of a sudden downpour. And this girl, a dental technician in the next office, had come out and stood there waiting with him. She was about thirty-two, he guessed, a Scandinavian with all the frank, healthy grace of her kind. They had stayed there talking until the rain stopped, talking about skiing and New York and where she'd come from in Norway.

Then he'd told her how he had enjoyed talking to her and she'd said, "Call me up if you ever want to talk some more. I'm in the book."

So here he was. His finger moved the dial.

"Hello, Ingrid?" he said softly, when he heard her voice. "It's Theo Stern. Remember me?"

❧{39}❧

The car hummed northward through the glittering cold that Theo loved. Winter had always been his time. He loved sifting snow in gray air; the spare design of branches, so Japanese; the expectation of fires, thick soup and quilts. Crossing the line between Massachusetts and Vermont, he thought that it was not very different from Austria.

He leaned forward, trying to adjust the radio, but the farther he got from the city the more it faded and Mahler's Ninth was scratched out by static. When he switched it off there were no sounds but the click of the windshield wiper and the clack of the tires.

It would be good to have Ingrid riding along. Her presence was pure ease and had been so for almost a year. Neither her laughter nor her silences demanded anything of him. Once every week he went to the city to teach and, taking the rest of the day and evening off, spent the hours with her. He was so absolutely free there in those two small rooms! She'd have good music playing and bread baking in the oven. The bed was next to the windows where hanging plants, which were the only curtains, dropped their green shade and moist fragrance onto the bed. Sometimes they lay all afternoon listening to music, while Ingrid smoked the sweet cigarettes that he had come to associate with her. When he left he was enlivened for the rest of the week.

But it would have been foolhardy for them to travel and arrive together. You never knew whom you might meet, although he had chosen this little ski resort because it was out of the way and he had never met anyone who had even heard of it, much less been there.

He had mentioned to Iris, knowing that she would refuse to go with him, that it would be nice to take a few days off for skiing. "There are pleasant things for you to do while I'm on the slopes," he'd said. "You could take walks around the village and look for antiques." But she had declined.

"You go, it will do you good," she had said, with the polite concern one has for one's friends.

Things were like that between them.

But he could think of no way to change them. Iris' mood had gradually dimmed. (Clouds drift one by one across a sunny sky; you look up after only an hour or two and are surprised to find that the sky has grown completely dark.)

She hadn't moved out of their room because all the others were occupied; but had instead removed their bed and bought twin ones. She had waited for him to make comment but he had made none. If that was the way she wanted it, Theo had thought angrily, that was the way she would have it. Everything that could be said about what stood between them had already been said, anyway. He remembered having heard stories about couples a generation or two ago, who lived out their lives beneath one roof without speaking to each other. He had never believed it was possible to live that way, but he saw now that it might be. Not that they lived without speaking, Iris and he; they were both far too concerned as parents to inflict anything like that on their children. No, they made decent conversation at the table and went to P.T.A. meetings and local dinner parties with unsuspecting friends. (He almost never went to the club anymore. Iris had been right about that; it wasn't the atmosphere he really wanted, and his weekly day with Ingrid more than made up for its loss, he thought now, smiling to himself.)

So that's the way things were. He hadn't been able to change Iris' thinking, nor had she changed—but she *had* changed his a little, he reflected. Yes, in an odd way some of her convictions had begun to influence him. Things she had said, dredged out of what tortuous channels, chambers and coves of her mind, had begun to seem true. Or to have some truth in them, at least.

Perhaps she is right and I didn't really want to be married? Sometimes I think —and I'm sad and ashamed of thinking it—that I really didn't want to be. I was so tired, I remember. I just wanted rest. Maybe all I wanted was some sunny rooms, a piano in a bay window, birds in the trees outside the window, and there wasn't any simple, efficient way of having these things without being married. Could that be?

Yet I did want children, another little boy—as if anything could bring back that first one! But these were beautiful children: Jimmy, a bright rascal; sensitive, thoughtful and sometimes difficult Steve; Laura, pink and curly—but how does a man begin to describe his darling, only little girl?

I wish it was enough for Iris that we have all this, and that life is—was—good together. Because it *was* good together! But that's not enough . . . she wants something I don't seem able to give her. I feel—I have felt—sometimes as if I had given coins to a beggar who needs more than I have to give. She wants me to *adore* her. I don't *adore* her.

Before they were married Iris had trembled in his presence; he had seen that she was in love with him and been very moved. He remembered having thought that he would be so good to her (then perhaps, after all, he had really *wanted* to marry her?), and, in turn, enjoy her quiet ways, the refinement of her face. A lovely lady, she was. Stuffy concept in America, but still valued in Europe, or at least it had been when he had lived there. Reason enough in Europe, the best reason, in fact, for choosing a wife.

But he hadn't expected the intensity of her love. Those trusting, worshiping eyes! A man could feel guilty without having done anything. Her soul was in her eyes. All that grave emotion! It was almost frightening. To be responsible for the survival of another soul!

He frowned. His thoughts had made his head ache, or perhaps it was only the woolen cap that was tight. He pulled it off. If he had met Iris away from the vitality and welcome of her home—the first home he had been in for so many years—if he had met her in an office, say, sitting with pad on knee, her dark, pensive eyes looking past him to the corners of the room—would he have been as easily drawn to her? The truth was: no. Yet, once having known her subtle and resilient mind, her shy pleasure in being with him, he had quite simply wanted to be with *her*. They had slipped into a pattern of understanding, and a common language. It wasn't that often that two people were able to walk so easily in the same rhythm through the world, including the rhythm of sex.

They had had all that, and yet he was unable to talk to her about this obstinate, fixed idea that he must feel for her and toward her in just such and such a way, just so and so and in no other way nor for anyone else, either present or past.

Women! But not all women.

That first time with Ingrid she had told him, "You have the body of a dancer or a skier. V-shaped, tapering from the shoulder to the hips. Especially marvelous for skiing."

Theo had been amused. "I happen to be fairly good at skiing."

"You see? I could tell. So different from a boxer's body, for instance."

"You're an expert on male bodies?"

She'd laughed. "I've seen enough of them!" And when he didn't answer, "You're not shocked?"

"Of course not. Just surprised. You don't seem to be—"

"A tart? But how provincial of you! Does one have to be vulgar to take pleasure in what was made for pleasure? Must sex be either sanctified or else damned?"

"I don't know. But most people, especially most women, see it that way, don't they?"

"It's a simple pleasure, that's all, that's what I believe. Like wine or music. When you tire of it you change the brand, or turn off the record."

"I hope you don't tire of me too soon," he had remarked another time. They were eating fettuccine Alfredo. She had a wonderful appetite. That was another thing that made him feel good to be with her. She wasn't always whining about calories the way most women did these days, and how she'd have to starve all next week to make up for tonight. The fettuccine kept slipping off her fork and she began to laugh. Then he laughed, and it had all been so completely silly. He hadn't laughed with such foolish high spirits in—how long?

"I don't expect to tire of you," Ingrid had said franky. "I still love Beethoven and if you don't believe I still like Château Mouton Rothschild, you can try me."

"All right, I will," he had answered and summoned the wine steward.

Then she had grown serious. "But when you tire of me, do me a favor, will you? Call me up and tell me so. Don't lie and make considerate excuses for not keeping dates. Don't try to break it to me gently. Just say, Ingrid, good-by and it's been great, but good-by. Will you do that, Theo?"

"All right, but I don't want to think about it. We've just begun," he'd said.

Still, the freedom, the freedom, like an invigorating breeze! If women only knew!

He had been able to talk to her about Liesel. For the first time he had been free to spill everything out, with no modesty, with no hesitation. Everything. And Ingrid had carefully listened. He had talked for hours while she lay on the bed, smoking cigarettes. He had talked and talked. He had told how, at first, he hadn't been able to believe in the death of Liesel or their child; how once, in a London restaurant during the war, he'd heard a woman at a table behind him speaking with a foreign accent, an accent he'd fancied Liesel *would have had* if she had known how to speak English. He had made an excuse to get up from the table and look at the woman. That was how mad he had been!

He had even recalled that young chap in London whose wife had been killed in the bombing of their house and how he, Theo, holding the fellow's hand, had sworn to himself: No, it's crazy to love and make yourself so vulnerable. I don't ever want to be so vulnerable again.

He told how, after the encounter with Franz, Liesel's face, which had faded, now returned and hung in the air before his vision, clear in every detail: the white scar where a cat had scratched her neck, the crooked tooth about which she was self-conscious, the fact that her lashes were dark and her brows blond. That face had been before him all the time, *all the time!* Sometimes he had welcomed it, aware how much he had been longing for it; sometimes he had covered his eyes and cried out, "Go away! Stay away from me! Go away!"

He had told Ingrid all of that and, in the telling and her hearing, had found relief, a softening, and ease.

He did not ever speak of Iris and Ingrid never asked him to. So much was understood between them! She quenched his thirst, appeased his hunger and was herself satisfied. They could let their minds go empty in a tide of sleep after joy and no worry about what anybody *wanted* or *needed.* Care-less woman! Woman-without-care!

Iris would never understand anyone like her.

Nor would my father-in-law, Theo thought grimly. He would want me stoned to death. Endless love as long as you don't transgress; no mercy if you do. The only reason he forgives me for my irreligion is that I'm a doctor. The thought amused him momentarily.

"Your work is holy. You do holy work," Joseph said often.

Well, in a sense there's truth in it, if you want to stretch the word "holy" a bit. Theo lifted his hand from the steering wheel, flexing it inside the glove. An intricate weaving of fragile bones, and what it could do! He was proud of the work he could do, and also humble about it. Holy? Well, perhaps.

But then, all labor is holy and the body is miraculous. Labor of bent backs on mountain slopes, tension of dancers or players of the violin. What a mechanism, man! A brute at worst, and at best a self-centered, pleasure-seeking organism.

And yet, why not? As long as we don't hurt one another! (I'm not hurting anyone, am I?) Just let us flourish for our little time with our small greeds and our small sins, and die without struggle when our time is over.

"What will you do with your life?" he'd asked Ingrid one day.

"I don't know. And that's the beauty of it! To enjoy the beauty of it! I like my work. I like being healthy and young and I shall try to stay both as long as I can. Also, I like music and good food. And I like you. I like you very much, Theo."

"I'm glad," he'd said.

"But I don't want to own you. Don't be afraid. You can get away any time you want. Because I don't want to be tied either, you know."

And it was for just that reason that he had no wish to get away. Wise woman! Perversity of man!

He came now to the fork off the main road and stopped to look at the map. Right for five miles at the fork, past the general store. . . . His heart began to pound with anticipation, a nice, painless pounding. The car crept up the mountain. There were few tracks. The road hadn't been traveled much, so the place had been well chosen, after all. He drew up at the inn, which was set in a stand of spruce. There it was, her little green car. She'd got here ahead of him; she drove like a fury.

The snow was firm and deep. It wasn't too cold. With luck, there would be some sunshine in the morning. Meanwhile there were food, a fire, a bed and a gay, strong, wise, sweet girl.

WEAK FEBRUARY LIGHT fell on the rug near the window and over Iris' hands, which were holding a book she wasn't reading. She was just sitting there, Anna saw, looking out at the weather. She tapped at the open door and Iris turned around.

"Hi," Anna said cheerfully. "I've got my marketing chores over with and I thought I'd take a walk. I needed some exercise."

It was the best excuse she could think of for this unusual forenoon visit. The truth was that she had detected, running through their mundane telephone conversations of the past few days, a new and alarming depression of the spirit.

"Well, sit down. Do you want some lunch?"

"Thanks, no, I'll not be staying that long." She sat down, perched rather tentatively on the chair, and wondered how to comment or what to inquire. It was always so difficult, with Iris, to find the reaching word.

"If Nellie doesn't shut off that radio in the kitchen," Iris cried suddenly, "I shall go mad, or go in and smash it."

"Too bad you're not up in Vermont with Theo. You really need a little change, Iris. It gets on a woman's nerves, being constantly with children, and no relief." Platitudes, for lack of the truth.

There was no answer. And Anna said softly, "Iris, a moment comes when we have to cut through our reserve. I've known for a long time that you're in trouble and I've been too polite, too hesitant to ask. Now I'm asking."

Iris looked up. Her face had no expression at all. It looked empty. Her voice was just as empty. "Sometimes I don't care whether I live or die. Now you know."

"What has Theo done?"

The question struck Iris like a blow. Her mouth crumpled and twisted into the grimace of tears.

"What's Theo done? Nothing, really. Just gone away, left me. We've left each other. We're in the same house, but we've left each other."

"I see." Anna spoke carefully. "Will you tell me the reasons, or don't you know them?"

"Oh, I know all right! It's because of me. I don't come up to standard . . . I don't ski, I'm not a delicate blonde, I'm only mediocre at the piano. Let's face it, I'm only mediocre, period."

So that's it, Anna thought. I might have suspected it.

Iris stood and walked up and down the room. Then she sat down at the desk again, facing Anna.

"Mama . . . I know I'll be ashamed of myself for asking you this, but I have to know. Was she as beautiful as her picture?"

"I haven't seen any picture," Anna evaded.

"Please. Don't treat me like that. You saw her when you were in Vienna."

"All I remember is a pretty child. . . . Iris, darling, why are you doing this to yourself?"

"I don't know. I don't know."

A long time ago, years and years—when?—Anna had had a flash of thought: If ever I have a daughter I will not let her be vulnerable and unworldly.

"You see," Iris cried, "you see that I haven't even got self-respect anymore! I'm a mean and petty soul. To be jealous of that poor woman who went through the fire of the century and died in it! To begrudge her the only thing left: that someone who loved her should mourn for her! I'm so ashamed of myself, of this worm inside of me! Do you see what a nasty person I am?"

"You're not nasty. You never were. But you think too much about everything, yourself included." Surely there had to be some combination of words that would sound natural and wholesome and comforting. "It's normal to feel a little jealous and normal to be a little guilty about it."

"No," Iris interrupted. "You don't see what I mean. How can you? Papa adores you; there was never anybody else but you."

Anna winced, as pain cut through her, then attempted to seem casual. "Your father's a man; how do I know he tells me everything? And I don't sit around worrying about it, I assure you."

"But you do know," Iris said impatiently, "that he's not up at a country club surrounded by women or sitting alone downstairs grieving half the night. I am absolutely superfluous, don't you see? Thrown away. And I don't know how long I'll be able to live like this."

"Do you want to leave him?"

Iris stared at her. "I wish I could want to. But I don't want to, I don't think I could live through that, either."

"I wish I knew how to help you."

"Help me! You could have helped me by not giving me such a ridiculous name, for one thing! 'Iris!' Look at me, do I look like an Iris? What reason could you have had to think I would grow up and fit such a name! Unless, of course, you hoped I would look like you!"

"I'm sorry. We thought it was a lovely name, that's all."

"Oh, God," Iris said.

Her balled fists pounded the desk. Then she lowered her head to it. Such wretched suffering! Broken open. The nape of the neck was so weak, so tender, even on an adult; Anna put out her hand to touch it, then drew back, afraid to intrude.

Oh, I love her, I love her, and yet it has never been what it was with Maury. Golden Maury. Those first years on the sidewalk, the women on the camp chairs, the toddlers with pull toys, his laughter, his bright hair. An old grandmother had put out her hand and touched his head. *"Wunderkind,"* she called him. Wonder child.

But how could it have been like that for Iris? God knows I never felt joy because of her, either before or after she was born. Such misery, such despair, such guilt, must they not wear off on the child in the womb? And afterward, looking at her, searching her face for signs—crazy as it seems—that through her I would be punished. That she might be, heaven forbid, retarded, crippled, marked. So she's not retarded or crippled but without a doubt she is marked. Pallid, timid. Oh, she is valiant, poor soul, she tries for happiness and she can attain it, but then something happens; an ill wind comes and knocks her down. My fault. There must have been some way I could have taught her to be strong and sure of being loved, mustn't there? But I didn't do it. . . .

It's all vague, the past. Iris' past eludes me. She grew up, I worried. She never gave any trouble. I remember that she never was young.

Damn Theo! What has he done to her?

Perhaps if she had married that stubby, timid schoolteacher who had hung about during the war, perhaps life would be less complicated for her. He had been a humble man and Iris would have been his queen. But then every man and woman can ask how different his life would have been if he had married someone else. Surely everyone at some time or other wonders about that? A graying couple walks past my house each afternoon. They even come out in their trench coats in the rain. The woman has a ruddy face; her hair is tied back with a ribbon. They take steps in unison, talking, always talking. What can they have to say to one another? "I hate chatter," Joseph says. But that man and woman lean toward each other, laughing. Would I be different if I had married a man who had so much to say to me? If I had married Paul?

Iris looked up and wiped her eyes. "Tell me, would you have wanted to die if Papa hadn't asked you to marry him?"

My God, such questions! "No. No man is worth that."

"Now I'm sure you're not like me and I'm not like you."

"I suppose not."

On a shelf above the desk stood a model of Rodin's "The Kiss." Odd that Anna had never noticed it in this room before. Fine for a museum, but, my goodness, wasn't it queer to have the naked, embracing pair exposed like that in one's house, especially with children running in and out? Iris must be far more "free" than I about things like that. I still undress in private. Joseph is amused. I don't know why I do that. I've not been embarrassed to stand naked in front of Paul.

Anna's thoughts swirled slowly. She stood befogged, as if dazed, unsure of where to go, of what to say. How would I feel in Iris' place? I don't think I'd be as distraught as she is. Theo is the center of her life and "the centre cannot hold."

Just now I told her that no man is worth dying for. Yet I've always said that if some tyrant were to demand my life or Joseph's I would say "take mine." Would I do that for Paul, I wonder? I wonder what Paul is doing this minute. What would he say if I could speak to him about his daughter's anguish?

But she had to deal with Iris' life, not her own. "You must speak to Theo. Speak to one another, break through the wall. You may find that he's ready, after all these months, to listen and to change." Anna's speech began to gather momentum, spilling out clichés. "Time is the great healer, you know. Especially when you've done right. The only thing it doesn't heal is the wrong you've done to somebody else."

"What do you know about that? What wrongs have you done?"

"I'm human."

After a moment Iris said, "I don't think I've done wrong to Theo."

"Perhaps not. But can you try to forget what he's done to you?"

"I don't even know that you can call what he's done a 'wrong.' He's simply grown tired of me. He can't help that, can he?"

"You don't know that for certain. Again I say, my dear, you analyze too deeply. You may imagine motives that aren't there. Or exaggerate them, anyway. I used to watch you doing it when you were a child."

"You were always watching me. Searching my face as though you were looking for something."

"I was? I don't remember that at all. Don't mothers always look closely at their children?"

"This was different. I always used to think you looked as if you didn't recognize me, as if you weren't quite sure who I was."

Anna was silent.

"*Do* you know who I am?"

"I don't understand!"

"An outsider. That's what I've always been."

"Aren't we all, to some extent?" Anna parried.

"Of course we're not. Look at yourself, at all the friends you have. You don't have to be alone five minutes unless you want to be."

"Friends? It depends on what you mean by friends. I know dozens of nice women, but real friends? There's Ruth, of course." Anna counted on her fingers. "And Vita Wilmot, and I'm very fond of Mary Malone. There's Molly and Jean Becker and—that's it. The rest are just good company, nice people. You expect too much from people, Iris. They won't give it and they'll always disappoint you."

"That's pretty cynical, coming from you."

"Not cynical. Just realistic. One can't expect too much, that's all."

"I don't expect anything anymore," Iris said dully.

"Come! You're a young woman! Look ahead. Think positively." (I sound like the Rotary Club. It's because I don't know what else to say.)

The doorbell rang and Iris started. "It's the children, home for lunch. Do I look as if I'd been upset?"

"You look all right. They won't notice." They were too young to see the wan face, the wrinkled skirt and blouse. Anna sighed. "I'll run along. I've a beauty parlor appointment this afternoon. Shall I make one for you?"

"You're being tactful, Mama. I know how I look and I couldn't care less."

"Then I haven't helped you at all? I did want to help you!"

"I know you did, Mama, and thanks. But as I told you when you came in, I'm beyond it. If it weren't for my children I wouldn't care whether I lived or died."

"You don't feel well today, Mrs. Friedman?" Mr. Anthony, who had been doing her hair for years, was still young enough to be Anna's grandson.

"A headache, Anthony. That's why I'm not talking."

She closed her eyes, then opened them, disturbed by brassy voices from across the room. An over-ornamented woman with a handsome, aging face was fretting. Her little fat lower lip was thrust out like a coral cocktail sausage.

"A bit further over here at the temple; tease it up, Leo, over the ear, can't you see?"

Patient Leo moved a strand of hair another fraction of an inch. Anna watched the little play. It quieted her churning thoughts to watch the woman fidget and pose, studying herself in the mirror as though she could eat herself up.

Another woman got out of the dryer and went over to sausage-lip. "How was your ski trip?"

"Very nice. We had great weather and the children loved it. We stayed at a little place in the middle of nowhere. Didn't meet a soul we knew, for a change. Oh yes, one. Dr. Stern, the plastic surgeon. And not another soul."

"Theo Stern was there? Who with? Not with his girl friend?"

"I don't know him. Jerry knows him. Why, has he got one?"

"Sure has!! It's been going on for ages. People think they can get away with things, it's really funny. The way I know is, my son Bruce has an apartment in town and it's across the hall from this tall, stunning Swedish gal. So one night, we were at Bruce's place, we go to change our clothes for theatre, we see Stern going in. He used to be at the club a lot, with his wife, mousy kind of person. Anyway, I didn't think anything of it, but when we bumped into him again a couple of weeks later, I said to Bruce, I said, 'Say, is anything going on across the hall?' And Bruce said, 'Yeah, it's his girl friend, he's there every Tuesday.' "

"Tall blonde Swede?"

"Yes, I saw her once. With hair coiled to one side, you couldn't forget her."

"My God! She was *with* him! He tried to pretend he had just met her. Wait till I tell Jerry!"

Mr. Anthony put the comb down and crossed the room. When he came back to Anna the voices had been stilled.

"You told them who I was," Anna said.

"No. Not who you were. I told them to drop the subject. I'm sorry, Mrs. Friedman. Such dirty, clacking tongues."

Out on the street a wind had risen, a wind with a threat in it, fitting her fear and anger at the woman who, by disclosing what Anna didn't *want* to know, had now forced her to act. She had been presented, furiously, with a demand for action.

She fought against the bruising wind to her front door. Home was shelter in bitter weather; the blurred, stained-glass colors of books, the bowl of yellow roses on a waxed table, had always shut out whatever was raging in the world outside. She came in and stood for a moment looking at these things, seeing now, perhaps for the first time, that walls are no protection, are so easily plundered, are fragile as an egg shell against the menace of the world.

I have to fight for her, she thought in terror. I have to fight for her.

A MAGAZINE SETTING, Theo reflected. An imitation colonial crane and iron pot hung at the hearth. On the loom in the corner someone had started a few feet of woven cloth. Cheerful fakery. But the fire was real, and so was the drink. The cold flesh tingled with heat and expectancy. Where was she, anyway? She took too long getting dressed; all women did.

"Stern! What are you doing here? I thought I was the only one who knew about this place!"

"Hello, Nelson," Theo said and rose to greet the man's wife. Bad luck! The first time he'd ever run into anybody he knew when he was with Ingrid and now it had to be Nelson from the hospital pathology department.

"Here with the family?"

"No, I took a couple of days by myself. My wife thought I needed the rest," Theo said.

"We've brought our girls with us. Join us at dinner, don't eat alone."

"Thanks, but I—on the slopes this afternoon I met a young woman, I think she's a teacher, and not wanting to eat alone, I asked her to join me. I don't know how I can get out of it now."

"Bring her along, there's room for six at the table."

"Very nice of you. Ah, there she is now." Ingrid was coming down the stairs. Her hair swept to one side in a bronze coil, fell over a yellow shirt bright as lemons. People were looking at her. She came straight to Theo.

"Well, here I am! Did you think I was never coming?"

"Dr. and Mrs. Nelson," he said, "Miss—excuse me, but I'm so bad at names, Miss Johnson, is it?"

She took the cue. "Johannes. How do you do?"

"Miss Johannes is an expert from Norway. Really an expert, you must watch her tomorrow."

"I told Stern here, let's make up a table. My wife and I are planning the North Cape cruise next summer and maybe you can give us some pointers about Norway."

"That's very nice of you, but I've already reserved a table and I don't want to upset the dining room arrangements," Ingrid said, looking at Theo.

He was flustered and annoyed with himself for being so. "I'm sorry," he began, meaning to address Nelson.

"That's all right." Ingrid's voice was pleasant and cool. "Quite all right, Doctor Stern. Of course you'll want to be with your friends."

He saw as she walked away to the corner table for two that she was furious.

Nelson leaned toward him. "Say, you move fast!" he whispered. "Get the shape of that babe!"

Theo ignored him.

Fortunately, not much conversation was required of him. Mrs. Nelson was one of those women whose monologue can fill an evening. Ordinarily he despised such trivia of restaurants, shops and travel, but tonight he was grateful. He had only to swallow his food and get rid of the Nelsons who were all going over to an inn where the girls wanted to hear a "chantoosy" come up from a New York nightclub. Against their insistent urging Theo pleaded tiredness and got up to Ingrid's room as soon as they were out of sight.

She was sitting in bed reading. He saw at once that he was not to be invited into the bed.

"I'm sorry," he began. "But I couldn't think of any other way to handle it. The man's a pest. He works in the hospital and lives not too far from me." He threw up his hands. "What else could I have done?"

She didn't answer. He felt her anger and went over to the offensive. "You could have carried it through and had dinner with us. It wouldn't have hurt you."

She laid the book down. "Not hurt me? You fool, I've never been so hurt in my life!"

He was truly astonished. "Tonight? By this?"

"Tonight. By this."

He sat down on the end of the bed. "Tell me why," he said, gently.

"It hurts more that you don't know without being told."

"I'm very puzzled. You know me well enough to know that hurting is the last thing I want to do. I've seen so many wounds; God knows I don't want to make any more."

"Very fine words," Ingrid said bitterly. "Very fine. I've heard you say them often enough. 'The only things I guess I believe in are not causing any pain.' Isn't that what you said? And, oh, yes, 'We're like insects; our lives can be wiped out in an instant.' And so you believe in laughter, and the joy of each day, and being good to one another. Oh, you can be eloquent, Theo, so eloquent!"

He was perplexed at her mockery. "You still haven't made clear what this is all about."

"What it's about is, we're finished. You and I are finished. You and I are finished."

"You can't be serious! What have I done?"

"It's what you've not done. I've been feeling a lot of things for a good while now, though I haven't told you. And tonight just brought my feelings to a head."

"You should have told me what was going on in your mind."

"Maybe I should. But it's been vague, and I wanted to be patient, I thought maybe it would go away or something would happen in our lives. But tonight when I had to hide from those common people, I felt dirty. You were ashamed of me! I wasn't good enough for you! You couldn't dare let those people know we knew each other!"

"Ingrid! The words you use! 'Not good enough!' 'Ashamed!' When you know it was only because I have a wife and I couldn't—"

"Exactly! She doesn't have to hide, does she? But I do!"

Theo threw up his hands. "But you knew from the beginning that was how things were! Didn't you say you wanted to be free, that there'd be none of this heavy emotion—"

"No emotion! You *have* been damaged, haven't you? No emotion!"

"Well, of course, I didn't mean it just that way but—oh, you knew what I meant. What we both meant. The sort of thing that ties you hand and foot." He got up and stood there, looking at her. He felt totally confused.

She didn't answer.

"You knew what we both meant, didn't you?" he repeated.

"I guess," she said in a small voice, "I guess I'm not being fair to you. You did make it clear. And so did I."

"Well, then?"

"But the fact is, Theo, lately I've been thinking that I might like to be tied down. Hand and foot, as you say. I never thought I'd want that, but all of a sudden I do."

He didn't know what to say.

"I'm thirty-four. And I want someone who belongs to me. Someone on the street and in restaurants and home in bed . . . someone who belongs to *me*, not on loan from another woman."

Suddenly he began to laugh.

"What in hell are you laughing at?" she said angrily.

"Sorry. I'm not laughing at you. It's only that—you're all alike, aren't you? Why should I have thought you'd be different?"

She smiled wanly, but he saw that her eyes were wet. She reached for a cigarette, lit it and looked up. "So what do we do, Theo?"

"I don't know. I've been very happy with things as they are, and I'd be happy to go on as we are."

"You wouldn't leave Iris? Theo, if you tell me that you will, I'll go mad with joy. Otherwise, you see, this is just a dead end for me."

He walked to the window and looked out. In every crisis of his life he felt a need to get out beyond hampering walls and, if that wasn't possible, at least to look out at free space. He stood there now, watching a fresh fall of snow swirl in the circle of light at the front door below. He was hypnotized as the flakes went spiraling; they seemed, by some trick of the vision, to be rising instead of falling.

The day comes inevitably. Always there comes a day of reckoning and decision. Nothing lasts in its first simplicity. Not marriage, not this. He sighed. Behind him the sweet smoke puffed into the room. He turned around. Ingrid was still lying on the bed, with her ankles crossed. She looked limp and he felt terribly, terribly sad.

"I can't leave Iris," he said quietly. "I don't know what's going to happen to us eventually, but I do know I'm not ready to do that."

"Will you ever be ready?"

"I don't know."

He took her hand and it lay in his, not moving. A glossy tear rolled down her cheek as she turned her face away. He felt his own eyes fill. Why did women always make a man feel sad?

"You have a whole world to take, dear Ingrid," he said. "So take it and bless you."

THEO SAT BEHIND his desk, between a row of diplomas and the photographs of Iris with the children. Handsome devil, Anna thought; that's what they used to say when I was young. That little bit of gray, and so supple from all the skiing and tennis! Handsome devil.

He rose in surprise. "Well, Mother-in-law! What brings you here? You're much too pretty to have come for a face-lift."

"Thank you. Not this trip, anyway. You enjoyed your holiday? You came back early."

"Yes, the snow was mushy and I'd had enough."

Now that she was actually here, her bold anger ebbed and she was afraid to begin. But Theo helped her.

"You didn't come to ask me about my skiing holiday."

"No. I didn't." She sighed. "I was at the beauty parlor yesterday."

He raised his eyebrows and waited politely.

Anna looked out of the window. A pigeon was sitting on the air conditioner. She had set herself an impossible errand. But it had to be completed.

"You know, that is, you've heard that a lot of gossip goes on in beauty parlors?"

He straightened slightly in the chair and waited again.

"So it happens that I learned of something I would be happier not to know. . . . You weren't alone on the trip, Theo. You have, shall we say, a 'relationship' in New York?"

"I have?"

"People, various people at various times, have seen you with a—lady. A tall, blond lady. Unless, of course, they are lying. If they are, forgive me for what I've said."

"They're not lying."

"I'm sorry. I was hoping they were."

"I could insist that they were, but you would find out the truth quite easily. And anyway, I would despise myself for the lie." He struck a match for his pipe. She saw that his hands were trembling.

"Is that all you have to say, Theo?"

"What else is there? I could say I'm not the first man and I won't be the last. I could tell you that probably two out of three men do it. But I won't. I'll just say I'm not terribly proud of it."

He pushed his chair roughly back and stood up. He walked to the window where the pigeon was preening and stood with his back to Anna.

"I admit I went a little bit crazy when all that happened last year. And Iris couldn't cope with it. I don't blame her, I guess; though I don't know, I'm not sure whether I do or not. Anyway, it began to snowball, and we just kept on down hill until we came to the bottom."

"Some snowball. Some hill," Anna said dryly.

"Then I met this girl and it happened just at a time when we—"

"I'm only concerned about Iris. I don't want to hear a word about anyone else."

"But let me just tell you. I'm sure you'll want to hear that it's all over between me and the girl—"

"When did that happen?"

"The day before yesterday. It's really over, no question about it. Finished and done with."

"I'm thankful for that . . . I think Joseph would kill you if he knew."

"You're not going to tell him?"

"Of course not. But not for your sake. For his. And for Iris'."

"And you? Don't you feel like killing me, too?"

Anna answered slowly. "I can't sit in judgment. I suppose people do what they have to do."

Theo turned and stared at her. "That's quite a free concept for your generation."

"Perhaps so. But all the same, I'm not going to let you crush my daughter, Theo."

"Mama! You think I want to do that? This was something entirely—all right, you don't want to hear about it. But I have to tell you: I care about Iris. I suppose you can't understand that."

"Believe it or not, I can. But the problem is, she can't."

"You've talked to her."

"Yes. Also, the day before yesterday."

"Did she tell you that we haven't been—living together? She had our bed taken down."

Anna flushed at this intimacy from him. And she said with some defiance, "Very well. That was wrong. But a woman doesn't do that without reason, even if it isn't a justifiable reason. You were going around like walking death for too long. At least, she felt it was too long. And then drowning your sorrows with the 'smart' crowd at the club! I'm not blaming you, but after all, there has to be an end to it, hasn't there? Iris is alive, she has her own life; she can't have your memories." Tears started in Anna's eyes. She pressed the lids shut. "Some women could weather all this without much damage. But she can't. I beg you to understand, Theo, she can't help herself! It's the way she's always been. She thinks she's homely and not good enough for you. She thinks you're dissatisfied, that she's been a failure. She needs rebuilding, Theo. I tried and I'll keep on trying, but I'm not the one to do it, am I? It's you."

"You make me feel like two cents," Theo said, very low. "As cheap as that."

"It wasn't my intention. I only want to throw light into a dark place, so you can see where you're going. You have three children and their home is about to fall apart. That can't happen, Theo! Do you understand me?" she cried, hearing the passion in her own voice. "The family always comes first! Always!"

"I do understand you, Mama, and I've told you, it's over. I'll go home tonight and tell Iris that it's over."

Anna looked up in horror. "Theo! She doesn't know about—the woman! If you add that to what she already thinks it will ruin her."

"But I'd like to make a new start. I'd like to bring some honesty into the situation."

"Yes, your honesty would make you feel heroic, wouldn't it? No matter what it would do to her. Theo, I swear it, you'll have a lifelong enemy in me if you don't give me your word right now that you will never, never, never, in any circumstances, tell Iris about this. She's in a very bad way, Theo." Anna's voice quivered. "I'm afraid for her. I'm frightened."

"I tell you again, Mama, it's over. And Iris will never know about it, since that's your wish."

"Thank you. And remember, I was never here in this office talking to you."

He nodded. "I'll try to straighten everything out. I want to. You don't think I get any enjoyment out of living this way?"

"I don't think you do. But I have to tell you, I'm not sure you'll be able to straighten everything out. It's pretty late. And Iris isn't easy to handle. That I know."

Theo smiled ruefully. "I know, it too."

Anna rose, drawing her coat about her. "But don't get the idea that I won't fight for my daughter, stubborn and difficult or not. Because I will, if you two can't patch it up and it comes to that."

"You're deceptive, Mama. Iron underneath. You can be dented and scratched, but never pierced."

"Oh, yes, of course. Iron."

Theo walked with her through the outer rooms where patients were already waiting. She saw herself in the mirror as they passed it: tall, with bright hair lying against the dark collar of her fur; saw a man's eyes raised to stare at her. Not bad, she thought grimly, not bad for my age and the troubles I've seen.

"Mother-in-law, don't take it amiss," Theo said at the door, "but if I had been older or you had been younger when we met— Anyway, you are a remarkable woman, are you aware of that?"

She flipped her hand at him. "I wouldn't have liked your type." (But very probably I would. For you remind me, Theo, with your dash and grace, you remind me of Paul.)

ANNA CLIMBED THE stairs to the sitting room where Nellie had said Iris was at her desk. She walked in boldly.

Iris looked up. "I didn't expect you."

"I know you didn't. I came to find out how you are today."

"The same as I was the last time you saw me."

The girl's voice was hollow. Strange to be still thinking of her as a girl, and she a woman of thirty-six. But there was a girlishness about the slender neck, the grieving eyes.

"I hear that Theo's home."

"He came back yesterday."

"And?"

"And nothing. He should never have married me, that's all."

"That was and is for him to judge, isn't it?" (I went about it all wrong the other day; I shall take desperate measures and win or lose.) "And suppose it were so, suppose I say, it's a little late to be thinking of that now, isn't it? A house filled with children and you talk like this? It's nuts, that's what it is!" Anna's voice rose and, remembering Nellie downstairs, she lowered it, although not the passion and intensity which mounted and filled her. "Look out there at that sky, at that world with all the sparkle! It's gorgeous, and you sit closed in here, mourning because it's not exactly what you wanted! Do you think even lucky people ever get all of what they want? Who are you that you shouldn't have a burden of some sort to carry, even one of your own making? So many of our burdens are of our own making, anyway." She stopped, thinking: Retribution? Punishment? Punishment for me, through Iris, as I once thought it might have been through Maury? Absurd. A superstitious concept. Joseph would say it wasn't. Yes, he would say, everything has to be paid for before we're through.

"You know I was happy," Iris said softly. "There wasn't a woman anywhere in the world, I swear it, who was happier than I was."

It was true, it was true. Damn Theo again! The girl was dying inside because of him. Her pain could be as clearly seen as a burn on the flesh.

This thing between a man and woman— Now, in the presence of her daughter, the ache of youth came alive again.

"How long can you go on like this?" she asked abruptly.

"I don't know. I don't know anything anymore."

"Have you talked to Theo since he got back?"

"No. He's miserable too. The holiday didn't do him any good either." Iris laughed curtly.

"Can't you feel sorry for him, then? Can you have so much feeling for the poor and oppressed of the world, and so little for him?"

Iris gasped. "You're taking Theo's part?"

"I'm not 'taking part' at all." What were Theo's words? 'A little bit crazy,' he had said. Anna went on, "It seems you've both gone a little bit crazy. Not that Theo didn't have reason enough. And maybe you did, too. I can't get inside your soul. All I'm saying is, we mustn't be beaten by the pressures of life. The pressures of life," she repeated and, caught in a whirl of thoughts, heard her voice die off in a minor key.

After a moment she went on thoughtfully, "Iris, people don't like martyrs. You must learn to act, if you're to save anything, including yourself. When you don't feel joyous, pretend that you do. After a while you may actually start to feel that way."

"That advice from you? A cheap subterfuge? Is that what you've been doing all these years? Pretending?"

"What do you mean?" Anna stared at her daughter.

Iris flinched from the stare. "I don't know, if you don't."

But, Anna thought, I do know what she means. She has always had strange feelings about Paul, ever since he sent that picture years ago, perhaps even before that when Joseph and I had arguments about the Werners. No matter. I can't help what she may have thought about me, and she has enough troubles of her own just now.

Suddenly everything came together: panic, pity, impending doom, impatience and anger at having this mess dumped in her lap. Everything, but chiefly panic.

"Listen to me! Come out of your cocoon and look at the real world out there! What if you were to lose him? You, who told me two days ago that you couldn't face the thought of living without Theo! You think, if he should finally get sick of all this and walk out, that there's going to be a line of men waiting to take you and your three children? Do you? Yes," Anna said cruelly, hacking at herself as well as at Iris, "and what if he were to die? What if he were to leave one morning as usual, and a little while later some stranger rings the doorbell, the way they came to tell us about Maury, and you learn that Theo is dead? What then? Tell me!" Her breath came fast and she couldn't stop the ugly words, although she saw that Iris was horrified. "Yes, in three seconds it would be all over. For good. And you left here alone in this house with your silent dignity, your wounds, your pride and your children who have lost their father. Well, it could happen!" Iris had put her hands over her face. "And don't come to me, if it should! Don't come to me for sympathy! Because I've had enough trouble to last me a lifetime and I'm not about to take on any more."

The rotten thing was that she was taking pleasure in what she was saying, taking *pleasure* in hurting Iris! (You have no guts, Iris, that's what's the matter.) And at the same time she was so afraid. My God, if anything were to happen to you! Iris, my girl, my girl, why do things have to be so hard for you? You don't deserve it.

"I don't care if you hate me. I'm saying what's right for you to hear. I don't care if you never speak to me again. Well, of course, I do," Anna said. She was losing her breath and weakening; she gripped the frame of the door. "But if you choose not to speak to me I can't help it. Now, listen to me, go out and get your hair done! And throw away that gray—that *dustrag* you've got on. I don't want to see rags like that on you ever again. Put a smile on your face when Theo gets home. Put one on, damn it, if you have to paste it on! Now call a taxi for me. I want to go home."

Iris looked up. "That's a good idea. I was just going to ask you to leave my house."

"Well, I beat you to it."

For the first time in her life Anna went to bed early without being ill with a fever. But she had never been so exhausted. It had been like pushing an enormous round load up a hill; it kept slipping back and you had to push harder to regain what you had lost.

Fortunately Joseph had gone with Eric to the city for dinner and a hockey game at the Garden. Eric always saved a day out of his vacation for his grandfather. Really, they ought to give him a great party for his twenty-first birthday, she thought, lying back against two pillows and warming her hands around the cup of tea. A beautiful party, with a little band, a group of youngsters to make live music.

We've come a long way since that day we drove home from Brewerstown with a terrified, brave little boy. Thank God for that. And pray that this trouble with Iris works out as well. But I don't know, it's so far gone. Theo's awfully independent, not easy to handle, and she's impossible.

I wonder when you can ever stop eating your heart out over a family? I hope the children haven't overheard or sensed things. Stevie especially: he's so bright, he sees everything. Sometimes I think he has a worried face, although probably that's just because he's the first child and the first child is supposedly more sensitive, more attuned to what's going on among adults. Although Maury wasn't —oh, yes, he was! You forget, you didn't find out until much, much later what had been going on under the sunny manner. Still, it's true he was never as complicated as Iris, I think.

Everybody's difficult. I, too. My God, am I difficult!

I can't agonize anymore. I want another cup of tea and haven't the strength to get up for it. I've done what I could for everyone. What counts most now, what has to count most now, is Joseph and me. I wish once more that I had his absolute faith. Still, since I know he has it, why do I guard him from all this trouble? He ought to be stronger than I. And he is, in so many ways. Only not where Iris is concerned.

The front door opened. "Anna! I'm home!" Joseph called.

"I'm upstairs, in bed."

She heard him coming up two steps at a time, like a young man. "In bed already? What's the matter?"

"Just a chill. Start of a cold. I've taken an aspirin," she fibbed.

"You're always running around with your errands and charities! Why don't you think of yourself and take it a little bit easy?" His voice was irritable and anxious.

"Don't yell at me, Joseph. Besides, look who's talking about running around. Did you have a good time?"

"Sure did. I dropped Eric off for a 'late date.' There's a crowd over at some girl's house near the Point."

"That's good. I was thinking, we ought to give him a party for his next birthday."

"Great idea! Shall I get you another blanket? Are you cold?"

"No, I'm fine. Really. I'll be perfect again in the morning," she said cheerfully.

He drew the blanket around her shoulders. "Well, I hope so. I just hope you've caught it in time before it turns into anything worse. God forbid."

"I think I have," she said. "I think perhaps I've caught it in time."

THEO CAME IN and saw that the two narrow beds had been taken away. The old bed with the white and yellow spread was back in its place. Iris came out of the dressing room. She was wearing a robe of some sort, a hostess coat, they called it, or something like that. Anyway, it had a kind of pretty ruffled thing like daisy petals around the neck. She had been at the hairdresser's.

"Good evening," he said. A small laugh like a bubble rose in his throat. "I see there have been some changes in the furniture."

"Are you pleased?" she asked, without looking at him.

"Very." He waited a moment and when she looked up he moved and put her head on his shoulder. She didn't come nearer, but she didn't go away, either. They stood like that for a minute or two. He remembered the night not so long ago, when it was he who had rested his head upon her shoulder and she had tried to give comfort to him. Well, that was past.

His hands moved over her.

"Not yet," she whispered. "Not just yet."

"But soon?"

"Yes, all right. Soon. Quite soon."

❈{40}❧

On a day in the early fall of Eric's senior year at Dartmouth he met his cousin Chris Guthrie for lunch in New York. It was Chris's first visit home from Venezuela in three years.

"I've saved all your letters," he told Eric. "They're real nostalgia for me. I feel I'm back on the campus, snow in the air. You write extremely well. You know that, don't you?"

"They tell me I do."

"What are you planning after graduation?"

"My grandfather has a place ready for me in the firm."

Chris stirred his coffee. Then he looked up acutely. Eric reflected that all "men of affairs" had that look. He'd been watching them at neighboring tables, in their dark suits and English shoes; they had a way of concentrating keenly, of making the moment *move*. Their eyes never *dream*, that's what it is, he thought; they never rest on anything for more than a second or two. They don't see that beyond the window the September haze is dusty amber and the city is waking to a brisker season—

"I asked you," Chris said, "I asked you whether you'd like that?"

"Excuse me. I didn't hear you. I hope to like it all right. It's an opportunity most people don't have, isn't it?"

"Starting at the top in a family business? I should think not!" Chris went on thoughtfully, "You know, when I drove you down from Brewerstown seven years ago—now I can tell it—I was as sorry for you as I think I've ever been for anyone in all my life. And now that my own kids are growing up and I look at them and think of what happened to you—well, I wouldn't want them to have to face what you did."

"On the scale of world suffering I rank pretty low, in spite of everything, Chris."

"Well, if you mean hunger and want, that's something else. But there are other kinds of suffering. You had an awful lot of courage, and—"

"Chris, I'm fine. I really am."

"I can see you are. Tell me, when you think back, are things very different from when you lived with Gran and Gramp? No reason for asking, except curiosity."

"Well, the personalities are different. Very. But as to feeling wanted and all that, it's the same."

"Good. Let's see, what else can I ask you? Have you got a girl?"

Eric laughed. " 'A' girl? No."

"Good again. Don't tie yourself down too young. But to get back to the work business: tell me, have you ever considered *not* going in with your grandfather?"

"Not really. I haven't got any special ambitions. What makes you ask?"

"I'll tell you. I'm being given a tremendous job. A promotion. It'll mean four or five years in the Middle East, based in Iran."

"Gosh! Cloak and dagger! Lawrence of Arabia!"

"You can kid, but there really is a helluva lot of that stuff going on. Anyway, I was thinking: I'm supposed to get a staff together, four or five bright, young eager beavers. So I thought of you. I'd have no trouble getting you approved, that's sure." He lit a cigarette and waited a moment. "How does it sound?"

"What would I have to do?"

"Sales. Contacts. Politicking. You name it." Chris waited again, then added, "It's a fantastic part of the world. Literally. I've been there and it really got to me. When you see your first Bedouin in his *kaffiyeh,* riding a camel—"

The restaurant, the dark suits, the table with its cloth and cutlery dissolved into a bazaar of burning colors and a gaudy sky. Eric had to smile at his own extravagance.

"It's very tempting, very alluring and very sudden, Chris," he said cautiously.

"Of course. You don't think I expect a decision this minute, do you? I'm coming back around Christmas and we can talk some more then. But I do want to leave one thought with you, Eric. No, two. The first is obvious: that there's a real future in a company like ours. The second ties in with your ambition to write."

"In what way?"

"Well, in order to write you have to have something to write about, don't you? You have to know people and cultures and conflict. Think of the memory bank you could establish on a job like this! Enough to draw against for the rest of your life! And I'd see that you had plenty of time for exploring."

Again, that quick look of estimation. Eric answered it slowly.

"It would be such a—a *defeat* for my grandparents."

"Yes, but they've had their lives and done what they wanted. Now it's your turn, isn't it? In time I'll have to be moving over myself, to make room for my own boys. I'm almost forty-two, you know." Chris summoned the waiter and took out his wallet. "I've got a train to make. Eric, it's been great. Every time I see you I realize how much I've missed you. Think it over; there's no rush, but I truly believe this could be the start of something great for you. I'll get in touch. And oh, yes, remember me at home."

For the last year he had been feeling that his life was sliding steadily toward the unknown. Except for the few who knew that they were fated for something definite like law or medicine or engineering, this feeling was common, Eric knew. It wasn't strong enough to be called panic; it was just *there,* a kind of scary drift into a world in which perhaps one would never be entirely at home. He tried to imagine himself sitting in the office every morning of his life, conferring with bankers and mortgage brokers, then driving out to an enormous tangle of construction out of which would emerge another grid of look-alike, boxy houses. Not that it wasn't a decent product and therefore a productive life, but as far as he was beginning to understand, it wasn't something to which he could look forward with any exhilaration. When a man has completed a thing he had wanted with all his heart to do, he sits down to rest and says, "There, that's over. I wanted to do it and I've done it!" It wasn't like that at all, at least as far as he could see.

So he kept thinking about what Chris had offered.

He certainly hadn't intended to mention it to anyone, yet one day when he was home over Thanksgiving he found himself telling Aunt Iris.

"Maybe I'm rationalizing the whole thing because I want the adventure," he concluded.

"There's nothing wrong with wanting adventure, is there?"

"I suppose not. And ever since Chris planted this seed the building business has looked duller and duller."

Iris said slowly, "Without actually thinking it over, I've sort of assumed you would write. I don't know how or in what form, but I've just thought of you that way. Perhaps because your father and I both had vague desires to do something with words . . . only, neither of us had any true gift and I believe you have."

"One doesn't just rent a room, buy a typewriter and begin to write," Eric argued and, paraphrasing Chris, "you have to live first and have something to write about."

"True. And writing isn't what you're asking about right now anyway, although it might well tie in, as your cousin says."

"You're avoiding an answer. What I want to know is, should I consider the offer?"

"Should you hurt my parents, you mean. That's what you're asking me, isn't it?"

"I'm sorry. It's not fair of me to expect you to be neutral, is it?"

"No, it isn't. Because I know what it will do to them. And still I know that you've a right to be somebody yourself, not just somebody's beloved grandson." Iris sighed. "So I guess I'll just have to throw the decision back in your lap."

Eric nodded soberly. "Only don't mention it, please? Not even to Uncle Theo. I need time to sweat this out myself."

"Not a word. I promise."

Just before Christmas he and Chris met again at the same place.

"I haven't made up my mind," Eric told him.

Chris was surprised. "What's the obstacle?"

"I keep thinking about Grandpa and Nana. He's had me down at the office telling everybody I'll be working there next year; he's even got my room set aside. *She's* bought Early American prints for the walls." And when Chris began a gesture, he went on hurriedly, "I know, you'll say it's my life and that's true, but it's a big decision and I can't make it in such a hurry."

"Listen," Chris said, "I want you to come in later this week. I'll get an appoint-

ment with the people here in New York for an interview. Then whatever questions you have they can answer and you won't be making the big decision just on
my say-so. Only one thing—" he lowered his voice and glanced at the adjoining
table, "when you give your name, spell it the way you used to, will you? Freeman? It's more American that way. I've told them that's your name."

"Why did you do that? What difference does it make?"

"It makes a difference. Take my word for it. Particularly in the Middle East,
everything heating up between the Arabs and Israel."

"You mean that I shouldn't appear to be Jewish."

"Well, you aren't, are you? You were brought up an Episcopalian and you're
my cousin. Who would think of asking whether you were Jewish?"

"I'm also Joseph Friedman's grandson."

"Of course, of course. But listen, Eric, it's a chilly, practical world and you've
got to be practical to survive in it. I strongly advise you to play that side down for
business purposes. Especially this business."

Eric grimaced. "Lousy. Dishonest. And worse than that, cruel."

"Why cruel? You aren't doing or saying anything hurtful. It's just a case of *not*
saying something, a case of omission." And when Eric didn't answer, he added
urgently, "Besides, aren't you forgetting the other side of yourself? Gran and
Gramp and all the life you had with them?"

"Chris! You think I could forget them?"

"I certainly don't. And after all, it isn't as if you were a religious Jew. You
haven't gone over to the religion, have you, Eric?" Chris asked abruptly.

"To tell the truth, I haven't any religion at all," Eric said. His voice sounded
somber to his own ears.

"Well, that's the fashion these days, isn't it? So shall I make the appointment
for this week or do you want to put it off till my next trip?"

"Put it off," Eric said. "As long as there's no hurry."

After leaving Chris he walked down Fifth Avenue toward Grand Central.
Christmas lights in shop windows and out of doors rippled and streamed like
moving water. "Adeste Fideles" clanged from a loudspeaker above the entrance to
a department store. The citadel of Christmas, emporium of glitter, cathedral of
twentieth-century America. The department store. He felt unusually depressed.

A bank advertised its loan service under the smiling photograph of a young
couple admiring an expensive sports car. Was that the measure of contentment,
the measure of a man, his ability to provide a sports car? Or a motorboat, a
diamond, or any of the things for which people put themselves in hock? Worth
his weight in gadgets, a man was.

Climb, forge ahead, acquire, be smart, even if you have to lie a little, even if
you have to deny the truth about yourself to do it. Why not?

He began to walk faster, to breathe more deeply of the icy air. Morbid today,
misanthropic. The world really isn't all that awful. Just my own personal riddle,
needing to be solved. That's all it is.

If this offer had come, not from one of his mother's people, but from one of
Grandpa's cronies, Mr. Duberman, let's say, or some other of the pinochle group,
would it be much less of a problem?

He tried to imagine the scene, a party perhaps, everyone around a table crowded with crystal, with flowers, with silver platters and bowls of meats, half a dozen kinds of meats, half a dozen kinds of smoked fish, salads, molds and puddings, spicy condiments and pungent sauces, glossy, twisted loaves, fruit, cakes—

"Eat, here, pass the salad to Jenny, she eats like a bird—"

"If you don't taste that pudding you'll insult my wife," Grandpa would roar, and pile a ladleful of steaming noodle pudding on someone's plate.

Nana's bracelets would clash; she'd smile with pleasure and pride, diamond pinpoints flashing in her ears.

"Did you know that Eric will be going abroad next year?" Grandpa would inquire of the table at large. But everyone would be talking: on this side two of the men having a vigorous political argument; on the other side someone telling jokes, people crying with laughter. Grandpa would clink on a goblet with his knife and call above the noise.

"You've heard about our Eric? You haven't heard?"

With amusement and tenderness he constructed the scene in his mind: the sudden silence, his grandfather's announcement, the cries of congratulation; his grandmother getting up to hug him, squeezing his head against perfume and warm silk; an old man gripping his hand.

"What a smart boy! A treasure! Joseph, Anna, a treasure of a boy—"

Of course they would shed tears because he would be going away; of course his great opportunity would have to be anywhere else but in the Middle East, where now, at the end of a second millennium, people of this blood were again being threatened with slaughter. Granting all that, he knew it would still not be such unacceptable pain as this return to his mother's people, reminding them again of their losses. He wondered suddenly how it must have been for his father, making the decision which was to take him from them for good.

Pain. How do you measure it? Doctors measure it in dols: much pain, middling pain, less pain. . . .

He went back to Dartmouth the following week, with graduation only five months distant, with no decision made and sure of nothing.

GREAT-UNCLE WENDELL DIED in early April and was buried from the home which had been in his family since the first Guthrie had come to Massachusetts three centuries before.

Eric drove down from New Hampshire, meeting as he went the first uncertain gusts of spring that blew warm whenever the sun struck through the clouds. In spite of his errand he felt exhilaration as the car rolled between stone-walled fields, down aisles of elms on old main streets, past the white, square, ample houses of his childhood. He knew exactly how these houses would look inside, the corner cupboards flanking the fireplace in the dining room, the tall clock on the landing midway between floors. The shapes and patterns of Brewerstown.

When they came back to the house from the churchyard where the Guthries lay, the faces that gathered, faces of relatives and strangers, were familiar, too. How odd that you got used to other types and faces without real awareness of the difference and the change! Now suddenly he realized that he hadn't seen faces like these in a long, long time.

Generalizations were totally unscientific. There were almost as many exceptions as the rule, and yet he could know, here in this room, that he was not among his father's people. Less tension here perhaps, less animation, color, noise? No matter; it was different.

They were an unmistakable breed, these people, shaped narrowly and of a healthy toughness that went with hardy skills like rough-weather sailing or cross-country skiing. The women, even those who weren't pretty, who had long, craggy faces, wore the marks of their kind: skirts and blouses, gold circle pins, a strong, no-nonsense manner. He would have recognized one of them if he had encountered her in Patagonia. He stood there watching the group around the coffee urn, listening to the crisp accents and gentle voices, feeling as if—as if he had just walked into his own home after a morning's absence. And quite suddenly he understood what it was that moved him so, in a way that was probably not entirely reasonable, that was just simply because—

Because they looked like Gran.

Chris was there with his wife and older boys. Chris's brothers were there also with young, pregnant wives.

Hugh came over to introduce Betsey. "I've heard you're going on an exciting venture with Chris," Betsey said. "We're all so delighted that you'll be together."

Eric flushed. "I haven't quite made up my mind," he answered.

Chris had come up behind them. "I don't know what you're waiting for," he said. For the first time he sounded impatient. "It's already April and if you want to come along you'll have to see the people in New York by the end of the month. I can't stall any longer for you, you know."

"I know."

"For the life of me I can't imagine why you don't jump at the chance!"

"I guess because it's for five years. One wants to be absolutely sure of a commitment like that."

"Well, don't think too long, that's all." Chris walked away.

Now Hugh introduced an old man who had been standing near the fireplace. "Cousin Ted, this is Eric. You've never met, I think."

Eric took hold of a hard leathery hand, looked into a pair of concentrating eyes.

"I knew your mother when she was a baby. Never saw you, though. Never see much of my wife's family since she died. But I wanted to pay my respects today. I live over in Prides Crossing since I retired." He rambled, moving toward senility.

"I met your father once. Came to me for a job at the bank, I recall. Couldn't give him one, though. Depression, you know. No jobs. You look like your mother," he said abruptly. "A fine, pretty girl, your mother was. Died too young. Look at me, I'm eighty-seven."

Someone came and led him away to the coffee urn. Eric thought, All these people know more about who I am than I do. The thought caused a bleakness and at the same time a soft wish to reach out to them.

"Remember us," Gran said.

If I turn my back now and cut myself off that'll be the end, the final end. The old people are dying or dead. Chris will go away and when he comes back we'll be strangers. At least, there's a little something between us now, a little flame that can be fanned.

Arabia. Riding with Chris of that old, first life, into a new life. . . . Someone had put pine cones in the fireplace; the sweet, sharp scent of them sifted through the warm air. Fragrance and flavor, like those of Proust's madeleine, were potent instruments always; he could smell Maine's salty coves again and Brewerstown's gilt Septembers, its fires of fall. Oh, remembered places, remembered faces! Flesh of his flesh and quiet ways; Gramp's birds and a white horse grazing, and so much more. So much.

He found Chris talking at the far end of the room. He tapped him on the shoulder.

"Chris, I'll go with you," he said.

DURING THE WEEK of spring recess he opened his mouth a dozen times to tell his grandparents and closed it again, feeling weak and cowardly.

"I want to buy you a good car," Grandpa said. "The jalopy was good enough for a college boy, but you ought to have a better one now. So be thinking about what you'd like and we'll take care of it after commencement."

He said, "Why don't you take a month or two off before you start putting your nose to the grindstone? Drive out to California or something? Have a ball."

Nana said, "I was thinking, would you like me to fix up your room at the office or do you want to pick out your own things? Jerry Malone just refurnished, so maybe you'd like to take a look at what he bought for some ideas—"

Grandpa said, "You haven't seen the new shopping center since we finished up, have you? How about taking a ride over with me? I have a couple of people to see there this afternoon."

Eric went along and strolled through the long expanse of malls, turns and alleys, up a level and down a level, marveling at the enormity of it all and trying to observe enough to make, later, the intelligent comments that would be expected.

But all he could feel was a pervasive sadness. So many aimless couples drifting through the afternoon with their children tugging at them, looking for amusement! Anxious men in lumber jackets, tired women with hair in curlers, wandering with their desires through mazes of stores piled with shoddy trash that they couldn't afford and didn't need! And Eric knew that if he were to express all that to his grandfather he would only stare in astonished dismay.

They got back in the car. "Well, what did you think of it?" his grandfather asked. There was a sparkle in his voice.

"It's a busy place, all right."

"Wait till you see what we're building in south Jersey. It's still only on paper but we expect to break ground in September. Maybe I'll let you work on it. I'll send you down with Matt Malone to get the feel of things. Matt's a smart boy. You can learn a lot from him."

Eric's left hand lay on the seat and suddenly his grandfather placed his own over it. He spoke very low, so that Eric could barely hear him and knew that the old man was embarrassed by his own emotion.

"For years I've envied Malone. It was wrong of me, I know. *Thou shalt not covet. . . .* But I did, all the same. All those fine sons to go into business with him! To carry on what he had built out of years of sweat, while for me it was all going down the drain. Into nothing, as if I had never existed. Until you came. I don't mind telling you, you've taken years off my shoulders. Or put years onto my life, however you want to say it. Do I make you feel uncomfortable, Eric? Forgive me this once, if I do."

"That's okay, Grandpa." My God, my God, how am I going to say it? With what words? Where? When?

On Friday evening his grandmother called him aside. "Eric, I want to ask a favor. Would you come to temple with us tonight? It's the anniversary of your great-grandfather's death and Grandpa has to say Kaddish for him."

"Yes, surely, I'll go."

"Thank you, I'm glad. I know it's not your prayer, but still it will make him feel good to have you there."

He sat through the sermon not hearing it, heavy with the weight of his dilemma. He was aware from time to time of plaintive music, but only half aware. The name of Max Friedman was called in a long list of names; the sounding of its syllables made a small shock in his head and it came to him for an instant that the blood of that totally strange man—for if he were to be brought back to life what could they have to say to one another?—that strange man's blood was in him, nevertheless. The congregation rose. He felt the rustling and stood with them through the murmuring of several hundred voices all in unison. His grandmother's head was bowed, her hands were clasped, her face was serious. His grandfather's old hooded eyes were partly closed. He swayed as he held the prayer book but he was not reading it; he knew it by heart. They know I won't be saying this prayer for them, Eric thought. One of Aunt Iris' little boys will have to do that when they are dead. And yet I mean so much to them.

And now the blessing: "The Lord bless thee and keep thee; the Lord cause the light of His face to shine upon thee—"

Then "Good Sabbath," the people turning to each other in the neighboring pews, families, friends and strangers kissing or shaking hands.

"Good Sabbath." Joseph kissed Eric and kissed Anna; Anna kissed Eric and kissed Joseph.

They moved slowly in the press going down the aisle. Grandpa rested a hand on Eric's shoulder. He saw that his grandmother watched the gesture. He thought irrelevantly that her red hair was too youthful for the expression that she wore. He looked at her while she looked at her husband's hand. Something was being weighed and balanced behind her thoughtful, clever face, something of delicate complexity, spun of unspoken things. He felt, he could almost touch, an emotion so tense that a move might shatter it, whatever it was: a question held back, a plea, perhaps, for which there were no words?

He knew then, in the throb of that instant, that he couldn't go.

*   *   *

"You're not angry, Chris?" he asked, when he had finished his story. They had met in New York for the purpose, so Chris had expected, of taking Eric to the interview.

"I won't allow myself to be." Chris smiled but his eyes were angry. "I'll just say you're rather young for your years, completely inexperienced and far too sentimental. You're like your—" he broke off.

"Like my parents, you were going to say."

"Well, yes, I was. However, it's hardly unusual for a person to be like his parents."

"Like which of them?" Eric persisted.

"Like both. Too idealistic for their own good, each one of them."

Chris took Eric's hand. "I'm always in a hurry these days, it seems. So let's just say, 'Good luck to us both.' And if you ever need me, Eric, you'll know where I am. Keep in touch, will you? All the best," he said. His face changed; a look of gravity and softness came over it, and for an instant Eric was back in the boat, bobbing behind a curtain of willows, and Chris was saying, "Your Gran is going to die." He shook off the illusion.

"Thanks, Chris, for everything," he said, and, releasing each other's hands, they parted among the hastening crowds on Forty-third Street.

Later that week Iris told him, "I'm not sure it was the right decision for your own self-interest. But it surely was generous, Eric."

He didn't answer. Now that he had made the decision he felt that it hadn't really been generous of him at all, that actually he had been and was—would always be?—too divided to be entirely content either with staying or with going.

"I think I'd like to wander around Europe for a couple of months this summer," he said suddenly, the idea having just come. "I've never been much of anywhere."

A small inheritance from Gramp was to be given to him at commencement time. It was a legacy, literally and figuratively, from an era when a young gentleman was expected to make a tour of Europe before he "settled down."

"I wish I could go with you," Iris said. "But Theo says Europe smells of decay. I'm hoping someday he'll change his mind."

"This wouldn't be your summer to go anyway, would it?" For Iris was pregnant again, at thirty-seven; he wondered how pleased she could be about it, and rather thought it must have been an "accident."

"The baby'll be here by the time you get back, I guess. It's due around the middle of October."

"I'll be back," Eric assured her.

In mid-June, after commencement, they helped him pack. His grandmother brought home a set of fine luggage, a traveling umbrella and a travel bathrobe, all highly impractical, and all a way of saying, "have a wonderful time; we love you." He had learned that much about them during his time in their house.

On the last night they went to Theo's and Iris' for dinner. The two boys had pooled their allowances and bought film for his camera.

"I would like some pictures of Stonehenge," Steve told Eric solemnly. "I have a book about it. Nobody seems to know who built it, do they?"

Jimmy asked Eric to find out how you play rugby and how it was different from football. Laura had helped her mother make a package of fudge, "to eat on the plane for dessert." And Eric felt the poignancy of departure.

Anna cried a little. "I don't know why I'm crying! I'm so happy that you're going to have a marvelous summer. I don't know why I'm crying."

She cried so easily. Gran would never have done that. He thought that he had been cursed with ambivalence. In some ways he was closer in feeling and expression to this woman than he had ever been able to get to Gran, and yet Gran was a part of his fibre and his life as this other grandmother could never be. She had come too late. A part of him would always be withheld from her and awkward with her.

Suddenly it occurred to him that that was what she was feeling too, and that was why she cried.

In a little town near Bath one afternoon he bought a cheap notebook at a stationer's and began to write.

I think sometimes that what is bothering me is that I no longer believe in anything. Perhaps, coming from an urban, halfway educated American in this secular age, that sounds absurd. But there it is, all the same.

Perhaps if I believed in something I would know where I belong, or where I want to belong, and among what people. You may ask, what has belief, which is so absolutely personal, got to do with belonging to this, that or the other social group? Nothing, really.

I sat half the afternoon in a Saxon church in a Thomas Hardy village. Saxon! Imagine how old! It was cold behind those thick walls, with a hot summer hush outdoors. I walked out to the churchyard. There was no one in sight except some cows chewing and drooling in the field next to the graves. Sound of bees. I read the names on the headstones where they weren't rubbed out by centuries of rain. The same names on plaques in the nave; the same on doors in the village. Thomas Brearley and Sons, Cobblers since 1743. Live here all your life; work; sing hymns on Sunday. Same work, same words, over and over. Baptized in this church, cold water on the infant's forehead, squalling at the font. Die and be buried a few steps away. Must be some truth here? If all these generations, in grieving or rejoicing, felt there was Something here, must there not certainly be Something?

In the silence, in the old, old place so small and plain and human, I could see myself on the edge of believing.

At nine or ten, going to church with Gran and Gramp, it was different then. So much awe. Used to come home to big Sunday dinner, roast and pie, wearing my best suit, feeling everything in order. Wish I could feel it

again. Wish I could feel like my grandfather and Aunt Iris in the syna-
gogue. Not so sure about Nana; I think she's trying to be like them.
Naturally, she wouldn't say, or maybe doesn't even know herself. Asked
Uncle Theo once about himself: had he lost faith? I never had it, he said.

Ireland. Fearful damp and chattering teeth. Fog and rain in cold stone
slums. I watch old women in black shawls doing the Stations of the Cross
in roadside villages. My great-great—many greats ago—came from Ireland,
Gran said. Like one of these women in the shawls? But first a girl, walking
the roads. So poor. Decaying teeth. Eyes like turquoise. Superstitious.
Clustering, dark legends: elves, gnomes of the woods.

I go into a church. Tawdry frescoes, calendar art in candy-box colors.
Effeminate figure on the cross, insipid woman holding the infant. Think of
high art: the Pietà, the Mother and dead Son. The accumulated agony of
the centuries: above all, human.

That's all it is: human. Need to lean on something while we stumble
through life. That's all it is, isn't it? Any thinking man knows that's all it is.
Father, I believe. Help Thou mine unbelief.

Gramp always wanted to come back here and couldn't. Now I see why
he wanted to. Plane trees, hill towns, old olive orchards of Provence. Snapshot of my mother, sitting in front of a vineyard. Her eyes turned to this
same light. Roman faces. They've been here since then. No, before then;
the Greeks came first. Marseilles was Marsallia. Ruins of a Greek city at
Glanum. All these flowing rivers of life. The Rue des Israelites in a medieval town; another flowing river, but of blood. The Judengasse in Salzburg:
all over Europe, locked up, chains at the two ends of the street. A unique
history among peoples, myself at the tail end. Fierce beliefs. They died for
them. I don't think they were worth dying for. I don't think any belief is
worth dying for. Do I? Maybe I'll find one that is. Then it will be worth
living for, too.

I pose myself a question, a cliché by now. Would I give my treasure, my
small worldly treasure (large to me) for the lives of a thousand unknown
yellow (or any other color) men on the far side of the globe? Another
question: what is the value of my immortal soul (assuming that I have one)
compared to the immortal soul of a squalid pimp in a New York alley? I
don't know the answer to either question.

These things trouble me.

Weeks later

Juliana stands before red flowers in a window box. The house has a
gable roof and a canal runs in front of it. She eats from a box of Dutch
chocolates. I think I am falling in love with her.

I know I am falling in love with her. She has been working on a kibbutz in northern Galilee and is home for vacation. Why? I ask her. Why Israel? She says she wants to see the world. She says the Dutch have been good to the Jews (that I know); she says it is exciting there. Ideals in action, she tells me. A place for the young. A new country. She wants me to go back with her. Just to see what it's like, she says. I'm going. I would go anyway, even if it was to Timbuktu.

Oh, lovely Europe, your flowers and your wine, your bread, your music. We're flying southeast, over the ancient, warm and violet Mediterranean lands. I shall remember the sweetness and delight of Europe.

And I shall remember its concentration camps, Uncle Theo says.

❖{41}❖

So narrow is the northernmost tip of Israel that a giant of ancient legend would be able to straddle it with one foot in Lebanon and the other in Syria.

The river Jordan, mighty in the imagination of the Western world, was only a stream, Eric thought with surprise, and the falls at its source, which were held in awe by the natives, were only a faucet's trickle when compared, not with Niagara, but with any modest waterfall at home.

Nevertheless, the land was lovely.

At the crest of a low hill stood the wooden buildings of the kibbutz: dormitories, dining hall, library, school. Barns and sheds ringed the slopes; below them stretched wide orchards, and beyond these lay a flowing sea of grain.

Reapers moved through that golden sea. Young men and women climbed the trees, picked and packed the fruit. Cattle stamped in the barns. Fresh-mown grass sweetened the air. From the dining hall one heard the sound of someone practicing on the piano; from the machine shop came the clang of iron against iron. In the big kitchen from morning to night meals were in preparation. Children splashed in the swimming pool: the second generation, building on the foundation of the pioneers, had added this touch of luxury. Out of rock and the neglect of barren centuries, vision and toil had made a way of life.

And all of it lay within gunshot of the Golan Heights.

"The Syrians have crack troops up there," Juliana said, pointing eastward to bluffs that rose like a wall. "Anything that moves in the fields or on the road is a target, whenever the notion takes them. Last year, just after I got here," she said bitterly, "it was a bus going in to town. The driver was hit and of course it smashed. Eight killed, two of them children under five."

They were walking through the yards between the buildings. Juliana was very serious. "Come, I'll show you something else. On this side we're only two miles from Lebanon." They slid on slippery grass between lines of thin young pear trees. At the lower edge of the orchard she raised a screen of leafage and they looked into the ugly reptilian mouths of a row of guns.

"This is our second line of defense. The wire fences and the guards are at the border."

"It's rather sobering, to think we sleep with guns in our back yard."

"It's a safer feeling, I'll tell you that! Still, now and then they slip through anyway. You must have read about the raid on the school? It was in the next town, only twenty minutes from here. Down there through that grove, that's the border and the wire fence. If you walk straight down you'll reach it."

Eric thought, If I had gone with Chris I would have been on the other side of it. He wondered fleetingly what sort of lives were being lived on that other side, but in the short weeks he had been here he had become so much identified with these lives that he found it hard to imagine those others.

He slept in the dormitory for single men. On the wall opposite each bed hung each man's gun. Pants and shoes lay on a chair alongside the bed. You could be dressed, downstairs and out of doors in sixty seconds.

He thought of stories that Gramp had told about their ancestors who had settled the wilderness of New York State. Energy and guts. Making something out of nothing. Perhaps that was the pull of this place for him—that, and Juliana.

"Do you really like it, Eric? Do you feel anything of what I told you about when we were in Holland?" she asked.

"I'm beginning to. And I do know what you meant."

They sat down on a rock in the lowering sun. It was the Sabbath and a hush lay over everything. Work had stopped. There was deep quiet except for mild stampings and lowings from the barn.

"When I first came—I had wanted for years to come—it was because I felt an obligation. Lots of young Europeans do, Germans, too. Now I stay because I love it. But the obligation came first."

"Tell me about it."

Juliana shuddered. "Those years of the war when I was nine, ten, eleven, we saw such things—" She was silent for a minute or two, then resumed, "A neighbor of ours, a determined woman, with convictions—"

"Like you," Eric interrupted, with a smile.

"She was a brave woman. She had a Jewish family hidden in her attic behind a camouflaged door. Just like Anne Frank. You've read the book?"

"Yes."

"Well, it was like that. Only a few people knew they were there. Whatever food we could spare, an extra apple, or some cereal at the bottom of the pot, my mother took next door. We children weren't supposed to know but I heard my mother telling my father that there were two brothers and their wives, some children and a baby. They had to hold the baby under a blanket to muffle its cries.

"So, one day the Germans came and took them away. They went straight to the hidden door. And they took our good neighbor, too, in a truck filled with people on the way to the camps, most of them to the furnaces. The husbands were separated from the wives and children from their own mothers. We heard them all the way down the street as far as the corner, crying, crying—" Juliana covered her face with her hands. "Do you think, Eric, that I shall be able to forget things like that? I don't think I will. One day the Nazis took my two uncles, my mother's younger brothers. We never heard from them again. They had been working in the underground, you see."

"And someone reported them?"

"I guess so. We were so afraid all the time for my father. I wasn't supposed to know that either, but you know how children always find out what's going on in a house. So I knew that my father was also in the underground. And at night, whenever it was late and quiet and you heard the sound of a motor or footsteps pounding toward the house, I was sure they were coming to take him away, too."

"Do any children anywhere have the kind of life children are supposed to have?" Eric burst out.

"I'm sure they do! They must or the world would be a total madhouse! Why, was your life so hard?"

Some other time, perhaps. Not now. "No," he murmured, "actually it was warm and beautiful." And it was true, in most ways, wasn't it? No self-pity; self-pity stinks, he thought roughly, and repeated with firmness, "it was warm and beautiful."

From the dining hall came music, a piano sonata played with fervent hands and spirit. Eric looked up questioningly.

"Shh!" Juliana motioned, and they waited in the violet dusk until the music had ended, waited even a moment longer until it had died away on the air.

She said softly, "That's Emmy Eisen. You know, the woman who helps me in the nursery sometimes? She was a piano teacher in Munich and hid there all through the war. She's so blond, they thought she was an Aryan, you see. And she had good friends, Catholic people who said she was a relative and got false papers for her. She was one of the lucky ones; she didn't get caught. But her husband did and her two sons. That's why she doesn't talk very much. I don't know whether you noticed."

"Ah, yes," Eric said.

"It's a pity she can't have a good piano for herself. The kids wreck this one. Eric, you haven't been thinking about a word I've said!"

"No," Eric said.

"Well, what have you been thinking, then?"

"I have been thinking, if you really want to know, that I love your lovely mouth and your round arms."

Farther down the hill was a hollow; tall grass and a curtain of heavy shrubbery made a small green cave, entirely hidden. Besides, it was almost dark.

"Come," he said.

She rose and followed. The soft green curtain swayed shut behind them as they passed through.

HE HAD CHOSEN to work in the barns. He learned to operate the milking machines; he cleaned stalls and hauled feed twice a day. This labor too reminded him of Brewerstown and of his people's past. Other than that there was little in this motley world to remind Eric of any other place.

When they were gathered at supper in the dining hall he could observe the people in all their variety. First there were the old ones, who had come here from the cities of Russian Poland and had taught themselves to work the land. Then there were their children, the sabras, blond, husky women and men: earnest people for all that they could dance and jubilate. A determined and tenacious people! Last, there were the visitors, mostly students from everywhere: a Christian girl from Australia who had come out of curiosity and for a summer's adventure; boys from Brooklyn, English Jews and German Gentiles, come for a month or two. Few intended to stay, as Juliana did.

She worked in the nursery, since in Holland she had been trained as a kindergarten teacher. Every other night she had to sleep in the nursery, which, Eric was shocked to learn, lay underground. Actually it was a bomb shelter behind a pretty blue door. He was very moved. The world had no knowledge of how these people had to live! He wondered whether even his grandparents, who cared so much, knew what it was really like. "One fears for these children living under the guns," Juliana said. "Of course, it doesn't bother the little ones. But the older ones know. They understand very well."

Many of the fifteen- and sixteen-year-olds had survived the concentration camps and wore, would always wear, the outrageous number stamped upon their arms. The boys wrestled and punched as boys did everywhere. The girls tied ribbons in their hair and practiced flirting, as girls did everywhere. But their eyes were anxious.

Juliana was good for them. She was young enough to know the current popular songs and to teach them how to use a lipstick with skill. She was just enough older to give them some of the mothering they had lost, most of them having lost it when they were still so young that they could barely remember it.

And while Eric watched her with these young people, while he walked beside her under the wind and in the sunlight, he thought: was there ever, could there ever be, another woman like this one? With the other half of his mind he knew that every man who loves a woman thinks the same. Yet there was not and never could be another one like her.

Sweet, so sweet, with her hair bleaching and her skin turning to café au lait under this searing sun! She was healthy and sturdy, and almost as tall as he; she seemed never to be tired. He didn't admire "delicate" women, nor ruffled fragility. It pleased him now to think that with a woman like Juliana a man could go anywhere in the world; nothing would be too daring or too new for her.

He hadn't followed her all this way with any thought of marriage. At twenty-one none of his friends was married and he'd had no wish to be, either. He'd had no wish to be committed to any place or any person with certitude enough to say: next year at such and such a time, in such and such a place I shall be doing this or that. Not at all. (And that, he had sometimes thought, was odd of him, because so often, talking philosophically with a friend, he'd heard himself saying that what he needed most was something that lasted.) But permanence had been for his future. He had simply wanted to follow Juliana because, of all the women he had known, she was the most enchanting.

Yet, as the summer wore on, he began to feel a sense of looming loss.

Two weddings were celebrated on the kibbutz within one day. Eric had naturally seen more than a few weddings in his time, but never so much emotion: so many tears and embraces, so much reckless dancing, so much wine. For a while he played his customary role as a wedding guest, observing with curiosity and feeling a human sympathy with their pleasure, but no kinship. And then all at once, standing among the crowd that waved the brides and grooms down the road on the way to their short seaside honeymoons—he could not have said what had been happening inside his head—but all at once the whole business seemed very, very lovely and quite inevitable. He began, in private, to think about it, and was surprised to find himself doing so. Also, he was a trifle pleased and proud. Then he began to edge toward the subject, to walk around the farthest reaches of it, testing the ground, not quite ready yet to walk straight through.

"Tell me," he asked Juliana one day, "do you plan to stay here very long?"

They were sitting on the ground, near the pool. Everyone else was in the water, but he had held her back, wanting to talk.

"Well, it does seem like home to me."

"Yes, but," Eric pressed, "do you plan to stay always?"

"That's a word I don't use. I've told you, I don't like to think that far ahead."

"I do. I want to find a place and people that are going to be right for me forever. There has to be something in the world that's forever."

"Like what?"

"Well," he said, "a house, for one thing, that you won't have to leave. Where you can plant trees and stay to see them grow old."

"Tell me what else you dream of," Juliana ordered, gently outlining his nose and cheeks with a long blade of grass.

"I dream—" he hesitated. "I dream of writing a book, one that might be remembered after I'm dead. A really great book. And I'd like to write it in a room in a house like the one I grew up in." He wanted to add, and was perhaps about to add, "And with you in the house with me," but she interrupted.

"I hope you do! Oh, I hope you get everything you ever want as long as you live!"

People usually say such things out of perfunctory kindness. So the anxious urgency in her voice startled Eric. "Do you?" he asked.

And she answered, "Yes. Because I love you, Eric. So of course I do."

Certainly this was not the first time either of them had told that to the other, but now he went further, wanting and also fearing to know. "Has there—was there ever anyone—"

Juliana looked away, beyond the noise and busy motion at the pool. "There was one, just one, but that was a long time ago and different from this."

He wasn't satisfied. "What happened?"

She looked back at him, blinking as if she were recalling herself from a distant place. "He wanted—he bothered me too much about getting married. So we quarreled and ended it. It was just as well."

Even that did not satisfy him. "And that's all?"

"All that's worth talking about."

"But tell me," he persisted, "what would have been so terrible about getting married?" And added, trying for a light touch, "I thought that's what little girls aim for, from the cradle on."

"Yes," she said, "they do. And such a pity. Poor women! Don't you feel sorry for women?"

"No," Eric said honestly. "Or rather, I never thought about it."

"Well, think about it, then! The miserable marriages they make because they're afraid of waiting too long and being passed over! And the miserable marriages they stay in. And the miserable children—"

"How bleak you sound! As if there were no happy marriages. That's not even sensible!"

She threw her hands up. "It's sensible for me, and that's all that counts. I like my life the way it is."

His heart sank. A year or two from now would she be telling some other man about him: "Yes, there was a young American, but he bothered me about marriage and so we—"

"What about children?" he asked lamely. "You're so wonderful with them. Surely you want children?"

"Right now it's wonderful enough to take care of other people's children."

"But you can't go on doing that," he argued. "That's only a substitute for the real thing."

Juliana jumped up. "I'm boiling in this heat! Let's swim!"

"Go ahead. I'll come in a minute."

What was it? Why? She was so free in loving when they lay in their "green cave," so free with her thoughts, whether glad or sober, as long as they didn't touch on any personal future. She baffled him. It would have been easy to understand and cope with, if there had been another man. Once he had had a girl he liked tremendously; then she had started to become involved with someone else, and Eric had come straight out before the two of them, demanding, "Who is it to be? He or I?" Funny thing! He smiled, remembering. She had chosen Eric, and then after that he hadn't especially wanted her.

But that had been different. That girl hadn't been Juliana. And the rival now wasn't another man. What was it, then?

At summer's end the young foreigners left to go back to the universities and back to jobs. Only a few would return; this had been an adventure, but next year they would try a different place, Nepal, perhaps, or Sweden.

"Aren't you supposed to go back to the States?" Juliana inquired of Eric.

"I can take a while longer. I was promised a trip before I go to work, so this can be it," he said.

Besides, he thought, the timing of all these departures was unfortunate. Everything was at the harvest, and just when more hands were needed for a few hectic weeks of twelve-hour days, suddenly there were fewer. If he were going to leave, this surely wouldn't be the right time to do it.

The truth was, he knew he couldn't leave her. Not yet.

When the harvest was finally in, holidays were taken. Eric had not seen Jerusalem. It occurred to him, since Juliana had told him how marvelous the city was, that she might like to go there with him for two or three days. So he arranged for a ride with some other people and told her, when they met at noon, what he had done.

She was indignant. "Now what gave you the right to plan my time for me?"

He thought at first that she was joking, but when he saw that she was not, he was astounded. "I should think you would thank me for having got us a lift, and saved you the trouble of scrounging for one."

"What made you so sure I wanted to go with you?"

"Have you by any chance gone out of your mind?" he demanded.

"No. I just don't like being taken for granted by a man!"

"Well, you needn't worry about that anymore," he said furiously. "I shan't take you for granted again. I shan't take you at all!" And he strode away.

He was sore with his anger all that afternoon. Women! "Sorry for women," she had said. Capricious, moody, childish, ungrateful, stupid— He ran out of words.

Could there perhaps be someone else? Anything was possible, yet he couldn't imagine who it might be. They'd been together so much, she hadn't had time even to talk to anyone else! Still, anything was possible.

At supper he sat purposely apart from her. But when it was over and he had to go down to the barns for the evening checkup, she followed him.

"Eric. Eric, I'm sorry." She laid her hand on his arm.

He didn't answer.

"I get that way sometimes. I know it's stupid and wrong. It wasn't decent when you were being so nice."

He melted. "Yes, but—what was it all about?"

"I just get a queer feeling sometimes about being owned. Independence is very precious to me. I get scared. I can't explain it."

"Well, all right then," he said awkwardly, far from understanding.

"And you're not going to stay angry with me? Please?"

"Well, all right," he repeated. "You want to go on Sunday?"

"I want to. Very much."

The minibus was filled. Half the passengers were children and young teenagers. Their singing was shrill and deafening and gay. The road cut through brown fields already being plowed for winter sowing. It passed through new cement-block towns, bare, ugly and clean.

"It's all they can afford," Juliana explained when Eric made comment. "They've neither time nor money. Beauty can come later."

For beauty had been in the past, and in Jerusalem was there still. The car stopped at the crest of a hill. Below lay the pale amber city, spreading to farther hills and up their sides.

"It isn't gold," Eric remarked wonderingly, "as in the song. It's amber. Yes, that's it."

"There's an old tradition," the driver said. "One is supposed to walk into Jerusalem. Who wants to get out here?"

A few of the boys and girls got out. Juliana jumped out with them.

"I was hoping you would," Eric said.

For three days they celebrated. He followed where he was led. They needed no guidebook, for Juliana knew the city well.

"It's a great pity we can't see more," she told him. "East Jerusalem is all Arab; they don't allow us to go in. And the old Jewish quarter that had been here for two thousand years was wrecked and captured when the Arabs attacked in 1948."

Still there was more than eyes or feet could cover in three days. Museums and archeological digs. Crowded alleys of the Old City, foul to smell and vivid to look at. Arab women in black veils and Arab men in *kaffiyehs*. Narrow shops where men hammered brass and cut leather. They followed the Way of the Cross. They heard the *muezzin's* eerie cry in the early morning, and heard it again at noon when they went to a mosque to watch men kneel at prayer, facing toward Mecca.

In rocky fields at the city's edge goats climbed with bells jangling. A man led a string of shabby camels whose great eyes blinked patiently as they waited, tethered in the blinding sunlight. They listened to the melancholy twang of eastern music. At night they danced the hora. They wandered through dark, old shops.

"This is a street of Yemenites," Juliana explained. "Most of them are jewelers, silver crafters."

"I want to buy something for you," Eric said.

"I didn't mean that!" she protested. "I only wanted you to see because it's interesting. They've come here from Yemen—"

"Buy one of these bracelets," he commanded. "No, not that one, it's not nice enough. Pick an important one."

The shop's owner held up a handsome bracelet, its silver filigree as fine as lace.

"That's the one," Eric said firmly. "That is, if the lady likes it."

"Oh, yes," Juliana said, "the lady does!"

When they were outside she asked, "Eric, are you so rich that you can spend money this way?"

He was touched. It hadn't cost anything much at all.

"No," he said, "I'm not, although people here might think I was."

On their last day Juliana told him, "I've saved the best for now. I'm going to take you to a synagogue."

"Oh," he said, amused, "you forget! I've been in them many, many times before."

"Not like this one, you haven't. At least I don't think you have."

At the end of a long alley they stopped. "This looks like medieval Europe!" Eric exclaimed.

"Well, it is. It's been transplanted. One can find everything in this city. Didn't I tell you?"

In the box-shaped synagogue of ancient stone they separated, Juliana climbing two flights of stairs to the women's balcony where hidden women read their prayer books behind the lattices. Squinting through a minute hole she could see the men at their prayer desks below, wrapped in their shawls, and chanting. Eric must be among them but she couldn't see him.

They met again just outside the entrance.

"They all looked so old!" Eric said.

"It's only the beards and the black clothes that make them seem so."

"To think they've been praying this way for three thousand years!"

"Maybe longer."

"My grandfather went to a place like this on the lower East Side before he became 'modern.' " Eric laughed. "You know, I've an idea he would still prefer it. But my grandmother wouldn't."

"Do you realize, these people don't care about politics or wars or anything that's happening beyond their doors?"

"They're waiting for the Messiah, who'll set the world to rights."

Juliana shook her head. "They'll go on praying like this through raids and wars, and heaven forbid, even through defeat."

"That's faith. They believe. I wish I did," Eric said.

She looked at him curiously. "Don't you believe in anything?"

"Do you?" he countered.

"Yes. Freedom and individual dignity."

"Well, if that's all, why, I'll buy that."

"Maybe that's all the belief a person needs. Worth living for and dying for."

"Yes. Only, I don't want to die right now!"

"Nor I, of course not!"

"Ask me what I do want," Eric commanded.

"What do you want?"

"To live where you are. To be near you forever."

"Nothing is forever," Juliana said darkly.

"Do you really think that? I don't like to hear it."

"I know you don't."

"I want to marry you, Juliana. You must know I do."

"Ah, you're very young for your age, Eric!"

He stopped in the middle of the street. "That's a rotten thing to say!"

"Don't be annoyed with me. I only meant—I'm older than you. I'm twenty-four."

"Don't you think I figured that out? And what difference does it make, anyway?"

"None, I guess. But I also meant—you're too trusting. You scarcely know me and still you want to offer me your life on a silver platter."

"It's my life," he muttered. "I can offer it where I like."

"Ah, don't be annoyed!" she repeated. She leaned over to kiss him. "Let's buy some ice cream. My feet are tired and I'm hungry. We can sit in the park over there and eat it."

They sat on a bench in the park, eating ice cream out of the container. Children went chattering home from school, their bookbags slung over their shoulders. Tourist buses passed. In a yard across the street a family was decorating a succah for the Feast of Tabernacles; gourds, squash and wisps of grain were hung from or piled on the rafters. Eric followed Juliana's gaze.

"It's the harvest festival," she explained. "They take their meals outdoors in the little booth."

"A pretty custom. All people have their pretty customs."

"Of course."

Two old men passed, looking in a book together. Their beards and their hands waved in earnest discussion.

"My grandfather would love to see all this," Eric said. "I was thinking, if he had a beard and a broad black hat he'd look just like these old men. You see the same face here, over and over."

"Yes, you do."

"Is anything the matter?" Eric asked. She had laid down the ice cream spoon and was sitting with her hands in her lap.

"No. . . . Yes. . . . I have to tell you something."

He waited, but she didn't begin.

"I don't want to tell you."

He saw her agitation. "Don't, if you don't want to."

"No," she contradicted, "I do want to tell you. That is, I want to tell someone. I've always wanted to tell someone and I never have. And I can't stand it anymore! Do you know what it is to have something burning inside you, something you want to talk about and can't, that you're so sick of, so ashamed of—"

He couldn't imagine what she might have done and he was frightened.

"Do you know what that's like?" she demanded again.

"No. No. I don't."

"Do you remember that I told you about my family, how they helped those poor Jews in the attic, and how my uncles were taken by the Nazis?"

"Yes, you told me about your parents, and—"

She interrupted. "Not about my parents. About my mother." She turned her face away, addressing the air. "My mother and her brothers." She stopped and Eric waited.

A fire engine went clanging by. A police car followed with screeching sirens. For a few moments it was impossible to be heard. Then quiet returned to the little park; deep quiet: crooning pigeons pecking at crumbs, a woman calling once across the street. But Juliana didn't begin again.

He waited and was about to say, "Go on," when he saw that her eyes were pressed tightly shut and her fists were clenched in her lap. He didn't know what he ought to do.

Presently she said, steadying her voice, "My father . . . when the war ended the Dutch authorities came for my father. He had been a counterspy for the Germans. One of the leaders. An important man." She opened her eyes and looked at Eric. "An important man! It was he who had turned in my uncles and the neighbors and our minister and all those others who worked in the underground. Can you believe that? My father!"

Eric drew his breath in.

"I thought my mother would lose her mind."

"Perhaps," Eric said, "it wasn't true? And the charge was false?"

Juliana shook her head slowly. "That's what we hoped. But it was true. He didn't try to deny it. He was proud of it. Proud of it, Eric! He believed in it all, the master race, the thousand-year Reich, all of it!"

Eric reached for her two hands and held them.

"Yes, I thought my mother would lose her mind. To have lived with—and, I suppose, even loved—a monster, who sent her own brothers to their death. To have lived with such a man and not known what he was."

He stroked her hair. He had no words.

"And he was kind to my sisters and me. We always had things, toys, some candy—when the country had nothing. We went out into the country together. He loved us. And he sent those other children to die."

"I'm sorry, I'm sorry," Eric said. It was all he could think of to say.

" 'Tell me,' my mother used to ask me after it happened, 'tell me, can you believe anyone, trust in anyone?' I was fourteen . . ."

"She didn't mean it that way," Eric said gently.

"I suppose not. She's doing well enough now. She has my sisters and me; she works, she lives. But still, if you could live with someone and not know what he really was, why then—" Her voice faded away.

"So that's it," Eric murmured to himself.

"What? What did you say?"

"Nothing important."

It began to grow dark and street lamps came on.

"I'm glad I told you," Juliana said. "I feel better."

"You can tell me anything," he answered, meaning it.

Yet in a way he was sorry she had told him. For he had met the rival now and seen that it was fierce and would be hard to vanquish.

"There's a child who troubles me," Juliana told Eric a few weeks later. "Do you remember, I told you about the bus that was shot at last year? There were a few children who survived but their parents were killed."

"I remember. You showed me the spot."

"Well, this one child—perhaps you know Leo, who follows me around? He's nine now, a little boy with glasses."

Eric nodded. "I shouldn't think he'd be any trouble."

"He's much too quiet. He never bothered anyone, even right after it happened. We had so much hysteria here. We were up all night with some of the children, and it went on for weeks, nightmares and crying. But never with Leo."

"Maybe you're too concerned. Have you talked to anyone about it?"

"Oh, yes! And people just say that he's very mature and very brave. And that's true, but still something bothers me."

"I'll talk to him if you like. I was a camp counselor. Maybe I still know how to talk to kids."

"I hoped you'd say that," Juliana said gratefully.

She brought Leo to him one afternoon while he was feeding the calves.

"You said you needed some help and I thought Leo might be able to help you. He's strong and tall for his age."

Leo said nothing, just stood there, neither scowling nor smiling.

"These calves," Eric explained, when Juliana had gone, "have just been weaned. And I'm trying to get them to drink their milk out of a bucket. But the problem is that they don't understand and they try to knock it over and—whoa, there—see what I mean? Now, if you could hold the bucket while I stick his head in so he can get a taste of the milk, why, we—"

There were five calves. When they had all been fed, Eric said, "That was kind of fun, wasn't it?"

Leo shrugged.

"Would you like to do it again another day?"

"If you need the help, I'll do it. People are supposed to help."

"Never mind that. Do you *want* to?"

"I guess so."

"I'm going down to the pasture to bring the cows in. They're far out today." This time Eric didn't ask whether Leo wanted to go. He simply said, "Come with me."

The boy obeyed. They picked their way down the path. The wind made a thin whistle as it passed and moved on through the grain fields.

"It's beautiful, isn't it?" Eric said. "You're kind of lucky to live in such a beautiful place."

"Yes."

He tried again. All he could come up with was that trite question with which adults plague children: "What do you want to be when you grow up?"

"Whatever the country needs. A soldier, probably."

The priggish answer puzzled Eric. "Leo, I wish you'd tell me what you really think, not what you believe I want to hear."

The boy stopped on the path, opened his mouth as if to speak, then closed it and went on ahead.

Pathetic shoulders! Skinny legs! Baby, boy and man! And out of some remote corner of time and memory another question came.

"Leo—you must think a whole lot about your father and mother, don't you?"

A second time the child stopped. But now he looked at Eric sharply. "You're not supposed to talk to me like that!"

"Why not? What's wrong?"

"Because I heard the doctor say and the nurse say, they have to get our minds off what happened. And that's what I try all the time to do, and now you come and ask me a question like that!"

"Come here," Eric said, "sit down a minute." He perched on a large rock at the edge of the path. "You're supposed to get your mind off it, is that what they say? But you haven't been able to do that, have you?"

"Most of the time I do," Leo persisted. "I'm not a baby, you know."

"I know you're not," Eric said gently. "But I'm not either, am I?"

Leo was puzzled. "What do you mean?"

"I mean that I lost my father and mother the same way you did, or almost the same way. In an automobile. And I still think about them, and I know I always shall."

Leo was silent, watching Eric.

Eric went on, "Yes, and often when I was younger, I cried. I thought how unfair it was that I, of all the boys I knew, had such a thing happen to me. I cried."

"It's not brave to cry," Leo said. A quiver ran over his face.

"I think it is. I think it's quite brave to be honest about the way you feel."

"Do you? Do you ever cry, now that you're old?"

"Look at me," Eric said. His eyes were filled with tears.

The child stood staring at him in wonder. And suddenly he dropped onto Eric's lap, shaking and digging his wet face into Eric's shoulder.

For a long time Eric held him. Pictures, pictures, flashing in his head . . . Gran. Chris. Nana. . . .

Then he thought, They'll be wondering why the cows are so late. But he didn't move.

At last Leo raised his head. "You won't tell anybody?"

"No."

"Not even her?"

"Who? Juliana? No, not even her. I promise."

Leo stood up and wiped his nose and eyes.

"Is there anything else you want to tell me, Leo?"

"Yes."

Eric bent down and Leo whispered, "I'd like a big toy sailboat for the pond."

"I'll make one for you. I'm pretty good at that sort of thing. Now hurry. We're late with the cows."

ARIEH, WHO SLEPT in the bed next to Eric's, remarked, "I notice something about you. You don't talk much lately of home. Of the country house where you grew up, or anything else."

"I guess that's so," Eric admitted.

Arieh was a sabra, born on the kibbutz. He was a country man, with a country man's slight roughness and silences.

"Everybody likes you here," he said abruptly.

"Do they?" Eric felt the flush rising on his neck. These people had few flowery social graces. You had to earn a compliment and even then, he had noticed, you often didn't get it.

"I'm glad," he answered, "because I like people here too."

"Juliana says you've done a wonderful thing with the boy."

"He's a fine child."

"Nobody else knew what to do with him. How did you know?"

"I don't think I really *knew* anything," Eric said slowly. "It was just something that came to me."

Arieh nodded. "That's good enough." He reached for the light. "Mind if I turn it out? It's been a long day."

Lying there in the quiet dark he thought about these simple days of his new life. Nourishing days they were, like mild and good bread eaten under a tree at noon, or perhaps in a kitchen on a winter's night, such frozen country winter as he remembered from his childhood.

He labored and with each week the labor became easier, his body leaner and faster. Sometimes, passing back and forth from fields to barn, he caught a glimpse of Juliana outside with children, or on some errand alone, walking with strong rapid stride, her fine long hair lifting from her shoulders. And then the day would linger interminably while he waited for the night.

"A sound mind in a sound body." He felt that his mind was also very strong, that there was nothing he couldn't cope with. It wasn't that he had made any stupendous decisions about himself; he was putting them off, and he knew he was. But when the time came for decisions he would be able to make them.

Then he scoffed at himself for this euphoria. "Because you're living a 'natural' life," he scoffed, "because you feel healthy, you think you can solve everything." If only she would marry him! But he knew he mustn't ask her again, knew that he would have to wait for the fear that was in her to ebb away, whenever and if ever that might be.

So the warm fall passed. Winter is sharp in Galilee; it came to Eric that shortly there would be no more evenings in their "green cave."

Their need for one another was so strong by now that there was seldom any preliminary talk between them. He would meet her where they had arranged, outside of her door, and walk down the hill, through the orchards.

"Come," he would say. She would spread her shawl on the tall grass and they would lie down in the shrubbery behind the great guns.

One soft night while lying there, they heard the sound of Emmy's piano carried down the hill by the wind. It rose and fell, sang and died. Music, Eric thought, drawing the word out in his mind's ear, how clearly it speaks to us! With a hundred voices it speaks: of hope and courage, of old sorrow and new joy, telling without words of how man loves the earth, of his fear of dying, and of his awe beneath the stars.

Something caught in his throat, a little gasp, and Juliana turned to him.

"When will you marry me?" he asked her, entirely forgetting his resolution.

And to his absolute, incredulous astonishment, she answered, "As soon as you like."

"Oh," he said. "Tomorrow?"

In the faint light from the sky he could see her smile. "Would you wait until my mother can get here? It shouldn't take more than a few days."

He felt, as when pain has abruptly been relieved, or as when the flesh is warmed after searing cold, a deep, deep comfort. For a little while, in complete tranquillity, they slept. When they awoke the moon was up. Hand in hand, as they so often walked, they went quietly back together, up the hill.

A BURST OF fire and thunder tore a hole into the sleeping night. The men were out of their beds and instantly awake, as though they had been expecting Armageddon.

"It's the gas pumps!" Arieh cried. "They've hit the pumps!"

No question who "they" were. . . .

The tanks caught, lifting the earth in clods, raising a tower of fire. A carpet of flame fell over the roof of the cattle barn, then the garages and the stables. By then the men were into their pants and shoes, and with rifles and grenades were halfway down the stairs.

"Where to?" Eric whispered. "Follow you?"

"Yes," cried Allon. "Head down!"

There was a crack and a ping! Then another ping! and a snapping of splintered wood as bullets slammed the walls.

"Out the side door," Allon ordered. "Then around by the back way to the dining hall! Quiet, heads down, on the double!"

Eric understood. From the hall they would command the quadrangle, nerve center of the community. Anyone who tried to cross there would be in their range.

They slid along the rear wall. From the stables came the human shrieking of the horses.

"Can't we—oh, Christ—can't we get them out?" Eric whispered.

"Are you crazy? Quiet!"

With side vision he saw the frame of the cattle barn outlined for an instant only in a square of fire. Then it collapsed: the hay had caught. The cows! Dumb creatures. Their mild eyes.

Guns were cracking and ripping all around them now as they ran. But whose guns, theirs or ours? A man ran out somewhere ahead and was struck down screaming, spinning like a top. There was unearthly howling from every building. Where were they, the attackers? The muffling darkness protected the enemy as well as themselves.

They reached the dining hall and felt for the door, which was opened from the inside, where others had already gathered. Crouching, they crept in single file: Ezra, Arieh, Allon, Eric, all of them.

And will I come through this? And will I know how to fight?

The huddled leaders whispered. The room was quiet. Outside the guns still crackled and snapped. Where? Where were the attackers? Was there no plan to counter them? But there had to be. . . . Eric's lungs burned. They had raced all the way uphill to the hall. His head itched; it was soaked with sweat.

"You," Allon said, "I want one of you at each window. Zack's men are holding the south dormitory, so they can't help here. There are twenty-nine of us altogether, but we don't know how many those devils have. So we've got to send to town for help. They've cut the phone wires. . . . Ezra, can you get to the truck and roll it down hill without making a sound? When you're on the road you can start the motor and then go like hell."

"I'll do it. Where's the dog? Get him out of the kitchen for me."

"He'll make noise!"

"Who, Rufus? I want him with me. He can tear a man's throat out."

Ezra and the dog slipped out through the kitchen door.

Diagonally across the quadrangle lay the nursery, with a cluster of firs beside its blue door. Juliana would be frantic in there, hearing all this without seeing or knowing—

Terror almost took Eric's voice away. "And the children? The nursery?"

"Dan's men are supposed to be there."

"I don't see them." Eric strained into the darkness, lit now to a smoky yellow by the dreadful light of the fires.

"You're not supposed to see them!" Allon spoke impatiently. "But they are there."

So there was a plan. Of course, of course there was. But suppose it hadn't worked? If Dan's men had been trapped or—?

Again there was silence in the hall, except for loud breathing. They waited. Waited.

"Where do you suppose they are?" Eric whispered to the man beside him.

"Who?"

"The Arabs."

"I don't know. How should I know? Everywhere." Avram was frightened, pretending not to be, pretending to be experienced and expert. "They'll try to rush us, thinking we're all holed up in here for defense. We'll mow them down as they come."

There was faint scratching at the door, very faint. Allon, with readied gun, pressed himself against the wall, and opened it a crack. The dog Rufus dragged himself in, whimpered and fell: a pile of bloody, ragged fur, his belly slit open.

"Oh, my God," someone said. "Then Ezra—"

They stood there, staring at each other. Someone called from a window at the front: "The south dormitory's on fire! Oh, Lord, they're jumping from the win—" The voice was cut off with a shattering blow and then a pretty tinkle of glass. Arieh—

Allon crept to him on hands and knees and turned him over. "He's dead," he said flatly, without looking around. "He shouldn't have been standing up."

"How do you know?" Eric cried, without thinking. "Maybe he—"

"The top of his head is shot away," Allon said. "Come and see for yourself."

Eric thought, We played chess last night. Then he thought, I'm going to vomit. But I can't be sick now.

"Listen," Allon said, "we have got to get to town. I'll go, and I need three, no, four with me. Who'll come?"

"But if they got Ezra they must be guarding the road," someone objected. "So how can you possibly—"

"Down through the orchard, and around to the road half a mile past the gates."

"It won't work, Allon! It's committing suicide! The orchard's where they must have got through in the first place!"

"Is there any other way?" Allon asked. Crouched there on his knees, wet with the blood of Arieh, he had immense authority. "Well, then, we'll have to chance it. Who goes?"

"I will," Eric said.

"No, you don't know the way well enough. Ben, Shimon, Zvi, Max, we'll go. If any one of us is hit the rest won't stop for him. One of us has to get through. Marc, you take charge here while I'm gone."

As if in reply another window was smashed out at the front; glass sprayed the floor, falling on Arieh, at whom none of them dared look.

Again they waited. Marc stood in the corner, flat against the wall, from which at an angle he could see through the farthermost window.

"They're crossing the quadrangle," he whispered suddenly.

"Who are?"

"I—it's too dark. For God's sake lower that gun!" he cried to Yigel. "They may be ours!"

They waited. Somewhere, in a history of the First World War, Eric recalled having read that the soldiers' chief complaint was the interminable waiting. With dry mouth. Wet hands. Needing to pee.

He crawled to the window and peered an inch or two above the sill at the side. Yes, there were men walking through shadow, crossing the quadrangle. They were heading toward the nursery door. Some of ours? Dan's men? Reinforcements? But then why so openly and upright? They can't be ours— His heart lurched. They must be—

At the nursery door the men stopped. There were—he counted—five of them. No, seven? It was too dim to see. They were just standing there. Why? Who?

A bullet slammed into the room, then another and another, a fusillade. Marc screamed, shot in the thigh. David fell; dead or wounded? There was no time to find out.

"They're on the roof!" Avram cried. "They've got up on the roof of the extension."

The devils! The fiends! Now they could shoot in through the windows while no one could shoot back upwards into darkness.

There were only three whole ones left: Avram, Yigel and Eric. They crawled to the back of the room, dragging Marc with them out of reach of the bullets which were coming in now like rain.

Suddenly the rain stopped. Into total silence a voice rang, speaking in accented Hebrew.

"You in there! We have a proposition to make! Can you hear?"

Avram, Yigel and Eric stood gripping each other's arms.

"Listen, we know you're there! Will Allon the boss speak up? Answer! You don't have to show yourself!"

"How do they know Allon?" Eric whispered.

"Arabs in town. Contacts across the border. Who can say?"

"Allon the boss! You'd better listen! Or we'll burn out the rest of the place. If you give us what we want we'll leave you in peace."

Avram whispered, "Shall we answer?"

"No," Yigel said fiercely.

"Yes," Eric argued, "if we can kill time talking back and forth maybe Allon will have got through to town and we'll have help."

"What do you want?" Avram called then.

"Are you the boss Allon?"

"I am. What do you want?"

"Six children. Any six. We take them back with us and hold them until your government gives back our six freedom-fighters who are in your jails."

"The freedom-fighters are the ones who attacked the schoolhouse two years ago," Yigel said to Eric. And to Avram, "Tell them to go to hell."

"You know we aren't going to do that!" Avram called back.

"You might as well! Otherwise we can kill all the children, and the rest of you, too. Look, our men are already waiting at the nursery door."

"You won't get away with that!" Avram shouted. "There are over a hundred of us on this place . . ."

"Maybe there were. But there aren't anymore."

Silence.

"When we get in that nursery there won't be one of them left alive. Allon boss! You'd do better to let us have six now. Any six."

The little ones' beds were painted with ducks and rabbits. Clowns and baby elephants danced on the walls. And Juliana slept there. My girl.

Somebody rattled the lock at the back door of the kitchen.

They jumped.

"Be careful. Don't open it."

"Who's there?" Yigel cried, pointing his revolver.

There was a loud whisper. "It's me! Shimon! Open up!"

Yigel opened the door enough to admit a young Arab, with his hands in the air and a rifle, held by Shimon, in the small of his back.

"We got this guy coming up the hill with a knife in his hand." Shimon handed the knife to Avram. "Zvi and Allon are dead. Max and Ben kept going. Maybe they'll get through to town."

"If we knew how many there were," Eric said, "maybe we could—"

"Could what?" Avram demanded scornfully.

"Ask him how many there are anyway," Eric said.

Yigel said something in Arabic and translated. "He says he doesn't know."

"Give me the knife," Eric said, and took it from Avram. He held it against the Arab's naked throat. The man pulled back in horror, gurgling, his eyes wild. "Yigel, tell him that if he doesn't answer I'll cut the way he cut the dog—and probably Ezra, too. Tell him."

Yigel spoke. The man mumbled, and Yigel translated, "He says 'four.' "

"There are at least six or seven in front of the nursery alone, and more on the roof. Tell him we want the truth," Eric commanded.

"He says five. He had forgotten to count himself."

Eric slashed the knife lightly over the Arab's shoulder. The man screamed and Eric withdrew the bloodied knife. "Answer me," he cried, "or the next time it will be your throat!"

The Arab trembled, cried out, and Yigel translated once more.

"He says there are two on the roof. He doesn't know how many at the nursery door. The rest are dead."

"All right. Tie him up," Eric said. It surprised him that Avram and Yigel obeyed without argument.

"Allon boss! What are you waiting for? Until we set fire to the nursery?"

"You won't get away with it!" Avram called back.

Christ, where were they, Max and Ben? And if they had by some miracle got through, how long would it take to reach here from town with help?

Eric crawled to the front window. A torch had been lit at the nursery door, no doubt to fire the place. In its tossing light he could count them: five, no, seven, poised at the door and waiting. He could hear their screaming laughter. The ruffians, the savages. And those piteous women on the other side of the door. Juliana— It came to him that he had never known such anger, such outrage.

He stood up yelling, not recognizing his own voice, not knowing that he was yelling. "I'm going to get them! I'm going to get them!"

"Get down!" Yigel cried. "Eric, fool, get down!"

"The dirty, rotten, murdering scum!" Eric screamed.

Yigel pulled him down. "Shut up! You can't do a thing! There are seven of them."

"I have one grenade—"

"But it's too far! They'd shoot you from the roof, those others up there! You'd never get near enough to throw it, don't waste your life—"

Spots of red and yellow rage flickered before Eric's eyes. The terrors of the world flashed through his mind as, it is said, in the instant before drowning a life flashes past. They knotted in his chest, all that were anguished, cruel and wrong: lost children, violence, corruption and early death. All of them, all of them—

His shirt ripped down the back, leaving a piece of khaki cloth in Yigel's hand as he tore out the door and down the steps with the grenade.

The survivors told it this way: He sprinted across the open space toward the nursery like a football player running for a goal. He dodged and darted while bullets slashed the earth around his feet. About five yards away from the gang at the nursery door a bullet tore into his back and he fell dead, but not before he had thrown the grenade into the middle of the gang and killed them all.

It was over. The two snipers fled in terror from the roof and were captured in the orchard. By the time help arrived from town the fires were out and everything was quiet, except for the crying of the women, preparing the dead.

On the other side of the world, in America, a cablegram brought the news. It was a week now since it had come, and Joseph had aged ten years. He sat at breakfast, his first full meal in days. He finished his coffee and pushed away from the table, but didn't get up, just sat there with his mouth hanging open. Like an old man. Anna hadn't looked in the mirror at herself. God knew what she must look like! And what difference did it make?

And then (as though they hadn't had enough), Celeste came in with the mail, bringing, among the piles of bills, advertisements and letters of condolence, a letter in Eric's handwriting. It had been mailed ten days before.

Anna's hand shook, but she spoke steadily. "I have to tell you, Joseph. There's a letter from Eric."

"Read it," he answered in a flat voice.

She swallowed and obeyed. "Dear Grandpa and Nana, I have just come in from planting oats. From where I sit the dark, wet fields stretch away to the horizon; it is so beautiful." He had sat at a desk, his hand had rested on this paper only a few days ago. No, not a desk, more likely a rough, unpainted table. There were fine wrinkles around his eyes; he strained them; he would need glasses early. His eyes were so light and brilliant when his face was tanned; he would have got quite brown, working in the fields. "I don't want to seem affected or some sort of oddball, and I hope no one thinks I am, but if they do I can't help it. It's as if something were behind me, pressing me on to do something, really do something for a good cause. I hope you can truly understand."

Joseph groaned and she stopped. "Go on," he said.

"I can really feel I belong in this place. For the first time since I've been old enough to think abut such things," (since he came to live with us, he means) "I feel no conflict about who I am. I'm just another pair of willing, needed hands. . . . I know you hoped so much that I would carry on your work and your name. Thousands of young men would be so grateful for a chance like that, and I *am* grateful, really I am. But it's just not for me. Since I've come here, I've been sure it isn't."

"He wasn't ever going to come back," Joseph said wonderingly. "Not ever going to come back."

Anna looked at him sharply, but he was sitting quite still.

She resumed, "You two, of all people, will understand that there's something different about this country. It's not charming or graceful like Europe, not rich and strong like our own country which I love so much. But come visit me here and see for yourself what I mean and what I'm doing.

"Also, I should tell you that I have a girl. I don't know how we will resolve things between us, but I love her. She's Dutch; you'd like her at once. You know how kind the Dutch were to our people during the war—"

She finished the letter and put it down. Then she opened a thin airmail envelope, addressed in a foreign hand.

"It's from a girl, Juliana. She must be the one he meant."

"Read it."

". . . he had written to you, I think, only a day or two before it happened. But at that time he hadn't known we were going to be married. Not that it makes any difference to you now—" Anna stopped and, steadying her voice, went on, "but still you might want to know what he was doing up to the end. He was very brave, which others have told you or certainly will tell you. But more importantly, he was happy. I wanted you to know that. Also that he spoke of you often and loved you so much.

"My first thought was of running home to my mother, to my people. Then I thought no, not while this evil flourishes. But I'm going to leave here to pioneer in the Negev. I'm going to the desert, to a harder place."

There were a few more lines and good wishes.

"Poor girl," Anna said.

"Yes—poor girl."

So they sat unmoving. The morning paper and the coffee cups lay on the table between them, as on any ordinary day. Then Joseph put his head down on the table.

God, God, where are you? Anna cried silently. Why do You torment this good man? To say nothing of all the rest of humanity! The world aches and crumbles; people are eaten by cancer, they scream in madhouses, machine guns are turned on children, the landlord takes half a month's earnings for the right to live in his hovel. Tell me, why do You in Your wisdom permit all this?

And why do I still believe in You in spite of it? Theo says because I need a father image. I don't know, I don't think so. I can't think at all. I don't know why I still trust You. Yet I do. I have to, or I couldn't live.

But I ask You all the same, when will You stop torturing us?

The telephone rang and she rose to answer it. She spoke a minute and came back to the table.

"That was Theo," she said quietly. "Iris has just had the baby. A boy. They're both well."

BOOK FIVE

"ALL THE RIVERS RUN INTO THE SEA..."

ECCLESIASTES

❈{42}❈

They told him it was a slight attack, a mild coronary. "You're better off, in a way, than a man who hasn't had a warning and goes right on doing the wrong things. Why, you'll last for years," they assured him, "as long as you exercise and eat right." But he always had done both of those things. "And don't worry," they said. Hah!

His mind wandered. Came from having nothing to do. He'd gone through the *Times* twice today and now had climbed upstairs to his round room and spread plans on the table. They were assembling the land for a shopping center in Florida. It ought to be a bonanza with all the building going on, the condominiums and retirement colonies. Now his mind sharpened, narrowed to specifics. As soon as they'd let him out of the house, by the first of the month, they said, he'd have to round up some of the chain stores. They'd want a five-and-ten, certainly; a drugstore; one of those popular shoe outfits and then a few assorted boutiques. They'd need some spectacular landscaping, an alley of royal palms down the middle, perhaps. They could call it Palm Walk.

He moved restlessly around the room. Anna had been right—it was a wonderful little place for him. He liked looking down at tree tops. He liked hearing the sounds of the household two floors below; he could hear just enough to feel he was at home, and still not be disturbed.

He felt well again, and looked well too, even had a lot of hair left without any gray in it. Anna had to dye hers: he insisted. Her face was still so firm; why should her hair be old? It was dyed the burnished russet it had been naturally. She looked fifteen years younger. She was still strong, walked gracefully. You could tell a lot by the way a person walked. As for himself, he couldn't believe he was seventy-three, that it was seven years since Eric died— But better not to think of that, or of a lot of other things. Now was now. True, he had a load on his mind, a huge business with a couple of hundred men and their families dependent on him, but he could cope with it. He wanted to cope; that's how you knew you were alive. When you had one problem after the other, you solved one and moved on to the next.

Malone, now, he'd got very old. His lips trembled and his eyes watered. He won't last as long as I will, Joseph thought. Malone had been ready to retire, hadn't been up to the pressure, and fortunately had had enough sense to know it. He was better off out in Arizona. Besides, Malone had sons.

We should have had more children, he protested for the thousandth time. Iris' young boys were the only future: their own future, not their grandfather's. As it should be. But it would be good, all the same, to have one of them take over, one of them who'd care for the work and the name he had made! Land. He'd been right about its being the basis of all wealth. If you managed it correctly. But Jimmy's going to be a doctor, like his father; you can tell already. He chuckled: last week Iris found a mouse cadaver under his bed. They all say Jimmy's the apple of my eye; well, Philip's the other apple, then. Philip, my joy, my darling. Coming downstairs in his pajamas to hear Theo's quartet, and we thought he'd come for the cake! They laugh at me, but I still say, who can tell? Rubinstein and Horowitz were young once. I think he plays like an angel. We never had anyone like him before in our family. Except that niece of Anna's, that poor girl Liesel. Maybe the music comes through her, some strain way back. Not from my side, goodness knows. So Philip won't want my business either, that's for sure.

And Steve: hah! Set a bomb under it more likely, with all that socialism of his, or anarchism, whatever you want to call it! No, that's not fair. He's only a boy, not sixteen yet, and the times are radical. It's a fad. He's got a long way to go. Still, very troubling.

Thank goodness, Laura's okay. Anna all over again, with that look on her face as if the world had been made brand-new every morning!

They'll all go their ways without me. Everything will go on. These trees will get taller. People will come and go to school and the office and the supermarket; I won't be here. Kid yourself, if you want, about your energy and your ambition and not looking your age; kid yourself and let other people kid you too—as if a man can't tell when they're soft-soaping him! But the drift is there. Drifting, that's the feeling.

You just don't seem to need much anymore. Sex—forget about that! And food. You don't enjoy it, at least not the way you once did. Even sleep: how sweet it is to sleep all night through! You don't realize it until you start waking up every morning before dawn. It's still dark outside and you lie there with your eyes open, watching the light come through the blinds and hearing winter wind or else birds' first calling, like questions in the darkness, minutes apart. It's the loneliest time. Anna's still asleep. Her shoulder is fragrant; she puts perfume on before she goes to bed. We're separate after all; every human being—separate and alone. You never know that, or maybe don't admit it, until the time comes near to die.

Anna says: "Why don't you take it a little easier? You could leave more to the Malone boys. Just keep a hand in one or two days a week to see how things are going."

No. What would I do here all day? Sit around and listen to my arteries harden? Work is—it's cheerful. When I'm away for more than a couple of days I have a kind of creeping melancholy and it scares me. That's why I never liked to take trips. It's the one way I disappointed Anna, because she'd have gone hiking all over the globe and up every mountain if I'd been willing. Work and the company, Friedman-Malone; they're my *life!* Anna knows that.

He moved to the television set and switched it on. The voice came first, then a picture flaring gradually into the great blank eye of the screen. It was a replay of the Kennedy funeral the previous week: the dirge, the celebrities walking across the bridge toward Arlington and the horse with the stirrups on backwards. The horse.

Eighteen years since that other president had died. . . . He remembered the stores on Madison Avenue displaying the black-bordered portrait. Eighteen years! And this was worse: the young man with his head shot away. He turned the television off.

Death and violence. Violence and death. When your heart gives out it can't be helped, but deaths like this one! Kennedy's and Maury's, the smashed-up, bloody deaths. And Benjie Baumgarten's drowned face. What had made him think of that now? Then Eric. All unnecessary.

Oh, Maury, oh, my son, if I could have you back again I wouldn't care what you did. If I'd made it easier for you and that young girl, taken the pressure off, then maybe— Almost twenty-five years ago. And your son. I tried to make up to you through him, as if perhaps you could know I was loving and being good to your boy. But he didn't want it, not what I had to give. He didn't know what he wanted, Maury. He didn't know where he wanted to belong. Maybe in a world where everybody was the same. (Hah! When was there ever, when will there ever, be a world like that?) When he was with one kind he felt guilty about turning his back on the other. He never told us, but we knew. Your mother was the one; she figured it out, and she was right. He felt more guilty about turning his back on our side because we're the sufferers, the weak ones. Yet he was tempted toward the sunny side, the Gentile way. Who can blame him? And then he felt guilty all over again. He had no roots. That's one of the overdone words of our day but I don't know another that fits as well.

Still, Eric wasn't the only person in his position. Perhaps he made too much of it? Should just have put it in the back of his head and *lived*? But he was sensitive; he *minded* more, about everything. It seems we're a family like that, too soft, thinking too much about ourselves and everyone around us. (Not me; I'm tough, I'm the only one not like that.)

Even my father and mother. They had nothing, they knew nothing. But my mother wanted me to be a doctor. We stood on the tenement roof. I carried the basket of clothes up for her to hang. Her eyes came straight out of history, deep eyes of Rachel and Sarah. She was younger than I am now, and she seemed so old. Their hard, hard lives. Sleeping in the dark cubby back of the store. Worried about what they'd have to put on the table: water in the child's milk again? Oh, God, to live like that!

And yet, how simple! Only one worry: money. They wouldn't believe it, if they could come back to see what people worry about now. Iris and all that child psychology, sibling rivalries, permissive schools, progressive camps. What poppy-cock, nothing to worry about at all.

A good thing she's gone back to teaching. I didn't think so at first, don't believe a woman should work if she doesn't have to. Seemed to me it might look as if Theo couldn't support his family. But it's really worked out all right. Iris looks as if she's doing what she wants to do. She acts more—important. Even wants to go on for a master's in special education. Guess she got restless with the usual suburban business, P.T.A., scouts, dentist, dancing classes. Always was a bright girl, Iris.

"You want me, Celeste?"

"I've brought these." Another pot of chrysanthemums. "Here's the card."

"Where're we going to put them all? There's no room for them here." Besides, the damned room looked like a funeral parlor with the flowers and potted plants, and those piles of get-well cards to be acknowledged! He'd gotten so much stuff, books and brandy and letters, even a letter from Ruth. Well over eighty now, she was. Her crabbed hand, the letters sliding downward off the page: "Dear Old Friend, We all love you."

She loves me. But I didn't help Solly. I let him die. . . .

Celeste was waiting. "I'll take it downstairs and let Mrs. Friedman put it someplace. You're feeling all right, Mr. Friedman?"

Always looked so scared, Celeste did, opening the door by inches as if she expected to find him lying dead on the floor. . . . Made you cranky, a scared face like that. And then ashamed of himself, he said heartily, "I ought to be sick more often, I get so much attention!"

"Oh, don't do that. We'll take good care of you without your being sick."

"I know you will, Celeste, I know you will."

"Would you like a cup of tea or anything?"

"Thanks, I'll take my tea when my wife comes home."

"She'll be back soon. Want the door closed?"

"You can leave it open, thanks."

Good to hear the sounds of the house, Celeste talking to the day worker downstairs. Good woman, Celeste. Member of the family. Steve ought to talk to *her,* ask *her* what she thinks! She'd tell him she had it pretty good! Beautiful room. TV set to herself. Paid vacation. The best food, all she wanted to eat. Steve ought.

Anna should be here soon. He'd made her go to the luncheon of the Hospital Guild. She hadn't wanted to leave him but she hadn't been out of the house in weeks now, since his attack. Do her good. Looked fine when she left. She dressed well, Anna did, and it wasn't just the expense; you had to know what you were doing. Some of the richest men's wives looked awful. "Clothes, where are you going with the woman?" That's the way they looked, with their hair puffed out like watermelons and all the dangling bracelets. Gaudy and vulgar, they were. Anna's taste had taught him that.

She had taught him many, many things. Everything good in his life had come from her, all charm and fragrance, all gentleness and joy. Maury and Eric had come from her. And Iris—

He frowned, winced. That ugly, insane flash of thought again! He was so certain he had wiped it from his mind, but here it was back, like a stain that can't be got rid of.

That Iris may not be mine! My darling, my dear! It—it chokes me. . . . I think of how unforeseen she was: five years between births, and I'd been so troubled then, I hadn't been near Anna very much. Yes, and I think—crazy thought—I've even thought that Iris looked a little like that Werner fellow. Crazy, crazy thought that I've got to drive out! That I will drive out! I ought to be ashamed of myself.

Yet there was something between the two of them, if not that. Some thing. I don't know how far it went, but I know. Before our marriage or after?

When? Perhaps that day when I sent her to borrow the money? If it was, I have only myself to blame. I should never have made her go, never put her in a position where she— Alone in that house. All those dark stairs, dark wood banisters going up and up; a tall mirror at the end of the first flight to the room where the piano stood. Anna showed me once, and I never forgot the first time I had been inside a rich man's house.

Or perhaps a meeting on some dusky winter afternoon? In an ornate hotel, the traffic marching down Fifth Avenue ten floors below. Glasses and bottles twinkling on a table: champagne, for Anna drinks no whiskey. Yes, a table. And a bed.

He closed his eyes, pressing them shut.

As for me, there could have been women. It's so easy, especially when a man can buy things. Girls in the office. A lady lawyer at a closing once: tall, black hair coiled over a white collar. So easy. But there was never much time, I climbed so fast. Not enough time for that sort of thing. And I never really wanted it enough or I would have found the time, wouldn't I? Never really wanted it enough.

Anna.

I didn't think, when I asked her to marry me, that she would consent. There'd been nothing between us, no look, no slightest touch of the flesh to make me think I had any chance at all. Yet I asked and she said yes. In a way I knew that wasn't how it usually happens between a man and a woman. In a way I knew even then that there was *something*.

She was so young. Naïve, not of the world. And still is, to a certain extent, though she would be annoyed to be told so. Never let her guess, never let her suffer because of my darkest thoughts. Understanding. Forbearance. Whatever you want to call it. For I have had so much, that she has given me. And we have had such a life together, she and I.

Anna, my love. My love.

There was the car now. He looked at his watch. She'd come home early, not wanting to leave him so long. He heard the garage door go down, then her steps on the gravel drive. Another car came, and a door slammed. More steps. Whose?

Then Theo's and Anna's voices, coming upstairs, the voices of Jimmy and Steve below them.

"Good afternoon." Theo's mock-professor voice. "How is the patient today?" And in his normal voice, "We drew up to the stop light at the same time and the boys and I got the idea of coming along to see you."

"You're always a sight for sore eyes, you people. How's everything, Theo?"

His long-established greeting. It meant: How are you doing at the office? Busy enough but not overworked, I hope. Paying your bills with something left over after taxes. It meant: Is everything smooth at home? No troubles with the kids?

Theo's long-established answers reassured him. Yes, yes, everything was fine and there was nice news: Jimmy had made the tennis team.

"Well, congratulations!" Joseph said. "And you, Steve? You upset about something?" For Steve was frowning, with what Anna called his "buttoned-up" expression.

"No."

"Go ahead," Theo said. "You can tell Grandpa." And, since Steve stayed silent, he went on, "Steve was at my office just now to do some papers on the copying machine. And he happened to overhear a conversation with a patient, a girl who's going to have surgery because she doesn't like the shape of her nose. Steve's disgusted, not just with her, but with me! He thinks I should have booted the girl down the stairs along with her nose."

Steve spoke up. "I said, with all the wounded and suffering people in the world you should be ashamed to waste your work on a spoiled bourgeoise."

"Suffering is a matter of degree," Theo said. "If her nose makes her miserable, even though that may seem ridiculous to you, it really isn't ridiculous at all."

"I don't go for that argument. The fact is, you treat people like her because you make money doing it and that's the only reason. The profit system again."

"What's wrong with the profit system?" Joseph demanded.

"What's wrong? The profit system is wrecking the environment and destroying the human spirit. That's all."

The stance of the boy, his slight figure leaning against the wall, the proud lift of his head, angered his grandfather.

"Destroying the environment! What the devil do they teach these kids in school, anyway?"

"School!" Steve was scornful. "I do my own thinking! School doesn't teach anything, except cramming for high marks."

Joseph threw up his hands. "Bah! Socialist poppycock! It all comes down to one thing, this sort of talk. Envy. All this leveling business, pass-fail grades and that stuff; it's the people who get Cs and Ds who want it. They may give you all sorts of high-flown moral reasons, but the plain fact is they envy the people who get As."

"That doesn't apply to me," Steve said stiffly and accurately, for he had always been an A student. "I'm not envious of anybody or anything. What I am much more is guilty, and you all should be too."

Jimmy swung his tennis racket. "Aw, come on, Steve, lay off, will ya?"

But Joseph had been goaded and wanted to pursue the subject. "Guilty about what?"

"About living the way we do. You ought to be guilty about living in a house like this while millions of human beings live in shanties!"

"It took brains and hard labor to earn this house! Don't you think a man deserves some rewards for his brains and labor?"

"There's a lot of luck involved in making money." Steve spoke quietly now, while Joseph could hear his own angry panting breath. "Luck and a little chicanery here and there, besides."

"Steve! That's going too far!" Theo said furiously.

Joseph raised his hand. "Leave him! Chicanery, is it? I want you to know that your grandfather has never been party to a crooked deal! Do you hear that? Not a thing to be ashamed of. I've built honestly. People need shelter and I build it for them. Most of them never lived so well before. And I'm supposed to be a louse because I make some money doing it?"

"Joseph! You're getting too excited!" Anna cried. "You're not supposed— Boys, why don't you go outside for a while and practice serves against the garage wall?"

"Or start walking home," Theo said. "I'll catch up with you on the way." And when they had gone downstairs, "I'm sorry. Steve is tough to cope with. We have this all the time."

"He's angry inside," Anna said. "Maybe because Jimmy is taller?" she questioned thoughtfully. "That can be very hard, having your younger brother grow taller than you. And now he's breaking out with acne besides."

"My wife, with the excuses," Joseph grumbled. "With the psychology."

"Never mind," Anna said. "There are things going on inside of a child that we can't guess at. Iris said the guide told her Steve's IQ is a good bit higher than Jimmy's, and still Jimmy does just as well, and he seems so much more interested in things, his stamps and animals and tennis and—"

"Jimmy!" Joseph interrupted. "Jimmy's always been easy on the nerves. His own and everybody else's."

"Jimmy has always had an accepting attitude," Theo said. "He enjoys life. No credit to him, he's very, very lucky to have been made that way. He just seems to look at things clearly and calmly. A couple of nights ago he asked: 'If you and Mother should die what would happen to this house?' I was taken aback for a second and then I realized it was a perfectly reasonable question. But Steve flew into a rage with Jimmy. He had furious tears in his eyes. I'm sure it wasn't because of thinking that Jimmy might have hurt our feelings. Goodness knows, Steve never takes much heed of other people's feelings! It must have been because he's terrified of death, poor guy, of our deaths and being left alone." Theo sighed and no one spoke for a moment. Then he stood up. "Ah, well, they don't know when they're well off, do they? I suppose we didn't either, at that age. But it will all pass. I just hope Steve doesn't get involved in anything too deeply before it does. He's been talking about going south this summer on one of those marches."

Joseph intercepted Anna's distress signal. "Anna, stop protecting me. I'm not dead or dying yet."

"Of course you aren't! It's just that you get too upset. You always do!"

"Mama's right," Theo apologized. "I shouldn't have brought the subject up. Don't worry, I'll handle things."

"I know you will, Theo. But it isn't easy. What we do for our children! We spend our life's blood—"

"There was a very fine speaker at the luncheon," Anna said. "The subject was hospital costs. You would have been interested, Theo."

Joseph smiled. Transparent! Keep the conversation impersonal. Don't upset the old man. We'll just take up the time until the visit's over.

Anna and Theo forgot how clearly words carried up the stairs, even though, a few minutes later, they spoke so quietly at the front door.

Joseph could hear Theo say, "He's rather low in spirits today, isn't he? To be so upset about Steve— I don't think it can really just be Steve's nonsense."

"No, no, I know him. I should, shouldn't I? He's thinking about Maury and Eric. He gets this way sometimes, even before the attack, he did." Anna's voice lowered. "He can't bear to hear the mention of their names. I always try, when the day comes around that either of their names is called on the roll of the dead at temple, I always try to make some excuse not to go. I say I don't feel well or something."

"And does it work?"

Anna laughed. "Of course not! But I try."

You never know with Anna, what she's hiding, what planning, always to spare me. She thinks I don't know that for a time years back things weren't going well between Iris and Theo. They all covered up, but I knew. I didn't ask because I guess I was afraid to know. Anyway, they wouldn't have told me.

Thank God it's all right now; I can tell that too. He's a good man, Theo is. I like to see him come walking up from the tennis courts with the kids, talking French or German with them. And good to Iris: his voice is gentle when he speaks to her. I hear that. He'd better be.

My dear, my heart. From the day she was born, the homely, tender, appealing little thing. . . . Yet she's done well. She's turned out to be a good-looking woman in her way, not in the popular fashion, but different looking, distinguished. That's the word: distinguished. Iris.

That kid Steve had better not cause her any heartache. I'll tell him so one of these days, too. Chicanery, he said. What a word! Luck! He makes it sound so cheap, like crapshooting or slot machines. Luck! All that labor, getting up before five to reach the building sites in those early years! Scrambling for contacts and financing, sweating out the mortgage payments, that was luck?

He says we don't give value for the money. Granted, we don't give the value they gave in this house that I'm living in. How can we, with the building trades unions getting more and more every year? Squeezing the bosses dry. Still, I know a man wants his family to live decently, wants to give them things. I ought to know! So what's the answer? That I don't know. I'm sorry I don't.

I understand in a way what Steve means, even though he thinks I don't. He's a smart boy, the smartest of the lot. But I can't take to him the way I do to the others, my baby guy Philip or Jimmy. Jimmy has merry eyes. I just thought of that. Maybe because of Steve's stringy long hair? And I like immaculate fingernails, especially when I'm eating. I can't help it, I hate dirt. Damned arrogant kid! And still, you can feel something. So unhappy. Poor Steve. Wish I could get to him. Poor kid.

Anna came back with a tray, two cups of tea and a small plate of biscuits. "You're to have this and then a nap. Doctor's orders, so don't grumble."

"Who the hell needs a nap?"

"You do," she said calmly. "You want to get back to the office, so do what you're told."

She sat down, stirring the tea. Her face was placid, dignified. Firmness in the softness. Remarkable woman! Why do I always think of what my father would have said? Quality, he'd have said. He used to pick up a fine piece of cloth and smooth it between his thumb and finger. "Quality. You can always tell," he'd say.

"What are you thinking?" Anna asked.

"Of you. I didn't make a mistake when I saw you sitting on the stoop at Levinsons'."

"I'm glad."

"Are you, Anna? Sometimes I wonder. I've had too much time to think, this past month. You remember, just before I had the attack, we were at that benefit for the blind? You were talking to that fellow who publishes the art books, and I thought, 'There's the kind of man she ought to have married, the kind of man who speaks her language.'"

"You want to get rid of me?"

"Don't make a joke of it! I'm serious." He reflected: ought he to tell her the rest? Yes, yes, have it all out, all of it. "I know I promised you once never to talk about the subject again, but lately I haven't been able to put it out of my mind. About you and Werner—he was a man who spoke your language, wasn't he?"

Anna sighed deeply. "Oh, Joseph! Not again?"

"I'm sorry. I know you assured me there never was anything, but so many things don't fit: words, gestures, incidents. I needn't go over them again, because you know them and I know them. But they don't quite fit, and my sense, my instinct—"

"Senses and instincts don't prove anything," Anna interrupted. "I gave you rational answers. I can't do more than that. I feel as though I were using a sword against cobwebs when you talk about 'instincts.'"

Even in her quiet denial he heard defiance. If he were not still an invalid she would have been more vehement, he knew, more angry. He mustn't press too hard, mustn't look for trouble. He was lucky, after all, to have had her all these years, he told himself for the thousandth time. A woman like Anna could have had anyone.

"Don't torment yourself, Joseph. Don't ask me these questions. Even if you can't believe me, and I'm sorry you can't, just don't ask me anymore."

So he would never really know, never *really*. To wipe out his doubts, to know that she was totally his and always had been, that there had never, never been anyone else—what he would not give! The remaining years of his life, that's what he would give.

"I would like to be truly at peace," he said aloud.

"Then be at peace. I can't say any more than that." Anna finished her tea and stood up to stroke his forehead. Her hand was warm from the teacup, and he smelled her perfume again.

He didn't move, enjoying the sweep of her hand across his forehead, hoping she wouldn't stop. "It's beautiful here, isn't it?" he said, wanting to detain her.

"Very. It's home."

This quiet house, the view of trees, he thought suddenly, these go always to the people at the top. In Buenos Aires or Peking, no matter what the system, the quiet rooms and view of trees belong always to the people at the top.

"If anybody thinks there can ever be a world where you can get this without effort he's crazy," he said suddenly. "I sweated to get it, Anna, I sweated."

Anna thought, I sweated for it, too. She said, "I know you did. And that's why it's time you stopped, isn't it? Look, here's George come up to see you."

The door, which had been left ajar, was pushed toward the wall and the huge black dog came lumbering in.

"It's chilly for May and he hates the cold."

"He's getting old," Joseph said glumly. This was George the Second, son of the George who had come with Eric to their house. And George the Second had a son, Albert, born just before Eric went away.

"I know. The young one wants to be outside, though. Would you like it if George took a nap with you?"

"Apparently he intends to, whether I like it or not." For George had stretched out on the couch, considerately leaving just enough room for Joseph.

"All right, lie down now. Philip will be here before you know it. And Laura said she might come too."

He lay down obediently and Anna closed the door behind her. Two or three times a week, Philip stopped in on the way home from his music lesson or religious school. What a schedule for such a little fellow, only seven! But that's the way they did it these days. And come to think of it, it hadn't been so different for Maury and Iris, either. We all push our children to excel, we want the best of all worlds for them. Only this child, this Philip, is really something special! I worry about him when they drop him off at the corner. He's got two streets to cross, and so much traffic. Of course there's a light. But he's such a little fellow.

As soon as I'm out and around again I'm going to stop in at F.A.O. Schwarz and I'm going to buy the most lavish, expensive, magnificent toy they have in the place. Anna and Iris won't approve but for once I won't care, I want to buy something for a spoiled rich kid. Something I never could have dreamed of when I was his age. I don't know what, but I'll find something.

He couldn't fall asleep. Too much rest, that was the trouble. Maybe get up and read. Anna had had a book up here the other day. She'd said something about beautiful essays by some important guy, and he'd seen she wanted to talk about it, so he'd asked her to read him a page or two. And it had been rather pretty. For a moment he had seen what she meant.

Too bad he hadn't read anything, all his life. He'd always admired scholars, but you had to be born a scholar, not made. Yet those teachers Iris was always having over at her house, nice people all of them, so genteel and with so much knowledge, poor bastards! They couldn't even afford the ten dollars it took to buy one of the books they loved so much. What sense did that make? Still, it would be a good thing to have had both worlds. There was so little he knew. Living with Anna, he was always aware of it, although she never allowed him to talk that way about himself. That time they'd been in Mexico City and her relatives had taken them to see those tremendous ruins: what a feat of construction! Anna had known all about the builders. Aztecs, were they? She had read about their palaces and priests and what the Spaniards had done to them. Yes, Anna knew so much.

Was that the book she'd been reading the other day? It had had a red cover;

she'd left it on the chair. He got up. Yes, a book of essays. He'd glanced at it after she'd left the room. There had been one on growing old which she would certainly not have let him see, would have hidden from him. But he remembered it, page forty-three. Your memory is still pretty good, what do you think, hey, Joseph? The arteries can't be too hard with a memory like that.

Here it was. "On Growing Old." His eyes scanned the page. ". . . taut strings loosen, knots untie; the fingers open and drop what they have been holding to so tightly. The shoulders lighten, freed of what they have been carrying. Go, let go; where the wind sweeps and the tide takes, let go."

❧ {43} ❧

Anna walked up Fifth Avenue in shafted light, from October gilt to shadow and back again. She was youthfully exhilarated and enjoying it.

A week ago she wouldn't have believed it possible that Joseph would take a vacation! They had just broken ground for a new apartment complex in south Jersey; his little round room was awash with papers and blueprints. But then the Malones had arrived home to visit their newest grandchild and, with their descriptions of the West's great spaces, had at last caught Joseph's fancy. He had agreed to go back with them.

She could have been a wanderer. The Painted Desert, the Petrified Forest, the Navajo reservations—she had wandered through all of them in her mind. This would be a journey to known, desired places. Perhaps Joseph could be persuaded, since they would have come so far anyway, to continue on to the coast?

Eleven o'clock. She was to meet Laura at Lincoln Center at twelve-thirty for lunch and the ballet. Anna had been in the city since nine, too early for Laura; young people liked to sleep late. She had finished her shopping: just walking shoes for herself, and no new clothes, since Mary Malone was not a fashion plate. One didn't feel with her the often tiring need of looking perfect. She'd stopped at the men's department and bought some sport shirts for Joseph. He really needed them, although he would argue that his old ones were good enough. How he still resisted spending on himself! She must remember to take the price tags off these so he wouldn't see and make her return them.

Thank God, he was feeling so well lately. A sudden picture out of nowhere stood in the air before her: he was reading the real estate section of the Sunday *Times*. His hands were really beautiful for a man, long-fingered, the way a pianist's or a surgeon's are supposed to be. This trip might be a start. It would be marvelous to go to Europe again, and then to Israel. Sometimes he spoke of seeing those places Eric once wrote about. True, he spoke only vaguely, yet the thought must be in his head. Her own thoughts ran faster as she strode uptown.

There's another case of gold charms. I got a better buy on them this morning for Laura's birthday, to add to her bracelet. It's hard to know what to get for her. One can't always give books. She's certainly not a child, yet not a woman either. Try to remember what I was like at fourteen. But my life was so different, living at

Uncle Meyer's among strangers. Still, I must have had some of her confusions, in addition to my private ones.

I wonder, I wonder about people. There's so much I don't know. If I'd been born here and had a chance to learn, I'd have liked to study psychology. That couple now, standing on the corner quarreling. She's about to cry. He's actually walking away. What are they doing to each other? And why? Those two old women walking ahead of me; they're at least as old as I am, even older. Withered, painted faces. Legs all knotted with veins. Dressed like young girls. Fancy, pretty shoes. A young girl's innocent dancing slipper. How absurd. How—sad.

Maybe everyone is scared, scared they'll never get what they want or, if they've got it, scared that somebody will come and take it away. (If nobody does, time will.) Yes, we're all afraid of things we don't talk about.

There's a dress in the window, clouds of pink. That would be for Laura a few years from now, and was for me years ago . . . that dress Joseph bought in Paris: was there ever anything as enchanting?

Lovely, lovely day. Growing warmer, the last of Indian summer. Walk westward through the park toward Lincoln Center. Laura's never seen *Swan Lake*. She'll love it. The time I first heard *Tristan*. Soft air now, dust on the trees. Old men playing checkers on the benches. Children roller skating. Not in school? Of course, it's Saturday. I'm forgetful lately. I've been noticing that.

Out at Seventy-second Street on Central Park West. Overshot the mark. Oh well, walk back again. Here's the street. No harm going through. Just to see. The street is filled with dark children. Puerto Ricans playing ball. They played stickball on the lower East Side, the street always loud with cries, I remember. All kinds of cries. Here's the house: is this it? Yes, it is. So small! Tall and narrow, two windows wide. A rooming house now, probably, like all the others. People sitting on the stoop. Last sun of the year. The shades are torn. Water-green velvet hung in the "parlor." Between the windows was a low table where the tea service was laid at four o'clock. And above that, Paul's room with the riding boots, the Yale banner and all his wonderful books.

Am I the person I was then? I don't recognize myself at all. Still, as time moves, it wasn't that long ago that I came uptown from Ruth's house and entered this one.

Blot it out. What sense is there in thinking of what might have been? Or in wondering how Paul is now? No sense, and yet I wonder. I'm still not used to thinking I may never see him again. As if he were dead.

I'm not used to the thought of Ruth's being dead! Didn't know I'd miss her as much. She'd gotten tart and envious. But she was always *there* and you could trust her. "I'll take care of you," she said that first day when I stood with my bundle and shawl, knowing nothing. I trusted her then and I wasn't wrong.

Hers was a twisted road. Sitting there that night when Solly died, and everything else was gone, not Solly only, but everything. It would have been easier if she had never had the apartment where they lived for those few years with carpets and a silk shawl on the baby grand piano. On Washington Heights when we went there last summer after her funeral, the first floor had been turned into stores. She lived above a hand laundry and a bar. Was it as depressing when we lived there? No, it's changed. And certainly I've changed. Everything has.

Dan's dead too, in Mexico. I saw him only twice in fifty-five years. I wish I could have seen him just once more.

We're going down hill.

Laura ate the bacon omelet. Her long red hair, which, Iris reported with amusement, she pressed on an ironing board, fell over the plate. She pushed it back and looked up. "I'm starved," she said.

"It smells good."

"Bacon's delicious. You've truly never tasted it?"

"Never. I remember when I came to this country, the first time I saw bacon cooking I was disgusted."

"Because you'd been taught it wasn't to be eaten. Why don't you try some?"

"Sometimes I think I might. But then your grandfather—"

"You needn't tell him. Does one have to tell a husband everything? Does one?"

"I've always thought one should." God forgive me for the lie.

"Well, then, tell him. Shouldn't a woman be free enough to do something her husband doesn't approve of?"

"I suppose you're morally right."

Laura thought a moment. "But then," she said gently, "but then, it wouldn't be worth it to you, would it? To take a *stand* on something that upset him so—you'd only be sorry afterward, wouldn't you?"

Anna smiled. "You've said it for me, better than I could have."

A perceptive child. An instrument: I play a note and she makes harmony. More of a daughter in that way than Iris ever was, although I know Iris isn't unique. I've heard enough daughters talk, and mothers, too. How would I have been toward my mother, I wonder, if she had lived? I must be careful not to be too giving to Laura, not draw her away from Iris. It's too easy for a grandparent to do that.

"Daddy played all the music from *Swan Lake* last night and we talked about the plot. You know, it's the first ballet he ever saw. His parents took him to see Pavlova dance it in Vienna. We went *thoroughly* over the music and the story. *Thoroughly.* You know how Daddy is." She laughed. "When I was young, about eight, I used to think I would become a ballerina. I really thought all you had to do was want something and you could get it."

"But now you know better."

"Mostly. At least, I believe I do. Maybe I still am childish and don't see myself. Except that sometimes I already feel grown-up."

"I know. This morning, when I saw a pink dress in a window, I forgot I was an old woman."

Laura didn't make the absurd protest that people make: *Oh, you're not old. . . .* She said instead, "It must be awful to be old. Is it really awful?"

"If you think about it too much it can be. I try not to think about how little time is left."

Laura put her chin in her hands. They were waiting for dessert, Anna's coffee and Laura's pie with double ice cream. You never knew when you took the child out to eat whether she was in one of her starving periods or on an eating binge. This week she was on a binge.

"Tell me, Nana," she asked seriously now, "have you been, are you satisfied with your life?"

"Oh, my," Anna said, "oh, my, that's much too grave a question for this nice, bright Saturday! Besides, it's impossible to answer." The questions the girl asks!

"Try."

"I can't. If you mean, am I happy in this life that I have, I should answer, yes, very. I love you all. I have friends and do interesting things, some of them a little useful, I hope. And I have pleasures, like taking my granddaughter to the ballet. But if you ask whether I might have liked another life, Pavlova's, or perhaps to be a Madame Curie— Don't you see that's what I mean, that it's impossible to answer?"

"Sometimes I'm terribly sorry for people," Laura said, with a mouthful of ice cream. "My father, for instance. I'm often sorry for him."

"Why are you?"

"He must think a lot about that other family of his, Liesel and their little boy. But he never talks about them."

Anna was silent.

"I suppose he feels that Mother wouldn't like it."

"Why do you say that?" Anna asked, making a little shrug, as if to say, I'm quite casual about this, not particularly interested.

"I don't know. I just think she wouldn't."

I wonder, wonder what they know or half know, half remember. They were all so young. No harm done, thank heaven! And anyway, who ever said a child must sail in sunny waters every day of his life? Not even natural. Still, one speculates about what's in their heads. Delightful children, all of them. Even the boys, if you can use the word about boys. And why not? Jimmy, of course, Mr. Unflappable . . . and Steve, moody, dark and bright as quicksilver; he's the one I find most appealing. Isn't that strange? Joseph can't understand it. Steve bothers him and I can see why. He bothers me. Yet there's something I want to reach out to, something very, very warm. Philip, the dividend when we hadn't expected any more. And this girl. God keep them all. Incongruous, blessing them here in this place with the clattering of voices and dishes. God keep their soft flesh unharmed and their hearts from grief. No, that's impossible . . . well, God keep them anyway.

"It's time to go in," Laura said. "Everybody's going."

"Yes, yes," Anna said, looking at her watch. They stood up and moved through the slow crowd in the lobby. People looked at them, Anna knew, at the tall redheads, the old one and the young one.

The chandeliers, flashing ice and diamonds, rose toward the ceiling. The great hall darkened. The overture began. When the curtains drew back at last upon Prince Siegfried's forest and the enchanting waltz, Anna heard beneath the music the sigh of Laura's pleasure.

*   *   *

Laura hummed. "It was marvelous, marvelous! Thanks so much! I loved it!"

The taxi stopped in traffic on a seedy street of dance halls, bars and dingy movies. *Girls, Girls,* the poster read. *Miss Dawn La Rue and Miss April La Follette. Fiery Passions, Burning Loves:* that was the movie advertisement. Anna hoped Laura might look the other way but naturally she was staring at the photographs. Not burning love at all, Anna thought, just cold sex, as mechanical as pumping pistons. Not that I'm the last word on that, God knows. But still, there's no feeling in all this, no caring, and it ought to be the most alive thing in the world, oughtn't it? Wonder what makes girls do this? What makes Miss Dawn LaRue do what she does? Or what makes anybody, for that matter? For some utterly unfathomable reason, she had a vision of Miss Mary Thorne, in shirtwaist and skirt, handing to Anna a copy of *Hiawatha.*

The taxi moved away toward Grand Central. It occurred to Anna that Laura might have a question about what she had just seen, or else that she, the responsible adult, ought to have something to say to the girl about it. A dirty business! It angered her that this dirt should be foisted on a mind like Laura's. Still, you couldn't keep a girl in the dream of *Swan Lake,* either. Really, she ought to say *something.* But what? I can talk to her about anything else, but when this sort of thing comes up, so do my barriers. As they always have, all my life.

On the East Side the scene changed to clean streets and middle-class shoppers going home. Small theatres discreetly advertised foreign films.

"Oh, did you see that, Nana? I saw it last month with Joannie. It was great."

"I saw it too. It was beautiful," Anna said.

"You know what I loved about it? It was so real. French pictures always are. I mean, the girl wasn't a fabulous beauty. She had a big nose and her hair got all messy when she went swimming, the way mine does. She had the most beautiful smile, though. And the boy did too, the way he looked t her. You remember when they were going along the street, carrying one of those long loaves of bread without any paper on it, and all of a sudden he stopped and turned her face up to his as if it were a flower?"

"I remember," Anna said, although she didn't.

"When the picture ended I was crying. Then the lights came on. I hate the way they come on suddenly and simply smash your mood. My nose was running and while I was fumbling for a Kleenex this woman going out beside me looked at me and giggled. I was so furious I said, "Why don't you mind your own business?" And she looked absolutely shocked. Then I was so ashamed of myself, I could have died. Couldn't you just *die* when you do something awful like that?"

Sometimes, Anna thought, when they were in the train, they don't talk at all. They won't "communicate," as Iris says. And sometimes everything spills out.

"I really have to make a fresh start in school this year and do better in math, even though I don't give a damn about it. When am I ever going to use a quadratic equation, for heaven's sake?"

"I'm sure I don't know. I don't even know what it is."

"There, you see what I mean? And you're just as well off without it. Anyway, that's one of my resolutions for the year. The other is to get rid of the flab about my waist. It's disgusting."

"I don't see any flab."

"You can't when I'm wearing a dress. But I got new dungarees last week, and after I'd worn them in the bathtub to shrink them they fit all right, but you could really see that my waistline's awful. I've got to do something about it. You've got a good figure for your age. I don't suppose you ever had to worry about it. What kind of perfume do you use?"

"Nothing in particular. Your grandfather's always giving me presents of it so I use what he brings."

"I use Calèche. It's really marvelous. Sexy, but also refined, if you know what I mean."

She could go on prattling for hours and I'd never get tired of listening to her.

". . . I've got this enormous new blowup of D. H. Lawrence in my room. It covers half the wall."

". . . pimple cream, it actually works, but I look as if I had smallpox when it's dabbed all over my face."

". . . loved every minute of it today, although of course you can't get the same feeling after Tchaikovsky that you get, say, after Handel, can you? I mean, it's just not the same language, is it?"

If one wanted to label this fraction of time, this segment of space, it would be *eastern seaboard suburban, upper middle-class.* Grandmother treating granddaughter to the Saturday matinee. An American phenomenon. And a lovely, lovely day.

The train slowed toward their station.

"You know, Nana, I'll remember today. I'll say to my children, the first time I saw *Swan Lake* I went with my grandmother. It was a beautiful warm afternoon and we rode home together on the train."

I needn't worry about her, Anna thought. Not this child. "We'll get a taxi," she said. "I'll drop you off and then go straight on. Your grandfather will most likely be home by now."

In the taxi she gathered her packages, feeling rich with the pleasure of giving things, the charms to be hidden away for Laura's birthday and the new shirts for Joseph.

Malone's car with the Arizona license plate was parked in the driveway. Joseph must have asked them to dinner. Would the roast be big enough? She dismissed the cab and was halfway to the front door when Malone opened it.

"Hi," she began, "what a nice surprise! I wasn't expecting—" and saw his face. "What is it? What's wrong?"

"Anna, take it easy. Joseph—his heart. He fell over in the office; just fell over at the desk. We called a doctor down the hall, but—"

"Oh, God," she said. "Where is he? What hospital? Take me, hurry—"

Malone held her shoulders. His tears were running. "Oh, Anna, Anna, no hospital. It's too late."

IRIS SWAYS. HER face is gray. "I'm all right, Theo," Anna says, for he is holding her arm. "Take Iris."

The chapel is full. Noon light pours through the stained-glass windows of which Joseph was so proud. It bobs on the floor of the aisle in dots of ruby and gold. How can I think of such things? Anna wonders. But I must think of them and of the faces, mustn't look at the coffin, mustn't think of him lying in it. Look in the second row; there's Pierce, our congressman; Burgess of the Provident Bank; What's-his-name from the National Council of Christians and Jews. Faces, faces. I must remember them. Joseph would remember every one and thank them afterward. There are all those people from the hospital's board of directors. That short man coming in, he's from the building trades union; Joseph always dealt decently with working men and they knew it. Faces, faces. Women from the temple sisterhood. Tom and Vita Wilmot. There's Celeste's friend, Rhoda. To think she would bother to come! And Mr. Mozetti, the gardener. The Malone boys and their wives. Ruth's daughters; how fat they've all grown! And Harry; he looks shabby-sad; strange, he's still driving a taxi and Solly was always so proud of his book-learning. Strange.

Must think, must think. The rabbi is taking my arm now. I'm fragile. They're afraid I'll fall apart. But I will not. Joseph would be ashamed of me in front of all these people. The rabbi is saying that he left a good name behind him; a most priceless treasure, it can be purchased only through the labors of a good life. He means what he says, the rabbi does. He's a kind man and he knows that, this time anyway, what he's saying is true. It isn't always, but then, he has to say something good of the dead, isn't that so?

Suppose they could hear; suppose they knew what was being said about them? *De mortuis nil nisi bonum.* Maury was amused that I could remember his Latin proverbs without knowing any Latin. But I always had a good memory and a good ear.

"He lives on in the hearts of those who loved him," the rabbi says. His voice is gentle and earnest. He looks at the widow, speaking to her. "He was devoted to his faith." Yes, yes; he was. "An inspiration to his grandchildren; he gave them a sense of their identity." All along the row the grandchildren sit with scared, upturned faces. Laura is crying softly. Will they remember what he gave them? Only time will tell, a lot of time.

The beautiful, familiar words ring their stern and regal music. "Fear God and keep His commandments, for this is the whole duty of man."

Music. "O God full of compassion, Eternal Spirit of the universe, grant perfect rest under the wings of Your Presence to Joseph who has entered eternity."

We go out and get into a long black car. It looks sinister. There is a motorcycle escort: Who arranged that and why? Joseph wouldn't like it. Even in death there are status and pride. Humble people have pathetic funerals, not like this one. Now we ride through the cemetery gates. There's the Kirsch family mausoleum; it's like those royal tombs we saw in Europe. Wealth and hierarchy, even in death. Joseph would never allow anything like that . . . "Just a slab," he told me once. I'll have it put down next year, and mine next to it . . . "Anna, wife of Joseph," it will say. What a crazy person I am to be having these thoughts while they help me out of the car, holding me up by the elbows. All that green cloth draped to hide the fact that it's only a hole in the ground. All these dead, acres and acres of them. Wouldn't it be strange if they knew we were standing here? *Knew,* as they lie in the dark under the flat mown grass, under the weight of the heavy earth on their egg-shell skulls and their helpless hands. Suppose they could hear and people were saying things about them; their keen ears could hear but they would be unable to defend themselves: *Yes, but I was right! You didn't understand, I tried, I only meant—*

De mortuis nil nisi bonum.

And is that what it was all about, Joseph, that we nurtured our children and loved them and lost them, that you did nothing but work all your life, even though you said it was a pleasure to you? What was it for? That we should walk away like this and leave you in the ground? Is this what it was all about?

There is a rustle. People rise and murmur the Kaddish: *"Yit-ga-dal ve-yit-ka-dash she-mei ra-ba—"*

Iris is sobbing when Theo leads them back to the car. Why am I not crying, too? Joseph would be proud that I'm not. Still, I ought to cry.

Someone whispers, "I thought he spoke beautifully." Someone: "She's holding up well . . . she always had dignity."

The sky goes wintry. Before we reach home the rain comes, a somber, gusty, spattering rain. Lights are on all over the house. Friends and neighbors have come with pink chrysanthemums, baskets of fruit and chocolate cakes.

"Come," Celeste says, "have a cup of tea, you've had nothing all day." She leads me to the dining room, and I allow myself to be led. In spite of everything the body cherishes its comforts: the tea, the fire, the windows tight against the rain. I let them put half a chicken sandwich on my plate.

Why don't I cry?

It was the hat that brought tears. After that long day it was the sight of Joseph's crumpled rain hat, forgotten on a chair in the upstairs hall. She went into their room, holding it to her cheek—his old hat that he would never wear again—and stood there weeping, swaying in the ancient way of mourning women.

Empty, empty.

She got undressed. The bed was turned down, such a wide bed to lie in alone. She had a quick flashing picture—from what storage space in her head?—of Joseph playing at the beach and Solly with him . . . they were throwing a ball . . . "Poor Solly . . . all of his young brightness quenched," Joseph had said once, not seeing himself.

Somebody pushed open the door. It was only the old dog, George the Second, who had slept with them ever since—since Eric went away. He raised his head, turning his mild eyes toward Anna, asking where Joseph was . . . and receiving no answer he settled on the mat at Joseph's side of the bed to wait.

I wasn't good enough for him. I said that yesterday, and Iris stroked my hands. She said, "Mama, that's not true. You made him happy. You know he was happy!"

Yes, he always told me he was. It must have been hundreds of times during all our years that he told me so. And still it's true; I wasn't good enough for him.

Oh, I tried, I tried. I wanted to, and I owed it to him.

That priest who, besides Paul, is the only other being on earth who knows what I know—I wonder whether he's still alive? We never even told each other our names.

Theo knocked. "I've brought you something. May I come in?" He had a glass of water and a pill in the palm of his hand.

"I never take tranquilizers, Theo." She hadn't meant it to sound stiff-necked or proud, but it came out that way.

"Just once, tonight. You've been a good girl and you deserve a little help."

"I want to face it with my own strength."

"I know you're strong, but you're also stubborn. Now, the doctor says, take it . . ."

"All right, all right. I thought you had gone home."

"We're sitting downstairs."

"Take Iris home . . . it's been so hard for her."

"I know. Now she'll really have to finish growing up, the whole way."

"You've known that, too?"

"Of course. She was her father's little girl."

"Yes. His little girl."

After a moment Theo said, "Laura's here, sleeping in the room across the hall."

"Oh, no, why?"

"Oh, yes. She'll come back tomorrow after school and sleep here for the next few nights."

"You shouldn't burden the child with me."

"Laura's not a child. And *she's* not to be her father's baby girl, Anna. Besides, she wants to stay."

I'm overwhelmed with your love and I can't speak.

"That's what families are for," Theo said firmly. "Now, sleep."

❧{ 44 }❧

With pride and pleasure Jimmy observed Janet across his parents' Thanksgiving table. It had been a wonderful vacation so far, except that he'd missed sleeping with her as they did back on the campus. She was in a bedroom just down the hall from his, but he wouldn't enter her room while they were in his family's house. Was that hypocritical? But he just couldn't have. Anyway, he didn't want his parents to have the slightest reason to find fault with Janet.

She was laughing now, flinging back her dark, curly hair. She hated that hair. No matter how strenuously it was brushed, it always fell back into a shape of its own, a round crest above a round face. Her arms, breasts and hips were round. (She would have to watch her weight in only a few more years.) Even her blue eyes were round. In all that curving softness one would expect the eyes to be naïve or vague, but they were not. They slid up from under heavy lids with sharp awareness, keen as the brain inside the curly head.

It amused him to think that she had come with the highest references, being the granddaughter of some vaguely distant relative of Nana's, that old lady, Ruth, who used to visit his grandparents before she died.

"How did you two ever meet in that huge place?" Dad inquired now. "Well," Jimmy explained, "since we're both pre-med, naturally we have a lot of the same profs. And one day after zoology lab this guy Adam Harris gave me a message. You tell the rest, Janet. I never get the relationships straight."

"It's the craziest thing!" Janet began. "It seems that Dr. Harris' grandfather—he's dead now—was some sort of fourth cousin to my grandmother Levinson. And that year, at some other cousin's funeral, a whole group of relatives got talking and found out that Jimmy and I were at the same university. So they decided that Adam Harris ought to introduce us. All of this in a cemetery, imagine!"

"Adam Harris thought it was very funny," Jimmy added. "Incidentally, he's the best thing that's happened in college. A gifted research man who also likes to teach. A rare bird. And human, too. A regular guy."

"I'm told that our grandfathers, yours and mine, grew up together on the lower East Side. I never knew that; did you? Well, anyway," Adam Harris had said that day, "I've delivered the message and done my duty."

"What's she like?" Jimmy had wanted to know.

"Judge for yourself, my friend. I will tell you this, though, she's damn smart. One of the best in her section. And that's all I will tell you."

It hadn't occurred to Jimmy to ignore the request, for he had a strong sense of courtesy and social obligation. So he had intended simply to call, take the girl out once for coffee and then not call again.

Janet had laughed when he'd told her. "You know, I was supposed to look you up, too. My mother'd been bugging me about it. She still exchanges New Year's cards with your grandmother since mine died, and I think that's how she learned we were both out here. My mother's impressed with your family. She thinks they're important."

Only Janet said things like that, coming right straight out with them. At first her manner had startled Jimmy, but then he grew to like it. She didn't fumble or hint; you always knew what was on her mind.

"We're fairly poor," she had told him directly. "My dad owns a shoe store. Oh, I guess I shouldn't say 'poor,' exactly. What I mean is, I can't go to med school unless I put a lot of the money away for myself. I work every summer and I've got a scholarship for college now."

"You make me feel pampered," Jimmy had admitted. "A little ashamed."

"Why? I wish I didn't have to struggle so hard. I'd be glad to have my parents give me money or get married and have a man buy things for me."

"You know I live on Washington Heights around the corner from the apartment house you used to live in," Janet was saying now to Nana. "Your husband was so good to my grandmother," she went on. "She was always talking about him. When my Uncle Harry's grandson was sick he paid for everything. She used to say they don't make people like Joseph Friedman anymore."

Nana's eyes looked wet. Ever since Grandpa died her eyes had been quick to tear at the slightest few words.

She seemed to be very interested in Adam Harris. "You admire him so much?"

"Oh, yes," Janet said. "He'll talk to you and he'll listen. He's really great."

Nana shook her head. "Strange. When I think how different the grandfather was—"

"In what way, different?"

"Well, I never knew too much about him, only that he was once a boy in your Grandpa's neighborhood and ended as one of the biggest liquor distributors in the country."

"Funny background for Dr. Harris," Jimmy remarked. "He's such a simple person. Drives a Volkswagen and wears the same suit every day."

"Interesting," Nana said, and Jimmy wondered what she was holding back. With his grandmother, you never knew. Then she inquired of Steve, "Do you know him too, this Adam Harris?"

"I don't take sciences. But I know him a little, see him around with guys at lunch. He's a sentimentalist, a phony defender of the status quo, like most of the faculty. Full of crap."

"It seems to me," Dad said, "you don't have a good opinion of anyone at college, do you, Steve?"

"Actually, no. They're all tools of the system, hirelings paid to train the young for the corporate rat race. What's there to approve of?"

"I'm sorry you find it all so miserable."

"Oh, I don't really give a damn."

Their mother, Jimmy saw, glanced at their father as she passed the cranberry sauce, and had just opened her mouth to change the subject when Steve dropped his bomb.

"And the reason I don't give a damn is that I intend to quit at the end of the term."

"What's that you said?" Dad asked.

"I said I intend to quit. Drop out. Leave."

"Oh, really," Dad said politely. When he talked that way, there was fire under his ice. "Oh, really? And what do you plan to do with two years of college to your credit?"

Steve shrugged. "Before I do anything else I want to stop this war."

"They'll draft you, don't you know that?"

"Not me, they won't! I won't go."

"You'll go to jail?"

"Could be," Steve said carelessly. "Or Sweden or Canada, more likely."

Their grandmother gasped and started to say something, but Mother warned her with a look. Everybody in the family knew that Dad's rare anger was not to be interfered with. Steve liked to call it the Prussian in him, although it seemed to Jimmy that he had always heard that Austrians and Prussians despised each other.

"Let's leave the war out for a moment," Dad said carefully. He laid his fork down, although the dinner wasn't half over. "Or let us assume that the war has ended, which, please God, I hope it soon will be." Dad always said "please God," while denying that he believed in God. "Would you still feel that an education was unnecessary?"

"This kind is. They don't teach anything you can't pick up by yourself if you want to. And I don't want to. I don't intend to train myself to spend a lifetime making money."

"You don't approve of money?"

"Not the way it's exalted in this country. Not when it's put ahead of love."

"You're very glib, but your glibness doesn't stand up under analysis. Do you think, for instance, that because a man makes money for his family he doesn't love them?"

"That's not what he said, Theo!" Mother objected, defending Steve.

Her defense of his brother was as old as Jimmy's memory. Even years before, when Laura teased him and Steve hit her, although they both were scolded, the scolding voice was different for Steve. Did their mother hear her own anxious plaint when she spoke to him, or about him?

Steve murmured now, "If you want to get personal, I'd say it would have been better if you had cut your practice in half and given us more time."

"Cut my practice in half! I couldn't possibly have kept you in this house if I'd done that! Would that have been love?" Now his father's voice rose and although it still wasn't loud, it vibrated and seemed to shake the table. "Here you sit with good white teeth, fifteen hundred dollars at the orthodontist's—oh, I know it's vulgar to mention money, but I'm not the one who brought it up, you are. Money is part of love and don't say it isn't. Every time I wrote out a check for something you needed or something that would give you pleasure, I felt your pleasure. A piece of my love went into every dollar. Yes, and a piece of my gratitude for the country that makes it possible for me to be generous with you. Can you understand that?"

"I don't share your jingoism," Steve said.

"Jingoism! Because I speak of gratitude to this country?" Dad pushed his chair back. "Listen to me! I owe everything I am to this country that took me in. Fools like you who were lucky enough to have been born here don't know how lucky you are. I kiss this ground. I say this before all of you. I'll go out on the sidewalk in front of this house, and I'll kiss the ground! You hear me? Yes, and your grandfather felt the same way, too."

"My grandfather was a money machine," Steve said. "I'll give you this much credit: at least you do have other interests, music and tennis and reading. But he did nothing at all with his life except make money. And you know that's true."

"Oh!" their grandmother cried. "Oh, I don't understand what's happening here, never at the dinner table—"

Jimmy glanced at Janet, but she was carefully looking at her plate.

And Mother said, "Steve, I'm saddened and ashamed that, no matter what you may think, you should have so little feeling, that you should—"

"Feeling!" Dad interrupted. "Feeling! Yes, these left-wingers weep their tears for every underdog and malcontent in the four corners of the earth, but for the family that breaks its back and heart for them, no tears at all. Nothing. So you'll drop out of college; never mind asking your parents what *they* think or how they feel about your throwing your life down the drain—"

A mess.

Upstairs, later, Jimmy went into Steve's room. "What the hell ever got into you? Christ, I don't care whether you want to act like a damn fool! Drop out, do what you want, but will you tell me why you had to wreck the dinner?"

"You're sore because your girl was there."

"You're damn right I am! It could have waited for a private time. There was no real reason for doing it then."

"No real reason not to, either. I didn't make the uproar, remember! I just quietly said what I was going to do and it was Dad who hit the ceiling."

"Yes, and you had a pretty good idea he would. You used to do that when Grandpa was alive too, say things that you knew were like waving a red flag in front of a bull."

"Grandpa!" Steve said scornfully.

"You didn't like Grandpa?"

Steve shrugged, loosing from his shoulders, in a gesture of total rejection, all unwanted burdens. "It's like saying I don't like Tut-ankh-amen. We hadn't communicated in years. Actually he was dead years before he died, only he didn't know it."

"Sometimes you're awfully hard, Steve."

"I'm not hard. I only want the same right that everybody else in the family has to express my opinions, which seem to shock them to their foundations. They never think how I'm shocked by theirs."

"That's not so. I've heard you and Dad talk about things, politics and social justice, lots of times."

"Okay, I'll admit Dad means well. He tries to be open-minded, now and then when he's in the mood to be. He'll listen and try—or he says he tries—to understand. But basically, you know as well as I do, he's as uptight as any Wall Streeter about getting ahead and having things, cars and new carpeting and crap like that. He doesn't really care about people in places like Harlem who have to worry about food instead of carpets. And Vietnam. Sure, he thinks it's wrong, but does he do anything about it, put himself on the line? God, it stinks, the whole business, you know what I mean? Sometimes when I hear them talking about insurance and tax-free bonds and all that garbage I could puke. I could honest-to-God puke!"

"So, okay, I get what you're driving at, but all the same, it is their house and I guess they can talk about what they want in it, can't they? Hell, I don't agree with them half the time but I don't go around making waves. Let them think what they want and I can think what I want, for Pete's sake."

"What kind of relationship is it where you can't speak your mind? That's why I hate to come home, if you must know. At least on the campus I can talk freely. It's like breathing fresh air again when I get back there."

"I thought you were going to quit!"

"Yeah, and a lot of my friends are, too. I don't mean the whole campus is free. Christ, no. I meant my crowd."

Steve's crowd. Earnest, gesticulating, wrathful. He supposed they were all ultra-bright like Steve, although he didn't really know any of them except by sight, orating on the campus, gathered under the trees or in club rooms. They were names he recognized from the *Clarion Call,* flying here and there, to congressional hearings, to vigils, parades and strikes, an uneasy flock in constant flow and motion. He wondered how they ever got any work done or passed exams. After all, you had to spend *some* time cracking the books . . . even if you were brilliant like Steve. It puzzled him.

"Where there's genuine love there's understanding, isn't there? Well, isn't there?" Steve demanded now.

"Steve, you see perfectly well what I mean but you pretend you don't. I can't win an argument with you. You've got a trick way of talking and twisting things against all common sense, against what any man in the street would simply *feel* was right."

"Yeah, *feel.* Think with your blood. Like a fascist," Steve said.

He had a slow, faintly mocking habit of shutting the lids down over his eyes, dismissing you. Sometimes when he did that Jimmy wanted to hit him. Then other times, when he looked at his brother, at the blue veins that stood out on the temples under the thin, fair skin, he felt a tenderness more moving than any he ever felt for their little brother, Philip.

"I didn't want to come home for Thanksgiving, anyway," Steve said. "You forced me to come."

"I'm sorry I did," Jimmy answered quietly. "Well, okay, then, I've had enough for tonight. I'm going to bed."

"The sleep of the just," Steve mocked.

His snapping sarcasm had always been infuriating. Yet it was only a cover-up. Jimmy remembered having thought that years ago. He remembered other things, too.

There was the time when Jimmy had broken his leg and Steve had got all his assignments, brought books from the library for his project, typed his papers, fed his gerbils and tended his plants for the experiment on Mendel's Law. He remembered how, when they were very young, Steve used to get so mad about being weaker than he; never able to win a fight, he would fall into such a frenzy of outraged despair that the fight would end with Jimmy's being sorry for him.

My brother's debtor, and his keeper. It sounded so pompous. Yet there it was.

THE NEXT AFTERNOON, to Jimmy's relief and his parents' concern, Steve left to attend a peace rally in California.

Nana invited Jimmy and Janet to lunch. He knew that she must have been very pleased with Janet or she wouldn't have invited them. They sat in the sunny, lofty dining room, the women chatting easily, as women always seemed able to do. With half his mind he heard them discussing Janet's family, college and skirt lengths. The other half of his mind was listening to different voices.

The dinners he had eaten at this long, polished table! It seemed as if all of them had been ceremonial, although there must have been many that were not. What he remembered, though, were song and prayer, flowers, candlelight and enormous quantities of sweet-and-sour food.

"We're boring you," his grandmother said suddenly.

"No, no. I was just letting my mind wander. I was thinking of how we used to be dressed up for holiday dinners in our best suits and how everyone was so punctilious."

"Did you hate it?" Janet asked curiously.

"Oh, when I was very young I was impressed. But from about fourteen on I used to be so bored. The meals took forever. I spent the time hiding my yawns."

"People are easily bored at fourteen," Nana observed. "But you know? It was beautiful, wasn't it?"

Yes, very beautiful. Now, having been away from home and childhood, far enough away in space and time to see it as it had been, he could think of it as a way that he would like to live over, to repeat when his turn should come.

"I wonder whether Mother feels the loss?" he asked. "She was so attached to Grandpa. And Dad doesn't or won't keep the holidays like that in our house."

"I imagine she misses it," Nana said quietly. "I know I do."

The silence held faint sadness.

Then Nana asked surprisingly, "Are you a religious person, Janet?"

"Yes, the tradition means a great deal to me. It always has."

His grandmother smiled. Then she said briskly. "If we're finished, why don't you show Janet through the house? She said she wants to see it."

They started in the music room. The Bach *Goldberg Variations* lay open on the rack of the piano.

Jimmy remarked, "I guess Philip's been here."

"Yes, he was here for supper last Sunday and he played for me."

"Do you remember how no one dared even cough when Philip was playing?"

"I do."

"With all respect, I don't think it was because Grandpa understood or even liked music."

Nana laughed. "He didn't."

"It was only because it was Philip playing."

The fierceness of that love! Jimmy wondered whether the kid had minded being displayed like that. But he guessed not. Philip was at Juilliard now and, after all, what use was it to play an instrument without an audience? Thank goodness, though, he wasn't a "different" or outlandish boy. In fact, he was a great deal better adjusted than most people were, having a sociable, almost placid nature which didn't fit with the platitudes about musicians and temperament.

They climbed the stairs to Grandpa's round room. The humidor still held the scent of rich Havanas, although it had long been empty. Blueprints lay rolled in sheaves on the shelves. A handful of fresh marigolds stood in a little cup on the desk, Nana's flowers, the same as the ones that bordered the terrace and framed the lawn on this pearl-gray day of fading fall.

Janet stood at the window. "What a lovely house!" she cried softly.

"Yes," Jimmy said. "In some ways it seems more like my childhood's house than the one I actually lived in."

Below on the one-story wing of the library, Virginia creeper climbed thickly on the walls. It took a generation for creeper to grow like that. It was so strong now you would barely be able to pull it off if you should want to. The whole house was strong.

"I remember sleeping over once when I was very little," Jimmy said. "I was terribly afraid of thunder and on that night there was an awful storm. You knew I was afraid, Nana, and you came into my room where I was lying awake. But for the first time I wasn't afraid at all, and you were so surprised. I told you that I wasn't afraid in *this* house, that nothing bad could ever hurt or scare me in *this* house. Do you remember that?"

"I don't remember it and I'm glad you told me." Nana was pleased.

Presently they kissed her good-by and rode away.

"You have a wonderful family, Jimmy," Janet said. "I love your grandmother especially. She does seem strong, like her house. She gave me—oh, I don't know exactly—a feeling of permanence. I'm the sort of person who likes things to last, Jimmy."

"I am too," he said.

In his dormitory room, Jimmy lay sprawled on the bed in a jumble of blankets, clothes and textbooks, watching Janet get dressed. He imagined that his flesh still glowed, as though the air that touched her flesh was warmed by it and brought the warmth back across the room to him. He foresaw the bleakness of the room when she would have left it, and him alone in it, until next time. In the year he had known her she had become as near to him as his pulses or his breath.

"Don't go," he said.

"Jimmy, I have to. If I stay here I won't study and I've a chemistry quiz on Thursday."

"We'll both study. I won't bother you."

"You know we won't study."

He laughed. "All right. You win."

She drew on her jacket. "Okay. I'm going. You can come to my place Friday. My roommate's going home for the weekend."

"Okay. Wait, let me get something on and I'll walk you over."

He ran around the room picking up clothes, a shirt flung over the typewriter, pants on the floor.

"Janet?"

"What, dear?"

"I'm sorry there was a scene at my house. A helluva thing, on your first visit! And honestly, we never have big fights like that one, only small ones now and then when Steve starts them."

"I didn't mind. I only felt bad for all of you, especially for your grandmother. I liked her so much."

"Yeah. It's been hard for her since Grandpa died. She's really great, Janet. Sometimes she can sound like somebody in a fairy tale, as if she hadn't been paying attention to the world at all. Then other times you think, She's no fool, that lady. Did I tell you she's an opera buff?"

"Do you really think Steve will drop out of college?"

"Yeah, I really do. I really do. You know," he said slowly, "Steve's kind of a genius. I mean, he could be if he wanted to. He can do languages, math, everything. Did I tell you he got in the seven-nineties on his Boards? And he never has to study the way I do. I mean, I kill myself studying. With him I think it's a question of memory; he reads a page once and the whole thing sort of prints itself on his mind. He's fantastic."

"What is he interested in?"

"Nothing. He used to be a history buff, but then he started saying it was all crap, all slanted, the books don't tell the truth. After that he got involved with philosophy, that's his major, but I don't know whether he cares about it that much or what he plans to do with it."

"Teach is about all, isn't it?"

"He doesn't want to teach. Anyhow, the new wrinkle is that the universities are all fake, irrelevant, feeding the war machine, you know that." He thought of something and laughed. "I remember one time he told my grandfather about the philosophy major and Grandpa asked him what he was going to do with it. With Grandpa everything had to be practical. So when Steve didn't answer my grandfather said, kind of making a joke, 'Well, you could open a store: Steve Stern, Philosophy.' Everybody laughed and Steve was so mad."

"Not much humor in him."

"Not much. Especially now. It's this damned Vietnam. Seems as if that's all some people talk about."

"It's important enough, Jimmy," Janet said very seriously.

"I know. But it doesn't have to *poison* a person's whole life, does it? I plan on going ahead and being a doctor, regardless. And so do you, don't you?"

"Of course I do."

They opened the door onto an altered world. Snow, which had been sifting finely all the day, had turned into floods of sleet. It rattled like gravel as it fell. The wind slammed the door shut behind them and bent the trees, sending a shower of icicles cracking to the ground.

"The world looks angry," Janet said.

Probably you had to be born here on these midwestern plains to live easily with such savage winds, such dark gray, frozen winters. The sleet stung their cheeks. With eyes pressed half-shut against it they stumbled and slid. Janet fell. Jimmy pulled her up and they struggled on to her door. Light from the building showed her curls salted with white.

"You look sweet with the snow on your hair," he said.

She put her hand up to his cheek. "I love you, Jimmy. You're so soft, I must remember never to take advantage of you."

"I'm not worried about that."

"Don't study too late."

Walking back against the wind and sleet, he lowered his face into the woolen scarf. He felt deeply tired. It wasn't a physical fatigue. He hadn't realized how tense he'd been about the weekend at home, either because Janet might not like his family, or, more probably, that they might not like her and that she would then turn against him. But everything had worked out well enough. Now he was feeling the aftermath of tension.

He'd been especially glad that Laura and Janet had gotten on together. He thought of his sister, now that she had passed through the audacious moods of adolescence, as a kind of "norm." She had such a friendly attitude toward life. If he had been asked to characterize her he would have used words like "reasonable" or "accepting." He supposed he might be oversimplifying but anyway, that was how he saw her. She was rather like their father.

Steve was like their mother, he mused, although whenever Jimmy had remarked it he had been contradicted. And he could see why. On the surface no two people could have been less alike, his mother being so courteous, so anxious (one read anxiety in her eyes, in the two vertical lines between the eyebrows), so concerned to please. She had always been afraid to lose her temper. (Because she feared that her children wouldn't love her?) She had let them get away, very often, with far too much. Yet her same anxiety was in Steve.

Perhaps, Jimmy thought, I am more perceptive than I think, and shall not lack for understanding when I become a doctor.

Dad had treated him and Janet with serious respect as he took them on a tour of the hospital on the day before Thanksgiving. Back at his office he had had lunch sent in and they had sat with him for an hour or more talking earnestly about doctors and medicine. After a while the conversation had drifted unexpectedly into family, perhaps because of having seen Grandpa's name on a bronze plaque in the lobby of the hospital.

"I miss him," Dad had said. "We were two very different people and we disagreed about many things. Yet there has never been a man whom I respected more or loved more." He had gone on talking and recollecting. "His family was everything to him. And, you know, he was right. There was a time in my life when I didn't want to be vulnerable because of family, when I wanted to put all that away. Yet without it there's nothing. Only the black hole of the spirit."

Jimmy had seldom heard his father so solemn. He had sounded like Grandpa. He hadn't even been sure he understood what his father was talking about, but he sensed that Dad had honored them by revealing a part of himself.

Yes, Jimmy thought now, I come from decent people.

He would have liked to ask his parents specifically about Janet, but he didn't dare. They wouldn't approve of such an early marriage. They would say that at twenty he couldn't know his own mind or make a decision that would be permanent. But if he was mature enough to know that he wanted to be a doctor and so to dispose of the rest of his life, then why was he not mature enough to make a decision about Janet? They would think otherwise, however. Most parents would.

Anyway, there was the question of money. He couldn't ask them to support a wife for him. Dad made a fine living, but there were four to educate and he had to work very hard to keep up. No, it was quite impossible.

He trudged up the stairs to his room. Steve. Janet. An enormous work load. And admission to medical school. But mostly Janet.

The room was cold without her, as he had known it would be. Five years! Who knew what five years might do with their commitment to each other? A couple of hours together here and there, now and then? It could take the very life out of their relationship.

Five years. It was like saying: a century. It was like saying: never. He felt deeply tired.

"ALL WARS," STEVE repeated. "Not only the Vietnam war. All wars are fought to benefit a few who get rich or richer. The rest just die in them for nothing." The veins were prominent again in his temples. They looked bruised. One of them twitched, Jimmy observed.

It was an incongruous group at the table in the coffee shop, haphazardly come together. Jimmy and Janet had come in out of the perilous cold for a hot drink, and had been joined by Adam Harris, alone. Shortly afterward, they had seen Steve shove in, just back from the peace rally in California. He must spend all his allowance on travel, Jimmy thought. His coat was torn. It lay now, flung on the floor with a pile of paperbacks: Kafka, Fanon, Sartre.

"All wars?" Adam Harris queried. "You remind me of the student groups who vowed they wouldn't fight in any war, even though Hitler was arming under their noses. What can you say to that?"

"It was basically the same thing. If the world's financial interests hadn't fostered Hitler there would have been no need for a war. Don't you see that war and the system are reverse sides of the same coin? That the one can't exist without the other?"

Exhausted, he put his head down on his folded arms for a moment. The others stared at him and shifted restlessly. He had been with them for half an hour and the tensions he had brought had now begun to affect them, too.

Suddenly he flung his head up. "I was thinking on the plane flying back: everybody on it was dead, do you know that? Ask them about Vietnam, the schools, Latin America—you think they give a shit? No, who's going to win the next Series, can we keep the blacks out of the union, should I get out of the market, that stewardess would be a great lay. That's all they were thinking."

Adam Harris said patiently, "You're not discovering anything new or startling. People are naturally and always concerned first with themselves. Social change is slow. But it comes. Eventually, when enough people want to get out of this war in Southeast Asia, we'll get out of it. That's the way democracy works."

"Democracy! Anybody who thinks this country is a democracy needs a shrink!"

Adam Harris smiled slightly. "Do you know of a better system anywhere?"

"No, that's just the point. We have to create one from the bottom up. And we start by stopping this war. That's the first step." Steve confronted Jimmy. "Why don't you do something about it instead of just sitting on the sidelines? We've a meeting Sunday afternoon in Loomis Hall. Why don't you come and hear what it's all about?"

"I know what it's all about. I read the papers."

"Danny Congreve's going to speak. Do you know he's one of the best minds, the clearest thinkers we have? If we could have men like him running the country—"

Jimmy had thought of Congreve as a rabble-rouser. Perhaps, though, that wasn't fair? Congreve was a kind of disciple of Harold Clifford, an erstwhile Quaker and theologist who was sweeping the country from coast to coast with his antiwar fervor.

But he shook his head and with effort met Steve's blazing look. "Sunday afternoons I hit the books. You forget, I have to keep my grades up."

"An evasion," Steve objected. "You could find some time if you wanted to."

"What I want most is to be a doctor. I might just be able to do some good for the world in *my* way."

"And incidentally pull in fifty thousand a year doing it. Or will you aim for a hundred."

"Listen, since you keep badgering me, I'll tell you one reason I don't want to get involved. I've been reading too much about overturned cars and broken bank windows. I know you personally don't go in for that sort of stuff—at least I hope you don't. But I want to stay away from it altogether and, if that's your idea of cowardice, make the most of it, Steve."

"What you're afraid of is your true self," Steve said.

Adam Harris interposed. "I happen to think the war is very wrong. But I don't think that overturning people's cars and breaking people's windows is the answer. Violence never is."

Steve stood up and wriggled into his jacket. "Violence is what we're against, don't you understand? You talk about a car or a window as if they were significant, when they're only incidents. The real violence is the shedding of blood in war, the strife in industry, the raping of nature. What we want is to bring the world back to decent values, to do away with competition and envy and anger."

He picked up his books, an abrupt, surprising shyness returning to his manner. When he wasn't passionate about his beliefs, it flashed through Jimmy's mind, all conviction went out of him. This was how he usually looked.

"Well, so long," Steve murmured. "So long." And clutching the books, with shoulders bent, he scurried out into the dimming afternoon.

The others stood up and moved toward the door. "A passionate young man, your brother," Dr. Harris remarked.

"I know," Jimmy acknowledged. "I wish—" he hesitated. "I wish he would think a little more about himself, about where he's going. We worry about him at home."

"I don't think you need worry. A great deal of this talk is only talk. People like Congreve, for instance, they sound like young wolves who want to tear the world apart, but they don't and the world goes muddling on as always."

They stood a moment on the sidewalk. "Yes," Adam Harris said, "they'll find out about violence. It's the tragic mark of our time. But eventually they'll learn that it can't accomplish anything, not in the lives of nations or individuals. It always fails in the end. Well, it's been nice talking to you two about something other than advanced vertebrate zoology."

When he had left them Janet spoke for the first time in the last half hour.

"Amazing how such a brain can be so innocent, isn't it?"

"What do you mean, innocent?"

"Well, for Pete's sake, Jimmy, all power, whether of nations or families, is founded on violence! From the oil dynasties to the British Empire, to the country's private fortunes. His own family too, I'll wager, although he may not even know it. Everything! You name it. Everything."

"But he did say," Jimmy countered, "that they all fail in the end."

Janet stared at him. "Yes, of course they do! When they're beaten by an adversary that's more ambitious, clever and—more violent. Don't you see?"

"At this point I don't see anything. My head's spinning."

"I don't say it's right or good, but that's the way it is."

"I'm confused. This sort of argument isn't for me. I think I'll go back to the room and tackle vertebrate zoology. It's easier."

Somebody on the floor had been using his portable television and forgotten to turn it off. From the little box with the four-cornered eye there came a tumultuous, hysterical shrieking. One thought immediately of a street accident or some other sudden horror. But it was only a quiz show. The curtain had just been drawn back to display the prizes.

Hot-eyed fools, licking their lips over a refrigerator, an electric broom, a—a *gadget!* Disgusting! he thought, switching the television off. And then: not disgusting. Pathetic. But why pathetic? Because they needed these things and it was so hard to afford them? Or because they oughtn't to want them so badly in the first place? Which? I'm getting like Steve, Jimmy thought, addling my head with impossible questions that have no answers. He sat down in the armchair by the window, suddenly tired, with a kind of drained breathlessness.

Yet so much of what Steve preached was true. The trashing of America. Litter of broken metal, rims, cans, frames of unrecognizable defunct machines. Seen from train windows: a blasted, withered landscape. Elevated highways over heaps of rusting cars among dying weeds as tall as a man; greasy puddles and smell of burning rubber, where once in the duck-filled marshes gulls had risen from the plume grass and flapped toward the sea.

Gray. Mud gray, rain gray; gray of ashes, old tires and wet cardboard boxes. And over all a stinging, mucky smog.

The trashing of America.

And a similar trashing of that small country in Southeast Asia, except that there the ruin was overlaid with blood. He felt his brother's anger, the righteous rage that sparked and shook the body of his brother.

Yet there was something wrong with that anger, too. Jimmy strained. He was not used to thinking very hard about things unrelated to his own difficult, demanding goal. It had never been easy to find fluent words for his thoughts. He had heard and observed that science majors often were like that. Perhaps that was why patients complained that doctors didn't "relate" to them?

Yet now he knew well enough what he felt. A strong apprehension swept through him, so that he shuddered and was chilled. He understood that those who saw what Steve saw with such searing conviction, and what he himself half saw, could be as blind, as narrow and as ruthless as that which they fought against. He saw that their righteous anger could be dreadfully and easily perverted, that in its fanatic drive it might only end by tearing the world apart, like the wolves that Adam Harris had talked about.

ALTHOUGH IT WAS close to ten o'clock and the icebound campus was deserted, with all its windows shut tight against the cold, within minutes lights flared, telephones rang, voices called, doors banged and the quadrangles filled. Everyone raced toward the science building where more lights blazed from bottom to top, so that it looked like an ocean liner on a gala night.

The stunned crowd was quiet. Voices murmured in the circle of flashing lamps, the ominous red warnings of police cars and ambulances.

"I didn't hear anything," Jimmy said, inquiring of someone standing next to him, "did you hear anything?"

"I thought I heard a thud or a thump, but I didn't pay any attention to it until some guys came running down my floor yelling that there'd been an explosion in the science building. I never thought—"

Other voices rose and faded.

". . . the building was empty!"

". . . all the ambulances?"

". . . army contracts, of course."

". . . no right to use the campus for the war machine!"

". . . aren't we part of America?"

". . . you're full of shit!"

". . . geez, there was somebody in there!"

Silence, except for small shufflings and rustlings. Among those standing near the door an aisle was cleared, so that men coming carefully down the slippery steps with the stretcher could pass through.

"My God, who is it?"

"Is he dead?"

"No, not dead." Moving, with an arm flung out from under the blanket that has been put over him. The blanket slips. It is picked up and laid back, but not before it can be seen that the lower half of the body is soaked with blood and wet, mangled cloth: a mush where two legs belong.

". . . it's Dr. Harris! Oh, Christ, it's Dr. Harris!"

". . . who's he?"

". . . biology. He musta been doing papers late in his office."

". . . geez!"

"He's not dead? I mean, the face all gray and—"

". . . that's shock. Not dead. Not yet, anyway."

". . . oh, my God!"

Jimmy's knees buckled. He sat down on the steps. There was no one he knew in visible range, just a lingering crowd of strangers, watching for something else to happen. The ambulance whined down the street with its red lights revolving.

". . . the watchman saw two guys here earlier tonight. He says he can identify them."

". . . bah, rumors! I don't put stock in that stuff."

". . . I heard they found a body in there. I heard it was Dan Congreve."

". . . you're out of your cotton-pickin' head!"

". . . no, he's right, I heard two cops talking and they said so."

". . . they found two of them. You'd think they wouldn't get caught by their own explosives. They don't know the other guy's name."

". . . one body, two bodies. Soon they'll be talking about twenty."

As soon as he could control his knees Jimmy got up. His chest hurt. He wondered whether you could have a heart attack at his age. He thought of what had been under the blanket and his stomach turned over. (You'll never be much of a doctor like this!) But yesterday in the coffee shop Adam Harris had said that violence was something young people only talked about, not meaning it. The last man in the world to suffer from it! Wouldn't hurt a fly, you had only to look at him to see that. Jesus! A liquid collected in his mouth, like vomit.

He had to see his brother. Could it possibly be? No, of course not. He quailed. Ought to be ashamed of myself for harboring—funny word, "harboring"—such a thought. Still, there was another body. Unidentified. *Steve said: one of the best minds we have, come hear him.*

Could Steve possibly—? No, of course not. Steve was no doubt still in his room, dreaming over a book, too absorbed to have heard the excitement. Besides, his room faced the other way, toward the lake. You might not even be able to see or hear anything there. Anyway, he had more likely been asleep. It was after midnight. Yes, Steve would be asleep. He always went to bed with the chickens. It was one of his traits. Of course.

Steve wasn't in his room.

He knocked and kept knocking, disturbing the people across the hall.

"What do you want?" someone called out crossly.

"I'm looking for my brother, Steve Stern."

"He's not there. He went out a couple of hours ago." The door slammed.

Now breathing was really painful. He panicked again: could a person his age really have a heart attack? There being no place else to sit, he sat down on the floor. A couple of fellows coming back to their rooms looked at him curiously, thinking, no doubt, that he was drunk.

The grandfather clock downstairs, gift of the class of 1910, went *bong!* One bong. One o'clock. He leaned his head against the door and stretched his legs. They reached almost across the width of the corridor.

Once, sitting with his father, he had watched a television play about the Nazis and the resistance in France. They had caught some woman and tortured her by pulling her toenails out. She hadn't talked, had refused to talk, just kept repeating in such an awful voice, "I have nothing more to say! I have nothing more to say!" He remembered now that he had thought: "This is a helluva thing for Dad to be looking at, bringing everything back to him. I ought to turn it off but I don't dare. Why doesn't he just get up and walk out of the room?"

But his father had just sat there. When it was over he'd been silent for a few minutes and Jimmy had been silent too. Then his father had slammed his fist into the palm of his hand so loudly that Jimmy had imagined a fist cracking into a defenseless jaw must sound like that. He had kept sitting there, not knowing how to get up or what to say, feeling his father's anguish.

Then his father had sighed and said, "It's a great storm wind shaking the earth. It began in my youth and then a lull came, but I think the storm will rage again. I feel the grit and dust coming in the cracks."

Jimmy shuddered. He looked at his watch. It was six o'clock. He must have fallen asleep, and he ached all over. Steve hadn't come back. What he must do became entirely clear to him. He must go to his room, wash and shave, then take the seven o'clock bus downtown and go to the police headquarters. Either that other, unidentified body was Steve's, or else Steve would have to be sought somewhere. Yes, it was entirely clear.

He flexed numb legs, went downstairs and began walking toward his room. Outside the science building, where a black hole, broken glass and tumbled bricks were now visible in the daylight, was a police car with four police on guard. He walked deliberately in their direction and stopped in front of them.

"Is is true that Danny Congreve was killed in here?"

One of the policemen looked at him coldly. "You that interested?"

"Yes. Dr. Harris was a friend of mine."

"Oh. Yeah, it was Congreve. And one other in the morgue. Up to now they haven't identified him, or what's left of him."

Tears wet Jimmy's eyes. He wiped them away with his glove, but not before the others had seen them.

One of the cops said, kindly now, "They say the prof will live. He'll lose a leg, though. Maybe both."

Jimmy stood there.

"Bastard!" another cop said. "And the damndest thing—they didn't even know how to do the job properly. Killed themselves with their own dynamite."

The police radio crackled in the car and they stopped to listen. Jimmy walked away.

Lose a leg. Maybe both. He was a tennis player, Adam Harris. A good one, too. The other's in the morgue, what's left of him.

Again the pain came, a hot tightening in his chest. *My brother. A brother of mine.* My parents' son. Christ almighty!

He pushed his way up the stairs. Better get a cup of coffee before going; that way he wouldn't feel so faint. Maybe. He came around the corner of the hall, toward his door.

Steve was standing there.

They stood there looking at each other.

"You thought I was mixed up in it," Steve said.

"My God! I didn't think you— But I didn't know."

Steve's face was white. No, not white, a dreadful color, like the underside of a frog.

"Come in," Jimmy said, unlocking the door. "Come in and sit. Where were you? I've been outside your room all night."

"I was undressed, studying, when I heard all the noise and running outside my room, so I got dressed and went over. And I saw, I saw your friend." He put his hands over his face. "Jimmy, I'm sorry. So awfully sorry."

"Where were you last night?"

"I couldn't stop vomiting. So I went to the infirmary and they kept me there. One of the nurses told me this morning about Danny Congreve. Jimmy, I never thought, I could have sworn, I would have trusted him, I did trust him. I feel totally incompetent, unworthy—"

A vast relief swept through Jimmy. "Don't, don't. You're not the first person to have misjudged—"

"*This* wasn't what I wanted, what I talked about!"

"I know that, Steve."

"I've gotta get away and think."

"About what? Think about what?"

"About everything. Myself, mostly. I've got to."

"Where will you go?"

"I don't know. Some empty place. A guy I know, quiet guy, not political, just into conservation and the earth, you know, he's got a place north of San Francisco, said I could come any time I want. So I guess that's what I'll do."

"When will you go?"

"Now. Tomorrow. I want to get out of here. I've been wanting to, you know that, only now it's for different reasons. You understand?"

"I think I do." He didn't, really. He could feel pity and sadness, but he couldn't understand. Perhaps he never would.

"You'll call the folks and tell them after I've gone? I don't want to go through the hassle of talking to them right now."

"I'll call them," Jimmy said gently.

THEY WERE AN hour early. They stood in the lounge at the wall of windows, looking out upon arrivals and departures, baggage carts trundling back and forth, mechanics checking, pilots boarding with their little black bags en route to Paris; Portland, Oregon; and Kuala Lumpur.

"I'll miss Philip," Steve said.

"He'll miss you, too. We all will." Do all words that are torn out of you, yes, torn and ripped, do they always sound so banal? "Miss you": what did it mean?

"Don't crap me up, Jimmy. It'll be a lot more peaceful in the family with me gone."

Why did he feel like crying? You'd think he was seeing his brother off to certain death, when all he was seeing were things past: Steve hunching up the hill after school (why was just this such a persistent memory?); Steve and he as kids in the bathtub together, and long before that, Laura with them; three in the bathtub until they got too old, he and Steve staring at Laura, laughing about her after they had been put to bed, wondering what it feels like not to have a penis; Steve casually offering to go over his math with him, knowing he was stuck and ashamed to ask for help; Steve in the hospital with pneumonia and his mother crying in the bedroom, pretending she wasn't.

"They tried to be impartial but they always loved you more, Jimmy."

"Not more. Just differently. Because we're different, aren't we?"

Steve didn't answer. A crowd of tourists came through when their flight was called. Bound for Hawaii, with tour signs pinned on their shoulders, they were middle-aged and raucous, wearing Hawaiian print shirts under their overcoats; the men were bald or balding; the women were freshly curled and blue-rinsed. They clamored out of sight with their cameras, bags and merriment.

"I feel so sorry for people," Steve said suddenly. "For their struggles and their sicknesses, and all knowing they're going to die. I feel their pains so badly sometimes. Yet I don't like them," he mused, almost as if Jimmy weren't there. "I don't really like them, do you understand what I mean? With their transistor radios and their guffawing. They're such small-minded buffoons, most of them. I don't have anything to say to them."

It seemed to Jimmy that if you tried, you could surely relate to anybody, even to a bald old guy in a Hawaiian shirt. He was human after all, like yourself, wasn't he? But probably that was too simplistic. If it were that easy Steve wouldn't be what he was.

"How's Dr. Harris? Have you heard anything?" Steve asked.

"He'll live. One leg's off at the hip, the other at the knee."

"Christ," Steve whispered. He bit his lip. "He was a gentle, decent man, Jimmy."

"Yes."

"I don't know how I can ever get over it."

"But you weren't involved! It had nothing to do with you."

"On the periphery I was, and it did."

"You didn't know what those people were going to do!"

"But I should have known, that's the point. You see what I mean about myself? I don't understand people. They never say what they mean or mean what they say."

"Do you feel that way about me?"

"No, it's funny, you're probably the only one I can read clearly."

"I must be pretty empty, then!"

"Don't joke. I know you're trying to make the moment easier. I think if I get away, just get out where it's warm enough to be outdoors all year and plant things, work in the earth, use my hands, I think maybe that will help. Maybe I'll straighten out in my mind what I want to do."

"Yes, yes, it ought to be a good thing," Jimmy said awkwardly.

"The land needs healing, too," Steve said. "Maybe I can help heal it?"

The question, rhetorical, hung in the air.

Mother said once of Steve that there are people to whom living comes hard. They see the world as it ought—or so they think—it ought to be. But they are never at home in it as it is, for what reason neither they nor anyone else can say. Well, that was a neat enough summing up. But what was to be done about it?

The flight to San Francisco was called and Steve picked up his bag.

"Well, Jimmy?"

Jimmy put his arms out. They hugged each other. Steve felt so light, so light and frail in his arms. Then Steve turned and walked abruptly away. It seemed to Jimmy that, of all the crowd pushing toward the plane, Steve was the only one traveling alone, although that was probably not so. He only looked that way, hurrying with his rapid walk, his shoulders forward and, although Jimmy could not see his face, the expression of anxiety that he so often wore.

The loaded plane slid down the field to the takeoff point, where it went out of sight behind a wing of the terminal building. Jimmy watched until it came in sight again, taxiing to the far end of the field where it waited for takeoff. Even from this distance he imagined he could see it trembling, an insect with two rows of seats in its thorax, and a roaring heart too big for its skin. He thought he could even hear its mighty whir as, gathering all its strength, it tensed itself and leaped, rose into the lurid air and headed west.

BACK IN HIS room he waited for Janet. The hour moved so slowly. He ought to be using the time. The pile of books, the assignment notebook on the desk, were urging him to use it. But a lethargy had come over him, lying on him like heavy, pressing hands.

He ought to call his parents. They would take the news with an assumption of calm, not wanting him, Jimmy, to know the force of the blow. (Would they always, all their lives, shield and protect him, or would a time come when it would be their children who would shield them?) They would go into the dining room at the next dinner hour and tell Laura and Philip, keeping their manner light, that Steve had gone but would surely be back, that while they thought it was a grave mistake, people had to make their own mistakes and were sometimes the better for having learned from them. (That would be Mother talking.)

Afterward, upstairs in their bedroom, she would cry, and come to breakfast the next morning with slightly swollen eyes and claim a head cold. (Was this a harbinger of years to come that, already while they were still only in late middle age, not really old at all, already he could feel this way for them? And feel the end that was inevitable? A tooth parting from its socket, a wrenching of bone out of bone, that's how it would be.)

The telephone rang. He got up to answer it, hoping it wasn't his parents, because he hadn't yet framed what he was going to say.

It was his grandmother. She had never telephoned him at college and a fear of some disaster shot through him.

"It's all right, everything's all right," she said, as though she could read his fear. "Except that we've heard what happened on your campus."

"Yes. It was awful." Inadequate word, so far from the unspeakable truth.

"Has Steve gone yet?"

"Well, yes. As a matter of fact, I just came back from the airport. What made you ask, Nana?"

"I just had a feeling. I felt he might go in a hurry because of all this."

"That's just how it happened."

"You haven't told your parents yet?"

"No. I'll do it tomorrow. I sort of wanted to get myself together first."

"I know. I won't say anything. Besides, that's not why I called. I wanted to talk about you."

"About me?"

"About you and Janet. You know, Jimmy, she's a marvelous girl."

"You think so?" Jubilance in his voice, and a little cracking sob. Exhausted. Too much of everything, this whole long week.

"Yes, I do. When are you going to marry her?"

Jubilance faded. "We've another year of college and four years of medical school, Nana."

"Five years are too long to wait. It's waste and a sin to put off living while you're young and when you have the capacity to live. So many people haven't got it."

He threw his free hand helplessly into the air. "What can we do?"

"You can let me give you the money to marry her."

Years before she had come into his room during a thunderstorm, sensing his fear. Now again, across more than a thousand miles, she had sensed his need. Tears burned and he blinked them back, as though she were able to see them.

"It's too much to take from you," he said quietly.

"I'm the best judge of that, don't you think?"

His parents wouldn't like it. They liked—his father especially liked—to be self-sufficient. They wouldn't even let him take it from Nana, he was sure. They were always saying she did too much as it was. And they were right.

Hope sank.

"Jimmy? Are you there? Well, what do you say?"

He thought of something. "Would you, do you suppose we could borrow it from you? We could start to pay you back as soon as we go into our internships." Hope rose. "Interns get pretty good pay. Would you consider that?"

"Listen, I called you, didn't I? I want you to get married. I want to give, I mean lend you, enough so you'll be able to."

"With interest, it would have to be," he said proudly.

"Of course, with interest, what else? A business deal is a business deal. Right?"

She was playing a game, humoring his pride. He was quite aware of what she was doing, and yet this was the only way he would have it.

"How much interest?" he asked.

"Well, five and a half, six percent. The same as I get from tax exempts."

"The ordinary rate's much higher."

"I know. But a grandmother and a grandson, after all! I don't want to get rich on you. So, five and a half, all right? And you figure out what you'll need for light housekeeping, two rooms and your monthly expenses, above your allowances. You do that and mail it to me this week. Hear?"

"I hear. Nana, Janet's coming any minute and when I tell her, she won't believe it! I'm so grateful, I can't start to tell you, I—"

"Then don't. Listen, this call's getting expensive. My telephone bill is a disgrace this month. Write me a letter, Jimmy." The receiver clicked.

He stood there wiping his wet eyes and shaking his head. A dollar more on the telephone bill, and thousands to support them for the next five years!

There was such a great churning, such a twisting in his knotted chest. Steve, Adam Harris, Nana and Janet, all of life past and to come, churning and twisting. He wished he could sit down and weep with it as a woman might, without shame.

Before the knock came he knew by the footsteps in the hall that it was Janet.

"I'm so sorry," she cried. "Oh, I'm so sorry about Steve!"

Through all the thicknesses of cloth, through her quilted jacket, he felt heartbeats. At least, he felt his own. Wave after wave of comfort rolled over him, just standing there like that. The knot in his chest untwisted itself in a wash of sedative and healing warmth. He held to her as though she were a tower, and he almost a foot taller than she!

It came to his mind that he could give her the news now, but he didn't want to speak just yet. He unbuttoned her jacket and then her blouse, loosened her skirt and led her willingly to the bed.

He thought he heard her whisper into his shoulder, "Don't worry, don't be sad about anything, not about your brother, not about anything, I'm here, I'll always be here." And then he heard nothing, saw nothing, just sank into a bliss like summer night, as warm and throbbing, and lay there in that night until at last he raised his head into what might have been the dawn of morning, into a gold so luminous that it flickered into silver and a silence so vibrant that it trembled into music.

❦{45}❧

"Will you please make iced tea?" Anna asked, coming into the kitchen. "And bring out the walnut cake? I'm having a guest this afternoon."

Celeste turned from the stove. "My, that's a nice dress! I was saying to Miss Laura just last week, your grandmother looks like herself again."

During these few years since Joseph's death she hadn't paid much attention to appearances. At the beginning she had worn mourning for a year, although her friends had insisted that people didn't anymore, and that Joseph wouldn't have wanted her to. But she had known better. He, who had cared so much about old conventions, would have wanted her to.

Now she adjusted the dress where her narrow gold bracelet had caught in the sleeve. It was fine, cream-colored linen, a dress for summer, that brief, beloved season, and she took pleasure in it.

"The gentleman and I will have our tea outside," she added. "It's much too nice to be indoors."

"Gentleman!" Celeste repeated. "Gentleman!"

Anna smiled. "Yes, an old friend," and went out, leaving Celeste to wonder.

She had not long to wait. The car paused at the entrance to the drive—he would be looking for the number to make certain of the house—then started up, crackling over the gravel, and came to a stop not far from where Anna stood. It was a small foreign sports car, a young man's car. The door slammed and Paul Werner came up the steps.

Anna didn't move, forgetting to offer him her hand. He stood there, looking at her.

"You don't change at all," he said.

"You haven't that much, either."

He had gone gray, but his hair, still thick and smooth, shone silver against tanned skin. The eyes—the family eyes—were brilliant, like the young eyes of a child.

Suddenly Anna felt a dreadful awkwardness. What had she done? Why ever had she allowed him to come here? Leading him to the terrace, she murmured, "Sun or shade?" and when he had chosen shade, sat down and could think of nothing more to say.

433

But Paul spoke easily. "What a lovely place! It suits you. Old house, old trees, and so quiet."

"Yes, we've been very happy here."

"I'm glad you answered my note. I was afraid you might not."

"Why shouldn't I have? There's no reason anymore why I shouldn't."

"I was sorry to learn of Joseph's death. He was a fine man."

"Yes." *Fine man*. A banal expression, gone meaningless through thoughtless overuse. All dead men became fine men. Yet in Paul's mouth, at this moment, the words had impact, the flavor of truth. Yes, he had been, Joseph had.

"You knew that I also lost my wife?" Paul asked.

"No! I'm sorry. When?"

"Almost three years ago."

"As long as that! I'm sorry," Anna repeated.

"Yes. Well." He crossed his legs, his foot swaying into a path of sunlight. His shoe was new and polished. She remembered—such an absurd thing to remember—that he had always worn fine shoes and had narrow feet.

She stood up. "I'll just remind Celeste. You'd like iced tea? Or something else?"

"Tea will be fine, thank you."

She was grateful, returning with the tray, for the small fuss of the tea ritual, serving the lemon and sugar, slicing the cake. It gave one something to talk about.

"A long time, Anna."

She looked up. Paul was smiling at her, and she smiled back. "For people who —knew each other rather well, we're both pretty tongue-tied," he said.

She shook her head wonderingly. "Where does one begin?"

"Suppose we begin with Iris. How is she?"

"She's a middle-aged woman, Paul. That's hard to believe, isn't it?"

"Our two lives are hard to believe. But go on."

"She's grown so strong and competent! And a great help to me! Joseph left a good deal of property, and Iris is the only one of us who seems to know how to talk to lawyers and accountants. She's got a marvelous head for business. I think she surprises herself. Goodness knows, she doesn't get it from me!"

Paul smiled again, without comment.

"And the children are grown. Jimmy is going to be a doctor and—"

He interrupted. "The husband? It's still a good marriage?"

Anna nodded. She could have told him volumes, couldn't she? But the thought of putting into words the myriad complexities of all those lives was exhausting. There wasn't enough time and anyway, the effort would be futile. It wasn't possible to make them real to him: Iris, Theo, Steve and all the rest. People he didn't know at all.

"Nothing to tell me?"

She threw up her hands.

"I understand I'm asking you to give flesh and life to phantoms. To sum up years in a few minutes."

"I know you would like to see them, Paul. I know that."

"And I know I never can. Unless—" he stopped.

"Would you like to see some pictures, at least? I've just fixed up an album of new ones. I'll bring it out," Anna offered.

He bent over the album. He had a graceful back, his body unthickened and unslowed by age. He would live to be very old, quite likely, remaining supple to the end. She had a flash of memory: the day she had first seen him, still almost a boy, dashing up the steps of his house, with arms full of gifts from abroad.

"The girl looks like you, Anna. She's lovely."

"She's a lovely person, Laura. Kind and sensitive and gay."

"Fine-looking boys, too. Who's the young one?"

"That's our Philip." (Joseph's little genius, she thought wistfully. Oh, he's good, but he's not that good!) "I'd forgotten, he wasn't even born when I saw you last." The words rang mournfully. She wanted to defy the mournfulness. "Iris has a happy household," she said. "All growing up well." Why mention Steve's crisis or the worries over Jimmy's acceptance at medical school or the worries about Laura's boy friends? These were all normal nowadays, anyhow, more's the pity.

"It seems like madness when I realize that these are all partly my people," Paul said.

"I know." She felt a darting pain in her chest. Or had she only imagined it? They said one could. Psychosomatic.

He put the album aside. It occurred to Anna that it was rude to keep him sitting outdoors. "Would you like to see the house?" she asked.

He nodded and they went into the coolness, through the dining room where Joseph in his dark suit looked soberly from the wall, and finally into Anna's favorite sitting room at the back of the house. Here the light was caught and held in every season. It was the room where she lived now; magazines lay on the tables, and a ski sweater that she was knitting for Laura lay on the white and yellow sofa.

"This room looks familiar," Paul said.

She didn't understand. "Familiar?"

"You don't remember? My mother's sitting room was always yellow and white. They were her favorite colors," he said quietly.

That room! Oh, yes! She felt a prickling flush from her neck to her forehead. She had forgotten.

Paul was examining the watercolors that covered one wall. "These are very fine. Did you select them yourself?"

"Yes, years ago. Joseph always left things like that to me. He wasn't interested in art."

"Very good taste, Anna. You could get triple what you paid for them. Not, I suppose, that you care about that."

"No, I bought them because they make me feel contented. That's the only reason."

They were simple works, spare of line: pond lilies and water weeds; a long vertical painting of a dead tree raising its arms into a thunderous sky; a small square picture of lichen on a wet, black rock.

"Charming," Paul said. He walked to the window again and stood looking out at the shimmering afternoon, just stood silently looking.

When she followed his gaze she saw only the tea things on the garden table and the tops of the phlox, their towered flowerets showing mauve and cerise above the wall. A breath of their pungent fragrance came through the open window.

Anna sat down and waited. How strange it was that he should be standing here in her house! How briefly he had entered her life, only a few weeks' worth of hours at most, if you were to add them all together! And he had done as much to change her life as anyone could. She recalled now what had not crossed her mind in years, for she had buried the memory, locked it away in a top drawer and hidden the key; those nights in his parents' house, so long ago, and her own dry sobbing, the swallowed tears, the fist in the mouth. Youth, its pains more piercing than any of the deeper griefs that come later!

"You've had some good in life, when all's said and done." Paul spoke into the stillness. "In spite of the trouble I gave you, haven't you, Anna?"

"It wasn't only trouble," she said gently.

"Wasn't it, Anna?"

"There were moments of great, great joy."

"Moments!" he exclaimed. "Moments! Out of a lifetime! That's all I was able to give you."

"Are you forgetting? You gave me my daughter as well."

"And how are things between you?"

"She is a real daughter to me. I couldn't want more."

"I'm glad."

He sat down facing her. She began to feel tense, and, picking up her knitting, twisted the yarn mechanically around the needle.

"I'm glad I could do something besides make life hard for you, Anna."

"I never thought that. But you know, I have just thought of something else."

"What is it?"

"I've never had a chance to tell you and thank you. After that time at the opera, when Joseph was so terribly angry and I told you I couldn't see or hear from you again, you never betrayed my trust, or subjected me to the smallest risk. And you could have. Another man might have."

Paul looked at her steadily. "I would have cut my right arm off first. You know that, Anna."

She put her hand to her cheek. "Oh, God!" she cried.

There was a silence. After a moment he spoke again.

"So that's how it's been for us. I wish it had been otherwise."

A locust rattled like a rivet and cut itself off in mid-rattle. From the tall wild grass beyond the lawn came the steady chirp of grasshoppers. Sounds of summer past the halfway mark: full bloom of summer moving toward its close, while late roses curled at the edges, scorched in the heat.

"The sad end of summer," Paul said as if he had been reading Anna's mind. "When the locusts make all that noise you can be sure it's almost over."

"Until next year," she said.

"You always were an optimist, weren't you. You find the cup half full."

"And you find it half empty."

"Often I do."

She smiled at him. "Then you must rush to fill it, mustn't you?"

"As a matter of fact, that's what I plan to do. I came to tell you about it. I'm going to go abroad to live."

"Abroad? For good?"

"Yes. I've been, as I needn't tell you, the most loyal American. Yet a part of me has always been in love with antiquity. I have a longing for one of those old villages in southern France where the ruins go back to the Greeks. Or else perhaps someplace in Italy. The lake country—Lugano, Como. Have you been there?"

"No, I missed those."

"Ah, you'd love Lugano, Anna. It's not tropical, but golden warm, with great, great peace. Yes, I'd like to buy a place there. Would you come with me? Would you?"

"Why," she said, astonished. "I really—"

"I know I've dropped a bombshell. And it's late, I know that too. But that's all the more reason why one ought to salvage something."

Why was it that the distant past was so much clearer than things which had happened only a few years ago? She was able now to feel herself, yes, actually to feel herself, back in the posture of the adoring greenhorn girl when he, a young god descended, stood so high above her. Yet here he sat, supplicating, and she could have wept for him, wept for them both.

"It could be very lovely for us to be married, Anna, even now."

Lugano. Stony, narrow streets and blossoming trees. The two of them walking the streets, under the trees. A table on a terrace in the sun and a bottle of wine and the two of them. A room in an old house, with the night breeze coming through the windows as they fell asleep together and the morning breeze flowing when they awoke together. She couldn't speak for longing and delight.

And yet she already knew the only possible answer.

"You know," Paul said, "that something sprang to life between you and me at the very beginning. And it's still alive. It's lived through every kind of disappointment and mistake, through time and distance. Nothing's killed it. Can't we give it a chance to flourish at last? Can't we let it go free?"

"If we were alone in the world—" she began. "But we never are. There are always others."

"Tell me what you mean."

She met his anxious eyes and spoke with utmost tenderness. "There are those who came before and are gone. There are those who came after. It's just not possible. Not possible."

"But why?"

"Because this is Joseph's family, Paul. Don't you see?"

He shook his head. "No, Anna. No."

She rose and came to stand before him, putting her hands on his shoulders. "Look at me. Listen, my dear, my very dear. Can you imagine yourself at Theo's and Iris' table, facing them and me and their children? Can you see how I could possibly bring you into this family, in which your daughter doesn't know she is your daughter and your grandchildren don't know who you are?"

He didn't answer.

"Iris has always had vague, uneasy thoughts about you and me, I know she has. And if they were to be sharply awakened again—can you imagine that?"

Still, he didn't answer.

"It would be madness. Don't you know that it would be? And that I couldn't bear it?"

"You couldn't bear it," he repeated, very low.

"And you couldn't, either."

She broke away and walked to the end of the room. Tears came and, with her back to him, she rubbed them roughly away on her arm.

I mustn't touch him again, mustn't let him touch me.

"Again the family," Paul said. "Always the family, coming ahead of everything else."

"But you do understand why, don't you?"

"Yes. Still, if I could change your mind, I would. And to hell with them all."

"You don't mean that."

"No, of course I don't." And then, abruptly, he said, "You know, I envy Joseph."

"Envy him? He's dead!"

"Yes, but while he lived he—lived."

The mantel clock chimed in the next room, marking the hour—that indifferent, cheerful little clock which his parents had given—as it marked all the hours, whether of pleasure or pain, of coming or going. All the same, no matter.

"Is this truly final, Anna?" Paul asked.

She turned to look at him. This was the last time, really the last. Oh, the eyes, the marvelous blue eyes, the laughter, the strength, the gentleness; the wonderful mouth, the hands—

"Is this your final answer?"

"Paul, Paul—it has to be."

No tears, Anna. You've said good-by to people you love so many times and in so many ways, all your life long. This is another good-by. That's all it is. No tears, Anna.

"Well, then. I shan't see you again. I shall be in Europe before the end of the year."

"I'll think of you. I'll always think of you."

She gave him her hand and he held it for a long moment between both of his own. Then he dropped it.

"No, don't see me out. Good-by, Anna," and he left through the tall door to the terrace, stepped over the low wall onto the grass and out of sight.

The engine started up; the gravel spurted. When she knew he was gone, she went out to the terrace. The glass from which he had drunk was on the table; his fork lay on the plate. She looked at the chair where he had sat.

All, all a mystery. Our contradictory loves and loyalties. What we want to do. What we ought to do.

The clock chimed through the open window, chimed the half hour and the hour. Shadows laid long blue-gray streamers on the lawn and the sun had gone far west before Anna finally stood up again and went back into the house.

❊{46}❊

⸻

Some call it the Sea of Galilee. The Israelis call it Kinneret, the harp-shaped lake. The hotel is crowded with people come from all over the world to see it: Americans; Japanese with their cameras, two or three apiece slung over their shoulders; a party of French nuns whom Anna and Laura have encountered three or four times by now, from Eilat northward through Jerusalem.

Laura is already asleep. Light comes through the windows; light of the moon or stars? Anna gets up to look out where the lake lies below and trees droop like dark blue fountains. There is a diamond glitter on the water, the scattered radiance of phosphorescence. She thinks she hears the splash of fish.

Sleep comes quickly to her but so lightly that it doesn't last. She remembers how Joseph used to complain about that and about early waking. For a long time she lies now, hearing Laura's soft breathing from the other bed, thinking of the morning. As soon as she falls asleep again she dreams.

Some are old, troubling dreams. There is the dream in which two people are one and one is two: Maury and Eric are each other. There is the dream in which Joseph comes driving up in his car, and she runs to him with impulsive joy, but he turns his head coldly away. He will not speak to her; she knows it is because she has wounded him and there can be no balm for the wound.

She dreams a new dream about Laura and Robby McAllister. He is a nice boy, intelligent and friendly, with freckles and thick blond eyelashes. Laura has been living with him in college. He is of the wrong religion. Besides, he won't marry her, anyway. Men don't marry women who are had so easily. Or is that no longer true? Life has been changing so fast that she is often not quite sure whether a thing is still true or not.

She stirs and wakes again.

And if he should want her, his parents won't. They will surely reject her. Fear dries Anna's mouth. In the first morning light she sees Laura's shirt and jeans on the chair: childish clothing for a child. Careless, foolish little thing!

Iris knows about it. "Does your mother know?" she asked Laura. "Oh, yes, she knows, she's a little afraid I'll be hurt. She hopes I know what I'm doing." Is that all? Nothing about right and wrong, nothing at all of the truths we've been living with, or trying to live with, for all these thousands of years? What can be the matter with Iris? What kind of mother is she, anyway?

440

I sound like Joseph.

Laura said in Paris, "Mother told me not to tell you, that you'd be shocked."

"Then why have you told me?"

"I like to be honest about everything."

Honest about everything! The byword of this generation. It doesn't matter what you do as long as you come out in the open with it.

"Does your father know?" Anna asked her.

"No, he'd be too upset. He believes in the double standard, you see. It's natural for men, but nice girls mustn't."

"I quite agree with him."

"Nana, I don't *understand* you! Why? What's the difference between men and women. I mean—"

"Women get pregnant," Anna said scornfully. "That's the difference."

"Not these days, they don't."

Can you believe it? Can you believe it? Anna thinks now. She moves quietly around the room, getting dressed. Throwing themselves cheaply away, cooking and washing for and sleeping with a man who owes you nothing in return, no loyalty, no responsibility; who can walk out between now and an hour from now! Good God!

Loud voices go down the corridor. People have no manners anymore, no consideration, making a racket at seven o'clock in the morning.

Her foot hurts where the new shoe has raised a blister. Outrageous, at the price you have to pay for shoes. Nobody gives honest value anymore. Everything is, as the kids say, a "rip-off." Yes, it is, and they're the worst of the lot, ripping off their elders.

She knows she is tired, irritable and cross. In two more days she'll be home. She'll take a book out into the yard, a book about any century except this crazy one in which she lives, and sit there. Just sit and let the world stew.

She oughtn't to have put off traveling for so long. Five years ago she would have been steadier on her feet. She had resisted cruises, because of all the old widows she knew whose families put them on ships to pass time in luxury and to get rid of them safely. (There are doctors on cruise ships and Mama will be well taken care of in case anything happens.) Then this summer the desire came to go abroad. She wanted to see France again, having never forgotten its allure. And she wanted to see Israel.

"But Mama, why this summer?" Iris objected. "You know I'm finishing the dissertation for my doctorate. I couldn't possibly take time off."

"I'm not asking you to. I'm quite capable of going alone."

"Mama! You're seventy-seven!"

"I might die, you mean. So they'll send the body back."

"Mama, it's disgraceful to talk like that! Can't you wait till next summer? I promise I'll go with you then."

"As you said, I'm seventy-seven. I can't take the chance of waiting till next summer."

She wore them down. So it was arranged that Iris would "put her on the plane" and Laura, who was hosteling through Europe with a group of girls, would meet her in Paris and go on with her to Israel.

She was more excited than she admitted to herself, so that the reality turned out to be anticlimax. Flying to Europe! It sounds dramatic but it is really almost like sitting in an inter-city bus and doesn't take as long as some bus trips. That trip to Europe in 1929—ah, that was something else! You bought a diary and a steamer coat and dinner dresses; the orchestra played while you danced with the thrilling tremble of the engines underneath you, as the ship pressed on, pushed on across the ocean, the tumbling sea, the world. The very sound of it! Long, mournful vowels: across the world. Now that is all gone.

Still, Paris was what it was the first time. It pleased her that the room had the same view and that there were tall gladioli in the lobby. With delight she heard again the sound of the language, crisp sound of taffeta, ripple of water plunging into water. She watched the people going in and out: businessmen walking briskly, carrying their briefcases; women with poodles in rhinestone collars, patient little animals yawning under the tea tables.

Laura arrived. Darling Laura! Thoughtful enough to have worn a dress, for which Anna was grateful. Although, to tell the truth, if she had appeared in that handsome lobby in her dungarees with the backpack, Anna would have been so overjoyed to see her that she would have forgiven her.

She wanted a bath. Like a waif, she exclaimed over the enormous tub in the enormous bathroom. She came out of it all fresh and fragrant with Anna's bath oil.

"Nana, is it all right if I invite a friend to dinner?"

"Is it all right! I've been expecting you to. Several friends, if you want."

"Just one. We've been traveling together all summer."

"Fine. Do I know her?"

"Not her. Him."

And that was how Anna learned about Robby McAllister.

Laura opens her eyes and blinks into glorious light. Her skin is moist and pink with sleep, like a baby's when he wakes from his nap. And that boy, Anna thinks, that boy sees her like this every morning, takes it as his right, as if he owned her! Anna is outraged at the boldness of him and outraged at Laura.

Fool! Fool! Wrecking your life when you have everything and are too stupid to know you have it!

I sound like Joseph.

"Did you sleep well, Nana? I'm starved," Laura says.

"Well, don't take too long stuffing yourself. The driver will be here for us at eight-thirty," Anna orders, hearing the sharpness of her own voice.

Laura gives her a strange look and says nothing. She dresses and eats a quick breakfast in silence.

The cemetery is on top of a hill. Having been guided through the kibbutz—nurseries, library and dining hall (here he walked, ate, worked)—past the cattle barns, the great, clumsy, gentle animals staring solemnly as they go by, they begin the climb.

It seems that everything you want to see in foreign countries must be reached by a mountain of steps. Still, she's doing well enough, trying not to hold too hard to Laura's arm.

"Careful, Nana," Laura says. She has been told to watch out, that old women fall and break their hips and get pneumonia. Anna almost hears Theo's warnings and cautions to watch for failing heart, exhaustion, stroke. The young must take care of the old.

But unbeknownst to the young, the old also take care of them. Anna has been watching Laura, never leaving her alone with the room waiter at breakfast or with male guides; guarding her against bold eyes and impertinences (there's an old-fashioned word that you never hear nowadays: impertinence). Although to guard a girl who has tramped all through Europe with a boy she's not married to does seem rather absurd, doesn't it?

The graves lie in a level square of grass cut out of an evergreen grove. Laura finds the marker.

"What does it say?" Anna asks.

"Just the name and the dates of birth and death according to the Hebrew calendar."

The guide says in English, "You know Hebrew, and your grandmother doesn't?"

"In my time," Anna replies, "the sacred tongue was for boys to learn."

She tries to sort out what she feels. This is, after all, the true reason she has come so far. She remembers how she and Joseph spoke of coming here, how they dreaded the moment when they would stand where she is standing now.

"Did you by any chance know him?" she asks the guide.

"No, I wasn't here then. But I heard about him." His hands move in a gesture both rueful and fatalistic. "Our history is ongoing, you see. We need to remember our brave ones. And so on this place we all know about the American boy and what he did that night. Although it was a long time ago."

It was almost noon. A voice calls in the barnyard and another briefly answers. Birds, which have been flurrying and whistling through the morning, fall still. Heat pours on the scrap of earth where Eric lies, and all over this hardheld land between Syria and Lebanon, whose very tree tops can be seen from where they stand.

"So terrible." Laura speaks into the stillness. "So terrible, when he had finally found the place where he was happy."

"He wouldn't have stayed," Anna says, with sudden knowledge. "He would have become disillusioned with this, too."

"You surprise me, Nana. I should think you would have thought this was the right place for him."

"No. He was looking for something. He would have spent the rest of his life looking for a place to belong, a perfect place, and never finding it."

"Does anyone?"

"Find it? Oh, yes, some people never even have to look. Your grandfather was one. He was blessed that way."

Laura's mouth opens, as if to ask, "And you?" But she doesn't ask it.

Anna stretches her hand out into the burning air. Blue veins and brown spots disfigure the hand, as with some disease. But it is only age. My flesh, she thinks, mine lying here. Joseph's and that of his old mother whom, for no reason at all, I never liked. And Agatha's. Delicate Agatha and her people with their cool, Gentile austerity. Out of that poor young pair, their love and their anguish, came this boy.

"I don't understand very much," she says out loud and clearly.

Laura and the guide turn to her in surprise. Then the guide says, "Your driver's waving. It's time to go if you've a plane to catch."

"Wait a minute, wait a minute. I'm coming."

The others walk to the gate. With consideration and respect they leave her alone. Memorize it before you go: loose sweep of evergreen branches over the wall; two half-grown laurels at the right and a row of geraniums along the path.

Peace, Eric, son of my son, wherever you are and if you are. Shalom.

"It's always sad to leave a place that's so beautiful," Laura remarks, "even when you've only been in it a few days."

They are coming down out of the hills in late afternoon. Below lie the Mediterranean and orange groves cleft by a highway, along which traffic is speeding toward the airport.

"So it's meant something to you, being here?"

"Oh, yes! You feel, you can't help but feel, there's something here. After thousands of years! It's lasted so long, it gets to you. I didn't think it would," and Laura touches her heart.

"Yes," Anna says. "Yes."

"Nana, tell me something. I've been feeling that you haven't said anything because you wanted harmony on this trip, but that you've been very angry at me all the same. Have you been?"

Anna turns to her. "I was. But I'm not anymore."

"Why not?"

"It just all went away, the anger, hurt, or whatever you want to call it."

"I'm glad," Laura says simply.

As always, Anna sees both sides of the question. (Joseph used to complain that she never kept firm opinions.) She knows one thing, though, that you can't live by slogans. What's honest for one is a lie to another.

The main thing is to live. Foster life. Cherish it. Plant flowers and if you can't pull the weeds up, hide them.

"L'chaim," she says, speaking aloud for the second time that day.

The driver smiles through the rear-view window. "You're right, Mrs.," he says. "I'd drink to that if I had anything to drink. L'chaim. To life."

❧{47}❧

It was not what anyone could call a "proper" wedding. Joseph would have been horrified for more reasons than one. Still, Anna thought, it's very moving. Laura had wanted to be married in Anna's garden and she hoped Iris' and Theo's feelings weren't hurt, although they didn't seem to be. But Iris had never bothered about a garden and Anna's was lovely, the pears heavy on her famous espaliered trees, the phlox full-crowned in mauve and violet, and on the air a sweetness like cinnamon or vanilla, the bouquet of summer.

The judge was a woman, mother of one of Robby's college friends. The two young people stood before her, hand in hand, he wearing slacks and an open-necked shirt, she in a long white cotton shift, with her red braids hanging over a white shawl. Like me as a greenhorn, Anna thought. Laura's face turned up to Robby in simple worship. Just yesterday Iris had stood like that, her solemn gaze framed in lace. Robby began to speak the poem which they had chosen for their wedding service, while Philip played very softly on the portable organ.

> "Oh the earth was made for lovers, for damsel and hopeless swain
> For sighing, and gentle whispering, and unity made of twain.
> All things do go a courting, in earth, or sea, or air,
> God hath made nothing single but thee in His world so fair!"

"Emily Dickinson's one of our favorites, Nana," Laura had said. "You've read her poems, I'm sure?"

Flattering that her granddaughter had been sure! It just happened that she had read some, Emily Dickinson having been one of Maury's favorites, too, along with Millay, Robinson and Frost.

Now Laura answered.

> "Approach that tree with caution, then up it boldly climb,
> And seize the one thou lovest, nor care for space, or time!
> Then bear her to the greenwood, and build for her a bower,
> And give her what she asketh, jewel, or bird, or flower—
> And bring the fife, and trumpet, and beat upon the drum—
> And bid the world Goodmorrow, and go to glory home!"

445

No one stirred. The judge began to speak. One wondered what the assorted guests might be thinking of all this. Iris had been terribly troubled, Theo not as much so, yet more than one would have expected from a man who claimed to have no beliefs and no allegiances.

"There'll be none of us left at the rate things are going," Iris kept saying. "And when I think of Papa I could cry."

It was true. Joseph, watching his darling Laura married in such fashion, Laura for whom he had no doubt already imagined a stately wedding of the ancient tradition in the chapel he had built!

But Robby was a remarkable young man, and Joseph was dead. There was no fighting the times; it would be like fighting the tides to try. This was the way it always had been, in greater or lesser degree. Waxing and waning. Some stayed, some went.

For Robby's people, conservative small-town folk standing quietly in their print dresses and white gloves, for them too this surely was not a first choice. But this was a different time and generation. People didn't fight to the death for their first choices anymore.

Anna's eyes roamed over the group, over the young New York girls with flat shoes, and long, straight hair. Their faces were as unmade-up as in Anna's own youth and as different from their fashionable mothers' as it is possible to be. Full circle.

Ah, there were the Malones, come all the way from Arizona! He must be—let's see, Joseph would be eighty-two, so Malone must be eighty-five. And Joseph always worried so about his health, always said Malone wouldn't last.

Too bad that one had to wait for a funeral or a wedding to see people whom one didn't see for years, or never had seen. She had seen the twins—twins again after two generations!—when they had visited Mexico in 1954, but Rainaldo and Raimundo had only been a little more than one year old.

Anna had had a letter a month before, enclosing, as always, snapshots of the increasing family. So many of them, generation after generation! Prospering, too, to judge by the façade of a house which looked more lavish than the ones they had visited, and those had been very handsome houses, indeed. Dena looked very old. The paper was splotched; her sight was failing. But she had wanted Anna to know that her granddaughter's twin sons were going to be in New York on their way to Europe, and wouldn't Anna like to see them?

So here they were, one of them speaking no English at all, the other just able to understand and be understood. They also spoke a little Yiddish, learned from their grandparents, but only a little, and Anna's Yiddish was rusty enough. In their fine, dark suits with black velvet yarmulkes on their curly hair, they stood courteously and correctly. From where she was Anna could watch their dignified, skeptical expressions. She was ruefully amused. They were strictly Orthodox: what could they be thinking? Thinking it wasn't a real wedding at all, no doubt.

"And so, by the authority vested in me by the State of New York—"

Man and wife. They kissed, as if nobody else were there. Oh, my! And then the congratulations and laughter, more kissing, and it was over. Darling Laura.

She'd wanted bare feet, said she liked the natural look of it in a garden. There had been such a fuss over that, Theo being the most scandalized. "How far out can you get?" Iris had wailed, Iris who was always the first to excuse the innovations of the young. Fortunately, a pair of sandals had come as a present from Steve, handmade white sandals, with a bag and belt to match. He was "into"— loathsome expression—leather handwork on the commune. And because Steve had made the sandals, Laura wore them, which had settled the matter, thank goodness.

Theo walked beside Anna into the house. "It was very lovely after all, Theo," Anna said.

"It was cockeyed, and you know it."

"I don't. It was honest and poetic. Not my style or yours, but theirs."

"These kids today! These kids!"

"At least your daughter is married, and that's more than a lot of parents can say these days."

"Steve could have come to his sister's wedding," Theo remarked darkly.

"He'll come home one day. Maybe sooner than we expect."

"I don't know that I can forgive him for not being here today."

"He wanted to come, can't you see? That's why he sent all those things. They're so carefully made, it must have taken him weeks of work. But he just couldn't face everyone. That's the reason."

"Messed up his life," Theo muttered stubbornly. "An unforgivable mess."

Suddenly Anna felt Joseph's presence, felt in her mouth the words of authority that he would have used if he had been convinced he was right.

"People get into situations they never wanted to get into. And it's hard getting out. You know that, Theo." It was the first and only time she had reminded him. It hurt her to do it. But she knew by his silence that Steve would have no trouble from his father when he did come home.

"Look at your Philip!" she cried gaily. "He's become a man overnight! He seems much older than sixteen, don't you think? And I thought he played beautifully."

Laura and Robby hadn't wanted a reception line, so people simply clustered around them, wandered about the garden and drifted into the house where the champagne had already been opened.

Anna took a glass and handed another to Theo. "Come, drink! Every man's upset at his daughter's wedding. There's nothing wrong with you, in case you're thinking it's odd to be feeling depressed."

Theo grinned. "As a matter of fact, I was."

She patted his arm. "You've an awful lot to be happy about, Theo," she said, not meaning to lecture him.

She saw that he understood. They were both looking over at Iris, who was standing at the fireplace talking to Janet's parents and some others. She could have been photographed for one of those "social" magazines in which gracious ladies stand before fireplaces or under the curve of a stairway. How Iris would have been amused at that!

"What are you laughing at now?" Theo inquired.

"I was thinking about that woman who asked you one time why Iris didn't have her nose fixed, since you were 'in the business.' "

"I wouldn't have done it even if Iris had wanted it."

Yes, Ruth had been right, all those years ago. Now in middle age an authentic beauty *had* come upon Iris. It was at this moment almost astonishing and she understood that Theo was seeing it, too. Iris' dark hair, which had gone only a little gray, was parted in the center. She had worn it that way for so long that Anna couldn't remember when it had been different. . . . Her face was all pure curves: the high strong arch of the nose, the eyebrows, the fine mouth. When you looked away you wanted to look back again at her face.

Now people were crowding in from the garden, thrusting out hands to shake and cheeks to kiss, giving greetings and compliments.

Someone, some friend of Theo's?—(Too old.) Friend of Joseph's? (Too young. My memory certainly isn't what it used to be.)—paused for conversation.

"What a marvelous house! And the grounds! One doesn't expect to see grounds like these so near New York these days."

"Ah, but it's changed! When we first moved here, it was so quiet you could sit outside at night and all you'd hear was katydids. Now you hear the traffic on the highway."

The man sighed. "I know. They're building a development in what used to be an apple orchard across the road from me. It's very sad," he said, and moved on.

For a moment she was left alone. When I die, she thought, they'll sell this property. No one wants these big houses anymore. They'll tear it down and build garden apartments or else turn it into some sort of business. There's an insurance company at the corner already.

It had been tactfully suggested that perhaps Anna might want to sell the house and take an apartment. It was the suggestion she had herself urged upon Joseph when he had the first heart attack. He had resisted as strongly as she did in her turn. No, the house was home; she was able to afford it and she wanted to stay in it. She had planted trees: birches, locust and firethorn. There were all those books in the library, and the things in Joseph's round room that mustn't be disturbed, his collection of pipes that would go to the grandsons. And what would she do with Albert? Such a big dog, in an apartment! No, it was unthinkable.

Iris was still talking at the far end of the room. She must have been saying something amusing, because people were laughing. Then she laughed too, clapping her palms together in a pretty gesture. How far she had come! Truly, truly, prayers are answered, Anna thought. Well, sometimes they are, at any rate.

But to think that Iris would be the one to manage things! No one else in the family had any idea of business. Dear Theo never knew whether he had a nickel or a dollar in his pocket. So it was Iris who had learned how to deal with property and investments for the estate. No doubt she would know what to do with this old house when the time came.

I hope it won't be torn down, Anna thought. Perhaps there will be someone who can use it. And there will be a child's swing under the ash tree again. They'll keep the feeders filled for the winter birds.

"Nana," Laura said, "have you met Robby's aunt? This is Aunt Margaret, his favorite. He talks about her so much, and I talk about you, so it's only right for you to meet and know each other."

"Margaret Taylor." A stout, friendly woman, with the dignity that large women can have, took Anna's hand. "Your little bride is darling. We all love her already."

"I'm glad. Sending them so far away when they get married, one can only hope they'll be loved."

"They're going to New Mexico, I understand. They'll adore it. The most marvelous colors, and all that space."

"I've heard. I've never been farther west than Pennsylvania." Strange. In all these years. And we could have afforded it. Why didn't we?

"You grew up in New York, Mrs. Friedman?"

"I came to this country when I was seventeen and I've lived in New York or near it ever since."

"Such an exciting city! I wish we could manage to come more often, but somehow one never finds the time. When I was young I used to visit; my older brother, fifteen years older than I, had a friend from Yale who was just wonderful to us all. For years, at Christmas, when we'd come for a week of shopping and opera, they'd insist that Mother and my sister and I stay at their house. Paul Werner, his name was, and they lived in the most sumptuous apartment on Fifth Avenue, near the museum. I've never seen such a place. Perhaps you knew the family?"

"I know who you mean," Anna said, and the woman sped on. "They had quite marvelous art. I was an art major at college and I was so impressed! It was all Hudson River School; it went out of favor for a while, but I needn't tell you how it's prized today. He had so much charm, Paul Werner. Young as I was, I sensed it. Too much charm for the woman he married. She was a fine person, but awfully dull, I thought."

"You haven't seen him since she died?"

"Oh, no, not since I was in my twenties. But my sister's kept in touch; she saw him just a couple of years ago, in Italy. He had a villa on Lake Maggiore, you know, an old house filled with Renaissance furniture and modern art. That's the style these days, to mix incongruous things, isn't it? Oh, Donald, come meet Laura's grandmother; this is my husband."

"And whom are you ladies talking about? Paul Werner? I couldn't help but overhear."

"I was telling Mrs. Friedman about him. I don't know how the subject came up; we just drifted into it."

"My wife never got over him. Her closest brush with royalty."

"Oh, Donald, you're the worst tease! You know you were just as impressed as I was! One felt so *alive* with Paul, and he did have a touch of the regal, in a very nice way."

She turned to Anna. "But you said you knew him?"

"I was a maid in his parents' house," Anna said. *Now, that's a shocker, isn't it?*

They did look, for an instant, shocked; but they pulled their faces together and said pleasantly, almost simultaneously, "Well, it's a real American success story, isn't it, your life?"

"I guess you might call it that," Anna replied.

Her reaction was a slight one, not piercing-sharp as she might once have expected it to be, but a small painful twinge, and quite controlled.

Yet, without being noticed, she went upstairs to her room. The heavy earrings had begun to hurt. Iris had made her get all her jewelry out of the vault for the wedding. It was proper to be adorned for the wedding of one's granddaughter, and yet in a way it was silly to dress up such old hands and such a wrinkled neck. Sighing, she removed the earrings, easing the pressure, and leaned forward to look at herself in the mirror.

Funny, when you get old your nose droops. My nose was never this large. Theo says it has something to do with cartilage. But I don't look too awful. I've held up well enough. I look calm. I always did. Faces deceive. Even after that conversation just now, I still manage to look calm. Only my head aches. She put her hands to her temples; there was a stronger beat there than usual.

The great diamond, Joseph's marvelous ring, lay like an oval teardrop on her finger. It had the pink fire of sunlight and rainbows. Strange to think that it had been torn out of the deepest, darkest earth with all that light in it. When I'm put into the earth it will go on living in the light, its pink fire blazing on some other, living hand: whose? Not Iris', nor Laura's . . . neither of them would wear a thing like this or want it any more than I did. Joseph's marvelous ring.

She got up slowly and went back downstairs. People were moving through the lovely rooms in their bright dresses and white summer suits. It was the last time the house would glow like this. Philip was sixteen. She could give a wedding party for him too, but it would be amazing if she were still here when he was old enough to be married. And as for Steve, who knew?

From where Anna stood at the foot of the stairs she could see directly into the living room where her portrait hung. So young in the pink dress, with that faint look of surprise which she was certain she saw and which no one else had ever admitted to seeing! Wouldn't she really have been surprised if she could have foreseen the things that would happen! Yet how could she have foreseen what it was like to be seventy-eight years old? One never imagines oneself that old.

"Nana!" Jimmy cried. "Janet and I have been looking for you. Everyone's going in to eat."

"I've been admiring the house," Janet said. "Every time I come here I see more gorgeous things, your china, and all the silver— Well, someday."

"Someday what?" Jimmy asked.

"Someday we'll have it, too. With both of us working we'll be able to have a nice home," she said confidently, and quickly added, "I don't mean like this, of course, but nice."

Joseph would have approved of this girl. The work ethic, he always said. You worked and you were rewarded. A bright, practical girl, not lazy, not ashamed to say what she wanted. Two more years and she'd be a doctor. All that and a brand-new baby asleep upstairs. *She* would love the diamond! She would wear it with joy. So she's the one who shall have it. Time to divest yourself, the lawyers said tactfully, which was a way of saying that you can't last much longer and you ought to be thinking about inheritance taxes.

"I'm going to leave you all the silver," Anna said suddenly.

Janet flushed. "Nana! I didn't mean—"

"Don't be silly, I know you didn't mean anything. But things like these should be enjoyed. Iris calls them dust collectors and Laura's going to be digging on a Navajo reservation, so she won't want them. That's why I want you to have them."

"You'd better keep some for Laura just in case," Janet said, adding mischievously, "they may get tired of archeology in a trailer and decide they really do want some of the things they've been scoffing at."

Anna smiled. "You may be right. Anyway, I'll start making my list tomorrow."

"What morbid talk at a wedding!" Jimmy protested.

"Not morbid at all. Just practical."

Jimmy took her arm. "Well, practical or not, we're going in where the food is."

At once her obligation as a hostess came to Anna's mind: the special menu for the Mexican twins, who were as strict in observance of the dietary laws as any of their ancestors had been. She summoned Celeste to check. The young men had been seated with Anna, all other guests being free to sit where they chose, which was yet another of Robby's and Laura's innovations.

It pleased her to see that so many of the young, including the bride and groom, had already settled themselves at her table. All these beautiful young people in their astonishing variety! Robby, pink-cheeked, frank and not too unlike Jimmy. Raimundo and Rainaldo, looking positively Spanish, and just three generations out of the Polish village; how to explain that? The reserve, that was it; that Latin formality which made them seem so much older than these American boys, although they were the same age.

What irony! Vain, good-hearted, ambitious, clever Eli; all his line had been eradicated, while Dan the schlemiel, the humble, lived on in these handsome boys and many more. Landed in Mexico with nothing, in an unknown country which these his descendants take for granted, no doubt, as though it had always been theirs. And those who come from me take this America for granted, too, instead of seeing the miracle it is. My mind wanders. Strange, timeless people, I think, so contradictory, so tenacious.

Fragments of conversation float like balloons above the table. Young people are so earnest these days. In my time you danced at a wedding. How they love to talk! Well, fashions change, round and round. That much I can see from my vantage point; it's one of the rewards, the very few rewards, of being old. Everything passes. The revolution of only a few years ago, the dirt, the fury, even the beards all gone or going. So something else will take its place to worry and confuse us!

Jimmy was saying, explaining to one of Robby's friends, "Janet and I don't observe all that." (They are talking about Rainaldo and Raimundo.) "But we do think the religious tradition should be selectively maintained. One doesn't step out and away from such a long, gallant history. Besides, it's important for children to have a sense of identity."

High talk, fine talk. They have to analyze everything, give reasons for everything. It's the disease of the times. But never mind their reasons, as long as some of them stay with the tradition.

Robby said, "I've been learning a lot from Laura about the immigrant generation. It's fascinating to think that when they came here at the start of this century they were really skipping two or three hundred years in one stop. Out of the late middle ages, actually. Some hadn't even seen a railroad!"

Quite true. I was ten years old before I saw one, nice boy. Nice boy with bright green eyes, so serious and interested in everything! Only I do hope you decide to buy a suit sometime. You can't apply for a job wearing slacks and a shirt. Or maybe you can these days?

A very pretty girl spoke from the far end of the table. "There'll have to be changes. We can't just go on exploiting people and destroying the environment. It's simply too late for 'every man for himself.' Otherwise there'll never be any peace on earth."

As if there ever could be, anyway! But no, I shouldn't say that. What do I know of the future? One has to try. Maybe the vision and energy of these young will do what we didn't do, didn't even try to do or concern ourselves with. For us it was enough to take care of ourselves!

So I don't know. It's all for them to solve if they can.

Rainaldo—it must be he, because he spoke a little English—caught Anna's eye. How rude of her. She'd been neglecting them. She smiled. He smiled back and, by way of making conversation, pointed to the candlesticks.

"Very beautiful silver, Aunt. Very old. Two hundred years, I think."

"You're right. They belonged to my great-grandmother. That's your—let's see, great, great, how many greats, four, no, five?"

Rainaldo threw up his hands. "Fantastic! It does something—" he pointed to his heart—"to think about it."

"Yes," Anna said, "it does."

"In Mexico we also have very fine silver. I am used to see it. That picture—portrait, painting? That is Uncle Joseph, I think? My grandfather told me about him."

The portrait hung behind her. From his end of the table Joseph had always faced himself. She turned.

"Yes, it's a good likeness. I mean, he really did look like that."

Not when he was young. In youth he had had an anxious look. But here in this portrait he was confident, a little stern perhaps. A patriarch presiding at the family table.

"Laura talks about him so much," Robby said. "I wish I could have known him."

"He was a simple man," Anna explained, as if she had been asked to sum him up. "All he wanted, really, was to keep the family together. I think that everything else was just a means to that end."

There was a little flurry of voices and laughter. A group stood up and came over to Anna's table. Theo called out. "I want to ask everyone to drink to my mother-in-law. May she live a hundred and twenty years!" The glasses touched and he added, "It isn't every man who can wish his mother-in-law long life and mean it." His eyes met Anna's and stayed in a long look.

"And I would like to drink to the memory of Papa," Iris said softly. "On a day like this especially we remember him."

It was inevitable, at any and every gathering, that the resemblance game be played.

"Do you look like him, Iris?" Doris Berg inquired. "Standing there beneath his picture it seems to me perhaps you do look a little like your father."

Iris asked, "Do you think I do, Mama?"

She wants to be told she looks like him. "I'm never very good at seeing resemblances. I always think everyone looks like himself."

Doris Berg persisted. "Oh, I don't think so! Some people are carbon copies of each other. Jimmy looks just like Theo, and Philip looks like Iris. Iris does have a high forehead, something like her father's, but still," doubtfully, head on one side, "still it's hard to say . . . maybe you don't look like him. You *are* a mystery, Iris."

And Mary Malone said, "But our bride is her grandmother all over again! The red hair and the eyes, you couldn't mistake those! What curious, wide eyes you had, Anna! I remember when I first met you, you looked as if you couldn't see or know enough, as if you were just in love with the world."

It was over. The bride and groom had driven away on a camping trip. Celeste had appeared at the front door with boxes of rice. That was another tradition which Laura and Robby had wanted to dispense with, but Celeste had had other ideas and they had run down the driveway to their car through a rain of rice. Theo and Iris stood next to Anna until the car was out of sight. Their hands were joined.

Anna touched Theo's arm. "She isn't gone, Theo. You haven't lost her."

"How do you know?"

"Because. They go their separate ways, but there's a chain that holds them to you all the same." She almost, but not quite, believed it herself.

When the guests and the caterers were gone and only the family was left, Anna went upstairs.

"I've got to get this rig off," she complained.

"I'll help you," Iris offered. "It was a lovely wedding after all, wasn't it? I thought it was going to be so hippie. . . . Oh, that darn dog again!" For Albert had pushed the door open and greeted Anna with wet nose and dripping whiskers.

"Look at your dress!"

"It can be cleaned, I don't mind. I'm worried about Albert. He's apt to outlive me, and you don't like dogs."

"Mother, you're so morbid!"

It was the second time that day that she'd been told that, and she didn't feel morbid at all. Didn't people ever want to face facts?

"Still, I do believe Laura and Robby would take him. They'll have plenty of space. . . . I must write and ask them."

"Do please allow them to have their honeymoon first before you start talking to them about death. Let me put your corsage in water."

Hideous things, orchids. I always liked cheerful flowers, like dahlias and asters, almost anything but orchids. Joseph always bought them for occasions; he seemed so pleased when he gave them to me. I never told him they remind me of snakes.

"Here, give me the necklace. I'll just put it in this box overnight and take it to the vault for you in the morning. What's this?"

"That's not my jewelry box." Anna was embarrassed. It was a fancy tin box that once, long ago, had held candy. In it she had hidden the last cutting of her own long red hair.

Iris lifted it out, a shining spiral that fell almost to her knees. "Mama, what hair! It's beautiful! I'd forgotten how beautiful . . ."

"A long time ago."

"It doesn't seem so long. I remember at my wedding, you wore a pink dress. You used to wear a lot of pink, so clever with your hair. You were the most striking woman there. Nobody looked at me; they all looked at you."

"Iris, I hate to tell you, but you do say the most idiotic things. You were a lovely bride, as lovely as any," Anna argued firmly.

Iris' eyes filled. My daughter looks at me and I can tell what she is thinking as clearly as though the bones of her forehead were transparent. She is remembering childhood and mothering and she's guilty because she always loved Joseph more than she loved me. I put out my hand; she lays hers in it, but she doesn't feel comfortable with my touch. She never has, though I don't know why. But it's something she can't help, any more than she can help loving Theo.

Janet knocked on the open door. "May I come in? I thought I'd bring the baby to visit."

She laid the baby in Anna's lap. Anna put her finger out and the tiny hand wound around it. The baby's eyelids were shut like two fragile shells. Oh, to be young again, to produce a thing like this!

She felt a sudden panic. Something had gone absolutely blank in her head. She couldn't remember: was it a boy or a girl, this child of Jimmy's? I can't remember, she thought in horror . . . I can't shame myself by asking. They'll think I'm senile and I'm not that at all, not yet, although God knows and I know that my arteries are hardening. A pity, because otherwise I can see things in a clearer light than ever.

"The baby's not too thin?" She drew the blanket slyly away. A pink sweater. Ah, a girl. Of course. My great-granddaughter.

"The doctors don't want them to be fat, Mama. You know that."

Rebecca, that was the name. Rebecca Ruth, after Janet's two grandmothers. Too bad Ruth couldn't have lived to see her. Isn't it funny that we should be great-grandmothers to the same child? A good name. Thank heavens, they hadn't given her one of those phony names that people used these days, like Judy with an "i" on the end or Gloria with a "y" stuck in it for no good reason. Rebecca Ruth, you've just arrived and I'm about to leave. We'll overlap by a few years at most. I'd like to live till you're old enough to keep some memory of me. What vanity!

But I'm the link, the only one in this house tonight who ties them all together, Rainaldo and Raimundo, Philip and Steve. . . . I hold up my hand. Is it true that some of the cells in me are the same as in this baby? I wish I knew more about biology. I wish I knew more about everything. Think of the things Rebecca Ruth will see and know! Things I can't even conceive of. And my mother stood at the door of our house, talking of a marvelous time when every woman might learn to read.

But one thing was true then that's still true now. I told Theo there's a tie that holds us all together, and I said it to comfort him, but I meant it. It's there, or nothing has any value at all. And I know *that's* not true. It's the lifeline of the family, and if we can hold to it then we can make good children and the world will be better. Maybe that's putting it all too simply in these tangled times, but then, the truest things are always simple, aren't they?

Oh, I'd like to stay a little longer to see what Philip does with his talent, to watch over Iris (though I'm certain she doesn't need it anymore). How can I die and leave them all? I worry so! You silly fool, you think they can't manage without you? Anna, the indispensable!

The baby stirred and puckered her peach face. "I'll take her," Janet said, "it's feeding time again."

Anna thought of something. "I should like to have my picture taken with her. It will be a fine thing for her to have. Not many people can know what their great-grandmothers looked like. Why, I've been curious all my life about the people who came before me! And there was never any way to find out. Certainly no pictures."

"We'll have a photographer come in the morning," Iris declared. "We'll take the boys from Mexico—I never remember those names! We'll take the whole family. Here's Philip. You played wonderfully, darling."

"Nana," Philip said, "I've come with the tape recorder. I hope you haven't forgotten. Nana and I," he explained to Janet, "are doing the story of her life for posterity. It was my idea. Because of what Nana always says about families and people knowing their ancestors. All that stuff."

Anna clasped her hands. "I don't know what to say! It's not as if I'd had a heroic life or anything."

"Nana! You're not backing out?"

She was suddenly quite, quite tired. But he looked so disappointed! He has my father's pale eyes, set far apart, and he moves like him, clumsily. How can he understand what life was like for his great-grandfather, maker of boots and harness? For him it's a story, picturesque and touching. For him my father is truly dead, as we all are when the last person who knew our faces and heard our voices is gone. The most we do is to save a little part of the life that was.

"No," she said, "I'm not backing out."

"Great!" He straightened up from the machine. "Just sit back comfortably, Nana, and begin at the beginning."

The beginning? Sometimes it was so cloudy and far away that she thought it had never been like that at all. Then again, it was like the morning of today, so that you could reach out and touch it, could feel it and smell the air. Soft, foggy, fragrant air of Europe. Keen American air. Beautiful America, more wonderful, painful, generous, difficult and kind than she could have dreamed when she had been a child and longed so much to see it.

"Just say whatever comes into your head, as far back as you can remember. It doesn't matter what. Only don't leave anything out."

She wanted to laugh, but the boy-face was so earnest, so eager.

"Relax, Nana. I'll tell you when I'm about to start."

She closed her eyes. The lamp light shone through her lids, making a tracery of red. Veins, like a design in lace. Yes, think. All a brilliant muddle, a heap of flowers, or colored paper blown in the wind. Eric, coming bravely toward them over the grass. Maury in the Yale processional and Maury on the kitchen floor, eating an apple. Iris, frail child, holding Joseph's hand. Birdsong over Eric's grave. And Joseph's whisper: *How lovely you are.*

A jumble and a flickering, far, far back. Do I really remember that my mother wore a dark blue shawl with a small white pattern? Can it be possible that I remember her voice at prayer, that it was low for a woman? *Blessed be Thou O Lord, King of the universe,* she said, in that childhood room for whose warmth and safety we search all the rest of our lives and never find again.

"Are you ready, Nana? I'm starting the tape."

"There was a town. Yes, that's a good beginning." The words were rapid and clear. "It was on the other side of the world and not much of a town, just one wide, muddy street running to the river. It may be there still, for all I know, although my people are long gone. There was a board fence around my father's house, and in the kitchen a black iron stove. There were red flowers on the wallpaper, and my mother sang."

RANDOM WINDS

To my children,
and to the memory of my parents

"For where there is love of man,
there is love of the art."

DAY OF WRATH

On Adirondack lakes ice boomed and cracked. Grainy snow, melting at last, slid into the ditches along mired roads. Dr. Enoch Farrell drew his watch out of his vest pocket: he had made good time. Once past the Atkins's farm the road flattened and there were only three easy, level miles to home. He drew the buggy's curtains tighter against the sweeping rain that threatened his fine, polished bag. The best black calf it was, with brass fittings, the parting gift, along with a well-bound Gray's *Anatomy,* of Dr. Hugh MacDonald, who had been his preceptor in Edinburgh. He never went anywhere without the *Anatomy,* although surely he must have memorized it by now! He never went out without his current reading either, for this hour trotting home at the end of the day was his best, perhaps his only, truly private time. And rummaging, he searched for *Bleak House.* To think that Dickens was dead these thirty years or more and now, in this first year of a new century, his work was as alive as if it had been written yesterday!

Things were heaped in the bag. Jean was always straightening it, but it never stayed that way. Opium, laudanum, stethoscope, Hop Bitters—fine stuff, good for any dozen ailments—no Dickens. He must have left it home. Damn, he was always forgetting things! If it weren't for Jean . . . . Well-matched they were: she so practical and precise, while he—could he dare think of himself as a leaven, bringing brightness and humor to the household?

So his thoughts ran.

Left now, and across the wooden bridge where the river, which had been iced over only last week, was running fast. The little mare began to speed, and there was home with its twin chimneys, front porch and two square office-rooms. Very nice! Nicer still when the mortgage should be paid off, whenever that might be! It didn't look imminent. A man could count himself lucky to keep abreast of the daily expenses: four children with another on the way.

Enoch climbed down in the barn, unhitched Dora and led her to the stall. A couple of hens, disturbed in their straw, rose squawking. The barn cat rubbed against his ankles while he covered the mare with a dry blanket. It gave a man a good feeling that even these poor, dependent creatures were safe and warm under his roof. And speaking of roofs, he ought to get that leak mended before it got much worse.

The children were halfway through supper. Alice, the baby, clattered on the high chair tray when she saw him.

"I thought you'd be even later in this weather," Jean said. "Heavens, your cap's wet through! Your knickers are soaked! Sit down, while I get the stew. I've kept it hot and there are biscuits, too."

"Ah, those'll hit the spot on a night like this."

He washed his hands at the sink. A fine convenience it was, to have water running in the kitchen. Easy on the woman of the house and sanitary besides. He took his place at the head of the table, said grace and picked up his fork.

Jean's hands rested on the apron beneath which lay her growing baby, in its seventh month. Her pink, anxious face was flushed from the kitchen's heat. Four child-faces turned toward Enoch, mixed of his flesh and hers: her bright almond eyes in Enoch Junior and the baby, Alice; his temper and his laughter in May; her quickness, her reserve in Susan.

"Well, anything new happen around here today?" he inquired.

"Nothing much. Oh yes, Mrs. Baines came. She always manages to come when you're out."

"What's the trouble?"

"Walter again. Sounds like the quinsy sore throat, the way he always gets."

"I suppose I'd better hitch up and go back over there."

"Indeed you'll not, after the day you've had, and in this rain! Besides, they never think to pay you. It's always 'next time, Doc.' "

Enoch sighed. "I know. But he tries, Jean. The man works awfully hard."

"So do you." She rose to put more stew on his plate and poured coffee. "I made brown Betty for dessert." Then she added mischievously, "Anyway, I told her what to do for the throat."

"You did what?"

"I told her what to do. I've heard you tell it often enough to know it by heart, haven't I? Red flannel around the throat, goose grease on the chest, soak the feet in a tub of hot water, powdered mustard and camphor ice to keep the fever from cracking the lips. Right?"

"Dad! Dad! I did elevens and twelves in the multiplication tables today and I—"

"Enoch Junior," Jean rebuked him, "you're interrupting. And anyway, this is grown-ups' time. You're not supposed to talk at the table."

"Let him talk, Jean. What'd you want to tell me, son?"

"I wanted you to hear my multiplication."

"Tell you what. You go start your homework on the parlor table, and soon's I finish my supper, I'll join you. May and Susan, you're excused, too."

The room grew quiet. Alice sucked on her bottle and Jean dished out the pudding. A coal fell softly in the stove.

"Had a nasty business today with Hettie Simpson," Enoch remarked. "Did I tell you this would have been her eleventh? Just as well she miscarried, I suppose. Except she might have bled to death if I'd been much later getting there. I packed the uterus, but I'll need to go back early in the morning. It worries me, she looked so white."

"She can't be more than thirty, can she?"

"Thirty-two, and looks nearer fifty."

If she lives this time, he thought grimly, it'll only happen again, unless the consumption gets her first. And Jim Simpson? Why, he'll cry a bit and have another wife in a couple of months, some strapping girl of seventeen who'll start a family for him all over again. Yet you couldn't blame a man. Who would do the work and look after the children if he didn't marry in a hurry?

"You look so tired," Jean said softly.

"I didn't know how much till I sat down, I guess."

She peered through the window into the dismal murk, out of which the wet tin roof of the shed glistened like dull silver. "This weather's enough to exhaust a person. Seems as if spring'll never come and it'll never stop raining."

When they went to bed the rain was still beating mournfully, persistently, upon the roof. For a long time Enoch lay awake, listening to the ominous beat.

In the morning they were astonished that the rain had not slackened. All through that second day it never varied in its determined steady fall, neither speeding up nor slowing down, just marching evenly, like soldiers' stern and solemn feet.

And the third day.

Then came the north wind. It struck with fury and the night was loud with complaint. Water poured like a river through the gutters; the house shuddered. The rain swayed as the wind gusted and died, gusted and died. The roof was lifted from the toolshed, the torn wood screeching as it parted. From the tight house where his children were asleep, Enoch peered into the yard and saw that the chicken coop was holding. But he went back to bed with uneasy thoughts of planets rending, flung away from the sun.

Just after midnight, there was an almost imperceptible slowing of the rain. Alert ears could isolate the sound of individual drops, with a fraction of a pause between them: cessation, then a violent spurt, and another cessation. Finally came a startling stillness in which one heard, regular as a metronome, great drops plopping from the eaves and the shaken trees.

At last in the morning the sun came out with a burst of spangled light. Water stood in a pond two inches deep in the yard. Under the porch roof, soaked sparrows clustered, chirping through the daily family prayers. Jean had lit the Franklin stove, but the parlor was cold and Enoch hurried the prayers.

"The sun will soon draw all this water up," he observed, closing the great Bible with a bang. The children wanted to know whether there would be school that day.

"Of course there will, but the road will be a mess. You'll need your high galoshes," Jean told them.

"I'll try to get back early enough to do something about the toolshed roof," Enoch said. "See if you can dry off the tools before they rust, will you?"

Jean packed the lunch boxes and tied May's scarf, fastening it down with a large safety pin on the chest. May, like her father, always lost things.

"Now, Enoch Junior, mind you don't run on ahead. It's slippery wet. I want you to help your sisters through the muddy spots so they don't fall and dirty themselves."

"Aw," said Enoch, "why do I always have to?"

"Because you're a big eight-year-old boy, and your sisters are small."

The parents watched their three march down the road, the boy obediently between his sisters. There marched the future! Yes, and the sum of the parents' pasts; such love, such hope encompassed in those chattering three, so carelessly kicking pebbles on their way to school! They watched until the children were out of sight, then smiled at each other. Jean went back into the kitchen and sat down heavily in the Boston rocker by the window to enjoy a second cup of coffee. Enoch went to the barn and hitched the horse. The storms had set him three days behind with his house calls and he would have to cover a lot of ground.

At noon, just as the children were having lunch, it began to rain again. But it was a very light rain this time. No need to send them home early, the young teacher thought as she glanced out of the window, especially since they had already missed a couple of days that week. The younger children played indoors during the lunch recess, while some of the older boys, wearing rubber mackintoshes, went outside. In any case, by two o'clock, shortly before school was dismissed for the day, the drizzle had stopped.

And at two o'clock, a mile and a half upstream, in one incredible, unexpected instant, an old earthen dam collapsed. Rumbling and crumbling, with thunderous roar and colossal surge, it burst, it fell apart. A blinding spray rose into the air, tumbled, splashed and crashed, leaving a dazzle of fine mist upon the ruins. The lake behind the dam, swollen by tons of melted ice, poured into the river. And the river slid over its banks. It plunged through the narrow valley. It gathered strength and speed. Like a merciless, violent army come to pillage, it advanced.

At two-fifteen the children were dismissed from school to walk home. A quarter of a mile behind them the mighty wall of water rushed, flooding the whole valley now, flooding the houses up to the second story, wrecking and smashing. It gained on the little flock of children as they meandered and as the seconds passed. They heard its distant rumble before they saw it. Towering doom rose high at their backs. They began to run. Horrified and screaming, they scrambled and raced. But the water raced faster.

Late in the afternoon Enoch came down from the hills and beheld catastrophe. He pulled on the reins and stared aghast. Water lay where farms and roads had been that morning. Stagnant at the edges, it was torrential in the middle, speeding in a dirty brown froth.

My God, the schoolhouse! That was the schoolhouse roof, the only red roof in the neighborhood! A dreadful faintness almost toppled him. Then panic came. He thought he heard himself screaming at the mare. He whipped her, which he had never done before, and the mare sped.

Here the road lay on an elevated ridge from where he could look down on the water, some twenty feet below. Treetops poked up from the swirling current, strewn with terrible debris: here a dead cow, its stiff legs spread as if beseeching the sky; there, drowned chickens in a coop; an ice-chest; a parlor table with a square marble top. On a flimsy branch a terrified cat clung, its mouth strained open in a wail too far away to be audible.

Enoch trembled and went cold.

His own house lay beyond the place where the river curved sharply to the east, and he saw as he approached that the water had risen over the front steps. The stable, lying on lower ground, was covered to the eaves. One of the three strong, young maples that fronted the road had been ripped up. Flung into standing water in the yard, its fibered roots protruded like torn ligaments.

He jumped down, waded thigh deep to the porch, and banged the front door open.

"Jean! Jean!"

Water had seeped into the parlor, soaking the Brussels carpet, trailing long feelers down the hall toward the kitchen. Over everything lay the foul stench of wet wool.

"Jean! Jean!"

He ran upstairs, bounding two steps at a time.

"Jean, for God's sake, answer me! Where are you? Jean?"

He went back to the porch and stood in his waterlogged boots looking wildly around, up at the sky and down. Under his tongue there was a burning and the salt taste of blood. It was so quiet! The yard was always noisy. The first things you heard were the cackle of chickens and the dog's bark. Then he realized that the chickens had been drowned and the doghouse was underwater.

He climbed back into the buggy, wrenching the mare's head roughly, lashing her toward the road leading to the village center, which lay beyond the curve of the river and the flooding.

The crazed man and the terrified horse tore down the road. So quiet, he thought again. Eerie quiet. Even the birds were still. April, and no birds.

At the church there was a crowd of buggies and wagons and people on foot. He pulled into the yard.

"Where—Do you know where—" he began, addressing a man whose face he knew. But the man looked blank and hurried past.

People filled the narrow stairway to the basement, going down and struggling back. A fainting woman was being carried up. All about was a murmur of sound, soft crying and low talking.

Enoch pushed his way down. The taste of blood under his tongue was still salty sharp. He put his finger there and drew it out to look at it.

Against the back wall on the floor, the bodies lay in a long double row covered with sheets and blankets. A young man knelt on the floor next to a body from which the sheet had been drawn away. Enoch recognized the dead face. Madeline, he though, Madeline Drury; he felt nothing.

Beginning at the left, he lifted the cover from the faces. Nettie Rogers. The old woman who lived with her—he'd forgotten her name. Jim Fox's boy Tom, the one who had had infantile paralysis last summer. He moved faster, hurrying down the row.

"Doc! No!" Someone caught his sleeve, pulling hard at him. "Doc! No! Sit down! Reverend Dexter's been looking for you. He wants—"

"Damn you, leave me!" Enoch cried, wrenching his arm free. And then—

Oh God! Almighty God! His children! Enoch, Susan and May lay side by side in a row. Like dolls they lay, stiff as Christmas dolls, May in the pink scarf, the cotton-candy pink that Jean had knitted, still wound about her chest and secured with a safety pin.

My girls. My little boy. He heard a voice, a mad voice, his own, as if from far away, from another country. He sank to the floor, rocking on his knees.

"Oh my God, my girls, my little boy!"

Strong arms came at last and drew him away.

THEY HAD TAKEN Jean and Alice to a house near the church. Reverend Dexter led Enoch there.

"Have they told you about Jean?" he asked.

"What?"

"Jean," the parson said gently. "The shock, you know. But the women knew what to do. They took care of her."

"The shock?" Of course. Jean was in her seventh month. He hadn't thought— But he must think. She would need him. And he quickened his steps.

In the kitchen of a strange house Alice was sitting in a high chair while a stout woman spooned cereal into her mouth. She seemed to spend her life in a high chair, being fed.

"She's in there, sleeping," the stout woman said, nodding to Enoch.

He knew the woman, as he knew everyone in the village, but again he couldn't think of the name. He walked to the bedroom door, then turned back, hesitating.

"Did she—did she see them?" he asked.

"Not exactly," the woman said. "Reverend here, he wouldn't let her see."

"I'm grateful to you for that, Reverend," Enoch told him.

He stood looking at his wife. Her face lay in the crook of her arm. Her dark hair was loosened. He drew the blanket up softly over her shoulder. Currents of rational thought, which in this hour past had been stopped, began to flow again. So tender, a human body, a human life! Nothing more to it than a few pounds of fragile bone and soft tissue. Yes, and years of nurturing and thousands of hours of loving care. Wiped out, gone as if they had never been, like last year's leaves! And the marvelous years of youth, the dignity of adulthood and learning—all these forfeited, all these now not to be— Oh, my children! A cry caught in his throat.

"Doc?"

The man of the house—Fairbanks, yes, yes of course, that was the name— came to the door.

"Doc, have you got a minute? Me and my brother Harry was over to your place already. You know your pantry ell? Well, the roof is stove in where the maple fell on it. But we was thinking, if you can buy the material, Harry and me'll fix it. Harry owes you a bill, anyway. Did you know the branch breached at Lindsey Run? It flooded out for six miles downstream."

"Thank you," Enoch said.

"Think nothing of it, Doc. We all want to do what we can for you. Say, it's a good thing you had your mare with you. The stable almost got drownded."

A mare. When my children— Get out! He wanted to cry. Kind fool, get out and leave us!

"I'll go ask my wife to make some tea when your missus wakes up," Fairbanks said.

Jean opened her eyes. "I'm not asleep," she whispered.

Enoch knelt on the floor, laying his face against hers, his cold, wet cheek upon her wet cheek, and stayed there like that.

"God's will," she whispered after a long time. "He wanted them home with Him."

God's will that their babies should drown? Son of a minister he was, reared on the Bible, but he couldn't believe that. God the Creator, yes! And God the giver of righteous laws; but God who decrees the individual fate of every living creature on the planet and orders the death of a child? That was hogwash. Hogwash! Yet it gave her comfort.

"Yes," he murmured, "yes," and with his free hand smoothed her hair.

"I love you," she said.

I love you, she says, out of her blood and grief. She reached up her arms to draw him near, but they fell back weakly. He understood that she wanted him to kiss her, and he bent down and pressed her lips.

Then he said, "Jean, Jean, my girl, we'll start again. We'll have to love each other so— And I'll take care of you and Alice and me. We're all that's left."

"You're not forgetting him, the new one?"

"Him?"

"The baby, the boy. You haven't seen him?"

"But I thought—"

Mrs. Fairbanks, coming with the tea, overheard.

"You thought it was a stillbirth? No, no, Doc. Look here."

She raised the window shade. A sad lavender light slid into the room from the quiet evening sky. On a table near the window lay a box, and in it one of the smallest babies Enoch had ever seen. Scarcely larger than a raw, young rabbit, he thought.

"I bought a new pair of arctics on sale last week. Luckily, I still had the box," Mrs. Fairbanks said.

And Jean called out, "I want his name to be Martin!"

"Not Thomas, after your father?"

"That'll be his middle name. I want him to be called Martin."

"Well, all right." He looked at the child. Four pounds, if that. Nearer three and a half, he'd guess.

"Poor Jean, poor lamb," Mrs. Fairbanks whispered. "Likely she'll be losing this one, too."

The baby fluttered. Its toy hands moved, and under the blanket its legs jerked weakly. Then it wailed, the doll's face crumpling and reddening, the eyes opening as if in protest or alarm.

Mrs. Fairbanks shook her head. "No," she repeated. "He can't live. That's sure."

Something welled up in Enoch, and he shook a furious fist at the universe.

"No!" he cried fiercely. "No! Look at those eyes! Look at the life in those eyes! He will live, and he'll be strong, too. So help me God, he will."

BOOK ONE

THE ASCENT

❈{ 1 }❈

$\mathbf{A}$t the top of the long rise, Pa guided the horse toward the shade and drew in the reins. He pulled off his woolen jacket and laid it on the seat next to Martin.

"Professional dignity be darned!" he said. "The next patient will have to look at me in my shirt-sleeves whether he likes it or not."

The sun was ahead of the season, Ma had remarked that morning. Shadbush was still in bloom, and barn swallows were barely back from the south in time for Decoration Day.

"We'll just wait a minute here," Pa said, "and give the mare a rest."

The sweating animal stamped, slapping her tail. She had been making a strange sound for the last half hour, more like a plaint than a whinny.

"Something's bothering her, Martin."

"Black flies, do you think?"

"Don't see any, do you?" Pa climbed down to examine the mare. He pulled the harness aside and swore.

"Damn! Damn, look at this!"

The flesh along the horse's back was rubbed bloody raw in a line as long as three fingers put end to end.

"Laid open with a whip," Martin said.

"No doubt, and left to suppurate."

Martin nodded, feeling a twinge deep inside at sight of the wound, feeling also a certain pride at being the only boy in the fourth grade who knew the meaning of words like "suppurate" or who, for that matter, had a father like his.

"Poor little livery stable hack!" Pa cried. "At the mercy of every drunken lout who has the money for its hire. Reach in my bag for the salve, will you?"

The little mare quivered, her muscular back rippling and twitching.

"Now a wad of gauze, a thick one."

When he was finished, Pa got the water bucket. The mare drank gratefully. Martin gave her an apple. Then the two stood watching, pleased with themselves, while the mare chewed, salivating in a long, thick rope.

"She's a nice little thing," Pa said. "Wish I had the money to buy her and give her a decent home."

"But we've got Star, and she'll be ready to take out again as soon as her foal's a month old, won't she?"

"You're right. I daresay the man would want thirty dollars for her." Pa sighed. "Well, might as well start. One more call at Bechtold's and then home in time for the parade."

They moved on again. "Just look up there, Martin, at the side of that far mountain! You can gauge the height by the kind of trees you see. At the bottom there's oak, but oak won't grow more than twelve or thirteen hundred feet up. After that, you get balsam. Way up top there's spruce, all that bluish-green stuff." He leaned over Martin, pointing with outthrust finger. "Those are the oldest mountains in the United States, you know that? See how the tops are rounded? Worn away, that's why. And I'll tell you something else." He pointed to the left. "Down there, all that level land was once buried underwater. Can you believe that?"

"You mean the ocean was here once?"

"Yes sir, that's just what I do mean."

"When the ocean came, what happened to the people? Did they all drown?"

"No, no. That was millions of years before there were any people here."

At the foot of the hill, making a wide S-curve, lay the river.

"Pa, is that the river that overflowed and drowned Enoch Junior and Susan and May?" Martin knew quite well that it was, yet he always asked.

His father answered patiently, "That's it."

"Then I was born, and you had me instead of Enoch Junior as your boy. Do I look like him?" To that too, he knew the answer.

"No, he was small and sandy, like me. You're going to be tall, I think, and of course you're darker, like your mother's family."

"Do you like me more than you liked him?"

"The same. A man's children are the same to him, like his own ten fingers."

They drew into the Bechtolds' yard.

"Wait out here, Martin," Pa said.

"Can't I come in and watch?"

"I have to change a dressing. It might make you feel bad to see the cut."

"No it won't, Pa. Honestly, it won't."

What his father didn't know was that Martin had already seen much blood, having peered many a time through the shutters of a first floor window when he was supposed to be amusing himself outdoors. He had watched Pa set a compound fracture. (The little gray tip of bone pierces the flesh; the ether cone silences the screams.) He had seen the mangled stomach of a man gored by a bull. He had also seen his father wrestle down another man who had been beating his wife, and this last had impressed him most of all, although he had known it would be wise not to mention having seen it.

"All right then, come in."

A scythe propped carelessly in a dark corner of the barn had sliced Jake Bechtold's leg to the bone. Pa pulled the nightshirt up. Carefully he unwound the bandage, revealing a long, blood-encrusted gash, black and crisscrossed with stitches. He studied it for a moment.

"It's doing well. Better than I expected, to tell the truth. No infection, thanks be."

"We're grateful to you, Doc." Mrs. Bechtold wrung her clasped hands. "You always seen us through."

"Not every time, Mrs. Bechtold," Pa said seriously.

"Oh, that! That was in God's hands. There wasn't nothing you could've done more than you did do, Doc."

When they go back in the buggy, Pa sat in silence for a while. And then he broke out. "Oh, it's hard, it can be so hard! Sometimes such awful things happen, you can't put them out of your mind as long as you live!"

"What awful things, Pa?"

His father paused, as if the telling would be too difficult. Then he said, "It was in my second year here, almost into the third. I never go to Bechtold's without living it all over again the way I did just now."

"Was it anything you did?"

"No, it was something I didn't do. I wasn't able. Jake had the flu. While I was in the bedroom examining him, their little girl, just three years old she was, pulled a washtub full of boiling water off the stove while her mother's back was turned. We laid her on the kitchen table. I can still hear how she screamed. Once in my life I'd ordered a lobster. It was when I first came to this country and stayed those three days in New York City. A lobster is bright red when it's boiled, you know, and I remember I couldn't bring myself to eat it. The child looked like that. I thought, 'I don't know what to do. I'm supposed to know and I don't.' A lot of people came running in, wailing and crying. They poured cold water on the child. I didn't think to tell them not to, although really it wouldn't have made any difference what they did. The child was sure to die. Finally I found something to do. I got a scissors and began to cut her clothes off.

"Her body was one terrible blister. I couldn't even look at the face. When I pulled off the stockings, the skin came with them in long strips, like tissue paper. I took some salve out of my bag. It had gone liquid from the hot sun, so I dribbled it all over the child's body. Everybody was looking at me, just standing there watching, as if there were some magic in the jar of melted salve.

"The child lay moaning on the kitchen table all that afternoon. Someone asked, 'Why not put her in a bed?' 'No,' I said. 'Best not to lift her.' We put a little pillow under her head. Her pulse was so faint, I don't think she felt anything. At least I hope not. We waited. Nobody talked. I heard the cows lowing, wanting to be milked. I'll never forget the sounds they made, they and the child's moaning. All the neighbor women came. Shortly before dusk the little girl died. I pulled the cover over her face. I still hadn't looked at it."

Martin shivered. Pa's tales always made him feel he had been there when they happened. He had been in that kitchen with him and the dying girl; he had been on the deck with him when he sailed away from Ulster to America, out past the breakwater and the headlands, out to sea.

"I shouldn't be telling you this, should I?" Pa asked. "Your mother would be angry. She'd say you're too young to know how hard life can be."

"I'm not too young. I'm nine."

"You're a lot older than nine in many ways." His father's arm, which had been resting on the back of the seat, slipped to Martin's shoulders. His father's hand felt warm and firm, making a union between the two of them.

"Pa," he said, "I want to be a doctor."

Pa looked at him carefully. "Are you saying so because you think I'd like to hear it? Is that it?"

"No. I really mean it."

"You may change your mind."

"I won't change my mind."

Pa had a little twist at the corner of his mouth, not a real smile, only the start of one, the way he did when he was pleased about something, or when he and Ma had a secret.

"Well, you're smart enough," he said now.

"Alice is smarter."

"Maybe so. But she's not going to be a doctor, that's for sure. There were a couple of women in my class at medical school, and they were pretty bright too, but if you ask me, I don't think it's decent. There's man's work and there's woman's work. Doctoring, to my way of thinking, is man's work."

"You always say it's God's work," Martin said shyly.

"Well, of course it is that. Take Bechtold's leg, now. It's true, we've learned a lot about sterilization; twenty years ago you'd thread a needle and stick it in your coat lapel. But even so, you can still have infection. With all our knowledge, we must remember to be humble. Never give way to pride in your skill. Another time you might not be as lucky."

The buggy rumbled across the bridge. Martin leaned over the side, where the water was high with springtime flooding. Close to the bottom of the bridge it swirled, jewel-green, beautiful and dreadful. The power of water! Power to drown or to freeze or scald. Yet it could be so soft, closing over you on summer afternoons, all silky cool while you floated and were so gently borne.

Pa said suddenly, "I'm going to buy this mare. He'll sell her if I offer enough."

"You said we didn't need her and we couldn't afford her."

"We don't and we can't. But I can't send her back to the livery stable, either."

Martin smiled. In a way he could not have put into words, he understood that this tenderness toward the animal was connected with the sharp, cruel things they had been talking about.

They circled through Cyprus. Men were putting red, white and blue bunting around the bandstand and all the stores were closed, except for the soda fountain. Martin could anticipate delicious flavors: teaberry, chocolate and Zip's root beer. Oh, the smells and music, the feel of a holiday!

Now they were trotting down Washington Avenue, from which the side streets led to open country. These were shady streets; iron deer stood on their lawns and porches held stone urns filled with red geraniums. You wondered what lay inside the lofty houses where maids in striped aprons swept the steps and gardeners clipped the hedges.

A woman in a white dress and a light, flowered hat was coming out of a house. Two little girls, all white and lacy like her, walked beside her. They were

younger than Martin. One of them looked very queer, he saw. There was something wrong with her shoulders.

Pa halted the buggy and tipped his hat.

"How are you, Mrs. Meig?"

"Very well, Doctor, thank you. And you?"

"The same, thank you."

"Is this your boy, Doctor?"

"Yes, this is my son, Martin."

"He's going to be a handsome man."

"Handsome is as handsome does."

The lady laughed. Even her laugh was pretty. She had come quite close to the
buggy so that you could smell her perfume. Narrow silver bracelets flashed on
her wrists. Martin stared at her, then at the daughter who was just like her, except
for the bracelets: the girl had a gold locket lying in the hollow of her throat. He
looked at the other girl and quickly looked away; you weren't supposed to stare
at a cripple.

Pa tipped his hat again and clucked to the mare. It had all taken half a minute.

"Who was that?" Martin asked.

"Mrs. Meig. That's their house."

He twisted around to look back. The house was strong and dark, built of
stone. It had a curlicued iron fence and starry flowers scattered on the grass.

"Did you see all those wild flowers, Pa?"

"Those are daffodils, and they aren't growing wild, only made to look that
way. It's what they call 'naturalizing,' " his father explained. He knew everything.

Suddenly Martin knew what was exciting him. The house looked like a castle
in a book about knights! It was smaller, of course, but it was secretive like that. It
made you want to know what went on inside.

"Have you ever been inside, Pa?"

"Yes, once. The parlor maid was sick and they couldn't get Dr. Pierce. That's
how Mrs. Meig came to recognize me." Pa grinned. "It was a miserable, wet night,
I recall, and I guess Dr. Pierce didn't want to go out just for a maid."

"What's a maid for, Pa?"

"Why, when you have a big place like that you need people to take care of it.
The Meigs own the Websterware factory down by the canal where they make pots
and pans, you know. I guess half the men in Cyprus work there."

But Martin was thinking of something else. "What was wrong with that other
little girl?"

"She can't help the way she looks. She has a curvature of the spine."

"What's that?"

"Her spine wasn't made right before she was born. You can be thankful it
didn't happen to you."

True. It would be terrible. The kids would make fun of you in school. He
shuddered.

Ma and Alice were already waiting on the porch when they drove into the
yard. They had summer dresses on and white shoes. Alice wore a broad blue sash
and bow.

"Don't they look pretty, standing there?" Pa asked.

"That lady was prettier than Ma. And the little girl was a whole lot prettier than Alice."

Pa rebuked him. "Don't you ever say that, Martin, you hear me?"

"I only meant Ma and Alice haven't got big white hats like those." It was not what he had meant, however. "I wish they did, don't you?"

"It's not important," his father replied.

His mother was in the mood of the holiday. She ruffled Martin's hair, grazing his cheek with the harsh skin of her fingertips.

"Hurry up, you two!" she cried gaily. "You've ten minutes to wash and change."

Ordinarily, passing his sister as he went into the house, Martin would have pulled open her sash. Just because she was a year and a half older, she needn't think she was queen of the roost! Now, though, some sudden tenderness kept him from spoiling Alice's careful bow. He could not have explained what it was that he saw in his mother and sister just then: something vulnerable and wanting, perhaps, although they were smiling at this moment and happy. He only felt the dim confusion of contrast: that startling glimpse, just a few seconds' worth, of a house, of a fragrant, slender woman and a flowery girl-child; then this house and these two whom he knew so dearly. Something stirred in his heart, a kind of longing, a kind of pain.

Some days are marked for recollection, days which, on the surface, are not very different from all the other thousands in the chain of years. But seeds have been sown which will lie hidden quietly until their time, until a commanding shaft of light breaks through; then all the concentrated life in the seeds will stir and rise. Perhaps it was unusual for a boy only nine years old to make a resolution and have a revelation all in one day; perhaps more unusual still for him to know, as they were happening, that he would remember them.

Yet it was so.

⚜{2}⚜

Long before sunrise Martin awoke with instant awareness that this morning was different. He was leaving home. The college years close by at Hamilton had been little more than an extension of home, but this, he knew, would be a final departure. After four years at Cornell Medical College, after four years of New York City, the life of this house would be unfamiliar and he would be someone other than he now was.

The suitcases stood near the door, black shapes in the graying dawn. When they had been fastened shut and taken away, what would be left in this old room to which he had been brought on the day of his birth? The bed, with its loopy crocheted spread, the ink-stained desk and the maple dresser on which his toilet things had been placed in parallel lines, equidistant from the edge. Like his mother, he was compelled toward neatness and precision. He could never think constructively until everything was in order, notes arranged alphabetically in the notebook and papers in their folders. A neurotic trait! But one couldn't help the way one was made.

Guilty and melancholy thoughts crossed his mind sometimes. If it had not been for the deaths of those other three, especially of the brother, he would not have been going away to become a doctor. Oh, then, what would he have become? Death and survival! One life thrives on the destruction of another! He had been thinking more often lately about those three. Perhaps it was because they lay in the graveyard not half a mile down the road, and would be lying there this morning when he passed to meet the train that was taking him away.

Pa knocked on the door and came in just as Martin swung his legs out of bed.

"You realize I haven't been in the city since I arrived on the boat from Ulster? And I wouldn't be going this year if riding down with you didn't give me a reason." He yawned widely. "Excuse me. Didn't sleep well last night."

"Excited?"

"Partly, and overtired, too. I was up most of Wednesday watching old Schumann die."

"I remember him. Alice and I used to think he looked like Santa Claus."

"Yes. Well, it's sad that after eighty-seven years a human being can't go out without a struggle. Even morphine didn't help much."

Martin, pulling on his sharply creased new trousers, thought: How will it be for me when I witness my first death?

"He went through some hard times, too. For a while there during the war some folks wouldn't talk to him because he came from Germany. Said he kept the Kaiser's picture on his parlor wall, which wasn't true. Did I tell you I delivered his granddaughter's baby last week? A hard birth, a breech. Takes some doing, a breech. I remember when I had my first one. That was back in the nineties. I'd never seen the patient before. There were no X-rays then, and I remember when I reached in and realized those were the feet presenting, I was scared to death. Never been so scared in my life."

"And?"

"And I lost the baby. The mother was all right, but—it's an awful thing to lose a new life, perfectly formed! They blamed me. Two of the woman's friends deserted me after that. Went to Doc Revere, who didn't know as much as I did. Had filthy hands, black fingernails. He hadn't even heard of Semelweiss and gloves. But they thought it was my fault."

"And was it?" That was one thing about his father: you could be straightforward with him.

"Might've been. A skilled man might've been able to turn the baby—I don't know." Enoch shook his head. "There's an awful lot I don't know." He stood up. "Let's go down for breakfast. Your mother's got pancakes and sausage." At the door he turned back. "Just one thing more I want to say. Martin, I envy you, born in a time when you'll learn things I couldn't dream of! The answers to dark secrets will come as clear as day. Maybe even cancer in your lifetime. Well, I'll see you downstairs."

Martin stood still in the center of the room. Point of departure. Yes, yes, he wanted to be a doctor! Yet he feared. What if he didn't do well? Suppose he were to discover that it had been a mistake; that, after all, he wasn't fitted for it! How then would he turn back? How would he face his father and face himself?

Sunlight, moving westward now, stained the whole rug bright blue. The closet door stood open, revealing empty hangers swinging from the rod. A child-sized baseball bat lay on the floor, along with a photo of the Yankee team and a pair of old sneakers. He stood a moment in the doorway, touching these things gently with his eyes, before leaving them behind. It was like what they said about drowning: a rush of memory, a whole life up to the last minute. Did everyone, departing, feel like this? He knew they must, but also that they didn't, exactly. For each one is unique. Each one's thoughts belong to him alone, and the way he will take belongs to him alone.

❈{3}❈

In a copybook, between thick cardboard covers, Martin kept a diary. He liked to believe that when he was older, in more leisured hours, these pages written in the rapid hand that hardly anyone except himself could read with ease, would keep time from consuming him without a trace.

Turning his pages, then, flipping and skipping at random, the searching eye perceives the intimations and the forecasts.

My first week in New York is over. Pa stayed a day and a night, long enough to see me settled in. We had a very good dinner at Lüchow's. I watched him counting out the bills. These years will be hard for him.

I took him to Grand Central to catch "the cars." (He still uses that old-fashioned expression.) I never realized until we stood there together how small he is compared with me. The only feature we have in common is the nose, a profile like the ones on Roman coins. It gives the face an ascetic look. He says our noses are the result of the Roman occupation of Britain!

I waited until the train had left and all you could see was the taillight moving down the track. I shall miss him with his ragtag quotations, his stars and rocks and Greek mythology. There can't be anything quite like him. Tender, feisty, absentminded little man!

I am on my own.

This was my first day in the dissecting room. I thought I would vomit and the humiliation scared me. Then I looked at my partner, Fernbach—we were assigned alphabetically to share a cadaver—and he looked sick, too. So we both began to laugh, a stupid, embarrassed laugh.

I tried not to look at the face. You can make believe that the rest of the body is a machine: it has no individuality. But the face is the person.

Maybe for the first time in my life I am really aware of man as a perishable thing. I guess I've just accepted without challenge what they taught in Sunday school—all those lofty, consoling words about man's immortal soul. But the body of man can be crushed! It rots like any animal that has been run over and thrown to the side of the road. There is no dignity. All privacy is stripped away. The sphincters relax. I find a scar, a white rip across the shoulders. Was it from a childhood fall, a drunken scuffle or an accident while decently supporting a family? No matter now.

How ugly the body, on the table under the strong lights, invaded and marauded by strangers like me! Yes, and beautiful, too, as an equation or a snowflake is beautiful. Design, evolving and altering with subtle patience, for a hundred thousand years.

My floor is a league of nations. There are Napolitano, Rosenberg, Horvath, Gault and a fellow from Hong Kong, Wong Lee. His father owns a bank there. He doesn't mention it, but everybody knows it.

My best friends are going to be Tom Horvath and Perry Gault. Tom reminds me of my father. That's funny, because no two people could look less alike, Tom being six feet tall, with what they call a leonine head and a big homely face. His father's Hungarian, his mother's Irish. "Makes me a typical American," Tom says. He's a little bluff and opinionated, but I feel his honesty and gentleness. It is the gentleness that is most like Pa.

Perry is the brain. He's got a photographic memory for everything from anatomy to baseball scores. He's small and quick, with enough energy for any three people, a hot temper and a soft heart.

They think I'm superstitious because I have "feelings" about the future. I feel that Perry and Tom and I are going to be involved in life together, perhaps even in great struggles. Ridiculous? Maybe!

Six months already fled. I've been trying in such free time as I have to learn something about this enormous city. I have so much to learn beside the fine print in all my fat texts. There's so much out there in the world! Went down to the Fulton Fish Market yesterday. Shoving crowds and red faces. Piles of iridescent fish, pink and gray under a gloss of wet silver. Thought of that Flemish artist Breughel I saw at the museum one Sunday.

Then I walked over to Fifth Avenue past the library lions—there's a place where I could lose myself—and on uptown. What a treasury! Paintings in gilded frames. A model room with tall windows and a view of gardens. Pyramids of books. Photographs of Rome—umbrella pines and marble. Freud's *Interpretation of Dreams:* Was he right, or is the brain just chemistry, I wonder?

New York is a feast and I am so greedy, I want to know it all. After an hour of roaming I don't want to go back to my small room and memorize the course of the brachial artery. But I do!

My second year! I've been watching some surgery and it's very, very sobering. There are stars here: Jennings, Fox, Alben Riker. Saw a radical mastectomy on a woman about my mother's age. Quiet, resigned face. Knows she will not beat this illness. Watched Riker remove a tuberculous kidney yesterday. A master, with golden hands.

Wouldn't it be marvelous to be a surgeon? But where and how to get the training? One has to make a living. Who can afford it? I do believe, though, that the day will come when there will be more specialists than general men. Medicine is growing more and more complex, Tom disagrees. Anyway, he says he can't wait to be finished, to open an office and marry his girl, Florence. He says I'm lucky to have my father's practice to step into. He's right about that, I know.

TOM WORRIES BECAUSE at the end of my second year I still don't have a girl. The thing is, he's happy with Florence—they've been going together since high school —and thinks I ought to do the same. It's generous of him, but I don't want a girl right now. Problem is, "nice" girls want to get married. It's understood that if you hang around with one for six or seven months, she has a right to know what you plan to do next. Even the parents get that look on their faces, either too warm and friendly or else ever so slightly cool. In either case, you know what they're worried about, that she's wasting her time. To be fair about it, I can see their point.

But I'm not wasting my time, either—what little time I have! Met a nurse up from North Carolina—Harriet, red-haired and rosy-pink. A strawberry. Looked so innocent. It took me all of twenty-five minutes to find out she isn't. Luckily, she's got an older sister with an apartment in the Village.

MY TIME IS racing so, I can't believe it! I'm three-quarters of the way toward writing "Doctor" in front of my name. They say young people think they have all the time in the world, but it's never been like that for me. Sometimes I feel as if I'd just been born and other times I'm in a panic because I'm already twenty-four —a third of my life gone by—and I'll never do or see everything I want to do and see. I didn't know there was so much; how could you know, living in a place like Cyprus? Yet, it's true that there are people living here in the city who could be happier living in Cyprus.

I've heard Edna St. Vincent Millay read poetry in the Village. I've gone to the opera—standing room, of course, but it's worth it. My God, how splendid it is! The lights and the sudden darkness; the curtain rising and the music pouring . . .

I've been reading about a man in Canada, a Dr. Banting, who has discovered help for diabetes through injections of insulin. He's had astounding success. Imagine being a discoverer, a benefactor like that! How must he feel with the whole world's eyes turned on him? To be like that! Oh, not for admiration, but to know! To know that you know! Martin, Martin, is there an ugly streak of vanity in you? I hope not.

But I wish I didn't have this itch. I feel that if I don't do something big, discover something or develop some stupendous skill, I will have failed. They say, of course, that most beginners are romantic about themselves, that it's only naivete and youth. I wonder.

THE FOLKS WANT me home again for the vacation. Pa says I can ride around on house calls with him and that now it will all mean a lot more to me. Two months will be too much, though. I figure on a month before I come back here and gird myself for senior year. They're reorganizing the main library and I can get a job lugging books. I need the money. Can do a lot of reading, too.

*   *   *

Home on vacation. A curious thing happened today. I went with Pa on a call to
one of those fussy Cyprus houses with the turrets and the iron deer that I used to
think so grand. The man of the house had a bad case of grippe. I waited in the
library while Pa went upstairs.

It was a dreadful room with too much heavy oak furniture and, over the sofa,
an awful picture of a barefoot running nymph with windblown scarves carefully
arranged to cover genitals and breasts. I was staring at it when someone spoke.

"Horrible, isn't it?"

I jumped. Then I saw who it was: a small girl barely five feet tall. She was
about twenty years old with a sweet face, a fine head of dark curly hair and a
curvature of the spine.

"Sorry I scared you," she said. "I'm Jessie Meig."

I told her I was the doctor's son and she wanted to know whether I was a
doctor, too. I said I was going to be, this time next year.

I don't know why I'm writing all this down, except that it's been such a
strange day.

"I thought you were calling on my sister," she said. "If you want to see her,
she's in her studio across the hall."

I told her I didn't know her sister.

Then she said, "Well, when you do know her you'll probably fall in love with
her."

"Why on earth should I?"

"Because men always do. But nothing ever comes of it. At least, not yet. Father
will keep them away until he finds someone he approves of."

I was so dumbfounded by all this that I didn't know how to answer.

And she said, "Anyway, Fern's not really interested in men right now. She
wants to be a great painter. Besides, she's timid to start with. If I looked like her, I
wouldn't be timid, I can tell you that."

"I would hardly call you timid," I said.

She laughed. "You're right, I'm not. For a person like me it would be fatal. I'm
not afraid and I don't worry. Now take you—you're not afraid, but you are a
worrier. I see it in your face."

Perhaps she felt she had to be startling, to entertain? I don't really know. But I
was beginning to be amused.

"I guess I am," I said. "It runs in the family. My father worries about the
progress of mankind and my mother worries about the roof over our heads."

"I suppose you're poor," she said.

By this time nothing surprised me, so I said: Yes, we were, fairly so.

"Too bad. Country doctors work so hard for so little."

I was actually beginning to like the bite in her speech! Most of the time people
talk and don't say anything real, anything they truly mean. You could see this girl
was honest and intelligent. What a foul trick nature played, attaching that bright
head to such a body!

And suddenly something came flashing up from the bottom of my mind.

"Why, I remember you. We were in the buggy—that's how long ago it was—

passing this house and you came out with your mother and sister. I can see you clearly."

What a stupid, bumbling idiot I was! Because, of course, what I meant was: *I remember the crippled girl.*

So I tried to cover up quickly. "I especially remember your mother."

"She died seven years ago."

Then I tried to cover up some more and moved to the bookshelves. I must say, they did have a lot of great books. And I started mumbling about Sandburg's *Lincoln* and how that was one of the first things I was going to buy when I could afford it.

We talked some more about books until Pa came downstairs and we left. I'm still feeling red in the face. A strange encounter.

A WEEK LATER Pa found a package on the front porch. It was for me, Sandburg's *Lincoln,* with a card from Jessie Meig! "Anybody who wants anything as reasonable as a book shouldn't have to wait for it. So please accept this and enjoy it."

I suppose I could have written a note of thanks, but since I almost had to pass the house on an errand in Cyprus, I thought it would be nicer to stop by with my thanks. So I went in and asked the maid for Miss Meig, but instead of seeing Jessie, I was taken to the sister. She was at work before an easel and I could see she didn't want to be disturbed, so I said I was sorry about the mistake and backed right out.

It's queer, though, how much I remember of the few seconds I stood there! The most startling face looked up at me: dark, almost olive, with extraordinary pure blue eyes. I've never seen such eyes. Her hair is curly, like Jessie's, but shorter. I thought of the way curls are carved on ancient Greek statues. She wore a white smock. There was a drop of paint on her sandals. And that's all, except that I don't understand why the picture stays so sharp in my mind.

That nonsense Jessie spoke about people falling in love with Fern?

No need to worry! I can't afford to complicate my life for a good long while yet. I shall probably never even see the girl again.

Still, I feel a sense of drama, sitting here, writing these words.

❖{ 4 }❖

The senior year flew by faster than any of the years before it. Martin really began to feel like a doctor. A subtle power came to life in him, as though he could instinctively smell out disease; could feel it pulsing under his fingers and glimmering before his eyes. He began to plan an intellectual game, even taking notes on the subway.

"A laborer, large man in a yellow Windbreaker. Italian. Must have been a good-looking, powerful youth. He is eating a doublenut chocolate bar, crunching and chewing with pure pleasure. Putting on fat. In a few more years his strength will ebb. At fifty he'll be jelly and flab. Hypertensive already, I'll wager, although he doesn't know it.

"A man of forty. Somber, intelligent face. Anglo-Saxon. A green pallor. Cigarette-stained fingers. Reaches for cigarettes, observes 'no smoking' sign, shoves them back into pocket. Ulcer type. A lawyer, perhaps? Underling in a large firm. Burdened with responsibilities and nightwork."

His mind stretched. He felt himself reaching with new curiosity into far corners, to the Academy of Medicine to hear a psychiatrist lecture on hypnotism, to listen to new theories about cancer and new procedures in the operating rooms.

One man, a neurosurgeon, attracted him especially. He was a Spaniard, Jorge Maria Albeniz, trained in Barcelona, a frail, elderly man with a formal European manner. Behind his back the nursing staff spoke of him fondly as "The Duke." By the medical staff he was thought to be talented but odd. It was said that, if he had wanted to, he could have made a fortune. But most of his time was spent in his basement laboratory or at the clinic where he treated the sick and taught. He liked to operate only when the case was so difficult that other men were reluctant to take it.

Martin watched one day while he removed a pituitary tumor from a young woman. The tumor was too far gone for complete removal.

Albeniz spoke as he worked.

"With X-ray treatments, she may have a few more years. Her children will be that much older, nearer to being able to take care of themselves. We're buying time, that's all." He looked up at the silent young men surrounding him. "As you see, there is a terrible lot we still do not know how to cope with."

This simple honesty touched Martin. Brainwork, he thought, must be the most challenging field of all. And he looked in wonder at Albeniz. How did a man get to be like that?

He began to feel a new and unfamiliar restlessness.

It followed him home on vacation. Suddenly he noticed things he hadn't seen before. His father had some absurd and ignorant opinions.

Of a man with chronic headaches he said that they ran in the family. "I remember how his Uncle Thaddeus used to fall into rages from them. He'd be so sorry afterward. You've got to keep spices out of the food. They thicken the blood and you get congestion in the head."

Martin made no comment. So much for the temper headaches that might have been caused by anything from sinus to migraine to allergies, tumor or incipient psychosis. Or maybe only worry over the mortgage. Spices in the food!

He went with Pa on a house call. The family had a fat little four-year-old boy of whom the mother was proud.

"He's a bruiser, ain't he, Doc?"

"Hello, there, Dale," Pa said. "Yes a fine, fat boy. Anyone can see he gets plenty of your good rich cream and butter."

"Only thing, all last winter, I don't know why I forgot to mention it to you, he complained that his arms and legs hurt. Not real bad, I could tell, because he didn't cry. It just ached him, you know."

"Where? In the joints?"

"Knees and elbows."

Pa waved his hands. "Nothing. Just growing pains. He's growing too fast, that's all. I wouldn't worry about it."

When they were outside, Martin observed, "Don't you think you ought to consider rheumatic fever? And the child's too fat besides."

"No, I don't and he isn't," Pa said shortly.

Well, some sort of father-son rivalry was only to be expected! They had been singularly free of all that up until now. He certainly didn't want a rivalry to pull them apart. So again he kept still.

On the third day at the noon meal, his mother inquired about someone's baby.

"A lot better," Pa told her. "Dover's Powders and an enema. That does it."

This time Martin couldn't resist. "Pa, we don't use Dover's Powders anymore."

"What do you mean 'we don't'? Why, I've been using that stuff since before you were born!"

Martin opened his mouth to retort. Then he thought: An older man must be allowed to keep "face." If I'm to show him anything new, I must do it carefully and in private. We'll need to work well together, we must and we will—

Still, a restlessness, the same that had been with him for weeks now, or for months, came over him. He could hardly sit still for the tingling in the solar plexus. The meal, with second helpings for Pa, with coffee for his mother, seemed endless.

"How about my borrowing the flivver this afternoon?" he asked. "Thought maybe I'd run up to Cyprus on a couple of errands."

When he had finished at the drugstore and the hardware store, he got back in

the car to go home. There was, after all, no place else to go. It was a day of
January thaw, with dripping icicles overhead and slush underfoot, a good day to
go home, bring the restlessness under control and do some studying for
midterms.

That being his intention, it was never quite clear to him how it happened that
on Washington Street, heading toward home, he suddenly swung the car around
and found himself, three minutes later, parked at the curb facing two iron deer in
front of a dark stone house.

THERE WAS THE same shocked disturbance of equilibrium as the first time.

"Why are you staring at me?" she asked.

"Because I've never seen a face like yours."

"It can't possibly be that unusual!"

"You must know it is. Blue eyes don't belong in such a Spanish face, such a
Greek face."

"There's no Spanish in me, or Greek either."

He supposed she was not "beautiful," in the accepted sense; she was tall,
almost as tall as he, and her coloring was too strange. But there was something so
—so *dreaming* in her soft expression, as if she were seeing things he couldn't see!

In the left hand she held her brushes like a fan. Now, choosing one, she bent
to the easel and laid a stroke of red on a bird's wing: three scarlet birds sat on a
wire fence against a background of snow.

"Am I interrupting your work?" he asked.

"No. This one's finished. At least, it's the best I can do with it."

He knew almost nothing about art. Perhaps this was merely a sentimental
postcard? But it was vivid and it appealed to him. So he said sincerely, "It's a
pretty piece."

She considered it, frowning slightly. "I can't really tell. So far, I've only imi-
tated, you see. Look at this, for instance."

This was a small square of canvas covered in many tones of pink, whirling
from fuchsia to pearl. Looking closely, one saw that these were trees in blossom,
their dark forked branches buried in the billowing pink.

"Monet. I was trying to be Monet. The water-lily thing, you know. And over
there, those boats drawn up on the beach, that's Winslow Homer."

" 'M.F.M.,' " he read in the corner. "What's the 'M' for?"

"Mary. My name is Mary Fern. They call me Fern at home because Mother's
name was Mary. But I'd much rather be called Mary."

"Then I'll call you Mary. I saw you once when I was about nine years old," he
said irrelevantly.

"I know. Jessie told me . . . She says you'll be a wonderful doctor. You
weren't embarrassed, the way most people are when they meet her. They never
seem to know how to talk to her."

"There shouldn't be any different way of talking to her."

"There shouldn't be, but there is. People are sorry for her. And of course she
knows it."

"How hard it must be for her, having to live so close to you all her life!"

Instantly Martin regretted the exclamation. But Mary answered simply.

"I know. We don't get along very well."

"She can't be much older than you?"

"Younger. We're thirteen months apart."

There was a stillness in the room. Airy and white as it was, with its white walls and the view of the winter day through uncurtained windows, it had no relation at all to the rest of the cluttered house.

"I like this room," he said. "I feel peace here."

"There is peace here. Most of the time. Except when I'm in one of my rebellious moods." Mary laughed. "I'll bring coffee. Just clear those paint pots off the table, will you, and we'll have it by the window."

The sun struck glitter from the gilt rims of the cups and from the ring on her finger, moving round and round as she stirred the coffee. The ring was a topaz set in curiously twisted gold. Her nails had sharply marked half-moons. There was a small mole in the center of her cheek. He had never felt such tremendous, intense awareness of another human being. It became necessary to speak very calmly.

"What did you mean by 'your rebellious moods'?" he asked.

For a moment she didn't answer. Then she said, "You see—maybe it's entirely foolish, this thought of greatness in art—but how can I know unless I'm taken seriously?"

"And no one does?"

"My mother did. If she were living, I'd be in New York or somewhere studying. But Father thinks it's all 'nonsense.' If I had any money of my own—"

"You'd go away?"

"Oh yes! Yes! I do so want to see somewhere else!" And she made a free gesture with her arm. "Haven't you ever wanted to—get beyond?"

"All my life, as far back as I can remember."

"And have you done it?"

"In a way. My beyond is my work. Medicine."

"Ah, then you're very lucky! I don't even know whether my work is any good! I've done nothing yet. Nothing. And I'm already twenty."

"You're in a great hurry. I understand."

"Do you? Do you ever feel you want to hear all the music ever written, see all the great cities, read all the books, know everything?"

He smiled. "All that and art, too?"

"Art, too. I have to find out who I am. Because I'm surely not Monet or Winslow Homer, am I?" Then with sudden embarrassment she said, "I'm sorry. You can't possibly be interested."

"You're wrong."

"Well. You did ask about my 'rebellion,' didn't you? It's not very savage or successful, so far. And sometimes I'm even ashamed of it."

"Why should you be?"

"Because of Jessie. After all, I have so much. She has so little."

He nodded. What conflict must be within these walls!

His eye fell on a watercolor hung on the wall between the windows: a girl in a swing, her curved back half hidden by a fall of leaves.

"That's Jessie?"

"Yes. She didn't like it. But nobody sees it in here."

"It's very good, I think."

"It's the truth, anyway."

"People don't always want to see the truth."

"Oh, Jessie sees it well enough! It's Father who doesn't, or won't. She needs so much to talk to somebody about her life! What's to become of her? Father's not a person one can really *talk* to. He wants to pretend there's nothing the matter, while all the time he's so afraid."

Martin didn't know what to answer.

"What will become of her?" Mary repeated.

"Won't she just stay here as she is?"

"Father won't live forever. And I'll do what I can for my sister, but I probably won't stay here, either."

He felt absurd alarm. "Suppose you were to be married?"

"I doubt I shall marry anyone from Cyprus."

He wanted to ask, "Why? Is there anyone? Do you—" But that, too, would have been absurd.

When they went to the door, he told her he'd be back for a while in the summer after graduation and asked whether he might come again.

"Come. But come and see Jessie, too."

"Do you always think of Jessie?" he asked curiously.

"Wouldn't you, if she were your sister?"

He considered, feeling the moment with acute and sudden pain: the allure of the girl, the melancholy of the house and, over all, his old familiar sense of time eluding.

"Yes," he admitted. "I probably would. So I can just be a friend to both of you, can't I?"

Spring came and commencement and he was home again. His mind was filled with Mary. He thought of all the clichés in the language. "Head over heels." "First sight." "Chemistry," whatever that might mean. All were expressions which he had once found unbelievable.

He was, of course, too easily moved; he knew that about himself. He was embarrassingly given to tears not easily blinked away. Only a month or two ago, for example, passing an exquisite baby in a carriage, a Della Robbia cherub with bright hair, he had stopped. The baby had given him a smile so miraculous, and he had been so touched, that the mother, seeing the absurd rise and glisten of his tears, had hurriedly wheeled the carriage away, thinking no doubt that he was some sort of madman and possibly dangerous.

Now joy pierced him through: his own, and the joy of the eyes in that dark, poetic face.

But he hardly ever saw Mary alone and the summer days were vanishing. Birds flash among dense trees; fish flick into deeper water, out of sight. So their interrupted minutes fled.

Twice Martin took her to the movies. The third time, at the father's suggestion,

Jessie went along. Once there was a picnic, a family affair. In the evenings the family sat together in the library, Jessie and the father playing chess.

Mr. Donald Meig was a pale tan presence. He wore impeccable pongee summer suits and his pale tan hair showed the even tracks of the comb. His smile was courteous and faintly supercilious. Clearly, Martin's presence was not welcomed. It was tolerated because he was the doctor's son.

"Fancies himself an aristocrat," Pa said.

Meig was not a money snob—for he would despise that as vulgar—but a "family" snob. He liked to talk about "good old stock." As if all human stock weren't equally old! At his table he sat among a clutter of Irish silver and English porcelain, with a stuffed swordfish over the golden oak sideboard—a big fish himself in the little pond of Cyprus.

"Your mother's people were Scotch-Irish?" he inquired once of Martin, and without waiting for an answer, "I've some of that myself. It's not the usual strain around here. Most of the Scotch-Irish went to the Appalachians. There's a branch of my family there still. Went west through the Cumberland Gap to Kentucky, you know."

Martin hadn't known. His mother's people had gone from Scotland to the north of Ireland and, after a couple of generations there on the farms and in the cloth mills, had come here shortly after the Revolution to work again on the farms. Pa, of course, was a much later arrival from the same part of the world. These simple histories were taken for granted at home; one neither concealed them nor boasted of them.

Meig concluded pridefully, "People tend to settle near their own kind, naturally. Like the Dutch in the Hudson River Valley. We've some Dutch in our family, too. No landowners, no Van Cortlandts, just small farmers, poor and hardworking."

Well, Martin thought, everyone has his quirks. Nevertheless, he asked Mary, "Is your father the absolute authority in everything, always?"

"I suppose you could say he is," she told him. "I don't want you to think he's a tyrant, though. Aunt Milly says he ought to have got married again, it would have been better for his disposition. Only, he's afraid to marry someone who wouldn't be good to Jessie. So you see, he's really a good father. I try to remember that."

Martin wondered what the mother could have been like. Probably she had been like the daughters, for even Jessie had gladness, with her energetic, tossing head, her opinions and her curiosity. Meig was so profoundly different! The woman must have been suffocated in that house, he thought.

"May I ask," Meig said to Martin, "why you call my daughter 'Mary'?"

"Because she likes the name," he answered.

"Well, I'm sure I don't know why. She has always been called 'Fern' at home."

His mouth closed in disapproval. As if the world and all the people in it were too common, too intrusive?

And yet, sometimes, Martin had caught him looking at Mary as though he were wondering that such radiance could have come from himself.

"Why are you smiling?" Martin asked her once.

"I was watching that bee," she said. "See how greedy it is!"

Its burrowing body was furred with gold dust, buried in the flower, in its damp and tender warmth. And Martin flushed at the parallel image which flashed into his head. He felt the tingle of heat in his neck. Could she have such thoughts too? For the first time in his experience he felt he knew too little about women.

They walked in warm rain. He had never known anyone beside himself who didn't mind being soaked in rain. Outside of someone's open window they stood hiding behind a wet syringa, listening to the Quartet from *Rigoletto* coming over the radio.

"I remember," Martin said, "the first time I knew that music could make you laugh or cry. So many different kinds! The organ in church, all waves and thunder, or the band in the town square that makes your feet dance. And once at Reverend Dexter's, I heard four men playing violins. I remember wishing I could hear music like that again."

"My mother played the piano," Mary said. "We used to get out of bed and sit at the top of the stairs to listen. The house was different, then."

"You really want to get away, don't you?" he asked gently.

"I think I do, Martin. And then I think: It's home, I'd miss it. I'm confused . . . . What I really want, with all my heart, is to paint! To put everything down that I feel in my heart, in here! The meaning of life!"

How young! he thought, with tenderness.

"I think, if one can do that, one will never be lonely. But then, you would first have to experience life, wouldn't you, before you could paint it?"

How young, he thought again.

Grape summer, dusky blue. Rose-red summer, deep in clover!

"I HOPE YOU don't have any ideas about that girl," Pa said at supper one night. "You've been spending a lot of time over there."

"Enoch!" Ma cried.

"No, no, Jean. Martin knows I don't interfere. It's only a cautionary word or two, which he can take or leave. They're not our kind, Martin."

"What kind are we, Pa?" Martin spoke mildly, yet there was a tension in him, not of anger or resentment, but apprehension over being told something he might not want to hear.

"Why, it's self-evident," Pa answered promptly. "Can you see that girl washing dishes in this kitchen? The worlds don't mix."

Worlds. Are we then destined to stay in the one world for which we were made, like pegs in holes or keys in locks? The design cut and not to be altered? Yet, look about you, it is often so.

"I wonder how long the Meigs will go on living like that," his father said. "They say the plant's gradually going downhill."

Martin was surprised. "Websterware? The backbone of the town?"

"I've some patients who work there, and they tell me the business has been running on its own momentum for years. Meig isn't the man his father and grandfather were, you know. He's in over his head and too proud to acknowledge it."

His sister Alice remarked, "Rena works in the office at Webster's. She says people all know Mr. Meig keeps Fern shut away here until he finds the right marriage for her. Disgusting, isn't it? As if a woman were a prize racehorse to be mated with a prize stallion."

"Alice!" the mother cried.

Alice tittered. Ever since she had been "going with" Fred Partridge, she had become bolder, almost smug in her new security. Soon she would enjoy the status of a married woman. Fred, who taught gym at the consolidated school, was a decent fellow, as neutral as his own eyes and hair, and totally incurious about everything. Once Alice had had yearnings. She had been serious and enthusiastic. Now her enthusiasm was visibly draining away. She was "settling" for Fred Partridge.

Martin felt sadness for his sister, as for all eager, young and shining lives, all women who were not Mary Fern.

His mother was saying, "I hear the crippled one is smart. Is that so, Martin?"

"Her name is Jessie," he corrected stiffly. "Yes, she is."

"And is the other one really so good-looking?"

Alice cried, "I can't imagine who told you that, Ma. She's thin and much too dark, and—"

Martin stood up, murmuring something, and fled.

IN THE MOTIONLESS air the candles made stiff tips of yellow light. Moths struck with a fleshy thump on the screens. Conversation, on this last night before Martin's departure for the city and internship, moved around the table between Jessie, Donald Meig and an aunt and uncle from New York. Only Mary and Martin were silent.

He was ill at ease and his feet hurt. He had bought white shoes, an extravagance because they would be so seldom worn, but he couldn't have come to dinner here without them. Clothes were insurance, a kind of statement that a person "belonged," whatever that meant. Idiotic! But that's the way it was and always had been. "Costly thy apparel as thy purse can buy." Shakespeare knew about people like Donald Meig. He knew everything about people.

Mary was serving a salad from the bowl which had been put before her. The gauzy, cherry-colored sleeve had fallen away from her bare arm. She had the look of someone who had strayed by accident into that room and that house.

Jessie was laughing; she had a hearty, appealing laugh that sometimes brought tears to her eyes. It was really a pleasure to watch her! It occurred to Martin that in these few weeks he had become accustomed to her, sitting with her summer shawl gathered in stiff, concealing folds, her rapid hands moving as she talked, her bright eyes observing everything.

And recalling suddenly what she had said about her sister at that first meeting, he wondered what she might be guessing, what she knew . . .

A sharp ache shot through Jessie for the young man in the cheap suit and the stiff, new shoes; the earnest young man with the proud, quick face and the eyes looking so hungrily at—someone else!

Oh, if I had Fern's body what I would do! she thought. Soft, dreaming thing, she lives in fantasy. I would make sure of that young man. He's worth a dozen of

any others I've seen. The way he looks at her over the top of the glass when he
drinks, pretending not to!

Oh, if I had her body!

Long ago, the maids talked, two of them standing in the bathroom. "Poor
child," they said.

I looked around for the child before I knew the child was I.

In the mirrored door, I saw myself, naked and pink. There were Fern and
Fern's friend, come to stay overnight. And I saw they were alike, and I the
different one. How old was I? Four? Five?

The seamstress came to make my dresses with wide, embroidered collars.
Berthas, they used to call them, and they were so pretty, ruffled or pleated for
concealment. They didn't conceal. I took the hand-mirror, and twisting, I could
see my back, could see how the cloth where the ruffles stopped was stretched
over the sharp knife-blade of bone.

I remember those long rides in the car and the doctors' waiting rooms where
Mother read *Heidi* aloud while we waited. Heidi was a brave girl and I must be
brave, too. Then the doctors came in their white coats. They were kindly and tall,
touching my back with cold fingers. There was much talk, and after that the long
ride home.

"Tired?" Father would ask Mother, and she would answer, "No, I'm all right."

At the best toy stores they stopped to buy new dolls. They never knew I didn't
care that much about dolls. I had rows of them, stupid-looking things with long
yellow hair and patent leather shoes. I used to undress them, taking off their lace-
edged panties and petticoats. Their backs were smooth and straight from their
shoulders to their little round behinds. They looked like Fern.

Once at school I stood with a circle of children dancing around me. I can hear
them now: they're laughing and pointing. "Jessie is a—" they chant, but I don't
remember the word. Don't want to, perhaps? I remember the teacher, with her
indignant, trembling voice, coming at a run. The children flee and I walk inside
with her, hand in hand.

In the playground I had been so fierce and proud, but now at her gentle
comfort, I sobbed on the teacher's shoulder. She reached in the drawer and gave
me her clean handkerchief. It smelled of eau de cologne. I can smell it still.

Aunt Milly wants Fern and me to go to Europe with them this winter. They'll
stay at the Carlton in Nice. Me at the Carlton with Fern! Tea-dancing. Steps
leading down. You stand at the top of the flight, waiting to be seated. Eyes turn
up to see who you are. And I shall be standing next to Fern. No! Thank you. And
thank you again . . .

Mary stirred uncomfortably. If only Jessie would take that look off her face! A
moment ago she was laughing and now she looks thunder-dark. Will I never
grow used to her?

"Jessie's handicapped," they told me so seriously, long years ago.

I must have been still a baby. I thought "handicapped" meant there was
something wrong with her hands, until the day I noticed her back.

"What is that? Does it hurt?"

"No," Mother said, "it hurts only in her mind."

I remember thinking that, if everybody looked like Jessie, then I would be the queer one and people would stare at me.

"They don't mean to stare, they don't mean to be unkind, they're only curious. But she will have that all her life," people said.

Yet she was always tougher than I. Peppery as she was, it was she who did the hitting.

"You must never hit her back, never," they said. "You're so much stronger! Suppose you were to hurt her? To break a bone? What then?"

And I could see her tumbling, shattered on the floor, like that Oriental vase which Uncle Drew had brought from China and which a maid had broken, bringing lamentation to the morning.

I hit Jessie. She struck the table edge and a great reddening lump like an egg rose on her forehead. Feet came running—Carrie, the cook, Mother, Father. I was stiff with fright. She wailed and they picked her up. Father whipped me, me, his favorite, as I knew even then. He was so proud of me! His fierce voice, his fierce face were like an ogre's.

"Don't you ever hit Jessie again! Don't you touch her! Do you hear?"

Uncle Drew took me aside. He was the only one who felt sorry for me. I stood between his knees while he sat on the sofa, his hands on my shoulders.

"You haven't hurt her, Fern. Everyone's excited, but you haven't hurt her, Fern. Remember that. It's only a bump and will go away in a day or two."

I didn't want to go away to school. I had friends here. And I didn't want to leave my dogs! But Jessie had no friends. A small, private school would be better for her, they said.

Mother said, "We can't send Jessie away to school and keep you here, can we?"

And Father said, "You will meet nicer girls in boarding school, anyway."

But the girls all came from New York or Boston or Montreal. It was the same as having no friends at all.

Now she doesn't want to go to Europe this winter. If she doesn't go, Father will want me to stay home, too. But I'm going. No matter what, I'm going.

I shall be sorry to leave Martin. I might fall in love with him if I could know him a little longer. And still in a way it seems I've always known him. Even his silence speaks to me. Is it possible that he loves me already? But he's going away tomorrow . . . But he will come back. It's only a few months, after all. Maybe, then . . . And I shall see Europe . . . all the sparkle . . . I've never been anywhere at all.

I think Jessie has fallen in love with him, though. I'm sorry if she has. I hope she hasn't. Life is very, very harsh . . .

"It will be such joy having you with us, Fern," Aunt Milly was saying and then, addressing Martin, "We've invited Fern and Jessie to go to Europe with us, did you know? We shall leave just after Labor Day and spend the winter. I do wish, Jessie, you would change your mind and come along, too."

Jessie shook her head.

"It would do you the world of good, you know. Take you out of yourself. You really do need—"

"I really do need a new spine," Jessie said, and laughed.

Aunt Milly blushed. "Oh, Jessie, I only meant—"

"I know what you meant, Aunt Milly. You meant well."

"Nice is wonderful in the winter, very mild," Uncle Drew observed. "You can always change your mind, Jessie. Up to the last minute."

The voices crossed the table in a neat little fugue.

Aunt Milly said to Fern, "You'll be seeing the great art of the world. It'll help immensely in your career, you know."

"Career!" The father was irritated. "Don't, please, give her more grandiose ideas than she already has. It's a pretty hobby and that's all it is."

"Excuse me, but you're hardly a judge," Mary said.

"And you think you can judge?"

"No, but there are other people in this world who can."

"Was that thunder I heard, by any chance?" Uncle Drew asked, changing the subject.

Martin smiled at him, receiving a knowing, answering smile. A kindly soul! Worlds removed from the heavy-handed petty tyrant at the head of the table!

"Mary, let's go for a walk," he proposed when they had left the table. "And Jessie come, too."

"I don't want to," Jessie said.

Mr. Meig frowned. "It's going to rain any minute."

"Rain won't hurt anyone," Aunt Milly told him.

"We'll not go far," Martin said.

The town was closed for the night. Houses wore shut faces; their windows were drooping eyelids. A horn blew somewhere, a forlorn, far call in the silence. They circled through dwindling streets from pavement to asphalt to dirt, and where the fields began, turned back, talking of this and that and of nothing in particular.

"So you'll be going away," Martin said. "I'll miss you, Mary."

The words were unforgivably banal. He wanted to say such beautiful, extravagant things: I'm enchanted, I think of you all day. Why was he so awkward, so tongue-tied? Was it the family, the gloomy house, the gloomy father? Perhaps, in another setting more private and free, or if he were a few years farther along and had something definite to give—

The smell of rain was in the air when they came to the gate. Eastward, the clouds were darkening with approaching storm, but in the west the afterglow still streaked the sky in lines of copper and rose and a yellow like the inside of a peach.

"Oh look!" Mary cried. "It sparkles! Martin, look!"

But he was not looking at the sky. He was looking at her, standing there with her hand held to her throat and the wonder on her face. There was a pain in his heart that he couldn't have believed possible.

At the front door they stood cramped between overgrown laurels. And quite suddenly the rain came, spattering on the leaves.

"Well," he said. "I guess I'd better start."

"I'll think of you. We all will."

He had meant only to kiss her good-bye. But when he had caught her to him, he was unable to let her go. How long he would have held her there he didn't know, but someone stirred in the vestibule as if to open the door. So she turned quickly into the house and he went clattering down the steps into the rain.

❈{5}❈

This was the way of it: He was Dr. Farrell, intern, responsible for lives. Agitated relatives waylaid him and the squawk-box pursued him. His irrevocable signature went on every record. Pray it wasn't written as witness to a mistake he'd made! Best not to think about that, though; just step forward and begin, the way a child learns to walk.

THE EMERGENCY ROOM stayed in motion all night. One lived on black coffee. He slept on a cot or dozed off, rather, for a few minutes until a nurse came to shake him awake again. The doors would swing open, and another stretcher come rolling through. On the wards, the ominous nights were filled with sighs. Unbearable pain was unbearable to watch. He dreaded the terminal cancer patient most of all; the breakdown of personality in even the most stalwart was terrible. He had not known that desperate people, even the very old, call out for their mothers.

At times he thought he felt the weight of the pain-filled building, ten stories high, lying on his shoulders.

"WHAT'S DIFFERENT ABOUT you?" Tom asked.

"I don't know. What is?"

"You're only half here. Is there some trouble with your father or something?" Martin had often said his father worked too hard and his blood pressure was too high.

"No, no, I'm just a little tense, I guess."

There was no one in the world whom he could trust more than this friend who was searching him now with inquiring eyes, but he couldn't, he didn't want to, talk about Mary.

If only his mind were clear again as once it had been! If only the work were all he had to think about! But he trembled inwardly: trembled at seeing the name of the Meig plant in the weekly paper, forwarded from home; trembled at seeing a patient named Fern, a fat woman with a brogue and abscessed tonsils.

He trembled when the mail came. She sent a card from Lake Champlain: *Visiting here for a few days. Love.* He read it over and over, studying the shape of the words. She wrote in backhand. He wondered what that meant, whether it said anything about her personality. Then a card came that had a picture of an ocean

500

liner. It had been mailed from Cherbourg. He imagined her walking in the rain on a cobbled street. He ached for her. It was a definite physical ache in the chest. One could understand why the ancients had believed that the heart was the seat of the emotions.

His own emotions came close to the surface. He broke off with Harriet, in a scene that he had wanted to keep gentle but that she made angry. His desire for her, for anyone but Mary, had drained away, as if a sluice had been opened.

A tragedy took place in the hospital when one of the nurses killed herself. She had been going with Dan Ritchie, resident in orthopedics; he had promised to marry her, then changed his mind. The horror of this shook Martin deeply. How the suffering must have cut to make a human being want to die! But he thought he could understand it. He felt that he had grown enormously in understanding.

And he was thankful for being overworked. It was the only way he would get through the winter.

WHAT HE SAW first on the stretcher was a young girl in a tight pink sweater and skirt. It crossed his mind that she looked like a girl who would be named "Donna" or "Dawn." And on a necklace of cheap beads her name was spelled out: Donna. She had been run over in the rain. Her face was gashed and her arms, which she must have flung out to save herself, had been crushed.

Standard procedure, he thought, accustomed as he was by now to quick judgment and quick action. Neurosurgery later to save the ulnar nerves. Useless hands, otherwise. Patch the face while waiting. Sedation, of course. Local anaesthesia. He called out orders. Black silk. Fine needle.

"This won't hurt," he said.

Never did this before. Where to find a surgeon Saturday night? Common sense. Trick is: very, very small stitches. Careful. Careful. Suture. Tie. Knot. Cut. Again. Suture. Tie. Knot. Cut.

When he was finished, the pathetic face was crisscrossed with black silk and he was sweating. He leaned down.

"Donna? I'm all through."

She was, mercifully, half asleep. "Will my face be all right?"

"Yes," he said confidently.

The mouth, large and cherry-colored, quivered. "Do you promise I won't be scarred?"

"I promise."

"Will I be a cripple, Doctor?"

"Of course not," he said. And forgive me for the lie because I really don't know.

They had cut the pink sweater off. Somebody began to cut the necklace.

"No," Martin said. "Don't do that." And he pulled the clasp toward the front to unfasten the beads. They would be precious to Donna.

After she had been wheeled upstairs he kept thinking of her, and the next morning was still thinking of her. Mentally, as was his habit, he constructed her life. She lived in a walk-up and worked in the five-and-ten. For lunch she ate a tuna fish sandwich and a chocolate soda. She stood in line at the funerals of

movie stars, chewing gum in wads. He felt an indescribable sadness. Some patients did that to him. What would become of her with paralyzed hands?

Dr. Albeniz was to operate in the forenoon. Martin arrived when it was all
over and the doctors were back in the locker room.

"It was very close," Albeniz said, replying to Martin's question. "But I'm fairly
sure she'll be all right." He seemed surprised. "Why, do you know the girl?"

"No. I was on duty when she came in. I sutured her face."

"You did?" There was strong emphasis on the "you."

Martin felt quick dread in the pit of the stomach.

"I'm afraid I'm the culprit."

"Culprit?" Albeniz, who was tying his shoes, glanced up. "On the contrary, I
asked because it's a superb job. By the looks of it she will have scarcely a scar."

Martin swallowed, disbelieving. "I guess I was just lucky then."

"You had your nerve, knowing nothing about it!"

"Yes, sir."

"You have good hands. Are you interested in plastic surgery?"

"Not particularly." He corrected himself, "No, I'm not."

"Well, it was a superb job," Albeniz repeated.

Martin flushed, both with pleasure and misgiving. What had he dared to do,
knowing so little? He had just been awfully lucky! Very generous, though, of
Albeniz to say what he had.

A week or two later, Albeniz ran past him in a corridor. Speed was his
eccentricity. It seemed that all the greats had some eccentricity or other! Jeffers
wore rubbers even when the sun was shining. Albeniz never took the elevator,
preferring in his haste to run up three flights of stairs. When he saw Martin he
stopped.

"Would you like to know how your patient is getting on?"

"Oh, yes," Martin said, pleased at being treated like a colleague.

"Well, for a while I had my doubts, but she will definitely have usable hands.
Also a presentable face, thanks to you."

It seemed necessary to say something polite in return. "After what you've done
for her, my suturing seems unimportant."

"Not so. It's not very good for one's mental health to have scarred cheeks, you
know."

"But your work is vital. I've seen you work and I've been—I guess you could
say I've been thrilled each time."

Albeniz smiled. "Well then, I give you a standing invitation to come and watch
whenever you're free."

THE OPERATING ROOM was fitted out in porcelain and stainless steel, gleaming silver-
gray. Beyond the great window, the winter sky was a darker gray. Albeniz and his
resident, the anaesthesiologist, the nurses, the assistants and the subassistants
moved quickly in an ordered pattern, their feet making no sound. It was a
subaqueous ballet, a serious dance around the table on which the patient lay, his
shaven head firmly clamped. The green curtain hanging on its frame separated his
head from the rest of his body. A profusion of tubes was connected to various

parts of that body; to someone who didn't understand them it appeared to be only a tangle of tubes. But they were the weapons of this little army which was fighting for the life of the man on the table.

The excitement was unlike anything Martin had ever felt before. He stood with the explorers, with Balboa sighting the Pacific Ocean and Magellan rounding the world.

Bare and exposed lay a human brain. Albeniz looked up from it to the X-ray, hanging directly in his line of vision. There the arteries turned and curved like grapevines or Virginia creeper. There lay the dark blot and clump of tumor. Martin's heart pounded. He tried to remember what he had learned about the brain; neurons, axons, dendrites—and could only think: There somewhere in that roughly corrugated mass, that lump made of the same stuff as stomach or liver, ran the electricity of thought. Out of it came words, music and commands to clench a fist or kiss beloved lips.

"Clamp," said Albeniz.

His hands in their pale gloves moved inside the patient's brain, moved among those billions of neurons.

"Cautery," he said. "Suction."

Five and a half hours later it was over. Albeniz looked up. His eyes, above the mask, were weary.

"I think I got it all out."

Martin knew he probably had, but no surgeon would ever say, "I know I have."

He was awestruck.

A fine surgeon is an artist, thought Martin. All eyes are on him. He may be a simple, modest man like Albeniz or a bully like some others I've seen. But either way he is respected: he has a great gift. What I should wish is to be like Dr. Albeniz.

What am I dreaming of?

In such limited free time as he had, Martin observed Dr. Albeniz. He went to his laboratory and to his clinic. With curiosity and fascination he followed some cases through surgery and into ultimate rehabilitation—or else to post-mortem. He asked questions, but not too many.

Someone asked, "You going in for neurosurgery? That why you've been hanging around Albeniz?"

Not very likely! Who could afford to go in for graduate work? Only very special people, types who could drift through Europe from clinic to clinic, spending a half year here and a half year there with the great authorities of Germany or England, steeping themselves, acquiring knowledge and finally, a name. For that sort of thing you needed independent means. Certainly you needed time. Probably too you needed a mentor to foster and advise.

He was about to go off duty one afternoon when he was summoned to Dr. Albeniz's laboratory. Perplexed by the summons, he went at once. The doctor was hanging up his lab coat.

"I was wondering whether you like Italian food. There's a place just a few blocks down Third Avenue."

"I've never had any," Martin said.

"Good! It'll be a new experience, and everybody likes Italian food, even Spaniards like myself."

Outside on the windy street Albeniz explained, "In case you're wondering about this occasion, it's just because I like to talk to the rising medical generation now and then."

"It's very good of you, sir." Martin hoped he didn't appear as awkward as he felt.

When they were seated with a clean, darned cloth and a basket of bread between them, Albeniz asked, "Would you like me to order for you?"

"Please do."

"All right then. Clams oreganata to begin. Pasta, of course. Salad. Do you like veal? Veal pizzaiola, then. Isn't it ridiculous to eat like this without wine? A fine, dry wine with the sunshine in it? You Americans are such Puritans with your Prohibition." He sighed, rubbing his hands to warm them and was silent a moment. He took off his glasses and rubbed the bridge of his nose.

"You know, I've been watching you watch me these last months. You find my work interesting, don't you?"

"Yes, I—" Martin began, but Albeniz interrupted him.

"Tell me why you wanted to be a doctor."

Martin said slowly, "It always seemed, as far back as I can remember, the most exciting thing I could imagine."

"Yes?"

"And I was curious. It's like solving puzzles. You want to go to the next one." He stopped, feeling the inadequacy of his explanation.

But the other man smiled. "I'm glad you didn't say 'to help humanity,' or 'because I love people.' Some such rubbish. I hear young men say that and I don't believe them."

Martin was silent.

"Of course you rejoice when you've done something good for another human being! And of course you feel pity when things go wrong! But if you feel too much pity, you break your heart. Or you go crazy." He waved an admonishing finger. "You have to be disciplined, controlled and expert, a puzzle-solver, as you just said. Then, when the mind is beautifully clear and very cool, then you can really do some good. Sometimes. You understand me?"

"I think so."

The clams were brought. Albeniz took a mouthful, then laid the fork down. "We know so little. Take my field. It's only for the last thirty years or so that we've dared to go very far into the brain. Neurosurgery is a new discipline and most of what we know we've learned since the war." He paused, picked up the fork and put it down again.

"Although, taking another point of view, it's very old. Ancient, in fact. The Egyptians trephined the skull four thousand years ago, using sharpened stones."

With a clean fork, he pressed a diagram into the tablecloth.

"You were in the war, weren't you, Doctor?"

"I worked in a British military hospital. My clinical training I had taken in Germany before the war." Albeniz shrugged. "Medicine knows no politics, or shouldn't. But that early work was crude. There were too many infections. We've come a good way since then."

"I see that."

"Did you know we're going to have a separate department starting in September? At last we'll be removed from general surgery. And high time."

"I didn't know."

"Well, it's just been decided. Of course, that will be only a start. What we ought to have, what I dream of, is an institute where neurosurgery and neurology could be combined. Then we could truly study the whole brain: its function, pathology, even the tie-in with what is called 'mental illness,' which has, I've long been convinced, a physical cause. Perhaps God knows how many physical causes." He sighed. "But, as I say, that's only my dream. I haven't the money or the influence to make it come true. I'm no good at medical politics. I'll just be grateful for this little new department and let it go at that." He made a small pyramid with his fingertips. "I'm talking too much. Tell me, what do you think about what I've just told you?"

Martin shook his head. "I haven't any right to think. I don't know anything about it."

"Well spoken! I like that! I detest these fellows who go on rounds and wisely nod their heads, pretending to know, when they haven't the slightest idea what it's all about. How do you like the veal?"

"Oh, great! Some change from the cafeteria!"

"I should hope so. Tell me, what are you planning to do when you finish in June?"

"Work with my father. He's got a general practice upstate."

Dr. Albeniz studied Martin. His austere face softened.

"Are you happy about it?"

No one had ever put the question like that. People assumed he was happy. You finished your internship; then you went into practice, and if you had one already waiting for you, why then, you were just very, very lucky indeed! So he waited a moment and then, for the first time, expressed the truth.

"No sir, I don't think I am."

"I see."

"I guess I haven't wanted to admit it, even to myself."

He turned away, looking at an amateurish painting of Italy, candy-pink roses against a white wall and a gaudy blue sky.

"Have some more pasta. You're thin enough to afford it."

"Thank you, but I'm not all that hungry."

"I've upset you with my questions, haven't I?"

"A little, maybe."

"More than a little. You know, or maybe you don't know, that I've been observing you? Ever since that time you sewed up the girl's face. It's strange that you should have come to my attention through work that's not in my field, but I knew that the hands which could do that without having been taught could do much more."

Martin waited. He became conscious of his heartbeat.

"And then you began coming to watch me, and you came to the lab and you asked intelligent questions."

The beat accelerated.

"You're aware, of course, that you've earned a reputation this year?"

"Well, I—"

"Come, come! Dr. Fields tells me you're the best intern he's had in his service in ten years."

"I didn't know that, sir."

"Well, you know it now. So hear me. I'm coming to the point. In this new service that I'm to have, I can train two young men. I already have one coming from Philadelphia in the fall. I'm asking you to be the other."

Martin looked at him dumbly.

"You understand what I'm driving at. I wouldn't have to waste words with you. I'm doing a lot of talking now, but the fact is, I don't talk much when I'm working. I'm an impatient man and I need people around me who grasp my meaning quickly. I could work with you, Martin." He paused, then added thoughtfully, "I want a man who will grasp the whole concept of the brain, not just a skillful surgeon-mechanic. I want someone who has curiosity. That's the key word, curiosity. What do you say?"

"Forgive me. I'm stunned."

"Of course, it's a new idea for you! This would be another world from the one you had been planning on—sore throats, measles and cut fingers. Not that we don't need good men who're willing to do that. Men like your father. What do you think he will say to this?"

"He'll be terribly disappointed, I'm afraid."

Sick over it. Dread sank in Martin like a stone.

"Yes, I can imagine. I've never had a son, but I can imagine your father would want you to come home. Still," Albeniz said quietly, "there are always some who have to break the soft family ties no matter how it hurts. In a way it's like being a soldier or a monk. I was forty before I got married. In Europe men marry later; it gives them time to develop. My wife knew she would come second to my work. Late at night, on Sundays if need be, I'm at the hospital. It is my devotion. Perhaps I express it badly, English not being my native language."

"No, sir, you express it very well."

"You think so? Yes, well, devotion, then. Look. I move my finger. An electrical impulse in my brain provides the energy with which I move the finger. Simple, eh? You think so? Of course you don't! What if the signal is given and the finger refuses to move? What if a finger moves when the brain doesn't want it to? These are the tantalizing mysteries. We still know nothing. Nothing. Talk of exploring the poles! Here's exploration for you!" He broke off abruptly. "You have a girl?"

Martin flushed. "Yes . . . No . . . I mean, there's nothing official, but—"

But her face floats over the pages of my textbooks and no matter what else I'm thinking of, part of me is always thinking of her.

Albeniz smiled. "Well, you'll work that out. There's always a way." He stood up. "You will get twenty dollars a month and your keep. You will live penuriously, unless, of course, your family has money."

"Oh no!"

"Then you will live penuriously. There are worse things. In time, you'll be rewarded for your work with some of life's comforts, but you will deserve them then, which is more than can be said for a lot of people who live in comfort. Well, I'm going back to the lab for an hour and then home." He shook Martin's hand. "The next time we come you'll try the spaghetti carbonara."

Martin was halfway back to his room before he realized that Albeniz hadn't even waited for his acceptance. He had simply taken for granted that no young man could do anything other than accept. And of course, he had been right!

There was such a beating and fluttering in his chest that he couldn't shut himself indoors just yet; he had to move, to walk. He went rapidly across town. Past Fifth Avenue, where the great stores were shut for the night. Past Sixth Avenue, where the last late workers were leaving the office towers. Westward and southward through shoddy streets. Blowing papers wrapped themselves around his ankles. A luncheonette released the smell of frying grease. Near Times Square a Chinese restaurant wore a garish red-and-gold faked pagoda front. The lights of a dance palace blinked in and out. "Fifty Gorgeous Girls. Fifty." And it was beautiful. Everything was beautiful.

After a long time, he turned back. He felt like shouting out his glory. Remembering his father, he pushed the thought away, knowing that he would handle things somehow because, as Dr. Albeniz had said, there's always a way.

Then he thought of Mary. She would be home soon and he would talk to her. How foolish of him not to have told her how he felt before she left! Not that she hadn't known! He smiled to himself. Well, in another month he would put everything into words; he'd buy her a little ring; the three years wouldn't be all that long to wait. Her father—there was another problem, of course, but not insurmountable, either. Donald Meig's displeasure was hardly the end of the world!

He sat down at the desk and began a letter. He thought of asking her then and there to marry him, but the words looked either too stark or too florid and he decided he'd rather wait to speak them aloud and hear her answer. For the present he would only describe the marvel that had occurred tonight.

When he had finished he stood for a while looking out of the window. The soft, cold air of February, faintly damp with the nearness of spring, washed over him. A light went on in the wing of private rooms across the street. An ambulance, its tires making a small sigh on the pavement, rounded the corner. He took a long breath and spoke to his empty little room.

"I am going to be a great doctor." It was half a declaration and half a wondering question. "I am going to be a great doctor."

By two o'clock in the afternoon of the following day everybody knew about Martin. He was the only intern in the program who would be going on to specialize. It was something to talk about, to be envious of or impressed by. Tom puzzled over it.

"Oh, it's a stupendous opportunity," he admitted. "But I don't know, Martin, it's a depressing specialty. The patients are all strangers, people you'll never see again. And most of them die, you know they do."

"But if we take that attitude, they always will. The idea is to keep them from dying, isn't it?"

"Well, I can't wait to get out on my own. Beats me how you can even think of another three years."

Tom and Florence were to be married in July and he was to set up practice in Teaneck, New Jersey, with three thousand dollars borrowed from their families. The early marriage Martin could understand and envy, but not the haste to leave the hospital.

I love it here, he thought. For me it's the heart of the world.

Never before had he experienced such euphoria, such joy. Everything blossomed. He found himself singing as he moved around his room in the mornings. All the faces on the street were friendly. He wanted to walk up to people, grasp them by the buttonhole and shout at them: Isn't it a wonderful life? There's so much you can do with it! So much work, so much love—if only there were more time! Yes, it's so wonderful and there'll never be enough time for it all!

Then one day he decided to tell Tom and Perry about Mary. Their goodwill, their good wishes for him brought the usual tears to his eyes and their usual jokes about those foolish tears of his; they knew each other well!

Tom asked, "Have you told your father yet about Albeniz?"

"No, not yet."

"Well, what are you waiting for?"

"I'm a coward, I guess. But I'll do it when I go home next month. When Mary gets back."

He'd had only a postcard since he had written his news. They had been moving about all over England; she would write a real letter soon. In the meantime she wanted him to know that his news was wonderful. She was happy for him and proud.

He stuck the card in the mirror above the dresser and read it over morning and night.

At last there came a thick envelope, postmarked "London." Cutting the lunch hour short, Martin went to his room, locked the door and sat down, enjoying his anticipation. His eyes sped over the pages—

". . . Alex's mother has been a friend of Aunt Milly's and Uncle Drew's for years. He's a wonderful person. You would really like him! His wife died when their baby was born, a beautiful little boy, Neddie. . . . The wedding will naturally be very small, but I don't mind. Jessie and Father will come over for it, and we shall have the ceremony at Alex's house—so old, deep country and yet not far from London. You can see sheep on the hills in back of the garden. . . . I know you will be surprised at the suddenness of all this. I am myself! But I am so very, very happy."

He thought at first that she was talking about someone else who was going to be married, a friend or someone met on her travels. He read it again. Then he went to sit on the edge of the bed. He put his head in his hands and felt ill: giddy, as though he were going to vomit.

You would like him, she dared to write! Like him!

Martin groaned. For an instant he had a crazy sensation: he was imagining this, it was a nightmare and in a minute he would wake up. But no, there it was, three compact pages in her own backhand script.

Why? How? Didn't she know what he felt for her? Had she felt nothing, then, for him? Could he have been imagining that, also?

Or had she measured him against this—this Alex and found him the lesser of the two?

Oh, Tom was the lucky one! A solid woman like Florence was what a man wanted! A woman who knew her own mind, instead of—

He pounded his knees with his fists. Timid, short-sighted fool that I am! To assume that she would be there, waiting, ready whenever I was ready! Instead of making sure, instead of saying, that last night on the front steps—

He went into the bathroom and was violently sick. Then he came back and sat for a while, staring at the wall. After a time he picked the letter off the floor and ripped it across, ripped it over and over, and flung the shreds back on the floor. His arms felt heavy. A great weight descended and he threw himself down on the bed.

Someone pounded at the door. Martin opened his eyes into weak, departing sunlight.

"Are you in there? Open the door. Where've you been?" Tom cried. "Didn't you hear the squawk-box? They've been calling you for an hour!"

"I didn't hear. I don't seem to be feeling well."

"Sit down. I have to talk to you." Tom's long, ugly face was suddenly sad, like Lincoln's face.

"What's the matter?"

"First tell me what your trouble is. Are you really sick?"

"Yes. No. I've had a kind of blow, that's all."

Tom studied him. "Is it anything you want to tell me about?" he asked softly.

"Mary's being married in England," Martin said, looking at the floor.

"I'm sorry! Oh, Martin, I'm so sorry!"

"I know you are."

"You don't deserve it—"

A fire engine clanged in the street below. When it had passed, the silence was absolute.

After a minute Tom spoke. "I have to hit you again, Martin. Have to hit you when you're down."

Martin looked up. Distress furrowed Tom's cheeks, furrowed and creased them.

"What do you mean?"

"Your sister telephoned. When you didn't answer, they told me instead. Your father's had a stroke."

⤳6⤵

He slid the flivver into the shed. Dean, their old, brown, calloused horse, thrust his head out of the stall. He'd outlived his usefulness and Pa was simply saving him from the glue factory. Hideous thought.

Martin entered the stall and laid his head against the hard, rippling shoulder. Its living warmth gave comfort. He felt such loneliness! With Alice married and gone, with his mother herself in need of strengthening, there was no one to talk to. And after all, what was there to talk about?

Should he talk about Mary? No use in that. It was over and done with. Strange how chemistry worked, how the flow of man's desiring could be extinguished by time and troubles as a fire is quenched.

Talk about his father, the withered flesh, the tottering walk? What is there to say about a life that's running out? Just running out, like this horse's life, old Dean's.

Anybody coming in would think he'd lost his wits, standing here like this. And abruptly repelled by his own sadness, Martin straightened and went into the house.

"Pa gone up to bed this early?" he asked.

"No, he had his supper and went to his desk in the office." Jean lowered her voice. "It seems to help him, sitting there looking at old records and things. I suppose he feels he's busy. Martin?" Something in her tone made him look up. "Martin, I didn't know he'd taken a new mortgage on the house, did you?"

"I? No. He's never talked business affairs with me."

"Well. The original mortgage had been paid off before you went to high school . . . I don't understand." His mother's lips trembled. "How could he have worked so hard all these years and we still have nothing? It just seemed to go as fast as it came in. It's not as if we'd had any luxuries. Well, yes, we did buy the new parlor suite last year; the old one was really a disgrace. And we put new linoleum down. But I wouldn't even have done that if I had known."

He didn't answer, there being nothing to say. She set his plate on the table, poured coffee and, attempting cheer, sighed, "Well, what's done is done I guess. No use bemoaning it."

If there is anything pathetic, Martin thought, it is penury in old age, the specter of dependency. Old age must be hard enough without that.

510

From the kitchen table he could see into the parlor, where above the brown imitation Chippendale sofa hung the new photograph of his parents, taken fortuitously only a few months before Pa's stroke. Alice had wanted it taken. Ma had resisted, but Alice had pressed. It was only because she was moving away, she had said. Privately she had told Martin of her feeling that something was going to happen.

"You couldn't have known Pa was going to have a stroke," he had argued.

And she had said no, she certainly hadn't known that. She had simply felt that *something* might be going to happen and she wanted the photo before it was too late. So they stood for all time together in a gilded oval frame, the mother wearing a silk dress and a gold watch on a neck chain, the father in his dark good suit, looking, for him, unusually dapper and spruce. He would never look that way again.

"You saw Ken Thompkins today?" Ma inquired now.

"Yes. He won't last the night. He's been vomiting from a strangulated hernia since last Wednesday and they didn't call till today. His wife thought it was colic." Martin could hear the exasperation in his own voice. "My God, what pitiful ignorance! I thought as a last hope we could rush him to Baker for surgery. I would've driven him the seventy miles myself, but he wouldn't go. Says if he's going to die, he wants to die at home." And Martin threw out his hand in a gesture of hopelessness, tipping the coffee cup.

His mother rose to wipe the spill and handed him two letters. "I forgot. Here's mail for you."

Martin propped the letters against his water glass, reading over a lifted fork. Tom wrote that he had opened his office. He had got privileges at a good hospital. Florence was keeping her job, and they were gradually furnishing the house. Martin must somehow get down to see them.

The second letter was from Dr. Albeniz. He was holding Martin's place open. He understood the circumstances, but hoped Martin would be able to set things in order at home within the next few weeks.

"Something wrong, Martin?"

"No. Tired, that's all."

"I don't know what we'd do without you," his mother said. "It would be disaster, plain and simple. Isn't it the hand of Providence, though, that if this had to happen to your father, it waited until you were finished and ready to take his place?" She stood frowning a little, wiping and wiping the spot, now dry, where the spill had been. Then becoming aware of his gaze, she brightened. "Oh, I hear my raccoons at the trash! They're almost tame, coming for their bread every night. I used to be annoyed with them, but your father taught me— You remember your pet raccoon, Martin? You were only about seven or eight when Pa found it along the road. Remember?"

He was not fooled by her brave prattle.

"Pa's doing better, you know," he said gently.

"Martin, you mean well, but I'd rather have the truth. I see him going downhill. Give me the truth: What's going to happen?"

"Ma, I don't know. I'd tell you if I did. I'd be surprised if he improved any, but he could go on no worse than this for years. Or he could have another stroke or a coronary tonight."

Her eyes widened. "Oh, it isn't fair! He was so good to everyone!"

The night-bell rings. Sleet clatters on the windowpane. Pa creaks down the stairs and out the door; the motor coughs in the garage. The time is two-fifteen . . .

"No," Martin said, "it isn't fair." (Not if you believed in just rewards, which he didn't and his mother did.)

Presently the collies began barking in the yard, subsiding as they recognized a familiar voice.

"Sounds like Charlie Spears," Jean said. She opened the door. "I thought it was you! Why, Charlie, what have you got there?"

Charlie Spears came in and set a carton of groceries on the floor. "Thought you might use some extras from the store outside of your regular order. A few delicacies for Doc. Doc Senior," this with a nod to Martin. "He was always partial to bananas, and here's Scotch marmalade, herb tea, water biscuits and some of that there smelly foreign cheese. I never liked it myself, but then, there's no accounting for taste, as they say."

Jean flushed. "Charlie, you're too good to us. You shouldn't, really you shouldn't. We're doing fine and—"

Charlie looked up sharply. " 'Twasn't charity, Missus. 'Twas because Doc was always real good to me and he's a friend."

When he had gone, Jean said, "People have been so kind. Sometimes it's hard not to cry, they've been so kind. It's one of the rewards of this kind of life. So you see, it isn't all hardship, Martin."

"I know that, Ma," Martin said firmly.

There were shuffling steps in the hall, and his father appeared in the doorway. "Who was that?"

"Charlie Spears. He brought you a package of goodies."

Enoch glanced at the carton without interest.

"I'm bored," he said petulantly. "Nothing to do here all day."

"You'll just have to learn to kill time," Jean told him, "until you get to be yourself again."

Enoch stared at her. "Kill time! That's the worst thing you could have said. It's time that's killing me. Well, I'm going up to bed. Good night, folks."

He struggled slowly up the stairs. It was difficult because the bannister was on the right and it was his right arm which had been weakened. Once when he faltered, Martin rose to help, but his mother waved him back with a signal.

"He doesn't want to be helped."

And Martin knew that this understanding was born of thirty-four years of life together.

So they sat, the wife and the son, not speaking, stirring the coffee in their cups. Chink. The spoon struck the cup, then ground around the sides again. Chink. Once more the collies barked, this time at the front of the house. Martin got up and went to look. There was nothing to be seen in all that darkness except the band of light that slid from the open door. Then his nose led him to the basket of apples, to the sharp, fresh scent of Greenings.

"Martin, what is it?"

"Somebody's left apples on the porch. There's no name. That's odd."

"Not odd. People do that lots of times when they can't pay and Pa's written them off. They feel they want to give whatever they can. No, leave them there. You can carry them to the root cellar in the morning." She went back to the kitchen.

He sat down on the porch step next to the apples, with a dog on either side. A fox barked from the woodlot across the road. Low on the horizon, just above the trees, Orion shone. You couldn't be Pa's son, he thought, without having learned something about the constellations. The sky looked lonely, the universe larger and more lonely than at other times and in other places.

If he could hear some music, it would be a comfort, he thought, remembering the soaring voices and soaring strings. All the lights! All the life! Why couldn't he just accept?

Alice had gone with Fred to live with his parents in Maine and she, a woman with no place of her own, was not complaining. Although, who knew how she really felt about it? Her letters were always cheerful. But then, Martin wasn't given to talking much about his feelings, either.

"You're letting the cold air into the house." Jean stood in the doorway. "I'm going to bed. You coming up, too?"

Martin and the dogs went in. "Soon. I thought maybe I'd go over some things in Pa's desk."

"Oh, I wish you would! If he had only let me take care of things! I always wanted him to, but he didn't believe in a woman doing all that. I know the bankbooks are somewhere in the desk. I guess you can find them." She hesitated. "I don't want to bother him by asking how much money there is, as if I expected him to die." Tears stood in her eyes, puddled there, but not overflowing. "So it would be a good idea if you'd look things over. Only don't stay up too late. You need your rest."

The old rolltop overflowed with paper. Out of childhood came the recollection of his mother's exasperated voice: "If you would just once let me straighten this mess up, Enoch!"

Under a pile of prescription blanks, old postcards, letters, calendars and samples of medicine in cardboard containers, lay a marriage certificate and birth certificates, Alice's and Martin's own. Also Enoch Junior's, Susan's and May's. Why on earth had Pa kept those? Here was the mortgage agreement, which should be in a safe deposit box in case of fire. Here was the disability policy, small at best, but invalid now at age sixty-five, just when you were most likely to need it. Martin swallowed outrage. And here three savings-bankbooks, tossed in the muddle. He opened them and added the sum. Four thousand, four hundred eighty-three dollars and seventy-six cents. He rummaged incredulously for another book, but there was none. This was it. This was all Pa had, after a lifetime of labor.

He sat in a kind of stunned despair. The pity of it! Four thousand dollars and this modest house, an upended box devoid of comfort or grace, that needed every kind of repair anyway. How often had he not heard the story, told with pride, of how this house had been acquired?

"I had my eye on it, at the crossroads, and only three and a half miles from Cyprus. The bank was glad to make the loan. I had a good reputation already; and I'd only been in this country six years."

So then, this house and a basket of apples left by a grateful patient. And who would take care of them now, except their son?

It must have been hard for his mother. He remembered the time Pa had dropped a hundred and twenty-five dollars. He'd had the money stuffed in his pocket on his way to town to pay bills.

"I even made you a leather purse," his mother had mourned. "Why don't you use it?"

And Pa had been ashamed. "I forgot."

There were the times he had actually given money to patients. "They had nothing," he would say, and his mother's lips would grow tight and thin, as though she were fastening them together with a pin. She'd been afraid to speak, having never got over the honor of being married to him. If she had ever had regrets, she had not admitted them, probably not even to herself. True to her stern beliefs, she would accept without complaint whatever burden the Lord might see fit to lay upon her.

For a long time Martin sat, then abruptly reached for a piece of paper and a pen. He could have poured out pages of his grievous disappointment, but nobody beside himself cared about that. Each man bore his grievous disappointments alone. So the pen slipped rapidly across a single sheet of paper.

"Dear Dr. Albeniz, Thank you for waiting until I could reach a final decision. I appreciate your patience and your understanding . . . grateful and honored by your offer . . . impossible because of my family situation . . . regret. Very good wishes."

Short and sweet. He put his hands over his face. His sadness was so vast it emptied him. He was hollow, floating in chill gray sadness, in shreds of vapor, fog and whispers. Everything that had been so bright and pulsing had just quietly slipped away, fallen from his outstretched hands. Gone. All gone.

A great wind rushed past the house. Wind of the world, carrying a hundred million hopes away. Not just mine. Remember that.

And rolling the top down on the scattered papers in the desk, he went upstairs to sleep in the maple bed which had been his ever since he had outgrown a crib.

THE YEAR HURRIED toward its close. The lakes froze; a thin film of dimpled ice hardened and thickened. Among the neighbors Christmas preparations made a pleasant bustle as tins of peanut brittle and homemade fudge were carried from house to house. Pine sprays with red bows were hung on front doors and small boys careened down the hills on their Flexible Flyers.

Christmas morning brought a sugary, fresh fall of snow. Shortly after six o'clock, Martin was called out. When he got back it was almost time for dinner. Pa looked up questioningly.

"Anything important today? Anything I ought to know?"

"I think I've finally persuaded Mary Deitz to have the goiter operated on."

"She's had that goiter fifteen years! Cut, cut, that's all you young fellows know how to do." Pa was having one of his cranky days.

"I'm not the one who's going to do it, more's the pity."

"Hmph. You were telling me something the other day about something in the —the ventricle . . . I don't remember. What was it again?"

"The ventriculogram, you mean?"

"Yes, that's it. How does that work again?"

"Well, it's—you remove the ventricular fluid and you inject air through a hole in the skull. Then you can tell by X-ray where the air has moved within the brain. That's putting it very simply, of course."

"Hmph. I dare say there's good in a lot of this new stuff. But these fellows don't know everything, Martin. Just because they fasten their names onto some high-sounding articles, don't let them fool you."

"No, Pa. I won't let them fool me." He looked so small and old, standing there. And also, in a dreadful way, he looked childish.

"What'll happen when you fellows have divided up the whole human body among yourselves, hey? One'll study the left ear, the other will study the right knee! Why, there won't be a doctor among the lot of you fit to treat a whole patient!"

Pa had used to say, "You will see such marvels in your lifetime, Martin!" But now illness and the hidden envy that can corrupt old age had changed him into someone else. And his son's heart ached.

The Christmas table was set in the dining room which was on the chilly side of the house. Pa felt the cold. "I don't know why we had to eat in here," he complained.

"I'll put the electric heater near you," Martin offered.

"No, wait, I'll get it," Jean said. "You carve the turkey, Martin."

That had been his father's job. All those years of Christmas and Thanksgiving turkeys, of Easter hams, eaten in this room! It would be Martin's job now, so he guessed he'd better learn. Strip the leg off first, take apart at the joint, now cut the wing. Now slice neatly from the breast.

"My, that's expert," his mother said heartily. "Enoch, will you say the grace?"

"Let Martin do it."

"For what we are about to receive, Father, we thank Thee," Martin murmured.

The platters passed between the three of them. Pa's plate was mounded with creamed onions, turkey, mashed turnip, mashed potatoes and cranberry sauce. He had not lost his enormous appetite. Silently, voraciously he ate, gazing with abstracted eyes at the sideboard array of Jean's best cut-glass bowls and her "good" dishes.

"Those dishes were given to us when we were married," Jean said suddenly. "And do you know, there's only been one broken, and it wasn't done by me. It was one of the neighbors helping clear the table. That's why I never like anyone to help me. Even if they don't break things, they chip them."

There was a silence. Martin tried to think of something to say.

"I do wish Alice were here," Jean remarked.

He understood that the remark was partly an expression of a real wish and partly an effort to break the silence. He tried to cooperate. "Do you suppose she'll have a chance to visit before spring?"

"I shouldn't think so. The roads are awfully bad and the train connections are dreadful. She'd have to travel all the way east to Boston, and then come west again."

"I imagine she'll do it all the same," Martin guessed.

"Oh, she might at that. She's a good daughter, Alice is. And I know she wants to see her father. Anybody like to try my mincemeat? I brought two jars up from the cellar. It's so good the next day with cold turkey. Enoch! Enoch! What is it?"

Pa's hands clutched at his chest. "I don't feel well." He pushed his chair violently away from the table. "I have a terrible pain. Terrible!" he cried, very loud.

And while in an instant of dumb shock they stared at him, he stood up, stretched tall and reaching, stiffened, buckled at the knees and toppled. His face struck the edge of the table with a dreadful, tearing sound. Then the chair broke, splintering as Enoch and the chair both crashed to the floor.

"Oh God!" Jean screamed. "Oh God! Enoch, get up! Martin! Enoch! Get up!" Her cry was to repeat itself in Martin's ears for the rest of his life, and Christmas was to be marked with the memory of it forever.

ENOCH WAS LAID out in the parlor between the two front windows. People came with proper grave faces, bending to the widow, who, her first spasms of weeping past, sat quietly acknowledging their hushed sympathy. They looked down at the dead man in his dark suit and his secret dignity: *I have gone beyond your small concerns and I know what you cannot know.* They stood looking with embarrassment and fear. They walked, risen on the balls of their feet, and with the same grave, tragic faces, left the room.

They stood in knots on the porch, on the walk and in the road, hailing one another, greeting briskly.

"Want a lift home, George?"

"Say, when'd you get the new car?"

Alone in the evening, Martin went back into the room. It was not his father's face that moved him most, it was his hands. Wasn't that strange? Yes, his hands, folded on the chest where the undertaker had arranged them, waxy and larger than life. Were they really that large or was it because of something the undertaker had done? Hands, that marvelous circuitry of brain to hand that can curve to catch a ball, clench to a smashing fist, or open to touch with gentle palm. Marvelous, marvelous. My father's hands.

And somewhere out of his most cursory readings in psychiatry, Martin remembered: Was it Freud who said that the greatest blow to a man is the death of his father? All the knotted, complicated web of memories, resentments, comfort and confidence, humor and wisdom and stubborn foolishness—everything, all of it that made me and that I shall carry through my years lies here. You try to make some order out of it, and there is none. It ends in this.

My father, you've gone so far away. I think that if I talk loud enough, surely you will hear me. I can't understand why it is that you can't hear. You lie there, but you've gone. Everything's *stopped* in you. It terrifies me, this death of yours. I've seen death so often by now, but not your death. There are things I would like to have talked to you about when you were yourself and well. In so many ways Ma has been the head of the household, for somebody had to try to manage things. But you were always the heart. You were the heart.

IN THE PILE of letters that arrived during the next week, there came a note from Jessie Meig.

"Father and I were so sorry to learn of your father's death. He was a kind, old-fashioned man. He will be missed. If you ever have time, would you come to visit us? Would the Sunday after next for tea at four be all right?"

He whipped the letter against the table's edge. Be damned if he would walk into that house again! What did they think of him, for God's sake? Why should he want to visit there? A small fury surged in his chest, and then receded. Very likely they weren't thinking anything. Then he felt foolish.

He looked at the letter again, at the blunt black strokes: an unusual script, individual and strong, rather like Jessie herself. He wondered what life was like for her now in that house with her sister gone. Not that they had been that warm toward one another! Still, a sister was a sister. He was tempted to accept. Admittedly, and not unnaturally, he was a little curious. Why not? But on second thought, he decided he really didn't want to go.

A few weeks later his mother reported, "Jessie Meig telephoned today. She wondered whether you had got her note."

He was ashamed of his rudeness. Perhaps he had been more than rude? Perhaps even terribly unkind, rejecting the well-meaning, outstretched hand? Then he had a mental picture of Jessie, seated in the enormous wing-chair, almost curled within it, as though she felt protected by the wings. He had forgotten how small she was, and he thought: Out of pure decency, I ought to go.

So, on the following Sunday afternoon he strode up the walk between the iron deer, stood under thawing icicles on the porch and entered the house he had never expected to enter again.

❖ 7 ❖

Jessie put the remainder of the lunch into a bag and capped the Thermos. "Do you want to drive, Martin, or shall I?"

"It's your car. You drive."

Summer had barely peaked and already the first small signs of its wane were beginning to appear. Blueberries, powdered with pale dust, were thick along the roadside. Queen Anne's lace stood stiff and starched in the fields.

Ever since winter's end, Jessie had been going along with Martin on his far country house calls. He wasn't quite sure how the habit had been formed; he thought vaguely that it might have been her father who had suggested it. At any rate, that negative, inhibiting person had been surprisingly cordial during these past months.

"It'll do you good to get out more," he had said.

Certainly that was true. Jessie's need for companionship was visible enough. Martin understood, because the same need was in him. He missed good talk, that quick comprehension which comes when the associations and the bent of mind are kin. Most of his boyhood friends had dispersed; those still here at home were married and there was no place for Martin in their households. After five close years, he felt the loss of men like Tom and Perry. It seemed sometimes that in all of Cyprus the one person to whom he could really talk was Jessie Meig.

The father went upstairs in the evening now, leaving the library to them. Martin had come to take his place opposite Jessie at the chessboard. She usually beat him! There was music on the radio; there was pleasant comfort.

"You're worried about something again," she said, taking the wheel. "I can always tell."

"I am. It's that place we stopped at before lunch. I'm still feeling sort of sick about it."

"The woman with the cough?"

"Cough and nausea. She's lost sixteen pounds in the last two months. I know it's a malignancy. I'm so sure I'd take a bet on it." He shook his head in recollection of the dreary young woman with the delicate face. "I told them she needs to go to the hospital for tests. I was as emphatic as I could be without using the word 'cancer.' I said she must go, that there was no choice. The husband kept saying, 'She's just weak after birthing and she'll be all right.' *He* assured *me!* And

518

anyway, the hospital was out of the question. Who would take care of the kids? Then he followed me outside and told me he'd be careful, he knew she'd had too many kids too fast. She wasn't strong like some women. He'd see she had no more. Oh, she'll have no more!" Martin said grimly. "She won't be alive nine months from now."

"Trouble started in the ovaries, I suppose."

"Why, yes, I've a pretty good idea it did. But how do you know? Were you guessing?"

"You told me something once about another case that sounded like this one. I would never want to be a doctor, but still I do like to listen to you and I do remember things."

"And I—if I couldn't have been a doctor, there's nothing else in the world I would have wanted to be."

Around a bend, they were slowed almost to a stop by a wagon with an enormous load of hay. From the top of the pile a woman called cheerfully, "Hi, Doc!"

"That's good fodder you've got there," Martin called back.

"Yes, and we'll be needing it before you know it. The older I get, the shorter the summers get."

"Just don't throw that back out again unloading!"

"They like you, Martin," Jessie said when they drove on.

"I like them."

In his few short months of practice he had been touched a dozen times with powerful emotion and the emotion of power. In their houses, in the beds where the fevered lay with brilliant eyes, they turned to him in trust. Touching their sick flesh, he could feel their engulfing gratitude and admiration. Something swelled in a man then: might one call it a kind of love? And yet he knew, although they did not, that what he did was often not enough and should be better.

"Most illness is self-limiting," he mused aloud now. "Fluids, bedrest and warmth will cure most ailments in a matter of days. But what bothers me, Jessie, is the other kind. This morning's case, for instance. I'm stymied, battling distance and lack of facilities and ignorance. The patients' ignorance and my own. Mostly my own." And he repeated his thoughts aloud, "What I do could be done so much better!"

"I'm sure it could," Jessie said.

On those infrequent times when he had expressed such doubts to his mother, her standard, uncomprehending reply had always been: "Oh, you belittle yourself, Martin."

"It must be marvelous to know and do!" Jessie cried vehemently. "To be your own person! Why do people think women don't want that too? They think you're some sort of oddity if you want what a man does, the same freedom to stretch your thoughts and learn things. You know, if I were whole, I would defy all that and try it anyway. Some women do and always have. George Sand, for instance. I've read her novels, and they aren't very good, but that's not the point. She was a free woman. That's the point." Her hands were tense on the wheel. And she finished furiously, "As for me, every thought I have, every breath I take, is influenced by this damned hump."

Martin tried to change the subject. "The next place we come to used to be the Brook farm. My father would tell me every time we passed it how, back in the nineties, when he made calls in a buggy, they had a big mean dog that would lie in the tall grass beside the road and jump out at the horse. One time it made Pa's horse bolt, and the buggy turned over in the ditch. Pa broke his arm."

They passed the Brook farm without event. Silage corn was tall in the fields and cattle chewed dreamily in pasture-shade. A man, recognizing Martin, waved a paintbrush from a ladder propped against the Grecian pediment of his house, on which the facade of the Parthenon or the temple of Sounion had been reproduced in native wood. Pa, the classics student, had never failed to remark on things like that or on the names of New York State towns: Ithaca, Syracuse, Rome. And Martin's thoughts drifted on with his father.

"Pa used to carry a wire-fence cutter with him on winter calls. The roads got snowed over so often, he'd be driving through fields without knowing it. He used to fold a newspaper under his vest to keep warm. Sounds like a hundred years ago, doesn't it? But it wasn't so long ago, really. Say, doesn't that look tempting?"

In Gregory's Pond, the confluence of three streams, a few small boys were swimming.

"Why don't we bring our suits sometime?" he proposed. "Oh, I forgot, you don't like to swim."

"That's not true. I really do like to."

"But you said—"

"I only said so because I didn't want you to see me in a bathing suit. Now all of a sudden, I wouldn't mind. Maybe because you're a doctor. But I wouldn't be ashamed anymore."

"Jessie, there's nothing to be ashamed of!"

"Well, not ashamed exactly. It's that I think people will find it—disgusting," she said, so low that he barely caught her word.

" 'Nihil humanum mihi alienum est.' You said you remembered your Latin, didn't you?"

" 'Nothing human is alien to me,' " she said quietly, and after a moment, "Thank you."

"You ought to put a higher valuation on yourself, you know."

"I suppose I should. But then, so should you."

"What do you mean?"

"You ought to be doing what you *want* to do. Something more important than what you're doing."

"But what I'm doing *is* important. These sick people are important."

"Of course they are! But you're one of the movers, the advance guard, Martin. Listen! There are people who sing in the chorus, and we need them. Then there's the tenor lead, and we need him most of all."

"Maybe you overestimate me."

"Oh, I despise false modesty! What's that magazine sticking out of your bag? You've had it there since last week."

"This?" He drew out a copy of *Brain*. In a moment of high hopes he had taken a subscription to it. "Oh. There's a fascinating article this month about an operation for the removal of the frontal lobe. I'll lend it to you if you want to read it."

"I wonder what a person is like after that?"

"From what I've read they're recognizably 'normal.' They do lose some—mental energy, I guess you could call it—desire to figure out new undertakings, and so on. But I guess that's better than the alternative."

"Incredible! The whole business is, delving inside the brain."

"Yes. I used to watch Dr. Albeniz operate— It seemed almost magical to me."

"Isn't he the one who wanted you to train with him?"

"Yes."

"It's been horrible for you to give it up, hasn't it?"

"Well, not easy."

He would have to stop thinking about it, learn to accept reality and cultivate patience. He'd never had much patience and that was another flaw in him.

"I'm sorry I brought it up just now," Jessie said soberly.

"That's all right."

"It's not all right. It's like taunting you with your impossible dream, and that's cruel."

"I'm not the most deprived person in the world, after all."

"No, but you are depressed more than you should be."

Was it so evident then? And he was always so careful to be briskly cheerful!

"Oh, you don't show it. You needn't worry about that. But I've told you, I'm queer that way. I can sense hidden things in people."

Astonishing girl! For it was true. Melancholy, sticky and gray as cobwebs, had been clinging to him.

"There's something I've been wanting to say to you, Martin. I haven't done it because you're so reserved and I—"

"Reserved? Is that how you see me?"

"Of course. Don't you even know that about yourself? What I wanted to say is: I hope you have no thought that I'm running after you."

He was embarrassed. "Of course not."

"Most people wouldn't agree, I suppose, but I always think that men and women can be good friends. So I just wanted to set you straight, in case you might be thinking I was fool enough to think otherwise. These last months have been wonderful for me. You understand?"

"I understand."

The little car spun along. Jessie's keen face frowned at the road. Then she turned back to Martin.

"I've been wanting to ask you something else, too. Were you terribly in love with Fern?"

Ah, but this was too much!

"In love with her?" he answered curtly. "I scarcely knew her!"

"There's no reason to be angry."

"I'm not angry!"

"Offended, then. It was a natural question, wasn't it? Why all this so-called 'tact' and secrecy?"

No matter how blunt or shocking, this outrageous girl would say it! Yet, he thought, I am a supersensitive cuss and I know I am; my pride will be my downfall.

"But what made you think—"

"What made me? Because Fern is—Fern. If I hadn't had my own problems, I would have loved her myself." Jessie sighed. "As it is, I've almost hated her. I was rotten to her when we were children . . . Once I bloodied her nose, then when she hit me back they punished her, even though I'd started it. I have some mean memories, I can tell you."

He began vaguely, "Well, children—"

"Of course," she interrupted, "it's not bloody noses anymore. It's just feelings. As if she could help the way she is any more than I can help the way I am! I've felt so guilty sometimes, I've been sick with it."

He didn't want to listen. And he wondered whether this girl would be stripping herself before him if he hadn't been a doctor. People seemed to think that if you were a doctor you would welcome every possible confession.

"I've begrudged her very existence. Even her name, I've begrudged her that, too."

"Her name?"

"Yes. It sounds so cool and full of grace. 'Mary Fern.' 'I'm lovely,' it says. 'Mary Fern.' While I, I'm 'Jessie Gertrude.' It's a black-woolen-stocking's name. As if they took one look at me when I was born and gave me a name ugly enough to suit."

Jessie shifted gears to climb a hill. Then she said, "Fern's the total sentimentalist, you know."

Martin didn't answer. Below them the valley spread its wide, green peace. Jessie was spoiling the afternoon.

"Mother worried so about her! She used to say Fern would rather *suffer* than destroy her idea of perfection. For instance, she would never get a divorce and come home if she were to make a bad marriage. That would be an admission of defeat. Did I tell you she's pregnant?"

"No."

"They didn't lose any time, did they? But I'm glad for her, I really am. Alex is awfully nice; they've a marvelous house and a flat in London and he's really giving her encouragement with the art thing, for whatever it's worth. It should be a very good life for her at last, not having me to keep her from going places."

"Don't dwell on that, Jessie. Things probably weren't nearly as bad as you're making them."

"Yes, they were . . . You know, I've never told these things to anyone before. Do you think I'm a rotten, nasty person, Martin?"

"Of course I don't."

"I swear to you that I really, deep inside me, want everything to be good for Fern. Do you believe me?"

"I believe you and I think you're wonderful," he said gently. "Even with that sharp tongue of yours." He smiled. "You're perceptive and honest. I'm glad I know you."

She answered with untypical shyness. "Are you? Then I'm glad, too, because it's the same for me."

THE SECOND WINTER began. Still winters of the north! A branch cracks, snow sifts and falls sighing to the ground. For five months the ground is white and the spruce-covered hills are black. In the morning before you see it, you can smell the fresh snow that has fallen during the night. You hear the ringing silences of evening.

Martin's mother said suddenly, "You ought to be married."

A flush spread up her cheeks. She must have been thinking the words ever since they had left the supper table and not meant to speak them with such startling abruptness.

"There's no girl around that I want to marry."

"You haven't tried to find one, have you? All you ever do is work or go to play chess with that Jessie Meig. It's no life for a young man."

The telephone rang and Martin went to answer it. "Hello?"

"This is Donald Meig. I was thinking maybe you could run over tonight. Can you? There's something I'd like to talk to you about."

"Yes, surely, I'll be right over," Martin said, with some surprise.

Half an hour later he was in the familiar library.

"Excuse us, Jessie, will you?" Meig said. "I've a medical matter to discuss with Martin." He closed the double doors firmly. "Have a brandy. It'll warm you. You're wondering why I called you."

Meig sighed, and Martin waited. "You have problems. I have problems. Or I should say I have one problem. Yes. But I'd like to talk about yours first. I know you're not satisfied with your life here."

Martin felt ashamed. Jessie must have talked, making him look like some sorry malcontent. So he defended himself.

"I feel I've been doing a fairly good job, learning practical things that I needed to know."

Meig waved him aside. "Nonsense! Platitudes! You're not the average run-of-the-mill country doctor, and we both know it. So let's get to the heart of the matter. You've had some spectacular offers."

"One offer."

"All right. One spectacular offer. Jessie tells me it was the opportunity of a lifetime, and you've had to pass it up. Is that true?"

"True."

"A damn shame! The door opened to the future and then shut in your face for want of a few dollars!"

"A great many dollars, I'm afraid."

"All relative. What's a fortune to one man is pennies to the next. And compared with what you might earn if you could have this training, it actually is only a few dollars."

Surely the man wasn't offering to lend him money? Martin felt a peculiar distaste.

"It's not because of the dollars, however many, that I would have taken the training," he protested.

"I'm aware of that," the other man said shortly. "You've heard of Hugh Braidburn in London, the neurosurgeon?"

That was almost like asking whether one had heard of Darwin or Einstein! "Of course. He's coauthor of the textbook. Cox-Braidburn."

"Well, I'm acquainted with him. His father-in-law was the head of our plant in Birmingham. We sold the plant about ten years back, but the contacts are still there. As a matter of fact, Braidburn had dinner with us on his last trip over just before my wife died." Meig sipped the brandy thoughtfully, twirling the snifter, tilting the little amber lake. "I could get any favor I asked him for."

On a table behind the sofa stood a photograph that Martin had never seen before. Framed in silver, Mary held an armful of calla lilies, a lace veil swirling to her feet. He tried to decipher her expression but could see only the calm, reflective smile of the traditional bridal picture.

"I said," Meig demanded, "what do you think of the idea?"

"Excuse me. I wasn't—I didn't quite understand."

"Good God, man, pay attention! I asked you how you'd like to spend a couple of years in London, studying with Braidburn."

What sort of a charade was this? To study with Braidburn? Why, even Dr. Albeniz would be awed at the thought of it!

"Like it, Mr. Meig? It would be—it would be paradise! But it's impossible!"

Meig laughed. It struck Martin that he had never seen the man laugh until now, hadn't ever seen his teeth.

"It's not impossible at all. I told you I could get any favor I asked him for."

Yes, yes, Martin thought, I suppose people like these always do know somebody who will do them a favor. It's a chain, a network all over the world. If I had a voice and wanted to study for the opera, he'd know the best voice teacher in Italy, one who didn't take any more pupils but who would take me. And he became aware that his heart was beating very fast.

Meig leaned forward now, lowering his voice. "Of course, I can't expect you to understand without giving you the whole story. So now let's go to my problem. I have angina."

"I'm sorry. I didn't know."

"Nobody does. I go to a doctor in Albany because I don't want anyone around here to find out. Most especially not Jessie. I mustn't frighten her."

"If you'll excuse me, do you think that's wise? If anything were to happen to you, it would be harder for her not to have been prepared, and Jessie is nothing if not a realist."

"You know her rather well, then."

"We've had a lot of talks this past summer and fall. I can tell you I think she can cope with things far better than most of us."

"She's a bright girl. Both my girls are. They're like their mother. Soft, too.

Especially Fern. Curious about everything. Music. Pictures. Books. Jessie's got all that but not as soft. She's got a little of me in her."

Jessie would be amused to hear that. "Father's a Babbitt," she'd told Martin once, not unkindly. "He calls Uncle Drew 'arty' because he collects books, although he does make allowances since Uncle Drew is rich, after all."

Now Meig looked away at a point on the wall above Martin's head. "Damned injustice! My wife never drew a happy breath after Jessie was born." He looked back at Martin. "It's been hard, all around, very hard. We weren't always fair to Fern, either, I suppose, keeping her away from lively places where young people meet each other. But we were always torn between her and what was best for Jessie."

Martin moved restlessly. All of a sudden, it seemed to suit this cool and haughty man to confide in him! All of a sudden, and why? And what did it have to do with neurosurgery in London?

"Now let me tie all this together. I have angina, I have a daughter who will be alone in the world on the day I die. Fern has a life of her own now in England, and there are a couple of relatives in New York who also have their own lives. So what's to become of Jessie? That, young man, is my problem."

Martin was silent.

"When I'm gone and she's lonely, some clever operator will think she has millions, which she hasn't, and he'll marry her. After a while he'll leave her. Oh, there's little you can tell me about the world! I've seen it all." Meig stood up, poured more brandy and sat down again. "If I could only see her well and wisely married before I die— Marriage used to be, and in Europe among some groups even today, still is, a family contract. It's a sound, planned arrangement involving friendship and mutual interests. And that's not bad as a foundation, when you consider it carefully."

Was it possible he was going to say what Martin thought he might be going to say?

"Well. I've turned this over and over in my mind for a hundred hours, and I want to make an honest proposition." Meig took a deep breath. "Marry Jessie."

Martin felt his mouth drop open.

"I'll see to it that you get the best medical training in the world. I'll subsidize you until you can support yourself. And I'll give you enough to maintain your mother. She won't have to know it comes from me. She can think you're getting paid over there and it'll save her pride. I understand all about pride, you see. Yes, marry Jessie, and make a life for yourself."

One couldn't just get up and stalk out of a man's house. One couldn't tell him he was out of his mind. Martin was stunned.

"You don't have to give me your answer now. Think it over. Take plenty of time. On second thought, not plenty, because I don't know how much time I've got, and I'd like to close my eyes knowing that she's cared for and protected by a man of decent character. I'm a keen judge of people, and I would put my life's savings on this table in front of you and leave the room."

"I appreciate that, Mr. Meig. But I have to tell you that I hadn't thought of marriage for years yet. As you say, I am—at least I hope I am—a responsible man, and marriage isn't something that one just—"

"Martin, let's do without diplomacy, shall we? This is a time for plain talk. You're thinking, and I don't blame you, that Jessie Meig isn't precisely what you had in mind when you thought of choosing a wife. I'd be a fool if I didn't know that! But I also know, and you do too, that burning love affairs usually go up in smoke anyway. Now, Jessie is an unusual human being. You've said so yourself. She's intelligent, she's good company and she thinks the world of you. Anybody can see she does. She'd be a trusted companion all your life." He paused. "And she'd have reason to be grateful to you."

Martin winced and Meig saw it.

"Yes, I did say 'grateful'! What's wrong? But you'd be grateful to her, too, wouldn't you? Because without her you'd spend the rest of your life here, going to waste."

Martin stood up to get his coat.

"Will you at least think about it?"

"I understand what you've said, Mr. Meig, but—"

Meig waved him aside. "Your impulse is to say 'no, absolutely not.' You think if you accept, you'll be selling yourself. Dishonoring yourself. Isn't that so?"

"I feel—" Martin began and was interrupted again.

Behind the strict, rimless glasses the eyes were shrewd. "Sentimentality, Martin, sentimentality!"

Martin had one foot out of the door.

"Of course she doesn't have the remotest idea of what I've been saying and must never find out, whatever you decide."

Martin was horrified. "No need to worry about that!"

"Very well, then. Just give it some thought, that's all I ask."

It was such a cold night that, unless you knew better, you could lose an earlobe. In spite of the arctic air, Martin sweated. The shame of it! He looked back at the house, wondering which of the second-story lights came from Jessie's room. And with flashing insight, he thought he could feel how it would be for her, proud as she was, if she could know what had just passed between her father and himself.

The proposition was, of course, unthinkable. Yet it had been well-intentioned, born of desperation. That this arrogant, private man should have revealed himself like that to a stranger! What must he have seen in that stranger? Ambition, obviously, but much more also: loyalty and kindness and honor. No question about that. He trusts me, Martin thought. Then his thoughts veered.

He dares to think I can be bribed!

Don't be a pompous ass, Martin; he didn't mean it that way!

It's a bribe, all the same!

He's terrified and wants to see his house in order. A human being has revealed his sorrow before you, Martin!

But the thing's impossible. And now a fine friendship has been spoiled for good. How can I feel free in that house anymore?

It was the most weird encounter, weird and sad! The wind rushed and the night was inexpressibly lonely. The planet was small and shriveled with the cold. And he went to bed thinking of loneliness.

For two weeks he stayed away. Then it occurred to him that such an abrupt disappearance would be a cruel hurt to Jessie. And indeed, it had been.

"I thought maybe my father had made you angry the last time you were here," she said, looking anxious.

"No. Why should you think that?"

"Because he can be so superior and cold. He antagonizes people."

"Well, he wasn't. Anyway, I don't antagonize so easily."

"That's not true. The truth is exactly the opposite."

"You're right, as usual," he admitted, and she laughed.

Seated as usual in the great wing chair, with her cheeks gone pink from the fire's heat, and the pinpoint sparks of gold in her ears, she could have been so lovely! If only—And he wondered whether anyone would ever marry her. Would anyone ever love her? Respect, admiration, companionship—these would come easily in all the virtuous ways through which human beings relate to one another. And surely even tenderness could come. But love?

She said softly, "You're very quiet, Martin."

"Sorry. I didn't mean to be." He brought himself back into the moment. "By the way, I finished *Main Street.* I meant to return it tonight, but I forgot to bring it."

"Did you like it?"

"Yes. It has the ring of truth. Depressing truth."

"I've something else for you, quite different." She ran across the room to the shelves. She always ran. Did she think it made her less visible to run?

"Here. It's Rolland's *Jean-Christophe,* a beautiful story of a musician in Paris. Especially good for you."

"Why for me?"

"Because it's a story of a struggle. Always, even when he was a child, he knew he was going to be a composer, a great one. He faced everything—loneliness, poverty, rivalry; but he never gave up."

"And did he win in the end?"

"Read it." She forced his eyes to meet her own. "You're a tenacious man, you know? You'll get what you want. I feel it in you."

A sudden brightness came into the little face, a fervor so glowing that it seemed he was seeing past the frail barrier of her forehead, seeing deep into her with shocking clarity.

She loved him.

Good God! He hadn't intended that! Hadn't intended to weaken or mislead this vulnerable small girl! What had he done? How had this come to be? Clumsily he flipped the pages of the book she had put into his hands.

"Seems like something I'll hate to put down," he said.

"Yes."

Did he deserve to feel such guilt and shame? Truly he hadn't been aware that this was happening. Nor perhaps had she. Well, it would have to be stopped, that was all. Brought abruptly to a halt before any more damage was done.

He simply wouldn't come here again.

And swiftly, with such grace as he could summon, he escaped from the house.

THERE ARE DAYS on which troubles accumulate and peak. One oversleeps and there is not time for breakfast. One is late for the first appointment and for all the others after that. It rains on the wet snow; then the rain turns to sleet and the roads turn to ice. It is March and one is sick of winter, but there are weeks and weeks of it still ahead.

The office was crowded all the morning with coughs, sore throats and a rampant case of measles that should have stayed home instead of polluting the waiting room.

The last case in the afternoon would have broken Martin's heart if he had allowed it to. Elsie Briggs was thirty-four, unmarried and the youngest of a large family. Hers was the old story of the daughter who stayed home to take care of her parents, wearing herself out for the senile and incontinent, locking herself away from life behind four dismal walls. And Elsie Briggs was finally breaking down. They would be taking her to the state hospital on Friday because there was nothing else to do with her. There was no outpatient care; there was no place other than the bleak state institution. Martin shuddered. In this mood he closed the office for the day and went to the car.

Ordinarily, he would not have answered a summons fifteen miles north in the mountains, especially in weather like this. But these were old patients who had bought a remote farm and moved away. Their parents had been his father's patients. Pa would have gone, he told himself grimly.

Sliding and struggling up the hills, each one more steep than the last, the flimsy car shook through fierce crosswinds. The windshield wipers clacked. All was gray: dim fields, gray air, steady snow. After two miserable hours, he pulled into a yard to find what he had expected: unpainted boards, a ramshackle porch, no light poles. If anybody needed cutting or stitching he would turn the car to let the headlights shine into the room. Rural poverty like this in the twentieth century!

In the bare kitchen stood a huddle of five runny-nosed babies and a thin mother, terrified because her husband was sick. Who was to tend to the man's work?

The man had pneumonia. Martin left medicines and a sheet of instructions.

"Keep taking his temperature regularly," he told the woman. "Can you get out to a phone to call me tomorrow?"

She was concerned about his bill. "I can't give you anything now, Doctor, but I'll be at my sister's right near your place in a couple of weeks. I'll bring it then."

"Don't worry about it," he said gently, knowing quite well that he would never be paid, knowing also that he wouldn't want to be paid. For who could touch dollars that would deprive these children of something they needed? And heaven knew, they must need everything from oranges to shoes!

So he left to slide and slip, downhill this time, the fifteen miles homeward. In the city or under some better system—though God knows what system in places as remote as these—this patient would be taken care of in a hospital. At least, somebody would see him tomorrow. In this weather he surely couldn't get back soon enough. And this frustration, along with so many others, nagged him as he drove.

I don't know anything. I'm not an expert obstetrician, cardiologist or orthopedic surgeon. I'm not an expert anything. That arm of Wagnall's that I set last week wasn't done right, I know it wasn't.

My father's kind hands lay folded over his black vest in the coffin. He gave the best care he could. He tried. My God, he did! And that's better than nothing, better than no care at all! A man has to be satisfied with it. My father was satisfied.

Quite without warning, not fifty feet ahead of the car, a tremendous limb, almost a quarter of a giant elm, split from the weight of ice and crashed on the road. In pounding panic, Martin swerved. If he'd been a few feet farther along, all his problems would be over! And he laughed at his own macabre humor. Indifferent nature! Savage world!

The wind whipped the trees as he carefully skirted his near-disaster. March was the most dismal month of all. Yet his father had loved it, had liked to talk of the stately cycle of the year, its rhythm and its grandeur. The road curved around the lip of a plateau from which, through beating snow, he could see a spread of white fields and hills folding back to the mountains out of which he had just come. Grand, yes! Eternal. Majestic. All the orotund words. A man might well stand in awe of it. He understood that deeply. But everybody wasn't meant for it, and he hated it, hated the loneliness, the monotony, the awful cold. He had never said it aloud before, but he said it now.

"I hate it."

And he could have wept.

Six miles from home in sleet as slippery as grease, the car slid off the road. He swore, then rocked the car, trying to get traction. He revved the engine over and over, to no avail. At last he got out. It was so cold, thirty below he'd guess, that his lungs burned with the small pain of each indrawn breath. The hairs prickled in his nostrils. Taking the shovel from the back seat, he tried to dig. The snow was so hard that the tip of the shovel bent backward. He sighed.

"Goddamned junky old car! Goddamned winter!"

Suddenly recalling Pa's advice, he got the burlap from under the front seat and placed it beneath the rear wheels. Then he started the engine. It roared and whined. The wheels spun furiously. It's rubbing the tires to a thread, Martin thought. But at last they caught hold and the car lurched back onto the road.

When he crept into the yard an hour later, the house was dark and he remembered that his mother had gone to an afternoon at the church, followed by a supper. She had left his meal on the coal stove in a covered dish. It was stone cold. Then he saw that the kitchen fire was out. The house smelled dank and musty. He ran down to the cellar where the furnace stood like a hungry monster beside a hill of glossy coal and flung the door open.

There was no fire here, either. The monster hadn't been fed and ashes were thick in the grate.

Blasted boy! His mother had arranged with Artie Grant to tend the fires today

while she was gone, but obviously he hadn't come. He went back upstairs to the
rear porch for kindling wood. Each ice-incrusted piece had to be dislodged by
sheer force. Now, back to the cellar with newspapers and matches. But first the
ashes must be cleaned out. Martin's head pounded as dust from the ashes set off a
fit of coughing. He sweated and shivered, shoveling the ashes out, then shoveling
the coal in. Last he shook down the grates, making a lonely rattle in the empty
house. From the head of the stairs the collies stood observing him, while he
watched the fire take hold.

Finished in the cellar, he went back up to the kitchen. His mother had just
come home. For an instant she was framed in the doorway, her pretty eyes
anxious. She wore her old, black "good" coat; the black feather on her hat was
turning green. Humble. That's how she looks, he thought. Mean word. Humble.

"Goodness, look at you! You're all over ashes!" she cried.

"Yes. Where in blazes was Artie Grant?"

"He's usually so dependable! I guess the weather was just too bad for him to
get here."

"It was, was it!" Martin was furious. "Wasn't too bad for me, though! I only
traveled thirty miles round trip to Danielsville and back!"

"Martin," his mother said mildly. "Martin, you're tired and hungry."

"Of course I am. Why not?" After a day like this one, was it too much to ask
for a house that was warm so that you could at least rest when you came in?

When his supper was ready Ma sat down in the rocker near the table. "That
shutter keeps banging. Hear it? The hinge is loose. If I get a new hinge, will you
put it on sometime?" And without waiting for him to answer, "Your father never
cared about things like that. Never cared about things at all, you might say. The
world of ideas, that's what he lived in, all that he cared about," she reflected,
sighing a little. The light fell over her head, over a smooth streak of gray that lay
like a ribbon on her still-dark hair. She was talkative tonight. "Yes, he was a
student of the world. He read everything. I'm sorry I never had much time, and
now it seems to be too late. I'm out of the habit of reading." She rocked: creak,
creak. "Anyway, I would never have been like him. I do like things so much. I
like *having* things. You never knew that about me, did you?" she asked shyly, as if
she were making some astounding confession.

"It's no sin to like things, Ma."

"Do you know where I always wanted most to go? I used to wish I could go to
Washington, to see the Lincoln Memorial and the Capitol and all that. But we
could never seem to get away."

"You could go now. It's outrageous that you should have to think twice about
having such a small pleasure."

"More than twice. We don't have the money to spare. You'll be needing a new
car by summer. It's a wonder this one has lasted as long as it has."

Never in all the years Martin had known his mother had she expressed any
desires. It hurt him to hear her. Yes, and made him strangely angry, too. He felt a
whole jumble of restless feelings.

"Your father was so content. He'd sit here rocking by the stove when the front
room was too cold to go over his records, and he never complained. Sometimes

he'd read aloud about places far away. Places like Afghanistan or the Amazon. And I'd ask him, 'Don't you wish we could go there?' 'I am there in my mind,' he'd answer."

"I'm not like him," Martin said.

"That's true. I've never known anyone like him."

In the hall the old clock struck with a tinny bong. Ashes tinkled in the stove. His mother coughed, a thick phlegmy cough that she hadn't been able to get rid of all winter. It wasn't her fault, surely, but it was exasperating. And he had a sudden projection of himself on long, dull, winter nights like this one, sitting in a shabby room like this one with a faceless woman: not his mother, of course, but a woman who would be his wife, since inevitably a man acquired a wife.

The future was a dull road going endlessly uphill, downhill, uphill, stretched through an unchanging landscape; at last, when one no longer hoped for any change, one would come to the final hill and just drop quietly off into the unknown. Life would have passed, never having counted for very much, or not what one wanted it to count for, at any rate. It would have gone by without color, without sparkle or aim.

But all the time, in other places, some men would have been doing what they wanted to do! They learned, they lived, they moved ahead! And there came again that old sense of rushing time which had haunted and beset him since adolescence. He was already twenty-eight! Without meaning to, he smashed a fist into his palm and sprang up as if he had been shot. There was such tension in his solar plexus that he had to move, he had to—

His mother looked up. "Where're you going?"

"I don't know. Just out."

"In this weather?" For it had begun to sleet again.

"I've been in it all day. I'm used to it."

"Oh, I forgot to tell you. While you were down cellar, Jessie Meig telephoned. Odd for a girl to telephone a young man, don't you think so?"

"No. Just natural and honest."

"Her sister didn't do it, did she?"

No, Martin thought, she never did.

"It's not even very clever, if you ask me. She must be a strange girl, that Jessie Meig."

"Why do you always say 'that Jessie Meig' as though you had something against her?"

"How could I have anything against her? I don't even know her."

"You know she's crippled, and that's what you've got against her."

"Martin, I don't understand you sometimes! You're so blunt and bluff lately, so outspoken! You've no tact anymore."

"I'm outspoken, I'll admit." It came to him that indeed he was more candid than he had used to be, that he had learned it for good or ill from Jessie. "Say what you mean and mean what you say. What's wrong with that?"

"Very well, then. I can't for the life of me understand what you can see in a poor, crippled girl. It's pitiful, of course it is, but here you are, a tall strapping fellow, and you could get any girl you wanted if you set your mind to it."

"I've told you, Ma. She's a friend, one of the best I've ever had outside of Tom, and there are things she understands about me that even Tom doesn't. How she's managed to know so much about the world, living the way she has, I have no idea. And I like being with her. What more can I say?"

His mother looked surprised. "Why nothing more, I should think."

And he went on, vehemently, "Because she has a few misshapen bones, is she any less a woman? Is she to be put away as damaged goods, returned to the manufacturer, because of that?"

His mother was silent.

"By the way, what did she want?"

"Just to know why you'd been staying away and whether you might want to come over this evening."

Twenty minutes later Martin stood in the Meigs' library. It went very quickly. His mind had simply made itself up, and he didn't have to think about words. The father grasped Martin's two hands in both of his.

"You won't be sorry. It's probably the wisest decision you'll ever make." There were tears in his eyes and at that moment Martin began to like him. "God bless you both."

Jessie's answer to his question was surprisingly calm.

"Are you sure you know what you're doing?"

"I'm sure."

"Because I don't want to be an albatross around your neck. I couldn't bear it."

"You will never be that, I promise!"

She had a pretty mouth and when she smiled, two charming dimples appeared at the corners. Taking her face between his hands he kissed her gently.

"I'll make life good for you," he said.

He meant it, with all his heart.

BOOK TWO

THE WEB

❧{8}❧

Fern always teased Alex that she had married him because she loved his house.

"Well, naturally," he would answer, "how could anyone help but fall in love with Lamb House?"

Among its oaks and orchards it lay as though, like them, it had been planted there; so farsighted had they been, those Elizabethans with a sense of home and long generations.

Through diamond-paned casements one looked south toward the village of Great Barrow. Little Barrow lay three miles to the west. On the tilted slope above the valley, pear trees flowered and the hills rolled back into a haze.

Fern turned from the easel. The spaniels, sprawled with noses to the grass, raised their heads in question. They had followed her across the Atlantic and shadowed every move she made.

"No," she told them, "I'm not finished yet."

And she raised her eyes to the living picture beyond the easel. In the upper left-hand corner lay a green square dotted with pinpoints of white which seemed scarcely to move, although they were live sheep on the Ballister farm. Everything was small and perfect, as in a meticulous Book of Hours. The valley was the merest hollow in the swell of the land.

"As if God's finger touched, but did not press, in making England," she said aloud, and was pleased with herself for quoting Elizabeth Barrett Browning. She had been studying the English poets from Chaucer to Eliot, for if one were going to live in a country, she believed, one ought to know its poets.

"Now that I know you well enough, I'll confess," Alex's mother had told her only a few weeks before. "I wasn't very happy about having an American daughter-in-law. So many American girls are simply not ladies; I can't help saying it. But you are, and so very charming, Fern! Everyone says so."

They had been standing in the upstairs hall, which, like the great one downstairs, was blazoned with family portraits: squires in eighteenth-century breeches and lace cuffs, clerics in grim black, an admiral with a three-cornered hat, two cabinet members—Tory, nineteenth century—and over one fireplace, the original Elizabethan with beefy face and sleepy eyes to whom this manor had been given for favors rendered the Crown somewhere in the West Indies. They were all Lambs.

Alex's mother came from a decent undistinguished family of schoolteachers.

"Naturally," Alex said with some amusement but no unkindness, "all this ancestor business means more to her." His late father, though, had been bored and sometimes irreverent about it.

On a table in the angle of the stairwell stood a group of photographs in silver frames.

"That, of course, is Edward VII as Prince of Wales," the elder Mrs. Lamb had informed the younger.

Fern had dutifully bent to read the scrawled inscription.

"My husband often went on shooting parties in Scotland with His Royal Highness."

"Went whoring with His Royal Highness too, I'll wager," Alex had remarked in private.

"I had this photo of Susannah put up here in the hall while you and Alex were on your wedding trip. It used to stand on the piano in the drawing room, but I should think that too conspicuous, not fitting, now that Alex has married you."

Fern had murmured that she wouldn't have minded, which was true. She felt no jealousy, although her mother-in-law apparently expected her to. The girl was dead, after all. Here she sat for all time in her patrician simplicity with hands on lap and a pearl rope looped around the little finger. The one memorable feature of her neat face was a timid expression in the prominent eyes. Could she perhaps have had some foreboding that she was going to die and leave her week-old boy?

"To tell the truth, I was never very happy about Susannah, although she was English to the bone."

Perhaps she had only been intimidated by this mother-in-law!

"You are far prettier, you know."

What an unnecessary, heartless thing to say!

"It's a good thing Neddie has no idea about his mother."

"He'll have to be told I'm not his mother."

"Why, yes, sometime, of course. But he does love you, Fern."

"And I adore him."

Sometimes there is immediate bonding between two human beings. It has no connection at all with age or circumstance. It is simply there.

"You've handled him splendidly, everyone says so."

She knew it was said she was "marvelous with Neddie," making no difference between him and her "own" infant girl. They didn't understand. Neddie *was* her "own."

"He's not been jealous of the baby at all! Usually they carry on dreadfully when a new baby comes into the house, or so I hear. Unfortunately, I never had more than one. You're sure you're not rushing things in that respect, Fern?" This last had been spoken with a glance, a light progression of the eye as it blinks in its rhythm and recovers from the blink, toward the midsection of Fern's body, where the new swelling was just barely visible. "After all, Emmy's not a year yet."

"The doctor says I'm quite healthy."

Fern's own patience surprised her. Two years ago she would have had to swallow exasperation; now she was learning to see beneath the surface of people and things. Behind this pallid face with its indrawn lips, behind the accent—which, even here in England, was a fairly blatant imitation of the royal family's accent—she saw a lonely woman who had striven foolishly all her life.

So she said gently, "If this one's a boy, we shall name him Alex, of course. Will he be the fifth or the sixth?"

"He will be the sixth Alexander Lamb. Should you want me to come a week or two ahead of time to plan for the christening, I'm sure I'll be able to manage it. And I can stay on afterward, as long as you like."

Poor soul! She was waiting to be invited to live with them at Lamb House. But that, Fern thought, I will not do. She's perfectly well-housed at Torquay with all the other prosperous widows. No, that I will certainly not do.

"You know," Mrs. Lamb had complained, "it's Neddie who should have borne the name. Don't you think it's disgraceful that Susannah insisted on naming him for her father? True, her father had died that year, but even so, the firstborn son should be named after his father."

"Well, anyway, he looks like Alex," Fern had assured her, although it was probably not true. Neddie would be narrower and darker than Alex. But it was what the older woman wanted to hear.

Pregnancy, like love, she thought now, can be calming to the nerves. The doctor said some women became euphoric. This inner radiance then, this vitality and warm contentment with her own body, the home and the people who surrounded her—this must be euphoria. And, taking up the brush, she corrected some greens with a stipling of gilt where the sun had glazed them.

A little group came in sight around the corner of the house: Neddie, running ahead of the nurse who was pushing Emmy in the perambulator. Fern held out her arms and the little boy ran into them. She put her face down on his crisp hair which smelled of pine shampoo. It pleased her that this child who had been shy with strangers had so readily accepted her and loved her.

He wiggled free.

"Shall we have music again, Mummy?" he asked.

"Mummy's busy," Nanny Hull admonished.

"Later this afternoon, darling. We'll put a record on."

"The singing man?"

She laughed. "Yes, yes, the singing man."

Neddie had come into the room when Alex had a Caruso recording on the phonograph. Without making a sound, he had sat down to listen, and then had waited while Alex wound the phonograph again to repeat it.

"And will I have yellow cake, too?"

There had been a cake with yellow icing that day, and now they were turning into a ritual, the singing man and the cake.

"You'll have cake, if you promise to eat your supper. You mustn't stuff on sweets," Nanny said.

"Of course he mustn't."

The baby Emmy was asleep. She was blond and already long for her age. She would be large-boned, as if she belonged entirely to Alex and not at all to her mother. With curiosity Fern touched the pink hand that lay curled like a shell on the blanket. I don't know her yet, she thought. Everything is closed up, a gift in a glossy box. It is delivered at the door, and one can only guess what is possibly inside. But it is all there, and there's little we can change.

Still, at the same time, we could teach her anything, couldn't we? Mandarin Chinese, if we wanted to, instead of English? Everything is so confusing. I feel light-headed.

"Have you had a bit too much of the sun, Ma'am? If you don't mind my saying so, you ought to put up your work for a while today. You've been at it since noon."

The woman spoke considerately and probably sincerely, except for her use of the word "work." She couldn't possibly conceive of what Fern did as "work."

"Yes, thank you, Nanny. Perhaps I shall."

"It's fearful hot today."

Funny what the English called fearful heat! It couldn't be more than eighty. Still, she obeyed, as Nanny drew the wicker lounge chair into the shade and plumped the cushions.

"There you are! A nice bit of nap will do you good. I'm to take Neddie down to his pony and he'll go for a ride with Mr. Lamb."

Fern closed her eyes, letting the drowsiness of pregnancy have its way. She was so catered to, so loved and cared for! How many women with two children had leisure to go all deliciously relaxed and limp? One could feel so guilty thinking about one's unearned privileges.

Old Carfax, stirring in the perennial border, struck a stone with his hoe. He was being careful not to wake her. He was a wiry little man, pasty-skinned in spite of a life out in the weather. For thirty years he had been tending this garden: it was an extension of his back, of his roped and sinewy arms.

Fern opened her eyes just as he stooped to remove a thread of weed which would have marred the perfection of the rosebeds. She watched him move on through the perennials: violet steeples of campanula, gold coreopsis, dusty dark-blue globes of echinops. Fragrance of stock and musky spice of phlox hung in the sweet air. Behind the border stood a solid wall of yews, still wet with last night's rain.

"The yews are as old as the house," Alex had told her the first time he had brought her here. "We've a priest's hole on the third floor behind a false wall. I'll show you. Part of the family was Catholic, you know, but it got to be too dangerous for them, I suppose, and we've all been C. of E. for two hundred years at least. They also say Cromwell slept here, but I don't know whether that's true."

"It's like all those houses at home, where Washington's supposed to have slept while he was chasing you or you were chasing him."

They had been sitting on the stone bench, the one where Carfax had just now set a flat of Michaelmas daisies. They'd sat there talking for an hour or more, then quite suddenly Alex had asked her to marry him and as suddenly she had accepted.

Yet they had really been leading up to that moment from the time they had been introduced in the winter. Aunt Milly had pursued her purpose with utmost tact, to be sure! And ordinarily Fern would have been outraged by any such "scheme," but because she herself was so strongly drawn to Alex, she hadn't objected.

He was delightful. It was, quite simply, good to be with him. It was heartening —was that the right word? Yes, heartening was a very good word, she decided. There was a kind of crinkling good nature in his face even when he was being earnest, and she had told him so. She was not used to men who laughed. Certainly Father had done very little laughing!

He had a fine curiosity about practically everything. At dinner he could listen to Uncle Drew's talk of securities and German reparations. He could ask pertinent questions of a guest concerning blight-resistant roses. With a cricketeer he talked scores and plays. One felt that he could manage anything. And he had a certain reserve; Fern was comfortable with that. Traveling through Europe, she had had to fend off too many young men on dark hotel terraces. To a girl whose life had been unusually reclusive, that sort of thing could be flattering at first, but after a while one got tired of having to decide between accepting sticky kisses when one felt nothing for the man or, by resisting, risk being labeled "prig." But Alex had been satisfied to go slowly, sensing her wish to feel the way, to move as a river flows, deepening to the place where all the streams gather in a final rush, which would be the more marvelous for having come gradually.

So she had read, and so she believed.

Obviously he was affected by his responsibilities. He had inherited a substantial business in maritime insurance; but unlike many young heirs he had not turned it over to managers; he ran it himself. The greater responsibility, of course, was to his child.

She remembered the day he had first brought Neddie to the hotel. They had been on the way to the zoo. She had opened the door and there they stood, the tall man and Neddie, who was just two. She had knelt, putting out her arms, and the little boy had come quite willingly, while she murmured the things adults do.

"What a fine big boy you are! And is this your bear? How are you, Toby Bear?"

She had been fourteen, almost grown, when her mother died. The loss had seemed to mark her more than any other happening in her life until then, and perhaps that was why she had been so moved by Alex's child, when he put his hand in hers.

"Strange," Alex said. "He's usually quite timid with people he doesn't know."

Alex's eyes had been very soft and in that instant Fern had known he could be trusted.

All during the late winter and early spring they saw London together. Alex had friends in a variety of circles: business, music, society and art. They ate with a pair of schoolteachers in Soho and dined at Claridge's before the opera. They walked in the parks and on streets which Fern had visited with Jane Austen, with Thackeray and Galsworthy. And, as so many Americans do, she fell in love with the grand, old, mellow city.

In a mews near Curzon Street Alex had a flat furnished, as she was later to learn, like Lamb House. Oak and yew were seventeenth-century; mahogany was eighteenth-century; the landscapes were nineteenth-century. Here was the progression of the family, marching through history.

Alex had discerning taste. She told him he ought to be in some business having to do with the arts—antiques or a picture gallery. He had been pleased.

"But maritime insurance is more lucrative. I can always buy art. Some day I'll be buying a Meig, you know."

"You've never seen any of my work. How can you say that?" she had replied.

"Just a feeling I have about you."

They had been having dinner at the flat, so he was a host being courteous and that was all. Yet she could remember everything that had been said.

She had sighed. "I'm so confused in my mind. I wish I knew whether I had any potential."

"There's only one way to find out. By doing. It's a shame you haven't had more encouragement."

"More? I've had none at all."

Except for Martin Farrell's. He, admittedly knowing nothing about art, had nevertheless urged her to struggle on. And sitting there across the table from Alex, she had become aware of the letter in her purse which had arrived from Martin just that morning.

It had been written in a state of joyous excitement. She, with her own hopes, had understood that a door had been flung open for him, a wide and generous entrance to the future! And she was very, very glad for him.

But there had also been a faint sense of shame. She had thought, all the weeks of that hot, lovely summer in Cyprus and especially on the last night, that something was growing—that given time, perhaps when she came home . . . She had obviously been mistaken. Three years of further study! Very likely he wouldn't marry until long after that.

Women, herself included, tended to be foolish about doctors, as about pianists or romantic actors, whom young girls pursue and old ladies adore.

Foolish. Foolish.

"London suits you," Alex had remarked abruptly.

And looking out at the shine of the expensive street, she had reminded him: "I'm also a country person."

"What you need," he'd said, "is to have a home in a quiet country place where you can paint, yet be near enough to the city for first-rate classes."

And he had reached across the table to press her hand.

Not long afterward they had driven to his village. It had a cobbled High Street, a chemist's and tobacconist's and an ancient church.

"There's where the Lambs are christened, married and buried. That's the lichgate. They used to rest the bier there, but now we trim it with white flowers for brides. There's the riding club where I keep three horses. It's only a stone's throw from home, and it's just as easy to stable them there. Do you ride? Yes? Oh, there's nothing like riding just after dawn when everyone but birds and roosters is still asleep!"

So they had rounded the corner of the lane and come upon the house, drowsing in hazy, filtered light. There it lay, sturdy, secure and most of all so brightly cheerful. It seemed like a place Fern had always known. It seemed as if there could be no deeper joy than to stay here with this gentle, loving man, in this golden peace.

Promptly then, cablegrams went out to Father and Jessie at home. Letters went back and forth across the ocean. Lists were written and arrangements made. Aunt Milly rejoiced. Alex's mother rejoiced. An engagement solitaire was bought at Asprey's.

Fern sent instructions home. Father must bring the photograph of Mother in her room. They must crate and ship her books and all her paintings. They were to bring the sterling which had been put aside for her, Tiffany's *Audubon Birds*. ("Animals, naturally," Jessie had remarked, with her usual tart humor, which happened to be accurate, for Fern had also asked them to bring along her collection of dog etchings as well as the two spaniels, who would have to remain for six whole months in quarantine.)

The wedding was held at Lamb House. Just as Alex had said, the lich-gate had been trimmed with white flowers. They had ridden back from the church in a carriage, also decked with flowers. Neddie had worn a powder-blue velvet suit and had his picture taken with the bride and groom, while old ladies wiped their tears.

Everyone in the village had been invited. There was champagne for all in the great courtyard square and there was dancing indoors under the enormous chandeliers. The dining hall was illuminated by silver candelabra as tall as a man. The vermeil dinner service, taken from the vault for the occasion, glittered between bowls of old Carfax's prize roses in bridal pink and cream.

"Positively medieval," Jessie remarked. "I didn't think they still did this sort of thing." Then more softly, she said, "But it was beautiful, Fern, and I shall want all your photos to remember it by."

The honeymoon was a voyage to India. For Fern Meig, who had never been anywhere and had so longed to go "beyond," the very thought had been intoxicating. In the eyes and ears of her mind she saw and smelled enchantment: red lacquer, gold thread, frangipani and patchouli, jasmine, burn and blaze.

Unfortunately, Alex had been seasick most of the time. She had felt sorry for him, not only on account of his physical misery, but because she saw he was humiliated.

Then at the end of the sixth week, she too became a victim, but for a different reason: she was pregnant. It must have happened almost immediately, on the night they spent ashore at Gibraltar, visiting some friends of Alex's father. That, and the few other nights they had slept on land, had been the only normal ones on the trip. So it had been rather a queer honeymoon! Poor Alex! Thank goodness, though, for his sense of humor, he had finally been able to make a rueful joke of it.

Now, with Emmy not yet old enough to walk, she was pregnant again, and still having spells of nausea, so that on many nights she had to disappoint him. But he was considerate and patient. Not all men were, she knew.

He was patient in other ways, as well. He had taught her how to run the unfamiliar household. He had taught her about bills and bank accounts, things difficult enough to master in a strange currency, especially hard for her who had never handled money at all. He'd been so good about all that! And so good about her work: True to his promise he had arranged for the best classes in the city, in particular an outstanding class in oils with Antonescu. For the first time she had been able to feel she was learning.

"Well, how are you doing?" Alex came around the house and laid a hand on her shoulder.

"Painting or stomach, do you mean?"

"Both."

"Stomach's queasy unless I remember to keep a sweet cracker in my pocket."

"Biscuit."

"Well, someday I will remember to call a cracker a biscuit, I promise. How was the ride?"

"Marvelous. After this baby we'll go every morning when I'm home. And when I'm in London you should go with Daisy or Nora or somebody. I took your mare out just now for exercise. I'm rather too heavy for her, though."

There wasn't an ounce of extra weight on Alex. He glows, she thought; from his boots to his bright hair and outdoor skin, he shines as if he had been gilded.

"We'll make a rider out of Neddie, too. You should have seen him on his pony this afternoon."

"He wasn't scared at all? He's only four, Alex!"

"That's the time to start. And he loves it." Alex examined her picture. "You know, you've got the perspective on the hill just right! Do you realize, incidentally, that you don't imitate anymore? You're developing a style of your own."

"Maybe. Antonescu says I still pay too much attention to detail, though. It should sweep more, it should feel more careless. I understand what he means, but it's not easy to do it."

A bicycle bell tinkled up the drive. In a moment Mrs. MacHugh from the village would appear around the curving shrubbery, bringing the afternoon mail.

"I'll get it," Alex said.

It was past time for a letter from home. Of late, Fern had been troubled by thoughts of home. Aunt Milly had written that Father had seemed unusually tired on her last visit to Cyprus. There'd been a history of heart trouble among the men in the family. If Father were to die, what would become of Jessie? And Fern had a vivid recollection of her sister sitting with the cards spread out for an elaborate game of solitaire; the little face, surrounded by arabesques of curls and lavish folds of scarf, was proud and lonely.

She stood abruptly and walked to the front of the house, where Mrs. MacHugh, having just handed the mail to Alex, was turning the bicycle back down the drive.

"Letter from America! Two of them! Looks like one from your father and one from Jessie. The rest—just advertisements and an invitation from the Mercers."

She sat down on the step to read. The note from Jessie filled just one page.

"I shall be in England a week after you receive this." In England? But how? But why? "Read Father's letter. He will explain it all. He can do a better job of writing than I can just now."

Prick of pin, quiver of apprehensive chill as when a running cloud covers the sun. Tiny shudder as when a jangling note is struck on the piano. She opened her father's letter and read it quickly through. Then she read it again.

"Oh no!" she cried.

"Oh no what? What's wrong?"

Fern laughed. The sound was harsh and queer.

"What is it?" Alex repeated.

She gave him the letter, then leaned back against the doorpost, fighting a sudden heaving of nausea.

"Well," he said, "this is news, isn't it?"

"I don't believe it!" she cried.

"Why? Is it all that strange?"

"For goodness sake, don't you think it is?"

"Well, I suppose one mightn't actually *expect* Jessie to marry, and yet she—"

Fern sat up. The wave of sickness had subsided.

"I think it's—I think it's disgusting!"

"I don't understand. Do you know the man, by the way?"

"Yes, he's a doctor, as you read. A country doctor. It's—farm country, hills, something like Scotland. Yes, it looks something like Scotland," she said irrelevantly.

"But do you *know* him? What is he like?"

Fern swallowed, as if a lump of some tough substance stuck in her throat. "It's hard to describe him." She shook her head, frowning. "He is a very intelligent man with a wide-ranging mind. A quiet man with a lot of restless energy. But that's contradictory and complex—"

"We're all contradictory, some of us more than others. Anyway, if he and Jessie love one another, I don't see why you call that disgusting."

"She may be in love with *him*. I've no doubt she is. But as for him, well, could you be in love with Jessie?"

"I'm not, so I can't answer for myself. That doesn't mean some other man couldn't be. And I did like her a lot, you know. I thought she had wit and heart."

"He can't love her! It's impossible."

"You don't know his feelings, Fern. You really ought to be glad for them. For Jessie."

"Did you read the whole thing? They're taking a flat in London. He'll be working here for the next three years."

"So then he won't be a country doctor, after all, will he? They'll have a whole other life."

"Yes, a whole other life."

Alex got up and drew Fern to her feet.

"Let's go in. I need to shower and change. Then I want tea. Yes, you ought to be glad for them," he repeated, climbing the stairs.

Fern lay down on the bed. Water rushed in the bathroom shower, fogging the mirror on the open door so that she saw herself in a blur. Lying there in the middle of the enormous bed she looked forlorn and she felt ashamed. Why should she begrudge Jessie this miraculous deliverance?

Whenever she thought of her sister she saw her small and huddled, sometimes even crying with a lump on her forehead that was Fern's fault. Jessie was a measurement, a symbol of deprivation and unfair disadvantage.

Her thoughts went to Martin. "A quiet man," she had told Alex a few minutes ago, "with a lot of restless energy." She might have added more: a sensitive man, perceptive, tense, reserved, intellectual, kind, proud, ambitious—yet not one of these words, even the word "ambitious," made clear how he could have married Jessie.

She was bitterly angry.

"After they're settled in," Alex said, rubbing himself dry, "we'll give a party for them." His eyes crinkled with friendliness. He liked parties. "We'll have a little band and string lights in the trees. Welcome to England and all that. What do you think?"

"Lie down here with me," she said.

"I thought you didn't feel like—"

"I only meant, hold me. We don't have to make love unless you want to."

He drew her head down to his shoulder. "You don't feel well. I can wait. There's more between us than only that, I should hope."

Yes. And she thought: I do wonder what all the mystery is for? One gets the idea that it is the purpose of everything, this entrance of the man into the woman, when actually it is such a quick thing, not at all like the fuss that's made over it. What's really best is to be held and loved, to wake up in the night and not be alone. To be cared for as Alex cares. He's done so much for me. I've grown so much with the things he's taught me.

Her hands went to the rounded hill below her ribs. The baby fluttered for the first time. Its new life, thumping, had knocked at the door. How wrong of her to feel anger or anything but thankfulness and—and gladness! She had everything. Everything!

"Have a nap," Alex said. "We've an hour before tea."

The sky suddenly had gone dark and chilly. A gust of rain battered the windows. He drew the coverlet about them both, while her head still rested in the curve of his shoulder. So warmed, her tremors eased.

Ah, foolish, she thought. Alex is right, it is no business of ours! As long as we're here together, with Ned and Emmy and whoever it is that's stretching and turning inside me now, why should I care what other people do?

In a few minutes, she drifted into the sweetest sleep.

⚜{9}⚜

Martin stepped outside into a fragrant morning; the air was damp on the skin. Here in England June still had the feel of spring. It was a long walk to St. Bartholomew's, but he enjoyed starting his workday at the hospital with the vigor and well-being that came after exercise. And with this sensation of well-being he crossed through the park and turned down the Mall.

It had been, beyond expectation, a good year. He smiled, still warmed by the hour he had spent since he had got up, in the pleasant flat above the square of chestnut trees and sycamores. Jessie and he had breakfasted at the bow window that overlooked all the bird-filled greenery. His last sight before leaving was of her puttering over some last-moment touch on the little room which had been readied for the baby who was due right now—perhaps even today!

He hadn't really planned to have a child this soon. But apparently Jessie had! She would be an excellent mother, he reflected. He hadn't thought much about that until now, but on these solitary walks all sorts of thoughts streamed through one's head. . . . Yes, she would be excellent, with all that energy, remarkable energy for so small a body. Well organized, too; everything was planned out beforehand so that the actual doing seemed always to be easy. He marveled at this ability of Jessie's to manage things, and could imagine her directing in her capable, cheerful way a household of children. *Cheerful.* That was Jessie. If you had to think of a single adjective that above all else described her, *cheerful* would surely do as well as any.

Suddenly he recalled the day they had moved into the flat; it was a furnished sublet, drably decorated; it had been raining that afternoon and the drabness, combined with the pelting rain, had depressed him so that he'd almost wanted to turn around and walk out—he who never really cared that much about possessions or the appearances of things! But what wonders Jessie had done with those rooms! She'd filled them with flowers, inexpensive daisies in bright blue glass bowls. She'd hung travel posters on the walls, delightful scenes of golden places: the Fountains of Vaucluse and Venice and Segovia. She'd become a devotee of the flea markets: one day she'd come home lugging a tarnished, wretched old pot that turned out to be a splendid silver tea kettle. She'd been so pleased with herself! She knew how to enjoy the hours, Jessie did, and knew how to stretch her mind. She'd stretched his mind, too, leading him through every gallery and museum in the city. They had gone to Elizabethan plays and the ballet and of course to the opera that he loved so well, and rummaged through old bookshops.

In the fall they'd gone to Paris; there had been a neurological conference at the Salpetriere; they'd walked their feet off down every alley and into every corner. Christmas week had been celebrated in Rome. They had seen palms growing in Cornwall. They had traveled to Ulster and visited the stony village where Martin's father had been born and a long line before him had died. Martin had been immensely moved by its loneliness and dignity. Yes, it had been a remarkable year and he had Jessie to thank for it.

Not that he hadn't had some trepidation at the beginning! Once having passed the first shock and splendor of the opportunity with Braidburn, he had come to the awareness that in England he would see Mary again; the thought had plagued him all the way across the Atlantic Ocean. He had felt—he hadn't known quite what it was he had felt, other than a decided discomfort and a wish that he might somehow avoid the whole business, which was, of course, impossible.

They had been driven straight to Lamb House. It had been one of those gray-green English afternoons, halfway between rain and heavy mist. The sky had been filled with noisy birds, starlings and rooks; the country looked soft, he had thought.

"I like this kind of day. I've grown used to it," Mary had said, answering some comment about the weather.

Queer that he should remember such a slight remark!

She had been standing in the doorway when they drove up. The boy Neddie had been on one side and a tiny girl, just able to stand, had been on the other. And he had wondered whether she was aware of the picture she made, blooming with her two children and her pregnancy.

Yes, he remembered that day. They had gone walking about the grounds. Naturally, Jessie had described Lamb House beforehand, but no description could have done justice to it in Martin's mind. He had had no frame of reference for such a place.

Intending nothing, truly intending nothing by the trivial words, he had remarked, "This is a long way from Cyprus, isn't it?"

And with unmistakable anger, Mary had repeated, "Yes, isn't it?"

Surely she couldn't have been jealous of Jessie? After all, she hadn't wanted him for herself! So it had come to Martin's mind that she must be resentful over the marriage because she thought him some sort of fortune hunter. This idea had stung him, and still would have done so if he allowed it to. For he was, after all, living on another man's money, wasn't he? And living well. Perhaps, then, he did look like a—a fortune hunter?

But not for long! Jessie's father would be repaid for everything. They would live better yet on what he, Martin, would provide. His wife and children would depend on no one else but him.

Fortune hunter! And what of Mary's motives? Ah, but that was unfair! Alex was a man to be desired by women, a kindly, generous, intelligent man who happened to have wealth. Martin himself could surely have been bitter at the sight of him, not because he had any remnant of desire for Mary—she had rejected him and that was the end of that!—but because of normal resentment toward the winner. Instead he had come to like Alex. You couldn't help but like him.

Occasionally, still, he could remember his first anguish over Mary, how painfully and slowly it had ebbed into anger and how the anger had finally seeped away into nothing. Oh, there was some small disturbance yet—embarrassment, that was all. He was still and probably always would be so damned touchy! A regular prickly pear, he was.

But he was forcing himself to get over this embarrassment. Mary too had evidently got over it, or over whatever it was that had made her so cold when he and Jessie had first arrived. Perhaps she saw now that he was working hard, and would get somewhere in the world and was in the meantime making a good life for Jessie.

So the relationship between the two couples was cordial enough, although it was not a close one. Every now and then they met in town for dinner or theater. Two or three times Martin and Jessie had been at Lamb House amid a bustle of guests and children. Jessie had declined the last few invitations and he had concurred. He really didn't have the time to spare; he wasn't his own master as Alex was. Besides, the Lambs' was a different world. Alex, the Englishman, naturally had friends in many circles. Jessie and Martin, strangers both, were very slowly enlarging their little group one by one, or rather, two by two. Alex and Mary ran an expensive establishment; she was busy in the domain of art; he had countless business obligations. Their lives were complicated. The Farrells' life was simple. And they were satisfied with its simplicity.

"You're happy, Martin, I can see," Jessie liked to say, not questioning or doubting, merely taking pleasure in his pleasure, and expressing the euphoria which had bloomed with her pregnancy. He, in turn, took pleasure in seeing that euphoria, and in the calm, fine trust between them . . .

He looked at his watch and quickened his walk. He was due in the operating room at eight. This was Mr. Braidburn's day. "Mr."—funny English mode of address to a doctor! And now Martin's mind leaped ahead, away from his own concerns, toward the hospital where he had spent the larger part of this past year. Even when he was away from that building, his heart was still in it!

"What happened to the Eldridge girl over the weekend while I was away?" he would ask himself. "To the ironworker with the third-degree burns who'd got a piece of steel in the brain?" And his memory would go back in time to the story Pa had told so long ago of the scalded child in the farmhouse kitchen. Poor Pa! He'd had the will to help, but not the tools. Now Martin had those tools in hand.

There were just three young Americans and half a dozen Englishmen working in the wards and clinics, examining and selecting the patients to be discussed on the following day. Often Martin wondered how much these patients understood, as they were wheeled in before the instructors and assembled students. Most of them were simply too frightened to understand very much, he thought, which was just as well. God pity them: the paralyzed; the afflicted with their jerking limbs and senseless laughter; the soon-to-die.

Most of them were poor and inarticulate, struggling for words even when they must know clearly enough what they wanted to say.

"Doctor, will I walk and talk and be a person? Will I die?"

Their shabby imitation-leather pocketbooks, clasped stiffly on their laps, were sad to him. He dreamed of his mother. She had owned that same kind of shabby black bag. He dreamed that it was lying on the kitchen table at home. His mother was crying, "I've lost my pocketbook," and he was telling her, "Why, here it is, Ma. Don't you see it?" But she only kept on crying and wringing her hands. The poor moved him so.

He pitied animals. So soft he was! He must learn to hide it! In the laboratory he worked on monkeys and dogs. It made him sick to touch their fur, to win their trust only to terrorize them later. Yet it had to be done. How else to learn what cells do after stroke or how brain wounds heal? How else to learn anything? Fortunately, Evan Llewellyn, wiry dark Welshman, great neurophysiologist and patient teacher, was kind to the creatures. He kept suffering to a minimum. Otherwise Martin could not have stood it.

It was a privilege when he was allowed to share a small basement laboratory with Llewellyn. Jessie, having overheard Martin talking about microscopes, had bought him a beautiful Zeiss, and there with Llewellyn and the Zeiss, during long afternoons and often late into the evenings, he laid the foundation of all he was to know about the pathology of the cell. He was becoming increasingly convinced of what Dr. Albeniz had said about the unity of all brain study: surgery, neuro-cytology, and even psychiatry were parts of a single discipline and ought not to be separated. The practitioners in these divisions must know what the others were doing.

"Too many neurosurgeons blunder into the brain," Llewellyn declared.

He was nearly eighty, with cheerful eyes and a face remarkably unlined. "Never stop learning," he would say. Whenever he was challenged for coming in on holidays or Sundays, he had an answer. "When you stop working, you're dead, or might as well be."

Martin thought: That's what my father used to say. And a truer thing was never said, he added to himself, as he rounded the corner and made his way to Saint Bartholomew's door.

BRAIDBURN TALKED AS he worked, his steady voice instructing and explaining. This was the third hour and he was tiring. A drop of sweat stood on his forehead; a nurse stepped forward to wipe it before it could slide.

"Look here. The size of an orange."

Martin blotted seeping blood with gauze. A year ago he had been puzzled at first sight of these absorbent squares, each with its dangling black thread. Now he knew so much; also he knew how much he did not know. And he remembered his fear when a brain was first exposed beneath his own hands, when he was first permitted, under supervision, to take the knife.

"Sponge," Braidburn ordered.

The patient was young. Martin had seen him first at the clinic, waiting on a bench with his wife and a couple of whining children. He had a wizened city face, a clerk's face, respectful and scared. Relating his symptoms, his mouth had twisted.

"I can't seem to stand up straight. I feel like vomiting. The headache's splitting and my eyesight's queer."

Through the ophthalmoscope Martin had observed the hemorrhaging retina and the enlarged head of the optic nerve.

"See anything, Doctor?"

"Well," he'd answered kindly, evasively, "we'll need to take X-rays, you know. Then we'll see about straightening you out."

He had known then what the pictures would show: a tumor pushing up under the temporal lobe; slow growing, he would guess. Also, he had thought, or felt, that it would be nonmalignant; he had not voiced the thought to anyone. There was something odd about the appearance of the person when malignancy was present. Again, that was only a feeling he had. Pa used to have feelings like that about patients, too. But Pa had often been wrong.

This time Martin had been right: the tumor was benign and encapsulated. A little thrill went through him, remembering the pale wife and children. Also, he was pleased with himself.

"The rest is up to the gods," Braidburn said now. "We've done all we can." He looked up. "Close the flap, Farrell, please. Jasper, assist. I've finished."

There ought to be applause, Martin thought. Some of his fellow students complained that men like Braidburn were arrogant and difficult. Braidburn in particular had been labeled "manic-depressive." But he was merely a man of moods. Martin loved him, as he loved all these men and loved this place.

A few hours later, he had just taken a seat at the bench downstairs with old Llewellyn when the telephone rang. Martin spoke a moment and hung up.

"My wife's at the hospital in labor."

"Hurry up, then, what are you waiting for?" Llewellyn cried.

Martin tore upstairs and started to race toward the taxi-rank. Mr. Meredith intercepted him.

"Llewellyn called upstairs. Get in. We'll drive you."

So it was that Martin went in a limousine to the meeting with his firstborn.

Meredith was considerably silent. Martin wondered what he could be thinking. Perhaps the same thought that he himself had been stifling and that now had abruptly shot up again from some buried place in his consciousness. It had been foolhardy to permit a pregnancy! What if the child were like its mother? How terrible and cruel! The child would despise them, and rightly so, for having brought it into the world. And Jessie—poor Jessie—would be destroyed by guilt. Martin shook with fear. All the day's contentment shivered away.

Meredith was saying, "I met Fleming once. Looks like anybody else. Penicillin will absolutely revolutionize medicine . . . although some patients are allergic to it. But I shouldn't bother you with medicine today, should I?" He tapped Martin on the knee. "Just watch that Achilles heel."

"What?" Martin asked in confusion.

"We all develop one, you know. The moment the child is born. Whatever

happens to it after that will happen to you, every cut and bruise. Ah well, here we
are. Good luck."

At the desk they told him Jessie was already in the delivery room.

"Make yourself comfortable in the waiting room. We'll call you as soon as we
know anything."

The waiting room was vacant except for a woman reading a book. When
Martin entered she put it down and he saw that the woman was Mary Fern. She
smiled.

"You were operating, so Jessie called me when the pains came very suddenly.
I've been with her until just now."

"Thanks awfully. Is she all right?"

"Very excited. Very happy, between pains."

Martin sat down, took a magazine and couldn't read it.

"You're reading the same words ten times over and you don't know what they
mean," Mary observed.

"I know."

"Try a picture magazine, it's easier." She added gently, "I know you're a doctor, but when it's your own baby, I suspect you forget you're a doctor, don't you?
So let me tell you, it's not so bad having a baby. She'll be all right. She really will."

"Thanks again."

"I'm glad I happened to be in town. We're staying in overnight."

It occurred to Martin that he hadn't been alone in a room with Mary since—
since Cyprus, and seldom enough even then. This thought created an intimacy in
the commonplace, impersonal room. Absurd! He smelled a slight fragrance: her
perfume. When she turned a page he heard the faint jingle of an ornament on her
gold bracelet. For some reason the sound was irritating. He wished she would go
home. Then he was ashamed of himself, and spoke to her pleasantly.

"The country must be beautiful this month."

"Yes, it's heavenly. But you're making conversation. You don't really feel like
talking now. Don't bother about me, please . . . I'll just sit here and read."

The stillness was oppressive. An hour ticked by. At every passing step in the
hall he looked up, thinking it was for him. Mary looked up too; they exchanged
anxious glances. She returned to the book, rustling the pages. The bracelet jin-
gled. He wished again that she would leave.

Her presence, as he sat there with nothing to do but let his mind wander,
brought him a mean recollection. At a luncheon table when he had first arrived at
St. Bartholomew's, Henry Barker had unknowingly humiliated him. Barker was
Braidburn's associate, a garrulous, informal man, rather un-English. Martin remembered every word he had said.

"To tell you the truth, when your father-in-law wrote to ask a favor of
Braidburn, I thought probably a loan was being called in, a return for old friendship, you know. I can't say whether Braidburn thought the same. We had no idea
we were getting a gifted man. For you are that, Martin!" And he had gone on, "I
look forward to meeting your wife. Only the other day we were talking about our
visit to America with the Braidburns when we met your wife and her family. A

lovely child she was, about fourteen, I should think. Tall for her age, with the most extraordinary blue eyes. I never forgot."

Martin had said evenly, "That was Mary Fern. She's married to an Englishman, and they live in Oxfordshire when they're not at their flat in town."

Mr. Barker had been confused. "Oh? How many sisters are there, then? I seem to remember only two."

"There are just two. I married the other one."

Why did he remember, keep remembering, such things? Why did he not expunge them like a chalk scribble on a blackboard? Just wipe them out?

Mary stood up. "I'm supposed to meet Alex's mother and bring her home for dinner." She looked at her watch. "Will you think it awful of me if I leave you?"

"No, no, go ahead. And give my best to Alex."

"You'll call me the minute you hear? We'll be at the flat all evening.

"Of course."

He watched her go down the street. She still had that slight sway in her walk. Her skirt swung gracefully. It was funny, a few years ago women all wore dresses to the knees. Now their skirts were three-quarters of the way to the ankle. How quickly one grew accustomed to change!

"Don't you think Alex has done a lot for Fern?" Jessie had asked recently.

He had answered that he didn't know what she meant. But he had known. Lamb House, status and freedom had made a woman out of a girl.

He watched her as far as the corner. A man turned to look after her as she passed; struck, maybe, by the blue eyes in the dark face? A mere accident of coloring and charm, and men, poor fools, were beguiled!

But what should all that matter to him? And he felt abruptly angry. It did not matter! His life was filled. He had his work, his home and now a child. And the child would be normal! Of course it would! By the law of averages it would; he ought not to have let himself succumb to any morbid thought that it could be otherwise, or to morbid thoughts of any sort. Such thoughts were wasteful and therefore stupid, and he knew better.

Think of bright things, good things, purpose; think not of the past, but of the years to come . . . . I'll come back again to Europe one day, he promised himself. I must see Epidaurus and the Temple of Aesculapius. I'll bring my son with me! Yes, my son! I'll teach him and show him things I never saw, never had. I'll give him things I did have, too. My father's arm would rest around my shoulder, drawing me to his heat when it grew cold. We'd sit on the steps and watch the sky light up from the first solitary spark to the streaming of the Milky Way. My father and I. Now my son and I. He'll be tall and easy, not tall and rigid like me. He'll have broad shoulders. I can hear his voice, its first deepening when he starts to become a man. This is what life is all about—

A man in a surgeon's white coat was walking toward him. "Mr. Farrell?"

Martin stood up with a question on his lips, afraid to ask it.

"A healthy child, and your wife is all right, too. Just coming out of anaesthesia. You may see her now."

They entered the elevator. "We had to do a Caesarian section," the other man said. "Tried not to, but there wasn't enough room. The spine, of course."

Martin followed him down the corridor. He was struck with the oddity of himself in the role of follower. Was this how people felt toward him, waiting for his words to fall?

"I would not recommend having any more, Mr. Farrell." Sober eyes admonished Martin. "I'm very, very serious about that."

"I understand. Certainly not."

The man switched to sympathy. "You've had a couple of bad hours."

"Yes," Martin said, and to his own shame was suddenly aware that his terrors had not been first for Jessie, but for his boy, his son. He wondered what anyone who could know that would think of him.

He went in to Jessie. Her face was white as the blankets, but her eyes were triumphant. Filled with tender contrition, he stooped and kissed her forehead, and stroked her damp, curly hair. Murmuring, she closed her eyes.

"She'll sleep now," the nurse said. "Would you like to see the baby?"

At the nursery door he was shown a bundle wrapped in a pink blanket. He remembered that he hadn't even inquired the sex of the child and he felt a draining disappointment.

"A lovely girl," the nurse said.

He stared at the baby. She was unmarked by struggle through the birth canal, and she had long dark hair.

The nurse was jovial. "You could almost braid it, couldn't you?"

He knew he was supposed to respond with the usual comic, awkward pride of the new father. But there was only a sinking in his chest. His little son! And this was the last chance.

The baby opened her eyes. It was impossible, of course, but she seemed to be staring straight back at Martin. For more than a few moments they regarded one another. Then she yawned, the pink mouth making a perfect O, raised her hand and dropped it in exquisite relaxation.

"She's bored with our company," the nurse said, laughing.

Against all rules, Martin put his finger into that miniature palm. At once the miniature fingers curled around his thick one. How strong she was! Already reaching out to life and grasping! The tiny thing! He felt a lump in his throat. The tiny thing!

And she was perfect, without a flaw. A rush of gratitude went through him; he felt the old warning tingle of rising tears. At the same time he wanted to laugh. Perfect, without a flaw! Beautiful, too, with a straight little nose, strong curved chin and thick lashes, lying now on cheeks whose skin was fine as silk. His girl.

"What will you name her?" the nurse asked.

He had to think a moment of the name they had selected for a girl.

"Claire," he said, between the laughter and the tears. "Her name is Claire."

THAT NIGHT HE sat down and wrote a letter. "Darling Claire. On this the day, almost the hour of your birth, I want to tell you how I feel before many of my thoughts can slip away. We don't know each other yet, but already you are part of me, like my hand or my eyes. I wouldn't have believed it possible. I love you so . . ."

❦{10}❧

Sometimes Fern thought of the bed as a kind of throne, raised as it was on a shallow platform in the middle of the long wall. Everyone came to her here, where she leaned against fresh white linen pillows under a canopy upheld by carved mahogany posts. Neddie and Emmy climbed up to be read to; the baby Isabel was placed here in her arms to be fed.

Alex had said, "I read once that home is where the furniture has stood in one place for a century. You're sure you don't mind moving into a house that was finished long ago by other people?"

She had not minded, as long as she could have her books from home; art books, history, poetry and books her mother had read to her when she was a child. They all stood now on shelves in the yellow sitting room across the hall. Everything else in Lamb House had been there before her, except for the bed. She had not wanted to lie with her husband in the bed where his parents had conceived him. So the original had been taken down and stored away. In a London antique shop she had found a replacement almost like the first, but without any personal, known history and therefore, new.

Sometimes she thought of the bed as a ship, a great safe ship floating all night on a quiet sea until morning. Waking early, she would open her eyes in the familiar haven of the lovely room, into which first light shook itself through white, trembling curtains and dappled the copper bowl of orange roses on the table. And for a few minutes she would lie quite still, feeling that fine brightness of the spirit, that tranquility of the flesh, which is called, for lack of any more apt definition, "well-being."

But all this was of the past.

For months now, she had lain most of the time alone in the bed, on sheets gone cold and pillows crumpled by her restless, sleepless head. Alex slept on a narrow cot in the dressing room next door. He had first begun to sleep there during the winter when he'd had the flu. Its aftermath of coughing had lasted for weeks. Then, in order not to wake Fern after late meetings in town, he had kept on using the cot . . .

She was finding it impossible to talk about. That was puzzling, because Alex and she had been able to talk about anything. Women in particular had often remarked, with some curiosity and much frank envy, on this free and lively interchange of theirs. It was such a wonderful thing to be able to *talk* to a husband! Their husbands came home from work and read the newspaper—

Given, then, a relationship like this there ought to have been no reason why she could not have said: "What's wrong? I want to know." Yet she could not bring herself to say it.

Instead, humiliation knotted in her chest; she felt a prickling, inhibiting sense of shame. She was perfectly aware that this was only false pride and a wife ought not to have false pride. Yet she had it.

One day she bought a book about married love and left it on the table at the foot of the bed, next to the folded London *Times*. Alex riffled through it and put it back.

"Good Lord," he said, "you'd think people never could have got married and lived together without having somebody write a book of instructions for them!"

The remark was so unlike him, to whom openmindedness and intellectual curiosity were essential virtues, that Fern was astonished and said so.

In answer he laughed and went back to the *Times*. And she, rebuked and made foolish, said no more.

"By the way." He lowered the paper a few minutes later. "At the Baker's dinner Malcolm said you were the most striking woman in the room."

"Very nice of him."

"Well, you were! You should always wear either white or blue." He yawned. "I'm wrung out. I could drop right off to sleep. Had a meeting about the blasted German insurance today. Terrence made the report and you know how long-winded he can be. If you want to read some more, I'll sleep in the dressing room."

"I don't want to read anymore," she said flatly.

The darkness had a hollow feel as if she were alone in a cavern. How could everything have changed so quickly? Briefly Alex stroked her shoulder and brushed her earlobe with his lips.

"Good night. Sleep well," he said tenderly.

In a minute he was asleep. She *willed* him to turn back to her, but her will had no effect. Yet, if he had turned and opened his arms, she would not have come into them. For was she to exist only to satisfy his odd whim? What could he be thinking of? And didn't he wonder at all what *she* might be thinking?

Rain spattered the leaves close to the windows. Rain again! No wonder the English drank so much brandy and so much boiling tea! The dampness shuddered in her marrow. She got up to take another blanket and lay awake while the rain quickened and darkness deepened in the hollow cavern.

There was another woman: there had to be. Who, then? That cousin of Nora's, she of the false voice, chirrup and chirp? She had a very convenient flat in London. Maybe even Nora herself? Shameful to think of one's friend; kind, strong Nora. Still, one never knew; one heard incredible things. That Irish girl, Delia somebody, who won the jumping trophy at the horse show? She was dark and the women he admired were always dark ones. The girl couldn't be more than eighteen. She had the most absurd way of stretching her eyes, slanting them at a man even when he was no taller than she. Alex had danced with her at least five times at the Elliot's.

Maybe it was none of these at all. Maybe it was someone he had known before they were married, some woman he couldn't have married, because she wouldn't have been a proper mother for his child.

She must find out. She would find out.

Alex sighed in his sleep and turned over; one relaxed arm brushed Fern's rigid shoulder. He smelled of cleanliness, of shaving lotion and Pear's soap. And she slid away, out of touch.

Her mind sped. He'd gone riding with Delia last Thursday afternoon. They were out two hours, at least. She would have gone, too, if he'd asked her, but when she got back from errands in the village he had already left. And when she went down to the stable to saddle Duchess, they were just coming in.

"We went all the way to Blackdale. It was marvelous!" Delia cried. "You should have been with us, Fern."

Yes, I should.

Her hair falls like black silk . . . It's not possible. Things like this happen to other people. Like auto accidents and cancer, they happen to other people.

On a Sunday afternoon in dark and threatening autumn weather, Alex stood up suddenly and stretched.

"I've a yen for exercise. I think I'll take Lion for a canter up to Blackdale. Not far."

"Not far! An hour and a half there and back. And it's going to rain."

She knew she sounded critical and cross. But he answered pleasantly.

"I'll be home before the rain comes, I think. And if not, I shan't mind."

"Well, suit yourself. I've no wish to get soaked."

"Shouldn't want you to," he said, still pleasantly.

He had been gone half an hour before her thoughts took clear shape, and a decision was made. What sort of fool did he take her for? A country canter in this weather? And he'd been on the telephone three times before lunch today.

From the closet she pulled a mackintosh and rain hat, for the rain had begun. Then she went into the hall and called softly up the stairs. "Nanny? Let the children have tea without us this afternoon. I've an unexpected errand."

She would be waiting for them at the stable, standing in the lane as they rode up. She would smile, smile dangerously, and then see what Alex would have to say.

But afterward—what would come then? She couldn't think that far ahead. Vague images of daring courage came to mind: of those men who last summer had gone up the sheer face of a mountain in the Himalayas. The vertigo! The horror of falling! Could they have felt such panic in the pit of the stomach? No. They wouldn't have been able to do it if they had.

Step forward. Get through it. The rest will follow.

She walked swiftly. There was no one on the road, the villagers being either at the radio or sleeping Sunday dinner off. Even the clattering crows of autumn had taken shelter from the wet.

The fools! They would be soaked! Unless they knew of some place to hide away in—she couldn't imagine where. There was no one about in the stable yard,

either. The horses had all been taken indoors. From the little office next to the
tack room where Kevin, the head groom, had a desk and kept his records, came
an oil lamp's weak glow. It wouldn't do any harm to wait inside with Kevin. She
would still be able to hear them trotting up the path. Let Kevin hear or think
what he might.

The window was next to the door so that, standing with one's hand on the
knob, one's face was almost pressed against the pane, and one's eyes were drawn
into the room. Something caught Fern's attention before her hand had turned the
knob.

A cot, covered with a plaid horse blanket, stood opposite the desk along the
farther wall. Someone was lying on it. She leaned forward. Blinked. Stepped back.
Leaned forward again. Frowning, she flattened her nose on the wet glass. It was
like looking into an aquarium. The shape on the cot—no, there were two—the
shapes slid, pale and slippery, like great, gliding fish, underwater creatures
twisted in some unfathomable embrace. And for a minute or two she stood there,
failing to understand. She saw, yet did not grasp the meaning of what she saw.

Then a face came into view. It moved into the path of the lamplight. It was a
face and a bright head that she knew . . . Alex spoke. She saw a flash of naked
white as Kevin sat up. And she understood.

She gave a harsh cry and clapped her palm to her mouth and fled from the
shaft of light into the shrubbery. She heard Alex crying, in a voice of terrible
alarm, "Who's there? Who's there?" And she ran.

Crouched and stumbling in the failing afternoon, under a sky grown eerie as
moonlight, she ran, hidden from the public road behind hedges and walls. A
bramble ripped her leg. She fell. Pebbles ground into her palms. She had a crazy
thought that someone was pursuing her.

"Oh my God!" she gasped. Her heart beat so! It beat so! And she put her hand
to her chest. Was there some stoppage there? Even at her age, the heart could
stop, couldn't it?

She reached the house and banged the door open. A child, hearing her steps,
called from upstairs, but she raced to her room. She threw the soaked mackintosh
and hat upon the floor and lay down upon the bed. Her throne! Her ship! She
was dizzy, sick, delirious. It was all unreal! Untrue! She had not seen, could not
possibly have seen it!

Yes, she knew of such things, but very vaguely, for there was nothing in print
except for some sparse definitions in the dictionaries. A girl in school had overheard her brother talking. There had been tittering, shocked laughter, so that
dimly and half-comprehended, a conception of something awful and unnatural
had been formed. She had been perhaps fifteen when these things had happened.
And she knew now very little more than she had known then.

If only her heart would stop *pounding* so! It felt as though a volcano were
swirling and burning in her, as if she were too full to contain the swirling and
burning.

Downstairs the front door opened and then was closed with the muffled thud
of solid wood. Footsteps sounded: Alex's familiar tread. He came in and stood
beside the bed.

"So it was you," he said softly.

Fern's dry, scared eyes stared up at him.

"Well, now you know."

She kept on staring at him. He looked the same. The strong shoulders in the handsome riding jacket, the humorous tilt to the eyes, were the same.

"Why?" she whispered.

He shook his head. He sighed.

"I'm sorry. Oh God, I'm sorry."

New terror passed over her, a terror like the cold wind of abandonment. She was alone. Alex was not Alex anymore. Then who was there?

"I thought it was Delia," she whispered.

How much better if it had been Delia, after all!

"You thought it was Delia? That rattle-headed, empty fool?" He laughed.

There was no mirth in the laugh; it was only bitter, nervous, agitated. But the sound of it, and the look of his easy stance, with the riding crop in his left hand and his right hand thrust into the jacket pocket, were too much. Everything burst in Fern. Everything that had been held back for months, added now to this, burst open in one long, wild, frenzied scream. It rose and filled the room; it emptied out into the dusk.

"Stop it! Stop it, Fern, stop it!" Alex cried.

She wasn't able to. Her mind was working clearly; she understood that this was hysteria, her first experience of it. What she had read of it was true. You slid down and down and down, hearing from some far distance your own appalling screams. Over the edge you went, over the edge.

She struggled for air. And struggling up, she ran to the window to push the casement wide.

Alex, misinterpreting, pulled her back and pinned her on the bed.

"You fool! I'm not worth killing yourself for!" He opened her collar. "Quiet! Quiet! Whatever's happened, it's not the world's affair . . . People can hear you."

She wept now, beating the bed with her palms. "I don't care who hears! Let them!"

"You'll terrify the children. You care about them, don't you?"

The children! Ah yes, the children! And this, their father.

"Take some," Alex said. A decanter and small green glass for his nightcap stood on the tray. He filled the glass. "Take some," he commanded again.

She twisted away. "Don't put your hands on me!"

"All right. All right. But talk to me. Please talk to me!"

Silently now, her thick tears rolled as smooth as glycerine.

"I know you can't understand. I can't expect you to be anything but horrified. And I'm so sorry, Fern. Oh my God, just so sorry!"

She thought, I can't stay here. And for one mad instant she saw herself walking out, just walking out, leaving everything behind—this house, the children, her pictures—and most of all this loathsome man. She saw the strapped trunks and the suitcases waiting in the hall. On the top of the pile lay the patent leather traveling case which had come with her from home. The car waited in the driveway. Neddie, Isabel and Emmy stood at the foot of the stairs, their bewildered eyes asking why she was leaving them.

Alex was speaking softly, soothingly. "At least, though, you must see that Kevin's no threat to the marriage, as Delia would have been."

"Threat to the marriage? What marriage? If I could walk out tonight, just walk down the road in the mud; if there were a train going out, a train to anywhere, I don't care where, I'd go. I'd go this minute."

"You're forgetting something."

"Forgetting?"

"Your children—"

"They'll go with me wherever I go."

Alex shook his head. "No," he said. "No." In the straight-backed chair beside the bed he sat erect, as if in the saddle, except that one knee was crossed high on the other thigh. This easy posture alarmed her, as she recognized something she had seen before, although it had never yet been directed at her. It was an iron will in casual disguise. It was determination, not to be diverted.

"What do you mean? You're not fit! Do you think you're a fit father to rear a family? Why, any court would—"

"Any court would if any court could. But it would be your word against mine. Whose do you think they would believe?" He got up, walked the length of the room and strode back. "Whose word? They would say you were a demented, vicious woman."

"I'll find a way! There has to be a way for truth to make itself known. This is a civilized country."

Alex held up his hand. "Wait. And if you were able to prove it—you wouldn't be, but for the sake of argument, let's say you could—then of course, this being a civilized country, I would be relieved of my post. How do you think we should all live then? If you have any idea that inherited wealth alone supports us, you're terribly mistaken. You know very well what's happened to investments here since the crash in America. I *need* to work, Fern. Keep that in mind, if you care about your children."

"Then I'll simply take them and go, that's all. You can't very well set a guard over us whenever you're out of the house."

He raised his eyebrows. "Where will you go? Your father's been almost wiped out in the market and his factory's running on one cylinder. He'd hardly welcome a returning daughter and a brood of children, would he?"

She wiped her eyes roughly. "Alex, tell me, if you can, why? Why?"

"Why what?"

"Why did you marry me? Or marry anyone?"

"I thought it would work. I wanted it to, how I wanted it to! From that first time at your aunt's dinner . . . Fern, you were the loveliest thing I'd ever looked at. Everything, everything about you, your voice, and the quietness in you, and all the life . . . You think like me. We go so well together. I wanted it to be so good for us." His face twisted as if he were going to weep. "My heart aches for you; I wish I could love you as you ought to be loved. Oh my God, how I wish I could!"

"In the name of decency, then, will you give me a divorce? On any grounds you want. Any."

He shook his head.

"Alex, for God's sake, why not?"

He wept. His tears repelled her.

"Why not?" she repeated.

"I would never see my children again."

"I would let you see them. I swear I would."

"I want to live with them, as much as you want to live with them."

"You have no right! You've forfeited the right."

"It's the point of view," Alex said, bringing himself under control. "Society's point of view. In the society of ancient Greece, if you were living there, you would see this differently."

"I'm not living in ancient Greece."

"Well, but listen to me, I'm a good father. You know I am. This other thing—this has nothing to do with it."

"You disgust me," she said.

"Is that all you have to say?"

"I want a divorce. That's what I have to say."

"No, Fern, no. Freedom, yes. Live as you will. I'll ask no questions. But the household stays as it is."

The rain shines on the window. The pale bodies twist like sea creatures underwater.

A shudder rippled down Fern's back and contorted her face. Her teeth began to chatter.

"When you're more calm in the morning, I'll explain to you—"

"I don't want explanations," she cried. "Just get out! Get out where I don't have to look at you. Get out!"

When he had left the room, she crept under the blankets. It was fearfully cold. She remembered a hot beach in Florida years before, walking on the sand with her mother and Jessie, picking up shells. How good to be so young, to know nothing!

A BIRD TWITTERED in the blackness and a breeze puffed. It was the subtle stirring of the earth that comes just ahead of the dawn. She remembered that they had had no dinner last evening. Her dry eyes ached. She would be appalled to see them in the mirror, and at the sight of her own stricken face the tears would start again.

What am I going to do? she thought.

The door opened. Past the window the black had turned to gray. She could see him as he approached the bed, and she stiffened. He was still dressed except for his boots and the coat of his riding habit. Like her, he had been awake all that long night.

"Fern, can't we even try to be reasonable about this?"

"Reasonable!" she cried scornfully. "You really like that word, don't you?"

"It's a good word, one of the best."

She didn't answer. She felt hopeless, burnt out.

"I'll fix a room across the hall. I'll spend more time in town. I should anyway. The business needs it."

Fern got out of bed and walked into the bathroom while his voice followed her.

"Plenty of couples live this way. They rear their children, they're good to one another. Share things—everything but sex. It's not ideal—but it happens. I could give you names that would surprise you. Some of the artists you most admire. M.P.'s. You've even been in their homes. Why, I could tell you—"

"I don't want to hear!"

And on the icy tiles she knelt down, something she had not done in years, not since passing through the religiosity of early adolescence. Yes, once since then, on the night her mother died, she had knelt and prayed: God help me, please. So now on her knees she murmured again: God help me, please. But she had been reared in a household of skeptics, and nothing moved inside.

When she realized that Alex was standing there watching, she struggled to her feet.

"You find this theatrical, I suppose?"

"No, I've done it myself on occasion."

"And did it help?"

"No."

She picked up the bathroom glass and threw it at him. Falling short, it smashed on the floor, scattering its pointed shards with a tinkle.

"Damn you," she cried, "get out! Get out of my sight!"

When he had gone, she got down again on her knees in the splintered glass and cried and longed to be dead.

Alex's mother, accepting a second portion of pudding, remarked, "I'm so sorry to have missed Alex. If I had known he was going to be busy in town all week, I'd have postponed my visit."

The women sat together at one end of the long table. The three days' visit had been interminable for Fern. Ordinarily it would not have been hard to endure, for by now she was used to Rosamund. (Such an odd name for this woman! "Rosamund" should be young and careless; these Alex's mother could never have been, even in youth.) But she was far too desperate to cope with small talk, although she made the effort.

"You'll stay for dinner, won't you? We'll have it early. You'll have plenty of time to catch the evening train."

"No, I'll take the five o'clock. Thanks anyway. I'll be back next month for Neddie's birthday, though."

By next month, Fern thought, it may all have been too much. Perhaps I shall have fallen apart by then. Can't you see what's happening?

Rosamund whispered, "Fern, you're not expecting again? You don't mind my asking? But you do look a little peaked."

"Oh no, no I'm not."

Rosamund laid her hand on Fern's arm. The heat of her hand came through the woolen sleeve. Her warm breath smelled of minted mouthwash.

"I used to envy my friends who had daughters. I used to say, 'A woman needs at least one daughter.' But you know, I don't say it anymore, not since I've had my daughter-in-law. In this slipshod, devil-take-the-hindmost world, I can rely on you. You're so good to me! I tell everyone."

This undeserved, pathetic praise caused disquiet in Fern. What had she ever given, after all, to this poor woman, so hungry for affection? Visits and presents, perfunctory, expensive knickknacks that one picked up without effort or thought.

"Fern, will you come up while I pack my suitcase? There are some things I want to show you."

In the few days of her occupancy Rosamund had made the room her own. There was a clutter of magazines on the bedside table next to a photograph of Alex's father. On the round table in the bay window lay an elaborate, interrupted game of double solitaire, and this last spoke to Fern. As Rosamund gathered up the cards, it spoke of Jessie, of long evenings and long silences.

"In my spare time," Rosamund said now, "I've been making a surprise for you. I thought you might like this."

And she placed on Fern's lap a heavy picture album covered in dark blue velvet, embroidered in silver thread: Alexander Lamb V.

"I'd intended to keep it for your Christmas present, but I'm too impatient to wait that long."

Fern turned the pages. There was Alex at three months, lying naked on a fur rug. Here he sat in a high chair, there in a rowboat. Wearing an Eton jacket, he stood between his parents. "Smile!" the photographer had commanded and Alex had smiled. The label read, "First Day at School." Here, some years later, he was on the soccer team.

"Can you tell which one was Alex?" and as Fern pointed to the wrong one, "I thought you wouldn't be able to tell! Wasn't he chubby? But he has such a large frame! I wonder that he stays so thin now, with the meals you serve."

"We don't eat this way all the time. And of course, with all the exercise, especially riding, you know—" She stopped.

"Well. I wanted you to have it."

"It's beautiful," Fern said. "Thank you so very, very much."

"Wait. I have something else." From her bulging handbag Rosamund withdrew a silk purse on a drawstring. "I've been meaning to give you these, and now is as good a time as any. That's my mother's garnet bracelet. It's eighteen carat. Not that I'm boasting, but so much Victorian jewelry isn't real gold, so I thought you ought to know. And my ruby ring. Try it on. It'll fit your little finger."

Fern was frightened. "You mustn't do this!" she cried. Wasn't it odd that these things should frighten her? "I can't possibly take all this away from you."

"You're not taking; I'm giving. Who else will I leave my things to when I die but to you?"

"Yes, but leaving them is different. You've plenty of time yet to wear them and enjoy them."

For the second time that day Rosamund laid her hand on Fern's arm. Fern looked down at the blunt arthritic fingers.

"Child, the ring won't even fit me anymore. I want you to wear it. The ruby's small, but it happens to be flawless. I was always so proud of it."

"I don't know what to say," Fern began.

People who trusted you, who were good to you, controlled you. You were helpless before them. This woman expected to be loved. She assumed that her son was deeply loved. She weighed you down. The air in the room became as it was in her own home—heavy with habit and obligation. In Rosamund's parlor the mantel was cluttered with snapshots from old holidays, with Christmas cards and theater programs. It was like living in a museum or an ossuary.

"I don't know what to say," Fern repeated.

"Don't say anything! I'll have more for you the next time I see you. My husband was so generous toward me! They're good men, the Lambs. We're lucky, you and I. Alex is a one-woman man like his father. You'll never have to worry the way so many do these days. And did even in my time, too; oh yes, they did! What some of my friends put up with! Because of pride, of course, and also for the children's sake. What's a woman to do? I often think of Lucy Hemming. She's dead now, so I can talk. Walter Hemming kept a singer, pretty enough in a common way, took her to the best places where all Lucy's friends could see them. Disgraceful! But you're crying, Fern! Have I said anything? What is it?"

Fern stood up. She had to get out of that room.

"Nothing. It's foolish of me. I was just touched at your giving me so much."

"Why, my dear, you are softhearted, aren't you?" Rosamund was pleased. "Just enjoy them. I'm so sorry I missed Alex. Kiss him for me."

She thought, rushing down the hall, that she wouldn't be able to stand much more. There had to be someone she could talk to. Someone.

SHE LONGED FOR her mother. It was humiliating that, at this age and herself a mother, she should feel such need. If only her father were a man one could go to! But you could never talk to him of *interior* things. He had always been concerned with externals: proper appearances and material goods. He would never understand this. She could even imagine his fury, an outrage almost childish. There would be no rational analysis from him, no comfort. Her mother would have given comfort even though she might not have known what was actually to be done.

As for talking to Jessie, the roots of alienation were too deep. Perhaps alienation wasn't the right word; indifference might be a better definition. Or unease? Whatever the term, things were as they were.

Since the birth of her child, Jessie had drawn farther away. Within the real world she had made another world into which few were admitted and these mostly old people, or women who, because they were dowdy or scholarly or both, were no threat to Jessie. Fern saw this clearly, pityingly. And she wondered what place Martin had in that little world. Her mind, opening the door of his and Jessie's bedroom, retreated in shame and closed the door at once.

So she couldn't go to her sister. They hadn't even seen each other since they'd had an American Thanksgiving together and now it was almost February. No, not Jessie.

Who, then?

And she knew even as she put the question and denied the answer—because the meeting would be awkward at best and probably futile as well. She knew nevertheless that the answer was Martin.

Why? There was a subtle coolness between them. She still felt discomfort in his presence, although not what she had felt when he first arrived in England. Certainly she wasn't angry anymore. She had made herself behave like a mature, accepting woman. Perhaps, she reasoned, Alex had been right. People looked for different things in marriage and, after all, theirs was not the first such marriage. Martin was most tender with Jessie. And quite mad about the little girl! A lovely child, she was. A firebird. Quicksilver. Curiously, she reminded one of Neddie. Emmy and Isabel would be large, placid women, easy to live with. Martin had been so wonderful with poor Emmy that time they happened to be visiting and she broke her arm. A gentle doctor. Alex called him a born physician. Rare. Strange, but the doctor and the man seemed *separate*.

The man didn't reveal himself except when he talked about Claire. When one overheard him from the far end of a table or a room, he was usually talking about her. But more of the time he didn't talk at all. She didn't remember him as such a silent, private person. At home in Cyprus she had thought him spirited and eager. How things changed! But she herself had changed since then! One could call it learning or aging. No matter. But Martin was kind; that hadn't altered. He would surely listen to her. He could be trusted. Maybe he would even know some way to help her. Was there any help?

A coal fire burned in the grate. The walls were covered with black and brown books bound in frayed and powdering leather. Everything in the room was very old; it looked like Sherlock Holmes's office on Baker Street. Actually, it belonged to Mr. Braidburn. Martin had explained that he sometimes saw patients here for Mr. Braidburn when he was away.

Fern kept looking around the room, aware that Martin also was considerately looking elsewhere, giving her time to calm herself. There was a Turkish carpet. There were heavy curtains, printed in dark red and tan. The room was warm. One could forget that it was on the ground floor of a hospital, that on the floors above people with hideous things growing in their heads lay dying. On the desk there was an open folder with a pen beside it. But Martin had written nothing and said nothing, only listened.

Now he said, "You were beginning to smile a moment ago. Why?"

"For some reason or other, I was remembering the day you told me my eyes don't belong in my face."

He didn't answer.

"I think of myself as having been very childish for a girl of twenty."

"Not childish. Inexperienced, which is quite a different thing."

He lit a cigarette and leaned back in the chair. She was conscious of every sound, of the little scrape of the match and the creak of the chair. A small pain flashed through her temples.

She said abruptly, "People don't know anything about each other when they marry. It's absurd. It's all artificial. We go to the hairdresser. He brings flowers . . ."

"Yet you must have loved him."

"I didn't know anything about him, as you see."

"The part you knew, you loved. Didn't you?"

"Why do you say that?"

"I think—you wouldn't have married him otherwise. Would you have?"

She felt as though she were undergoing an inquisition. He was *pressing* her. Why? And she passed her hand wearily across her forehead.

"I don't know. It's just the time, the place. Feelings rush over us. It's just—tricks. Yes, tricks."

"You shouldn't be bitter. Shouldn't deny the feelings you had. That is, if they were true ones."

He laid the cigarette in the ashtray from which smoke rose in a straight column toward the ceiling. Raising her eyes with the smoke, she saw that he was looking at her for the first time since she had come into the room.

"Were they?" Martin asked.

"I'm sorry. Were they what?"

"Your feelings. Were they true?"

"Yes, yes. I don't know." These last weeks she had grown thinner, and her rings were loose. She twisted them. She faltered: "If you had asked me before all this, I would have said, 'Yes, I loved him.' Now I think it's possible I thought so because I didn't know what I was missing."

Martin got up and went to the carafe that stood on a table.

"Would you like some water?"

When she declined, he poured a glass for himself and stood with his back to her drinking it slowly. His back, his shoulders, even the way he stood, were subtly different from what they had been three years before. They had the look of authority. She was thinking that when he went back to his chair and spoke again.

"Are you saying that you were comfortable with Alex because he made no approach to your sexuality? Is that what you're saying? Is that one of the reasons you married him?"

"You've no right to say that!" she cried, in immediate anger.

"Why haven't I? I'm a doctor. You asked for my opinion."

"That doesn't give you the right to humiliate people."

"If you feel humiliated, I'm sorry. That wasn't my intent." He spoke quietly. "But you don't have to stay if you don't want to hear me."

"All right. Go on."

"You've said yourself, often enough, that you were very young for your age. That means you had no knowledge of sex and as yet apparently no real need of it. Also, what little you knew about it you feared. And I think you still do."

"Do you mind telling me what you're driving at?"

"What I'm driving at is that you're not hurt because you've been deprived of sex and love. You're hurt because your life's been turned inside out."

She wanted to slap him. In her need she had come to him for aid and comfort;

he was giving her a scolding and scorn. Tears started. Biting her lip, she controlled them.

He stood up again and went to rearrange some books on a table. He was strangely agitated. Then he came back and sat down.

"I'm sorry. I'm not being fair to you. I sounded angry, I know."

"Yes, you did. Why?"

"I don't know why. One doesn't always understand oneself."

" 'Physician, heal thyself,' " she said with bitterness. And quite suddenly she saw before her, not the man of authority who had risen when she had entered the room awhile ago, but the young man in the shabby suit at the dinner table in Cyprus, a youth with something burning and bright in his face, and with a certain pathos. She spoke gently now.

"We're quarreling—"

He collected himself. "Mary, I don't want to. I want to help you."

"You still call me Mary," she said irrelevantly.

He lit another cigarette and leaned down to replace the pack in a desk drawer. When he raised his head he had resumed the professional manner: kindly, reasoned and firm.

"I want to help you," he repeated. "You're scared to death."

She twisted her rings. "I don't know where I'm going, don't understand anything. I have no patience with the children, can't work, can't paint, can't bear to look at Alex—he disgusts me."

"Tell me, Mary. What do you know about homosexuality?"

"Not very much."

"There have been times and places in which it was an honored form of love. Did you know that?"

"They didn't teach us that in history class! But I suppose I knew."

"Some of the world's best minds—Leonardo, Michelangelo. Even Shakespeare, they say—'How like a winter hath my absence been from thee?' That sonnet was probably addressed to a boy. Does that shock you?"

"Maybe, a little."

"Well, the Church says it's wrong, of course, but—"

She interrupted, "I wasn't brought up with much religion."

"I was, though. I've had to discard a lot of it and yet the core—" He stopped. "What I wanted to say was, the Bible also tells us not to judge. And that I believe is right. Not to judge."

She was silent.

"People hate anything different from themselves. There are people who hate Jews without ever having known one, or else having known one bad one."

"This is different."

"Not really. All the goodness that was in Alex—isn't it there still?"

"I don't know."

"You do know."

She sighed.

"He's not *wicked*, Mary! And let me tell you, he suffers. It's obvious he can neither change himself nor accept himself. If he could accept himself it would be easy for him. But this way, it's very hard. Can't you see how hard?"

"I haven't thought about it."

"Well, think about it. Maybe you'll come to understand."

"My father never would!"

Martin smiled slightly. "I'm sure he wouldn't."

"When I found out about Alex," she said slowly, "it was as if a trapdoor had opened up and I'd been dropped, just dropped, out into the weather. Violently. I'd been living all my life in a cocoon. Tell me now. Tell me. What am I to do?"

"No, you tell me."

"I?"

"Yes. You tell me what is the most important thing you have to do from now on."

For an instant she wasn't sure of his meaning. Then it came to her with a rush. "To take care of my children. Is that what you meant?"

"Of course."

She smiled warily. "That certainly isn't all one gets married for."

"People marry for many reasons. Because they're lonely, or need a particular kind of understanding or a companionable mind. Many reasons."

Now he was looking straight at her again, dropping the professional manner as one slips out of a sweater and leaves it on a chair.

"Please, don't say anything to Jessie, will you?"

"I don't discuss other people's confidences."

"Excuse me. I should have known better."

"And excuse me. I was pompous and rude just now."

Neither spoke for a moment. Then Martin began.

"Work. Work is always the salvation, Mary. You have a gift. Use it. Fill your days with it."

"No," she said. "I've no true gift. Father was right about it. It's only a very little talent that I have."

"You can't be sure yet. Give it time."

"Time! I'll have plenty of that—"

"You'll need a great deal of courage. But I think you have it."

"Thank you."

He added thoughtfully, "A very good thing, although maybe you can't see its importance right now, is your home. As long as you have to stay there and have no choice. There's great comfort to be had from 'place.' It doesn't happen to be like that for me, but for some people it's—as they say—the essence. It's true for you, isn't it? And Lamb House is the place?"

"Yes," she said. "I walk around sometimes just *touching* things. There are certain trees, an old sycamore where I can sit and feel the world breathe. One can feel such peace among trees."

Suddenly she was very, very tired. They had said everything there was to be said and gone as far as there was to go. She rose to leave.

"Wait. I'm giving you a prescription for sleeping pills. Just half a dozen. Take one only if you need it badly."

"I shan't kill myself, you know!"

"If I thought you had such an idea, I wouldn't give them to you at all."

He stood up, but did not come from behind the desk or offer to shake her hand. It crossed her mind that he hadn't touched her when she had come in, either, and that perhaps in spite of the professional kindness, he really disliked her after all. She put the prescription in her handbag and thanked him.

"Perhaps I haven't helped you, but I did try," he said.

"It's helped me to talk to you. Yes, it has."

"I'm glad." He might have been expected to say, "Come back anytime if you need me again," but he did not, and so she repeated her thanks with a correctness to match his own, and went out.

On the rattling suburban train, she fell asleep. She had always been one of those rare, contrary souls for whom sleep in time of trouble was a psychological escape, and there would be no need for pills.

When the train swayed around the last curve before the home station, she woke up. Martin had been right: there was comfort in "place." The High Street gave cheerful assurance. The butcher, florid and garrulous, came out on the step to remark, as always, upon the weather. The seed store had hung out its little packets of nasturtiums, delightful scraps of orange and yellow silk with a sharp, enticing perfume after rain. Fern thought wryly: But they are usually covered on the underside with black pinhead bugs. It is the underside that surprises.

Neddie came around the house. "Guess what?" he cried.

She widened her eyes, responding to his gaiety, his dare.

"I can't guess. What?"

"We had ice cream at Rob's house. It was his brother's birthday."

"You did?"

"Yes, and it was chocolate."

He pranced, jiggling the green pompom on his woolen cap. Oh my heart, my darling! How could I ever leave you?

"Chocolate!" she repeated brightly before, remembering some other errand, he sped away around the corner.

The house enfolded her. She went slowly up the stairs, sliding her hand on the smooth old bannister. At the top she paused before the photo of Susannah.

"There was never any love between us," Alex had told her, "after the first month or two." He had been ruefully amused, making a joke of it. "That's when I found out that the books in her family's library had false backs. Only, I found out too late."

Had Susannah also found something out too late? But the cool face told nothing.

Alex, coming upstairs a moment later, knocked on the frame of the open door. "May I?"

"Yes, come in."

They faced each other, Fern at the closet where she had been hanging up her coat, he in the doorway.

Then, astoundingly, he said, "You've seen Martin."

"What? What makes you say that?"

"You know I sense things. You've told him everything, haven't you?"

"Yes. Are you angry?"

"No. What did he say?"

"I don't know exactly. That is, it's hard to remember." She stammered. "I suppose—he tried to explain, to help me understand."

"I'm very grateful to him. I've always liked him, anyway."

She raised an eyebrow.

"Don't be nasty! I was referring to intelligence, compassion, humanity."

She saw that Alex had imagined mockery in her expression. "I only meant, you don't know him well enough, do you, to feel much of anything toward him?"

"I told you I can sense things. I judge people very quickly. For instance, I know that he's in love with you. I've known it for a long time. He's the man you should have married."

"Don't be absurd!"

"Haven't you seen how he always manages to leave a room the minute you enter it?"

"What on earth are you saying?"

"You mean you haven't noticed?"

"No, I haven't," Fern said tightly.

"Well, it's true."

She turned away. "I've got to get this hot dress off. It's miserable."

In the dressing room she put on a robe. That pain again, the little pulses in her temples! She touched them lightly. He oughtn't to have said that about Martin! There were enough terrible things for her to think about already without adding more. She had mountains to climb! Mountains! And anyway it wasn't true! Martin was responsible and serious; he wouldn't— Suddenly, involuntarily, she gave a little cry.

"Are you all right?" Alex called.

She came back to the bedroom and sat down. "It's been a hard day, and I'm worn out."

He knelt on the floor and took her hand.

"Fern, I'll be the best friend you ever could have."

He moved his cheek until it rested on her limp hand, and she could feel his tears. She wanted to draw away, yet did not; they sat unmoving through an expectant silence.

At last Alex raised his head. "I've been through hell," he said.

"Have you?"

"Don't you believe me?"

"I believe you."

"Hell for you, too. I know that, Fern. I hope . . . I don't ever want you to think that I—that what I am has anything to do with you. It's just me."

Silence again.

"It didn't work with Susannah. But then, she was a sharp-tongued bitch and I thought it might have been partly her fault. I hoped it would be different with you. And I tried, Fern, you know I did."

She was seeing herself objectively. She was looking through a telescope, to the end of a long, long corridor of time, during which she would mature into understanding. It was as though she were looking at some other woman, surely not at herself, who would have to endure a purgatory of fruitless, unending analysis, while anger and pain would slowly evaporate like salt in the sun, leaving—leaving what? A desert?

Alex spoke again. "I try to remember how it began. My music teacher, perhaps? He had strong fingers. Supple brown hands. I couldn't stop looking at them.

"And there was a boy in school. Lewis was his name. He sat at the next desk. He also had brown hands and thick beautiful hair. Strange, troubling twinges went through me, very slight, I remember, very puzzling. Little devils, sitting with hot pitchforks somewhere at the pit of my brain.

"I didn't understand yet. You were supposed to have girls' pictures in your room, a snapshot of your own girl, or actresses, all breasts and thighs and glossy mouths. I kept thinking maybe I just wasn't growing up as early as boys usually do, that pretty soon I'd get to be like the others. But I didn't know, and there was nobody in the world I could ask, least of all my father . . . And then suddenly I was in the last form and during the long vacation a lot of chaps went up to town and brought some girls over to somebody's flat. And the girl I was with"—now Alex was almost whispering—"the girl laughed because I—I didn't want to. She laughed. And the news got around when we were back at school. It was a huge, splendid joke! Except for Lewis. He came to me, and we talked. He was so fine, so decent, so different from the others . . . He became my only friend, and I was his. In a way you might say we suffered together."

He looked down at his hands, turning them over and back, as if they could offer him some explanation.

"There are memories, so minute and sharp they ought to have been absorbed years ago, but never have been. A burly ruffian with hairy ears and a shattering voice, saying, 'Alex pees sitting down.' Why isn't it possible to forget things like that? Why should a boor's taunt have power to torment you a quarter of a lifetime later?"

So that's the way it is, Fern thought. She had not wanted to be so moved. She had wanted to keep the hard anger, to hold the insult which had been dealt her, to hold them both fast and neither weaken nor give in. But give in to what?

In these few minutes, night had come, and from the triangle of sky that filled the upper corner of the window, there poured an iridescent afterglow. It fell upon the man's bowed head. Feeling her gaze, he looked up.

"Fern, everything I have belongs to you and the children. I don't mean just things, this house or money. I mean caring. My devotion. I can't help what I am. I'll have to go on just quietly being what I am, you know. But I'll never ask what you do with private portions of your life. I'll never ask.

"So we could live here, couldn't we, with our children, and be happy in other ways?"

"Happy!" she cried silently.

And Alex repeated, "Couldn't we?"

In the simplicity of the words and in his face she saw, not so much a plea for pity and understanding, as a kind of wonder that they two were here like this, having learned what they both now knew. That much she saw, and also she saw disbelief, as when a man has been wounded, so she had read, and stares at the shattering, not able to believe that he is himself and the wound belongs to him.

Then pity came, after all, and she bent down to rest his head against her shoulder, rocking and swaying as if he were a child and she his mother. Or as if she were the child, panicked and lost, and he her comforter. Or as if he and she, strangers just met, survivors of some awful cataclysm, some rage of nature, avalanche or quake or firestorm, must cling together out of need and then, because of common humanity and common trust, must stay.

BOOK THREE

PASSAGES

❖{11}❖

No self-respecting institution at home would have put up with so ancient a building, Martin reflected, as he prepared to leave for the afternoon. In America this would have been torn down, or more probably abandoned for a new building in a newer part of the city. These steps on which he stood to regard the blossoming day had been laid down in the eighteenth century. The wings to right and left of the central structure were Victorian, darkly bulbous, with beetling fenestration. It amused him to imagine that they looked like the women of their era, stout in bombazine and bustles.

"Making your plans for the day?" Mr. Meredith drew on gloves and tucked his umbrella under one arm.

"Great plans. I'm going to the park with Claire."

"Taking a bus?"

"Later. I want to walk a little before I catch it."

"Fine. I'll go part way with you."

Through speckled sunlight and shade under the lime trees, they fell into step. Each man was sturdy with well-being and aware that the other was the same. A small boy came galloping with an enormous borzoi on a leash. A young woman in a yellow suit came out of a house, carrying a sheaf of tulips wrapped in green tissue paper.

"Splendid weather," Meredith remarked with a sigh of pleasure.

Martin said, "I can't believe I've been here three years."

"Does it seem longer to you or shorter?"

"That depends on mood. Longer or shorter, it's been wonderful. It's opened worlds for me."

"I must say, you've taken good advantage of it. Your cytology paper is impressive, Mr. Braidburn tells me. I confess I haven't read it yet. I'll have to wait until it's published. You're going to the conference in Paris next week, of course."

"I wouldn't miss it. Dr. Eastman's coming over from New York and I'll have a chance to see him again."

"Have I congratulated you on your association with him? Great fortune for you."

"I'm indebted to Mr. Braidburn forever. After all, when Eastman wrote that he was looking for a new man, Mr. Braidburn could have recommended any one of half a dozen others, and I know it."

"What have you been offered, may I ask? Full-time association?"

"Yes, on a trial basis, naturally. If things work out well, why then it will become permanent." Martin's voice trailed off. The whole prospect had an air of unreality. Everything had gone so smoothly, one deliberate step after the other.

"You've got just two months more, haven't you? You must come for a weekend in the country with us before you leave. Well, I turn off here. Enjoy your afternoon."

Glancing after him, Martin thought: Funny, in the beginning, the formal manners, the bowler hats and accents put me off. He smiled, recalling some of those first impressions.

They had taught him much, those men: Meredith, Braidburn, Llewellyn and the rest. All those dark winter afternoons under electric lights in the pathology lab! Those early mornings watching Braidburn in the O.R.! And the lunchtime discussions on clinical neurology; the diagrams drawn on the backs of menus; the questions; the arguments! Yes, he would take good memories back with him.

From the top of the double-decker bus, he enjoyed the panorama of the city. How the northerners of this foggy little island worshiped the sun! This was the first real warmth of the season today and here they were already, stretched out wherever there was a plot of grass, turning their pale faces to the light. Here came the Victoria and Albert Memorial, a wedding cake in stone. He had a glimpse of a deerhound on a stone frieze, pursued by men wearing classical togas. Absurd! A large stone lady perched on a kneeling elephant; an elaborate necklace fell between her naked, spherical breasts, and that was absurd, too. But the breasts were exquisite. He stared at them until they were out of sight. Now came the turn into Kensington High Street and a few blocks to walk home. He got off and began to hurry.

Claire was dressed and waiting for him. They started for the park, she riding ahead of him on her tricycle, jangling its bell. Her dark curls just touched the velvet collar of her tiny coat. Jessie dressed her in fine taste, but then, Jessie's taste was always fine. He couldn't take his eyes from Claire. And he wondered whether she would ever have any comprehension at all of what she meant to him. Her bright voice, her vigor! There was such a softness in him! That nothing, nothing, should ever happen to this child! No one ever hurt her! And although he knew that this cherishing of a child was the most universal emotion known to man, still it seemed to him, no doubt foolishly, that what *he* felt must be unusually intense.

How irrational life could be! Now, with the way lying clear before him to support a family, he could have but one child. Alice had sent snapshots of her three, the girls not nearly as pretty as Claire. Fred taught at a village school in the potato country; it must be a struggle for them. Yet Alice was about to have another child.

Once in the park, past the Round Pond and the ducks in the Serpentine, Martin led the way to the statue of Peter Pan. (He had read the story to Claire; Jessie said it was too advanced for a three-year-old, yet he was sure she had understood it.) And, finding a bench, he settled down to watch Claire riding back and forth on the path.

Not far from the statue they were taking pictures for a fashion magazine. Lanky and lean, the models posed smartly with arched back, thrusting pelvis and long, striding legs. Their purpose was ostensibly to seem indifferent and aloof. Yet sexual invitation was written on their lovely, haughty faces.

Under a spreading bush a couple lay in uninhibited embrace for anyone to see. And it was said that the English were "cold"!

Martin breathed deeply. A tart, bitter fragrance blew from behind him: out of dark earth had come an explosion of huge geraniums, blazing and blooming like none he had ever seen at home. And these also were sexual in their exuberance.

Primeval, burgeoning spring! Fragrance and moisture of new life, bursting, reaching, wanting. Wanting so! Until it—it hurt!

He became aware of his heartbeat. It happens now and then: you hear your own heartbeat and suddenly, for no reason that you can explain to yourself, you are reminded that someday it will stop. The sturdy, steady heart will flutter and gallop, will flutter and slow. There will come a final beat. And the amazing little pump, which has been serving without an instant's rest for all your years, will halt.

And now the old, familiar melancholy seeped in Martin: the veil, the cloud over the sun, the shade drawn down on the day which had been so blithe and charming up till a moment ago. And he remembered that this melancholy had been lying upon him for many months past.

There had been such cheer when Claire was born! So much purpose and joy! What had happened to them? And when? But it was impossible to set a time, to say "There, that's the moment we began to be unhappy."

Back in Cyprus it had seemed remarkable that Jessie could be possessed of such practical good humor, so much realistic common sense, such strong optimism. "Wholesome" had been his word for her then, often a priggish word when misused, but actually a fine one, meaning "healthy" and "whole." Now that wholeness had split. How? Why?

There had been "scenes." He hated them. It might be supposed that no one enjoyed them, although maybe some people did, dramatic types who flaunted emotion to gain attention. But Martin cringed at the thought. And Jessie was always miserable afterward. Yet they happened, again and again. They were very hard to live with.

A few weeks before they had gone to see *Gisèle*. A new ballerina had been dancing, an exquisite girl who was being talked of all over the Continent. A dream of a girl—unforgettable. Her dark red hair, caught in a tail, fell tossing to her shoulders. She rose *en pointe,* her white arms reaching in a perfect curve, her mauve skirt drifting—Splendor and grace to catch at one's throat in awe and linger, smiling, on one's lips!

And all the while Jessie had been watching, not the dance, but him.

Coming into the bedroom later that night, he had caught her standing naked in front of the mirrored door. She had turned on him furiously.

"Why don't you knock? Do you have to come in here to stare at me?"

"I wasn't staring at you! But for Heaven's sake, I'll look away if you want me to."

"Yes, do! It's a lot more pleasant for you to look at anyone else but me, I'm sure it is. Ballerinas, waitresses—almost anyone but me."

Wanting to be patient, he had yet said the wrong thing. "Jessie, can't you try not to think about yourself? Other people really don't pay all that much attention to your—"

"To my what?"

"Your—disability."

"You can't say it, can you?"

"Say what?"

"Hump!" she cried. "I can say it well enough! H-U-M-P. Hump. Go on. Say it!" He sat down wearily, covering his eyes with his hands.

"You didn't think I heard," Jessie said, "that time in Vienna in the shop where we bought the porcelain tea set and the saleswoman said to you, 'You'll be glad you bought it. Your mother will love it.' She thought I was your mother!"

"Oh, if you're going to let a shopgirl's stupid mistake haunt you like this, what can I say to help you? I want to help you, Jessie," he said gently.

So he had tried and in the end, when she had exhausted anger, she had apologized, in shame.

"Oh, you are patient with me, Martin, I know you are! I ought to be grateful for what I've got, and I really am. It's just that when we're out together—you have no idea how I steel myself to go places with you! I feel the thoughts in the air, the messages passed from one to the other. And I know what they'll say after we're gone, how the women will talk on the telephone the next morning."

For a week or two after that particular time they had gone nowhere, except on Sunday to a country inn where they had sat on a high-backed settee near a fire and watched the locals play Shove Ha'penny. No one had paid any attention to them. For those few hours it had been as it was when they rode around Cyprus on house calls, talking about the state of medicine and everything else under the sun. He understood now that these things had interested Jessie because she could hide behind them: they were not about *her*. But she couldn't hide in anonymous places forever. She must know that.

Could he ever think of her as other than a poor bird with a broken wing? Her strength had been deceptive: the bird could flutter bravely in the cage but the wide world frightened it. Then his mind closed, unwilling to confront yet another analysis.

He looked for Claire. She was safely pedaling down the walk, her short legs working like pistons. He looked at his watch, which was a handsome one, last year's Christmas gift from Jessie. She was always buying things for him, caring about his clothes—he himself cared almost nothing about clothes—seeing to it that there were books on his night table, making plans for the office he would have. Next year at Christmas they would be in New York and he would be earning. He would have to find some splendid present for her, something, even, that he couldn't afford. A ring? She had slender fingers. A sapphire?

Now memory made one of its implausible and senseless associations. Mary wore rings. Mary still wore that curiously fashioned topaz ring. Only a few weeks ago, coming home earlier than usual, he found that she had dropped in for tea, something she hadn't done in half a year or more. She had risen as soon after Martin's entrance as decent manners would allow. He had been aware of that. Every nerve in him had been aware of her. And he had observed that she wore the topaz ring. White lilacs circled the brim of her straw hat. Her shoes were delicate. He had seen that her eyes avoided him, looking toward the wall, or resting on her hand, the one with the ring, which lay on the arm of the chair.

He concluded that she was embarrassed before him. People often were after they had revealed their intimate miseries. He had only seen her perhaps six times since that day, more than a year ago, when she had sat before him and told, with more dignity than most women would have been able to muster, the story of wreckage. He had, for a bad few moments, been harsh with her that day; for some reason he had wanted to hurt her; and at once he had been terribly ashamed and tried to make amends. He hoped he had made them adequately.

There had been no way to find out, or to find out how she was faring at all. From the outside, seen at a Thanksgiving dinner or a Christmas party, everything looked handsome enough, with a patina of wealth and charm and family unity.

"Fern would never get a divorce," Jessie had remarked once, a long time ago. "It would shatter her image of perfection."

But that wasn't true. She would have got one if she could have.

And he wondered about many things: whether Alex had any idea how much he, Martin, knew of the Lambs' affairs; whether Mary had someone else by now; whether she lay alone at night and how troubled she might be because of it—

Surprising, though, how one could get used to being "alone." He had thought of himself, and indeed had been, a man with strong and frequent sexual needs. yet now a very little went a long way. Lying down at night next to Jessie's immaculate, light body, he could fall instantly asleep. When a man has worked under pressure all day he is too tense to want anything but sleep, he told himself —and at the same time knew this for the rationalization it was.

Oh, it ought to be otherwise! It ought to be the core of a man's life, its force and heat!

If only he could get rid of the images that lay on his brain as though they had been printed there! Mary, in Braidburn's office, struggling against tears. Mary, proudly pregnant, standing at the door of Lamb House. Mary, in Cyprus, painting three scarlet birds on a wire fence. Fantasies! Soon, if he didn't curb them, he would become obsessed by them again as once he had been. Foreboding and alarm began to flutter in him now. It was humiliating not to be able to direct his mind at will . . .

Claire climbed up on the bench between him and a proper British nurse who was tending a baby in a perambulator.

"Read to me," she commanded.

He opened the little book which he had thrust into his pocket before leaving home and she explained earnestly, "It's about dinosaurs. This is Allosaurus. He eats vegetables."

"And very good for him, too."

"I hate vegetables."

"I know. That's why I said what I did."

She laughed. Only three, and she could already share a joke with him!

"Shall I read about him, or about this one?" he asked.

"This one. He's Tyrannosaurus Rex. He eats people. Look at his teeth, Daddy."

"Oh, he's fierce all right," Martin agreed. "We'll read about him, then."

When he had finished, she went back to the tricycle.

"That's a bright little girl, sir," the nurse remarked.

"Thank you."

"A child with spirit. She knows what she knows."

Martin dutifully praised the baby in the perambulator.

"I often see your little girl here with her mother. This is my favorite place in the whole park."

"It's a beautiful spot."

So this woman had seen Jessie, too. The nurses must have gossiped: "The child's mother—poor thing . . . No, not the father . . . Very odd, really." He could hear them. Then he felt ashamed. Good God, he was as bad as Jessie! People did have other things to talk about, after all.

"You'll be going back to America soon, I hear."

"Yes. In the fall." He corrected himself. "The autumn."

"I expect you'll be happy to go home."

"Yes, home is always best, isn't it?" Martin answered tritely.

The sky was what one called "mackerel," spotted and clouding over toward a sudden English shower. He stood up and called to Claire. Holding the child's hand, he guided the tricycle across the street.

"Home is best," he had said. Yet here he had had perhaps the best years of his life. Here he had grown farthest and swiftest toward what he wanted to be. "Why don't you stay in London?" people often asked. For it was a civilized place. Always he would remember its moist, foggy air and its mild light lying on greenery and gray stone.

New York, on the other hand, was aggressive. The searing summers drained your strength. The tearing February wind, blowing off the rivers, was fierce enough to spin you around in your tracks. And all the time, one was battered by noise of traffic and hammering rivets. If they were not tearing something down, they were putting something up. A restless, unsettling place!

Yet he had felt its lure and power from the very first. There was no place like it, so challenging, so—alive! It called to him; it dared him to do his best. Yes, time to go back. Time, too, for Claire to know she's an American. She speaks now with a pretty birdlike chirp, the accent and inflection of the English upper classes. So that's another reason to return. But the true reason, the real one? The answer struck Martin like a slap across the cheek. Because it will put an ocean between *her* and me.

"IT's *OTELLO* TONIGHT, isn't it?" he called from the shaving mirror in the bathroom.

Jessie didn't answer. When he came back into the bedroom, she was sitting at the window, looking out into the street.

"Why, you're not dressing! We haven't got all that much time!"

"I'm not going to the opera," she said.

"Not going! What's wrong?"

"I've nothing to wear."

"What can you be talking about?"

"About having nothing to wear. I refuse to go out anymore in makeshift clothes."

"You always look fine," Martin said, too heartily. "That white lace cape-thing you bought—"

"Capes! Scarves! Creeping in, crouched under a cape!"

Swallowing impatience, he said reasonably, "I don't know anything about fashions, but perhaps a good dressmaker—"

"I'm tired," she interrupted, "of having you ashamed of me."

He almost shouted: "I have never been ashamed of you, Jessie!"

"If I looked like Fern, you wouldn't have to be."

"I am not ashamed, I tell you!" He was so weary of having to cope with this again! Maybe in the morning when he felt fresher he would do better, but not now at the end of the day. He sighed and recited, "Actually, you do look very much like Mary. You've said so yourself."

"Why will you keep on calling her Mary?"

"She likes the name."

Jessie's mouth twisted. "You know, Martin, you don't fool me. You never have."

"What in blazes are you talking about? Who's trying to fool you?"

"You never say, 'I love you.' Do you even realize that?"

"I'm not much for words. Maybe that's a fault. Yes, I guess it is. But actions are something else, aren't they? How do I treat you? You should ask yourself that."

"You've been—exemplary. You made a bargain and you've stuck with it to the letter. Honorably. You couldn't get my sister, so you took me."

As it is said, the best defense is a good offense. "I am not, positively not, going to stand here—" and catching a glimpse of himself in the mirror, with one half of his face covered in shaving lather, Martin felt ridiculous and irritated with himself. "You're making trouble where there is none, Jessie."

"Don't fence with me. Father warned me before we were married. People don't know how shrewd Father is, because he's closemouthed when he wants to be. But he knew it was Fern you wanted and he warned me not to marry you. He was right."

"He warned you?" Martin was totally confused.

Jessie twisted a hankerchief. She began to cry. Two red blotches appeared on her cheeks. "Yes, yes, he only wanted this for me after I convinced him. Maybe he wanted to be convinced, I don't know . . . You were, after all, a solution for me, weren't you?"

He was stunned. For a moment there was no sound in the room.

"Why am I telling you this? I'll be sorry tomorrow—"

Anger surged in Martin and quickly died. After all, what difference did it make now who had or had not conceived the marriage?

"I loved you, Martin. We were alike in a way; we were prisoners. Your prison was poverty and mine was my body. And I thought—I thought perhaps we could make each other happy. It would be a kind of trade-off."

He stood in a fog. Thickly it settled, a heavy weight of hopeless fatigue, so that it seemed he could never make the effort to move through it.

"I thought—oh, I gave it hours of thought, believe me—I thought, although you didn't love me, as you might have loved Fern if she hadn't gone away, or loved some other woman, still you liked me tremendously. I knew you did. I believed we could manage with that. It's been done before." And Jessie looked up half timidly, half in defiance.

Prison, she had said and it was true, except that he had already escaped from his and she never would.

"Jessie," he said softly, "Jessie . . . you're wrong. You think I don't love you . . . but I do." And that also, in its way, was true.

A small doubting smile fled from her face. "Don't, Martin, I'm too smart for that."

He made a helpless gesture. "Then I just don't know. If you won't believe me—"

She sighed. "It's my own fault. I took advantage of your need. It was my fault."

"Who's talking about fault? We're here, now, today. And we have so much—" Suddenly his energies revived and he began to speak eagerly. Holding his fingers spread, he counted, "We have a home. We have friends and will have more. We have a beautiful child. We can't allow this sort of thing to go on, for her sake, if for no other reason."

"That's true."

"Well then?"

She stood up and laid her head in the hollow of his shoulder. "I'm drifting. I'm floating with nothing to hold to."

He put his arms around her and held her gently, as one holds a troubled child. "You have me to hold to." He stroked her hair, the jaunty curls on the sad, bent head. "I wish I could make you feel the way you did when we used to ride around on house calls. Remember how we'd talk and talk? You had ideas about everything in the world."

"I felt I was a part of things then. It's different here. You're gone all day, climbing up in the world, and I'm left out."

"But this is what it was all for! It's what you wanted, isn't it?"

"I know. I planned the whole thing, and at the start I was happy; I was! But now it's all got complicated . . . I don't make any sense, do I?"

"Well, plenty of people don't make any sense. But you'll climb out of the slump. I'll pull you out of it. Now let's hurry, shall we? How fast can you dress?"

"I don't want to go tonight, Martin. Truly. You can go without me. I won't mind. And I'll be all right. Really."

She expected him to stay with her, he knew. And, pity or no, he felt suddenly perverse. He wasn't angry, he wasn't being stubborn; he was simply weary of yet another "scene." Moreover, he had wanted to hear *Otello.*

"All right then. I'll go," he said. "Have a good sleep. You'll feel different in the morning."

THE SINGERS HAD taken their final bows, and the departing crowd moved slowly through the lobby. Alex Lamb touched Martin on the shoulder.

"Hello there! Where's Jessie?"

"Didn't feel up to par tonight. She went to bed early."

"Come back to our place for a spot of supper. It's my birthday and some friends are coming."

"Well, I really ought—"

"Come on, you can spare an hour or two for your brother-in-law. Jessie must be asleep by now, anyway."

The Lambs' table was bright with iris and narcissi, flowery porcelain, laughter and wine. The women were so lovely! Even the older ones had a pearl glow, not from the candlelight, but from something within. And in Martin, too, a subtle warmth began to stir.

"Fern hasn't been able to shake the cough." Alex was speaking to someone at the far end of the table. "The children had it first, and it's gone from one to the other. So I'm insisting she take a week on the Riviera to get over it."

"You're not going?"

"I can't. There's too much on the fire at the office. But she'll be happy on the beach with a pile of books."

A woman called, "That's the most splendid necklace, Fern! I've been meaning to tell you all evening."

Everyone turned to look at the necklace; a filigree of gold and garnets, it rested as in a velvet case on Fern's naked shoulders; the heavy pendant lay on white silk between her breasts.

"Her present for my birthday," Alex explained, with a smile of a fond husband.

Observing that smile and Mary's answer, Martin felt, among all the converging streams of his emotions, a current of soft compassion. Of all the people in that room, he was almost surely the only one who knew their truth. How capricious, how reckless was life! Once he had seen it as a steady journey: for some a dull plod, for others a triumph, but in any case something with direction, that one *controlled*. He had, of course, been very young when he had thought so.

For nothing he had done or willed had brought him to where he was now. And where was he now? Quite simply, he was a man in love, a man obsessed with loving, filled with it, driven by it. Something had forced him to love this woman from the first moment. And never, in spite of all his self-denials, had he ceased to love her.

How was it possible? Who could say? It was, after all, the human condition! A natural phenomenon: a simple thing! But light and water were simple things, too, as long as one didn't try to explain them.

And, sitting at that festive table, Martin had now a sense of total recall: the white room with her pictures on the wall; her face raised to his when he came in; that incredible blue gaze; the paint spot on the sandal. The moment, the arrested moment, in which everything had changed, although he had not known then how much.

But she? What of her? He had no way of knowing, dared not try to find out. And he thought of her, living her sham; he thought of Jessie—and he thought his head would burst with futile thinking. The warmth and sparkle seeped out of the room, seeped out of his spirit.

Someone was addressing him. "So you'll be leaving us, going back to America, I hear?"

"Yes, soon," he replied.

Someone remarked to Fern, "You'll miss your sister."

She made some acknowledgment. Glancing up at the sound, he caught her gaze. And a strange thing happened: she did not turn away. Eyes normally move toward the sound of voices; they come to rest on one face, then another; they flicker over a table and across a room. But hers did not. They fastened on Martin's eyes and held there.

Talk bubbled around the circle as wine bubbles in a glass; still the eyes held to each other. His—his heart was in his eyes, that's all he knew. Hers—hers had such a look . . . He wanted to believe it, had to believe it. Unmistakably it said: If you want me, I shall not refuse.

Wild, tremendous, reckless joy surged in him.

His right-hand neighbor, an agreeable, gray-haired lady, looked concerned. "Is anything wrong?"

"Wrong?" he repeated confusedly.

"You put your fork down so abruptly, I thought you weren't feeling well."

"No, no. I just remembered something, that's all."

"Well, as long as it was something happy," she said brightly.

The talk kept on swirling. He did not hear it. At last people pushed their chairs back and left the table. Then someone put music on the record player. Dancing began in the hall.

From the arc of the bay window in the drawing room a balcony projected, a little space affording room for no more than two or three to stand and look down upon the square. Mary leaned against the railing. When he stepped behind her she did not move.

The square was still. It was late; distant traffic only murmured now, as distant water rushes in a country place. Light globes hung among the trees like white balloons and a powerful scent of wet earth rose from the shrubbery.

"Who stole my heart away? Who—" The little tune floated with a poignant sweetness from the room at their backs.

In the tiny space among the potted plants their shoulders touched. Still neither of them moved. Someone inside turned a lamp on; the beam of its light fell over a blossoming azalea in a tub, turning the white buds rosy, the color of flesh.

"My God," Martin said. He was shaking.

She looked at him.

"What are we going to do?" he asked.

"I don't know."

"We have to do something about it. Don't you know that?"

"Don't," she whispered. "I'm starting to cry. I won't be able to turn around if someone comes."

He understood that tenderness would bring more tears. So he waited a minute or two and then spoke quickly.

"I'll be in Paris at a conference next week. I can leave after the second day. Will you—"

"Yes . . . Yes."

"Where will you be staying?"

"At the Georges Cinque . . ."

Voices passed and passed again in the room behind them. Still they stood, hostess and guest, looking out at the lovely night.

"Darling," Martin said. It was the first time he had said the word aloud. "Darling Mary."

❦{12}❦

They had six days. Eastward through the Provençal spring they drove, past olive orchards and round hills dressed in lavender. On cobbled squares they parked the rented car and drank cassis while old men played boules. They came down out of the hills to the sea on a morning when light showered from the sky and broke into a hundred thousand sapphires over the bay.

How beautiful, oh God, how beautiful!

And they came to a white town, to a house with tall, blue-shuttered windows, where the air smelled of lemons and everything glittered in the sun.

"We're here," Mary said. "Menton." She laughed. " 'Glücklich wie Gott in Frankreich.' "

"What does that mean?"

"It means 'Happy as God in France.' It's one of the few things I still remember in German."

"Do you remember enough French to ask for a good room?"

"We already have one."

"Then shall we go upstairs right away?"

"Do you want to?"

"You know I do."

Light, coming through the blinds, drew bars of dusty gold across her thighs. Outside it was still afternoon, but within the tall old room dusk had settled.

She made a little sound, an indrawn breath, part sigh, part cry. He turned in the bed and put his lips on the soft hollow where the sound had caught in her throat. His thudding heart had slowed; now it started up again. They had been lying in that sweet peace which follows ultimate attainment. Surely no other woman in the world, he thought, had ever or could ever—Over and over they had dissolved and merged and become one. There were no words for it. All the millions of words that had been written came down to nothing.

In the evening, they sat and talked. They went back to the beginning.

"What did you really think, Mary? Didn't you *know* I wanted you? Why didn't you come home? Why did you marry Alex? Tell me. Tell me."

"Oh," she said, "what had I seen or known? I had never been touched by anyone. Yes, you touched me . . . I thought when I came back from Europe, we'd see each other again and after a while—"

"But I was dying for you, Mary!"

"But your letter! You were so proud and glad about Doctor Albeniz—"

"You remember the name!"

"I remember everything. I understood then that your work would always come first. I thought perhaps I had imagined the other—about me. And I felt ashamed. Then that same week I met Alex."

Martin was silent. Yes, of course she would have welcomed Alex then, with all his cheer and strength, with all the color and movement of the life he offered! Offered without postponement!

"I understand," he said.

"Would your work really have come first, Martin? Would you have asked me to wait three years?"

He wanted to be completely honest, both with her and with himself. "I don't know. I've thought about it, foolishly I suppose, asking myself whether you would have waited for me, whether I would have given up the offer if you hadn't been willing to wait or what I would have done if my father hadn't died. My God, what a tangle it was—and is!"

"And I," Mary spoke so low that he could barely hear her, "I wanted to get away from that dim house. Would I have waited three years more? I don't know. You can't imagine how I wanted to get away and—and live!"

"I can," Martin said.

"Yet I ask myself, was it really as bad as all that? I've told you before, one has no right to be a fifteen-year-old romantic when one's twenty."

"You've made up for it," he said gently.

"Oh yes, I'm a hundred years older!" She clasped her hands under her chin; her rings flashed in the darkness. "How easily one throws oneself away! As if one could replace oneself and all the lost days. I would do differently now."

"You can't be sure of that. We torture ourselves, all of us do, with questions that can't be answered."

"I wonder," Mary said, "whether my children will ever wonder about me someday and ask whether I've been happy."

"That's a strange thought."

"Not really. I often think about my mother. You would have liked her, Martin. She was so different from Father. I never knew why they married. I think he was overawed just because she was so different from him. Sometimes at the table she would talk, and I knew he wasn't even listening. He didn't care about any of the things she loved."

Martin looked down into the trees. The dark pines and her evocation of old memories were suddenly oppressive.

"Don't," he said.

"Don't what?"

"Talk about sad things."

"I didn't mean to be sad. You do the talking, then."

"No, I'd rather hear you. I don't know you enough, Mary. I should need a lifetime to know you and I won't have it."

"Now you're the one who's talking of sad things."

What's to become of us, he thought, now that we have begun something that can't go on and also can't end?

He roused himself. "Come. We'll go down and walk on the beach. It's too beautiful to waste a minute of it."

In Nice they walked on the Promenade des Anglais, while a stream of smart, snub-nosed Renaults went by. Stepping quietly in the hush of grandeur, they looked at shop windows and marble lobbies. From a terrace they observed a nineteenth-century panorama: wide effect of water and gauzy sky, of sails, white dresses, pillars and balustrades. Sprightly music played and no one, Martin saw, noticed that the musicians had threadbare cuffs.

"Let's go back to Menton," he said abruptly.

"You're a funny duck! We just got here!"

"Do you mind? If you really do, I'll stay."

"No. We can have a country lunch if you'd rather."

"Then I'd rather."

At a market in a walled village on the Grand Corniche they bought food: cheese, fruit, bread and the shriveled black olives of the region. On the side of the road they stopped to eat.

"Better than all that splendor," Martin remarked.

"It made you uncomfortable?"

"Yes, that sort of thing's a snare. A doctor must never let himself forget ordinary people. It's only too easy."

"For you, do you mean, or for anyone?"

"I'm no different from anyone else. Or maybe I am. I want beauty terribly, and beauty in this world can be expensive."

"I think you're too hard on yourself."

"That's what Jessie always says."

Mary looked away. Her face was sad. "I'd managed for at least two hours not to think of her until just now."

"We're not going to hurt her," he protested. "Neither of us wants to or will."

"But I'll know when I look at her, or at you, or at myself."

He closed his eyes, shutting out the noon brightness. "We couldn't have helped it—the whole thing, from the beginning."

"I'm so sorry for us all!"

"For Alex, too?"

"No, he's as happy as possible, in his circumstances. You know," she said, "I've accepted all that . . . Did you ever think I really would?" There was a spiritual beauty in her face as the sadness ebbed into grave calm.

"Yes," Martin said, "I did think you would. I remember, on the day we met, how compassionately you spoke of Jessie."

"But to be truly compassionate, one needs to have suffered. One needs to have been alone. I know that now. I didn't then."

"Mary . . . tell me, is it terribly hard for you now, the way things are?"

She was silent for a while. He did not interrupt her silence.

Then she said, "You might say it's as if I were a widow, living with a kind brother. Not the worst fate in the world, I suppose. Thank God, I have my children and my art, such as it is."

But if she didn't have the children, she would be free. Yet, if she were free and he not free, how would he feel about that? Guiltily, Martin repressed the selfish thought.

"Listen to me," he said. "We're overanalyzing. Let's just accept, instead. What's past is past. There's nothing we can do about it now."

She stood up. "You said we mustn't spoil our days here, and you were right. So, no more talk! Let's go back to the beach and pretend we have all the time in the world."

THREE MORE DAYS. For long hours they lay in a hidden hollow of the beach, under the escarpment of the hills out of whose rocks these ancient villages had been carved. On a promontory, like a finger thrust out into the sea, the tearing wind had bent pines into the attitude of prayer. But in this windless hollow the warmth was kindly, the air was like silk on the skin and the sand like silk.

He took her hand. It seemed to him that strength flowed from one to the other through their hands. And he thought that ultimate joy would be to lie forever in this sun, to float in this sea—for was the sea not once our home?—and to wake in the first light with this woman next to him.

Coming back to their room one day they found the maid cleaning. "I saw you walking yesterday," she said. "M'sieur and Madame looked so happy." She spoke with the awkward boldness of one who is naturally shy. "I watched you laughing, and I felt happy, too. I'm going to be married on Saturday."

"Oh," Mary cried, "we shall be gone by then! Is he the young man who waited for you at the end of the drive last night?"

Blushing, the girl nodded. "You could have come to the wedding in my village. It's not far from here."

Mary reached into the closet for her dressing gown, white silk embroidered with red Chinese poppies. "I want you to have this," she said and, as the girl protested, "No, I want you to. I've been so happy wearing it. It will bring you luck."

"I wonder what sort of children they'll have," she said when the girl had left. "She, with her round face and pug nose? The boy is thin and has a craggy nose. He looks gentle."

"You wonder about everything, don't you? You're probably the most curious person I've ever known," he answered, smiling at her.

There was a radiant joy in her eyes. He saw that for the moment her spirit was unencumbered. He wished it might always be so . . .

"I would like to have gone to that girl's wedding," Mary said.

"Why would you?"

"I saw a country wedding here once. The bride was a farm girl in a homemade dress. After the ceremony she laid her bouquet at the feet of the Virgin in the side chapel. I think they pray for many children, I'm not sure. I would pray that I had chosen the right man . . . Afterward they drove away in an old car with daisy streamers tied on. It was very touching . . . I cried."

Could it have been like that for us? Martin wondered.

ONE MORE DAY. In the afternoon they went walking inland. Everything drowsed. Birds were silent. Houses with closed shutters lay sleeping in the heat. Plane trees in long alleys were quiet in the windless air.

"Siesta time," Mary said.

"I know. But we can't waste it." And he said, "I've never made love on the grass."

She laughed. The sound was happiness, and this happiness was beautiful to Martin, seductive and yet pure.

"Why wonder? Let's find out."

They walked on past a field where cows rested in the shade, then climbed a fence into a dark little grove. Still the world slept; there was no one in sight. Behind a curtain of living green they lay down, in the hush and murmur of the breathing meadow.

THE LAST DAY. Late in the afternoon Martin came out to the terrace and paused in the doorway. Unaware of his presence, Mary sat with bowed head. She had changed into traveling clothes; their neutral tan was sober in the pastel afternoon. And this sober color, the curve of her skirt and her bent head created a melancholy which, if you were to translate it into music, would quiver into a minor chord and die on the air. He stood there looking and looking. There was something in his throat. He kept swallowing, but it wouldn't go down. Then she saw him.

"The bags are downstairs," he said.

She nodded.

"They've taken the car. We'll get a taxi to the station." He sat down and took her hand. It lay limply in his. "There's time for something to eat," he said.

"I can't."

"But you must," he said and asked the waitress for a tureen of soup.

And he sat there wishing, wishing that they were just beginning, that they were going away somewhere, to Afghanistan or Patagonia, where they would shed everything: names, past, everything.

"What have we done?" Mary whispered.

"Nothing," he said. "Nothing to hurt anybody, since that's what you mean."

"Nobody?"

"No. Alex wouldn't care and Jessie will never know."

"And what about you and me? What is to become of us?"

Below them lay eternal blue, azure and turquoise, blue upon rippling blue. He stared out over the water.

And Mary repeated, "Tell me, what's to become of us?"

"I don't know . . . I'll think . . . There must be something."

"Oh God!" she cried.

"Dearest. Dearest. Don't."

She turned her face away.

The waitress came back with the tureen. "Careful, it's hot! Shall I bring a salad?"

"Madame is not feeling well. This will be enough," Martin said.

"So now we just get on the train and go back," Mary cried. "Nothing more? And that's all? I'm twenty-eight," she said, and he understood that she meant "I'm too young to settle for 'nothing more.' "

The wheels of daily living turn regardlessly. So he paid the bill and tipped the waitress, checked in his pocket for the train tickets and summoned a taxi.

The train clattered northward. At a rural stop, a couple with three children entered the compartment; the youngest was asleep on the father's shoulder. The man's face was tender; his hand cupped the small head.

When a rag doll dropped to the floor from the girl's sleeping hand, Martin picked it up. And he remembered Claire, who slept with a doll in a tattered orange dress.

At the same moment Mary said, "Emmy and Isabel have dolls like that. Alex bought them in France." Her lips trembled.

If Mary's children were mine, Martin thought, and Claire belonged to Mary—

She laid her head on the back of the seat. He remembered that she had told him how she found escape in sleep. Rest then, he thought, drawing the shade to keep the light from flickering on her face. Her breasts rose and fell under the tan silk. He remembered their perfume. If they had been alone in the compartment, he would have put his head next to hers. But now these strangers were here, sitting like monoliths on Easter Island. Every time he looked up, he met the curious eyes of these innocent strangers, and he hated them.

All through the long trip to England, to the parting place, his thoughts went round and round like a poor blinded mule at the threshing floor. There must be a way . . . There is no way . . . There must be a way . . . There is no way . . .

They were astonished to be met at the railroad station in London by Alex Lamb. Even before the train had come to a halt under the glass roof and the iron fretwork they saw him scanning the carriages, then running toward them.

"Nothing wrong with the children, it's all right!" he called. When they came up to him he lowered his voice. "But you have damn well made a mess of things! All hell has broken loose."

"What? What are you saying?" Mary cried.

"Good Lord, Fern, I don't mind! But dammit, if you had only told me! Then I would have known what to say."

On the platform, surrounded by luggage and hurrying feet, they heard the story.

"You see, Jessie got the idea that it would be jolly to call the hotel in Paris and let Claire talk to her father. And the concierge told her—" Alex turned to Martin. "He told her that you had left. Or rather, he said that Monsieur and Madame had left, that he himself had got them a reservation on the Blue Train for Nice.

"So then Jessie, having thought that over, telephoned my house and asked for Fern. And I said, quite naturally, that you'd gone to Nice for a week's rest from the children and me. How could I have known? You really ought to have told me!" Alex repeated.

"Jesus Christ!" Martin cried.

"I hope you're not upset about me," Alex said. "You've been told that I'm not likely to play the role of outraged husband. Jessie, of course, is something else."

"How is she now?" Martin asked.

"Now? I really couldn't say. She was rather bad off when I saw her on Saturday. I went right up to town to talk to her, but it wasn't any use. She and the child left Monday on the *Leviathan* for New York."

❈{13}❈

The double doors of the familiar library had been slammed and the curtains pulled tight, trapping Donald Meig's anger in the shadowed room. His words beat the walls like fists.

"You Goddamned scum! Her own sister! I wouldn't have cared if it had been anyone else! What the hell. I wouldn't even have blamed you all that much. But to shame the family that took you in and—No, let me talk. If it weren't for me, you'd be doling out aspirins and driving thirty miles in the middle of the night for two dollars—if and when you could collect."

Martin trembled. It had been a hard voyage through ferocious seas, with the ropes up in the corridors and the passengers vomiting in their cabins. After disembarking, he had rushed at once to the train. Now, tense with a poisonous mixture of humiliation and foreboding, he stood before a man who appeared to have gone mad with rage. Meig's eyes glittered like the glass lumps in the deer-head on the wall.

"All right, Mr. Meig. You've said it a dozen times and I've answered you. I'll answer just once more: It was terribly wrong. I have no excuse." He threw out his hand. "Still, I ask you again: I want to go upstairs and see Jessie. After all, this concerns her more than anyone."

"Jessie doesn't want to see you. Jessie wants a divorce. And you"—Meig leveled a forefinger as though it were a pistol—"you are going to give it to her. You are going to make no problems. Do you understand?"

"That's between Jessie and me. We have a child."

"A child? Yes, you damn well have! And my English society daughter might have remembered that she's got a house full of children herself. Oh, a wonderful pair, the two of you! My God, I've seen degrading things in my time, but nothing lower than this! His wife's sister—"

A door in the hall above closed with a thud. Running feet, a child's feet, crossed the floor.

"At least I want to see Claire," Martin said.

"No. No. You've seen all you're ever going to see of Claire. Listen to me! I've consulted lawyers, all last week I spent with lawyers, and do you know I have it in my legal power to keep you away from that child forever on grounds of moral turpitude? Do you? And I suppose you think Dr. Eastman would take you on as an associate when the tabloids got through with you! A doctor and his sister-in-law! Juicy reading! The public would drink it up! And I'll do it, make no mistake. I'll do it if you throw one obstacle in my way. I'll ruin you and I'll ruin Fern, too. I want nothing more to do with her. No, you've seen the last you're ever going to see of Claire."

Martin's stomach churned. He hadn't eaten all day, and his head throbbed. Feeling sick, he stared at the glass lumps in the deerhead.

"You're an unforgiving man, Mr. Meig. Haven't you ever heard of a second chance?"

"An ax murderer doesn't get a second chance, and that's what you are: an ax murderer. You've axed my family. You've driven two sisters apart and robbed me of Fern and her children. Yes, I know it took two of you, but you're older. You're a man and a doctor. You had the greater responsibility. And when I think that you owe me everything you are!"

"As far as that goes, you needn't worry." Martin spoke quietly. "You'll get back every cent with interest."

"Oh, interest, is it? Make it five percent. It's the going rate. That's all the more reason, then, why you'll get out of here without any fuss. Go to New York and pay me what you owe. After that, we want no more to do with you."

THE TRAIN WAS full. He rode back to the city, smothered by a haze of cigar smoke and the roaring jollity of a crowd celebrating Repeal. Bracing his head in the corner between the seat and the windowglass, he closed his eyes.

His child. His Claire. He thought he would lose his mind if he couldn't see her.

Her curls, finger-wound, lie on the collar of her yellow coat. "Allosaurus eats vegetables," she informs him seriously.

Surely, if he wrote to Jessie, she would feel some compassion!

"You couldn't get my sister," Jessie says, "so you took me." Her face is swollen with tears.

She would be most unlikely to feel compassion.

Suppose he were, somehow, to contest the divorce?

It wouldn't work and he'd have been destroyed for nothing.

What did that mean—"destroyed"? And why should he care? He only wanted his daughter. His child.

Jessie's child. She'd come full circle, Jessie had. Out of that house of gloom he had taken her, and back to it he had sent her. Oh, not wanting to! Wanting truly —and he examined himself, for the hundredth time turning a searchlight into the darkest corners of his spirit—truly to cherish her as he had so carefully done until that night on the balcony at the Lambs' house.

Oh, wasn't it strange, that if he had had some common affair of the streets, the world would have shrugged and pretended not to see?

Mary Fern. The night wind rises, rattling the palms, and we go inside together. She comes through a door at noon with an armful of marguerites; she drops them on a table. She laughs—

The train jolted toward the city and Martin dozed. He dreamed that he was walking on some great avenue, Fifth or Park, that he went to call on Dr. Eastman and found the doctor staring at him in horror and dismay because he had no trousers on.

In fact, Dr. Eastman welcomed him. "I've been looking forward to this ever since we met in London," he said graciously. "I'm forty-eight and overworked. It will be good to have you share the burdens."

He was a tall man, looking younger than his years, with the long, handsome face that seemed indigenous to old American wealth. Did the wealthy breed handsome children through a process of selection, or did handsome people find it easier to grow wealthy? More importantly, though, one could sense good nature in Eastman, which was fortunate, because people who looked like him were often frosty and stood on their authority.

So he emerged from the meeting with some tentative confidence in one area, at least. He began to walk fast, striking hard at the pavement. Early in life the patterns are set so that, mechanically, one follows in their grooves. When Martin Farrell is distressed he walks, or else sits down somewhere to listen to music. He flexed his hands. They were his capital, all he owned, they and the new knowledge in his head, gain of the years since he had last walked in this city.

Gains and losses . . .

"Loss," he said aloud, without meaning to, so that a child trundling a toy on the walk looked up at him. And the word sounded in the air like the sorrowful whistle of a train going past in the country night.

Through shreds of moving clouds, a needle spire appeared and hid again. It was the great building of the Empire State. When he had left for England, only a few years before, it had been an enormous wound in the earth, and he had had a new young wife who believed in him. And no child. And no broken love on the other side of the Atlantic. No ache of longing. No remorse.

Change. Much change.

OFTEN HE WONDERED how they would appear to him, those first few years, after they had passed and he could look back on them. There had been such a piercing in his vitals that he had sometimes been certain he could not survive it. He had sat with his wretched head in his hands, thinking, always thinking. . . .

The wrongs he had done, not wanting to! The lives touched by his life and damaged by the touch!

Alex wrote twice to him. A large-minded man, Alex was realistic enough and selfish enough to look after his own interests first, yet decent enough to include others in the scheme of things.

He wanted Martin to know that Fern was enduring. She was most terribly distressed about Jessie: all her life she had been so careful of Jessie! Alex was doing his best to hearten her; she must paint again and go to classes; must see friends and go riding; fortunately, the children were demanding and could fill her days.

It would not be necessary, he wrote at last, perhaps it would even be unwise to write again. He trusted that Martin would understand.

Martin understood.

And he wrote to Jessie. He thought of her, sitting in the old familiar chair in the old shadowed room while their child slept upstairs. The tone of her reply was calm enough, but the denial of all requests was firm and final.

"We will leave things the way they are. You have many possibilities ahead of you. I have only Claire."

And that, too, Martin understood.

In the end it was work that saved him. Purposely, now he exhausted himself. In the office, thanks to Martin's long hours, they were seeing far more than the doubled number that would have been expected by the addition of one other man. Eastman remarked that Martin worked like a demon.

As the months increased, inevitably and mercifully the memories blurred; they always do. Now and then he had an unexpected vision of Lamb House in soft fog; or a vision of blue Mediterranean glitter; or of steam puffing from the locomotive at the railway terminal in London. The last thing he had seen was her back in the tan traveling dress hurrying away, leaning on Alex's arm. We never got to say good-bye, he thought.

And sometimes still, a woman with a swaying walk would pass on the street; foolishly, knowing quite well it was not she, he would turn around and stare.

Sometimes a child passed, a girl who would be—and he would estimate the time—about the age of Claire. And if the child happened to have dark curls he would wonder whether Claire still wore hers long and how tall she was and whether she remembered him at all or ever spoke of him or missed him.

So, close the chapter, Martin. Close the book. It stands on the shelf and you can reach it anytime and read it over if you wish. But it is better not to.

❧{14}❧

The picnic had been cleared away, the remains of watermelon and potato salad stowed in the kitchen and the last of the children put to bed. Now, in the pleasant somnolence that comes when one has overeaten, they sat on Tom's narrow porch, watching the slow approach of summer night. Across the street a garage door rumbled and shut with a thud. A girl's voice rang out once and ceased.

Perry spoke out of the darkness in the corner. "If I didn't know New York was just across the George Washington Bridge I'd think I was back in Kansas."

"I've come to love small-town life," Flo said. "I never thought I would."

"I'm not surprised. I should say you and Tom were made for it, both of you," Martin observed.

Flo had been born middle-aged, predictable and kind. He could feel the warmth of her, as if she had reached out and touched him. As for himself, he had easily assumed the role of bachelor uncle, coming out here on holidays and Sunday afternoon with toys for the children and pastry from the French bakery near his apartment. Bachelor uncle! Well, there were worse things to be.

"I wish you'd stay for the rest of the weekend," Flo said. "You'll miss the fireworks tomorrow."

"Can't. Eastman's leaving tonight to join his family in Maine and I'm on call."

"You surely don't have many emergencies!" She meant, it can't be like Tom's life; people call him out any old time.

"You'd be surprised. We get gunshot wounds, all kinds of nerve damage. And car accidents, of course, especially on holiday weekends. Tell her, Perry."

"It's a fact," Perry said. He mused: "I was thinking, we go back a long time, don't we? Ten years since med school! It doesn't seem possible."

"Say, Martin," Tom added, "do you ever see anything of your first hero—what was his name?"

"Albeniz, you mean?"

"Yes. Albeniz."

"Not much. He still works at Grantham Memorial and I'm at Fisk. My first hero, did you say? My only one, on this side of the Atlantic."

"Why? What's the matter with Eastman? Not a hero?"

"No. I suppose that sounds strange, though."

"He's a great surgeon," Perry said quickly. "You've got to admit that, Martin."

"I do admit it! He could operate on me anytime, but—"

"But what?" When Tom got hold of something, he held on doggedly.

"I don't know, really. Something subtle. Oh, maybe I'm being entirely unfair. Maybe it takes the edge off heroism to be so damn rich!"

"I read in a society column," Flo said, "his wife comes from the Harmon Motors family."

"A lot of us were invited to their place in Greenwich over Decoration Day," Martin said. "It looked like a movie set—butlers serving drinks around the pool. Didn't seem like a doctor's house at all." And he added somewhat sheepishly, "I had a good time, though."

"That's a helluva long way from Emergency Relief!" Tom said. "We only get a dollar a call, you know, but at least you're sure of the fee. Only thing, I wish patients wouldn't get scared in the middle of the night and call three doctors at once. We usually meet on the stairs and have to toss to see who gets the call, and then the losers have lost sleep for nothing. Oh well, we keep our heads above water and that's something!"

"Speaking of Albeniz," Martin began. He hadn't talked about him in a long time, and suddenly for some reason he wanted to. "Albeniz was a prime mover in my life. He made a difference in it. And the thing that bothers me is that, outside of his own hospital, you don't hear much of him. He doesn't get his just due at all."

"And why would that be?"

"I don't know, really."

"Yes, you do!" Perry said. "It's simple; he doesn't write enough or travel to meetings to blow his own horn. He doesn't play the social game, either. There's an awful lot of that in a big medical center, you know." He spoke earnestly, explaining to Tom. "I never realized how much! Hospital committees, racket and tennis clubs, golf—that's how you build a constituency."

"Sounds like a bunch of stockbrokers, not doctors!" Tom's old indignation flared. "If you want to become rich, you don't belong in medicine. You can always go in for real estate or wholesale plumbing fixtures, for God's sake."

"Remember what Wong Lee used to tell us? You can't crusade against the world, Tom. You'll only bang your head on a stone wall." Perry stood up. "Listen, I've got to pick up my girl. Do you mind if I run? I'll just make it."

Martin looked at his watch. "I ought to be going soon, too. By half past, anyway."

They watched Perry stride across the grass to his car and drive away.

"Salt of the earth," Martin said.

"Always was."

"He's rising to the top, too. One of the best anaesthesiologists around. You feel secure with him there."

"Listen," Tom said abruptly, "I want you to do me a favor. I've got a three-year-old boy I'd like you to see. I could have him over now. They're only a few blocks from here."

"Tom," Flo protested, "it's a holiday! You've no right to put Martin to work."

"Martin's a doctor, and this might save these folks a trip into the city."

WHEN MARTIN HAD examined the boy and the parents had taken him away, Tom asked, "Well, what do you think?"

"There's a positive Babinski on the right. There's got to be some sort of lesion in the cerebral cortex." He paused, collecting his impressions. "It could be a tumor, a congenital defect in a blood vessel or—"

Tom interrupted. "In any case, you ought to see him this week."

Martin hesitated and Tom urged, "No delays, Martin, please."

"Of course not . . . They've got no money, I suppose?"

"Hardly! The father delivers for a laundry."

"Eastman would see him as a clinic patient, then. Or I would, since he'll be away for the next few weeks."

"So?" Tom waited. "You can handle it, Martin."

Something in Tom's voice and his respectful silence while the little boy had been examined touched Martin poignantly. Here in this simple office, so like Pa's except for more modern furniture—a flat-topped desk and leather chair, an electrocardiograph and sterilizer—stood the friend who had started out with him, who had done just as well as he had and who must now turn anxiously to him for help. It made him feel apologetic about knowing more. He hoped Tom had no such feelings about it.

"You know," Martin said, "between ourselves, I'd rather you sent him to Albeniz's clinic than ours."

"For Pete's sake, why?"

"Maybe this is disloyal of me, but I owe you the best, and I can talk honestly to you. Eastman's clinics are perfunctory. He's in too much of a hurry to do a real job. The private practice is just too big, and that's the fact of it."

Tom shook his head in disapproval.

"I can't complain because—well, I can't."

Tom's eyes seemed to bore into him. "You were saying about the clinic?"

"I was saying—Tom, send the kid to Albeniz! People come from all over the city to present cases and ask questions. He's a *teacher*."

"Do you ever go there anymore yourself?"

"Not for the last year or so. It's impossible for me. We're too busy—" One day on impulse he had made what he told himself was a social visit to Albeniz; in truth he had some vague hope that Albeniz might offer him an association. But Albeniz worked alone in his modest office, which had never been very busy. Money, apparently, didn't interest him that much—

"Gosh, look at the time! Let me just say thanks to Flo and then I'll rush."

Tom followed him to the street. "Oh, you've traded in for a Nash! Rumble seat and all! This is a nice little boat."

"Don't use it much in town. Got it mostly for when I run out to see you."

Tom's hand went to Martin's shoulder. "There's a lonely look about you, Professor."

Martin smiled. "I know. I ought to get married. You are, and Perry will be next month and everybody is. You've been telling me that since the first year in med school."

"Yes. And you don't listen."

Martin wiped the smile off. "You're forgetting, I've been married."

"But that's over," Tom said gently.

"Well, I'll give it some thought one of these days. My love to the kiddies."

He turned the little car toward the George Washington Bridge. The weekenders had departed long since from the city and traffic was light. He drove slowly. A sudden tiredness, wholly emotional, washed over him. Visits to the Horvaths were usually an antidote to the weariness which could befall a man who had to grind through a heavy routine week after week. In their simplicity, Tom and Flo gave comfort. They were bread and butter; they nourished and soothed. Their house was a cheerful place, with its heartening, practical bustle and no time or need for introspection. This time, though, the visit had not quieted him. Leaving them, he had felt a kind of evanescent melancholy in the region of the chest.

Envy of Tom? No, no! He would require, when at last he should be settled in life, something quite different from what he imagined Tom and Flo possessed in one another. And he wondered as he crossed the bridge, where the river ran silver under the evening sky and the downtown towers were pink and all the city's scruffy soil was concealed for the night, whether Tom might ever feel he wanted more or whether everything had indeed turned out as neatly as he and Flo had planned and packaged it.

So it might have been for me, he thought with sudden wrenching, if it hadn't been for Mary. Mary Fern. In England now, the sun would soon be rising. And probably rain would fall before the day was over. It almost always did. She would collect her paints and easel and go inside. She would stand at the door, taking delight in the sound and smell of the rain.

Swerving, he missed an empty hearse by inches. An omen or a warning? Smiling wryly, he pulled himself back to the present time and place. He had come full circle now, back to the days of Greenwich Village and the Harriets. He wondered where his particular Harriet might be. A respectable wife and mother, he supposed, home in Wilmington, North Carolina, and remembering Martin only vaguely, if she did at all.

Now there were others. There was Muriel, who taught school and was separated from her husband: no entanglement there. There were Rae, a clever girl who called herself modern—meaning without illusions—and Tina, supervisor at a hospital far out in Queens. One never got involved where one worked.

Once last year he had come close to another sort of girl, very young and cheerful, with charming freckles on her nose. He could perhaps have committed himself, if her parents hadn't objected because he was divorced and had a child. So it had ended before it had begun, which was just as well because he hadn't really wanted it very much, anyway.

Surgery began at seven. When, in the early afternoon, Martin and Eastman got back to the office, the waiting rooms were already crowded. Three secretaries juggled appointments at the telephones. The examining rooms were filled.

Records and files in their manila envelopes were piled on the desks. The patients, terrified under brave, assumed calm, were led in.

O Excalibur, the magic sword! He carried the magic sword, and it was knowledge.

Turning the car left off Riverside Drive, he drove eastward past the brown, Romanesque monument which was the Museum of Natural History. Now the city's poor were ambling homeward from their holiday in the park. A beggarly decade, this of the thirties, a time of meagerness and grief. He wondered whether the forties would be any better: they were always saying prosperity was just around the corner.

Yet, in medicine, the thirties would be remembered as years of rich discovery. The pace was accelerating, as his father had predicted it would. Already the sulfonamides and penicillin had changed the face of disease and routed the horror of infection in surgery. He could feel a palpable excitement on entering an operating room, knowing how greatly increased was the chance of success. A patient wheeled in on the stretcher was an unopened gift package, he thought suddenly. A preposterous concept? Not at all! For if one could send that patient home, able to walk and to talk, his words coming sensibly and clearly, why then, wasn't that a gift to yourself, the doctor? The most splendid gift of all? There was nothing like it, nothing in the world!

He was fortunate to be working with Eastman. The man's technique and speed were marvelous. And Eastman liked him. There was, of course, no reason why he shouldn't, for Martin not only worked well, but he worked hard. Still, those qualities were no guarantee of anything. Many an association broke up because of nothing more than some obscure difference of personality. He remembered that year in medical school when it had seemed that Dr. Humphrey, the anatomist, had been his enemy from the very first day in the classroom. Just didn't like the cut of my jib, Martin thought. It was hard when, very young, you first learned that there were people in the world who didn't like you. But then, there were people *you* didn't like! Women with nasal whining voices; all people who lick their lips between words, their wet tongues slipping in and out like snakes' heads; sloppy people who forget things and come late.

We're all hard on each other, he reflected. Jessie's father never liked me. He used me. I never liked him, either, although for a while I tried to. And I suppose you might say I used him, too.

He had been hoping to "use" Dr. Eastman, not for any benefit to himself, but for that idea which was coming to seem more and more imperative of late. Working in the laboratory on cell pathology and neuroanatomy, he became aware that the idea was never absent from his thinking. So on a resplendent spring afternoon, walking from the hospital to the office, he had spoken of it to Eastman.

"We'll never abolish useless, even dangerous surgery, until the surgeon knows more neurology. In England Mr. Braidburn's been trying for years to found his own separate institute. Unfortunately, they can't raise funds over there. But in this country, Depression or not, it seems to me there's still a lot of untapped wealth. One only needs to get the right people together."

"I daresay. Raising funds is a hard business. I'm afraid I'm too middle-aged, too busy and tired to embroil myself in it," Dr. Eastman answered, fending Martin off.

He had persisted. "Dr. Albeniz used to talk about it when I was in med school. About true progress coming only when all the neurological specialties are joined in one discipline under one roof."

"Albeniz is a fanatic, Martin. He's exceptionally talented and as fanatic as a monk. For him there's no world beyond the hospital." Eastman laughed. "I believe he'd sleep there if he could and if his wife would let him."

It seemed to Martin that Eastman had spoken too carelessly, as though the subject were of small importance. That anyone should speak so lightly of a man like Albeniz astounded him.

Eastman, reading disapproval in Martin's face, had admonished him good-humoredly.

"Don't be so solemn, Martin! You're advancing and making a damn good living. What more do you want? Leave well enough alone."

Yes, he was advancing. He owed no man! Donald Meig had got every cent back with interest. A check went out each month to his mother. He lived in an excellent small apartment, halfway between the office and the hospital. There he had everything he wanted—four walls of books, green plants and some Shaker furniture. Pure lines, no clutter, only space and quiet and a good record player. He had surprised himself with how little he had wanted after all.

Yes, he was fortunate. He had a coveted place and no right to feel unrest.

After putting the car in the garage he walked home through a gritty, warm night breeze, telling himself how fortunate he was. When he entered the apartment, the telephone was ringing. Over the wire came the familiar, short command.

"Dr. Farrell? You're wanted in emergency."

"A̲N AUTO ACCIDENT way out on Long Island," the resident reported. "A young girl. They're bringing her in now."

Rows of heads in the emergency waiting room turned curiously, and he lowered his voice.

"It was a wedding party, riding from the church to the reception. The girl was a bridesmaid, the bride's sister, I think."

Martin grimaced. "A rotten memory to keep!"

"They ought to be here soon. We'd been trying you for half an hour before we got you."

"Sorry. You tried Dr. Eastman? He mightn't have left yet."

"Yes, he had. We called you next."

The wait took Martin back through years to his own stint in emergency. Hurried, harried nurses and interns kept method and order. Two little boys, wounded by firecrackers, were brought in. A mother with a sick, swaddled baby expostulated in an unknown, foreign tongue.

The ambulance wailed, and Martin started up while the doors swung open, and a stretcher rushed past carrying a blue-gray man, having a heart attack. Not for him. Then the siren wailed again, and this time it was for him.

From under the blanket trailed the blue silk skirt of a summer dress made for rejoicing. The contrast of this dress with the bloodied young, blond head of its wearer was outrageous and obscene. And he thought how absurd it is that in one careless, brutal instant a life can be deflected from its peaceful course.

Having made his light-fingered, swift examination, and ordered X-rays, he stepped out into the corridor, still sick with this absurdity, which had never struck him so forcefully before.

A man wearing striped trousers and a dark coat with a carnation in the lapel, some proper uniform that was not a part of Martin's life, came up to him.

"My daughter," he began and stopped.

Martin took his arm and led him to a bench. He looked into an anguished face.

"Mr.—"

"Moser. Robert Moser."

"I'm Dr. Farrell, Mr. Moser. You want to know what we found," Martin said gently.

"I want you to answer one question, Doctor. Will she live?"

"We'll do everything we can to see that she does."

"I'm a man who wants the truth, Doctor. No soft soap."

"Well, Mr. Moser, we're doing X-rays now, but I can tell you already that your daughter's skull is fractured in several places. And there's almost certainly extensive pressure on the brain. Just how much damage, we can't tell until we look."

"Then you'll have to operate?"

"Yes. Right away."

"There wouldn't be time to get my wife here? She—they've given her a sedative, and my chauffeur is driving her in. I came in the ambulance, but she would want to see Vicky."

"I don't think we ought to delay. We've got to relieve the pressure."

"I see." Mr. Moser stared at the floor. His lip went twitching toward his left cheek. He looked up.

"Dr. Eastman should be here any minute, shouldn't he?"

"No sir. Dr. Eastman's out of town. I'm his associate, and I'll be taking charge."

The twitching ceased and the lips firmed. "You're very young. How long have you been with Dr. Eastman?"

"Four years. Before that I trained in London. I'm perfectly qualified, I assure you."

"Excuse me, but your assurance won't be enough. This is my daughter's life. You're positive you can't reach Dr. Eastman?"

"Positive. He's gone to Maine. He's a sailor and will be gone for two weeks."

Mr. Moser stood up. He was of equal height with Martin. They were almost toe to toe, as in a confrontation.

"Maine isn't the moon. He could come back."

"Not in time, Mr. Moser."

"I'm a trustee of this hospital, do you know that?"

"I didn't know it."

"I want an experienced man. I've no wish to insult you, Doctor, but I've no time to waste on the amenities, either. I ask you to give me a list of neurosurgeons on a par with Dr. Eastman."

"We don't have yardsticks to measure doctors," Martin said, and immediately regretting the hot-tempered reply, amended it. "But I can name some competent surgeons for you. There's a Doctor Florio on the staff, and there's a Dr. Harold Samson."

"I'll call them."

"I can do it for you."

"I'll do it myself."

Martin waited. He could see Moser in the telephone booth, dialing, hanging up and dialing again. He felt a strong current of compassion and at the same time anger, at the stinging rejection. What did the man think he was doing on Eastman's service? Polishing shoes?

Mr. Moser came back. "Neither one of them is home. What do you doctors do, abandon the city because it's a holiday?"

Martin didn't reply.

"That's all there are? There must be dozens of neurosurgeons around!"

"You said you wanted the best."

"Well, give me second best, then."

"You're looking at one right now."

"You're pretty damned impertinent, you know that? Dr. Eastman ought to be told about you. I asked you for another name, or I'll call my internist and ask him, although God knows where he is tonight."

Martin controlled his anger. "There is a man . . . He doesn't work here at Fisk, but he has privileges here, and I believe he'd come."

Mr. Moser sank onto the bench. He looked as though he had used his last strength.

"His name is Albeniz. It's in the book."

"Damned foreign name. I can't think how to spell it. You call him for me."

Dr. Albeniz listened to Martin's brief summary. "I would come for you," he said, "but it's impossible. I'm in bed with a cold and fever. Why don't you do it yourself?"

"I'm willing to, but the father wants someone better-qualified."

"You're perfectly qualified, Martin."

"Not well enough, he thinks."

"Well, if he can't find anyone better and won't accept you, you have no more responsibility in the case. Tell him so and let him go where he wants."

"I'll do that," Martin said.

When he came back from the telephone, Mr. Moser had put his head in his hands and his shoulders were shaking. Martin stood over him.

"I can't get Dr. Albeniz," he said quietly. "He's ill."

Mr. Moser did not raise his head. "Then go ahead. I can't do any more. Go ahead with whatever has to be done and God help you."

Martin wasn't quite sure, as he walked away, whether that had been a prayer or a threat.

*   *   *

Midnight lay beyond the windows when Martin entered the operating room. At the edges of white light, the world was gloomy green. Green walls and rumpled cotton. Green, refracted from the bottles in cabinets. Green, the sterile cloth on the table where, glittering like silver at a palace banquet, lay the tools: knives, drills, forceps and mallets.

Perry looked up, waiting, his eyebrows rising like parentheses above the mask. He had been fetched out of a movie theater where he had been with his girl. Martin was thankful they had found him. There was something reassuring in the sight of those familiar eyebrows.

The assistants waited. A nurse put a second pair of gloves over Martin's first pair. A fine calm came to him: I can do it.

On the girl's naked skull, brown coagulated blood clumped in dark beads along the crooked wounds, like branching rivers on a map. Such strange thoughts he had, selecting a knife from the service row! His eyes narrowed; he could feel them tightening and sharpening. His lips pressed shut. And he brought the knife down, into a spurt of fresh, red blood, which was at once sucked up and sponged away. Down through the scalp the knife sliced, until the scalp was folded back on glistening bone.

Electric drill. Press hard, down through the bone. A drop of sweat starts on his forehead under the cap. Alertly, a nurse steps up to wipe it away. He remembers having seen the gesture in London. Braidburn sweated, but Eastman never does.

The drill stops. He moves it slightly and applies it again. He is drawing a pattern, a small circle on the skull. Press hard. Careful, careful, not to penetrate the brain beneath the bone! Complete the circle. Now he has made a disc of bone; lift it out and ease the pressure on the brain: that is the object. He is aware of voices, movements in the room, whispers and the swish of rubber-soled shoes. The clock lurches. A half hour ticks.

He asks Perry, "Everything all right?"

"Everything okay," comes the answer.

"Steel blade," Martin commands and it is handed to him. He flicks out the disc of bone and holds his breath, dreading, waiting for hemorrhage and gush of blood. No! For an instant, he is relieved. He calls for his magnifying glasses. When these have been strapped around his head, he peers in, and holds the breath back in his lungs again. He is conscious of his own heartbeat.

From the force of the blow, the smash of bone on metal, a splinter of that bone, needle-sharp, has pierced the dura mater. He perceives a leakage of the spinal fluid and sighs. Dietz, the senior resident, is peering in, too. Now he draws away. Dietz's eyes are very black—the rest of his face is hidden, but his eyes convey to Martin that he has seen and understood. It is somehow comforting to feel the comprehension of this intelligent young man. It is comforting to be surrounded by the whole quick, skillful team.

And carefully—oh, every movement is so tense, precise and careful—Martin eases, pries the needle-point of bone—he is almost panting now—and retrieving it securely between the bright tips of the forceps, hands it to the waiting nurse. He sighs, a deep, long involuntary sigh.

Now there is nothing to do but withdraw and wait. He has done all he can.

The leakage will cease of its own accord or it will not. The meninges will heal without infection, or they will not. There will be a scar, that much is certain, and the scar will perhaps be normal, or it may not. It may cause epileptic seizures at some later date, or it may not.

So he sutures the scalp. It is all over. Then he stands and looks down at the girl, while they wrap her head in folded white cloth: Hindu hat, lacking only a forehead jewel.

Her lashes lie on her childish cheeks. The purity of the unconscious face strikes him to the heart. He rips the gloves off and walks out and is terribly, terribly tired.

THE PARENTS WERE waiting in the outer hall. He was sorry that they had come to him before he could change his clothes, because their daughter's blood had spattered on him and he saw them looking at it.

"We've done what we could," he said, knowing it was not enough to tell them.

Moser opened his mouth to ask a question, but then the mother began to weep, and he led her away; it was a relief to Martin because he did not know what he could have answered if they had pressed him.

After he had changed his clothes, he thought of going home. But also he wanted to look at the girl again. He knew there would be nothing to see tonight. She would be unconscious far into the following day. Still, he wanted to see her again. So he went to the coffee machine and had a cup and then another, before going upstairs.

The family had taken a suite, and she lay in the center of a large white room like a carved stone queen on a tomb: a long white ridge under white covers, with calm white eyelids.

"Can I get anything for you, Doctor?"

He hadn't noticed the nurse sitting in the corner. "Just tell me the time, please. My watch has stopped."

"A quarter past two."

"You'll be here till seven?"

"No, sir. This isn't my shift. I go off at midnight ordinarily, but the supervisor asked me to stay."

The pitch and tone of the girl's low voice attracted his attention, so that he strained through the weak light to see her. What he saw was the full body of a Venus and a mild young face, too round for beauty.

"Have I seen you before?" he asked.

"I don't think so. I only came two weeks ago from Mercy Hospital." She stood beside Martin looking down at the unconscious girl. "I've got her bridesmaid dress hanging in the closet. Her mother said, 'Throw it out. I never want to see it again.' But I couldn't do that. Doctor, what's going to happen to her?"

"You know better than to ask that," he chided gently.

"Well, of course I really do. But this has really got to me tonight."

He saw brimming tears, and he went on as gently as before, "You mustn't let a case do this to you, or you'll be torn up all the time, won't you?"

"I know. I'm not at my professional best." She gave him a rueful smile. "Sometimes I go so far as to think I wasn't even meant to be a nurse! I take things too personally. And I wonder, are other people like me? You, for instance? You see this kind of thing all the time. What do you do about it? Can you just forget and go on to the next one?"

"I don't forget. I store it away with all the other evils that happen in a lifetime, and I learn not to take them out or look at them too often."

"I'm not always like this. Heavens, I wouldn't want you to think I was! I just haven't much resistance right now. You know the way you are after you've had the flu, for instance?"

"I know," Martin said.

When the relief nurse came, they walked down the corridor together. In an island of light, a charge nurse worked on charts; beyond that island lay dark blue shadow.

"And have you just got over the flu?" he asked.

"Not the flu. A broken engagement. That's why I transferred, to change my luck. Superstitious, I suppose. Would you like some coffee?"

"I don't need a third cup, but I'll take one anyway."

There was no use going home now. He had office hours at nine, and three hours of sleep would be as bad as none at all. He followed her into the cubicle where the coffeepot stood on a table.

A nighttime chill came shivering through the window. The girl drew a sweater from a hook and warmed her hands around her cup. The sweater had a name tag: Hazel Janos.

"That's me. Hungarian. People never pronounce the name right."

"My best friend is Hungarian. Tom Horvath. He taught me to eat palachinken."

"I make good palachinken, with cherries and sour cream."

He sat back and observed her. She had very white skin, the kind that burns painfully at the beach. Her brown hair was too fine and soft. She would be one of those women who always had trouble keeping it in order. Right now, pinned under the starched cap, it was tidy. She looked particularly clean. He wondered why nurses always did: surely they didn't bathe more often than other people did?

Resting her chin on her hand, she looked out into the night sky. The outline of a rooftop made an isosceles triangle at the lower end of the window. She sighed.

"I'm curious about you," Martin said.

"Why?"

"You're all knotted up, aren't you?"

"Yes."

"Want to tell me about it? Or shall I mind my own business?"

"You really want to know?"

"Only if you care to tell me."

So often people told him of their quarrels and debts and loves, and he usually wished they wouldn't. But now, for some reason, he wanted to hear this girl talk.

Why? There was nothing remarkable about her, unless a lulling voice and a very female softness were remarkable.

"There's not much to tell. It was only another case of a girl who wanted to get married and a man who didn't."

"I see."

"Walter lost his job almost four years ago. I told him we could live on my salary till things got better. My folks have three rooms on the top floor where we live in Flushing and they'd have fixed them up for us. But he wouldn't sponge, he said. So we just argued and argued and one day I gave him an ultimatum and I lost. That's it," she finished quietly.

"Perhaps he'll think it over," Martin suggested.

"No. He's gone to Kansas City. He has a brother there, and maybe his brother will find a job for him, I don't know. I think he was just tired of things here, of all the wrangling and of me. And he just needed to get away to a new place. I can't blame him, really. The juice seems to go out of things when you have to wait too long for them."

"That's true."

"I'm twenty-eight and a virgin. Do you suppose that could have been my mistake? I sometimes wonder."

Her candor touched Martin. "I honestly don't know," he said.

"Maybe in my heart I didn't trust him. Oh, why am I telling you all this? Because you're a doctor and people think they can say anything to a doctor that they wouldn't say to anybody else?"

Oh Lord, not again he thought, and answered, "I think people feel that way." He sensed that she was waiting for some positive statement, something that would be a comfort, so he searched for something and came up only with a cliché. "Time heals everything, they say."

"Do you believe that, honestly?"

"No," he said.

She laughed. Her lips curved back on strong even teeth and the laugh changed her face. Comely, he thought. That's the word. Comely.

"I'm not laughing because anything's funny. I think it's because I feel better for having told you. You're the only person I've told besides my father and mother."

He reflected, "I never do remember why laughter and tears are related. One of my professors in a philosophy course spent a week of lectures on the subject, but for the life of me I can't remember what he said." He bent forward, clasping his hands around his knees. "I have a little girl," he said suddenly, surprising himself. "I haven't seen her since she was three years old, and she's seven now." And why *he* should be talking like this to *her*, he had no idea. "Her mother and I are divorced and she has custody. I thought maybe she would relent, let me see the child. I've asked often enough."

"And?"

"And lawyers answered, reminding me of the terms of the divorce."

"But that's so cruel," Hazel Janos said softly.

"Yes. The divorce was." Not Jessie, he meant. There was no cruelty in Jessie.

He could understand her position quite well. And he sat still, thinking about that which would have been impossible to put into words and was yet so clear to him.

The girl said, "I rather thought there might be something else beside what they say about you."

Martin looked up. "What they say about me?"

"Well, of course, you must know that people—that nurses—talk about doctors, especially about the young, unmarried ones." She flushed. "But they say good things about you! That you're awfully gentle with your patients and really care, that even when you're cranky with the nurses sometimes, you're sorry afterward. They all like you."

"That's not what you meant before, when we were talking about divorce."

She said timidly, "They think you must be a chaser because you're not married. But I didn't think you were."

"You didn't?"

"No. I felt a quietness in you. And maybe some sadness."

It isn't sensible to talk about your private life, especially where your work is: a snobbish concept, maybe, but of proven practicality all the same. And even as he was thinking so, Martin began to speak.

It was almost as though someone else were talking and he were listening. Slowly and thoughtfully, he heard himself say aloud the names of people and places which he had scarcely used since they had passed out of his life. Menton. Mary. Jessie. Lamb House. Claire.

The night wind blew hard there on the fourteenth floor, so that Hazel drew the sweater closer. Her eyes never left his face.

"That's the whole story?" she asked when he had finished.

"The whole story."

"And it's over between Mary and you?"

"Yes," he said harshly.

He was angry with himself. Why had he spilled everything out to a stranger? All day he had been feeling a foggy sadness, and now, having been on his feet almost twenty-four hours, he had simply been carried away by fatigue. Damn, he ought to have gone home to sleep instead of sitting here pouring his heart out! He stood up. It was five o'clock. A milky light had risen at the windows.

"I'd better get home to shave and change before I go to work. By the way, when do you go back on duty?"

"At seven tonight."

"Then this was your time to sleep, and I've kept you up."

"I wouldn't have stayed if I hadn't wanted to." She touched his arm. "I just thought—you're probably sorry you told me so much. You're worried I'll talk about it all over the place. But I never will. You can trust me."

He looked down into a face so gentle that it pained him: it was like looking at a wound. One saw such faces on lonesome children, on certain rare old men and sometimes on women of radiant goodness.

"Yes," he said, "I trust you."

* * *

Eastman MOVED BACK from the respirator, stepping carefully between the oxygen tank and the tubing. In the transparent box which had been trundled over the bed, Vicky Moser lay unmoving, except for the slight rise and fall of her chest. He beckoned to Martin and they went out to the corridor.

"For the sake of my blood pressure, I had to wait a whole day before I could talk to you, Farrell," he began.

"I don't understand!"

"You had no right to take the knife to Vicky Moser!" Eastman's words were precisely separated, cut apart, as if he were teaching English to a foreigner. "You had no authority. What made you think you had?"

Martin was dumbfounded. "But you were out of town! And I *am* your associate!"

"You made no real effort to reach me. As a matter of fact, I had gone to my sister's house in Westchester before starting for Maine in the morning. I could have been back here in little more than an hour."

"How, in all fairness, could I have known that?"

"Well, in all fairness, perhaps you couldn't. Certainly, though, you could have called some other chief, couldn't you?"

"Dr. Florio and Dr. Samson were called and couldn't be reached."

"What about Shirer, then? These are prominent people, Farrell. Moser's a trustee. You don't fool around with people like Moser. I shouldn't have to tell you that, for God's sake."

Anger began to boil up in Martin, but he answered coolly. "In the first place, sir, I don't care a damn about prominence. In the second place, I didn't recommend Dr. Shirer because I consider myself a better surgeon than he is."

"What? Shirer has been on staff here for thirty years! And you compare yourself with him?"

"He's been doing mediocre work for thirty years, Dr. Eastman."

"Oh, I suppose you consider my work mediocre, too?"

"Of course I don't. But there are some procedures I *can* do as well as you can, and this was one of them."

"It was, was it?"

"Yes. I knew I could do it. I wouldn't have undertaken it otherwise."

"I call that arrogant. I don't know what you call it."

"I call it confident."

Eastman's cheeks reddened. "I'll want to talk about that again, Farrell. I'm not sure you and I can get along in the future unless certain things are clarified."

In Martin the anger now boiled over. He had done a thorough job! If it didn't work out, if the girl should die or should live and merely vegetate, why then, it would have happened anyway! It would have been "fated," "ordained," whatever that meant. I truly and honestly know my limitations, he thought.

And he said, with a calmness that surprised himself, "I don't think we will get along, Dr. Eastman, unless you give me the respect and freedom I deserve."

For a second Eastman stared at him; then, without replying, he turned about and almost ran down the hall.

*   *   *

For three days they poured glucose and oxygen into Vicky Moser. She was now Eastman's patient; Martin had been removed from the case. He wondered what was being whispered about the hospital. No doubt the news had filtered down to the newest student nurse on the floor. Nevertheless, he went in to look at Vicky. Hazel Janos was there one evening, but she made no comment, only watched while Martin pulled Vicky's eyelids back and found no change. The pupils were still enlarged and made no move under the pinpoint shaft of his pencil-light.

On the fourth day came momentary hope when normal breathing resumed, and she was taken out of the respirator. But still she lay inert, unresponsive to touch or light or the sound of voices.

Once, in the elevator, Martin saw her parents, two people grown abruptly small and old. The mother huddled and shivered, although July blazed outside. When they saw Martin, they turned away and he understood that they were holding him responsible and would always hold him so.

At the office he continued to hold regular hours. Eastman did not come in. Obviously, he had interrupted his vacation only for the Moser girl. It seemed to Martin that the secretaries looked at him with curiosity and compassion. Probably they had been told he wouldn't be with them much longer.

And for Vicky Moser the days rolled slowly through their routines: feeding tubes, spinal taps, antibiotics, anticonvulsives. If she lives, Martin thought, she may not be able to talk. She may not be able to move. Or she may be able to talk only nonsense and move with the violence of an animal. Even though officially the girl was not his patient, in his mind she was so still. With him she had entered the desert, so to speak, and he must see her out of it.

Whatever happened, they would say it was his fault. Eastman would see to that, had seen to it already. And it wouldn't be his fault. *Still, what if it were?*

He began to pray: O God, don't let her die; she's only eighteen. Strange that he should pray! He had had no interest in religion for years, being neither for it nor against it. He wondered whether his beseeching was not perhaps some sort of theatricality, watching himself at humble prayer in a fine old tradition, without believing a word of it. And then he remembered his father's rounded cadence in the moldy green parlor before winter breakfasts and he felt like crying.

O God, don't let her die!

At the hospital, late one afternoon as he was about to go into Vicky's room, Martin met Eastman coming out.

"Anything you want?" Eastman asked bluntly.

"Just to know how the patient is doing."

"My patient," Eastman said, "is doing badly. I plan to operate again in the morning."

Martin was appalled. "Operate again? But why?"

"Self-evident, I should say."

"I would guess there's hemorrhaging, which ought to subside. If you ask me, we should give it some more time."

"I'm not asking you. I'm of the opinion that there are splinters in there, and I'm going back for them."

"Doctor," Martin said earnestly, "let's put personal feelings aside for a minute. I give you my word there are none. I removed them all."

"Damn it! You couldn't have!"

No stranger would have believed that this man could ever be genial. His eyes were hostile; his lips folded inward, making a gash across the chin.

"I'm having X-rays in the morning, naturally, but I can tell you right here and now what they will show."

He swung around. His shoes slapped the floor smartly all the way to the elevator.

When Martin went into the room he saw at once that there had been no change. The very air felt cold, as if some chill were issuing from that poor body, as in a crypt where the dead have lain for centuries. He stood a moment, shuddered, and went downstairs again, out to the searing street. Here were the smells of life—gasoline and dog droppings and a sugary whiff from the open door of a bakery.

Why had she not revived? There were no splinters, he knew there weren't. *Still, suppose there were?* Eastman was going to operate again, and she wouldn't be able to take the shock. If she died—

He thought of the times he had been present when a family received the news of death. A husband, a mother or a child dies; some people can accept such loss in wordless despair; others scream, protest that it can't be true. It was the most terrible errand a doctor ever had to carry out, and one never would, never could, get used to it.

That night Martin scarcely slept. At five o'clock he got up and walked through echoing streets to the hospital. He half hoped Hazel Janos would be there, then recalled that she went off duty at midnight. A bulky, middle-aged woman in white was dozing upright in the chair beside the bed.

"Is there any change?" he whispered, and the woman answered, "None."

Gently, Martin raised one eyelid, then the other, and turned his flashlight on. There was no contraction of the pupils. He sighed.

Then he lifted the blanket, reached for a limp arm and stroked it. Was there, or did he imagine a very, very faint withdrawal of the flesh, a reaction to his touch? He felt a swift rise of expectation and as quickly stifled it. He pressed harder. Was there a movement, the merest fraction of movement?

"Did you see that, Nurse?"

She turned up the light and leaned over the bed.

"Here. I'll show you."

Again Martin pressed the arm, and now he was sure he saw a slight withdrawal.

"Did you see it? Did you?

"Yes. Yes, I think I did. Oh, Doctor, do you think possibly—"

And the two of them, the aging woman and the young man, stared at each other across the bed.

"I don't dare hope," Martin said. It may mean nothing at all, he told himself, only a reflex, a flicker in a dead brain. It probably does mean nothing. Yet he hoped.

At seven the shifts changed and a new nurse came. He heard the two women whispering in the corridor outside the room as he stood watching by the bed. Still the girl lay, the marble effigy on the tomb. At eight o'clock orderlies arrived to wheel her below for X-rays.

"I hear they're going to operate again," the nurse remarked with curiosity. She had a handsome, cold face. Martin didn't answer. Hazel Janos would *care,* he thought suddenly.

At eight-fifteen Mr. Moser entered the room, stopped when he saw Martin and frowned. "I thought you were off the case."

"I am. This is purely unofficial. I'm humanly concerned to see how my work turned out."

Mr. Moser sat down next to the nurse. They spoke in such low tones that Martin couldn't hear, but he wasn't supposed to hear. He was to be excluded.

At the window he looked down to aimless scurry and hurry on the street below. From this height human beings were no more than water beetles on a pond. Awesome to think how in each one, that man lifting the trash can, that one inching his car into a parking space, raged a private, daily struggle with the universe!

When Dr. Eastman came in, Martin did not turn around.

"We shall have to operate," he heard Eastman say in his quiet voice of authority. "There's undoubtedly a splinter in there, maybe more than one. We'll know, of course, as soon as the X-rays come up."

In the room there was total silence. Martin, still standing at the window, felt eyes on his back. At eight-fifty a technician came in with the X-rays.

"Thank you, Mr. Poole," Eastman said formally.

Now Martin turned around as Eastman held the X-rays to the light. The brain was a gray-and-white intaglio on the plate. Spare, Martin thought, like modern art. For a long minute or two Eastman studied it while Mr. Moser, puzzled and afraid, peered over his shoulder.

At last Moser spoke. "Well, Doctor?"

Eastman pursed his lips. "Perplexing. Perplexing."

"What is?"

"There's nothing. Unless—"

"Unless what?"

"Well, no splinters—that I can see."

A strange sound, part laugh, part sob, forced itself from Martin's throat. It was almost inaudible, but Eastman heard it. He looked over and then quickly away.

So I was right, Martin thought. But still, still there could be infection, couldn't there? We were absolutely sterile, and yet one never knows.

When the door opened and the patient was brought back, the little group reformed around the bed. Eastman was silent. The others waited for him to say something.

And Moser said softly, "My wife is falling apart."

Eastman nodded. "I know."

"What do you suggest now, Doctor?"

"I've been thinking—another set of X-rays. There's got to be something there. I'm still convinced. The ventricles aren't enlarged, the—"

"Look at this," Martin said.

"At what?" Eastman said coldly.

Martin turned the flashlight on. "The pupil. She reacts. And this morning I thought I saw—"

"Yes, what?" the father cried.

"It may have been nothing at all."

"What did you see?" Moser asked. "What did you see?"

"I am not sure. I don't want to give you false hopes—"

He pinched the girl's arm. He thought her lips moved but he couldn't be sure. And he stood there, stroking, then gently pinching, then pressing that thin white arm. And all the time, without seeing it, he felt Eastman's gaze upon him, scorning and challenging.

Mr. Moser sighed. "Nothing. Nothing," he murmured.

"I don't know. I feel—" Martin began.

What he felt was a slight, slight reflex in the arm.

"I don't know," he repeated.

And Vicky's lips moved. A little sound, a breath, the faintest groan came into the silence around the bed. Martin bent over the girl.

"Are you Vicky?" he whispered. The dry lips moved again, barely touching each other.

"Are you Vicky?"

The eyes flew open. For the first time in days they opened to the light; for a few tense moments they were blank, then subtle recognition gathered there.

"Have you been sick?"

She nodded. Her head barely moved on the pillow, but it was unmistakably a nod.

"You're going to get well now, Vicky."

She stared at Martin. Her eyes strained to understand.

"Yes, you are. Do you know I'm a doctor?"

Again she nodded.

Martin thought—he thought his heart was in his throat.

"There's someone here to see you," he said softly. "Look," and he motioned to Moser.

Moser leaned over the other side of the bed.

"Is this your father?" Martin asked.

It was a long minute. "Is this your father?"

The girl's eyes struggled to focus. The whole face struggled to come back from a far place. There was no sound in the room, no breath, no rustle, as the three men waited, their faces furrowed with their tension.

And finally, finally, into that agonizing silence came a word, very low, but audible and clear.

"Daddy," she said.

*   *   *

Bᴏʙ Mᴏsᴇʀ ɢʀᴀsᴘᴇᴅ Martin's hands. "I was half out of my mind, Dr. Farrell! For God's sake, you can understand that, can't you? If I was hard on you, if it was unforgivable, try to forgive it, will you? I'll never forget you till my dying day. I—we—all of our family—we'll never forget you."

So much emotion, so much gratitude, were both overwhelming and oppressive. As quickly as he decently could, Martin fled.

Eastman caught up with him outside of the solarium. "I don't mind telling you, Martin, this has been one of the worst experiences of my professional life. I just went off the deep end. It looked so bad there, just so bad."

"I understand," Martin said.

"I'm sorry if I was unjust to you. I sincerely am. I was wrong and I admit I was."

There was embarrassment in another human being's discomfiture. And Martin fidgeted. "That's all right. As long as it's turned out well."

"Turned out well? The girl's going to come out of this and what can you add to that?" Eastman beamed. Light twinkled on his glasses; his teeth twinkled in a large, affable smile. "So let's forget the whole business, Martin, and take up where we left off."

Martin began quietly, "I've been doing some thinking, Doctor."

"Yes?"

"And the sum total of it is—that I really want to go it alone from now on. It's been a fine opportunity, working with you, and I've appreciated it, but—perhaps it's a matter of temperament—I know I'd rather work alone."

"Martin, you can have all the freedom you want. That's what you're telling me, isn't it? I understand your position. I give you my word that from now on it will be the way you want it."

Martin shook his head. "Thank you, Doctor, but I've made up my mind. I can wait a few weeks until you find another man, of course. I'm sure there'll be a dozen knocking at your door to take my place."

"Don't be foolish. Don't cut off your nose to spite your face just because you're piqued."

"It's not pique. I'd been mulling it over long before this, without knowing I was doing so."

"There's a depression out there, in case you haven't noticed."

"Oh, I've noticed, all right! But my wants aren't very many. I feel I can manage."

"You're making a great mistake, Martin!"

"I hope not. But I have to try." Martin put out his hand. "Thank you for everything, all the same."

He walked on past the solarium. Wheelchairs stood against the walls. There was a rich smell of flowers; hospital bouquets were wistful, belying the very nature of flowers. He went on past stretchers in the corridors and visitors waiting in the lobby for admission cards. The loudspeaker called with urgence: "Dr. Simmons—stat, Dr. Feinstein—stat." My world, he thought.

Hazel Janos, powder-white from cap to shoes, was coming up the steps. Her eyes widened and brightened when she saw Martin.

"I think our girl's going to make it," he told her jubilantly. "She spoke this morning, recognized her father."

"Oh," Hazel cried. "I'm so glad! I prayed for her."

"Say a little prayer for me, too, will you? I've taken a big leap. I've left Eastman and I'm on my own."

"I will, but I don't think you'll need prayers. You've got success written all over you."

"Have I? Strange, I don't feel that way about myself. I don't especially want it, either, if it means being another Eastman."

"You'd never be like that. You're soft inside." For a moment she looked frankly into his eyes; then, flushing, turned away as though she had been too intimate, and went inside through the revolving door.

Martin ran down the steps. It might not be so easy, after all, to make his way without Eastman's protecting hand. But it was time, as he had said, to try.

And he felt more free than he had felt in a very long time.

❧{15}❧

We remember more than we think we do. We understand more of what we see than we are credited with understanding. Years after the fact, one day things fall into place and we say, "Ah true, ah true! I must have known that, really, when I was only five or six or seven." Flickering as interrupted dreams, the voices—indignant, earnest, mournful—sound again behind shut doors and across the lawn. Sudden tendernesses and secret glances repeat themselves in a dim land-scape at the back of a stage, behind a gauze curtain.

The child knew her mother was different from other mothers, from other people. How? When did she first perceive this shameful difference?

The child knew that her father had gone away and that there was something terribly wrong about that. She thought she remembered great height, someone bending down to her, always bending, and being picked up and hugged. There had been a statue in a wide green place, and they two had stood in front of it. There had been a tiny glass boat, hanging on a Christmas tree. She had put out her finger to feel the pointed masts. Gold walnuts hung on the tree. There was a huge glass ball, lavender, so smooth you wanted to stroke it or else to crumble and scrunch it, like that.

"You mustn't break it," her father had said.

It was he, wasn't it? Who else could have said it, then?

Dogs had come barking. The house had been full of dogs. And there had been children, some vague girls and a boy, quite big, who called the jumping dogs away. But she had been frightened, and her father—who else could it have been? —had picked her up and told her not to be afraid.

She asked her mother about this memory, but her mother had forgotten. Her mother had forgotten everything, it seemed, and although she always answered questions patiently, the answers never told anything. So after a while, Claire stopped asking.

One day at a friend's house after school, an old woman said, "And you're Claire Farrell! I knew your grandfather. He was a good doctor, a good man."

"My grandfather? He's not a doctor. He's sick at home. He stays in bed most of the time, or on the sofa in the sun parlor."

"Your other grandfather is the one I mean, child. Your daddy was a doctor here, too, but he didn't stay very long."

In the bottom drawer of a cabinet in the library, Claire found the photograph albums. Some of them were very old, bound in shabby red velvet with tarnished metal clasps. The people in these were strange; their wide skirts looked like lampshades. The men had full beards and solemn eyes. She could recognize none of them.

But there was another album, a black one with a broken spine. Here the pages were loose, and some of the pictures slid out of their pointed corners. These were familiar people: Grandpa, looking much the same as now except that his hair was dark; and Mother as a little girl, twisted even then. It was strange to think that a little girl could look like that. Here she was again, older this time, with a dress-up dress on and a pearl necklace, standing next to a laughing girl, much taller than Mother and not twisted. Claire carried the album to where Grandpa sat in the sun parlor.

"Who's the pretty girl with Mother? That's our porch they're standing on."

"That's your aunt, Mary Fern. We don't talk about her anymore. We don't think about her. You'd best go put that away."

"Why? Is she dead like Grandma?"

"No, she's not dead, but she might as well be."

"Why?"

"Because she was wicked. She did bad things."

"What bad things?"

"Stealing, for one. Taking things that didn't belong to her."

When Mother came in, she was very angry. "I will not have you talking to the child like that, Father," she said. It seemed to Claire that she was shaking.

"Why not? She might as well know the truth."

"At six?"

"She can start getting used to the idea. When she's older, she'll have been prepared for it."

"Never! Never, do you hear? It's my business, my trouble! Mine to decide how much of it I want to have known and talked about, whether all of it, or some of it, or none of it. And don't let me ever, ever hear you say one word to that child again, Father. I mean it, I mean it!"

Old Bridget, who had been listening from the kitchen, said to Claire—(but she was half talking to herself, Claire knew; she used to mumble in the kitchen: "The bread knife now, where did I put it? Oh, I am so sick of these rheumatics, my poor legs!")—old Bridget said, "Yes, that's what happens when you get old and sick. She would never have got away talking to her father like that before."

Mostly, though, Mother was nice to Grandpa even when he was cross. She always said she was sorry for him because he was old and sick. Maybe she could be very sorry for sick people because she wasn't made right and knew how it felt.

When you walked behind her you could see how one shoulder stuck up so much higher than the other and how the crooked edges of her bones stuck out from under the collars and scarves and all the clothes she wore.

Why didn't she look like other mothers? Why did a person have to have a mother like her?

Yet she could do things the other mothers couldn't do. She could make anything with her hands. She made a patchwork quilt for Claire's bed and silk flowers for the bowl on the hall table. She sewed a Tinkerbell costume for Claire to wear in *Peter Pan*. It was all feathery white, with hidden, tinkling bells that had come from a theatrical costumer's in New York. The teacher kept talking about Claire's costume. She didn't say so, of course, but it was the best costume in the class. Some of the other mothers had used nothing better than crepe paper. The pirate hats didn't fit and kept sliding off.

Today was the final dress rehearsal. Everybody was standing in the schoolyard after lunch waiting for the bell to ring. The teacher was on the steps watching her first-graders. She wore a dress with little flowers all over it. She had pink nails and a new ring like a pearl button, only it was a diamond engagement ring. She was going to be married next month as soon as school was out. Claire wished Miss Donohue was her mother.

They went inside and ran through the rehearsal. The teacher said it was practically perfect. Claire felt so beautiful and so clever, tinkling her bells. And suddenly, when they were just about to take the costumes off, something came into her head, something from that time long, long ago.

"I really saw Peter Pan once," she said. "There's a statue of him in the park in London and I was there with my father."

Jimmy Crater scoffed. "You did not! There isn't any such statue!"

"There is so and I saw it."

"You're a liar."

"I am not. Go ask Miss Donohue."

"Why yes," Miss Donohue said. "Peter Pan in Kensington Gardens. It's famous. Now, who'll help me stack this scenery in a safe corner till tomorrow?"

"There," Claire said, "I told you so."

"Ah, you're full of baloney."

"Am not."

"You never even were in London."

Now a little circle of allies and enemies gathered around Claire and Jimmy Crater.

"I was born in London!" Claire cried triumphantly. "I lived there with my father and mother. I ought to know where I lived!"

"You haven't even got a father," Andy Chapman said.

"I have so. Everybody has a father."

"Oh yeah? Where is he, then?"

"None of your business."

Under the Tinkerbell ruff and fluff, Claire felt the rising heat.

"Hasn't got a father, hasn't got a father!"

Claire stuck out her tongue. "You're mad, Jimmy Crater, because I can knock you down. I'm bigger and stronger and I'm a girl, but I can knock you down!"

Jimmy's fists went up, prizefighter fashion, churning under his chin. Andy, the ally, thrust his up toward Claire.

"Come on! Fight then!" they taunted.

"I don't want to fight, but I can if I have to!"

"Ah, you're scared! You haven't got a father, and your mother's funny-looking, and you're scared!"

Claire's fist struck Jimmy's nose. When he fell, chairs clattered. Andy shoved Claire. They all fell, ripping the Tinkerbell dress down the back. It made a sound as if the cloth were screaming.

Miss Donohue came running. "Boys! Boys! Oh, how awful! What's happening here?"

Claire got up. "Look," she said. "Look what they did."

Miss Donohue turned her around. Her cool fingers fiddled with the cloth at Claire's back, pulling and smoothing.

"I'm sorry, Claire. I'm so sorry. I'll sew it for you, dear, it won't show on stage, I promise. Claire, where're you going? You can't go, school's not out yet!"

But Claire had already gone. Out of the room, out of the building, around the corner she fled.

The streets were empty. Mothers were inside the houses, getting dinner ready. Fathers were away at work. No one would have seen her even if she had been weeping. But she was not weeping. She would not cry. Rage clenched her fists. If Miss Donohue hadn't pulled them apart, she would have beaten those dirty boys!

She took the long way, but she often did that, to pass the houses of her friends and those she had peopled with imaginary relatives. The yellow house with the privet hedge belonged to her best friend, Charlotte, who was home with a cold. If she had been there today, she would have helped Claire fight. Charlotte's house was nice to be in, much nicer than home. Sometimes Claire was invited there for Sunday dinner. They had scatter rugs in their parlor and hall, and after dinner Charlotte's father and mother would roll them up and dance to the victrola. They called it doing the tango. Charlotte's father said he would teach it to them when they were older.

The brick house with the rose garden belonged to an old lady who was always doing things to the flowers. She carried a straw basket and wore straw hats. She always smiled and said hello to Claire, and even though she was old, she was pretty. Claire liked to imagine that this woman was her grandmother. She liked to imagine going to that house on Thanksgiving. There would be aunts and uncles and cousins at the table.

The Hendersons lived across the street from Claire's house. Every Thanksgiving, Claire's mother would look out the window at all the cars driving up to the Hendersons and say, "My, they're having a crowd this year!" Then she would turn and go sit at the table with Grandpa and Claire.

Sometimes Claire would go to the kitchen after dinner and have a second dessert with Bridget, who could be very jolly when she wanted to be, but often wasn't. Mother said Bridget was cranky because all the other help had been let go, so she had everything to do herself. Anyway, she was getting old and would soon be going to Florida to live with her niece in a warm climate. And then they would have to find another maid because, afford it or not, Mother certainly couldn't be expected to take care of a big house like this herself. That's what Aunt Milly said, anyway. Mother said she could if she had to. She said you could do anything if you set your mind to it. Aunt Milly said Mother was a wonder, but she was too hard on herself.

Claire liked it when Aunt Milly came to stay a few days. She had a nice, chuckling laugh and always brought good presents, besides. She was visiting them now, sitting with Mother on the front porch. There was no way to get into the house without their seeing her. So she slid through the shrubbery, under the mulberry bush. If they saw her, there would be fuss and questions: Why had she left school early? Why was the costume torn? Her mother would scold and scold, as if it wasn't all her fault in the first place. I hate my mother, Claire thought.

The mulberry bush was like a little private house with soft, green walls. You could sit there by yourself and think, could swallow the lump in your throat until you didn't feel like crying anymore. You could listen to interesting conversations on the porch or watch ants building a nest. They were building one now, marching in a long procession through the tunnel they had made. Each one was carrying something, a seed or a dead bug. One of them had a piece of leaf bigger than itself! Uncle Drew said there were rooms underground at the end of the tunnel where they stored their food and kept their babies. He said it took them days to build all that. You could wreck it all, squash it with your foot, in a second if you wanted. But that would be mean. Poor things.

"Claire, is that you? What are you doing?" her mother cried.

"Sitting under the mulberry bush."

"I can see you are. But what are you doing there?"

"I'm watching ants."

"Ants! For Heaven's sake!"

"Why not? They're a whole lot better than dolls!"

"Well, come on out, will you? Goodness, your Tinkerbell costume! It's all torn! And your face is scratched! What happened?"

"I had a fight with two boys."

"Oh my," Aunt Milly said. "Oh my, I'm surprised! A dear little girl like you!"

"No, no, Aunt Milly," Mother said. "Claire, do you want to tell me what it was about?"

"No," Claire said. *It was about you, stupid. All your fault.*

"Well, but you know you mustn't get into punching fights. Girls don't do that."

"Why can't they? Why can boys do everything. It isn't fair."

"But you don't want to be a boy, do you?"

"No. I want to be a girl who can do the things boys do."

"It doesn't work that way."

"Why?"

"I don't know. It's just the way things are."

"Then I don't like the way things are."

"You will, though. You'll grow up and be very, very pretty. And a wonderful man will come along and want to take care of you." Mother stroked Claire's hair back from her forehead. "Come and we'll put peroxide on that scratch."

She followed the lopsided back upstairs. The little bells tinkled sadly. No man was taking care of Mother except Grandpa, and he didn't count. No man like

Charlotte's father danced with her. Because she was funny-looking, that was why, just as Jimmy Crater said. Claire's eyes filled with tears, and this time they leaked over.

"Ouch! You're making my eyes sting with that peroxide!"

"It's not this little bit of peroxide. You're crying."

"I am not crying!"

"Yes, you are. Is it because the costume's torn? It's too bad, but I can fix it. I'll have it ready for you in the morning."

"I'm not going to school in the morning."

"Not going to be in the play."

"I don't want to be in the play."

Mother shook her head. "I don't believe that," she said gently.

If her mother had been angry, Claire would have been angry right back. She had no fear. But sympathy brings more tears; already she had learned that much about her own emotions. So she stood there with her small chest heaving, an ache in her throat and a stinging behind her eyes.

Mother looked away. She seemed to be looking all around the room: at the floor, where bright spots flickered as the wind moved in the new-leaved maple at the window; at the walls and the ceiling; everywhere except at Claire. Then, in that same quiet voice, she spoke.

"I won't be coming to the play tomorrow, either, or to the picnic afterward. I've too many things to do at home."

But that's not true, Claire thought. She wanted to come! She's been talking and talking about it. Then why?

Her mother seemed to be thinking of something, making up her mind, the way she did when she was deciding on turkey or lamb or on whether Claire might go to Charlotte's house or not. She was so quiet for such a long time that Claire was suddenly afraid. Maybe her mother was going to cry? Mothers weren't supposed to cry; if mothers cried it meant that something must be terribly wrong and bad, something that would make you feel lost—

At last her mother spoke. Her voice was strange, not like any of her ordinary voices, scolding or in a hurry or simply telling something.

"Oh, you've had a bad time, a terrible day, haven't you? I know, I know! It's awful for you because I look so queer next to the other mothers. And you have no father. You can't even say he's dead, can you? Like the McMath children, whose father died and everybody went to the funeral, so they knew." Now she looked at Claire. She grasped Claire's shoulders and held them hard. "But I'll make it up to you. I owe it to you and I will. I don't know how, but I swear I will."

The words were almost angry, but Claire knew her mother wasn't angry. It was scary in a way. Yet in another way it was like the times her mother put bandages on cuts and made things all right, and was so strong.

"Come to the play tomorrow," she whispered. "I want you to come, Mama."

"Do you truly? You don't have to say so if you don't mean it."

"I mean it," Claire said. "I want you to."

⊰{16}⊱

Sky-glow come through the slatted blinds, marking the walls in zebra stripes. The city sky was never truly dark; the city never truly slept. A truck ground gears; a tugboat hooted on the river; pigeons clattered on the windowsill. Martin looked at the clock. It was five in the morning and he had set the alarm for six. This had been happening to him of late, this early waking, with troubled mind alert and turning. Softly, he slid out of bed into chill air, drawing the blanket back around Hazel's shoulders.

In the other room he went to the window and looked down onto the street. A couple in evening clothes got out of a taxi; the woman wore long, rich furs. For a moment or two, as they crossed the sidewalk, he could hear their bright voices. From a private house in the formal, nineteenth-century row on the other side of the street, a man emerged and got into a car. He was carrying a suitcase. A woman stood in the doorway, waving good-bye to him. Was he leaving early to attend the funeral of a relative in Boston, or embarking for adventure in Calcutta? The mystery of other lives, the barriers between them and his own life, the uncertainties of all lives, saddened Martin always, but more so in this dimmest hour of the night.

Kahn, the cat, climbed out of his basket, stretched, and coming to Martin, rubbed between his ankles in an S-curve, then sat back to regard him with a calculating stare. It was as if the creature felt his tensions. Its eyes glittered, two green light bulbs implanted in smoky fur. A child had placed the kitten on his desk one day when it was small enough to fit in a man's hand. He bent to stroke it, and the animal purred its pleasure. Then, having had enough, it walked off into the bedroom and leapt to the bed at Hazel's feet.

Light turned mother-of-pearl now at the edge of darkness. From where he stood, Martin could just discern the curve of Hazel's arm and the long spread of her hair on the pillow. Mild September brown, he thought: she was so warm, so absolutely warm! Most women had cold hands and feet; not she. Her body had deep curves, tempered a little to modern taste: powerful, rosy thighs, great firm breasts, strong shoulders. What dogged generations of survival it took to produce that vigor!

And yet the rest of her—spirit, psyche, whatever you wanted to call it—was total contradiction. You had only to catch her unaware to know that. Innocence, he thought, as intrinsic as the whorls on the fingertips. She did not even know that her flesh was voluptuous! How would you describe her? A simple person? She had such pleasure in small things—a row on the lake in Central Park, a movie and ice cream afterward. She took the complications out of living. She was restful. In her presence you could feel that people were good and the world a hopeful place.

And yet—and yet she was not happy. Her tears, or rather the traces of her tears which she always tried to hide, disturbed him, and he would feel obliged to question her, although he knew the reason quite well.

"It's nothing," she would say, denying because she was afraid of driving him away. She wanted him to marry her. She loved him: her twining arms when they lay together, her beating heart against his chest—she loved him.

She had scruples. It cost her much to do what she did not believe in doing, and to hide it from her family, besides. He had met the family twice. Grimly, he recalled the noisy immigrant home in Flushing: the parents; the sister; Rudy and Ernest, the huge brothers; all the other brothers and sisters-in-law. Hospitable, honest people, they were frankly impressed with the American doctor. They liked him. But they were straitlaced, too, and wouldn't take kindly to this at all if they knew. No, not at all.

Why hadn't he married her? Why was he holding back? Waiting for that old first longing, the sweet obsession? But perhaps the obsession was something one did better without. Four years since . . . He went into the kitchenette to heat water for tea, having acquired the English morning habit. Tea worked against the seeping cold on days like this. In the refrigerator stood a covered bowl of goulash, left from the previous night's supper, and a dish of cucumbers in dill sauce. Hazel was a homemaker, maker of a home. Such strange, delicious foods she provided! Such warmth in her kitchen, such fragrance of rich cabbage soup and cinnamon-scent of pudding!

Once, in some context or other, he had said to her, "Food is a way of giving love, you know."

And she had answered, "What difference does it make? Psychologists only put names to what everybody's known all along."

She had a way of coming to the heart of things. It had occurred to him momentarily that that was a trait of Jessie's, too, but then he had realized that in Hazel it was just naivete, which was certainly not like Jessie at all!

"It's so beautiful!" Hazel had remarked the first time he'd brought her to his home. And she had walked around the two plain rooms, looking and touching. She had been impressed by his books and his father's medical diploma from Edinburgh, written in Latin and festooned with ribbons and seals. She had admired the etching of the Parthenon, to which, in a rare moment of semiextravagance, he had treated himself.

"You're giving your plants too much water," she had informed him. "It drowns the roots. That's why the leaves look yellow."

He remembered everything of that first time. She had known he was going to take her to bed. Wanting it, she had also feared it. And he thought, as he very often thought: *Poor women. One can be so sorry for women.*

He felt much tenderness for Hazel, and believed he saw her clearly. She was a woman afraid she would never be married, or would have to marry some beefy fellow like her brothers. She was afraid of growing fat, like her mother. Afraid of being overdressed or underdressed; of having had insufficient education and not recognizing music or having read books that other people had read; of not possessing the virtues of the refined middle class.

At Christmas, Martin had brought his mother to the city for a week's visit. Christmas had been tinctured with a bitter taste ever since his father's death, and he had hoped to enliven it for her with the glitter of theaters and restaurants. One evening he had brought Hazel to the hotel for dinner, and his mother had immediately liked her.

"There's a girl who could make you very happy, Martin," she had told him.

Yes, his mother would see that! It had occurred to him lately that Hazel was quite like his mother—except, he thought ruefully, his mother, being of a different generation, was far less forbearing. (She had never asked about Jessie or what had happened. She was a lady, brought up not to mention painful subjects and not to want to hear about them either.)

On a spring Sunday he had taken Hazel to Tom's house. And afterward Tom and Flo had got onto the subject, too. Why didn't he marry her? You didn't find women like Hazel on every street corner! What was he waiting for? But he had fended them off with a feeble joke about Tom's being Hungarian, like Hazel. He wouldn't let anyone pin him down, and wouldn't pin himself down.

Certainly he was doing well enough to support a family—not splendidly—but who except for a glamorous few in this somber decade could think of splendor? He was doing surprisingly well. His name was appearing more and more frequently on the operating schedule at Fisk. He was acquiring a bit of a name. Among the younger general men he had made friends; they played handball with him and biked in Central Park on Sundays; they referred their patients to him because they respected his work. Also, they approved of his fees, which were surely more reasonable than Eastman's!

And remembering Eastman's ornate house, his office with its Circassian walnut paneling and its Oriental carpets, Martin felt a certain satisfaction. His own office in a modest building on a side street was functional. There were no excessive costs to pass on to the patients. He had time to spare for teaching, good teaching, and research. In a couple of years he might even be needing a second man, someone who might want to work with him on his dream of a neurological institute—his pipe dream.

Having drunk the tea, he went back to the living room, closed the bedroom door and put the new record player on very softly. Mr. and Mrs. Moser had given it to him on the anniversary of their daughter's operation, along with the happy news that she was playing tennis again.

He laid his head back while daylight crept and the Bach *Magnificat* sang. God, to be able to say it all as those old masters had said it! All the splendor, the beauty, the love! One wanted it so, and sometimes found a bit of it, and then lost it.

My life is half over, he thought. I'm thirty-seven.

On the bookshelf at his elbow stood a small framed snapshot of Hazel standing in front of a hydrangea bush. She was holding Tom's and Flo's newest baby.

"That becomes you, Hazel," Tom had said and Flo had frowned at him. The frown meant, "Don't embarrass the girl, for goodness' sake!" In the eye and ear of his mind, he recalled the day: Tom's dowdy, cheerful Dutch colonial, the scuffed woodwork, the tricycles and high chairs and all the noise. Why did it ache in him, in him who loved order and serenity and quiet?

In the park where he sometimes walked with Hazel on Sundays, a father and a little boy came to sail a toy boat. Other fathers slid and shouted at ball. And he would stop to watch them. Machismo, was it? A man wanting a son? Yes, yes, as old as time, that was! But a daughter, a daughter was—and he thought of Claire again. Not an hour passed on any day without some glancing thought of her. How much of him could she remember? Slipped from his hold, forever lost and gone, like Mary.

The music stopped. Carefully, he slid the record back into its cardboard case. I am overwhelmed with loneliness, he thought. Overwhelmed with it.

Hazel coughed. It was almost six, and she too must rise and go to work. She wasn't one of that spoiled lot that men complained of, telling in the locker room how their wives nagged when an emergency spoiled a dinner party. No, Hazel was solid, kind and durable. And in her flesh also, a man could find the oblivion which ends in ease.

She loved a wedding! He smiled to himself. She had invited him to her brother's wedding; the ceremony had moved him more than he would have thought possible. The bride was nineteen and pale at first under the lace cap, but afterward rosy as a child, and Hazel's eyes had filled, thinking—how well he had known what she was thinking!

"You'll have no trouble with the word 'obey,' " the minister had said, "although it is becoming the fashion to omit it."

Well, he wouldn't try to force 'obedience': Hazel needn't worry about that. How glad she would be! And how glad he, to be what he had never been: the giver. Giver, firstly, of material things. And don't, he thought grimly, don't ever sell that short. Would he ever forget the hard years, his mother's dread when the bills arrived? No, don't sell it short, for the peace and calm it brings. So he would be a giver of that peace and calm. Something swept through him, a fine resolution, a purity of hope.

He opened the bedroom door. Full daylight lay now over the bed. Her face was half buried in the pillow, but she heard him come in and stirred, and gave him her lovely, curving smile. He laid his cheek on the warm, spread hair.

"Wake up," he whispered. "Wake up. I want to ask you something."

❊⟨17⟩❊

Nineteen thirty-seven was the darkest year, the lowest year, when the stone struck the bottom of the well and sent a dismal echo. Jessie sat before the desk where bank statements, tax bills and accountants' reports were spread. Oh, the darkest year, in which Father's heart had finally given out and the Websterware plant, after three-quarters of a century, had closed its doors!

She raised her eyes from the papers to rest them, having been at the desk since morning. A monotonous winter rain poured from the somber sky, pitting the broken ice and mushy snow on the lawn. Where the snow washed away, soaked earth lay exposed like soft brown pudding. This was the fifth month of winter. It had come early, yet when had it not come early in this part of the world? And she thought, looking out upon the bleak day, that June could never have been in this place and would never come to it again.

Place where I was born, you have grown cold to me. You have a stranger's face. Once I belonged here and was intimately known (in London, or any other place, I was a sojourner, an observer). The genteel, passing on a Cyprus street, looked considerately into my face and never allowed their eyes to fall upon my crooked shape. The workmen in my father's factory would quickly tip their caps and turn away. Now they are unemployed and don't tip their caps, certainly not to me. My taxes are in arrears. There is really no excuse, Depression or no, for the mess we are in, Claire and I. Something could have been salvaged! How many times I told Father, I warned him, to cheapen the line to fit the times! Who buys copper pots, fit for the kitchens of aristocrats, in times like these! Better if he had given more thought to business instead of ranting these last years about Martin and my sister!

I remember the night I couldn't stand it anymore. I told him I wouldn't listen to another word and when he kept on, I threw a lamp across the room. I had never done a thing like that in all my life and I despise vulgarity, but I did it.

In the morning Father said, "I hope you will apologize."

The pieces hadn't yet been swept away. It was a hideous lamp, a Greek goddess with a fixture growing out of her head, ugly and expensive, like everything we own. Yet when I saw it shattered on the floor, I was terribly ashamed. But I would not apologize.

"No," I said, "I was driven. You drove. I've told you I don't want to hear any more about Martin."

And Father at last was silent.

I feel so sorry for Martin. Isn't that strange? *Sorry for him? Sorry for Fern?* But I knew about them from the very first, that's the reason. When they stood together in this dim house, in the corner next to the potted palm, I knew. When they came walking out of the orchard at Lamb House, I knew again. They might not have known, or wanted to, but I did. Those eyes of hers! Lapis lazuli, someone said. Just two eyes after all, and if they had been brown or gray, would that have made a difference?

Still, it would have been no good for Martin and me even if Fern had not existed. Oh, we would have stayed on and eked out a life, but what good would it have been? I'm too proud for that. Does it seem strange that a woman who looks like me can indulge herself with pride? Pride's a luxury, isn't it? But that's the way I am.

Yes, I cried my tears in the beginning, cried in bitter shame, in outrage and loneliness, even in despair: what was I to do with my life? Life, though, has a way of answering that; grief passes as other trouble comes to take its place.

So: I don't hate, but I don't love anymore, either. Let them live and prosper, far from me. Certainly my sister prospers in her English garden. And Martin? Well, let him make of his career what he can, and he will probably make a good deal of it.

But the child—the child is mine.

Across the hall, Aunt Milly had been fiddling with the radio. What ever could she have done with her time before the thing was invented? Kate Smith's hearty voice cheered her; Amos and Andy amused; the tribulations of King Edward and Mrs. Simpson enthralled her. Now, though, she switched it off and came to the door.

"Jessie, aren't you through yet? Why don't you give yourself a rest?"

"I have to go over these figures before the tax people come." She felt a wry smile stretching her cheeks. "They're coming here instead of my going to the town hall, as I rightly should. Deference to my crippled state, I suppose. Or else in memory of the glory that was once the Meigs'."

Aunt Milly's rosy old face puckered. "Jessie, I wish you'd let me help out. That's why your uncle sent me up this week, to see what we could do. We can't do a great deal, it's true, we've been hit like everyone else, but I'm sure we could manage something."

"No. Thank you, but no, Aunt Milly. I've got to stand on my own feet. Temporary help wouldn't solve anything, anyway. I'd only be worried about paying you back."

A car door slammed and Jessie peered out the window.

"They're here. Two of them. Donovan's from the tax office and the bald one's Jim Reeve, the new mayor."

"Would you like me to stay for moral support?"

Jessie shook her head. Poor Aunt Milly, whose very maids had always ordered her about, to give support?

"No, dear. You go read in the parlor. This won't take very long."

"AFTER ALL, YOU'RE now two years in arrears," Donovan said. He had the placid manner of the overfed, but his voice was not as mild as it had been half an hour earlier.

"I suppose I'm the only one in town who is!"

"Of course not. But that's got nothing to do with this case."

"Naturally," Reeve added, "there are plenty who've fallen on hard times. But sooner or later they're bound to go to work again and be able to pay up. In your situation, though—"

Jessie felt herself stripped naked before these men. Sweat gathered under her arms and on the palms of her hands. Four generations of Meigs had lived in this house, and during all those years no men such as these could ever have been invited to sit down in the parlor. Yet now, in the arrogance of their picayune power, they had come to tell her they had the means to confiscate the house itself! And enjoyed the telling too, without a doubt! Donovan, whose nails were dirty, was unconsciously picking at the brocade braiding on the sofa, loosening the strands. She opened her mouth to chide him and stopped; the thing was hideous anyway.

"I will not let you sell my house for taxes," she said instead, surprising herself.

"Now really," Donovan began, "we came here to talk sense. We don't want to argue. This is no pleasure for us, I assure you."

"Oh, it's a pleasure for you, all right! You can't flimflam me! It's the best fun you've had in a long time. But let me tell you something. I'll burn the house down before I let you take it away." She caught her breath. "Don't look so amused. I know quite well I'd be arrested for arson. But that wouldn't help you, would it? And what worth is a vacant lot in these times?" She turned to Reeve. "Listen, I happen to know you've had your eye on this house. You'd like to live in it."

Reeve had a nervous twitch and now his eye jumped. "I don't know where you could've got that idea. I never—"

"Come on, come on. Let's not waste each other's time. This is a small town and word gets around. I know your wife wants this house. Very well, then. Give me a fair price, and she can have it."

There was silence. Donovan lit a cigar, and Reeve stared down at the floor. Then he asked. "What's a fair price?" His eye had gone quite wild and there was a hot flush on the crown of his head.

"Twenty-eight thousand dollars. That's what the Critchleys got down the street. Theirs is a twin house to this one."

"That was a year ago. Prices have fallen since."

"Twenty-eight thousand dollars," Jessie repeated. "Less the back taxes."

Then Donovan said, "You're forgetting. We can take the house for taxes and put it up for public sale."

He owes Reeve a favor, she thought instantly.

"Public sale!" she said with scorn. "You don't expect me to believe that? You think you'll get the house for half-nothing, don't you?" She lowered her voice. "Listen here, my great-grandfather gave employment to half the people of this town. Where did your father work, Mr. Reeve?"

Reeve smiled slightly. "At Webster's."

"And your grandfather?"

Reeve sighed. "At Webster's. What's the point of all this?"

"The point is that you wouldn't be mayor, you probably wouldn't have gone beyond the eighth grade, if it hadn't been for that job. You'd be raising potatoes, and you wouldn't have the faintest chance at a house like this."

Donovan took out his pocket watch. "You still haven't got to the point."

Jessie breathed deeply. "Well, I'm getting to it. You either give me a fair price for this house, or I go to the newspapers and tell them you've got a private deal to take it for taxes and buy it cheap yourself. Then you'd have to put it up for public sale, and I'd get a decent price after the tax lien had been paid. And you'd have a lot of explaining to do."

Donovan put his watch back in his pocket and looked at Reeve with a silent question. Jessie stared out the window, watching the rain, listening to its thirsty gurgle in the gutters. Maybe it won't be so bad to get out of here, she thought. Except that, for the life of me, I don't know where I'll go.

Presently Reeve said, "I'll bargain with you. I'll give you twenty-five, less the taxes."

"Twenty-eight, Mr. Reeve. Take it or leave it."

"Twenty-six and that's overpaying."

"It's not and you know it. Twenty-eight, Mr. Reeve."

Reeve got out of the chair. "Twenty-seven and not a cent more."

She saw that he had gone as far as he would go and thought quickly: So, a thousand less. I didn't expect to get what I asked, anyway. That's how business is done. She held her hand out.

"We'll shake on it, then. And good luck to us both."

Aᴜɴᴛ Mɪʟʟʏ ᴛʀᴇᴍʙʟᴇᴅ. "Jessie, you were marvelous! I couldn't help but hear. Oh, to tell the truth, I listened at the door, I was so worried. I don't know how you did it. I couldn't have, not in a million years."

"It only worked because there were two of them. Reeve obviously thought over what I said about the newspapers. He's in a worrisome position, after all. There've been rumors that Donovan's brother-in-law, the contractor who built the new high school gym, gave them a kickback. So naturally they don't want the papers to have anything else to probe into. The timing was right and my little stratagem just happened to work, that's all."

"You were so splendidly furious, Jessie!"

"I was furious, all right. I've been half-crazy with worry and angry over being worried. That's how I was feeling when those two walked in, so I just took it all out on them."

"Well, you were splendid," Aunt Milly repeated, adding, "But where will you go?"

"Believe it or not, I haven't the faintest idea."

"Oh, dear Heaven!" Aunt Milly murmured. Her chubby hands clasped and unclasped. "Your father—I know he was troubled about the way things were, but I'm sure he never dreamed the plant would actually shut down! And your mother! When I think of her, so delicate and cared for, I'm just so upset . . . . Don't you think you really ought to ask for help now? For Claire's sake?"

"If you mean I should go to Martin, you can save your breath. We made a bargain: a painless divorce in return for his not coming near us ever again."

"But—" Aunt Milly argued faintly, "times change, and you know he'd want to do everything he could for the child; you know how he adored her."

"Yes, and I don't intend to reawaken the whole business just because I need money. It's a closed chapter." Jessie's voice quavered, and she thought: It's been a terrible day; I could just lay my head down and cry. She steadied her voice. "I have to be independent. I have to."

"Only one more question. I don't know why you never want to tell me, but do you ever hear from him?"

"In the beginning I did, but not anymore."

"You know he's married again? I heard quite by accident from a woman who lives in the same apartment house."

Jessie made no answer. A burning soreness which had been absent a long time spread in her chest. Aunt Milly lit another lamp, drawing an amoeba shape of sickly yellow light on the floor. The glass eyes glittered in the deerhead on the wall and the room wavered in gloom.

"God, I hate this damned room!" Jessie cried suddenly. "To think we spent most of our lives in it!"

"You're upset, and no wonder. Come out on the sun porch and unwind a bit. Then we'll talk about what you're going to do." The clear little voice chirped kindly, "Goodness, what you've done with this porch! It's like sunshine even on a day like this."

The old wicker furniture and the floor had been painted. A round indigo rug with a scalloped ruby border lay in the center of the floor. Ferns flowed out of hanging baskets at the windows. A brass Indian jug held knitting needles and wool. The room had the boldness and cheerful confidence that is unconcerned with fashion; because everything in it was inexpensive and of purest taste, it looked like a rich man's simple country retreat.

"I'm glad you got rid of those depressing palms. Uncle Drew always said they belonged in a funeral parlor. And the rug is handsome."

"I hooked it myself. Have to have something to do in the evenings besides read."

Aunt Milly looked thoughtful. "It's really different, Jessie! Original and bright. Somehow it belongs to this century. Do you know what I mean? I do believe you're an artist, my dear!"

"I'm certainly not an artist."

"Well, I think you are!"

Jessie closed her eyes. The adrenaline having poured, exhaustion now followed. Nevertheless, her thoughts spun.

At least there would be some money from the house: a respite of sorts. But it

was no permanent solution. Oh, if she were a man, she would have been educated for something! But being a woman and a cripple—loathsome word, although the euphemisms were no better—you were supposed to stay home and be
taken care of. Yes, but what if it didn't work out that way? What then? I could
have run the plant much better than Father did, she thought. I'm not being
conceited, either. I know my defects well enough! I'm sharp-tongued; I tend to be
bossy. I've got to watch that. But I know I could have run the plant much better
than Father did. I can handle people. I'm not afraid of them, at least not as much
as to let it show. And I've always had a head for figures.

"I never liked it here, do you know that?" Aunt Milly startled the silence. "I
always felt sorry for your mother, gay as she was, having to hibernate in Cyprus.
It's only a factory town, plopped down among the farms. Fine if you're a farmer
or you work in the factory, but otherwise there's nothing here. Especially for you,
Jessie. Let's speak frankly. Small towns like this are narrow-minded. They put
people in slots. You've always been that 'poor Meig girl.' And now you're poorer
than ever."

"What are you driving at?"

"I think you ought to leave, that's what. You have nothing in Cyprus except
memories. And some of those you'd be better off without."

Always, there was perversity in Jessie. She had never really liked it here and
yet since it was, after all, home, she felt obliged to defend it.

"We had some good years before Mother died. You forget," she said stubbornly.

"I know, but they're over. You know what? You ought to come to New York."

"And what would I do in New York, tell me that?"

"For one thing, Uncle Drew and I would be there, so you wouldn't be entirely
alone. And you know what else? I think you should go into the decorating
business."

"Decorating! For Heaven's sake! You think that's easy? I couldn't just put a
sign up and open the door!"

"Well, of course not. But you do have marvelous taste. And you've always
made a hobby of antiques; you must have taught yourself a lot."

"I've had no training! I couldn't possibly—"

"You could take courses toward a degree while you were working. It's been
done."

"And where would I find customers?"

"I could start you off. I know two people already. There's a Mrs. Beech who
has a little summer place in the Berkshires. A room like this one would appeal to
her. Then there's a friend of mine whose daughter's being married. They're pretty
strapped financially, but I know you could fix an apartment for her without
spending too much." Aunt Milly held two fingers up. "That's two, possibly a
third. And those women would recommend you to their friends; that's how it
would grow. Jessie, I believe you could do it."

For the moment, Jessie had nothing to say. The idea was so foolish, so daring,
that no sensible answer could weigh against it. On the floor near her chair, Claire
had left a half-done jigsaw puzzle of George Washington at Valley Forge.

Thoughtfully, Jessie studied it, then leaned down and fitted a piece of Mad Anthony Wayne onto his horse.

"You'd have the money from the house to start with," Aunt Milly urged.

True. And perhaps with very good management and very good luck, it might work. As Aunt Milly said, it had been done before. No. No. It was crazy!

"The world isn't waiting for me, for Jessie Meig," she said.

"The world isn't waiting for anybody."

That was true, too . . . To be one's own mistress! Never to have to ask anybody for anything! Imagine it! Ah, but it was crazy, impossible—

"It would be a whole other environment for you, Jessie. Cosmopolitan people are so much more tolerant. You wouldn't be an oddity, if that's what you're afraid of. A thousand circles crisscross the city with all kinds of people—foreign, artistic, old money, new money—all kinds."

True. True. And there were such fine schools in the city. Enrichment. Small classes. Claire at Brearley or Spence. That bright, busy mind being fed. Expensive, but what could be more worth working for?

Here the tail went onto the horse; there went a piece of an officer's tricornered hat; a gilt button; a section of split-rail fence. After long minutes, Jessie looked up. A kind of daring, scared excitement raced through her, catching in her throat.

"You know, Aunt Milly, you may be right! And after all, I don't have a wealth of other choices, do I?"

On the final morning, she rose early and threaded her way through cartons and barrels to the kitchen. For the last time, she put the coffee on and in a kind of mental fog, waited while the water purred. Two pairs of mourning doves, colored a rosy fawn in the first light, were at the feeder. Fern's favorite birds, she thought, with a little stab of memory, and stood there listening to their plaint until, something having startled them, they flew off with a squeaky rattle and twitter.

From the farms a quarter of a mile away, a rooster cried its clarion command to the sun and was answered all around the countryside with jubilant and pompous yawp: Behold the day! The old and peaceful, common sounds of home!

"I'm a teary mess," she said aloud, "and I don't want to be. I can't afford it. I've got to make sense and order. God, how do I know I can?"

For the last time, she went outside to walk around the house. The gravel crunched and the wet grass was fragrant. Above her rose the tower with its gingerbread carvings: carpenter-gothic was the style. Its attic had been emptied of three generations' flotsam: Grandfather's motheaten billiard table, a chewed wicker puppy-basket and Father's gold-tipped walking stick from his dapper youth. Also Fern's bridal photograph, which Father had tossed there when Jessie came home.

She went back into the house and stood in the bay window where the minister had married her to Martin, she knowing all the time that it was wrong.

So he had married again! A beauty this time, a beauty like Fern? A woman whose naked body he could adore, not pity or shudder at? And what of Fern, whom certainly he had adored? Who loved her now? Did he, still? And if so, why then— Dammit, enough of this! You'll get nowhere, Jessie! Some things are for you and some things are not. Haven't you learned that yet?

Six o'clock. She went softly up the stairs. Outside Claire's door stood a carton of books with ice skates and a child's tennis racket on top. A terrible, crazy panic started in her. What if anything were ever to happen to the child? What if she had died during the night? Oh God! She pushed the door open and went in.

Claire's long legs lumped the blanket almost as far as the end of the bed. Normal! Tall, straight and perfect! Her mother's affliction, thank Heaven, was no inherited thing, but only one of nature's little miscalculations. Like an albino elephant.

The small hand gripped the corner of the pillowcase. Such a vigorous child she was, curious and determined! Not the easiest to rear, but a treasure. A treasure. She shall have everything, Jessie thought, all the joys: dresses, dances, lovers and trips to the stars. And they will all come from me. Damned if they won't.

She leaned over and touched the child on the shoulder. "Come, darling. Time to get up. Time to go."

❈{18}❈

From her place at the breakfast table Claire couldn't see the back yard, but she knew that the skimpy forsythia had stretched weak yellow strands over all the board fences between Park and Lexington Avenues. In their own yard, a few scattered hyacinths, left over from what must once have been a lavish garden, had poked through the hard earth. Sparrows chittered and fought. They always grew more strident as spring approached.

Jessie mused across the toast and cereal. "Someday I want to do the whole yard, build a terrace and plant trees. Oh, what jewels these old brownstones are! Just look at those tiles! You'll never see work like that again."

Blue tiles covered the fireplace wall. Painted on each was a musical instrument: violin, flute, drum or horn—ten in all, before the pattern was repeated. Claire had counted.

"Portuguese," Jessie said. "The man who owned this house before the bank foreclosed was a music critic or professor, I think. Poor man." She sighed. "This room must have been his study."

Every day Jessie just walked around admiring things: the ten-foot ceilings, the pineapple newel posts, the pegged floors.

"This house was built with love," she would say.

Claire was bored by such preoccupation with the house. The only thing she really admired was the dumbwaiter on which the meals were hauled up from the kitchen. They ate on the third floor because the dining room was occupied by the business.

Jessie reflected now, "Funny, I had to pay about as much for this little place as we got for the big house and one and a half acres back home. You know, I've been thinking, I may rent a proper shop over near Madison Avenue. I saw one that's fairly cheap. And the business really needs more space. Then we'd have the whole house to live in." She sighed again, but this time it was a satisfied sigh. "You know Mrs. Brickner, the one who comes with the Pekinese? She wants me to do an apartment for her in Palm Beach. Things haven't gone too badly for us, have they Claire?" And, without expecting an answer, Jessie picked up *The New York Times*. "It's not polite to read at the table, but breakfast is different," she said.

Claire had expected her to say it, since she did so every morning. She waited for her mother to hand over the second section.

"Here, you read, too. You ought to know what's going on in the world, now you're in fifth grade. Yes, look, the ad for that store is in again. Maybe I'll ask your Uncle Drew what he thinks. Or maybe I'll just go ahead myself and take it. These bad times can't last forever, can they? And I could be ahead of the game with a long lease at low rent. Anyway, the people who have been coming to me don't seem to be suffering from the bad times, I must say." The paper crackled as the pages were turned. "You know, sometimes I wake up and for a minute I think I've just been dreaming about these last three years."

Claire didn't hear the rest. Out of all the thousands of black letters on the spread page, her eye had fastened on a handful, the few that spelled a name: *Dr. Martin Farrell*. First there was something boring about speeches at the Academy of Medicine, then a short list of names. *Dr. Martin Farrell* stood out from the rest as if it had been printed in red.

This name was never spoken at home. She had not thought about it for a long time, either, not since she had been quite young. The image "father" came to mind when it did, without specific features, in a sort of blur made up of large-ness, tobacco smell and harsh wool. Her concept of "man" came, naturally, from the men she knew: friends' fathers, the school principal, the doctor and the dentist, with something also of Uncle Drew, a pale figure who sat back while Aunt Milly did the talking and who, in a restaurant, added up the bill and paid. Of course, there had been Grandpa, but he was dead, and she had been only six when he died in his upstairs room with its sour smell. These, then, were the models out of which "father" was constructed and it existed in some vague recollection, some old sense of loss, long ago.

Surreptitiously, she passed her hand over the print: *Dr. Martin Farrell*. It must be the right one. There wouldn't be two, would there?

"It's eight-fifteen," Jessie said suddenly, lowering *The Times*, "and you haven't finished your breakfast."

Claire picked up the spoon and began swallowing cereal. Something had fixed itself in her head, something so hard and solid that it was surprising that she had not thought of it before. She drank the milk and got her coat. Jessie tied her tartan scarf and kissed her forehead.

"Be careful at the crossing," she admonished, as she did every morning. "You coming right home after school or going to Carol's house?"

"Carol's got a cold. I'll come home," Claire said.

She went downstairs. From the front hall, you could look into the shop, which took up the whole first floor. Along one wall were dark shelves with shining objects on them: a marble head of Shakespeare, a clock with a gilded face, candelabra and a porcelain tureen with blue roses on it. Pieces of beautiful cloth were spread like fans on the backs of chairs. There were old, carved chests of drawers and many little tables. There were lamps and pictures and a crimson velvet sofa. All of these things were for sale except her mother's desk with its tidy, stacked papers and its telephone. Aunt Milly and Uncle Drew said Mother was very clever, and it was astonishing what she had managed to do in only three years. Yes, her mother was very smart. But she was not thinking of her mother.

She hurried down the front steps between the two stone urns, each with its evergreen like a toy soldier in stiff salute. Under the bay window was a neat, small sign: Jessie Meig, Interiors. It still bothered Claire that her mother's name was different from her own. Sometimes people asked about it. Her mother said it didn't matter, that here in the city divorce wasn't anything to be shocked about. Claire knew that was true. There were three other girls in school whose parents were divorced, so it was not at all the way it had been in Cyprus. Still, for some reason, it bothered her this morning.

She went down Sixty-seventh Street swinging her bag of books, arrived at school, sat at her desk and went to lunch as on any ordinary day. But a curious excitement stirred in her all that time.

THE SUBWAY SWAYED and roared. She had never been alone in it before. She had copied the address out of the phone book, shown it to the man in the change booth, and been told to take the Lexington Avenue line, get off at 125th Street, then walk two blocks east and one block north.

This was adventure! Being alone and going somewhere was adventure. She thought of Boadicea, blond and bold with her crown, commanding troops against the Romans. She thought of an Indian princess with coarse black braids as glossy as a horse's tail, riding in prairie wind toward where the Rockies rose.

Suddenly in the window across the aisle, her own reflection flashed. With the green school skirt hanging below the hem of her coat and the plaid wool scarf around her neck, she bore no resemblance to Boadicea or an Indian heroine, either.

Suppose he didn't want to see her? Suppose he had a lot of other children by now and hadn't told anyone about Claire? He might even be terribly angry! Yet something drove her on. She had the directions firmly fixed and didn't even need to read them again. It puzzled her, when she climbed back up to the lofty afternoon, that all the people on the streets were Negroes. The boys jostling home from school and the women carrying grocery bags were all black. It didn't seem like New York at all. But she walked briskly, found the correct address, and sure enough, there was a sign in the first-floor window: Dr. M. T. Farrell.

She rang the bell and a tall black man with curly white hair, wearing a white coat, came to the door. He seemed surprised.

"I'm looking for Dr. Farrell," Claire said.

"I'm Dr. Farrell. Come in."

She wasn't sure what to do next, but she said politely, "I'm looking for my father, Dr. Farrell."

The man smiled. "Well, it's too bad, but it seems you've come to the wrong place."

She had worked up so much courage and energy and now this! All the courage and energy oozed away like air from a balloon.

"Sit down," the man said, "and let's see if we can straighten this out."

In the cramped, vacant waiting room there were four rows of wooden chairs, one against each wall. Claire selected a chair in the middle of a row. The doctor sat opposite.

"Suppose you tell me about it," he began.

"Well, you see, I haven't seen my father since I was three and I'm not sure what he looks like. But his name is Dr. Martin T. Farrell. I think the 'T' stands for Thomas. I'm almost sure it does."

"Now that's a coincidence, isn't it? Because I'm M. T. Farrell, too. But my name is Maynard Ting Farrell."

"When I looked you up in the telephone book, it said 'M. T. Farrell.'"

"Yes, I use initials, I don't know why. I just always have. Why don't we get the telephone book again? Perhaps we'll find Dr. Martin."

· He had a soothing voice. Colored people have nice voices, Claire thought.

"Yes, yes. This must be it. Dr. Martin T. Farrell. It's just five lines above my name. You skipped it when you were looking."

She giggled with relief. "That was stupid of me, wasn't it?"

"Not stupid. You must've been in a hurry or had a lot on your mind. Where do you live?"

"On East Sixty-seventh Street."

"You know, you could have walked to where you were going. It's only seven blocks."

"Oh!" Claire said.

"Does your mother know what you're doing?"

"Of course she doesn't! But I wanted to see my father. You're not going to tell her?"

The dark man looked at her for a moment. "No," he said gently. "I'm not going to tell anyone. Have you got a nickel for the subway back downtown?"

"Oh, I have a lot of money. I get fifty cents a week. Look, it's in this pocket."

"Well. Just stick it deep down while you're on the street and only take the nickel out when you get to the subway. Why are you staring at me?"

"I was thinking how nice you are," Claire said, "and that you look like chocolate with whipped cream on top."

"Why, that's a very pleasant thought, isn't it? And you remind me of the opposite—vanilla with chocolate on top." He opened the door. "Now, you'd better start before it gets dark."

On the stoop he stood looking after her. "Good luck, good luck!" he called.

The people you meet! Claire thought. It's a strange world. One minute you're lost and feel like crying and the next minute you feel so friendly.

STREETLAMPS CAME ON just as she arrived. The dusk was shadowy. She felt afraid. What if it were the wrong place again? The apartment building looked like the ones where many of her friends lived: white stone with a green awning that reached from the door to the curb. A doorman with brass buttons opened the door and directed her.

This waiting room, like the other, was vacant. But unlike the other, it had a carpet, pictures, lamps and magazines. A lady with a permanent wave sat behind a small desk. She looked annoyed in that well-mannered way people have when they are in a hurry and you are delaying them. She was probably getting ready to go home. Claire marched right up to the desk.

"I want to see Dr. Farrell," she said, holding her fear in.

"Have you an appointment?"

"No. I only just decided to come."

"Well!" the woman said, with a deep, indignant breath. "Well—what is it about?"

"A personal matter," Claire answered. Mother sometimes said that on the telephone.

"I'm sorry, but I can't take up the doctor's time unless you will state what—"

She felt a sudden strengthening of nerve. *I don't like this woman and she doesn't like me.*

"Just tell him—just tell him that Claire is here. He'll know who I am."

HE HADN'T CRIED out or jumped up and squeezed her, which was a relief. It had occurred to her on the way that he might do that and she didn't want that, although she could not have said why. He had started to get up and come around to the front of the desk, but then he had sat down again, as though he hadn't been able to get up. His face had gone very pale. She had seen how white it looked against his dark blue suit. Now it had gone red.

From the opposite side of the desk, she regarded him furtively. She didn't want to seem to be staring at him. She didn't want to meet his eyes. It felt—it felt too *sudden,* meeting his eyes as she had had to do when she came into the room. Yes, too sudden. So she kept glancing at him and then quickly away at the wall of books to the left. Her hands were twisted together in her lap and the palms were wet. She took a handkerchief out of her pocket and wiped them.

He was medium. He was neither very young like her friend Carol's father, nor bald and tired like some of the other fathers in the houses where she went to play. He had nice hair, brown and thick. He didn't wear glasses and he looked, she thought, like a doctor. Perhaps it was because he wore a dark tie. Doctors always seemed to wear dark clothes; at least Dr. Morrissey did whenever she had the grippe and he came to see her. Yes, he looked like a doctor and he was her father, her real father, sitting here.

A cry came out of her. "I feel scared!"

He answered softly, "Yes. Yes, I know."

"No matter how calm you make yourself on the outside, there's nothing you can do about the inside, is there?"

He replied with a question. "Does your mother know you're here?"

Why did people always have to ask that, as if your mother had to know or be told every time you took a step or spoke a word or ate a mouthful?

"No. I came from school by myself."

"From school? You go to school here in New York?"

"Yes, of course, since second grade. I'm in fifth grade now. I go to Brearley."

"You live in New York?"

"Yes. We didn't have any money in Cyprus and we came here so Mother could earn some. She went to school and she has a degree now. A.I.D."

Her father took a handkerchief from his pocket and wiped his forehead. Then he took a drink of water from the pitcher on the desk. She could see he was very upset. She didn't see why he should be *that* upset.

"Tell me about it," he said.

"Well, you see, Grandpa lost all his money and then he died and the factory closed and we couldn't afford to stay in our house anymore. So Mother learned to be a decorator and Uncle Drew and Aunt Milly got a lot of customers for her and then more came and Uncle Drew says she is a very smart woman."

All these words with which Claire had lived so long in her mind sounded aloud with a moving sadness. She had never felt their whole meaning until this moment. Her voice quivered, telling the story. At the same time, it was pleasurable and dramatic to be part of such a story.

"Your mother ought to have come to me. How could I have known? I would have given you money."

"She wouldn't have taken it."

"How do you know that? Did she say so?"

"She didn't ever talk about it, but I knew just the same. She doesn't like you, does she?"

On the desk lay one of those paperweights that you turn upside down so that snow falls over a country village and a white church with a steeple. Her father played with it, turning it up and back, up and back again.

Then he said, "No, I suppose she doesn't. I'm sorry about that, too, because I like her. And you I love, Claire. I've never stopped loving and thinking of you, every day of my life. Every day," he repeated, putting the paperweight down with a thump and looking at her, looking straight into her eyes.

She looked straight back. "Why don't we live together, then? Why did you go away? I used to ask and ask and I never got any answer, so I stopped asking. But somebody really ought to tell me."

Now her father raised his eyes and looked at the wall behind her, above her head.

"The simplest thing I can tell you is that people sometimes change. First they expect to be happy together. Then they find out they've made a mistake and aren't happy, so it's just better for each to go his own way."

"That's not the whole story," Claire said impatiently, feeling the old indignation at being put off. "You haven't really told me anything at all."

Her father sighed. "You're right. I really haven't."

"Then why don't you?"

"I don't like to say this because you seem so much older than ten, but—"

"Ten and a half."

"Ten and a half. Perhaps you really aren't quite ready to understand it. Sometimes I don't even understand all of it myself."

"I think I know why. It's because Mother is—has a hunchback. She looks funny, so you didn't want to live with her anymore."

Her father got up from his chair. "Oh no! Oh no! I can't help what else you may think, but you can't be allowed to think that of me. Never, Claire. Never. Your mother is a wonderful woman, and I knew when I married her that—"

"Then it's because you wanted to be a famous doctor. That's why you went away."

"Who on earth could have put that idea in your head?"

"Nobody. I'm only trying to figure things out."

"Well, that isn't true, either. Besides, I'm not famous."

"Aunt Milly says you are, almost. She says you will be someday."

"Your Aunt Milly talks about me?"

"Only sometimes when Mother's not there. Once we went to a movie together and afterward to Hicks' for a soda, and Aunt Milly said it was wrong to hide things from a child and never talk about you, as if I had no father and never had had one. She says it's wrong to keep so much hatred."

"It's not a question of hatred. Not that simple."

Her father turned around and stood facing the window, which was odd, because there was nothing to see outside except a courtyard and walls. Anyway, it had got dark by now. Then she realized that he was crying.

"Are you crying?" she asked, and when he turned to show that his eyes were wet, he smiled and said, "It's all right for a man to cry sometimes, you know. It's nothing to be scared of."

And he came and laid his cheek on her head. She sat very still. He whispered. She felt the warm breath on her head.

"I hope you haven't been too sad about all this."

"Oh no. I mean, it's not the very worst thing in the world that you went away! It's happened to some of my friends, and they get along fine. Only sometimes, well, you know, sometimes I get in a thoughtful mood about life. With me it's usually around five o'clock when I'm getting ready for dinner. Isn't that odd? Then things go around in my head and I feel bad for a while. Mother says I think too much, anyway. Maybe I do."

"Tell me, can you remember anything at all about when we lived together in England? Can you?"

"Not very much. Just odd things, here and there. I remember the Christmas you gave me Reginald. We were in a house, not our own, because it had stairs. You took me down on your shoulder and you gave me a doll with a lace dress. You said it was from Santa Claus. I believed in him then. And still, I don't know how it was, I knew that that present wasn't from him. It was from you."

"You named her Reginald."

"Yes. And there was a man—I guess he had been invited to Christmas dinner—who laughed when I told him my doll's name. He said Reginald was a boy's name, and I couldn't name her that. But you said I could if I wanted to."

"I remember."

"I wonder whose house it was. There were children there, bigger than I. One was a boy, I think. And it must have been a country house because there was a lot of snow outside."

"Yes, it was snowing."

"The dining room was down a long hall, and the Christmas tree was in the hall," Claire said proudly.

"Yes. Yes, it was. I'm amazed that you can remember all that."

"Whose house was it?"

Her father said slowly, "It belonged to your aunt, Mary Fern."

"I thought it might have! She's Mother's sister, isn't she? And why is she a secret, too? Why will Mother never answer a question about her own sister?"

"I can't help you, Claire. I'm sorry."

"I wish I had a sister. I hate being an only child. Hardly anybody I know is an only child."

Her father said quietly, "You have a brother."

Astonished, she cried, "I have?" And, following his glance to a photograph which stood on a bookshelf near the window, she saw a woman holding a little boy on her lap. The child wore a short suit, and he had a toy duck or chicken in his hand.

"That's my brother? That little boy?"

"Yes. His name is Enoch, after my father. Your grandfather."

It was too much. It was almost overwhelming . . . Then she thought of something.

"I know about your father. Home in Cyprus sometimes people told me he was their doctor a long time ago. The postmaster told me and our maid Bridget said so. Is that your wife in the picture?"

"Yes. Her name is Hazel."

Claire considered that. "What shall I call her when I visit your house?"

"Let's ask her what she'd like, shall we? But then, your mother may not allow you to visit, you know."

"I'm going to, anyway. I really do obey almost all the time, but this is different. Besides, if you want me to come, I'll obey you. You have a right to say what I may do, haven't you?"

"Not really, Claire."

"Why not?"

"Well, because—well, I haven't ever done anything for you up till now, have I?"

"You can start, then."

"Oh, I want to. Is there anything you need? Tell me."

"I don't need any *things*. Mother's making a lot of money. Well, not a lot, but enough. Every time she fixes up somebody's house, they tell their friends, and then the friends call her."

"Remarkable. A remarkable woman."

There was a silence before her father spoke again. "And are you interested in decorating, too?" But it was as if he really didn't care to know and was only saying something polite to fill a silence.

"No, I don't care about doodads like that."

He laughed. "Doodads! Where did you get such an old-fashioned word? Your grandfather used to say that just the way you said it now."

Proudly Claire affected carelessness. "Oh, I don't know, I read it someplace. I read a lot. I've just started *The Count of Monte Cristo*."

"Ah yes."

"But what I like even better than reading is science. Leaves and bugs and all that. It's my best subject. I'm going to be a doctor."

"You are? And when did you decide that?"

"Oh," she said, still feeling that proud carelessness, "about a year ago."

"But you'll marry and have children when you grow up."

"Not if it interferes with being a doctor. Did you know we were all descended from monkeys?"

"Yes, in a way. It's not exactly like that, though. It—"

But her thoughts came rushing, and she had to interrupt. "Tell me, do you believe in God? My grandfather did. He even got angry when I asked him once. But Mother isn't sure, and I wondered what you thought about it."

"Well, I think, the more we learn about the universe, the more we have to believe in some design. It can't all be just an accident, can it? So in that way, I call the plan God, and I believe. But that's not the same as the bearded old king with a crown and a throne."

"The anthropomorphic God," Claire said quickly. Her father blinked surprise.

"I read that in *The Times,* and I looked it up in the dictionary. You didn't think I knew it, did you?"

"No, I didn't. I have a lot to learn about you, I see."

"Do you know what I'm thinking of now?"

"I can't in the world imagine. You keep my head spinning."

"I'm thinking of the clock with the gilded angels. I suppose talking about God reminded me of angels. It came from Switzerland. Don't you remember?"

"I never saw it, Claire."

She flushed. How stupid. How unthinking. Of course, it had been long afterward.

"I'm sorry! It was Grandpa who bought it for my birthday, just before his first heart attack. He was sad that year."

"Was he?"

"Yes, I think he was sad because nobody liked anybody anymore."

Her father was silent again for a little, and then he said strangely, "You're only ten."

"Ten and a half. You keep forgetting."

"Yes, yes. Ten and a half. Enthralling Claire! You always were. Enthralling." And he kept looking at her.

When the desk clock rang six chimes, he jumped up.

"Your mother will be worried sick about you! We've been sitting here, not thinking of the time at all. Come, I'll walk home with you."

Claire drew her coat on. "Better not come near the house, though."

"I'll only walk to the corner and watch until you're inside."

When he had got his own coat, he came and put her head on his shoulder. Then he laid his cheek on top of her head again. She did not ordinarily like close contact, having had very little of it. Her mother seldom gave more than a good-night kiss, and Claire had long ago sensed that this reluctance of Jessie's had something to do with thinking that people might not welcome her embrace. So this was the first time she had ever known the actual feel of someone else's emotion; it was more intense than any words that could have been spoken. And she held very still with her head on her father's shoulder until they heard the traffic start far off on the avenue. Then he let her go.

"God keep you, Claire," he said.

Jessie stared into the darkness past the window. Claire waited. After the furious preliminary scolding, having come home past six o'clock and frightening her mother to a frenzy ("I was about to telephone the police!"), they had sat down in the little room with the blue tiles and Claire had told the whole story. Now, dry-mouthed and scared, she waited for anger and punishment. Her mother scarcely ever punished, but then Claire had never done anything as monstrously daring and defiant as this.

Jessie laughed.

First her mouth opened with the sort of disbelief that comes after some particularly crazy practical joke. And then she laughed out loud. "Good God!" she said. "Good God!" And then, "Well, I guess I've no real right to be furious. It's just the kind of thing I would have done."

It couldn't possibly be going to end as easily as this! Nevertheless, Claire's heartbeat slowed.

"So, then, how is he, your father?"

How was he? That was another question you couldn't answer, like some of the other questions grown-ups asked: "How are you doing in school?" "What are you doing with yourself lately?" But some sort of answer was expected.

"He said I was 'enthralling.' "

"Did he?" For an instant Jessie looked pleased. Then she pulled in her smile and looked somber again. "And so, what did you think of him?"

Another question you couldn't answer! But Claire thought of something. "I thought he would be older."

"He looks—he looks well then?"

"I guess so."

"What did you talk about?"

"A lot of things. He has a little boy. I saw his picture."

"I see."

"His name is Enoch. That was my other grandfather's name. Did you know?"

"Yes, certainly I knew. And now you'll be going back to visit, I suppose."

Something forlorn had come into her mother's voice, something hollow and sad, like an echo. Claire looked up quickly, but Jessie was just sitting there as usual, with the pearls glimmering in her ears and the crocheted scarf about her shoulders that she wore every night because she said the house was chilly. Melancholy seeped like shadows in the room.

"Don't you want me to?" she asked.

"You can imagine I'm not happy about it. But you'll do what you want, anyway."

"I wish you wouldn't mind too much, though."

Jessie didn't answer that. Instead she asked, "You've been thinking about your father for a long time, haven't you?"

"How did you know?"

"I didn't until now. But obviously I should have known."

"I'm sorry I scared you," Claire said. "We got talking and forgot to look at the clock."

"Well, next time let me know where you are, that's all."

Her mother stood up. "It's time for your bath, and you haven't done any homework," she said.

At the door, Claire turned around. "Mother?"

"Yes, Claire?"

"Don't worry. I'll still love you."

"I won't worry."

"Things will be the same. This won't make any difference."

"Of course, dear. I know it won't."

But of course, she didn't know it. And Claire, trudging up the long stairs to her room, didn't know it either. For it could never be exactly the same again. It wasn't just the two of them, anymore.

❧{19}❧

Martin moved his chair back from the table. "Well, this was a great dinner. Had enough?" he asked Claire.

The devastated Sunday roast stood in its cooling gravy on the sideboard with the peas, the sweet potatoes, the homemade rye rolls and the apple pudding. He ate too much, as his father had before him. He resolved to watch it.

"I'm stuffed," Claire said. "You're a better cook than our maid, Aunt Hazel. You can cook better than any maid we ever had."

Hazel smiled. "If you still want to take Enoch to the park, Claire, you'd better start. It gets dark and cold early."

"I want to go to the park," Enoch said at once.

"I'm ready. I'll just get my pea jacket."

"All the buttons are off it," Martin observed.

"Not all, only three. How come you noticed? Mother's always noticing, but I didn't think you would."

"You think I'm blind in one eye and can't see out of the other?"

"Give them to me. I'll sew them on," Hazel offered.

The three stood watching while she sewed the buttons. Her soft hair kept falling over her forehead. Whenever she pushed it back, she looked up at them and smiled.

"You're really so nice," Claire told her. "You know, my friend Alice's parents got divorced, and her father's new wife is nasty and Alice hates her, but I certainly don't hate you."

"That's too bad," Hazel said. "About Alice, I mean. I'm glad you don't hate me, though."

"I was supposed to wear my good coat today. It's rose-colored, sort of, and has a gray fur collar. Mother made me buy it, but I don't like it."

"Your mother has beautiful taste," Martin said. "You can learn something from her."

"I know, but I'm not interested in things like that—clothes and keeping my room neat and stuff. I'm just not interested."

"There. That's done," Hazel said. She bit the thread off between her teeth. "Now you look better. I'll get Enoch's snowsuit on. Be sure to hold his hand very tightly; he can slip loose before you know it."

644

"You can trust me," Claire assured her.

"She likes coming here," Hazel observed when they had gone. "I guess it's fun for her to be with Enoch. Her own house must be very quiet, I suppose."

"I suppose," Martin answered.

"She really is an odd character, Martin. In a wonderful way, I mean. So—different."

"That's true."

"Do you ever think you would like to see her mother?"

"Not particularly."

Hazel wanted to talk about Jessie, to probe in dark places. But the truth was that, yes, he would have liked to have seen Jessie, to talk about Claire, to find for himself whether the sore had healed at all. However, Jessie did not want to see him.

"Well, I guess I'd better clean up the kitchen. You going to work?"

"Just for an hour before the Philharmonic comes on. I've a few patient-reports to check."

He had fixed up a room for himself and his personal treasures: his desk, his books, records and the little radio on which he listened to the Sunday broadcast of the Philharmonic. The rest of the house was Hazel's, the woman's province in which he did not interfere. She had done with it as she liked, and the result Martin would have characterized, if asked, as cozy: somewhat tasteless, but inoffensively so. There was a clutter of pillows and fringe and draperies in cloudy colors which tended to cloud his mood. Old rose, reminding him of rotting flowers, and tans like stale tea stains. In Martin's little study the walls were white. The dark floor was bare around the edges of an old Persian rug patterned in gold and cream like sun on sand. There were no curtains, only shelves of plants, so that from his desk he could see the sky, and this gave him freedom and lightness of heart.

Someone last spring had sent them an azalea in a wooden tub. The flame-colored petals had fallen, but the shining leaves thrived, and it would surely flame again in season. Hazel had nurtured it. She had a green thumb.

The afternoon was murky and still. He looked down to where, three floors below, bare gingko trees stood in a row along the curb, each one enclosed in its low fence of wire scrollwork. Claire, holding Enoch by the hand, had just crossed Seventy-third Street and headed toward the park. He watched them, the tall, curly-headed girl and the little waddling boy, until they turned the corner. Tenderness filled his chest. That they might know grace and mercy all their lives! Their flesh was so soft. He yearned for them: more for the girl than for the little boy? No, no! How could he? And after all, one couldn't measure. They were different, his feelings, neither more nor less, just different.

He suspected—he was almost certain—that Jessie could not be at ease with this new development. He hoped her resentment was not too acute. He suspected she would not have let Claire know if it were. At any rate, Claire never said anything about it.

She had invited herself to dinner this Sunday and Martin had asked, "Doesn't your mother want you to have dinner with her on Sundays?"

"She has a cold and has to stay in bed, so I'd have to eat alone anyway."

He tried to fathom their relationship, and concluded that Jessie, pragmatic as always, had adjusted to living with a good, but strong-willed, very adult child. In short, Jessie would know when she was beaten! It took rather a good deal to beat Jessie, too, Martin reflected now, with a touch of amusement and more than a touch of admiration. The world had not confounded her yet. Professionally, she was doing very well. Hazel reported that at one of the hospital auxiliary meetings, some of the women had mentioned Jessie's name as though they were impressed. An extraordinary twist of fortune!

Extraordinary, too, that after all his own despairing, fruitless efforts, his daughter, without any act or effort of his, should have been returned to him. His entrancing daughter!

His mother had come to visit again for her birthday. Meeting Claire for the first time, she had wept.

"She's different from the others, from Alice's girls," she had told Martin. And he had asked her in what way.

"It's hard to say, exactly. More curious, for one thing. And very strong. Yes," she had repeated after a moment, "yes, very strong."

As Jessie had done, Claire would say whatever came into her head. She had been like that when she was three, he remembered. (Enoch, at three, was still a baby.) He was thankful that what came into her head caused no disruption in the life of his household. She had with frank simplicity liked Hazel at once, and Hazel, loving soul, had liked her. Hazel would be especially charitable, he knew, because Claire was a "victim of divorce" and because her mother was crippled. Hazel tended to think in clichés. But they were kind clichés.

He was thankful that, for whatever reason—most probably her own pride—Jessie had said nothing to Claire about the truth of their divorce. Someday, inevitably, he supposed she would have to know and he dreaded the prospect of being diminished in his daughter's sight . . .

Ah well! Sufficient unto the day, et cetera. He pulled out his writing pad and a pile of reports. A reminder had been propped against the bookend: "The Mosers have invited us for next Friday dinner. Are you free? Shall I accept?"

As it happened he was free, yet he knew that if he had not been he would have made an effort to become so. The Mosers were amiable and decent people. They were all gratitude. Vicky was in fine health: Martin was given detailed proof of her fine health at every meeting. Moser wanted to believe in Martin's special genius, a belief that was as ill-founded as his first refusal to believe in Martin at all. But it was difficult, even impossible, to change a layman's opinion of a doctor, once he had formed it. And generally he formed it on the strength of something read in a popular magazine, or on the experience, probably misunderstood at that, of a relative or friend.

"An acquaintance of mine has a son," Moser had been saying recently, "out in Dayton, Ohio. Same situation as Vicky's was, after an accident. And the surgeon botched it. He's a useless lump of flesh, poor boy. An outrage."

"Well," Martin had said, feeling an obligation toward the unknown surgeon who had probably not botched it at all, "it might have been a different thing entirely, you know."

"No, no, it was the same thing. It only made me realize more and more what we owe you, Martin. Yes, it was the hand of God that led us to you. And nothing you or anyone can say will change our minds."

He hoped the dinner would be nearby at a hotel. It would be a long drive out to the Mosers' Long Island place on a winter night, after having worked all day. Still, Hazel liked to go there. It was no average experience, of course. You turned in at the great iron gates, traveled half a mile up a driveway between immense walls of shrubbery and were greeted by a servant at the top of a flight of steps. Double doors opened onto an octagonal hall. You walked on pastel carpets through lofty rooms filled with mirrors and brocade furniture, past a polished mahogany library whose shelves were filled with uncut leather-bound sets and silver golf trophies. Through the casements you looked out on terraces descending to the Sound at the base of a shallow bluff.

"It's an English manor house," Mrs. Moser liked to explain. "Elizabethan. We had an architect who was famous for English design."

Mrs. Moser had come from Iowa and married Mr. Moser long before he became president of his tool and die company. She wore many diamonds, but she was a simple person, somewhat intimidated by her husband and his status. Hazel felt comfortable with her.

Now Martin started at the top of the pile of reports, read through one and wrote corrections in the margin. His mind wandered: too much dinner, or maybe just the Sunday letdown after a week of split-second activities and meals on the run. His mind went back to the Elizabethan manor. The Mosers would not have recognized a real one or liked it if they had. He thought of Lamb House.

Why was it that, on days when he was with Claire, he thought more of—of her? Were they at all alike? Not the eyes, for Claire's were dark. Never in any other human being had he seen just that pure and lucid blue. But there was something, some joyous movement of the head, something in the child of eleven that reminded him they were of the same flesh, after all.

No, Martin, no.

In the kitchen, Hazel was singing. "I hear music when I touch your hand," she sang, and the sound was sweetly, faintly mournful, like herself. She wanted so much to make everything between them perfect. By preference she read romances and women's magazines, but the better to resemble Martin, she made herself read whatever he had just been reading, and asked him to discuss it afterward. He often did and found her comments apt. She was not especially fond of music, either, but would go with him to the opera and had bought a book to learn about it. She was convinced that all the other doctors' wives were educated, although he had told her that was not true, and in any case it didn't matter, because he was satisfied with her as she was.

What Hazel really liked was domesticity and the company of women like herself. Flo had become a trusted friend, and that pleased him; it would have been hard for him and Tom if their wives had disliked one another. Also, she liked being with her family, especially her sister Tess, whom Martin bore only because she was Hazel's sister. Tess was an incessant talker, and her voice was excruciating.

Hazel knocked on the door. She always knocked on the door when he was working, although he had told her she needn't.

"I thought I'd remind you the concert will be coming on in three minutes. You get so busy, you might forget."

"Thanks. But I wasn't busy, I've been daydreaming."

"About what?"

"About what a good year it's been."

"I'm glad. If you want me to listen to the concert with you, I'll stay. I won't talk, either." Her eyes were innocent, holding more innocence than Claire's, by far.

He said fondly, "Only if you want to. You needn't pretend with me. I don't mind that you don't like music."

"I want to try to like it, Martin, so we can share it together."

Try to like it! Mozart and Bach, their celestial mathematics! The glory and the peace, like stroking fingers, like quiet hands.

"All right," he said and turned the dial.

There was a buzz and scratch of static. A voice rumbled. Then it came clearly.

"At seven fifty-five this morning, a large force of Japanese planes attacked the United States naval facilities at Pearl Harbor, inflicting great damage on Ford Island, as well as at the Army Air Base, Hickham Field. Casualties are mounting—

"My God!" Martin cried.

"A large number of Army Air Corps planes was destroyed on the ground. Winging in over Oahu, Japanese torpedo and dive bombers destroyed hangars, docks and—"

Hazel's hand went to her mouth. She always covered her mouth when she was frightened. "Does it mean—" she began. They stared at each other and her broken question hung unanswered in the air.

Ask anyone who was alive on that day and is old enough to remember what he was doing and where he was at the moment he heard the news, and he will answer you with a kind of awe in his voice.

"We were on our way to the beach."

"I had just taken the roast out of the oven."

"We were getting dressed for my brother's wedding."

So these two also would remember the day that shook the world, that changed the world for them, as for their countrymen, and indeed, in the end, for all men everywhere.

The last thing Martin saw before he turned the bedside lamp out was his uniform hanging in the closet with his sober civilian suits. The suits looked queer, like relics of some other man or life. He felt he would walk awkwardly in them if he had to wear them, and it had been only half a year since they had been his daily garb.

The room was strange, too, this room in which they had conceived their child and spread the Sunday papers on the bed and, warmly covered, had lain listening to the wind. Home on a three-day leave, he thought it might have been better not to come, not to be reminded of what he had already grown unused to and would not have again for no one knew how long. Or ever? The last medical contingent to go overseas had been torpedoed in the North Atlantic. Young Prescott had gone down with them, and for some reason—he had not known Prescott well at all—but for some reason he could recall his face most vividly, plump and soft, eager to please and worried. His wife had been pregnant with their fourth child.

From down the hall came a sharp little cry. Hazel sat up and waited for the cry to be repeated, but it was not. "Enoch's dreaming," she said.

What did a three-year-old dream about, this gentle baby with his mother's anxiety already written in his eyes?

"Martin," she whispered into the darkness, "how long will you be at Fort Dix?"

"Dear, I haven't the least idea."

"But it's a staging area, isn't it?"

"Hazel, please."

"I know you're not supposed to tell anything, and I understand why, but—" She clung to him. He could feel her lips moving against his neck. "Martin?"

"Yes, dear?"

"I'm trying not to cry. I'm so ashamed of myself."

"It's all right to cry. I don't want to leave you and Enoch, either."

How old would Enoch be when he came home? And Claire, whose years with him had been so few? And in how many rooms, how many houses all over this land were men and women lying awake tonight, holding back the hour of departure?

"Martin? You won't be angry if I ask you something?"

"Of course I won't. Ask me."

"It's something we've never talked about. I really haven't ever thought about it before, except that now—well, if you should go to England—I mean, I'm not asking whether you are, but it does seem possible from all one reads that you will be going there—"

He knew, he knew what was coming.

"Well, suppose you should be sent to England. Would you ever want to see her again? Mary?"

It was the first time in years that anyone had spoken the name aloud to him. Now, in the column of air where the door stood ajar and the hall light intruded upon darkness, suddenly the name took shape and hung there in a curlicued script, colored, he thought, a kind of silvery green. Mary. Mary Fern.

"You know that's over," he said softly. "Long before I met you. And now we're married." He tightened his arms around her. "Weren't you once engaged to someone else? I could be jealous of that, couldn't I?" He didn't know why he was talking so much. He was prattling and it was absurd.

Hazel said faintly. "Not really. That was different."

Of course. They both knew it had been.

"We are married," he repeated with emphasis.

"Yes, we are truly, aren't we?"

She picked up his hand, laid the palm to her cheek and kissed the palm. So soft! And he was responsible for this soft life! Why did women, good women, and it seemed to Martin that the women he had cared for were all good women, make a man feel as if he held their lives in his hand? He'd better be worthy of this trust! He wanted to, and he would be. He would cause no pain and no tears, ever. No, never, never.

Deep into the night he lay, long after she had fallen asleep, listening to the little puff of her breath, tensing for another cry from their child. The pallid light of his last day at home was already sifting out of the sky before he slept.

⊰{20}⊱

First he put the lamp out, then pulled the blackout curtains aside. The windy autumn night was Elizabethan, Shakespearean. He half expected to see the witches of Endor come sailing over the woods, or horsemen in cloaks come clattering up the road.

The outline of the main building was inked against the sky. Once it had been a sanitorium for the nervous diseases of wealthy Englishmen, casualties of the peace. Now it had been turned over to casualties of the war. Martin stood a few minutes listening to the soughing wind, then sighed and went back to his desk to write.

"Dearest Hazel, I'm in the country, about half an hour out of London." *Omit that, the censor won't allow it.* "It's good to be on dry land after what they say was one of the worst crossings ever. What it could have been like on a smaller ship, I can only imagine. It was bad enough on the *Queen Mary.*" *Omit that, for Heaven's sake, take everything out after "ever."* "I am a good sailor, I discovered. I was born in a flood and survived. There is an affinity between water and me. One jokes about seasickness but it is no joke, I can tell you." *Poor guys piled high, deck upon deck on bunks stacked one above the other, vomiting their guts out.* "There really ought to be some sort of medication for it. I daresay there will be one day.

"For those of us who stayed well, it was an exhilarating experience." *Exhilarating? Without lights we zigged and zagged across the ocean. Dark ship, dark ocean. I went out on deck where the silent watches were posted, hoping for clouds to cover the infernal brilliant moon. Exhilarating!*

"I have to tell you a funny story." *Keep it light, keep it cheerful. Besides, it was funny.* "I shared a suite, the bridal suite maybe, with two men, one a dermatologist from Des Moines, good-natured, a sort of jokester; the other, a psychiatrist, wasn't a bad sort either, except for being somewhat pompous and all-knowing.

"Well, the psychiatrist assured us that seasickness is a mental state, that if you don't want to be sick, you won't be. You know the sort of talk some of them can go in for. Anyway, on Thanksgiving Day we met the worst of the storm, waves over the topside portholes, ropes up along the corridors. Our psychiatrist, claiming a slight headache, elected not to go to dinner. He looked sallow and faintly green, like the tinge on a cauliflower. My friend from Des Moines thought it

651

would be kind to bring a tray back for him, but when we got to the room, he was flung out on the bed like Raggedy Andy.

" 'Look what we've brought,' Des Moines said. 'Didn't know whether you liked dark or white, so we got some of both. And a great stuffing—better than Mother used to make, better than my mother's anyway. Cranberry relish, pumpkin pie with ice cream—why, what's the matter?'

"The psychiatrist waved us away. His eyes were rolling.

" 'Come, come, you're not seasick. Bring yourself under control, man! It's all in the mind! Try some creamed onions.'

"I got the basin just in time to save the carpet.

"So here I am, and very busy. We have a first-class hospital with every piece of equipment you can think of and some you can't. The worst wounded are brought here." *Change that "wounded" to "cases." At Oran the Vichy French fought the American landing like tigers. How especially hard to think that the terrible wounds on these boys of ours were inflicted by Frenchmen! Sad and mad. But then the whole business of what men do to one another is and always has been sad and mad.*

"Dearest Hazel, I wish I were more articulate. But then they always say doctors are nonverbal people, don't they? Whether true or not, it's true of me. You will just have to imagine how it is for me without you and Enoch. And, of course, my Claire.

"You have been so understanding about her. I know there are women who wouldn't welcome her as you do. Have I told you, have I thanked you enough for it? If not, I do so now. Now I'm going to end this, read your letter again, and go to bed."

He picked up Hazel's loving scrawl.

"My darling, You asked me to tell you what kind of big present you should bring me when you come home. 'When you come home.' I read those four words over and over. I'll tell you: I shall want another child. There's nothing else I want." *She never asked for things. Other men here had already been up in London to spend their pay on earrings, silver tea sets and Lord knows what else.*

"Oh my darling, we all miss you so! Enoch gets to look more like you every minute." *He doesn't. He looks like Hazel.* "I have gone back to nursing. You said you wouldn't mind. I'm on the seven-to-three shift. Josie is still with us, and she'll get Enoch off to school in the morning after I leave. Then I'll be with him from three on, so you see, I'm not going to neglect him.

"I do have a good feeling, though, about helping out. The hospitals are so dreadfully shorthanded. Also, I shall be earning money, so we won't have to dip into savings, and there'll be a head start for you when you come back.

"Your mother is well. I spoke to her on the telephone, and I won't forget her birthday.

"I went to hear Ezio Pinza in *Boris Godunov*. I'm really learning about opera. I do wish they sang all of them in English, though.

"Claire comes every other week or so. We've become good friends, I think. But it's no effort on my part, so don't thank me. You know, Enoch will do things for her that he won't do for me? Last week he was sick and I couldn't make him swallow his medicine, but when Claire arrived, he did it for her. I asked her whether her mother knew how often she stopped here after school, and she said, 'I don't tell her, but I'm sure she guesses.' And then she said, 'She'd just as soon not hear.' Imagine such insight at her age! She's a lot older than her years. Sometimes I almost feel she's older than I am. Certainly, she's more determined."

Smiling to himself, Martin got Claire's letter out again, and skimmed the pages.

"Dear Daddy, I'll be going into eighth grade in September! Brearley is a great school, but the science class is very babyish. I don't mean to say I'm so smart, but one of my friends has a sister in high school, and I can understand her biology book. I'm in a big hurry to be a doctor. Were you like that too?

"Do you ever pass the place where we lived and the park where I rode my baby bike?

"Aunt Hazel is very nice to me. Of course, that's only because I'm your daughter and she loves you. I think it's hard for her, living alone. She says she has trouble balancing the checkbook. If everything wasn't always so mixed up, I could ask Mother to teach her. Ha! ha!

"Are you staying anywhere near that house in the country that belonged to Aunt Mary Fern, and does she still live there? I still can't imagine why she's such a big secret when she's Mother's sister."

Martin put the letter away. That child! Ferreting and probing, persistent and blunt as ever her mother had been.

Someone had left a touring map of the British Isles in a drawer of the desk. Merely out of curiosity, because Claire had asked the question and he had nothing better to do, he unfolded the map. Lamb House was sixty-odd miles away, a long distance over the twisting lanes that in this country passed for roads. Not that it mattered. Long or short, it did not matter. He put the map back and slammed the drawer shut.

Occasionally, one panicked. How many years might this war not go on? One had a confusion of emotions as the wounded were brought in: thankfulness that one was not lying destroyed on a stretcher, and then shame that one was not. Argue as you might, and it was true that you had no choice (a neurosurgeon belonged behind the lines, not aiming a gun at Rommel, the Desert Fox), the shame was there. Even Tom, a first lieutenant in the South Pacific, was facing danger under fire, while he, Martin, was safe in this first-class place, not very far from the Eisenhower headquarters at Bushy Park. Also, guilt was there. Out of the suffering of the maimed, he was being educated, increasing his skills. And this disturbed him most of all.

Under a shrapnel wound he discovered a proliferating prior growth, which, without the wound, would have gone undiscovered. Having written about this oddity for a professional journal back home, he received a flood of letters and some publicity, which had not been his intent. He was deeply, perhaps unreasonably, troubled about things like that.

He spent long hours with his patients, hours when he could have been eating or sleeping. Some of them touched him so that he thought they would live inside him for the rest of his life.

A boy from a tobacco farm in North Carolina, a chubby kid no more than nineteen, told him, "You know, Doc, I was sure I was going to be killed in this war. I never thought about anything like this."

"This" was a shattered arm and a ruined face. Martin had been more successful with the arm than the plastic surgeons had been with the face, although it was no fault of theirs. Their repairs were masterly, but still they were repairs. On the left side the patched cheek had the tight, immovable gloss of patent leather, while out of a raw socket glared a glass eye fixed in its glitter; the right side crinkled with speech and its eye could still weep tears.

"Tell me, Doc, will people be—well, will they know me when I get home? Tell me the truth, Doc, please?"

Martin said what he could. "I didn't know you before, but they've done a splendid job. And of course, it will improve as it heals."

"Do you think—this is probably a dumb question, but—well, if you were a girl—I mean, do you think that girls will—"

Girls will shudder and pretend and be very, very tactful, at least most of them will, I hope.

"Sure, sure. Why not? You're a kind of hero, son, and don't you forget it."

Could he tell these young men the truth of what he felt, that their wounds were a personal affront to him? An outrage? We are outraged when vandals destroy a painting, but *this*?

Sometimes men weep. They turn away so that I will not see. And sometimes they don't turn away. I pat a hand or a shoulder. I'm awkward. "I know," I murmur, "I know." But I don't know. How can I, whose turn hasn't come? How can I really understand a twenty-five-year-old man whose genitals have been shot off?

There is a kinship of pain so worldwide now, Martin thought, that it has almost become a part of the natural order of things.

A few months more, and he would have been here a year. His life had evolved into a routine, a continuing order, as if he were a bank clerk or an insurance salesman, except that his work was to mend the dreadful wreckage of the war. When the working day was over he would wash his hands and go to dinner or, now and then, up to London for a night out. It was absurd, surrealistic. The only remedy was not to think about it much. Just go ahead, he supposed, and do what you can and take your promotions. He was a full colonel now, as if he were on a battlefield, where, in a certain sense, he really was.

LONG AFTERWARD, MARTIN couldn't recall where he had been going, only that he had been hurrying down a London street, and then, suddenly looking up, had seen in a gallery window a watercolor on an easel: three red birds sat on a wire fence. He stood quite still.

It's not the same, he thought, collecting himself. That other had a background of snow, and this picture was dark green, full summer. Yet the resemblance was unmistakable.

He went inside. A genteel elderly lady came forward and he asked about the picture.

"It's a nice piece, isn't it? Rather better than most of them here." And seeing that he seemed surprised, she explained, "We've turned the gallery over for the month to an amateur exhibit and sale. It's part of the war effort, the proceeds going to needy children. Would you be interested in that one?"

He stammered. "It looks like one I've seen before. Is the artist perhaps—"

"I can look it up for you. Wait, here it is. *Three Red Birds*. A Mrs. Lamb. A lovely person; she's given us quite a few things, as a matter of fact. She works in charcoal, too. This head of a child is hers. Now it, I think you'll agree, really is rather good."

That must be Ned, Martin thought. He'd be a young man now, eighteen, fighting for England, no doubt. But here he was only about ten years old, with his chin held between his hands. The hands were poorly drawn. But the eyes had life and spirit; the mouth suggested humor. And Martin stood, holding the sketch and feeling—he didn't know what he felt.

"It has a certain quality, hasn't it? It could have been sentimental, but isn't." The woman smiled. "It's the sentimental things the public wants, of course. Although why not, when you come to think about it?"

"Yes, why not?" Martin echoed.

Apparently the woman had a need to fill up silence. "Most of this amateur work is pretty bad. But sometimes you find a person who's almost got it, whatever 'it' is. I've dealt in art for thirty years, and usually can tell the real thing when I see it, although for the life of me, I can't define it! Now, this woman comes very close. She may have it, or she may not, I'm not sure."

"I'd like to buy it," Martin said.

"Which? The head?"

"No, the birds."

"Oh. Well. How very nice. The lady will be so pleased. She brought it in from the country just last week."

On the train returning to the hospital, he had a strange sensation that he was carrying contraband and people were staring at it, staring through the paper. For a moment he thought of leaving the parcel on the seat.

When he got to his room, he propped it against the wall in a corner without unwrapping it. Why the devil had he bought the thing? There it stood, making a disturbance in the room. There were enough disturbances in the world without any more.

It was three days before he took the picture out of its wrapping and held it to the light. In the lower left-hand corner, she had placed her initials: MFL. The bottom of the F turned up in a flourish; the L had a curlicue. Slowly he traced the letters with his fingernail. So she was still living at Lamb House with Alex! But of course, he had expected nothing else. And he wondered whether by now any other man had come into her life, and if so, who and how.

He went outside. The night was still. In the west lay a low streak of hazy, lingering pink. No bombers had gone out yet. On most nights at about this time a flight roared overhead from the airbase only ten miles to the north. In early dawn, you heard them again; they never seemed as loud on the homeward flight and you wondered how many had failed to return.

He stood leaning against the cottage wall. The cruelty, the haphazard idiocy of men's lives! The planet was a ship on an uncharted sea cleaving a way through infinite cold space. At least, they said it was infinite. Who really knew what the concept could mean? Perhaps, like a ship heading toward a hidden reef, it was even now careening toward its doom in some unimaginable celestial wreck. All we know is that we are whirled through our short days and our transient delights, so quickly over and lost.

SOME THREE WEEKS later on a Saturday afternoon, Martin stepped out of a train and walked down a standard village High Street. The church, he recalled, was on the left. There one turned into a country lane, and after a short walk, arrived at Lamb House.

No sooner had he arrived there, he wanted to go back. He felt that his presence must announce itself to everyone who saw him, that someone surely must turn to challenge him. He passed a few women carrying market baskets, a Tommy home on furlough and some girls on bicycles. But no one even glanced his way.

The tiny door-gardens had been planted in vegetables. Only one scrap of earth, too small for vegetables, bore any reminder of what life had been before the war. It was a patch of mignonette, like late snow, next to a clump of larkspur.

He ought to go back. But he hadn't come here to entangle anyone; he had only come to see how she was! What could be wrong with that?

The front lawn had been planted with cabbage. He had taken no more than a few steps up the lane when he saw Mary. Her back was toward him but he knew her, nevertheless. She was hoeing the cabbage. And again he felt a powerful urge to go away. Afterward, he was to ask himself whether he might not truly have done so if she had not happened that moment to see him.

She stood quite still as he approached. She wore a white shirt and a brown skirt. She was sunburned and had a smudge of earth on her cheek.

"I bought your red birds. In a gallery in London," he said.

She looked at him, not understanding.

"I saw the sketch of Ned, I think it was Ned. Was it? So I came here." He stopped. "I'm not making any sense."

She let the hoe drop. "What are you doing here?"

"Here? Or in England, do you mean?"

"You've just come to England?"

"No. Since last fall."

They stood looking at each other for a minute.

"You've not grown any older," she said.

"Eleven years older."

The years had told on Mary. There were some lines on her forehead which had not used to be there; also a thinning of the cheeks so that the enormous eyes were deeper.

"Is Alex here?" he asked.

He hadn't planned the question; indeed had had no thought of what he would say when he got here. But the question sounded normal enough.

"With Montgomery in North Africa. He volunteered."

There seemed then nothing to say.

"You're well?" she asked. "Your family's well?"

How queer and formal she sounds! he thought. The questions confused him. "My family?"

"Your wife. Your boy. Aunt Milly writes to me sometimes. That's how I know."

The word "wife" flustered him. "Oh yes, yes, everyone is well," he answered awkwardly.

"You've been seeing Claire again."

"Yes, yes, I have."

"I was glad to hear it."

Again he thought: How correct she is!

The sun, glittering in his eyes, gave him an excuse for looking away. He felt that he hardly knew this woman. He felt quite numb inside.

"Will you come in, Martin? We have five children now and I have to help with the supper for them."

He was astonished. "Five?"

For the first time she smiled. Faint lines fanned from the corners of her eyes.

"No, no, mine are away. Ned's in the RAF and the girls are at boarding school. These are evacuees from the bombing."

"Then you must be busy. I'm keeping you."

"You're not keeping me."

He followed her into the house.

"Sit down while I set the table," she said.

He sat down stiffly with his cap on his knees and watched her laying the places at the carved oak table, an earthenware plate and mug at each plate. He remembered her sitting at that table, wearing velvet. He shouldn't have come. How could he tell what feelings she might have toward him now? Embarrassment, no doubt. Perhaps even anger. It was possible. Anything was possible.

"Have you come by car?" she asked abruptly.

"No, I took the train."

"Then you'll have to stay the night. There're only three trains a day now, and the last one's already left."

"I'm sorry! I never thought! Perhaps there's a room somewhere in the village."

"No need. We've plenty of room here, even with the children."

He tried desperately to think of something to say.

"All these strange children. They're quite an undertaking."

"Not really. I've reared three of my own, after all. These keep me company."

"Ah, yes."

"I'm afraid you'll find it bedlam here until they're all fed and sent up to sleep," she said politely.

"I shan't mind," he answered as politely.

It seemed to him they were behaving like relatives, who, meeting after long silence, had found that they didn't like each other very much anymore.

IT WAS IMPOSSIBLE that a bloody war was being fought! Or that there could be places like the operating room where Martin bloodied his sleeves every day. A fire was snapping on the hearth. The tough old sycamores creaked in the wind at the corner of the house. Country noises out of a Victorian novel! Nothing in the room had relevance to what was happening in the world outside it, neither the framed ancestor in the plumed hat, nor Alex's copper-and-silver riding trophies on the mantel, nor the needlepoint bellpull to summon servants who were no longer there.

A door closed above. There were steps on the stairs, and Mary came into the room.

"I'm sorry I took so long. Hermine—she's the youngest—still cries sometimes for her mother. It takes a while to comfort her."

"I didn't mind. It's peaceful in here."

"Peaceful and chilly."

Kneeling, she stretched her hands out to the fire. An enormous sheep dog came in from the hall to flop down near the heat. The tall clock ticked, making a lonely sound in the stillness. At the supper table, the children had created distraction. Now again there was nothing to say.

Mary stared somberly into the fire. Presently, she looked up.

"Are you happy, Martin?"

The question, following the stiffness of their first hours, startled him. And he evaded it.

"Can anyone be happy in 1943?"

Her eyes said: *That's not what I meant.*

"Forgive me," he said. "I know you meant something else . . . I suppose I am."

"Tell me about your children. First, Claire."

"Oh," he answered, relieved at a question he could answer with ease, "Claire's going to be *somebody!* Whatever she does will be on a large scale. She'll have a great deal of joy or a great deal of pain. Probably both."

"That's rather like you, isn't it?"

"I don't know. I can't see myself. But she's like her mother, too," he said thoughtfully.

"Tell me, what do you know about Jessie?"

"Only secondhand reports from Claire, and not very many of those. But I can tell that the household is cheerful; that says something."

"I think of Jessie all the time; I suppose it's just conscience nagging."

"Eleven years," Martin said softly, "and it still nags?"

"Why? Don't you ever feel it?"

Now. Now they were approaching the heart of the matter.

"Yes," he said, "I do. But talk about something else. There's nothing to be done about what's past."

"All right. Tell me about your little boy. What is his name?"

"Enoch, after my father."

"I remember your father. He was a plain man and very kind."

"Well. My boy was three when I last saw him, a quiet baby with a kind of sweetness. Very different from Claire."

Mary rose from her knees to sit near the fire, resting her hands on the arms of the chair. "You're not wearing the topaz," Martin said.

"Topaz?"

"That odd, carved ring you always wore on your little finger."

"Oh, you remembered that! I gave it to Isabel. It was my mother's, and Isabel is like her, even though she looks like Alex."

"So—Alex volunteered, you said?"

"Yes. He had strong convictions about the Nazis long before most people did, and he wanted desperately to go."

"He's a man of spirit."

"If he weren't, I don't think I could have stood it all these years."

Back again now to the heart of the matter. This time he was less afraid.

"Has it been so terribly hard, even so?"

She clasped her hands. He had forgotten that passionate young gesture of hers.

"I don't know. What I mean is, you come to love life more when it's been hard, isn't that true? There are balances. Maybe I wouldn't have been as close to my children if things had been different. Maybe I've learned to care more about other people."

There was a change in the room. Suddenly he became aware that his heart had begun to race . . . The fire snapped. In its twisting flames flowers burst open, surf tumbled, castles towered and fell. And Martin sat quite still, letting himself be hypnotized.

At last he said, "You've been very strong, Mary."

"You do what you have to do," she said quietly.

"Do you look into the future at all?"

"Not beyond this war. When it's over—whenever that may be—then I'll think about the future."

She got up and put another log on the fire, making a small thud and a rush of sparks.

" 'Man is born unto trouble as the sparks fly upward,' " Martin said. And, as Mary looked puzzled, he added, "I don't usually go around quoting Job. It just came out of my head, stuck there after all those Bible readings in the front parlor when I was growing up. Anyway, it's glorious poetry, even if you can't take it all as literal truth."

"You think man is born to trouble? Doesn't he make his own?"

"You could argue that till doomsday. Whatever the cause, though, I wish you hadn't had so much of it."

"My sufferings rank pretty low next to what's happening in the world right now."

She smiled, and with that unfolding, courageous, lovely smile, time contracted. Eleven years was yesterday. Today was eleven years ago.

"Blue eyes don't belong in such a dark Spanish face. Or is it Greek?" he said.

"There's no Spanish in me, or Greek either, Martin."

He stood up. She was so close that he could see the pulse in her throat, could see the dark line where the lashes grew out of the fine, white shells of her lids, could even see a glistening of tears.

"I shouldn't have come!" he cried out.

She didn't answer.

"I didn't come here to begin it all again. I swear I didn't."

"Oh my dear, I know that."

Enormous happiness flooded. It surged in him. He could have shouted to the skies. He could have sung.

❧{21}❧

How could he ever have convinced himself that it was over? He had wanted to believe that those few days on the southern coast of France so long ago had been simply an interlude, one of those delights, mingled with a piquant grief, that life occasionally bestows. Now he knew that those days had been not an end, but a beginning, or more exactly, the end of that beginning which had occurred when he had first walked into a room and found her there, long ago.

They met in London or at Lamb House or at an inn near the hospital. When they were unable to meet they wrote letters.

"Dear My Love," he wrote, "All music and all grace are yours. If I could write a poem, it would start like that. I sit at the window of your flat and wait for you. It is night. I can't see you coming down the street, but I know by the sound that it is you. The front door opens softly, not with the crash that other people make who enter here, and you come up the stairs.

"I am never irritable when you are with me, I, a man always in a hurry, who runs instead of walks, who am impatient for people to complete a sentence.

"The little sounds you make are pure pleasure to me. I close my eyes and, half asleep, I listen to you turn a page. Your heels make a delightful click on the floor between the rugs. When you draw the curtains, I hear leaves rustle.

"I open my eyes and watch you pour tea. I am entranced by your hands, by everything you do.

"All this past year that we have been together, all these odd hours, are the reality of my life. The hospital and the war are its dark background.

"What have we not done together? Heard music often, sat in a bomb shelter through eerie hours, lain in an old bed in an old room at Lamb House and tried to believe that there was no time earlier or later than our long, deep, lovely night.

"Oh, Mary, it's been a long time coming, this acknowledgment. Did you have the same long sense of loss? Like dreaming of some perfect place, some cool blue place that could be forever home, and then waking to find you're not there and never will be?

"But why do I write like this, when I am awake and I am here now?"

THE LESS ONE has of money or time, the more skillfully one learns to use them. An hour for a supper, one night in the London flat or at an inn near the hospital, rarely a whole day's and night's leave—these were the equal of weeks in an ordinary life. Everything was heightened, sharpened and quickened.

They walked on country lanes and rested under trees. At Canterbury, struck to silence and awe, they stood before the altar where Thomas à Becket died, went out afterward into Kentish fields, smelled the hops harvest, passed the aristocratic pile of Knole and had dinner by candlelight in a room where Dickens had dined. They rode the trains to nowhere and back. In stormy weather they took shelter in museums or stopped to watch Lady Cavendish, Adele Astaire, dancing with GIs. They wandered the streets. One day Mary took him to the place where Alex's mother had been killed in the 1940 blitz. The very earth was mutilated, an open wound filled with a rubble of blasted stone and tumbled brick.

"She was on her way to the Anderson Shelter in the yard. She was hit not six feet from the entrance."

Half a house stood at the far end of the enormous hole, and over it all had crept the lovely purple willow herb, a veil drawn on a disfigured face.

"It was September seventh," Mary said. "A warm day, I remember. The leaves were blown off the trees. It was like green shredded tissue paper, all over the streets. And then there were the fires. Ships on the Thames were burning. It looked as if the river were burning too. And the streets were full of cats, isn't that queer?"

"Cats?"

"Yes, they were lost, looking for their homes. But their homes weren't there anymore."

"Come," Martin said. "Come now."

Back in the flat they sat down to their plain supper, boiled potatoes and eggs, eaten with wine and by candlelight on the gleaming table which had once held crystal and flowers. Luminous pale fingers touched Mary's forehead and fell across the white lace at her neck.

"The lace comes from an old teacloth that belonged to Alex's mother. I rescued it," she said.

The homely remark touched him. Her hands, which had once worn polished nails, looked rough. One nail was darkened from a bruise. The naturalness of these things made him feel married to her.

"You look tired," he said. "With that house and those children, aren't you doing too much?"

"There are only two left. The others have gone back to their families. Anyway, I could say the same to you about doing too much."

"I have no choice. Besides, I'm used to it."

"And I'm not. I've been spoiled all my life."

"That's not a word I would ever use about you."

"But it's true, Martin! All that life we had before the war, all the privilege which made things for people like me so charming, that's over, you know. Alex has been saying so for years. He saw the war coming long before any of our friends did, and he was right. So I believe him when he says it will never be the same again. And perhaps it's just as well that people like us won't have so much and others will have a little more."

Yes, Martin thought, remembering the waiting room in the hospital where that other England brought its ailments, seeing again the wizened clerk-faces, sickly white, with rotting teeth.

"Only I do wish, I hope, we'll be able to hold on to Lamb House," Mary said.

"I hope so. I know what it means to you."

"Oh, not for me! For Alex and the children. It's their heritage."

"Not for you?"

"When the war's over," she said quietly, "I'll leave Alex. The girls will be grown by then, and it won't matter anymore."

Something opened up in Martin like a taut spring releasing.

"Leave Alex?"

"I don't say that easily. We've lived under the same roof so long, he and I. My friend: that's how I've come to think of him. My friend. But it's time, or it will be soon."

He wanted to say, to cry out to her, *Then you and I?* But a packet of unopened letters lay in his pocket, like a warning hand upon his flesh. That morning, a moment before he had left his room, they had arrived from home. Home. So long ago! So far away! Press the eyelids shut and try to imagine oneself back across that ocean, try to hear American voices. Faces dim and fade. They blur and vanish. So long ago! So far away!

From the radio in another room came the BBC's music: the majestic andante from Schubert's great C Major. It lifted and swelled like a vast, calm, moving ocean.

He shook his head, shook himself free of complex thoughts. Not now. There's time enough to think. She hasn't left Alex yet. The war isn't over. So, not tonight. Just let pure sweetness flow tonight. Drink the wine, a bottle of sunshine taken from a vineyard on the Rhine before the war. There ought to be flowers on the table, but there are none. Imagine them, then. Imagine iris, and roses so darkly red as to be touched with blue. Think of Mary wearing velvet again. Remember night birds, lemons, the sigh and crash of the sea . . .

H E DOZED. MARY stroked his forehead. He had been on his feet in the O.R. for eighteen hours straight. Her fingers soothed and soothed. He was half aware of the mohair afghan being lightly settled over his shoulders. A pity to waste our little time in sleep, he thought, and struggled to keep awake, but lost.

He dreamed. His mind roved. At the same time, he knew he was dreaming.

A letter had come from Tom; at least it seemed to have come from him. He had had a terrible spinal wound, yet he wrote that he had seen Jessie somewhere in the Pacific. Jessie's back had grown perfectly straight. She was tall and very rich, with a bag of gold coins at her waist. She was married, and her husband's name was Alex. Claire appeared. She had a baby, a boy named Enoch, but Enoch was bigger than Claire. He was already in college. Now he was on a tanker going to Murmansk. The tanker went up in flames, while he, Martin, stood watching, unable to move. *Jump!* he screamed. *Jump! You didn't save him,* Hazel cried. *You knew he was Claire's baby.* Her face was so sad; he had never seen such a terrible sadness. But perhaps it wasn't Hazel's face? Was it hers or his mother's? It was such a sad, old face. It was the first thing he had noticed about her. *I'm going to Germany to look for you, Martin,* she said, *because it's so lonely here without you.* The word was drawn out so he could hear the wail in it: *lonely.*

He woke abruptly. One lamp was bright in the room, on the table next to the telephone. Mary was sitting there with her head in her hands. He saw that she had been crying.

"You didn't hear the telephone," she said.

"No. What is it?"

"They called from home. My friend Nora did. She didn't want me to walk in alone and find the telegram."

Ned, he thought, the boy. Oh God, no, not her boy.

"It's Alex. He's dead. Oh Martin, Alex is dead!"

Kneeling on the floor, he put his arms about her waist. "I'm sorry. I'm so sorry. He was gentle, he was kind."

"It's so rotten cruel! Hard! Cruel!"

"I know. I know it is, my darling."

"You see death every day. But I—"

For a long time he held her with her head resting on his. At last she spoke.

"How am I going to tell Ned and the girls? I won't be able to think of any words."

"You'll think of them."

"Emmy's been homesick. I've spent hours on the telephone with her. They've been so afraid for their father."

"You'll know what to say. Tell me, isn't Ned stationed near me?"

"About an hour's drive, I should think. Oh, do you think—could you?"

"I'll switch hours with someone. And there's a fellow in transport who'll get me a car. You remember, he's dropped me off a few times at Lamb House?"

"I remember." She began to cry again. "Martin, I've just thought, what if it were you? How could I bear it?"

"People do. And you would. But it isn't likely to be me."

"I know you feel guilty about not being overseas."

"I do . . ."

Yet—if he had to go now and leave her, how hard it would be. All, all a welter of conflict, the whole damn business of living! A man's guilts and his desires, pressing and pulling at him.

He caught her to him. In the midst of death, life clamors. Something like that went through his head.

"Unhook the collar of your dress," he said. "The lace. I don't want to tear it."

He picked her up. Almost as tall as he she was, but so light, so firm and light, so supple and fine. My lovely. Never, never anything in all the world like this! Never. Oh Mary, life clamors.

Winter fog hung in the trees. The car was an open one, and the cold beat about their heads as Martin drove. The boy sat staring straight forward. His first tears had been shed and swallowed. Only a prominent Adam's apple bobbed now and then in his thin neck. They sped through villages, down High Streets deserted, as afternoon neared evening and people went indoors to shelter. And Martin recalled the day they had buried his own father, on just such a still day between Christmas and New Year's, with the dry ground frozen and no wind.

This boy's father, though, would lie in no coffin among flowers, with hands that the undertaker had neatly clasped. This boy's father—was pieces blown somewhere in the desert air, fragments in the desert sand.

"You know he's to get a medal for heroism?" Ned spoke unexpectedly.

"No, I didn't."

"Mother's friend has a relative in the War Office and he found out. My father saved four lives. Crazy, isn't it?"

"Crazy? I don't understand what you mean."

"He didn't have to go to fight, that's what I mean. They wouldn't even have taken him if they'd known."

"Known what?"

The boy turned a clear and earnest face to Martin. "Why—what you know. He wasn't—he wasn't—" The Adam's apple bobbed. "Don't make me say it when you already know about him, please."

"I see." Martin was appalled. Was there no innocence left in the world at all? And he asked, "Who told you?"

"I heard it around the village when I was still in school. I've known for years."

"I see," Martin said again.

"People are rotten about it."

"I know."

"Some boy said he couldn't fight his way out of a paper bag. They won't be able to say that now, will they?"

"It would be a rotten thing to say even if it were true."

They rode on silently until Martin said, "We're almost there. We'll make it by six, I should think."

More silence. Then Ned spoke again. "Isn't there anything you want to ask me?"

"What should I ask you?"

"I thought you might want to know whether—whether I'm like my father. I'm not. I've had plenty of girls already, and they're what I want."

"What you want isn't any of my business, is it?" Martin responded quietly.

"You're very decent. My father said you were. He said you were the only person who'd really understood."

"You spoke of this with him?"

"Yes. After I'd first heard talk, I went and asked him. And he told me. I guess it was one of the hardest things a man might ever have to tell his son. But he did it."

"And, may I ask, how did you feel?"

"Sick about it. I ran out of the room and cried. I couldn't talk to him or even look at him for days. But then after a while, after I had thought about it, I went back. He was my father, and a better father to me than most of my friends had."

A boy like this one could make a lot of people ashamed of themselves, Martin thought.

"I felt sorry for Mother, though," Ned went on. "She stayed because of us, the girls and me. I knew that. The girls didn't and don't. There couldn't have been much in it for her, could there?"

I love your mother, Martin wanted to say, and imagined the boy replying, I know, my father told me that, too.

But he said only, "She loved her children. You were worth it to her."

At Lamb House lights were on, the driveway was full of cars. With his arm around Ned's shoulders, they walked together, Martin with Mary's boy, into the house.

A WEEK OR more before the sixth of June in 1944, Martin had gone south on medical affairs and stood where one could look across Southampton water to the Isle of Wight. From Weymouth Bay across to Portland Bill lay a thousand ships or more, destroyers, landing craft and mine-sweepers. So in his bones he had known, and was therefore not surprised to be awakened toward morning on the sixth of June by the sweep and drone of hundreds of airplanes flying overhead. It had begun.

In the wards expectant faces look up from the beds. "It's here," they say, and then, in some primitive ritual of denial, are silent. For if it failed—one dared not think of that.

First announcements, oddly enough, come over the German radio, sounding as if nothing much has happened. "The Allies have attempted a small landing on the coast of France."

Later in the morning comes a short statement from the BBC: "Allied naval forces under the command of General Eisenhower, supported by strong air forces, began landing Allied armies on the coast of France."

By noon the churches are filled, from Westminster Abbey and St. Paul's in London to the smallest village chapel. Under Gothic stone lace, facing the pale tips of lighted candles, old men and women with sons, and young women with husbands, bow their heads to pray.

Martin would give much to be part of that day in France, even as he knows that its first casualties will soon be rolling down the road to his door.

Through summer and autumn, the momentum quickens. The train gathers speed, it tops the hill and goes roaring down the long straight track. Paris is liberated; De Gaulle strides down the Champs Elysées. The Germans withdraw. The Allies pursue and cross the Moselle River.

In dark December the Germans gather strength for their last stupendous effort in the Ardennes. At first the radio brings bleak reports for the Allies from Bastogne, from Namur and Liège. But in the end, the stupendous effort fails and, late in the winter, the Germans are driven back. The Allies cross the Rhine at Remagen Bridge. The war in Europe is as good as over.

Now orders begin to arrive. Major So-and-so is to proceed to Michigan or New York to receive the wounded from the Pacific theater. Captain So-and-so is to proceed to California to embark for the Pacific theater.

One day, Mary speaks what for many weeks has been unspoken between them.

"They'll be sending you home soon," she says.

It is both a statement and a question. Martin doesn't answer.

He went outside and lay down in the grass. At the top of the rise, he could see the wheelchairs on the terrace where convalescents had been let out to gaze at a spring that some of them had thought never to see again.

At the foot of the modest hill, a stream curved under an arched stone bridge. Gilded catkins hung from the willows, which in summer stood like young girls with streaming, long pale hair. A hawk sailed over Martin's head, paused in the sky and plunged behind the rim of the trees.

He closed his eyes. The air was full of sounds, blending into one long hum of afternoon, of bees, wind and larks. There was a rhythm to lark-song: five beats long, two short. There was rhythm and music in all things. Passionately, he wished he could know more about music.

Someone was playing ragtime on the battered piano in the hall. It was the boy from Chicago, no doubt, the one whose arm he had repaired so well, except for one lost finger. The boy had been worried about the piano; it meant a lot to him, he said, although he was no musician. He was playing pretty nicely in spite of the lost finger! Boom da da-da, boom da da-da.

From the porch came the click and tick of Ping-Pong balls; there was a cadence in the volleys. All his senses were so sharp today! Most of the time, he thought, we are only half alive, missing things. But perhaps it was better so, better not to feel so sharply.

The dog beside him licked his hand. He had forgotten that the dog was there, he'd grown so used to it. One cold night in the previous winter, he had found it sitting outside the local pub where he had gone for a beer. It was only a shabby mongrel of a type so common as to have become almost a breed in itself, with pointed ears and a setter's tail meant to be carried in pride and gaiety. But some pleading in its face had caught at him, and he had stopped to talk to it. Two villagers had come out and warned him away.

"It'll bite you," they said. One had picked up a stone. "Get out of here! Get the hell out of here!"

The dog moved a few steps and sat down. It had been desperate enough for food to risk the stone.

"People abandon them," Major Pitman remarked. "It's a disgrace."

The man who had picked up the stone rebuked him. "They don't have rations enough for themselves. What do you want?"

They had started to walk back to the hospital. At the end of the street, Martin had realized that the dog was padding behind them.

"I'll have to get him something to eat," he'd said.

"You'll never lose him if you do," Major Pitman had warned.

"I know."

At Martin's door, the dog had stood on the step waiting to be asked in.

"Oh, no," he'd told him, "I've nothing for you."

And the wretched creature had licked his hand.

"What am I to do with you?" he asked now. "It's soon going to be over between you and me."

The dog raised sorrowful brown eyes. I *understand,* they said, and he crept closer. A grasshopper, with green transparent wings like finest paper, lit a few inches from his paw, but the dog took no notice of it.

You will not abandon me, he told Martin; *I believe in you.*

Martin laid his hand on the warm flanks where you could no longer feel the ribs. "Yes, you know, don't you? You know I can't turn you out."

The dog's tail thumped the ground.

"Mary will have to take you. I'll leave you behind with Mary."

And Martin sat up. *Leave you behind?* Was he, then, really to go away? Twice in a lifetime? Haunted, haunted! A fairly intelligent man, supposedly in charge of his own life, he had been obsessed since the very first day.

What was it all about? Why were we here? What was history but a history of turbulent past griefs? Crackle of fires as Troy burned, he thought; splitting timbers as Jerusalem fell and Rome was sacked, weeping of parents when the Black Death emptied Europe, agony and shame of the concentration camps, thundering of bombs on burning London. So little time to flower in the sun and live and take one's love!

Mary, Mary, I can't leave you again. I can't.

The dog crept closer still and licked his hand.

HAZEL wrote, "LORRAINE Mays tells me your unit is to be brought home by summer. She was surprised you hadn't let me know, but I understand, darling, that prudent as you are, you didn't want to raise my hopes until you could be absolutely sure."

There were only three weeks left before departure. In the morning, every morning, while a crowded day still lay ahead, he assured himself that at some point in that day, everything would suddenly be resolved. And always the night came without solution. Well, tomorrow then?

There were two weeks left.

One day in London he passed a toy shop and saw in the window a wooden horse like one that Enoch had played with. Later he had an errand that took him past the Brompton Oratory, where he had pushed the newborn Claire in her perambulator. Here in these old, old places, past baroque stone, through mews and Georgian squares, she had first learned to walk. Always he saw her in that yellow coat and bonnet.

He felt weak, aware of his heartbeat. Turning into a cardiac neurotic, he thought, scornful of himself. But he was trembling when he arrived back at the hospital.

"Don't you feel well, Colonel?" his new lieutenant asked.

"No, I've been fighting a blooming cold all week."

He sat down at his desk before a sheaf of records which had been left for his signature. The words made no sense.

Was there any possible way he could request postponement? Any way orders could be rearranged, so that perhaps some other man who was in a hurry to go home—as who was not?—could go in his place? He needed time! Time to think! But of course, that was nonsense. This was the army. And shutting the door, he put his head down on the desk.

Write to Hazel? Take courage and put it all on paper? A lot of men in this war were doing and had done just that. For one sharp moment, he saw her sitting in the chair at the kidney-shaped desk where she used to read the mail; he saw her eyes crinkling in a smile, her face softening, as she opened the letter. He shivered.

Go home and tell her then. Give her as gently, as kindly, as reasonably as you can, the truth. But what of Enoch? What of Claire? *Carpe diem,* it is said; seize the day, seize life. It speeds away while you watch. And I'm forty-four years old.

H<small>E KNELT ON</small> the floor beside their chair where Mary sat knitting. Narrow blue veins crossed and merged in delicate webbing on her wrists. He took the wool away and kissed her wrists. Had he been asked what he was feeling, he could have said it was not worship, it was not comfort, it was not joy, it was not desire. It was all of these and it was beyond them. It was beyond the farthest reach of longing.

"I can't," he said.

"Can't go away?"

"No. Can't go away."

After a few days another letter came. "Enoch will be in the second grade next fall, imagine! He's so like you, Martin, always reading. People say he looks like you, too. He wanted to have a picture of you in his room, so I had a duplicate made of the one on my night table. It's the last thing I see before turning out the light and the first thing I see in the morning when I open my eyes.

"I think sometimes that if you were to stop loving me, I couldn't bear it. But then I know that couldn't happen any more than I could stop loving you. I don't think there can ever have been two people who understand each other better. I feel that, even though you're three thousand miles away, we're still together. And soon, please God, we really shall be. I'll turn in bed at night and you'll be there, and it will no longer be a dream."

Martin put the letter down. A dull sadness seeped into the room, like fog. He read on.

"I've saved so much of your allotment, you'll be surprised. Living alone like this, a woman doesn't need to spend much. I hardly ever go to the stores except for Enoch's clothes. And yesterday I bought a necklace for Claire's birthday, seed pearls on a gold chain. She's such an amazing girl. It's hard to believe she's only fifteen . . . Now that you're coming home, though, I shall treat myself to some new clothes. Would you like to see me in a black lace nightgown?"

She had used to sit up in bed and wait for him when he was called out. She always said she couldn't fall asleep until he was home. If only there were some meanness in her, some sly and reprehensible selfish streak which could assure her survival while it gave him an excuse! But no, she had wanted only and always to please everyone, even her exasperating relatives. God knew what fears, what chained resentments even, underlay that anxious love of pleasing!

And suddenly Martin heard his father's voice. So often in the crises of his life, he had recalled that voice, not necessarily its words, rather its tone of earnest conviction. He remembered, too, the expressive movements of the hands, so uncharacteristically Mediterranean for a man from Ulster. And he thought of his own little son. What would that boy remember of his father?

He went down to the street. He needed to move. Mary was to come in later from the country, but she had her key. The night was gray and the scudding clouds threatened rain. His footsteps pounded so that he startled himself and made himself walk more softly. He walked across the city and came to the river.

In the middle of the bridge, facing the Victoria Embankment, he lit a cigarette, then threw it down into the iridescent, oily water and watched it blink out. The sky behind the Houses of Parliament blackened as the storm approached. A flash of lightning brightened the long, even facade, the fretwork pinnacles, oriels and turrets of this place where men sat and made rules to keep themselves from consuming each other. He lit another cigarette, threw that one, too, into the water and began to walk home.

Some soldiers passed, their laughter stilling to a startled salute when they saw the American officer. Hearing their muttered "Had too many, that one!" as they passed him, he realized that they had heard him groan. Did he look as wretched as he felt? As woebegone? Yes, his head was bent, his hands were knotted behind his back as though he were pacing the floor of his own house. He straightened up.

Mary was asleep on the sofa when he let himself in. Dismayed, he remembered that he had left Hazel's pages scattered. She had picked them up and placed them neatly on the table next to the lamp.

She opened her eyes. "I didn't read it," she said.

"I didn't think you did."

"It's from home, isn't it?"

"Yes."

And kneeling down, he put his head on her lap. Then, ashamed of his wet eyes, he couldn't raise his head. The price a man paid for manhood! Valor and steel, the ramrod back, the stiff upper lip!

"You're going home to stay?"

"Yes," he murmured.

She got up and, going to the window, pressed her cheek against the cold glass. At last she said, "A commitment. I understand."

He couldn't answer. What words could he have found? He thought perhaps dying would be easier, going down into oblivion and rest.

"We deserve something better . . ."

"Who knows what anyone deserves?"

"Our timing is always wrong."

"God knows that's true."

"Bitterness is ugly, Martin. And I am so damn bitter."

THEY LAY IN bed, talking.

"There was a couple who lived near Alex and me. He was twenty-eight, and he died one Saturday morning after playing tennis. Before the war, people of twenty-eight weren't dying. It was a grief so terrible that you turned away from looking at her. And still I couldn't have understood it . . . Tonight I do."

He took her in his arms. The last time, the last time. He thought he had cried the words aloud; perhaps he had only heard them in his head. A swelling tide of blood crackled and surged as he lost himself in her; never draw apart, he thought; never, never . . . and then he did fall away and lie apart at last, seeing shadows, hearing the sound of rain.

It must have started while they lay in love. Trucks were passing at the corner, a rumbling convoy of army vehicles, each one guided by a being as filled with his own essentiality as Mary and he. The little room trembled with their thunder. The clock struck three. A few hours more, and it would be over.

W HEN SHE CAME out of the bedroom in the morning, he had already collected his things.

"Just your clothes, Martin? Not the Churchill mug or the Rowlandson prints I gave you or anything?"

"Only your *Three Red Birds*. I don't want anything else."

They stood in the little hall.

"Do you think we'll ever be in the same place at the same time again?" Mary asked.

"I don't think so."

"If we ever are, I'll walk quickly away, and you do the same. Will you promise me, Martin?"

"I promise."

"It's eight, and you'd better hurry," she said.

But neither of them moved.

"I'll go down the stairs, Martin. I won't look back. Wait two or three minutes until I've driven away."

"No. I'll see you into your car."

"Please. I can't just drive off with you standing there. Please. Help me."

"I want to go down together," he insisted.

In the instant before he put the light out and shut the door, she began to look like a stranger. She was wearing a skirt he had never seen before. It had grown chilly, and she had put a sweater over her shoulders, a complicated knit of the kind people receive as gifts. Yet, under the skirt and sweater was the flesh he knew so well, more dearly than any he had ever known, or ever would.

And was he absolutely mad to be doing what he was doing, or was it the only way to keep from going mad?

They went downstairs and out to where her car was parked. It seemed to him that they ought to be saying something. He wanted to say: Understand, we are the kind of people who cannot step on other people's faces. He wanted to say: You see, the trouble with you and me is that neither of us has courage enough to preserve ourselves. For, isn't that the first law of nature? Yes, but nature isn't civilized, and we are, you and I. He wanted to say all those things, but he said none of them.

He might have done so—or again, might not have—but just then a man came out of a house and went to his car, which was blocked by Mary's.

"Oh," the man said, "you're going? Looks like a fair day! I suppose you will soon be leaving, Colonel, now that the Jerries have given up?"

"I suppose so, yes."

"It's been a long war. It'll seem strange here when all the Americans have left."

"I guess it will." Would he ever go, the fool? Couldn't he see he was in the way? But no, of course, he was waiting for Mary to move the car.

"Well, if I could just back out," the man said, politely enough.

"Of course."

The man got into his car and started the motor. Mary got into hers. She placed her hands on the wheel, then looked up at Martin.

"Are you all right?" he asked. "Can you drive all right?"

She nodded. He wanted to say—God knows, what he wanted to say. *Oh, my dear, my love, forgive me, take care of yourself.* And he said nothing.

She put out her hand and touched his quickly. Her little car began to move. Then Martin turned, and rapidly, blindly, walked into the stunning glare of the risen light.

BOOK FOUR

VISIONS

⋯⟨22⟩⋯

Over the northern shore of Japan's lovely inland sea, in early morning the *Enola Gay* came winging toward Hiroshima. And in one fiery moment of warm summer, the war ended.

In movie theaters across America, people sat with upturned faces, watching the mushroom cloud and the settling ashes of what had been Hiroshima, watching Tojo hand over his sword on the battleship *Missouri* in Tokyo Bay.

When the show ended, they got up and went out into Times Square's electric night, or else into Main Street's shadowed night to walk home under rustling maples. For the moment, there was only rejoicing. Some years later would come recriminations and defense. Some years later, tourists would visit the museum in Hiroshima and stand in shocked and grieving silence before the pictures of the maimed. But for now, there was the business of living to be resumed.

On laden ships, crowded in passageways, on bunks four tiers deep, the impatient men sailed homeward. Trains were jammed. And the stations which had, four years before, seen so many dreadful partings were witness to a million reunions of sons with parents, of husbands with girl-wives and children who had been babies when their fathers went away.

Of course, there were some who were not being met at the station. These had already been informed, or had informed, that absence had changed things: that she had found another man in the factory or down on the street, or that he had found a girl overseas. For such as these, the end of the war was as much of a shock, or possibly more of a shock, than the start of it had been.

But most came back home to the same wife and the same job at the gas station or the bank. And these, the wife and the job, might have been either balm to the heart or else a secret disappointment that the great adventure was over.

Everyone joined the scramble for goods, for everyone needed everything and everything was in short supply. Ration books were torn up and thrown away. Gradually, the shops began to fill again with nylon stockings, sugar, lamb chops, shoes and chocolate bars. OPA was taken off and prices jumped, but since wages did too, no one objected.

Pessimists like Tom Horvath, ever cautious, predicted a bust and a slide back down to the grim grind of the years before the war. It didn't happen. There began instead a long procession of the most plentiful, lavish, dazzling years in all the

history of America, indeed in the history of any land or empire on the planet,
since histories have been written.

MARTIN WAS PROPELLED by events. He needed only to stand still and be swiftly
moved as if on a conveyor belt, from that first moment of beholding Hazel's
radiance and hearing her glad shaking cry, then of catching the boy up in his
arms, the cheerful little boy in whom Hazel's effort had kept alive the memory of
Martin.

He got down on the floor with Enoch. Three years before the child had played
with blocks. Now he could read *Dick and Jane* and write the note tacked on the
bedroom door: "Dear Dady. Well come home. Luv, Enoch."

Claire came, quieter now, less impetuous, wearing a feminine blue dress and a
hairdo. He sat with her to talk about college. She was barely sixteen, but already
the rush was on. Should it be Smith or Wellesley? Where were the better science
programs? She wore glasses now. For some reason, they were becoming to her
alert and mobile features, and he thought: She is going to be a rare woman.

The telephone kept ringing welcome. Martin's mother called, her old voice
quavering with tears until Alice got on the line. Friends rang the doorbell. One
evening the door was opened to Perry, still in Navy uniform, back from the
Aleutians; a week later, Tom telephoned from California that he was on his way
home.

On the first Sunday they could borrow a car, Hazel and Martin went to visit
the Horvaths. Tom had gone quite gray. The men hugged each other, hiding great
gulps of emotion, then sat down to eat one of Flo's enormous dinners and stu-
diously didn't talk at all about the war. That would come later.

"You've still got your appetite," Flo observed.

And Martin answered that, yes, there hadn't been much good eating in England these last years, and the English had never been first-rate cooks, anyway. So
he filled himself, while Hazel watched, not able to take her eyes away, and he was
grateful that she was still so sweetly pretty, with so much joy in her face, and
hadn't grown older and fat as Flo had.

He was grateful, too, for Enoch, who demanded his attention and made, he
admitted to himself, a kind of natural barrier or buffer between himself and
Hazel's intensity. If she noticed at all that the child was in the way, she did not
appear to. So Enoch averted many moments which for Martin would have been
sorely strained.

He was in a hurry to be busy again. Work would be his salvation. And his
head whirled with the speed of reentry to the former life.

His old civilian clothes still fitted, but felt foreign, and the first day in the
hospital was queer, too, walking in and wondering whether he'd attract too much
attention, or perhaps none at all.

On a bronze plaque in the lobby, he found his name on a long list of names,
some of which bore stars. The stars gave him a thundering shock, recalling the
faces that went with them, faces that would never be seen in this building again,
while he could walk in, hale and straight, to be greeted like a hero.

For, indeed, they remembered him. Nurses came crowding up; the old ones, those over sixty, kissed him. Doctors came to shake his hand. Even Eastman was cordial.

"I read your article in the Archives. Extraordinary case! You must have seen more in your three years over there than we see here in ten."

"More than I ever want to see again. Not that kind, anyway," Martin told him.

THE FIRST THING you had to do was to open an office. Space was almost impossible to find. One consulted newspapers and agents; one canvased every possible doctor for news of space to sublet. In desperation at last, he agreed to share with an obstetrician of acquaintance, also back from the service, who hadn't yet found a place. It would have been an unwieldy arrangement for both of them. At the last minute the other man found something, and to Martin's great relief, he was left with an ample office all to himself on the fine East Side street.

Painters had to be found, at a time when it seemed that everybody in the city must be calling for one. There were furnishings to buy. Hazel wanted to help, but Martin told her mildly that, while the house was hers, the office was his. Here he would spend the larger portion of his days, and he knew what he needed: simple Danish chairs and desks. And on the walls, a series of fine photographs, views of the city done in sepia: a liner coming through the Narrows, an old man feeding pigeons on the Mall, rain on Fifth Avenue in late afternoon with the lights coming on.

He had been prepared to borrow from a bank the considerable money needed to get started again. But when Hazel, with simple pride, showed him the savings book in which his allotment checks were methodically recorded, and he saw that there was more than enough to pay the bills, he was much moved.

" 'She looketh well to the ways of her household, and eateth not the bread of idleness.' "

Hazel's admiring comment, "You do know the Bible backward and forward, don't you?" embarrassed him. But she was right about it all the same. He was his father's son.

They needed a new apartment. The old one had been cramped to begin with, and now, in the rear, a building was being put up which would have so darkened Enoch's room that he would have had to burn electric light even on the fairest day.

"The new apartment must be sunny," Martin insisted, which limited their choice even further in the limited market.

Of course there had to be more rooms, for without doubt, they would soon be having another child. Not a day went by without mention of it from Hazel. Martin had no real objection, although surely no desire, either. He had Claire and Enoch; they were enough for him. But Hazel's position was very different.

As with their first home, she had free reign. He had little time anyway to spend in the rose-colored living room with its flowered, middle-European embellishments. She liked it, and he was pleased with her liking it. Only his study was to remain as it had always been, a refuge for books and music and plants. For a moment he considered the possibility of hanging Mary's *Three Red Birds* above the bookshelves. But then he realized it would be an affliction to him every day, like a hairshirt, and wrapping it up again in brown paper, he laid it away at the top of a closet behind a row of old medical texts.

He began to fit back into the routines of home: the sounds of a little boy roller-skating down the hall; Claire's dropping in one or two afternoons a week after school; Hazel's resumption of her comfortable life among women, with classes in needlework, P.T.A. and recording for the blind.

"It's almost as if you hadn't been away, isn't it?" she remarked once during the third or fourth month. "I used to be afraid we'd never make up for our lost time, but it's not been like that at all."

It seemed to Martin that her thankfulness was an aureole about her head. She glowed with it. And his thoughts would flee to that other woman—his thoughts, like some poor chained dog, that in a sudden rush of glad anticipation, forgetting the chain, jumps forward at full strength and is jerked fiercely back at the throat.

In the fall Hazel knew she was pregnant. The following spring she gave birth to another boy, whom they named Peter after her grandfather. A good-tempered baby, resembling his brother, he gave promise of being, again like Enoch, a quiet little boy.

Martin tried to remember what he had felt on the day Claire was born. He seemed to recall a first aching disappointment that she was a girl, and after that, a surge of absolute exaltation, totally unlike the tender, subdued pleasure he felt now. Again, the circumstances were not at all the same.

They made plans to rent a house in Westchester for the summer, near the beach yet close enough to the city so that Martin could commute by train. On crowded days, he would stay alone in the apartment.

So they were on their way, he in the hospital and the office, Hazel in the busy home, and both of them in a mild bustle of work and children and meals, of coming and going and living. Apparently, out of first confusion, order had quite rapidly been wrung.

He treads the carpet softly, its rough pile prickling his bare soles. The old insomnia which has plagued him intermittently through life has come back. He steps into hazy, pink light: a lamp has been left burning in the hall, so that Enoch will not trip on his way to the bathroom during the night.

He looks in at the boy who sleeps in a tumble of blankets and toy animals. Then he goes into the baby's room. The infant has wedged himself crosswise in the crib, his head pressed up against the sides. Very carefully, the father readjusts his position, concerned for the pulsing fontanel in the tender skull, although he knows it is foolish of him. The baby is really not that fragile.

Quietly he recrosses the hall to his study. He closes the door and turns on the record player. Perhaps music will help him tonight. It always has.

The Cleveland Orchestra plays "Ein Heldenleben," doing it better than either the Boston or the Philadelphia, he thinks. He listens carefully to the solo violin, and with pleasure, recognizes the recurrence of the theme from *Don Quixote*.

When the music stops, he starts to reach for *Don Quixote*. It is consistent to stay with one composer, and consistency is part of his compulsive nature. How well he knows himself! But he pulls his hand back and turns the player off. It is no use. For the first time, music has failed him.

He looks at the desk clock. It is past dawn in England. He starts to switch the lamp off, but again halts his arm in midair, remembering suddenly a strange thing that had happened in the drugstore that afternoon, where a woman was buying perfume.

"La Fougeraie au Crépuscule," she had said, mispronouncing the words, and had asked the clerk what it meant.

"Don't know," the clerk had replied with a shrug.

Martin had answered, not intending to; the words just issued from his mouth, "Fernery at twilight."

"Oh," the woman had said, surprised that he should know.

"It's the only perfume I remember," he had added awkwardly, most foolishly, as if the woman had asked or would care what he remembered.

It is cold in the apartment now, and he goes back to bed. He hopes Hazel will not wake up. If she does, he will have to take her in his arms, for although she keeps saying everything is quite normal again, it is plain she still needs reassurance that they are as they always were.

He draws the quilt up over his shaking shoulders. The baby cries out, but it is only a startle, and is not repeated. He is just five months old, and Hazel is pregnant again.

She has brought this pregnancy about, allowed it to happen, without asking Martin. Now she presses and curves against him, like a spoon fitting into another spoon. He understands her needs. She is so good to Claire, he thinks, as he so often does. His thoughts run on, darting and colliding with each other.

Claire is tenacious, spirited and serious. I missed so many of her good years. Jessie has done a superb job. I should like to tell her so. I saw a woman ahead of me on the street who looked like Jessie from the back. When I saw she wasn't Jessie, I don't know whether I was sorry or relieved. I wonder what I would have said if it had been? Why, I should simply have told her she'd done a superb job!

Claire is a merging of Mary's blood with mine. I never thought of that until this minute. A stunning thought! I never had it before; I don't know why. It shocks me.

I've had a dream of Mary on a ship, a sailing ship out of some other century. She was standing on the deck or at the prow. At first I thought she was a figurehead. Things are like that in dreams. The sails were swelling and the wind pulled at her skirt. I was on the dock. We stretched out our hands to each other. The water grew wider between us as the ship moved away. Then the wind whipped the scarf around her face so that I couldn't see it anymore, and the ship went faster, straight out like an arrow, to the rim of the world.

It is said that loss grows dimmer with time. But is that true? There was a German-Jewish doctor in my company; Hertz was his name. He was a taciturn, persevering, thoughtful man. He had lost his wife and children. I used to wonder what he carried inside his head. Would it be easier or harder to know that Mary was dead?

It is also said one must force oneself to think of positive things. All right then:

my work. I'm grateful for being so busy. I truly am. Think of something beautifully lazy, of swimming to the float and drowsing in the sun. No good. I can't feel it. Think of something gay and funny. That day halfway between her house and London; I was late arriving at the country pub, and someone, some boorish old man, had been trying to flirt with her before I got there. We laughed so to see his face when I walked in. But it isn't gay and funny, remembering it now.

He feels himself beginning to drift finally toward sleep. Cold air seeps through the blankets. It is raw as only an English house can be. The casement bangs, and an air raid warden's shrilling startles him awake. He opens his eyes and stares into the street below. It is some sort of minor accident. This isn't England. He's home.

Hazel murmurs. She, too, is dreaming. And he feels so gentle toward her, as to a child lying there asleep, and so sorry, just so sorry. Now she stirs.

"What is it?" she asks. "Is anything wrong?"

"No, no," Martin says. "Go back to sleep. It's all right. Everythings's all right."

❊{23}❊

At the far end of the apartment's hall, looking on the courtyard, was a dank room used for storage. Even on the brightest afternoon, the bulb, which hung on a single wire from the ceiling, had to be lit. Three stories below lay the gray cement floor of the court where ash cans stood along a wall. Ten stories above, by twisting one's neck and pushing one's eyebrows up, one could see a corner of sky.

Inevitably, Enoch was drawn to this room. His mother, who almost never complained about anything and who, Claire thought privately, really did spoil the boy, objected that he messed it up. But since the room was only a jumble, Claire didn't see what additional harm the child could do.

There were cartons of dusty books, thick college texts of Martin's in dark green and brown. There were two old microscopes, one of which had belonged to their grandfather, with its old-fashioned jars and bottles, some still half-full of a desiccated ointment. An American flag, souvenir of a long-forgotten parade, drooped from a stick in a corner next to a dress form which Hazel had used in the days when she still made her own dresses. More busty even than Hazel was, the headless figure would have scared the devil out of you if you had come upon it suddenly in the dark. There was an old easychair from whose arms the dried leather rubbed off in ruddy pellets. There were thick black phonograph records of Galli-Curci and Caruso from the days of the windup Victrola, and a bicycle of Martin's which he had no time anymore to use.

Now to all these had been added some possessions of Grandmother Farrell's, sent on after the funeral by Aunt Alice so that Martin would have his fair share of things by which to remember their mother.

Claire sat down on a broken chair. It was raining hard. Some of the rain fell even in the narrow shaft between the buildings, trickling in the dust on the window.

"Gee," Enoch said, "look at these *National Geographics*! There must be a hundred of them. Let's take them all to my room."

"No, you won't. Your mother'll have a fit if you drag those to your room. You can look at them in here till they come home. I'll look at these old pictures."

Old photo albums still retained an aura of the forbidden, and she had to think for a while why this should be so, before she remembered the albums at the

681

house in Cyprus when she had been no more than five or six and found in them the pictures of her unknown pariah aunt. A mystery, Claire supposed, that would never be cleared up.

But in these snapshots of her father's people, there were no mysteries, or none that she could see, at any rate. There were only nostalgia and a sort of sadness, which she had thought a person would have to be old to feel. She hadn't expected to feel it when she was just sixteen. Yet she was feeling it. Probably it was because the death of that grandmother last month, a woman she had seen only four times in her life—and the last time when she was dying—had touched her deeply. She had known perfectly well that her mother had not wanted her to go with Hazel and Dad. Jessie would have liked to be able to forbid the trip. But since a death had been involved, she had very likely felt that objection would be shameful. So she had made none, except to indicate by her compressed lips and flat voice that she was not pleased.

Here was the grandmother as a young woman of the Gibson Girl era, her neck collared to the ears in boned net. The anxious, pretty eyes looked out under the brim of a stiff sailor hat. Living is hard, those eyes said.

In old age the eyes had been a faded, opaque gray, as if a curtain had already fallen between them and the living world. She had been sitting up in bed, awakening when they came into the room, and then drowsed off in the middle of a sentence with her mouth dropped open over her even, large false teeth. Just gliding gently out of the world, Claire had thought. It was strange to think that if this woman had not lived, *she* would not be living either.

They had buried Jean Farrell in the cemetery in Cyprus, and during the long ride from the place of her death at Aunt Alice's house, her son and daughter had relived their years.

"Remember the hot bricks in bed? Funny, when your feet are warm, the rest of you gets warm enough so you can fall asleep," Martin had said.

And Alice had said softly, "The things you remember! Maple taffy! Isn't that a foolish thing to be thinking of today?"

Martin had explained to Claire how maple taffy was made. "You collect the sap twice a day and boil it over a wood fire," he had said carefully, as though this were a piece of knowledge so precious it must be preserved. "Then you fill a soup plate with snow and pour the hot syrup over it. When it cools, it gets hard and sticky like taffy."

"Your father tells me," Aunt Alice had said to Claire, "that you want to be a doctor." She had spoken formally and politely, more formally to Claire than to Hazel, as though Claire were the stranger and Hazel were of her blood. "Your father used to keep mice and frogs in formaldehyde, under his bed. Do you remember, Martin, the time you had the dead snake there, and Mama found it when she was cleaning? And how she screeched?"

So it had gone. And at last they had reached Cyprus, driven down its principal street—"How it's grown!" Alice had cried—and out past the house where Alice and Martin had lived.

Martin had sighed. "It was all farms here then."

The town had spread around it. Across the road from the house had been an industrial park. "Light industry," the sign had said. Rows of muddy cars had stood in a gigantic parking lot.

"They've taken the porch off, or glassed it in, I see. They must live upstairs."

Martin had pointed to where, on a frame house with a boxy glass front like a protruding abdomen, "Guido's Pizzaburgers" was lettered large.

They came to the cemetery. Claire, having never been at a funeral before, had expected something intensely dramatic. But it had been very simple, just a short prayer before they lowered the coffin. Each of them had thrown in a handful of earth, and then walked away. And that had been all.

"I don't suppose we ever really knew either of them," Martin had said. He had turned Claire around and told her, "Take a last look. You may never be here again. Just remember that you come from decent people." He had stopped a moment, and she had understood that he was thinking old thoughts.

"Look," Enoch said now, "I opened it."

"Opened what?"

"It came off. The hinge broke off."

"That's Dad's old trunk. Don't go prying in it, Enoch."

He had already pulled out a uniform.

"Gee, look at the hat!" It came down over his little head, resting on his ears, while the visor grazed his eyebrows. "Gee, why didn't Dad ever show me this before?"

"I guess he'd just as soon forget about the war."

"Look at this! Dad used to be an explorer scout. Did you know that, Claire?"

"No. He did do a lot of climbing in the Adirondacks, though."

"And what's this? 'Washington High School, Martin Thomas Farrell'?"

"That's a diploma, what they give when you're all finished. You'll have one someday."

"Will you?"

"I'd better, if I want to get into Smith and then med school. What have you got there? Don't do that. Those are private letters. You're not supposed to read other people's mail."

"It's not letters. It's pictures."

"Here. Put them back in the envelope. You're tearing it, Enoch! Give it to me!"

A packet of snapshots fell to the floor. They had been enlarged so that the faces were clear: her father's and an unknown woman's. They had been taken during the war; her father was in uniform. The woman was slender; her hair was short and curly. In one of the photographs they were holding each other's hands. And one was an attempt at a portrait, for the woman was sitting on a garden bench, wearing a wide straw hat and a full skirt, like a Renoir lady. On the back of this was written: "You are everything to me and always will be." The signature read: "Mary Fern."

Those clustered words stood out as though they had come to life. Heat rose into Claire's face, up to her forehead. She was shaken. Mother's sister, Mary Fern! This, then, must be the reason one was forbidden to ask about her! Mary Fern and my father! He had intentionally kept these pictures, hidden them away; he so

meticulous, precise to a fault, who never left things lying around, who reprimanded anyone else who did! He wouldn't have kept them if they hadn't meant
"everything" to him, too!

"Look at these," Enoch cried. "There's a whole bunch of letters here, and look
at the snowshoes! Claire! Did you know these were snowshoes? You walk on top
of the snow with them. Golly, there's a lot of good stuff in this trunk!"

"Come, come," she said. "We're putting everything away."

She slipped the packet of snapshots into her purse, folded the uniforms into
the trunk, replaced the scout badges and all the memorabilia of boyhood; then
led Enoch out into the kitchen to feed him cookies and a glass of milk.

Darkness had come abruptly, giving a forest eeriness to the afternoon. Disturbed, without aim, she wandered through the rooms, turning the lights on as
she went. At Hazel's bedroom door she paused. All the cloying sentimentality
with which Hazel had furnished her home was concentrated here.

A hanging cabinet was cluttered with china figurines of men in powdered wigs
and women in hoop skirts. The carpet had blue roses all over it. A lamp was
shaped like a child holding a puppy. And on the desk there was a photograph of
Martin, his ascetic face completely out of keeping with the rest of the room.

On a table in the den lay a stack of magazines, professional archives and
reports of congresses, along with notes in Martin's crabbed writing.

". . . approaches to mental disease," Claire read. ". . . ambivalence of brain
and mind." She stood there, trying to fit what she knew of this part of her father's
life—analytical, austere and serious—with the man in the snapshots.

But it was naive, it was absolutely *childish* to suppose a parent was only what
one saw on the outside! Certainly one knew better than that. Still, one's father!
That there could be such—such taint in one's own family; things not clean, not
good!

"You come from decent people," he had reminded her at his mother's funeral . . .

The door opened, and Hazel came in with Martin. "We hurried back as fast as
we could." She was out of breath and anxious with haste. "You're a dear to babysit
for us, Claire. Was Enoch a good boy?"

"Oh yes. And the babies are still napping."

"I'll get them up," Hazel said, discarding her raincoat.

For a moment Claire stared at her father. It crossed her mind that, in the flash
of a few seconds, her concept of him had changed. It was the angle of view that
mattered. As the little boy with a scout badge, as the brother of Alice—that was
one way to see him. The woman who had written *You are everything to me* must
have seen him differently. Hazel had still another view. And Jessie? Whatever her
view might be was well hidden.

Hazel came back with the newest baby, Marjorie, drooped over her shoulder.
The mother and the child wore the same expression of innocent, domestic tranquility.

"You'll stay for supper, Claire?" Martin asked.

His eyes regarded her with affection. In them she read how much pride he had in her and how he would want her to have the same in him. She brushed at her own eyes as though cobwebs hung before them.

"Thank you," she said coldly, "I'm going home."

Only an hour before she would not have believed she could despise him.

THEY TALKED TILL past eleven. Jessie parted the curtains and stood thoughtfully looking out into the night. Over her shoulder Claire could see that the rain had stopped; a ghostly glitter lay on the walls and trees, matching her own fearful mood. The curtains fell back with a taffeta rustle as Jessie turned around.

"You shouldn't have taken the pictures," she said.

"I had stuck them in my purse and I didn't know what to do with them."

They lay spread out now on the coffee table. Claire picked one up, then slapped it down.

"How I would hate her if I were you! Both her and Dad, but her the most!"

"Oh, I've had my fill of hatred, make no mistake about that! But you can't keep it up, year in, year out. It's corrosive. I guess that's why I kept the whole business to myself until now. I didn't want you to be corroded. Also, to be honest, there was a little matter of my own pride." And Jessie smiled slightly, in the self-mockery that was her habit.

"She spoiled your one chance. She could have had dozens, couldn't she? And she took your only one."

"Damn it, yes, she did."

The love seat at the fireplace held small silk pillows, round as jewels: amethyst, topaz, garnet. Jessie fussed with them now, patting and rearranging. Presently she said, "Yet I always knew I'd been foolish to marry Martin. And after all that—happened—it would have been more foolish to hold him. I could have done it, you know. He wanted to stay. Because of you and a sense of obligation. But I didn't want that. I couldn't bear what I knew he must be feeling toward me, in spite of his merciful denials."

What could it have been like in bed? Claire wondered. All those books that were passed around among her friends—somehow one always thought of strong and handsome people doing the things that were described in those books. In sudden shame she flushed and could not look at her mother.

Jessie was moving around the room again, at the magazine rack now. She spoke abruptly.

"I heard from Aunt Milly that Fern's husband was killed in the war."

"How horrible!" And Claire had a quick flash, out of some old war movie, of a sky torn by terrible guns and battering rain, of a man lying in the mud with a leg torn away. "How horrible!"

"Yes. She's had her share too. But she ought," Jessie said somberly, "she ought to have married Martin in the first place. I knew it the first time I saw them together. Before they knew it."

"What? Love at first sight?"

"Don't scoff! It happens."

"Pulp magazine stuff."

Jessie smiled. The smile enlivened her mouth, but her eyes were still. "You'll find out."

"It's just not real."

"You're sure you know what's real and what isn't? You're sixteen and you already know that?"

"Well, I read, don't I? I see things, don't I?"

"But you haven't lived them."

Jessie played with the gold chains at her neck. She wore too many and they were too valuable. Why were they so important to her? Claire wondered. The thought was new. And all this business about love—how did Jessie know? Because she had gone through it herself? And this thought, too, was new.

"So what you're saying is that they couldn't help it?" Claire asked.

"I suppose I am."

"That sounds almost noble."

"Noble! Good God, I? You know better than that, after living with me all your life. No, it's just that I've had to come to terms with things or go crazy. And people like me can't afford to go crazy."

Jessie picked up the photographs and shuffled through them. "You can keep these or destroy them," she said, laying them back on the table. "Whatever you want. I don't care which."

"Not return them?"

Jessie shook her head. "They'd be a time bomb in that family. They'd wreck it."

"You care if they do?"

"There are children! How can one wish that on children? It was enough when you—" She stopped. "And besides, that woman—that Hazel—never did anything to me."

Ah yes, poor Hazel! Why did one think of her as "poor" when she was, after all, so snug and well off in her home? But there was something— She was so mad about Martin, it was embarrassing sometimes.

Jessie leaned over a photograph. She spoke reflectively, almost to herself. "Of course, I always knew he was an uncommon man. I always saw how far he'd go if he were given half a chance."

"He talks about you sometimes. I think he might even like to see you. Why don't you? People who've been divorced can still be civil to each other, can't they?"

"A while ago you never wanted to see your father again. Now you want me to see him."

The mind is so confused. You are old enough to understand how young you are and how contradictory everything is: other people, one's feelings about oneself, everything. How long will it be before you ever get it all straightened out? Will you, ever?

And, almost angrily, Claire cried, "I don't *want* anything! I only asked why—"

"All right, I'll tell you why. I'm peaceful the way things are, the way I am. I don't need to complicate my life with him or with my sister or anyone. I've nothing to say to him. I've made my way with no thanks to anyone except myself.

Listen, I don't want to hurt anybody, Claire; I only want to be let alone. I'm a realist. I've had to be."

Jessie's face, in the shaft of lamplight, was coppery gold. It burned. Intelligence was in it, and strength, and pain. Suddenly, through the opacity that separates one human spirit from the other, there came to Claire a flaring white translucence, an opening up, so that for an instant she entered into Jessie, lived as Jessie, was there in that other instant of shudder and shock when the young girl first truly saw herself and knew she had been condemned when she was born.

Jessie got up. "I'm weary." She stroked her daughter's hair back from her forehead. "Come to bed. You've had a hard day. You've done a deal of growing up today."

Alone in her room Claire stood brushing her hair. The rain had begun again, threatening the windowpane. Suddenly it came to her, so suddenly that she stopped the brush in midstroke, that she pitied, not Jessie only but her father, too. He—in all his competence and strength, he who was able to solve everything —she pitied him! And in this pity there was something new, another kind of love . . . Wasn't that strange?

And now she felt the tightening of things and people. It was a feeling new to her, who had been particularly free in doing and thinking whatever she wanted. Those two, she thought, my father and the woman, Mary Fern—what sort of woman can she be, she with the dreaming eyes beneath a shady summer hat, with the long fingers lying on the silk lap? Those two have changed so many other lives besides their own! Because of them my mother and I live alone in this house; because of them there are Hazel, little Enoch and the babies—

What may come to me yet, to all of us, bound as we are to one another?

<h1 align="center">❈{24}❈</h1>

The day the office had opened, indeed the day on which the lease was signed, Martin had been terrified lest he had undertaken too much and wouldn't be able to afford it. He was still, and probably always would be, a cautious heir to the Depression. But he need not have worried.

Very quickly the appointment book began to fill. Friends from the old bicycle and handball days had returned from the war and were sending referrals. More referrals came from new contacts in general practice and the specialties; his reputation was wider than he had known. So it became clear that, for the first time in his life, he would not only not be short of money, but would have it to spare, would have that freedom from constraint which comes when all one's bills can be paid without wrinkling the forehead over them.

He came to his desk one afternoon while the office was still empty.

"You're early," the secretary said. He always thought of her as the "little" secretary, although she was over forty and had a perfectly good name: Jenny Jennings. "There's no one booked till one-thirty."

"I know. I finished at the hospital." And he closed his door.

The truth was that he hadn't finished at the hospital in any way he would have wanted to finish. The patient had died. Thrusting aside the sandwich and coffee on the desk, he went over, for the third or fourth time in the last hour, the agony of the morning.

Even before the hemorrhage started, he had known. Disaster had a certain feel and smell. He had known its warning breath often enough, and would know it again. That was in the very nature of the hard and sorrowful work he had chosen. Sometimes you were given an extra bit of last minute luck to pull you out of a tight place, but not very often, and not today. From the evil growth attached to the carotid artery, the bright blood had just come gushing. Bearing down on the gauze packing, it had taken his whole strength in an attempt to stop the flow, but it had kept coming. And he had wished he were somewhere else, anywhere but there and then.

A circle of heads had surrounded him. He'd been aware of faces watching the open skull, watching him to see what he was going to do. But there had been nothing to do and they had all known it.

"The EKG is flat," Perry had finally said at Martin's shoulder. The words were

688

mournful, final, like the sound of the sea in a shell. "There's no heartbeat," he'd said.

"Oxygen," Martin responded, but it had already been brought. The tube was in the nostrils and someone was pressing on the chest of this young man who had been, so he had told Martin with pride, a varsity basketball player. Now he worked in a bank, and his wife had had twins last winter.

Martin had drawn off his gloves and slapped them furiously to the floor. Leonard Max, who was chief resident now, picked them up without a word. Then they both went to the locker room, where they put on lab coats to hide the tragic blood on their hospital gowns, removed the operating shoes and went down the hall to the waiting room to tell the family that the basketball player, the son, the husband, the father of the twins, was dead.

Later he had talked to Perry, protesting. "It need never have been if I'd got to him a year ago."

"I know," Perry said softly. Always he had been a foil when Martin was in trouble, offering some cheerful comment or remark to offset a stillness in Martin, offering as now his listening silence when events exploded.

"Idiots!" Martin cried. "Treating him for a neurosis when he complained of headache! Pressure of the job, the responsibility of twins, they said. My God, it's shameful . . . Talk of the unity of the neurological specialties!"

He remembered now the young man's courage and confidence, assumed, very likely, for who would not be terrified to know that an evil something was swelling and tightening in his brain? But he had been quietly brave, reassuring his wife, shaking Martin's hand, making a lame joke or two.

Ah, you saw so much death sometimes in this work, you wished you had become a dermatologist, or better yet, a math teacher, a car salesman, anything but what you were! Some deaths touched you with a knife-edge of anguish, just as some of the war-wounded still stayed visibly in mind, while others had faded, not because any were more worthy than the others, but because—well, they just did. And he remembered now the boy he would always think of as Chicago and how he hadn't been as concerned about dying as he had been about losing that one finger.

Pa, Martin thought. Pa had that terrible concern, so personal sometimes as to be almost unprofessional. He had tried to conceal it, but one always knew by the way he clenched his teeth on the pipe stem, so that his words came out all muffled. His mother would tell the children not to annoy their father that night because a bad thing had happened: a patient had died. And her eyes would be so troubled! Soft people, they had been.

Sometimes he could still feel flashes, for just a second or two, of the grief he'd felt when his father had died. And he was reminded of the day he'd met Leonard Max. It had been the young man's first day on the job. Martin had asked him something or told him to do something, and when Max hadn't responded at once, he had been impatient and spoken sharply. Afterward someone had told Martin that the boy had just got news that morning of his father's death. He was finishing the morning's work before taking the train home. And Martin, remembering his own father, had been so sorry and ashamed, more sorry than he could say. He had apologized to Max.

"I get impatient too quickly. I'm a damn-fool perfectionist. Forgive me."

Now the "little" secretary opened the door. "Thought you might want a second cup of coffee, but you haven't touched a thing," she said reproachfully.

"I know. I've been thinking."

"You've only got another fifteen minutes."

Obediently, he unwrapped the sandwich now and leaned back in his chair. This room was where he really lived. It was the core and center of his life, when you came down to it. Here he sat to hear one anxious recital after the other, the tales of symptoms that would end either in success and health or in disaster. Each began here on the other side of this desk. Each was a new and terrifying adventure.

What did these people see when they first walked in here with the damp palms and the dry mouth of fear? They saw a neatly furnished room with cheerful pictures and many books. They saw a man with a calm, professional manner, a stranger on whose reputation their hopes were fixed. They could know nothing of *his* fears, his private guilt, empty longings and high ambition.

Jenny Jennings had put a sizable stack of mail before him to be answered. On top lay a still-unanswered letter from Mr. Braidburn. Martin hadn't heard from him in years, hadn't even gone to see him during the war. Why? Probably, to his shame, because he hadn't wanted to be asked about Jessie or Claire.

Anyway, here was his letter, asking whether Martin had any suggestions for a most excellent young man who wanted to go to America. He had been doing some fine research in neuropathology and would like to combine that with further surgical training. Could Martin find a place for him in his laboratory?

Research! A kind of angry shame crept over Martin. What had he to offer such a man? Very little, except, as the practice kept growing, what Eastman had offered him: a chance to do important surgery and make money. There was nothing wrong in that. But it wasn't what he had had in mind at the beginning, was it?

And suddenly he thought of Albeniz, who had wanted his own institute, who had deserved it and who would have done a greater service to the sick if he could have had it. Then it occurred to him that he had been so hurried lately that he hadn't thought of Albeniz in months. So he picked up the telephone and, reaching the number, was told that the doctor was dead. He had died of a heart ailment almost a year ago. Martin must have missed the notice in the paper and so, apparently, had other people. *Sic transit gloria.* You are here, you make your little mark and you are forgotten.

Miss Jennings knocked at the door. "There's a man outside," she said, "without an appointment. He says you operated on his son-in-law this morning. The one who died." She looked worried. "He seems all right, but do you want me to stay?" *People have been known to be distraught and threatening,* she meant.

"No," he said, "it's all right. Let him come in."

Martin stood up and put out his hand. "I'm so sorry," he began, "I can't even begin to tell you, Mr.—"

"Ambrose. I was at the hospital this morning." The man was slight, tired and apologetic. "I just took my daughter home."

"Oh," Martin said again, "I'm so sorry! He was a fine young man."

"We know you are, Doctor. But you did the best you could."

"It wasn't good enough."

"It was too late. I knew that. The poor boy didn't; at least, I don't think he did. Maybe he had thoughts and didn't want to worry us. Who knows?"

The voice trailed away and Martin felt the heavy weight of sorrow in the room, the old familiar sorrow of his work, so acquainted with grief. "Acquainted with grief," that poignant phrase from the *Messiah*, he thought, and then was aware that the man had said, "I knew." He came quickly to himself.

"You knew? How could you have known?"

"No reason." The man held his gray fedora on his knees and kept smoothing the crown with the palm of his hand, round and round. "It was just a feeling. So we talked about it, my daughter and I. We thought, if Michael dies, we want to know why."

Because, Martin answered silently, the diagnosis was delayed. It wasn't malpractice, it was just bad judgment, all too common. And there's not enough cooperation between the fields.

"We want to help so that it won't happen again. We're not rich, but I have a few dollars put away, and I want to make a donation. I read in the papers about all this research in brain diseases, so I've written you a check, and we want you to use it wherever you think best. Put it where it will work so they can learn more about these things."

The shining innocence, the goodness, the courage!

And gruffly, because those damned humiliating tears of his were rising, Martin said, "It's five hundred dollars. I don't want to take it. There are children, the twins—"

Mr. Ambrose stood up. "It's all right, Dr. Farrell. We've decided. It's the way she—we want it. And he would have wanted it, too."

So they stood there looking at each other with the presence of the dead boy between them. Then Mr. Ambrose shook Martin's hand. "Thanks, Doctor," he said again, and Martin watched him go out.

Damn it to hell and back! Maybe that boy wouldn't have died if— But maybe he would. Don't play God, Martin. Yes, but maybe he wouldn't.

He got up and walked around the room, picked up a book, put it back, went to the window, looked out and saw nothing but a dazzle on the street. Then he sat down at the desk again and vaguely saw the snapshots, old and new, under the glass: his children with Hazel; himself with Claire in front of an old wall on a proud visiting day at Smith; his father wearing a duster, standing on the running board of his first car.

"You will see things I haven't even dreamed of," Pa used to say, and Martin swore again.

Braidburn's letter still lay on his desk. Oh, if he had a place to take in that young man, he knew exactly what it would be like! He'd planned it, outlined it on many a sleepless night.

Once he'd begun a study of pituitary tumors and abandoned it in the middle when he left old Llewellyn, years before. The whole problem of circulation in the brain—there was so much he wanted to find out! And it would have to be, need to be, combined with surgery. Then, of course, the psychiatrists would be welcome too; they'd be needed in problem-solving—

He thrust a fist into his palm. There'd be room then for Braidburn's protégé, and many more. Perry, of course, to head anaesthesiology; good, dependable Perry at one's side. And Leonard Max. Now there was a fellow in whom intelligence and devotion were written tall!

Jenny Jennings opened the door. "Seven waiting outside already," she said accusingly.

Martin sighed. "All right. Send the first one in."

He walked slowly home. On a Madison Avenue corner, a discreet display in a window caught his eye. Behind a very fine antique desk, French, eighteenth century, stood a lacquered Oriental screen; an old engraving hung above it; the whole was most quietly elegant, made vivid with a splash of violet fabric. He stopped a moment to admire. The sign read: "Jessie Meig, Interiors." He stood there gazing at the sign and remembered that Claire had said Jessie was expanding into new quarters.

Baffling and extraordinary, this life! So strange the ways in which we act on one another! There was Albeniz, now dead, who had lit the spark in him. There was this woman, Jessie, who had fanned the spark and given him Claire besides, the pearl, the treasure of his life. Then Hazel, the warm and tender. And always, always that other, hidden, and beloved— What am I doing in return for these? Martin thought, and, standing momentarily outside himself, saw himself in all the complexity and contradictions of his nagging, Calvinist conscience, his zeal and his zest.

As soon as he got into the house he went to his study, picked up the telephone and quickly, before his nerve should fail, called Robert Moser.

"Hello, Bob? This is Martin, Martin Farrell."

"Everything all right with you?"

The voice held surprise. Martin had never called Moser at his home or anywhere else. Such contact as the families had was made by the women, by Moser's wife calling Hazel, to be exact.

"Yes, all right, but I want to see you about something."

"No trouble, I hope."

"Not really. Or rather yes, in a way. I need money," Martin said bluntly, and correcting the clumsiness, explained, "Not for myself. You may remember years ago I mentioned my—well, sort of pipe dream, I used to call it, of a neurological institute here at the hospital?"

"I remember."

And Martin detected impatience, masked by courtesy.

"Well, something happened this morning. No need to go into details. But I've been galvanized into action. I've been thinking, when you want to do something, do it."

"Can't quarrel with that." Amusement now, and a trace of skeptical suspicion.

"And since you're a trustee, the only one I know, it seemed logical to begin with you."

"Money's not plentiful, Martin. We're operating at a deficit. You know that."

"Hospitals always do, don't they? And somehow they always find what they need."

"Yes, but you're talking millions. Prices have soared since the war."

"I know all that. But there are always the foundations. Maybe even government funds. Matching funds, if only we could get started and have something to show."

"Why do you want this, Martin? Have you any idea what you're letting yourself in for?"

"The answer to the second question is yes, I think I know. As to why I want it, that goes way back. Let's just say I'm convinced we need it. The profession needs it. The patients need it."

"There's no lack of neurological centers, as far as I can see."

"True. Although they're not exactly what I have in mind. But aside from that, don't you think our hospital, one of the finest in the city, or the whole country for that matter, deserves this honor, this crown on its head?"

Moser smiled. Martin could hear the smile in his voice. "You put it well. You'd like to run the whole shebang, naturally."

"I'd like, Bob, to teach and do the research I've been missing. That's what I'd like."

"You'd have to give up a lot of time from your practice, wouldn't you?"

You're doing very well, you can make a pile for yourself. Why don't you let well enough alone? That's what Moser was saying in effect, exactly as Eastman used to say it.

"Bob, I want this," Martin said.

"You want the moon, too?"

"Call it impossible, call it what you will, I want it because it's right."

"I'd never get the trustees to go along. The world's full of nay-sayers."

"Once the building's up, ten, twenty years from now, no matter how long, and the patients start coming and the work is being done, they'll be the first to applaud, I promise you."

"Maybe so."

"Bob, I'm going to do it, even if you won't help me."

"Talk sense, Martin. You don't know the first thing about finance. How in hell are you going to do it?"

"I don't know. I'm going to begin. You built up Phoenix Tool and Die. You didn't sit around, afraid to take a chance, did you? You began with nothing, didn't you?"

"Well, you might say I did, yes."

"Okay. Enthusiasm I've got. And I'll get others behind me. I know I will. I'll go to meetings, I'll talk. We'll get contributions from the public, too, you know."

"I doubt that."

"I already got my first check this afternoon. And I know we can get more."

"How much?"

"Five hundred dollars."

There was a silence.

"Five hundred dollars from a grateful patient who had no reason to be grateful."

"You're not serious, Martin?"

"About what? The patient? Of course I am."

"I meant the money. Just what the hell do you think you can do with five hundred dollars?"

"The Chinese have a saying, 'Every journey begins with the first step.' "

"Well, all right, but—"

"We need a campaign. We need to organize. You have contacts in industry. I'll tackle the foundations; maybe you can, too."

"You've absolutely no idea how hard it will be. The foundations are inundated with appeals."

"Bob, I know it can be done." And suddenly inspired, Martin cried, "If there hadn't been this kind of drive and confidence all through the history of medicine, if they hadn't found the means to build hospitals and fund research and train people, your daughter wouldn't be playing tennis now."

Again there was a silence, much longer this time. Martin, holding the phone, heard traffic noises, noises from the kitchen and Moser's silence. At last there came a tired sigh.

"Okay, Martin, you've got me. We'll need to do a lot of talking, though. You'll need to get some tentative figures together, very rough, so at least I'll have some idea of what we're talking about."

"I'll do that."

"Better get advice on those figures before you bring them to me. I have no confidence in you at all as a businessman, I must tell you that."

"I couldn't agree with you more. But I can get the facts you want. Give me three weeks. I'll call you."

"Fine, Martin. You do that." And Moser hung up.

A sense of unreality was left in the room. Martin's head went light, as if he were going to be sick. He looked at his hands as if they belonged to someone else. What had he done? And he sat there thinking: Perhaps it will be too big for me after all.

Then, after a long while, reality flowed back. A bag full of apples or potatoes rolled over the kitchen floor and a child shouted. Trucks stopped on the street below, the workmen cursing cheerfully at each other. Life was proceeding in all its noisy, brave confusion.

Can do, he resolved. Anyway, I need to be overworked. It's the way I am. Otherwise I think too much. It's always better to be doing and trying, even if I fail.

He got up from the chair. Every journey begins with the first step.

❈{25}❈

Arrivals and departures made a modest bustle in the lobby of the Connaught. Fern, waiting for Simon, could identify by clothing and accent the varied travelers: Americans, West Germans and British country people spending a few days in town. He hadn't wanted her to go upstairs with him to meet the customer, who assuredly would have been flattered to meet her. The man was a haggler, he said, and he'd be able to get a better price for her work if she wasn't present.

The money would be very welcome, she reflected with an unconscious sigh. Alex had told her often enough that there wasn't sufficient inherited wealth to live on, and there certainly wasn't.

Yet she would be sorry to part with the picture, a quiet, cloudy seascape which she had done while on a visit to Isabel and her husband in Scotland. It had been one of those rare, remembered days when everything had seemed to fit, and she had thought, observing the happiness of her newlywed daughter, that life would probably go well with Isabel, that unlike her mother, she would see it through into hearty middle-age with little conflict.

They had been very close that afternoon, and the memory was all there on canvas: the gauzy, cloud-striped sky, the enormous loneliness of the dun beach and the kindness of three who were friends.

Paintings, she thought, and not only her own, were like children being shunted between foster homes. To sell them was to demean them. One felt such tenderness for them, as one peered close to marvel, especially at a Turner or other masterwork, to study the way in which the brush had been applied, the way in which color could be used to hold the life of light! It pained you when all that love—yes, it was love that went into it—fell into the hands of people who didn't understand it, who perhaps didn't even like it very much but knew it would be talked about because it was expensive. Or worse still, knew it would rise in value so that in a few years it could be got rid of, traded up!

She opened the newspaper to the critic's column which had so delighted Simon that he had telephoned her an hour before breakfast that morning to read it aloud.

"Not to be missed," she read again, "is the retrospective exhibit by M. F. Lamb at the Simon Durant Gallery. Once past the collection of her earlier works, sensitive foreground figures, all seemingly in mourning in a gray-black world, and influenced, it is rumored, by depression after the loss of her husband in the war, one can allow oneself to be enchanted by a lyricism which recalls the young Matisse. Her landscapes and interiors alike display a balanced organization and taut harmony. Empty space has indispensable meaning for this painter. It must be said that, unlike Matisse, the somewhat tender colors produce a dreaming, feminine effect which is fortunately never sentimental.

"Of particular charm is the *Girl with Flute,* the muted reds giving a fragile—" And so on.

Well, it was all very fine, very wonderful. It would never have happened if she hadn't met Simon at a quite casual supper in the country a few summers before. He'd given her a tremendous push, had brought her forth at a time when she had relinquished the possibility of being anything more than a Sunday painter. And in bringing her forth, she saw clearly, he had forced her to grow. Recognition was tonic. She *was* doing better work. And for the first time in years, she could feel the stirring of new possibilities.

The elevator opened and a young couple came out. Their glossy leather bags were already waiting for them at the front entrance. These must be the people. Bolivians, Simon had said, honeymooning on a mining fortune. Yes, they were speaking in Spanish. The girl was very young and shy. He was handsome and tough. An arranged match, perhaps? They still did that among important upper-class families in South America.

So that is where my Scottish afternoon is going, Fern thought. I don't think it will bring him any joy!

The elevator opened again, and here was Simon. By his smile she knew that negotiations had gone well. It had probably been trying, since the richest people could drive the hardest bargains.

"Sorry to keep you so long," he said.

"I haven't minded. I've been watching the crowd. So it went all right?"

"Splendidly. We got our price. It's a good thing you didn't come up, though. He even sent his bride out of the room. Apparently money is a dirty subject to discuss in front of women. Shall we have lunch?"

"But I've got the car in town, and I wanted to drive home this afternoon."

"Can't we at least have a quick salad or a sandwich someplace?"

It touched her whenever his cheerful animation subsided into disappointment. His generosity merited generosity in return.

"All right," she said, "a quick salad."

"I never get to see you."

"You do. We had dinner only last Sunday."

"Well, but this is Friday, isn't it?"

She took his arm and they went out onto the street.

"Goodness, there must be a million foreigners in the city this summer, don't you think?" she said gaily. She was fending him off, leading away from the personal. And a little chill of guilt went through her, as it does when one has ignored a child or been sharp to someone who doesn't deserve it.

They sat down at a table in a bay window. Fern busied herself mixing oil and vinegar for the salad. Simon gazed out to the street, his lively face gone still, the heavy eyelids dropped like hoods so that he could only have been seeing the bottom half of the passersby.

Ordinarily, he had so much to say. He talked better than anyone she knew, with a great deal of sophistication and yet very little skepticism—an unusual combination of traits. It was not easy to be an optimist without being also something of a simpleton.

He was an attentive listener, too. But sometimes he would look at her with such close attention, as if he were seeing far inside, as if she could hide nothing from him, that she would feel her thoughts coming to a fumbling halt.

She stole a troubled look across the table. A few gray strands had come into his sandy hair; she had never noticed them. He would stay young for a long time, being of the thin, supple type that at eighty or thereabouts has thick white hair and wears good tweeds and remembers how to dance.

So they sat for a little while until presently Simon found something to say.

"Everyone all right at home?"

"Oh yes, thank goodness." Fern grasped at conversation. "I heard from Emmy yesterday. She still adores Paris. I don't suppose she'll ever come back."

"You never know."

"No, you don't, do you?" she agreed.

"She may marry some sturdy British businessman, and you'll have her back here again."

"Maybe so."

Silence. Why was it especially awkward today?

"Strange how different my daughters are from one another. And they look so alike," she remarked, feeling instantly embarrassed at her own banality. As if Simon could care about the personalities of her daughters, whom he had seen perhaps half a dozen times! But she went on, "Emmy knows four languages, so she's perfect in the European business world. I can't see her satisfied living Isabel's life, having one baby after the other."

"I didn't know Isabel was—"

"No, not yet, but I'm sure she will be. They both want lots of children."

"The way it looks," Simon said, "you'll be rattling around alone in Lamb House, won't you?"

"Well, I don't know about rattling around. It was left to Ned, naturally, although I have the right to live there as long as I want. Maybe sometime Ned will marry and come back. Then, of course, I'll move out. Although, I don't know really." Now her thoughts ran seriously, for the subject was of genuine concern. "He doesn't show any signs of settling down. He's due back from Egypt soon, does well in every job he's had, but right now someone's put a bee in his bonnet about America. So many of the young men want to go where the 'action' is. That's their expression."

"Where the money is," Simon said. "I daresay you can't blame them."

"I wouldn't say that was true of Ned. He's creative and imaginative. I really think it's just change that he wants, something new. He ought to do splendidly in advertising."

"Of course, New York's the base for that."

"So very likely he'll be flying off again. I miss him," she said simply.

"From what I see, children are ungrateful wretches. You put everything you've got into them, and all they do is forget you."

"They have to live their own lives, Simon."

"I suppose so. Still, I've never regretted having none. Margaret did. It must be a much deeper need in a woman, after all. Almost the last thing she said to me before she died was that she was sorry she wasn't leaving me with a daughter or a son to remember her by."

"But you remember her anyway," Fern said softly.

"Shall I tell you something? It's been ten years, and by now I really don't remember very much. Yes, I recall how loving and good she was, and that we lived well together. But I don't really remember her. I can't quite see her face anymore. Do you understand?"

Fern didn't answer. Alex's face? It came back to her only in some swift movement of Emmy's mouth or when Isabel threw her head back to laugh too loudly. She had never seen Alex in Ned. He might have been of different stock, so different was he, with those musing eyes and that odd half-smile, reminding her, improbable as it was, of Martin.

And suddenly she was aware that her fork was half-raised to her lips. She laid it down.

"I've upset you," Simon said kindly. "I didn't mean to, Mary. I'm sorry."

"You just called me Mary," she said. "No one ever does."

"You told me once you liked it better. I try to remember that. I try to remember everything you like."

"You're so good," she said. "Just good. There's no other word."

"Am I?" He shrugged. He took a cigarette from the pack, choosing it carefully, tapping it, lighting it, pursing his lips and blowing the curled smoke toward the ceiling. Then he ground it roughly out, twisting it in the ashtray, and reached across the table for her free hand. His own was trembling.

"Marry me," he said. "I've been on the verge of asking you so often and you know it, don't you, Mary? I've all but said it a dozen times."

"I know." And lowering her eyes away from his gaze which was so intense, so strong that it frightened her, she thought: I am not ready for this.

"With a little push, even a glance, a bit of something in your voice to encourage me, I would have said it long ago. Well, now I'm saying it. Marry me."

It was too bad, too bad, that tears should spring into her eyes.

"I know I'd always take second place."

"You shouldn't be satisfied with second place."

"But if I'm content, Mary, isn't it for me to choose? Besides, it's not like a recipe, is it? Loving, I mean? You can't measure it: a cup of this, a spoonful of that. Loving is different every time."

She murmured pointlessly, "I don't know."

"So even though I understand how you loved Alex, this would be different."

She didn't answer.

"Besides, Alex is dead."

The waitress came to take the plates away. Simon released her hand and she put it in her lap, not wanting to be held, not wanting to be fastened.

"I'm not ready yet," she said, looking down at her hands.

"You're not a girl anymore. There's not all that much time."

"That's true."

"When will you be ready, then?"

"I don't know," she said again.

"I would be good for you. I've been good for your work already, you've told me so."

"Yes. Yes, you have. You would be." She looked up. He was so grave, so fine and grave. "Oh, I wish I could," she cried, and now it was she who stretched both hands across the table and took his. "Oh, Simon, whatever you say about not caring, not minding, you deserve so much better!" Her tears rolled over and slid.

"Don't cry here," he said gently. "We'll go now. I'll take you to the car."

The top was down and the rushing wind, the sound and touch of it, calmed her grieving spirit. That Simon's proposal should have been so painful! Dear, trusted friend! Considerate, tender, and demanding, too, as one wanted a man to be! What was wrong?

In the late afternoon when she kissed him good-bye on leaving the gallery, his cheeks were rough, for his beard grew quickly. He was clean, so very clean. She knew so much about him. She knew what he liked to eat and to read, the kind of friends he chose. What was wrong?

That ache. That other. Still she saw him as on that last morning when, through the rearview mirror of the car, she had watched him walking down the street in his American uniform, walking out of her life again, going away. She had not been on that street since, had taken care to avoid it. The flat where they had said good-bye had been given up, the excuse being, and it was the truth, that it was too expensive to keep.

Her thoughts ran in tangents. Even Lamb House could only be maintained by opening it to the public two days a week. American tourists came crowding to see how an English country family lived, or had lived. But she had an obligation to keep the place for Alex's children. The girls wouldn't want it, but perhaps Ned might one day. He had understood his father's feeling for it. My feeling, too, Fern thought. The house speaks to me. Martin saw that. "You love each tree," he told her once. He had understood. It always came back to Martin. Everything always came back to him. Everything joined in a circle: Alex's house and Martin and Alex's son. Her son. Where did it all end?

Circles don't have an end, she thought. And life is linear, with a beginning and an end, somehow, sometime. I'm very tired.

At the toll booth, an elderly man with an automatic smile took her change. For some reason he made her think of an animal at the zoo, imprisoned without having committed any crime. To think of spending your life in a little cage, taking coins! Nothing that lived, animal or human, ought to be confined. She hated zoos and belonged to a committee for their abolition. Alex had always laughed, in a nice way, with mild amusement, and so had Martin, because she had joined so

many causes: against the slaughter of whales and seals; for the preservation of the
forests; against drug abuse; for foster homes and battered wives. Well, as long as
you lived in the world, you owed it something, didn't you?

And she felt a piercing compassion for everything that lived, the sort of feeling
that flashed through you now and then with such dear intensity that you couldn't
possibly feel like that all the time, or even most of the time. It would sicken your
soul. But shall I ever clear my own way, she thought?

The little car moved off the highway and slowed around the curve of the road.
It was a lane, really. She still had enough memory of America and its roads to call
this a lane. The car crept up the drive at Lamb House and into the garage.

In the burning afternoon the house lay shadowed among hovering beeches. It
opened its arms. When she had stepped inside, it would close them around her
again, walling the world away.

And she stopped a moment to listen to the infinite buzz and hum of a thousand little creatures busy in the grass. A butterfly, Parnassius, pale crystal gray, lit
on her arm, its frail folded wings trembling there before it fluttered off into the
light. And a leaf fell, a very small leaf, oval and yellow, spiraling slowly through
the quiet air.

Oh, lovely, blooming world! Birth into life, life into death, the leaf and the
bird in me, I in the leaf and the bird, unending round of radiance and darkness.
But shall I ever clear my own way? she thought again.

The maid, Elvira, one of the last remaining village girls who hadn't preferred
the factory, had seen her from the window and came running.

"There's a young lady in the hall. She asked for you. She's been waiting. An
American, I think."

Now, in the summer before their final year at Columbia College of Physicians
and Surgeons—known informally as P. and S.—five young women were traveling
through Europe. They followed the route trod by generations of students since
the days of the eighteenth century's Grand Tour: through Italy's museums,
cathedrals and ruins and up over the Alps, westward and northward to the
chateau country in splendid summer leafage, and at last across the Channel to
London. Together and on foot they went down the guidebooks' lists, from the
Tower and the palaces to Samuel Johnson's house.

Alone, Claire made her personal and private explorations. With some reluctance, Jessie had given the address of the house where they had lived when Claire
was born: an austere white house of expensive flats in what had once been an
aristocrat's town mansion. The street was quiet under its linden trees. Having no
exotic attractions for tourists, it seemed yet as foreign as a hill town in Tuscany.

Claire felt a mingling of excitement and nostalgia. She stood there for a while
and then, following the city map, walked over to Kensington Gardens to see the
statue of Peter Pan. She had perhaps not realized how intense had been her need
to see these things, for under the neat and capable exterior of this young woman
—neat, now that she had learned the requirements of simple grooming—lay a
core of sentiment. A sentiment, she thought humorously, a sentiment almost
Victorian.

The group was to spend a week in Scotland before going home. On the morning of the day they were to depart from London, Claire made a decision. Then, having prepared herself in advance with a railroad timetable, for she had been playing delicately with the idea ever since they had left New York, she proceeded to the station and took a train into the country.

These little villages straight out of Thomas Hardy followed a design: two rows of cramped, quaint cottages flanking a broad street which ended in a country road. Then, that branched off into three or four lanes, each leading to a fine, great manor at the back of a field on which one was not at all surprised to see a flock of sheep cropping the grass. So it was easy enough to find the place.

She stood in the high, square hall of a very old house. A young maid had admitted her, then left her alone among dark portraits, a vista of long rooms and smells of flowers overlaid with a pungent whiff of brass polish.

Now that she was actually here, Claire felt her first sinking apprehension. How could she have dared to come? It was an impudent intrusion upon a past that didn't belong to her, an invasion of privacy. One would have every right to order her away—

Someone asked, "You wanted to see me?"

A thin, dark woman stood in the doorway. An instantaneous impression flashed in Claire's mind, as when a picture snaps onto a screen: lady of refinement. She wore the delicate, plain dress that such ladies wear to the city in hot summer. She could have been a young woman aging too soon, or an older one who had stayed young.

"You don't know who I am," Claire said, trembling a little. "But—"

"But I can guess. You're Jessie's daughter. You look like her."

"I've startled you most awfully, haven't I?"

"You've startled me, yes. Why have you come?"

"No reason except curiosity. My own. No one else knows I'm here."

"Well, curiosity's a good enough reason, I suppose."

The eyes, Claire thought; those strange, light, startling eyes, at once dreamlike and perceptive, they—they struck you!

And she said softly, "A family feud! All that secrecy and for all those years! Do you never think how strange and sad it's been?"

The fantastic eyes swept Claire from head to foot. "Oh yes, oh yes, I think!"

The eyes looked away for a moment and then returned. "It's rather awkward just standing like this. As long as you're here, you might as well have a cup of tea with me, don't you think?"

Claire followed into the kitchen. The little maid had disappeared. Fern poured water from a copper kettle into the teapot. A huge white cat slept on a chair beside the table where a tray of violets flourished. She moved the cat and the violets.

"Sit down," she said.

Her tan, long hands were clasped tightly and nervously in her lap. Then she loosened them and put them on the table, as if commanding herself.

"I used to wear my hair like that when I was your age."

"I've seen pictures of you. They didn't do you justice. You're beautiful."

"Thank you."

"What shall I call you? Aunt Milly and my mother call you Fern; once, a long time ago when I asked him about this house, my father spoke of you as Mary."

"I didn't know I was spoken of at all." And this was said with a slight rueful, humorous turn of the lips.

"Well, you aren't very often. But you still haven't told me what I should call you."

"Whatever you choose. I don't mind."

"Well, Mary, then. Aunt Mary. It suits you. It's an ordinary name, but not on you."

"You may even drop the 'Aunt,' you know."

"All right, then. Mary. Although it doesn't make much difference, does it, what I call you for one afternoon, since I shall probably never see you again?"

Mary poured more tea. The cat slept on, and the old clock chattered on the wall. A stranger entering the kitchen would have thought that these two women were carrying out a daily ritual.

Mary said abruptly, "I wish sometimes I could see Jessie again." Her hand moved round and round the cup, stirring the tea. "I wrote to her. I wanted to explain, if I could. But she never answered."

"What could she have said?" Claire defended. "After all, you couldn't have expected her to answer, 'It's all right, forget it, I understand.' She couldn't have done that, could she?"

"That's true." And the two plain syllables, spoken in minor key, touched Claire with a sense of finality.

"I hear," Mary said, "I hear from Aunt Milly that Jessie has made a great name for herself."

"She has. It's amazing what she's done."

"I'm glad. If you care to tell her you've seen me, say that I'm glad."

"I'll do that. Is there anyone else you want to know about? Anything you want to ask me?"

"No," Mary said.

There was a little silence until Claire spoke again.

"My mother has no ill will toward you anymore. That's past. I thought you might want to know."

"Is that really so?"

"Quite so. Not that she would want to see you . . . just that she has no anger."

"And you?"

"I? Well, I would hope to have some understanding of people. It would be a pity if I hadn't, wouldn't it, since I'm a doctor, or will be by this time next year?"

"Yes, I know you are."

"Aunt Milly, I suppose?"

"Of course. The town crier. That was what we called her when we were children. How is she, by the way?"

"Failing, since Uncle Drew died. She's long past eighty, anyhow."

Silence again. What should she say next? When ought she to leave? And frowning a little, Claire squeezed more lemon into the cup, fussing to occupy her hands.

"Elvira thought you were an American tourist come on the wrong day."

"An American tourist? The house is open to tourists?"

"Yes, it's the only way one can afford to keep a place like this."

"It's an enchanting house," Claire said.

"You haven't seen it. If you've finished your tea, I'll take you around."

They walked down three steps into what must once have been a banquet hall, Mary explaining, "It hasn't been used in years, it's so enormous."

"But I remember it!" Claire cried.

"You, you were here a few times. Can you remember Emmy and Isabel, too? And Ned?"

"Only vaguely."

"Come, I'll show you their pictures. This one's Isabel in her wedding dress." Claire observed that the girls looked like Valkyries.

"Yes, don't they? Ned's quite different. Would you like to see the grounds? At the gates there, those are temporary kennels for the visitors' dogs. The English always take their dogs when they go tripping, you know. And over here, back of the orchard, is the byre. We only keep four cows now, and of course, I hardly need all that milk. But people want to see the place as it was in its best years."

It was that time of late afternoon when in northern countries the sun slants at so acute an angle that the grass is gilded, and trees in the middle distance are washed in silver light. On the path ahead of Claire, Mary's silhouette was dark against this ecstatic flare of light.

Fey, Claire thought suddenly, recalling the word her mother had once used to describe Mary Fern. She belonged in this place. No proper reserve of dress or manner could belie the different and secret thing that was hidden in her. And she remembered the destroyed and long-forgotten photographs of the woman on the garden bench, the shadowed face under the straw brim—

"Here's where I work," Mary said.

She opened the door of a small brick structure in back of the main house. At the far end of the single room, a glass wall faced the northern sky. The other three walls were covered with paintings. Even at first look, one saw that they were of important quality. Claire was stunned.

"Surely not all yours?"

"All mine."

On an easel stood an oil of a very old man in front of a stone shed. The man was as strong and winter-gray as the stone; the whole was without a single superfluous line or stroke of brush. For a few minutes Claire studied it.

"Lonely," she said.

"Yes, that's Jasper. He's almost ninety, and he comes to milk the cows."

"The end of an ancient way of life. That's what you're saying, aren't you?"

"Of course. You can't blame the young people for wanting to go to the towns. And yet the old country people seem so cheerful. I don't know. But then, there seems to be more all the time that I don't know."

Claire walked slowly around the room, past the fair head of a genial girl, Isabel or Emmy perhaps; past a spray of reddening oak leaves in a copper bowl; a slum street, semiabstract, with animated crowds under lines of hanging wash; a mourning woman with her head on her arms.

"My God," she said. "You did all this? Nobody ever told me."

"They didn't know. And if they had known, why should they have told you?"

"But you're no—no talented amateur! You must be a name."

"They tell me so," Mary answered quietly.

And standing there in the sudden stillness that fell between them, something went all soft in Claire. This woman had lived through passions of which she, Claire, still knew almost nothing. She had endured and had come through to create all this. As Jessie had come through also, in her way. And Claire thought: *Women survive.*

There came then an acute, abrupt awareness of blood tie. There had been so few in her small separated family, and she had always suffered from their lack. She had a swift recollection of the house in Cyprus, a mental picture of every dim, high room. She fancied, although no one had told her which bedroom had been Mary's, that the one at the top of the stairs must have belonged to her in childhood. From its windows one would have looked down on the side lawn and the table to which, on sultry afternoons, the lemonade was brought . . .

"What are you thinking?" Mary asked.

"I feel sad here," and Claire touched her heart.

"Yes." Mary held out her arms. "Oh yes! We could have loved each other, you and I."

Afterward it became clear that if Mary had known her son was to arrive from Egypt, she would not have invited Claire to stay overnight. But Ned had not been expected until the end of the month.

Shortly after breakfast, an athletic young man in a sober business suit came striding up the driveway carrying in each hand an enormous travel-worn suitcase. Five huge dogs clamored all over him in exuberant and loving welcome. When the greetings were past and the clamor had died, Mary made the introductions.

"So you're the American cousin. I remember you," he said.

"You couldn't possibly. I was only three years old."

"And I was eight. You cried because of my dogs. I had to put them outside, and I was mad as hell."

"I don't blame you. You must have hated me."

"I did," he said.

The top half of his face was earnest. He wore tortoise-rimmed glasses like Claire's. The bottom half contained a well-marked, cheerful mouth, strong teeth and a square chin made gentle by a touching cleft. He was a boy come home to shelter and food ("Hotels for six weeks! I'm starving!"). He was also a man come back from conquest.

This combination of positive competence with lively eagerness was extraordinarily attractive. It was a perfect reflection of Claire herself. She saw that instantly.

Perhaps this is one of the meanings of "love at first sight," although no doubt there are more meanings than one . . . .

By the end of the first hour they had learned everything that was important about one another.

"There's nothing else I ever wanted to be except a doctor. It's my life," Claire had told him, along with the facts that she loved animals, music, travel and art, although she knew very little about either music or art; she was a nightperson, very sloppy and forgetful, and hated to cook.

He told her that he loved dogs, music—about which he knew rather a good deal—cooking, history and old houses. Business, its competition and expansion, fascinated him. He despised "social" people and "class." He thought he would be at home in America because there was so much less of that sort of thing there.

"I've seen half the world, anyway. Now I want to see the States."

"It's so funny to hear people say 'the States.' "

"Why? What do you say?"

"America. The United States."

"I like your accent."

"You do? Most Englishmen don't. I like yours because it's so neat, which sounds funny coming from me."

"You're free and easy. I always think Americans are like that. But I've never known any very well."

"Your mother is American."

"Not really. She's been here so long, she even speaks like an Englishwoman."

After a moment, Claire said thoughtfully, "I shouldn't have come here."

"Why shouldn't you have?"

"Because. The air's thick with things we mustn't mention. Chiefly, my father. Do you know what I'm talking about?"

"I know."

"If I did the right thing, I would leave here now."

"Do you want to leave?"

"No."

"I don't want you to either . . ."

They bought a Wedgwood plate for Jessie in the village, bicycled to a country pub for lunch, climbed the belfry, read on stained glass windows the distinguished names of military heroes and, in the churchyard, deciphered the eroded names of the humble unknown. And they talked.

"My father doesn't know I found those photos or that I know anything," Claire told Ned, "not even why he and my mother were divorced. I'm supposed to think it had something to do with money—or just generally not getting along. I guess," she reflected, "Mary thought he would stay on after the war."

"I don't know. I remember hoping for her sake that he would."

"But there was Hazel! He couldn't have stayed."

"Some men would have, even so."

"Not my father. He's steadfast."

"Mine was too, in his own way. Are you shocked over what I told you about him, Claire?"

"Not *shocked*. But, tell me, has it made any difference to you?"

"What do you mean?"

"That you might feel you have to prove you're not like him?"

"I should wish to be like him in every other way. He had a fabulous mind and was one of the kindest men I ever knew."

"Well, then, as for the other, it's no crime, Ned, or shouldn't be."

"A lot of people wouldn't agree with you."

"I'm a scientist. We look at things without judgment, without cobwebs. My father taught me that, I think."

"You're very proud of your father, aren't you?"

"He's a great doctor. They send patients to him from all over the country. It's so strange that I can't mention him here! Or do I only imagine I can't?"

"You don't imagine it. There's a locked room in the house. It's in my mother's head, and you mustn't ask for the key."

"Dad's got a locked room, too, now that you put it that way."

It seemed to Claire that she had never spoken as easily to anyone in all her life.

Of those few, swift weeks, only disjointed scraps remained, frames in a moving picture running backward and too fast, as on returning from a journey, we forget the lecture in the museum of antiquities, recalling instead a shabby restaurant where a girl sang "Plaisir d'Amour" in a heartbreaking voice; remembering a family grouped on a railroad platform with a basket of tomatoes and a feeble yellow dog.

In Ned's small car they toured the south of England. She was to remember wet ponies in a downpour on Dartmoor; a flat tire on the road to Stonehenge; a dinner by firelight in a room with a seven-foot ceiling. She was to remember— later they would laugh about it—hearing footsteps outside of her door one night at an inn and hoping it was Ned. It had been.

"I had my hand on the doorknob," he said, "but then at the last minute I lost my nerve."

For a long time Claire had been concerned about herself. Many of her friends were married, some were living with a man and a few "slept around," which last would have been repugnant. She had had proposals enough, both for living arrangements and for marriage. In each case the man had been personable, intelligent and kind. Yet none had reached her and she needed deeply to be reached. She was a romantic in spite of herself and she knew it.

So, when the day came, she was ready.

It was a day on a Devon hill, an afternoon of bee-hum and heather, with great cumuli boiling in the sky. Flat slabs of glacial rock thrust out of the earth, making wide, warm beds on which young lovers must have lain together for unrecorded centuries.

Claire spoke through the wind-rush and the hum. "I'll remember this place. Sometimes I do that, promise myself to remember a place or a time, and I always do."

Ned didn't answer. He was playing with a blade of grass, twisting it around his finger. Then he looked up. There was something in his eyes, something radiant, eager and at the same time reverent, which she had never seen in anyone before. So how could she have known what it was? Yet she recognized it.

"Have you ever?" he asked softly. "Claire, have you ever?"

"No."

Imperceptibly he drew away, but she put her arms out and pulled him down. "I shouldn't have told you that. I want to, Ned. I want to very much."

"And you never have before?"

"I never wanted anyone before."

"You never loved anyone before?"

"Never."

He stroked her hair. He took her face between his hands and kissed her eyelids, kissed her mouth . . . Everything was at the zenith: the season, the day and the years of their youth. That was the beginning.

"You'll marry me, Claire," he said when he brought her back to London.

"Is that a statement or a question?"

"A statement, of course."

The blood ran high in her veins. She felt light, triumphant, flirtatious. "How do you know I'll say yes?"

"The same way you knew I was going to ask you," he said, laughing.

There was so much laughter in him! He took such pleasure in small events: a game of Scrabble, a walk in the rain, an amusing conversation with a barber. He was astonishingly observant. Once after a ride on a bus he remarked on a couple who had sat across from them.

"She hates him, didn't you see?"

"Why, how can you know that?"

"All the time he was rattling the newspaper she never took her cold eyes off him."

"Really? Why do you suppose she does?"

"Oh, I've no crystal ball! Still, he was an earthy man, with that full red face; likes his ale, I should think, while she was beaten, so drab and shrunken. An implausible pair," he said compassionately.

"Ned, you're amazing!"

"No, I just like to observe. Now over there, that house, the one with the smashed Georgian portico and the peeling paint—there's a story behind that. Divorce or some family scandal or bankruptcy."

"How on earth can you tell?"

"Because. This is a wealthy row and it's the only house on the street that's run down. There has to be a reason."

"Ned, you ought to write! Really write a novel or a biography or something. You describe things so vividly, you've a gift."

"It's not that easy. But someday, maybe."

Life with Ned would be sunny, filled with the vigor of the unexpected. Whatever came, he would manage it and make some good come out of it. In this most curious way he reminded Claire of Jessie and she told him so, assuring him that he would like her mother. It never occurred to her to ask herself whether Jessie would like him.

"I remember your father," he told her. "I saw him once or twice. It was a long time ago and I was very young, but I remember liking him."

"He's a wonderful man," Claire said soberly.

"And you are your father's girl, aren't you?"

"I suppose so. He's a wonderful man," she repeated.

It never occurred to her to ask herself what her father would think about this whole affair, either.

They parted in London with Ned's promise to be in New York in the fall. So closely had they grown together that the parting was a tearing. It crossed Claire's mind, although she did not say so, that it had probably been the same for her father and his mother. For a moment she thought how strange and sad that was; then immediately, as befits the normal, healthy selfishness of youth, she forgot it.

IN THE TROPICS there are certain plants which grow half the height of a man during a single night. They reach for the sun. So can a man and a woman reach for one another. Those whom this incandescence touches are not necessarily unusual people; it is only the heat of their yearning which is unusual.

❧{26}❧

Pink dots, like the crowd faces in a photo, Martin thought, observing the audience while he waited on the platform for his turn. The first speaker had addressed this Pan-American conference in Spanish, the translation coming over earphones. The second was speaking now in accented, fluent English. A blackboard hung behind him, and when he stepped back to chalk a diagram, Martin, craning to look, could see through a part in the draperies the slanting rooftops along the San Francisco street, as it pitched sharply downhill.

He looked back over the audience, wishing that Claire were there to hear him. But she was still in England, or had possibly just got home. Hazel was sitting with some other wives about six rows back. Catching his eye, she smiled slightly and shyly.

He had expected to be nervous as his turn approached. Because he was himself intolerant of error, including his own, he needed to be sure that what he said was beyond challenge. He hoped—he thought—he had here today a gleam, albeit a small one, of something new, an original fragment to add to what was known about the convoluted mystery of the brain.

Now his name was spoken. He was being introduced. He stood to meet a few seconds of applause, and waiting for it to cease, felt a merciful calming of his heart and a flow of confidence. His mind cleared of blur. He looked out at all the faces tilted upward like plants turned toward the light.

"I shall make three points," he said clearly, "beginning with the nutrient arteries to the midbrain. It is generally understood that—"

In plain, crisp words he made his three points, observing with a fraction of awareness that one listener's forehead was knotted in thought, another looked dubious and a pair were nodding toward each other as if to say: Yes, he's got something there; do you agree?

So he came to the end, and feeling a warm internal glow, sat down to long applause. He had done well.

Later in the lobby, a little crowd gathered with compliments and handshakes.

"You speak the way you write," one man told him. "You don't waste words. I like that."

Another said, "You had something of your own to tell. It was no mere rehash, no cut-and-paste job."

And Hazel cried, "I'm just so proud of you, Martin! So proud! Even though I didn't understand a word." She added generously, "I wish Claire could have heard you."

They walked out into full sunlight, Hazel observing that it was their first day in the city without fog. The fair light, the excitement of the morning and the alluring, unfamiliar streets filled Martin with euphoria.

Everything, everything had come together! He thought of his work bearing fruit. He thought of climbing a long hill to stand now at the top and be crowned.

"Too bad we can't start for Carmel now," Hazel remarked.

"I can't get the car till tomorrow morning. But you can have a swim in the hotel pool this afternoon, you know."

She had been a counselor at the Y during girlhood and was a strong swimmer, unlike himself who had learned by splashing around in a swimming hole. It was a pleasure to watch her in the water; he always admired professional skill, whether at chess or piano or anything else.

"You don't mind one or two stops on the way? Marjorie wants a Japanese doll, and I saw one in a window. I can't for the life of me think of anything for Peter, though."

"A chess set," Martin said promptly, the image of chess having just passed through his mind.

"Oh, do you think?" Hazel was dubious. "He's only eight."

"I'll teach him. It will exercise his brain."

For Peter, who was tender-hearted, jolly and surely not unintelligent, had as yet not much ability to concentrate. Neither does Enoch, Martin thought, with a dimming of euphoria. He writes poetry, he dreams. Does well enough in school, but not the way Claire did. Oh, not fair to set her up as a measure!

"Here's the place," Hazel said. "I won't be long."

He stood at the entrance and watched her. After great effort, she had lost ten pounds, and this loss revealed angles in her face which had been hidden by that roundness of youth which had so touched him when he first knew her. Yet perhaps he liked this more; it gave strength to her face.

She wore a becoming dark-blue linen dress. It occurred to him that her clothes had been different lately. She had become acquainted the previous winter with the Roman wife of an American doctor. The woman belonged in one of Hazel's glossy fashion magazines, in some photograph of a beak-nosed, thin aristocrat from a papal family, sitting in her marble palazzo wearing a plain expensive dress with some splendid jewel at the throat. She was certainly not a beautiful woman; yet she was arresting. Possibly Hazel had been learning something from her.

But still she smiled too eagerly, too timidly. Now she was thanking the saleswoman for the fourth time. He kept telling her not to apologize her way through life. Of course, she denied that she did it, and his telling her so only made her defensive.

Ah Hazel, dear and loving Hazel of what are you afraid? Do you sense something that lies too deep for you to understand? There is such sweetness in you, and yet beneath, there must be so much anger, too! How can you not be angry at a world that has somehow forced you to be so good, so thoughtful and mild? Was it your people who made you like this, or were you simply born that way? You pretend. Often, simply to please me, you even pretend to have pleasure in sex when you aren't feeling any. I never tell you I know because it would humiliate you.

And, with a kind of shock it crossed his mind that, for the second time, he had married a woman who, although for a different reason, was unsure of her own worth. Might it have been because of some insecurity in himself? There was so much one would never comprehend, even about oneself.

What if he had been living all this time with Mary? Then he asked himself why, for God's sake, he should have thought of Mary at just this minute, while standing in this store in San Francisco between the doll counter and a shelf of toy cars? He never *really* thought about her anymore! He didn't permit himself to! (She was just always there, as his past was there, his room in Cyprus with the slanted ceiling; his mother's voice; the dark hills and all else that had made him what he was.)

Hazel handed him the packages. "We ought to get something for your sister, don't you think so?"

"What did you have in mind?"

"I saw a little bracelet in a window near here. Alice never really gets anything, does she?"

"Fine," he said, and suddenly saw his mother coming in at the kitchen door with her "good" hat on, its sorrowful feathers raveled and drooped; saw her, then, and Alice, now, as though they were one figure. "Get something for Alice's girls, too," he said quickly.

"Yes, of course."

"And don't you want anything for yourself?"

"I have everything," she answered simply. This simplicity of hers was always poignant.

"Last night in the hotel arcade, you were looking at a tablecloth."

"The Venetian lace? It was awfully expensive, Martin."

"You loved it. I could tell."

"Well, but, can we afford it?"

"Yes," he said, "I think we can," and was pleased at the smile that came and went on her mouth.

From the terrace outside their room, he could hear her singing cheerfully while changing into a swimsuit. He had been concerned that she would regret having come on this trip, that her mind would be at home with the children. They were her center, as they were not for him. (Yet, hadn't he always seen himself at the head of the table surrounded by the wealth of family?)

To tell the truth, at fifty-plus he was over-age to father such young children as the last two were. When he came home at night, he was tired, and quite naturally, they were noisy. He was sometimes impatient with them. Hazel never was. She was so patient with Claire, too! Once, not long ago, she had even spoken up when he had scolded Claire for something.

"I'm surprised," she had said. "You so seldom criticize Claire, even when she needs it. This time she didn't need it."

Suddenly, now, he remembered that. And he wondered whether Hazel ever thought he might favor Claire over the others. Because in his heart he did, and he knew he shouldn't. He had such hopes for Claire! And up to this minute, every one of his hopes had been fulfilled.

She had done brilliantly, had even written a paper on genetics which might possibly see publication. For such a girl one was justified in having extravagant hopes. She qualified for the finest training, the best internship. After that a neurosurgical residency, or perhaps her interests might lie more deeply in neurological research. Whichever she might choose, there would be a place for her on his team. Father and daughter; she would—

"Sure you won't change your mind about a swim?" Hazel inquired.

Through the open robe he could see her full breasts, her strong thighs in the swimsuit, a figure no longer young, but firm still and sturdy. She looked like health itself.

"No, you go. At the moment I feel too lazy."

"Good. It's what you need, to feel lazy." She smoothed his hair. "I do worry about you, Martin. You never have any private time. Between patients and teaching, working three nights in the lab, and now this institute business—" She reminded him more and more of the way his mother had used to worry over Pa. "And writing another textbook on top of it all!" she added.

"Not writing," he corrected. "I'm only contributing a chapter this time. The rest is a symposium."

"Well, whatever it is, I don't know how you do it all."

"Go along with you," he said, "and work up an appetite for dinner. We're going to Trader Vic's."

He lay back in the lounge chair. The good warmth of the sun went through to his bones. How he loved it, and how he hated the cold! It shriveled his spirit and always had, even when he had been a child in Cyprus.

The beach, that was what he loved. Tomorrow they'd go down to Carmel, and for a whole week he'd get up early every morning, he promised himself. While everyone still slept, he'd go down to the beach and stand there looking out at the endless blue, the sea blue and the diamond dazzle. At dawn there would be no footprints on the sand except the ones he would put there. All others would have been washed away during the night. In a cleansed and pristine world there would remain only the pure curve of sea and the parallel curve of sky.

I could have been a beach-bum, he thought, and was amused at himself, knowing that that was one thing which he, the precise, the exacting, the apprehensive and conscience-laden, could never, never be.

Even here, even now in this hour of solitary peace, while the wind hummed in his ears and his eyes were bemused by two sailboats on the bay heading outward under the Golden Gate Bridge, his thoughts were traveling back east. They'd made tremendous, incredible progress! After almost six years of arduous effort they'd reached the Dobbs Foundation at last, and now finally were moving in high gear.

In part the crucial contact had been brought about through efforts of Bob Moser's, but the decision to make the grant had come because of Martin.

"I've gone as far as I can go," Moser had told him. "The ball's in your court, now. You'll have to put the idea across."

And he had done so. In one fateful evening on the Moser's terrace after dinner, Martin had been able to convince Bruce Rhinehart, then the acting president of the foundation. Rhinehart had been a careful listener. There had been something southern about him, with his long, narrow face and pince-nez, his way of inclining the head in courteous deference. Bob Moser was obviously in awe of him. The control of millions, even though they are not your own, commands respect, Martin thought. The power of money. Human nature.

First he had produced an estimate of the cost. Then, restraining the tremble of his hand, he'd shown the rough sketch, dog-eared by now, which he always carried in his pocket.

"You're familiar with our old two-story wing on the side street, Mr. Rhinehart? Our thought is we'd tear that down and build ten floors up, with entrance into the main building, of course. We'd have laboratories and auditoriums for teaching on the first two floors, with patient floors above." He'd kept his voice even, not too boldly confident, but not pleading, either. "I've got a lot of thoughts about the operating rooms. There's been so many improvements since ours were built. We'll need facilities for photography of the brain, somewhere near the Department of Encephalography. See? Over here on this end."

Rhinehart had inquired when and how Martin had first got his idea. He recalled now that he had answered, "It's been a dream of my whole life, my life as a doctor, that is," and hoped that hadn't sounded grandiose, because it was the simple truth. "We're an old, honored hospital," he'd explained. "I've felt deep loyalty to it ever since I first came to work here under Dr. Eastman. I believe we need and deserve this institute."

They had talked until midnight, Rhinehart listening all the time with that attentive courtesy.

"It's gratifying to see how much we've been able to raise from private contributions, Mr. Rhinehart. Three hundred thousand dollars."

At that moment Bob Moser had injected humor.

"That includes fifty from a friend of mine, a plastics manufacturer looking for a tax deduction," he'd said with a grin. More soberly he had added, "We've a long, long way to go, Mr. Rhinehart, and I hope you'll see the road ahead as clearly as we do. We—I—that is, Martin here, Dr. Farrell, is in my opinion, for what it's worth, one of the outstanding—"

And Rhinehart, perhaps observing Martin's embarrassment, had put in quietly, "Indeed I know of Dr. Farrell. His text on neuropathology is the current standard. We do so much medical philanthropy, we have to keep abreast of these things." And he had turned to Martin. "I assume, of course, you will expect to head the institute."

Martin had made a small gesture of assent.

"It would be a question, then, of our gambling on you."

"To an extent, yes. Although I would hope the project would encompass a broader span than any one personality, and last a good deal longer."

He had asked Martin in what ways this institute would differ from existing ones.

"Naturally, every man has his individual methods," Martin had told him. "This has been part of me for so long, this conviction that I have about encompassing mind and brain in one study— Yes, it's done elsewhere, of course. But I have worked out my own ideas about modes of research and patient care."

"Well," Rhinehart had said, and there had been something so decisive in the syllable that Martin had stopped with a tug of fear that he had perhaps over-reached himself. "Well, Dr. Farrell, I'd like you to come before my committee next week and tell them everything you have been telling me."

And so they'd be laying the cornerstone, if all went well, sometime next spring!

Hazel wanted the date to coincide with his birthday. She loved grand celebra-tions. Half drowsing now, he lay back in the chair, reflecting on birthdays. What a great fuss Hazel always made! They, like holidays, were an excuse for having a crowd, from friends like Perry and Tom to distant cousins whom one never saw during all the rest of the year. She would cook Martin's favorites: roast beef, corn pudding and apple pie. The bought and fancy decorated birthday cake was for the children's benefit, so each one could have an icing-flower. He could see them now: Enoch, so cautious and agreeable, that you wondered what he might truly be thinking; the little ones, Peter and Marjorie, who had more of Hazel than of himself, although Marjorie looked like him. And Claire. She seemed to bring air into the house with her. She'd fling her coat to a hall chair, and Hazel would hang the coat up in the closet, for Hazel was neat like Martin. Where did Claire get her careless ways? Why, from Pa, of course!

And he thought, with smiling rueful remembrance, of Pa's desk and his mother's sighs over things forever mislaid or lost. Yes, of course, from Pa. Genes were a funny business.

A liner was coming in at the Golden Gate; coming from Japan, perhaps? He'd like to see Japan sometime.

What had he been thinking? Oh, yes, that genes were a funny business. Families were a funny business. You'd never think Hazel belonged in hers! When they got talking, the whole lot of them, it sounded like the rattle of machine guns. It made you aware that English is a guttural language. Tess, her sister, had the drone and sibilance of a nonstop talker.

But he had been, and would go on being, good to them. One of them was always in some need or other, either because of illness, or simply because of having more children than he could afford. He never minded helping them, even rather liked it, in an odd way. Because their need made him feel superior to them? Yes, because after all these years, he still smarted over having needed the help of Donald Meig. He could still feel half-naked shame at the memory of standing in that room.

"If it weren't for me, you'd be peddling aspirin tablets." That was what Meig had said, and the worst part of it was that it was true.

So it was good for the ego, it was salve and balm, to be a kindly, tactful giver when one could just as easily say to one's brother-in-law, "You're a fool and you're lazy; you shouldn't have had seven children when you can't even support two."

No Meig, he! And Martin wondered what Meig would think if he were still alive and could know about the institute.

Hazel came out onto the terrace. "Oh, did I wake you? We've a letter, or rather you have. You won't believe it—it says Jessie Meig on the envelope."

He sat up instantly and opened the letter which had been forwarded from his office.

"Dear Martin," he read, "No doubt you will be astonished to receive this. I thought it better to write because, frankly, it's less of an embarrassment for both of us than the telephone would be.

"I'll be brief. Claire has returned from Europe with shocking news. While in England she took it upon herself to visit Lamb House. There she met young Ned Lamb. They spent three weeks touring together and have now decided to be married. He is to come to New York in the fall—has a job in the offing. The wedding will take place next summer after Claire's graduation.

"You have influence over Claire, maybe more than you realize. You need not answer this. I shall simply assume you will do what you can to prevent this folly. Sincerely, Jessie Meig."

"Whatever's the matter?" Hazel cried.

Martin crumpled the letter. Did anything ever go smoothly? Was there ever a time when you could sit back and say to yourself: "Come now, rest a little. You've earned it"? Only a moment ago he had been feeling fairly satisfied; perhaps he had been *self*-satisfied and this was to be his rude punishment?

"Talk to me, Martin!"

He came to. "It's all right. I mean, it's Claire. She wants to get married."

"I thought someone had died, you looked so stricken!"

"She met him in England. Went to visit Lamb House. Goddamned crazy thing to do! It's Ned, her aunt's son."

"Oh? But then, he's a cousin, isn't he? How can they marry?"

He realized he had never given her any more than a few barest facts at their first meeting, so long ago.

"They're not. His mother died when he was born. She—Mary—brought him up."

"I see. Well?" Hazel touched his arm. "Martin, you look dreadful. Does it really matter so?"

He turned on her. "Of all the stupid questions! It's an insane folly, and you can ask me—"

His vehemence appalled her.

"I'm sorry," he said. "You didn't mean anything. But oh, damn it, one's children can wreck things!"

"You're thinking of Jessie, aren't you? Yes, I can see why. It would be awful for her, wouldn't it?"

He pressed his lips together and leaned against the wall. He felt like a traveler in a depot in a strange city, uncertain where to go.

What the hell had she been doing, going to that house? She shouldn't have gone abroad this summer! But how in blazes could he have guessed, when he made her a present of the trip, that she'd do a crazy thing like that? And then he remembered how the child Claire had come to him. Independent as hell, she did what she wanted and the devil take the hindmost! Well, the devil had taken it now, that was sure.

How in God's name to bear with this, when he already had so much to crowd his brain: the institute, the daily round, the family? For so long he had stifled memory, by sheer force he had crowded it down. Would "anguish" be too strong a word for what he was feeling at this minute? He thought not. There would be grandchildren. They would belong to him and to Mary. Also to Jessie. It was—it was unthinkable! He groaned.

"Oh," Hazel cried, "I've never seen you like this!" She mourned over him. "But surely if there's nothing wrong with the young man, it can be worked out somehow. I mean, you don't even know him, do you?"

"He's her son. That's awkward enough."

"Yes, of course, but much more so for Jessie than for you. After all, you only had a few days'—affair—and never saw her again. My goodness, it's ancient history! Anyway, there's nothing you can do to stop it, is there? I mean, Claire's a woman. You can't very well order her around, can you?" She gave a small, nervous laugh. "Especially not Claire."

He knew what she wanted to say: "Claire's headstrong and obstinate. She always has been and you ought to be used to it by now."

Jessie must be in a fury! Or would she have swallowed her wrath and grown silent instead? As though it were yesterday, he remembered that Jessie could do just that.

He tried to recall the boy: sensitive, decent, thoughtful and pitifully young in the RAF uniform. Yes, but that was ten years past! And anyway, what difference did all that make? What difference could anything make beside the fact that he was *her* son?

Suddenly Hazel's hovering presence annoyed him. He wished she would go inside and leave him alone.

"What are you staring at, Martin?"

Controlling himself, he answered evenly, "There's a gull on that balcony. It's been there all afternoon."

"Perhaps it's got a nest." She kept standing there, troubled and hesitant. "I hope you're not going to grieve too much over this business with Claire."

"Let's fly home in the morning," he said abruptly.

"But we were going down to Carmel and Big Sur!"

"I don't feel like taking another week. I've got a hundred things to do at home, anyway."

"You mean you've got to see Claire."

"Well, what if I do?"

Her lips trembled. Then he thought: She asks for so little . . . And he felt torn, pulled this way and that.

"Let's compromise," he offered. "Four days at Carmel. We'll go to Big Sur another time. I really want to get back sooner, Hazel."

Her eyes softened. "Fair enough. I understand." She put her arms around him. "Let's dress for dinner, shall we? And try to take your mind off things a little? I've heard so much about Trader Vic's."

THEY WERE EATING chicken in coconut sauce when a couple came to sit at an adjoining table. The man hailed Martin.

"Colonel! Colonel Farrell! It is you, isn't it?"

"Why yes," Martin said, hesitating.

"Dickson. Floyd Dickson. Don't tell me you don't remember?"

"Of course I do. For the moment I couldn't think."

"Yeah, I've put on thirty pounds since then. Meet my wife, Dot."

"And my wife, Hazel. Dr. Dickson and I were stationed together in England."

"I was a crummy lieutenant. Used to hang around and watch the colonel stitch the boys together."

Martin sighed inwardly. He was especially in need of a quiet dinner on this night! And of all people now, he'd had to encounter this loud, restless individual whom the years seemed to have made louder than ever.

But he inquired politely, "Living in San Francisco?"

"No. L.A. We come from Minneapolis, you know, but I got sick and tired of shoveling snow. I've got a pediatrics practice in L.A. Dot likes 'Frisco, so we run up now and then. You been to Carmel?"

"We're going in the morning for a few days."

"Where you going after that?"

"Home. I'm due back in New York."

"What you should do is, you should hop on a ship or a plane and go off to Hawaii, as long as you're this far. After that, the Orient. Say, waiter, how about pushing these two tables together so we don't have to shout? That is, if you don't mind?"

"Well, no," Martin said.

Scraping and shoving, the Dicksons settled down.

"I hear you're making a name for yourself," Dickson remarked. "I always thought you would."

"Thank you."

"I met a fellow in the hotel lobby this noon who'd just come from your speech. He was telling me something about you heading a new institute in New York. Neurological research, he said."

"Yes," Martin said quietly, "it's underway."

"Well, they all say you're the man back east! But seriously now," Dickson addressed Hazel, "you ought to make him have a little fun, too."

She smiled. "I try."

"Sure. Take a couple of months off. You're a long time dead."

Dot Dickson asked whether they had children.

"Three," Hazel answered. "Two of them are only seven and eight. We can't leave them yet for any length of time."

"We went to Greece last year. Left the kids with my mother-in-law. Took the cruise around the islands. Beautiful, beautiful," Dickson said.

"I'd like to do that sometime," Martin admitted. "Greece is the place I've most wanted to see. All my life."

Mrs. Dickson assured him he would love it. "And the shopping's incredible," she told Hazel. "You can get gold jewelry for practically nothing. Oh, I adore traveling! Two years ago we took a fjord cruise out of Copenhagen. I almost bought a silver service. They're handmade, you know. But then I thought it probably wouldn't go with our dining room—it's French provincial. What do you think?"

"I really don't know," Hazel said. "I'm afraid I'm not very good at things like that." She fell silent.

And Martin thought how much he appreciated a quiet woman. Even a woman like Flo Horvath, who was otherwise dear to him, he couldn't have tolerated for a week. All that chatter and twitter!

Then Hazel, apparently feeling a need to be more sociable, remarked, "I've always wanted to see England, but Martin doesn't want to."

"Oh, really? I just love England," Mrs. Dickson said enthusiastically.

"I guess the men saw enough of it during the war," Hazel responded.

"I feel that way," Martin agreed.

Two years ago, flying to a conference in Geneva, they had come down through clouds; England had lain on the left, with the sun just setting over it, and he hadn't wanted to look. He had turned away and got a magazine.

"I wouldn't mind going back," Dickson declared. "In fact, that may be our next trip. Dot here is wild about antiques, old houses and all that. Of course, we don't have much of that here in California. Say, Martin, speaking of old houses, you remember that place you used to visit out past Oxford?"

"No," Martin said, startled. "I saw a lot of places and it's a long time since."

"Sure you must! I drove you there a couple of times and picked you up in the ambulance on the way back. Talk of old! That house must have been three hundred years old if it was a day."

Martin asked Hazel, "Would you like a salad? I forgot to order one. Waiter, may we have two green salads, please?"

Dickson turned to his wife. "You would have flipped over that place, Dot. Martin said somebody said Oliver Cromwell slept there once. I never got to go inside, though."

There was no malice in the man. Martin himself had covered so skillfully, had made his visits appear so innocent, that Dickson could have had no idea what he was doing.

"What did they call it again? Lion House? Cockeyed names, all their places have names. No, what am I saying? Lamb House. That was it. Lamb. Wasn't it Lamb, Martin, where you used to go?"

Martin raised his eyes. The anguish in them must have communicated itself to Dickson, bringing a sudden, terrible comprehension.

"Maybe I'm thinking of somebody else," he said quickly. "I rode around with so many guys, you get mixed up, your memory goes back on you."

A flush like a scald rose in an even horizontal line from the man's throat to the hairline. It looked like water rising in a glass. And strangely enough, Martin felt sorry for him.

A queer silence fell over the table. Martin looked back at his plate, moving the rice around with his fork.

Presently, in a flat voice, Hazel spoke.

"Ask for the check now, Martin, please."

"No dessert?" Mrs. Dickson remonstrated. "You don't know what you're missing! They have the most fabulous desserts! The pineapple—"

But Hazel had already risen. "I don't want any," she said steadily. She walked to the door. Martin excused himself and followed her. They got into a taxicab.

"Hazel," he began.

"I don't want to talk," she said.

In the hotel elevator, she faced forward. He tried to place himself where she would have to look at him, so that by some expression, perhaps, he might convey to her what words could not. But she did not let him meet her eyes.

In their room she took off her coat and hung it in the closet. Then she went into the bathroom. Martin walked to the window. Lights festooned the great bridge. Lights quivered on the bay, where little boats moved festively and people were all free of care. He turned back into the room, the quiet, pearl-gray room that spoke of money and the serenity that can go with it. His lips were dry with dread.

Hazel came out of the bathroom. She stood leaning against a table. It shook, and her purse fell to the floor. She didn't pick it up.

"So you did see her when you were in England," she said at last.

"Yes."

"Why did you lie to me?"

"I didn't lie. We just never talked about it." And immediately he was ashamed of the cheap evasion.

"You made love to her."

He had a sense of standing at a crossroads. With one syllable, "yes," he would take a turning from which there could be no retreat. Also, he had a feeling of déjà vu, as if he had always known that this might happen, although really that made no sense. The chances of its happening must have been one out of a thousand, at least. Yet here he was.

"You made love to her," Hazel repeated.

"Yes," he said.

"It wasn't just one time. You stayed together."

"Yes."

She clapped her hands to her face and dropped them.

"I wouldn't have minded other women, prostitutes least of all! Believe me! I understand that a man can't be away for three years without— But her! Why did it have to be her?"

She began to weep without changing expression. Her face was smooth and uncontorted, a fixed face, with streaming tears. And this strange control dismayed him more than a frenzy would have done.

"Why?" she cried.

He trembled. What could he say? He thought of something.

"I came back, didn't I? Doesn't that tell you anything?"

"Yes. It tells me that you loved your children. Especially Claire."

"No, no. It was more than that."

"Your career, then, your precious career."

"I thought of you," he said.

"Oh, I believe that one! I surely do believe that one!"

"But it's true."

Hazel began to speak rapidly, with mounting pitch and force. "You were my whole life, do you know that, Martin? You were what I lived for. And to think that all the time, every loving word you ever spoke to me was a lie! That everything, everything was an act and a rotten lie! Oh my God, I understand what that poor cripple went through! What is this woman, anyway? What sort of whore is she, that she couldn't leave you alone? Not once, but twice?" She sobbed now, she pulled at her hair. Her mouth was twisted in the mask and grimace of grief. "A whore, that's what, a whore!"

"Ah, don't," Martin said. "Ah, don't."

"First her sister. But it wasn't enough to ruin one marriage, was it? Oh, I could tear her eyes out! If it weren't for my children I would kill her. Oh my God, I hope she dies in agony with cancer! Cancer!"

"I want," he began, "I want to tell you—" and stopped.

What did he want to tell? Had it been anyone other than Mary, some WAC or nurse or English village girl he might have said: *I couldn't stand being alone anymore,* and might have expected to be half understood. But Mary was different, and more's the pity, Hazel knew it.

Yet he tried again. "I can only beg you to understand my conflict. My weakness, if you like. Weigh this against our years. I've been a good husband to you, you know I have—"

"Claire's marriage," she interrupted. "I see it now. No wonder you can't bear the thought of it! No wonder!" She flung herself on the bed. "Get out. I want you to get out."

"Be reasonable, Hazel. Please. I'll get you some medicine, a pill, to help you get through this tonight."

"I don't want a pill. Do you know something, Martin? I hate you. I wouldn't have believed a human being could change as I have in just five minutes. Whatever I felt for you all these years is gone. It left me at the table in that restaurant. Just left me."

"You're frantic and I don't blame you. But can you try to put everything aside till the morning? We'll talk it over more calmly, we'll straighten it out, I know we will."

"I don't want to talk. In the morning I'm going home to my children."

"All right, we'll go home, then. Will you lie there quietly while I go out for medicine?"

"I'm not taking any."

"You have to pull yourself together. Never mind how you feel about me. You've got three children to think of."

The crowded street was almost as bright as day. It was easy going down the hill. One almost had to hold back to keep from hurtling forward. Two prostitutes with crayon pink cheeks approached him. Except for their hard bright eyes, they looked like children. They couldn't have been older than sixteen. Their scornful laughter followed him.

In a shop window he saw the bronze Kwan Yin which Hazel and he had looked at on their walk that afternoon. It seemed now to have been a month ago. It seemed to have been a month ago that he had read the letter about Claire. And he stopped again to study the merciful goddess, perhaps to find in her benign expression some comfort for his raging pain.

Ah, he would give anything, anything, even his precious hands, not to have done this to Hazel!

Mary, Mary, he thought then.

"That one's had a bit too much," the soldier had said when Martin passed that night in London, all those thousands of miles away and so long ago.

Too much.

When he had got the medicine, he walked back up the hill. Cable cars were still running, but he forced himself to climb. It took the last of his breath.

She was undressed, lying in bed, neither reading nor sleeping, just lying there. Her eyes were swollen. She looked ugly, and this moved him terribly, the fact that she looked ugly because of him. He came over to the bed and stood looking down at her.

"Is there anything I can do? Anything that can be undone?"

"I don't see what." She spoke quietly now. "You never got over her."

"But I love you," he said, not denying the other. "Can't I make you believe me?"

"No, Martin, you never did."

"You're wrong. I did and I do." He knelt down at the side of the bed so that his face was level with hers. "Please, Hazel. Please."

"Please what?"

"You know. Understand. I never *wanted* it to happen."

"You couldn't help it, you mean?"

"No."

"That makes it worse, doesn't it?"

He didn't know what to answer.

"You spent two years with her. Two years out of your life while you were married to me."

How to explain? How to say that there are different kinds of love? That there are circumstances, timing, fate, enchantments—ah, call it what you will. He stroked her head. He wished he could feel the way she wanted him to. Indeed, he did feel something very deep, but it was not what she wanted and he knew it.

In the morning they packed their belongings and flew home. On the way to the airport, the cabdriver was chatty, which would ordinarily have been an annoyance. But this time, Martin found relief from awful silence in the flow of talk.

They boarded the plane. Their seats were three abreast, Martin at the window, because Hazel never liked to look out, and on her other side, a man, a lawyer or accountant, very likely, who was deep in documents. Martin had a newspaper and a paperback, but couldn't concentrate on either.

As clouds parted, one saw the speeding shadow on the plain in ink-blue wash. Ahead, clouds curved like the drooping petals of enormous peonies. A river ran in a red-rock canyon where ocean fossils lay five thousand feet below the surface of the ancient earth.

What matter any of our transient sorrows in the face of these?

Hazel was crying again. He didn't dare to look in her direction. He heard the click of her purse as she got a handkerchief out, and hoped for her sake that the man on the other side wouldn't notice. The embarrassment would crush her.

Long hours later, somewhere over Pennsylvania, the sky grew dark. The plane lurched and the "Fasten Seatbelt" sign came on. Then began the long descent toward the million lights of eastern cosmopolis. Thunder crashed around the rocking plane as they came down into the storm, and a woman in the seat behind cried out in fright.

"Don't be afraid," Martin said to Hazel. "We aren't going to crash."

She turned to him. He saw that she was dry-eyed. "Do you suppose I care if we do?"

He thought of the ride out to California, of yesterday's euphoria and elation. And now this.

Oh God, help our fevered struggles.

BOOK FIVE

LOSSES

❖❂{27}❂❖

For two months gloom like a heavy shroud had lain on the house. On an evening in mid-September, Martin sat alone on the screened porch. It was hot, but not with the sweet heat of summer. This oppressive heat was lasting past its season into the time of fleeing birds and silence. He wished they were back in the city. With no particular logic, he thought it might be better there. At least he would be able to walk over to the office at night and do some paperwork. Anything to get out of the house. But school would not open for another week, and Hazel had wanted to stay here as long as possible, obviously because she could hide more easily in this place where they were merely summer transients and very few people knew them.

He could hear her moving about in the kitchen. Every evening now after the maid had gone upstairs, she found occupation in the kitchen cooking and baking. He got up to stand in the doorway. Ginger and sugar scented the warm air. The complicated paraphernalia which Hazel had brought from home—pots, molds, terrines and cookbooks in glossy jackets—shone in a yellow light. And still it seemed to Martin that rot lay over everything.

She took a pie out of the oven. It had a high meringue, colored delicately brown, like toast. He wished she would stop filling the children with stuff like that! Marjorie was big and rawboned like Hazel's mother and had already gained ten pounds over the summer.

Hazel set the pie on the counter. "Can I make you a cup of tea?" She spoke politely as one does when a neighbor has unexpectedly dropped in.

"No, thank you."

Her eyes, with their round, pure whites, had always in their mild innocence been appealing. Tonight they were dull. Stubborn, he thought, and was ashamed of the thought. Suddenly he saw that she had grown very thin. She must have been losing weight for weeks.

"You've lost weight," he said.

She wiped the sink and hung the dish towel on the rack. "What difference does it make?"

"A great deal. If you lose any more, we'll have to check into it."

"Why? You think it's cancer? I'd be out of the way, then, wouldn't I?"

"Don't be a fool! This sort of talk won't work, Hazel. There's a limit to sympathy, as with anything else."

"You want to know something? I really don't care whether I have your sympathy or not."

"What do you care about, then?"

"I should think anyone could see what."

"The house, you mean? The children? Yes, you're doing everything according to the book and better. But there are other things."

"Yes, there are other things, and it's a little late for them." She pushed the loose hair back from her forehead. "I'm going up," she said wearily.

He understood that the subject had been switched off again. "I'll stay and let Enoch in. And Claire. You remember she has two days off this week?"

"The room's ready for her. And you needn't wait for Enoch, he's staying overnight with his friend Freddy."

The ceiling light made hollows and shadows on her cheeks. For a moment she stood there as if she were looking for something and had forgotten what, and Martin felt a mixture of pity and exasperation.

"Well, I'll be going up," she said again. "Good night."

"Good night." He went back to the portable television on the porch. A heated drama was taking place on the screen, a drama about doctors. He recognized the hero and could have written the plot, in which the intern, pure in his astounding brilliance, solved with no trouble at all the problem that had been baffling the most renowned specialists in the world. Idiocy! He switched it off and wandered into the living room, picked up the newspaper, and finding it filled again with repetitious litany of murders and burglaries, of bankrupt cities, defense budgets and election speeches, put it down. He sighed and wondered whether the returning owners would feel any emanations of his frustrated spirit in their house. He thought he could feel theirs, from the faded cretonne with its stiff maroon chrysanthemums, to the Victorian desk in the corner with its rosewood fretwork, solid as a cathedral and inherited from either his or her great-grandmother.

He reconstructed the family. It was a game, a pastime for him. Their silver would be inherited with their politics—Republican, naturally. On their inherited Lenox china they would eat their formal meals of thin roast beef, clear watery soup and mint-green gelatine dessert. He hadn't liked this house when they rented it because it had the spirit of bleak, repressed emotions. The man in the yellowed photograph wore a nineteen-twenties' straw boater at a jaunty angle, but the face was no Scott Fitzgerald face of celebration: the lips were pressed too thin. Furthermore, the house had smelled of wet bathing suits and tar-stained sneakers on the day they had walked in. Still, it was on the water, and after all, that was what they had sought for the summer. One good thing, though: the master bedroom had twin beds. He wondered how they would have managed during these past weeks if Hazel and he had had to share a bed. Next week back home they would have to.

He had been trying to straighten things out. Oh, how he had been trying, since that ghastly night at the restaurant in San Francisco! She would sigh. "Why are you sighing?" he would ask, and she would answer, "Was I? I didn't realize it."

Maybe she didn't. Often a sigh was only unconscious relief of tension. Her tears brimmed unexpectedly. They'd gone to the movies a few times, and there in the darkness he'd heard that snap of the pocketbook opening and shutting as she got out a handkerchief. In the reflection from the screen he could see the wet glisten of tears and had known they couldn't possibly have been caused by the banal and silly story on the screen. Sighs and tears. Two or three times he had gone over to her bed and put his arms around her. She hadn't pushed him out, only lain there like an unresponsive lump as if to say: "Take it or leave it; it means nothing to me." He had grown quite empty of whatever complex feelings had brought him to her in the first place: need for sexual release, tenderness, sorrow, a wish to heal. All had simply drained away and he had lain stiffly beside her thinking of what he might say to break through, and then finding no way, for he had many times used up all the words he could summon, had gone back to his own bed.

He wondered now how long a family could hold together like this. Enoch, at least, must sense something. This summer he'd been counselor at a day camp for retarded children. He related to the rejected and the weak. He wasn't—fortunately—one of them; still, he would never make an Ivy League college or be on Law Review. He wasn't the type to lift his head high above the crowd. He'd be a good teacher of the young, especially the troubled young. He wouldn't sympathize with me if he were to know the truth, Martin thought. Youth can be awesomely puritanical. It takes seriously what we teach, till it discovers what we really are.

But surely Enoch must know something? he asked himself again. There'd been one quarrel when they'd first come back from California, during which Hazel's voice had been loud enough to be heard across the road. She had been in a rage, pounding her fists on the wall. He hadn't known she was capable of such passion, of whatever sort. Afterward she had been contrite and trembling, as if ashamed of having given such offense. And this docility had sickened him as much as the rage, which was, after all, not abnormal in the circumstances. For he had pulled the rug out from under her emotional security.

They had sat down at the dinner table and Hazel, smiling, had served the salad and sliced the cake. But her eyes had shown pink swollen lids under the heavy powder. He wondered why Enoch had never asked about that, and then thought maybe the boy didn't want to know. He had an instant's flash-view of supper tables, millions of supper tables all over the country, of families sitting with a man and a woman and the children in between. How thin the fabric which held them together! My God, you know nothing from an outward view! And he remembered that doctor across the hall in his building, a distinguished obstetrician, an amiable grandfather with a refined and pretty wife. One afternoon he had suddenly closed the office door for good and gone to Arizona with his secretary. Was anything, was anyone, ever simple, direct and clear?

He got up and, from the drawer of the desk which he had appropriated for the summer, took out a folder. "The Institute," he had scrawled on the cover. This at least was direct and clear. Every detail had its purpose, whether scientific, technical or artistic. Across the entrance, below the pediment, he wanted a single sentence to be carved in the stone. Searching, he'd gone back again, as he had always done, to the Greeks. No other culture before or since had been able to express either in words or stone, probably in music also if one could only know, such fundamental truths with such comely grace.

He thought now he had reached a decision. *"For he who loves man loves the art."—Aesculapius.* These few words above the door would say it all, he thought again. He would submit it to the trustees at the next meeting, although most certainly they would be willing to leave it to his choice. Men like Moser, and most of them were like Moser, wouldn't know very much about the Greeks and would care less.

Also, there was the question of a mural for the lobby. Martin wasn't at all certain that one was indicated—you didn't want the place to look like a post office or a courthouse. Yet there were those who pressed for it. And the idea might not be a bad one if the right artist were found to do it. He'd been collecting photographs of samples. Thoughtfully now, he held them to the light, visualizing the proportions, the way they might appear to visitors turning left from the corridor, as they would do. The figures mustn't loom too large, or they would be lost in detail . . .

He had begun to enjoy himself, his tension loosening, when he heard Claire's brakes screeching on the gravel drive. She drove too fast! No matter what you said, people of her type never learned. Impetuous, slam-bang, charming! Capable of stunning surprises, too. He was still not, maybe never would be, over the shock of learning that she had known about Mary and himself since she'd been sixteen and discovered those photographs.

In the beginning, he knew, he'd had Jessie to thank for their daughter's discretion, and perhaps for her compassion. Now he had Claire herself to thank.

He opened the door for her.

"Hi, Dad, how's everything?"

"Fine. I've just been going over designs for a mural in the lobby. Want to see? Or want coffee first? There's some kept hot in the percolator."

"Coffee first, please." She followed him into the kitchen. "Have some, Dad?"

"No. It keeps me awake. I'll just watch you."

She studied him. "You're a bit charged up, aren't you? Well, I don't blame you. They've really been racing along with that foundation. I watched the cement mixers and all the rest of the stuff today, and I got sort of charged up myself. Or choked up, thinking that it's really happening at last, and you did it."

"I and a few hundred others."

"Oh, don't be modest!"

Martin reflected, "Jessie always used to tell me that."

"Anyway, it becomes you. You may be sleepless with excitement," Claire said cheerfully, "but it becomes you."

Blind, blind. She's so happy herself that she sees nothing else. Happy over that fellow! He'll be arriving soon, Martin thought with a sinking in his chest, and I'll have to see him. Funny how things change their proportions. Since this trouble of my own, I haven't had time to think about that affair. I'll have to, though.

"I did a delivery today," Claire was saying. "It's the happiest part of the hospital, isn't it? Dr. Castle was there, but I did it all myself. The kid was dark blue and I was scared, but I put the suction tube in and the kid turned a nice pink and let out a good loud howl. I felt great."

"Not sorry about turning down the Chicago internship?"

"Well, I did want it, but that was before I knew Ned. He'll be here next month, you know." As if Martin didn't know! "He's landed a terrific job: White, Davis and Fisher. They're one of the three biggest in the business." Claire got up and went to the cake box. "What a baker Hazel is! It's a wonder you're not fat."

"I think I'll have a cup after all," Martin said. He poured the coffee and took a few swallows. Then, forcing cheerfulness, he inquired, "So, you're growing sure of yourself, are you?"

"Yup. No butterflies in the stomach. There's something about even a little clinical experience that gives you confidence."

"For a woman who ranked number five in her class last June, I should think you'd have plenty of confidence."

"This business of measuring people against each other is a mean thing when you think about it," Claire reflected. Then she smiled, "Still, I must admit it's kind of exhilarating when you happen to be at the top of the list."

She wore contact lenses now and Martin wasn't yet used to her face without glasses. It seemed less earnest. Could "genuine" be the right word for her, with the still-boyish curls and the charming tilted nose and the long neck? She has the world before her, he thought, including, damn it, Ned Lamb. I wish to Heaven—

And suddenly she turned somber. "Dad, I wish people wouldn't make everything so hard for Ned and me. Mother simply will not open her mind."

Small wonder, Martin thought grimly.

"It seems to me one ought to be able to come to terms with the past. Why should a new generation be tied to a past it had nothing to do with?"

Nothing to do with? Where did these young think they had come from? Risen out of the sea or sprung from the head of Zeus? He managed to murmur, "It's not so simple. You've revived old pains. It's not only the young who feel." And he thought: I wish I could talk to her about Hazel . . . But some parental dignity and pride was shocked at the possibility.

"Oh," she said quickly, "oh, Dad, I know." He could see the frank compassion in her eyes. "You'd be surprised if you could know how well I understand many, many things."

Martin smiled dubiously. "You think you do?"

"You and Mother both think you're being asked to give up the peace you've made. Mary thinks so, too. Ned wrote me."

"Well, wouldn't we?"

"Yes, but— Oh, I grant it would be easier to start clean with a new family and no skeletons in the closet. It's not ideal that nobody speaks to anybody else."

"Can't you see what this means? Shall I give you all the old clichés about how marriage is hard enough without starting in with problems? How they come along fast enough through the ordinary business of living? I can give you those clichés, but you know them already. What you don't know is that they're all true."

"I suppose they are, but they've never deterred anybody yet, have they?"

A cricket set up frantic, repetitive chirping in the kitchen. Like human chirping, Martin thought. We repeat and repeat, but we don't change each other's minds.

"How about some sleep?" he said kindly. "We'll solve nothing tonight."

Claire yawned. "I've been looking forward to these two days. I plan to spend every minute on the beach tomorrow. The last of the year."

He watched her go up the stairs. Superb product to have come out of so strange a marriage! And with an ache of understanding, he fancied he knew how Jessie must feel about this daughter of her flesh. Then he turned out the lights all over the first floor and stood a while in the dark hall before going up to bed. Over the creaking in the old walls and the swish of passing cars on the quiet road, he seemed to hear voices filling a vast room. All the voices in a foreign, low cacophony were saying urgent, serious things to one another, yet, heard all together, they made only a contradictory buzz and murmur so that you could make no sense of anything. You knew only that many things had gone wrong.

"I'm tired of thinking," he said, as he went up.

He woke with the uncomfortable sensation of being looked at. Hazel was sitting on the other bed in her nightgown, staring at him.

"How long has this been going on?" he demanded.

"Why? Can't I look at you?"

He got up out of bed without answering. From the closet he took a suit and from the dresser drawer, a shirt. Then, returning to the closet, he selected a tie, took his shoes and went into the bathroom to dress. He was trembling. Another day. When he came out of the bathroom, she was still sitting there.

In the dining room Esther, the new maid, had put his orange juice, coffee and toast on the table. She was from the South, a young brown girl who actually looked pretty in a pink cotton uniform.

"Eggs or cereal this morning, Doctor?"

"Eggs, please," he began. Then, the thought of eggs suddenly sticking in his throat, he changed his mind. "Neither. I'm not hungry."

When he had swallowed the coffee, he remembered that he hadn't shaved. He ran his hand over his chin to feel the bristles and went back upstairs. Hazel was still sitting on the edge of the bed.

In the bathroom he scraped once over, a sloppy job, but he was already late and it would have to do. He had left the bathroom door open so that the bedroom was reflected in the mirror: the unmade beds, the clutter on the dressing table, and then Marjorie coming in to have her braids done. She had thick mouse-colored hair, the kind that she would probably want to bleach when she was sixteen.

"Hi," he said through the mirror. "What are you doing today?"

"Jane's mother's taking us to her grandmother's. They've got a pool."

"That ought to be great." He spoke heartily. The heartiness was a form of condescension to the child, not like his usual manner, but he was conscious of trying to brighten the atmosphere. He wondered whether the child saw anything odd in the way her mother had been sitting on the edge of the bed, still in her nightgown.

The little girl stood patiently with head bowed to the brush and comb. There was such pathos in the nape with the center part ending in those babyish wisps! He watched as Hazel worked the braids. How many hundreds of mornings would she have worked these braids before Marjorie had grown up or cut them off? Now Hazel fastened the ends with rubber bands and a narrow black ribbon tie on each. For an instant she put her face down between the girl's frail shoulder blades which, in spite of the baby fat, were outlined beneath the thin cotton of her summer dress. It looked to Martin as though she had placed a kiss there. Then, turning the child about, she kissed her again on the cheek.

"Have a good time, darling," she said.

"Have a good time," Martin called and they heard Marjorie clattering down the stairs.

When he came out of the bathroom, Hazel stood up. She seemed to have lost more weight during the night, her eyes were so large.

"Hazel, how long will this go on?" he asked.

"I don't know."

"It's been weeks. What do you want of me? I've said a hundred times how sorry I am. What else can I do? How can I make it up to you? I've asked and I've asked. Tell me what you want of me," he said desperately, "and I'll do it."

"What I want you can't give."

"What is it?"

"I want it not to have happened," she whispered.

Martin threw up his hands.

"Oh God!" she cried. "What does a woman have to do to be like—like Flo Horvath, or the woman next door, or practically anybody up or down this road, with nothing to think about except what to have for dinner or what dress to wear next Saturday? Should it be the blue with white dots or the yellow with brown stripes?"

"Listen," he said. "You've got to stop feeling sorry for yourself. You try my patience, Hazel. You do."

"I can't."

"How can you know what any other woman has to think about? You think you're the only one who's had any trouble? People don't—don't—" he stumbled, "dine on champagne and strawberries every day. That's not life."

She clasped her hands. "Champagne! It would be good to have a taste of that. Oh, I know one needs bread and meat and you've given me that, and I've always been grateful—"

"Bread and meat? What are you talking about?"

"I mean, you've given me a home and you're a good father: you've been kind, very kind. At God knows what cost and effort! Oh, how my heart goes out to Claire's mother!" This must be the fiftieth time she's said that in these last two months, Martin thought. "I always felt so terribly sorry for Jessie. It was such a sad story. So many errors that ended in sadness. Why, I even felt sorry for—for Fern, Mary, whatever you call her. Isn't that a joke? Sorry for her?"

Martin stood with a hand on the doorknob and that queer weakness draining through him again. It would follow him all day. Sitting in the train he would be unable to read the newspaper. At the office and in the hospital he would dread the homecoming, and yet at the same time look forward to it with the hope that this day, maybe at last, something might have changed while he was gone.

"I remember the first time you talked to me, the night you operated on the Moser girl. I remember every word. 'I have a little girl,' you said. 'I haven't seen her since she was three.' And then you went on and talked about how it had happened. You were so honest that my heart hurt for you. 'I was overwhelmed,' you said. Those were your words. 'I was overwhelmed.' But it was all over, you said. And I understood. Those things happen. An infatuation comes and it goes, like a storm that passes. How was I to know that every word was a lie?" Her voice went up an octave, harshly, resounding as if she were calling through a tunnel. He was certain it could be heard through the closed doors and the walls.

"The children," he warned. "This is our business, not theirs."

"No, we certainly don't want the children to know, do we, that their heroic father spent the war years with the woman he loves while his wife was three thousand miles away, unable to defend herself? I wouldn't have cared, I say again, if it had been some casual affair, I would have understood. I've told you."

"Yes, you have, six dozen times." And Martin thought: Strange, that's exactly what Meig said to me. He asked heavily, "What do you want me to do?"

"What do you want to do? Claire says she isn't married. Maybe you want to go back to her. Yes, maybe that's just what you want to do, go back." She had affected a taunting posture, hand on hip, with a sly expression. It drove him to sudden fury.

"Ah, you're obsessed! There's no talking sense to you, Goddamn it!"

"I should never have married you! My sister always says—I never told you—you think you're too good for our family, anyway."

Blab-mouthed pest with the bell-clapper tongue! After he'd been so decent, so generous, to them all! Surprising though, that the woman could have sensed, in spite of all his careful tact, what he thought of her. Coldly, he said, "You're in pretty bad shape if you have to take your opinions from your sister."

"I know what you think of her! Maybe I shouldn't have married anyone at all, or just picked out a man from the phone book to have children with and to share the expenses. We'd have no pretense of loving each other. It's a worthless trick of nature, the whole business, anyway."

"You don't believe a word you're saying, Hazel."

"I believe it now. Then, then I was so in love with you I wasn't thinking clearly! Maybe I wasn't even altogether sane."

He thought for an instant: Then why can't you understand how I— And in the next instant thought: But you do understand, that's the whole trouble.

"I believed in you, Martin. How can I ever believe anyone, how can I ever trust anyone again?"

It was true. How could she? But he said, "You can believe in me. It's just that you ask too much. I don't say you had no right to ask it. You had every right. I simply wasn't able to give it, that's all. And I'll be sorry till the day I die."

She put her face in her hands for a moment, then flung her head back. She looked, he thought, like a woman coming out of shock after an accident. "So where are we?" she asked.

He wet his lips. "We are—we are here, a family, together. We've a whole future," he said, speaking deliberately, "years and years, I hope. Even though the past hasn't been exactly what you wanted, can't you put it behind, since it can't be altered? I do love you, Hazel."

"Fine words. I wonder. Nights when you stay in the city, do you bring your women to my bed in the apartment, or do you go to theirs?"

Outrageous accusation! He'd always felt a certain fastidious scorn for an habitual chaser. It had only been one he'd ever wanted, one other.

"You know that's crazy," he said.

She sighed. "Yes, I suppose it is. I'm sorry."

"All right then, we're back where we started. What can I do to end this?" He caught her hand, but she pulled it away. "Tell me. I'm deadly serious, Hazel."

"It's all ruined. I'm a second choice. What can you expect me to feel for you?"

"You're not a second choice. I came back to you."

"We've gone over this again and again. You came because of your children."

True. Yet if there had been no children, might he not have come back to her anyway? Son of his parents and child of his times that he was, would conscience have driven him? After all, Hazel hadn't *asked* to marry him. There was no answer.

"I can't work and come home to this, spend the rest of my life with someone who is so miserable, Hazel."

"Then leave! Go on, leave!"

"Damn you, I'm not going to leave and you know damn well I'm not, so cut it out!"

"I don't care," she said very low, "whether I live or die."

"Ah, you've gone crazy!"

"Damn you! Do you hear? I don't care whether I live or die!"

He stood at the top of the stairs. "You're crazy!" he shouted again. "And I'm sick of it!"

She slammed the bedroom door. The vibration shook the walls. Below in the hall, the chandelier swayed, the prisms tinkling.

"Hazel, open that door! I want to tell you something. I have to go to work. I can't leave like this, and I have to catch the train."

No answer.

He looked at his watch. Seven minutes to get to the station. The hell! He fled down the stairs and out the door.

CLAIRE WOKE EARLY. The curtains were swaying in the damp wind off the Sound. Once the first haze had burned off, the day would be bright. That was her first thought. Her second was of Ned. She had always believed that sex was talked to death, everywhere from learned texts to movies. Now she was certain of it. How or why pull apart, dissect and analyze that loveliness, for which there could really be no words any more than you could describe music or— One thing, though, you could say: sex feeds on its own appetite. She had been dreaming of it every night she had left Ned behind. There was such an emptiness, such an ache! A sweetness now which she could not have imagined before that first day on the warm rocks there on the Devon hill! And it seemed to her that October was a measureless, unbearable age away.

If only Jessie would accept with generosity! "I don't want to be reminded of home," she complained. Strange that she should still think of Cyprus as home, even at this remove. And Claire remembered the weedy canals, thick with the green murk of algae, the bleak snow banked head-high along the streets.

"I've become a new person with another identity. This marriage will draw me back into the old." Jessie had spoken like a petulant child or a wheedling woman, neither of which roles befitted her or was at all familiar to her daughter. "When you marry him it will all come back," she cried. The incredible selfishness of such words, as if you could ask someone not to marry because it would bring unpleasant memories to someone else!

"He's not even her son," Claire had protested.

"He grew up in her house, so he is her son. He has her touch all over him. He has her ways."

Ways. What ways? It was all ephemeral, like trying to grasp a cloud.

"It'll pass over," Jessie said, reassuring herself. "You hardly know him."

But it will not pass over, Claire thought now, angrily.

"How was I to know that every word was a lie?"

Hazel's voice pierced through the wall. She was crying, and Claire sat up. Martin's voice came now, an angry rumble. The voices rose, becoming more distinct.

"What do you want me to do?"

"I should never have married you!"

Embarrassed and alarmed, Claire got out of bed and moved noisily around the room. She ran the water in the shower. This was not her affair and she had no right to hear it. A door slammed. It made a vicious noise. She thought of a finger being caught and winced as sympathetic pain shot through her own finger. Then she heard her father thudding heavily down the stairs, heard the front door close sharply and a few moments later the car backing down the drive with an impatient spurt of gravel.

She went down to the dining room. Esther opened the swinging door from the kitchen.

"Will you have eggs or cereal, Miss Claire?"

"Cereal, please. Has Mrs. Farrell had breakfast yet?"

"No, ma'am."

Oh, why this artificial, stupid, servant-employer relationship? Claire spoke forthrightly.

"That was pretty awful this morning. Does it happen often?" And as the girl hesitated, "It's all right, Esther. They're my family, after all, and I love them. I've just never heard anything like that before. I thought maybe you could tell me something that might help."

"No, ma'am, I only been here three weeks and they seem like real nice quiet people. I never heard nothing."

"Well," Claire remarked tritely, since some answer was required, "these things happen, as they say, in the best of families."

"Oh yes, married folks is bound to have their troubles. I was married once and it ain't easy. These muffins are nice and hot."

Hazel came in from the porch. "I thought I heard you. I'm sorry I wasn't up to greet you last night. I wasn't feeling very well."

"All right now?"

"Oh yes. It was nothing, after all." Her eyelids were red and her lipstick hastily smudged. She wore a terry robe. "I've got a suit on under this. I thought I'd go for an early swim," she explained. She sat down decorously, clearing her throat like a nervous old lady making an afternoon visit.

Claire thought: Good heavens, Hazel, you needn't put on an act for me! Why don't you just cry or swear or get up and leave the room if you feel like it?

Hazel asked, "Have you got everything you want?"

"More than I should have, thanks. These muffins! I'd be fat as a house if I lived with you!"

Hazel contradicted her. "You'll never be fat. You'll be like your Aunt Mary." And as Claire looked astonished, she added, "Of course, I've never seen her. Of course, I've never seen your mother either."

"No," Claire said.

"Do you think you look like your mother?" Hazel persisted.

"I don't really know whom I look like." Very odd, these remarks! And what could be their purpose?

"Life's been hard for your mother, I imagine."

In all the years they had known each other, Hazel had observed the strictest tact concerning Jessie. The nearest she had ever come to acknowledging that Claire had a mother was to inquire, "Everybody well at home?"

"She's managed quite comfortably," Claire said, sounding cool without having intended to.

"I saw one of her model rooms at the Antique Show last winter. I went with a friend of mine one afternoon. I don't know much about those things, but I thought it was the best room there. A red-and-white library, it was. She's very talented."

"Yes. Are Marjorie and the boys gone for the day? The house is so quiet."

"They've all gone off. Their last freedom before school starts next week."

"You've got marvelous children, Hazel. I hope I'll be as lucky as you."

"You've got time for children, haven't you? I suppose you'll want to wait until you finish your residency with your father."

"Your father" came out with an edge of sharpness. But why not, after the morning's events?

"Well, Ned and I will have to work that out," Claire replied cheerfully, the words "Ned and I" making a fine warmth in her chest. "You know, sometimes I feel so young, I think I have all the time in the world. Then some days it seems as if I ought to hurry up and do right away whatever I'm going to do, like having children, for instance."

"You're twenty-six, and I'm forty-six," Hazel said.

"You don't look it." That was mostly true, although not this morning.

"I feel seventy-seven," Hazel said.

She got up and went to the sideboard, picked up a saucer, examined and replaced it, then walked to the porch door and stood looking out.

Martin's not easy to live with, Claire thought suddenly. No, that's not fair! I never lived with him, so how would I know? He's compassionate, kind and perceptive; but he's difficult, too. And he's driven. That's it, he's driven. He's obsessed with this institute business. He wants perfection and he's tireless in seeking it. Yet he could shut his eyes for hours; all alone, listening to music. She'd seen him sitting there with that half-smile on his face, just letting the music pour over him, and she had wondered what he might be thinking. Complex.

Hazel's drooping posture and bleak words made gloom in the room. Claire sought to enliven it, but found only hackneyed words.

"Everybody feels old sometimes. We all have our days."

Hazel turned to her as though she had said something profound. "Oh, do you think so? Do you think people are fundamentally alike? I ask you because you're a doctor, you must have had so much experience."

"Well, the differences can be amazing sometimes. I've been on pediatrics up to this last week. I've seen mothers frantic over a minor cut, and then last week I saw a woman come with not one, but two mongoloid children. She was so courageous and accepting! I thought: I don't know how you bear it."

"If I could have had more education," Hazel said, "I think I would have liked to be a doctor. As it is, nursing was as far as I got and I loved it. Except," she reflected, "except sometimes I'm afraid I got too personal. Some patients just touch your heart. Cancer patients, especially. I never did know which was right: to tell them they're going to die or let them think they're going to get better. What do you think?"

"Most of the psychiatrists and the chaplains say to tell the truth. They guess it anyway. And you can always tell them that many people are cured, which happens to be so."

"Sometimes I'd turn the light out after the night's last medication and I'd think, as I left the room, how frightened they must be, lying there in the dark and wondering how much longer they had to live. But other times I'd think it may not be hard at all to die. After all, there's mercy in nature, too, isn't there? Maybe when people have to leave, they're ready to leave. Don't you think so?"

"So far in my experience I've actually seen just one person die. He'd had a heart attack and I can tell you he wasn't ready. He was damn scared."

"Well, I don't know," Hazel said vaguely, turning back to the door.

Over her shoulder and through the trees Claire saw the white sheen of water. A feathery wind moved the leaves. It was hard to think of a morning when you wouldn't be here to feel all this or hear Beethoven or lie in bed with a man's arms around you.

"Why think about things like that?" she cried impatiently, almost angrily. "Your time won't be here for years! Do you often have thoughts like these?"

"No, no, of course not. I'm sorry. It is a stupid conversation, especially for a young woman in love."

Claire stood up. "I think I'll go put my suit on. I've a great book and I'm going down to the beach. You coming too?"

"I'll meet you there," Hazel answered.

They swam the length of the beach and back, Hazel slowing for Claire's benefit.

"You could be a pro," Claire told her as she spread a towel and propped herself against the seawall.

She had brought binoculars. It amused her to watch boats crossing the Sound. "There's a yacht to end all yachts. Must belong to a Greek shipping tycoon. Here, look, Hazel."

Hazel took the binoculars. "Could you cross the ocean in that?"

"I'm sure you could. Which reminds me, I've been thinking, Dad and you really ought to have a vacation from children. Why don't you go to Europe this fall? All those old, old places! They do something to your heart."

"I'm sure they do."

"Of course, I know it's hard to get the time."

"Oh, I don't think that's the problem. Certainly it isn't for me. I don't do anything."

Something in her tone, something oblique, touched Claire. "What do you mean, you don't do anything?"

"What do I do? I'm just Dr. Farrell's wife. I go to meetings of the Wives' Auxiliary. I'm on a committee to raise money for this or that and I'm treated with respect because I'm his wife. Otherwise I'm nobody."

There was some truth in what she said. This was the status of women and had been so for centuries. Yet it was not altogether true. Hazel might see herself that way; yet there were plenty of women in her position who didn't see themselves that way at all. Hazel had simply lost her *persona*.

"That's not so," Claire said emphatically. "You *are* a person in your own right. Your job is bringing up children, and they're fine children, too. What's more important? You've sunk into routine, Hazel, that's what's the matter with you. You have got to get away."

Hazel stood up. Her hair streamed out in the wind. "I'll get away. Feel how strong the wind is? I'm going in again." She put on her cap, tucking the hair back. "Coming?"

"Not now. I feel like reading."

Hazel walked into the water and turned over to float.

No life except through her husband, Claire thought. Poor thing. It's all right if you're satisfied. Apparently she isn't. Thank goodness Ned will never expect that of me. We're a different generation, she thought.

The beach was empty. Summer renters had returned to the city and year-round residents didn't feel such eager need to use the beach, especially in September. Claire read a few pages before growing drowsy. The sun burned through the clouds and she turned over to let it bake her back. Last sun of the year until next summer.

Hazel's dog was barking. "Oh do stop, you fool!" Claire cried crossly, having been jolted awake. Fritz, a black dachshund with a shattering voice, was standing at the water's edge. Esther must have let him out of the house to follow Hazel.

Claire sat up. Hazel had been swimming parallel to the shore, up and down the length of the beach. Now, though, she was swimming away from it. What was she doing? Claire took up the binoculars. The red cap rose to the top of a swell, sank out of sight and rose again. She could clearly see the raised arm of Hazel's strong, determined crawl. No doubt of it, she was swimming out! Swimming away! Claire looked up and down the beach. There was no one in sight. She stood up and ran to the shore.

"Hazel!" she called, cupping her hands. "Hazel! Come back!" and knew as she called that she couldn't possibly be heard. Good God, what was the woman doing? Claire stood there. She looked down at the dog as if he might know. He had stopped barking. He looked back at her with pathetic, questioning eyes. She frowned, squinting through the binoculars. The cap and the arm were growing smaller, moving with astonishing, deliberate speed away and away. What could the woman be thinking of?

And suddenly Claire knew what she was thinking of.

She thought of plunging into the water and following. But she wasn't a good enough swimmer, and wouldn't have been able to catch up with her anyway. She began to run toward the house, her shocked heart thudding, but there was no one at home except Esther, and what could she do? She looked up and down the beach. The club was a quarter of a mile away. There was no time, no time! Then she remembered the Mayfields, two houses down. They had a speedboat, moored at a little dock.

Sinking into the sand with every step, she ran. A boy of fifteen or so was pumping a bicycle tire in the driveway.

"Please!" she cried. "You've got a boat! The lady! Mrs. Farrell! I think she's drowning! Please get the boat!"

The boy dropped the pump and stared.

"Hurry! Please, for God's sake, hurry!"

"Miss, I'm not sure I can run the boat. I only learned just now, and my dad said never to take it out without him."

"Is your dad home? Who's home?"

"Nobody, just my grandmother. You can use the telephone."

"There's not time. Please! Try, please!"

The boy climbed into the boat and tried the engine. It sputtered and died. Claire got in. The boy bent over and tried again. It sputtered, coughed and died.

"I only learned," he apologized.

Two minutes. Three. Claire scanned the open water. The sun had come out again and there was only a vast gray dazzle, a sheet of steel.

"There, I've got it!"

Triumph. The engine had set up a regular putt-putt-putt. Claire pointed the direction. Hazel's dog marked the place, shrilly barking again at the water's edge.

"There! Out there in a straight line from where I was sitting! Exactly straight. Hurry!"

Clouds rolled back over the sun. The air grew chill. The summer sweetness had gone out of it and the water had roughened. The prow pointed to the sky, then fell as the little boat rose and sank through great swelling hills and troughs. Claire shaded her eyes, straining and peering.

"Sure we're going right?" the boy asked.

"Yes. Yes, I'm sure." Claire gripped the seat. "You look to the right, I'll look to the left. She had a red bathing cap."

"But what would she have been—" he began, and fell silent.

The water came alive as if some huge creature far below were rolling and turning. How could anything as frail as a human being contest its power? Claire hadn't known the Sound could turn so evil so quickly. Nor had she ever known such terror, such absolute sheer terror.

The boy, holding fast to the tiller, looked around at her, asking doubtfully, "Could she have swum this far, do you think?"

Claire looked back at the shore, where a line of houses stood white and no larger now than scattered boulders.

"Or this fast?" the boy said. "Even though we started later we'd have passed her anyway."

Claire's teeth were clenched. Panic, as well as the rocking of the boat, had churned her stomach. But she commanded, "Let's go a little farther."

The boat pitched like a roller coaster. "We've gone a mile and a half," the boy said.

"Yes."

"We'd best turn back."

"Yes."

They stared at each other, the boy's face scared and wondering. Claire began to cry.

"Was she—is she your mother?"

"My stepmother. Oh God!"

The boy became practical and manly. "We've got to call the police, I think. And the Coast Guard. That's what you're supposed to do."

The boat tore back toward shore, slapping the water, Claire still scanning the surface from side to side. Nothing. Nothing. Far out, heading north, a cruiser took its leisurely way. People in vacation mood were sitting on the deck, very likely, eating and drinking, maybe even singing in their gaiety, while, only a mile or two from them, another soul had cared so little about life that she had thrown it away. How was that possible?

I didn't see, Claire thought. All the time she was talking to me, this crazy, desperate resolve was inside her, and I didn't see. Oh Hazel, poor foolish, suffering Hazel, why did you? What made you? Out here, beyond the surf and at the bottom, they say this turbulence grows quiet. Anything which falls to the bottom lies there quietly. Or do the currents carry it away? Claire closed her eyes. The nausea mounted. At some spot, perhaps here where they were now, the exhausted, driven body had made its last effort, the arms made their last curving

stroke, the legs given their final flutter-kick. The heart and the lungs had strained.
How had she gone down? Struggling and crying, perhaps, having changed her
mind, screaming for help?

The water was dark green, opaque, like sculptured glass. She would have
cleaved it narrowly going down, and then it would simply have closed over to
resume its rhythm—moon rhythm, wind rhythm—as before. All this morning I
was irritated with her. Yes, she bothered me with her queer remarks and her
mournful, ghastly air. I wanted to get away from her. I got away from her,
politely, with my book. Not that it would have made any difference if I hadn't. Or
would it have? Could it have?

Objects on the beach were growing larger. Some children had come out to
play with an enormous ball. The dog was still there, running up and down with a
lopsided bounce. Claire and the boy went up to the house. She heard the boy
taking charge, heard him at the telephone and in the kitchen, talking to Esther.
She sat down on the stairs. She felt empty. The little dog came in and lay down
on the bare floor where it was cool. Meat was roasting in the oven. The house
looked normal, as it did every day, as it had looked only thirty, maybe forty-five
minutes ago, before everything changed.

Esther began to cry, a high, terrified wail, keening on one note. From nowhere
out of a quiet morning, the empty street filled. People came to stand on the lawn
and murmur. Cars drew into the driveway. Men came to question Claire. Someone led her to the sofa and brought a cold drink. She looked at the clock. It was
noon. Dad would be leaving the hospital for the office just about now. On his
desk he kept an oval photo of herself in gown and mortarboard at the Smith
commencement. Next to it stood a large color picture of Hazel and the children,
wearing Sunday clothes and nice smiles. The telephone was placed to the left of
these in front of a comical wooden figurine of a surgeon which someone had
given Dad years ago. He would pick up the telephone.

"Claire?" he'd say.

"Yes, it's Claire," she would answer. And then what?

Oh, how could Hazel have done this thing and why did none of us know? If
I'm a doctor, I ought to understand, oughtn't I? Then perhaps no one can know
what lies inside another, and to say you ever can is a pretentious lie. In the most
ordinary people, and some might claim that Hazel was such, for she had no
particular distinction, in each of them lie secrets. Such secrets! Old childish hurts
that make us what we are, powers that are never exercised, visions of what life
ought to give.

The answer is, of course, there are no ordinary people.

❊⟨28⟩❊

The odd thing was that Martin knew so clearly what was happening to him. He understood his own progression from first numbness to most awful pity and self-accusation—(If I had gone back upstairs to talk to her that morning instead of going to work)—through sleeplessness and then sleeping-to-escape, through all of these in a long slide to the somber place where at last depression closed around him darkly, like a curtain.

He had thoughts of falling, of crashing down the cellar stairs, or worse, of opening a door and stepping into an elevator shaft. He could hear his own screams borne away in the wind of the fall. He had nightmares of interminable stairs—stairs again!—only this time going up and coming out at the top to stand on a beam ten inches wide. He was alone, ninety floors above the beams: thin as wires, they were. He woke in a sweat of terror.

He dreamed he was addressing a meeting in some great city, in some enormous, echoing hall. He mounted the rostrum. Hundreds of dark suits and white faces waited respectfully. There were coughs, chairs scraped and programs rustled. He opened his mouth. No sound came. People were staring at him. Oh panic and shame! From the back of the room came the first embarrassed, nervous laughter. It spread, that tittering laughter, that high and hooting laughter, it ran all up and down the hall. Oh God! He woke with a pounding heart.

His children turned to him at table, searching his face. Their eyes asked: Why?

"Eat your vegetables," he would answer kindly, "if you want to grow tall like Enoch and me."

It wasn't fair to link Enoch with himself in the rank of adults. He was only sixteen, and seemed younger. Martin tried to remember what he had been at sixteen, but was unable to. There are times when the past closes over like waves, is hidden and drowned.

Oh, drowned.

"You spoiled my doll's hair!" Marjorie wailed at Peter, "and I'm going to tell Mommy!"

Shocked, Enoch looked toward Martin. But Peter spoke first, scornfully.

"Mommy isn't here anymore. Mommy's dead, don't you even know that?"

"Well, when she comes back, I mean."

"She isn't going to come back. Don't you know what 'dead' is?"

Enoch choked on his food, put the napkin to his mouth and left the room.
Martin heard him go clattering up the stairs. Should he go to the boy with
comfort of some sort? Words were needed, many words, and there were none. To
die in bed of pneumonia, even to die in a crashing car or plane was acceptable.
But to will to die! How to explain to his son that mother had wanted to die?

Nevertheless, he got up from the table and went upstairs. Enoch lay on the
bed, his face twisted by weeping denied. Martin laid a hand on his shoulder.

"Don't hold it back," he said. "It's always better just to let it out."

But Enoch struggled. Like my mother, Martin thought. Like me. Everything
held in to the bitter end—disappointments, grief, desires—all held in. So history
repeats itself.

"Why did she do it, Dad?" Enoch whispered.

"Let's not talk about that, shall we? She simply swam too far out and probably
didn't realize."

"Don't treat me like a child, Dad, will you? Everybody knows it was on
purpose. Please don't treat me like a child."

"You're right. I won't then," Martin said softly.

"Then tell me why. Don't you know?"

"Son, I don't. I wish I did." Well, it was half a lie, but only half. Truly, he
didn't understand. How could that business have mattered so much, weighed
against this boy and those two downstairs? How could anything have mattered
that much? Yet it had. "Son, I don't know," he repeated.

From the yard came the long dry rattle of a locust. The evening sun, dark and
sickly yellow, glared at the window. Martin wiped his forehead. Fall would be
welcome. A chill gray misty morning might be more cheerful. Any change might
be more cheerful.

"Let's go down and finish dinner," he said. "We have to eat. We can't afford to
get sick."

Yes, the dinner hour was the worst. Esther had thoughtfully removed Hazel's
chair. It stood now between the windows, facing Martin. And he knew that his
puckering mouth and racing heart were symptoms of a panic state. He sat quite
still, knowing that in a minute or two it would pass and ease. He studied his
plate. Surrounding the mound of string beans, potatoes and meat ran a key
design in gold. There were sixteen repetitions around the rim and, in the center of
the plate when the food was pushed away, there was another design, some sort of
geometric enclosed within a circle. A mandala. Buddhist. O jewel in the heart of
the lotus. Something like that. He shut his eyes.

The weight of everything! These poor three! And Claire, too, adult as she was
and on her way, but still a responsibility of his. That young man, Mary's boy,
would be arriving soon, and then that would need coping with, God only knew
how. All these lives, all such a weight upon him, as if he had to lift them, pushing
them up a steep enormous hill.

Things bothered him that never had before. Esther hummed in the kitchen,
with a tuneless maddening drone. He wanted to scream: Quiet! You're driving me
out of my mind! In the early mornings, gardeners arrived to mow the lawns all up
and down the road. Lately they had introduced a wicked new device, a leaf

blower with a sustained blaring howl. Then came the garbage truck and its infernal grinder. Wherever you went in this frantic world you heard metal grating and power vibrating; cars, planes, radios, lawn mowers attacked the ears, the head, the very soul of a man. He could have gone out and smashed them all. And he longed for an empty place, anywhere at all, with no one or nothing in sight, just wind and trees.

Hazel's dog came whining. It was always sniffing at her closet, although Claire had removed the clothes. Claire had been so tirelessly strong and sensible during those first terrible days, caring for the children, the house and telephone and all the letters to be answered. He had made her take Hazel's new fur coat, scarcely worn, and a pearl necklace. The rest of the jewelry was in a safe deposit box to be kept for Marjorie. Not that there had been all that much! He worried that he had not been generous enough with Hazel. She had so rarely asked for anything. He ought to have insisted. She'd been such a simple woman. Simple! Oh, my God. So his thoughts ran, like a fox pursued, darting, hiding, running to cover and dashing to escape.

But he must pull himself together. He must. If only he had someone to talk to, someone to hear everything from the beginning! There was no one. He certainly couldn't talk to Claire, not to his daughter. He thought of Alice, his sister, so much like himself, or so she had been when they were young. Flesh of his flesh; she would, if she were here now, put her hand on him in mercy and love, without judgment. Yet had she really been all that much like himself? So long ago it had been; still he could recall in her a strain of Puritan abstinence. He thought of Jessie. Curious that he should think of her now! And yet, in those long days when they had first known each other, there had been no mind more responsive to his own.

Tom ought to have been the one. Damon and Pythias, David and Jonathan: yes, up to a point, they were. Trust and loyalty lay between them. Kindly Tom would claim to understand, but he wouldn't understand. For he had never wanted very much. Smallness contented him in all things. But he, Martin, had wanted everything—an exquisite love, exalted knowledge, the warmth of a family, all the color and music of the earth. He had been born wanting them.

His hands bore down on the arms of the chair where he sat through that first dreadful week; the pressure was wearing the cloth away. There came a spell of rain. It sluiced through the gutters and splattered on the roof. It dropped in gusts from the trees and churned the Sound. And he sat on, listening to the many sounds of rain. Was there a motif of water in his life? Storm and flood had torn him too early from his mother's womb and killed those other children, whose faces in old hazy snapshots were so real to him. How had his parents survived their loss? He thought, too, of the story of the scalded child, which, of all his father's tales, he had never forgotten.

How Hazel had loved water! Sometimes they'd gone in the winter to walk on the beach; he, hating the cold, had done so for her sake only. But she would tie a babushka under her round chin and laugh at herself. "I look like my own great-grandmother on the farm in Hungary."

"I hate this house," Martin said aloud, "and all this water. I'll never go near water again."

Friends came to help. How many friends they had! People brought food and offered to take the children. It was astonishing how good people were. And still there was no one to talk to. The words they spoke were mechanical, as were his answers. None of them came near the heart of things.

Back in the city, he thought: Everything is loose, life has come loose. I must tighten it up again. I must. Do things with my children. I'll take them to the zoo, he resolved, buy books and read together. So his mind ran.

He could sit at his desk across from a tense and frightened patient, listening and replying, but all the while, at the bottom of his mind, were his children: I robbed them of their mother. He was offered reassurance: children forget. But that was certainly not true. Anyway, Enoch was no child. He suffered, Martin suspected, daily, hidden lacerations. His mother's son. Mine too, Martin thought.

In the elevator, on the street waiting for the light to change, his teeth were clenched and his jaws ached with the tension. Would he be able to manage everything? The office, the looming responsibility of the institute, the house, the children? Yes, of course he would. He would have to. Yet an evening came when, from his chair in the den, he heard them quarreling fiercely over a bag of doughnuts, which their mother would not have allowed them to eat before dinner. He knew he ought to rise and go in to stop the uproar, but he only stirred in the chair and didn't go. Let Esther handle it as best she could! It was suddenly too much for him to cope with.

The telephone rang. "Just to remind you," Leonard Max said, "we've got the Devita woman at seven-thirty in the morning."

Martin had been going regularly to the office and the hospital, working automatically and well. But perhaps he hadn't really been working all that well? And all at once he knew he wasn't prepared to operate in the morning. He heard himself saying, "I don't think I can make it. You'd better get someone to help you."

"I can get O'Neill, I'm pretty sure," Leonard said quickly. Too quickly? "Martin, maybe you should take a rest. People have been saying maybe you should."

"They have?"

"After what you've been through, a few weeks abroad would do a lot for you."

"I couldn't leave my family to go abroad, you know that."

"Well, then, how about a rest at home? Sleep late, relax, spend some time with the kids. You could say you'd gone away on vacation and nobody would bother you."

Falling, falling.

"Yes, I could do that," Martin said.

Leonard Max was hearty. "You'll be back better than ever."

"Thanks, Len," Martin said, hanging up.

He's thinking that I'll never be back, I can tell by his voice, so comforting, so cheerful. I'm finished, everything's ebbed out.

He got up and locked the door, then put a stack of records on the turntable, three hours' worth of Beethoven, Schubert and Brahms. He pulled the curtains shut, so that the room grew soft and dark. Like the inside of the womb, he thought scathingly, and lay down.

It was surprisingly easy to hide. For a week he feigned the flu. Claire kept telephoning, but he warned her away from his contagion.

At the beginning of the second week, on a raw November afternoon, he got up on sudden impulse from the chair, where he had listlessly been reading the news —all discouraging, nothing but strife—put on his coat and went out. He had walked blocks down the avenue when a wind came up and it began to sleet, so he turned around and went home. It was not the weather that had driven him, though. It was rather a peculiar sensation that had overwhelmed him. The world was too large, with too many people in a hurry. There was too much empty air. He knew that these feelings were bizarre, and he was frightened.

Now he had an excuse to stay inside for another few days. He had foolishly gone out too soon and was running a fever again. Claire scolded him by telephone with threats of pneumonia. He ought to be ashamed of himself, she said. He promised meekly not to do it again.

But he couldn't maintain this pretense, couldn't stay in hiding. He would have to force himself, find something pleasant to do. Yes, that was it, find something happy. Surely there was something colorful and happy left in the world? Christmas shopping, perhaps, before the season got too late and crowded? It was a long time since he had bought anything or even been in a store.

So, with a careful list, he set forth. He would walk downtown. Exercise, that was the thing; the healthy body, the fast walk. Make the heart work and breathe deeply.

A truck, swinging around a corner, almost ran him down so that he jumped back in terror. "Why the hell don't you look where you're going?" the driver swore.

A fat man got out of a taxi, fumbling in the pocket of his bulky overcoat, while traffic behind the taxi blared furious horns. And these sounded like swearing too. Everyone was so irritable, so angry!

He thought he would buy a sweater for Claire, but he wasn't sure of the size, and wasn't sure whether she would like a plain one or a cardigan with an embroidered collar. He stood a long time looking at the sweaters, knowing he was taking too long and unable to make up his mind. The saleswoman, a dry creature of outrageous hauteur, left him for another customer. "Well, when you've decided," she said. "I really can't—"

Oh go to hell, he shouted at her silently, full of hatred. It seemed to him that the arrogance of these expensive goods, which she merely handled and would never own, had been transferred to her person. Strange. Very strange. And he left without buying anything.

On the sidewalk in front of the store, he stood and watched the women going in and out. They were like animals on the prowl for meat with their slouching walk and their darting, avaricious eyes. Parasites and predators, he thought contemptuously, spending the hours away while their husbands labored, and half of them not even grateful, he'd guess. Hazel had never been like that.

He was terribly tired. His overcoat weighed him down. Turning toward home, he walked a few blocks north and then east. Everyone seemed to be hastening in the opposite direction, so that he was constantly bumping shoulders and grazing people who were annoyed with him for having done so. He felt out of breath.

A little crowd stood before a pet shop window looking at a display of parakeets in ornate cages that were too cramped. Poor marvelous creatures! Turquiose and jade and topaz, brilliant as any jeweler's art! A masterwork, each one, with its powerful, tiny heart and net of tiny veins; an imprisoned marvel, meant to ride the bright air. And as so often, tears came. A man leaving the shop looked at him with alarm, but being well-bred, looked immediately away.

He must go home. At the corner he tried to hail a taxi, but they were all occupied, and he began to walk. Faces wavered as he passed. He tried to focus on them, growing queasy with the effort. He began to walk faster. Something was at his back; he was being pursued. Now he was almost running. The thing was coming closer, reaching to grasp the small of his back. And at the same time he knew that there was nothing there, that he was having what the layman might call a nervous breakdown, or at least, the harbinger of one.

When he arrived at the apartment house, he was panting. He thought the doorman, young Donnelly, pink-faced and fresh out of Ireland with the class deference still in him, looked at him strangely. But all he said was, "Good evening, Dr. Farrell." The upholstered elevator cage took him to his floor. He was safe, then, in his own apartment, in his own room.

But his heart kept pounding. Perhaps there were symptoms he didn't recognize? After all, he was not a cardiologist. Heart attack. Taste of salt, of blood under the tongue. The chest squeezed in an iron fist. Swirls of red and yellow lights before the eyes like a Jackson Pollack picture: daubs they were, in spite of fashionable opinions! What if he were dying? He would vomit on the carpet, Hazel's good rug. Or struggle to the bathroom and fall on cold tile, clutching the smooth porcelain sides of the tub. Pa had died clutching the dining room table.

He lay down on the bed without taking off his overcoat and thought: I'm dying.

"You can't go on like this," Claire said.

Martin opened his eyes. "I fell asleep. What are you doing here?"

"Enoch called me. He looked in and saw you. He was scared."

"No need to be. I'm weak from the flu and I fell asleep, that's all."

"Dad, you're not fooling anyone, so don't waste your breath. Sit up," she ordered. "Let's get your coat off. Now lean back." She moved briskly. "You're shivering. I'll get you a brandy."

He felt, in the face of her authority, like a child. "Claire, Claire, I'm falling apart," he said suddenly and for the first time was not ashamed.

She took him in her arms. "Dad. Dear, dear. No, we're not going to let you."

"There are things you don't understand."

"Do you want to tell me about them?"

"I don't think I can."

"Don't then, if you think you'll be sorry afterward. But," she said steadily, "you really ought to talk to somebody and get it off your mind."

Off your mind! As if you were excising a tumor! That would be easier. A tumor can at least be seen, not like this amorphous, secret pressure in the head where, so they say, almost any unsuspected thing can lurk: desires to rob a bank, rape a neighbor's wife or assassinate the president, God only knows what.

He began, "You don't know why Hazel—"

Something in his daughter's expression—oh, he had from the beginning been so sensitive to the slightest nuance of her expression—something said to him that she might know.

"I've a pretty good idea. She found out about you and Mary."

Martin sighed. He put his hands on his knees, turned them over to regard the heartline on the palm and the whorls on the fingertips, then back to the cuticle. No pair of hands in the world like any other pair, no life like any other life.

"It was in California. We met a man I'd known during the war."

Claire said softly, "If I were a man I would fall in love with Mary, too, I think. Maybe you should just have stayed there after the war. Ned thinks you should have."

"Ned does? He's very young."

The room was still. No sound came from the apartment. It was as though the household had suspended its life in wait for Martin. And suddenly anxiety came uttering back like bird wings in the air, like those poor, caged creatures he had been looking at that afternoon.

"Ah, Hazel!" he cried. "I destroyed her anyway! Didn't I?"

"No," Claire said. "She did it herself. You are the only one who can destroy yourself. Other people can't, unless you let them."

"You believe that?"

"I do."

"I hear your mother talking."

"Well, she's got a lot of strength. And Hazel didn't, no fault of hers, God help her."

Years ago when he was an intern and that nurse—Nora, was it?—had killed herself, he remembered thinking how he'd hate to be in that man's shoes.

"You make it all sound very simple," he said.

"I don't mean to. Listen to me. Listen. You've been stumbling along with a load of guilt enough to break your back. But you were good to Hazel! You gave her good years! She was totally content till the very end."

"If I could undo it," Martin began.

"Well, you can't. You know what your trouble is? You think you ought to be a saint and you're only a man."

"You think so?"

"I know so. Everything in your life has to be perfect, and it can't be."

Martin laughed. It flashed through his mind that he hadn't laughed in months. "You've analyzed me pretty cleverly, I think. I hope you'll do as well with Ned."

"Does that mean you've decided to approve?"

"No, it just means I've decided not to fight it."

"Because you know you'd lose."

"Not only that. I want you to be happy, Claire. As long as you're bent on doing it, I don't want you to start off with bad feelings, that's all."

She gave him a look of purest gratitude. "Thanks, Dad. I'll bring him here, then."

"Have you brought him to your mother's?"

"For a short visit. Naturally, Mother was correct but cold as ice."

"The pain's too deep, too old. And Claire, on my part I want to say—"

"You want to say you don't want to see Ned's mother. You won't have to, I promise."

They sat for a while without speaking.

"I wish it could be different—joyous and warm," Martin murmured.

"It's all right, Dad. For me things don't always have to be perfect."

He felt something soft and calming in his chest: strength, pouring in some occult way from this child of his back into him. It was a fine tingling, a rising of hope, anticipation. Whatever it was, it was a benison. And just as he had known when he had been falling into sickness, now just as surely he recognized the first faint start of healing.

The door opened and three heads appeared around its edge.

"Come in," Claire called. "Don't be afraid. Dad's feeling much better. He's going to be all right."

❖{29}❖

The new apartment was complete a month or more before the wedding and Ned had officially moved in. Most of the time, Claire stayed there with him, too. She was perfectly aware that Jessie knew. They simply didn't talk about it.

With a certain amount of reverse snobbism, or perhaps only to be different from her mother, Claire had always liked to say that she cared not a whit for things. Yet now, because these particular things were really her own, she liked to walk around touching them or just to look at them in the light that poured from the afternoon sky when the curtains were drawn back. Many of these new possessions were actually old: her grandfather's leather set of Thackeray and Trollope, brought from Europe long before the century had turned and handed over with appropriate ceremony by her father; the blue-and-white quilt made by Grandmother Farrell that Aunt Alice had generously parted with for Claire; a lacquered Chinese chest that Jessie had been saving for a client, but had given to her when she saw that of all the objects in the shop, it was the single one that Claire really wanted.

Then of course there was a bed, the center, the heart of the new home. They had bought it together after days of searching: an outsized Victorian relic, large enough to make babies in blissful comfort and later to nurse them and play with them on winter Sunday mornings. They liked to fantasize.

"We used to think our parents' bed was a ship or a castle," Ned had told her. "Those shadowy halls could be a forest or an ocean full of scary things, and we'd run through them as fast as we could and pounce on that safe bed in the lamplight."

Except for the children, Claire thought, there hadn't been much joy in that bed. Not much joy anywhere for Mary Fern.

Ned's key turned in the lock, and he came in looking, now that he had given up the umbrella and the bowler, like any prosperous, young American coming home from work. He hadn't expected her so early, and she was pleased to surprise him.

She laughed, "You're the only person whose face wreathes in smiles. I always thought that such a silly description, but you know, your face does wear a smile like a wreath. A conquering hero's wreath."

"Idiot," he said, kissing her.

"I've brought stuff to eat, sandwiches from that great deli down the block. And Mother's cook made a cake. I snitched it because Mother's up in Vermont and there's nobody at home to eat it."

"When you said 'stuff to eat,' I thought you meant you'd cooked a dinner."

"Heavens, no! I can't cook, Ned. That's one thing I never fooled you about. But I will learn. As soon as I've more time, I'll really learn." She had set the table in the kitchenette, and now she put out the food. "Here's potato salad, here's cole slaw, a French bread and a beautiful melon."

"Leave that a minute and sit down. I want to tell you something," Ned commanded. He sounded so serious that she turned at once from the refrigerator, but his eyes were smiling with excitement.

"There's another silly expression that fits you. 'His eyes danced.' Isn't that ridiculous? Have you ever seen eyes dance? I never have except for yours. They're dancing right now."

He grasped her hand and pulled her down. "Listen. Listen. Anderson called me in today and said we were going to the president's office. For a minute, I got cold. Jergen never sees anybody. I didn't think he even knew me except maybe from seeing me in the elevator or the men's room. No, not even the men's room— he has his own. But as we were walking down the hall, Anderson told me what it was about. They're reorganizing the offices in Hong Kong. The operation there has been falling way behind and the top man is due for retirement anyway. So Jergen asked Anderson to make a recommendation, and—and, Claire, I'm it! I'm the one!"

Claire put her sandwich back on the plate. "I don't understand," she said.

"Me! Us! I'm to be head of the office! We're going to live in Hong Kong! They know we're being married and they were very nice about a honeymoon and all that, so we won't have to be there until September first. Also, of course, they'll pay for moving our stuff. What do you think of that?" And he sat back with his face wreathed in smiles and his eyes dancing.

She was perfectly sane and she had heard it all correctly. Still, the thing was totally unreal.

"I know it's a shock. Here we were settled with a fine view of the East River, and instead we'll be on the other side of the world with a view of the junks in Hong Kong Harbor."

Claire wet her lips. Then she took a swallow of water. "But aren't you forgetting something? I've got one of the most desirable internships in the world here at Fisk and a Fisk neurological residency next year. So this can't make any sense to me, Ned."

"Darling, I know it must be awfully upsetting to you. Anything as totally unexpected and sudden as this—I know." He put his arms around her, his safe arms. She laid her head on his shoulder. Then she remembered something.

"You talked about writing. You used to dream about being an investigating journalist, probing in hidden places, exposing wrongs, you said."

"Yes, I know, that was all very fine, but I've come up against hard facts and the hard facts are that you have to seize your opportunities. And this is my opportunity. A bird in the hand, as the saying goes. Darling, I'm sorry. So sorry to be confusing things like this for you when you've been so efficient, working so hard and still managing to get this apartment together and . . . and just doing the work of two people. I'm just damned sorry to do this to you."

"Well then, do you have to?"

"A man wants to get ahead, Claire." Ned spoke softly. "A man needs to. I want you to depend on me. That's what being a man is all about."

She drew away. Depend on him? Yes surely, in a way, but—

"Can't we just rearrange our thinking and look at this as a great adventure?"

" 'Our' thinking? I'm the one who is being asked to give up—"

Now Ned interrupted, "I'm not asking you to give anything up, Claire. We won't be there forever, because I most certainly don't intend to live in the Orient for the rest of my life, and anyway, that's not what they plan. I'm sure we'll be transferred. In fact, Anderson said, speaking unofficially, of course, it wouldn't be more than four or five years."

"Four or five years!"

"Yes. And you'd still be young enough to begin a residency then. Your father would get one for you. We'd have a lot of money saved up, too," he said enthusiastically. "There's extra pay for working overseas, you know."

He didn't see that she was devastated. There'd been a photo in the paper that morning of a woman who had come home to find her house burned down. All day that anguished face had kept rising in front of Claire's eyes. And now her own face must be looking like that . . . But Ned was sitting there, looking as fresh as he always managed to look after a day's work, not perceiving her at all.

He reached out to unwrap a sandwich.

"You must be crazy," she said.

"Crazy?" he repeated mildly. It took a good deal, she knew, to ruffle him, and this steadiness, this calmness in storm, was a quality she had cherished in him. "Crazy?" he said, and this time he sounded hurt. "I thought you'd be thrilled for me. I don't think you know how unusual this is. I'm the youngest man ever to head a foreign office for the firm, and I'm new on the job to boot."

"Oh," she cried, "oh, Ned, of course I know! I'm terribly proud of you." Actually she hadn't thought about it until just now. "I do see what a fabulous honor it is, I really do!"

"It's more than an honor. I'll be earning thirty-five thousand a year, plus all the extras!"

"It's wonderful, of course it is! But what about me? I can't just table my work, can I? I can't just put it aside for a while and pick it up again sometime later when it's more convenient, can I?"

"You could." He spoke gently. "I know it's not the ideal way, but it's not impossible, especially in these circumstances."

Dumbfounded, she made no answer. And he went on, "After all, you're not a man. You don't have to get through with it as fast as possible to earn a living."

"Earn a living!" she cried now. "That's not what it's all about for me! I thought you understood me better than that! Medicine is all I ever wanted. Ned! It's my— my life!"

"I do understand you. You know I do. And yet I thought I was your life. Your love and your life."

Claire got up from the chair and leaned against the refrigerator. The hard slick metal cooled her burning shoulders and back. "Oh God!" she said, closing her eyes. When she opened them, he was staring at her. He looked frightened. She tried to speak very quietly now, with seemly control. "What I mean is, we can't, we mustn't lose contact with each other over this. You see—oh, I don't want to sound conceited, but perhaps you don't know how hard it is, don't understand that this residency is an—an achievment. And it wasn't my father's name that did it. It was my own record. Dr. Macy's daughter was turned down, and—and others were, and it's not something I can possibly walk away from and begin over in five years." She went suddenly weak. "Five years, Ned! Five years out of my life! I would never go back, and in your heart you must know it."

"You could if you wanted to."

She couldn't answer. It occurred to her that the little supper, the fruit, the iced tea and the sandwiches looked pathetic, lying untouched on the table, waiting and wasted as she would wait and waste.

"If I don't accept, I'll stay an underling in the firm. Once you refuse a thing like this, they never offer you anything worthwhile again, don't you understand?"

She did understand; that was the hard part of it. She knew it meant a harsh, continual struggle to survive out there in the world.

"My father left no great legacy, Claire. I've got to make it on my own."

"I know you do."

"I have a feel for this work. At any rate, it's what I've got my start in and I can't very well become a—a lawyer or a civil engineer, for Heaven's sake, can I?"

"No."

"And I like the work. Naturally, people like what they do well. But it's really incredible to be paid so much for doing what you like—putting together words that can change people's minds."

"I see."

"You get a feeling of power. Strength and power in a worldwide enterprise."

"I see."

There was silence. Lowering her eyes to the floor, she studied their feet: Ned's still in his good English shoes, russet with a fine gloss; hers in the summer sandals she had put on when she came home. They were careless, happy shoes made for running on grass or sitting beside a pool with a drink in hand. Her thoughts ran at this odd tangent. Then she raised her eyes.

"What shall we do?"

He stood up and strode into the living room as if the kitchenette were too confined for his feelings. Two or three times he walked the length of the room. She understood by the pounding of his feet that frustration was turning into anger. Then he turned upon her. It came to her that she had never before seen his anger.

"How can you ask what we shall do! I've been trying my best to explain! How can there be any question? We'll go where I can carve out a future for ourselves. It's the man who supports the family, after all."

"Not always, Ned."

"Well, it's still the pattern. The primary income is the man's."

"That will change. It's changing now. Why am I not entitled to use my energy and brain as much as you are? Tell me, why?"

"Listen, Claire, I don't want to get into an abstract argument. Sometimes, though, I wonder whether your mother really gave you the best example."

"I'll say she did!"

"Not if this is the result."

At ten-thirty they agreed to stop wrangling and went to bed. Exhausted, Claire fell immediately asleep but in the middle of the night woke up. The wind was blowing the shade. It was snapping, as if it were angry, which was absurd; but still it seemed as if the world were threatening at the window. She got up to close it and went back to bed and lay there thinking. She thought about all the hundreds of millions of men who had been born and died and will be born and die, so many transient little lives, each lifting its tiny head above the mass of the rest, each seeking out one other tiny body to cling to. With such fierce, tiny strength, they were drawn to one another as the magnet pulls toward the north. Why just this man, this woman, and no other?

I want a fabric to be woven between us, a strong, unbroken tissue, unblemished from beginning to end, not like Martin or Jessie or Alex and Mary.

Ned moved, making a sound like a mutter or a sigh. His dream was troubling him. What was his dream? She reached out her hand to wake him, to say, "Oh Ned, my dear and darling, what shall we do? Don't leave me!" But thinking then it would be cruel to wake him from merciful sleep, she drew her hand away.

"WHAT DOES HE think?" Martin cried. "That medical training is something you put down and take up like a piece of knitting, as simply as that?" And she knew he was thinking: My girl, my brilliant girl, after your grades, your record, your potential, and you're to give it all up so he can go off to an advertising job? An advertising job, compared with medicine?

"He could get a job elsewhere, after all," Martin said more calmly. "Inconvenient, perhaps, but not impossible."

"That's exactly what Ned said about me."

"Well, it's entirely different, and I'm astonished that he doesn't see it."

"Dad, don't turn your anger against Ned. Help us. Advise us. We've spent three days talking, and I don't know how to solve it." She wiped her eyes roughly. "I don't want to cry. You know I hate crying."

"Yes. Yes, you're between a rock and a hard place, as my father used to say." Martin sighed. "Sometimes I think we doctors ought to be like priests: don't marry and don't have children. When there's no one you love and have to care about, then you can do what you want. Nothing can hurt you."

"Well, we're not priests, are we?" And she thought as she pressed him, of all the secret things written inside us, as on a scroll, unrolling back and back.

"Ah, you know in what direction my hopes lie! You're my own and I want so much for you. How can I think clearly, fairly? For you I want 'the world and all that's in it.'"

"Then you don't know how to solve this," she murmured.

"You will have regrets either way—how I wish I could spare you!" he said gently. "Only remember that you're not alone. I'm here, for what I'm worth."

She thought: All of a sudden he looks the way he will look twenty years from now. He raised his eyes to hers. She thought she had never seen eyes of such soft, penetrating sadness.

THE ARGUMENT HAD gone into the second hour of the fourth day. "Machismo, Ned," Claire cried. "That's what it is! You have to play the dominant male to show you're not like your father."

"That's a Goddamned rotten thing to say!" Ned cried.

She was instantly contrite. "I know it. I apologize. I didn't mean it that way. But you are being a heavy male, you really are."

"When you break free of your father and his ambitions for you, maybe you'll grow up and be a woman," he said coldly.

She was furious. "Maybe one day you'll learn there's more to being a woman than just taking care of a man."

"Don't dodge the issue. Ever since I came to New York I've seen and thought —I haven't spoken out but I'm going to now—you're letting your father plan your life! How do you even know you wanted to be a neurosurgeon? *He* decided it for you when you were some sort of a child prodigy and now you—"

"You're crazy! Nobody ever said I was a prodigy. Don't make a fool out of me! Putting words in my mouth, or my father's!"

The air quivered between them with the intensity of a summer storm.

"I'm going for a walk," Ned said. "I need to get out. Maybe it will clear our thoughts, being quiet for a while."

She heard the elevator door clash open, followed by the whir of its descent. "Whither thou goest," and so forth. Ought she not go to the ends of the earth with him? Had she not come from a long line of women who had done just that, following their men across oceans, bravely leaving home and parents, all the dear, familiar places? "Whither thou goest . . ." Yes, but women were different then, and I am different; certainly not better, only different. I am a doctor first. Secondarily, I happen to have female organs. Why should I be controlled by a uterus and a pair of ovaries? Why should these make all the difference?

Maybe, maybe, he will come back from the walk with another point of view. Maybe he will come to an understanding of what I mean. You love a man, and suddenly you're fighting. He turns into a stranger.

She got up and put a record on the player. This need for music, this, too, was a legacy from her father. Laying her head back, she willed herself into another place and time, while Respighi's "Birds" rustled in Rome's cypresses. Thousands of birds fluttered and wheeled against a background of triumphant Sunday bells. The birds filled her head. Most living of all living things, so free, whirling and beating through the windy sky! So free!

The door opened and Ned came back. He turned the record off.

"We've talked it all out," he said, not looking at her. "We've gone as far, I think, as words can take us. So for the last time I ask you. Have you changed your mind? Will you come with me?"

She took a deep breath. "No, Ned. I can't."

His face was closed up tight, like faces at funerals. Who knows what regrets and terrors lie behind the faces you see at funerals?

"You see," she said, "I have to do what I have to do."

He looked at her. "Well, that's it, then isn't it? I suppose it has to be. I'll take my things in the morning when you're out. It will be easier that way."

"Yes," she said.

Once she had been standing on a sidewalk where a dreadful accident had happened in the street. Someone had been run over. She'd had the same sense of unreality then, queer and remote as voices heard across water or snow.

"Well," he said and stopped. He opened his mouth again to speak and closed it without another word and went out. Again she heard the clash of the door and the whir of the elevator as he went down. But this time was the last. And silence fell.

THE APARTMENT LOOKED abandoned although, two months after Ned's departure, Claire was still living there. The cleaning woman had been in, leaving fresh towels in the bathroom and the morning paper on the coffee table. It was cold in the room, even though on the street below heat blasted yellow-hot as if from an untended furnace. She turned down the air conditioner and sat huddled, shivering and swaying. I must look old, she thought. Bitter old, and as desolate as I feel.

For almost a month now, she had known she was pregnant. And she sat with her secret knowledge, looking around the room as though in some corner of a cabinet or shelf lay an answer to her questions.

A closet door had been left ajar, and on the top shelf she saw a forgotten hat, that crushable Irish country hat which he had worn in England and brought with him when he came here. He had come here to be with her. That hat looked sad. In Hong Kong now he would be wearing a panama hat, wouldn't he? Or maybe one of those tropical topees? Or did they only wear those in India? He would be wearing a white suit and drinking a gin sling in a garden, or else in some cool room where a ceiling fan turned slowly. No, that was Somerset Maugham in Singapore, half a century ago. In Hong Kong he would be in an air-conditioned room like this one, fourteen floors above the street. Would he be working late and thinking of Claire?

My nerves, she thought. Good God, my nerves! I'm a moth beating and bumping on a windowpane, trying to get out. Get out where?

Feeling ice-cold, she ran a tubful of hot water. But her shoulders and knees, protruding from the water, were still cold. And she wondered whether the creature inside her, the tiny, fishlike thing, could feel the cold. Some said it wasn't really alive yet, but of course it was. There might even be a way in which it could sense the misery in its mother. Who really knew? It sleeps. It rocks in the warm pool and already contains within itself all that it will ever be: a cherub with curled lashes and a cleft in its chin like its father's; a fleet running boy; a timid, good girl with large feet. To destroy these possibilities? Yet, to be a child without a father?

She got out of the tub and dressed herself, then began to cry. A tabloid writer would describe "heart-rending cries," she thought disgustedly. I'm sick of tears. But the truth was that they were heart-rending. My heart is rent. I hope they can't hear in the apartment below because I can't stop. She slid to the floor and knelt with her face on the seat of the chair. I'm crying for everything. Why have I spoiled everything? Why has he spoiled everything? Damn him! Still, there's nothing else I could have done. And now, this baby—

Think! Don't let tears and fears carry you downhill! Fear rides a toboggan over the ice; once it slips past the brim of the hill, it can't stop. So hold on, Claire, hold on.

Across the park in the heart of the city there waits a man with an expert knife, a skilled and sterile knife that can solve the problem, that can destroy or save, whichever way you care to regard it. Sub rosa he works, but he is well recommended. Doctors send their wives and their mistresses to him. Medical students send their friends.

Nevertheless, fear followed at her back. It pursued her into a waiting room which was no different from a dentist's, with an etching of the Cologne Cathedral and a neglected sansevieria in green pot. It reminded her of those places where you take a crucial examination, where a pencil sharpener grinds, a proctor assembles a pile of blue books, and their crisp rustle tells you it is too late to run away and claim to be sick. Too late.

"Mrs. Blake," the nurse called. For a moment she forgot that was the name she had given, so that the nurse had to repeat it. All heads in the room turned to Claire as she rose. They were all scared. And they all knew that was not her name.

It was done with extraordinary speed.

"Well, that wasn't too bad, now, was it?" the doctor said.

He was three-quarters of the way out of the door. He hadn't spoken a word up till then.

"No, it wasn't," Claire said, unclenching her teeth. Actually, the pain had been quite bearable. She remembered the sound of scraping and willed herself not to think of it.

"You can go home now," the nurse told her.

"Can I do anything?"

"Well, I wouldn't suggest a ten-mile hike. Rest today and take it easy for the next few days, that's all."

Heads went up again when she came out into the waiting room. She felt so sorry for them all. She wanted to say: Don't be afraid, it's not so bad. A young girl sat there, a child no more than fourteen. A couple sat there; they were no longer young. He was shabby in a crumpled summer suit. Probably they already had more children than they could afford. She felt so sorry for them all.

Out on the sidewalk she stood hesitating. Suddenly she didn't want to go back to her apartment alone, which surprised her, for she had imagined herself, when this was over, going back to her own place and quietly resting, pulling herself together, not so much in body as in mind.

Mother was still in Vermont. She decided to go to her father's. Having overcome his dread of water, he had rented a summer house again near a beach. She hailed a taxi and drove to Grand Central.

There was no one but Esther in her father's house when she arrived. Claire sat down in the kitchen.

"You want something to eat, Miss Claire?"

"No thanks." I only want not to be alone. "You just came back from visiting your folks in Florida, my father says."

"Yes. Tarpon Springs. My kids live there with my mother."

"It's beautiful there, isn't it?"

"Yes, but you can't earn enough to support the kids."

"How many do you have, Esther?"

"Me? I only have two. But my sister, she's got eight here in New York. Six born since her man left her."

"How do they live?"

"Oh, she on the Welfare. Gotta be."

"Tell me, Esther. Why does a girl have all those children? I mean, because she's all alone and—"

Esther raised her eyes. The lashes rolled slowly scornfully up from her cheekbones as if she were reluctant to reveal a deep, old enmity. "That's just the reason. A girl gets lonely."

Lonely, Claire thought, wondering. I'll need to learn so much about people that I don't know at all.

She got up and walked to the kitchen-door, looking out at the lawn where stood the picnic table, the string hammock and the barbecue, the apparatus of American suburbia. At the bird-feeder a cardinal feasted on sunflower seeds, while his partner picked up the overflow on the grass. Suddenly into the silence came a running flash and a flurry of desperate shrills.

"Oh, Esther, come!" Claire screamed. "The cat's got the cardinal! Come! Run!"

Esther ran outside and came back. "It's too late. Don't look," she said with surprising gentleness. "There's nothing you can do." And she turned Claire away from the pathetic heap of scarlet feathers. "Don't you feel well, Miss Claire? My, you feel very hot. I'll make you a cold drink."

Without curiosity and disbelief, the girl looked into the face of this strange woman who could cry so over the death of a bird.

Toward dawn, Claire woke. A shaft of light fell into her eyes, making her head ache. Then she became aware of another ache, deep in some pit between her spine and her stomach. Something was knotted, tight and hard and sore. She felt her forehead. It was hot. Then she remembered yesterday, and alarm struck. Could there be anything wrong? No, no, surely there was nothing. It was only the natural effect of an unnatural procedure. It would certainly take a few days to feel normal again.

She drifted back into sleep, turning her head away from the irritating light. When she woke again, the soreness inside had turned to pain. She was shivering and her head was hot; it felt hollow. No, this surely wasn't right.

She sat up in bed just as Marjorie came through the door. The girl's long hair fell like a curtain over her shoulders.

"You said you'd do my braids for me."

"Of course. Sit on the bed." Claire raised her arms. They were weighted at the shoulders. She raised herself in the bed, forcing her strength, forcing cheerfulness. "Got plans for today?"

"Lisa's mother's taking Peter and me to the beach."

"Oh fine!"

People were thoughtful of these two who had no mother. Children without mothers. Mothers without children. Would hers have been a sturdy peaceable child like this one? An affable boy like Peter? No. These were predominantly Hazel's children. Hers would have been someone different. But who? Her arms fell.

"I seem to be tired this morning," she said. "Maybe you'd better ask Esther to finish."

She lay back and dozed again. When she woke, the house was quiet and she had a sense of morning lateness. And she stumbled out of bed, calling, "Dad! Dad!"

Esther appeared at the foot of the stairs. "It's ten o'clock. Your father left on the seven-forty-five," she said in some surprise.

"And the children? Where's everyone?"

"Enoch's gone to his job and Miz Baily took the kids to the beach."

"Oh yes. Marjorie told me."

"You're sick," Esther said accusingly.

"I know. I'm sick."

"I told you yesterday I thought you was."

"I know. I need to see a doctor. I'll get dressed."

"You came all the way to Jersey in a taxi?" Tom Horvath repeated.

"Yes." A surge of pain shook Claire, cold sweat dampened her hands. "First I thought of Dad. Then I thought better of it. Maybe we needn't upset him with this."

Tom Horvath looked at her seriously. "He will have to know," he said.

"I'm very sick, aren't I, Uncle Tom?"

"I'm afraid you are, Claire." There was no reassurance in his homely face. "I'll have to take you to the hospital."

"Oh, can't I go home? Tell me what medicine to take and—"

"Come, you know better than that. You've an infection, dear girl. You've got a hundred and four fever."

"Peritonitis?" Her voice trembled and chirped. Suddenly the room went dizzy with stripes and blocks of brilliant color. The chairs bent in the legs. The floor tilted, and Uncle Tom swam slowly toward her, curving his way through heavy water.

"Yes, Claire. Peritonitis."

*   *   *

"WHO DID THIS, Claire?"

"I can't tell you."

Her body twisted in the bed. Her stomach twisted. Was something holding her head in a vise? Was she vomiting or only feeling the need to?

Dad's face came close. The eyes pinched up and there were knobs on the forehead. Then the face vanished. Hands did things. Nurses' hands, delicate and chilly. Voices and echoes sounded at the end of a long corridor or somewhere in an empty auditorium. The ceiling spun like a top slowly wobbling before it falls.

She ripped, she tore and split. Cloth tore. Trees cracked open and animals shrieked. I can't stand all the noise in this place, all this noise and all these bright lights in my eyes, she said. Ah, bloody froth and bubble of pain, rising and cresting! Hold on, hold on until it passes. Will it pass? Slide now as it ebbs, down and down, into a dark, burning trough. So hot, the glowing fire! Now rise again, splinter and crack. Rise up and up. Ah! Hold on! Hold on and twist. Oh God! How much? How long?

She opened her eyes in a later time. An hour? A year?

Lightly, quietly, she lay on clouds, on seafoam, in a white bed in a vast landscape where there was no sound: land of the dead?

Her father's face leaned over her again. Blinking, she looked and looked again to make sure it was he.

"What day is it?" she whispered then.

"Tuesday."

"Tell me what happened."

"It's the fourth day and the drugs have taken hold. Your fever's down."

"I'm going to be all right?"

"Yes, thank God, you are."

"I almost died, didn't I?"

"Yes, Claire."

"I've made so much trouble for you," she said as reality rolled back.

"You surely did. Oh my darling, why did you do this to yourself?"

She sighed. He would want a lot of words, so many words, and in the end, they would say nothing. For how could she begin to explain it all?

"Tell us at least who did it."

"No."

"Claire, it's your obligation to tell. The man's outside the law."

"I was, too, for going to him."

"That's true, but he's a butcher. He's got to be stopped."

"No. He's very skilled, I'm sure, but there's always a risk. You know that. There's a risk when you operate, too."

"I operate to save life, not to take it."

"Don't be proud, Dad. And don't make me feel more guilty than I already am."

"I don't want to. But talk to me! Don't make me feel as if I'm facing some sort of conspiracy between you and this—this nameless person."

"But it is a conspiracy. It has to be. It's a conspiracy of trust," she murmured. "I trusted him to help me and he trusted me not to talk."

In anguish, Martin cried, "He didn't help you!"

He took her hand. She felt the pressure of his hands on hers, although she had no strength to return it. Cool sunlight flickered peacefully over the walls and it pleased her to watch it.

"It's so good not to have things hurt inside," she murmured.

"Nothing hurts, Claire?"

They could understand each other's most elliptical remarks. She answered, "Something always will, I guess."

"You didn't want to let him know, to call him back?"

"No." She spoke with pride. "He made his choice once, didn't he?"

"So did you," Martin said quietly. He released her hand, got up and changed chairs. "I liked him in spite of myself. You know that."

"Yes."

"But I hated the marriage. I couldn't help hating the thought of it. So in a way I'm relieved it's not going to be. And also, because you loved him, I'm guilty as hell over being relieved. It's so damned complicated! I can't unravel anything."

"Don't try. It doesn't matter anymore."

"We seem to do everything the hard way, you and I, with the best of intentions."

"I know." She felt the smart of starting tears and turned her head away. "Dad? Let me sleep, please. Let me sleep now."

Jessie stood by the side of the bed. Her lipstick was smeared. She must have been in an awful rush to go out like that.

"Well, Mama," Claire said and remembered that she hadn't said "Mama" since she had entered first grade.

"So, Claire. You've messed things up a little, I see."

"I thought you were in Vermont."

"I was. Your father telephoned me there. He got the number from my office."

"He called you?"

"Yes. I've been here every day."

"You've seen Dad, then?"

"No. There isn't any reason to see him, so I take care not to."

Like a child of separated parents, Claire had for just an instant a fleeting picture of Martin and Jessie standing together again; an unfounded, useless, silly hope, it was, the result, no doubt, of her own exhaustion.

"Well, what do you think of me?" she demanded. "I'm waiting for your opinion."

Jessie regarded her. "What do you want me to tell you? That you've been wicked, or that you've been a fool? Or neither? Or both?"

"Tell me whatever you're thinking."

"I'm not thinking anything. I'm just glad you're alive. Other than that, I feel numb."

The nurse came in with a drink and a right-angled straw. "Lemonade for you. Drink it all, you need plenty of fluids. Can you manage?"

"I'll help her," Jessie said.

Claire made the introduction. "This is my mother, Miss McGrath."

"Oh, Mrs. Farrell, pleased to meet you," the nurse said, careful not to look at Jessie.

Jessie braced Claire's head. There was surprising strength in her arms. It seemed to flow right down into Claire's spine.

"Finish it," she commanded.

When she had done so, Claire leaned back on the pillow. "Have they told you," she asked, "that I may never be able to have a child after this?"

Jessie closed her eyes. When she opened them, her face had sunk into sadness. "They've told me."

The room was still. The crash of a tray in the hall reverberated like an explosion.

"What else could I have done?"

"You could have had the baby," Jessie said. It was more a question than a declaration.

"Without a father? I had my own experience of that."

"You could have gone with Ned."

"I'm to be a doctor. I have a life as a doctor. I'm Martin Farrell's daughter."

"I understand. Also you have your pride. I understand that, too."

Claire smiled faintly. "Yes, you would."

"I'm not sorry you didn't marry him. I don't have to tell you that. It would have been a miserable all-around situation—and not just for me."

"I've told you, that old business had nothing to do with us."

"So you say. But there's no need to argue it anymore, is there? I'm only sorry it ended in the way it did for you."

"It's crazy," Claire said, very low, "that I've been trained to save lives, yet I took a life away." And after a minute, she repeated, "What else could I have done?"

"I can't tell you. There're just so many things I don't understand. There's just so many things I can't solve, and this is one of them, and I never shall."

"Do you know how I feel this minute?"

"Tell me."

"As if nothing I may do after this can ever matter very much, as if the world were empty."

"Empty? No, no." Jessie shook her head so that the long gold earrings swayed like tassels. "It's too full, Claire. Full of opposites and contradictions. There's charity and hatred, there's art and vandalism. There's loving and not being loved. Oh my God, it's so crowded with wanting things and fighting for them! And sometimes it's sheer hell." She sighed. Her eyes went vague. She seemed to be dreaming into the space above Claire's bed, beyond the window and far out. Then abruptly she jerked her head back, crying cheerfully, "Empty, Claire? Never. Soon you'll walk back into the world again and you'll find out."

❧{30}❧

Judy was eight years old, and the first thing Martin had noticed about her was her curly hair, his favorite kind that springs between the fingers. She was not a pretty child, but more poignant than any prettiness was her bright humor. Or perhaps she only touched him so for the simple reason she was just eight and she was going to die.

He had been keeping her alive—he and the hand of God—for eleven months. Sharply, distinctly, he could recall his grief when on the day of the first operation he and Leonard Max had opened her skull and discovered the gluey, spreading glioma multiforme. She had asked him whether he would fix her up so she could skate again. She was a very good skater, she said, and he could come and watch her some Saturday morning at the Rockefeller Center rink. Her parents had promised figure-skating lessons, but her left leg had been too weak this past winter. He had given her an evasive answer which could be interpreted as comfort and hope, but not too much of either.

It was very hard to look into a child's face and to parry her questions when you knew what was going on inside her head. Of course, she had not been on skates again: walking was difficult enough. The entire left side was going. He had left an opening in her skull, covered only by scalp, so that the growing tumor might have room to move outward instead of farther in upon the brain. Like seed in fertile earth, the tumor grew, bulging into a lump like a potato surrounded by a new growth of curls. In a few weeks at most, they would have to operate again. And then one Sunday afternoon Leonard Max telephoned.

"Martin? I'm at the hospital with Judy Wister. They called me from home for morphine, and of course I told them to bring her right in. The intracranial pressure's shot up. We can't wait till Monday."

"I'll be right over. Get the O.R. ready and call Perry, will you?"

"What if I can't get him? It's Sunday. He may not be home."

"Then get anyone you want but I always feel better with Perry for anaesthesia."

"Of course."

Martin hated this operation. When he came into the operating room, he knew everyone would see how much he hated having to do it to this child. He knew that he was not like most surgeons, who managed to keep a cool, professional dispassion. But it was not the way he was, never had been, and it was too late to change now.

The child lay on the table under the lights. So quick, so small, with her little monkey-face; he could imagine her on skates, her toothpick legs under a whirling short skirt of yellow or red; could see beyond her to her home, an apartment in the more respectable reaches of the Bronx, where you pressed the buzzer to get in at the front door and then went through corridors that smelled of onions to the bedrooms where five children slept and where you would look past the courtyard into other people's bedrooms.

The parents were waiting now at the foot of the hall. They knew she was going to die long before skating time next winter. He hadn't told them so, but they could understand what he had not told them. And he thought of them going back to that apartment without her, of how they would remember her flashing on her skates; he saw the father plodding back to the telephone company where he labored for the rent and the food and the shoes and the dentist. All this went through Martin's head while he took the few steps from the door to the table where she waited for him.

Leonard Max was ready. Martin wondered whether it had been a disappointment to Max that he had returned, able and well from a dark depression. Otherwise Max could have got the practice and hired an associate to be junior to *him!* Yet he might be doing Max a terrible injustice in thinking so. You never knew about people. Never again would he presume to understand the workings of the human mind, including his own; so delicate, subtle, secret and precious it was.

Perry came in and took his place. It seemed to Martin that he was panting, as though he had been fetched in a hurry. But it was so good to have him there, he and Leonard and the familiar, competent, swift nurses.

So he picked up the scalpel and began. He cut through the fine silk sutures that he himself had sewn in the scalp. Blood, as was to be expected, came spurting into the automatic sucker. He cauterized the surface vessels. Now farther, farther, knowing all the time that the thing was too deep for hope. How it had grown in these few months! Like weeds in a week-long spell of rain it had flourished, spreading roots and arms, branches and tentacles, and from each of these the finest, toughest fibers. Hopeless. Hopeless. Still he worked on, cutting away at the yellow, bulging brain and tumor, so interwoven now that they had become a single entity.

Doggedly he cut. *But why are you doing this?* The answer is the same as the mountain climber's famous reply: Because it is there. Until the last breath has left the body, you do whatever you know. Everything you have ever learned or practiced, you do. Given another few months of life, so the theory goes, who can say that some miraculous therapy may not suddenly be discovered, so that at the very last second, this child might be pulled back from the grave? So you work, even when you know it is too late for any theory or therapy to be applicable here.

The room was unusually quiet. Everyone remembered that this little girl had been here before. All knew that the most Martin could do this time was to remove as much more of the tumor as possible to relieve the pressure on the brain. Then he would close up the scalp and wait for the bulge to form again. Maybe once, or at most twice more, this would all be done again, and after that would come the end.

At Martin's elbow Perry's eyes and freckled forehead turned copper under the lights. Like some priest of an ancient rite, Martin thought—queer thoughts he was having today—Perry stood beside the silvery metal cylinders of anaesthetizing gas and oxygen, listening to the stethoscope, monitoring the pulse, announcing, at regular intervals, the blood pressure. Occupied with his own exploration, Martin was still always alert to everything else around the table, from the nurses handing instruments and gauze to the gas bags expanding and contracting with the child's indrawn and outgoing breath. Suddenly it seemed too long since Perry had last spoken.

"Blood pressure," Martin called.

From the corner of his eye, he looked up. Perry was standing there with a kind of absentminded, dreaming look. For an instant Martin followed his gaze to the window and the sky, where evening crept.

"Blood pressure, Perry!" he called sharply now. And at almost the same moment, he saw that the oozing blood from the wound he had been excavating was turning dark, turning blue.

"For Christ's sake," he cried. "Oxygen! For Christ's sake!"

Perry leaped. His arm appeared to leap through the air, turning one cylinder up, the other one down. Oxygen purred with a soft, liquid rush: whish, whish. He looked up at Martin. Such a strange, helpless look! It crossed Martin's mind: something's the matter with him; his eyes are swimming.

Then Perry said, "Erratic pulse."

"Adrenalin," Martin commanded.

"I don't think I can get the pulse," Perry said.

"Oxygen," Martin commanded.

"I definitely can't get the pulse," Perry said. It sounded in Martin's ears like pleading.

"Cardiac arrest!"

There was a swift, disciplined scurrying in the room. Someone jumped on the table and began to thump on the child's chest.

"Two amps bicarb!"

"Let's get the paddles."

"Open up the fluids!"

"Open the intravenous line!"

These low commands went back and forth; arms and hands reached back and forth. The needle of adrenalin pierced the heart; it seemed like hours and was, actually, minutes.

"The EKG is flat," Perry said, and then, finally, "It's finished."

Someone was still working, working desperately on the chest.

"No," Leonard Max said, "it's no use." And he repeated, "It's finished."

There was a tired silence until Max broke it again. "Perhaps it's a mercy," he said gently. "She hadn't very long."

Martin didn't answer. He had gone through it before and would go through it again; each time was a separate agony. And in a familiar gesture, he drew his gloves off and threw them on the floor.

They went out into the hall to the waiting room where the second act was to be played, the act of notification. The three paced down the corridor abreast, Martin and Leonard and Perry. Martin wanted to ask, "What happened, Perry?" But then he wasn't sure he ought to because there was a fuzz of confusion in his mind right now, and anyway, there was this to be got through, and he was exhausted.

The mother went mad. She had been standing with her hand over her mouth as the three men approached. Possibly, he thought afterward, the news had been written in their eyes or their walk. And he knew he would always see her face out of a long line of such faces going back years and years. It was wide across the top like a cat's, with a delicate pointed chin and round pale eyes. Her scream was the most terrible sound one could ever hear, worse than the cry of an animal being slaughtered or a woman in labor. Her husband and some other young man, a brother or brother-in-law, took her to a room. Nurses came running. Someone gave her a hypodermic. It was over.

And Martin went home to have supper with his children, who had, as far as he knew, no alien things growing in their heads, and he was thankful for that.

Later, in bed, he tried to reorder his thoughts. Had the child become cyanotic because of the surgical shock or had Perry in some way failed? He recalled that in the flurry he had sensed something strange about Perry. But then, perhaps it was only his imagining as a result of the flurry. Everything had happened too fast to remember the sequence of events. He often thought he'd make a bad witness to an accident. It had been proven that three people could witness the same event and give three completely different reports of it. So his mind went spinning and rotating toward sleep.

In the morning at the office Leonard said, "That was some rotten Sunday afternoon yesterday."

Martin, going over mail at his desk, had a sense of Leonard's hovering halfway to the door, as if he were waiting to say something more.

"Did you see Perry afterward?" Leonard asked.

"Afterward?"

"Yesterday, before you left."

Martin looked up. "No, I went straight home. Why?"

"Well, there was something odd about him."

Martin waited.

Leonard sat down. "I think—Jesus, I hate to say this—but I could swear he'd had a couple of drinks."

"You know what you're saying. Leonard?"

"I sure as hell do! I'm not saying it to anybody else, Martin, for God's sake. I'm telling you. He was talking to one of the kid's relatives, the uncle I think. The young guy with the parents. I saw him in the hall after I got dressed and he just— well, he was talking too loud and too much and— Well, you know that faint something you can detect, not drunk exactly, but—"

Martin interrupted. "Did you notice anything in the O.R.?"

"I only thought—well, I thought he wasn't paying attention. The kid should have got more oxygen. He wasn't monitoring."

For a long minute neither of them spoke. Martin tapped a pencil on the desk. Certain things came back to him more clearly now: Perry looking out of the window; the sky streaked rust and claret. He felt the slow thud of his heart.

"Yesterday was his anniversary, they were having a party at his house."

Perry was not a drinker, but at an anniversary party, surely he would have had a couple? "I just don't know," Martin said again.

"Well, of course, little Judy's days were few and cruel. When you consider, it's just as well. Merciful, in fact."

"True. Undoubtedly true. But not the issue exactly."

"I wonder," Leonard began.

"Wonder what?"

"Whether we should— I mean you or both of us, or whether we should—"

"Say anything to Perry?"

"Yeah. What do you think?"

"Or wait. Maybe he'll say something. Maybe something will—"

Leonard stood up. "Right. Nothing hasty. It's all vague. See whether he says anything."

PERRY SAID, "TOUGH about the little girl, Martin. But I guess you knew before you started how it was going to end, so it was no surprise to you."

"It was a considerable surprise," Martin said distinctly.

Perry's expressive eyebrows rose to his freckled forehead. "I don't understand. You honestly expected her to survive the operation?"

"I certainly did, and maybe another one like it a few months down the road."

They were in an empty corridor, waiting for the elevator. Nevertheless, Martin lowered his voice.

"Perry, were you feeling all right yesterday?"

"What the devil makes you ask that?"

"Because. Level with me. You weren't monitoring."

"The hell I wasn't!"

"I don't think you were. She went cyanotic."

"So? That's never happened before?" A bright flush of anger inundated the freckled forehead.

"Yes, but this time I—"

"Just what the hell are you trying to prove, Martin?"

"I'm not trying to prove anything. I'm only asking. Don't get excited."

"Don't get excited! When you're practically accusing me of negligence, you expect me to—"

"I'm not accusing you of anything. I repeat, I'm only asking whether you can clear up something in my mind. If friends can't talk frankly with each other—"

The elevator came. It was crowded. The two men stood abreast, not touching, Martin aware of Perry's fast angry breathing. He regretted having spoken. The whole thing might be a dreadful error on his part. If so, Perry had every reason to be hurt and furious. Yet—

On the third day Leonard came into Martin's office. "You know Perry's car, that imported job he bought last month?"

"What about it?"

"The front fender's crumpled up like a handkerchief. I saw it in the parking lot this morning. So I told him, I said, 'That's some fender-bender. How did you manage to do that?' And he said it happened Sunday afternoon, backing out of the lot, after the surgery."

"That doesn't prove anything," Martin said.

"No, but it adds up."

Martin didn't answer. He felt like a cheap detective, one of those matrimonial snoopers. Then he thought of something and rang for Jenny Jennings.

"Did I remember to have you send flowers to the funeral home for Judy?"

"You did. I sent a spray of roses from you and Dr. Max."

"Good. Good. Thanks."

So she's at peace. No more vomiting, dizziness and pain. No more shaved head, medicines and bandages. At peace. But I'm not. Still, can't play detective, prosecutor and judge. Too difficult. Drop it. What's done is done.

T HE NURSING SUPERVISOR met him one morning in the lobby and drew him aside. "I've had a call from a lawyer, a Mr. Rice. He wants to see the record on Judy Wister. It looks like trouble."

So it's come! was Martin's first reaction. All these years he'd gone without a suit for malpractice. It was bound to come once in a lifetime anyway, he thought grimly. Still, he had done his best for the child. He would have said, naively no doubt, that the Wisters of all people would never do this to him. They had seemed to worship him, to be so grateful. And he felt a small, sad hurt.

"Well," he said, not wishing to let the hurt show, "I guess my turn's just come. I've got plenty of company, that's for sure."

So he was quite prepared when a few days later Jenny Jennings informed him that a Mr. Rice had called on behalf of his clients, Louis and Martha Wister, and would be in to see him at three that afternoon.

Mr. Rice was a garish individual with oiled hair and a rasping voice. Two strikes against him anyway, Martin thought, feeling some amusement at his own surprising calm.

"Well, Mr. Rice, what is it you want to know about me?" he began.

"Nothing about you at all."

"You're not here to serve papers, to sue me?"

"No, no. Mr. and Mrs. Wister specifically exclude you from any culpability in the death of their child. The matter concerns the anaesthesiologist alone. We want your testimony to the effect that he was negligent as a result of being under the influence of alcohol."

"Oh, no," Martin said. "I've known Perry Gault for years, and he's the best man in his field that any surgeon could want. As a matter of fact, I don't like to operate without him. He's completely reliable." He heard himself babbling.

"That may all be true, but the fact is that on this particular day, he had been drinking. Mrs. Wister's brother, Arthur Wagnalls, had conversation with Dr.

Gault and smelled alcohol on his breath. Furthermore, the doctor had an accident in the parking lot on the way out, and the man whose car he hit believed either that he had been drinking or wasn't feeling well, he wasn't sure which. Also—"

Martin raised his hand. Something in him was frightened for Perry and wanted to defend him. "Wait. This is all unsubstantiated. The child's uncle is not an impartial person, after all. And anyone can say anything about anyone, can't he? You could go out of this office right now and say I'm drunk, couldn't you? And it would only be your opinion."

Mr. Rice smiled. It was an all-knowing smile. It said, "I am a step ahead of you and no matter how fast you run, I shall always remain a step ahead."

"We have an impartial person, as you say. One of the nurses, Delia Whitman, has already given a statement to the effect that Dr. Perry had been drinking."

"Delia Whitman? There was no such person in the operating room, and I'm well acquainted with them all."

Mr. Rice said patiently, "She's a student nurse. You probably wouldn't know her. She was attending Mrs. Wister and was present when Dr. Gault and Mr. Wagnalls were talking. Afterward Mr. Wagnalls remarked on Dr. Gault's condition, and she answered, she told him, yes, it was clear to her, too."

Martin, stunned, resorted to pencil-tapping.

"Furthermore, the record of the operation says a great deal. The girl became cyanotic. Anaesthesia was hurriedly lowered and oxygen increased after you, the surgeon, ordered it. Dr. Gault had not been monitoring the flow."

Ugly, ugly! The only other brush with law that Martin had had in all his life had been his divorce and he had come away from that with no love for lawyers. Wordmongers, sophists and procrastinators, they were; their aim was to trip you up, to trick you into saying what you didn't mean.

"I'm not a lawyer," he said somewhat brusquely, "so will you come to the point? What do you want of me?"

"I want you to be a witness for the Wisters in a suit for malpractice against Dr. Gault."

"No, no," Martin cried. "I want to be left out of this. I don't have time, I'm a busy man. There's a roomful of patients out there. I'm concerned about them and only about them."

"Exactly. And you want them protected against this sort of thing, don't you? Isn't it your duty to protect them, since you're so concerned?" Mr. Rice stood up. "I won't take any more of your time now, Doc. Think it over. When you do, you'll do the right thing, I'm sure." He backed toward the door. "I'll be calling you again."

I'm sure you will, Martin thought with enormous distaste.

Perry looked large and clumsy in Martin's little den.

"I'm sorry to come busting in on you like this," he said, "but I was sitting around after dinner tonight and I thought, 'Well, why don't I go see Martin and talk it all out?' We've been avoiding each other. I was hasty that day in the hall, very upset, but as you see, it turns out I have reason to be upset. I'm so damn sorry, Martin," he finished.

"Yes. Well—"

"You know, of course, you've heard they've served me with a suit?"

"I heard." He estimated that the entire hospital had heard within an hour.

Perry leaned forward. "Martin, I'm going to level with you. I did have a couple of drinks. You know I don't drink much. A little goes a long way with me. Too long."

Oh Jesus, Martin thought.

"I shouldn't have gone to the hospital at all. I know I ought to have told you to get somebody else, but the thing is, when you're a little bit dazed, under that thin edge of sleepiness, you don't know you are. Martin, you're not going to testify against me? She was going to die anyway." There were tears in the friendly copper eyes and Martin couldn't bear to look at them. "You don't know how I feel. That kid— If I could bring her back! But nobody could. How long did she have? Three months? Six at the most? So when you come down to it, what great difference did it make?"

Martin was silent.

And Perry continued. "It should never have happened and you can bet everything that's holy, it never will again. Never. Martin, what are you going to do?"

Martin spoke very gently. "I don't want to do anything to hurt you. Do I have to tell you that?"

Perry stood up and began walking the length of the little room: twelve paces to the bookshelf at the far end and twelve paces return. "Martin, for myself— Oh, I won't say anything grandiose and tell you it wouldn't matter, because of course it would. But the truth is, there's more than myself. The truth is I've got the two boys in college and Leonore's having a mastectomy. A radical, I'm afraid."

"I didn't know."

"Well, we just found out last week. Now I've got to put this on her, too. You see, what I'm saying is, I'll need all the support I can get from my friends. Martin, I'm scared as hell."

"Take it easy, Perry, take it easy. Things have a way of working out. We all want to help you get through this, stand by you."

What was he saying? Words, cheap, smooth, easy words, meaning nothing. How was he going to "help out"? Just what, exactly, was he going to do? His head whirled with it.

A WEEK AFTER that the lawyer came from the company that insured Perry, that insured them all. This one was a gentleman. He wore a nice dark suit and had a nice quiet manner. He was from Harvard Law. You would like your son to grow up and be like him.

"What is it you want of me?" Martin asked for the second time in as many weeks.

"To testify on behalf of Dr. Gault. The child died of natural causes. There is no convincing proof of anything to the contrary."

"Convincing," Martin thought. *Semantics. All law is word-twisting. Convincing to whom?* He passed his hand over his forehead.

"I'm not cut out to be a lawyer," he said apologetically. "I'll confess my head's beginning to whirl."

"Of course. Let me get in touch with you in another few days, to go over specifics. I'm sure we can work things out with satisfaction, and dispatch this nasty business as quickly as possible." And with a pleasant smile and handshake, he, too, departed.

THE CASE SEEMED to fill Martin's life. He wished it would go away, wished he'd never seen Judy Wister or Perry or anyone. It was becoming uglier, with a creeping element of vengefulness. The Wisters telephoned him at his home—he ought to get an unlisted number, damn it!—to plead. The mother wept. Well, he couldn't blame her! Perry's wife came to his office late one afternoon and walked five blocks with him toward his home, red-eyed and begging all the way. Couldn't blame her, either.

One afternoon the hospital superintendent called him in. "There's talk that you don't want to work with Perry's lawyers," Mr. Knolls said.

Martin answered slowly, "It's not that I don't want to work with them. I don't want to work with anybody. I want to be left out."

"You can't be. You won't be."

"Why?" Martin burst out. "Why can't I mind my own business and be left alone!" The instant he had said it, he knew the lament was puerile.

Mr. Knolls didn't even deign to answer it. He said instead, "Of course, I can't tell you what to do, and I'm not trying to tell you. I've known you a long time, though, and I feel free to point out a few things you may have overlooked."

"Such as?"

"Perry's had twenty-two years here at Fisk. A distinguished record."

"I certainly know that."

"Unblemished. The publicity of this affair, the strain, the emotional damage can wreck a man after all those good years."

"I know that, too."

"Now he needs all the help he can get. Don't condemn him. It won't bring the child back, anyway."

Martin looked at him.

"He's suffered enough from this already. His wife's undergoing—"

"He told me."

"Well, then, I'll say no more."

Martin nodded. "I understand."

He began hearing unpleasant things about himself. "You're acting like a boy scout," he was told. "The guy had one extra drink. We all agree he shouldn't have come into the O.R. But he's never slipped before, and he'll never slip again. So what's to be gained by crucifying him? What?"

Purpose. Abstractions. A man's whole professional life versus a dead child who was going to die anyway.

"You'll be a great hero to no one but yourself, Martin. Perry's going to win the case. He's got prestigious people to testify for him. And the O.R. nurse is sweet on him; you know the chubby blond, what's-her-name? And that resident Maudley is scared shitless. He'll say what he's expected to say. So where does that leave you if you go to the other side?"

He spoke to Tom. "Awful, awful," Tom said, sighing and shaking his great leonine head. Then he said cautiously, "It puts you in a bad position. Tough on you."

Martin waited.

"Yes. Tough. It's always hard to testify against another doctor, I guess because you never know when it could be you. There but for the grace of God—that business." He paused. "Any one of us could make one slip in a lifetime, couldn't we?"

True. And Braidburn long ago had warned not to be too quick to judge: you never knew when it might be you who'd make a fatal mistake. One mistake out of a lifetime of good service . . .

At night he lay awake conducting internal dialogues while shadows flickered over the ceiling.

Tomorrow the lawyers will be calling again. I've told Jenny Jennings to stall them off, but that can't go on indefinitely.

Cold, stony looks in the hospital now. I used to think it's simple. One side or the other. Angel of truth, versus monster of corruption. Not like that at all! Generals on the battlefield lose thousands of men through miscalculation, errors of judgment, quirks of behavior. Nothing happens to them.

You're comparing canaries with alligators.

Not so. Death is death, whether of one or thousands.

She was going to die anyway, remember that.

But if it hadn't been that child, that case; if it had been a benign encapsulated tumor, a meningioma, something relatively easy and Perry had not monitored, what then? Then there would truly have been disaster.

Yes, but it wasn't an easy case. It was death-writ-large.

They won't recover, the Wisters won't, whether you're for them or against them or if you take a boat to China and disappear. The biggest names in the county medical society are going to testify for Perry. So you'll be a boy scout! You'll lose a friend and make more enemies.

You could retrieve a lot of goodwill by agreeing to testify for him. You could. You have tremendous prestige, which is respected. Don't underestimate it.

So the long nights passed.

After dinner the doorbell rang. Enoch came into the den where Martin was at his desk. "There's a lady wants to see you, Dad."

He hoped it wasn't Perry's wife coming again, but probably it was. And, suddenly very tired, he made a decision. He would just simply say "yes" at last. Throw in the sponge and say, "Okay, how do you want me to help?" Get it over with. It made sense, really.

Instead a young girl walked in and sat down. He didn't recognize her.

"Delia Whitman," she said. "I know you but you don't know me. I'm a fourth-year student nurse." She swallowed hard. "I'm the girl in Dr. Gault's case."

Oh, not more of that! "Why have you come to me?"

"Because—I don't know. I wanted to talk to somebody, some doctor. And I thought—the things they say about you, the nurses, I mean, a person gets a reputation—" Her voice trailed off in tears and she took out a handkerchief.

"Don't cry," Martin said, forcing patience. "Just tell me what's on your mind."

"Well, it's— This is what happened. After the operation when the little girl died—the mother went to a room. She was crying and Miss Hannigan called me to come and help. Stay with her, you know?"

Martin nodded.

"So, then I had to go out in the hall for medicine, and this man, the uncle, was talking to Dr. Gault, and he called me over and asked me how his sister was, and I said we were getting her some medicine, and I'm awfully sorry about the little girl. And Dr. Gault started to talk. And Doctor, he was acting awfully funny. He was talking loud, not very loud, but the thing is he was just—funny. And afterward, when they were taking the mother home, the man saw me and he stopped me and said, 'That guy, that doctor, he'd been drinking, hadn't he?'

"And I said, 'I guess so.' And he said, 'You smelled liquor on him, didn't you?' and I said yes, I had, because it was the truth, I did smell it. And now, now the lawyer for Dr. Gault—he's an awfully nice young man, but he keeps coming around and they want me to say I had only been joking, that the man had put the words in my mouth, that I had thought he was kidding." The girl wiped her eyes and blew her nose.

Jesus, Martin thought, will this business never end?

"The thing is, I just don't know what to do, Dr. Farrell. And I haven't got anybody to ask. Some of the girls say one thing and some say the other. And it seems to me what they say is all according to whether they like Dr. Gault, and it seems most of them do. Or else what they tell me depends sort of on my looking out for myself and not getting the doctors offended with me. And it seems the doctors are mostly all sticking up for Dr. Gault. So I've come to ask you what I should do." She finished, balling the wet handkerchief in her palm.

It surprised him that out of this confused narration, a single threat could emerge so quickly and clearly. He had no hesitation at all in replying to this troubled, honest, childish girl.

"Why," he said softly, "you must just tell the truth, mustn't you?"

"Just like that?"

"Just like that," he repeated.

Explanations and justifications would only confuse her some more. What she had come for was plain direction, as when a child, needing to obey, asks to be told what to do. When she had thanked him, too apologetically and too effusively, she went out. Strange how easy it had been to tell *her* what she must do and so difficult to tell himself what *he* must do!

He opened the window. The night air washed over him, bathing his hot face. Then he turned on the record player where a record had been left, the *Reformation* symphony. For long minutes he stood listening, while his unfocused eyes rested on the sky over the river. The music was a shaft of light. It was a great plea and answer. And in some absolutely crazy way it seemed his father's voice was mixed up in it.

Suddenly everything was very simple.

He went to the telephone book. A pleasant young man from Harvard Law School would live somewhere in Manhattan, on the East Side. Yes, here it was. Might as well do it now, get it over with before the morning and be able to sleep tonight. I'm very tired, he thought again. I haven't slept well in so long. And he picked up the telephone.

"This is Dr. Farrell," he said. "I'm sorry to disturb you at home, but I'll be brief. I've made my decision. It's a painful one. I want you to know that it is, and I should hope perhaps you might find a way to tell Dr. Gault it is. But I cannot, I simply cannot, help you. I couldn't do it and rest."

❧{31}❧

Martin, having changed from operating clothes to street clothes, looked in for a moment at the door of the doctors' lounge. It reminded him of the passing glimpses he'd had of London clubs where old men napped on brown leather chairs. The walls held Piranesi etchings of broken classic columns with vines trailing over the stumps. Why did dentists and doctors always seem to go in for broken classic columns?

Young Simpson, he of the good cheer, called out, "Going back to the office so late, Martin?"

"No, waiting for my daughter. We've a party on the Island."

"Enjoy yourself," young Simpson said.

Going down on the elevator Martin felt the smile still on his mouth. It was remarkable how even the most casual proof of being liked and accepted could freshen and support a man. As for enemies, you could hardly get through life, he supposed, without garnering some. And he thought regretfully of Perry, who having won his case without Martin's help, now ignored him whenever they chanced to pass; of others, too, whose greetings, if any, were noticeably cool.

In the lobby he waited for Claire. The rotunda was solemn, like an edifice of ancient Rome. A new bronze plaque, glossier than the rest, displayed the names of the most recent benefactors. He was standing there reading the names almost mechanically when his daughter appeared. He watched her before she saw him. Her face was set in gravity; as soon as she saw him it bloomed into a smile. Real or assumed? he wondered.

"Reads like Dun & Bradstreet, doesn't it, Dad?"

"I don't like this lobby," he said. "It's pompous. The institute will have quite a different feel."

She patted his shoulder as if to say: I know it will be the zenith of your life. They went out into a benign spring afternoon and walked toward the parking lot.

"Up to the second story already," Claire observed as they passed the new construction at the end of the block.

"Right on schedule. Yes, we ought to be functioning a year from this month."

For the sake of some obscure and foolish dignity, Martin tried to keep the jubilation from his voice. Two months ago they had laid the cornerstone, a great chunk of mauve brown marble set in a row of granite. There had been a committee to select the artifacts which in some distant, unimaginable century would be uncovered; the city might be rubble and ruin by then. And as always, Martin thought of the schoolboy poem: "My name is Ozymandias, king of kings. Look on my works, ye mighty, and despair."

Anyway, Braidburn's text had gone in, he'd seen to that. Now almost fifty years old and much outmoded, it was still worthy of honor as the great pioneer. Outmoded! Every five years a text became outdated, so fantastic was the explosion of medical knowledge, a proliferation like leafage in a rain forest!

Thinking aloud, which he often did when in Claire's company—it pleased him that she found nothing odd in his doing so—he said, "It's the most challenging intellectual field of all, medicine. More than any science, as far as I'm concerned, including space exploration. What's more important than humanity? Each step, each advance whets your curiosity so you have to go on to the next. I sometimes imagine a composer must feel like that when a symphony unfolds in his head."

And for some reason Judy Wister popped into his own head, the skinny, trustful little thing who had lain down beneath his hands. He recalled the lawyer, that well-dressed, affable young man who had told him, "You're a man of probity, Doctor, after all." Probity!

The suffering, he thought, you could never rid the world of it! Even on this brief walk, in these few blocks, you saw its symbols: a dirty old woman mumbling to herself; a lost, bony mongrel foraging in a trash can; a drained young man, sallow-cheeked, climbing up out of the subway.

How we are driven! We prate of free will and of course it is a fact, but what of accident, chance meeting, timing, health, the very luck of the genetic draw? On another day, for instance, Hazel, even given what she was—and I don't suppose either she or I really knew what she was—might not have done what she did. It was just that moment, that particular day. He could think of it now, could even talk about it, although he seldom did, without that terrible choking inside.

They got into the car and Martin took the wheel. Claire sighed. "I can't say I'm looking forward to the Mosers' little shindig."

"You're doing me a big favor. I like to show you off, you know. Besides, it doesn't hurt you to become known. The world doesn't beat a path to anyone's doorstep."

"The people you meet at their place—they're all such wastrels."

"The Mosers are decent people," Martin protested.

"They may be, but the crowd you meet there just isn't real. You get the feeling, at least I do, that everybody's out for something."

"We're all 'out for something.' We all want recognition, to stand out from the crowd."

"Don't mind me," Claire said. "The fact is I'm starved and I get cranky when I'm starved."

Martin said, "The crankiest of all was your grandfather. He had an appetite like a bear."

"Well, that's another way I'm like him then. You always say I'm like him."

Martin looked over at her. "Yes, you are, rather. You don't give a darn how you're dressed. You'd better catch that button, it's hanging by a thread."

"Oh damn!" she said. She pulled off the button and stuffed it in her pocket. "You know, I think I would have liked the way he lived: simple, no pretenses."

"You don't know what you're talking about. It was a life so hard you couldn't begin to imagine it."

They drove along in silence for a minute or two, during which with swift recall Martin saw again the snowfields and poor dark houses, felt the brutal cold, heard the voice of the kind ascetic, so devoted to his work, and of the wife who paid her full share for that devotion.

Claire asked, "Did the orthodontist send you the report on Marjorie's teeth?"

"Yes. She needs the work. They'll start next month. You've been so awfully good to the kids, Claire, with all you have to do. Do I thank you often enough?"

"You don't have to. They're good kids. Peter's sweet and so serious and Marjorie's a housewife, already." Claire sounded amused. "I swear she knows more about keeping a house in order than I ever will."

"She's like—" Martin began, and stopped. For an instant he had forgotten that Hazel was dead. He thought of something. "I forgot to tell you. You know that man from Salt Lake City I operated on last winter? The one who owns half a copper mine? Well, I got a letter from him today. I'd been talking to him about the institute, and he hadn't said a word, but now in a letter he wants to know how much we'd need to pay for an operating room. An entire operating room! Imagine!"

"A true G.P.," Claire said.

"A what?"

"Grateful Patient. And you've certainly had loads of them, if anyone has."

They were riding now along a maze of highways, past clusters of apartment houses twenty stories high; and these clusters were like islands in a sea of cars. This crowding gave Martin a vague melancholy. Then glancing over at Claire, he realized that the melancholy was because of her . . .

There was something remote about her these days. Oh, she was talkative as always, enthusiastic about her future with him, and so appreciative! But there was —something. No use asking her to talk about it, because she would refuse. Just as I, he thought, am unable to talk about Mary. Especially now, after Hazel— Sometimes a thought leaps, a thought of seeing Mary again, and my mind clamps down, just shuts down sharply. So it must be for my daughter, with Mary's son!

Apartments gave way to grids of tiny houses, row on row and all alike among flat fields, with no trees. Baby carriages and tricycles were scattered on their tiny lawns. Each house must hold at least two tiny children; and in each house a woman was living a life so different from Claire's— He wondered whether she would indeed ever have a child, and if not, how the lack would affect her. He would have liked to talk to her about that too, but he dared not.

The suburbs became the exurbs. There was restful space between the houses. Behind brick walls and wrought iron gates the overarching trees were budding so that the land was veiled in pale green lace. When Martin's car rolled up the Mosers' driveway it came to a stop among Mercedeses and Rolls-Royces. Chauffeurs stood about talking. From the water side of the house a choir of peepers piped and trilled. And Martin, moved by some old nostalgia, stopped to listen.

"Another spring," he said. "Every year I'm glad I've lived to see it again."

Hundreds of daffodils were scattered over the lawn. "Naturalized," Claire observed, and Martin thought: Where did I see this before? In some place far off— and suddenly remembered the lawn in Cyprus and Pa saying, "They don't just grow like that. Somebody put them there."

It WAS WARM. The press of people, the fires under the great carved mantels and the good Scotch produced this hearty warmth. The chatter might be a silly waste of energy, as Claire had remarked, but it was good, nevertheless, to be here. Martin stood with his little plate of canapés and his drink, listening to tag ends of three conversations at once.

"He gave two floors to the new wing in Tulsa. Oil people, of course," someone said.

"My wife's cousin is on the board of directors, and that helped. Frankly, his grades weren't all that good."

"There wasn't time for a wash-and-set between lunch and my tennis lesson."

Claire had found a young couple whom she knew. They were at the far end of the room. Martin was relieved that she had found people her own age to talk to. Most of the people here were too old for her, as he had known they would be. He watched her in her quiet dress standing among all the bright silk plumage. Distinguished. The authentic article, he thought, wanting so much for her. Academic honors, yes, those she had; and he was so proud, thinking of that. But she needed someone, he thought again; she oughtn't to be alone. Men ran after her, he knew they did; yet she didn't seem to care about any of them—

Bob Moser came up with a drink in hand. "Having a good time?"

"Very. It's a spectacular party, as always."

"I'd like to talk to you for a minute if you don't mind. Let's go in the library, it's quiet there."

They sat down. Moser's head was framed by a row of golf trophies, and above them a shelf of smooth leather-bound sets. He seemed to be studying Martin. There was an odd pause which Martin found necessary to fill.

"This house was meant for parties," he observed pleasantly.

"Yes," Moser said. He took off his glasses, revealing tired eyes. "I suppose this isn't the right place for what I have to tell you. I had thought of ringing you on the phone, but one can't talk properly on the phone. And then I thought we might go out to lunch together, except that you're so busy."

Martin waited attentively.

"We've been friends for a long time, Martin."

Martin nodded.

"Christ! I don't know how to start." Moser's mouth made a queer twist as though he were about to cry. "I feel, I feel the way you must feel when you have to tell a family the patient has died." The familiar open face closed up and Moser shut his eyes.

Alarmed, Martin asked, "Is anyone ill? What is it, Bob?"

"I wanted to be the one to tell you. I didn't want you to get it coldly at a meeting or by letter or however they planned to do it."

And suddenly Martin knew. He thought: It's crazy, but I know what he's going to say. He set his glass down and waited.

"You know Dr. Francis? Stanley Francis?"

"From San Diego. I've met him at meetings."

"I understand he's a good man, done some fine work."

"Yes, he's head of the department out there. Does a lot of teaching."

"Like you. Kind of a duplicate of yourself, if I may say so, only younger."

"About five or six years, that's all."

"Yes. Well." Moser got up from the chair. A large globe stood in a corner. He placed his hand over the top, the splayed finger covering the Bering Sea and the North Cape. He twirled the globe.

"Christ, Martin! I haven't slept these two nights. It was decided—this is still confidential, of course, but the trustees had a meeting the day before yesterday and it was decided—the fact is—oh hell! They've offered the directorship of the neurological institute to Stanley Francis, and he's accepted. That's it in a nutshell." And giving the globe a violent twirl so that it rattled as it spun, he walked away and stood with his back to Martin.

Martin trembled. The room had a feeling of unreality. The ripple of voices in the next room was suddenly remote, like fading voices heard when one's hands are held over one's ears.

"I see," he said. "I see . . ."

Moser turned back to him. "New blood," he said dully. "That's the reason they gave to make it sound convincing. You can make anything sound convincing, can't you? But it was yours by right." His fist slapped into his palm. "You're the one who dreamed of it and worked for it; your patients gave funds for it; you set up the teaching program, attracted the young men to train and be trained. It was yours."

"Yes," Martin said, feeling faint. "Yes, it was."

"I'm sick!" Moser cried. "Sick over it! Jesus Christ, I tried! I tried! I was two hours in there fighting for you, Martin! And I want you to know the vote was very, very close. I don't feel free to tell you who voted how, naturally, but—"

"You don't have to," Martin said, breathing deeply. "I pretty much know."

"I suppose you do. Well, you made enemies, Martin. What can I tell you? You made enemies. You threw it away." Moser spoke angrily. "I don't want to say it again, I don't want to rub salt in the wound, but I can't help it. You were a fool, a Goddamned fool!"

"You think so?"

"I know so! My whole life experience tells me so. Look out for number one, it says."

"Maybe you're right. At this point I don't know. I don't know anything."

"Yes. But I'd still go to hell and back for you. What are you going to do?"

"First, get my balance. My head's spinning."

"Want another drink? Brandy?"

"No, that's just what I don't want, thanks."

"Want to lie down?"

"No, no, I'm all right, Bob. I'll be all right."

"Want me to send Claire in?"

"No, no, I'm okay, Bob. Really."

Moser looked doubtful. "Positive?"

"Positive. Just leave me. Please. Please."

"Then I'll go back in. And, Martin?"

"Yes?"

"Maybe you can spare an hour for lunch with me one day, especially—"

Especially now that I won't be working my head off for the institute, you mean? And Martin answered, "Sure, Bob, sure I will."

French windows led to a terrace. They were ajar. After long minutes he got up from the chair and went outside. Light from the house stretched long gilded fingers among Moser's cherished, nurtured trees. Beyond this small enclave of light and safety lay unknowable darkness, the menacing water gurgling on the rocks below the bluffs. And over all was the vast cold sky.

A world of danger. You get on a plane and it crashes in flames the way that one did last month, a plane full of vacationers with their cameras and new bathing suits. You go to swim in warm water and under that warm, bright indigo lurks a shark. You walk to the post office and the shoe repair shop doing your friendly, simple errands, while all the time a cancer grows secretly within you, corruption and death waiting quietly for their hour. It is a world of danger. You can depend on nothing except yourself, and sometimes not even on that.

He walked to the edge of the terrace and leaned on the balustrade, looking downward on Italianate descending terraces, an imitation of the Villa d'Este outside of Rome. And this ostentation, to which he had grown moderately accustomed, chilled him now as it had when he was young.

Beyond the terraces lay rough and marsh grass, out of which the peepers were still trilling. They would still be there a thousand springs from now, long after the terraces had been worn away and the balustrades crumbled. "Look on my works, ye mighty, and despair." He thought: I ought to be full of hatred, but I'm not. And isn't that strange?

It began to rain and he heard the chauffeurs behind the shrubbery scurrying to the cars. From the deep shelter of the doorway, Martin stood in a trance of exhaustion, watching the branches dripping in the squall, watching the steady rain. It was almost tropical, the way it fell, so fast that it seemed not to be moving at all, as if it were a solid, luminescent curtain hanging between himself and the outer world. He thought again: I ought to be full of hatred. Why am I not?

"I've been looking for you everywhere," Claire said. "What have you been doing out here in the rain?"

"It's letting up. I've been smelling spring in the air."

"I thought surely you'd be where the food is. They've got great lobster mousse that's like nothing Esther feeds you at home. Why, what's the matter?"

"Will you not get excited if I tell you?"

"You look white. Are you sick?"

He told her. She leaned against the wall as if she had been struck.

"No! I don't believe it! I simply don't believe it!"

"You can believe it. It's true."

"The bastards! The lousy bastards! It's because of that case, isn't it? You betrayed the club, the good old boys, the old school tie!" She began to cry.

"Ah don't, Claire! It's not worth it."

"Yes it is! It is worth it! Oh, I could murder, I could kill them all! It's immoral, it's obscene. And I'm so helpless."

"Don't, Claire. Don't take it so hard."

"But, Dad, you earned it! You earned it."

I did, he thought. By God, it hurts. Like a knife, it hurts. Punishment, because I did what I know, *and they know* was decent. Yet it doesn't seem as much of a punishment as I would have said an hour or two ago it would be.

And he reflected, "Do you know, I'm not as crushed as you'd expect?"

"That'll come later."

"I don't think so."

"Why? All your life, as long as I've known you, I've heard about the neurological institute."

"So it's come to pass, hasn't it? It'll flourish and I'll work in it, without the status and the name, that's all."

"That's all? Well, I'm crushed, if you're not! Why don't you get out and fight? Why doesn't Mr. Moser get out and fight for you?"

"It wouldn't do any good. He did fight. And one has to learn how to lose with a little dignity."

"That's Eastern fatalism. Resignation. That's why they never accomplish anything in those countries. They're resigned to misery and loss."

"I shan't be miserable, my dear. Anyway, I didn't speak of resignation. I spoke of acceptance, and there is a difference."

"Yes? What?"

"You accept what you can't change. A good thing to learn, Claire."

"You mean *I* need to learn it?"

He thought—or perhaps he only imagined?—a certain bitterness. And he answered gently.

"I only mean, it's a good philosophy. Use it as you see fit."

Claire rested her head against the stone. With eyes closed, her face was classic. It was eloquent. How blessed he was for having this daughter! He mustn't let himself be too proud of her, or too careful of her if he could help it. For there was nothing that couldn't be taken away. He should have learned that by now. He thought then, Maybe, after all, I'll have more time now. Forgo the glory, but forgo the endless committees and the dreary wasteful paperwork, too. More time to teach—to teach Claire. More time for the quiet lab, the way it was all those years ago in London, down in the basement with old Llewellyn.

And he stood wistfully looking out at the trees, dripping slowly now that the rain had stopped, and at the sequined lights along the shore.

Claire murmured, "You know who's going to be furious about this? Mother."

"You think so?"

"Yes. You know she always says you were born great. Annointed, you'd think, the way she talks."

"She still talks about me?"

"Not about you the man, but about you the doctor."

"How is she?" Martin asked. "I don't inquire often enough."

"She's fine. Making money hand over fist. Busy all day and half the night."

From somewhere in the room beyond came a bright gust of laughter. Curious, Martin thought, but I'm never part of the laughter. I'm on the outside rim of the circle looking in, and always have been.

"What are you going to do?" Claire asked, just as Moser had.

What did they think he was going to do? "Go home, for one thing," he answered.

"All right then, let's get out of here."

"Shouldn't we go in and say good night and thank you?"

"Ah, the hell with them," Claire said. "In that crowd we won't even be missed." She took his hand, and they went together across the grass.

BOOK SIX

TIME AND TIDE

·{32}·

All that winter Jessie had been admonishing, "You're overworked. You don't even rest on your days off, what with running around on errands for those children of your father's."

Quite truly, Claire, like every other intern, was overworked. It was not uncommon to go twenty-four hours without sleep and, when sleep came, it was like being drugged. Once she had been so exhausted, she'd started to laugh at nothing and hadn't been able to stop. Yet all that was to be expected. No one ever complained with any seriousness.

But as for the children, well, Jessie was simply jealous of them! Ever since Hazel's death, Claire had felt poignantly their need for patient hours of childish things: museums and walks and ice-cream treats. A life of Martin's kind was inevitably paid for by the family. He tried to care for his children but it was very hard: he had so little time and, never having been with them all that much, his beginning attempt was bound to be awkward.

Now, too, since her own—loss, should one call it euphemistically?—she had felt more sharply not only the children's needs, but also some new need within herself. The wholesomeness of children, still so removed from the ugly agonies of adulthood, gave basic comfort. It was like warm food, like milk and bread after sore sickness.

All this crossed her mind one free morning while she stood in the operating room watching Martin at work. He had suggested that she ought to witness as much neurosurgery as possible, so as to get a head start on next year. So she stood now among a group of residents, interns and even some fourth-year students who liked to wander into the operating rooms where big names were at work. Her eyes went from one face to the other: all wore the absorbed expression of total interest and respect. Her eyes went to Leonard Max and rested kindly on him. He had been so devastated by Martin's defeat that he had sworn he would refuse to work under the new man from California. Fortunately, for the sake of Max's fairly young career, Martin had been able to dissuade him from such beautiful, impractical, fierce loyalty.

And Claire felt a thrill of pride: strip a man of title—as they had—but it made no alteration in his true value, and even the enemies, those who had stripped him, knew it and had to acknowledge it.

Now she watched the small vertical line between Martin's brows as he worked with the loupe. With utmost delicacy, with excruciating concentration, he labored among the most minute nerves of a leg that had been mangled in an accident. The process was exhausting to watch. She could barely imagine what it would be like to do it. Not until the procedure was finished was she aware how her hands had been clenched, how painfully the muscles of her neck had tensed.

She waited in the corridor for Martin. The nurse at the charge desk looked up with a pleasant remark.

"Pretty soon we'll be seeing you up here every day."

"Next year."

"What a privilege to learn from your father! Nobody needs to tell you that, I'm sure. I've known him since I was capped. Downtown at Fairview it was, that's where I started and he was an intern. Yes," she reflected, "he used to come up and watch Dr. Albeniz, just the way young people come to watch him now. He was one of the greats, Albeniz was." And taking her sheaf of charts, she went down the corridor.

A privilege, Claire thought. Not a day passed without someone, some nurse or intern or clerk in the clinic or even her mother, reminding her of the privilege. She had begun to be tired of hearing it.

THEY SAT AT lunch in the doctors' dining room. The paper napkin, on which for her benefit and instruction Martin had diagramed the morning's procedure, lay alongside Claire's plate.

"Well," he said, "enough of that for today. Got any plans for the weekend?"

"Thought maybe I'd join you and the kids and go skating on Sunday afternoon."

"Sure, fine. But I meant—social life is what I meant." His smile was anxious.

"Oh, I'm going out Saturday night. Maybe Friday, too, if I still feel like it when the time comes." She knew he wanted to ask, but wouldn't ask, with whom she was going and how she liked him, and was she doing anything foolish again?—he hoped not! He wanted, of course—parents always wanted—to be told that their child was safe, was happy. And feeling sudden compassion for his anxiety, she added gently, "Don't worry about me, Dad. I'm really, really fine."

She was rewarded by the relaxing and brightening of his face. "That's all I ever want to hear," he said.

"And I'm not doing anything foolish."

"I know you're not."

Actually, the opportunity for doing anything "foolish" had scarcely presented itself, certainly not as frequently as Martin might be thinking. There had been relationships since Ned, of course there had been. One didn't live in a convent! Yet there was no life in any of them. She had relapsed into the years before Ned, to that era of intelligent, agreeable men, most of them inevitably doctors, who didn't *reach* her. The current companion, Patrick Moore, had considerable charm with his Irish sparkle and cheer, but even he was petering out and they both knew it. She supposed she was waiting again for the feeling she had first had on that hill in Devon.

Martin shoved his chair back. "Well, I'm off."

"Back to the office?"

"No, it's Tuesday. The neuropathology conference."

"Oh, of course, I have the GYN clinic." Finishing her coffee, she watched him go down the room, saw nods and a few greetings exchanged on his way. Perry Gault, among others, did not look up as Martin passed. That anger would remain, no doubt of it. And she wondered how deep, actually, the wound must lie in Martin, how deep the multiple wounds, the whole affair of the institute. It was plain that he gave himself now completely to teaching and to his own long solitary hours in the laboratory. These things that he loved he would talk about with eagerness. About the wounds he would not speak, and one had to respect his privacy.

The clinic and emergency rooms were already filled. In the corridors waited babies, the sick, the old and the healthy who had brought them here. A small Puerto Rican stood up and smiled.

"Hello, Mr. Filipe," Claire said.

"This time I brought my daughter Angela, Doctor."

"Good. I'll tell Dr. Milano. She'll see her in a few minutes."

Dr. Milano was a handsome woman in her forties, who seemed able to manage with great calm a large practice as well as a household of two teen-agers and a husband. From her Claire was gradually absorbing a manner and feel for the ill.

"Mr. Filipe's outside. He's brought his daughter, can you believe it?" Claire said as she went in.

Dr. Milano smiled. "I can believe it. It's happened before."

Mr. Filipe had made a memorable scene only a few months ago when his wife had died. She had been a patient of Dr. Milano's. The man's grief had been one thing, but his fury at Dr. Milano had been another, a fury based on the fact that women had no business practicing medicine and that if Dr. Milano hadn't been a woman, Mr. Filipe's wife wouldn't have died. A woman should stay home and raise kids. Everybody knew that. A doctor should be a man.

It had taken a good deal of effort and some hours before he had been quieted. But something, time or goodness knew what, had done an effective job, because here he was actually back again, bringing his teen-age daughter for treatment.

"You're the one who won him over. You know that, don't you, Claire?" Dr. Milano said.

"Oh really," Claire began.

"Yes, yes you did. You have a way with people that's very warm, my dear. Well, let's begin, shall we? I have to quit at three. I'm going up to do an abortion. Want to see it?"

Oh no, Claire thought. Oh no! "I don't think so. I've never seen one," she said.

"Well, then, it's time you did. All right, start calling them in." '

So they came filing in, the old known faces and the new ones who would in all probability become familiar too. Most of these women's troubles were not of the kind that could be solved overnight. One came to know them and their pains quite intimately before one was through.

There was the diabetic girl whom they had warned against becoming pregnant. But her husband wanted children, so she had gone ahead anyway, only to produce a monster who, luckily for itself and its parents, had been born dead.

Now came an unmarried, pregnant addict, accompanied by one of her four children; this was a twelve-year-old boy, also plainly addicted. Outside the door he waited for his mother, as if afraid to let her out of his sight. He had sly, sliding monkey's eyes. Like a monkey's, too, were the dark sadness and the wordless questioning.

And there was the girl who had been impregnated by her brother.

And there was the girl whose infant was born with sore eyes from gonococcus.

Was there no end to the ignorance, the helplessness, the need? Poor women, Claire thought. Poor women!

All these foreigners, she thought, too. Sometimes it almost seems as if I'm not in America at all. The fact is, I really resented them at first. The language difficulty makes such a tiring struggle. And they're so confused, so scared. And they mostly smell of garlic. But I should be ashamed! After all, they came here driven by the same needs that brought my grandfather out of his poor village. Oh, it's a disgrace the way some people treat them! Clerks, lower middle class themselves, feeling superior because these people can't speak English and have nothing, not even pride anymore, what they had of it having been knocked out of them. I spoke sharply to a clerk who was being nasty to some poor woman yesterday. Now she'll have it in for me if she ever gets a chance. If I dared, and of course I don't dare, I would say something to Dr. Norris, too, one of the few obstetrical residents who have no compassion for these women. He's so arrogant, you'd think he was a vet handling a cow!

In a curtained cubicle, Dr. Milano was examining a woman. On a straight chair near the desk where Claire was filling out a form, sat the woman's friend, who had come with her. They both looked up at the sound of soft weeping.

"Then she must be pregnant," the woman said. "That's why she's crying."

Claire could have predicted the comments that followed.

"She's my sister-in-law. Her husband's a devil. They have five kids already, and he don't make enough to buy their shoes. Sometimes I help out, even though I can't afford it, but the kids have to have shoes, don't they? And she's all nerves, Doctor. She's forty-two, and the boys are wild sometimes. I keep the two big ones at my house for a couple of days. She can't manage, she gets so nervous, she cries. Doctor," the woman pleaded, unconsciously clasping her hands, "she can't have another baby! It will kill her or she will go crazy, either one."

Victims. Victims. Women and their children.

"I understand," Claire said. "Someday it will be possible to take care of things like this."

"But now what?"

Claire shook her head gently. "Not now." Except for the rich, and even they take a chance. And she thought, looking at the clock, at three I have to go upstairs and watch. God, I don't want to. But I have to.

*   *   *

THE WOMAN IS covered with a sheet that has a hole where it lies on her abdomen. Why is she here? What ailment, pretended or true, permits the doing of this thing today?

Dr. Milano has been overly rushed and that is Claire's excuse for not asking her to explain. The truth is, Claire doesn't want to ask.

She is required to look. The area where the doctor is to work has been rendered antiseptic and has been anaesthetized. The doctor takes a needle. Claire has read what is to come, yet she trembles. The doctors plunges the needle into the abdomen, into the uterus where the baby lies growing in the warmth, in the dark. His head is bent; he rests so comfortably. Each day, each hour he expands into a complexity of fingernails, eyelashes, delicate, convoluted shells of ears . . . The doctor takes a syringe and injects the stuff which will, a few hours from now, contract the womb and force him out of his warm home to die.

Claire's fist is clenched on her mouth. My baby, too, she thinks.

Dr. Milano looks up. Her eyes tell Claire she understands her questions. How can a woman, herself a mother, do this thing? Or how, when she has seen so many of the hungry, unwanted and abused, can she not do it?

Oh God, make everything more simple, so that I can know, finally, and for all time, what is right.

THE SMELL OF snow was in the air when she reached Madison Avenue. She began to walk a fast mile toward her mother's house. They drifted into the habit of a weekly dinner together, on any day convenient for Claire. The sky was smudged in somber gray, but at street level was spread the glitter of approaching holiday: Santa Claus and wreaths, gilded angels, velvet robes and brocade evening bags. Wafts of perfumed air came through revolving doors along with segments of canned carols: "It Came Upon a Midnight Clear."

With heads bent against the looming wind, people brushed into each other. Some were too tired and hurried to look up and apologize. Others, having just come from office parties, were too crocked to look up or care about any tidings of comfort and joy.

Claire had visions, sentimental visions, of people caroling around fireplaces or on doorsteps, in places where people all knew one another. In such places the carols would really mean something. This world was so hurried, so enormous and indifferent, that one could almost feel afraid in it. "Lonely world," she said aloud, and was surprised at the sound of the words and the feel of her own warm breath caught in her coat collar. "Lonely world." (That baby will never see it, lonely or not.)

And passing a flower shop, she stopped impulsively to buy a dozen dark-red roses. Mother had a greedy need for flowers and she, Claire, had sudden need to make a tender gesture. Waiting there while the roses were being wrapped in green tissue, she felt this tenderness at the vision of herself mounting the steps of her mother's house with a gift in hand.

And then, above the exuberance of trailing fernery and roses—color of blood, color of life—among all that moist, triumphant burgeoning, she unexpectedly caught sight of her own mirrored face. For an instant, she did not recognize it. So white! So old! But that was absurd. She was only twenty-eight.

Outside again in the cold, the lonely mood came flooding back. She had been sleeping poorly, waking in the middle of the night with oppressive thoughts. Tonight, surely, she would wake up to think of a baby. But whose? That woman's today or her own?

There are no answers to most things, Claire. You're gradually learning that, aren't you? Answers, that is, which are always right or always wrong.

How strange to think that she and Jessie, both at work in the same city, only a mile or two apart, could exist in such different worlds! Jessie's ladies concerned themselves with silks and marble. But those poor women who came to the hospital, the ones who scrubbed the city's floors while others slept, what of them? How did they bear the injustice of their lives? (Yet who is to keep the floors clean? Answer that!)

You belong with Dr. Milano's women, Claire, not with the silk-and-marble ladies, decent and good though many of them may be. You were made to belong with those others.

In Jessie's house the lights were lit. Grateful light, grateful warmth, she thought as she went in. Above the hall table where she laid her hat and gloves hung a portrait of somebody's eighteenth-century ancestress, not Jessie's, although it had hung there so long that possibly Jessie had by now convinced herself that she was. The woman had a handsome, critical face in which there was no sympathy for Claire's modern malaise.

"Well," Jessie said, holding out her cheek to be kissed, "how are you? You look worn out again."

"I am, a little. You're not, I see."

"I don't allow it. Nobody thanks you for it. Sherry?"

"Yes, please."

"What are you looking at? The jewelry? It's new, if that's what you're wondering."

"It's magnificent."

Jessie's taste in jewels was exotic and conspicuous. Tonight she wore jade in ornate gold filigree. The chain glowed on her dark dress, and the earrings swung halfway to her shoulders.

"I know I attract attention. I will anyway, so I might as well make a bold job of it." With a twist and jab, Jessie snuffed out a cigarette. "By my possessions, I can show I have accomplished something. Vulgar, I suppose," she said, regarding Claire's blouse and skirt and ringless hands.

"No, I understand it," Claire answered quietly.

Twirling the sherry glass slowly between her hands, she stared into the fire. When you have been reclusive all through girlhood, tolerated, pitied and excluded, you were entitled to enjoy your release, especially when you had achieved that release by your own strength and efforts. She could imagine the sort of perverse thrill that must come to Jessie when a new client, one who had not been forewarned, crossed the carpet to face her at her desk. She could even imagine her mother's silent amusement: Yes, this little person is the Jessie Meig you've heard about. Yet in spite of this bravado, Jessie never went out on social occasions unless a client was along. It was true that she was too busy to build a social circle of her own, but actually she wanted the company of important clients because at parties they gave her the shelter of their physical presence and prestige.

"You saw the article in the magazine section last week?" Jessie inquired now.

"Yes. I was going to mention it. Only there've been so many, that I'm quite used to seeing your name."

"I had so much publicity on the Arizona place that they've asked me to do a small Bermuda inn for the same people. I shall enjoy that. I'll get away from the tropical, I think, and do it in pure eighteenth-century English with a lot of color." She mused. "I'm seeing it in my mind's eye already."

"It's getting so I should think one almost needs an introduction from a friend to persuade you to do a house."

"Not quite, but almost," Jessie smiled. "Let's go in to dinner. Tell me what you did today."

"Very different things from what you did. I watched an abortion."

Jessie raised an eyebrow.

"Sometimes I feel so sorry for women! Their poor bodies, all their conflicts! I saw a young woman who had a botched abortion. She'll never have a baby, short of a miracle, that is."

Jessie was silent.

"I don't believe much in miracles," Claire said somberly. Suddenly the food was hard to swallow and she put the fork down.

"You're not hungry."

"I was when I came in, but now I'm not."

"Ah Claire, Claire, you have more in your heart than you'll admit!"

Claire felt the threat of tears. Lowering her eyes from her mother's gaze, she stared at the flowers on the center of the table: anemones, each as rare and languid as an Edwardian beauty. Their pale stems curved in the water, which trembled slightly in the shallow bowl. The stem was the beauty's neck, and the spreading petals were her head, top-heavy with piled, glossy hair.

"Ned would have loved a child," she said softly. "How he would love a proudly pregnant little woman waiting at home for him every evening after his exciting day!"

"Most men would, you know."

"I know most men would. There's nothing wrong with it . . . So, he'll find somebody, if he hasn't already, who'll be glad to give it to him, I'm sure."

"I hope you're not too bitter, Claire?"

"You've been bitter often enough, haven't you?"

"Yes, but that doesn't mean I want to see bitterness in you. Anyway, mine was different, it couldn't have been helped. The circumstances, I mean."

"And mine could. I made my own. You don't have to tell me."

"I won't tell you anything. It wouldn't do any good anyway. But I will say, come stretch out on the sofa. Take the pillows away and stretch out."

The fire had settled down and purred softly now, like a cat. "Smells good, doesn't it?" Jessie remarked. "Cedar logs."

"I was rummaging today," Claire began, after a minute, "and found my Brearley yearbook. God, how fresh-faced and hopeful everybody looked! With all the sentimental sayings under the pictures. And when you think of what's actually happened—"

"What has?"

"Well, Lynn's a model, living in Beverly Hills with a squat, rich old man. June's already had two divorces. Paula broke her neck diving into a pool that had no water in it."

Jessie shuddered. "Do tell me something cheerful, will you? You're not yourself at all tonight."

"You don't think so?"

"As a matter of fact, though, maybe you are yourself. The self you've been for quite a while now. I don't know exactly when you became what you are, but I suspect when."

Claire didn't answer. Her head ached with the held-back tears, with weariness and the weight of things. The room was weighty, heavy with the accretions of a way of life that was going, she suspected, if not gone. Jessie's independence was no first choice, but had been forced to birth out of courage and desperate need. Jessie would have rejoiced to be cherished and guarded by a man.

"I want to go away," she said suddenly. "To India or Brazil, some place. Any place."

"What? Why? You don't want to train with your father?"

She began to cry. "No! But I don't dare let him see it."

"I don't understand! Such a fabulous opportunity, Claire!"

"Yes, only I don't want it."

"Good Lord, whyever not?"

" 'We are such stuff as dreams are made on.' Our parents' dreams for us."

"Never mind the quotation. Tell me why you don't want it."

"Because I hate it. It's awful. The whole atmosphere is awful." Claire shuddered. "The shaved heads and the people who can't talk afterward. All the physical therapy and phony—no, not phony—the contrived cheer because somebody can take one step. And you know he'll go home and maybe take six steps after a while. To say nothing of the ones who die under surgery. It's just too depressing, and I can't see myself spending my life with it."

"Well!" Jessie cried, throwing up her hand. "I just don't know at all! When did you start to feel this way?"

"I don't remember. It just grew. I don't think I ever really *thought* about it at all until I began to get into it, don't you see? And found out what it was like?"

"You wanted to please your father. You always have," Jessie said, accusingly.

"No, I don't think I even thought that much! Not consciously. It just seemed to be the thing I was naturally going to do. After all, if one is a doctor and one's father happens to be Martin Farrell, one is sort of expected to—I mean, you expect yourself to—it's not as if he were any ordinary man, just anybody—" And to her own dismay, Claire began to sob. Everything just surged up and burst. "I hate Dad's work! I'd be no good at it! Everybody says, 'Oh, you're so unbelievably lucky!' And I know I am. I'm so proud of Dad and so guilty, and— I know you're shocked."

"Claire, I'm not shocked. Surprised, but not shocked."

"He's been so wonderful to me. And I've been so depressed because apparently I don't appreciate it enough."

"All the same," Jessie said quietly, "I think you ought to tell him."

"I can't! Oh my God, I can't do that! Don't you see? He's counted on it for years! He's already had so many failures! How can I give him one more?"

"How? You're not obliged to compensate for his disappointments! Or for anyone's."

"You say that because you—"

"I say that because it's the truth and not for any—any personal reason you're thinking of."

"I'm so ashamed!" Claire gasped. "I don't know why I'm crying like this."

"You're entitled to cry! You don't have to be so damned brave! Shall I leave the room? Would you feel better if I did?"

"No, no. Stay."

Presently Jessie laid her hand on Claire's forehead. "Move over. I'll massage your neck. You're all knots. Does that feel good?"

"Yes."

"Tell me what you want to do in India."

"Oh—go somewhere with one of those agencies that sends medical help to people who haven't got any. I don't want too be a medical great. I'm not cut out for it. I'd like to bring primary care, simple care and hope to people, especially to women, because they're the most trod upon. They're at the bottom of the heap. Wherever you go, women are at the bottom of the heap." And to her own horror, she began to cry again. "But there's no use talking about it, I can't do it. I'll stay here and—and petrify."

"You were speaking of Ned a while ago," Jessie said softly.

"What about him?"

"You still think about him."

"He treated me badly. *Badly!*"

"Why don't you just forget him, then?"

"Oh!" Claire cried. "A good question! Why don't I? I don't know . . . I don't sleep. I wake up every night and I'm scared. I don't understand why I'm scared. Maybe of being so alone? But I do understand how it was for Dad when Hazel died . . ."

Jessie's fingers soothed and soothed. "It's not the same, darling. No one's died."

"Our baby died. I made it die."

"That's not the same."

Claire sat up. "What else could I have done? Should I have gone after him?"

"Certainly not," Jessie said stoutly, "not then and not now. One doesn't run after a man!"

They both sat looking into the fire. At last Claire's tears stopped, and the fire flickered out.

"I guess I'll go home," she said.

"No, stay here for the night. Take a sleeping pill and get a good night's rest."

"I never take pills, Mother."

"Well, Doctor, take one tonight. Just one mild pill."

"No pill. But I will stay. That I'll do." It would be good to avoid the apartment tonight, and the bed where she had slept with Ned, and the sight of his Irish woolen hat, which he had left on the shelf.

Like a little girl, she followed Jessie up the stairs and into her old room, where a doll from her tenth year still stood next to a first-year Latin text and a souvenir birchbark canoe, those innocent relics of easy years before real life had begun.

A GREAT SQUARE desk covered with papers, medical periodicals and sundries stood between Jessie and Martin. How many of life's salient encounters take place among three, two people and a desk?

He still looks like a doctor, she thought, and that's odd, because what does a doctor look like? Yet he does.

For the last half hour and for two weeks before that she had been resisting a confusion of emotions: stubbornness and pride, worry and embarrassment and cowardice, along with anger at the circumstances that were forcing her into a supplicant's position. Still, she reminded herself, she was doing this for Claire: for Claire she would take sword against monsters if need be. Happily, Martin was no monster, she thought with a certain grim humor; he was Claire's father and as concerned this minute as she was herself.

"It's cost you a good deal to come here, Jessie, and only serious need could have brought you. I want you to know I understand that."

"Quite so."

Once more the doctor had spoken: comprehending, kindly and firm. Through Jessie's head went scraps of flitting thought: *It seems a century (another age of man) since we walked in Kensington Gardens while Claire in her yellow coat rode the tricycle. It seems yesterday since Cyprus.* A bit of poetry went flitting, something about "time in its flight." *That summer he bought painful new white shoes. The little car jounced over the back-country roads and the doctor's bag lay on the seat between us. Fern wore blue linen and our mother's pearls.*

There was a queer turmoil in her chest. Weakened, she sat up, straightened and spoke decisively. "Claire mustn't know I've been here, or ever know I've told you how she dreads your kind of work. This must come from you as if it were your own idea. That is, if you agree."

"She really hates the work all that much?" Martin repeated with disbelief.

"Apparently so. It's tearing her down." And I'm tearing you down by telling you, but I can't help it.

"When—when did she first know this about herself?"

"How can anyone say exactly 'when' anything happens inside one's head?" Like falling in love or out of it: does anybody know exactly 'when'? Answer that if you can, Martin. "It's tied up somehow with Ned, that I know. Maybe that's when it started. I don't know. At any rate, it's been growing more and more—the conviction that she doesn't want your kind of work. She's absolutely devastated at the thought of a lifetime of it."

"Why hasn't she ever told me? For God's sake, why?"

"She knew it would be a terrible wound."

Martin was looking at his hands, which gripped the edge of the desk. She understood that it was difficult for him to look at her. Her eyes, too, avoided him, as they circled the room. On a shelf near the desk stood the photograph of a woman with a quiet face, a trifle too round, and timid, pretty eyes. Claire's description of Hazel had been remarkably accurate. Yes, Jessie, thought, he's had trouble enough for one lifetime, whether of his own doing or not doesn't matter.

"Such a waste of her skilled mind!" Martin cried abruptly. "She'd be doing the most rudimentary medicine. Does she know that?"

"Of course she knows it. It's what she wants."

"She'll deliver babies, but if there should be complications, she'll fail because of not knowing enough. She'll set a broken bone, but if it's a compound fracture of the shoulder, she'll be unable to cope with it. She'll do a lot of things passably, but nothing expertly."

Jessie replied with patience, "She understands all that."

"I had been counting on her more than I knew. Looking forward to something so special! Father and daughter. She, in a way, beginning where I, in not too many more years, will leave off." He tapped a pencil. With a small shiver of recognition, Jessie remembered the habit. "There's so much new. Every day it comes piling in. One would need five lifetimes to learn it all." His face sank into a tired sadness.

Again she looked away and was silent. A typewriter clacked in the outer office. A fire engine screeched past the windows. The stillness when these sounds ceased was bleak and lonely.

At last Jessie spoke. "I'm remembering something," she said softly, "that you may have forgotten. I'm thinking of you and your father." It was the only personal remark that had passed between them.

And now Martin gave her a long look. "I haven't forgotten . . . What you're reminding me is that every human being must develop in his own way. And that I ought to be the first to see it."

"True, isn't it?"

"Yes. Yes. You always did like to get at the heart of things in a hurry, didn't you? Well, you're right, of course. And I'll tell her. You can depend on it. I'll tell her that I've been thinking it would be better for us both if she were to go her own way. I'll find words to make it convincing."

"I thought you would. Otherwise I wouldn't have come."

"What about that—other affair? She never talks to me about him."

"Nor to me, until that night. It shocked me so! Claire almost never cries, you know she doesn't."

"Everything's bottled up inside."

"That's what worries me! Not that there's anything to be done about him, to be sure."

"He was a fine young man. I tried hard not to like him, but"—Martin threw out his hands—"it didn't work."

"A fine young man? It was an impossible situation! Impossible!"

"I grant that. But then—human situations often are." Martin hesitated. "I suppose there's no way of finding out where he is? That old aunt of yours?" He broke off and Jessie understood he meant that Aunt Milly could write Fern and find out.

"Aunt Milly died last year. Anyway," she said, suddenly indignant, "I wouldn't dream of asking! Claire would never forgive it and I wouldn't blame her. Pride is the last thing a woman wants to lose." Martin would be thinking, no doubt: *Well, you ought to know.* And well I ought, Jessie said to herself. Aloud, she went on, "With a little effort I could hate the fellow for the mess he's made of her life."

Surprisingly, Martin replied, "It was Claire's fault, too."

"You don't mean you would welcome him back, for Heaven's sake?"

"He's not my first choice. But if she wants him?"

"This is all academic, and may I add, I'm glad of it?" She stood up. "But I might as well bring you something pleasant along with all the bad before I leave. You remember a patient named Jeremy from Tucson?"

"Yes. I operated on him a few months ago."

"His sister-in-law is a customer of mine. She's been singing your praises everywhere."

"That's nice to know." The quick smile was youthful, as though praise were an embarrassment.

"She was telling everyone he'd been given up. Something about the tumor being in both lobes and six other doctors said it was impossible, but you said you could do it?"

"Well, yes."

"She said his doctor came from Arizona to watch you. He'd been convinced it couldn't be done."

"Yes."

"So those people all think you're something of a hero."

"Hero? I know my work and I love it, that's about all."

"That's enough, isn't it? Well, call me if there's anything I should know about Claire. Otherwise, of course, I won't expect to hear from you."

"Of course," Martin said courteously.

He came from behind the desk and opened the door. It was like taking leave of one's lawyer or banker, and she was grateful for his calm tact which had so eased the difficult meeting for them both.

She put out her hand. "So, having told you what I came to tell you, I'll be going."

"I'm thankful you came. I had no idea, none at all. But I'll set her free—for India or wherever she wants to go. Without guilt or any looking back."

"India," Jessie murmured, going through the door. "Of all places."

For long minutes Martin sat looking at the wall, the bookshelves and the windows all blurring in the wintry light. He was vaguely aware when the typewriter fell silent and when Jenny Jennings poked her head in at the door to say good night. The sight of him sitting here in a fog of abstraction aroused no concern in her, for his people were used to seeing him puzzle over his problems.

But this problem hurt so much! He turned it over and over in his mind, examining it as though it were an X-ray. Jessie would never have come to him, after all these proud years, unless it were really serious and she were really alarmed. It took a good deal to alarm Jessie, too. Well, he would break the tie, that was all! How could he have known it had become so painful? Never by one word had Claire revealed herself. Poor little soul! May this be the right thing for her! May she never regret it! May I get over my loss with good grace!

Then he thought of that other pain of hers, the man-woman thing. What it could do to a human soul! So she wanted him still, that boy! There was no sense in it, when the world was full of young men who would gladly have her. Claire, with all that life in her, that bright life! And her eyes, with their grave gaze, and their soft lashes, flashed through his memory. No sense in it at all!

She wanted Ned Lamb. He could see them still: handsome couple! They had looked as though they belonged together. There had been something between them which, although one might not wish to admit it, one recognized. Little Claire, so proud, so foolish! And remembering how close she had come to dying, he trembled. Her longing—if it was anything like what he had suffered over that boy's mother—was dreadful. He tried to remember how it had felt and could only recall that he had felt it, been sick with it, almost overcome by it and that every day had been a struggle against it. And remembering, he actually began to feel it again. A soft ache, creeping, settled like a lump in his throat . . .

It had grown quite dark. Suddenly he sat upright and turned on the desk lamp. He looked in his telephone book for a number, and dialed it.

"I want to leave a message for Mr. Fordyce," he said. "He always books my trips. Can he get me a flight to London toward the end of the week? Yes, Thursday or Friday would be fine."

❈❴33❵❈

From the hotel window Martin looked out on a dull sky, out of which beat a steady rain. An English winter: he had forgotten. He had ordered breakfast in his room. The rented car would be delivered shortly so he could make an early start. The route was clear in his mind. That he had not forgotten.

Night had just faded away. A car with headlights on moved slowly in the street below, the light picking out the remains of a discarded Christmas tree that had been tossed in the gutter. It was a mournful sight so late in the winter, those broken branches with tinsel scraps still clinging. A cat came prowling, foraging for food perhaps, and finding nothing, set up a bitter wail. Hunger? Or hunger of another kind, a tomcat crying for a female shut up somewhere in a house?

Thoughtfully he drank his coffee, still not sure he ought to be where he was. On the plane above the Atlantic, he'd had his moments of thinking he'd made a mistake, that he would just turn right around at the airport and take the next plane back. He'd had moments at home, too, in which he'd tried to extricate himself from his own undertaking. Calling the New York office of Ned's firm to ask whether he was still in Hong Kong, all he'd found out was that Ned wasn't even with them anymore. Only the remembrance of Jessie had spurred him to persevere. Sheer guts it had taken for her to have come to him! But she had done it for their daughter, and he could do no less than try, at least, to straighten things out for Claire, if it was not too late, and if he could.

And thinking with some pity of his daughter, he recalled something Mr. Meredith had said on the day she was born, something about the Achilles heel: "Whatever happens to that child will happen to you," he'd said. Yes, yes. If Jessie were correct in her report, and there was no reason to think she wasn't, how Claire must suffer! Fantasies of reunion: imagining what you would say if you should meet by chance; imagining yourself walking haughtily away, wanting to hurt, leaving him or her staring helplessly after you. Or imagining outstretched arms and healing tears.

Fantasies! Had he not had more than a few himself? He had meant to do right; yet had he not wronged all the women he had known? He should never have gone back to Mary during the war. In his heart he must have known what was bound to happen. He had only made it hard for her to find someone else. His fault.

He looked at his watch. Too early. Now that he had made up his mind, time was going too slowly. And he sat on, brooding and mulling over, denying and reconsidering, a thing he had never dared to examine in the light of day. It began to take shape. It grew so rapidly that he knew instinctively it must have been lying there, stifled inside him, for longer than he could know.

They called from the desk to say that the car had been delivered. He went downstairs and took the wheel. A sudden enormous excitement possessed him, an astounding surge of energy. The tension made him hot and he lowered the window, not minding the rain.

The last he had heard, she was still living at Lamb House alone. What if, as long as he was going there to speak for Claire, what if he were to speak for himself as well? Why not? Was it absolute madness? Why not?

The rain ceased. Fog lay in shreds and tatters, snagged on the lower branches of the trees. A pure light touched the tops of the worn old hills. The wind rushed in his ears like ringing silence. He was almost there. And he had a curious sensation, an expectation of reward as at the theater in the moment before the curtain rises.

The maid said, "There's only Mr. Ned at home. He's in the studio. Shall I fetch him?"

"Thanks. I know where it is."

For a moment Martin stood in the doorway, watching Ned who, in shirt-sleeves and work clothes, was removing a painting from a crate. At the sight of this stranger, who could possess such power over his daughter as to bring her father here to beg for her, strong feelings of resentment, shame and grief churned up in Martin. With them was mixed the memory of Claire lying ill and drained, of Claire so hurt, so still. Strange! It was only after Jessie had pointed it out to him that he remarked how the stillness had lasted. She had always been so vigorous; why, then, had he not noticed the change? And all these feelings were so strong in Martin now that they pounded in his head; he felt almost ill with the pressure of them as he stood there.

Ned saw him. Astonishment spread over his face. He didn't, or more likely couldn't, speak.

"No," Martin said, "you're not imagining things. I'm sorry to have startled you."

"Well—well I—"

"I've come looking for you. I didn't expect to find you so easily. I rather thought you'd be in Singapore or somewhere."

"No, I've been home awhile."

They stared at each other. In their looks were anxiety and wariness, puzzlement, embarrassment and a certain hostility.

"Come in. Sit down."

Martin took an uncomfortable straight-backed chair. Ned sat on a packing case. It seemed to Martin that he looked tired and older than one ought to look at his age.

He began resolutely. "I'll come to the point. I want to talk about Claire."

Ned's expression was unreadable.

"It's not, as you suppose, the easiest thing I've ever had to do. But first I have to ask you something: Is there another woman in your life? If there is, I'll go about my business and you can forget you saw me."

"There's no one."

"Then that's one hurdle past. The next is: No matter what, if anything, should come of this conversation, I want your word that my daughter will never know I've been here. She's proud; I don't have to tell you that. Perhaps too proud, though I'm sometimes not quite sure what that means. Anyway, I want your word."

"You have it."

"Because if she were ever to find out, I'd have your head."

"I said you have my word." Ned waited.

"Now the hard part. The fact is, she's still in love with you. She's miserable. She's never told me, but her mother knows. She's made herself miserable ever since—" And idiotically, he felt tears skimming over his eyes. He swallowed. "Ever since she lost the baby."

"The baby!"

"Yes. You left her pregnant."

"Oh my God!" Ned cried. "A baby! But when? It died?"

"Yes," Martin said. "Or, I mean— Oh damn the language! It didn't die, she had an abortion and *she* nearly died of it. There's the whole thing in one sentence." And taking out a handkerchief, he wiped his eyes unashamedly.

Ned let out a long sigh. "I would have come back. She knew where I was. I would have come back."

"Yes. Yes. Well, it would take a Solomon to figure out what went on in your two heads. Nowadays they call it a breakdown in communication or some such stuff."

Ned put his head in his hands. The room was very still while he sat there, not looking up.

"I wish I knew what happened," he said at last. "I've asked myself and asked. I wanted to go to her, but she sent me away. Somehow I couldn't get over that."

Martin felt a flare of anger. "You could have written."

"Yes, it was small-minded. We hurt each other so." Now he looked up at Martin. "I thought about her . . . I'd take a girl out, and driving away, I'd see Claire's face. It's been like that ever since. I'd get to thinking perhaps it would always be like that, and I'd always see her face. You know how it is?"

Martin said steadily, "I know how it is."

Ned flushed. "Where is she? What is she doing?" he asked.

"She wants to go to India or Brazil or some far place like that. Probably India."

"Not going to work with you?"

"No. She has very different ideas which I wasn't aware of. Another failure of communication. Life seems to be full of them. I don't understand why they happen. Is it pride or stubbornness, or both?"

"Claire and I, we're both proud and stubborn. Both of us, I mean."

Somehow, the rueful half-smile was appealing, Martin thought. And Ned added, "Machismo. Do you suppose I overdid it?"

"Ah well, she's a feminist! Was one before she was old enough to know what the word meant. Still, you asked an awful lot of her, you know. And times are changing. You can't treat a woman like a child anymore."

Martin thought again: What am I doing here, pleading for this reunion which will only complicate my life, unless—unless what I thought of this morning were possible? And the thought came leaping back. Mary and I. How improbably tidy! How neat, how perfect! And yet, why not? Why not?

Into his thoughts, swirling like flares in a dark place, came Ned's plaintive question. "What can we do now, do you think?"

"That's rather up to you, isn't it?"

"India," Ned repeated.

"Yes. She wants experience working with the poor, women in particular. Women and children." He added sharply. "I think you ought to know, she may not ever have a child."

"I understand."

"You'd have some mending of her spirit to do if she can't, I should suppose."

"I understand."

"This India business—you might well guess it's not my idea for her. But then that's hardly relevant, is it?" And Martin hoped he didn't betray the remnant of his bitterness. "How could you manage that if—if you should straighten things out with her? She determined to go, you know."

"Oh, I'm a free agent now. I quit the work in Hong Kong. I was miserable there, thinking of her—" Ned cleared his throat and stopped.

Martin thought: *I have really hit him where it hurts,* and was keenly sorry.

"I found that I didn't really *like* advertising anyhow. It seemed suddenly much ado about very little, persuading people to buy things they often don't need and can't afford."

"Rather a sudden revelation, wasn't it?"

"Not really so sudden, when I piece it all together. I'd always wanted to write. To write truly, I mean, without tricks. To use words honestly and well. Claire knew. She never told you?"

"She mentioned something. But then you were so enthusiastic about the job—"

"Yes, well you see, doing the kind of journalism I had in mind, reporting on things I cared about and felt people ought to know about—conditions in slum schools or saving the whales or revolt in Iraq or whatever—you don't just break into that whenever you feel like it. So I'd got a bit discouraged and then side-tracked into advertising, making a lot of money—a lot for me, at any rate—getting this great promotion, very flattering to the ego—" Ned threw up his hands.

I like this man, I really do, Martin thought. He said aloud, "A man's ego. That always figures."

"Perhaps it figured too much with me." Ned looked away. "Claire told me at the end—we were wounded and angry with one another—she said I was trying to compensate, to be the man my father wasn't. Yet I had always, or so I'd thought, been very proud of my father, while overlooking that other business. So

I couldn't forgive her for saying that." Now he looked directly at Martin. "But perhaps she was right. Perhaps I did want to feel big and powerful and manly, climbing up in the corporate world, running around to important meetings with my briefcase."

Martin asked gently, "So you've quit that world?"

"Yes, I've taken a chance and it seems to be working out. I go abroad on contract and report on things for newspapers and magazines. I've an article on changes in Spain coming out in the States next month."

"Congratulations, then!"

"Thank you." Ned added abruptly, "I don't need a great deal of money to live. I never did, even when I was earning it."

"Come to think of it, Claire doesn't either. She buys a pair of shoes when the old ones have worn out." Martin smiled, remembering worn shoes and missing buttons.

"I could go wherever she went." Ned spoke thoughtfully. "We could work our schedules on an equal basis."

"You're really ready to accept that 'equal basis' business? I'm not sure I could. But then, I keep forgetting, you're a new generation."

"Yes, sir, I have to remind myself of that sometimes, too, and I'm not all that old."

No, you're not. You're very young. You've a long way to go. Pray it will be easier for you than it has been for me, Martin thought, with surprising tenderness. Then he thought of something else.

"I don't even know whether she'd have you after all that's happened. Her mother says she would, even though her mother's not enthusiastic about it herself! On the strength of that, I came here. A wild-goose chase, perhaps, but I must warn you."

"I'll chance it. I'll go and find out . . . But I haven't asked you about yourself, sir. I suppose the institute is open by now and running under your hands?"

"It's open and running well," Martin said, adding unemotionally, "but not under my hands."

Ned's eyebrows went up.

"That's another story. Now's not the time to go into it." And wanting to turn away from the subject, he looked around. "These pictures, they're all—"

"All Mother's. They've been sent back from an exhibit. We're rehanging them."

Martin got up and walked around the room. Claire had said something once, quite briefly, about Mary's achievement, but he had not imagined anything like this. An embarrassment of riches, he thought, given as he was to remembering phrases. Beautiful, beautiful! Grace and love shone in these trees and human figures, these faces, this fruit and running water, that ragged child, this tired old woman, those clouds like flowers in the sky. And he remembered all those years ago when she had told him with such young wistfulness, "I don't know yet who I am."

Ned touched his arm. "This I would call a masterpiece. Do you agree? It's called *Music of the Sphere*."

On a tall vertical canvas, she had drawn the earth as one might behold it from another planet. Glowing, golden-green and silver-blue, it hung or seemed, rather, to be spinning in a gentle rhythm through vast darkness. A jewel it was, a living heart, sending a radiance into the frozen universe. Around it an aureole of tender light was shot with sparkle of tropical rain and of petals that might have been musical notes or musical notes that might have been petals. A work of most sumptuous and subtle imagery, it could only have been conceived by someone who was in love with the world.

Profoundly moved, Martin could find just commonplace words. "Magnificent. Magnificent."

"The critics thought so. People have been calling to buy it. But this is one she won't sell, which, of course, I can understand."

Martin's heart hammered. He looked straight into Ned's eyes. "How is she?" he asked.

"Happy in her work, as you can see. Happier all around than she's been in a long time, I should guess."

"I wouldn't want to shock her by walking in without warning." And yet if she were to walk in suddenly upon him, it would be a shock to rejoice the soul, he thought with a small rise of joyous laughter. "Claire's told me that you knew, of course, about Mary and me. Not that we've talked much about it. We're all too reticent, I sometimes think. But—well, I thought, coming here, that maybe after all this time, she and I—" Something in Ned's expression stopped him.

"I'm not sure I understand your meaning, but if it's—"

"I think you do understand," Martin said.

"Oh, then . . . Oh then, I'm sorry! You didn't know . . . Mother's been married almost a year."

"Married!"

"Yes. Simon and she have known each other a long, long time. He owns a gallery; he's done wonders for her in every way. I'm very fond of him."

Married! It crossed Martin's mind that he must look ghastly, for with extreme kindness, Ned added, "Things can be a muddle sometimes, can't they, sir?"

"Muddle?" Chaos and storm, more likely!

Devious and strange is the heart of man. Certainly his own was. And feeling dreadfully weak, Martin sat down again on an upended packing case, thinking of that bright thread that had been woven through all the twisted, turning patterns on the loom of his life.

Married.

She, she, from the first day, with the eyes and the dreams and the dark, lovely face—

"Fey," Jessie said. "Fern is fey."

Married.

"I thought you would have heard through that old aunt, Milly."

"No, Milly's dead."

"I'm sorry." Ned looked considerately away.

Sorry about the old woman's death? Or about— Martin pulled himself together. "I'll have to be going. I've done what I came to do. The rest is up to you."

"Can I give you a lift to the station?"

"Thanks. I have a car."

He was going out when the door opened and a man entered. He was a tall man, of middle age, wearing country clothes and a pleasant outdoor face.

"Simon," Ned made the introduction, "we've a visitor from America. This is Dr. Farrell, Claire's father."

Simon shook Martin's hand. "I'm glad to know you. But you're not leaving?"

"I'm afraid so." Martin felt weakness and dizziness again. "I only came for a word or two with Ned. I have to get back."

Ned explained, "Dr. Farrell came about Claire. I may be going to New York next week, Simon. I'm going to see her."

Simon looked from one to the other. "So that's it, is it? Why, I'm delighted, Doctor! I've been suspecting it was Claire all along, if you want to know the truth of it." His pleasure was genuine. "You see, I understand what it is to know what you want and not get it. Have you ever met my wife, Doctor? But of course, you must. How clumsy of me! Her sister. Forgive me, I forgot for the moment."

"Quite all right. It was a long time ago," Martin murmured.

"This is all her work. Perhaps you've heard of her reputation? She's not well known in America yet, but we may show some of her work there sometime."

"Ned's been showing me. It's very, very beautiful."

"Has Ned shown you this? It's her portrait. I had it done by Juan Domingo. He's a Mexican, a very fine artist. He's caught her to perfection, I think." Happiness exuded from the man. He guided Martin to the far end of the room. "Here it is. She must have been a young girl when you saw her last. Would you recognize her from this?"

There she was, full length, next to a table on which stood a bowl of flowers, some large, white flowers, hydrangeas or hyacinths. His eyes swam so he couldn't tell what they were. One hand rested on a pile of books. Her dress was a subtle clash of ruby and flame, but all he really saw were the great, wondering eyes looking out at something far away.

"Would you recognize her?" Simon persisted.

"Yes," Martin said. "I would recognize her."

"I had this done ten years ago, but she hasn't changed much since then."

"You've known her ten years," Martin repeated, for no reason at all.

"Yes. It took me that long to persuade her to marry me. But I'm a persistent man." And Simon laughed with the contentment of a man who can afford to laugh.

Martin looked up and saw the pity in Ned's eyes. "An excellent likeness," he said, it being necessary to say something more. He moved again toward the door. He was an interloper here, a trespasser and a thief who ought to run before he should be discovered.

"Mary will be here soon. She only went out on a few errands," Simon said. "Can't you possibly stay to tea?"

"Thank you. You're very kind, but I have an appointment at my hotel and I really can't."

They shook hands. Martin nodded to Ned: "Perhaps I shall be seeing you in New York." And he went out.

At the top of the rise where the road curved, he stopped the car and looked back. Through bare trees one could see the roof and one wing of Lamb House. There it lay, as it had lain for centuries. To the passerby it was a fine and honest house with nothing extraordinary about it, surely not the shimmer and glamor of the forbidden. Well, he had come for Claire, hadn't he? And he had done his best. What happened next would not be of his making. As for the rest, the other business, he didn't know. He couldn't say. He could hardly feel. He was numb.

MARY CAME INTO the studio where Simon and Ned were still arranging pictures.

"We had a visitor, darling," Simon said. "If you took a hundred guesses, you couldn't guess who."

He looks so happy, Mary thought, it's like coming home to a warm fire just to see his face when I walk in. "Well, then, you might as well tell me."

"It was your former brother-in-law. From America. The doctor. Isn't that strange? I invited him to tea, but he couldn't stay."

"Martin!" And she repeated softly, "Martin was here?" She looked at Ned.

He nodded. "He came to talk about Claire." Ned spoke steadily and she understood that this tone was meant to steady her. "I think, Mother, I'll go back and see her."

Mary sat down. Her mouth trembled. She hoped no one would see it. And she said almost apologetically, "I'm just—stunned. I—seem to be shaking."

"Well, of course!" Simon cried. "Oh, you've worried your mother, Ned. She may not have let us see it, but I've known it all along."

"She oughtn't to worry about me at my age."

Mary said, "Of course I wasn't happy about it at the beginning . . . Jessie and I . . . But, oh I do think Claire's exceptional, and if you can work things out, why . . ." Her voice left her.

"Her mother didn't like me at all."

"Not you yourself, I'm sure," Simon interposed. "Why would anyone not like you? I'm sure it was only because of that miserable feud. How a family can split itself apart over money! I've seen it time and again—it's always a pity. And the longer you let a thing like that continue, the more impossible it is to mend it."

Mary managed to collect herself. "Well, if it's my sister who stands in the way, if that's all, she'll come around, Ned, no matter how she feels about me. She'd do anything for Claire, as I would for you."

"And the father likes you, I could see that," Simon observed. "An awfully nice chap, Mary! He took a great interest in your paintings, too."

Ned spoke lightly. "Well, naturally, anyone who admires your work ranks on top with Simon."

"So you'll be leaving us! It'll be restful here without you," Simon joked back.

"Go to Claire," Mary said, "if she's what you want. Even though being a doctor comes first with her, Ned, go to her. That's what you first admired and why you were drawn to her, after all. Perhaps you've never thought about it like that."

Ned bent down and kissed his mother. "I understand," he said. "Thank you." For a moment they looked into each other's eyes before Mary turned away.

"I'm going up to the house," she said. "That is, if you don't need me here, Simon?"

"No, no. We're almost finished. Go ahead."

She went slowly up the path. Suddenly, not wanting to go inside, she sat down on a bench near the wall where in summer perennials would bloom. The beds were covered now with a mulch of dark wet leaves. She laid her head on the back of the bench.

Suppose he had come last year before I married Simon? What then? Oh, Simon is everything that's steady and good and male. There's such peace and ease now in my heart. But if he had come last year?

So many, many ifs! When we were young and that doctor with the Spanish name invited him to go on for three more years: if I hadn't been willing to wait and he had chosen me instead, would he have come to hate me for it afterward? If. If. And if we had spent our lives together, would I still feel this softness going through me at the thought of him? I wonder. Could there possibly be any joy now between us after so much grief: after Jessie, and then that poor dead woman Ned told me about? Could there?

Always, always, what we could have done or should have done, and what we blame ourselves for having done or not having done. Do we truly have choice? Or is it all written beforehand in the stars or the genes? God knows.

Two small hot tears gathered in the corners of her eyes and she wiped them away with her knuckles. At least she could hope: maybe it will turn out well for Ned. She's an extraordinary girl, that Claire. You have to admit that, even though the union of those two will be a burden for the rest of us. But they must do what's right for them. They'll only know whether it was right long years after they've done it.

And I? Simon and I will stay here, in this house that I love so much. After we're gone, some movie star will probably buy it. But until then, we'll be here. Alex would be glad to know that. Perhaps, where he is, he does know it. I used to think that was nonsense, but now that I'm older, I'm not so sure. I'm not sure of anything anymore.

"I thought you'd gone inside," Simon said.

"I was going to, but it's so warm and lovely here. One can almost imagine it's summer."

He bent and kissed her. "Mary. Mary Fern. Are you pleased about Ned?"

"Whichever way he wants it, if it works out well for him, I will be."

"You're a good mother, the kind of mother everyone should have and the kind of wife. Do I tell you often enough?"

"You do, my dear, yes you do."

"I've been thinking, would you like to go to America?"

"I don't know. I haven't been there since I came here to marry Alex. They say it's so changed."

"What doesn't change, my darling?"

"Highways and tract houses—all built-up, I read. And still, the fall must be the same, and those hot Augusts when the grass burns brown and the locusts drill all afternoon."

"We'll go to California, take some of your work to show and have a bit of vacation at the same time. And stay in New York for a while."

"Not New York," she said quickly. "Let's just pass through it. I never liked New York."

"Whatever you say, as long as we're together." And he sat down on the bench beside her. In the windless afternoon not a twig stirred. A mild sun broke through the clouds, and above iron-gray winter hills, pale fire striped the sky.

❧{34}❧

Ned and Claire were to be married very quietly on a Saturday evening at Jessie's house. Two of Claire's friends from Smith, along with the husband of one of them and a London friend of Ned's who was on business in New York, made the sum of the guests. Because of the smallness of this group and the resultant intimacy of the occasion, there had been tacit agreement that Martin would not be present. Instead, he was to give a little dinner for the bridal couple at his apartment the night before. To this, and for the same reason, Jessie had not been invited.

"It will be much more *comfortable* for everyone that way," she had said sensibly, and Claire had agreed.

"That's just what Dad said, too."

The mantel in the library had been cleared of its ornaments. On the afternoon of the wedding Jessie covered it with a flowery spray of white: stephanotis, roses and carnations, twined together with narrow white silk bows. Claire had insisted on wearing a very simple suit, but Jessie had managed to persuade her that it ought at least to be white and silk and adorned with one of Jessie's own handsome necklaces.

Jessie hummed. She would not have believed, some months ago, that she could actually feel happy at Claire's wedding to this particular young man; but her terrible concern over her daughter had outweighed everything else and the sight of that daughter's face during these last weeks had brought enough joy and ease to cancel out whatever doubts or regrets still lurked.

"The rest," she said now, half aloud, "is in the lap of the gods. So far so good, anyway—" and she fastened the last bow.

The house was quiet. The cook was busy in the kitchen, Claire was out having her hair done and Jessie was placing the flowers on the dining room table when the doorbell rang.

"I'll answer, Nora!" she called.

She opened the door. Her hand was still on the knob and that steadied her in the instant of recognition.

The woman on the doorstep smiled uncertainly. "Jessie, may I come in?" asked Mary Fern.

*　　*　　*

808

Jᴇssɪᴇ ᴡᴀs ᴄᴜʀʟᴇᴅ in the wing chair. She must be lost in a room without a wing chair, Fern thought.

"I didn't come for the wedding," she said. "I didn't even know this was the day. Ned's letter mentioned sometime this month but in the circumstances, naturally, we didn't expect to be asked."

"You have a right to come to your son's wedding if you want to. No one told me you might want to."

Of course. Jessie would be correct in all things. They had, after all, both been brought up to be. But what were the real thoughts in that elegant, small head and behind that cool face? Suddenly Fern was sorry she had given way to her unreasoned impulse.

"Perhaps I shouldn't have come. If I'm not welcome, Jessie, just say so and I'll go."

"Have I said you were unwelcome?" Jessie asked brusquely.

"No, but—well, you see, we're only passing through the city . . . We're flying to California Monday morning . . . And I was sitting at lunch just now . . . I had such an overpowering sense of your presence . . . You were not a mile away . . . I got up and walked out of there thinking I must see you, even for a minute, even if you were to slam the door in my face . . ." She stopped. Tears stung her eyes.

"Well, I didn't slam the door in your face."

A basket of needlepoint stood on the floor next to Jessie's chair. She picked up the unfinished work. "I have to do something with my hands. I don't ever seem able to sit still and do nothing."

"Then you haven't changed."

"None of us ever do, do we?"

One could take that remark in many ways. Fern made no answer, and silently the two women sat, Fern stiffly and uneasily, while Jessie poked the needle in and out.

Presently Jessie spoke. "I'm told you've made a great success with your paintings."

"Yes," Fern replied simply.

"So Father was wrong! A pity he didn't live to see himself proven wrong for once." She looked up at Fern. "You think I'm vindictive? Maybe so, but the truth is the truth, all the same."

"He would have been proven wrong about you, too," Fern said gently. "Ned's told me about you."

"Has he?"

"Yes. And this house is lovely. Mellow, like Lamb House."

"Hardly like Lamb House! So you're still living there?"

"Still there. For me, after all, it's home. And Simon loves it too."

"You're happy with Simon?"

"He's very good to me. He's strong and kind."

"That's not answering my question, is it?"

Fern threw her hands out. "Oh Jessie," she said.

Jessie thrust the needlework away. "I'm sorry. I shouldn't have said that. I'm upset. You've upset me."

Fern started to rise. "I know. It wasn't a good idea. I'd better go."

"No! Stay there! I wouldn't forgive myself if you were to leave like this. Now that you've come we must finish what you've started."

"Finish? How?"

"Clear it up. Freshen the air. Whatever you want to call it. What I want to say is, I'm not angry anymore. I don't hate you, Fern. And I haven't for a long, long time."

Fern got up and walked to the end of the room. On a round table in a corner stood a group of photographs, mostly of Claire from babyhood to the present; among them was one of Fern's and Jessie's mother, her pensive face surmounted by a World War One feathered hat. For a long time Fern stayed looking at the remembered face. At last she turned back to her sister. Her voice quivered.

"I don't know whether you'll understand—but you've relieved a pain that has been so sharp—so sharp, Jessie. You can't know."

"Maybe I can." Jessie stood and put her hand on Fern's arm. "Maybe I can."

Fern's arms went out and Jessie's head, which reached no higher than Fern's shoulder, came to rest on it. Fern's hand moved over the curly head; her other hand lay on the misshapen little back. So they stood, holding one another, while something miraculously, slowly, eased in the heart of each.

"It's so simple after all, isn't it?" Fern murmured. "Why didn't we do it before?"

"I don't know. Damn fools both, I suppose." Jessie wiped her eyes. "Sit down and talk to me. I want to hear about your daughters. I want to know more about the man who's going to marry my daughter. In one hour give me the story of the last twenty-five years. Can you do it?"

She can still charm, Fern thought as they talked. The wit was there as it had been years ago in Cyprus; the eagerness was there along with the laughter.

"Remember when Aunt Milly came to visit and we put the kittens in her bed?" Jessie cried.

"I wonder what Cyprus is like today?"

"I passed near it last summer on my way to a client in Buffalo but I didn't drive through. I want to remember it as it was for us, with the tower and the iron deer and lemonade on the lawn."

So they talked, while the hour passed. They spoke of everything and everyone except the man whose name would best remain unspoken.

Then Jessie said, "You'll need to go back and dress for the wedding. You and Simon be here at seven, will you?"

"It's been—it's been beautiful, Jessie."

"Beautiful. Bitter and sweet."

Yes, sweet to be together after so long, and bitter that it had taken so long to happen. Old wrongs and ancient grievances! Like climbing weeds they cling, twisting, twining and thickening until the day that somebody gathers the strength to pull out all the roots—or almost all of them.

❊{35}❊

Their plane was leaving for India tonight. Martin had already bid good-bye to Ned and Claire, but it came to his mind that he would like to see them just once more. They were, after all, going to the other side of the world.

It was a fine spring Sunday with a flush of pink in the light. He walked south toward the Waldorf where Ned and Claire were staying. Strollers pushed British perambulators and led dogs of exotic breeds like puli and briard. Expensive children and expensive animals, he reflected. A group of hearty boys, not expensive, zoomed past on roller skates: iron ground on stone. A Hindu couple passed, she with a gold-edged sari and red caste mark. The variety and vigor of this most marvelous of cities! He passed the Institute for Neurological Research. On the shady side of the street it stood in modest elegance, like some quiet scholar in resplendent cap and gown. Unnamable sensations flowed through Martin.

"A lot of water under the dam," he said aloud, surprising himself.

Yes, a lot of water. And he thought there ought to be a better way than that tired cliché to express what he felt about the changes and crises of a single life, not just his own, but any life, every life.

With Claire gone it would all be very different for him now. At least he had tried not to let her know. He was sure he had kept things festive for her.

The little dinner he'd given had been gay. Enoch had come in from Brown; the Horvaths and a few friends of Ned's and Claire's had been invited. He had even brought his sister and her family to New York. (Dear Alice! His gift of an annual trip to the city was the high point on her calendar.) Esther had prepared a fine meal and Marjorie had arranged the table. Already she had developed her mother's domestic gifts, and Martin actually had been able to smile a little at the sight of Hazel's fine ruby glass, so long unused. But the lace cloth, bought that day in San Francisco, had brought a twinge of sadness.

He'd been alone with Ned for a few minutes during the evening, and Ned had offered assurance. "I want you to know, sir"—his English courtesy—"I want you to know that everything will be all right this time. You can depend upon it."

And Martin had replied cheerfully, "I know I can. I'd be raising hell otherwise."

Her boy! Out of all the young men on the planet, it had had to be *her* son who, having grown up in her house, with her touch on him and the sound of her voice in his ears, would bring so much of herself into Claire's life, and so inevitably, into Martin's own. But he was a decent young man. And Martin remembered that long ride through the winter afternoon after the boy's father had died. A decent young man: he had compassion, that was one good thing.

Yet only time would really tell how it would work out. Perhaps even a couple of generations before one would really know. The modern woman! Mary and I, Hazel and I, we came from the old times. You made a compact, you gave your word, and you stayed with it at whatever cost. This was all new, this uncertainty, this flux. Jobs, marriages—you tried them on for size; if they didn't fit perfectly, you simply changed them.

"Take care of her. Love her," he had told Ned, hoping he wasn't sounding too old-fashioned, too protective. Well, the devil if he did!

Love. From all he read and saw on the screen and heard people say, it didn't seem to have the passion and intensity it had had when sex was hedged about with rules and mysteries. The concern then was for the other, the object. It was a kind of—yes, it was—adoration. Today the concern seemed to be with self, with the act of sex as if it were a game. Is my partner giving a full, fair share? Am I performing well? Obtaining the satisfaction that the experts say I should? Pleasure-measure, that's what.

How do I love thee? Let me count the ways. I love thee to the depth and breadth and height my soul can reach.

And yet, in his living room, he'd seen his daughter and the man she loved holding each other's hands with such a look in their eyes— They've been through the fire, Martin thought, and come out safely on the other side. God bless.

In the hotel lobby there was the usual genteel flurry of arrival and departure. Luggage and messages and florists' boxes moved back and forth. A little man at a counter was raising a storm about theater tickets. The seats were way over on the side, he said, and he'd be damned if he was going to pay those prices.

"Well, but—" replied the harassed young fellow on the other side of the counter, "you wanted them for the same night, and those were the only ones left."

Why did people contend so savagely over trivia? Maybe one needed to have gone through fire, as he had been thinking a moment ago of Ned and Claire, to weigh the true worth of things.

Dr. Farrell and Mr. Lamb were still upstairs. Their bags were to be taken down at half-past five, the clerk said. In the elevator Martin shook his head with rueful amusement. "Mr. Lamb and Dr. Farrell," indeed!

At the fourth floor, he got out and stood wondering in which of three directions to find the room. Across the corridor a man and woman were also hesitating, with their backs to Martin. The woman was tall, almost as tall as the man. She wore a suit of thin wool the color of wheat. Her hand, in a light glove, rested in the curve of the man's elbow. Her hair, worn in a curly cap, was lightly touched with gray. And he knew her at once, even before he heard the unmistakable voice which he would have recognized anywhere on earth.

"It's number eleven, I think," she said.

Turning just then, she caught Martin's look. Her own glance swept down the corridor beyond him, swept lightly back and paused. Eyes recognized each other in that fraction of an instant and spoke: spoke what? Such messages as may circle through space and touch and vanish. He thought her lips moved, but perhaps it was only the quivering of his own vision.

"It's this way, Mary," her husband said, "left."

The elevator came again, and Martin got in. There was a roaring in his head. He needed to sit for a moment in the lobby, but there were no vacant chairs. Then he thought he needed to get away, but there was a scramble for taxies at the hotel entrance; he hadn't the patience or the nerve to wait. He began to walk, almost to run. He felt as if he had been struck.

"If we ever see each other again," she had said, "walk away, do you promise?"

"Yes, I promise," he'd told her.

And he thought that possibly the best proof he loved her was his wish that she might be happy now. He was not noble, he knew he was far from that; yet he could wish it for her. A good man and kind, was Simon. He'd seen that at once: a manly man who would know how to make a woman happy.

Mary Fern. Mary Fern. A distant glimmer, fading and brightening, fading and brightening. For how long? For always? Until the end of his days?

He had walked two blocks when a car drew up just ahead of him. It was a foreign limousine, driven by a chauffeur in a maroon uniform. A little woman, wearing a loose cream-colored coat, got out and dismissed the car.

"Jessie!" he cried.

"Martin?" She hesitated, then put out her hand. "How are you, Martin?"

"I'm fine, thanks. You're going in here?" he asked, indicating the apartment house before which they stood.

"No, walking home. I need the exercise, so I sent the car back to the garage."

It seemed necessary to say something further, so he remarked politely that the car was handsome.

Jessie smiled. "What you really think is that it's too lavish. I know your spartan tastes."

"No, no."

"You don't fool me, Martin. But I love that car. It means a lot to me."

"Well, it's certainly handsome. And I like your coat, Jessie."

"Rats! It's the same outfit I wear year after year. The same cape to cover the hump. The only things that change are the color and the fabric."

Little Jessie! Tart, plucky little Jessie! And something touched Martin sharply near the heart, some old memory and a sense of déjà vu. Oh, but his heart was vulnerable today!

"Do you mind if I keep you company?" he asked her. "We seem to be walking in the same direction."

"Come along, of course."

They had gone a block before either of them spoke. Jessie said, "You've been to see Claire, haven't you?"

"I went to the Waldorf, but then I didn't go upstairs."

"Because you saw Fern instead."

"Now, how did you know that?"

"You have a faraway look. Didn't I always know when something was on your mind?"

"That's true. You always did."

"No, you never fooled me, Martin."

He didn't answer. He was remembering something he'd seen only a few weeks ago, a painting in a Chicago museum: Albright's *That Which I Should Have Done I Did Not Do.* It was a simple picture of a funeral wreath hung on a wooden door, and it had touched him profoundly, reaching into dark places far within.

"I did you a very great injustice," he said now. "Not that it helps you any for me to tell you so. But I've carried the guilt of it with me every day of my life."

"I'm sorry to hear that! Very sorry, Martin. In the last analysis you did me an enormous favor, you know. I've got Claire because of you, haven't I? And you know as well as I there was no Prince Charming waiting in the wings to carry me off and 'get me with child' as they say in the fairy tales."

He looked down at her. Her hair was smartly cut. Her face, which had some-times seemed older than her age when she was young, now seemed younger than her age. It was alert and keen as ever.

"Did you know Fern was in New York?" she asked.

"No," he replied and couldn't resist asking. "Did you?"

"I didn't know she was coming. Nobody did. She arrived in time for the wedding."

"She was at the wedding?"

"Yes. She came to my house that afternoon. I'm glad she came. I would never have asked her to, not in a hundred years. But I'm so glad she did. We had a good, long talk."

Martin was so astonished that he could think of nothing to say.

"The wonderful thing is that seeing her didn't hurt me as much as I would have expected it to! I suppose it's because I've made something out of my own life. I don't have to feel like—like *nothing* anymore! Oh, it went back so far! To when I was still in a high chair, probably, and she was running around with a beautiful, straight back . . . You understand?"

"I think I always have, Jessie."

"I don't say it still doesn't hurt. And always will, a little . . . Sometimes I think how queer and sad it is that I never loved anyone enough. Not even you, for if I had loved you enough I wouldn't have had so much pride, would I? And if I had loved Fern enough I could have forgiven her for being herself." And she reflected, "I don't count Claire, because that's just biological."

Martin said painfully, "You're a very loving woman, Jessie. Make no mistake."

She ignored the little protest. "It's natural to think it's on account of the hump that I was inhibited from loving. But what if it had nothing to do with that? What if I was just put together without the capacity to love?"

"No, no. I can't believe that. Can't buy it, as they say."

"Well, buy it or not, that's how it is."

Martin was silent. They walked on, their steps brisk on the pavement.

And suddenly Jessie said, "I'm sorry about what happened with your institute. Claire's told me how they cheated you."

"One gets used to things."

Jessie smiled wryly. "Not to everything."

No, one would never accept a hump on one's back, never, he thought, relinquish the longing to be graceful and beloved.

"We shall miss Claire terribly, shan't we?" she said.

"Yes."

"You, at least, have three others."

"True. But she—" He stopped. It sounded theatrical to say, although no doubt Jessie would believe it. "But she is my special child, my heart."

"You have awfully nice children, Claire says."

"Gentle. Like their mother," he said soberly.

"Like you, too."

Wishing to return the honest compliment with equal honesty, he said, "You did a fantastic job, bringing Claire up. I've always wanted to tell you."

"You had something to do with that yourself, you know. You were her hero from the start. How I suffered when she went to claim you!" And Jessie raised her eyes to Martin with a look of pure and simple honesty. "I had so wanted to keep her all for myself!"

"You've kept her, Jessie. She loves you, and has such admiration for you! Believe me, I know."

"Yes. But now this marriage! It seems like another loss. We won't be seeing her much at all anymore."

"It's lucky we're both busy."

"I didn't cling to her when she was with me, that's one good thing. I hadn't the time, and I wouldn't have done that to her anyway." Jessie sighed. "Oh drat! I never could stand mournful people and that goes for myself. Here's my place. I won't ask you in because we really have nothing more to say to one another today, have we? But it's been nice, all the same." She held out her hand. "Luck, Martin."

"And to you, Claire's mother."

Streetlamps flared on and the sky above the craggy rooftops turned dark green. He walked home more slowly now, through a clement, deepening dusk. His thoughts roved loosely. Strange day! A day in which the past had rushed forward to tie up with the future. In some ways, he thought, Jessie always understood me the best. Yes it's true, she did from the very beginning. A sound like a chuckle of amusement rose in his throat. Barely five feet high, and the strength of her! But then, Mary is strong, too. And Claire. My Claire. Enormous strength in all these women! Poor Hazel didn't have it. No blame to her: you're made the way you're made. For that matter, I don't even know how much strength I have myself. Pity one can't ever see oneself.

A LIGHT SHONE through the crack of Peter's door long after supper. When Martin opened the door Peter was sitting at his desk.

"Math again?"

"Algebra. I hate the stuff." The boy's troubled mouth puckered like a child's, yet on his upper lip there was the faint beginning of down.

"Just do the best you can. Try to relax over it," Martin counseled sympathetically.

"I've got to do better on the next test."

"There's no 'got to.' No one person is expected to excel at everything, Peter."

"Claire always does. I wish I was smart like her, Dad."

"You are smart in your own way."

"Not like her," Peter said stubbornly.

"We're all different."

A fine boy, Peter was, a serious, responsible child. But it was true, he'd never have the intellectual fire of Claire. Too bad! And he thought: A boy needs it so much more. Then he thought: Claire would be furious if she could hear me say that.

He put his hand on the child's shoulder. And something of the tenderness that was in him must have been conducted like a current through his touch, because Peter looked up anxiously.

"Are you unhappy, Dad?"

"No, no, of course not. Why should I be?"

"Well, I thought— Enoch says you'll miss Claire so much. Will you?"

How many more times would he be required to answer that question?

"Yes, we all will, won't we?"

"But you will especially."

The boy's eyes, trusting and shy, rested on his father's face. And for the first time, Martin did not turn away from that reminder of Hazel, that quiet gaze.

He cleared his throat. "Gosh, you're growing. Is that the only sweater you've got to wear?"

"What's wrong with it?"

"The cuffs are halfway to your elbow."

"I grew three inches since last year. Haven't you noticed?"

No, he hadn't noticed, he'd been so absorbed with other things.

"We'll go shopping next Saturday morning. I guess you'll need practically everything, won't you?"

"Marjorie's been wanting things ever so long. Her dresses are too short, and last year's spring coat doesn't fit at all."

" 'Ever so long'? Why didn't she ask me?"

"I guess she thought you were too busy."

"She could have gone shopping with Claire again."

"But Claire's been getting ready to go away."

"Gosh," Martin said doubtfully, "I don't know anything about what little girls should wear."

"You could just get what the other girls in her class have, couldn't you?"

"You're right," Martin said.

The boy's kindness struck to his heart. Ever since their mother's death, it seemed these children had been gradually drawing together. And he thought of the adult fears they must have, these good children of his. They had still so much to go through: teeth to be straightened, homesickness at camp, sex education with its wonders and dangers. (How to convey to them some rudimentary knowledge, when you knew so very little yourself?) Then college boards, and after that, the earning of a livelihood. How to do that without being trampled in the crush, and still refrain from doing any trampling, still keep some of that first, clean Sunday-school decency?

Claire sees the world the way my father saw it, Martin thought suddenly. She thinks she's sophisticated, and in some ways, superficially, she is. But fundamentally, she is like my father.

He looked at the clock. They would have taken off by now, headed eastward toward an old, poor, dangerous land. No, he couldn't allow himself to grow old even if he wanted to. He still had too many people to think about.

He smiled at Peter. "Well, we'll take care of everything. Now I suggest you go to sleep. It's late and tomorrow's Monday."

He went into his den. All the little objects in the room, the lamps and bookends, the ashtrays and the clock, glowed like jewels in the light of the naked white walls. Suddenly and for the first time, he understood why he had surrounded himself with whiteness. That first room of hers— And he opened the closet, where on the top shelf, still in its English wrapping paper, gone dusty and brittle with years, stood the *Three Red Birds,* summertime version. Taking it down, he propped it against a shelf, then stood a moment, studying the rhythm of the birds and the background of that living green which she so loved.

"Among trees," she used to say, "one hears the world breathe."

So tomorrow he would hang it up at last and face reality. Had it, though, been all real? Sometimes it seemed unreal, an enchantment that couldn't possibly have been as he remembered it. And if they had lived together, sharing a roof, childhood diseases, plumbing bills and fatigue, how would it have been then? How endured?

That, my friend, you will never know.

It was time for sleep, if he was to do his best in the morning. Tomorrow's surgery was going to be tough. The patient was a student, a young physicist, already possessed of awesome knowledge beyond Martin's comprehension. And something was growing in his head, something which Martin would reach in to find, probing deeper and deeper, not knowing until the very last whether his most educated conjecture had been correct. How could a man ever get used to such a venture? Each time was like the first time. And on the slipper chair in his bedroom he sat down to go over the steps and possibilities for tomorrow.

When he had reviewed his mental diagrams to his satisfaction, he allowed his mind to wander and ate an apple. Hazel had always provided a piece of fruit for him at bedtime. Now Marjorie continued the custom. He sat back to enjoy the comfort of it: a fine tart apple, a Northern Spy, he'd guess. There had been a tree outside his room. Oh, the life in that tree! Midsummer rustlings and rapping all night at the house wall when polar winds drove. The apples of boyhood: Russets, Greenings, Gravensteins. Wasps in sweet, rotting piles of apples on the grass. Basket on the porch when Pa sickened and died.

When I die, my patients will bring neither apples nor tears to my house. Some of them will not even remember my name. "Some big doctor did the operation," they will say. But my father—how they loved him! And he loved them! They never knew—how could they?—how little he knew. And he, even he didn't know how little he knew. Not his fault, of course. He wouldn't believe it if he could come back and see what I am going to do to that young man tomorrow morning.

So one pays for everything. We know more, we can do more; but we are not the fathers to the sick that my father was, and they do not love us.

He walked to the window to pull the curtains shut. Under a white sky glow, the city throbbed. Even from this height, Martin could hear its murmur. Only yesterday he'd stood at a window looking down at the crowd pouring in for his medical school commencement. The cap and gown, so regal and austere, had hung ready in the closet. Alice had sat between his parents in the second row. The parents had looked small and gray. He could remember thinking that some of the parents had been young. He could remember Tom being solemn and Perry, lost now, choking on laughter. Dr. Perrault gave a long speech about medical advances, great changes coming. Names were called. He'd had an awful feeling he'd stumble up or down the step getting the diploma. Then majestic music, marching out. Pa shook his hand. Had those been tears or only blinking into the light, into the sun? "Dr. Farrell," Pa had said, the first to call him that.

Thirty-five years, he thought now. There's still so much I haven't done. And as always came that sense of rushing time, like the wind in a boy's ears as he runs downhill.

He pulled the curtains and picked up the telephone. "Who is this? Miss Kerrigan? My patient Bateman in Room 1002, is he still restless?" (Restless, yes, why not, poor boy, on this long, long night, this speeding night, not long enough for him?) "Have Dr. Cotter come in to look at him, will you? Yes, thank you."

He was worried about young Bateman, so bright, so eager, so terrified. When a man didn't expect to recover, Martin had found out, he often didn't. There really was such a thing as the will to live. Once he had thought it an old wives' tale and had said so with some scorn when his father had told of it.

"There are some things we'll never know," Pa had said, and it was true. Body and mind are interwoven. Or call it soul, if that is the name which satisfies you.

Sighing, Martin drew off his shoes. You could relax a little when you had a resident like Fred Cotter watching over things. It didn't happen often. Once in a blue moon, among the waves of perfectly competent, willing young people, came one who had that special feel, a sort of inner birthlight, so bright, so flaming, that nothing would ever put it out, not age, nor wealth, nor prestige, nor even love. A man like that is a partner in the universe, you might say. Albeniz would have approved of Cotter.

He had got his old diary out to show to Claire before she went away. It lay now on the table, opened at the frontispiece where he had written that quotation from Aesculapius which, forgetting that he had known it long before, he had chosen again for the pediment of the institute. And he saw himself on the bed under the sloping roof of his room in Cyprus—sweet scent of warm wood shingles in July—writing with the book propped on his knees.

That Greek physician, alive in a time and place so different from this as scarcely to be imagined anymore, had perceived the truth. The lustrous sky of Attica, Martin thought; he had always fancied it as having been particularly blue.

Oh, he would go there yet, take his children someday and see it. "Yes, yes," he murmured, turning out the light. Then clearly, loving the sound of the old words, he spoke them aloud into the darkness.

"For where there is love of man, there is love of the art."

EDEN BURNING

*To the garden, Earth, man's only home, and
to all those who would save it from the vicious
tyrannies of fascism and communism*

AUTHOR'S NOTE

There is, of course, no island of St. Felice in the Caribbean area. Yet, as a composite of all the lands in and around that lovely troubled sea, one might say that St. Felice does indeed exist. So, then, and notwithstanding that its characters are entirely fictional, the tale told here is a refraction, a reflection, of the truth.

PROLOGUE

On a winter afternoon in the year 1673, a fifteen-year-old indentured servant named Eleuthère François, of the family later to be known as Francis, saw the island of St. Felice rise up between clouds and sea. He was a waif from a peasant's cold home in Brittany, and despite all the sailors' yarns he had been hearing, had never imagined anything like this entrancing blue of water and sky, this warmth, this soft, unceasing wind. White sand lay spread like a silk robe, he thought, astonished at himself for having the thought; he was not in the habit of making comparisons, had indeed found little need in his life to do so. And stammered to himself as the island grew larger, It is a flower lying on a pond. Or the jewel in the bishop's ring that Sunday? The dark green shining, the deep, dark shining . . .

He knew nothing about the island where he was to remain and found a great family; knew nothing most certainly, of that primordial heaving of the earth's hot crust which had produced an arc of such islands between two continents. He had, very likely, no conception at all of a volcano, or of coral, or of the red-brown man who had preceded him there, the red-brown man with high cheekbones and black hair straight as a horse's mane who had come across the land bridge from Asia some thousands of years before to wander eastward and southward, to scatter from what we now call Hudson Bay to what we now call Tierra del Fuego.

Eleuthère François thought of himself as a first-comer, although it had been a century since the first priests, armored soldiers, and buccaneers had arrived from Europe on their sailing ships. Under the tranquil leafage of these forests men had already been crucified and roasted alive for gold. In the ramshackle taverns of Covetown sailors and their whores drank out of emerald-studded stolen cups, gambled and stabbed each other for the possession of gold. He could not have known as he waited at the rail, while the ship moved in toward the wharf, that even now another kind of wealth was beginning to outmatch the metal: human wealth this time, black, out of Africa. He could certainly not have imagined how this wealth, so brutally seized, would in time produce such refinements as a stately portrait under the ceiling fan in a governor's mansion, or the tinkle of porcelain teacups on an English lawn, or a girl of his own blood dancing in white silk over a polished floor.

The anchor dropped. Men shouted. Gulls cried and swung about the rigging. Ignorant, hopeful, daring, and afraid, Eleuthère François stepped ashore.

BOOK ONE

BROTHERS

⍣❀{ 1 }❀⍣

Teresa Francis, called Tee, was six years old when first she learned that St. Felice was not the world—and fifteen when she fled from it in fear and shame, for reasons that the most flamboyant imagination could not have foretold.

"The world is enormous, child," Père said. "It's a great ball spinning around the sun, and St. Felice is only a fleck of dust on the ball."

Père was her grandfather and her friend, more so than ever in that winter of 1928 when her father, he who was Père's son, had died. She understood Père's sadness, feeling it as a graver pain than Mama's was, in spite of the black dress and the tears.

"Look carefully, there—those two dark curves like clouds, you see? Those are St. Lucia's peaks. That way, there's St. Vincent. And Dominica, and Grenada—"

The child had a sudden image of these islands, drawn out of who knew what remembered words, an image of green turtles, mottled and domed, like turtles dozing by the little river where black women were even now beating clothes clean on the rocks.

"And down there's Covetown, follow my finger—you can see the careenage, and I think I can just make out a liner coming into the roadstead."

A liner. A great ship with smoke twirling from the funnels and a lovely name like *Marina* or *Southern Star*. When the ships came they brought good things: bisque dolls with real hair, Mama's beautiful hats and her kid gloves ("Unbearable in this climate," Mama said, "but a lady can't go very far without them, can she?"), and the glittery things in the Da Cunha shop on Wharf Street, and Père's books and Papa's suits from England—only there would be no more of those; his suits had been given to the servants.

She stood there thinking about all that, stood in a silence of wondering and trance, in a remote and midday silence, until a woman far below at the river broke it with a whooping laugh and Père spoke again.

" 'Full fathom five thy father lies, of his bones are coral made.' Our first ancestor here became a pirate. He came as an indentured servant and ran away from a cruel master to join the buccaneers. Have I ever told you that, Tee?"

"Yes, but Mama said it wasn't true."

"Your mama doesn't want to believe it. His name was Eleuthère François. When the English took the island the name was changed to Francis. . . . It was my great-grandfather who called this house Eleuthera, after a city in ancient Greece. He was an educated man, the first in our family to study at Cambridge. . . . I love this place. Your father loved it. It's in our blood. Two hundred years of it and more."

Père was tall. A child had to crane her head to see his prominent, thin nose. He carried a gold-knobbed cane, not to lean on, but to flourish. His name was Virgil Francis. He was master of the rising hills that mounted in tiers of jungle and cane toward the summit of Morne Bleue; master of all the looping fields that swept to the shore. Lands and houses miles away across the island were his also: Drummond Hall, Georgina's Fancy, Hope Great House, and Florissant.

For all this ownership, Tee knew, he was respected. In later life she was to wonder how she, a child kept in an unworldly ignorance so profound that it nearly destroyed her, could have known that ownership commands the most respect of all.

"But why ever he chooses to stay in this shabby, far-off hill place," Mama complained, "I will never understand." Her earrings sparked. Now that she was in mourning she wore jet instead of pearls or gold, but still they sparked. "Drummond Hall would be so much nicer, even though it's run-down, too. A pity, he's no manager."

Tee defended him. "He speaks Latin and Greek."

"Much good that does when it comes to running a sugar estate!"

But Mama would never have dared say that to Père. In all the pictures taken during those slow, long days it is he who sits in the fan chair on the veranda, Mama and the others who stand around him. Looking backward with these photographs (mounted in a black imitation-leather album with frayed corners), Tee, in another country where snow falls through gray afternoons, strains to recall the faces and the place which after so many years have grown unreal, yet which at moments can still be as painful and sensitive as fingertips.

Here she is herself in a dark skirt and a sailor blouse, the uniform of the convent school in Covetown.

"We are not Catholic, of course," Mama said. "But the nuns have the best school here, and as long as you go to the Anglican church on Sundays, it doesn't matter."

The twelve-year-old face is earnest, timid, and plain. She has inherited Père's proud peaked nose. Only her lavish hair is beautiful, lying dark on her shoulders. Later she will be told that this hair is aphrodisiac; certainly she would not have understood that then.

Here are the wedding pictures, the day Mama married again. Mama wore an enormous pink hat. There had been roast suckling pig and hearts of palm. A whole palm tree had been cut down to make the salads.

"A sin," said Père, who would lay his hand on a tree as though it could speak to him.

Mama's new husband was Mr. Tarbox—Uncle Herbert, Tee was to call him. He was a neat man who still spoke of England as home, although he had been living on St. Felice for twenty years. The servants said he was wealthy; he had been a commission merchant in Covetown, and now was to be a planter, which was a much more distinguished thing to be. He had money to invest in the Francis estates and perhaps he would make them pay more richly; he was known to be smart. They hoped he would get along with old Mr. Francis. Miss Julia was, after all, not a daughter, only a daughter-in-law. Still, there was the girl Tee to hold them all together. So they spoke.

Mr. and Mrs. Tarbox were to live at Drummond Hall. In loving memory of his son and to provide a home for Tee, Virgil had given a grand house to his daughter-in-law. But it was too echoing, too lofty for Tee.

"I don't want to leave Eleuthera," she said stubbornly. "I won't ever see you, Père."

"Of course you will! But you belong with your mother. And don't forget, Agnes will be going with you."

Agnes Courzon had come years before from Martinique, to work for the family. She had coffee-colored skin; her hair was fastened sleek-flat; she had gold hoops in her ears and on Sundays wore a flowered turban and a necklace of large gold beads. Tee supposed she was handsome.

She liked fine things. "When I worked in Martinique at the Mauriers'—oh, là! What a gorgeous house! Such damask and silver you never saw! But for the eruption I would never have gone away. Destroyed, that wicked Mount Pelée destroyed it all. It hurts my heart to think of it. But wait," she said, "wait and see what your mama and Mr. Tarbox will do with Drummond Hall. It won't be like this old place, tumbling down—"

Tee looked around the room. Really, she had never noticed that the plaster garlands were falling from the ceiling. Books were heaped on chairs. A small coiled snake lay preserved in a jar on the windowsill. Père studied snakes.

"I'll be glad to leave," Agnes said. "I should think you would be, too."

There are dozens of photographs of Drummond Hall. At the end of a lane it stands, between a row of royal palms. Twin staircases join at the top on a veranda, from which one enters into the gloss of parquet and dark mahogany.

The house was Mama's pride. But Uncle Herbert's thoughts moved out beyond the house.

"We shall need new rollers in the mill. And I'm thinking about turning the east hundred into bananas."

Mama said doubtfully, "I don't know why, I still think of bananas as a kind of Negro peasant crop."

"Where've you been these last twenty years? Have you any idea how many tons the Geest ships carry back to England from Jamaica alone?"

"But the old sugar families here—"

"Julia, I am not from an aristocratic sugar family, you forget. I'm a middle-class merchant." Uncle Herbert was not indignant, merely amused. "We're way behind the times on St. Felice and I mean to catch up. There's relatively no care with bananas. You plant the rootstock and in twelve months you're ready to harvest. There's no processing, nothing to do but pick, grade, and ship."

"It'll throw a lot of people out of work, cutting down on sugar," Père told Tee privately. "He doesn't care, though. A new man come to run things."

"Don't you like Uncle Herbert?"

"I like him well enough. He's a worker and he's honest. It's just that I'm too old to learn new ways. They don't agree with me."

But they agreed with Mama. Here in one deckle-edged snapshot after the other stands Julia Tarbox, gay and charming as Tee will never be: ruffled and flounced for a ball at Government House or smiling on the veranda with her two new babies, Lionel and little Julia, born only a year apart.

Tee knew, of course, that the babies had come from inside her mother, just as puppies and colts came out of their mothers. The question was, How did they get there? It was frustrating that there was absolutely no way to find out. Nothing was written anywhere and no one would talk about it.

"We don't discuss things like that." Mama's rebuke was gentle and firm. "You will find out when the right time comes."

No one at school knew, either. Vaguely it was understood that men had something to do with it. But what? Some of the girls used to gather around a daring, arrogant girl named Justine who could whisper odd things, but one morning the nuns caught her and after that she wouldn't tell anything. So Tee was troubled by unanswered questions. Of course, as Mama said, she would have the answers sometime, just as sometime she would wear high heels, or be invited to Government House. Until then she must simply try not to think about it too much. . . .

Meanwhile, here she stands with Mama and the two little ones. Père has taken the picture with his box camera; she is about to spend the summer of her fifteenth year at Eleuthera.

"The whole summer!" Mama objected. "Why on earth do you want to do that?"

Mama wanted her to go to the club, to be among girls from the right families, to be popular. Mama didn't understand, or didn't want to understand, that you couldn't make yourself be like that if you hadn't been born like that.

"But I love Eleuthera," Tee said. You could ride bareback into the hills; you could float on the river, just float and think; you could read all afternoon with no one to interrupt you.

"Well, you may go on one condition. Agnes will have to go along. You're too old to be without a chaperone."

"My books are getting mildewed," Père complained on the day he came for Tee. "I've got a cabinetmaker coming to build cases for them."

"Buckley doing it?" Uncle Herbert asked. "He repaired a settee for us. Did a splendid job."

"His apprentice is better than he is. A colored boy, no more than nineteen, I should think. Clyde Reed. He'll stay at Eleuthera. It'll take him most of the summer, I expect."

"All summer!"

"Yes, I shall want dentil moldings. And glass doors to keep the damp out."

"Still, the whole summer!" Julia repeated idly.

"Why not?" Père stirred his coffee. It was a way of ignoring Julia. "A most unusual boy, actually. I caught him reading my *Iliad*. I don't suppose he understood it. A pity, he wants to learn. Of course, there's a lot of white in him." He leaned toward Uncle Herbert. "Some of the best blood on the island, very likely."

Tee caught the whisper, caught Julia's frown. So there was something hidden here, something ugly?

"Reed," Uncle Herbert reflected. "Weren't there some Reeds who owned Estate Miranda for a short space? Gambled it away at cards in London. No scholars in that lot, I should think."

"Well, this Reed is, or could be, if the world were different. But it isn't. At least I can lend him some books, though."

Uncle Herbert said carefully, "If you'll allow me an opinion, with all respect, Père, I always feel that sort of thing's a kind of teasing. Offering an equality that you'll have to withdraw the moment it seems the offer might be taken up."

"Well," Virgil said vaguely, "we'll see." He stood up, ready to go. "Anyway, Tee and I will have a time for ourselves. It's a lot cooler in our hills than it is here, I can tell you."

"See that she invites some friends, do, please," Julia urged as they drove away. "I don't want her spending the whole time with horses and dogs. Or reading on the veranda. She is so like—"

Like my father, Tee thought defiantly. But I shall just read all day long if I want to. Or spend it with the dogs if I want to.

She knew nothing, nothing at all, that summer.

In the blue shade of the late afternoon Père spread a large notebook on his lap.

"Quitting time, Clyde! You've been hammering and chiseling since breakfast. Would you like to listen to what I've got here?"

The boy Clyde came and sat down on the steps. It was odd that one called him "boy" in one's mind, for certainly he was a full-grown man. Tee thought, It is because he is colored, which seemed answer enough. Still, she mused, he is not very colored, is he? He was a shade or two lighter than Agnes, and like Agnes, quite clean. He wore a freshly washed shirt every morning and carried with him a pleasant scent of the wood on which he worked; sometimes a papery curl of wood shaving caught in his hair, which was thick and straight. White man's hair, it was. His narrow lips were the white man's. Only his eyes were Negro. White people's brown eyes were never that dark. It occurred to her that Clyde's had a wise look to them. Or perhaps a mocking look? As if even when he was being most respectful—and he was always respectful, Père would not have allowed him to stay if he had not been—as if his eyes were saying, *I know what you are thinking.* But then, she thought, that's probably silly; I am given to silly observations, Mama always says.

"This is a translation I made," Père explained. "From the French, naturally. The original is in my vault in town. It's crumbling, ought to be in a museum. Well, I'll get to that one of these days. Here it is: 'Diary of the First François.'

" 'We sailed from Havre de Grace on the English ship *Pennington* in the year of our Lord 1673, I being fifteen years of age and indentured for seven years to a Mr. Raoul D'Arcy on the island of St. Felice in the West Indies; he to pay my passage and clothe me, he to pay me three hundred pounds of tobacco at the end of my service.' "

Père turned some pages. "Fascinating. Here, listen to this. 'We labor from a quarter of an hour after sunrise to a quarter of an hour after sunset. I share a cabin with two black slaves. They are pleasant enough, poor creatures. They suffer, but I suffer worse than they do. My master admits to working the white man harder because after seven years he will part with him; but the Negro is his for life and must therefore be kept in health.' "

"I thought," Tee remarked, "our ancestor was a buccaneer."

"Oh, yes! He ran away to join the buccaneers. You can hardly blame him. And yet—what a devilish thing is human nature!—he became more savage than the master whom he had escaped. Listen to this. 'We came alongside the *Garza Blanca,* a merchantman sailing for Spain, sometime before moonrise. We boarded without a sound, surprising the watch, whom we threw overboard into a heavy sea. We bayonetted the captain, seized the guns, and put to shore, there to dispose of a goodly cargo: gold, tobacco, hides, and a great prize in pearls.' "

"I don't think," Tee shuddered, "I want to know any more about this François." She stretched out her arm, turning it over to regard the small cluster of blue veining at the elbow. "I can't believe his blood runs in my veins. . . . A savage like him!"

"Many generations removed, my dear," Père said complacently. "And anyway he became a gentleman before very long." He flipped through a few more pages. " 'I have resolved to become provident, having seen my lads squander a year's gain on brandy and' "—Père coughed—"other things. 'I mean to buy land and live on my property like a gentleman, to marry well—' " He closed the notebook. "And so he did. He married Virginia Durand, daughter of a well-established planter who had apparently no qualms about giving her to a reformed buccaneer. He lived, incidentally, to make a fortune in sugar before he was forty. Sugar's not a native plant; you did know that, didn't you?" Père frowned. "Tee, I'm feeling the signs of age. I was about to tell you about sugar and all of a sudden the facts have fled. Would you believe it possible that I can't name the place where it originated?"

"Excuse me, Mr. Francis, sir," Clyde said. "It was the Canary Islands. Columbus brought the first cuttings from there."

"Why, yes, you're right; of course you are."

"Yes, sir. I read it in the *National Geographic.*"

"You read the *Geographic*?"

"I've a friend. He was my teacher when I went to school. He keeps it for me."

"I see."

Clyde spoke eagerly. The words came out fast, as if he were afraid someone would stop him before he was finished. "I read a lot. I guess I've about read everything in the Covetown library. Well, not quite. I like history the best, how we all got to be what we are, you know—" He stopped, as if this time he feared having said too much.

He wants to show us how much he knows, Tee thought, sensing now not only the mocking pride which had been her first impression, but also something humble. It made her uncomfortable.

But Père appeared to be delighted. "Oh, I know you're a reader, Clyde! And

that's wonderful! Reading is all there is to knowledge. Reading, not classrooms.
. . . Oh, I've been collecting books all my life. I've got books from as far back as
when the English took this island from the French in—"

"In 1782, when Admiral Rodney beat the French at the Battle of the Saints."

"Listen to that, Tee! Listen to what the boy knows! Didn't I tell you Clyde was
smart?"

He is treating him like a performing monkey, Tee thought.

Père stood up. "Well, Clyde, you may borrow all the books you want from me.
Any time. As long as your hands are clean when you touch them. Come, Tee, it's
time. We're having guests at dinner."

"Père," Tee said when they were inside, "that was insulting. Telling him about
clean hands."

Père was astonished. She had never spoken to him that way. "You don't
understand," he said. "They don't mind. They're not as sensitive as you are."

How could he know? How could he say such a thing? And yet he was so kind,
Père was. Who else would invite a colored workman to sit down with them?
Mama certainly would not, nor would Uncle Herbert.

"Bigotry, besides being stupid and cruel, stains the personality," Père liked to
say. Yet there was this contradiction in him.

Another thing to puzzle over! The world, as you grew older, kept presenting
things to puzzle over. There were many vague thoughts in her head, circling there
like bees: thoughts about places beyond the island and times before the island
and how people came to be what they are . . .

"You are much too serious," Mama complained, not unkindly. "I wish you
could just learn to take pleasure out of life."

And Tee would think, Your pleasures are not mine. I'm not pretty enough for
your pleasures anyway, even if I wanted them. And if I had your beauty, I
wouldn't know what to do with it, how to laugh and touch Uncle Herbert on the
cheek when he stands there adoring you in a room full of people. What I need is
someone to talk to, really talk, without having to be afraid that I'm boring, or
childish, or asking too many questions.

Père was growing too old for her. Suddenly that summer one saw that he was
losing vigor and patience. Often he forgot what he was saying. He began to sleep
away the afternoons. Eleuthera grew lonely.

So now, after the noon meal, Tee would wander into the coolness and sweet
wood scent of the library to read or watch Clyde chisel a floral wreath on a
cornice. There was something soothing in the tapping noises of the little hammer
and in his soft whistle of concentration . . .

One day she read aloud from the ancient diary.

" 'July, seventeen hundred and three. Time of great woe. My wife's brother and
four of his children dead of the fever. There is scarcely a family that has not
suffered dreadful loss.' Whatever made people come to this wilderness in the first
place, Clyde? I can't imagine myself doing it!"

"Poverty, Miss Tee. There was no work in Europe and what there was paid
badly. These islands weren't populated by the rich."

He was reminding her that her ancestors hadn't been aristocrats. She saw the humor in that and didn't mind. Sometimes, lately, she surprised herself with her own insights.

"Also, a lot of convicts were sent here. It was called transport." He put the chisel down. "But you didn't have to be a criminal to be a convict. You could go to prison for stealing a few pennies, or for being in debt. You could be innocent, really. The innocent poor," he said queerly.

In the pause that followed, the words repeated themselves in Tee's head with a kind of grave dignity: the innocent poor.

"Well," she said, wanting to break this gravity that verged on sadness, "well, ancestors are fascinating, don't you think? You must wonder about yours"—and instantly flushed with the awareness of having said something awkward, something *out of place*. She apologized: "I'm sorry, I didn't mean—" making it worse.

"That's all right, Miss Tee." He picked up the chisel, setting to work again. "Yes, I wonder about mine. Not that it does any good."

"You could be a teacher," she said after a minute, wanting to make amends. "I think you know as much as my teachers know."

"I left school too early. My mother got sick and couldn't work, so I took to this trade." He turned around, his shoulders gone proud. "There's no shame in working with your hands, as middle-class people, even among my people, seem to think."

"No, there certainly isn't. And has your mother got well?"

"She died."

"Oh. And your father?"

"I don't know whether he's alive or dead. I never saw him."

"Oh. My father died when I was six. Would you believe I still think about him? I feel as if—I miss him, even though I couldn't have known him well. I suppose it's because I'm not very close to my mother."

Clyde looked at her. His eyes were kind. "That's a great loss for you. And for her."

"She has two new babies and a new husband, so it probably doesn't matter." Her voice sounded bleak in her own ears.

"There have to be more reasons than that, Miss Tee."

"Oh, there are! We're very different, you see. My mother cares about clothes and entertaining and being invited places. She knows what families are important and who's going to marry whom and who's going abroad next month. But I don't care about that sort of thing at all!"

"What do you care about, then?"

"Oh, books and dogs—all kinds of animals, actually, and riding, and of course I'd like to go abroad, too, not to see the fashions but—"

"To see how other people live. To see Rome and London, the crowds and the great buildings— Yes, I'd like all that, too! And I mean to do it, someday."

"But then you'd want to come back here, wouldn't you? I know I'd always come back. This is home."

"It's different for you than for me," he said quietly.

Yes. Of course it was. His life and hers, both lived upon this little island, were different, indeed. And she had those queer feelings again: pity and a certain guilt —which was absurd; none of this was her fault!

Agnes remarked indignantly, "I never saw such an uppity boy, talking away with you by the hour—you'd think he was part of the family or something!"

"He isn't 'uppity,' Agnes. He's very polite. And he's one of the smartest people I've ever known!"

"Hmph," replied Agnes.

Agnes was jealous. Tee understood. Having no children of her own and having been scorned for it, Agnes had taken possession of Tee and couldn't share her. Yes, she was jealous of Clyde.

How strange it was that, outside of Père, a person like Clyde should be the easiest friend she had ever made! At school she had no deep friendships; there had once been a girl who read poetry with her, but she had gone to live in England and now there was no one.

Clyde appreciated poetry.

"Listen to this," she said. "It's by Elizabeth Barrett Browning and it's the loveliest of all, I think. Listen.

> *I thank all who have loved me in their hearts*
> *With thanks and love from mine. Deep thanks to all*
> *Who paused a little near the prison-wall*
> *To hear my music—"*

The room was very quiet. He had put down the tools. She was intensely aware of the quiet and the pure round tone of her own voice speaking.

"I wasn't quite sure at first what she meant by 'prison-wall,' and then I realized she meant her loneliness."

"She had a good deal of guilt, too. The family's fortune came from the West Indies, you know, from slave labor. That didn't disturb her father at all, but she was sensitive."

Clyde's face was soft. He's quite different when Père isn't here, Tee thought suddenly. Not stiff, nor humble either. Just probably himself.

"You read that very well," he said.

"Yes, Mama says I read with expression. I often think, if I were better-looking, I might be an actress."

"But there's nothing wrong with you, Miss Tee! You—"

"Look at me— No, no, you're not looking." For he had glanced quickly once and turned away. "Don't you see my nose? I've got my grandfather's nose. Can't you see?"

"I've never really looked at your grandfather's nose."

"Well, next time look at it carefully. Only I'd advise you not to let him know you're doing it."

The absurdity of this caution struck her then, and she began to laugh. Clyde standing there staring, measuring her grandfather's nose! And now Clyde, having, no doubt, the same picture in mind, began laughing too.

"You know, Clyde, I'll really miss you when you've finished these cabinets."

"It's good of you to say so."

"Not 'good'! True! I never say things I don't mean. I wish we could stay friends. Maybe we will!"

He didn't answer. Intent again on his work, he bent to refine the spreading petals of a wooden flower. She thought perhaps he hadn't heard.

"I said I wish we might stay friends."

"That would be nice, Miss Tee."

"Clyde, you don't have to call me Miss. Don't you think that's silly? We're the same age, almost."

"It's the custom," he answered, blowing the sawdust away.

"But a custom can be silly, can't it?"

"You're not going to change it, Miss Tee, even if you want to. You'll only make trouble for yourself if you try."

Now it was her turn not to answer. Instead, she stood over him, watching the chisel flow along the soft wood, shaping a vine. He was right, of course. There was a rigid order in this world. A person knew where he stood in that order and how he must behave, how he must speak. In their different ways each fell into his place at birth, whether it was Mama's place or Père's or Agnes's. Money was part of it. Color was part of it. But—and this was very strange—mind, which should be most important of all, was not part of it.

A mind was a queer thing. Père had a book with a sketch of a brain, a gray lump, ridged and corrugated; you would have expected a brain to be more colorful, more like a mosaic, patterned with the pictures that your particular life had printed on it. And it seemed to her as if Clyde's mind and her own were of the same print, so that you could have set them beside each other in a continuous design, and there would be no jarring, no interruption.

Only their skins were different—and not all that different. Her sunburned hand, resting on the shelf a foot away from his working hand, was almost as dark as his.

He came to the end of the vine, curling it upward into a joyous flourish.

"There, how do you like that?"

"It's lovely. You're an artist, Clyde."

"Not really. I wish I were." But he was pleased. "There's a man in Spain, Antonio Gaudi, who does these flowers in stone. He's building a cathedral in Barcelona, all leaves and vines and even animal faces, a whole forest in stone. . . . The world's full of beautiful things."

How did he know of such things? He must have lived, must still live, in some village hut a world removed from Covetown, let alone Barcelona! And a soft compassion moved in Tee.

"That's all for today," he said, putting the tools away.

"See you tomorrow, then?"

"See you tomorrow."

So the weeks passed, and Tee was curiously happy, not lonely at all anymore. In the mornings at her bedroom window she watched the crows descending from the mountain to eat the *palmiche* of Père's royal palms along the driveway. The calm days stretched ahead. In the warm evenings after rain she stood at the window in her nightdress and heard the toads singing in the tree tops. She was so peacefully happy! She had no idea why. She did not even question why.

THE HAMMOCK ROCKED gently between two acoma trees behind the house; so tall were they that their tremendous tops were shaken by a breeze, although at ground level the burning air was still. Yawning, Tee laid the book facedown on her lap; in the house Père was taking his long Sunday nap; the whole world dozed.

She came awake. On the path beyond the rose beds Clyde was walking fast, swinging a bamboo birdcage.

"What have you got there?" she called.

"A parrot," he called back.

"Let me see!"

He set the cage down beside the hammock. In it stood an enormous parrot, two feet tall, a king of birds, marked splendidly in amethyst and emerald.

"Sisseron," he said proudly. "The imperial parrot."

"Where did you find him?"

"Caught him this morning. It was some job to catch him, I can tell you."

"What are you going to do with him?"

"I have a buyer. A sailor on an Italian ship, due back this month. I promised to get one for him, last time he was here."

The bird raised its wings and, there being no room in the cage to extend them, wearily dropped them again to stand in an attitude of patient waiting. Yet its round, alert, and curious eye seemed to respond to Tee's attention, and this aliveness was piteous, as though through the eye alone a plea were being communicated.

"He's so quiet," she said.

"He's not used to the cage yet. He's frightened."

"It's awfully sad, don't you think?"

"In a way, Miss Tee."

"When you think of how fast they can fly, how they love to fly! . . . They can live to be sixty years old, Père says."

"That's true. This is a young one. Two years, no more."

"So then . . . He has maybe fifty-eight years to spend in prison!"

Clyde looked down at the parrot, then looked away across the lawn.

"How much did the sailor promise to pay you?"

"I'm not sure. But a good price."

"Whatever he'll give, I'll give more."

"But—you want this parrot?"

"Yes. I want to buy him and let him go free."

Clyde was troubled. "If you feel that way about it, I'll let him go now, right here. I don't want any money."

"No, I'll pay. It wouldn't be fair otherwise. And we mustn't let him out here. We must take him home."

"He'll find his own way. Its just up the Morne."

"I want to see where they nest."

"They nest high up, in old palm trees. See his strong beak? He can bore a hole with that in a couple of minutes."

"I know. But I want to see where."

Clyde said reluctantly, "It's an awfully hard climb."

"You don't want to go? Then I'll go alone. Here, give me the cage."

"Miss Tee, you can't climb up there all by yourself. You'd get lost or fall or something."

"Come with me, then."

The way narrowed through ragged banana groves, then mounted steeply among palms and tree ferns which, fanning and crowning into the upper light, formed a crowd of green umbrellas under the sky. In somber shade, the path lay underfoot, dark as the bottom of the ocean. Tee climbed and stumbled. Ahead, Clyde strode easily, swinging the cage.

"I'll have to rest a minute!" she called.

He waited while she leaned against a tree.

"You know what kind of tree that is, Miss Tee? They call it candlewood because you can make a good torch with it for night fishing."

"Père says you're an expert fisherman."

"I like to fish, that's all. I like the sea."

"You like a lot of things. I wish I knew as much as you do, especially about this place where we live."

"Well, I do know this mountain like the back of my hand, anyway. I could show you things! I'll bet you've never seen the fresh water lake in the crater. Right inside the volcano. I've seen it."

"I haven't."

"And there's a pond not far from here, too hard a climb for you, though. A pond full of blind fish. It's in a cave. I went there with my teacher. There's a film on the water that looks like ice—my teacher's been in Canada so he knows—only it isn't ice, it's lime dissolving from the roof. You crack this film and you can see the fish beneath. Hundreds of them. They're blind because it's pitch dark in there and they've been there for generations. Come on, are you rested enough?"

Some minutes later there came a change, a feeling of great height. Coolness rippled through the air; the ground was wet and the rocks were covered with moss.

Clyde pointed. "Just about here is where the cane stopped. You can still see some of it, run wild."

"Cane, up here?"

"Oh, yes! In slavery days the cane covered the islands, halfway up the mountainsides. But now grass and jungle have grown back over whole plantations, whole islands even. Little out islands like Galatea and Pyramid, places like that, where they only pasture sheep today."

"What a wicked thing that was!" Tee cried.

"Wicked? What?"

"Why, slavery, of course! To own another human being! When I can't even bear to see this parrot locked up!"

"You're softhearted, Miss Tee. Don't you know there are people even today who wouldn't lift a finger to abolish slavery if it still existed?"

"I can't believe that! I can't think who would! Can you?"

"I can imagine, all right." Clyde laughed slightly. "But there's no sense talking about it."

She felt chastened, as if she had been scolded, the rebuke coming not so much from him as from herself. It had been really thoughtless of her to speak of slavery, to remind him of that terrible past! And she imagined that the knowledge of that past must be a secret, angry shame, attaching itself to a person like a painful burr. Yes, it would have to be like that.

Clyde whistled. Only a fragment of a tune, the few bars quivered into a plaint, thrusting a question into the neutral air. No, you will not get what you want, Tee thought with pity and foreknowledge, as if she were replying to his question. You're asking for music and color and brave things. I understand what you want. But you will probably die on this island with your tools in your hands. Père called you a scholar. Yet who will help you? If I could, I would. Yes, yes, I would.

The path dwindled and failed. Cracked limbs and trailing branches impeded their way. Great loops of lianas, thick as an arm, swooped overhead. Out of dark hollows, ferns cascaded like fountains. This was the world as God first made it, before man came. She felt their presence as intrusion here and was silent.

At last, abruptly, they broke into a clearing. It was a circular space about the size of a medium room, its floor a matting of low growth, its walls the embracing palms and acomas, tall as the cathedral in Covetown. From the topmost branches, a hundred feet above the ground, hung strong, green ropes.

"Kaklin roots," Clyde said, squinting upward. "Would you believe the roots are up there in the tree forks, while the plant grows down? The reason is, the parrots eat the kaklin fruit and drop the seeds in the trees."

"These look like roots in the ground, though," Tee said doubtfully.

"Yes, because they take root again. It's all planned out. You'd think the parrots knew what they were doing."

"Is this the place where you caught him?"

"Right here. Shall I let him go now?"

"Yes, do. Poor thing. Open the cage."

The door slid up. The bird, released, stood still a moment blinking into a shaft of light, as if not yet convinced of his freedom; stood flexing and stretching his brilliant wings; then, with a harsh and hideous cry, seemed to catapult himself into the air. Craning their necks, they watched his almost vertical flight: up he soared and disappeared into the crown of the highest palm.

An instant later the air was crisscrossed by a flight of parrots, a flapping and beating, a gorgeous flash and rush of wings. In seconds it was over and gone. And the stillness fell back.

Tee was awestruck. "This place is—is magic. I'll never forget it as long as I live, never. Or forget you for bringing me to see it." She took Clyde's hand. "Aren't you glad you let the bird go?" she whispered.

"If you are."

"Oh, I am! Can't you see I am?"

He looked down at her, murmuring as if to himself, "You're like ivory. Like those little statues your grandfather keeps on the shelves."

"Oh, those! Those are white jade. They came from China, ages ago. We had a great-great-uncle in the China trade."

"White jade, then. Or milk," he said. "Yes, pale as milk." And taking her free arm, he turned it over, to stroke it gently from elbow to wrist.

She was surprised, so surprised as to know no affront, only confusion. No one had ever touched her like that, with such tenderness, for theirs was not an affectionate family; they did not demonstrate. This was almost hypnotic, this soft stroking. It made a warmth in her cheeks, it made a weakness in her. She wanted it to continue and at the same time wanted to pull away: there was a kind of embarrassment in being examined as closely as this, in not knowing how to respond. And as if casually, she tried to withdraw her arm, but could not: he had tightened his hold and taken the other arm, too.

"You're lovely," he said. "You're one of the loveliest things in all the world."

The warmth burned now in her cheeks, burned all through her veins.

"I don't know. I never thought I was—"

"You never thought you were beautiful because you're not like all the others."

How does he know that? she wondered.

"Because you don't chatter and preen and do your hair according to the fashion books—"

She looked down at the ground where dark stems and leafage frothed like ocean spray around their feet. From somewhere a fragrance blew, vanilla-sweet, clove-sweet, making her head swim.

"You have heart, you have spirit—"

He drew her to himself, holding her up; she had no strength; he had it all. Never, never had she felt like this, so helpless, so selfless, floating as in a dream. Her head fell back.

"I'm not going to hurt you," she heard him say. And she looked up into a face gone unfamiliar, gone stern and strange. She did not understand.

"I would never hurt you," he repeated softly. "I love you . . ."

Then suddenly alarm shot through her. Why, why? Something was wrong here, something— She came out of the dream.

"No, no!" she cried, but the cry was cut off by a hand on her mouth. She was picked up, laid down, stretched upon the ground among the froth and foam of green. Not roughly, but with gentle and determined strength, she was held fast.

"No, no," she cried again, struggling against the hand upon her mouth; the other hand had worked quickly, so quickly, on the thin fabric of her dress, beneath which, but for the thinner fabric and lace of her underclothes, she was naked. Her mind ran, clicking like a frantic, racing machine: Yes, yes, this is what it is. Of course it is. This is what Justine was punished for talking about in school. This is it, this was it all the time. And I not knowing. How could I not have known?

Pinned down, pinned, nailed, thrashing, with her yellow skirt over her head. Birds, now squawking in the trees. Awful pain, awful pain and shock. Her own voice muffled against the cotton skirt, against the weight that bore upon her. Terror. Outrage. Disbelief.

In a minute or two it was over. She felt release. She could look up to where he stood above her, where he stood horrified, looking down where she lay naked and weeping.

"Oh, my God," he said. Oh, my God."

She heard him crashing down the mountain, heard the terror in his feet. A stone struck a rock; branches snapped. The heavy silence fell again. She stood up. I, I, she thought, and stopped crying. She pulled at the skirt, smoothing, smoothing, reached back then for the ribbon that had fastened her hair. In the morning Agnes ties the bow in my room where by eight o'clock the sun strikes between the jalousies and makes a dazzle in the upper right-hand corner of the mirror. Her hands trembled now but she managed a bow, not as neat as Agnes's. The bow and skirt are self-respect. It is all over and will never happen again, by God, now that I know what I know. But they will punish me for this.

And she began to run, run as though terror were still at her back, falling over a log where swarming ants stung before she could dash them away, speeding like mad down, down to where the trees ended and high razor grass whipped her legs. Ran and ran.

"Your dress is all grass stains! Where were you?" Agnes demanded. "Where were you?"

"I fell. There was a boulder on the path."

"Path? What path?"

"Up the Morne. I went for a walk."

"Up the Morne alone? Whatever for?"

"I wanted to. Isn't that reason enough?"

"Reason enough," she repeated arrogantly, and Agnes stared without answering, silenced by this voice of command which she had never heard from Tee before.

Of course, the arrogance was only terror and self-defense. For if I let go they will get the truth out of me. But why am I afraid if it was not my fault? But it was mine, partly, wasn't it? Oh, I could kill him, see him shot before my eyes, torn to pieces, and be glad of it. Still, it was partly my fault. Coaxing, inviting, stupid. Yes.

It crossed her mind that whenever there had been an accident, a near-drowning or a fall from a horse, they gave you brandy. Père kept it in a tantalus on the sideboard. It had a dreadful taste, bitter and burnt, but maybe it would stop the trembling. So she went to her room with the brandy glass, heard the evening-stir from the kitchen wing when dinner preparations began, heard wood pigeons coo on the lawn, and did not move. The brandy put her outside herself, so that she could see herself, withdrawn and secretive, curled like a cat, with a cat's wily, secretive face. . . .

Mustn't think of it. You can will a thing not to have happened. If you never think of it again, then it never was.

*   *   *

Père was heard, that day and the next, asking all over the house, "Where the devil is Clyde?" He was furious.

"He left me with half a wall of unfinished shelves and tools all over the floor. Irresponsible," he kept saying when, after two weeks, Clyde had not come back.

"I always told you," Julia declared over the telephone, "you can't depend on any of them. And you always said in another time and place he'd be a scholar."

"Well, I still think he would. What has that got to do with this?"

A terrible heat seared the earth for the rest of the month. Then storms came, thunder, lightning, and torrents of rain.

"What queer, unseasonable weather we are having," Père remarked. "Is it the weather that's making you so silent, Tee?"

"No," she said.

I only want to feel the way I felt before, when Clyde and I were friends. I hate the anger that's in me! Why did he do that? He's spoiled all the goodness we had. He knew how stupid and ignorant I was, yet he did that to me. And now there's no one to talk to anymore, not about anything and certainly not about this. I have so many questions. Whom can I ask? No one. No one.

Inside the house, the walls crushed down. Outside, the dark Morne towered and threatened. The sea glittered harshly. And there was no place in which to hide from loneliness, none, anywhere.

When the storms ceased, the heat came back to punish the land all that long, long summer. Tee woke in the mornings with her hair wet on the pillow, although she had pinned the mass of it to the top of her head. She sat up and, feeling dizzy, lay back again. Things buzzed in her head, buzzed and throbbed like crickets, like frogs. Saliva gathered in her mouth.

"I feel like vomiting," she said when Agnes came in.

"Again! It's pork. I tell them and tell them not to serve pork in this weather, but nobody listens to me."

A strong scent came from the vetiver mats on the floor. "No, it's these mats. . . . They're sickening."

"They never bothered you before! Why, they've a sweet smell! Tee!" Agnes cried sharply, for Tee's nightgown had fallen off her shoulders, revealing breasts grown noticeably larger. Tee retched in the basin and fell back weakly, the mound of her belly stretching a nightgown too tight.

"Let me see!" commanded Agnes. "Don't be silly, you've got nothing the rest of us haven't got! Oh, my God!" Her mouth opened in an enormous O. She pressed her hand against her lips, swallowed, and then, after a moment, spoke very quietly, very deliberately. "Listen to me, I'm asking you: When did you last have —you know—when was it last?"

"I'm not sure. Well, May, probably."

"Oh, my God! Not since May?"

"I think so."

"You think? You don't know? You don't know what's the matter with you? You haven't looked at yourself?"

"What is it? What, Agnes, what?"

"Jesus and all the saints, what is it, she asks! You're going to have a baby! You don't know that? Who was it? Where have you been?" Agnes screamed, shaking at Tee so that the gold earhoops swung. "Why, you've hardly been off this place since we came here!"

Tee could not speak for terror, and Agnes's eyes spread wide, searching the girl's face. "It's not—it couldn't be—it's not that devil Clyde? Talk! Talk!"

Tee stood up, swaying.

"Oh, my God, I told you, Tee, I told you—" And putting her arms out, the woman took the girl in, offering strong shoulders, soft breasts, incoherent comfort.

"You guessed this, didn't you? You must have. And were afraid to think it. Oh, you fool, you poor baby, poor child . . . that devil . . . what are we to do with you?"

She heard herself wail, "I didn't know. . . . Nobody ever told me."

And Agnes keened, "Oh, what are we to do with you? Dear God in heaven, what?"

The woman's terror infected the girl, so that gooseflesh rose on her arms and her teeth chattered.

"You're freezing, look at you!" Agnes drew the blanket over Tee. "In all this heat you're freezing." She rubbed Tee's back. She swayed and lamented. "Men! I told you—"

"You didn't tell me—"

"You're right, I didn't tell you enough. Men! You can't trust them, not the best of them, not any one of them. And the sooner a girl's taught that, the better for her. Oh, but this world's a rotten hard place for women, yes, yes—"

"What's going to happen to me, Agnes?"

"I don't know, but I know one thing, I'm going to take care of you, don't you fret a minute about that. Agnes will take care of you."

There, in the flowered room, in the ordinary morning, with the ordinary morning sounds of voices, mowers, and birds beyond the windows, the two cried themselves out, the girl weeping fear, the woman, wrath.

Like an animal afraid to leave its cage, Tee cowered in the room all week. Agnes brought food on a tray, but she could not eat.

"What does Père say?" she kept asking.

"What is there to say? His heart is broken."

"Will he ever talk to me again?"

"He will, he will."

She had to know what was going on, what was going to happen. Standing behind her door when it was ajar she could barely hear Père and Agnes talking in his study across the hall.

"At least our girls are taught how to be careful," Agnes lamented. "We teach them to carry scissors and hatpins in their dresses." Then she laughed. "It doesn't always work, but at least when something happens they know what's happening! Young white ladies—this poor child—stupid as babies until the day they marry!"

There came more inaudible talk, and at last Père said, "Well, be that as it may,

Agnes, this is the situation. . . . We love her, and we'll help her. If her mother were ever to find out—"

"Oh, God and all the saints, she'd kill her!"

"Not quite that," Père said somberly. "But her life wouldn't be worth living. Not around here, anyway."

No, nor Père's life either, Tee thought. She rested her head against the door. If I would just die and get it over with. . . . But I don't believe it, really. . . . There's a mistake. Something has got to happen to make it all right again. . . . Something . . .

"They found Clyde over on the other side of the island," Agnes said. "In Lime Rock. I think he's got family there."

"They have, have they? I want you to get word to him, Agnes. Tell him—tell him I want to see him. I need him to take me fishing. He knows how to handle my boat."

On the sixth evening Père came at last to Tee's room. She was just sitting at the window looking out into the dusk when she felt him standing in the doorway.

"May I?" he asked softly. He came in and sat in the opposite corner. "I've something to tell you, before I say anything else. I went fishing today. Clyde took me. There was—an accident. The ocean was unusually rough. He fell overboard and I wasn't able to reach him in time. . . . He never could swim very well."

She didn't answer.

"I thought you might want to know."

She looked at her grandfather, who was waiting for a response. His tired eyes held questions and concern. Her answering look was dull. She could feel the weight of the dullness within her. Clyde was dead and Père had caused his death. That was a simple fact, but her mind worked so slowly that it took some minutes to assimilate the fact.

Père stood above and behind her, stroking her hair. "A complicated business. Justice and mercy. Yes," he murmured, talking to himself. "Hard. Very hard."

So he was dead. Dead, too, were the Brownings, the imperial parrot, and Gaudi's stone flowers in Barcelona. Dreams. A boy's dreams. Why did you spoil it all, not only for me, but for yourself? You had so much to live for; even if none of the dreams were ever to come true, you still had so much inside yourself.

Strange, she thought, I don't feel the same anger I've been feeling. Some of it's there yet, but it's changed. Père's glad he's dead. But I'm sad, it's all so terribly sad.

Père said, "Tee, little girl, I've made my plans. You'll go to France. I have an old friend in Paris, an artist. He would do anything for me, and so for you. I trust him."

"France," she repeated.

"The French don't care about things like this as much as we do."

Scandals, he meant. Despite all his proud French blood, he always said they had no morals.

"And afterwards?"

"We'll see. One thing at a time. Agnes will go with you. On the ship she will dine separately, of course, but in France she can appear to be a friend. You can live together and eat together."

"At the same table with Agnes?"

"Yes, in France it can be done. They don't have the same ideas about color as other people do. She will take good care of you. She knows what to do. Shall we go and have something to eat? Agnes says you've been starving."

"I'm never hungry."

"Come, Adela is still in the kitchen. She can fix you some biscuits and fruit, at least. Come. They think you've been ill with a fever, that's all."

"Père," she whispered, "I don't know how brave I can be."

"You'll be brave. This family is tough."

"But I'm not." She was the timid and bookish one; hadn't they always told her so?

"Yes, you are. Tough inside. It's the slender tree that stands up in a hurricane, you know."

He put his arm around her shoulder. In the soft dusk, dark as it was, she could see the shine of his tears.

SHE WAS TO leave from Fort-de-France in Martinique at the end of the month.

"But she's too old to be sent away to school now!" Julia protested, meaning, She's fifteen and it's almost time to start meeting young men. She had already said this a dozen times and now, on Tee's last Sunday before departure, was saying it again.

Tee moved the soup spoon around the bowl of black crab pepper pot. This was a soup reserved for feasts, as were the turtle and goose waiting now on the gadroon-edged silver platters where the servants stood at the sideboard.

"In France you'll see snow," Virgil observed, making neutral conversation.

"It's like sand, in a way," Uncle Herbert explained energetically. "If you can think of sand coming out of the sky and being cold and white."

"You're not eating anything at all!" Julia cried.

"She's excited," Père rebuked Julia. "It's only natural before such a journey, isn't it?" But his eyes begged Tee.

For his sake she took another spoonful of soup. What shall I do without you, Père? I'm so afraid of going—and more afraid of staying.

So the dinner was got through and, two days later, the sailing.

High as the deck rose above the quay, Tee could still see the faces: Julia's tears and Père's persistent smile. They had been fueling the ship since first light, the women, bearing the coal on their heads, weaving a long line from the sheds to the hold. Now they were finished and the gangplank was taken down. *Compagnie Générale Transatlantique* was printed on its side. The ship trembled and backed away. From the fort the farewell gun boomed, sending a flock of gulls and boobies into frantic loops above the harbor. The ship turned in a great arc toward the open sea.

"I'm never coming back," Tee said.

"You will! Of course you will!" Agnes cried.

"No, never. Except perhaps to be buried. Yes, they'll bury me at home."

"What kind of talk is that at your age? Come below for coffee. There's a box of almond cookies and a cake."

"No, not yet."

Staring, staring, I stand at the rail. I'm leaving you, Père. I'm leaving you, Mama, and I'm sad about that, for in your way you love me, too. So many thoughts go round in my head! Who will ride Princess when the morning's still cool and bring sugar to the stable? Who'll sail the *Lively Lady* past the headland to Covetown? Will anyone ask about me when the new term starts at school, or wonder why I've gone? All my books—I suppose they'll give them away, like Papa's things when he died. And then there'll be nothing left of me on St. Felice, nothing at all.

So, now, good-bye. Good-bye to the Morne and the little Spratt River, to the wind and the sun and the girl I was. I'm not sure where I'm going, but I know I have to go.

By midafternoon they had doubled back northwest, passing St. Felice. It was too far away to be more than a curve against the windy sky. Or a turtle, Tee thought, as she had done when she was a child, a domed and sleeping turtle, resting in the sea.

❧ 2 ❧

A burst of wind rattled the north window of the attic studio.

"It's too bad we had to be so gray and gloomy on your first day in Paris. It must seem terribly forbidding after St. Felice," said Anatole Da Cunha.

Tee raised her eyes from where she had been looking at the tips of her dusty shoes and saw that he was studying her. His own eyes were mild and reddish brown, like his hair and the tips of his paint-stained fingers.

"Here, you may read the letter," he said.

Père's script was black and vertical, his signature like dark trees in a grove: Virgil Horace Francis.

"I don't need to. I know what it says."

"In that case, let's get rid of it. Watch me."

Torn paper fluttered into the fireplace, flamed at the edges, and was eaten up.

"So, Teresa, no one here knows anything at all about you except your maid, whom you trust, and myself, whom your grandfather trusts."

"Why does he?"

"Because I owe him something and he knows I won't forget it. When I was eighteen—I'm forty now—he befriended me. No need to go into details. He befriended me, I a Jew of no importance on the island—"

"You, a Jew? The Da Cunha family—"

"Is Jewish. Or was. They came from Portugal via Brazil in sixteen hundred and something. Traders, merchants, all over the islands. Of course, they're all Anglican now, except for my branch. I'm the last twig of a thin branch that hung on, for some reason or other. I haven't seen your grandfather in twenty years, the last time he was in Europe."

Everything overwhelmed, this day in which she had entered for the first time a great, pressing city, such as she could not have imagined: the incredible traffic, miles of houses, and this house on a street of walls so high that one saw only the roofs behind the walls. One felt trapped. Here in this chilly room pictures were stacked everywhere one looked; on an easel in the corner stood a portrait of a woman entirely naked, brazenly naked, no concealing shadow anywhere. Yet Père liked this odd man, so it must be all right.

"Marcelle!" Anatole raised his voice. "Come in now, Marcelle. Teresa, this is my friend, my lady. She lives here with me."

Tee put her hand out. Marcelle's long, pointed nails pricked her palm. She kissed Tee's cheek. Her sharp, intelligent face was unmistakably the face of the naked woman on the easel.

"Ah, yes," said Anatole. "Marcelle is the only other who knows why you're here. But don't worry. She has arranged everything for you in her village, a little house where you can be comfortable and you will not run into anyone who knows your family. No one will question you. Country people don't bother with strangers except to gossip behind their backs and why should you care about that? Tomorrow we'll be taking you there."

At THE END of the single village street lay the house, the last in a row of ancient houses between the church and the *mairie*. It consisted of a simple kitchen and two sleeping rooms.

Agnes sniffed haughtily. She had taken an immediate dislike to Anatole and Marcelle. "I must tell you, monsieur, Miss Teresa isn't used to places like this."

"I'm sure she isn't," Anatole said calmly. "But in the circumstances, first things first. You'll be warm and cared for, Teresa. In a few months—it's easy to say, I know—but in a few months it will all be over."

THE SEASON DEEPENED into an icy winter. Darkness settled in the old trees, and the lamps were lit early. At home now they would be having tea with chocolate cake, or at Drummond Hall, those wonderful crisp elephants' ears that Uncle Herbert brought from the patisserie in town. The four o'clock rain would have left a bright drop on the lip of a scarlet canna and the air would be cool on the back of your neck. In the stable yard Princess would be drinking from the trough, raising her aristocratic head to snort her pleasure, then dipping it again to drink. And Mama, with Baby Julia and Lionel—Tee blinked.

She had been reading the same sentence for the last five minutes. Her mind was three thousand miles away—or maybe it was four thousand? Sighing, she put the book away and folded her cold hands together.

Agnes was reading a newspaper. It was strange to see her thus at leisure. It occurred to Tee that she had never seen Agnes when she was not hurrying about at work. Up until now, she had never even seen Agnes eat! The business of eating, when you came to think about it—and in this time of waiting and isolation Tee had come to think of many curious things—was a very personal and serious business. Agnes ate delicately, reflectively, without sound. One wondered about her thoughts. Julia had once remarked that Agnes was surprisingly refined, *élevé au chapeau:* brought up to wear a hat, to have manners like a white girl. In the dusk now the gold beads, her *collier-choux,* gleamed against her brown neck.

"You're looking at my beads, you admire them? My lover gave them to me when I was fifteen, a little younger than you. It took him three years to pay for them." She laughed. "A good thing they were paid for by the time he got tired of me."

"You—lived with him—your lover?"

"Well, certainly I did! Naturally!"

"But you call Marcelle a bad woman because she lives with Anatole."

"Well, naturally. Because that's different. You shouldn't mix with people like Marcelle. You're not like me, you're a young white lady of good family. You're not like me," Agnes repeated. Her mouth twisted, as if in anger, or perhaps in sorrow.

I don't know her at all, Tee thought suddenly, aware of confusion in the other. I've never seen her except as a person who was there to do things for me.

Gloom crowded the room as cold seeped through the walls. The weight beneath the folds of her woolen skirt grew heavier. She wanted time to hurry; she wanted it to stand still so that the thing which was about to happen would never happen. But the clock rattled steadily, deepening both the silence and the dread.

When a bird whistled in a barren thicket at the window, Agnes looked up.

"Listen! *Siffleur-de-montagne!*" She sighed. "My God, I didn't know they had birds in this place. It's not fit to live in, even for birds."

Tee made an effort. "Oh, yes, in the spring they come back, thousands of them, Anatole says. And everything is green again."

"So then, we'll see. By spring your troubles will be past, anyway. That's one good thing."

Her troubles past! If they would just stop telling her that! Tears leaked, slid under closed eyelids and rolled over the trembling mouth from which no cry came. Her fists clenched as if to control her panic that those tears would never cease, that she would never end in a corner of some dim room shut away, curled knee to chin on a cot or sitting upright in a chair, just staring, staring with the useless tears brimming, like that poor cousin of the Berkeley family over at Belleclaire, the one it wasn't polite to mention.

"I'm sorry. I'm sorry, Agnes. I don't want to be such a nuisance, it's only that —that we're so alone here in this silence, it's like the end of the world."

"Ah, don't! You don't have to hide your wet eyes from me!"

"I really try—"

"Yes, yes you always did. You'd come in the house with a bloody knee, biting your lips so you wouldn't cry, poor baby! Listen, it's good to cry things out, then the lump in your throat won't choke you."

Agnes stood, letting the newspaper fall to the floor. "What a crazy world! Poor Tee, poor little Tee! If I could take what's in your belly and put it in mine! Forty-eight years I am and nothing to show for it! Can you imagine that? And how I wanted it, while here you are—"

"I hope I die."

"You're not going to. You're young and strong. You'll be walking around the next day."

Tee plucked at her swollen waist. "I hate this thing. And I'm sorry for it because I hate it. Can you understand that?"

"Yes. Yes. I'm sorry, too."

Agnes mourned. The little room was filled with mourning. Unbearable. Tee stood up, went in to the bedroom, and lay down. In the dimness she could barely see Anatole's half-completed painting propped on the dresser.

"Will you do something for me?" he had asked. "I should like to paint you as you are. I've never had a pregnant model."

Compliant, indifferent, she had sat for him, or rather, reclined, close to dozing, while he worked and talked.

"The fruitful body. It's beautiful, you know. Don't shake your head! Some day
you'll feel what I mean, you'll have wanted children, you'll be proud. You don't
think so now, but you will."

He rambled, musing, thinking aloud, as if he did not care whether she heard
him or not, and indeed she had not cared, either, whether she heard him or not.
Yet now there were echoes in her head.

". . . a strange history, our bloody little island. All the islands. At one time
they used to fine a planter who fathered a mulatto child. Two thousand pounds of
sugar, I think the fine was. And the woman, with the child, was confiscated and
given as a slave to the monks. That was when the French were in control. Well,
there was always a shortage of white women, you know. Back in the seventeen
hundreds they even sent a shipload from Paris. Poor wretches, gathered up from
God knows where, their only qualifications that they weren't pockmarked and
were young enough to bear children! Talk of your island aristocracy, your first
families! Yet there came a time when a touch of dark had a certain *style*. Like
Alexandre Dumas. And they say even the empress Josephine, although I'm not
sure—"

Now Tee rocked her head from side to side on the pillow. It was all too much,
too much thinking. Two Clydes, the gentle, feeling, comprehending—and then
that other. Two Pères, the generous, the tender—and the one who had killed. For
her. He had killed for her. And all this horror had come out of those few minutes,
only an inch's worth of clock ticks; all this dread, because of a caged bird and a
drowsy afternoon, and—and a stupid, ignorant girl who hadn't even understood
her own feelings!

With cold hands she covered her burning face. In the kitchen the clock
struck, sounding distant and faint, so that with part of her mind she knew that
sleep must be on the way. Oh, the comfort of sleep and the long nights of escape!
If only they could be twice as long, to envelop the days and blot them out! Past,
present, and future, all blotted out!

There are those who cannot sleep when they are beset, but Tee was able to,
and perhaps it was that which saved her.

WHEN THE INCREDIBLE pain was past, she heard low talking in the kitchen. Then
the voices grew louder.

". . . a strong boy. Could pass for Syrian or Greek." That was Marcelle.

There came a rich sound, part cooing, part singing. That was Agnes.

Presently Anatole spoke. "Wrap him up and take him to the nurse. Just till we
can get her up in a couple of days and back to Paris."

Three voices rose together, with a certain agitation in their mingling. Raising
her head, Tee could see, through the partly open door, long shadows moving on
the kitchen wall.

"Listen," Anatole said. "We arranged it all before and there's nothing more to
discuss. She's not to see him! It's humane, it's sensible, it's what's done in cases
like this. She can't keep him, so why start up? Take him away, Agnes. Right now."

"But shouldn't I?" Tee murmured. "Mustn't I?"

"Shouldn't you what, my dear?" Marcelle had come in and was standing by the bed.

"Look at the—"

"No." Marcelle spoke firmly, her lips snapping shut on the word. "No."

Now came the infant's first cry. Quavering and long it held, then broke for the intake of breath, quavered into a strong wail and ended in a sob. The sound tore at something in Tee's chest. Here he is, after the long months; unsought for, unwanted, already he weeps—

"I want to see him," she whispered.

"No, I said. There's nothing to be gained by doing that, and much to lose. Now lie back and rest, there's a good girl, and leave everything to us, will you?"

Conscience, guilt, relief, all clamored in Tee's tired head. Still she protested. "But isn't it monstrous of a mother"—and stopped at the word *mother,* so incongruous, so impossible, applied to herself.

"Monstrous!" Marcelle was indignant. "Yes, that a girl—a child—like you should be in a fix like this, that's what's monstrous! Listen here, Teresa, you've got to look out for yourself from now on. Self-preservation, that's the main thing, always, and don't you ever forget it."

"You listen to her, she's right." Agnes came in and bent over the bed. "Better you don't look at this baby. He go his way, you go yours. No way you can walk the same road together. Not in this world, the way it is. Here, let me fix your ribbon, lift all that hair off your neck."

Yellow ribbons, pink ribbons, taffeta and velvet; blue shadows from the Morne leaping from the window to the mirror; Agnes tying the bow—

"Don't cry, Tee. You've cried enough. Now get your strength back. You're all worn out."

"Stop torturing yourself, stop worrying," Marcelle admonished. "Haven't I been telling you Anatole would see to things? You're not to bother your head. Anatole has got instructions and plenty of money, and Agnes is going to keep the child. Tell her, Agnes."

"Well, you know me, you know what I always wanted. So now I can have what I want, can't I?" Two warm, wiry hands held Tee's between them.

"Yes, it's a fine solution all the way around, don't you think?" Marcelle spoke cheerfully. "Agnes'll pass him off as her own. Probably they'll stay in Marseilles. It's a polyglot place with all kinds of people always coming and going, so she won't feel strange there. Don't you agree it's a good idea?"

"A good idea," Tee repeated. So the need to think and decide had been taken away from her. Better so. She wasn't thinking clearly and hadn't been able to for a long, long time.

"Your lips are cracked. Take some water. So," Marcelle said briskly, "it's all over. All over, Teresa."

Tee looked up into the alert, strong face. Such faces belonged to people who solved things, who knew their way in the world.

"Where am I going to go?" she asked softly. "What am I going to do now?"

"Well, do you want to go back home?"

Home to Père and the silent knowledge that would forever lie between them. Home to Julia. Home to Morne Bleue. You could scarcely go anywhere on the island without looking up at Morne Bleue, unless you stared straight out to sea.

"No. I'm not going back. I'll never go back again."

"Never is a long time. Still, it's understandable. So you'll stay with us, that's all. Anatole will think of something," Marcelle said with pride. "He always does."

THE ROOM ON the top floor of Anatole's house had a balcony on which stood three pots of geraniums. From it one could look out and watch the city wake up, that city of which Père had so often told, city of flowers and delights. But there was no temptation in it.

Tee shivered, although the late spring sun was warm. She passed her hand over her waist, which was flat and firm again.

"That comes of being young," Marcelle said cheerfully. "The muscles snap back like rubber."

Tee thought again, I should at least have looked at it—the words *he* or *him* being impossible to form in her mind. Yet she knew that if "it" had been brought to her, she would have been too terrified to look. So of course she had done right. Where would you go with it? What would you do with it? Marcelle and Anatole had said, over and over.

"When will you get this girl some clothes?" Anatole inquired one day.

"Whenever she's ready. I've asked you often enough, haven't I, Teresa? I want to teach you how to dress, so you won't look like a provincial when you go places."

"What places am I going to? I've nowhere to go."

"No, only the entire city of Paris. Or do you expect it to come to you on your balcony?"

Tee was growing used to Marcelle's sharp tongue and able to smile a little.

"Do you know you're very, very pretty when you smile? Do you know that?" Anatole demanded.

"I'm not pretty."

"Who told you?"

"No one. I've just always known it."

"Well, you've known all wrong."

"I'm awkward, too serious, too shy. I—"

"Awkward? You have extraordinary grace! You are too serious and shy, that's true."

"Leave her alone, Anatole. Will you go out with me tomorrow, Teresa? The first thing we ought to do is get your hair cut."

"Oh, what a shame!" Anatole protested. "That hair—it's positively aphrodisiac."

"Yes, but nobody wears it like that anymore. This is 1938."

So now in the mornings they would descend the steep flight before Sacré Coeur and go down into the streets, Marcelle guiding Tee as though she had been ill or were blind, and talking, always talking, at the hairdresser's, the shoe store, and the milliner's.

"Watch that young girl, Teresa."

"Who? Where?"

"That one, in the blue dress with the fortune in pearls around her neck. That old man, in case you want to know, is certainly not her father. Pay attention, Teresa my dear, you're always dreaming. What were you thinking of, you were so far away?"

"Thinking how odd it is never to see a dark face."

"I shouldn't think you'd miss them."

"I miss Agnes. I think of her."

"Well, she was good to you, I must say, although she got paid for it. But she's well provided for and content. What we have to do now is to provide for you."

They walked on silently for a little time until Marcelle spoke again.

"Anatole and I have been talking it over. You will have to get married soon, Teresa. It will be the best thing for you. There's really nothing else for a woman, anyway. Yes, you're thinking, 'She's a fine one to talk about marriage!' But you're not me. You saw where I came from. I'm better off with Anatole than I ever was, even though he won't marry me. Yes, I'd like to be a respectable married lady, only I can't be, and that's that. But it's different for you."

"Strange. That's what Agnes always said."

"Of course. She's a realist. Negroes have to be. They know what the world is, how the machinery works."

A young couple passed and entered a park. The father carried a young child astride his shoulders.

Looking after them, Tee said bitterly, "Who would marry me? Who would want me?"

Marcelle stopped still. "My God, what kind of ten dozen fools are you? You don't actually mean you would tell a man what happened?" Then, more softly, she went on, "Listen, Teresa, you've had bad luck, a bad deal, and the sooner you put it behind you the better for you. Lock it up at the back of your head. Do you think every girl who marries a duke brings a notarized personal history along? Women have to be very smart, Teresa. Never be fooled into thinking you can bare your whole soul to a man. Any man who knew the truth about you would throw you away like a paper handkerchief after he'd blown his nose in it. That's the injustice of being a woman. A man may tell you he loves your soul, but what he really loves is your body, fresh and unused, your hair, your breasts, and the ribbons on your charming hat. Remember that."

"It's so terribly sad," Tee said. And she understood that if Julia had been one to speak her true mind, she would have spoken like Marcelle.

"Well, yes, if you want to think so, but that's the way it is, all the same."

"You're beginning to feel better," Anatole remarked that evening and, without waiting for an answer, "Come, I want to show you something. I've finished it. I've put you in a grape arbor, you notice."

Already framed, beneath a splendor of leafage and clustered grapes, sat a girl, a stark and simple shape in a brown woolen dress, her face half concealed by the fall of her rich hair; her thin, cold, blue-white hands were folded over the huge curve of her belly in an attitude of patience which she had not felt.

"The grapes are ready to harvest. A nice parallel, don't you think?"

"It doesn't seem as if I could ever have looked like that."

"Perhaps I shouldn't have shown it to you?"

"It's all right. I can't hide from myself forever, can I?"

Anatole's red-brown eyes puckered in a smile. "You're growing up. A few months ago you were sixteen, with the mind of a twelve-year-old; now you're even a little older than your age. You really have changed, Teresa."

Well, changing anyway, she thought, if not changed.

"I think you're ready now," Anatole said next.

"Ready for what?"

"There's a young man I want you to meet. An American. He's a stockbroker and an art collector. That's how I know him. He's been coming here for the last few summers."

She waited a moment or two before replying, "I know why you're doing this."

"Of course. I'm thinking he would be a good man for you to marry, if it should work out that way."

"No, I mean I know *why*. You really don't believe in this sort of thing."

Tee surprised herself with her own words. Only a few months before, she had not known enough to "size up" anyone, nor would she have spoken so candidly if she had. But a bold instinct for survival was now rising within her.

"You have two sides," she said. "One for yourself, the artist who lives the way you do and believes what you believe, but the other is practical, like the rest of the world. You're doing this because it's what Père would want you to do for me."

"Not bad!" Anatole laughed. "Then you'll meet him? He's healthy, decent, and has enough money of his own not to be attracted to you for yours. His name is Richard Luther."

AT FIRST SIGHT of him, so finely dressed and out of place in Anatole's studio, she thought that Anatole had made a foolish mistake. This blond, assured young man with the easy smile and the air of always getting what he wanted could not be for her, nor she for him. The world, and Paris most certainly, was full of lively, confident girls who knew where they were and where they were going. What would he want with Tee Francis? So she gave him her hand and avoided his eyes.

But later in the room upstairs Marcelle said, "Anatole was right. Frankly, I didn't think you'd be his type. He likes you, though. He wants to take you to the theater tomorrow."

They went to a play and afterwards to supper, at which he ordered oysters, raspberries, and champagne. From a vendor on the corner he bought an extravagant sheaf of gladioli for Tee to bring home.

"Tell me about St. Felice," he urged. "It sounds so strange to me, like Patagonia or Katmandu. Who lives there? Is it all sugarcane? Do they have pineapple? Telephones? Do you have great parties on the estates? Tell me about it."

She laughed and was pleased at his curiosity, pleased at having been given something to say. And while saying it she understood that St. Felice had been the cause of attraction, that St. Felice—and therefore she herself—was exotic to Richard Luther, something new. He was a person who would want the different and the new: the latest fashion, the artist about to be discovered, the master chef in the tiny restaurant at the end of the hidden street. Having taken from all these what he wanted, then he would be off to something newer. So it would be with her, she saw.

Meanwhile, though, Richard gave her what she needed that summer, what she had not even been aware of needing. He gave cheer. Life was to be enjoyed. He was kindly (sugar lumps for the drayhorse at the end of Anatole's street); generous (a pocketful of francs for the flower vendor and an admonition to go home out of the rain). They were constantly on the move: a picnic in the country, a boat ride, the races, the art exhibits, the auctions, where he bought beautiful, expensive objects, which did not surprise Tee, for had not her mother also been a buyer of extravagant objects?

She went with him, then, a quiet presence, an observer, almost, of his enthusiasms, carried along, bemused and soothed.

Anatole asked no questions, but Marcelle probed for him. "What do you think of Richard, Teresa?"

"I don't know."

"You are the strangest girl! What do you mean, 'you don't know'?"

Actually, Tee was thinking, Is he, or is he not, just a little conceited? Is his face, so handsomely symmetrical, a little weak? And puzzled, she answered with a question.

"I have no means of comparison, have I?"

Marcelle softened. "True, true. I keep forgetting how young you are. Well, take it from me, he's ready for marriage, it's the right time for him. He's twenty-five, he's done all the sampling he wants. And you're different from anyone he can have known. Only sixteen! There's charm in that."

"I suppose I am different." What did he call her? Dark child, aloof—

"Your family would be pleased. He'll make a good husband."

"He hasn't asked me." In fear her heart accelerated, partly because he might not ask her (for what was she to do then?), and partly because he might.

Late in the summer, when it was almost time for him to go home, Richard Luther did ask her. They had left the bookstalls, where he had bought two old volumes, when he stopped and took a flat box out of his pocket.

"Open it," he said.

On gray velvet lay a triple strand of tenderly shining pearls.

"For you, Teresa. Pearls for the young and innocent. Diamonds for a little later."

"But I can't accept a present like this!"

"I know you can't, not from a stranger. This is just my way of asking you to marry me."

"You hardly know me!" she cried.

"I know enough. Teresa—it's a gentle name, like you. I'd be very good to you. You know that, don't you?"

"Yes," she whispered.

"I've lived in New York with my mother since my father died. My mother would be enchanted with you," he said confidently. "But of course we'd have our own place. We could have a country house, too. I've been thinking about New Jersey; there are miles of soft hills; they might even remind you of your mountains at home."

Still she hesitated.

"Are you thinking that you want to go back to St. Felice? Is that it?"

Her hands went unconsciously to her throat. "Oh no, oh no, I don't want to go back, ever!"

"Yes, now that you've started to see the world, I can understand that. Well, then? I do love you, Teresa."

They were standing at the river where the bridges, in both directions, arched like loops in stone, time-stained, yellowing and streaked. For minutes Tee looked down. So long ago, in another age, she had stood watching a river twist to the sea, watching the same slow flow of water, the little froth and bubble, the water, like time, maybe, carrying things away, the self with the flow.

Oh, I can, it can be, I want—she thought, as she turned to him. He's a good man, so lively and kind. He's a happy man. You feel happy yourself when you're with him! You feel as if nothing would ever hurt you. You'd never be alone anymore.

He put his arms around her. Smiling, he stroked her cheeks and her hair. His face glowed with his smile, making a glad hope surge in her. Perhaps this, after all, was love, the real and true, and it would keep on growing forever. Oh, she would return his kindness, his goodness, ten times over, be everything he wanted, surprise him beyond his expectations.

And at the same time she was thinking, We have nothing to talk about, and I don't know if we ever will have. . . .

They were to be married quite simply in Anatole's small, unkempt garden. There were, in the preceding weeks, moments that stabbed her.

"Will I ever make this work?" she cried to Marcelle. "Tell me, how can it possibly work?"

"Why not? Why shouldn't it? Listen, you'll be a good wife, you couldn't be anything else, and he's crazy about you. Have many children, that's what will be best for you. You're the type for it and it'll keep both of you busy and happy. Above all, no guilt, no looking back! Never. Do you hear?"

So, on a gilded autumn day, just one year after she had arrived in France, Teresa Francis married Richard Luther. The very next morning they sailed for New York.

Richard's mother was indeed enchanted by the bride. "How young! How shy and young!" she said, and everyone marveled, "Born on an island in the West Indies, imagine!" And someone whispered, "There's no end to the wealth those people have there. . . ."

Well, anyway, they gathered her to themselves, and even in a New York winter, they warmed her. Richard went back to the brokerage office and was gone all day while Tee furnished a house. This world now was so different from St. Felice that one could forget its very existence. Besides, she was already pregnant. . . .

Eleven months after the marriage, she gave birth to a fine, large boy, fair like his father. Sitting up in her flower-filled hospital room, Tee held the child close, laying her cheek on his head. Here, here was repayment for everything! Hers now, her own! Never to love anyone as much as him; never to be loved by anyone as much as by him. She would be such a mother to this child! Nothing would ever hurt him, not the rough sleeve of his father's coat, nor the faintest draft from the door to the hall. There was something special between the two of them.

And indeed it was to be so, although she could not really have known it then.

On the day of his christening the baby wore the lace robe that had been in the Luther family for five generations. Afterwards they brought him home and took his picture with his parents on the velvet sofa in front of the fireplace, then laid him lovingly to sleep in his nursery upstairs.

His name was Francis Virgil Luther.

BOOK TWO

COMING HOME

{3}

He knew he had been born far across the sea, but he had no recollection of the long voyage back to St. Felice, eighteen days from Marseilles. His mother said, "I didn't like it over there, Patrick. Too many strangers and too cold. So I brought you home."

His mother was Agnes, pronounced, as he later learned, with the accent on the second syllable, in the soft French way. She was strong. Her tongue could be sharp. When she gave him an order, she wanted immediate obedience. Yet, from her dark hands with their pink palms, he received, it would seem to him when he was old enough to think about it, daily and continual blessing: food, bandages for the bruised knees of childhood, and comfort when he was afraid. Sometimes he was very much afraid: of what? Of nameless things, of spirits among sighing trees, of being lost and losing her.

He was never very far away from her. As soon as he learned to walk, he followed her everywhere, from early morning, when they woke in the cabin, through the day in the big house, where she worked, and back to the little room again, where she gave him his supper and put him to bed.

The big house was vast and open, with tall doors, verandas, and wide halls through which breezes blew. The house had a shine to it; he had an impression of silver and shine. Even the dark tables and chairs had a silver shine when Maman polished them. It seemed to him that that was what she did all day, rubbing things to a glow: floors, teapots, and mirrors.

From the first he understood that this was not Maman's house. She was different there. *Shush,* she would say when he spoke too loud. In their own room she never said that. There she was loud herself, singing and rocking him. When other women came by in the evenings, they laughed together in high, shrill voices, talking fast, clapping each other on the back, swaying with laughter. And he would stand wondering at their laughter, not understanding it, yet in some nameless way enjoying it.

Little by little he learned to place himself in the world. The big house belonged to Mr. Kimbrough, a quiet man with a dry, white face and a white linen suit. Mrs. Kimbrough was white too; her hair was like chicken feathers.

In the kitchen of that house the faces were dark. The kitchen people were not nice. Tia, the cook, sat at the head of the lunch table; Loulou, who did the laundry, and Cicero, who served the Kimbroughs' meals on that other table in the dining room, sat across from Patrick and Maman.

"He certainly doesn't look like you, with that complexion," Tia would start slyly. She would shake her head while Patrick lowered his face to his rice and peas, away from her stare. "No, he certainly does not."

And Maman would answer, "How many times I tell you he is the son of a Frenchman? Born in France, you know that as well as I."

"A Frenchman, hey? And rich too, I suppose?"

"Rich enough, anyway, so I don't need to worry too much about this boy here."

"Why you working in this place then? You have so much money, why don't you quit?"

"I just might. I just might open a little shop somewhere, when I find the right place. Not in Covetown, though. The price is too dear."

Now would come Loulou's turn. "You boast too much, Agnes. Why didn't you stay in France, you had it so good there?"

"Because"—spoken scornfully—"because I came home to show off my boy, my baby you all thought I couldn't have."

Laughter, then. Years later he would recall it, only then comprehending the cruelty of such laughter, the sting of pleasure at someone else's expense, someone else's weakness or humiliation.

"Well, good you had him at last," Loulou would say. "If a woman never have child she bound to have troubles up here," and would tap her head significantly.

Then Tia: "Let's see how many more you can have, old as you are." Tia herself has nine children whom she talks about freely and rarely sees; they are cared for by her mother on the other side of the island.

Then Maman firmly: "I don't want any more. This one is precious enough. I want to bring him up right. Can't do that with too many pulling at your skirt."

He would remember a feeling which later he understood was confidence and safety. *This one is precious enough. I want to bring him up right.*

And he would remember old, disconnected moments, probably not in the right order or in rank of importance, though what was important was not always easy to know.

There was a house on a hill at the end of a long drive. They had been riding in cars and busses, riding and walking all day, looking for a shop to buy, Maman said. His legs ached.

"What place is this now?" he wanted to know.

"It's called Eleuthera."

"What does that mean?"

"I don't know. It's a name, that's all."

Eleuthera. He liked the sound of it. Words were pretty. On Sundays the preacher talked too long with a kind of dull roaring, so that he usually fell asleep, but sometimes proud words woke him up: celestial, eternity, paradise. Now: Eleuthera.

A tall thin man stood on the veranda.

"I was passing," Maman said. "I thought you might want to have a look at this boy."

The man didn't speak. He was silent for so long that Patrick looked up at him, questioning.

After a while the man said softly, "You shouldn't have brought him, Agnes."

"You've nothing to worry about, you know that," Maman said. "I won't bring him again."

The man put his hand on Patrick's head. "You'd like some cake and milk, wouldn't you?"

"No," Maman said, "he doesn't want any." But he did want some.

"Well then, some money for toys when you get back to town?"

He would remember of that day that she did buy him some toys, but he forgot what they were.

One day she said, "I'm going to open the shop now, at last."

"Like Da Cunha's, will it be?" For he had already remarked on the shops along Wharf Street: the bakery where you bought sweet rolls; the candy shop with whistles and balloons; then, at the far end near the hotel, Da Cunha's, where, peering in, you saw in the cool dimness, under the slowly whirling fans, tall shelves of bottles, clocks, glass, and china, all the gleaming things that reminded him of the Kimbroughs' house.

Maman laughed. "No, of course not. Those things are not for us. No, I mean to sell shirts and dresses to our own folks. And I can alter free of charge. That's one thing I learned when I was growing up. I can handle a needle."

"Will it be on Wharf Street?"

"No, not in Covetown. In Sweet Apple. It's a fishing village, and we'll be living right across from the beach where they pull the boats in. You'll like it there."

She had bought a good house, the best in the village. The owner had labored in America, had come home to build it and there died. It had a foundation, not stilts like the other houses; it had two bedrooms, its own well in the yard and running water inside. In the front room Maman put a counter and shelves. This was to be the store, their livelihood, the place where she was to spend her years.

Now he could venture out into the life surrounding. On certain days he saw the farmers bring their mangoes and bananas from the hills to market. He stood at the green to watch the older boys play cricket with palm-branch bats. Down on the beach he saw how nets were mended, how a circle of boats was drawn to trap a school of lobsters. Schooners came and went from Grenada and St. Lucia; he wondered what those places were like, whether the trees were the same there or the sky the same. . . . Sometimes a new boat was launched and that was a whole day's excitement, the men tugging the boat inch by inch on great logs across the sand, while a steel band played and somebody got to break a bottle of rum and people danced.

Sometimes, when his mother gave him a penny, he liked to go to Ah Sing's grocery store, the Chinaman's store. There were rows of canned goods with bright labels and a shelf of candy in jars. Soon he was aware that Ah Sing gave him more than his penny's worth. He had a nice smile and sometimes took a walk far up the beach with Patrick, talking with an accent that made Patrick miss every other word. Ah Sing taught him how to open a conch shell, how to watch out for the claw that can be hiding there even though you think the creature's dead; how to pull the body out of the shell, cut off the sickle, and clean it.

"Take it home to your mother and remind her to mix half sea water with the fresh when she makes the stew."

He remembered that. And Ah Sing taught him to swim and how to raise a pig, which he kept with the chickens in the yard behind the house.

But mostly, as befitted his age, he played, and his days passed sweetly, circling through unchanging seasons without aim, except as a plant stretches toward the sun or butterflies circle in the afternoon.

Then one day he was no longer a baby. He started school. Not everybody started school; you didn't have to go if you didn't want to, if your mother complained that she didn't have the money for uniforms, or if you were needed to help on the sugar estate in crop time. But Patrick had a supply of dark blue shorts and white shirts; his mother wanted him to go.

"Learn," she commanded, with her hands on his shoulders. "Learn, so you won't grow up and have to work on a sugar estate. Listen to the teacher and behave yourself, hear?"

That was strange, because sometimes she said, "You won't have to work on a sugar estate, thank God for that." Anyway, he didn't know what was so wrong about working there. The men in the village, those who didn't fish for a living, all worked on Estate Sweet Apple, the plantation from which the village took its name. So he left for school with a certain confusion, a feeling that he was being sent off to do something hard, that he would naturally hate.

Instead, it turned out to be delight. The whistle of the schoolmistress, bringing the class to attention, became in those first years a summons to a new kind of pleasure. On the long bench under the trees he plowed obediently through arithmetic so as to get it over with quickly, waiting for the big books with their stories of knights who fought with swords and rode their horses in places with strange names. All those things happened a long time ago, he wasn't sure when, probably before he had been born.

Sometimes the teacher held up pictures. There was a stone church much bigger than the one in Covetown.

"An abbey," she said. "Westminster Abbey."

"What is an abbey?" Patrick asked, but she didn't answer.

Then there was a long car called a railroad and this, too, was in England. There was a picture of a man with a pointed long face and large, pale, bulging eyes; he was the king, George the Sixth, and you were his subject, you belonged to him.

"That means you are English," said Mistress Ogilvie.

"We are English, did you know?" he asked his mother.

"Why, who told you that?"

"The mistress."

"Ah, well. We were slaves of the English. Did she tell you that too?"

"I don't know."

"You didn't know we were slaves?"

"I think somebody told me. But there aren't any more now, are there?"

"No slaves? *They* make the laws, *they've* got the jails! And so, what are *we*? I ask you, what are *we*?"

He stood there, feeling the knotted frown on his forehead, uncomfortable in the face of her strange anger.

"Ah," she said abruptly. "I shouldn't talk like that! There's nothing I can do about it, and it only gives me a headache, anyway."

She could say such odd things, things to make you think she hated the people who owned the estates; then, at other times, she would admire some white lady they might see on a trip to Covetown.

"Ah, but there's quality! So well dressed, such fine manners!"

It was confusing. So much, it seemed, depended upon skin: what people thought of you and said about you. He knew, for instance, that people whispered in the village about his mother and about their house. She never told him, and he understood that she never would, yet here and there he overheard enough to bring him some vague understanding that her little money had come from a white man, the man who had fathered him.

Over the dresser in his mother's room there was a mirror. Standing on a chair, he could see how light he was compared with the people he knew, excepting, of course, people like the Kimbroughs. None of the children in school was as light.

So he wondered about color and faces, Ah Sing's, for instance, with his peculiar, narrow eyes.

"That's because he's Chinese," Maman said, which was no explanation at all. It was confusing.

ONE EVENING SHE told him a story. He had been lying, for hours, it seemed, too hot to sleep. Lightning flared; the air was heavy and he felt the melancholy of oncoming storm. At the window where his bed stood he could see the yellow, flashing sky. Yellow is always angry, he thought. It was not the sort of thought he would express aloud; it would seem a stupid thing to say. Still, he always thought that colors were saying something: orange, for instance, looked surprised, as though something nice had happened unexpectedly. It was amazing what you could do with words.

Thunder rolled and cracked; rain pounded the tin roof; a terrible crash shook the house. Maman came over and sat on Patrick's bed. He moved nearer to her, ashamed of being scared.

"You think a storm like this is anything? I remember when Mount Pelée blew up. That was in 1902, the eighth of May, and that boom was bigger than any thunder you'll ever hear! People thought it was Judgment Day. They even felt the ground shake here on St. Felice, can you imagine that? No, you can't, nobody could imagine what it was like. A cloud came out of the mountain; first it looked like smoke from a burning house, but it kept on coming, until it filled the sky"— in the three-quarter dark Patrick could see that she was leaning forward and gesturing with her arm—"filled the sky all purple and red as blood, a fearful, ugly thing. It made you think of hell. . . . Then the ash came, falling hard as rain. It smelled like rotten eggs. Sulfur, they said. We closed the shutters tight, but the ash got in anyway and covered the floors. And centipedes got into the house, a foot long some of them, trying to get away from the ash upriver. We poured boiling water on them. I was a maid at the Mauriers' then, my first position. I was hardly more than a child, but it was good working there, better than being a porteuse, I can tell you."

"What's a porteuse?"

"You know, the girls who load the ships, carrying the coal or rum or sugar on their heads. They worked twelve hours a day, then, got four dollars a month. . . . So I was well off at the Mauriers'. We kept right on working, everyone did in St. Pierre. The mountain stopped rumbling after a few more days and so we thought the ash would soon stop falling. But the country people kept coming in. They thought St. Pierre would be safe. Farther up the mountain, they said, the hot mud was rolling still, choking the rivers, and the ash so thick on everything that the birds were dying in the trees. Then suddenly in our yard the birds began to die, too."

"Why didn't you go away?" He sat up now, so interested that he had forgotten the storm.

"Well, Mr. Maurier took his wife to Fort-de-France, but the servants had to stay and guard the house. The city was full of thieves, people sleeping in the streets, stealing from the shops and fighting. It was terrible, terrible." She paused. "Then came La Veretta, the smallpox. So many died, they ran out of coffins. It's funny," Agnes reflected, "how people think that nothing can ever happen to them. Not brave, I think, only stupid. Leon, the butler, had such a nice room in the Mauriers' house, he didn't want to leave! Just sat there with a bottle of the best wine from the cellar. 'Sit tight,' he said. 'It'll pass.' But I wasn't so sure. Fires were breaking out all over town. Leon sent me in to buy things; *he* wouldn't go on account of La Veretta! It's good he sent me, otherwise I wouldn't have seen the mud coming. I saw it sliding down the mountain and I knew as well as I know my name that that was the end of St. Pierre. So I found a man with a fishing boat and I gave him the five dollars Leon had given me. I told him to get me away, anyplace, I didn't care where, but get away.

"We were just out of the harbor when the mud wall hit the sugar factory. You would have to see it to believe it, Patrick! It covered the factory—and that was a big place, let me tell you—covered it up. It was gone in a minute, gone with all the people in it. Oh, God! And the mud kept rolling into the harbor, driving the sea away. When the water came rushing back, it lifted the ships in the harbor like chips of wood and drowned them, drowned the whole city before it pulled back into the bay. Behind the city the cane fields burned and I knew the Mauriers' house was gone, too, with Leon drinking wine in his nice room. The sky was black as night. I never saw St. Pierre again," she finished, very quietly.

"Don't you ever want to?"

"I could go. I've got a piece of land there, family land that was given to us when the slaves were freed. My cousins live on it, but I've got the right to go back any time I want, of course—I'm family. I don't want to, though."

"Why? Was it a bad place?" Patrick liked this talk. It was grown-up talk and he wished it would go on.

"Oh, they say it was a wicked city, the theater and dancing and all that. They say it was like Paris. But that's not true. I've been in both places and I know. Ah, but it was a grand life! Sundays when the family went calling, Madame Maurier wore her diamond bracelets over her kid gloves, and they'd ride in the coach with their fine horses and the coachman with his gilt buttons—"

"Did you ride in the coach, too?"

"Who, I!" She laughed. "Of course not! I worked my feet off for the Mauriers! I had the job because my maman had been parlor maid there and when she died, they gave me a position. My maman died with her fifth baby, you know."

"And your daddy?" (He half expected the answer.)

"He went away."

Patrick nodded. Daddies usually did. His mind sped on. "Tell me what happened on the boat?"

"Well, then, we landed here on St. Felice and found everyone spoke English! I stood on the wharf and wanted to cry. But I wouldn't, because a crowd was there waiting to hear what was happening in Martinique and I was too proud to cry in front of them all. I didn't know where to go. Then a white man came and leaned out of his carriage and spoke to me in French, queer French, though he told me later that was the way they spoke it in France. I didn't believe that but I found out it was so. . . . Well anyway, that's how I came to work for the Francis family."

"At Eleuthera?"

"What? What do you know about Eleuthera?"

"You took me there once."

"Lord, you're ten now. You couldn't have been a day over three!"

"Well," he said proudly, "I remember it. Mr. Virgil Francis died at Eleuthera. I read it in the paper a while ago."

"Yes, I know."

"It was a beautiful house, wasn't it?"

"Beautiful? Falling apart! That house hasn't been fixed up properly since Lord knows when."

"It was beautiful," Patrick insisted. "On top of a hill. Were they nice to you?"

"Oh yes. . . . Young Mr. Francis, so gentle he was, reading all day till his eyes hurt. He fell sick soon after he married. I helped nurse him till he died and then I—"

"He died?" Death interested him.

"Yes. Oh, that's enough, I'm running off at the mouth. Listen! The storm's over."

It had passed and crickets had started their music.

"Tell me about France," he said suddenly.

"I don't remember much about that. It was a long time ago."

"The volcano was much longer!" he cried.

"Anyway, I don't remember."

"You don't want to! And I like to hear about true things that happened—you know I do!"

She ruffled his hair. "Sometimes you're like an old man." And as if she were not talking to him at all, but into the air, she said, "I hope things will be easy for you."

"That I won't be caught in a volcano, you mean?"

"A human being is so small," she said, still talking to the air. "You can squash him like a bug."

He persisted. "The volcano, you mean?"

She looked at him now. "No. Life is what I mean. So go to sleep."

Those were the years of his childhood.

❧{ 4 }❧

At thirteen or fourteen a boy became a man. Then it was that he might earn his first wage, cutting fodder for the animals on the sugar estate. He would become aware of the ways that were open to him. The most frequented led through the estate, first doing odd jobs on a day-work gang, planting and weeding. If he did well he would probably be hired permanently. By his early twenties he would have learned enough and his arms would be strong enough to cut cane. There would be, then, years of that, the larger portion of his life. When he grew too old to cut cane he would go back among the young boys to care for the animals. All this, of course, depended upon whether he was "taken on" by one of the local estates; if not, he might sail away to try his luck on some other island.

The other path was narrower by far. If a boy was ambitious and smart at his lessons, and if the money could be found somehow, he might go on to Boys' Secondary School in Covetown. Then someday, wearing a suit and tie, he would go to work in a shop or bank or perhaps in the customs office or the courthouse. Boys' Secondary was a white building set among tended lawns, with a Church of England chapel and a fine cricket field in back. The headmaster wore an impressive black gown and a clerical collar. The masters were of the white race, but since planters usually sent their sons overseas to school, few of the students were. Yet the atmosphere was loftily British and a bookish boy from Sweet Apple, passing by and staring within, could not be sure whether his heart was beating with prideful hope or apprehension.

Oh, it would be foolish to set one's sights so high! One might not, probably would not, even pass the entrance examinations! So Patrick told himself and told his mother too, who did not want to hear.

"I've saved the money, and you'll go," she said.

Yet, on that first morning while she waited with him for the bus, the bright pink "Jamboree" loaded with laborers and women taking their produce to town, there were tears in her eyes.

Suddenly it became clear that a human being can be of two minds. Much as she had wanted it for him, so much did she fear the step that he was taking into the larger world, among people who would make him different from the boy she knew. This awareness touched him with brief melancholy, even on so triumphant a morning. Here was a passage, a passing out.

Yet it had already begun a long time before. Ever since his first day at the village school he had been changing, leaving her. This now was only a further step, toward what he did not know.

At thirteen one often does as much thinking and inner growing after school hours as in school. If the school stimulates, so much the better—the two parts of the day can complement each other.

Patrick did well. The masters were serious, disciplined men. Some of them even had some humane comprehension of how a boy from a village shack would need to struggle for survival amid unfamiliar order and decorum. For Patrick it was easier than for many: Agnes had already taught him the social graces.

In the sciences and mathematics he held his head above water. But in the Latin class, in history and literature, the realms of words, he swam with the best. His favorite class was history, taught by Father Albert Baker, a celibate, overweight Anglican priest with tobacco-stained teeth and keen, kindly eyes.

It was through Father Baker that his friendship with Nicholas Mebane came about.

"You boys should get to know one another," he said one day after class. "You'd like each other, I believe."

Patrick stood awkwardly. Nicholas, he knew, was the son of a doctor and had his own group of Covetown friends among the light-brown aristocracy. The school—the world, he was already able to surmise—was tightly partitioned; here, in addition to Nicholas's group, were the clustered whites, sons of bankers and middlemen not in a class with planters, who did not necessarily go abroad to school; here, lastly, was Patrick's group, most of them quite black, these the brightest boys from the villages. Patrick, except for his color, did not fit with Nicholas.

But the latter put his hand out. He had a frank manner.

"Glad to," he said. "I know you don't live in town, but maybe you'll stay in later some afternoon?"

So easily did it happen, so easily can two people surmount all differences when the chemistry is right. Certainly Patrick had never had a friend like Nicholas, and it soon appeared that Nicholas had never had one like Patrick. It was not just because they were both good-looking, capable at sports, and clever at their studies, for these things were mostly true of all the other boys; they would not have been accepted at the school otherwise. It was a sharing, a point of view, a mutual admiration, an indefinable.

Through the eyes of Nicholas, Patrick saw Covetown as though it were entirely new to him. At the wharf Nicholas pointed out the moored yachts and identified their owners.

"There aren't many here now, but before the war the bar of Cade's Hotel used to be filled with planters and millionaire yachtsmen, my father says. And of course the Crocus Club." He grinned. "Funny, our country club has everything they have; in fact, our tennis courts are supposed to be better." He looked at Patrick. "You know what? I bet you could get into any white man's club." He put his head on one side. "Well, maybe not. You *almost* could fool them, though."

"As if I would consider trying!" Patrick was indignant.

"I didn't mean you would."

They stood looking out over the harbor. Sugar lay on the quay ready for shipment. Square-sailed fishing boats had drawn up to unload.

"I used to see destroyers here during the war," Nicholas said. "Painted in zigzags. Camouflaged."

For Patrick the war had been so far away that it seemed unreal, except when his mother's newspaper ran a picture of wreckage in London, of houses blown apart, and then he would wonder what had happened to the people in the houses.

"It's funny," Nicholas said. "There was all that modern stuff here, planes and bombs and submarines like the one that came to Grenada. My father was there when it came." A German submarine had sunk a Canadian passenger ship near shore, and then quite coolly had moved out again into the ocean. "Then you think how, on this island, the quickest way to get from Covetown to the other side is still by sailboat! And some of our roads are so bad that it's easier to travel by mule than by car. We're not much changed from what we were two hundred years ago."

He's only quoting his father, Patrick thought, liking his friend none the less for that.

Turning back to Wharf Street, they paused to peer in at Da Cunha's glitter.

"You think they've got a lot of stuff in there? I was in their cellar storeroom once. Loaded from floor to ceiling with things from all over the world! A lot of these merchants—I don't say Da Cunha—but a lot of them make a fortune in smuggled goods, especially whiskey; did you know that?"

"Even today? I thought all that ended with the pirates."

"You'd be surprised," Nicholas said wisely.

They went on up the hill past the government buildings. Patrick had never thought about government before. It had only taken shape for him in the form of a mailbox or the sight of a policeman in his white, tropical hat and his red stripes, standing in front of the courthouse. Once when the king had sent a new governor from overseas, he had watched the crowd at Government House, the dignitaries in their fancy clothes passing through the gates. That was government.

"My father goes there all the time. He's a member of the Legislative Council." Nicholas made a pyramid of his hands, wiggling his fingertips. "At the top you have the governor. We're a crown colony, which means we're responsible to Parliament in London. We've got a legislature with two houses, just like Parliament. There's the elected House of Assembly—my father started out there—and then there's the Legislative Council, which is higher. Half of its members are selected by the governor. My father was selected by the governor," he added with simple pride.

Such matters of election and appointment were of little interest to Patrick. Regarding the union jack as it floated above the great white mansion, he had a physical sensation of awe, that was all. Councils and assemblies were too complicated to master, and somewhat dry; it was enough now to master Covetown, let alone London.

"The British Empire won't last much longer." Nicholas said then, solemnly.

"What do you mean? There won't be any more king?"

"It's more complicated than that. My father says there will be what he calls a loosening. It won't happen all at once. But people aren't going to work for half nothing anymore. Look at the riots they've had in Barbados and Jamaica."

Patrick hadn't heard of the riots but, nodding, pretended that he had.

"There've been more labor laws passed since the war than they'd passed in a century. They know in London that they've got to do something about conditions. . . . Why else do you think they sent Lord Moyne's royal commission to look into things? They haven't made the report public yet, but I'll bet you—my father says—it will favor federation of all the islands. Naturally, the business people and the planters will fight it, but it will come. Anyway, my father says independence will come one day, too, and the English know it. It's only a question of time. When it comes we'll need educated men to run things. That's why I'm going to be sent to England to study law."

The school taught to the Cambridge O level, and a sizable group of boys, working toward the overseas certificate, were planning careers in medicine and law. Patrick felt the allure of such a future but very little envy. There was in his nature an element of fatalism, of acceptance. He was not a Mebane and that was that.

The Mebanes lived on Library Hill, just under the pinnacle on which stood Government House. Here, in a row of stucco houses, each with its fenced-in yard, its boisdiable trees and its porch with a fine view of the harbor, lived the leaders of the black upper class: Dr. Sprague, the dentist, for example, and lawyer Malcolm Fort, and the Cox brothers, undertakers.

Dr. and Mrs. Mebane were handsome coffee-colored people. Their quiet clothes and the furnishings of their house were refined, Patrick knew, although his experience of refinement had been limited to the headmaster's rooms at school, where he had been asked to tea, his oddly vivid memory of the Kimbrough house, and his mother's nostalgic descriptions. All of these had been "white" homes. He was astonished, therefore, to see what he saw in his friend's house: so many pictures and books, elegant china, and the supper brought in by a servant.

They made him welcome. Dr. Mebane had a positive manner of speech, as though he were trying to convince the listeners of something important.

"My father was a doctor before me. I don't know whether you boys can realize how exceptional that was in those times. The only other two doctors on this island were white men, come out here from England. Both of them were alcoholics. My father, with half the training, was the one you'd want if you were really sick. He'd go way up into the hills at night anytime he was called, riding his horse, carrying a lantern.

"He worked like two men to educate me and my brother; I don't know how he did it. My later brother Edgar became a barrister and was one of the leaders of the Pan-African Congress in Paris right after the war. Nineteen nineteen, that was. They had a brave agenda, most of which didn't come to pass, although some of it did. Well, things move slowly. One learns patience. Anyway, it's men like him, educated men, who bring about the changes, never forget it." The doctor knocked his pipe out. "Am I talking too much, boring you?"

"No, sir," Patrick said.

He was honored at being included in serious conversation, even though he did not understand all of it. He felt great respect; he felt himself in the presence of a new way of living.

"What do they talk about?" Agnes wanted to know. She was pleased and curious whenever Patrick was asked to stay overnight at the Mebane house. Also he was aware of a certain resentment that she was trying to conceal.

"I don't know. Everything." He never meant to make his answer come out irritably. But it was hard, impossible, to explain to Sweet Apple what Library Hill was like. Oh, he could answer to her satisfaction what color the curtains were, and to please her he took care to remember—but the ideas and attitudes were something else.

There was a vague and growing disturbance in his mind. How little he himself knew compared, for instance, with Nicholas, who was his own age! It was as if he had been living in a cocoon.

"They say he sees white patients in town after office hours," Agnes remarked. "People who don't want to discuss anything too personal with their regular doctor."

"I don't know."

"I wouldn't expect you to know that. Haughty people, though, aren't they? All that kind are."

"They aren't haughty to me."

Yet there were things he would have been ashamed to let them see. Not his poverty, his simple house, for there was none of that particular kind of falsity in him, but other things: the ignorance.

Agnes kept the windows tightly shut at night. On each window she had painted a red cross. From earliest childhood he had known that this was to keep a loup-garou from getting into the house and sucking the blood from people's throats as they lay asleep.

"Sometimes it flies over the trees," Agnes had warned him. "You can easily mistake it for a bat. It's especially dangerous to babies."

When Patrick was about nine years old it had become clear that this was absolute nonsense. They had had a quarrel about it.

"You think you're too smart to listen to what I tell you, hah?" Agnes had berated him. "Getting too big for your boots, you are."

Afterwards, as always when she had been short-tempered, she had come to stroke his head. "Well, all right, maybe it isn't true. But suppose it is? How can one be sure?" That was the sort of thing it would have been embarrassing for the Mebanes to know.

But it worked the other way, too, an odd reversal. Dr. Mebane said things he would not dare to repeat before Agnes.

"My great-great-grandmother was a slave for the Francis family," he told the boys one day. "There's an old estate on the other side of this island—you may have seen it—Eleuthera. Well, the details are vague, 'lost in the mist of time,' I

believe the poet says. All I know is, her name was Cupid and her father was a
son, or maybe a nephew, of the Francis family. This was toward the end of the
seventeen hundreds. She must have been a beautiful girl. White women were
scarce on the plantations, you know, and life was very dull. So the white master
went to the slave woman and naturally he chose the best-looking, the healthiest.
Sometimes there was a lasting love between them. He'd buy jewels for the
woman, dress her in satin and lace. When there were children, the father freed
them, manumitted them. It would have been scandalous not to do so. Some of
these fathers were generous with money, with land or an education. So after a
century or more, what have you got? You have a brown class. Brown, less brown,
least brown." The doctor smiled ironically. " 'Least brown' even acquired the
dignity of being addressed as Mr. or Mrs. Well, anyway, that's the explanation of
why the people who work on the sugar estate today are coal black and why," he
said, with a certain mocking tone, "why I am invited to teas at Government
House. Not to private little dinner parties, mind you, certainly not. But when
you're in government you're as good as anyone. Yes, it all goes back to the bed,
when you think about it."

Patrick was silent. Grown people didn't talk about "beds" in front of boys. At
least, Agnes didn't. She would have washed his mouth out with soap if he had
done so. "Dirty talk," she would have called it.

"Color," the doctor resumed. "We think about it all the time, don't we? Even
when we don't want to admit it."

"I don't think about it," Patrick said untruthfully.

"I don't believe it."

"We never talk about it at home," Patrick said.

"Don't tell me you don't think about it, though. You're lighter than any of us
here."

Of course he thought about it even more than he realized. It was just always
there. When he looked around the class and saw that his features were exactly
those of the white boys, only the skin betraying the difference . . . . How easy life
would be, he thought, if one could remove the last trace of that *other* from the
skin. And on the other hand, he could recall how it had thrilled him when
Nicholas won the debate from a boy just out from England, a freckled red-haired
boy with a haughty accent barely understandable. The triumph had thrilled him,
not just because Nicholas was his friend, but because it had been a victory for
color.

"You are lighter than any of us here," Dr. Mebane said again. "How do you
suppose that happened?"

Patrick felt a flush of shame. Whose shame? Not his own, surely. What had he
to do with it?

The doctor leaned forward. "You're embarrassed. You shouldn't be. There is a
proper way to talk about these things. They are a part of life. And anyway, we are
all men in this room. You shouldn't be embarrassed," he repeated kindly.

But the doctor could not have known the full reach of his thoughts. He was
thinking of his mother. That business about the white man and the mistress . . .

She had been in France; the man who had fathered him had deserted her. And he was filled with anger toward his unknown father.

Now color was becoming totally confused with sex. Yet they were two different things. His mother ought to have hated whiteness, after that. But there was a contradiction in her, the contradiction of which he had so long been aware. She was proud that estate workers coming into her shop called her Miss. He had asked her once why she was more polite to customers who were brown like herself, and so often curt with those who were very black. He had received not only a denial but such a lashing of her tongue that he never mentioned the subject again.

But it was all around, in the very air. It came to him, lying awake one night, that even Dr. Mebane, for all his talk and insight, had betrayed his secret pride in his own light skin. A certain satisfaction had revealed itself in his smile and voice, belying the righteous indignation in his words. He is proud of those invitations to Government House, Patrick thought, and he felt an odd compassion, which would no doubt have astonished the doctor if he had known of it.

Also, he saw that his pride was really shame. It was like despising oneself.

THE FEW YEARS of schooling passed, flashing as they always do, so that when a long time later one looks back over them, only a few bright areas stand out in a sometimes serene, sometimes dull, sometimes fretful expanse of routine. In Patrick's case, the particular brightness, in spite of anything, was Nicholas and his father's cheerful house. Secondly it was Father Baker, who could always find time for a boy after school, who gave him hard things to do, long lists of books "to stretch the mind," he said. "Read Gibbon's *Decline and Fall;* hard going, but without it you won't understand how we came to be where we are."

Father Baker supplied the lists, but Nicholas supplied the books, a glorious boxful each Christmas. ("Patrick, don't be shy about accepting a gift. Don't let's be self-conscious with each other. I happen to have more money, no credit to me; it's not important and don't let it be.")

So he grew, in those vital years between thirteen and seventeen when it is said the best learning is done. Wandering about the island, he began to connect the things his eyes saw with the things he read or was being taught, all of these weaving and interlocking with each other into something that as yet had no design, but seemed to point toward one.

DURING THE LONG holidays before his final year, Father Baker gave an assignment: Write something about St. Felice, anything old or new, geological, commercial, anything. Father Baker gave difficult assignments.

Patrick had at first no idea what to write about. He worried over it. Then one day it came to him. At home in Sweet Apple he had wandered down to the beach and there encountered his old friend Ah Sing. And for no reason he could explain, regarding the stone-black eyes slanted above the Chinaman's cheekbones, it came to him that Ah Sing could just as well be taken for one of the Caribs who lived in their reservation on the far remote slope of Morne Bleue. But they have always been here! he thought, astonished. And Ah Sing comes from the other side of the world! How could that be?

He resolved to learn more. Father Baker liked to talk about "intellectual excitement." Patrick had probably never experienced what the teacher had meant, yet now, walking on the hard wet sand near the water's edge, he thought he might be feeling it. "It is a kind of fire," Father Baker had said. Yes. Yes. I want to say something about this place where I live, a strange place, when you think about it. All these so various and different people, living here, each in his layer, like those bottles of colored sand that is laid in stripes, apart! First there had been the Indians. This place had been all theirs, yet there was only a remnant of them left. You never heard much about them, other than the comment made by blacks that they had "good hair." Sometimes you saw them fishing at night by torchlight at the river. Now and then you saw the men on the roads with their loads lashed onto their backs, it being beneath the dignity—that much he knew—of an Indian man to carry anything on his head. It was all right for women, but not for men. You saw them bringing their baskets to the market for sale, or more rarely, carrying bananas down the mountainside to Covetown. They didn't go in for hired labor very much, and almost never worked on the estates. They gave an impression of silence and independence; a superior reserve was on their faces.

Once he had made his way on foot to the place where they lived. He had expected no profound revelations, so he had not been disappointed to find merely what he had seen in any other inland village: two rows of shingled huts with tin roofs, some goats and some chickens scratching in a little garden plot behind each house. Some things were different: women pounding cassava in gourds and men hacking a canoe out of a cedar trunk. He had observed all these things, both the resemblances to and the differences from the life around them, and having done so, had not felt any further curiosity. Yet now he did.

He went to the public library in Covetown. It was a fair-sized room, dusty in shafted sunbeams, up the stairs from the tax office which had once been the courthouse from which buccaneers were sent to the gallows. Happily, it contained an encyclopedia and a moderate collection of history books. On the shady side of the room Patrick sat down with a pile of books and began to take notes.

The original inhabitants of the Leewards and the Windwards were the Arawaks, who came in canoes from what is now Guiana. They were a pacific people, farmers and fishermen. After many centuries—no one knows how many or how remote—they were followed by the Caribs, coming possibly from what is now Brazil. These were a very different people, warlike and ferocious. Indeed, the word *cannibal* is said to be derived from their name.

It has been fairly well established that many thousands of years ago, when a land bridge between Asia and America existed in the region of the Bering Sea, the ancestors of both these tribes had wandered across and slowly, gradually dispersed themselves . . .

So it was true, then! These people and the Chinaman Ah Sing! He had observed it! And it was true!

H<small>E READ ON.</small>

> The Caribs slaughtered the Arawak men and married their women.
> . . . For many generations the men continued to speak the Carib language among themselves; although they understood the Arawak tongue, which the women continued to speak, they would never use it themselves. *Hammock* is an Arawak word. *Hurricane* is another.

With a feeling of recognition, Patrick paused a moment. What pleasure in words! Written, the word *hurricane* even looked like the haste and ruin of the real thing which he had seen once, a few years before: whole villages blown to pieces and great palms uprooted like weeds, as the wind came roaring at 160 miles an hour from the east.

He went back to the book and picked up the pen.

> With whiskey and some cheap ornaments, the European bought island after island from the Caribs. Not satisfied with ownership of the land, he pressed on for ownership of the native, but totally without success. The Carib would not be enslaved. Through mass and individual suicide, he defied the conqueror.

Glorious courage, proud courage! Patrick was youthfully and deeply moved.

After a week of diligence, he completed his notes, went home and began to write. He worked all day; when darkness came he set an oil lamp on the counter of the store and kept on.

His mother complained. "You've been up half the night for three nights now!"

"I have to," he answered patiently.

He had set it all in orderly mental sequence, so that his pen ran easily: history, adaptation to change, daily ways . . . ,

> At the top of the palm is a bush which looks like cabbage. Used as a shelter or a garment, it will keep a man dry in the heaviest rain.
> . . . know how to hypnotize an iguana by whistling to it so it can be tied up.
> . . . can shoot fish with a bow and arrow. Their bowstrings were made of liana vines, and the poison for their arrowtips, in warfare, was made of the sap from manchineel trees. . . .
> Early explorers report on their swimming feats. It is said that they were fast enough to knife sharks undersea.
> . . . can still weave reed baskets fine enough to hold water.

And their inner life:

Long before Christianity, they had a belief in one central spirit of good, commanding the universe. Also, they had a concept of evil not unlike the early Christian belief in the devil. . . .

To sum up, I admire most their love of liberty. This is the reason, I think, why even now they will not work *for* anyone. They have no concept of rank, either. Again, even today, their chief lives in a house no better than anyone else's. They never understood the European's sense of hierarchy. . . .

When he had finished, it was the last night of the holidays. Having made a careful copy of his work, with no erasures, he went to bed, feeling tired, exhilarated, and also worried about the worth of what he had done.

Two days later Father Baker summoned Patrick to his office.

"Who helped you with this?" he asked.

"No one."

"Are you sure of that?"

"Who could have?" Patrick questioned simply.

"This is a scholarly piece of work," Father Baker said. Thoughtfully, he riffled Patrick's neat pages. "I never expected anything as thorough as this. You must have spent days on the research. What made you do it? Can you tell me?"

Patrick hesitated. "It started because of the Chinaman Ah Sing. I've known him since I was four or five"—and he went on to tell about his first puzzlement over the Chinaman's resemblance to the Indian. "Then I've been thinking, I guess I've always been thinking, about my own ancestors. You imagine Africa, you know—I suppose very inaccurately—but still you do. You think of cathedrals and those little English villages in picturebooks. All of that is in you. St. Felice makes pictures in your mind." He was ashamed to say how he still thought in colors, so he said merely, "People like the Da Cunhas—Nicholas said the first ones here were Jews, the wanderers, the Bible people. What could have brought them here, too?"

He gained confidence. "This island where we live is so small! Yet there are so many different kinds of people living here, come from all over, living together, and yet apart, not knowing one another. I was thinking: Can the whole world be like this, too? With people wandering from one place to the other, really all part of each other, but not wanting to be?"

Father Baker was looking at him so intently that Patrick stopped. Had he been making an idiot of himself?

Then Father Baker looked away. Patrick observed the ropy veins at the man's temples, the soiled and shabby gown, then followed his gaze out the window to where voices were competing on the playing fields.

Soon I shall be gone, he thought, and felt a painful emotion. Gone from friends and books, gone from the civility of this crowded little office and the man, the sort of men, who sat here.

Father Baker turned back to his desk, picked up a pencil, and made a little circular design. Then he spoke.

"What do you plan to do with your life, Patrick?"

"Well, get a job . . ." He had thought, or his mother had thought, he might apply at Barclay's Bank. The tellers were mostly light blacks, which would be, of course, anybody's definition of Patrick. "Maybe in a bank," he said.

"Is that what you want to do?"

Suddenly a new thought came. It was so powerful that it must have been in him for longer than he knew. "What I'd really like is to teach. To read a lot and teach. Like you—not the priest part, though," he finished awkwardly, and was ashamed that he had perhaps been tactless.

"I understand. You'd have no difficulty getting a certificate to teach grade school when you graduate from here. But a boy like you should really go to England, to university. It would be a nice thing if you could go with your friend Nicholas, wouldn't it?"

Yes it would. But maybe Father didn't know how little he had. Maybe he thought Patrick was another Nicholas.

But no. "You surely would be able to get a partial scholarship."

That wouldn't be enough. His thoughts flew, then stopped. No matter. What-ever he would need, it would be more than he could afford.

"Well, think about it," Father Baker said as he stood up.

The new idea burned within Patrick in spite of himself. He did not speak of it to Nicholas, partly because he was a private person, even with his best friend, and partly because he was realistic and it made no sense to waste time talking of impossibilities. But he walked down to the wharf and watched the ships, even the interisland schooners, with a kind of longing that he had never felt before.

One evening at home something compelled him to speak. "My teacher said my paper about the Caribs was excellent."

Agnes nodded. "Very fine. Very fine."

"He thinks I ought to go to England. To university."

"He does? Maybe he'll give you the money for it?"

"I could get a partial scholarship."

"And the rest?"

"I don't know."

"Well, I don't know either. I think you'll stay here and get yourself a nice job and be grateful. Get foolish ideas out of your head."

Patrick flushed. Yes, it was only a fancy, a thing to be dismissed. But it clung to him. And he thought of Mistress Ogilvie, herself barely educated, teaching by rote the kings and generals of Europe—nothing, incidentally, of that great "dark continent" on which her pupils had originated; he compared her with the masters at Boy's Secondary and was shocked by the comparison. But if you were to set those masters beside the great scholars at Cambridge? What then? All the knowl-edge in the world, just bottled up in a few small places, uncorked for the few to drink! He thought of the laborers in the cane fields, who knew nothing. He wondered whether the folk in the great houses, men like old Mr. Kimbrough or— or the Tarboxes of Drummond Hall, for instance—might not, in their way, be as ignorant, knowing nothing much beyond the walls of their fine houses.

He felt a restless, cold discouragement.

"You want to go, don't you?" Agnes asked abruptly one night.

"Go?" he repeated.

"To England! To university! What are we talking about?"

"We aren't talking at all," he said angrily, "because it's not possible and I know it isn't."

"Maybe you're right," she said, a few days later.

"Right about what?" he asked, raising his head from his homework.

"Nothing. I was thinking out loud." Then she resumed, "What I meant was, right not to talk about your going overseas."

"I am right. And I don't want to hear it again!"

"Don't talk to me like that. I don't like your sassy voice."

He didn't look up and she went out of the room.

But a week or two afterwards she said to him, "I'm going away for a while, closing the shop. There won't be much to see to, but whatever there is you can see to it while I'm gone."

His first thought was, She must suddenly be homesick for Martinique. "Where are you going, Maman?"

"To New York."

"New York!" he cried, in astonishment.

He saw by her familiar sly smile that, in spite of her brusqueness, she was enjoying his surprise.

"Yes. I've business there."

"Business in New York? How will you get there?"

"On a freighter."

"Are you coming back, then?"

"Well, naturally I am! I have a little personal business, that's all! Do I have to tell you everything?" she complained. Then she touched his head. "There's nothing to worry about. You just stay here and do your work properly. I'll come home in a few weeks. And when I do, things will be different."

❧ 5 ❧

Teresa, long afterward, was to remember the day by its colors: dim greens blurred through an intermittent, melancholy rain over the low New Jersey hills. It was her habit to see places and persons in color: her husband a troubled, cloudy gray and her children rosy, tender as petals. Eleuthera had once been a blue luster, but was no more.

Now a scattering of amateurish, poorly focused snapshots lay on the desk next to the window where she stood with her back to the room. Having been forced to glance at them, having touched them with her eyes, she had pulled away, as one pulls the hand from a hot surface.

"You don't even want to look at him properly." Agnes spoke quietly, yet Teresa felt challenge. "I'd like to know what you're thinking right now. Yes, I'd like to know."

Somewhere below, around the corner of the house, came the flutelike call of a child. Teresa trembled.

"I feel—I want to sink into a hole where no one could see me. Or get on a ship and go as far as it sails."

"As far as it sailed it couldn't take you far enough."

Teresa turned around. "How did you find me here?"

"Easy enough. In the New York telephone book. And somebody said you were in the country for vacation week."

"You always did know how to manage things."

"I had to learn. I never had anyone to manage them for me."

Delicately, without sound, Agnes placed the teacup in the saucer. Her feet, in their neat black shoes, were crossed at the ankles. Unobtrusively, she had already examined the room: the pale carpet, the marigolds in the dark-blue ginger jars and the photographs, these of an intimacy that belongs in an upstairs sitting room. Plainly she approved of what she saw. *Élevé au chapeau,* Teresa remembered suddenly, irrelevantly.

Agnes raised her eyes. "Don't be afraid of me," she said gently.

Afraid? No, terrorized. This must be the true experience of terror: the second before the fall through empty air . . . the strange footstep coming up the stairs at night . . .

"I'm not here to harm you. I could have talked long ago when I went back to the island, couldn't I? But I'm not cruel, I'm a decent woman. Besides, I want to protect my son, my Patrick. You don't think I want him to know the truth, do you?"

"Patrick," Teresa repeated.

"Well, you never gave him a name. So that's it, Patrick Courzon."

"I didn't know you had gone back home. Père never mentioned in his letters."

"He saw the boy once. I took him there when he was three, then never again. . . . You've broken your necklace."

Her cold, sweating hands had been twisting and twisting. Now blue beads rolled across the floor.

Agnes bent to pick them up. "Your nerves. But I keep telling you, I haven't come to ruin you. What good would that do anyone? I only need help for him, for his education. He wants to go to Cambridge."

Something throbbed and stabbed in Teresa's head. That figure printed on film. That quick impression of tallness and thinness, of teeth, of a white shirt—all of it lived and had been taken out of her, was of her. And if someone had asked—but Agnes had just asked a moment ago! *What do you feel?*—she could have answered only, I feel ruin. I taste the poison. Nothing left: no children, no home, no *name*. Richard would—it did not bear thinking of, what Richard would do.

"Seventeen years!" she cried out. "After seventeen years you come to me with this! My God, do you know what you're doing to me?"

Agnes said evenly, "Give me what I ask for, then, and I'll never come near you again."

Could one believe her?

"You do want to know what he looks like, don't you? Only it's hard for you to say so. All right, I'll tell you. He has the Francis nose, like you and your grandfather. And he's light. I've seen Italian sailors in Covetown not much lighter. I think really it's only his hair that gives him away."

Agnes had not oiled her hair that day; it coiled and crimped—one sensed the primitive, looking at that hair. Such curious and devious tracks does memory follow: one thought of drums, looking at that hair. Of drums? Years ago on the plantations, so Père had said, you could hear them all day Sunday, and once the child Tee herself had seen the African dance, the heat and stamp of the calinda, powerful and hot.

She wiped her forehead, pulling herself back into the present. "I can get you the money. I will."

Richard took charge of the investments and the bank accounts. But she could always sell a bracelet. There were so many of them. He bought too many expensive, unnecessary things.

"Yes, I'll get it for you. Then you'll leave me alone? After all, he's yours, isn't he, yours?" *It's only his hair that gives him away.* "I have four children of my own, my husband's and mine. Three girls." *Long, silvery hair like limp silk on their shoulders.* "And my son, my first." *My lovely boy, my strong and gentle boy; I have never said so and never will, but he knows and I know, he is my heart.* "I can't let anything happen to them!" she cried harshly.

"Of course you can't."

"If—he—were ever to find out, it would all be over." She flung her arms out. "He would pull this house down! He's not the kind of man who would even try to understand . . . forgive . . ."

"What man is?" Agnes regarded her with grave, sad eyes. "I tell you, put this out of your mind. I was a mother to you, do you forget? More than Miss Julia ever was."

"That's true." There was no real memory of Julia, other than a pastel presence. No joy, nor conflict, either. And Teresa thought, Is that, perhaps, why I am what I am? I suppose, if I cared enough, I could be analyzed—goodness knows it's the fashionable thing to do these days—and then I would know; know, too, why I can be repelled by the Negroness of Agnes and a moment later find warmth and comfort in her.

"My little girl, Margaret, is retarded," she said suddenly, not having intended to. "Not a normal child. She will never grow up."

"I'm very sorry, Miss Tee."

"You know, sometimes I've had the craziest idea—that she might be a punishment."

Agnes nodded. "Not crazy. I've seen things like that."

But of course it was crazy, absurd. Only a peasant from a place like St. Felice could believe it: a lingering atavism out of centuries long past, flitting through the mind in moments of gloom.

Agnes touched a photograph on a table. "Is this your husband? A handsome man."

"Yes." When she was angry, she thought of him with contempt. An advertisement for hand-tailored suits. A male flirt, a chaser.

She was not in a position to complain.

"You're happy enough? He's good to you?"

These were less questions than statements; the fine polish of the room, the long fields and graceful trees beyond the windows would, for someone like Agnes, who had nothing, very likely be compensation for almost anything.

"He's good to me. I'm happy."

For in his way, Richard was fond of her. The strange allure of the "different" young girl from the foreign island had long ago, and predictably, worn off, but he was basically kind and had, moreover, grown up among people who seldom divorced their wives. He had no reason—none that he knew of!—to desert her.

With their children he was good-natured, patient even with poor Margaret's sticky hands and silly laughter; proud of the other daughters and of Francis, the precocious, lively boy. How had they begot such a boy? There was nothing of Richard in him except for fair hair and a certain way of smiling.

And she thought, sitting across from Agnes's soft, penetrating gaze, *We never talk about anything true except the children. We have never entered together into the heart of anything.* But it didn't matter. Even the "other women" really didn't matter. She had given her life to the rearing of children, much as a botanist concentrates on his experiments, the temperature of the greenhouse, and the chemistry of the soil.

She wanted, suddenly, to talk about Francis. "My son, my son Francis reminds me of my father."

"You can remember him?"

"A little, I think. I remember the stories he read to me. His voice was beautiful."

He was a long, tired shape under white bedclothes, lying in a room where the shutters were always closed against the glare of light. A black hearse, pulled by two sweating horses with black plumes on their heads, carried him away.

"He died bravely. He suffered and never complained."

"Père always said the Francises were tough. He said I was, too, even though I didn't think I was. He said it makes life bearable, that toughness."

"Your grandfather certainly had it," Agnes said grimly. "You know what he did to Clyde. Not that it wasn't to be expected, a colored boy—"

"You think that was the reason? That he wouldn't have done the same to anyone?"

Agnes smiled. "No. He had hatred, Miss Tee. He only thought he hadn't."

Tee was silent. Clyde, his life and his death, but most of all his death, must be stifled and buried under layers of secrecy and trembling.

"Still," Agnes reflected, "I don't curse him for what he did. There's murder in every one of us. I know I would kill for Patrick if I had to."

The silence thrummed and hummed.

"Tell me, Miss Tee, do you ever see your mother?"

She wet her dry lips. "They've been here twice to visit."

"But you? You never want to go there?"

"No, never." Again the silence hummed. In a moment the humming would burst in Tee's head, would roar and crash into a scream. And laying her fingers on her quivering mouth, she looked past Agnes's head into the mirror that minutes ago had reflected only a pastel mosaic of flowers and books, but now thrust back into the room a fearful face, collapsed in a repression of tears.

She ran to Agnes. A shoulder received her; a hand soothed her back. She spoke, muffled, into the shoulder.

"I can't afford to cry."

"I know. Otherwise, I'd say 'cry it out, you'll feel better.' But you can't dare to."

Tee raised her head. "I've been lying to you. No, not lying, either. It's just—I don't know how I feel. I never do. I don't really know what the truth about myself is. Oh, I do want to know what he's like, I do! And still I'm afraid to know. Afraid because—because of what he is. Forgive me, Agnes."

"You don't have to say that. You think I've lived all these years in the world without knowing a few things about it?" There was grieving in the voice, voice of an old woman who has seen too much. "All right, I'll tell you more. He's a quiet boy, gentle, thinks about things. Half the time I can't figure out what he's thinking. Ambitious, too, only it's not money he wants. And proud. Light as he is, he's proud of being black. Prouder than some who're coal black. Queer, isn't it?"

"Oh, yes." Sad and queer.

"And is he happy, Agnes?"

"He has friends. People like him. Yes, I'd say he's as happy as anyone. . . . I don't know what else to tell you. It's hard to describe all these years in a few words. But he's been the best part of my life, he has."

"I remember the day you took him. I wanted to look at him—and I didn't want to. And I've been ashamed of the not wanting to, ever since."

"There wasn't anything to be ashamed of! You were barely sixteen and frightened to death. You had plenty of courage, though, never think you didn't."

"I often think there are two kinds of courage. There's the kind that holds on, just quietly endures, has a plan and clings to it. That's my kind, that's what my life is. But the greater courage is being able to risk, just plunge off the path into the unknown. And that I'm not able to do."

"Come out with the truth, you mean."

Tee nodded. Suddenly she was aware that she was breathing hard, winded as though she had been running.

"You'd be a fool to do that. And I'd say it even if I didn't want Patrick for my own. You'd be exchanging him for all this." Agnes waved her arm at the room.

"You know I don't care about things that much. I can get along with much less than this, Agnes!"

"The four children? The husband?"

"The children," Tee said, very low.

"I see. That's how it is! You should have had more. You should have had a man to love all your life."

Tee's smile was faint. "So should you."

"I don't need it as much as you do. I never did. You had a heap of loving in you from the time you could walk. You were born like that."

"I loved you, didn't I, Agnes? You and Père. And now I've got Francis. I wish you could see him. Everything you said about—Patrick—I could say about him. He's quiet, gentle, curious . . ."

From below stairs came sounds of doors and feet. Agnes stood and put on her hat.

"I'd better leave before somebody comes and gives you questions to answer. But you will take care of that?"

"I will. And I hope—I wish everything that's good for him. I'll think, somewhere, making his way in the world, there's this boy who—" She stopped.

Agnes took Tee's hand between both of hers. It was an old gesture, long forgotten, now suddenly recalled.

"Agnes? After you've left I'll think of so much more I should have said. About everything you've done for me and what you are and how I love you."

"You don't have to tell me all that. I know."

They went downstairs to the door. On the threshold Agnes turned back, her gaze directed past Teresa into the hall, dim now in the fading afternoon.

"I see things. You remember how I could always see things."

"What things? What do you mean?"

"He'll come back into your life, Patrick will. Not through me, no, never through me! And maybe not into your life, I'm not sure. But into your children's. Yes. I see that clearly."

Teresa made no answer. Again the primitive, she thought, reassuring herself. Superstition, out of Africa. That, too, was part of Agnes. But her hands shook so that she could barely close the door and slide the bolt.

LATER FRANCIS ASKED, "Who was that colored woman with you this afternoon? I passed your room when I came upstairs."

"My old nursemaid. I guess that's what you'd call her."

"From St. Felice? What was she doing here?"

"She has a cousin working somewhere nearby, I think."

"I'm writing about St. Felice for economics, did I tell you? All about sugar prices and the competition of European beet sugar. People are always curious— even my teacher was—when I tell them my mother grew up on St. Felice."

"There's nothing so strange about it," Teresa said patiently.

"Well, they think it's all pirates and volcanoes, I suppose. But you know, when I read that diary of the first François, it was thrilling, actually."

Actually was the fad word this season at school. The youthfulness of this, the innocent boast of the basketball letter on his sweater, these as well as the two parallel lines across a forehead only sixteen years old—touched her sharply. She wanted to respond to his enthusiasms.

"I suppose, too, they think we're all sugar millionaires?"

"Oh, of course! And," Francis added, somewhat shyly, "they've got a lot of ideas about interracial sex. But I tell them"—he laughed—"I tell them we're all white, there's none of that in our family."

She was aware that her hands flew to knot themselves in her lap, then moved to twine on the dressing table among the combs and powder boxes.

"I mean to go there someday, even if you won't go."

"It's not as romantic as you think it is. You'd be disappointed. And"—prodding gently—"you'd do better to concentrate on getting into Amherst year after next, since that's where you want to go."

"I'll do that, don't worry," Francis said with his father's stubborn, charming smile.

Of course he would. He was a scholar. And Agnes's voice sounded in her head: *A scholar. Never a minute's trouble . . .*

"You're frowning," Francis said.

"Am I? I didn't mean to."

"Things go hard with Margaret today?"

"No harder than usual."

Francis thrust his hands into his pockets, jingling coins, as masculine a gesture, she thought, as girls' fishing for their shoulder straps was a feminine one.

"Want me to help you get her to bed?"

"That would be nice. I am a little tired tonight, really. And she does behave better for you than for any of us."

He looked thoughtfully at his mother. "People say you're wearing yourself out."

"Who says?"

"Oh, friends and Dad's family and even the maids. Just about everybody."

"They think I ought to put Margaret away someplace."

"Just a special school," he said gently, lowering his eyes.

"I wish they would all leave me alone!" she cried.

The boy was troubled. "Some people say you seem to be punishing yourself."

"Punishing myself! For what, I ask you?"

"I don't know, Mother."

A punishment, she had said to Agnes.

"Dad asked me to talk to you about it again, because you won't listen to him." Now Francis raised his eyes. Clear, beautiful, candid eyes they were, the only ones in all the world that could *speak* to her. "I said I would, but it wouldn't be any use. I told him you couldn't just desert a child like that. It's not her fault that she was born the way she was."

"You think that, too," she murmured.

"I think it would be easier for you to send her away. Most people would, but you wouldn't. You wouldn't do that to your own child."

There was such hell in her heart! And she turned away, so that he should not see its reflection in her face.

"Shall I go bring Margaret upstairs?"

"Yes, do, please."

Desperately she looked around the room, a room to which, as to the whole house, she had given her love, expressing it in the homely shapes of dear, familiar things: Francis' old, stuffed bear on top of a cabinet, a photo of the girls in party dresses, a framed snapshot of her first beloved Airedale, a row of garden books. There was no comfort tonight. Shadowed, alien, the room drew back from her, the walls receding, vanishing, so that the world's chill swept in. . . .

Margaret shuffled at the door. "Mama?"

"Yes, darling?"

"I don't want to go to bed." The loose, helpless mouth puckered toward tears.

"I'll read you a story first. I'll read you *Peter Rabbit.*"

"No, Francis read!" And the great girl, taller than her brother's shoulder, stamped her foot.

With enormous effort Tee summoned energy. At least the tussle would be easier tonight with Francis helping.

"Come, Margaret darling." And taking the girl's hand, she gave a grateful smile to her son. "Sometimes I don't know what I'd do without you."

W HEN THE HOUSE was quiet, she lay down. Richard would be coming home late, but she was thankful to be alone. She was often alone, he having an independent life in the brokerage house and the galleries. A faintly bitter smile touched her lips. He saw himself as a fascinating man, a financial wizard and a connoisseur of art. Yet, to be fair, he really did understand paintings.

"Anatole Da Cunha is one of the greats," he had told her. "Wait and see, his work will be priceless after his death." Acting upon this conviction, he had bought four of Anatole's landscapes. "His best work comes from his memory of the Indies. But you should be able to judge, Teresa: Does it have the living spirit of home for you?"

Yes. Oh, yes! Now, between the windows, in the path of the lamplight, hung Morne Bleue; in the foreground, under an oyster-colored sky opaque with heat, lay a stretch of familiar rippling cane, twice a man's height, and weaving through the cane a line of cutters, their black arms curved in the sway of labor like dancers on a stone frieze.

Richard had put it there for her pleasure, but she had not wanted it, had not wanted anything of St. Felice, not even Père's books when he died, although they had sent them to her anyway, sending too, without knowing that they had—how could they know?—the click of croquet balls on the lawn, the twinkle of candles in the Catholic cemetery, and the smell of rain.

Now too, outside on the New Jersey hills, it had begun to rain, an even, pattering, all-night fall. In St. Felice the rain comes plunging, pounding the earth and ceasing as suddenly as it begins, leaving a vapor to rise from the steaming ground.

Down at the wharf when the banana ship is moored, through the steaming wet come lines of barefoot women, bearing their loads on their heads.

"See," Mama says, ""how gracefully they walk! It's the same as the nuns teaching you to walk with a book on your head."

But it is not the same; the child Tee sees that clearly. It puzzles her that certain things should be so, that the heavy work is always done by blacks and that they live as they do. She goes to town with Agnes to bring some medicine to the cook's old aunt; the hot street stinks, the gutters run foul; the house holds merely a cot and a table. Why? No one tells her. Perhaps no one can.

Père talks with pride of Cambridge, of boats on a quiet river, of choirs and Gothic arches, of *gentlemen*. How can all that merge with Covetown?

Agnes says, "This boy needs the best. He deserves it."

Père says, "Three generations of our people have gone to Cambridge."

Now comes the fourth, and he doesn't know he is.

Teresa's head tossed on the pillow. Oh Francis, Francis my son, is this the real reason why I love you so much? Too much, maybe? That I want everything for you? Is it because I need to expunge, to *wipe* that other away, to wipe all the pain away, so that I might say, Here, you are my son, my only son; I have no other and there never was another? Is that why?

Oh, hell, hell in the heart.

She balled her fists at her sides. She firmed her lips. Listen, Teresa, this is the way it is. You just keep on doing what needs to be done, you hear me? And close your mind. You can do that. You've been doing it for a long, long time now.

Strong words, strong resolution. And yet you know—how well you know!— the days and the years when fear will flood again in gray afternoons, and the mouth will go dry and you will close your book to get up and walk around the room.

Agnes asked, "Are you happy enough?" Was that deliberate discernment or only the chance use of a word, that difference between "happy" and "happy enough"? For what is "enough"? For that matter, what is "happy"?

Oh, you can recognize happiness in other people! My mother is happy because she's not touchable, not breakable. When Papa died, her tears gushed and the wound healed. Richard? Yes, surely, Richard is happy. He has all he requires out of our marriage. I don't think he can even imagine what it is to be lonely.

As for me? When I walk in the rain I feel contentment. Books keep me company. My house is warm and safe on a windy night. There are two or three friends who are dear to me and I to them. Thankful that I can, I help the sick and the poor. And Francis—ah, Francis is my joy of joys! Without him, there would be no one under this roof to talk to. Poor, mindless Margaret. Two other girls who are like Richard, such glossy surface: good girls, just different from me, that's all.

I remember once I wanted to die; they say most people do at some time or other. Yet they get over it, as I did. You fall, but then you struggle up again. At least if you're worth your salt, you do.

Besides, "The Francis family is tough. Remember that," Père said.

Francis, too, lay listening to the rain. Tonight was one of his "anxious" nights, when he had trouble falling asleep. Often he had been told that he was oversensitive, and he supposed he was, if by that was meant a sharp awareness of other people's moods.

His thoughts kept circling. His mother had been troubled. Of course there was always Margaret, but somehow or other he didn't think it was Margaret who had been the reason. Ordinarily he would have asked her for the reason; they had between them a frankness that was both serious and humorous. There were certain times, though, when something held him back—and this was one of them —when a darkness crept over her, as when a cloud moves on clear water. These times came oddly, unexpectedly; she might be standing with the other mothers at some school function where he could be so proud of her, smiling quietly among the fashionables with their nasal twitterings—and suddenly the darkness would sweep over her. And he would know that for those few minutes she had withdrawn, that she had not been *there* at all.

Once, when he was very young, he had heard two maids talking about her.

"She's kind of a queer sort, but nice enough," they'd said.

And he had asked them, "Why is she a queer sort?"

"Oh," they had answered him, "we only meant, she is so far from home. She must be homesick."

He had pressed her, then, with questions. "Why don't we go to St. Felice? Why can't we visit?"

"It's too far . . . your sisters are too little . . . I get seasick . . . maybe someday."

She would never tell him anything important about the place, just odd little facts about, for instance, "mountain chickens," which are really enormous frogs that people cook like chicken. He wasn't sure what it was exactly that he wanted to know, only that it was more than she was willing to tell, which was strange because his father always talked so freely about his childhood.

Two times his grandmother Julia had come to visit. She was an important-sounding woman who kept complaining of the cold, although it was June. The child Francis hadn't liked her, even though she smelled like flowers and brought wonderful presents.

"Your mother despises us," she had told him. "Our backward little island."

It was untrue. Francis had known that even then, for his mother was not a person who despised anyone. On the contrary, she was always excusing people, even when they were wrong.

Last week the gardener had smashed up the station wagon.

"There was no possible excuse," Richard said. "Wool-gathering, not paying attention to the road."

"It's easy to condemn," Teresa said. "One never knows what is *behind* anyone." She hadn't said it to be pious or for the sound of it, but Richard had been annoyed. And Francis had been sorry for her.

He wondered whether, in spite of all concealment, she might be aware of his father's "escapades." He was old enough now to understand that there must have been, must still be, others like the one that had so disgusted him when he was fifteen. At dinner with a friend and the friend's parents in a restaurant he had encountered his father with a woman, a common, gaudy young woman, at the next table.

Richard had pleaded. "Don't tell your mother, son. It would only make everybody miserable. There's no harm in it, you know; I wouldn't hurt your mother for the world."

Why did people make these foolish marriages? Couldn't they tell beforehand that they wouldn't work? You had only to be with Richard and Teresa Luther for a couple of minutes to know how different they were.

Richard was extravagant and fond of himself. Packages kept arriving at the door although the closets were already overflowing. Money poured.

"Like French wine," said Teresa, who tended to be frugal. "Wanton waste."

Richard liked hunting and the parties that went with it.

"Wanton killing," Teresa said fiercely when he came home with a bleeding, limp deer hung over the car. "I can't bear to see it." She rescued stray animals.

Much of this had been barely overheard. There was never any overt quarreling. But children know these things. There is a coolness in the air of a house where the marriage is faltering.

In some vague way he felt a need to make up to his mother for all this. That, when he thought about it, was the real reason for his particular patience with poor Margaret, so that, unlike his other sisters, he didn't allow himself even to feel exasperated when she wet her pants or upset her plate.

His mother was grateful. "You're so kind to her, Francis," she would tell him, with a look of astonishment.

"You have a Presbyterian conscience," his father said, laughing, but not unkindly. "And the soul of a poet. A strange combination."

He did sometimes feel removed from other people, that was so. It was a kind of shyness that he had, inherited, he was sure, from Teresa. He knew that this shyness would have deprived him of his peers' approval if he had not luckily been given also a strong, tall body and the ability to excel at sports. In such random fashion does fate play with us!

Lately he wondered more often what, indeed, fate might be preparing for him. At seventeen you had to look toward the future. Richard naturally assumed that his son would work in the firm when the time came. His was one of the more prestigious firms on Wall Street; a young man might consider himself fortunate to start there at the top. But the prospect was already distressing to Francis: a lifetime under electric lights on a shelf in a vertical box counting money—for that's what it all came to, really, counting money. And no air, no sun!

Yet he had no alternative in mind. How simple it was when you were possessed by some passionate talent for music or medicine or—or anything! To be just a "bright student" who did well at everything, yet to be without distinction or direction, was burdensome, a somber prospect to a young man who was too serious, anyway.

He had thoughts, sometimes, of going off to be a rancher in the West—he'd been there once on a vacation trip—or of being a forest ranger or a dairy farmer, or just of writing a book in some quiet, leafy spot, although he had no idea what he would write about. Perhaps some sort of history? The past allured him. Before that, though, he'd like to see some more of the world, the places with fantastic names: Bora-Bora, Patagonia. And St. Felice. Yes, certainly, St. Felice, he thought in that last lucid moment before sleep. And he turned on the pillow, finding a comfortable hollow. Let sleep come now, softly. There were, after all, a few years left before he must decide what to do with his life!

The rain died and in its place the night wind rushed. Wind of the world! It shifts and rises, it drives, it goes where it will.

❧6❧

Four years. As always, there had been periods when time sped away like a bright bird; at other moments it plodded heavily and Patrick couldn't wait to get home. Years afterwards, he liked to say that it was England's cold fog that had brought him back to St. Felice, and perhaps there was a kernel of truth in his little joke.

The ship rose and sank with the swells. Standing at the rail, feeling the spray on his face, he realized that he had forgotten how soft the air could be. Overhead, the stars were blue; they looked warm enough to hold in the hand. In the north their glitter was hard and one could believe that they were millions of miles away.

The man beside him, a white man, a civil servant on his way back to Jamaica after a leave, resumed conversation.

"And so you're glad to be home again."

"Yes, as glad as I was to leave four years ago."

"Were you not—comfortable—in England, then?"

The man was middle-class English, reserved and courteous. If they had been anywhere but on board ship, he would not have permitted himself so much curiosity. But then, on land they would not have been conversing at all.

"I was quite comfortable. It was a new world. That is, you can read about a place, but it's never the same when you come to it, is it?"

How to describe the richness, the splendor, the confusion, the strangeness, and the disappointments of four years, when he was still organizing the memories of them in his own head? "I met South Africans, Hindus, Arabs, Japanese—"

The man laughed slightly. "And Englishmen?"

"Yes, yes, of course. My first friend was a miner's son from Yorkshire. He had the room next to mine." Now Patrick laughed. "My first winter they had the worst snow and cold they'd had in thirty years. It was inhuman. I didn't go out for two weeks. He brought me sandwiches and coffee."

He had been a short, ruddy fellow, Alfie Jones, with the congenital indignation of a rooster. The education of the poor, or lack of it, outraged him.

"We had a lot in common, it developed. We're both going home to teach in the poorest district we can find. That won't be difficult on St. Felice, at any rate."

"I should have thought, don't most of—your people—study medicine or law when they go abroad?"

894

"Well, they do. My best friend from home, Nicholas Mebane, is reading law in London. He plans to go into politics. You'll be hearing of him throughout the West Indies, I expect."

The man didn't answer that. Probably took it as a challenge, Patrick thought, although he had not intended it as such. But everyone, especially a civil servant like this one, knew that drastic changes and upheavals were coming.

Now clouds closed over, wiping out the stars in minutes. The sky turned deep gray; the moving water shone like jet. There would be a squall before morning. The contrast between humanity's scrambling and scrapping and the powerful rhythms of indifferent nature could make humanity appear ridiculous, Patrick thought, and then as quickly: But that is ridiculous, too; there are some things you can only get by scrambling for them.

"I have no desire to be political, though," he heard himself say.

"You could go far. In Jamaica there are many good posts for—" The man stopped, having been suddenly afraid, no doubt, that his remarks might be too personal, or even taken as an insult.

"Because I am almost white, you mean?"

"Well, yes, no offense, only facing the reality of the situation. Fair or not."

In England he had been taken for Syrian, for Greek or Hindu. Only here, here at home, there would be no mistaking what he was, or what was his place.

"But in the kind of government that is coming, not what you are running now, such things will not matter," he said evenly.

That silenced the man, who now reached into his pocket for a cigarette and had a time trying to light it between cupped hands against the rising wind. And Patrick felt a contradiction within himself: pleasure at having countered a smug attitude and regret at having embarrassed someone who had intended no hurt.

This contradiction was nothing new. He wished he could get rid of it. Because of it, many an otherwise congenial occasion had been spoiled, at least in part. There had, for instance, been that sumptuous wedding reception to which an English fellow classman had invited Nicholas and him. The bride had lived in a lordly house—three thousand acres of forest and lawn, lofty halls, splendid terraces—built by her eighteenth-century forebears with the proceeds of a West Indian sugar fortune. Standing beside Nicholas on the lawn, he had thought of his mother, come to serve in the Mauriers' house and dazzled by its wealth.

"I feel so black here," he had told Nicholas.

Nicholas had been amused. "Black? You? How should I feel, then? No, it's not race that is bothering you, it's economics. How do you think Alfie Jones, or ninety-nine whites out of a hundred, would feel in this place? You're too self-conscious, Patrick. You ought to get over it."

The man beside him now flung his cigarette into the water. "I'll be turning in. If I don't see you tomorrow—you'll be leaving at Martinique, you said?"

"Yes, I change there to a schooner."

"Well, then, good luck. You're almost home."

"Yes, thank you. Almost home."

*   *   *

AGNES WEPT. "LET me look at you! Let me look at you!"

She was much older than he had remembered. White threaded her hair. She had shrunk. Patrick kept looking at her, searching. They kept looking at each other all day, across the table where they ate and afterwards on the porch, where she rocked in the wicker rocker and people passed in their Sunday clothes with the Methodist Hymn Book under their arms.

They talked and they talked.

"You'll be glad to know it wasn't wasted," he said. "I worked hard. My ideas have jelled. I feel more strongly than ever that education is the answer. We have to build a generation with a whole new system of values. Get rid of stupid learning by rote and total bias toward things European or English. We need imaginative, gifted teachers. When I think of my own poor, ignorant Mistress Ogilvie—"

"You mean you're going to take a place like hers, nursing"—Agnes was scornful—"a pack of babies all day?"

"It can't be news to you that I want to teach, Maman."

"Yes, but I thought in Jamaica, maybe, since they've opened the University College. Certainly not *here* on St. Felice!"

He smiled. "You're sorry I came home, then?"

"You know I'm not! I'm thinking of you; you're too educated now for this measly little place. I prepared you for the world, I didn't think you'd come back here!"

"You came back, didn't you?"

"I'm different. I'm an ignorant woman."

"I'll be fine. Don't worry about me, Maman."

In the morning he took the bus into Covetown, seated between a pregnant woman with two young ones on her lap and another woman with two crated hens on her lap. The rickety-rackety bus careened dangerously over the abominable road, past cane fields and villages of daub-and-wattle houses where the privy stood at the back of the yam patch and naked babies crawled among tethered goats. He regarded it all in partial amazement, as though he had never really looked at it before, and partially with plain acceptance, because it was just the old familiar way of things.

The bus halted in the market square. He got out and walked down Wharf Street past the banks, the sugar brokers, and Da Cunha's, before whose windows tourists stood pricing cameras and watches. The undertaker still advertised coffins made to measure. Climbing the hill toward Government House, he passed the library, smiling at the memory of that far-off boy who had sat there writing his "masterwork" about the Carib Indians. Boys' Secondary came next. Father Baker's office was in the left-hand wing. He went up the path and almost collided with Father Baker.

The priest's round face wrinkled with surprise and pleasure. "Patrick! Don't tell me you're back already! How are you? How are you? Come on and talk to me, let me introduce you to an old friend, Clarence Porter; but of course you know who he is, everybody does."

Patrick looked into the face of a sturdy black man in late middle age. "Forgive me, but I'm afraid—" he said, and was interrupted.

"No need to apologize, young man. My work came long before your time, and if you'd known about it when you were at school you probably wouldn't have cared, anyway." And Porter took Patrick's hand, giving it a rough shake.

The teakettle was on the electric burner in the study; the cups were the same blue and white, stained tan on the inside, from which Patrick had drunk only four years earlier. Father Baker's gown was still spotted. Cries floated from the playing fields beyond the windows as he questioned and Patrick replied. One might never have been away.

While he was giving his account of himself, the big dark man—shades darker than a walnut—sat quietly. He wore a workman's clothing; his hair was gray; his eyes were watchful. When at last there came a lull in the questions and answers, he spoke.

"I was in England myself, many years ago. I could have stayed there, but I chose to come back. I'm glad you did, too."

"Clarence won't tell you much about himself," Father Baker began.

"Who says I won't? There's no virtue in false modesty. I've done my share and I'm not shy about it!"

"No more you should be. But let me tell it. Clarence has lived all over the world, Patrick. He's been a chef's helper in Europe, a travel agent's clerk in New York, a carpenter in Jamaica—"

"And an inmate of five separate jails," Clarence interposed. "Don't forget to put that in."

"I won't forget," Father Baker said quietly. He turned to Patrick. "They were honorable incarcerations. Clarence was jailed for leading strikes against inhuman conditions. He organized the first island-wide union here on St. Felice forty years ago."

Patrick wondered, "How is it I never knew about a thing like that?"

"To our shame," Father Baker said, "we never taught and still don't teach them in our schools. Not even at ours, which is supposed to be, and is, superior."

"Well," Porter said, "it's all ancient history. I'm taking it easy now. Just do a little carpentering when I feel like it, and go to union meetings, but leave the heavy business to the young." He tipped his chair back on two legs. "Oh, if I could write, I could tell—but you'd need a lot of skill to get down on paper all the courage, the fear, and the bloody brutality of those first years. I can remember the deportations and the all-white vigilantes. I can remember when they brought the Royal Wessex Regiment out from England to calm the countryside— But enough of that. Tell us what you're going to do with yourself now," he concluded.

The alert, remarkable eyes now fixed on Patrick made him self-conscious. But he answered simply, "I'm looking for a teaching post in a country district. Somewhere over beyond Morne Bleue in some little place like, well say like Gully, or Hog Run or Delicia."

Porter looked surprised. "You really want to rough it, don't you? I grew up on that side till I was twelve and left home. They still went whaling over there in those days. Used to put lookouts on the hills; when they saw a whale spout they'd signal to the boats and the harpooners would give chase. But all that's changed. Suppose you'll have any trouble getting a post?"

"Jobs are scarce, I know. But I'm well qualified. And I feel sure I can do some good. That's why I want it so much, because I really believe I can."

"You're an idealist, then," Porter said.

Patrick ignored that. "I have a friend—he's my best friend's father—Dr. Mebane. He'll help me. He knows a lot of people."

"Oh, he knows a lot of people! The right people, too." Porter's irony was unmistakable. Nevertheless, he shook hands as Patrick stood to depart. "And if I can ever help you, in some other way, remember me. Or if you just feel like having a talk. My place is on Pine Hill, other side of the harbor, where the working class lives. Name's on the gate: Clarence Porter, carpentry, it says."

"I SHOULD THINK," Dr. Mebane observed, "that Father Baker or one of the other masters might take you on as an assistant. Or something. Teaching in a country school seems rather a step down for you."

"I don't see it as such. 'Give me the child before he is six'—don't the Jesuits say that?"

"You could do more to mold the mind in secondary school."

"How many of our children ever get to secondary school?"

Dr. Mebane looked out over the harbor where two white yachts rode gleaming in the sun.

"The pay is much less," he said.

"I don't require much to live."

"You're an idealist!"

Patrick laughed. "That's what Clarence Porter said yesterday."

"How do you know him?"

"He was with Father Baker when I went to call."

"That figures. The good father is a sympathizer."

"Sympathizer?"

"With labor."

"Isn't that a good thing?"

"Of course. But there are ways and ways. Porter has always been an angry man. Too angry."

"There's much to be angry about, isn't there? Or sad. You know what, Doctor? There are times when I am so sad, when I think of our history, our long history in this place—"

"I hope you're not affected that way too often. You're very young. If you can't enjoy some lighthearted selfishness now, when can you? I detect a tendency in you to be too emotional, Patrick."

The clock struck the half hour. Its delicate *ping!* befitted the fussy room, the tasseled pillows heaped on the sofa and the dyed feathers in a glass vase on the bookcase. Once he had thought this house was the zenith of elegance; now he had learned better. It merely yearned toward elegance.

"Besides," Dr. Mebane resumed with vigor, "you have another history on this island. An English history, a French, or both. Their blood runs in our veins, too. And it's proud blood: explorers, aristocrats, Huguenots fleeing the Terror."

Patrick was silent.

"I keep that in mind whenever I sit in the Council or in any official capacity."

It is the pomposity of old age, Patrick thought. Even Nicholas had remarked it once, not unkindly, of his father.

"Things are improving all the time and further than I thought possible. Federation is almost upon us. I was a delegate to the Representative Government Association at Roseau in Dominica in 1932 when all we hoped for was popular representation in the legislatures, an expansion of the suffrage. I have stuck with the movement ever since. Three years ago I was in Montego Bay—that was in February 1956—at the invitation of London to discuss the Moyne Commission report and to draft a federal constitution. So far have we come in these few years! I'm an optimist, Patrick, it's the only way to survive. . . . You don't want to go into politics with Nicholas? You'd make a fine team, the two of you."

"Politics don't interest me in that way. I'm a teacher."

"Well, then, we'll just have to get you a job, won't we? But you'll need some recreation, too; would you like me to put you up at the Crocus Club? We've just bought a boat for deep-sea fishing and—"

"It's too expensive for me, I'm afraid," Patrick murmured.

"It isn't; you'd be surprised. Of course, the social business can get silly; it's the tennis that really attracts me. Still, you do meet interesting people. The movers and doers."

"Thanks very much, but if I could be settled first at work, then—"

"I'll do everything I can, Patrick. I miss my son—you can take his place this next year. Then, when he comes back, I'll have the two of you."

I am too critical, Patrick thought, going home. Mebane had his quirks, as who of us had not? That particular quirk about ancestry was one that Patrick had remarked in him a long time before. He ought to be grateful for the man's friendship. And he was grateful. Yet, the doctor was a small man. Like his house, he seemed to have grown smaller since Patrick had grown up. He had remembered them both, the house and the man, as large and impressive. They were neither.

HE HAD BEEN teaching for three months, living at Gully, a village hung halfway between a mountaintop and the sea, in a meager one-room house on stilts no better than the homes of his pupils. Sometimes, preparing the next day's lessons by the light of a kerosene lamp, he was flooded with a sensation of virtue which he immediately stifled as being ugly, unjustified, and smug. For the most part he was still exhilarated; the minds of his appealing little children were the emptiest possible slates, and as his were to be the first marks upon them, he felt like a great experimenter, a messenger, literally, from abroad.

One Saturday he went down into Covetown to do some shopping, stopped for a beer, looked for Father Baker, who was out, thought how pleasant it would be when Nicholas was back again, roamed some more streets, and found himself on the far side of the harbor in the section called Pine Hill.

At one time, obviously, the hillside must have been covered with pines; now it was covered with flat-roofed bungalows, each with its fenced-in cement square that passed for a yard, some bougainvillaea vines, and some sort of vehicle in a shed—a Ford car, a light truck, or a Honda. It was a wage-earner's neighborhood, in which the prosperity of an owner could be gauged by the tidiness of his possessions and the freshness of his paint.

Suddenly Patrick remembered Clarence Porter. He walked on, searching among the names on the gateposts. Porter's house, no more costly than those surrounding it, had a grass yard, bright blue shutters, and tubs of flowers on the front porch. Porter himself was sitting on the porch.

"Remember me?" Patrick asked. "You said I might drop in for a talk sometime."

"Sure, sure! Come in. Draw up a chair. Anything special you wanted to talk about?"

"To tell the truth, no. I guess I was just feeling a little lonesome. Wanted some adult conversation."

"That's right, you're with kids all the time now, aren't you? Have a beer."

"Thanks, I just had one downtown."

"Have another."

Porter fetched the beer. Patrick began the conversation in the conventional fashion.

"You've a nice house here."

"Built it myself. Built two, as a matter of fact. That yellow one up at the end of the street is mine, too. I rent it out. You get a good view from here, good breeze, same as they get on Library Hill, only it costs half as much."

Patrick acknowledged that that was so. Far below, the boats were dots in the harbor and Covetown's business section was a cluster of white rooftops. He had not realized he had climbed so far.

"My wife loved it, being up this high. She's dead now. I live here with my daughter Dezzy. Name's Désirée, but I call her Dezzy, which she hates." Porter chuckled. "She works at Da Cunha's selling things she can't afford to buy. Maybe you've seen her—very tall, almost as tall as you, long hair."

"I don't go to Da Cunha's. I can't afford it, either."

"Guess not!" Porter chuckled again. He struck a match, lit his pipe, and lounged back. "So! Dr. Mebane got you what you wanted, I see."

"Yes. I appreciate it."

"Aside from that, what do you think of him?"

The blunt question was discomfiting. "Well, I've known him since I was thirteen. I was always welcome in their house. I was from Sweet Apple, you know; my mother had a little store there, still has; Dr. Mebane was very kind to me—"

"Of course he was! Look at yourself! Your color, I mean. Has he invited you to join the country club?"

"Yes. I'm not going to, though."

"My daughter couldn't join his club. She's too dark."

There was a silence. The man's sense of injury was palpable. And Patrick said gently, "Perhaps she doesn't want to, anyway."

"The funny thing is, she would love it. Just as she would love to buy the stuff on Da Cunha's shelves. But that's natural. Women always want things. I myself couldn't care less." He tipped forward and knocked his pipe out on the porch railing. "It all stems from the white man and his concubines! These light-brown people like to think about how they've descended from the aristocracy of Europe. They don't want to remember Africa. A seat in the legislature, a collar and tie, being invited to a reception at Government House—that's all it took to buy them off. And the British Colonial Office has done just that!"

"Surely—" Patrick began, but Porter was not to be stopped.

"Do you know how many of these so-called upper-class browns owned slaves themselves? They were cruel masters, most of them, as cruel as the whites. They had learned well, let me tell you. Why, even as recently as the nineteen twenties — Listen. I remember there was a white man, an Englishman who came out here with a company that was to put streetlights downtown, a socialist he was, serious redhaired fellow; he went around making friends among the blacks here, the working class; made a few speeches, harmless enough. One night a gang beat him up. After that, they got rid of him, shipped him back to England, and who do you think applauded, who was behind it?"

"The planters, naturally?"

"Of course, the planters, the powerful families, men like old Virgil Francis. But never think the Mebanes and their kind didn't go right along. They've got their little vested interests, too, and the lower wages are, the more stays in their pockets."

Patrick said doubtfully, "But this is nineteen fifty-nine. People think differently now. I know that Nicholas Mebane isn't like his father, if his father is altogether what you say he is."

Porter stared at him a moment. "I hope you're right. I don't know. I get heated up. I'm not very tactful, am I?"

"Not very." Patrick laughed. Porter's vehemence was interesting, anyway.

"I shoot my mouth off. I'm self-educated. I read everything. Father Baker helped me. He's a man, a real man."

"Even though he's white?"

"Even though he's white. He thinks a good deal of you, by the way. He tells me—"

"I'd rather hear about you. About the early unions. I know almost nothing about them."

Porter looked pleased. He cleared his throat. "It's a long story. But in a nutshell, this is it. We had small unions as far back as the eighteen nineties, mostly in the construction trades. They didn't get far then because picketing was against the law. Also, a union could be sued for damages resulting from a strike. It took a world war, the first, and then a world depression to change things. You're too young to recall the bloodshed in the thirties. Strikes and riots from Trinidad to St. Lucia, from coal bearers to sugar workers. Slow, slow progress. But it's only the labor movement that's put another meal on the table, remember that."

The man's voice swayed Patrick, drew pictures in his mind. Sweet Apple, years ago, and the eight-year-olds working in the cane. Gully now, the children walking shoeless in the rain, bringing a lunch of lard on bread to school.

"But," he said, "when federation comes, economic progress will come with it. You condemn Dr. Mebane—and I do understand some of what you mean—but still, it is men like him who are bringing this great change about. With the end of colonial rule will come wider social justice. It's bound to come."

"Perhaps. Perhaps. Oh, I don't want you to think I'm an embittered man, prejudiced against people because they have more money than I have or their skin is lighter than mine—I wouldn't be talking like this to you if that were the case, now would I? But what I fear is this: We'll get our political independence only to have a new class step into the Englishman's shoes, and the workman will be no better off. Or not much."

The gate clanged. Against the glare of five o'clock sunlight Patrick could see only a tall, thin figure, obviously female, coming up the walk.

"Got the soapbox out again, Pa? I could hear you halfway to the corner."

"Come in out of the dazzle, it hurts my eyes. This is Patrick Courzon, a friend of Father Baker's. My daughter Dezzy. I told you, she hates being called Dezzy. She likes to be called Désirée."

"Why not? It's my name."

The girl set her packages down on the table.

"What have you got there, now?" Porter wanted to know.

"Dishes. A set of Spode."

"Good God! You hand them back all your wages on gewgaws!" It was a reproach, but a tender one.

"We needed dishes. The old ones are a disgrace. And these are seconds. You'd never know the difference, though."

"Well, I certainly wouldn't!"

She reached into the box and held up a cup. "There! Isn't that a lovely pattern?"

Patrick was not looking at the cup. He was looking at the pleasure in her face, the most beautiful he had ever seen. It was a classic face with narrow, sculptured lips, large, round-lidded eyes, and a thin, patrician nose—all of these cast in ebony. She wore a red blouse and a white skirt. She had a silver chain on her wrist. Something profound and powerful stirred in Patrick's chest. Afterwards he thought it must have been fear that she would vanish as easily and quickly as she had appeared.

In those few seconds he was changed.

She addressed him. "Has my father been bending your ear?"

"Oh, no, not at all. I've been enjoying myself." A stilted answer, schoolmaster-ish and dull, when he was capable of doing so much better! Her beauty had quenched his flow, silenced his wit.

Porter asked, "Why don't you invite Mr. Courzon to supper?"

"Patrick. Please, my name is Patrick."

"Patrick, then. You're invited," said Désirée. "I'll have it ready in half an hour."

The table, at one end of the front room, had been set with the new dishes.

Hibiscus flowers, cerise and yellow, floated in a crystal bowl. He saw that the bowl was very fine.

Clarence Porter followed Patrick's gaze. "Another Da Cunha special. Out of place in this house."

"Beauty is never out of place," Désirée said.

Patrick ate silently, while a pleasant banter crossed and recrossed the table. The girl got up to fetch the next course. From where he sat he could see into the large, clean kitchen. He watched her moving about, watched as she lifted her hair and twisted it into a coil on top of her head. That long, straight hair, heavy as rope—from where had she got it? From some Arab traders wandering south and west into Africa two centuries ago? Or from some Spanish buccaneer who had wandered into the slave cabins on this very island?

"It gets so hot on my neck," she complained, with a little petulant sigh.

"Désirée is part Indian," Clarence Porter said, as though he had read Patrick's mind. "My wife's great-grandmother was a pure Carib, off the reservation."

This time the father had given her the name that belonged to her. The name had a caressing sound, apart from its meaning. If you didn't know the meaning of *desire,* those syllables alone would tell you.

"And what do you think of the land settlement they are pressing for on St. Vincent?" Porter asked.

"Pa, don't!" Désirée turned to Patrick. "My father is too serious. Sometimes I simply have to close my ears."

Porter was amused. "All right, I'll be quiet."

"Too much heavy talk," she said. "Taste the ice cream. Look out at the evening."

Patrick followed her gesture. The sun was an orange ball, tipped on the long, even line where the sky met the sea. Covetown lay in cobalt shadow.

"How wonderful it is!" she said softly.

Her perfume smelled like sugar. Flowers and sugar.

"The time is today," she said, as if to herself.

Patrick looked up at her then. "You know, you're right," he said.

Too much heavy talk. Everything has grown too heavy. Ever since I was six years old, when Maman sent me off to school, it's been a competition. Work. Strive. Be earnest. But what of laughter? It's true. The time is today.

His courtship was short. He needed only a few weeks to learn what he wanted to know about her.

He took her to dinner at a place he couldn't afford, Cade's Hotel at the end of Wharf Street. It was a fine, square stone house with a high-walled garden and, if one didn't count boarding houses, the only place on the island where travelers could stay. In a quiet dining room, dominated by a loud tall clock and gilt-framed portraits of the royal family, one dined alongside English tourists and traveling salesmen on expense accounts. Locals, the whites and the near-whites, came occasionally for a change from their clubs.

Désirée had never been inside. Her pleasure was infectious.

"Look at that, Patrick, will you!"

"That" was a colored print of Queen Victoria at Balmoral, a scene replete with enormous yardages of plaid, fuzzy little dogs and a view of cold, foggy mountains.

"Scotland," he said. "I've been there."

Her eyes widened. "Oh, I would like to see it! I would like to see everything, anything. I've never been anywhere. Only once to Martinique and once to Barbados."

So, over drinks, he retold his English years as best he could, bringing color and drama to the telling, enjoying her attention. With a flourish of expertise he ordered the dinner: calalu soup and crab farci.

"I've never had crab cooked this way," she said.

"It's the French style. These are land crabs. They're fed for a few days on pepper leaves. Then they're baked."

"How do you know so much about cooking?"

"I don't. I only happen to know about a few French dishes because my mother is from Martinique and she's a wonderful cook."

Désirée was silent for a moment. Then, hesitating, she inquired, "Your mother —she came to Martinique from France?"

"No, she was born there and so were her people before her." And aware that this was not the answer that the girl was seeking, he said quietly, "What you're really asking is whether my mother is colored or white."

"I'm sorry! I didn't mean—"

"It's all right. My mother is dark, quite dark."

"As dark as I am?"

"No. Nor as beautiful, either."

He thought he saw her frown. Her face was lowered and he couldn't be sure.

"Is there anything wrong, Désirée?"

She raised her head. "You understand, I—we—don't go to places like this. Without you, I wouldn't be here. They wouldn't put us out, but they would make us so unwelcome that we wouldn't want to come."

"Of course, I understand."

An ant, crawling up the side of the water bowl in which the sugar bowl had been set, fell struggling into the water. Patrick shoved the whole contrivance to the other side of the table.

He laughed. "Look, it's not so fancy—you needn't be overawed. For me, in fact, the ants remind me of home."

She laughed, too. "You make me feel good."

"I don't think *you* need anybody to make you feel good. It's the other way around when I'm with you."

"Is it? Then I'm glad."

"You're a glad person."

"Well, I am most of the time. Or I try to be. The trouble with me is, I want things so badly."

"What things, for instance?"

"Oh, I don't know. Just a vague kind of wanting inside." She made a fist at the hollow of her throat. "When I see something beautiful . . . The Da Cunha brothers have pictures in their houses. There was one I loved, a ruined building, all columns and moonlight, you could feel you were there. Rome, Mr. Da Cunha said. He gave me a print of it for Christmas. I have it in my room."

The simple, childish recital touched him, reminding him of himself at age fourteen or so, reminding him, too, of the "blank slates" on which from Monday through Friday he struggled to write something that might inspire and endure.

"Désirée," he said softly. "I'll always call you that." Then realizing the implication of that "always," he added, "I'm going to know you for a long, long time."

In the evening they walked, carrying their shoes, on the long beach beyond the harbor. Between the ocean and the pine hills lay the salt pond, rose pink in the faltering light.

"This one has been here since the time of the Caribs," Patrick said.

"What makes it pink?"

"The algae. Red algae."

"You know so much. You know everything."

He glanced at her. For a second it flashed through his mind that such praise might be a mere feminine trick, the flattery that is supposed to ensnare a man; but no, her honesty was total. The quick-talking girl with the tossing hair who had subdued him at first meeting was, under the surface of a touching worldliness, only a naïve and tender child. And he knew that he had won her.

A pair of black-necked stilts came running through the shallow water.

"Hush," she said. "Watch them."

But he was watching her. In the still, unmoving air, her perfume was strong again: sugar and flowers. He touched her arm.

"Come," he said.

In a pine hollow, perfectly hidden, dark and soft, they lay down. He removed her white blouse and skirt. How many women had he known? As many as any man his age and as many varieties: the eager and lustful, the indifferently accommodating, those who had to be coaxed or pretended that they had. This one was different.

It was her first time. He felt an excess of tenderness on discovery, but no guilt or remorse, because he knew himself; knew, as his hands thrust the heavy hair from her shoulders, smoothed her firm breasts and long thighs, that he would never leave her. And he felt as they lay there together, both of them too overcome or perhaps too shy as yet for words, that she knew it, too.

When at last they stood up, it was quite dark.

"Shall we come here again tomorrow?" he asked.

"But it's a working day, isn't it? You have to travel so far."

He trembled. "Why? Don't you want to? Are you afraid?"

She laid her head on his shoulder. "No. I was only thinking of you."

So they will merge to make a whole. A serious man will respond to a sensual woman and to her delights, whether they be in a bauble or the music of rain or— or in himself. She grasps life with both hands and will teach him her way. While, he, born earnest, will draw her up to form, out of her young, captivating spirit, new tenderness and new strength.

*   *   *

AGNES WAS ANGRY. He had taken Désirée to meet her in Sweet Apple one Sunday afternoon.

"You're not going to marry that girl?"

"I haven't asked her yet, but I'm sure she will."

"My God, but the older you get, the more stupid you get!"

"I can't think what you mean!"

"You can't think? Well, look at her! A dark girl like that! A smart man marries up! He marries light, to improve himself and his children, don't you at least know that?"

He controlled himself. "I don't understand you, Maman. After all you have told me about the years of slavery, you can still talk like this?"

"What has that got to do with it? You have a way of twisting what I say, you always do."

"It's you who are twisting, you who're so confused that—"

But she had gone out, slamming the door.

He took a sheet of paper and wrote out something he had seen once in a history book about the slavery era.

> White plus black equals mulatto.
> Mulatto plus black equals sambo.
> Mulatto plus white equals quadroon.
> Quadroon plus white equals mustee.
> Mustee plus white equals mustafina.

He shouted, "What the hell am I?"

He looked in the mirror. Quadroon? Mustee? God damn! Who was the man who had fathered him? Three generations away from slavery, Agnes was, and still the confusion was entrenched, the pride and the shame intertwined like a nest of snakes. A stubborn woman who would not, simply would not, talk.

And yet, what difference would it make if she did talk?

In a burst of rage he threw his hairbrush across the room, splitting the handle of the brush and making a dent on the door.

Agnes opened the door. "I'm sorry," she said.

She stood there, breathing hard, holding on to the wall. For the first time he noticed her knobby, arthritic fingers. A lonely old woman, nearing the end of a lonely and limited existence. What could she know? His anger dissolved.

"I'm wrong," she said. "Go ahead and do what you want. Whatever makes you happy."

He knew she only meant it in part. Her feelings would not change. So this would have to do.

"YOU'RE MARRYING CLARENCE Porter's daughter? A beautiful girl," said Dr. Mebane. "Not radical like her father, I hope? No offense meant."

"No. She isn't interested in public affairs."

"That's good. A man's woman. When will it be?"

"As soon as she will." He had to have her. Suppose someone else were to come along one afternoon while he was away in Gully? He went cold at the thought.

"Why don't you wait a little? Nicholas will be home in a year and the two of you could have a little fun together. Spend a week in Barbados. Jamaica, even. Enjoy yourself. There's time before you need to tie yourself down."

"It's not being tied down when you want it," Patrick said gently.

"I just hope you're sure of your own mind. There are a lot of girls around." He meant, You could do better.

"I'm sure," Patrick said.

Clarence Porter was happy. "I knew it all along. I could tell the first day you laid eyes on her. And she on you."

They were to live in Clarence's other house at the top of the street. The present tenants were to move and Clarence would paint the place fresh for them.

"I'm so relieved we'll live in town," Désirée said. "I never liked the country."

"You couldn't live where I am now, anyway. I'll just get up an hour earlier each day and drive." He had bought a wheezing car, third or fourth hand. "We'll have to get a ring for you at Da Cunha's."

"Da Cunha's, Patrick? Where are you going to get enough money for that?"

"Don't worry, it won't be anything very large! But my mother sold a piece of land she had in Martinique and gave me some money a few years ago. Enough for my education and a bit left over."

"Then maybe we can have a better house of our own sometime."

"I don't know. Teachers don't earn much."

"Perhaps you won't always be a teacher."

He scarcely heard her.

THEY WERE MARRIED at the Anglican Church of the Heavenly Rest on the ocean side of St. Felice. It was a small Gothic building that might well have stood at a crossroads in the Cotswolds, except for the coconut palms along the edge of the graveyard and the breaking surf on the shore two hundred feet below the cliff. For fifty years now it had been more or less abandoned by the planter families who had built it, the advent of the automobile having made it easy to attend cathedral services in Covetown.

"But I would like to be married there," Patrick had told Father Baker. "I love the age of it, the way it has rooted itself like a tree."

The little group—the bride and groom, with Clarence Porter and Agnes— arrived ahead of Father Baker. They wandered along the nave. The filtered light of stained-glass colors, amber, rose, and lavender, lay on ancient, pale memorials, on florid script chiseled into stone.

In holy Remembrance of Eliza Walker Loomis, devoted Wife and Mother, a charitable and pious Example to her Relations.

Alexander Walker Francis, born in the Parish of Charlotte in the year of Our Lord seventeen hundred and fifty-two. Died in the service of His Majesty, King George the Third in the year of Our Lord seventeen hundred and seventy-eight. Valiant and honourable in the performance of his sacred Duty to God, King and Country.

In the dampness of the unused building lichen had begun to creep, obliterating the old words.

Borne aloft on Angel Wings. Here lie interred the Remains of Pierre and Eleuthère François, infant sons of Eleuthère and Angélique François, died and entered into Paradise on August the fourth in the Year of Our Lord seventeen hundred and two at the Age of eight Months. Our Tears shall water their Grave.

"Francis," mused Désirée. "And François. The same family, do you suppose?"
"It is the same," Agnes said.
Father Baker came. Patrick took Désirée's hand and they went to the altar. Through the poetry of the marriage service scraps of thought went in and out of his head: I wish Nicholas were here today with us. . . . It's not really Gothic, those are Corinthian pilasters. . . . I don't want to forget what he is saying.
He did remember kissing Désirée and shaking Father Baker's hand. He remembered the creak of the old door as they went out from dimness into light and drove away.
They circled the island, making a slow trip back to Covetown. On a hill where a little river curved to the sea he stopped the car to look at the view.
"See over there," said Désirée.
A columned house stood alone on the slope. Not large, it still had a simple grandeur.
"Imagine the view from those windows!" she cried.
"Perfect, I should say."
"It's called Eleuthera. It's empty now. I don't know why."
"Eleuthera! It seems to me I was there once."
"What would you have been doing there?" she asked him curiously.
"I don't know. Perhaps I only imagine I was."
"Oh, I should love to live in a house like that. Wouldn't you?"
He laughed. "I assure you I never give it a thought, my darling."
"Perhaps you could have lived in a place like that someday if you hadn't married me."
"Why, what on earth do you mean?"
"Who knows how far you could go? Without me you could join the Crocus Club, for instance."
He leaned over and kissed her. "I have absolutely no desire to join the Crocus Club. And this is no talk for a wedding day, or ever."
The sweet night fell in a jalousied room above the garden of Cade's Hotel.
She woke once from half sleep. "Have you ever had a white girl?" she asked him.
"No," he said, astonished.
"Why not?"

"I never wanted to." He could have had them, prostitutes, near-prostitutes, and once the sister of a Cambridge Fellow. Piqued by curiosity about him, no doubt. A novelty, he'd have been.

"Funny," Désirée said.

"Not funny at all. Anyway, I don't want you to talk like that."

He drew her to him. The dark, dark beauty of her! Warm perfume of wind-blown grass and sun, fragrance of night, of woman and earth! He had it all, all he would ever want, this one only, no other. Flowers, moist on a ledge in the unexpected corner of a desert. The blue eye of a lake on a towering mountain. Landfall after a long, long voyage.

❧{ 7 }❧

Ruin, on the day it descends, is actually no more sudden than is disease. The rot that is cancer was not created in the instant of discovery; slowly, unrecognized or only unacknowledged, it has long been making its secret way. And so it is with the secret disappointment in a marriage or with a financial collapse.

For some time Francis had been aware of trouble behind the closed door of the inner office. With hints, frowns, questions, and long silences, his father had revealed that something of consequence was happening within the company. It had to do with an enormous, risky loan, a grandiose project and unreliable people—in short, a gamble. Canneries and food processing were involved; as news leaked out and auditors, hastily summoned, moved in and out of the rooms pulling papers from file drawers, it came to be spoken of by some sardonic underlings (although never where they thought Francis could hear, for after all, he was a partner's son) as the Tomato Scandal.

It was as the Tomato Scandal that it burst at last onto the front page of the morning papers. In his newly furnished dining room above Central Park, Francis read: RESPECTED FIRM TO GO UNDER, S.E.C. INVESTIGATORS REVEAL.

My God! How had his father allowed this to happen? And did it really merit a two-column headline? At the same moment he knew it was naïve of him not to understand that the failure of such a house as Luther, Baines and Company was front page news, indeed. He broke out into a sweat.

"What is it, Francis? You look as if you'd been struck by lightning," Marjorie said.

"I have been." He handed the paper to his wife.

While she read, he watched her. They had been married for only eight months, and he was still not over his surprise at having won her, who was so smooth and assured, so different from himself. He was still not accustomed to the sight of her, fresh and animated as she was even in the mornings, wearing her silk robe and with her short dark hair perfectly in place. Her lips moved as she read— he always teased her about lip reading—and he wondered what she could be thinking about this failure of the family which she had so recently joined. She had very high concepts about duty and honor and status. Her own family was not rich, but it had distinction, and she was, he knew, very proud of that. He had met her at a cousin's party. Funny, he hadn't even wanted to go that night, either. But his father had been distressed when he had mentioned that he might not go, so he had gone, and there she had been.

His father had been distressed about him for more important reasons, too. He was thirty years old and he still hadn't done what was expected of him, namely, joining the firm. Instead, he had gone to South America with the Peace Corps; he'd taught school on an Indian reservation in New Mexico; he'd worked as supervisor on a dairy farm in upstate New York. He'd embarked on a master's degree in history. That's what he'd been doing when he met Marjorie.

A tall girl with magnificent dark eyes, she had a cool, quiet manner that said "quality." But it had been her voice that drew him. Funny, to be so moved by a simple thing like a voice, so that you kept coming back and back and couldn't stay away. It was like listening to the rush of water or staring into flames. Even her laughter soothed him, registering somewhere, he estimated, in the middle strings of a harp—he knew little about musical instruments—it soothed him, giving promise of tender and exquisite delights.

He had almost come to blows with his cousin.

"She's a cold fish, Francis. Not your sort. Can't you see she's not your sort?"

His cousin hadn't understood! He had common tastes; naturally, Marjorie's classic calm, her classic reserve, would baffle him. As for himself, he was entranced. She was like no girl he had ever known.

It had been only sensible, upon marrying her, to go into his father's firm. After all, he'd had his years of leafy wilderness and exotic places; having Marjorie meant, of course, supporting her. So he had been well aware of his good fortune in being able to embark so easily on the new life; to have this dining room with a view of the park where on Sundays they went bicycling or skating together, this bedroom where they lived their lovely nights.

Marjorie laid the paper down. "We ought to go over there," she said.

"Over where?"

"To your parents. It's only right that we should be with them."

Yes, of course it was. Marjorie would see that.

The scene in the dining room of his parents' house was the same as the one they had left. Coffee cups had been shoved aside to make room for the spread newspaper. His mother was reading it; Margaret was dribbling the milk from her cereal spoon. His father, who was standing at the window, turned around when Francis and Marjorie came in.

"Why didn't you tell me it was this bad?" Francis asked gently.

"You couldn't have done anything."

That was true enough. More to the point, he wondered what he could do now. He sat down beside his mother and put his hand on her arm.

Richard observed the gesture. "It's your mother I feel for," he said. "I thought we could get out of it quietly. But the damn newspapers—"

Teresa looked up. A familiar vein twitched in her cheek and her lips were tight, as if her hand had been pressing them shut so that whatever passion or rage was within might not be allowed to escape. Francis had seen that, often enough. It was nothing new.

After a moment or two she spoke.

"Richard, I don't care about that. Today's scandal will be forgotten next week. All I care about is that my children don't suffer because of this."

"I suppose," Richard said, in a shaky voice, "I suppose what I should do is commit suicide. Like Wayne Chapman. You remember when Chapman, Searls and Fitler crashed twelve years back and Wayne went out the window?"

"What would that solve?" Teresa asked.

Prattling, Francis thought. His father's appalling offer, which he intended to be so tragic, was only foolish melodrama. His mind turned and turned.

"There's the property on St. Felice. It's Mother's, so it won't be touched by all this."

Teresa spoke again. Her voice was flat, without accusation, and this very flatness made it all the more accusatory. "The property on St. Felice is gone and has been for a long time, Francis, except for one piece, my grandfather's rundown place in the north. I learned that this morning."

"Gone?" Francis echoed. "I don't understand." He looked from one to the other of his parents.

"Tell them, Richard," Teresa said.

"Well, you see, expenses were high and with so much tied up in securities—" Richard faltered.

Fool, Francis thought.

"I had to raise cash from time to time. So I disposed of the properties. Oh, I got a fair price for them, I didn't throw them away! Herbert Tarbox bought them for his son, for Lionel. I always got a very fair price—I can show you all the documents."

Francis ignored him. "So your brother, your half-brother, has it all," he said to his mother.

"Not everything," Richard corrected. "There's the place your mother mentioned—"

"Eleuthera," Teresa said, sighing.

Francis demanded scornfully, "Why didn't he buy that, too?"

"He didn't want it."

"And you did all this without Mother's knowledge? Just like that?"

"Not just like that. From time to time, over the years. I had power of attorney. She never knew anything about business, anyway."

Richard turned back to the window. Francis followed his gaze to the back yard, where a late, wet snow was falling on what in a month's time would be a showy bed of imported tulips.

And suddenly, the incredulous outrage in Francis melted into pity. His father was totally gray: his hair, his face, his flannel suit. His wrists, with the fine watch —"the most expensive watch in the world," he had boasted—were helpless as the hands of the dead. Poor, proud fool. The world, his particular world, would judge him with contempt; it had small patience with failure. Almost, Francis could feel more sadness for him than for his mother, who would, as always, weather what she had to.

Someone had to take charge. "So Eleuthera is left," Francis said. "We'll sell it and put the money in trust for Mother. Let's see what we can get for it."

Richard took up the idea. "Yes, yes, I can write to Lionel to put it into the hands of a local agent."

Francis made a swift determination. "No Lionel. No local agent. I want to take care of it myself."

His mother started. "What do you mean? Go there in person? Go down to St. Felice?"

"Why not? It's the only way to get anything done. Do it yourself."

"That's ridiculous! You don't know anything about the area! You'd be wasting time and energy. What do you know about property values down there? It's ridiculous!"

"Not at all," Francis said. Excitement mounted in him, the adrenaline of anger, adventure, and action. "How energetically will Lionel pursue your interests? Maybe he would and maybe he wouldn't. No, I'm the one to go."

"I don't want you to, I said." The pulses in Teresa's neck were visible. Her cheeks were dark red. "That long trip—it'll come to nothing—"

"I can't understand your objection," Richard spoke timidly. "Unless you'd prefer to have me go. One of us really should."

"You have enough to handle here," Francis told him.

"No one listens to me!" Teresa cried shrilly, pathetically. Her calm, that air of being able to stand up under any amount of pressure, was suddenly shattered. Certainly, she had had enough of a blow this morning to shatter it. Yet strangely, or so it seemed to Francis, she was more distressed by the prospect of his journey than by the crumbling of their fortunes. And why?

But he laid his hand on her shoulder. "Leave it to me, please, Mother," he said gently. "I'll work things out." Firmly he added, "Marjorie and I will leave next week for St. Felice. And you're not to worry, hear?"

THE LIGHT CRASHED down from the sky, stunning the senses like a bugle call in the morning.

"My God, how marvelous!" Marjorie cried.

They had been standing among bundles and crated chickens on the schooner's deck since dawn, watching the landscape emerge from the sea in a haze of lavender and gray where day encroached on night. A Turner, thought Francis, who like his father frequently conceived of reality copying art, rather than the other way around. Now, in one instant in this shower of light, everything clarified itself: a clump of roots, a line of surf, a steeple.

The man beside them at the rail, a seedy fellow of uncertain age with a wry mouth, had been talking for the last half hour. He was "in dry goods, shoes, overalls, nigger wares." Francis had started at the ugly word.

"Been coming here since before the Depression. Missed the war, naturally, but now I'm back on the old route. Things are no different. The nigger is still the nigger. A lazy animal. Give him rum and a woman, that's all he wants."

There was no place to move, or Francis would have moved away.

"You folks putting up at Cade's Hotel, are you? It's the only place in town except for some dirty boarding houses. You'll see some funny types at Cade's. Salesmen like me, of course, but mostly English tourists. Retired army people and professors. They come to hike around and study birds. You folks putting up at Cade's?" he repeated.

"No. We have relatives here. We're visiting."

"Now, I'll bet, I'll just bet, you folks have come for the wedding!"

"Wedding?"

"Some planter's daughter. Tarbox, one of the big owners, is marrying the governor's son."

Francis wished he were more adept at lies and evasions.

"We're related to the Tarboxes. And there is to be a wedding, but not until next month."

"Oh. It was in the papers, anyway. So you're related," the man said, with sudden respect.

Ah, well, poor guy, Francis thought, making the swift change from disapproval to forbearance which was so typical of him, poor guy. Now we have become important.

"You planning to stay long?"

"Not very."

"You wouldn't want to. It's a dull place. Hasn't changed in three hundred years. Why, there are parts here without roads, just trails into the mountains! Nobody comes here much, as I told you, except millionaires on their yachts. They like out-of-the-way places. They drop anchor in the harbor, go ashore for a drink with the planters at the country club or the men's club in town, no women allowed. Some of these planters, boiled-shirt types, are worth their weight in gold, but some of them are dirt poor, up to their ears in debt. I wouldn't take the whole island as a gift."

They were well into the bay. At one side stood the remains of a fort, surmounted by cannon, which even now pointed at the schooner as it approached.

"Used to take potshots at pirate ships," the salesman said, showing off for Marjorie. "Cannon like those look small, but they can do a lot of damage. Some of the planters used to keep one on the roof for when the niggers went killing on the rampage. It could happen again today, too; it's not farfetched, let me tell you. And when they do, it'll be bloody. You'd better hope you won't be here when it happens."

The words fell like a shadow on the morning.

"Yes, these islands have seen a lot of blood."

Francis shaded his eyes. The streets were steep, for the town had grown up the side of the hill. The center was a three-sided square, the street along the waterfront marking its fourth side. He could see arcades and wrought-iron balconies: the French had left their mark.

Someone was throwing coins into the harbor. Two black boys dove off the dock and retrieved them. The salesman, laughing, dug in his pocket.

"Nigger kids sure can swim! Well, I'll bid you good-bye. Enjoy your stay. One thing, you've got to hand it to the climate here. Always a breeze. And it won't start raining till June, but you folks'll be gone by then."

"He didn't paint a very good picture," Marjorie said.

At the foot of the gangplank a colored man tipped his straw hat.

"Mr. Luther, suh? Mr. Herbert sent the station wagon. He say welcome to St. F'lice and excuse him, please, it being banana day. They waiting lunch for you at home."

A fragrance, half-sharp, half-sweet, struck Francis in the face. There was languor in it, the perfume of blooming things, mingled with the sea smell of salt and tar. His heart accelerated.

How many generations since the first François had set his foot down in this place? "In the year of Our Lord sixteen hundred and seventy-three—"

He was embarrassed by his own emotion.

"But surely," said Julia Tarbox, for the third time since their arrival, "you knew young Julia's wedding was tonight."

"We thought it was next month," Marjorie said. She was flustered, which was unusual; Marjorie didn't fluster easily. But Julia had authority.

"I thought I had written Tee that we'd advanced the date. Not that it mattered, since she wasn't coming anyway. Of course it's marvelous that you're here. Shall we?" She pushed back her chair and everyone rose from the lunch table. "We'll have our drinks on the veranda. There's a breeze."

The long veranda faced a lawn so brilliantly green as to seem unreal. Beyond the flower borders and a low white fence five or six horses grazed in rich pangola grass.

"Oh, how lovely," Marjorie said.

"Yes, isn't it? Lionel's place is, too, in a different way. They've a view of the water. He and Kate were so sorry to have missed your wedding, but the trip would have been too much for her after her miscarriage." Plaintiveness crept into Julia's voice. "I never could understand how Tee could have stayed away all these years! And not to come for her sister's wedding! We managed to come up for yours! And yet, you know I wasn't even there when she herself was married. I don't know—her grandfather sent her abroad and the next thing I knew she was married. She was scarcely grown. I don't know." No one said anything. And Julia brightened, clasping her still youthful hands. "At least it will be festive tonight! You know, here in the privacy of the family I can admit there's something dream-like about it all. Julia marrying the son of Lord Frame!" She sighed, then turning to Francis, said abruptly, "So your father has managed to lose everything, has he? To tell you the truth, I'm surprised it didn't happen long before this."

Herbert Tarbox coughed. "Isn't that putting it too strongly, Julia?"

"The truth is the truth."

"The truth is not always easy to know." Herbert's firm voice surprised Francis; all during the lunch he had deferred to Julia. "I've known struggle in my lifetime. Women don't know what it is. It's not just getting money, it's holding on to it. You've got to have luck with you." His big red hand clutched the glass of rum on the armrest of his chair; his big red knees bulged from his khaki shorts. "I want to say something to you, Francis. You must be having some thoughts about the sale of all this property. I'd like you to look at the papers, so you'll know that I paid your father top price for every acre."

"I have no doubts on that score, Uncle Herbert."

"I don't understand why I never knew anything about it," Julia complained.

"Because Richard asked me to keep the transactions between ourselves. What his reasons were, I never asked. Had no right to ask." Herbert addressed Francis. "I bought it all for my son, for Lionel. I plan to retire. I've raised sugar and bananas for a quarter of a century, and that's long enough. Now let sugar and bananas support me. Next year this time, maybe before that, Julia and I will have a little place in Surrey. We'll raise a few roses, have a flat in London near young Julia, and maybe spend a winter in Cannes. Who knows?"

"You've worked hard and you deserve it," Francis said. It seemed to be what he was expected to say.

"You don't know how hard. The worldwide Depression began early in the West Indies. In 1923 sugar brought over twenty-three pounds a ton. By 1934 it brought five pounds. We had hunger and riots here. Fire and blood. Then the unions came. Can't blame the workers, it was inevitable. But they've grown too powerful, on your back, clawing at you. The last ten years or so—" He shook his head. "And you've got nature to fight. Floods. Hurricanes." He ticked off on his fingers. "Dampness. Spoilage. The trick is to diversify on export crops. I've put in a lot of cocoa. Lionel's put in sea island cotton and arrowroot. He's a better businessman than I am, and I've not been too bad, I think I can say that without being immodest. So I'll leave it all to my son. He was born here and he knows this life like the back of his hand. His wife does, too."

"Kate is like a man," Julia said sharply.

Herbert laughed. "Hardly! What you mean is, Kate knows agriculture. She gets along with the workers, which is a great help to Lionel."

"It's a good thing he keeps a rein on her," Julia said, "or she'd give everything away to the workers."

"You know, she always reminds me a little bit of your Tee."

"Of Tee? Nonsense! Tee was always quiet. Kate's got opinions about everything."

Herbert was chastened for the moment. "I meant, the way they both care so much about animals and growing things. I remember Tee was like that."

"You don't know a thing about Tee! What do you know about her? Come to think of it, I know very little about her myself."

Marjorie and Francis looked at one another. Herbert changed the subject.

"So you want to sell Eleuthera, Francis?"

"My parents need the money."

"I should have thought," Julia remarked, "that your father would have made a fortune with all the money from these properties. Investing in growing industries."

"Apparently," Francis said dryly, "he invested in ones that didn't grow."

Poor Father! Fortunate for him that he did not have to confront Julia face to face!

"It won't be easy to dispose of," Herbert said. "It's on the wrong side of the island, you have to go over and around Morne Bleue. As the executor when old Virgil died, I had the devil's own time knowing what to do. For a while I had it rented to a fellow who thought he could make it pay, but he gave up and went back to England. It's been lying fallow ever since." He stood up and walked to the other end of the veranda. "Come here, Francis. Look over this way. Thirty-three tons of sugarcane per acre every year. Machinery, that's what makes it possible. Eleuthera's mills, in Virgil's time, still used cogs of the lignum vitae that had come over in sailing ships. The old man never put ten cents into modernizing. That's why it'll be hard to sell."

Francis sighed. "I'll get what I can, that's all I can do. I want to put something aside for my mother and Margaret. You've seen Margaret, so you know what the need is."

Herbert laid a hand on Francis' shoulder. "You're a good son. Talk to Lionel after the wedding. He's got a head for business."

"If you haven't brought anything to wear, Marjorie, I can lend you something for tonight," Julia said. "We're practically the same size."

"Thank you, but I think I'm equipped."

"I thought you would be. I can tell the minute I lay eyes on someone. I like your wife, Francis. She's our kind. Life on this island," Julia continued, as they went upstairs, "has changed just dreadfully since the war. Before then you'd never go to Government House in the evening without black tie. Or to dinner at each other's houses, for that matter. Oh, but my grandmother used to tell me about real elegance! Why, the thermal baths on Nevis were more fashionable for Londoners than anything in Europe! They'd spend the whole winter at the Bath Hotel. That was a hundred years ago, of course. Well, things change and we must change with them. Tonight, though, you'll be meeting some of the oldest families on the island. I do wish Julia would come home, it's four o'clock, she'll be frazzled for the wedding—"

Her voice was still ringing in the upstairs hall when Marjorie and Francis closed their door.

"Well!" Marjorie said. "She's quite a character, your grandmother!"

"Is that all you'd call her?"

"But Herbert is rather sweet, I think."

"He's a decent sort. I don't know how he stands her, but he doesn't seem to mind."

"I'm curious about the daughter-in-law. Obviously, she isn't Julia's favorite person."

"If she's like my mother, as Herbert said, I can see why. They'd be oil and water."

Marjorie sat down to take off her shoes. "Funny that your mother never talks about all this, when it's so spectacular. It really is spectacular, don't you think? All these servants! I haven't counted, but we've certainly seen five since lunch. I love the way the chambermaid walks around in bare feet, don't you? Your grandmother showed me the original kitchen, detached so it wouldn't heat up the house. The paneling downstairs is perfect Adam. You wouldn't see anything finer in England." She flipped a brush through her short hair. Her face sparkled. "This house was a wedding present to a bride in 1778, did you know? Her father had the marble for the floors brought from Italy, and all the silver, the Crown Derby porcelain, came from—"

Francis was amused by her enthusiasm. "You'd like a house like this, wouldn't you?"

"Yes, if you could transplant it to Connecticut or someplace. This is a million miles from nowhere. I should hate it." She took a dress from the closet and held it up. "Darling, does this look all right for a wedding? Thank goodness I threw it in at the last minute. Will I do for tonight?"

He looked at her. She was perfection. He would never get used to having her, never believe the marvel of it.

"Oh yes, you'll do, you certainly will." His voice was thick in his throat. "Pull the spread off the bed, will you?"

"Francis! Whatever—there's no time!"

He looked at his watch. "We've an hour and a half. Pull the spread down."

❧{8}❧

In the lofty rooms of Government House, above the bride and groom, above Lord Derek Frame and Lady Laura, above the diamonds and the silks, hung the stern portraits of the regime: Victoria, wearing stomacher and diadem; Elizabeth the Second, youthful and grave; generals and admirals and judges in white perukes. An orchestra played "Tales from the Vienna Woods." The champagne was presented in fluted glasses on silver trays.

"What a pleasure to see champagne served properly," Julia exclaimed. "I hate those flat things. They're only fit for sherbets."

"This is absolutely fantastic," Marjorie whispered. "Could you ever have imagined a place like this, Francis?"

"You must be Francis and Marjorie," someone said. A hand in a long kid glove touched theirs. "I'm Kate."

Francis looked down, far down, at a small girl with a freckled face. Red-brown hair lay on her shoulders, too much hair for such a little person. Her wide eyes, with very clear whites, were alert and amused.

Lionel stood behind her. "I've been hunting for you everywhere in this crush. You're Marjorie. I always knew you'd find yourself a stunning wife, Francis." His gaze encompassed Marjorie from slippers to earrings.

"No more than you did," Francis answered with proper gallantry.

Marjorie said, "I can't believe we only arrived this morning! It's dazzling. Another world."

"My wife thrives on excitement," Francis remarked tenderly.

"I wish I had six pairs of eyes." Marjorie's own were brilliant. "That wedding dress! I thought mine was something—but this!"

"It belonged to me," Kate said. "Mother—my mother-in-law—had it altered for Julia. My father had no money, so Mother Tarbox bought it for me in Paris. It weighs a ton and the satin sticks to your back. Lucky for Julia it's a cool night."

"But I am sweating," Lionel announced. A large man, not much younger looking than his own father, he ran to early fat. "Shall we find a table outside before they're all taken?"

Fountains of flowers gushed out of stone jardinieres along the steps into the gardens. Flowers ringed the silver candelabra on the tables. Lionel led them to a table where two or three people were already seated and made the introductions.

"Mrs. Lawrence and Miss Lawrence, Mr. and Mrs. Prentice, from London. Father Baker. My nephew, Francis Luther, and his wife, Marjorie Luther."

The British ladies chirped. Father Baker remarked, "You seem more like brothers than uncle and nephew. Not that you resemble one another."

"There are only four years between us."

"So you've come all this way for the wedding," one of the ladies said, making conversation.

"Actually we didn't know the wedding was tonight. Francis came on business," Marjorie explained.

She was literal, Marjorie was. For some reason her reply irked Francis; he was not in the humor for explanations. Lionel leaned across his wife toward Francis.

"Father tells me you want to sell Eleuthera."

"Yes. Do you want to buy it by any chance?"

"I? No, no! I've got all I can handle. But someone will, if you let it go cheap enough. I wouldn't be discouraged," he added kindly.

"I'm not. At least not yet," which was not quite the truth.

"Virgil was fifty years behind the times. But Eleuthera was a poor choice for sugar in the first place. The family's first ancestor picked it out, I can't imagine why. Colonial plantations were usually situated near a harbor, or at least with good road connections to one. But it must have had some meaning for that old pirate," he said almost affectionately. "It certainly had for Virgil. He loved the place."

"It is beautiful," Kate said. "It is like a poem. A dream."

"A dream!" cried Lionel. "Good Lord!"

"There is an engraving of Eleuthera, made in the eighteenth century," Kate said, ignoring him. "The house is in the background. In the foreground it shows a sugar wain drawn by sixteen oxen, eight before and eight behind, to hold the weight going downhill."

"Kate is a history buff," Lionel explained.

"So am I, after a fashion," Francis admitted.

"Then you ought to see those engravings," Kate said. "There is another one, showing some imported deer in a fancy enclosure. There was a lot of extravagant living on these places once."

"A lot of heavy eating, drinking, and other things," Lionel added.

Kate smiled. A separation of two front teeth gave a certain good humor to the smile. Not really pretty, though, Francis thought.

"Kate is a music buff, too," Lionel said. "She plays the piano like mad. And that's not all. She rides a horse like the wind, can handle a sailboat, and on top of all that, she plays Lady Bountiful to the Negro."

The girl's smile left her face as though a rough hand had wiped it away.

Why is he doing this to her? Francis wondered and looked to Marjorie, who was always tactful in awkward situations. (She had, for instance, known how to "handle" Margaret at some difficult moments.) But Marjorie was involved now with the British lady and an elderly gentleman who had joined the group and was pressing a diagram of some sort into the tablecloth with his fork.

Father Baker spoke up. "Kate has a working conscience. She has been a great help to me in many ways."

"With all respect, Father," Lionel said, "I can only agree up to a point." A fine spray of saliva came through his loose, wet lips. "It is all a matter of how much and how far. Back in the eighteen seventies, I'm told, my own grandfather predicted most of the troubles we're having today. He always said"—Lionel looked around and lowered his voice—"said that the trouble would start with the mixed race. They have the intelligence of the white man and the temper of the Negro. With a little more encouragement of the kind some people give them, they will steam up the lowest elements and dispossess us."

"I believe you exaggerate," Father Baker answered.

"I believe not. Oh, I don't think we're going to have communism here, at least not for a long time. They're too busy organizing in more important places than this, like Jamaica and Trinidad. But look, they want one man one vote now, and that'll be the worst mistake ever made, letting people without property have a say in spending public monies. But we're going to have it, no doubt about that, and it's something to worry about. Why even the middle-class, educated browns are worried! You can't tell me they aren't, although they may not always admit it. Take a man like Dr. Mebane, he's a fairly wealthy man. . . . There he is, by the way, coming down the stairs."

Francis saw a dignified brown-skinned man descending the stairs with a brown-skinned woman in an elegant dress.

Father Baker observed wryly, "Quite true. You need not fear confiscation by Dr. Mebane."

"No, fortunately not. His son," Lionel told Francis, "his son is supposed to be brilliant."

"He is," Father Baker said. "He was my pupil."

"He's got a law degree and will run for office, they say. God knows what's going to happen. Maybe it will turn out all right. It's all confusing, to say the least."

"You are a colonialist," Kate said deliberately. "You are living in the wrong century and I'm sorry for you. You would have been so much happier in the eighteenth."

Lionel, laughing, patted his wife's cheek and stood up. "If you all will excuse me, I've people I ought to be talking to. A little politicking. See you later." He leaned over, whispering to Francis, "Don't take the priest too seriously. He's a fuzzy thinker. Bit of a rabble-rouser."

"I'm afraid," Father Baker remarked when Lionel had gone, "that we are boring you with our affairs, Mr. Luther. We island people tend to think we're so important and all the time we're so small."

"No." Kate was stubborn. "We are important. We're a microcosm of the entire world and what is happening to it." Abruptly, then, she changed her tone. "But if you'd rather hear of romance on such a romantic night, I can tell you the tales my great-grandmother told me. She lived until I was ten and she loved to talk about her youth, about quadrilles and mazurkas and traveling theatrical companies from France. In those days many of the older families still spoke French at home.

I could tell you about the staircases—there still are a few on the island—built so wide that three ladies in hoop-skirts could walk down side by side."

She puzzled Francis with her sarcasm and her passion. He didn't know whether he liked her or was sorry for her.

Marjorie had freed herself from the elderly British pair. "Oh, that's delicious, Kate! And do you live in an old house, too?"

"Very old. It's called Georgina's Fancy."

"There has positively got to be a story to a place with a name like that."

"There is, quite a story. The builder was a rich man, of course. He sent his sons to England to be educated, as they all did. One of the sons brought back a bride, Georgina. She was very young, and it's said she never wanted to come here to this far, lonely place. She was terrified of the slaves and with good reason, as it turned out, because she was raped and murdered in a slave revolt. Ten houses were burnt that night and their owners massacred before the revolt was put down."

"Good God!" Marjorie cried, shivering.

"There's a portrait at our house which we think is hers, a kind of imitation Gainsborough of a young girl in an ankle-length dress and black laced slippers, carrying a little dog."

"You're giving me goose bumps," Marjorie said.

"Yes, can you picture it? The sultry darkness, everybody sleeping, she in a great four-poster bed, and then the slaves creeping in at the windows, carrying machetes, no doubt. And they must have had torches, to fire the house."

"Savages!" Marjorie breathed.

"Yes. And yet one can understand. She must have been an ancestor of yours, Francis. Of course! Georgina's Fancy was a Francis estate! She might have been your great-great—don't know how many greats—grandmother. Or aunt, anyway."

It had grown quite dark, a violet evening. From a pond somewhere not far off frogs began to throb and trill. Two boys drew up chairs to Father Baker's side and talked about cricket. A young woman across from Marjorie started a conversation about auctioning the contents of a French manor house. Francis glanced at his watch. It was not yet time to leave. But it had been a long day and he was suddenly tired. Marjorie and the other woman changed to the subject of cars, or maybe it was cigars. The frogs and the orchestra drowned the words.

Kate Tarbox lit a cigarette. He ought probably to talk to her, since the man on her other side was busy with somebody else.

"Do you have children?" he asked, and was immediately shocked at himself for having forgotten about the miscarriage that had prevented her attendance at his own wedding.

She replied quietly, "No."

Then he said, "Well, you certainly seem to keep busy with public affairs, don't you?" Oh, Lord, worse and worse! He was saying all the wrong things.

She answered with a blunt question. "What do you do?"

"I've been in the securities business with my father."

"Oh, yes, surely, I remember. Do you like it?"

"Not particularly." He surprised himself with his reply, for he had thought, during this past year, that he did, after all, like it well enough.

"Why do you do it, then?"

"I don't know. I drifted into it. I guess that's the best answer I can give."

"It's an honest answer, anyway."

He tried to think of something else to say. "What is this tree we're sitting under? The roots are extraordinary, I've never seen one like it."

"It's a banyan. From India. Practically everything on this island is from some-where else, you know. The parrot and the sugarcane, coffee, bananas—"

"Bananas are not native?"

"No, Alexander the Great saw them first when he went to India. Europeans brought them to the New World. Carried by long tides from other places to take root here. Like me, and like us all."

"You speak poetry," Francis said. Imagining that he saw a small frown between her eyebrows, he added quickly, "I don't mean you're affected. I meant your imagery. Maybe you're not even aware of it."

"Oh, yes, Lionel always tells me my imagination runs away with me."

"What are you saying about me?" Lionel inquired, coming back to the table.

"Well, you do always say I'm unrealistic, don't you?"

"Lord, yes, you haven't the foggiest notion. But then, that's the charm of the feminine, isn't it? Right, Francis?"

"I'll let you know when I've been married four years, like you," Francis re-plied, giving Lionel the "social" smile which, since he had married and entered the social world, he had at last had to learn. Then, catching Marjorie's glance, the smile turned genuine. He was uncomfortable in this cloudy atmosphere of antag-onism, and suddenly grateful for the harmony in his own marriage, he reached over to take his wife's hand.

"I've a complication," Lionel said. "The fellow I was just speaking to has to leave tomorrow afternoon, so I'll need to spend the morning with him on busi-ness. And I had planned to drive you to Eleuthera. I know you're anxious to get it over with and go home yourselves."

"No problem," Francis said quickly. "If you can get us a car and give us directions, we'll make it on our own."

"You'd never find your way around the place after you got there, never know what you were looking at. Two thousand acres, rank as a jungle."

"I'll drive you," Kate offered.

Marjorie protested, "That would be taking up your whole day!"

"I don't mind that. I'll pick you up at half past eight."

She came bouncing down the drive in a canvas-topped Jeep. "A Jeep is what you need for these roads." She looked at Marjorie's white sandals. "You'll ruin those, or break your ankle. Haven't you anything else?"

"Only sneakers for tennis. But they'll look so silly with this dress."

"Put them on, then. No one's going to look at you." And as if aware that she had been brusque, Kate added honestly, "Not that you don't deserve to be looked at."

For the first few miles the road ran close to the sea. Fishermen were hauling in their nets. Laundry was drying on the rocks beside coves where salt water met fresh. Bare-bottomed children played in front of dilapidated, moldy cabins. Soon the road turned inland and began to climb as cane fields gave way to banana groves. Through the tattered leafage one caught here and there a glimpse of the sea below, calm and gilded in the morning sun. Laden donkeys plodded downhill. Women stood aside as the car passed, their faces without expression under the heavy baskets of produce that rested on coiled pads on their heads.

"How delightful! How quaint!" Marjorie cried.

"You think so?" Kate responded, somewhat dryly.

Here and there, among the notches and furrows of the rising hills, a lane ran to a grand white house.

"Estate Anne," Kate said of one. "Friends of Herbert's and Julia's. They race horses. Or rather, he races horses and she plays bridge. Not that I've anything against bridge, I don't play too badly myself, but it seems to me one ought to do something else, too, with one's life."

From the rear seat behind the two women, Francis had a three-quarter view of Kate's face. Changing its expression from moment to moment, it reflected, he saw, what was going on in her head. There was no deception in that face. Just now a cloud was passing across it, as though she had been reprimanded or were recalling a reprimand, some loneliness, some exclusion.

Then, in the next instant, as if remembering an obligation to be entertaining, she said, "Look at those mountain palms, over there, the smooth stems with the puff on top; don't they remind you of a Gay Nineties hat? Feathers and Lily Langtry, with the long neck?" And she went on brightly, "There are gorges high up here where you can actually see fossils and shells from coral reefs. All this was under the ocean once."

Mahogany and bamboo arched above the narrow way. Great ferns of the rain forest dripped and glistened where, in the proliferation of leaf and vine, no light could penetrate.

Kate expressed Francis' thought. "This place swarms with life. Crawling, walking, swimming, and flying."

"I shouldn't think anything could move through here," Marjorie said with a shudder. "Not that I'd want to. It's eerie."

"There are trails. People come up to poach. The most marvelous parrots breed here and it's illegal to steal them, but people do. They smuggle them out of the country in suitcases, and most of them die on the way. It's brutal. I get furious when I think about it," Kate said passionately.

Now began a gradual descent from the summit. The road wound and twisted. They passed a village, a handful of cabins, a patch of coconut and banana trees, then tilted fields and sunshine on the great mountain's flank, with sheep and cattle grazing in deep grass.

"Oh, what are those?" cried Marjorie, observing everything. Out of the distance she had picked what appeared to be white birds, standing on cows' backs.

"Cattle egrets. They eat insects off the cow's back."

"Well," Marjorie said, "curiouser and curiouser, as Alice remarked."

Suddenly Kate stopped the car. "There it is. Eleuthera."

Beneath them on a spacious tableland stood a long white house. At its back the mountain soared; before it, in enormous silence, lay the shimmering sea.

Kate spoke softly. "The end of the world, isn't it? A dropping-off place."

She released the brake and the car descended. Rusted gates were flung back against stone posts. The long lane between royal palms was overgrown. The aristocratic arch above the door had broken off; tall windows were shuttered; weeds were knee-high on the paths. Ruin, like a disfiguring disease, had eaten away.

They stared for a moment. Marjorie asked, "This is the house, isn't it, where your mother grew up?"

Francis nodded, unable, for the moment, to speak. He had not expected to be so moved, to feel such pain. People had sat and talked on this veranda; people had come up this driveway to the sight of flowers and the welcome of a barking dog. All of this had been alive.

His eyes went moist and he got out of the car to squint into the sun so that no one would see.

They went inside. In the great hall every surface was chiseled and adorned. The stair rails were elaborate twisted spirals; the newel posts were pineapples; the walls were paneled and carved. Through the open door the sun came shafting and a fine golden wood dust stirred in the warm air.

"It's like Drummond Hall, on a smaller scale," Marjorie observed.

"These great houses are cut pretty much to the same pattern," Kate answered. "Here's the library. That's mahoe, cabinetmaker's wood, and very precious. It's beautiful when it's polished."

"There are no shelves on this side!" Marjorie exclaimed. "It's only half finished! Isn't that odd?"

Francis felt that a man should assert practicality. "The roof's been leaking, look." He added doubtfully, "I wonder whether a thing like that ought to be repaired before we put the place on the market?"

"I don't think you ought to put a cent into it," Marjorie declared. "To begin with, we haven't got any money, have we? No, just mark it down and sell 'as is.' Clearance sale. That's that."

"Strange that the place hasn't been vandalized," Francis remarked. "It hasn't been, you can see that."

"People here are afraid it's haunted," Kate said. "The village people believe in spirits and witches, you know. You've heard about Anancy tales?"

"Yes," Francis said. "Old tales from Africa."

"Incredible ignorance in this day and age!" Marjorie commented.

"Not incredible, considering the way they live," Kate answered. There was a trace of impatience in her voice.

She really is too impatient, Francis thought. Yet it's true, the villages are miserable places. What can those people know?

"Shall we walk around the grounds now?" Kate asked. "There used to be roads to drive on, but they're too overgrown for the car."

"How do you know your way around?" Marjorie asked.

"I used to visit here sometimes when I was a child. My grandfather knew Virgil Francis."

"You knew my great-grandfather?" Francis was astonished.

"Not well. But everybody on St. Felice knows who everybody else is. You know, I think you must be like him. He was tall as a reed, and the one thing I do remember is his sort of beaky nose, like yours," she said, regarding Francis. "It's funny the things one can remember about people, unimportant things from years ago."

Marjorie had discovered a sugar mill, or rather, the ruins of one. The top layers of tile had broken off to a third of the original height. Their rubble lay in the long grass. An enormous rusty cauldron lay there, too.

"They used to bake cassava flour in that to feed the slaves," Kate said. "And here, look, here's the keystone of the mill. T.F. F for Francis, naturally. I don't know who T was. . . . The date's 1727."

Marjorie had gone on ahead, grasping things swiftly, as was her way, and passing on to the next. Francis, on the other hand, liked to linger, to savor and speculate. *Flour for the slaves.* Vividly, he could feel this place as it must have been, not silent as now, but busy with running feet and voices, tension and commotion, in the buzzing heat.

"There must have been a house here," Marjoie called back. "There's a foundation."

Kate called, "The overseer's house. He would have lived there with the book-keepers. And past them were the slave quarters, the barracoons. There would have been about fifty huts on a place this size. And then the factory compound, with the boiling house and the mill."

There was a sudden movement in the tall grass. A small flock of goats clattered into view, stared for a moment at the strangers, and went back to feeding.

"Gone wild," Kate observed.

"That stuff they're eating looks like cactus, for heaven's sake," Marjorie said.

"It is. It's called Turk's head, and goats are the only creatures who'll eat it."

Francis stood still. Let me feel this, he thought. Bee hum. Wind rush. Goats rip the grass.

A soft languor and longing, a peace that was part sadness, lay upon him. And he spoke it aloud. "Sad. Sad."

"Nonsense! It was based on slavery," Marjorie said briskly.

"I don't mean that, of course. I mean—" His voice fell away.

Marjorie's voice rang clearly. "They deserved what they got. In addition to owning other human beings, they were disgracefully incompetent. They exhausted the soil, spent more than they had, and let everything fall apart. Shall we go back to the house?"

They sat down on the veranda steps. Far below them, the river was a silver trickle. Around the point of the little bay one saw a fringe of cliffside trees bent inland by the ocean wind.

"That's where the Atlantic rolls, meeting the Caribbean. If you're the kind who gets seasick," Kate warned, "it's no place to go sailing."

Marjorie screamed and jumped. A small snake had slithered across what remained of the garden path and disappeared in the undergrowth.

"It won't hurt you," Kate said. "It's harmless."

"No poisonous snakes on the island? I've heard there are some who kill in a minute."

"The fer-de-lance. About five feet long. They'd hide in a bunch of bananas, and you would die in minutes if one struck you. There still were a few when I was a child, but there are no more now."

"I feel creepy here all the same," Marjorie said. "Let's go, shall we? Unless there's anything more you need to know, Francis?"

He considered. "What I need to know is, what persuasion can I use to sell this place? What are its assets?"

Kate made a sweep with her arm. "Its assets are all around you, aren't they?"

He looked at her. She was very serious. "Yes," he said gently, "the beauty. The beauty on this hill."

"You're not going to sell beauty," Marjorie said. "Here, I've got pencil and paper in my bag, let's make notes. Now," she told Kate, "it's obvious you know how to run an estate. What would you do with this if it belonged to you?"

Kate spoke promptly. "I'd begin by planting trees. On the higher slopes you have deforestation. That's pretty true all over the island, the result of improvident usage. From it you get soil erosion, droughts, and floods. As a matter of fact, we have been trying to educate the small farmer along those lines."

"Without much success, I'll bet," Marjorie said.

"Education takes time," Kate replied.

Francis was uncomfortable. Plainly, the two women disliked each other. He had no idea why or what to do about it.

And Kate continued, "After that, I'd plant bananas. Very little sugar, since you'd need too much new machinery for it. I would diversify with cattle, sheep, and fruit. And not just for export. There's tremendous need right here. Do you know that this fertile island doesn't even feed itself? It's a disgrace! Children, when they drink it at all, drink canned, imported milk. The people are terribly undernourished. A disgrace!" Kate struck her fist into her palm.

Marjorie regarded her coolly. "Go on, please. I'm making notes."

"I'd plant cocoa. This is the rainy side of the island, and it will do well here. Use the bananas as temporary shade when you set out new cocoa plants. And coconuts. We've a copra mill in town. The women here make cooking oil out of the milk and the dried remains you keep for cattle fodder. Then there's mace, which is the cloak on the nutmeg. You can raise that for export. See, there's some over there by the bamboo fence. Have I given you a few ideas?"

Marjorie had been writing rapidly. "Yes, thanks. Although it occurs to me, anybody who'd even consider a place like this would know something about how to run it, wouldn't he? These notes are probably unnecessary."

"You can't tell."

Francis stood up. "You're convincing, Kate. I should let you convince a buyer for me. By the way, have you any idea how I might go about finding one?"

"It won't be easy. But you could try Atterbury and Shaw in Covetown. They deal in properties. Shall we go?"

He stood for a moment with his hand on the door of the car. Great cumulus clouds had wrapped the peak of Morne Bleue in cotton and washed the house in pearl-gray shadow.

Kate looked at him curiously. "It's got to you, hasn't it?"

"It's a poem, as you said."

She smiled without answering, showing the gap between her two front teeth. He thought irrelevantly, I don't know why a gap between two teeth should be so charming.

U𝗉𝗌𝗍𝖺𝗂𝗋𝗌 𝗂𝗇 𝗍𝗁𝖾𝗂𝗋 room at Drummond Hall, Marjorie said, "You liked her."

"Liked who?"

"Don't play dumb," she said pleasantly. "Kate, of course. Who else?"

"Well, she's a very nice person. She went out of her way to be helpful."

"I don't mean that. You really liked her. You were attracted to her. You desire her."

"You're out of your head," he said fondly.

"She's your sort. Lusty and sexy," Marjorie said, undoing her bra. Above her white breasts the tan made a heart-shaped curve.

"Sexy? She's not even pretty. Well, not very."

"She's older than you are."

"Half a year!"

"They're not happy, couldn't you see that?"

"I know. I'm sorry for them."

"Yes, she's your sort. Outdoors. Animals. Spiritual, too. And she undressed you with her eyes."

"What!" he shouted.

"Yes, when she said that about how you look like your grandfather."

"I don't remember."

"Yes, you do! She said you had your grandfather's beaky nose."

"Great-grandfather."

"You see, you do remember!"

"Quit it, Marjorie."

"It's true, you desire her."

She was settling her breasts into a fresh brassiere, two lace cups on black ribbons.

"Listen," he said, "just wait till we get this damn dinner over and get back up here, I'll show you something about desire."

The pier glass reflected a supple girl with a quick, mobile mouth and clever eyes; the man beside her, although exactly her age, wore the soft look of a boy who is eager to please.

"W𝖾𝗅𝗅, 𝗇𝗈𝗐 𝗍𝗁𝖺𝗍 you've seen decay at Eleuthera, let me show you a thriving enterprise," Lionel offered one morning a week later. "Georgina's Fancy is half again as large as when I took it over, I want you to know. I've added a lot of acreage."

A tractor was loading cane stalks into carts, and some dark little boys, no older than eight or nine, were sweeping up the droppings.

"Shouldn't they be in school?" Francis asked.

"They leave in crop time to help out. They need the money." And as Francis made no comment, Lionel added, "Trouble is, these people have too many kids; they can't possibly support them all.

"We've got a central mill in town now, a big change from the days when each estate had its own mill. If the island were large enough, we could have a railway to get the stuff there faster. You can't let the stalks lie in the sun a minute too long or the juice will ferment, and then it's no good."

At the farthest boundary of the property lay the village, like all of them that Francis had seen. He had a quick impression of rotting wood, bare dirt, chickens and goats, before they moved on.

"I've got a tip-top manager, but even so, it's not the same as when you're on the job. Oh, I could get myself a house in town or on the beach and drive out here every couple of days, but I like to keep an eye on the ball myself. And my dad does the same. That's why he survived when so many others went under. You've got to know business, too, dealing with commission merchants; they take options on your crop and then at the last minute decide they've overbought and turn you down. It's tough." Lionel sighed.

I don't see him married to Kate, Francis thought, surprised that this intrusive thought should have come into his head, when actually he had been listening with real interest to all this information, so new and different from anything he had ever known.

They trudged on. "Yes, that's why you have to have at least two export crops to make it pay. Bananas are the best. They require very little care except pruning. Of course, nothing's perfect! There's a pesky little animal, the taltuza, something like a rat, that eats the roots. And we've had Panama disease—that's a fungus—but for once the government acted promptly and we wiped it out with lime."

They had walked uphill away from the cane toward the Great House. Two fawn-colored horses whinnied delicately behind a fence.

"Kate's pets. She's an expert horsewoman, but she treats those two like lap dogs. Comes of having no children, I suppose."

Francis was silent.

"The doctor says she can't have any. Took her ovaries out after the last miscarriage."

"I'm sorry," Francis said.

"Yes. Well. So, we were talking about bananas. It looks easier than it is, let me tell you. You're at the mercy of world markets, depressions, and wars. During the war you couldn't ship, at all, naturally. Now sometimes the ship is overloaded; you've got your load on the dock and they won't take it on. So you leave it there for the goats. And sometimes the inspectors reject your stuff—when there's nothing wrong with it, mind you; it's just that they've got too much and they want to keep the price up on the other side. Tough. Yes, we've had some hard times here.

And now there's all this talk of independence. I tell you, your head can swim. Still, it's home, it gets under your skin. I wouldn't leave. At least, I don't think I ever would."

"You'll be managing Drummond Hall for your father when he goes?"

"Yes, Kate will help me. She'll keep the books, ride over and look around. Another pair of eyes." They reached the steps. "I'll drive you back to Father's. I'd ask you to stay to lunch but Kate's in town. I'm to meet her at half past twelve."

Francis felt the sinking of slight disappointment. Ridiculous! "That's all right. You've given us a lot of your busy time. It was especially nice of Kate to take us to Eleuthera that day."

"Oh, she loved it! She loves traveling around, showing things to visitors. She's a good girl, Kate is. You know," Lionel said, with embarrassment sitting oddly on his bulk, "the other night at the wedding, maybe you thought I was a little hard on her. . . . You don't have to say whether you did or not. We get along fairly well, she and I, only her problem is she's a bleeding heart and it's going to get her into trouble some day. That's the fact of it, and it makes me sore as hell."

He did not want to see Kate exposed. And he repeated, awkwardly, "Well, you've all been very good to us."

"Anything we can do, just ask. Anything worrying you, just speak up."

"Nothing worrying us, except Marjorie's being afraid she hasn't brought enough clothes for all the hospitality!"

"That's no problem. Try Da Cunha's. They've got French dresses and what-all stuck away in the back. Marjorie could outfit herself for two years to come."

"We shan't be here that long, I'm afraid."

"You'll be here longer than you think. Unless you just want to go and leave things in the hands of Atterbury and Shaw."

"I may have to do that. But what I'd really like is to have a nibble before I leave. And I think—it's nothing short of miraculous—but I think we may possibly have one. I don't know whether he's a land speculator or what. Fellow from Puerto Rico. Well, we've cut the price to the bone, that's probably the reason."

Lionel nodded. "It's the only way."

And they drove back to Drummond Hall.

Mr. Atterbury saw Francis to the door. "My man expects to hear pretty quickly from his lawyers in Puerto Rico. I think it's fairly safe to say we've got a sale, Mr. Luther."

Francis, thanking him, held up two crossed fingers. He had left the borrowed car parked in the back of the building, but for some reason he did not feel like returning yet to the tennis-and-lunch regime at Drummond Hall, and he went on down Wharf Street, past the classic Georgian facade of Barclay's Bank to the square.

It was market day, and the town bustled with real life: he had already drawn a distinction between the "real" life of the island and the suave amenities of his relatives' homes. Busses from the country were still bringing people in, barefoot women wearing home-woven straw hats and cotton dresses in every imaginable electric color. Children of every age darted among mounds of bananas, breadfruit, fish, and coconuts. Yellow dogs—all the dogs here seemed to be of one variety so that, although they were mongrels, they had almost evolved into a breed—prowled in the shade and scratched at their mange.

Francis stood for a while observing this animation, then walked around the corner. At the orphanage he stopped to listen to a rehearsal of the children's choir; he had heard them sing on the previous Sunday at the cathedral service. The orphanage was opposite a cemetery. He walked across the street and leaned over the railing, thinking that this would be, after all, an agreeable place in which to spend eternity! Date palms and palmettos framed the space; the graves were elaborately trimmed with conch shells. In the cool, fragrant morning air, the pure child voices sang "Now Thank We All Our God." And feeling a pleasure serene as a beatitude, he waited until the hymn had ended.

Now quite familiar with the map of the little town, he turned into the arcades. The leaning houses with their narrow windows and crumbling iron lace balustrades might, were it not for the deep black shade of the fig trees in the yards, have been standing on the Place des Vosges in Paris. At the next small square he paused before a round bronze plaque set in the middle of the pavement. It was still legible: "In this place on the eleventh of July in the year 1802 Samuel Vernon, late a member of His Majesty's Council, died by hanging for the murder of his Negro slave Plato."

"Gruesome, isn't it?"

Kate Tarbox smiled from under a large native straw hat. "This one went a little too far. It amused him to watch men being beaten to death. Even his peers got disgusted with him, finally. So they tried him and hanged him."

Francis shook his head. "A very complex society!"

"Oh, yes! And it still is. What are you doing in town?"

"Just ambling about. And you?"

"I have a little office over there. The Family Counseling Service. Yes, I know it's like trying to empty the ocean with a soup spoon. I saw your raised eyebrow."

"Did I raise it? I didn't mean to."

There followed then that moment of indecision during which one can either speak the few graceful words necessary to terminate the meeting or else take up another subject which will prolong it.

Francis said, "I was thinking, as long as I'm here, I might pick up a few presents to bring home. I thought maybe, do you—would you make a suggestion?"

"There's always Da Cunha's. I don't know what you want to spend."

"Something middling, let's say. A pin or some beads, maybe."

"Da Cunha's, then."

They walked back through the market square. Francis felt conspicuous; he was so tall beside her, and he was used to walking next to Marjorie, who was almost his height. In high heels she was even with him; they were known as a handsome couple.

He needed to say something. "I don't recognize half these vegetables. Those are beets and cabbage, of course, but what's that stuff?"

"Akee. That's cassava. Those are pomegranates next to the melons."

"Pomegranates? Like the Bible?"

"Like the Bible. Those are tamarinds, that's sour sop. And plantains, they taste like bananas, but we serve them hot. And there's breadfruit."

"As in *Mutiny on the Bounty*."

"Right! Captain Bligh brought it from Tahiti. Easy feeding for the slaves. You can practically live on it. Here's Da Cunha's."

An exotic black girl with waist-length hair came forward.

"Désirée," Kate said, "this is my friend—no, my nephew. I'm his aunt by marriage, isn't that ridiculous? Anyway, this is Mr. Luther. He needs to buy some presents."

The thick, arched walls were of the eighteenth century. The ceiling fans, placidly whirring, were of the nineteenth. Singapore and Somerset Maugham, Francis thought. Liquor and crystal, porcelain and silver, made a lavish sparkle. In a glass-covered case lay a discreet selection of diamond watches.

His negotiations were few. Having quickly made his purchases, a doll for Margaret (who was twenty-four), three silver pins for his mother and remaining sisters, and some cigars for his father, they left the shop.

"Isn't she a beautiful girl?" Kate asked. "I always feel so insignificant beside her. An African princess."

"She is beautiful, but you don't have to feel insignificant beside anyone," he said, with automatic gallantry.

"She's married to a schoolteacher. Her father's a labor leader, Clarence Porter. A friend of mine."

"Of yours and Lionel's?" Francis inquired cautiously.

Kate laughed without mirth. "No, certainly not of Lionel's."

And he remembered having had, on the ride to Eleuthera some days before, an impression of melancholy, of loneliness and exclusion.

"How about lunch?" He spoke abruptly.

"I'd like that."

"You name the place, then."

"There is only one place outside of the country club. Cade's Hotel on the other side of the harbor."

From light they entered into the dimness of mahogany. A few men were seated at lunch among the dark portraits. They went out again into light and took a table in the shade of the garden wall.

Kate took her hat off. Her bright hair, released, curved about her freckled cheeks, grazing her chin. He had a sudden memory of Marjorie in the bedroom, of her clear pronouncement: *Oh, yes, she undressed you with her eyes.* He went warm with embarrassment.

But Kate's eyes now were on the menu. "The fish is always good. It's deep-sea, mostly. Abrecca, ballahou, salmon, grunt—"

"I'll have salmon. It's the only one I recognize."

They settled back. Her hand, resting on the table, displayed a large, square emerald ring which he had not noticed before. It was in perfectly good taste—son of a flamboyant father, he was critical of excessive display—yet it did not seem to belong to this particular woman, with her simple dress and sandals, her simple manner. Marjorie would have worn it with flair and style. Too bad, because he could not afford, and probably never would afford, to buy one for her.

"You've really got rid of Eleuthera? A lot quicker than we expected."

"I think so. Of course, the lawyers have all sorts of papers to go over, still."

"So then you'll be leaving."

"I should go home now, but if it's only a matter of another week or two before we get everything signed up, it's probably wiser for me to stay and see it through."

"You'll come back."

"It's not around the corner. What makes you think so?"

Her face crinkled in a smile. "Oh, those long tides will bring you. And the wind and the clouds on Morne Bleue."

"The clouds on Morne Bleue. I said you talk poetry, didn't I?"

"Seriously though, there's a lot you haven't seen. Christmas and Old Year's night, what you call New Year's Eve. Do you like calypso? Steel bands?"

He nodded.

"You ought to hear the real thing at carnival time, not what they give you in tourist hotels on the big islands. Everybody 'runs mask.' The costumes are marvelous, and the singers make up original songs; they'll make one up about you if you ask. The streets are jammed. It's a circus, a revel. You have to see it to believe it. Then on Ash Wednesday it's all over." She snapped her fingers. "All over, like that."

"Well, maybe I will see it sometime."

"How odd that your mother, who grew up here, never told you about it! But perhaps," Kate reflected, "she might have had unhappy memories. Not getting along with a difficult mother—"

"If I have heard that once," Francis interrupted, "I have heard it a dozen times: 'How odd that your mother never talked about St. Felice!' "

Kate was astonished. "I'm sorry. I really didn't mean to pry."

He was ashamed, then, of his irritability. "No, I'm sorry—"

She shook her head. "I do say things that are too personal, I know I do. It's a terrible fault. I should bite my tongue for saying that about your grandmother."

"Don't bite it. I haven't been fond of her either, the few times in my life that we've been together. I don't suppose it's easy being her daughter-in-law."

"She tolerates me, barely. That's because of my ancestry. I have excellent ancestry." She chuckled.

"Tell me!"

"Well, we were planter families on both sides, who lost everything when the slaves were freed. By the time I came along there was no money at all. My father had been beautifully educated, in England, naturally. He was a clergyman, a good friend of Father Baker's, who's sort of kept an eye on me since my parents died. He's a wonderful person, not one of those clergymen who *mouth forth*. He believes in works."

He wanted to ask, How ever did you come to marry Lionel? but of course did not.

And just then she said, as if he had actually asked the question, "Lionel wanted to marry a girl with colored blood. He's still in love with her. Naturally, that was impossible, so he married me."

"I see!"

"She won't admit it, which is shameful, although it's not her fault that she won't. It's the world's."

"Then how do people know?"

"Everybody knows everybody else's ancestry. And most people are related to each other if you go back far enough. For instance, I'm related to the Da Cunhas about six generations ago. One Jew, back there, and the rest Scottish and French since then."

He wanted to know more, but she said merely, "I used to go in for genealogy when I was young. I've more important things to do now."

"When you were young!" he mocked.

"I'm thirty. I've told you."

"So am I."

"You look older. I imagine you always have. You feel responsible for things, for people."

"As a matter of fact, I do," Francis said thoughtfully.

Noontime stillness lay like a warm hand on the little garden. When they had first sat down, birds had been flickering, but now they had gone to rest and there was no sound except the drip and splash of water from the mouth of a stone cherub set into the wall.

. . . *but of course that was impossible, so he married me.* The words kept repeating themselves in his head.

"Have I bored you with all my talk?"

Francis started. "Bored? No, keep on, please."

"Lionel says I'm a walking storehouse of useless information."

"Not useless to me," he said graciously. "Tell me, those odd trees on the other side of the wall, what are they?"

"*Sabliers.* Sandbox trees in English. They used to fill the seedpods with sand and use them to sprinkle parchment. Feel better, now that you know that?"

"Oh, much! Now another: What, exactly, is Creole?"

"It means someone born here who is purely European, that is, purely white. Anything else you want to know?"

"Dozens of things, but right now I'm enjoying the fish."

. . . *of course that was impossible, so he married me.*

"I suppose you do some traveling?" he asked.

"We went abroad on our honeymoon. Lionel is serious about work, though. So we don't go very far very often."

"Do you feel you're missing anything, do you feel that an island is confining?"

"Not really. People in large cities like to talk about all the things going on there—six orchestras, four ballet companies, a dozen theaters—but when you pin them down, actually most people don't do very much of all that. I have a record collection—it's my chief extravagance—and a good piano. Books are a problem, though. Our bookstore is small and things have to be ordered. It takes forever."

"I'd be glad to send you stuff when I get home. Or," he corrected himself, "Marjorie will, if you send a list."

"That's very good of you."

"Tell me what else you do besides reading and playing the piano and riding your horses and the—Family Counsel, is it?"

"You're not laughing at me?"

"Why ever should I do that?"

"Some people do, you know. I'm thought to be eccentric. Not practical." She folded her hands under her chin. Her nails were unvarnished; only the emerald glistened. "But I see myself as very practical. You've seen how people live here; aside from its not being morally right, it isn't wise to allow it to go on, because the day will come when they won't accept these conditions anymore. People like Lionel want things to stay exactly the way they are, but even a child can see that they won't."

"What do you propose to do?"

"Make the changes peacefully and fairly. We need schooling. Light industry and jobs. Housing. A decent hospital. I've tried to persuade Lionel to head a drive. He's got money enough, investments in hotels in Jamaica and Barbados. He could do it."

"But he won't?"

"He makes halfhearted promises and does nothing. Like the government."

"So you feel frustrated."

"Yes, I do. That's why I've got involved with family welfare. I feel I'm doing *something*. Teaching people how to feed their children. Handling problem children. They call them 'bad,' but it's really that they have no fathers to lead them."

Her eyes were prisms. As the light shifted through the leaves, they turned from violet to brown, then to a dark and austere blue.

"We also," she said, looking directly at Francis, "we also show them how not to have more children."

"Birth control?"

"Yes. You don't approve?"

"If people don't want children, they shouldn't have them. For the children's sake, if nothing else."

"Some people, black and white both, are outraged. They say I do this because I can't have children of my own."

"That's not only malicious, it's stupid."

"It's a terrible thing to want a child and not have one," she said softly, "but worse to have six you can't clothe or feed." She stood up. "You're finished? You've got things to do and so have I."

He walked with her to his car.

"Do you know," he said, with his hand already on the door, "do you know I have been having the strangest feeling? As if I had been here before."

"Déjà vu. It's common."

"I've always been sensitive to place: rooms, houses, streets. And not because they have beauty or grandeur or status. I've been in beautiful places that were cold to me, in which I've known I would be miserable. And I've walked down a street in some ordinary little town and thought I would be happy there."

"You feel that way here? That you would be happy?"

"Yes. Absurd, isn't it, considering that I don't know anything about it? And yet I feel like Brigham Young coming to Salt Lake City. There's a monument there where he halted the wagon train, looked over the valley, and said, 'This is the place.' "

"This particular place can be ignorant and cruel. You have to love it a lot to put up with all that."

"That's not what you said when you were telling about carnival and music and the rest."

"Every coin has two sides," she countered.

Yes, it is absurd of me, he was thinking.

"I don't believe Marjorie would like it," Kate said. "I see her as completely urban."

He came to. "Of course. I'm only fantasizing. Thank you for having lunch with me."

He did not say *Remember me to Lionel.* She gave him a little wave as he drove away.

That was impossible, so he married me. He would have given anything to know more.

Damn! So much stupid, unnecessary waste in the world!

Two weeks went by as they waited for word from the prospective buyer. Marjorie played tennis and went swimming. Francis, although there was no necessity to do so, went back to Eleuthera. Alone, he sat on the veranda steps, watching green lizards scurry up the columns. His eyes wandered out over fields and hills. Bananas on the hill, Kate Tarbox said. Fruit orchards. Cattle in the meadows by the river.

"I have founded a kingdom of my own," the first François had written in that diary which had so enthralled the child Francis, "where a pure river runs and the air is salubrious, far removed from the noisome crowding of towns."

A kingdom of my own! The old peasant, turned pirate, turned planter, had possessed a streak of poetry as well.

He leaned his head against the railing. Let's not get foolish, Francis, with that "streak of poetry." Poetry doesn't feed anyone. Yet he could feel again that old dread of the city, of the office on a shelf, the telephones and ledgers, counting money. It was all right if you were made for it, but he was not.

What, then, was he made for?

He thought, There's nothing to go back to. I should have to make a new start. Why not make it here? Why not?

And he sat up, excitement pouring like wine. Take charge. Create something. As a painter stands before a vacant canvas, or a sculptor contemplates a lump of stone, so might a man feel here before this wasted land. He would have been ashamed, reserved as was his nature, to put these feelings into words; they would seem puerile, vague, without value in the telling, although he felt, he knew, they were neither puerile nor vague.

So he marshaled arguments. Surely it could not be *all* that difficult! Surely he could learn as well as Herbert or Lionel had learned, enough to make this pay and enough for his parents while they needed it. He would do more; he would provide a better living for the people who worked the soil, build that hospital, show what intelligence and good will can create. . . .

So his mind ran, all that week and the next.

"You can't be serious," Marjorie said. "You can't be."

They were getting ready for bed. She sank back against the pillows.

"I really am. At first it seemed a wild idea, but I've been thinking it over for days. I've spoken to the bank about a mortgage, for cash to get started. They think, with hard work, I can do it. They've even put me in touch with a good manager, a fellow named Osborne, who managed a large estate in Jamaica."

Sweat came out on Marjorie's forehead.

"To my amazement, Julia has agreed to cosign a note so my parents will be taken care of until my father can get on his feet. Shows you never know about people."

"No, you don't," she said bitterly.

"Let me try, Marjorie. Please? I can make it work. I believe in my bones I can."

"It's that Kate who's talked you into this! All that stuff about fruit and cattle! If it's so easy, why hasn't someone else done it?"

"I didn't say it was easy. I said it was possible. And Kate had nothing to do with it."

He had not mentioned the lunch in town. It had seemed to him that would be giving it too much importance. Marjorie might not see it as the chance encounter it had been. When, on the following day, he had decided there was after all no reason why he should not have mentioned it, then it had seemed too late; she would think it odd that he had not mentioned it before.

She began to cry. He felt deeply sorry for her and put an arm around her shoulders.

"You know," he said gently, "you know, I never really liked what I was doing. I realize now how little I liked it."

"You never told me you didn't!"

"I guess I didn't really know it until now."

"That's ridiculous! You know how many young men would give their eyeteeth to have that job?"

"But they're not me and I'm not them." He looked out past the window; he could hear a rustle of leaves. "It was like being in prison, with good food and all the comforts, but still a prison."

"That's ridiculous!" Marjorie said again.

She wept and he put his arms around her.

"You're forgetting, I haven't got the job anymore."

"You could get another. Don't tell me you couldn't."

"Marjorie, darling, here's something I think I can do well. Call it an emotional decision, but aren't all big decisions emotional, when you think about them? The really big ones, like marrying you, for instance? Listen, Marjorie, listen, it's a challenge, an adventure. We're young enough to try anything. If we don't like it, we can always sell out. What difference if we sell now or a year from now?"

The argument went on for most of the night and the next day and the next. In the end, by dint of his promise that the experiment would be just that, an experiment and no commitment, by dint of that, with combined reluctance and valiant sportsmanship, Marjorie gave in, and Francis won.

❧ {9} ❧

The fragrance of raw wood was strong and sweet under a sultry sky. The heat in the lumberyard was stifling.

"Likely to pour any minute," Francis said.

The other man looked up. Clouds were speeding in over the roiling bay; the clouds were iron gray, rimmed with silver.

"October. We'll have had our two hundred inches of rain before the year's out. No hurricane warning yet, anyway."

"You'll deliver that stuff by the end of the week? I particularly want to finish the post-and-rail fence so we can let the horses out."

"You'll have it. We were saying, Mr. Luther, what a change! It's not much more than a year since you took the place over."

"Almost two."

"Well, if anybody had asked me, I'd have said it couldn't be done."

He felt gay as he headed out of town. The man's praise had been earned. No one had believed, neither Lionel nor he himself, how fast he would be able to pull shape and order out of chaos.

What a bombshell he had dropped! His father, at the time, had been numbly accepting of any new blow, but his mother had been shocked. When he and Marjorie had gone back to New York to arrange their move, she had implored, Why, why, when his future was before him, settle for a backwater? Was it fair to Marjorie? Did he want to rear a family on that speck of an island? Yes, he really did want to; was she not herself a product of the island? In the end he had temporized, as he had done with his wife: It need not, after all, be permanent; few things in life were, and he would very likely come back home eventually.

Ultimately his father's affairs had been straightened out. Friends had found a place for him at another brokerage house, and as his mother had declared, last week's scandal faded for some other to take its place in the news.

They had sold the country place and sent its furnishings on to Eleuthera, to Marjorie's great joy.

"We could never have hoped to collect all these things, wouldn't have had time or money enough," she said, as one after the other the cargo containers were opened upon carved beds and Oriental runners, Hepplewhite chairs, and Queen Anne silver.

Richard had not wanted to part with the Anatole Da Cunha island paintings, but Teresa had insisted that they rightly belonged in the setting of Eleuthera, and he had had to agree. So now, when Francis sat at his dining table, he could look behind him and see Morne Bleue in a gilded frame; when he looked before him, Morne Bleue itself, framed by the windows, rose into an arch of cloud.

Eleuthera being a large house, Marjorie had found it necessary to add to the furnishings. She was extravagant. The porcelain lamps, ordered through Da Cunha's, were the finest, as were the draperies and the old Venetian mirrors.

"You can't put cheap things next to what we already have," she argued, which was doubtless aesthetically sound, but costly. They were skating on thin ice, very thin, Francis told her, with debts to the bank, a banana crop barely taking hold, and some yearling beef sold at a profit, nothing more as yet. "Very thin ice," he kept repeating.

But in the main she had accepted the enormous change in her life, a change which she could never have anticipated, with great dignity. She liked to say that thoroughbreds didn't complain.

"Mrs. Luther has a head for practical affairs," said Osborne, who was himself a capable man, honest, respectful, and cold.

Francis had wanted to get busy at once on good living quarters for the full-time help, some sturdy cottages with proper sanitation. Going with Osborne into the villages to recruit labor, he had been horrified by what he saw. Some of the worst dwellings were made of beaten kerosene tins. Parents and children slept together in one bed, and sometimes on the floor.

"They don't know any better. They don't look at it the way you do, Mr. Luther," Osborne said.

"If they don't know any better, which I doubt, they ought to be taught. When they can afford it, they do live better."

"You can't do it now," Marjorie argued, as they went over figures with Osborne, who agreed.

"When you get on your feet financially, then you can think about indulging other people. Until then let them stay in their villages as they are."

He supposed that this made sense, but only for the present. He had made a mental list of the things he wanted to do, and housing had high priority on it.

To the left now lay the country club, deserted, for the sky had just released a drenching rain. He could see the turquoise pool ringed with white umbrellas. Marjorie spent a good deal of time at the club, as did most of the planter wives. Right after breakfast she'd get into the car and drive three quarters of an hour to spend the day at golf or tennis. Happily, she had been making friends here, more than he had made, and that not only because she had more time, but because she possessed qualities which he did not, an independence which attracted people, which they respected. She knew when to talk and what to say. Even her silences were confident.

He swung the car onto the mountain road and let his mind roam. It was not often these days that he had a solitary hour in which to do just that.

It will be better when we have a child, he thought. Children. Surely something must happen soon? And then: What did I mean by "better"? Just as surely, there is nothing wrong! Oh, Marjorie. Lovely, loyal Marjorie.

He ought to spend more time with her. But he was out at dawn, when the workers came trudging up the lane. With them he made the rounds from cattle barns to chicken pens, uphill to the new banana groves and back down to oversee new fences for the fodder corn. Later in the day there were the books to be gone over. A constant round.

He thought suddenly, We never see much of Lionel and Kate. Lionel is a good sort in his way, at least as far as I'm concerned. He's been cordial and helpful with advice. Sometimes in the evenings he would drive alone over the beastly mountain road to visit. "Kate's busy," he would say, although naturally no one had asked where she was. When he had gone, Marjorie would talk about Kate.

"Everyone knows she married him for his money. She didn't have a cent. You remember, she said the Tarboxes even bought her wedding dress."

"That's nasty gossip!"

"Don't be so holy, Francis."

He wondered what chemistry had produced such dislike between the two women. Marjorie was usually fair-minded. Yet a little thing like a voice, for instance, could set your teeth on edge, couldn't it? Or it could draw you near, as it had drawn him to Marjorie. Nor was jealousy a part of Marjorie. She wouldn't stoop to it, she always said; it was humiliating to be that insecure.

"She's really very odd. Not that the projects aren't well intentioned, but they won't work and she overdoes them. No wonder he's impatient with her."

He didn't want to talk about Kate. Well, she is a bit "odd," he thought, different from the mold, and probably that's why the women pick on her. He hadn't had a word alone with her since their lunch. There had been a Christmas party for the family, a farewell when Julia and Herbert left for England, and four, no six—he depressed his fingers for the count—other parties where they had met. Eight times in all. It would have been interesting to see her more often, just because she *was* different. Sitting there with her farmer's hat and her emerald, talking about music and tractors and clinics! Sitting there with the pluck and the spirit on the surface, the melancholy underneath. There was a lot more to her story than she had told, he was certain.

He had never repeated a word about Lionel's other woman, although Kate had made no secret of it. But it was no business of his. He wondered whether there was someone else in her own life. Again, it was no business of his.

The rain was coming so furiously that the wiper was unable to clear the windshield, and he bent forward to peer. Deep ditches flanked the road on either side, making it impossible to turn and go back to town. He had never seen such savage rain. It assaulted the car. He was afraid and ashamed of his fear.

After a while he knew that he had somewhere taken a wrong turn. The road didn't feel right; it was climbing more steeply than it did on the way home, and there were great boulders in its middle. This must be one of those branches that come to a dead end in some mountain village before trailing off into a mule track. The rain was as solid now as a curtain; the world reeled beneath the awesome power of the wind.

Then through the side window he caught sight of life: a banana station, a thatched shed about the size of a city bus shelter, where bananas were piled to await the pickup trucks. Two men were huddled in it.

He stopped the car and leaned from the window, calling over the roar of wind and rain, "Can you tell me where I am?"

A man answered, but Francis did not understand him. "I'm sorry, I didn't hear you! Can you tell me what place this is? Is there a village here?"

The man answered, and again he did not understand. The language was not English.

"Can you speak English?" he called.

The answer was a shake of the head, so he rolled the window up and went on, the car laboring now through a river of red mud. A few minutes later he came to a village, a short double row of huts with a schoolhouse at the far end. It was the usual rough board building on stilts, with a wide roof overhang that kept the rain from coming through the unglassed windows. With enormous relief he stopped the car and raced up the path.

The benches were empty, since it was already late afternoon. At his desk the teacher sat before a pile of papers.

"May I?" Francis called. "I've lost my way." He was out of breath and soaked. "I have no idea where I am."

"Come in, surely. Hang your wet jacket on a peg." He was an extraordinarily pale Negro with a thin aquiline face. "I've some papers to correct, if you'll excuse me."

Francis, with his usual sensitivity to voices, noted the cultivated accent. He took a seat, observing discreetly and alternately the man (pensive eyes, fine hands) and the rising fury out of doors (trees bent to earth, tossing and roar).

The teacher stood up and came close to Francis, making his voice heard above the gusting storm.

"I'm Patrick Courzon. You're in the village of Gully."

Francis extended his hand. "Francis Luther. I live up near Point Angélique. I seem to have strayed."

"You'll have to go back the way you came and take the next fork left, about two miles down from here. It'll bring you straight into Eleuthera."

"Oh? How did you know?"

"That you own Eleuthera? Everyone knows everything about everyone on this island. No, that's not quite true. But people are naturally interested in the revival of such an old, neglected place. It's somewhat romantic, isn't it?"

"I don't know about that. Mostly it's digging and grubbing or consulting books to learn how to dig and grub."

The young man put some books on a shelf and Francis asked, "Am I keeping you from your work? I'll just sit here until the storm ends, if it ever does."

"It will, in an hour or two." Courzon sat down. Apparently he wanted to talk. "It can't be easy for you, coming from the city, to start this sort of life."

"Fortunately, I've got a very good manager to teach me about bananas and fences and sheep and hiring—just about everything."

"Hiring? I don't suppose you've had trouble with that. We've a deal of unemployment." The face was bland.

"I know. I feel bad about that, and about the wages, too. As a matter of fact, I'm offering thirty cents a day over the standard, which hasn't," he added frankly, "exactly endeared me to the other planters." And added hurriedly to that: "Not that I'm trying to be holier-than-thou. It's just—" He did not finish.

"That's a substantial increase, considering that the farm wage is eighty cents a day in the cultivating season."

He could not tell whether the man was being hostile or merely straightforward.

Then Courzon asked, "What are you planning for your vacant land, if I'm not too inquisitive? But I, like others, am curious about you."

Francis decided that he was straightforward. "I understand what you're driving at. Estate owners leaving a tract out of cultivation so they won't have to pay taxes on it. That's a regulation which surely needs to be changed. No, I will cultivate and plant wherever the cane has gone wild, which it has done for what looks like generations. It should be a matter of conscience, when the need for food is so great."

"You astonish me, Mr. Luther."

There was a silence. Then Francis said, "On the way here just now I stopped some people to ask directions. They spoke no English, which surprised me."

"They speak patois in these places. A mixture of Carib and African words added to French."

"Yet the island has been out of French hands for a hundred and fifty years!"

"Longer. But these villages are removed from the world. Many of my children speak patois at home and are hearing English for the first time in my classroom."

"British English?" Francis asked with a smile.

"Well, I was educated by Englishmen in Covetown and after that I was at Cambridge, so I suppose a bit of the accent has worn off on me."

"You were born here on St. Felice, then."

"No, oddly enough, I was born in France. I was brought here when I was not yet two years old."

A French father? Francis wondered. Yes, probably. God knew what passions, heartaches, and shame had combined to produce this refined, this obviously sensitive human being! But then, that was probably true of us all in one way or another.

"My mother was born on the island," he said, "but she left it. And I came back to it. I sometimes wonder why. A wish to escape something else? The pull of history? I'm a type, Mr. Courzon, the kind of man who becomes an antiquarian, who putters about restoring old houses. I'm in love with the past, with roots. I've even made a start at writing the story of St. Felice, of all the people who came here and what brought them."

Courzon nodded. "If it's history you're looking for, we have it. Your own Morne Bleue—how the French and English fought over that mountain! Four times it changed hands in some of the bloodiest battles of the eighteenth century. There were the remains of a fort on the flank when I was a little boy, but that's gone now. People took the stone and bricks for use. The French built with stone —did you know?—and the British with brick."

"I didn't know."

Courzon stopped abruptly. "Sorry. I just overheard myself talking like a schoolmaster."

"Well, you are one, aren't you?"

At that moment the front door, forced open by the wind, slammed violently against the wall. Courzon got up and closed it firmly.

Francis was anxious. "Is this by any chance a hurricane? I haven't been here long enough to see one."

"You'll know one when you do, don't worry. When I was fourteen we had one that wrecked St. Felice. Our windows were smashed, a tree stove in the roof, and the floor was three inches deep in water. The island's entire cocoa crop was lost that year."

"A perilous dependence on weather," Francis said, shaking his head. "My uncle, Lionel Tarbox, tells me floods and droughts have come close to wiping him out a dozen times."

The other man said nothing to that, and in sudden comprehension, Francis flushed. "Of course, I know it is much harder for the poor," he said.

He looked around at the schoolroom with its shabby desks and meager shelf of worn-out books. There was a little blackboard on an easel and that was all.

"Yet you came back, too," he said, thinking aloud.

"Pardon?"

"I meant, it's a hard life here and yet you came back to it. You could, I suppose, have stayed in England."

"You mentioned conscience a while ago. I had to come home. Most of the children on this island stop their schooling after five years. Most adults are functionally illiterate."

"So now you are doing something about it."

Courzon looked out to where the rain had begun perceptibly to slacken. "Sometimes, lately, I have had my doubts. What sense does it make to teach Browning to children like these? 'Oh, to be in England now that April's there—' " His voice mocked the wholesome words.

Yet mockery, Francis thought, his interest growing, mockery would not be this man's typical mode or mood. His was a fundamental simplicity.

"I try to give them as much as they can absorb of their own history, the African and the West Indian. That at least has relevance to their lives."

Strange that he did not hesitate to speak this way to Francis, certainly he would not do it with—well, with Lionel, for instance, or with anyone else Francis knew.

"Are you thinking of politics, then?"

"I'm not sure. I'm not a man of action, that's my trouble. I am really not. But I have a friend, Nicholas Mebane, who has come back from England, too, and is starting a new party. He's working on programs to be ready when independence comes, and he wants me to work with him. So I'm thinking about it. Only thinking."

"I've heard mention of Nicholas Mebane. There was something in the paper, wasn't there? And it seems to me that a priest was talking about him the night I first came here."

"That must have been Father Baker."

"Perhaps. I don't usually remember names, and it was a while ago, but for some reason that one stuck in my head. The priest said he was brilliant, if I recall correctly."

"That's true, he is. He's a thinker and an orator. The two don't always go together, but when they do, it can be an unbeatable combination. Nicholas will achieve things. His achievements will spread outward from this one island like ripples in a lake."

Thrusting his hands into his pockets, Courzon walked the length of the room and back.

"Independence will give us initiative. From initiative comes character, a national character, with which to build democracy. But you have to begin with a strong leader, who can show the way. And Nicholas is strong—strong and large-minded. He will fight." He was exhilarated. "You've picked a time when great changes are about to happen, Mr. Luther."

"That's exactly what my Uncle Herbert told me." *Warned me.*

"From a different point of view, I imagine." Courzon smiled. "Do I offend you? I hope not."

"No," Francis said soberly, "if I'm to live here, I should know every point of view, shouldn't I?"

"It would be wise. That always has been part of the trouble, the ownership of the great estates by individual absentee owners—or worse, by foreign companies. They can't know, hence don't care, what is happening here."

"Well, I do care. My head is full of projects for cooperatives and—" Francis' voice trailed off, as he recalled a rush of ideas, Kate's ideas. "For one thing," he resumed, "I want to build some decent housing on my place for my permanent employees."

"I heard you did."

"You heard?"

"I told you, news travels on St. Felice. Well, if you can do that, just make a start at it, and if others will follow suit—which is to be doubted, I'm sorry to say —you'll be doing a great deal. Poor housing is certainly one of the reasons why the family structure is what it is. But we could talk all day"—Courzon threw his hands up—"I should end by discouraging you with all my talk! You'll want to clear out tomorrow and go home."

Francis shook his head. "No. Home is here now."

He was intensely curious about this man. Cambridge, nearly white, he had yet appeared to identify completely with the Negro peasant. He took a chance on a blunt request.

"Tell me something real about *yourself,* Mr. Courzon."

"Something real?"

"Yes," Francis said boldly. "What it's like for you, living here—as you are."

"Not being white, you mean?"

"I suppose I do mean that, partly. What is it you want most?"

"To begin with, I'd like to lift the restrictions on the franchise. One man, one vote. I don't own property, I'm a renter, so I can't vote. Listen, Mr. Luther, on this island as throughout the Caribbean, ninety-five to ninety-eight percent of the people are black, or some shade of it. Very few own property, so they have nothing to say about the way they are to be governed. Nothing at all."

"That's outrageous, of course it is. I'm told, though, that it's about to be changed. This year, even. What I meant was yourself, your personal life. You're married?"

"I have a wife, Désirée. We live in town."

"Désirée? Not the one who works at Da Cunha's?"

"Yes. You know her?"

"She waited on me for Christmas presents and for my wife's birthday. But I haven't seen her in a while, not that I do so much shopping."

"She's stopped working there. We have two children and they need her."

The rain had ceased entirely. Heavy drops splashed from the roof and the trees. The sun shone through a steamy haze. The two men walked to the doorway.

"I like to think the world will be better for my two children—and for all the others," Courzon said. "And I'm an optimist, I have to believe it will be. When you look back over history, making allowances for some bloody backsliding, the general trend, although you can barely discern it, the general trend, I believe, is upward."

"I hope so," Francis murmured.

A strange man, this, and a very strange encounter. And he had a sudden thought about history: it was power, history was, and that's all it was. Winning it and losing it. Power for good, but more often for ill. He could use power here, not with the greed which had brought the downfall of his poor foolish father, but with justice. Lionel and his kind would say he was as great a fool as his father had been! Yet he felt secure enough, this moment, to refute them.

He had begun his good-bye when something held him back. "A magnificent tree," he said, pointing to the sumptuous green bower beneath which he had parked his car.

"A flaming royal poinciana. Red flowers in June. You must have them on your place."

"None that large. They remind me of flamingos when they bloom."

"Speaking of flamingos, they used to be plentiful on this island. Not so long ago, either, when I was a child. You'll pass Flamingo Pond on your way home; they used to feed there on shrimp. There were fifty or sixty in a flock, a gorgeous sight. Bonaire's the only place you'll see them nowadays. Hunted to death."

"Change isn't always to the good, is it?"

"Not always. The whole world could be Eden if it weren't for the waste and destruction."

Francis folded his wet jacket over his arm. "I must say you've told me more about this place in half an afternoon than anyone has done yet except"—he didn't know for the life of him what made him say it—"except my relative, Kate Tarbox."

Courzon said simply, "She has heart."

"I forgot, you know her! Or your wife does."

"We both do. I got to know her through my father-in-law, Clarence Porter. They're involved in a good many projects, mostly through the Family Counseling. Clarence is helping raise money in the unions for a decent clinic, and Kate, of course, knows all the important families. It's hard, though. The people who could give don't want to, at least not more than tokens. But Kate's a rare woman, don't you agree?"

"I imagine so, although I don't see her that much."

Courzon shook hands. "It was nice to meet you, Mr. Luther. Good luck with all your projects."

"I'll tell you," Francis said, "I'll tell you—you ought to come visit," he blurted.

"Do you mean that? Or is it just 'drop in some time,' which I would never do?"

"I don't say things I don't mean." Marjorie would hardly be overjoyed, but no matter. He liked this man so much.

A smile spread from Courzon's quiet mouth. It was the first true smile of the afternoon, a smile without irony or melancholy.

"I shall call you. You're in the book in Covetown? Patrick Courzon?"

"I'm in the book."

He was still standing with arm upraised in a wave when Francis turned out of sight around the curve, downhill.

BOOK THREE

LOVERS AND FRIENDS

❧{10}❧

"Have I shown you this? I must have," said Francis Luther, offering a leather-bound volume. "It's the diary of my first ancestor on St. Felice."

"I've seen it, but Nicholas hasn't." Patrick glanced at a page before handing it over. " 'I mean to buy land and live on my property like a gentleman, to marry well.' This is original history, Nicholas."

"Fascinating," Nicholas murmured.

He occupied the seat on the window ledge with particular grace. His slim feet in their English shoes were crossed at the ankles; his patrician head was sculptured against the afternoon light. And Patrick felt some simple pride in having brought him for the first time to this house, even though the suggestion had come from Kate Tarbox. He saw himself as a link between the gentleman planter who owned the house and the brilliant black politician whose rise to prominence was unmistakably beginning.

"Books," Francis was saying, "are my one extravagance." He gestured toward a pile of new ones in bright jackets. "I keep having them sent down from New York. If there's anything you want to borrow, you're welcome as always."

"This is fascinating," Nicholas repeated, replacing the diary.

"If you want to borrow that, Mr. Mebane, you're welcome to. I've had several copies made besides that one. It's a curiosity, isn't it?"

"I'd like to, very much. Incidentally, I wish you'd call me Nicholas."

"Nicholas, then. Shall we have a drink before dinner? Or, I should say supper, since that's all it is on Sunday evening."

With a pleasure almost physical, Patrick observed the glimmering, small ritual of the drinks, the shimmer of ice and spurt of soda, the bubbles rising in the glasses. In the dozen or more evenings he had spent here in this library during the year just past, a sense of belonging had won out over a first suspicious sense of apartness. Not since that early boyish affection between himself and Nicholas had he felt so easily drawn to another man as to Francis Luther, come out of a world so different from his own and yet so like himself in mind and tastes and in that indefinable quality called heart.

None of this was true of Marjorie Luther. I am an invader in her house, he thought, and she despises my skin, although she'd be ashamed to admit it even to

951

herself. It was in her face behind the proper greeting. One knew these things. But no matter. His own Désirée had her resentments, too.

Through the tall windows at his elbow he could see the little group on the lawn, the women in the shade with Father Baker, who had preferred to stay outdoors. It was an Impressionist scene, or a good imitation of one, with the willow drapery arranged so airily and the women in petunia colors. Laurine, Patrick's ten-year-old, was sitting on the grass at her mother's feet. Kate Tarbox held Maisie, big as she was, on her lap. Marjorie Luther held a small white dog on hers. Impressionism, except for black skin, he thought now wryly.

"What a handsome room this is!" Nicholas exclaimed.

"Funny, it was only half completed when we moved in. I had it finished myself, which cost too much, but it was worth it. I practically live in here." And Francis nodded toward the large desk, which was covered with papers.

"Francis is writing a history of the Caribbean world," Patrick told Nicholas. "A great work, starting with the Arawaks."

"Judging by the progress I'm not making, I shall never finish it."

Nicholas asked curiously, "What is your inspiration? Your family history?"

"Oh, I should imagine so. I've been learning more about them since I came here. One, who'd been taken prisoner in the Battle of Worcester, came in Cromwell's transports. Another was a poor soul from a debtor's prison. And one was a governor. A mixed bag, as you see." Francis laughed.

"So you have really come back to stay, have you?"

"Yes, I've been in New York a few times to visit my parents, and each time the sight of the city did me in. Eleuthera! It's well named. It's my freedom."

"I wish," Nicholas said, "you'd finish what you were saying a while earlier, Mr. Luther."

"Francis, please, if you're to be Nicholas."

Nicholas inclined his head. "Francis. You were telling us about some of your plans for this place of yours. Of course you must know that your model village is already being talked about."

Francis interrupted. "Please! I've got ten houses up for my permanent workers, that's all I've done. Nothing for the seasonals. Nothing even worth talking about yet."

"Don't underestimate it. That's a fine beginning, an example to others."

"I'm not sure how much of an example it will be. I'm afraid, in my short time here, I am already thought of as a troublesome disturber of things as they are." Francis tapped the table thoughtfully. "However, it's my money, what little of it there is, and I can tell you there's little enough! Luckily I don't crave enormous wealth. I'd just like to pay off my mortgage one day, that's all."

"You see," Patrick said, "you see, Nicholas, why I wanted you to meet each other. It's a basic attitude, men of good will—" In his eagerness he floundered, feeling himself naïve, his emotion overflowing too visibly.

Nicholas leaned toward Francis. "Our good friends, Patrick and Kate Tarbox, brought me here out of the goodness of their hearts. Let me put things in a nutshell. Now that we've at last got universal suffrage, independence is only a few years away. Huge tasks await us. After political autonomy must come economic stabilization. Huge tasks! My party wants to come to power on this island. It's a democratic party, the New Day Progressives, young men with plans. But—and let me make this clear—we are not radicals. We don't want to confiscate. On the contrary, we want the support of the planter class, of those more enlightened members of it who will cooperate with us toward greater prosperity for all. And frankly, I need your help."

"My heart and conscience are with reform, but I'm not a political man," Francis objected.

"On the contrary, you are. A man who can see a need and take steps, even take one step toward alleviating it, is political. And as Patrick has just said, it's an attitude. An open-minded attitude. Oh, don't worry, I'm not asking you to make any immediate public declarations which would embarrass you! I understand your position very well," Nicholas said astutely. "All I want is to get acquainted with you and to feel that in you I have a mind and an ear to consult with. It's a gradual process, this building of a sympathetic understanding. May I, then, from time to time, have your ear?"

"That surely! I'm always glad to listen. I enjoy an evening visitor anytime. Patrick knows that. I believe I hear the supper bell."

Patrick's sense of ease evaporated in the dining room. Now, at this formal table, with Negro servants passing silver platters, he felt acute discomfort. And he wondered what the servants were thinking or would say out in the kitchen.

He looked around. An ill-assorted group, as the world saw it: the whites in their patrician home; the two black children—quiet and well behaved, or they could not have been brought here—with their tight braids; Désirée, silent in her pride and so vivid that the other two women faded by comparison. Marjorie Luther is frosted, he thought. A frosted woman, with fine skin, white as paper. Her silk was pale, her pearls were milky. He embarrassed himself with a flashing image of her in bed with Francis. She would be cool, he imagined, surely not like Désirée! Still, one never knew. And Francis had such great heart! He hadn't been ready for marriage. He was only now waking up out of ignorance. All this went through Patrick's mind while he unfolded the napkin and picked up the spoon.

Silence fell over the table. The incongruity of the gathering must have occurred to them all. And needing to break the silence, he addressed the hostess.

"Your cook, I would wager, is from Martinique."

"How did you know? Is the soup too spicy?"

"No, no, it's perfect. My mother came from there, and she's a wonderful cook. You must ask yours to make some of their recipes. Turkey with curry sauce—ah, that's something to remember!"

"Tell me some I should ask for, then." Marjorie Luther bent into the candle-light, pretending interest.

"Well, there are steamed *palourdes,* for instance. Clams with lime." He sought for something exotic to make interesting conversation. Actually, he had little interest in food. "*Acra de morue,* that's codfish fritters with green peppers. A typical dish."

"I shall certainly try that," Marjorie Luther said politely.

Silver clinked on china. Father Baker ate with an old man's greed, attentive to his plate, while Désirée fussed over the little girl and the others were apparently mesmerized by Morne Bleue, which filled the tall windows at the end of the room. This time it was Nicholas who rescued them from silence.

"Do I hear rightly that your mother has thoughts of going home to Martinique?" he asked Patrick.

"She talks about it. I don't want her to go, but she's getting older and seems to be feeling some pull toward her family land, or what's left of it."

"Do you all know about 'family land'?" And Nicholas explained. "It's a concept that has nothing to do with the legal code. It's custom, out of Africa. You can move away from the land for years, for a lifetime, but if it belonged to one of your ancestors, you have the right to come back and live on it and to eat the fruit that grows on it."

"And to be buried there," said Kate, turning away from the twilight on the Morne.

"You know that!" Nicholas remarked in some surprise.

"I've learned a few things in my time," she retorted with a smile.

"In the West Indies," Nicholas continued, "this land is almost always what was granted to a slave when he was freed."

"I should be making notes," Francis said, "for my history."

"That you'll never write," Marjorie added.

"Your husband," Nicholas said graciously, "has many irons in the fire. The day must not be long enough for him."

"I hope not too many irons," Marjorie replied.

"My wife is always afraid I work too hard," Francis said, apologizing for whatever it was that was going wrong at his fine table in the benign and mellow evening.

Kate threw out a question. "Speaking of irons in the fire, what about the new party? You men relegated us to the lawn, even though that's what I came to hear about."

"Oh," Nicholas said, "we talked a bit. No decisions yet."

"I'm sorry to hear that," Kate said, "because that's the reason Patrick and I wanted to get you together. Of course, I am always in too much of a hurry, I know."

Marjorie drank water, picking the glass up and replacing it with a harsh thump.

Kate went on speaking softly and rapidly. "We shall never get anything good done in this place without government. You all know that. Volunteer efforts just can't do what needs doing. That's something I never could get across to my husband. Not that he'd work with you people anyway, if I could get it across. He wouldn't even come tonight and sit at table with blacks, you know that."

Marjorie picked up her glass again and set it down so decisively that the water, tipping over, made a little puddle on the polished wood. It was as though she had drawn an audible gasp, although she had not.

"Don't be shocked, Marjorie," Kate said. "These are my friends. They know the facts of life. I speak openly with them."

"That you do," Father Baker agreed. "From the first words you ever spoke." He looked around the table with fond pride. "I knew Kate before she was born. With all her faults, I love her and I usually agree with her, too, although not always."

"Not on birth control," Kate said quickly. "Family planning, I should say. It sounds better and is more accurate, besides."

"It's a curious thing," Nicholas remarked, "how population has become the number-one issue in Central America. It wasn't always so. Most people, I think, don't know that during the slavery period there were more deaths than births. The difference was made up for by importation from Africa." His finely modulated voice took command. Everyone moved to face him. "I suppose to some extent it was undernourishment and overwork, but chiefly it was disease. Now medicine has rid us of yaws and cholera, of yellow fever and typhus. So as a result, we are crowding ourselves off the island. Off the planet, for that matter."

"Then would you be willing to include the subject in your platform?" Kate spoke earnestly.

Nicholas smiled. "With the usual ten-foot pole, I would," he said candidly. "After all, you have to get elected before you can accomplish anything. Isn't that so, Mrs. Luther?"

"Oh, of course," Marjorie acknowledged.

A consummate tactician, Patrick thought, as Nicholas continued, "It's a fortunate thing, I always say, when a community has citizens like you ladies. Active, educated women. . . . Women always have so much more concern for the basics, for the quality of life. I believe your husband said you're a graduate of Pembroke, Mrs. Luther? My fiancée went to Smith. Doris Lester, from Ohio. I should be honored if you would meet her after we're married."

Marjorie took interest. "When will that be, Mr. Mebane?"

"A Christmas wedding." And he added, Patrick knew, so that there would be no misunderstanding, "Her father is a minister of the African Methodist Church."

The atmosphere, thanks to Nicholas, had grown lighter. "And have you found many changes here after your time abroad?" Marjorie asked, addressing him but not Patrick, who had also come home from abroad. It is his charm, Patrick, thought, not minding.

"Not really. We've been asleep here for centuries. But"—and as if to warn, Nicholas raised his hand—"but let me tell you, change is on the way. We already have daily flights to the main cities of the Caribbean, with connecting flights to here. Eventually we'll have a jetport of our own, connecting us directly with Europe. All this will affect the way we live and the way we must be governed."

"It quite makes one's head swim, doesn't it?" Marjorie said smoothly. "Unfortunately, I am not at all political."

"That's what I said a while ago," Francis said.

"Everyone is political, or becomes so," Kate corrected.

"A profound statement," Nicholas observed pleasantly, as they left the table.

IN THE CAR, Désirée complained, "I'm exhausted! All that heavy talk! It's like carrying bundles till one's arms want to drop off. If you notice, I barely said a word."

"It was intelligent conversation," Patrick objected. "Your father would have enjoyed it."

"Oh, you and Pop! Tell the truth, weren't you feeling uncomfortable in there?"

"Maybe a little, but only because of her. Francis is an honest man, an independent. He didn't have to ask us. He wanted to. There's surely no advantage to him in having people like us in his house."

"No? You don't think he's counting on Nicholas coming into power? Maybe he's smarter than the rest of them. Looking out for the future."

Patrick said loyally, "Even so. There's more to it than that. Francis Luther likes me and I like him."

"It's a queer friendship," Désirée argued. "Your mother thinks it is. She keeps asking me. It bothers her."

"Probably," Nicholas suggested tactfully, "what's really upsetting her is that she's leaving."

"She doesn't have to," Patrick replied.

He didn't say that he had invited Agnes to live with them, now that she was too old to tend the store. No, she had told him, there was no room for two women in one house. Yet she was going back to live with a cousin. And he knew that neither time nor two babies had eased her resentment of Désirée. Indeed, he had once caught her comparing the skin of her arm with his babies' arms, which were many shades darker than hers. There lay the crux and cause of her anger! Yet in a curious way, and unjust as it was, he could understand and forgive her. Like so many, she was only a victim of universal prejudices. He felt a wave of sadness at losing her; he remembered her long-ago tale of Mount Pelée and how, only a child herself, she had fled to St. Felice.

Désirée spoke from the back seat. "Francis Luther made her have us there today. You can be sure she won't let any of her friends know she entertained us at her dinner table! Personally, Patrick, I feel humiliated in that house."

"Forget her," Patrick said impatiently. "What about Father Baker? Your father can tell you a few things about him. And what about Kate Tarbox? The few services we have, the little we have in the way of hospital care, are mostly her doing. Your father can tell you that, too."

"All right, Kate Tarbox. I'll agree," said Désirée. "But she's one in a hundred thousand." She laughed, reflecting, "Did you see Marjorie Luther's face when Kate said that about her husband not wanting to eat with us? I thought she would go through the floor, not that she doesn't agree with Kate's husband herself, Lord knows."

Nicholas chuckled. "She speaks her mind, that Kate. An interesting character. I have an idea she can be trusted, too."

"Trust Kate?" Patrick repeated. "Take my word for it, you can do that."

"The Luther woman is the much better looking of the two, though. She has height, for one thing," said Désirée, out of satisfaction with her own height. "And she knows how to wear clothes. That dress cost a fortune."

Patrick objected again. "You don't know what you're talking about. Kate has life! She has fire! Take a good look at her the next time."

"Listen to the man! Anybody'd think you were in love with her," Désirée told him good-naturedly.

Patrick was stubborn. For some reason it was important to defend Kate Tarbox. "She's *real*. One isn't used to a human being like her. Most people wear a mask. She doesn't."

"Well, if she doesn't wear one, she'd better do it soon, or the whole world will see she's in love with Francis Luther."

"That's ridiculous! Women!" Patrick said, shaking his head at Nicholas.

"Marjorie Luther knows it, too. That's why she hates her."

"Oh, women!" Patrick repeated, in mock despair.

Nicholas said quietly, "Désirée is right, you know. I sensed it, too. That's why I made an effort to draw Mrs. Luther out. The art of politics, my friend. You have to have keen perceptions or you won't survive."

"I'm not keen at all," Patrick said, feeling some wistfulness.

"You're not fair to yourself," Nicholas admonished him kindly.

They topped the last hill before the descent into Covetown. Pink and silver gilt and rose touched the rooftops, as the great red ball had begun to lower itself into the sea, and this final splendor rekindled some memory of the day's contradictions.

"Eleuthera," Nicholas said softly. "Freedom. A beautiful name."

"Yes," Désirée said. "You could certainly feel free in a place like that, couldn't you?"

"Freedom is relative," Patrick admonished. "You can live in a palace and have a mind so narrow that you might as well be in prison."

Nicholas teased, "You haven't changed since we were at school, my friend. I told you then and I tell you now, you should have been a philosopher."

"Oh, I never know what he's thinking," Désirée said affectionately. And as the car drew up in front of their narrow little house, "What I do know is, I could sit on that lawn forever, looking out at the ocean. Do you think people like them have any idea how lucky they are?"

Long stripes of pink and silver gilt and rose lay over the sea as the horizon tilted upward to consume the sun. The four, when the others had departed, sat out on the lawn with their faces turned to the radiance.

Marjorie was the first to speak, underscoring the nouns. "I don't know about all of you, but I found that exhausting! So much effort to manufacture *conversation*, especially with that *woman*. What on *earth* was there to talk about? That Nicholas was the best of the lot, a *gentleman*. He seems more like one of us, although of course he isn't really, either."

"That doesn't sound like you," Francis chided. And somewhat disturbed before the others, he explained. "Marjorie is too kind to have meant that the way it sounded. She's not a bigot."

"No," Marjorie insisted, "No. I did mean it just as I said it. I don't like having my house used for a political meeting. To me it was a false occasion. Artificial. What can we have in common with those people, or they with us?"

Father Baker answered calmly, "We may have to have—apart from any moral considerations—we may have to have much in common before we're through. They are going to be running the government here sooner than you think. The British Empire is being chipped away. India is already gone, and the rest of us are going, make no mistake about it."

Marjorie was in a mildly argumentative mood. "I don't see why you people are so ready to give up, to humor all these agitators! These people don't have such a bad life, you know. The climate couldn't be easier. You go down into the markets and see all those piles of marvelous vegetables and fish and—"

Father Baker interrupted. "Surely you must have learned by now that there's not nearly enough food to go around and not enough money to buy what there is."

"Well, there would be," Marjorie persisted, "if they didn't have such enormous families. It's really disgusting. All these children and no husbands. But of course there was no wedlock in Africa, so I suppose—"

"There are no jobs for the men, haven't you heard?" Kate put in. "That's why so many of them leave."

The women are sharpening their knives, Francis thought.

Marjorie digressed. "They're a childish people. One of the maids almost scared me to death last week. Shrieking that spirits were making her baby sick and spirits were throwing the furniture around in her house. I thought she was going insane till Osborne told me it was just obeah. What can you do with people like that? And they want to run the government!"

"You sound like Lionel," Kate said. Her jaw was set.

They despised each other. Francis moved restlessly in his chair, wishing the guests would go home. It was only seven thirty; in an hour they could decently take their leave. He felt annoyed with Marjorie and also defensive of her.

"Is it so bad to sound like your husband?" Marjorie asked. *Your husband* was accusatory. "I happen to admire him."

"Oh, he is admirable in many ways," Kate replied.

"I admire the way he enjoys life. He works hard and spends his money without all this heavy guilt about having it, which gets so tiresome."

The conversation went in waves. After each crash came a lull, in which the force of the wave withdrew to gather itself for the next collision. And he wished again that they would go home, and his wife go to bed, and leave him alone. They were upsetting him, which was a pity, for he had truly enjoyed the afternoon and the interaction between minds so different in experience from his own.

"They were both in my classes," Father Baker was saying. "I suppose I feel involved with their future because I always took special interest in bright boys of the other race. A mixture of compassion and, I'm afraid, some plain curiosity."

"Nicholas is obviously the smart one," Marjorie said.

The old man contradicted her. "Smart, yes. Clever, yes. But Patrick is the thinker. Slower and far less ambitious, almost without ambition, but— Well, time will tell."

"There is something very fine about him," Francis said. "I always have a sense of depth, of much unspoken. There is something in his eyes"—and, looking over, caught Kate's own eyes.

"Yes," she said, turning away.

"Do you hear from Julia and Herbert?" Marjorie inquired now of Kate. She was remembering her obligation as a hostess, in spite of all. "We had a letter two or three months ago."

"Yes, she says it's a good thing Herbert was brought up in England, otherwise they'd be just another pair of colonials. Colonials are never top-drawer, you know. It's all so funny really, these silly people sticking labels on themselves! 'I'm better than you; he's better than she.' Like those women at the club in town— especially the foreigners—acting so grand toward the help. They're almost worse than those of us who were born here."

"I haven't found them so," Marjorie said stiffly. "I've made good friends at the club. I wish we lived closer in. I wish Francis would buy a house in town, one of those lovely old ones with a walled garden in an alley."

"You know I have to be here," Francis said.

"You have Osborne. You always say he's so trustworthy."

"Yes, but not to wear my shoes."

Marjorie sighed and Francis thought again, She ought to have a child. The thought was always with him and no doubt always with her. Her nerves were going bad. During their visit to New York they had both had tests and the doctors had found no reason why she had not conceived. Everyone they knew had children, sturdy children with sun-bleached hair and rosy tans. Their joys and their tribulations were the inevitable subject of adult conversation. Sometimes he thought, although probably it was unfair of him, that Marjorie suffered more from a feeling of failure and deficiency in not having given birth than from the fact itself.

Yet he felt his wife's pain.

"It's getting damp," she said now. "Let's have our coffee in the house."

"Will you play for us, Kate?" asked Father Baker. "I remember when you were a little girl, practicing the *Liebeslieder* waltzes."

"I don't play very well anymore."

"But will you, anyway?"

She sat down at the piano. From his "own" chair near the window, Francis had an oblique view of her cheek and the curving hair which swayed like a curtain as she moved. He supposed she played with skill, but he was no judge; he only knew when music moved him, and Brahms always did. He had not worked, because it was Sunday, and had no reason to be so tired, yet he felt a need to soothe fatigue, and putting the coffee cup aside, he laid his head against the back of the chair and closed his eyes. The music rippled, telling of simple, country things, of May and streams, of gardens and first love. And the scents of frangipani and wet grass blew in with drenching sweetness.

Then, abruptly, the music changed. It paused and slid into a minor key. It was as though the shadow of some sorrow had darkened the spirit of the player. Just so, two or three times in the past, he remembered, had a visible shadow passed across her face.

. . . *but he married me instead.* He could still hear the cadence of the words, could see the sudden gravity and then the determined cheerful toss of the head. Funny, plucky little soul! A scrapper, he thought, afraid of nothing, and yet—

He had been thinking of her ever since. No, not thinking, exactly, just aware, as of a hovering presence at the back of thought, so that on an errand in town it would cross his mind that he might perhaps encounter her again on the street. It had never happened. Or entering a room at one of those crowded gatherings where you stand all evening holding a drink, it would cross his mind—oh, idly, very idly—that she might be there among the crowd. She never was.

All of this was meaningless, of course—aberration and whim! It came to all men at some time or other. It came and passed. And opening his eyes, he met Marjorie's rather thoughtful gaze, just as the music stopped and Kate closed the lid of the piano with a final thump.

"It's late," she said. "Come, Father."

It had grown quite dark. At the car Kate paused and looked up at the sky, where there was no moon and blue stars quivered.

"No wind up there. No sound," she said. "It seems so strange. Turning and turning, millions of stars in total silence."

He thought he saw tears in her eyes, but it might have been only their natural shine.

"We don't know anything, do we?" she said, and got into the car.

He went back up the walk to where Marjorie was waiting. Braced against the doorpost, she, too, was looking up into the sky.

"A depressing night," she said.

"Depressing?"

"Yes. Yes. Tell me, do you really think we'll ever have a child?"

With his arm around her, he could feel the rigid muscles under the soft silk.

"I don't know," he began. "Still—"

"But how stupid of me to ask! How can you know?" She began to cry. "I'm sick of myself, Francis! What excuse is there for a woman without a uterus that works? What am I to do with my life? Keep putting a good face on things with my friends? Run around like Kate Tarbox, making an idiot of myself?"

His fingers, which had half-consciously been soothing her shoulders, withdrew.

"What have you got against Kate? She's never harmed you."

"I don't trust her."

He spoke quietly. "Can't women have compassion toward each other? You know she's not happy at home."

"That doesn't give her a license to poach."

"Poach, Marjorie! That's total nonsense!"

Was it? Hesitating and denying, tentatively reaching and withdrawing, with their silences and their eyes, they had been communicating, he and the other woman. Yes, they had.

And, very troubled, very afraid, his arms went out again to his wife, but she had pressed herself against the door and shrank away.

"I've done you an injustice," he said, "keeping you here." When she did not deny it, he continued, "I suppose we ought to quit and go home."

"You know you're not going to do that, you're too committed here."

It was so. Now, would he have gone willingly with her if it were she who had committed herself to a labor and a way of life that fulfilled her need? With painful honesty he tried to answer Yes, he thought he would. True, this was a man's world, but there was in him a sense of fairness, and he thought he would. Then, was he asking too much of *her,* after all? He thought he was not.

As if she knew there was nothing more to be said on the subject, she sighed again. "I'm going in. Are you coming?"

"In a minute," he answered.

She wanted sex tonight, he understood. It was not only because of her now-frantic need to become pregnant. It was her need to receive her due, proof that she was desirable and that their marriage was successful, according to the books. He couldn't prove that this was so, but when he lay with her, his body knew it.

Something had happened, something had changed. And it was not just because they were living here; for here, as there or anywhere, one throve if all else were right. Neither was it her twinge of jealousy; he would give her, he vowed, no cause. He'd seen enough of that sort of thing with his father. Was it, then, simply because they had no children?

He became aware of an agitation in his chest, an altered heartbeat.

Far below, a sliver of sea gleam shone through the wilderness of leaves. A wind rose, moving through the high acomas. And Francis' memory, drifting without direction, plucked through some association with this sound of wind, a picture of Marjorie, standing with her arm in his, laughing, struggling as a gust blew the wedding veil across her mouth.

When had it changed, and why? He didn't know, he couldn't say, only that it had. It occurred to him that such must be the regret you know when you are old. He felt a lonely, chilling sadness. And he stood quite still, waiting, willing it to pass.

Ah, well, only a fool expects to keep forever all those first, mysterious raptures!

Then, then, there was always this, which alone would never change: he flung his arms out to the breathing night. All blue it was: the far pale stars were blue and the trees threw blue-black shadows on the grass. A bird, not yet sunk into sleep, called one clear, genial note and, falling still, stilled also some portion of the agitation in the young man's heart.

And he, too, sighed as Marjorie had done and went in and closed the door.

❧⟨11⟩❧

"There's so much to be done," Nicholas urged, tipping back from a spacious desk on which papers were ordered with soldierly precision, "while you're holed up in a village school, wasting yourself."

Around him the office walls held shelves of law books and well-framed diplomas. Above the windows hung a long green-and-yellow banner which proclaimed with spirit, NEW DAY PROGRESSIVES FOR A BRIGHT TOMORROW.

Nicholas followed Patrick's glance. "Like it?"

"It certainly catches the eye."

"Well, have you thought any more about our last talk?"

Now Patrick had to play devil's advocate. "No honest work is ever wasted. And I've always wanted to teach, you know that."

"You also understand what I mean. We've discussed more than once your sense of futility at teaching children what they'll never use."

"Still, if you can reach just one, light a fire in just one—"

"I know, I know. Pious hopes. but someone else could do what you're doing now. What I'm asking of you is far more demanding. You want to improve conditions? Then consider the power of the press! You write well, and our party needs a paper that will express its point of view. The island needs a paper, as a matter of fact. Here, listen to this." Nicholas picked up a copy of the *Clarion*. "Here's the front page: 'Miss Emmy Lou Grace was guest of honor at a party in celebration of her eighty-fifth birthday last Wednesday at the home of Mrs. Clara Pitt.' And here's what passes for an editorial: 'We must deplore the condition of the square on market day . . . fish heads attracting stray cats!'" Laughing, he flung the paper down. "Pap like this! And nothing about schooling, nothing about housing, nothing even about independence, which can't be more than two years away! Pap! Patrick, I've got money enough to start a paper and keep it going until it can support itself. When my father died last year he left much more than I knew he had. Look, I'm supporting this whole office, all this extra space I've taken for the party! I want you to take charge of a paper for me. I want to build a constituency before any of the other parties get ahead of us."

"They don't amount to anything. They've no real leadership, no programs except muttering discontent."

"Exactly. But you can't count on that forever. When independence comes—

962

before it comes—we want to be in first place. You're an idealist, but what good are ideals if all you do is talk about them? Here's your chance to bring some of them to life."

Patrick looked out the window, away from that pair of searching, vivid eyes. Across the cove an outboard skimmed, its wake a triangle drawn upon a clean page. Cathedral bells made a brief alto clatter and ceased. Sunday calm lay over the town, touching his ears and eyes with its languor, beguiling him away from the coiled energy of Nicholas and the decisions he was urging.

I am not a man of action, he thought again.

"Have you talked about me to your father-in-law?"

"Oh, yes." Patrick smiled mischievously. "He says to tell you he doesn't resent you because you wear fine suits and speak with an Englishman's accent."

Nicholas laughed. "So he approves?"

"Well, you know he wants a government that will represent labor. He says if you can do that he will certainly support you."

"Good. And what about the paper?"

"Obviously, it's important to have access to the press. The planters will no doubt fight all the way."

"Except Francis Luther and maybe a couple of other mavericks."

Patrick said slowly, "Clarence isn't even sure he trusts Francis. Needless to say, I don't agree!"

"Not trust him!" Nicholas exclaimed.

"Well, Clarence is getting older and has seen too much. He admits he's probably too cynical."

"He certainly is. Listen, it's our job to point out conditions that are insupportable, that can't go on. We need to persuade. It's stupid to assume that because a man is a planter and has white skin he's unteachable, or a natural enemy. And now there's something I haven't told you. I just found it out yesterday. Kate Tarbox wants to join you."

"How so?"

"She's left her husband. Finally. Should have done it long ago, or so the gossip goes." Nicholas shrugged. "Anyway, she's moved back into a house she had from her father. It's an unpretentious place, down that alley at the foot of Library Hill. And she wants to earn some money. She'd like to work on the paper, maybe even write something, under a pseudonym, if necessary."

Patrick whistled softly. Could this move of hers have anything to do with Francis? At once he decided not.

"Well, what do you think? It would be pleasant, I should imagine, to work with her." Nicholas looked at his watch.

Patrick stood at once. "Let me mull it over some more."

He went downstairs and got into his car, feeling the weight of Nicholas's pressure. The offer was complimentary, to be sure. Also, it had its temptations—chiefly, more money. Désirée would be pleased with that! A small knot gathered on his forehead. Deliberately, he smoothed it. No use fretting! She had a strong taste for luxury, and this taste had been encouraged since Doris had married Nicholas and come here to live. Doris, by Désirée's standards, perhaps by anyone's, was a sophisticate, a connoisseur of good things to wear and eat and be surrounded by. Doris and Nicholas were living in the house that had been his father's, but there was talk now, so Désirée reported wistfully, of their building a waterfront house on a hill about two miles from town. Very modern, it was to be, with much glass and open space. In the style of Le Corbusier, she had explained. She had very likely never heard of Le Corbusier until now, but she was an apt student.

His mind slid back to the paper and Kate Tarbox, who had walked away from a splendor which would have dazzled Désirée. . . . And his mind slid back to Agnes. She had sold the store and was ready to leave. He'd worried: What sort of place was it where she was going? What sort of house?

"Wattle and daub," she'd told him. "One of my cousins' husbands built it."

"But you've had running water here, you aren't used to that," he'd objected.

Her earrings had swung. "Why not? I was born under wattle and daub. I'm not too high and mighty to live under it again."

Funny how some people wanted things and wanted so badly, while others didn't care!

As for himself, he was comfortable, cleanly housed, and well fed. He was, for the most part, doing what he liked. And with a twinge he thought of "his" children, certain faces appearing to mind according to the bench they occupied. There was Rafael, restless and cunning as a monkey; just lately Patrick had begun to see some settling of his mood. Then Tabitha, a stammerer who, he was certain, had been beaten since infancy. And Charlotte, with a head for numbers more competent than Patrick's own by far. No, he was not about to abandon them! He could not! They challenged him and held his sympathies in their bare hands; they angered him, they tried his patience, and they loved him. Well, some of them did, anyway!

What Nicholas wanted was, moreover, a step into the dark. If it didn't work out, he would have forfeited his place in the school system. And if it did work out, he had no illusions about what it would lead to. Involvement in a tough political struggle, that's what. He had no taste for it, none at all.

And yet perhaps it was a grown man's duty to involve himself?

He thought, I really need to talk to someone. Almost at once, his car turned off the shore road, back up through the foothills, curving leftward toward Eleuthera. He wouldn't mind, Francis wouldn't; he might even be pleased to know that someone felt the need of his counsel.

In a state of heightened emotion, he was so intent upon himself that, as he was later to remark, it was a miracle he had observed anything beyond that self and the few feet of road ahead of the car. Indeed, he had actually driven some way past what his eyes had seen before the sight registered in his brain, so that he was not really sure he had seen it; something caused him to stop the car, to back it up over the narrow, twisting road, to find out whether he had imagined what he had seen.

No. It was quite real. Some feet back from the road, a child, a boy of nine or ten years, was standing, slumped and standing, tied by wrists and ankles to a tree. Patrick rubbed his eyes and shook his head. He got out of the car.

"What is it? What happened?" he cried. The boy must long ago have stopped crying. His eyes were dry. His lips were bleeding; he had been trying to gnaw through the coarse, frayed ropes that bound him.

Patrick knelt and, with his pocketknife, cut the ropes. He took the child in his arms. The boy had wet his pants; his tight black curls were sweaty; Patrick held him close.

"Who are you? Where do you live? Who did this?"

The boy struggled, not wanting to be held, perhaps in terror of being held, and Patrick released him.

"Tell me, tell me," he whispered. "What's your name?"

"Will. And I'm thirsty. I'm hungry." Still he did not cry.

"Get in the car there, Will. We'll find a place down the road and get you something to eat right away."

The boy climbed in beside Patrick. He sat quite erect and still, with two fists clenched on his knees. It would have seemed more natural if he had been hysterical, Patrick thought, but then, he was no psychologist.

"Who did this to you, Will?" he asked, very quietly.

"Bert did."

"Who's Bert?"

"Where I live. Bert."

"With your mother and"—he hesitated—"father?"

"I got no mother and father."

"Grandmother, then?" For that, of course, was a normal family pattern.

"No. She died."

"Brothers? Sisters? Who?"

"I had an uncle, but he went away. Took all my stuff with him, too."

"He did? What stuff?"

"I had pots. And I had two donkeys my grandma gave me. He stole them. Sold them and went away."

"I see," said Patrick. This tale of the abandoned child was not unfamiliar, only a more horrendous version of it than was usual.

"I want to eat, mister."

"You can call me Mr. Courzon. No," he said, looking down sideways at the dirty little fists so strangely knotted, as if to challenge the unfeeling world, "no, I'll tell you what: call me Uncle Patrick. I'll be your uncle, your good uncle, for today. Here's a store. I'll see what I can find to eat."

The store, actually the front room of a sagging house, had a few shelves of canned goods, some bags of rice and flour and sundries. He bought a chocolate bar, bananas, and a can of soda.

"Not the best lunch in the world," he said, with a cheerfulness he did not feel, "but it will hold you till we can get something better."

Will stuffed the food down. When he had finished, Patrick began again.

"Now tell me where you live, Will. I'm going to take you back. I'm going to ask a few questions, too, when we get there," he said grimly.

"Delicia. That's the place."

"Delicia! I ought to have asked before, oughtn't I?"

They had been traveling in the wrong direction. He wouldn't get to Eleuthera today, but first things first. He turned the car about and off onto a rutted track, not far from where he had found Will on the main road. I might have figured that out, he thought, irritated with himself.

"We'll have to put some salve on your arms and legs," he said. "Does it hurt very badly?"

"Some," Will said.

He was either too frightened to talk or too tired. My God, Patrick thought, swallowing outrage and pity, quite literally lumped together in his throat.

Delicia, he recalled now, having been there once when he'd got lost, was a remote and meager cluster of shacks in a humid wilderness of bananas. He could have written its history, he thought, stopping now at the place Will pointed out. There would be a core of strong and faithful women who remained to grow old on the estate, caring for the scattered children of the young who went off-island to work and seldom came back to claim them, or perhaps claimed two or three and left the rest or gave them away. There would be the men, the itinerants who stayed just long enough to father a brood and leave it; there would be those who, staying, had only cruel discipline or, at best, neglect for the children whom they or other men had fathered. A beggarly place, this, far removed from a village like Sweet Apple, for poverty, like wealth, had layers and levels: poor, poorer, poorest. Delicia was poorest.

Children, in shirts that left them bare from the belly button down, shared a dusty common yard with dogs and tethered goats. Sitting on the ground around a stone firepit, five or six women were eating breadfruit and salt pork out of a pot. Their heads turned to Patrick as he strode toward them, his footsteps angry on the ground.

"Whose boy is this?" he demanded.

Will had got out to lean, as if for protection, against the fender.

A woman answered, evading the question. "His mother dead. Estelle. She died birthing him."

"Well, who takes care of him now?"

"He had an uncle. Gone off-island. New York, I think."

"No, London," another corrected, "and never coming back."

"I don't care about that. Who takes care of him now, I asked?"

"We all do. I feed him sometimes with my kids," one said.

"Who tied him to a tree?"

No one answered.

Will spoke up himself. "You know. Bert did."

Patrick raised his voice. "Who's Bert? Where is he?"

"He not here."

"I see he isn't. Where is he?"

"Gone for the day."

A woman cried out defensively, some vague thought of lurking, imminent punishment having flitted through her head, "That boy there, he dig up yams! He dug up three yams. That why he got beat and tied!"

Will's roar startled the group. "I was hungry! Damn you, I was hungry!"

Patrick would have liked to cry outrage himself. Instead he put a hand on the boy's shoulder.

Then a young, pregnant woman went up to Patrick. "You want to take this boy? If he do misbehave again, Bert going to beat him, tie him up again. Bert or somebody."

She was telling him, asking him, to take the child away! Given her own dire wants, one could not have blamed her if she had simply turned her back indifferently; but no, concern and pity were alive in her, so that she cared enough to plead for this miserable, unwanted boy. As a naked bulb flares white in a dark room, comprehension flashed in Patrick.

Oh, if he had stopped to think further, to consider his own household, or measure the responsibility and problems that might ensue, then surely it would have made more sense to refuse, to drive away with a weary heart and in time to forget little Will Whatever-His-Name! But he did not stop to measure or weigh.

"Has he got any clothes? Anything to take?"

The woman nodded. "I'll show you."

They went into a house. In the front room, on the bare earth floor, chickens roosted and coconut oil—from stolen coconuts, I'll wager, Patrick thought—was boiling on a tin stove. In the other room were a bed and a pile of covers lying on the floor.

"This is his cover," the woman said. "Sometimes he sleeps in this house, sometimes anywhere, whoever has room that night. He can take these pants. And two shirts. One belongs to my boys, but he can have it."

"Just give me a pair of pants. He's wet the ones he's wearing."

They went outside. Suddenly it occurred to Patrick that he might be taking too much for granted.

"Tell me, Will, do you want to go with me?"

"Where you want to bring me?"

"Home to my house."

Will raised black unreadable eyes. They bored into Patrick's. "Do you beat your boys?"

"I have no boys. I have two little girls, and no, I don't beat them. I don't believe in beating children, or tying them up."

"Then I'll go with you," Will said.

So casually was the transfer made that, before the car had turned about, the women had gone back to their meal. The car bumped through the sultry shade of the banana forest and came out into the broad afternoon on the main road. It was like leaving some eerie landscape of surrealism—the clump of huts in that vast, dank jungle, the women squatting by the iron pot—to emerge again into such normal light. And Patrick shook himself, as if to make sure he was awake.

Will startled him. "Maybe Bert was hungry, too."

"What do you mean?"

"He wanted the yams himself. That's why he got mad and tied me up."

"You mean to say you're not angry at him?"

"I hate him. I'd like to kill him."

Patrick nodded. That was better, a decent rage. Still, what strange insight for a child to possess! *Maybe Bert was hungry, too.* How fathom the minds of men, or of a child?

"Put your head back," he said gently. "Or curl up on the seat and sleep a while. I'll wake you when we get there."

Oh, I've done a damn fool thing! he thought. Désirée will probably be frantic. And why not? Then, arguing with himself, came justification: I've wanted a boy, and Désirée won't have any more children. Her figure, I suppose. The girls are delightful, of course they are, but a man wants a son. Father and son. Do I want that so much because I never had a father? Anyway, a boy . . . And he glanced over at the sleeping child, a sturdy boy, tall for his age, Patrick guessed, and dark as Désirée. He had straight features, a nice-looking boy. Then the torn and welted skin on the thin, young arms removed the last of his doubts. He was prepared to do whatever battle might be necessary when he reached home.

SOME HOURS LATER he was on his front porch rocking in the dusk. Clarence had given Will a bath, and he had been put to bed in the spare room. If it had not been for Clarence, who had come over from his house when the news was brought, why then, it would have been a much harder battle, Patrick thought, feeling grateful to the old man.

The screen door swung open and Désirée came out on the porch.

"Are you furious with me?" he asked.

"I was, but I've got over it. Anyhow, it wouldn't do any good. You'll do what you want to do."

"Am I such a tyrant, then?"

"Not really. But I hope you know what you're doing this time, I surely do."

"I know."

She said quietly, "I'm the one who'll have all the work."

"What work? He's no infant. It's another plate on the table and a bit of washing, that's all." He put his hand out, drawing her to himself. "I've wanted a boy. If I were pious, which I'm not, I could say the Lord sent him. As a matter of fact, I do seem to be feeling a touch of religion now and then. Old age coming on, I guess."

"You're shocking!"

"Why? Because I said that about being religious—or not being?"

"Yes, and that about old age, when you're only thirty-four. And there's nothing old about you. Especially in bed," she added.

So he knew he was forgiven. "Nor you. You'll be young when you're sixty." He kissed her hand. "I want to thank you for being so good about this."

"What did you think I'd do?"

"I was afraid you'd raise hell and I couldn't have blamed you. Bringing a strange child into the house without a word beforehand! Why, most men wouldn't bring a puppy home without talking about it first. Still, if you could have seen him there, tied up—by God, you'd have done the same, you know you would!"

"He won't talk to me."

"Nor to me, very much. But what do you expect? He must be torn to pieces inside."

"He took a liking to Pop. Told him this house is beautiful. Like a king's palace, he told him."

"Now, what can he have heard about a king's palace, poor little thing?"

"But Patrick, what are we going to do with him?"

"Do with him? Why raise him, love him. What else?"

He went upstairs to the little room at the end of the hall, passing his daughters' room without looking in, for they would be sleeping quietly under their pink blankets. It was the unwanted boy who drew him. Discarded, he thought, and but for a good mother, I, too, was discarded. Freshly washed and full of a good supper, Will had fallen asleep. His hands moved, twitching, as if he were dreaming. And Patrick, standing over him, could only hope that whatever dream he might be having was filled with peace and trust.

Suddenly he remembered the morning's meeting. Yes, he thought now, yes, Nicholas was right! If you wanted a change, if a chance, however slight, were given you to change a world that could permit a life like this child's, then what right had you, what decent excuse, for refusal? Nicholas was right, and he would join him to do however little or much he could. He would call him now and tell him.

But at the telephone he thought first of someone else and called another number.

"I almost paid you a visit today," he said to Francis.

"Almost? What prevented you?"

"I've got a boy," he said. "We've got a boy in our family." And he went on jubilantly to tell about Will.

"I marvel at you!" Francis exclaimed, sounding glad.

"Yes, and there's something more. I'm quitting my job to go to work for Nicholas. He's going to start a newspaper and I'm to run it."

"Wonderful! We surely need a good paper around here."

Patrick hesitated. "Kate Tarbox is going to work on it with me."

"Is she?"

"Maybe you didn't know? She's moved back into town."

"When did that happen?"

"This week. Just now. She seems to have left her husband."

"Well," Francis said. "Well. It's been a day of news." His voice moved into a falling cadence. And Patrick understood that he wanted to get off the phone.

"I'll see you soon," he said at once. "Good night, then, Francis."

"Yes, yes, soon. And good luck, Patrick, in everything you do."

❧{12}❧

"It's almost nine o'clock," Francis said cheerfully. "Aren't you going to get up?"

He raised the shades. Lemon-colored light splattered the pillow into which Marjorie's face was buried. Receiving no answer, he repeated the question, careful to keep the cheer in his voice.

"Aren't you going to get up. I've made my rounds, had breakfast, and I'm ready to go."

"Then, go," she said, without moving.

The night before, when he had come home late from a meeting of the Agricultural Association, Marjorie had already gone to bed and they had exchanged only a few words, but those had been sufficient for him to recognize one of her moods. Confident, though, that it would pass as usual, that by morning the cloud would have lifted, he had turned out the lamp without more ado and fallen asleep.

Apparently, now, the cloud had not lifted. Inaudibly, he sighed and then, determined to proceed normally, went on, "I've a copy of the *Trumpet*. Want to read it over breakfast in bed?"

"The *Trumpet* is a rag."

"Oh, but the editorials are strikingly good! There's one here—it sounds like Kate's style, although it might be Patrick's—I'm not sure, anyway, it's about taxing vacant land, and I thoroughly agree. Why should anybody have the privilege of keeping land out of cultivation when there's a shortage of food and then be free of taxes on it to boot? It makes no sense, and I've said so myself many times."

Marjorie sat up abruptly. "Yes, you certainly have, haven't you?"

"What do you mean by that?"

"Oh, nothing, nothing at all. Except that you're being talked about as a troublemaker all over creation. Women were even talking about you at the club the other day after tennis. When they saw me they stopped."

"I can't help what a bunch of silly women who have nothing better to do decide to say about me."

"It's not just some 'silly women,' as you put it. You know very well they're quoting their husbands."

"You'd think I was a fire-eating bomb-thrower. All I care about is elementary decency, a tax structure that'll help clear up some of the mess you see around you." He tapped the paper. "These people are one hundred percent right."

"These people!" she mocked. "Kate Tarbox and your friend Courzon! A great pair! I shouldn't wonder if the two of them weren't—"

"Weren't what?" Francis asked, coldly now.

"Weren't sleeping together, for all I know."

"That's disgusting!"

"Why? Because it would be interracial? I shouldn't think you'd object to that, you're so broad-minded!"

"One can be 'broad-minded' without having sex with people. I meant that Patrick has a beautiful wife; he's an honorable man, and you've no right—"

"Yes, and Kate Tarbox is living alone in some miserable little house in town, having left her husband who always treated her well and would take her back in a minute. And you tell me there's nothing fishy there?"

"You can twist things around so I don't know which end is up! First you start in with editorials, and now we're on to Kate! Why don't you ask her, if you're so interested in her private life?"

"Why don't you?"

"I haven't seen her since the day she was here with Patrick and his family a year ago. Moreover, I don't care."

Marjorie lay back. "That makes two of us. Why should I gave a damn? Why should I?" She put her hand over her eyes, shielding them from the light, murmuring to herself. It sounded like "in the last analysis one is always alone," but he wasn't sure.

"What did you say?"

"What difference does it make what I said?"

"What the hell is the matter with you, Marjorie? Would you mind telling me what you're angry about now?"

"Not a thing. Not a thing. Should I be angry about anything?"

"I hate that answer you give me! With that hint that I ought to be feeling guilty! No, I don't think you should be. So why are you?"

She took time to reply. Their eyes fastened upon each other's in a long, hard stare.

"Let's just say I'm tired, shall we?" she said at last.

"From what? With a house full of maids?" Normally one who avoided argument to a point where he sometimes accused himself of cowardice, Francis could also be prodded into rage. "I'm sick of this verbal fencing! If you've got a grievance, come out with it, or else shut up. I'm not going to waste a day trying to probe into your head, Marjorie." He looked at his watch. "Come on, we should get to town before the crowds block the streets if we want to see the parade."

"I don't want to see it."

"You had a good time at Mardi Gras last year!"

"That was last year. Besides, you don't care whether I go or not, so don't pretend you do."

He could have slapped her—an aberrant thought, of course. Exasperation tightened in his solar plexus, a maddening knot. There had been too much of this kind of thing lately!

"Then I'll go alone. I want to see it."

"Go. Enjoy yourself."

He went downstairs and out to the car. The tires squealed as he wrenched the wheel, speeding around the curve, easing his tensions, taking a small revenge on injustice. Juvenile, he thought then; slow down. Be reasonable. It's not all that bad, having a blowup every month or so. Maybe it was her monthly cycle, after all? Maybe I want too much, some sort of impossible perfection. How do I know what it's like in other marriages, other houses? Except that in other houses there are children. . . .

Yet, during his own childhood in a house filled with children, there had been long strained silences as well as jovial warmth. So perhaps this was just the way things went between two people living a lifetime together, with or without children. . . .

The drive eased him. With the top down the wind whirred about his head. Once he had climbed the shoulder of Morne Bleue and begun the long descent toward Covetown, his anger sloughed away. Maturity is acceptance, he told himself. By evening things would have fallen into place again, he told himself, assuring himself. A faint sadness settled now in his chest where the anger had been.

Funny, he thought then, funny about Lionel and Kate. A queer couple, mismatched from the start. Did people see just such a mismatch between himself and Marjorie? He puzzled over that for a moment and thought not. Surely they were not like Lionel and Kate! Lionel said only, "It didn't work out." How much that hurt, or whether it hurt at all, one couldn't tell, for being a gentleman, Francis thought ironically, he would surely never show it. A gentleman didn't reveal his emotions. Oh, well! Oh, hell!

Covetown blazed with color and brass. There were bands in the squares and other bands marching with the long parade that wound and twisted through the streets. Indians in feathers, skeletons, Chinese dragons, crowned kings and queens rode on floats or walked and danced and pranced. Everyone was drunk with music and some with stronger stuff. Wearing one's mask, it did not matter how one screeched or capered, or what stranger one seized and kissed. It was all pure, reckless joy. Perched on a railing, Francis sat for a long time, watching the color and dazzle. He felt like a child before a Christmas tree and a pile of presents, and was suddenly aware that he had been needing this reckless joy.

After a while he got up and bought a rum drink, content to drink it alone, just sitting in the shade with his thoughts. He wondered whether he could be classified as a loner. He didn't think so, for there were always people whose company gave him warmth and light. They were selected people, though, not the "social" crowd among whom one was expected to take one's pleasure. He did not want to feel superior to them or anyone; nevertheless, they bored him with the monotony of their interests and opinions; they repelled him with their inbred selfishness. Or most of them did, at any rate. There were a few whose minds were open enough so you could say what you thought without raising eyebrows, but only a few. Lionel was patient with him out of a firm sense of family loyalty and also because he was a good sort in his way. Francis always thought of him like that: Good-Sort Lionel. Yet even he found Francis odd and off-beat. Concern for the whole community was a thing you just did not talk about; as long as the dogs were quiet, you let them lie. The idea was to live your own life as peacefully as possible.

And looking about today at all this gaiety under the sun, one might well shrug and think, Let it be! After all, why should I upset the peace? Except that the peace won't last, he thought, finishing the drink.

And now a sense of loneliness, as powerful as his earlier joy, swept over him. He had nowhere to go. He didn't want to go home. He would have liked to see Patrick. Yes, they'd sit and talk about things they'd read, and speculate and argue and get nowhere except for the pleasure of argument. . . . There wasn't really anyone else he could think of, when you came down to it, with whom he could so comfortably do just that. He walked on up the hill toward Government House and the library, fine old buildings among fine old trees. At the foot of Library Hill he turned off into a narrow alley formed by a double row of houses. Probably built for civil servants, out from England in the seventeen hundreds, he thought, recognizing the Georgian doorways and the narrow windows with their sixteen lights. He hadn't been down this alley in a long time.

Kate lived in one of these, he recalled now. Patrick had described a house in an alley, at the very end, the only one with a view of the water. Well, no business of mine, he told himself.

At the end, where the hill, abruptly rising, made a natural wall of green, a little house stood sidewise to the street so that one could see the back door and the yard. He stopped.

She was feeding birds, dumping a pan of crumbs on the flagstones. The birds, who had no doubt been waiting for her in their hidden places, came swooping down, not minding her presence. She had been wearing a hat, the same straw farm hat—or another one just like it—that Francis remembered. Now she took it off. Her bright hair shone red-gold in the light.

Then she saw him. "You've been spying on me!"

"Only for a minute. May I come in?"

"Use the front door. There are stickers on those vines, you can't climb over the fence."

On the front step he barely missed a bowl of water.

"For stray cats," she said, opening the door. "The neighborhood's full of them. It's a pity."

He stepped into a cramped little hall. Confusion made him awkward.

"You run an S.P.C.A. of your own," he said, needing to say something.

"I'm a thwarted mother. I like to nourish."

This childless woman could say that without bitterness! As though, quite simply, she had accepted the fact and was determined to live with it. "Besides, I'm terribly frugal," she said. "I can't bear waste. I suppose it's from not having had anything when I was young."

"I'm frugal, too, but with me it's because when I was young I had too much, which we couldn't afford. Only I didn't find that out until much later."

"You're in time for lunch if you want any."

"I've only had tea this morning and a rum cola just now, so I think I do."

"Come into the kitchen, then."

"It smells good," he said, following her.

"*Tourtière de la famille,* or not to be fancy, meat pie. You put in everything you've got, all the leftovers. There's ham and chicken, some veal scraps and vegetables. Shall we have it outside?"

A table with two chairs stood near the back door under an oleander bush, where a large homely mongrel and a haughty white poodle dozed together.

"A funny combination, aren't they? The big one I picked up along the road. He was on his last legs. Lionel gave me the poodle when he was a puppy and of course I love him, although I really don't care about poodles, they're too fussy. But I couldn't have left him behind, it would have broken his heart. Wait, I'll just bring out the cheese and fruit and then I'll sit down."

Well! Rather different from Georgina's Fancy, Francis thought, remembering Lionel's great dining hall. Rather different from my own place, too, he thought almost ruefully. But then, this was a doll house. Yes, a doll house.

"I've been following your editorials," he began, "and I think you're doing a wonderful job. Everybody's buying the *Trumpet.* Most of the people I know are annoyed with it and some are pretty angry over it, but at least they're reading it!"

"The credit goes to Patrick Courzon. And I'm not being modest, it really does. I'd like," Kate said earnestly, "to see this place, the whole of Central America, for that matter, governed by people like him and Nicholas. They could set things straight—or at least they'd try—and ward off a lot of trouble."

"I wish I could see Patrick more often than I do. I'm always glad when he comes over for an evening."

"He's awfully busy now. Ever since they got the boy, Patrick's felt obliged to do things with him. Désirée's not too good with him. She's a sweet person, maybe not smart enough for Patrick, not like Nicholas's wife! She's a little childish, and in any case, a better mother for girls. Besides, the boy's difficult."

"He didn't have much of a start, Patrick tells me."

"That's why he wants to father him. He's a strange, serious child. It's hard to make him laugh."

"You don't laugh very much, either," Francis said, surprising himself. He hadn't intended to say it.

"It's true, I haven't in years. But I do now. In the office. Ask Patrick. It's really quite gay there, and I love it. We've great young reporters, one bright black girl, two young cousins of mine, and then there's Robby Welch, the bank manager's son, home from England on vacation. His family had a fit at first about his working in an office with blacks, but they've come around. It's a good staff and I love it," she repeated. "It's really the best thing I've ever done for myself."

"I'm glad for you, Kate."

He wanted to ask about Lionel and her, but of course would not. One waited until one was told about private matters.

Grown of a sudden self-conscious, he avoided her eyes. His gaze fell upon her hands, from which the emerald ring was missing. His gaze fell upon a lizard, a quick green creature that, having slid up an unoccupied armchair, stood now a few feet away, staring with its jeweled eyes, while the pouch of its whitish neck throbbed in the heat.

"Gecko," Kate mused. "The name suits, doesn't it? Does one grow to suit one's name, or is it the other way around?"

"Well, let's think about that. Kate, for instance." And he forced himself to look at her. "Yes, Kate is the only possible name for you. Kate means freckles and bright hair. Someone small and lively and curious and earnest."

"Who talks too much and has too many opinions. While Francis—let's see— Francis has to be tall and rather quiet. His conscience commands him. He is also very, very kind."

"You're thinking of the saint, not me," he said with a lightness he didn't feel. "Here, let me help carry these inside."

Standing next to her, stacking dishes in the sink, once again words came from him that he had not intended to speak, perhaps not even thought. But they came, demanding and rushing.

"Do you realize that ever since that day we had lunch in town, the day you made me decide to stay at Eleuthera—yes, it was you who made up my mind— ever since that day we haven't spoken two words directly to each other? The few times we've been together, we've avoided each other. What are we hiding?"

"What?" she cried. "What are you saying?"

They stared at one another. She had the look of someone who is about to fall.

"You said I'm hiding something?" she whispered.

"I said you—" He faltered, murmuring something that blurred on his lips and in his ears; and then she did fall—fell toward him—and he caught her; he was drowned in an exploding surge of longing and immediate fulfillment, so that the longing and the fulfillment became one.

How long they stood in the kitchen, pressed and entwined, neither could have said, but when they drew apart the moment of astonishment had already passed and the blending, the merging, had been established. So it was, and neither spoke. She took his hand, guiding him lightly through the hall and up the narrow stairs. He felt himself floating, as if some great tide were bearing him forward.

After the sun glare her room was cool, a purity of gray and white. She pulled the shades, and in the shadow their bodies blanched. He was aware of a beautiful old bed, too large for the little room. He saw, as they fell back upon the quilt, red zinnias in a bowl on the dresser and, in the mirror above the dresser, the curving of her hips and thighs and the reach of his own rounding arms; then, closing his eyes, saw nothing.

THEY LIT TWO cigarettes and lay against the pillows. Two smoke spirals drifted in a newly risen breeze. Now words came, thousands of words, questions and thoughts so long held back and denied, now to be admitted and released.

When had he first distinguished her at all from other women? And was it true that she'd felt something from the very beginning, on that first day at Eleuthera? And had he really not known the truth until now, this afternoon?

"What made you finally leave Lionel?" he wanted to know.

"You had better ask why I married him in the first place."

"Why did you?"

She put her head on his shoulder. "It's not a pretty story. It hurts. I told you once, I think, that we were very poor in my family. An old name, and so much damned dignity! Oh, you must have seen some of these fine, land-poor families, with the paint peeling off the walls and the refrigerator kept in the drawing room because the kitchen roof leaks. No money to spend, just sitting on the veranda drinking the evenings away. We have them still, but there were more of them even a few years ago, before the corporations started buying them out." Kate sighed. "When your last pair of stockings has a run you wear them anyway, and you pretend, oh so gaily, that it just happened this minute and you simply can't be bothered to run upstairs and change them. I was so sick of it! Lionel was slender then and good-looking. Anyhow, it happened so fast I had no time to think. He took me to Da Cunha's and bought me a ring worth more than my father's house, this house we're in now, that I love so much and despised then. Well, I was very young, if that's any excuse."

The breeze had turned into a wind and the sun had gone around the corner of the house. Kate shivered. Francis drew her nearer, pulling the quilt around them, making a warmth into which she crept, closer and closer.

"His parents were wonderful, even my mother-in-law, your grandmother, was. She can be a terror, but she welcomed me. I didn't know why until much later, when I learned about the girl Lionel was in love with. Remember? Of course he wouldn't have married her, she has colored blood, but they were afraid he might. She's very beautiful. She lives in Barbados now, in Bridgetown, and he goes there to be with her.

"He did wrong to marry me, but I don't blame him. I wronged him, too. Neither of us loved the other."

"So it's finished? For good?" Knowing that it was, he yet wanted to be told that it was.

"Oh, yes. And my doing, not Lionel's. He would have gone on as we were. He was quite comfortable, but I've grown up. I know who I am. I don't need his money anymore and I don't want his kind of life." She laughed. "The only thing I miss—well, I do miss the horses! Can't very well keep them here. I support myself, though. Lionel wants to give me things. He's very kind; kindness seems to run in your family, doesn't it? But Nicholas pays me well enough and I have this house and I don't need anything. By this time next year we shall be divorced."

"You're brave. You're lovely. You're very lovely, Kate."

"Is it all right if I ask about Marjorie? Or would you rather not?"

"I'd rather not," he said softly. "Not now."

And he thought again, as he had too often lately, of how everything had changed. Yet Marjorie had not really changed. Comely, reliable, intelligent and graceful, she was, in essence, what she had always been. And he, wasn't he also what he had always been? Only the allure between them was gone, the passion and allure. So it was the marriage itself which time had altered, time working away, as the sea builds dunes and shapes the cliffs.

"Oh, God," he said.

"Francis, dear, dear, what is it?"

"I love you. I love you, and I don't know what to do about it."

She put her hand over his mouth. "Listen to me. Things solve themselves. Sometimes, after the first few months with Lionel, I'd lie awake looking up at the gray ceiling and I'd think, I've wrecked my life. I had no one, no place to go. But see how it's all unfolded! We'll grow old together, Francis. I don't know how, but I know we will."

Against his chest he felt the thudding of her heart. She had closed her eyes; the dark lashes on her cheeks were gilt-tipped. Lovely, lovely! This little woman, so pert and brisk, and still so soft, so soft! Innocent in her conviction that the world could be, and must become, a better place where no man turned a cold cheek to another and no one hungered and no one kicked a dog! Innocent.

And I, too, feel her indignations; I think of myself as one who wants to give; yes, there is all that in me. But also there is the very private man who cherishes his own domain. A cut above the men at the bar in the club, Francis, with your poetry and history? Yes, yes, you know you feel you ᵣe superior to them, and yet you're terribly ashamed of yourself for that glimmer of superiority. You chose a wife, you were drawn to her, because she, too, has that very private pride. . . .

Light fingertips smoothed his forehead. "You're frowning," Kate whispered.

"I'm thinking."

"Thinking of what?"

"Oh, scoops and pieces of things. You playing Brahms once on a quiet evening at Eleuthera. Of us in this bed. I'd like to wake up every morning in this bed."

But he was actually thinking of other things, of himself, at home saying, "Listen, Marjorie, it's no good, no good at all anymore." She would protest; he could hear her weeping that it was still good, it was, it was! And truly, if there were no Kate, he would know no better and it would probably still be good enough—as good as most people ever have, at any rate.

His thoughts fluttered away. Softly they lay, half sleeping, as day cooled into evening and the room turned dusky blue. Kate roused.

"I have to get up. Patrick said he'd bring some papers over at seven."

"Patrick. The salt of the earth, as my father would say."

"Yes, he's very, very special."

A book of poems lay on the bedside table. Francis flipped the pages.

"Emily Dickinson. A favorite of yours?"

"Yes, lately. I've gone back to reading her. A woman who lived alone. I thought I might learn how."

Something hurt in his throat. "You can't live alone. Don't you always say waste is sin?"

She smiled, not answering. He took a long look around the room, wanting to fix it in his mind: the wallpaper, arabesques within squares; the mat by the window where one of the dogs must sleep; her slippers, blue, with feather puffs on the toes.

Outside at ground level it was three-quarters dark, while at the top of the hill the great fireball still blazed in the sky.

"Look," Kate said. "The sun god! The Incas' priests used to throw kisses to him at dawn."

They stood on the step with their arms around each other.

"How can I leave you?" he asked.

"You aren't leaving me. You never will."

There was such an ache in him! They did not hear the creak of the gate, nor Patrick's footsteps on the path.

"I'm sorry to be early," Patrick said, not looking at them. He thrust out a sheaf of papers. "I'm in a hurry, I'll just leave these."

Francis said quickly, "I was just going."

The two men walked away down the alley, neither one speaking, until Francis said. "You saw. Well, now you know."

"I don't know anything you don't want me to. I'm an expert forgetter."

"Thank you for that."

They walked on. The parade was over, the streets had emptied. And the loneliness that had engulfed him in the morning came back to Francis now. He needed to talk and to hear another voice answer.

"You'll say it isn't any business of yours, but I want to tell you. Today was the first. It happened today, brand new."

"Not brand new," Patrick spoke gently. "It's been there for a long time, I suspect."

"You're right, of course, although I didn't know it, or want to admit it—The thing is, what happens now?"

"She's a special person, a beautiful person," Patrick said, meaning, Francis understood, "Be kind to her, be careful of her." And Patrick added, "There's no other man I can think of who's nearly good enough for her."

"I despise a cheat," Francis said suddenly, an unexpected memory of his father and the florid girl in the restaurant having flashed through his head. And as the other didn't answer, he went on, "I came here and fell in love with this place. There's nowhere else on earth I ever want to be. And now there's Kate and—I don't know how to explain it—Kate and this place are one in my mind. In my heart. My wife—" He stopped.

Patrick put a hand on his shoulder. "Sit down. You're shaking."

They sat on a stone wall at the side of the walk.

"Strange, isn't it," Francis mused, "that no one condemns, not really, a light 'affair,' a casual woman, but for this they'll throw stones?"

"Do you care if they do?"

"Not for myself. But for Marjorie—you don't like Marjorie."

"She doesn't approve of me," Patrick answered quietly.

"That's true. I don't think she can really help that, though. It's the way she's lived all her life. The shaping starts in the nursery."

"But you were shaped another way?"

"I can't tell. After all, you're the only one of your race I've known so well. So how can I tell what my shape is?"

"You're truthful, at least."

"I try to be. It's better, even when it causes pain. Anyhow, that's the way I see it. But I'm a coward, I dread having to look at Marjorie's pain."

"Listen," Patrick said gently, "you don't have to draw a map of your whole life tonight. Go home and try to sleep. Go to work tomorrow and let things turn over very slowly in your mind. They'll reach a level after a while."

Francis just looked at him.

"You think I'm speaking platitudes? Well, I am. Forgive me. It's because I don't know anything better to say."

Francis reached out and took his hand. "Believe it or not, I'm glad you found out. It would be awful to have to keep anything as tremendous as this locked up in myself. And there isn't anyone I'd rather have know, or could trust more." He stood up. "Now I'll go home."

Marjorie was sitting in the bedroom with a magazine at her feet when he came in. She had been crying, and her puffy eyelids were ugly. He was ashamed of himself for thinking of their ugliness before he thought of her self.

"Where were you all day?" she asked.

"You know I went to the parade."

"All day?"

"I met some people. We had lunch and a few drinks." He then realized that she was still wearing the robe she had worn that morning. "What have you been doing?"

"Sitting here, wondering why you didn't ask me what happened yesterday in town."

"I don't understand."

"You knew I went to the doctor."

"Yes, but—why, did anything happen?"

"Oh," she said with artificial calmness. "I would say it did. He told me I'm pregnant, that's all that happened."

Francis went cold. "In heaven's name, why didn't you tell me yesterday?"

"Why didn't you ask me? You came in the house talking about twin foals and never—" Again she wept.

"You knew it this morning and last night—"

"Yes, that's why I was what you called 'angry.' I wasn't angry! I was wounded —oh, my God, we've been waiting for years and you didn't even care enough to ask what the doctor said!"

He knelt on the floor beside her chair, putting his arms around her. "Marjorie, Marjorie, of course I care! But you'd been so many times before—How could I think it would be different this time? I thought it was another routine visit. Forgive me."

And at the same moment he was thinking: Kate.

"I can't believe it. I'm afraid I'll wake up and find it isn't true. People always say that, but that's just how I feel."

"I'm sure it's true. Wonderful and true."

"Do you care whether it's a girl or a boy?"

For so long he had been having fantasies about a son. But he gave the wise and decent answer.

"It doesn't matter. Just let it be well."

"You'd rather have a boy. Probably it's silly, but I have such a strong feeling that it is." Now she was chatting, comforted and exuberant. "What shall we name

it? I don't like 'Junior' at all. If it's a girl, I'd like 'Megan,' I think. Or maybe 'Anne'
—that was my favorite grandmother's name—"

Compassion struggled in him, not for Marjorie alone, but for the microscopic
being in her body, the life so desperately desired, that he went weak with it.

Oh, Kate, what shall I do?

He was stunned. He was numb. They went downstairs and ate a late supper.
Afterwards Marjorie wanted to walk outside and look at the sea. She was filled
with a tremendous ecstasy. He had not seen her like that since the day of their
wedding. It was far too soon for hormones to have done this to her; pure happiness had exalted her. Naturally, it would not last. No exalted state could. But he
wondered how long the residue would last. Simple joy was not one of her qualities, as it was one of Kate's. . . .

He did not sleep. Marjorie, having cried her tears of relief, slept deeply with a
hand folded under her cheek. Her face was tranquil, classic. How he had loved
her, or believed he did! If only one could go back and undo! Or if one could
simply go forward! But he was locked in. Too late. Too late.

And all night long a thousand tiny creatures throbbed and trilled in the trees,
all that pulsing life going on, century after rolling century, under the heavens.
Ignorant, happy creatures with nothing to do but grow and thrive and mate, into
whose cycle no anguish crept, no agonies of loss or conscience! All night long
they throbbed and trilled.

"OH, MY DARLING," Kate said. "You wanted a child."

"That's true."

"You're thinking that if it were yours and mine—"

"I am, I am."

"But I can't have any, Francis, not ever."

"I'm so sorry for us. So sorry for us all."

"Not grateful, even a little?"

He lay on the sofa in her parlor with his head on her lap.

"I don't know. I feel as if something had been given me by one hand and
taken away by the other."

"We won't let anything be taken. We'll find a way to keep it all."

"How?"

"I'll always be here. We can always be here like this."

"Secret afternoons aren't what I want for you or what you ought to have."

"But far better than nothing, my darling."

*In the den, between the humidor and the ship model, his father sat, beckoning.
"Don't tell your mother, son. You know I wouldn't hurt her for the world."*

But this was different. Here was no blowsy slut to be hidden away! Here was
his heart's love, to be announced to the world.

"I guess I knew," he said, thinking aloud.

"Knew what?"

"That there'd be no turning back, once I had made the admission. I guess I
really knew the day we had lunch in Cade's Hotel. But I wanted to spare you
this."

"And spare Marjorie?"

"Yes, Marjorie, too. God knows I'm not noble! It's only that something in me wants things to be open and clean. I hate concealment."

"So do I. Sometimes, though, there is no other way."

"Patrick said I needn't decide the whole future in a minute. 'Go slowly,' he said, 'and it will unfold itself.' But he didn't know about the baby."

"He was right, all the same. You don't have to decide anything. We won't hurt anyone. Just loving each other won't hurt anyone."

She bent to kiss his forehead and he put his arms about her. Here, here were his refuge and his desire. His whole being was warmed and the sweetest peace enveloped him.

❧ {13} ❧

In the hour before dawn the sea glowed with phosphorus. The pirogue lurched and the torch in Will's hand wavered as Clarence pulled in the seine to lay it on the bottom between their feet.

"Not bad for a nonprofessional. A fine haul of ballyhoo! We'll sell some, give some to our friends, and have the rest for supper." He took up the oars. "Hard work if you have to do it every day for a living, but kind of a good time like this, wouldn't you say so, boy?"

Clarence seldom waited for an answer, but not being himself a talker, Will didn't mind. He felt closer to the old man than to anyone he had ever known. And he settled back now in the stern, watching the first faint rise of dawn on the horizon and the seabirds soaring.

"This boat's the kind the Caribs made, with the knife-edge bow. Made out of a gommier trunk. They used to fell the tree when the moon was new, thought that would keep it from rotting. Old magic. Well, I guess we all keep some kind of private magic to believe in, don't we?"

The light grew and the torches were put out. A crowd of little boats turned back toward Covetown as the night fishermen headed home. They had all come a long way, skirting the island. A scalloped line of treetops became distinct as the minutes passed and the sky grew white. Cattle were moving dots on hillside pastures. Village rooftops glittered when the sun reached them. A fine house with lawns like a great, swooping skirt emerged from shadow.

"Chris-Craft," Clarence said, waving toward the private dock. "Look at that beauty. Fifty thousand, if it's a dollar."

Low on a bluff stood the house, the familiar porticoed and columned home of the West Indian planter. Its shutters were still closed; it slept.

"Florissant," said Clarence. "Belongs to the Francis family. Right behind it there's Estate Margaretta. Belonged to the Drydens. One of them married a Francis when I was a boy. Pooling the wealth, sort of. Colonel Dryden was my colonel in the First World War."

Will sat up. This was the first really interesting piece of information that he'd heard on the outing.

"You were in the First World War! You never talk about it."

"Don't like to. It was a bad time to remember."

"Did you kill anybody?"

"Never ask anyone a thing like that," Clarence said seriously. "If a person did, it wouldn't have been his fault and he shouldn't be reminded of it. As it happens, though, I didn't. I worked in the mess."

"What was so bad about it, then?"

Clarence considered. "It was just—oh, the whole business, the way we had to live. For instance, a black could never hope to be an officer in the British army, never be more than a sergeant, no matter how well educated he might be. At Taranto—that's where I served in Italy—we weren't allowed in the movie theater or the Y canteens. It's things like that that make you so mad, they fester in you. Some of the men wouldn't take it anymore. There was a mutiny at Taranto. It's an ugly thing when men get so mad." His voice dropped to a murmur.

"I can't hear you," Will said impatiently, wanting to hear.

"I said it's awful to see men maddened that way! They do terrible things and terrible things are done to them. I lost a younger brother there."

"Dead?"

"Dead. Shot in a riot. Then I came home. I worked on the transport ship *Oriana,* which brought the mutineers back here to serve out their sentences."

"And that was the end of it?"

"Not really. The end never really comes. Every end gives birth to another beginning, doesn't it? Well, in 1919, in Honduras and Trinidad, there were more riots. As soon as the troops were demobilized, they went rampaging, burning the homes and businesses of the whites."

Will was excited. "What happened then?"

"Oh, the riots were put down. They always are. That's why violence solves nothing. All the hopes and the fine talk came to nothing at the war's end. You know," Clarence said reflectively, "there'd been a lot of talk—in fact the British Labour Party had endorsed Du Bois's idea about making an African state out of the former German colonies, the colonies that we helped win for Britain. Reparation for centuries of slavery, he said, giving us back our own land in Africa, where we were taken from. Some people in Barbados even had a scheme to repatriate West Indian Negroes—"

"What is 'repatriate'?"

"To send you back to your fatherland. But," Clarence said with emphasis, "I'm not sorry that part came to nothing. This is my home here. My people have been here six"—he frowned, counting on his fingers—"seven or eight generations, probably. Two centuries, as far as I can count. The same for you, too, I imagine. Has anybody ever mentioned it to you?"

"No," Will said. Stupid question! Who would have told him?

"Well, you were too young to care about all that, anyway. You hungry now? Désirée made sandwiches and cake."

Will noticed he had recently stopped saying "Dezzy" after Patrick said he hated it.

Clarence unwrapped the box. "Coconut cake, your favorite. She's awfully fond of you, Will. You know that, don't you?"

Will nodded, feeling a small quick pain which was part anger. She wasn't "fond" of him at all; she was good to him because Patrick wanted her to be, and because one was supposed to be kind to an orphan. Curious how you could sit back, not saying a word, just listening and watching, and figure people out! It was really easy, he thought now, eating the sandwich. Easy. Désirée was lazy, in a way. She didn't want to have to think too much, just wanted to enjoy her peace, being loved and loving Patrick and the girls. She spent too much on clothes and fancy knickknacks for the house. Patrick complained, but he never did anything about it. Maybe he couldn't. Mentally, Will shrugged.

"Look," Clarence said. "Remember, I mentioned Estate Margaretta a while back? You can see the roof from here. It's an interesting house with a rotunda. I always thought I'd have liked being an architect, if the circumstances had been different. *Margaretta,*" he mused. "They used to name their places after their wives or after their daughters when the house was given as a wedding present. Yes, it must have been a great life for a planter way back then! Plenty of servants to bring you the best food and drink on a silver tray, gardeners to keep the house filled up with flowers, black mistresses dressed up in gold lace." He chuckled. "Not bad, not bad at all. But it didn't last. That's one thing history teaches—nothing lasts, not the Roman Empire, not anything. Say, have you read that piece I gave you about Wilberforce, who brought the slave trade to an end in the British Empire?"

"Not yet. We haven't come to it in school, anyway."

"Yes, and you may never come to it, the way the schools are. Read it for yourself."

The old man was a nut about history. Again Will felt impatience, but because he liked the old man he wouldn't show it.

"Yes, and then came the hard times for the estates. Debts, mortgages, and bankruptcies."

"Served them right," Will interrupted.

"My grandfather told me you could ride around and see great houses gone back to jungle with trees growing out of the rotting rooftops." Clarence stopped abruptly. "You're bored with all this, aren't you?"

Will grinned.

"You may be only eleven, but that's not too young to start understanding the past."

"Why?" Will asked, arguing the question.

"Because that's the only way to make the future better."

"Have you made it any better?"

Clarence looked at him sternly. "Yes, I have. Listen here, my grandfather worked a full year on a sugar estate for wages of five pounds. He lived on the estate and paid rent for his house—his hovel—and could be evicted at the owner's pleasure. And you ask whether it's better now? Yes, I'll accept credit for my part in the labor movement that has made it better, although not nearly good enough, God knows." He pulled on the oars and they creaked. "Now I'm too old. It's in the hands of men like Nicholas Mebane and your father. They'll push us still farther along. I'm glad your father left teaching. He can use his powers in larger ways."

Something bursting in Will's chest came out in a harsh voice, in harsh words. "He's not my father! Why do you always call him that?"

"He is! He's fathered you more than anyone else ever did! Sometimes you puzzle me, Will. You seem so critical, so sullen. But you're much smarter than your age and I think by now you should be able to see yourself and see the people around you for what they are." And letting up on the oars, he placed a hand on Will's knee. "It hurts me to hear you shouting out 'he's not my father!' "

"All right, I'm sorry," Will said.

"Then why do you keep doing it?"

"Look at him! And look at me!"

"The color, you mean? That bothers you? Why? Do you think you're pure African or I am? It's only a matter of degree. Listen, it took years to work out the resentments between the browns and the blacks. The browns had the good jobs, the money, and the vote. You know when they started to get together and work together? After the blacks got ahead a little bit and sweated themselves enough to buy a scrap of land, why then they got the vote, too, and the browns wanted their votes to get elected to the legislature. So," and here Clarence, laughing, leaned back while the boat drifted toward shore, "well, a black man, knowing that, would simply not pay his taxes; so he wouldn't be able to vote, and then one of these upper-class light skins would pay his taxes for him in exchange for his vote! Clever, wasn't it?" he cried, wearing a frisky expression.

Will was not amused. "Tricks. That's all it still is. Tricks, instead of having their rights. He and Mr. Mebane, hanging around Mr. Luther, up there in that fancy house! 'Eleuthera means free,' he tells me every time we go there. Free for who? Not for people like us! You think we'll ever live in a place like that? He gives you a cold drink and a piece of cake and thinks he's so grand."

"Who does? Francis Luther? It happens you've picked on one of the most decent men on the island."

"I heard you say once you didn't trust him."

"I didn't mean it that way, exactly. I was being wary. Give him a chance to prove he means what he says, that's what I meant. And so far he has. He's built houses, he's opened a dispensary with a nurse on his place, and a doctor comes out once a month for checkups. Nobody else has done what he's been doing. A very decent man," Clarence repeated firmly.

Will snickered, remembering something. "He shacks up with Mrs. Tarbox in town."

"What! What kind of talk is that? Where'd you hear a thing like that?"

"I heard Désirée talking to Pat—to Dad—in the kitchen. He said it wasn't true, but she said people see him at her house."

"People get me sick! Nothing better to do but spread lies and dirty gossip. I'm surprised at Désirée. And don't you repeat it, hear?"

"Well, all right." The old man was really angry, you could see that. "Well, all right. But still, Uncle Clarence, everything you said, sure it's okay that he has a nurse there and all that stuff, but still—"

"Still what?"

"Still it's only crumbs, isn't it? Like the kids diving for money in the harbor when white tourists come. They think they're so kind, throwing money away. The other day in town a man and woman, American, I think, by the way they talked, they stopped me on the street and handed me some candy. I threw it on the ground and told them what they could do with it."

"Will, Will, that was mean! You shouldn't have done it. The people meant well, they meant to be kind. Don't you see that?"

The crinkled face was distressed, its lines reaching up to where the white hair receded from the temples like cotton tufts. He's old, Will thought. Too old.

"No, I don't understand you, Will. It's hard to remember what I was like when I was your age. But I don't believe I was like you. No, I wasn't. You're a very bright boy, much more than I was. You don't study hard enough, though. Sometimes"—Clarence spoke slyly—"I catch you sitting over your books, just sitting there looking at nothing. What are you thinking of?"

"I'm thinking that you people don't do anything! You sit and talk about committees and elections and independence coming and how you can hardly make ends meet and shoes are so expensive. But in the Da Cunha shop they're selling wine from France and diamonds worth more than your whole house. Talk, talk!"

"What would you have us do?"

"Get out in the streets! Get out and shoot! Burn their houses down and take what you need. That's what."

"That sort of thing gets nowhere! It's not civilized. One works through government, through the labor unions! Ah, well, you're a child. Come, here we are, let's get rid of this fish and go home."

A small crowd awaited the catch on the beach, where an impromptu fair and barter had been set up. Homemade brooms and hats and baskets, baked goods and flowered cotton aprons were set up on improvised tables and upended boxes. Will took the net of gleaming fish and laid it in a box while Clarence fastened the boat.

"Better not let anybody hear you talk about burning houses, son," he warned, as he tied up.

Will stood there watching the old man fuss with the rope. Fumble. Fumble. Fumble your life away. He felt a strange softness toward the old man. He wanted to reach out and stroke him on the shoulder. Then anger filled him again, and he did not.

❧ 14 ❧

One day Teresa Luther went back to St. Felice. Tee Francis resisted still, but Teresa Luther gave in at last.

"How can you refuse?" Richard urged. "He's asked us so many times, and now, with our first grandchild coming—"

"I have responsibilities," she began.

"Nonsense! You have grown daughters who'll look after Margaret. They'll all get along without you very well for a few weeks," he said gently.

Adversity had softened and weakened him. Oddly enough, she often thought, it had given him a greater dignity, as well.

"Look," he said. "I got out this old album. Here you are."

There she was, serious and pale under the dark fall of her hair. Here they all were, Père with his gold-knobbed cane on the lawn at Eleuthera and Julia, in flounces, standing with Tee in front of the twin staircase at Drummond Hall.

"That must have been taken not more than a year or so before we were married," Richard observed.

"It must have been."

He said unselfishly, "Francis would be so glad! I can see his face when you walk in."

"And when you walk in."

The album rested on the windowsill. A flurry of dead leaves, driven in gray, chilled air, blew past.

"It's too bad we had to be so gray and gloomy on your first day in Paris," Anatole Da Cunha had said on just such a day.

"You're a strong girl, stronger than you know." That was Marcelle, who had taught her to survive.

Strange, I haven't thought of her in years. Not strange, I have made every effort not to.

"You can do whatever you have to do," Marcelle had said.

That was true. A marriage without love, a secret like a box of dynamite in the closet—one could manage anything if one had to. Now, finally, I am called upon to go back. There can be no excuse this time, I have run out of them.

"Then you'll go?" asked Richard. "I can make arrangements?"

"Yes, I'll go," Teresa Luther said.

*   *   *

IT WAS NOT very much changed. The public market, the cathedral close, the soft-drink stalls and the dusky, gray-green tamarinds were all the same. Raucous radios, more cars and horns, and a storefront movie advertising a cowboy picture, these were different.

And the house was different. They had built a new wing, with guest rooms and a nursery for the coming baby. Marjorie had renewed the house with a fitting and patrician charm that, in a way, resembled herself. It's not what it was when I lived in it, Tee thought, remembering crumbled plaster.

And she told her daughter-in-law, "It looks like you."

Marjorie was pleased with the comment. "Not, I hope, the way I look now," she said, touching her enormous belly, and pleased, Tee saw, with that, too.

Francis wanted them to tour outdoors with him. He walked ahead with his father, Tee following, up the slopes toward the banana groves.

"This is the major source of income," he explained. "Green gold, Father."

Richard was fascinated. He had never been in any part of the world like this one.

"The original tree is called the mother. New trunks grow out of the old roots. See this bunch? We call it a stem. See these? We call them hands. You get anywhere from seven to twelve hands in a cluster. The bananas are called fingers. You get over a hundred fingers to a stem."

The two men, framed by shaggy leafage, paused on the path, the one still wearing his dark city suit, the other in workman's khaki. Francis' hair had lightened and his skin been darkened in the sun; he shone. She wondered what Père would have thought about this young man of his blood. And with that extreme perceptiveness of him which she had always had, she recognized that something new, something vibrant and exciting, had come alive in him.

Richard, interested in finance, wanted to know how the crop was marketed.

"Well, Dad, I have to tell you I'm rather proud of something I've been able to do. We used to work on contract, you know, anywhere from one to five years with a big company; you'd give them a weekly estimate of what you'd deliver. Every planter, large or small, was on his own. But now we've got a cooperative. I had a hard time convincing people it would be a good thing, but now they admit it is, and we market through the cooperative, which gives us much greater bargaining power, naturally. Also, we help out in other ways, making loans for fertilizers, and disease control, and—there's a lot more to it, but that's the general idea, anyway."

Tee paused, letting the two men climb. Above, where the banana groves stopped and the jungle took over, one could see light playing in the upper branches of the dense acomas. Cathedral light, although one might very well put it the other way, remembering forest shadows in old churches at the place where the apse meets the nave. Mounting farther up the Morne, you would come to where the light, shafting straight as rulers, struck the ground and sifted up again into a mist, knee-deep. Yesterday. Yesterday.

And in the morning of childhood, yellowbirds with legs like two thin twigs came to the sugar bowl on the veranda. Each dark-gray wing bore a white mark, a beauty spot, she used to say. The afternoon drowsed in cicada hum until, at four, the rain came, leaving its sharp and bitter fragrance on the air. . . .

Returning, Richard and Francis roused her into the present moment and they walked back to the house. Humped Brahman cattle, grazing behind rail fences, raised their cream-colored faces toward the sound of voices, questioning with dark, languid eyes.

"First prize at the agricultural show," Francis said proudly. "Bananas are only what keep me solvent, you know. All the rest is what I really care about. I'm diversfying, trying to raise the island by its bootstraps. Lionel thinks I'm a fool to take risks and care so much. He'll probably tell you so. But he believes just in looking out for number one."

"There's something to be said for looking out for number one," Richard observed.

When Francis did not answer, Tee asked, "Don't you get along with Lionel?"

"We get along all right. Marjorie likes him more than I do, though. They think alike. He'll be here tonight at dinner."

"Marjorie said something in her last letter about Lionel's divorce. She didn't say why, just said it was 'civilized.' What sort of person is his wife? I mean, what was the reason?"

Francis looked away. "I don't know, really. A marriage fails: it comes down to that, whether there's one reason or a thousand, doesn't it? It failed." He stopped abruptly, then resumed, "I'm worried about Marjorie. The doctor says her pressure's too high. They may have to take the baby if it doesn't come soon by itself." He turned a troubled face toward his parents. "I'm glad you're here."

"We'll do anything we can, you know that," Richard said.

"And there's something else. A damned mess, just when you've come for your first visit! There's talk of a strike, a general strike. It could paralyze us. It could get very nasty." He squinted thoughtfully into the sun. "Still, maybe not. And I really don't think—in fact I'm sure they won't bother me personally. I've done so much and they know it. I've been on labor's side since the day I got here. No, I'm sure they won't bother me."

In the dining room, Richard sat opposite Anatole Da Cunha's painting of Morne Bleue.

"I have to admit it hurt to part with it," he said, "but it belongs here without question. Oh, he has the touch, hasn't he? Marvelous, marvelous! You can feel the sun on your skin! You know, I'm disgusted with some of the things the art critics write these days. Such as last week: 'A face representing a civilization in decline.' Now what the devil does that mean? Fuzzy personal impressions masquerading as analysis! When all that matters is whether you can feel the sun on your skin."

Marjorie got to the point. "It must be worth a good deal, mustn't it, now that Da Cunha's so old?"

"Oh, definitely. And when he's dead, the value will really shoot up. You know, Teresa, I should have had him paint you when we were in Paris. I wasn't thinking."

The mirror over the sideboard reflected Tee's face, very white in candlelight and dusk, a face still without lines, still sweetly curved, and yet not young anymore.

"Let's see," Lionel remarked, "you were fifteen, weren't you, when you left? So I must have been not quite three. Yet I always thought I remembered you, I suppose because Mother talked about you so much." He laughed. "You were a wild girl, she always said."

"I? Wild?"

"Oh, she only meant bareback riding and running around with animals—dogs and colts and parrots—all the things she never did, I suppose."

"Parrots!" As always, Richard was enthusiastic over anything new. "You have them wild here, don't you?"

"They nest way up the Morne toward the rain forest, and you don't always get to see them, but with luck we might. I've even seen the imperial parrot a couple of times. Sisseron. Amethyst and emerald, a glorious bird. If you're willing to climb," Francis offered, "we can go one morning."

"Oh, I'm willing!" Richard cried.

Tee thought, I should not have come. Her mouth went dry and she laid the fork down, then picked it up again and took some food, something without taste.

He could not possibly be here, could he? Patrick Courzon? The name made a sharp impact on her ear. And even if he were, she would never encounter him! The island was small, but not that small. And so stratified by color and caste into concentric circles which didn't touch. Surely, though, he was not even here! He would have stayed in England, or gone somewhere else to use his fine education. Not here.

But suppose he were? She tried to picture him: a year older than Francis, half of his blood, of her own blood, each of them alive and breathing at this very instant—now!—on this high, blue day; alike, so alike they must be, by the very law of averages! And still so different.

A maid poured wine for Francis, her thin, pretty arm, red-brown, dusky, stretched parallel to his pale one, making exactly the contrast that that other boy's would make, one supposed, if ever they should—Impossible! And yet, as fear trembled in Teresa for the thousandth time or more, something else trembled in her, too: pity, profound pity.

The young maid moved about the table, pouring the wine. There was proud grace in the poise of her narrow head; substitute for the blue cotton uniform a sweeping ballgown and you would have a princess, a dark princess. The girl, meeting Tee's gaze, smiled slightly.

Crazy world, with its strictures and classifications; all those gradations of mankind based on color and money, on legitimacy and class, when all we are is only—what? Protein, minerals, and water, mostly. Sea water. Yes, it's absurd, all of it, and still I haven't the courage to challenge it, or even to face it. If I could know what he is like, just quietly, secretly know, without anyone else's knowing, without ruining everything, facing rage. Sometimes I think I've been brave, but not brave enough. Sometimes I think I died here in this house when I was fifteen, and everything since has been a dream.

There came over her then an engulfing sense of unreality, of time so telescoped that the far past was only yesterday, and yet so long ago that it might never have happened. She gripped the edge of the table.

"Is anything the matter?" Marjorie asked. "You're feeling all right?"

"I? Just tired after the trip, that's all." And Tee smiled, forcing herself away, after long habit, from the ghost of a memory that had been keeping step with her since she was fifteen.

"You'll rest well tonight. Your room's in the new wing, very quiet, away from everyone."

"And you'll lunch with me tomorrow," Lionel said. "There'll be no hostess, but I'll give you a good lunch. I do all my own entertaining these days, now that I'm without a wife. But then, Kate never was very sociable anyway."

Richard, seeing that the subject was not taboo, inquired, "What did she do with herself, then?" He enjoyed gossip.

"Oh, good works. She was, and still is, on every blasted committee you can think of for the improvement of this, that, and the other. But to be fair, I shouldn't make light of it. She believes in what she does, and you have to give credit for that. In other words, she puts her money where her mouth is."

"She never liked people," Marjorie remarked.

Lionel contradicted her. "I wouldn't say that. She likes some of them too much. It all depends on what people you're talking about."

"Naturally, I mean our friends, the people we all know," Marjorie explained to Tee. "I've made wonderful friends here. They've been a saving grace for me, while Francis was busy with his bananas and cows and things." It seemed to Tee that she had bitten the words off.

Richard inquired. "Do you get many visitors from home during the winter?"

"Oh, yes, there are always a few yachts in the harbor. Last year the Crowes, friends of my mother's, the Standard Steel Crowes, dropped anchor and spent a day with us. And there are always a lot of chartered schooners in season. My cousins come every year and we have a marvelous time. They can't get over all the land we have and all the servants! They keep telling me you can scarcely find a decent cleaning woman at home anymore. So it's kind of fun, and I keep busy."

What does Francis talk about with her? Tee wondered. Marriage was a lifelong conversation, or it wasn't much of a marriage. And she wondered whether Richard would have noticed. No, he would not have noticed.

"So you're due any day now," Lionel said to Marjorie.

"I'm afraid I'm overdue. If the baby doesn't come in the next day or two, they'll have to take it."

Lionel frowned. "If I were you, Francis, I wouldn't wait that long. I'd take her in to town. You can't tell what will happen. If the strike comes, they're liable to block the roads."

"You really think so?" Francis was doubtful. "I rather think it will be settled quietly. I don't foresee violence, even if there should be a strike."

"You told us this afternoon," Richard reminded him quickly, "that it could be nasty."

"I meant verbal nastiness. Something unpleasant, not dangerous."

Lionel shook his head. "I'd feel more secure if Nicholas Mebane were in the country. He's one Negro with a white man's common sense. I've no love for him, mind you, or for any of them, but I have to admit he seems to be a man with the country's best interests at heart. However, he's at some sort of powwow just now, some meeting in Jamaica over federation or independence or some such. Without him, we could be in for a pack of trouble."

"These people aren't violent!" Francis argued. "It's simply a question of wages, a union affair."

"No? What happened right here last month?" Marjorie challenged.

"We had a little problem, nothing to do with what we're talking about. You see," Francis explained to his parents, "when you run a place like this, you're almost like the head of a family. Workers come to you with problems, when they want a loan, or have a quarrel with another worker. And it happened that one of the men lost his temper and slashed another with his machete, severing a finger. So I had to settle things down. It was disturbing, of course, but it has no bearing on the strike, none at all."

"I think it has," Lionel said. "These people are only one step removed from the savage."

Richard wanted to know what the unions were demanding.

"More money, naturally," Lionel answered. "They've a long list of grievances, wanting to be paid once a week instead of every other week—"

Richard interrupted. "That seems reasonable enough. Or am I wrong?"

"Very inconvenient and more expensive. Much more bookkeeping."

"Personally, I think they're entitled to most of what they're asking for," Francis said.

Lionel gave a sigh of exasperation. "Are you willing to raise wages?"

"I'll compromise. I'll meet them halfway. I've got good people, and if it costs a little more to keep them here in peace, I'll do it. I'm making a living."

"You would do better to be thinking of saving money for your own flesh and blood," Marjorie said quietly.

"My flesh and blood will be taken care of. No need to worry," Francis replied, as quietly.

There is nothing between them except the child in her belly, Tee thought. It was a sudden revelation. They had nothing! Quite possibly neither of them even knew it—and might never know it. That was the terrible thing: might never know it. If you were to ask Richard about his marriage, he would tell you it was good. He believed it was.

Too much, too much, she thought, feeling a great weariness. My son's marriage ought to be no affair of mine, but it will be, nevertheless; I shall go home with the burden of this, too.

Marjorie was pressing a question. "Will you drive me to Covetown tomorrow morning as Lionel advises?"

"I will, although I still don't believe there'll be any danger."

"When you've lived here as long as I have," Lionel said, "you'll know better. Good God, I remember when I was a child, there was an argument in a barbershop and a party of Negroes came in and cut the barber—he was a white man— cut him to pieces with his own razors. No one ever caught them, either. For all you know, they could be working for you here at Eleuthera." Lionel laughed. "Seriously, though, there's a lot of agitation out there, and don't think the fireburn went out with the end of slavery, because it didn't. Why, they burned half the estates on St. Croix back in my grandfather's time, and that's not so long ago! Burned them up because they weren't satisfied with their labor contracts. And things are more tense today than they were then, let me tell you."

Richard put his coffee cup down. "We're scaring the life out of these women. It's especially unfair to Marjorie. She's got enough to think about right now as it is."

Lionel apologized. "Sorry. You're absolutely right. So you'll have lunch with me Friday, if all goes well? Tee, do you remember the way? You won't get lost?"

"No, I won't get lost, and yes, I remember the way. I remember it very well."

As soon as he opened his eyes on Friday morning, Francis felt the unnatural stillness. Quietly, so as not to awaken Marjorie, he slid out of bed and pulled on his clothes. But she had heard him.

"Is anything the matter, Francis?"

"No. Go to sleep. You feel all right?" Her eyes, between heavy lids, had a bright sickly gloss.

"Dizzy, I think. I don't know how I feel, really."

Alarm jerked him more widely awake. "Stay there, then. I'll be back in a minute. We'll call Dr. Strand and drive you in to Covetown."

He went downstairs and outside. By half past six the milk cows should have been let out to graze; differing from many owners, he kept his cattle in at night to protect them from the damp. By half past six, in picking time, the men should have been in the groves. And hastening, he strode along the river gorge, up the steep path down which the stems were to be carried to the roadside for pickup. Except for the whistlings and twitterings of the forest, there was no sign of life. Thick as candles on an altar, the bananas stood on the trees, ready for picking. On the other side of the island the Geest refrigerator ship, like a great resting seabird, waited for the crop.

The strike had come then, with his own people in it! Betraying what he had liked to think of as a mutual trust! They had let him down, after all. The whole crop to be lost, all those months of steady bloom and growth! Anger clashed in his middle with his worry over Marjorie and still another urgent fear: he needed money. He needed it quite desperately, he owed the bank, another half-dozen cottages for the fulltime hands were only partially completed, he—

Osborne was running between the barns.

"So it's begun," Francis said. "With our people in it, too."

"I'm afraid so. Don't worry about the stock, though. I've got my sons milking and feeding. My wife's seeing to the chickens. We're slow, but we can do the necessary."

"What about the crop?"

Osborne threw his hands up.

"What do you mean? Just forget about it? To hell with it?"

"What else can we do?"

Oh, Osborne could afford to be calm! It wasn't his money. He'd get his salary and his house, regardless.

"Haven't I treated my people decently?"

"Surely you have, but—"

"But what? When my foreman's wife wants a new stove, I don't question. She gets it. Merton's baby has an ear infection. What do I do? I get in the car and drive him to the hospital myself. I don't want thanks, I tell you, I only want— Listen, Osborne, I've got to talk to somebody. There has to be somebody who can be talked to. Where is everybody, anyway?"

"A lot of men have gone to a meeting in town. And there's a crowd with picket signs outside the gates. You can't see them from the house."

"I'm going down there. I'm going to put it to them fairly and squarely. Biting the hand that's fed them better than anybody else on this island's ever done just makes no sense, no sense at all, and I intend to tell them so."

"I wouldn't do that if I were you, Mr. Luther. They've made up their minds. You wouldn't get anyplace. And some of them are union people from higher up. They don't even know you, and they could get pretty mad. This is islandwide. No, don't go down there, Mr. Luther."

Francis stared at the other man. A cold fish, with his calm counsel, who, for all he could tell, might have known perfectly well what was going to happen this morning! At a time like this, one could suspect anybody. But he must keep his head and save whatever could be saved. Keep his head! With Marjorie's condition, and— He turned abruptly.

"I'm going in to telephone. I'll reach someone who can do something. Damned if I'll just sit here and let that crop rot on the trees."

Patrick, he thought. Patrick's the one. They hadn't spoken for the past week or two. Francis' head had been filled with Marjorie and with his parents' visit, while Patrick had, through the newspaper, been involved with the strike, writing exhortations to both sides to negotiate, to be patient, and to keep their tempers.

Having called the doctor and been advised to bring his wife in before noon, he telephoned Patrick. Would Patrick possibly be able to rush out to Eleuthera right now? He hated to ask, but it was so important, and would he please come to the office next to Osborne's house. Yes, surely Patrick would.

Francis swung in the swivel chair and drummed on the office desk. His nerves were singing like telegraph wires. He'd had a teacher once who was all gone on the subject of relationships, of how everything was hooked on to something else and nothing stood alone. He hadn't comprehended it then, had been bored as hell by such dry abstractions, but now suddenly he saw what had been meant. Here was his child about to be born—pray God it would be well—and it was up to him to protect that child's security; but then, the workers wanted their own security, too!

"They've much on their side, you know that," Kate always said, and it was true; Kate saw things fairly; Kate—

He rubbed his hand over his eyes. Everything, everything circled round him: Kate and Marjorie and the baby, and money and justice, racing and colliding. Yes, the strikers had much on their side, their demands being neither impossible nor outrageous. If the planters had any sense, they'd accede and choose peace. In the end, they'd have to give in; couldn't they see that?

And he said as much when Patrick came rushing in.

"I'm glad you see it that way, Francis."

"Well, I do. Everyone must know I do. Then why are they punishing me, too?"

"It's not punishment. It's not personal. It's just that once a thing like this starts, there's a momentum. It took a long time to build. Now you can't stop it."

"That doesn't answer me! Haven't I been fair, been generous? I've plowed money back into improvements when I could have used it to pay off what I owe. I've a grocery store on the premises and put its profits into a welfare fund, I've— Why are they doing this to me?" He heard himself pleading.

Patrick spoke gently. "What can I tell you? It's not fair, of course it isn't. But they don't make exceptions. That's the size of it."

"Won't, you mean."

"Even if some of them should want to break the strike for you, they couldn't do it, you surely understand that. A union is a union. Orders come from the organization, from the top."

"Well, then, let's get to the top!"

Patrick shook his head. "Francis, it can't be done."

The patience in his manner irritated Francis. This was the stubborn patience with which one "handled" children, denying without explaining why. He struck the desktop with his fist.

"I have got to get this crop to the ship! It's an outrage, a wanton waste for the entire island, those ships going back empty, with space for a thousand tons!"

Patrick sighed. "I know, I know."

"I'll pay what they're demanding. Let the other planters do what they want, or say about me whatever they want. I don't give a damn."

"You've got courage and you've got principles. But you see, it's not the money alone. It wouldn't be, even if they could make an exception of you, which I tell you again, they can't. They've got to stand together."

"If it's not the money alone, then what is it? What do they want?"

"I suppose," Patrick said slowly, reflectively, "it's wanting to direct one's own life. That's the feeling that's been gaining strength here on these islands. These people have grown up. They've migrated overseas and sent back reports. They've seen how people live in other places and what they have. And now they're sick of being directed from abroad by foreign companies—"

Francis interrupted. "I know all that. I'm not a foreign company. I'm here every day working where they can see me."

Patrick was silent. He looked tired.

"You just said I have principles. You admit I've been a good guy. Go out to my gate now and ask those men to come back and harvest my crop."

"Francis, they wouldn't listen to me! I'm not even a union man. I only write for a newspaper."

"Then ask your father-in-law. They'd listen to Clarence Porter."

"Clarence is old. He's been out of things for years."

"Don't tell me he has no more influence!"

"If he has, he won't use it to break a strike, I can tell you that. He'd have my head for even daring to suggest it."

It was almost as though a game were being played, some board game, chess perhaps, in which Francis moved and Patrick blocked him and Francis moved again and Patrick blocked him. Once during childhood, when he had been losing at checkers, Francis had gone into a rage of frustration and thrown the board over. He felt that way now.

"Well," he said, controlling himself, "well, maybe you have some other solution for me." And he waited.

"I wish I had."

"Then," Francis said coldly, "it comes down to the fact that you really don't care about helping me."

"That's not true! But you're asking me to do the impossible. This will only be solved when the Planters Association signs a contract with the union, when contractors sign with their unions—it's spread all over, Francis. It's a movement, don't you see?"

Patrick's chair creaked. Osborne's porch door banged. The noises shuddered along Francis' spine and in his teeth.

"Well? Well? What do you advise me to do then?"

For a moment Patrick was silent, examining his fingers. Then he said gravely, "I have no advice. Except to sit and wait."

"And take my losses."

"What else?"

Francis could have struck him.

"What else?" he mimicked. "You and Osborne, with your quiet resignation! Oh, you talk, you people who've got nothing to lose! Have you any idea what I've put into this place?" He twisted his cigarette into the ashtray. He shot up out of the chair. "Yes, just sit here, I must, while they shut my place down, this horde that depends on me for wages and wants to be the master of my life!"

Patrick smiled sadly. "They believe, you see, that people like you feel entitled to be the masters of their lives."

The black arm of the wall clock moved forward with a jerk and click both visible and audible. Half past nine. Marjorie. He had to get her in to town before noon. Leave all this mess. Everything falling apart. No one helps. It's all on me. Again the clock jerked and clicked.

Suddenly something happened. He struck his hands together. "Illumination!" he cried. "I've got the answer! The Carib reservation! They'll do it! I can get a gang for a few days' work and pay them anything they want to pick this crop. It'll be worth it."

Patrick whistled softly. "Blackleg labor?"

"You can call it whatever you like."

"Apart from the rightness or wrongness, you ought to consider the dangers. How will they get the crop past your gates? The roads will be blocked—they'll never reach the dock."

"We'll chance it."

"There'll be a battle."

"If it's battling they want, let them have it."

Patrick had risen. The two men, of equal height, stood as if in confrontation.

"Francis, you're making a mistake. I know you feel you're being treated unfairly, not appreciated, and that may be true, but as they say in the labor movement, you can't make an omelet without breaking eggs."

"So, I'll break eggs, too!" Words came which ordinarily would not have fitted in Francis' mouth. "They've gone too far this time. This is my land. I've treated them well, and if they can't acknowledge that I'm the master here, to hell with them! And that's all I have to say."

Patrick's face hardened, surprising Francis, who had never seen hardness in that quiet face.

"I don't like the word *master,* Francis. It's ugly and it's out of date."

"Listen here, I've got thirty-six hours to get those bananas onto the boat. I haven't time to quibble over words."

"You've surprised me this morning. I didn't expect this of you."

Francis moved impatiently. "I'm sorry I haven't lived up to your expectations. But tell me about it some other time, will you?"

"I can tell you in one sentence right now. You are acting too grand, too feudal for this century."

Anger turned to fury in Francis. This—this *unknown,* whom he had befriended and liked and treated with so much respect, to turn against him, to rebuke him now, like a teacher scolding a child!

"Grand! Feudal!" he shouted. "After all I've done! You ungrateful son—" And he bit off the word.

"Of a bitch, you wanted to say?"

"Yes, son of a bitch!"

"The same to you, then," Patrick answered. He swung about and the door crashed.

For a minute or two Francis didn't move. The explosion in the little room, the voices of anger, left shockwaves trembling behind. A door had been slammed shut, not the sheet of wood that hung on a frame before him, but an invisible door which up to this morning had been open onto a warm communion between two men. He became aware of his own heavy breathing. He wasn't used to being this angry. Well, so, that's the way it is, he thought; I've seen his true colors. And then, ironically: True color? No, that's nasty, I can't mean that.

He raced next door to Osborne's house, across the veranda into the untidy living room where toys and newspapers littered the floor. You'd think, he thought irrelevantly, with the wages I pay, they'd manage better than this.

"Osborne!" he called.

"Yes, Mr. Luther?" Osborne came out of the kitchen. "Any luck?"

"No. I spoke to my friend and got exactly nowhere." He heard the bitterness in his own voice. "Listen here, I want you to get hold of some Caribs to pick that fruit. You know the chief. He knows me, too. You can pay whatever they ask and damn the consequences. We've got just thirty-six hours to get that crop to the ship."

Osborne's eyes were blank. He's not on my side, Francis thought, but he'll do what I order; he wants to keep the job.

"They can come down the mountain, in through the back way," he said. "I'll leave it all to you. I've got to take my wife into town. They may have to do a cesarean. Everything seems to have clobbered me at once today."

Osborne nodded. "Yes, sir. I'm sorry," he said, with proper sympathy. His eyes were still blank.

"You shouldn't have come. I tried to reach you but you had already left," Lionel said, adding crossly, "Francis shouldn't have let you, he ought to know better."

Tee explained. "He'd already left for the hospital with Marjorie by the time we got up." She worried. "I'm sure he'll call home or here the minute anything—"

Richard interrupted. "Maybe we should start back right now. The last thing I want is to get caught in a riot."

"There's been some trouble in Covetown," Lionel said, "but nothing out in the countryside. Yet. And maybe there won't be. Still, I'd finish lunch and get going fast if I were you."

He rang, and the servant came at once with the dessert and coffee. Conversation stopped as she moved around the table, her soft-soled shoes making the only sound in the noon stillness. The table was an island in the enormous, airy room. At the far end of the room glass doors opened to a terrace and a stretch of empty lawn. The house was an island, too, with no protection but a row of glass doors.

Tee rose abruptly. "I'm ready," she said.

They drove cross-island. "Looks peaceful enough," remarked Richard.

He didn't, naturally, know the difference. Not a soul was at work either on the roads or in the fields. The stillness was oppressive, like that ominous, waiting silence in the last sultry hour before storm strikes, when the wind dies and birds hide. And thinking this, Tee thought at the same time, It's my nerves, I am overreacting, as usual.

In a wide valley between the hills that roll toward Morne Bleue, only a mile or two beyond Eleuthera, they came, suddenly, upon a crowd. On foot, on muleback, in farm carts and battered cars, men, women, and children had converged upon a broad, mowed field. At its center a simple platform had been set up, from which a man was making a speech.

"I wonder what's going on," Richard said. "Let's have a look."

"I don't think we should. They might not like it."

"We can just sit in the car and leave in a hurry if we have to," he argued, curious as always.

Facing the sun as they were, it was difficult to see the speaker, but his voice carried clearly, for the crowd was remarkably quiet.

"For centuries the grandeur of England rested heavily upon these islands." The accent was faintly British and the tone reasonable, almost conversational. "The wealth that came from sugar was princely. Most of it went abroad. I saw great houses in England that make our grandest estates look like cottages, and they were built on sugar. People who had never laid eyes on St. Felice lived on the wealth drawn from its earth. And what was returned to St. Felice? Nothing.

Nothing. And what did you, who produced this wealth, get out of it? You know the answer: Not very much.

"It's true that things are a lot better now than they were back then, or even a few years ago. Some of you are old enough to remember when an estate worker earned twenty cents a day. On average we've come a long way from that, and some planters, a very few, are doing better than average. That's all true.

"Yet it's still also true that you are the victims of a system which leaves two thirds of you unemployed from January to June, once the peak season in the cane fields is over. So out of crop season you have to scrounge for work. Your women take jobs breaking stones on the roads. Your men leave the island to look for work elsewhere. And they say you have no family structure! No family structure!"

With scarcely any change in pitch the voice revealed, nevertheless, a passionate intensity, so that Richard whispered, "My God, the fellow's an orator!"

"When I was a teacher, I listened to the children. From them I learned more than you can ever tell me about drunken husbands and frustrated youths and babies who cry all the time because the houses are so crowded, so noisy, that they can't sleep. These are the facts of daily living.

"So then, what do you want? You want higher wages, and it should be simple enough to understand why you must have them. They say they can't afford to pay more. Well, the way things are run here that may be so. What is needed here is investment, is planning. Why, take coffee alone! We raise the beans, then we send them to England to be processed, and we import our own coffee to drink! Could anything be more absurd? Take sugar: why can't we refine our own sugar, make our own bags, manufacture molasses, rum, and bottles for the rum? Our people are crying for jobs; the population is growing. Ah, well, let me sum it up. With some intelligence and will, things can be changed. Now that every adult has a vote at last, you must learn to use it wisely." Here the speaker flung his arms out. "It's funny, I was asked to come here to talk about the strike and I've done so, but I couldn't help making a pitch for a bigger thing, for the kind of government which will be so responsive to your needs that strikes won't be necessary. I didn't intend this to be a political speech. I'm not a politician. I'm not a labor leader either, for that matter. I'm just a citizen who wants to improve things, that's all. And that's why I'm putting in a word for Nicholas Mebane, who couldn't be here today. I was asked to stand in for him and that's what I'm trying to do. Nicholas Mebane—you know him—and the New Day Party!"

Cheers came from the crowd.

"He's a white man!" Richard cried. "Look, Teresa! I think—no, no he isn't. Almost, though. I wonder who he is?"

The speaker raised his hand for silence. "What we want is a twenty percent raise. That sums things up for the moment. You'll refuse to work and you'll not give in until you get what you're entitled to. It's as simple as that."

He leaped down from the platform and was engulfed in the crowd. All was swirling movement, a pushing toward the center of the field, a streaming out and a noise of many voices.

Richard leaned from the window as he backed away, calling to a black man who was passing. "Who was the speaker? Who was that?"

For a moment the man in overalls regarded Richard in his linen jacket and Tee in her lilac summer dress. *Why do you want to know?* his silence challenged. Then he answered.

"He writes for the *Trumpet*. And he knows what he's talking about. Name's Courzon. Patrick Courzon."

FOR YOUNG WILL the long night had begun at the supper table. Patrick worried. "I don't like the looks of things. On the way back from my speech I passed two police stations that somebody's smashed up. It looks as if some tough elements want to take over."

Désirée changed the subject, just when it was getting interesting. This habit of hers exasperated Will. She always steered away from anything the least bit ugly. Fear was ugly, as were poverty and dirt.

"I'm so sorry I didn't get to hear you," she said soothingly. "You didn't tell me you were going to speak."

"I didn't know it myself. I was on the way back after that fiasco with Francis Luther this morning when they got a message to me. They wanted me to pinch-hit around the island in support of the strike. 'The New Day Party supports you all the way'—that sort of thing. I wish Nicholas hadn't left just now, though," he added darkly.

"You're more upset about Francis Luther than anything," Désirée said. "It's really not worth your being so upset, Patrick."

Patrick didn't reply to that.

Will was alert. "What happened? You have a fight with Mr. Luther?"

"Now Will, it's none of—" Désirée began, but was interrupted.

"It's all right, the boy can ask. I'm too tired right now to talk about it, Will, but when all this business is over, I'll tell you."

Laurine spoke up. "Pop-pop told me the police are thick all along Wharf Street. They must be expecting something to happen."

"I hope to God not," Patrick said. "A strike is supposed to be an orderly way of obtaining one's due, not a celebration for hoodlums." He got up from the table. "Anyway, it's a good night to stay indoors, just in case things do get out of hand. Where you going now, Will?"

"Just out to the shed to look over some stuff."

From the shed you could slip around the garage and down the hill without being seen. If there was anything going on in town, his friends would be there. Most of them didn't have fathers as strict as Patrick and could spend their evenings hanging around where they wanted to, anyway.

At the next corner he fell in with two of them going to town; by the time they reached the foot of the hill where several roads met, a stream of boys of every age from twelve to twenty was pouring toward the center. The stream grew wider and moved faster.

"What's up?" Will asked his neighbor.

"I don't know. Somebody said there was stuff going on downtown."

The boys began to trot, their shoes slapping the pavement. Evening was melting into night; lights went on and houses became alive. Doors opened; voices shot out into the streets. Excitement rang like radio waves in the air; it pulsed through Will's veins, tingled in his chest. He felt like laughing. He didn't know why, only that it was good to be running like this in the center of a crowd, all together, all one, running toward action!

Where Wharf Street cut across their path a line of police brought them sharply to a halt.

"Blocked off! Blocked off!"

"What for? What do you mean?"

"Order of the governor, that's what for."

From far down the street came a tumultuous shouting, car horns, the crash of glass, and the low whine of an ambulance.

"Da Cunha's!" someone cried. "Yeah, they've got the old man's diamonds! Da Cunha's, isn't it?"

The black faces under the proud white police helmets ignored all questions.

"Aw, let us through! Let's see!"

The uniformed line drew tighter. "Back, boys, get back. Nobody gets through."

Next to Will someone had an idea. "Round the square! We'll get in at the other end!"

The group swung about, raced past Nelson in his wrought-iron enclosure, whooped past the careenage, hurled a few stones gaily through the windows of Bata Shoes and World Travel, came out at the other end of Wharf Street, and once more were halted.

"Shit," Will said.

Another ambulance wailed by. Fire engines clanged; the street lights flickered over the jostling mob on Wharf Street. In his frustration Will's feet were dancing. For a minute or two the group stood undecided. Then, grumbling and frustrated, they began to disperse. With a couple of others Will walked back to the square. Out of the deepening darkness a fan of light from a streetlamp had spread open over Nelson. With what arrogance he stood on his pedestal, one hand on sword, chin lifted in surveyal as if he owned the place and everyone in it!

"Bastard," Will said.

His companion stared. "Who is?"

"Nelson. Nelson's a bastard."

The other boy shrugged, not understanding. "Where you going now, Will?"

Will didn't know. But he knew he wasn't ready to go home. Not tonight. He wouldn't be able to sleep, with so much happening or about to happen, in this place where nothing ever did happen.

A truck roared on the other side of the square. The driver leaned out.

"Hey, boys! Want a lift?"

Will and Tom Folsom ran across. "Yeah, where you going?"

"Home. St. Elizabeth's. You live out that way?"

"Yeah," Will said.

"Hop in back, then. I've got a crate of chickens on the front seat. Holler when you want to drop off."

"How'll we get back?" Tom whispered as they started out of town.

"I don't know. Get another lift, maybe. Or walk if I have to. Anyway, I'm in no hurry to get home."

The words were careless and grand. Tom looked at him with respect.

The truck, an open pickup, careened through the countryside, through tunnels of trees; the headlights, like two feelers, pierced the night ahead. Behind lay only darkness, dark sky over darker land. The wind raced through Will's hair; it seemed to him that he was flying, that he was powerful and could go anywhere, do anything.

At a crossroads, the driver slowed and craned his head around.

"Look there! Jesus, they sure broke that up!"

The police station had been smashed. The door had been kicked in and lay now on the grass along with a little pile of broken desks and chairs. Just beyond, where a row of cabins stretched on both sides, lights were on and people were gathered outside, far past the hour at which such villages were usually asleep. Will was wide awake.

"What's going on?" he called to the driver.

"Folks got mad, is all. You'll see two, three more like that along this road. And burned-out cane, probably too dark to see."

Tom wanted to know how far they were going. Scared, Will thought contemptuously.

Suddenly they stopped. "Hey, look there!"

At the edge of the road, half in the deep ditch, a truck lay on its side, its load of bananas flung into the road.

"I heard about that," the driver said. "Happened this morning. Fellow near here up at Eleuthera hired some Caribs off the reservation to carry his bananas to the boat." He laughed. "Straightened them out, all right."

Eleuthera. Lawns and flowers and pride.

"I turn off here, boys, road to Myrtle. You two didn't say how far you're going."

Something decided itself in Will. He could not have said why. Simply, it clicked. "I'll get off now. Got a friend lives just down the road."

"Let's go on to Myrtle," Tom said. "We can get a ride back from there. Come on with me, Will. It's late. I want to get home."

But Will had already swung down, so Tom followed. When the truck had turned out of sight, Will reversed his direction, toward Eleuthera. Plodding along through the empty night he struggled with his thoughts. Something had happened there today between Patrick and Mr. Luther; he wondered whether the overturned banana truck had anything to do with it. Patrick being the easygoing fool he was, most likely the argument was Luther's fault, he reflected. But however it had been, it was no concern of his.

"Where the heck you going, Will?" Tom complained. "I'm tired."

"Nobody asked you to come, did they? So put up or shut up, will you?"

The night was soft. The commotion in Covetown might have been taking place in another world. When Will's foot kicked a little stone, its clatter startled the silence. Alongside the road, behind a wire fence, he could make out the shapes of resting cattle. The air smelled sweetly of vanilla and hay. Stopping, he took a long, long breath. He walked on, with Tom padding silently behind. Still he did not know why he was walking, why he had come here.

A few minutes later he rounded a bend. And there it lay. To his right on a little knoll stood the house; for an instant, as the moon struck through dark and mounting clouds, its white columns glistened. Once when Patrick had brought him, he'd been given lemonade on that veranda. He remembered the woman of the house; she'd worn a lace collar and had been polite, but he had hated her. He stood there now, remembering.

A wind rose suddenly, making a sea sound in the trees. Below on his left the sea was making wind sounds; pale gray it gleamed; in a shaft of moonlight he saw a wave shatter itself upon the distant rocks. It was more beautiful than anything he had ever seen: beautiful, all of it, the water, the wind, the fragrance, and the stillness. Beauty like that could give you pain. And it could make you angry at yourself for feeling so. Angry. Angry.

Now again, clouds covered all the silver. It is going to storm, Will thought. In the house there were no lights. Yes, one, in an upstairs window. Bastards getting ready for bed. He stood looking at the window. Then he walked slowly up the path. He had no idea why, or what he wanted except just to look. Between hibiscus hedges he moved nearer.

A dog barked and another joined in. You could tell by the yapping that they were little dogs, some sort of silly pets.

"Quiet!" he heard a man's voice say. It was so still that the voice carried clearly over the rustling wind.

Will waited. For a moment or two a woman's shape appeared at the window, too far away to be recognizable, if he had known her. All he could sense was remoteness; beyond reach, in some long pale garment, cloud-white, flower-white, she stood high. Perfumed, he thought, cushioned like one of those jewels in a velvet box in Da Cunha's window. And his brain, which was so keen tonight, so filled with jumping images, brought him inexplicably the smell of kerosene burning in a battered lamp on an oilcloth-covered table in a littered hut. What would that woman up there know or care about that hut?

And he stood there, leaning against a tree, with his hands thrust into his pockets, watching that window even after she had gone. One pocket held a broken cigarette, left over from a secret smoking session in the shed. Also, there was a full book of matches. These he took out, turning them over in his hand. He fondled them. Then he had a queer thought, which he pushed away. The thought came back. It jumped in his head. And the tingling began again, just as it had in Covetown earlier, when he'd been running and the ambulance had clanged and glass had shattered. Once more his feet danced; hot excitement poured; it was wild, it was joyous, it was angry. Why not? Oh, why not? Be damned to everything. Why not?

And laughing now, laughing silently from deep in his chest, keeping out of the path of light that beamed from the bedroom, he crept toward the house. There was here, unmistakably, the smell of fresh paint. Under a downstairs window, which was ajar, a couple of painters' cloths had been left lying on the grass. He picked them up to smell them. Yes, turpentine and paint.

It was so easy! Some of the biggest things you could do were sometimes so ridiculously easy! Just shove the cloths in at the windows where they would touch the blowing curtains, then strike the match. That's all you had to do.

Frightened and fascinated, Tom watched. "What are you doing, Will? What are you doing that for?"

"Because I want to, fool. And if you ever," he whispered fiercely, "if you ever open your mouth I'll say we planned this together and you'll be—"

"Will, Will! You can trust me! What do you think I am? I swear I'll never—"

The fire ran up the edge of the curtain. Too bad they couldn't stay to watch! They sped down the driveway. Three or four miles down the coast, past the junction to Moorhead, they could probably pick up a lift. If anyone should ask, it would be plausible to say they'd been at Moorhead. And that was all there was to it. The last thing they heard when they reached the end of the drive was the shrill commotion of the dogs.

"Useless little things, Pekingese," Richard says. "I wish they'd stop yapping downstairs." He waits for a comment.

"I suppose they miss Marjorie," Tee replies.

She has gone to bed early because of a headache. Richard offers aspirin, and thanking him, she takes it. But aspirin will not assuage this ache. This is a terrible, terrible pain. She does not recognize herself through the chaos of such pain.

She is wracked with shame. Shame because of having borne him or because of having denied him? Truly, she does not know. She is heavy with pity for his young pride, the pride of Patrick Courzon. But her mouth is dry with fear. She scourges herself for her fear. Yet it is there all the same.

He'll come back into your life, Agnes told me. *Someday,* she said. Wise and good. Honest and strong. Agnes, who saved me.

Cursed, she thinks, oh cursed, like the island itself that I loved so much, as Père loved it, as Francis does and as now, so it seems, does—he!

How tough he was this afternoon! Tough and solid as Père. Everything intensifies in this isolation, this extravagance of light and heat. Anger is harder, grief is sharper and desire more keen.

Strange it is, although one's heard it often enough, that nothing can ever be forgotten. One buries and covers over, layer upon layer, but in the end it is no use. There are all those secret cells in the brain which remember even when one doesn't want to. Now, not piece by gradual piece, but instantly, "as in a blinding light," one sees . . .

Rape, you say? Attack? Yes, and also no. The happiness of that summer! Sun and wind and poetry. The astonishment of discovering one's own mind reflected in another's. How ignorant, how wise, how daring, and how young!

She took his hand and held it. The parrot, flashing royal blue and emerald and gold, fled upward into noontime silence. "I'll never forget you for this," she said, or something like that. She took his hand, she looked with tenderness into his face.

Attack, you say?

And that is what happened when she was fifteen, knowing nothing, but feeling everything, feeling what she had never felt before, or since.

Richard comes in from the bathroom to ask again how she is.

"Better," she lies, for her head is hot, and under the blanket she is shivering. She turns and twists on the pillow, her cheek rubbing her spread hair. *Aphrodisiac, said Anatole.*

"A very attractive room," Richard remarks.

"Red and white," she says. "Cheerful." He expects an answer. Yet it is good to keep talking of easy, banal things; it is a way to keep rooted in reality, as, when someone is hideously dying in the house, it helps to make coffee and slice bread.

"Not red and white," Richard corrects. He has such a fine, critical eye! "It's far more subtle. Crimson and cream. Those are Chinese peonies, you know."

He picks up the telephone and shakes it. There is neither hum nor buzz. "Seems to have gone dead. I've been trying it downstairs for the last half hour. I suppose it has something to do with the strike."

"I suppose."

"I'd like to know what's happening at the hospital. Our first grandchild," he says, with marvel in his voice.

Gone domestic now, in middle age, she thinks, not unkindly. Reformed. All the zest gone out of him, just leaked away. I never knew him, really. Maybe there was never much to know. He was always thinking of something else, someplace else, when you tried to talk to him. Only art moves him. I never did. Maybe it was my fault. But maybe no one else ever moved him, either.

"Francis says the doctor's excellent, trained in London. The first child is the hardest, of course. Although yours took no time at all, did it? But then, you were so young."

Lived a whole life like two strangers, he and I, and had all those children. A pair of friendly strangers, living side by side, but separately. Yes, for a long time I tried to make a union of us two, something solid and warm. I wanted it. I needed it. Only it didn't happen. So we speak now of common, daily things and I have known quiet happiness of a sort, yet there is always the silence, the secret silence, which he is not even aware of.

What if he were to be told *who I am?*

"Survive," Marcelle said. Hers was a lesson of cunning and courage. It has served well. Yet there is another courage that goes not with cunning but with truth.

"Richard," I shall say, "Richard, listen to me, there is something I must tell you—"

He is taking off his shoes. The room has gone pink in the lamplight. If I should speak those words, the peonies would explode into shredded petals on the floor and the lamps would shatter.

"I was thinking about that speech this afternoon," Richard says, taking off his shoes. "The fellow was eloquent, wasn't he? Must have had a fine education. In England, I imagine, on account of the accent. He was practically white, too. Must be hard for a person like that."

She thinks, Surely he had Père's nose, as Agnes said? Surely he looks a little bit like Francis?

Something dares her. Maybe she is losing her mind. But she walks to the edge of the precipice.

"Did you think he looked something like our family? My family?"

"Good God, no! What kind of an idea is that?"

"I thought maybe he did." It is like playing Russian roulette. Shall I? Shall I wait till morning or shall I never at all?

"You need to have your eyes examined." Richard yawns. "What are those two ridiculous dogs yapping at again?"

"The barn cats' prowling, I guess."

He calls the dogs upstairs. He strokes them and quiets them, then he gets into bed.

"That wind!" he complains. "I didn't know it could blow like that here."

"It's a northeast trade. I'll lower the windows a bit."

She gets up and stands for a moment looking northward to the Big Dipper.

"Eerie," she says, thinking aloud.

"What did you say? Eerie?"

"Yes. The way the night just drops down."

She goes back to bed. By his breathing she knows that Richard has fallen asleep at once. She is sorry for him because of what she must—might?—do to him in the morning. To him and all of them. If only there were some way of knowing what was right to do! It is this island that is at fault; one can't even think straight here!

The sad wind cries in the trees. She remembers these nights, the croak and peep and shrill of forest life, the sudden squeal of a small wild creature seized in bloody terror by some larger creature; all these have stayed with her except the sadness of the wind. She has forgotten how it blows all night off the Morne.

This will be a night without sleep. She does not even try to coax it. When morning flickers on the ceiling and birds rustle, she will be still awake. Perhaps, by that time, an answer will have been given her. She prays mercy for all who lie awake hoping for an answer by morning.

Perhaps, though, she dozes after all, or is so drowned in her trouble that it seems a sort of sleep. She starts up, aware of a change in the texture of the night. There is a sound of swishing under the wind rush. It is like footsteps in tall grass or tissue paper crackling lightly in a box. She thinks maybe Richard is making the sound, but he is lying quite still on his side in the other bed. A storm must be rising. She sinks back into crowding thoughts.

After a while she hears the roar of surf. That's odd, because the house is too far from the beach for surf to be heard. It puzzles her, but not too much. She is too tired. She turns again into herself.

Suddenly then, unmistakably, there is the salty tang of smoke. There is a new sound, a sizzle and snap as of meat frying and jumping in a pan. She gets out of bed and stands unsurely, dizzily, in the center of the room, trying to orient herself. Something is burning somewhere. Then all at once she understands. Jolted to panic, she rushes to the bedroom door and tears it open. A gust of incredible heat, like an eruption of the sun, flings her backward into the room. The entire hall and the stairway are blazing! Smoke flames into her lungs. With frantic force she tries to push the door shut, but the strength of the roaring heat is like the strength of a hundred men. She fights to breathe. Now the flames catapult into the room. They are taller than soldiers; they are an army advancing with their fearful weapons drawn. They catch the sheer curtains and the carpet; they reach for the ruffled shoulders of her nightdress and her long black hair. Her lungs are agony.

"Richard!" she screams.

Barely awake, he stumbles to the window, pushes the screen out and her out after it. There is a terrible mingling of cries in her ears, his as the sweeping fire sets him ablaze, and her own as she escapes it, to fall in fainting terror onto the net of the ancient boxwood hedge beneath the window.

❊{15}❊

Dr. Strand's private clinic lay on the outskirts of Covetown, above Government House. For fourteen hours Francis had been there, waiting. He had paced, attempted to read, and briefly, lightly, dozed. Now at midnight he stood at the window, looking down upon the harbor and the moving lights of cars.

The doctor came from across the hall with another report. "We're monitoring her pressure, Mr. Luther, and it's holding. She's fairly comfortable right now. The medication, you know."

Francis, wondering whether his confidence in the doctor was justified, nodded. The man had a good reputation and gray hair, which always bred a certain amount of confidence in the beholder.

"We've time yet to make the decision. Naturally, I'll avoid a cesarean section if I can."

One must have seen hundreds of cartoons and jokes about young husbands waiting outside delivery rooms. For some reason people found humor in the situation, God knew why, when in reality a man's head was plagued with doubts and questions. Some men must be torn with love of their wives and fear for them, while some would be praying first for the safe arrival of the child, though that was wrong, wrong, wrong . . .

"A good patient, plenty of courage," Dr. Strand was saying. "She wants this baby. No complaints, not a murmur out of her. A woman of pride."

"Yes, great pride."

But suppose this were Kate's child? Guilt ran hot and cold down his spine; his spine was naked, all of him was naked and exposed.

He hadn't been with Kate that often, a dozen times perhaps since Marjorie's pregnancy, not counting the time they had flown to a hotel in Barbados together. All night long the wind had rattled lightly in the palms. He'd got her a bouquet of gardenias—they grew almost wild down here—whose musky sweetness, reminding him of something, had kept him awake. It had reminded him of his father. Yes, yes. (*Don't tell your mother, son; I wouldn't hurt her for the world.*) And he hadn't hurt her. He hadn't walked out on his children, either. But then, his woman had not been Kate.

What do we ever know about anyone? he wondered now. I'd given up believing that my mother would ever come to St. Felice. For what subtle reasons, out of what fears she stayed away so long surely I never knew; maybe she herself never knew. His thoughts spun, driving, hurling him from Marjorie to Kate, back to his parents and to the child now struggling to be born. Oh, let it be safe and well, let it be a son who will be to me what my father and I never could be to each other!

He hadn't realized he was holding his head in his hands until the doctor touched him on the shoulder.

"You need a drink. If it weren't worth one's life out in the streets I'd go get you one."

At once he became alert. "What's happening? Have you heard?"

"Riots and demonstrations all over the island. A big tax protest over in Princess Mary parish. Somebody fired on the police, they fired back, and there were three killed, some wounded. More over at the south end too, I think. Anyway, Lord Frame expected this a week ago, it seems. There's a cruiser on the way from Bermuda with a detachment of troops. That'll straighten things out, if," the doctor finished glumly, "if they get here in time. Why don't you stretch out on the couch? I'll be back."

Francis lay down again. He was deeply tired. Far easier to labor in a field than to endure such pressure in the head and spirit! This could be disaster night, he thought, recalling old tales of rebellion, the night of the sword. Attempting to console himself, he reasoned that that sort of thing didn't fit the twentieth century, and was immediately aware of his own absurdity. Not fit the century of Hitler and Stalin?

He woke to the sound of rustling. In the lamplight, on the other side of the room, Lionel was reading. He moved his lips and strained his neck over the newspaper as a man does who is not accustomed to reading.

"Hello. Have you been here long?" Francis asked.

"Only a few minutes. I ran the gauntlet. The governor's declared martial law. The town's full of rioting drunks and scared merchants and planters who've rushed in from the country, afraid to be out there alone. Cade's Hotel is jammed. How's Marjorie doing?"

"We don't know yet. They'll probably have to operate. It's awfully good of you to be here, Lionel."

"That's all right. Family, after all. Besides, I happen to be fond of Marjorie."

"Well, she likes you, too."

I must be better at dissembling than I knew, Francis thought. He felt—he felt sly, in the presence of this bluff, bumbling man, having to hide his sometimes furious jealousy that the man had lived with Kate and "had" her. "Had." An antique, yet still expressive, use of that simple verb. Had. Possessed. Her dear flesh.

He became aware that Lionel was looking at him quizzically.

"Damned hard for you, Francis. May I say something frankly?"

"Yes, of course."

"I know about you and Kate. Don't ask me how. People find out things."

"I won't ask."

"That's what I meant by 'hard for you.'"

"Yes." And hearing his own laconic voice, like that of a stage Englishman, Francis thought, I don't know what else to say.

"If you had seen her first instead of—" Lionel began and stopped.

Instead of Marjorie? Oh, if only—! But it might not have made any difference if he had. Too young, without experience and so in awe of beauty, he had not been half the man he was now. And so the lovely, brief enchantment had simply slid away as imperceptibly as the change of seasons in a northern country.

"She would have been right for you," Lionel resumed. Not meaning to, he was twisting the knife. "What are you going to do?"

"Oh, God," Francis said and murmured, "We've a child now."

Lionel nodded. "Of course. And you don't want to smash Marjorie's world. Well, you can have it both ways, can't you? The family at Eleuthera and the little place in town. It's done all the time."

Kate had already offered that. Better than nothing, she'd said. But she ought to have more.

And he said so. "Kate deserves more. For that matter, so does Marjorie."

Lionel smiled. There was kindness and a certain amusement in the smile.

"You're really in a moral bind, aren't you, old man? I'm sorry for you. You know, I always have felt a little sorry for you, anyway. You take everything too seriously, too hard and heavy. I suppose you can't help it."

"I guess not."

"We both know I'm a rougher sort than you. I don't seem to feel about a lot of things the way you do. You suffer. To me you're a little soft in the head. Oh, I like you in spite of it, make no mistake! It's just that I think you'd be a whole lot better off if you stopped worrying about other people so much and looked out for yourself."

"Maybe you're right."

Words, words! You are what you are, and Francis could no more be Lionel than Lionel could be Francis. Still, he had looked out for himself that morning, hadn't he? Or perhaps it had not been on his own behalf that he had issued that defiant order to get the crop out; perhaps really it had been because he was now thinking of the child, of money and safety for his child. Already it made a difference. He hadn't yet seen its face, but it made a difference.

Lionel returned to the newspaper. And Francis sat on, straining for sounds from across the hall which might have meaning, but there were only passing footsteps, conveying nothing. He studied a row of "arty" photographs on the wall: horses knee-deep in pangola grass, which made him think of Kate; veranda columns casting shadows, as at Eleuthera; black children in a schoolyard, as at Gully, where he had first met Patrick . . .

The lights went out.

"Must have struck the power station," Lionel said. "They've already struck the phones, you know."

A nurse came in with a pair of oil lamps.

"There are fires all over the parish," she reported. "Our handyman just came in the back way and he says they've attacked the wireless station with stones and bottles, broken every window, smashed all the equipment."

They won't attack Eleuthera! Francis thought. They won't go after private homes. Besides, it's so far out of the way. He said aloud, "I had a hassle this morning." And he told Lionel what had happened earlier in the day. "I wish there was a phone, though. I'd like to find out what happened, whether they got any of the crop out."

Lionel shook his head. "You took a chance. Not that I blame you. Damned radical devils! So much for your fine friend Patrick, hey?"

"I don't know. I was mad as a hornet, but I've cooled off some. It's possible he really couldn't do anything, although I still think he could have bestirred himself a little for me."

"There you go, making excuses for everybody! Matter of fact, on my way here tonight somebody told me Courzon was out your way this afternoon giving a very inflammatory speech. Egging the crowd on to pillage and burn, he said."

Francis shook his head. "No. Impossible. That I won't believe."

Lionel shrugged.

"You don't have to stay here with me," Francis said considerately.

"It's safer here. Wouldn't dare go down into the streets now. Besides, where would I go? The hotel's full and so's the club."

The two men waited, one sleeping with his head back on the chair, the other wide awake, watching the maddening, slow advance of the hours. It was the longest night. The oil lamp flickered weakly. The silence was expectant; one awaited gunfire, and the crashing-in of doors, sounds that must surely explode in the next moment or two; one imagined also dreadful, perhaps final, things occurring in the room across the hall.

In the last hour of the night when, in spite of darkness, some subtle alteration of the atmosphere predicts the dawn, the doctor came back. He looked both weary and pleased to bring an announcement of importance.

"A natural birth. Hard, but we didn't need to operate, thank goodness. Come in and see them now."

Not yet out of ether, Marjorie lay with a look of peace on her lips, as if, in spite of her pains, she had gone under with a smile. Her hair curled on her temples as it always did when it was damp. She must have been soaked with the sweat of her struggle.

"She wanted this baby," Dr. Strand said, "and she fought for it."

Francis felt his tears collecting. "I'm so glad," he murmured foolishly. Or perhaps not foolishly: what else was there to feel but simple gladness? He smiled, for once not ashamed—he knew he cried too easily for a man from a northern culture—to let another man see his tears. He reached down and touched Marjorie's limp hand. She would be a good mother, too fussy, no doubt, as she always was, but a good mother, all the same.

"I'm so glad," he repeated.

"Don't you want to see the baby? She's down the hall."

"She? I thought you said—"

"I didn't say anything. You must have imagined it. Why, were you expecting a boy?"

"Well, I thought—" He stopped. He was as disappointed as a child who has been expecting a bicycle for his birthday and has been given a book.

"Sorry, but you've got a girl. A pretty one, with a cleft in her chin. Big, too, which was part of the trouble. Here, have a look."

She had her mother's dark hair, a whole head of it.

"Enough to tie a ribbon on," the nurse said.

Francis stammered. "Aren't they usually bald?"

"Usually." The doctor laughed. "I told you she was pretty. You'll have your hands full when she's sixteen."

"A girl," Francis said.

"She'll mean more to you than ten sons. Take my word for it. You'll come back and tell me so."

Well, true or not, she can't help it, he thought. And he reached down to touch the baby's hand, as he had the mother's. The scrap of a hand was warm to his touch. The fingers grasped his finger. Only a few minutes out of the womb, where it had been hanging upside down, a feeble creature floating in warm water, and here it was already making a demand of life! The fingers clung. He had the strangest feeling in his chest, in his throat. And he would not have pulled his hand away if the nurse hadn't put the baby back in the crib. . . .

In the waiting room Lionel looked up with a question.

"A girl," Francis told him. "And both well."

"Are they, then? Well, good luck, old man! And here's another good omen for you. Come and behold."

In three-quarter darkness the cruiser rounded proudly to port, lights glittering and gleaming from stem to stern. It seemed to fill the harbor with its authority.

"So," Lionel said, "that settles that. It's been a long night on both counts."

"Yes, both counts. Mother and baby," said Dr. Strand, who was literal.

"I meant," Lionel corrected him, "I meant the birth *and* our small revolt. In a few more hours, now that the troops are here, we'll have peace and order again, thank God."

"No, my friend, you haven't seen the end of this by any means," the doctor cautioned.

"You think not?"

"Oh, yes, for now, but this was only a skirmish. I'm looking ahead a few years. Yes, I'm looking ahead."

But Lionel was concerned with the immediate. "You're not starting home yet, Francis? Things can't be calmed down this soon."

"I want to get home and sleep. I could sleep for a week."

"Well, just be careful. It's been a long night, that's sure. Just be careful."

THE MORNING WAS almost still. In the mild breeze small ash puffs rose from a bed of cinders where the new wing had been. Only a few feet from the central portion of the house a miraculous and mighty rain had halted the fire.

"If only it had come sooner!" Osborne lamented. "We tried using the well, but the pump was too weak. And we couldn't stretch the hose from the river. We fought with buckets, we tried everything, Mr. Luther. My wife came out, and the maids and everybody. We almost killed ourselves trying."

"You did what you could," Francis said quietly.

"That fire went wild! I wouldn't believe it if I hadn't seen it myself. Of course, the wind was against us. That and the fresh paint. Thank God, though, the rain came, or we'd have lost the whole house."

Nothing, nothing was left of the new wing but some twists of metal—andirons or candelabra, perhaps.

"Terrible," Osborne said. "Terrible." He spoke with awe.

All that morning and all the day before people had been talking at Francis. Thinking to give comfort, they seemed compelled to talk.

"By God, I wish I knew how this happened, Mr. Luther! It was the only house on the island to be fired! Oh, some cane fields here and there went up, but that's to be expected at a time like this. We haven't seen a house burned, though, not since I was born and probably a time before that."

"No," Francis said. He had a pain in his chest. He wondered whether anyone as young as he could have a heart attack from grief. He couldn't afford to have a heart attack, leaving Marjorie with an infant in this chaos.

Osborne lowered his voice. "I keep asking myself, to be frank with you, whether it wasn't on account of the bananas. We got one load through the gates before the crowd could stop us. They were pretty mad, let me tell you! Still, I'd swear it wasn't any of our own people. Sure, they'd overturn a truck, but they wouldn't do a thing like this. There were a lot of gangs in town setting fires, you know, kids no more than fourteen years old, they tell me. Wild kids, slippery as eels. They'll never catch them."

For the first time in hours thought took shape in Francis' numbed brain.

"Not kids from town. Why would they come way out here to pick just my house? It doesn't make sense! No, it has to have been the strikers, Osborne, maybe not Eleuthera people, but hotheads from other villages. My uncle told me they'd been steamed up to pillage and burn. Why, there was a radical meeting right here in this parish, not two miles from our gates! I didn't believe him when he told me, but I do now. Because—here's the result."

Osborne did not comment. Instead, he held out his hand to catch a flurry of drops that had suddenly fallen out of the calm, bright sky. "Sun-shower," he said.

A rag had blown from the fire onto the grass. Scorched at the edges, the center still disclosed an arabesque of buds. Recognizing the fabric that Marjorie had had sent from New York, Francis bent to pick it up. How she had labored over her choices! The decoration of these new rooms had been the gladdest thing in her life here until her pregnancy.

He rubbed the cloth between his fingers. His father had died while that cloth flamed. A living torch, he had been extinguished among red and white Chinese peonies. Gone now were all the gaiety and kindness, the generosity and the foolish weakness; no one need fret or worry about him ever again. Bound and bandaged, his mother lay stunned into silence as if she had not yet assimilated the disaster, or as if she were remembering her own reluctance to come back here. It was only because of me that she came, Francis thought, over and over.

The sun-shower sprinkled his shoulders. For a long time he stood there crying in the warm, quiet rain.

❧{16}❧

In later years these events would be described by someone with a gift for imaginative language, someone, for instance, like Kate Tarbox, as a series of shock waves come and gone in a handful of days. There was, first, the shock of death, death of the innocent at Eleuthera, and then those killed in confrontations between police and citizens, along with one lone soldier from the cruiser, an ignorant lad shot by a wild bullet on his first trip out of England. But the greatest shock came from realizing the extent of anger, its depth, and the speed with which it could spread.

To be sure, the cruiser stood firm guard in the harbor. Order was restored. Shattered glass was cleared away and people went back to work. Passing on the roads and in the streets they gave greeting again as before; yet one had to wonder what rages and resentments still burned beneath the greeting.

All this passed outside of Francis' awareness. Beclouded, he moved through required hours and places. From the memorial service—that is to say, the funeral without the body of the dead—he went to the hospital. There Marjorie, half hysterical with fear and horror, alternately trembled, wept, and consoled herself with her new baby. There, down the hall, his mother, winning a valiant struggle for acceptance and control, recovered from burn and shock. Most of the time he sat at home in the cocoon of his library, staring at grief, which seemed to hover just beyond the window like some threatening, faceless dervish in whirling robes, waiting to descend and clutch.

He was sitting there like that when Kate came in.

"Oh, my darling," she said.

He put his head on her breast. Her fingers moved in his hair.

"Oh, my darling, what can I do for you?"

"Just stay here. Be with me."

"Yes, yes. I am. I will."

Opening his eyes, he saw the little rise and fall of her breast. Her neck and upper arms were scarlet.

"You're sunburned," he murmured.

"I was weeding. I should have worn a jacket."

He raised his head, reproaching. "You're so tired. You don't take care of yourself."

"It's just that I haven't slept. How could I sleep when all this was happening to you?"

Her eyes were troubled. Darkened, they were almost violet, a morbid color, color of pain.

"You love me," he said, as if the discovery were new. "You love me."

She swallowed hard. He could see the small lump move in her throat.

He had never been so near to another human being in all his life, so near that the very blood in their veins seemed to run together. And suddenly desire, which had been the farthest from his mind during these last hours, tore him into its current.

He got up and drew the curtains shut, making a wall of rippling green. The room, now dimmed, assumed an aqueous coolness, a forest coolness.

"Lie down," he said. "Take your dress off."

"Now? In here?"

"It's all right. I can lock the door."

Elsewhere in the house he would not have taken her. Some subtlety of judgment, some refinement of choice, would not allow him to do this thing in any room that had been adorned by Marjorie, in which her presence remained as though she herself were standing in it. He could not have done that to Marjorie, to Kate—or to himself. But this room belonged to him alone and there was no one here except himself, with Kate.

In her now he found all comfort and all healing.

Afterwards they lay quietly, not speaking. Slowly, the ceiling turned from white to luminous gray.

"It's getting late," she said. She sat up and put on her dress, then pulled the curtains back so that light slid across the floor.

Francis looked out the window. The whirling specter was gone; no threat was there, only the afternoon lying placidly among the trees.

"Did you know—could you have known—how I needed you?" he asked.

A smile began as a tender curving at the corners of her mouth and almost as quickly stopped. Her face fell into sadness.

"What is it?" he cried.

Her reply was so low that he barely heard her. "Suddenly I feel guilty. I don't know why. I've not felt that way before. It's this house, I suppose. Being here like this in her house."

It angered him that any shame should blight them, yet he didn't know what to say.

"Do you—don't you feel what I mean, Francis?"

"I don't know. I suppose I should. I don't know."

He unlocked the door and poured a drink from the bar in the cabinet.

"Have one? It'll steady you."

"No, thanks. Tell me about the baby, please." She had begun to steady herself.

At once laughter tingled in his throat. "She's pretty. . . . Funny how I wanted a boy. Maybe men always do? But now I don't mind at all. Her name's Megan. It's Welsh. Her mother's people were Welsh."

"I'd like to give her a wonderful present. May I?"

"Of course you may! Why do you ask? Why shouldn't you?"

"I don't know. I thought maybe, in the circumstances, it might not be—"

The laughter left him. "Oh Kate, Kate my love, why can't things ever be clean and clear and easy? Everything's such a goddamned tangle!"

"But we'll manage, won't we?"

"I've done this to you. I've complicated your life."

"No. You've brought life into my life. I'm sorry I felt grim there for a minute. I won't let it happen again. One has to—to take charge." And, jingling her car keys, she told him, "The first thing I'm going to do is buy Megan's present. The next thing—oh, I hate to pile another trouble on you, I wasn't even going to mention it, but I've no one else to ask, at least not until Nicholas Mebane gets back, and that won't be till tomorrow night, and it would be a shame to wait that long—"

"What are you talking about?"

Kate sat down again. "They arrested Patrick this morning."

Francis' heart jumped a beat.

"Can you imagine anything so idiotic, so criminal? Some utter ass must have decided to cast a net out for anyone and everyone who's ever opened his mouth to express an opinion! 'Incitement to riot!' Patrick of all people!"

He wet his lips. "What did you want of me?"

"Bail money. I'm awfully short or I'd never come bothering you with all you've got on your mind. I just hate to see a man like Patrick spend a night locked up, that's all."

He couldn't believe what he was hearing. And he tried to speak without betraying outrage.

"For my part they can hang him tonight," he said in a flat voice.

Kate stared. "You can't mean that?"

"My father was burned alive in my house, and my mother escaped by the grace of a miracle; you ask me whether I mean it?"

"It wasn't Patrick's doing, Francis! For God's sake, you don't think he crept out here that night and put a torch to your house, do you?"

"His were the brains behind the hands that did it. You can't tell me otherwise."

"I sure as hell can tell you! And I sure as hell will!" Kate's indignation crackled.

"He is not the man we thought he was. Open your eyes—"

"Maybe not the man *you* thought, but—"

"He could have helped me save my crop! At least he could have made an attempt. But he refused. And after that went about giving inflammatory speeches right at my doorstep. He knew the temper of the people, but instead of protecting me, his friend, he whipped them up—"

"Inflammatory speeches! He couldn't give one if he tried! He wouldn't know how to inflame anyone, he talks way over most people's heads, like a schoolteacher. If he ever wants to go into politics he'll have to learn to do better, let me tell you."

"He did well enough, apparently. Lionel told me—"

"Lionel!" Kate's scorn was hot. "Oh, *now* I see the connection! So it's Lionel who put his words in at Covetown, he's the one who's responsible! So he's turned out to be a rotten informer—I really never thought he'd stoop *that* low, no, I didn't!" She got up, snapping and unsnapping the clasp of her purse. "Francis, listen to me. Listen to me. To me; not Lionel!"

He didn't hear her. He was hearing, instead, Patrick Courzon's cool voice: "You're too feudal for these times." He was hearing Osborne's lament: "We did all we could, Mr. Luther." He was standing in mournful rain looking at cinders where his proud house had been.

"Bastard!" he cried. "Dirty, arrogant, ungrateful bastard! And you actually came here to plead for him! Is that why you came? Not to be with me, but because you were thinking of him?"

She was dismayed. "You don't mean that. You know I came for you! But I did think I could also ask you to help one of the best human beings you or I will ever know. I certainly didn't dream you had any crazy idea like this in your head."

"Crazy? It's one thing to have understanding, Kate, to be compassionate, to be"—in the turbulence of his anger he stammered—"to be *liberal,* but you carry it too far; you'll excuse anything in one of your underdog protégés. Arson. Murder. Anything!"

She put a hand on his arm. "Francis. Please. You're not talking sense. Don't fight with me. This is us, Francis and Kate."

"No, Kate. You can't get around me that way. I've had a blow between the eyes. Life doesn't hand out many blows like the one I've had this week," he said bitterly.

"Don't you suppose I know that? But we're talking about two different things."

"We're not. It's the same thing. You're making a hero out of someone who's partially responsible for what I've suffered. That hurts me, Kate. I can't forgive it."

She withdrew her hand. Neither of them spoke for a minute or two. Sounds of awakening activity, a slammed door and voices from the kitchen wing, announced that the afternoon was late and time was hurrying.

"I would like to talk reasonably to you," Kate said at last.

"I'll talk reasonably. But first you have to be loyal to me," he said quietly.

"Even if it means stabbing a friend in the back? An innocent friend?"

"He's not innocent. That's the whole point."

"But if I think he is?"

Her very stance was stubborn, her proud head and shoulders defied him. More now than in her first flaring anger he felt the force of her will.

"You've built a stone wall," he said, with a tired gesture. "I can't get through to you."

"There's a wide door in that wall. It's your narrow-minded prejudice that won't let you open it."

"Prejudice! What the hell are you talking about? You know very well I'm not prejudiced."

"You don't think you are, but you are, Francis. Suddenly I see it. You were enraged that Patrick Courzon, a mere native, could refuse you, when he ought to be so grateful for your attentions that he'd turn himself inside out for you. And that's the real reason why you're blaming him."

He was exhausted, wounded, and baffled. That she could turn on him like this! That she could fail to comprehend what was so plain! Enraged, he went to the attack.

"You're a blind fool, Kate. A fool and a fanatic. I hate to tell you, but maybe Lionel does see you clearly, after all. Certainly he's known you longer and better than I have."

"That's a filthy thing to say! Damn you, Francis!" Her eyes threatened rage. "If you can say a thing like that, we have nothing in common. I don't want to cheapen myself, or I'd slam my fist into your mouth for saying that."

"Perhaps," he said, "perhaps you'd better leave. We're not on the same side, are we?"

She went to the door. "God knows I'm not on your side! And God help me, I never want to be!"

He heard her heels clack furiously down the hall, heard the door close and then the sound of the car starting down the drive. The sofa pillows were disarranged where they had lain together. Thoughtfully, he put them back in place. Everything had happened so quickly, all that enthralling beauty, that sweet ravishment, turned into this sick churning in the pit of him!

The one time, the only time he'd needed her total devotion, in the greatest crisis of his life, she'd drawn back, withholding a part of herself to give to the very man who had hurt him the most! So he hadn't known her, after all, had he? Nor had she known him.

We are ensnared and beguiled.

You are singing to yourself in your car on a fair day; you are at the pinnacle of health, but around a curve, on the other side of a hill, a moment later you are crippled and ruined in a heap of crumpled metal. Or you are talking to a friendly stranger in some pleasant place; you are laughing, having a drink together, but a moment later his face turns mad and he points a gun at you. That's the way it happens.

He went inside and took a shower and then, because he still felt dirty, took another. A supper had been prepared for him, but he was unable to swallow it. Brandy went down more easily. He had never drunk very much, but he took the bottle into his bedroom, wanting numbness, wanting forgetfulness, and kept on drinking. There was a whirling in his head. Fire soared and glass crashed; black men hurled murderous rocks and Patrick Courzon sneered; Kate's mouth twisted with contempt; Marjorie withered on a hospital bed; his parents screamed for help; his mother's bruised eyes grieved. All whirled as the walls spun, until at last came vicious nausea, then exhaustion, and finally, sleep.

PATRICK COURZON WAS released, of course, along with all the union leaders. Only those who had committed violence were sentenced. The magistrate, an Englishman in a white wig, facing a series of black barristers in the same white wigs, made a graceful little speech about freedom of speech and the right to strike. The centuries-old system of justice, transplanted from the foggy north to the dripping heat and fly-buzz of the Covetown courtroom, worked.

The strike had not been altogether a failure, either. Some two weeks after it had been put down, the planters met and agreed to improve the wage scale by fifteen percent, which was almost, but not quite, what the workers had asked for in the first place.

IRONICALLY, THE TWO people who could most nearly relate themselves to Francis' emotions were Lionel and Marjorie.

Even Father Baker could offer only platitudes in the form of kindly counsel. "I know it's unspeakable for you, Francis. But hatred corrupts the soul. For your own sake you must try to conquer it. Especially since we don't really know who the guilty ones are."

Putting in a roundabout plea for Courzon! And Francis gave cold dismissal: "I know perfectly well who they are, Father."

Nicolas Mebane offered an alibi and self-exoneration with his condolences. Almost at once upon arriving back in St. Felice, he had come hurrying to Eleuthera, bearing in hand a splendid silver bowl engraved with Megan's name, from Da Cunha's collection.

"I can't tell you how much I regret not having been home when this tragedy— when all this mess—occurred." His mobile face bore a solemn dignity. "Perhaps I shouldn't say it, but, well, I almost believe it wouldn't have happened if I'd been here."

"Then you agree with me? You're putting the blame where I put it?"

Mebane said delicately, "It's difficult. . . . I find myself between a rock and a hard place, as my father liked to say. Maybe I would have been able to get your crop out without upsetting any applecarts, or rather, banana carts." He smiled. "Then again, maybe I wouldn't. It all comes down to knowing how to handle people, doesn't it? That's the true art of politics, knowing when to give in and when to demand. It's never, never easy."

The true art of politics was also double-talk and evasion. Francis felt a slight impatience.

"I know that," he said.

"Personally, I don't think I would have permitted that speech so close to your gates. Still, having the utmost sympathy with your position—if I were in your place I would certainly feel the same—you'll understand, I hope, that I must make other considerations, too. Patrick and I are closely involved. I have spoken to him, I shall speak to him—"

"Not necessary," Francis interrupted. "What's done is done. So you needn't upset your own applecart on my account."

"The art of politics," Mebane repeated, "is the art of compromise. And judgment, always judgment! I'm afraid my friend Patrick still needs to learn that." He sighed. "I sometimes feel I'm walking a tightrope, Francis. I have the organization, building and building with a great public good in mind. So I must keep the balance there. Yet the last thing I want is to lose your friendship over this."

"It's all right," Francis said. "My opinion of Mr. Courzon and your opinion of him need not influence our opinion of each other. It's all right."

"I'm wonderfully relieved to hear that." Mebane rose. "I can't tell you how much. Perhaps some day all this will straighten out. Who knows?" He added quickly, "But the important thing is that you and I are in a sense allied. We're both concerned with the future of this island, you as a producer, I, it's to be hoped, in government. And I think we understand each other."

Francis bowed his head in acknowledgment. "You will have my support when the time comes."

He meant it. Regardless of the double-talk—he was, after all, a politician!—Mebane was reasonable and decent, a practical man. One could talk to him. One had to respect him.

"If there is ever anything you need and I can do," Mebane said quietly, "you know where I am." His brown hand shook Francis' hand, his heavy gold ring bruising Francis' knuckles. "Your mother is coming along nicely, I'm glad to hear."

"Thank God, yes. I'm putting her on the plane to go home tomorrow."

"A stalwart lady. Give her my best, won't you? And the same to your wife. And the new young lady, by all means," he added in parting.

THAT WAS NICHOLAS Mebane. See what he brought for Megan." Francis placed the bowl on the bed, where Marjorie sat propped against white lace pillows.

"Oh, gorgeous! Handmade Danish silver, Francis!" Marjorie's fingers slid around the bowl, moving carefully with the grain. She turned it upside down. "Yes, of course, look at the stamp. Danish."

"Very generous. Overly generous." Expensive presents made him uncomfortable. A holdover, probably, from his father's careless taste for luxury.

"Why not? He's terribly rich, everyone says. Anyway, I really do like Nicholas. I always have. And that Doris of his. One feels sorry for a girl as clever and good-looking as she is, having that handicap. Being black, I mean. So you see, I'm not the disgusting bigot you always thought I was, Francis. I just never liked Patrick, that's all. I saw him as a fuzzy-minded troublemaker from the start, you know I did. And I was right, wasn't I?" she finished triumphantly.

He didn't answer. God knew he couldn't feel her sense of satisfaction! Disillusioned both in a friend and a lover, he could hardly find cause for rejoicing. He was a man who had misread directions and strayed into a wilderness. He had been wrong; he had been wronged. It had all moved so fast! Bewildered, he tried to reconstruct events, but the pattern of events was overlaid by the red blur of anger: Kate's, Patrick's, and his own.

A terrible sense of loss overwhelmed him suddenly, so that his eyes stung with burgeoning tears, and to hide his grief, he bent to pat and rearrange Marjorie's fluffy pillows.

"You look absolutely done in. It's been so awful for you," Marjorie said softly. "There's only one thing that could be worse: to lose one's child."

He was grateful to her, grateful at this moment for any human touch, any gentle word. Yes, in a pinch, in this pinch, he had to admit, she had been there when he needed her. Dependable and sensible, she had measured up, even calming her own first hysterical demands to leave the island, even accepting at last his reassurances, his determination not to be driven away. Call it a sense of duty or propriety, call it a rigid code of outmoded behavior, call it what you would, he was grateful for it.

Now he must measure up, too, must pull himself together.

"Yes," he said, thinking aloud, "yes, you remember what my father said? 'Look out for number one. That's the first commandment,' he said. Number one being, in our case, three-in-one."

"Elementary, I should think."

"Not what they teach in Sunday school, though. Well, I'll start in on that Monday, my dear. I've a lot to make up for on account of that crop we lost. Miss Megan needs new shoes."

Marjorie laughed. "Isn't she the cutest thing, Francis?"

"I think she has the Francis nose."

"Nothing wrong with that." Marjorie yawned and stretched.

He could not remember when he had seen her so happy, so expansive, so *soft*. Maybe things would be different now. Maybe, through some miracle, newness and youth would come surging back. That other business, that other woman, had probably been just an aberration, common enough, Lord knew. The man who didn't have such aberrations was the oddball, really.

"Oh, I'm sleepy," Marjorie said luxuriously.

"Take a nap. Want a cold drink or anything?"

"Later, thanks. Some lemonade in an hour or so. You are good to me, Francis."

"A woman who can produce a baby like ours deserves the best," he answered lightly.

Contentment felt warm in him as he went out and softly closed the door. It was only when he was halfway down the stairs that he remembered, queerly enough, that they hadn't kissed each other once since he had brought Marjorie home.

THE BABY WAS in a cradle on the veranda. Francis was watching her while the nurse went indoors, when a car came to a halt on the gravel drive and Patrick Courzon came up the walk.

"I've come as soon as I could," he began. "Kate's told me things. I had to talk to you."

Francis did not invite him to sit down. Instead he himself got up and stood leaning against a pillar. "There's nothing to talk about," he said.

"Francis, I was sick when I heard what happened here."

Sick, was he, standing there with his bland condolences?

"Were you?" he said dryly.

"Kate says you're blaming me. And blaming her because of me. She says—"

"I don't want to hear what she says."

"It isn't fair not to give me a chance to talk."

"You're scarcely one to talk about fairness."

A flush, red bronze, mounted in the troubled pale brown cheeks. One could almost feel sorry for the poor bastard! But no, no! And Francis glanced at his baby, who had made a small sound in its cradle. If she had come a week sooner into the world, she too would have perished in choking smoke. And he felt again that awful outrage, that first sickness at the pit of his stomach.

"One doesn't just throw away relationships—" Courzon began.

"Don't tell me what 'one' does or doesn't do!"

"I'm only asking for a chance to straighten out the confusion in your mind."

The arrogance of the man! Having identified himself—and Kate, too, yes, she too—with the scum who had literally brought his house down about his head, to dare to speak of "confusion" in *his* mind! To dare!

"I've told you I have nothing to say to you. You're lucky I'm managing to keep my temper at all. I advise you to leave me alone."

"I'm sorry to hear that, Francis."

"Yes. Well. You had better go. You're not welcome here."

For long minutes he sat watching the dust that had spurted as Patrick gunned his car. He sat there until the dust had settled. His eyes moved across the drive to the fields where his sleek white Brahmans had gone into their afternoon rest. Far down on the left there gleamed a sliver of beach and an angle of glitter where the sun struck the sea. Behind the house the hill rose in tiers, green on green, bananas and palms and varied groves, on upward to the Morne's peak wrapped now in cotton cloud. His kingdom, his benevolent small kingdom! Let storms roar outside, let the social rats race and the politicians moil; here, in this kingdom, peace and a reasonable plenty would continue, if he had anything to do with it.

And unconsciously he stretched out his right arm, flexing the muscles. He looked down again at the sleeping baby. No one, no one, by God, should disturb her peace!

"Scum! Wretched scum!" he cried, so loud that the baby's eyelids trembled.

And contritely, tenderly, he bent to adjust by a hairbreadth the soft, white coverlet.

❧{17}❧

Within three or four months Megan turned into a pretty child with remarkably fine dark blue eyes. They were both, Francis and Marjorie, a little bit crazy about her. But then, as everyone kindly remarked, it was only natural: they had waited so long and known so much disappointment before she finally came.

Francis kept saying that she had the family nose. He took a certain pleasure in that. Apparently it was a dominant characteristic; you couldn't breed it out. However, it was an attractive feature, giving a kind of pride to an adult face.

Marjorie ordered Megan's dresses from France, via Da Cunha's. From an expensive store in New York, via its catalog, came a marvelous pinto rocking horse the size of a small pony, a swing apparatus for the lawn, a dollhouse, and enough books to occupy the child to the age of ten. Yes, they were a little bit crazy and they knew it and they delighted in it.

She was almost two years old before they knew quite positively, or were forced to accept as a fact, that Megan was retarded.

Of course they resisted the knowledge as long as they could. An undesirable visitor knocks at the door and you do not open it; but when the knocking persists and the undesirable *will not* go away, the moment arrives when at last you open the door. So it happened to Marjorie and Francis.

At six months the baby didn't roll over. At nine months she didn't sit up or attempt to crawl, or say "mama" or laugh aloud. At one year she didn't even try to stand.

A woman at the club, one day when all the babies were playing in the wading pool, remarked quite seriously in Marjorie's hearing, "I can't imagine why they don't do something about that child. Look at her! She's just lying there like a vegetable!"

Megan was reclining in her stroller, content to do nothing. Her fair hair curled in the afternoon heat, which had flushed her face quite charmingly pink.

Alarmed and angry Marjorie reported to Francis what she had overheard.

"Some children are slower than others," he said. "It doesn't mean a thing. Haven't you read that Einstein didn't talk till he was three?" But with the thought of his sister Margaret, a terrible fear slid like cold slime down his back. And at the same time he knew that the fear had come quivering more than once during the last few months, had quivered and been put away.

"Maggie's had seven children and she'd certainly have noticed if there were anything wrong, wouldn't she?" Maggie was an upstairs maid who sometimes took care of Megan.

"I should think so. And certainly the doctor would have said something." He tried to reassure himself.

But certainly the doctor had said nothing, at least until they questioned him.

"I have had my thoughts about the baby," he admitted. "I've had them for quite a while."

Furiously, Francis attacked. "What do you mean? What thoughts? And why the secrecy?"

"To begin with, one wants to be sure. Children don't all mature according to textbook schedules. I didn't want to alarm you until it was necessary." An old man, and tired, he leaned back abruptly so that his chair squeaked into the waiting silence. "As a matter of fact, I don't want to *alarm* you at all, but I did intend to mention it at the next visit."

"It? It?" demanded Francis.

"A degree of retardation. What degree, I don't know."

Marjorie made a sound between a gasp and a cry. And Francis, flung back to the memory of Margaret, could not look at his wife.

"There's nothing actually to be done, anyway," the doctor said kindly, "except to watch developments. And to be patient and loving, which I know you are."

They knew then, that evil day, they knew. Yet they struggled to reject the knowledge. By the time they reached the gates of home they had made a hopeful decision.

"He's too old," Marjorie said, having wiped her first tears away. "He probably hasn't learned a new fact since he left medical school. We'll have to take Megan to someone at home."

"Home" was Boston and Baltimore and Philadelphia and New York. With each repetition of the story they lost a year of their youth.

"Don't tell them about your sister," Marjorie said. "It might prejudice their thinking. Let them evaluate Megan without prior judgments."

It was the first time she had spoken of his sister. That would be according to her code of good sportsmanship and courage: having married him with her eyes open, it would fit her ill to accuse him now. He looked at her with a certain awe. Sportsmanship! This was, after all, no tennis match! And he thought his guilt must be visible to the world, an affliction spread like leprous sores from head to foot.

"The IQ, as we all know," the experts told them, "is certainly not the perfect measurement. Yet some measuring stick is needed. So we say that roughly between fifty and seventy-five gives us mild retardation. Such people we call educable. They can learn to do simple, repetitive tasks and support themselves. Between thirty-five and fifty we call trainable, that is, they can care for themselves physically and—"

Marjorie interrupted once. "I've always read that most of the retarded come from homes where they're unwanted in the first place. Nobody reads to them or talks to them, there's no stimulation." She finished bitterly, "You couldn't possibly apply that to us."

"All true. However, there are many other genetically determined factors. Disorders of protein metabolism, chromosomal abnormalities—Not simple."

"So what do we do now, Doctor?"

"Take her home. Be gentle and encouraging. You'll need to spend time, teaching as much as she can accept. Later you'll see how far she can progress in school or whether she can go to a conventional school at all. It's too early to tell."

In the end, then, they learned no more from the authorities than the old man had told them in Covetown.

Before going back they paid a last visit to Francis' mother, who lived alone now with Margaret. His sister Louise was there with her two toddlers, both of whom, Francis noted, were active and well.

"I'm glad you came," Margaret said, with her gentle, foolish smile. She had grown strong and fat. Her stockings sagged and her nose was running. Francis wiped it.

Teresa was ashamed. "It's hard to watch every little thing," she murmured, almost defensively.

"Of course it is."

When Teresa had left the room for a moment, Louise said, "Margaret takes up her whole day. It's almost more than she can handle." Margaret had gone into the kitchen. "At the cake box again! The doctor says she shouldn't eat so much, or she'll be monstrous in a few years. But if you don't let her, she cries and screams worse than my babies do. The older she gets, the worse her temper gets. I don't know how Mother stands it."

Marjorie was staring somberly at the wall and Francis had no answer.

"Of course, a home is really the solution, but Mother won't hear a word of it. Mothers don't give up their children, she says. She has such a *conscience* about it! You know how she is."

"Yes," Francis said, "I know how she is."

They left Teresa's house with their future clear in their understanding at last. All the way back to St. Felice, a menace rode with them through the summer sky, muting their voices and breaking their hearts, while it darkened the sunny head of the child on their laps.

ONE MUST NEVER subordinate one's life to another's. That had been given on good authority and they both knew it. Nevertheless, they did it, for theory is one thing and practice is another. Emotion, of course, is still another.

It was a saving grace that they should both be of one mind. They had no need, even, to put their determination into words.

"How is she?" he would ask on coming into the house.

Or else he would have no need to ask, for Marjorie would be waiting in the hall.

"She picked up her cup by herself today."

And he would hasten to watch Megan repeat the achievement.

They did not bicker nearly as much as they had before. It was as if they had no more energy for it, or rather as if these things which had irritated them once were without importance now.

He was so bitterly sorry for Marjorie! It was his fault. Because of Margaret he ought to have taken thought; if she had married someone else, she would not have known this grief! And he felt more stricken because she did not blame him.

But sometimes he felt a curious *flatness,* as if there were nothing left to feel. It was as if he were a plow beast, stubbornly, with patient acceptance, pulling a load. Megan was the load. The sustenance he must provide for her was the load. The load was just something waiting when he rose in the morning to be put aside again when, tiredly, he went to bed.

The plow beast wore blinders. The events of the world beyond his toil were of no interest to him. When he read the papers with their news of endless conflict, both on the little island and the world abroad, he was not touched. He had had enough of all that, enough and too much. It was a relief not to care, not to feel passionate anger about anything or with anyone.

A relief not to feel passionate love, either, with all its honeyed anguish and suspense! You could, after all, live very well without it. You could simply take sex whenever you were hungry for it, just as you simply ate your meals without ado; one didn't need ravenous anticipation to take one's nourishment at table. So it was in bed. The child woke often in the night, crying for attention, and Marjorie had moved into the room down the hall to be closer to her. But he could go to Marjorie whenever he needed to, which was less often than he would have thought possible.

For some reason, then, he remembered the Indian summers he had known in the north; there'd been such fragrance in the air, such tranquil skies and shimmering trees. But it had been a time of withering, for all that.

It had not yet occurred to him that he was too young for Indian summer.

BOOK FOUR

ENEMIES AND FRIENDS

❖{18}❖

"We've asked for full and final independence now," said Nicholas Mebane, coming to the end of his remarks, "and when I return from the constitutional conference in London I shall have it in my hand. Or rather," he smiled, correcting himself, "we shall have it in our hands."

There was a burst of clapping, followed by a buzz of many conversations. Patrick looked around the office, which was now much expanded. The banner still hung on the wall of Nicholas's handsome room, but now across the hall lay a row of smaller rooms from which the rapid clack of typewriters was heard. Everything bore the mark and promise of prosperity. Union leaders, old and young, were all here this morning except for Clarence, who had not roused himself from peaceful retirement to come along. There were three white business-men, as well as the leaders of the black community, doctors, lawyers, and civil servants, representing the wealth and education of the race.

There sat young Franklin Parrish, just returned from London with a Gray's Inn law degree; his black, vivid face, on which was drawn, Patrick thought, a slight, possible trace of the Indian, was both keen and open. Surely a young man one would choose for one's daughter!

"The structure is ready for transfer," Nicholas was saying. "We have to admit we've learned a good deal from the British. The art of government is no small art."

Kate Tarbox stood and spoke earnestly. "I should like to say something. We are very small and I hope independence won't cause an inward turning. We need to look out on the world. We have all these links now, air service and radio. The Caribbean has been having its own small renaissance in music and writing and art. We've had exchange students and joint research in tropical agriculture. None of these things must be allowed to die when we become independent." With slight self-consciousness and a pretty flush, she sat down.

Nicholas applauded the little speech. "There speaks the power of the press! The *Trumpet* can do most to keep things alive, Kate, as you have done, and are doing so splendidly. The power of the press!" he repeated, "and of women!" And smiling, he nodded easily toward the next raised hand.

"You'll get nowhere with anything if you don't tackle unemployment." This came from a union man. "Since the mechanical loader was introduced in 1961 we've lost four hundred jobs in the cane fields alone."

Nicholas assented. "I'm familiar with that, although not as familiar as I should be and intend to become. My thought has always been that we ought to lessen our dependence on export crops and raise our standards of scientific agriculture. Our educators ought to get a handle on that." He turned to Patrick. "When I'm elected, and I will be elected, I intend to make you my minister of education. There will have to be a strong tie-in between education and labor problems. It will have to be worked out most carefully, and obviously I'm not prepared to do that this morning, or even tomorrow morning."

A white man, Elliot Bates, the banker, spoke. "One sees here the interdependence of all elements. To modernize agriculture you will need investment capital. I'd advise you to do nothing to discourage it. Just a reminder," he finished pleasantly.

Nicholas's reply was smooth. "We will surely not discourage anyone who can help us build the good life, Mr. Bates. Rest assured." He stood up. "Now I think we've had enough for one morning. Thank you all for coming."

Patrick and Nicholas went downstairs together.

"That was masterful," Patrick said with admiration. "You had all those different elements working as one. I could almost feel the gathering momentum."

"I love the challenge," Nicholas said frankly. "But let me tell you, the going won't stay this smooth unless we get some money. Plenty of money. Not just for the campaign, I mean, but support for the kind of projects everybody wants. As Elliot Bates said, we need investment capital. You need capital to build a damned chicken coop, for God's sake." They walked on down Wharf Street. "You may not want to hear this, but I was at Eleuthera over the weekend, talking to Francis."

"He let you in?"

Nicholas laughed. "I won't scold you for the sarcasm. Yes, he always lets me in; you know that. We have a very cordial relationship."

Patrick did not comment.

"I really need him on our side," Nicholas said.

"The planters all wear blinders." He could hear the bitterness in his voice and, disliking himself for it, tried to elevate his tone to one more matter-of-fact. "They prefer to believe independence isn't coming. Ignore it and it will go away."

"No, they know better. Anyway, Francis is different. There's a chink in his armor, a softness inside. And he's a tie with his class, don't forget. They're going to vote and I want him to help persuade them to vote for our side."

What I am feeling, Patrick thought, is jealousy, pure and simple. They never knew each other before I brought them together.

He said, "They'll vote for us. The other side's splintered, ineffectual, and they know it."

"I agree. Still, one should take nothing for granted. . . . He said he doesn't want to be involved in politics, although he did give me a nice donation. Maybe it was to get rid of me." Nicholas laughed again, with the confidence of a man who knows things are going his way. "Seriously, Patrick, it's a shame about you and him. A failure of communication, all the way round. I've told him so, too. I manage to mention it every now and then."

"Yes?"

"No soap! He thinks you're a rabble-rouser. He thinks Kate is, too."

He wanted Nicholas to drop the subject at the same time that he wanted to hear more. It crossed his mind that this was like wincing at an accident while being drawn to look.

"Pity about him and her, too. Oh, don't tell me you didn't know!"

Patrick's lips closed.

"Loyal in spite of betrayal?" Nicholas touched Patrick's arm. "Sorry, I wasn't mocking. Don't be hurt. You know I respect your standards. I respected them when we were twelve. But the fact is, news gets around this town and an awful lot of people besides you know about Kate and Francis. Or knew. Marjorie Luther seems to be one who didn't, though."

"Well, that's a mercy," Patrick said dryly.

"It really is. I don't like the woman much; Snow Maiden types aren't to my taste, although I must say she's perfectly friendly to me. And one does have to have a heart, after all. It's pathetic, the two of them are so wrapped up in the child. Must be hellish to bring something like that into the world and know you'll have to live with it the rest of your life. Ah, there's my wife now."

Waiting at the curb, behind the wheel of a European sports car, sat Doris Mebane. A row of bracelets slid down her arm as she raised it to wave.

"Patrick! Changed your mind, I hope?"

For a moment, after the last few minutes of agitating reminders, he could not bring his thoughts into focus. Then he understood.

"About Europe, you mean?"

"She would love it, Patrick! Oh, she's dying to go!"

"You would be doing me a great favor," Nicholas said. "I'll be busy with the conference in London, as you know, and I promised Doris two weeks in France while I'm working. I hate to have her go alone. Désirée would be company for her. And it wouldn't cost you a thing," he added gently.

"I know, and I appreciate the offer, believe me I do. A man doesn't have many friends like you two in a lifetime. Oh, it's hard to explain," he struggled, not wanting to seem ungrateful. "But every family's different, and I just don't see it working out for us right now. Some other time, maybe. And I'd appreciate it if you wouldn't talk about it to Désirée anymore."

"Well, it's up to you, of course," Doris said coolly. Patrick saw that she was aggrieved. "As you said, some other time. Want a lift anywhere?"

"Thanks, no. I'll walk. Need the exercise."

Selfish of him, he thought, going on toward home. But some instinct, and rightly or wrongly he trusted instinct, told him it would be a mistake for his wife to go. She was already drugged on beauty. The beauty of the natural world attracted her, but the charm of expensive objects enchanted her. And Doris would be buying her way through France. It wouldn't be fair or wise to tempt Désirée with things she couldn't own and never would own. This was his one reservation about the friendship between the two wives, a friendship for which, otherwise, he would have been totally thankful.

He passed Da Cunha's, where in the window there stood, as it had for several weeks past, a handsome five-branched silver candelabrum. Several times Désirée had casually pointed it out. He wished he could give it to her. Probably she couldn't help desiring such things any more than he could help wanting books, or someone else wanting music or women or drink.

Lovely Désirée! Again he marveled, again he wondered, at the peculiar chemistry which draws us one to another. Her blackness? As expiation for a subconscious pull toward whiteness? Ah, you analyze yourself too much, Patrick! He knew he did; he had been told he did. By whom? By Francis? Or had it been Kate? Funny how sometimes he confused the two of them in his mind and memory, even though the one had been removed from his life.

He went by the library and the courthouse. Just beyond lay Boys' Secondary. He stopped to catch his breath after the climb uphill. A mango dropped at his feet, just missing him with its thick splash of yellow juice, and his mind went back to the mangoes in the yard of the little house at Sweet Apple. Then he thought of Agnes. He had been in Martinique a few months ago; it would soon be time to go again, at least before Christmas. She had failed noticeably. He wondered whether it was simply old age or whether some sickness might be at work within her. Yet her spirits were high, her glance as shrewd and her tongue as sharp as ever.

"You're looking thoughtful," Kate said now, coming up behind him.

"I was thinking that we're finally on the way," he fibbed. They passed Government House. "He's a magnificent speaker, our honorable member from St. Margaret's parish. I listened to him last week in the Legislative Council. Very impressive, the whole business, from the silver mace and the bobbies' silver buttons right up to the queen's portrait, though that'll be coming down soon."

"Oh, Nicholas knows how, no doubt of that! He's a vote getter, if ever there was one. The voters will love it that he dresses like a white man, a rich one, and talks like one, too. He's all the things they never will be and wish they could be."

Patrick looked down at the vivid little woman striding beside him.

"That sounds mighty cynical. I don't know whether you intended it that way."

"I'm not cynical. At least, I don't want to be. I think I'm a realist, that's all."

"You don't believe in our party?"

"Of course I do. The others are a lot of self-seeking country bumpkins who wouldn't know how to run a government, and luckily, the people have enough horse sense to see it. As for Nicholas, he's shrewd as they come, but very, very talented. I wouldn't be working for him if I didn't think he was."

"I'm glad. I would hate to think you didn't believe in him completely."

"Completely? Who said anything about that? I believe in what I see from one day to the next. I can't look too far ahead. I've been disillusioned too often."

Francis, Patrick thought, feeling her bitterness as if it were his own. Well, in a different way, it was his own.

After a moment Kate resumed, "I only wish I could be sure he had your heart."

"Who, Nicholas?"

"Yes. His mind's brilliant. It's the heart that worries me."

"Oh, Kate, you're wrong! He's sterling. I'd stake my life on Nicholas Mebane. The man is sterling."

Kate looked up at him. "You're sterling yourself, Patrick Courzon." Then, abruptly, "Tell me, how's Will these days?"

"The same," he said soberly.

Against his will, he was perceiving things he didn't like in the boy who was now so near to manhood. Something ugly lurked there. Will had a quick brain and extraordinary memory. He could trip Patrick up over a fact or a date, even over something that Patrick himself had once said and then forgotten he had said. "I hate to admit I forgot," Patrick would tell him, laughing at himself as mature people should be able to do; yet the truth was that he always felt like squirming under the boy's bold stare.

Kate spoke gently. "I think of him as an empty vessel. He was dry so long, starved and dry, until you came to fill him."

"I try, anyway."

"That's all any of us can do. Try. Well, I'll leave you. I turn off here."

For a minute or two Patrick watched as she went up the lane toward her house. He knew her routine pretty well. First she would let the dogs out for a run, then replenish the bird feeders. She'd go inside and make her supper, which she sometimes ate at the table in the yard, with a book propped in front of the plate. In the evenings she'd write for the *Trumpet* or work on party accounts or make calls. Now and then, he knew, she'd go out dining and dancing with men who came over from Barbados or someplace, men she'd known through family, probably, or during her married years. What she did with them when they brought her home he didn't know; it was none of his business. Whether any of them wanted to marry her or whether she would accept if one should, he didn't know either; he hoped, at least, she had mostly got over Francis. She never said. But she was being wasted, that was one thing he did know. She was being awfully wasted. This was no life for a woman like her.

Thinking of women, he thought as always of Désirée. Thank God, *her* life was not being wasted! She held him with a thousand strands of habit and affection and sex still marvelously fresh; he chafed sometimes, complaining silently about one thing or another, yet knew how tightly he was held.

He smiled a little at himself and his memories. He remembered how he used to tease her over her devotion to the house. The truth was, he had grown most happily accustomed to the orderly comforts that she provided, the cleanliness of the linens and the pretty, appetizing supper table. More than that, much more than that, he had, quite simply, grown accustomed to her spirit, so that without her listening ear, her trust, her little touch of worldliness, her pleasure in every day, without all these and the balm of her understanding, he would have been parched grass, a withering tree. Yes.

And he went on now past the central square where Nelson stood with pigeons soiling his shoulders, past the careenage and out toward the savanna, where half a dozen glossy horses were being exercised by their grooms. On the veranda at Cade's Hotel a pair of pink-cheeked old Englishmen in white suits were enjoying their whiskey and soda. One recognized them as retired civil servants, taking a respite from the English winter. He reflected that someone who hadn't seen

Covetown for fifty years or more would probably find very little changed: the boats, the horses, and the winter visitors would all be familiar.

Yet change was here, not only the proud promise of meetings like this morning's, but another kind, tangible and visible, a creeping tide.

From where he stood the roof of the Lunabelle Hotel rose squarely over distant trees. A long concrete rectangle, a slab with hard edges, it was a machine-age intrusion upon the natural world of curves, in which hills arched against the sky and coves were scallops in the cliffs. He stayed there, looking at the tasteless thing which, not yet one year old, had already surrounded itself with its own small slum. A prediction of what might come unless it were controlled somehow; he must talk seriously to Nicholas.

In back of the Lunabelle a shantytown had sprung up. Here lived the little army that serviced the hotel, people who had come in from the villages looking for something better than what they'd had, but were now worse off. Here were no garden patches and no shade. In the glaring heat their shacks stood naked among pools of stagnant water, foul and glistening like sores on the skin. The place had acquired an unofficial name: the Trenches. In Jamaica, in Kingston, he had seen such a place, worse only because it was larger and, being older, had had more time in which decay could spread and young men, idle and angry, could collect, followed inevitably by all the vices.

Will had friends in the Trenches. The boy was so secretive! You couldn't ever get at him. Remote, and perceptive enough to understand that with his secrecy he was inflicting hurt, he didn't care whether he hurt or not! Patrick had so wanted to love him, did love him, and was not loved in return. He wasn't hated either, simply disregarded, mostly in that cool way just short of disrespect, as Will stood off, thinking his own amused and scornful thoughts.

In the yard, Laurine and Maisie were sitting among their friends talking about whatever it was that girls talked about, clothes probably. . . . They gave him joy, his girls. They were fond of him, which was, when you came down to it, most of the reward that parents wanted: that their children should be fond of them.

He kissed them. "Where's Will?" he asked.

"Back in the shed."

He needn't have asked. Will and his steel band had struck up again behind the garage. They had constructed their instruments out of spare parts, mostly rusty. Will played the tock-tock, the most important of the instruments. He had made it himself out of the bottom half of a kerosene tin. One of the boys had made a tom-tom out of goatskins and a rum barrel. Another had made his own shack-shack out of a bamboo cylinder filled with pebbles.

Patrick sat down on an upended barrel and watched. The watching was as much a part of the entertainment as the listening; the concentrated vigor of the players, their rhythm and sway were a dance in themselves. Sometimes on Saturday nights he'd pass the dance hall near the wharf where the young hung out and he'd wonder whether the girls in their earrings and bright skirts knew that they were basically dancing the calinda, brought out of Africa. Perhaps they did know.

The racket now in the shed assaulted his eardrums, but his feet were swinging in time, nevertheless.

"That's great!" he cried when the music stopped and the boys began to leave. "You practically set fire to that thing, Will! Almost burned me to a crisp just watching you!"

Tom Folsom poked Will. "Oh, when it's setting fires, Will sure knows how! Always did. Biggest and best fires of all time." He bent over, laughing.

Will's fist struck Tom a fearful blow between the shoulders. "Damn fool! Damn loudmouth son of a bitch of an ass!"

Tom straightened and sobered, his eyes aghast. And while Patrick stood astonished, the two boys stood staring at each other until, flinching under Will's fury, Tom picked up his books and sidled out.

"What the devil was that about?" Patrick asked.

"Nothing important."

"You were pretty mad about something unimportant."

Not answering, Will busied himself with a pile of music sheets. Patrick frowned, trying mentally to reconstruct the swift byplay.

"Fire. He said something about you setting fires."

"He doesn't know what he's talking about. He's an idiot."

"One of your best friends, isn't he?"

"So?"

There was a silence. Something lurked in the air. Something serious was being hidden. The least suspicious of men, nevertheless Patrick made a connection.

"You ever set a fire anywhere? Tell me, Will."

"Sure. Kids make bonfires all the time, don't they?"

"That's not what I meant." Oh, it was preposterous, what he had meant, too hideous to consider, and yet he was considering it!

"Then what did you mean?" Will looked up boldly.

" 'Biggest fire of all time.' Isn't that what he said? Like the one—at Eleuthera, maybe?"

"Bullshit!"

"I'm asking you, Will: did you have anything to do with that?"

"I did not!"

"Is that the truth, Will?" Patrick's palms were sweating. "Because if you had anything to do with that, I'd not only have to give you up to the law, I'd have to give up on you. And that'd break my heart."

"I said no, didn't I? What more do you want?"

I want to believe you, Patrick thought. Please God that you're telling the truth. Those hard, bright eyes of yours—I never really meet them, never get behind them. How can I know who you are?

And taking out a handkerchief, he wiped his hands, swallowed a painful lump in his throat, made an inner resolution to go forward hopefully, and changed the subject.

"We had a fruitful meeting this morning. Thought maybe you'd like to hear about it." Make contact with the boy, share your interests with cheer. Bury those ugly fears. "Nicholas will be leaving soon for the constitutional conference in

London. When he comes back he'll have it all signed, sealed, and delivered. Independence." The word fitted the mouth, a crisp, snappy, prideful word. He smiled, wanting to coax a smile from Will, but none came.

Will asked only, "And then?"

"Well, elections, of course. The New Day will surely get in, unless there's some unexpected coalition of all the splinter parties. No, we'll surely get in," he repeated, adding brightly, "and then our work begins."

"What part will you play?" Will inquired.

"Nicholas said this morning he'd want me to be minister for education, which would suit me fine. It's not all that political, or shouldn't be! I won't have a lot of speeches to make, thank goodness. Although I suppose I'll be asked to do a couple here and there during the elections. . . . Well, I'll manage that if I must." Feeling enthusiasm, he sounded cheerful to his own ears.

Will didn't answer. It could be like pulling teeth to get him to talk, but Patrick, accustomed to this reluctance, was usually patient. When a minute or two had passed in silence, however, he became exasperated.

"Well, haven't you anything to say?" he demanded.

"Yes. I spit on your elections."

Patrick was astonished. "Spit on them?"

"They have no meaning, your silly elections. They're just the old colonial farce with different actors. We'll still have the bosses. The white man will still have the money and people like you will front for him. Read Fanon. Learn all about it."

"I've read Fanon. There are truths in him and untruths. He's too angry, too violent for me." Patrick paused. "Frankly, I think you're rather young and inexperienced to have a valid opinion about Fanon."

Will looked at him. Often his eyes would slide away in avoidance, but at other times he would switch his head about like a whip so that the eyes came straight at you, narrowed and intent, with a cat's cold, powerful stare. You'd grow uncomfortable and look away, then be ashamed for allowing yourself to be intimidated by a boy less than half your age.

"I only meant," Patrick said delicately now, "you haven't had enough time to learn and judge, to evaluate and weigh. These men with the fiery messages— they're fanatics, Will. They can—and have—lured whole nations to their downfall."

"Downfall? How much farther down can we go?"

"A hell of a lot farther. We can go down into tyranny and bloodshed, a slavery worse than you can imagine. Yes, there's a lot wrong now, but nothing that can't decently be fixed. Think about it, Will. Look at your own situation, a nice home, an education—"

Will interrupted. He had risen and stood tensely, clenching and unclenching his fists.

"How many of my kind don't have a 'nice home'? You think I should be happy because I live here, but I'll tell you I'm not, I'm ashamed that I do!"

Patrick felt a rise of pity. Thin and tall now, the passionate youth took on again, for an instant, the guise of the terrified and beaten child, tied to a tree. He spoke quietly.

"Must you think so hard about these things, Will? You've so many years ahead to watch the world getting better, to help it if you will. Right now's the time to enjoy yourself, to—"

"It's all right for you to talk. Oh, yes! Pass-for-white! A couple of shades lighter and you'd have it made! What chance is there for anybody like me under this system? Enjoy myself!"

"That's foolish talk, exaggerated—"

"That's why you used to hang around Francis Luther, until he got rid of you the minute you wouldn't do what he wanted."

"That's unjust, Will. How can you know what's inside my head? Or anybody's? I don't judge people by their color, I'll tell you that, though. This morning I was with Kate Tarbox—"

"A fool of a woman! Can't have children of her own—"

"That's a cruel thing to say."

"—and doesn't want anyone else to have them. 'Overpopulation,' she says. Yes, of course, overpopulation of *our* kind! Genocide and nothing but!"

Patrick was suddenly exhausted. Rational argument had always been stimulating for him, a pleasurable challenge, but this blind 'thinking with the blood' had no direction and no end. It was a tiring, infuriating muddle. He got up.

"I've had enough for now, Will. I'm going inside."

He went down the hall. Will's bedroom door was open, revealing not only the usual jumble of sneakers, books and sundries, but also a large blowup of Che Guevara over the bed. Something new.

He went to his own room. Désirée was posing in front of the mirror. Her lemon-colored dress smoothed her body like a stocking or a glove. She knew how to move as models do, lithely and lightly.

"Pretty, Patrick?"

"Pretty," he said, for once not caring very much.

"Doris gave it to me. It's brand new but it didn't fit her. You have to go to New York to get clothes like this. If," she said wistfully, "you can afford them."

"Lovely," he assured her. He had no patience.

Clarence was reading the paper in the front room. He put it down when Patrick came in.

"Were you having an argument with Will? I was passing the shed and couldn't help hearing."

"He's steamed up over revolution and class warfare. It worries the hell out of me. Where will it lead?"

"I'm an old man and you're a young one, Patrick, but he's only a boy and his language isn't yours or mine. It's language, that's all it is."

"I hope you're right."

"Did I hear him say something about Francis Luther?"

"You did."

Clarence was silent for a moment, then said quietly, "I know how wounded you feel. Life hasn't toughened you up and maybe it never will. Remember, I told you long ago not to put too much trust in Luther, didn't I? Later, I got to know him a bit and changed my mind, but still later I found out I'd been right the first time. It's in the blood. The call of the blood—and the money—it's all the same. In a crisis, at a crossroads, a man goes with his interests and his own. As far as that's concerned, at least, Will may be right."

Désirée, still wearing the yellow dress, had come into the room.

"You talking about Will? Is he giving you trouble again?"

Patrick didn't want to involve her in the discussion. She was always too ready to turn against Will.

"Nothing much," he said. "Just a mood."

He didn't fool her. "I could take a strap to that boy! Poor Patrick, you wanted a son. Two healthy girls weren't enough, were they?"

Clarence intervened. "No I-told-you-so's, Désirée."

"I don't mean it that way, Pop. Patrick knows I don't. But it's been such a hard job with Will from the very beginning."

"He has his placid moments," Patrick argued.

"Yes. Like a hornet resting between flights."

"He'd had such hardship. I thought just loving him would rebuild him."

"Well, maybe it will," Clarence said cheerfully. "It's the idealism of youth, carried too far, maybe, but still, you have to remember the world would never advance without it. When the rough edges are sandpapered, what's left will be a building block, something solid in the structure we call civilization." He moved his old hands as he spoke, as if piling stones, setting them precisely, and pleased with his own metaphor.

But Désirée was disturbed by Patrick's mood. "Go on out in the hammock and read till I fix you some lunch. You never have any time to do nothing in," she complained kindly.

"I think I'll do that."

In the string hammock, under mottled, moving shade, he lay back with his book unopened. "Building the blocks of civilization," the old man had said. Well, perhaps. Or tearing them down? Destruction wearing the guise of justice? There was an awful lot of that in the world these days. And he lay there, frowning and troubled, wishing he could sleep.

On the front lawn the girls were still holding animated conversation. "He can't even dance!" he heard one say, and smiled to himself. Little women! He was reminded suddenly of Francis, whom he had glimpsed a week or two ago in town with his own little daughter, a soft little thing in a fancy pink dress. Francis, like himself, had so wanted a son, a friend of his blood, a healthy son. Instead, he'd got a sick daughter. The injustices of life, the cool indifference, the "luck of the draw"!

Then he was angry at himself for still thinking about Francis. It shouldn't matter to him! "A man goes with his interests and his own," the old man had said a few moments ago. Was that just nature, then, just bloody tooth-and-claw, when you came down to it?

A young man with his leg shot away in a festering jungle, a baby animal, still half alive, skinned to make a coat for a fine lady, a mother raped by special interrogators in a great stone city: just nature, bloody tooth-and-claw? Every man for himself and the devil with the rest? His head ached.

He woke with a smooth hand on his forehead.

"You needed that sleep," Désirée said. "Come inside, I've made cold cucumber soup."

She had changed from Doris's dress into a blouse and skirt. Her long hair was pinned up in hot-weather style and she smelled of flowers. He felt a swelling of desire, now in the middle of the afternoon! Oh, if he had any sense he'd take his own advice, that which he had given to Will, to enjoy his youth, or what was left of it, and let the world, including Francis Luther, take its time getting better. And swinging himself out of the hammock, he followed Désirée into the house.

❊{19}❊

From the high walls of Government House the portraits still looked down. Princes, queens, generals, and judges in the velvets and ermines of authority regarded the push and jostle of the crowd as serenely as though the world had not been turned inside out. Music buzzed and voices shrilled in Francis' ears. All day he had been pounded by the enthusiastic noises of oration, churchbells, and gun salutes from the warships in the harbor. The frenzy was still echoing in his head.

Today a nation had been born, an independent nation having its own flag, orange and green with a cluster of stars that rippled up the pole after the union jack came down. A duke had spoken, along with a dozen native dignitaries. Nicholas Mebane's clear voice had carried immense authority, so that it was quite certain, after elections were held three months hence, who the new prime minister would be.

Francis had not paid much attention to the verbiage, since on such occasions nothing new was ever said. Only noble and triumphant platitudes were called for. Problems would come later, in due time. Besides, everyone knew what they were: malnutrition, unemployment, electrification, imports, exports—one had heard them and read of them all before and would do so a hundred times again. The sun had blazed and he had wondered why he'd come, knowing, of course, that "everyone" had come and it would have been very queer not to have done so. His eyes had wandered, as had his thoughts—this old place had seen so many flags! —had wandered across the square to the careenage and the rotting capstan where great sailing vessels had been hauled up to have the barnacles scraped off, to the Nelson statue and then, at the far end, to Cade's Hotel, where he'd wished he could be having a cold drink in the shady garden.

He'd thought of Kate.

In that drowsy, dreaming garden it had begun, although he had not realized it then and probably she had not, either. The recollection had been extraordinarily vivid, even to the emerald ring, later to be discarded, even to her words. Something about "long tides bringing you back." It vexed him now that the memory should be so sharp. There were, after all, so many encounters, affairs, or whatever one wanted to call them, in any healthy young man's years: restaurant lunches in hidden little Italian places, drinks in neighborhood bars or extravagant hotels, "love" in cars and on ships, in bedrooms and on beaches; did one remember them all? Hardly! Why, then, should these particular reminders slide back to bother him, when his mind was so filled with other things, when they only made him angry, when he didn't *want* them?

He never saw her, which was all to the good. He never saw Patrick either, for that matter. He saw very few people, anyway. He hardly ever went to town these days, except for an occasional call at the bank, when he would park his car at the back of the building, transact his business, and be gone within minutes, or from time to time an evening function at the club, to which he went partly to please Marjorie and partly because it was unhealthy to be a total recluse. And there was small likelihood of meeting either Kate or Patrick at the club!

In the four years since everything had happened, the fire and the birth of Megan, he had drawn in, retreated behind an invisible wall of his own construction. He had learned to run the estate, as Lionel said with candid praise, "like a charm." His cattle had won prize after prize at the shows and were now being exported to Florida for breeding stock. In another few years his mortgage would be paid off. After that he'd be able to salt away every available extra cent for Megan, who would long outlive him and would need whatever he could give her. His mind whirled, thinking of these things, over and over.

His mind was in a constant whirl over Megan. Sometimes he would even drop what he was doing, and almost frantic with intent, run to fetch the child and patiently, urgently, repeat some simple number game, some little puzzle ("suitable for ages four through seven," it said on the box) as if through main strength and the power of his love he could *will* her into normality—knowing all the time that it was useless and absurd, knowing, too, that he would keep striving, as his mother still strove for Margaret.

Such were his days. The evenings were quiet enough. It was known that the Luthers were usually at home, so people dropped in from neighboring estates to sit on the veranda and watch the afterglow spread its rosy fire over the sea.

Often Marjorie entertained at dinner. She was pleased to display the house, to set a splendid table with heavy silver and thin French crystal. Surely one couldn't begrudge her this diversion.

As for himself, he liked it best when the Whittakers were invited, solely because they brought along a nephew who came from Chicago for long visits; the young man would play the piano all night if you encouraged him. Sometimes when the others went across the hall for bridge he would play for Francis alone, a Mozart divertimento, a Haydn capriccio or fantasia, music whose pure refinement, lacking all turbulence and bombast, could clear at least for a little while the turbulence in a man's heart and head. No one on this island could play like that —except Kate. Kate again!

"An exquisite piano," the young man said, stroking the keys.

"Yes. A Pleyel. My father bought it years ago in Paris."

"You know, of course, what he is?" Marjorie asked one night after the Whittakers had gone home.

"What he is? A music teacher, isn't he?"

"No, no. There's something wrong with him, I mean. He's a homosexual. Couldn't you tell?"

"I didn't really think about it."

"Honestly, Francis! You never notice anything! The way he uses his hands! And he's at least thirty-five and not married. Disgusting, isn't it?"

"No," Francis said.

Marjorie stared. "Sometimes I can't make you out at all. It's as if you actually try to take the opposite, whatever I say." And she had sighed, and he had gone to his desk in the library to work on his history of St. Felice.

He had surprised himself, these past few years, with his own diligence. Having put out his feelers in New York among rare-book collectors and dealers in out-of-print books, he had surrounded himself with piles of source material and was progressing well, stimulated by this rich hoard to explore and delve. Creeping back into minds and seeing through eyes long dead, he came to know the warriors and the traders, the architects and poets, the anthropologists, the governors and slaves, the flora and the fauna, all the myriad life of this small spot into which and out of which had radiated the energies of five centuries. It seemed sometimes as though he would never reach the end, and indeed he knew that inwardly he hoped he never would. For the work was a refuge and companion; only when he was immersed in it could he know such rare contentment.

Occasionally he thought of a time when it must finally be complete; he toyed then with the idea of embarking on another project, something he might call *Man at Work in His Environment*. Perhaps by then there would be time to travel and take pictures all over the world for such a book. And he bought from Da Cunha's a fine camera against such a day, only half believing that the day might ever come. But it was nice to have the camera waiting on the shelf all the same.

"Quite a change from the first time we were here," Marjorie remarked now, returning him to the present hour and place.

Yes, quite. To begin with, there were ten times as many people as there had been at Julia Tarbox's wedding to the Honorable Derek Frame. But it was the atmosphere that was most strikingly different, the air of jubilance today, written on the face of the black peasant in from the country in his Sunday suit, with his dignity and his hands held awkwardly, as if he didn't know what to do with them, while he stared about at the grandeur. And the brown middle class, here in its finery, was jubilant indeed. The women wore leaf-green and peach and crocus-yellow; their shoes and their hats matched their dresses; they chatted and drank champagne, they greeted and laughed. A spectacle for a Balzac, Francis thought.

"Have you noticed the necklace on Nicholas's wife?" Marjorie whispered. "Someone said Da Cunha had it brought from France."

Diamonds, turquoise, and gold flashed on Doris's coffee-colored neck. She was a handsome woman. The climate agreed with these women and they bloomed; white skin shriveled to leather in this sun.

Marjorie led him to the terrace. "Come, they've saved us a table."

"Who has?"

"Lionel and the Whittakers. I don't know who else. Oh, yes, they've stuck

Father Baker there, too. We always seem to get stuck with him, don't we?" She grimaced. "He irritates me, he's so benevolent."

"Perhaps we irritate him." Francis felt contradictory; he didn't know why, but then he felt that way with Marjorie too often. It wasn't decent of him. He must try to watch it.

Lionel looked up with a grin. "Great fun, eh? At least they haven't burned the prison so far."

Marjorie asked what he meant.

"Oh, you know, it seems to be the thing to do. All over the islands on Independence Day they burn the prisons and set the murderers free."

Marjorie shuddered. "Burning again! I suppose I'll always feel I'm living on borrowed time here. Now more than ever."

"Things aren't that bad," Francis assured her.

"I'm not that optimistic." Lionel shook his head gloomily. "I'm finally getting out, you know. I really am. The sooner the better."

"Getting out!" Marjorie cried.

"Yes, I made up my mind this morning, when I saw that flag go up. The trouble is, a lot of others feel that way, too, so who'll buy what I want to sell? Unless you will, Francis, since you want to stay. I'd make it easy, take back a big purchase money mortgage and let you have the whole lot for a price that might surprise you."

"No," Francis said, decisively. "I've no wish for large enterprises. What I've got is all I want."

Marjorie was eager. "Where will you go, Lionel? You always said you'd never leave!"

"I know, but things change. I'm tired of the uncertainty. So I'm thinking of a nice place in Surrey near my sister." He plunked his fist into his palm. "Damn it, though! I've got to sell fast before these people expropriate!"

Father Baker remonstrated. "Come now! Expropriate! Who, Mebane? He represents the rising middle class and no one else. They don't expropriate. You know that as well as I do."

Mrs. Whittaker's cheeks were habitually sucked in, with an expression of disapproval. "Rising, Father?" she objected, unpursing her lips. "Risen, I would say. Look at them, with their jewelry and cars! That whole section where Mebane's father lived has tripled in size. Have you seen some of the houses they're putting up?"

"You bet I have," Lionel said, "but middle class or not, you're going to see a huge increase in taxes. They've made promises to labor that have to be kept even if it hurts themselves. Expensive promises."

"I'm not too alarmed," Francis said. "Peace and order, that's all I ask for. As long as we have those, a few more taxes won't devastate us. Land taxes have tripled anyway since I came here, and that's been under British rule."

"Exactly," Father Baker said. "Even that government recognized necessity. The world is smaller now. Everybody knows what everybody else has got, and the ones who haven't got anything expect something, for which you can hardly blame them. And that's the crux of the matter."

"But where's the money to come from?" Mrs. Whittaker demanded. "With all respect to you, Father, if you were to strip us at this table and everyone like us besides of every cent we own, that wouldn't mean more than a few cents in the pockets of the poor."

"The answer, of course, is to produce more. Mechanize," Francis said promptly. "It takes us twenty man-days to produce a ton of sugar here. In Hawaii it takes about two and a half days. There's your answer."

"But the unions keep fighting these new machines," Lionel objected.

"True, and that's where education comes in," Father Baker began, but was interrupted.

"This is too gay a party for such serious talk!" Nicholas Mebane, accompanied by an ancient white man in an equally ancient suit, drew up two chairs. "Time enough to face all that business on Monday morning! I'd like to introduce Mr. Anatole Da Cunha. Someone happened to mention your name, Francis, and he wanted to meet you. He knew your parents."

Da Cunha took Francis' hand. "You resemble your mother. I remember her very well. I knew her in Paris. She was a shy young girl, very lovely."

"My father always talked about you. You introduced him to my mother," Francis responded.

Nicholas said proudly, "Mr. Da Cunha made this trip especially to be here on Independence Day. It's a great tribute, a great honor for us."

"I'm almost eighty," Da Cunha said, "and not very well. I wanted to see home one more time, and what better excuse than a day like this one?"

"Mr. Da Cunha is planning a gift for the new nation, a group of paintings that he will send if we will promise to start a small museum here."

"And to encourage the arts," Da Cunha added. "There's too much talent going to waste everywhere for lack of encouragement."

"I'll leave that to my wife. It'll be in good hands," Nicholas said. "That is, if I'm elected."

Laughter, flattering and polite, rippled around the table. Nicholas continued, "Naturally, she loves your island paintings the best. She tells me you always have at least one cabbage palm with its crown of thorns in every one. Is that correct?"

"Yes, that's my signature."

"How fascinating!" Marjorie cried. "We have a few of your works at home that Francis' father gave us. I must look carefully for the cabbage palms tonight." Her eyes widened with a new idea. "Would you like to spend a few days with us and see what we have of yours? We'd love it if you would!"

"Thank you, but I'm a guest of the Mebanes and I leave the day after tomorrow." He turned to Francis somewhat abruptly. "I hear you're a writer."

"An exaggeration. I've been working on a history of the island, of the whole West Indies actually, from Spanish galleons to Arawaks, parrots—and cabbage palms, too. But I don't call myself a writer."

"I didn't know you were living here. I lost contact with your parents years ago."

"Yes, I've become a native."

The old man smiled courteously. It struck Francis acutely that there was more than ordinary interest in the smiling courtesy. But why should there be?

"You're here alone? You're with your wife, of course; I meant, your brothers and sisters?"

"I have no brothers, and my sisters live in New York."

"Ah," Da Cunha said.

Yes, definitely he was curious. Well, he was old and probably eccentric to begin with.

Nicholas obviously wanted to draw him on now to another table, but Da Cunha prolonged the conversation.

"I bought a newspaper in New York. They're saying fine things about your new leaders. It's all very interesting to me. Franklin Parrish, they mention, and another one, Patrick Courzon. But you know them all, I suppose."

"Patrick Courzon is the intellectual," Father Baker said, tactfully enough, since Nicholas's attention had been diverted by a pair of enthusiastic pink-and-blue matrons.

"You know them? You know Courzon?" Anatole asked Francis.

"I know them both."

"Unfortunately," Father Baker said, "they've had some differences, Francis and Patrick. I must say I've felt very sorry about it, too, since this island needs all its best minds working together." And he looked reproach at Francis, who colored with anger. Father could be an interfering old fool.

Nicholas, released by the ladies, drew Da Cunha away. Immediately then, everyone began to talk about Nicholas.

"He really is rather likable, isn't he?" Mrs. Whittaker remarked. "One gets to thinking when one's with him that things may not turn out so badly after all."

"I don't know about that," Father Baker said, rather wanly.

"What, Father?" Lionel cried. "You should be jubilant today! This is what you wanted, isn't it?"

"I would be happier if Patrick were going to be running things instead."

"Nonsense! What experience has he ever had? Good Lord, Mebane is a barrister, he's worked on the Constitution, been on the Legislative Council, worked in the Development Bank during federation—you name it! He's a practical man! Mind you, I still want to get the hell away from here, but at least with Mebane one would stand a fighting chance of survival. He's got his feet on the ground and knows how to compromise. Courzon's nothing but a dreamer."

Lionel was right, of course. Oh, Patrick would have his place, Nicholas would see to that, for they had been like brothers since childhood. That was understandable. One had to admire loyalty of that sort. But Nicholas knew what he was about, and he'd picked the right slot for a man as imprudent as Courzon. Only last week he'd told Francis—obviously, he had high respect and regard for Francis to give him as many confidences as he did—that Courzon was to be minister for education. Well, he couldn't do any harm there and, to be honest about it, might even do some good. It was his sort of job.

"Why, even in the Guardian Club," Lionel continued now, "even among his own kind, the colored politicians, so they tell me, Courzon is called a dreamer. They don't think much of him, even there."

"And all the time the world is starved for dreamers," Father Baker said.

Francis turned away. Too much talk tonight, and the wrong talk, too! He was at his poorest in crowds and he wished they could leave now, but Marjorie would be among the last to depart.

She was laughing. Her laughter had always been infrequent; it was more so, naturally, during these last few years. Sometimes her laughter was genuine, especially her loving gaiety with Megan, but her "social" laugh was a high, affected chortle, straining the cheek muscles. It made his own cheeks ache to watch her. He could never see why it was necessary to make such an effort at seeming amused or to be amusing for the good opinion of people one didn't especially care about. Yet most people did it, so probably it was he who was the odd one.

Then he had a new and sudden insight: quite unlike himself, Marjorie *needed* the crowd and the approval in order to survive! When they were alone at home the silence often lay like a heavy cloth, shrouding the two of them and shrouding as well the room in which they sat. Her thoughts must be so heavy, then!

His own could run like quicksilver in his head. The other night he had been reading about Crete and the rosette motif on the murals at the palace in Knossos. For some reason he had needed to talk about it, to share his curiosity with someone.

"It must have meant something, don't you think? Or perhaps only a decoration?"

"I shan't lose any sleep for wondering about it, I assure you," she had answered, not unkindly, but with irony and boredom.

She had yawned and he had felt a profound and lonely sadness.

He drank his coffee, pushing the dessert aside. Tomorrow would be Sunday and a whole free morning with Megan while Marjorie slept late. Maybe they'd sail over to Spark Island. They could take Osborne's four-year-old grandson along— he'd be company for Megan. Or was that only a delusion? Roy was so far ahead of Megan. He tossed in the water like a dolphin; he saw everything and had his chatty opinions about everything; he could relate a photograph of a thousand-pound turtle to the newly hatched young crawling out of the sand holes on the beach where the eggs had been laid. He was a companion, that little boy, following his grandfather so closely that he was known on the estate as Mr. Osborne's shadow.

It was so hard not to be bitter, not to envy Osborne this wealth of his!

Yet just to look at Megan, not hearing the repetitious baby syllables, not knowing with what difficulty she was being trained out of diapers—just to look at her, you would never know she wasn't "normal." She with the soft blond down on the back of her warm, sun-browned neck, she with the double row of tiny, perfect teeth, the cobalt eyes, the—And behind his own eyes Francis felt the painful prickle of unseen, stifled tears.

How he was tied to that poor scrap of a life! And both of them tied to the scrap, the piece of earth on which they lived! Without making himself appear absurdly bathetic, he was never able to explain exactly how he felt about this tie, this solemn linkage both to his child and to the first of his blood who had built upon that land, or how he felt about the land: half guardian and ultimate shelter for that vulnerable child.

"You're in a fog," Marjorie said now, with slight impatience. "Where are you anyway, Francis?"

"In the middle of tomorrow morning," he answered, and she gave him her I-don't-understand-you look.

Something else troubled him. Could he possibly be "using" the child because there was no other deep affection in his life? No one else he would die for? For Megan he would die a hundred times over. Yet so would Marjorie. Often he watched them together, the mother and the little girl crossing the lawn at dusk, with their pale dresses like flowers or moths. In a way of which Megan could fortunately have no idea, it was she who held them all together. She, and Marjorie's compassion, too, for he could not have borne to lose Megan and Marjorie knew it well. Her standards might be rigid and unyielding, but she did live up to them herself; one had to grant that. In this respect, at least, he had certainly not misjudged when, on that first night so long ago, he had recognized the quality and honor that were Marjorie.

She prodded his ribs. "Oh, look! Look over there!"

"Over where?"

He knew instantly what she meant. Moving among the tables toward a large, reserved one at the center of the terrace were Patrick with his wife, a group of young white men and women who were friends and relatives of Kate's, two or three black politicians—and Kate.

"Clever of her to wear pink with that hair," Marjorie said. "Funny, she never did care much about clothes."

Lionel studied Kate frankly, as if it didn't matter whether she saw him doing so or not. "She never needed to care very much. Anything she puts on becomes graceful." The observation was surprisingly delicate to come from Lionel's lips.

"You never mention her," Marjorie said.

"Why should I? We're divorced. Besides, it would hardly be tactful in your house, would it?"

"What do you mean? Because she once had a crush on Francis?" Marjorie laughed.

Francis felt the blood rushing to his neck. "Don't be ridiculous, Marjorie!" His eyes met those of Lionel, who looked amused.

"You know she did!" Marjorie insisted. "I don't say it lasted very long, but—"

Lionel interrupted. "I never mention her in your house, Marjorie, because of the tragedy that happened to us all. You know quite well that's the reason. And also because she's involved with Courzon."

"Involved? I wouldn't be astonished at all," Marjorie said, "if someone were to tell me she's having an affair with him."

The blood was beating hard now in Francis' neck. But he spoke calmly and curiously. "You hate her, don't you, Marjorie? Why?"

Amusement still played on Lionel's face as he watched the little play.

"Don't be silly, Francis! Why should I hate her? Just a little gossip within the family, no harm in it," she said lightly, as if she had suddenly become aware she was going too far. "I'm quite open-minded, quite unjealous; you know perfectly well I always am. If I weren't, would I draw your attention to how attractive she is? Those earrings are stunning, by the way."

All one could see of Kate were her bared back, the reddish foam of curly hair and the glitter of swinging eardrops.

"They were her grandmother's. I found them in a safe deposit box awhile back. She'd forgotten about them evidently, so I sent them to her. They're not worth much. Pretty, but the stones are very flawed." Lionel lit a cigarette and leaned into his subject, as if he were quite at ease with it, enjoying it. "Kate never cared about jewelry except for funny old antique pieces. I remember the day she gave back the emerald ring. I really wanted her to keep it, you know. I came upon her in the bedroom, packing to leave me. She was sitting naked on the bed. It was quite a picture, stark naked except for the emerald. She threw it across the room at me. Yes, quite a picture. That fellow Da Cunha could probably paint it, make a big splash with it. He could call it *Naked Woman with Red Hair and Emerald,* or something like that."

The muscles in Francis' belly tightened with the old familiar shock and he felt again that outrage—although it was none of his business anymore—at the memory of Lionel and Kate, the memory with which, he knew, he was now deliberately being taunted. Lionel had rare nasty moods like this.

Lionel had "known" her. He had "had" her. But not as I once had her and as I knew her. Creamy and slippery under the shower. The mole on her left breast. That little gap between her two front teeth. Crying over an abused cat. Laughing in bed, that wonderful bed. The quilt has a different kind of bird embroidered in each square. . . .

Not that it made any difference to him! The past was past. She had written him off. She had failed him and he had written her off. His life was very different now. His head and his heart were filled in many different ways.

Lionel and Marjorie got up to dance. For a moment he watched as Marjorie's face appeared above Lionel's shoulder, a face still pure and smooth in spite of sorrow. He followed them until they were concealed in the crowd of dancers. Then his gaze fell on Kate's back; she was talking, her hands flying up in the animated gesture that he had forgotten until now.

A stubborn, fanatical, opinionated, bad-tempered woman, no matter what else! And so to hell with her.

But don't let anything happen to her. Keep her safe in the little house, with the doors locked and the storm outside. She's so small! She likes to think she's bold, but she's only a weak little thing and quite alone. Take care of her.

Something happened, Kate, between you and me. It can't be undone, can it? Something happened.

His hands were cold and he called for a second cup of coffee, really to warm his hands around the cup rather than to drink. His head throbbed so that the music's beat was painful, each crescendo crashing through his skull.

"Something happened," he said aloud.

Returning, Marjorie announced that it was time to go.

"I can see you're having a miserable time." It was a reproach in the guise of generous consideration. But he let it pass.

A wind had risen and Lionel, who had Marjorie's shawl in his hand, helped her on with it.

"Frankly," Francis heard her say very low, "I'm glad Francis refused to buy your property. Please don't offer it to him again, will you? I'm still waiting for him to get tired of all this and go home."

"Don't hold your breath while you wait," Lionel told her. "It's my guess he never will."

"Never's a long time," she replied.

But Lionel was right. He was not going to be driven out by politics or economics, by anything or anyone! He had lost enough for one lifetime: a kindly father dead and a dearly beloved mother left alone; then Kate, a woman out of a dream —until the dream broke; then Patrick, a Jonathan to his David, or so he had hoped; finally, finally an unhealthy child. Loss enough, yes, for one lifetime.

The land was all he had left. He had fallen in love with the land and it was like loving another life, so profound was the attachment. To abandon it would be to long and ache for it until the day he died.

No. Eleuthera was his and he was hers. There was nothing more to be said.

❖{20}❖

When at last you reach the place at which, reluctantly, you must accept some enormous, shocking change—as when the endearing child becomes the hostile adult or the enchanting lover turns dull and mean or the trusted friend embezzles and cheats you—then, looking backward, it suddenly becomes quite clear. Yes, yes, of course, that was the day, when he said this or she did that, of course, that was the first sign, the start, which you failed to recognize! Or did not want to recognize?

Nicholas Mebane entered office amidst a universal, roseate euphoria. Enthusiastic comparisons were made with Roosevelt's historic first hundred days. "We will not promise miracles," he said frankly, "but there will be immediate and swift beginnings. They will be visible and felt, I promise you that."

And Patrick's heart swelled.

Within two months of the accession ground was broken for a splendid recreation center, with soccer fields, a swimming pool, and basketball courts, a whole range of sports. With the turning of the first shovelful of earth, there was a collective jubilation among the people. At last they were getting something, something they could see and touch!

Next came the establishment of the St. Felice Museum in a great, stone eighteenth-century warehouse behind Wharf Street. Doris Mebane, whose project it was, had overseen the renovation. With taste as refined and graceful as her husband's, she had caused a dry moat along the building's sides to be filled with greenery, while in the lofty, quiet space behind classic arches Anatole Da Cunha's gifts to the nation were displayed. There were some dozen oils and two pieces of marble sculpture. Above the front portal Nicholas had ordered a grand inscription to be carved into the stone: *Pro bono publico.* In the official brochure it was explained that this meant: For the benefit of the people. The building was dedicated with the accompaniment of a string quartet and unlimited champagne in paper cups, the entire middle class of Covetown attending and admiring. A fine beginning, indeed.

Patrick had ideas of his own to offer. At the close of the ceremonies he drew Nicholas aside.

"Something occurred to me last night. It's a school children's project. I was thinking of giving out seedlings, young fruit trees or vegetables or both. We'd

1052

have instruction, and prizes, naturally, for the best results. It would serve a joint purpose, a fine activity for the children, and at the same time it'd point up our need to be self-sufficient in food. What do you think?"

"Excellent! Go to it! Draw up a rough plan and present it at the next executive meeting." Nicholas clapped Patrick's shoulder. "Did you ever think, or dare to dream, we'd come so far? Lord, I remember doing Latin verbs together! Not that they ever did us much good. Or maybe they did!" His laugh came from his lips and shone in his eyes, an upwelling of pure pleasure.

"Can we get to work on this, then?"

"Don't see why not. One good thing about it, it won't cost much. We're frightfully low on money. Frightfully." And having been hailed from across the room Nicholas began to move away.

"Give me a minute," Patrick said hurriedly. "I know how swamped you are, but I haven't had a chance for a minute with you in days. I wanted to add, what about giving tree seedlings to the farmers while we're at it? Some blue mahoe or Honduras mahogany? That last hurricane wrecked at least two thousand acres of government-owned forest and there's been no replanting at all. It occurred to me we could combine the projects. It shouldn't cost much."

"You're minister for education, remember? That would come under the heading of forestry."

"I know, but things do tie into one another, they overflow from one department to another."

"I've got to run now. Really. We'll talk about it some other time." Nicholas gave him another shoulder pat. "Just remember, Rome wasn't built in a day. Although I do love your enthusiasm!" he called back.

Patrick drank enthusiasm as if it were rich wine. So much needed to be done! He was too well aware how poorly qualified so many of the system's teachers were; better salaries and improved conditions were, naturally, the solution to that. Driving out past Gully one day he noticed that the roof, which had leaked so badly when he taught there that they'd had to keep a row of buckets on the ready, was still the same old roof, unrepaired. Textbooks, visual aids, the drop-out problem—so his mind ran.

At executive meetings he ran through his list.

"Whoa, not so fast!" Nicholas rebuked one day. "We'll get there eventually, you know."

"Yes, but when?" Patrick felt himself pressing.

"The money," Nicholas said, with emphasis. "Money. We haven't got it."

"But there's the World Bank loan. And you've just raised taxes. I'm not sure I understand why things are all that tight."

Nicholas winked around the room. The committee was a tight group, personally close; it was permitted to make teasing comments about each other.

"Money management, as I understand you, is not one of your talents, Patrick."

There were smiles and chuckles, so that Patrick, too, had to smile. Everybody knew that Désirée handled the money in his house, ostensibly because he was too careless to pay bills on time; he sometimes thought, though, that it was really because she spent everything as fast as it came in and had to rob Peter to pay Paul.

"No, you're no financier," Nicholas repeated, moving on to the next topic, a discussion of ways and means to "beef up" the police force on the streets of Covetown.

For a moment Patrick hesitated. Still unused to his role, it was an effort to speak up. But he did.

"The town's already full of police, it seems to me."

"We need them, don't we? We've too many pickpockets. They'll frighten tourists away if we get a reputation for being unsafe."

"The kids have nothing to do. You remember, we spoke about playgrounds—"

"Well, we've been giving them some, haven't we?"

"Only three in the lower parishes and the last one's still waiting for equipment." He went on thoughtfully, "Anyway, playgrounds aren't the real answer, are they? It all goes back to the economy. Everything does. And these aren't the nineteen sixties anymore."

"Exactly. That's why we need to encourage tourism and immigration. To do that, we've got to have law and order."

"Tourism and immigration aren't the whole answer, since you mention it. I've been wanting to talk about it, as a matter of fact. These people come flocking in for cheap land; they speculate and drive the prices up." Having once begun, his thoughts and his words flowed easily. "We shouldn't sell to speculators anyway, only to people who plan to stay and contribute to the country."

He thought he saw glances and lowered eyes. A sudden sensitivity to the change in atmosphere caused his skin to prickle.

"Hotel construction creates employment," Nicholas suggested mildly.

"Only temporarily. And for monsters like the Lunabelle and those others? No way! That's the kind of investment we don't need. They're wrecking the bay with all that dredging, destroying the natural marshland to make fancy beaches. Destroying the reefs, which kept the beaches from eroding in the first place. But they don't care. It's today's quick buck they're after and to hell with the next generation! Dumping raw sewage into the bay! When the wind's right you can smell the stink a mile away." And he looked around for some nod, some sign of agreement, but there was none; seven or eight faces circled the room, staring ahead without expression. "Look," he pleaded. "You all remember when the bay was full of lobsters and groupers. Now you have to go miles offshore for large fish. Pollution and spear fishing have done that. They're wrecking the seas. I've seen what's happened elsewhere and I've read Cousteau." About to finish, he thought of something else. "Go to the window and tell me we aren't on the way to ruining one of the most exquisite seascapes one might hope to see anywhere in the world! Remember what they did to Diamond Head in Honolulu? You've seen pictures—"

"You're jumping from fish to reefs to hotels," Nicholas interrupted. "We can't keep up with you."

"I'm not jumping. They're all part of the same picture."

There was a silence. Then Nicholas spoke, "Will anyone move that we take the previous remarks under serious consideration?" The motion having been made and passed, he added, "I shall appoint a committee to study land use with a view to preserving the character and ecology of St. Felice."

Three months later the sale of property for another bayside hotel was made public. Patrick went at once to Nicholas.

"I don't understand. I thought there was to be no more construction around the bay, at least not without discussion."

"We had discussion, a couple of hours' worth, at the last meeting, the one you missed."

"I missed?"

"Yes, I called an emergency executive committee meeting while you were visiting your mother in Martinique. I ordered the minutes to be sent to you."

"They were never sent, and to my shame I haven't been in Martinique in months."

"Queer! Well, someone was certainly misinformed. I'm sorry, I'm really sorry. And I do understand how you feel about aesthetics. It's just that we're badly in need of capital right now. I think I can promise that this sort of thing won't happen again, though."

Humiliated and indignant, Patrick nevertheless reined himself in. No sense jumping to conclusions! Nicholas wouldn't trick him! It was almost paranoid to suspect that he would.

Yet he left with the odd feeling that he had been placated, as one diverts a demanding child.

Désirée was stirring something at the stove. He could tell by her back and her stiffened shoulders that she was disturbed.

"I was at Doris's this afternoon. Nicholas must have had some sort of business going on at his house. The men were leaving just as we drove up."

He was startled. "Meeting? The executive committee, you mean?"

"No, of course not, although I did see Rodney Spurr and Harrison Ames. I didn't know the others. There were even some white men. One of them was that very heavy, short man who built the house on the cliff, the one with all the glass, you know."

"Jugen. He's making a lot of investments here, they say."

Désirée turned around. "Doris made me promise not to tell you, but Nicholas has been saying you don't cooperate."

Patrick was aghast. "Don't cooperate! What the devil does he mean by that?"

"That you—heckle."

"Heckle!"

"I hope you're not making any trouble, Patrick. You've been friends all your lives."

"And what sort of trouble would I be likely to make? Or do I ever make?"

"I don't know. Sometimes you do climb on your soapbox, though. You can be very stubborn when you've an idea in your head. You never give in."

"You mean I stand by my convictions? May I drop dead if I ever stop!"

"Don't get so excited! But you are stubborn, you know." Désirée's red mouth pouted. "For instance, why wouldn't you let me go to Europe with Doris that time? Quite frankly, she thought it selfish of you and so do I. I've never been anywhere and—"

"I couldn't afford the trip, that's why!"

"I thought surely with you being in government we'd have things easier. But it's really no different from when you were teaching or working on the *Trumpet.*"

"I didn't join the government to get rich."

"Well, you could at least have let me go once with Doris!"

"I'll be damned if I'll let you take charity!"

"Charity! Your best friend! It would have been doing Doris a favor. She wanted me to go. And they've loads of money, anyway. It wouldn't have meant a thing to them!"

"Loads of money," Patrick repeated, thoughtfully. "I don't know. Dr. Mebane wasn't all that rich and he had four children to divide among. I don't know."

"Nicholas is making money on his own! He's investing in hotels and beach front property all over the island. That new nightclub that opened off Wharf Street, the Circe—he owns half of that. Didn't you know? That new hotel they just announced—that's his!"

Patrick sat down. He was quite still.

Désirée continued in the high, petulant voice of Doris Mebane. "Why can't we get some pleasure out of life? Stuck in the same rut, when you could be getting ahead, like Nicholas?"

He answered coldly, angrily. "When do you plan to grow up? Or do you, ever?"

Her eyes filled and he was instantly sorry. She hadn't deserved his temper. This, today, was her first complaint. Although she had never had much of anything compared with many of her friends, she had, he was well aware, stifled her wants and been cheerful with the little he had been able to give her. Now, in their new situation, she must be feeling a certain bafflement. Doris's husband could provide things, while her own husband couldn't and didn't seem to mind that he couldn't. He wished he could explain it to her, but his own confusion dizzied him and he was silent.

With a full heart he went to bed, to lie long awake. So that was what Nicholas was doing! It was, very likely, what they were all doing and why they were silent whenever he spoke. They knew he wasn't with them. So he stood alone! To whom could he talk about it, where to turn? He felt a bewildered sense of betrayal. It would have been comforting to confide in his wife, but he did not dare. Her tongue was too loose, too innocent. The only human being he could talk to, when you came down to it, was Kate Tarbox.

On his walks home from the center of town he had to pass the office of the *Trumpet,* where from time to time he stopped off. He missed the place. It was so alive, with the news of the world flashing in, the typewriters clacking and the telephones ringing. And there was always Kate at the editor's desk. He'd used to catch himself, when he worked there, staring at her from across the room. She had the kind of face that is known as mobile, meaning, he supposed, that you could so easily read its moods as the light of humor moved across it, or as stern disapproval closed the lips, or as some lovely contemplation opened the eyes into a wide, soft gaze.

Sometimes, now, he would accompany her on the homeward walk to the corner of her street.

"You look glum," she remarked, as they climbed the hill, the day after the talk with Désirée.

He told her, half reluctant to reveal himself and half relieved to express what he had been stifling.

"I'm troubled," he concluded. "I feel as if I'm standing alone in the center of a circle, with everything vaguely falling away, and I can't reach Nicholas, I don't know why."

"Why don't you tell him what you know?"

"I can't. I promised Désirée. I don't suppose it would make any difference, anyway. It's not my business, is it, how a man invests his money?"

"This is your business. This is different and you know it. It smells bad to me." They stopped and Kate ticked off a list on her fingers. "Look. We were going to electrify the villages and put in a sewer system. On the north side they still dump night soil in the ocean every morning. Nobody talks about it, but we all know they do. We still collect water in cisterns and on rooftops. Nicholas spoke again and again of desalinization plants and hydroponic gardening and canneries. Oh, it was all so *energetic!* Our roads are terrible. We have more cars and more accidents. I know everything can't be done at once, but I'd just like to see some slight movement toward a beginning."

"I don't understand Nicholas," he repeated. His voice was hollow and sad in his own ears.

For a moment Kate seemed to be making up her mind. Then she said, "I want to show you something. Have you got an hour to spare, right now?"

"I'll spare it."

"You'll have to get your car. Have you ever been at the Lunabelle Annex?"

"Over the causeway, you mean? No."

"Over that little bridge you have to walk across, where the new cottages are."

At the remote end of the Lunabelle's beach, out of sight around the point and half a mile from the main building, they stopped the car. Tall grasses grew between the ruts of a secluded, sandy lane.

"Not used very much," Patrick observed.

The footbridge spanned a narrow channel. A circle of quaint, peak-roofed cottages bordered the white beach along the little island's rim. The backs of the cottages looked upon an oversized blue pool, amoeba-shaped. Parasols and expensive chairs stood on the silky lawn between the flower beds. It was very quiet. Only one couple, lying in the sun, looked up briefly as Kate and Patrick appeared and then went back to concentrating on the sky.

"Out of season," Patrick said.

"It's never crowded. This isn't for the public, you know."

"Isolated. One couldn't guess it was here."

"Exactly. Come, maybe there's an open door. Or we can peek in."

All the sliding glass doors were locked. But one could clearly see inside to rooms in which white velvet rugs lay on pink terrazzo floors and wide beds bore gilded carving; in one a lace robe had been left lying on a chair. A nineteenth-century, or possibly a twentieth-century, bordello must have looked or maybe still looked like this, Patrick thought, but did not say it.

"Bizarre, isn't it?" Kate asked, as they walked back between oleander hedges to the car.

"Yes. Who are these people?"

"You can't guess?"

He had some uncertain thoughts, but waited.

"The mob."

He stared.

"I can't prove it, although I suspect it strongly. More than suspect it. These men come down here from the states, bring their girls, do their business, and make their payoffs here in private where the government protects them."

"Payoffs for what?"

"Dope, I think," she said seriously, and as he still stared at her, she went on, "Why should you be surprised? Central America is ridden with it."

He couldn't answer that.

"You're crushed because it's Nicholas." She touched his hand. "Of course, I could be wrong."

"You've got to be wrong," he said. "You've got to be."

On the broad side lawn of Government House they passed a unit of police deploying, smart in their new gray uniforms with scarlet caps and scarlet trouser stripes.

"Stop a minute," Kate commanded. "What do you see?"

When he did not understand immediately, she asked, "You mean to tell me you haven't noticed them these last few weeks?"

"The style, you mean? Nicholas likes a certain amount of ritual and display," Patrick offered, almost sheepishly.

"That's not what I meant. Look again! When did we ever have so many police? Every one of them over six feet tall! They're tough, and they're all new men. There's not one old familiar face, the faces we all knew. I wouldn't be sur-prised—" she said and broke off.

"Surprised at what?"

"Oh, nothing."

"Women are so damned exasperating! Will you please finish what you started?"

"Frankly, I'm not sure I should have trusted you today."

"Well, thank you! Thank you very much! If that's the way you feel, don't bother to talk to me at all. Please don't."

"Don't be huffy. I didn't mean it the way it sounded. I meant that you're a very loyal person, and very close to Nicholas in spite of the things you've been seeing. How can I know what your conscience, nagging at you in the middle of the night, will tell you to do?"

He softened. "Kate, anything you've ever said to me has gone no farther. You ought to know that." It was the first time in a long while that he had made mention, however oblique, of Francis Luther.

She flushed. "All right, then." She looked around and lowered her voice, although the car was moving. "There are rumors that a national police force is being gathered. They've even got a name: the Red Men."

"Well, wouldn't that be more efficient?"

"Don't be dense, I'm speaking of a paramilitary force. Arrests in the night, mysterious disappearances, bodies dumped along the roads. Know what I'm talking about? You ought to know. It's the history of the twentieth century, isn't it?"

Shock went through him, down to his knees. "You can't be serious! Who told—" He broke off. "Excuse me. Of course you can't reveal it."

"Of course I can't. Let's just say I have—sources."

For a minute or two neither of them spoke. The car had stopped at Kate's house, but she made no move to get out.

"Patrick. I'm terribly afraid."

"It may not be what you think," he suggested softly.

"If I had any guts I'd put it all in the *Trumpet*. But I have none, that's the trouble."

"Kate! Are you out of your mind? Don't you dare!"

"You see, you do believe what you've been seeing, or you wouldn't say that. In a free country, the press has nothing to fear, has it?"

He didn't answer. Here were the old streets, the listless leaves, gray with dust, the muffling, sleepy summer heat, so long familiar, now as threatening as some queer, twisted alley in a foreign place where nobody speaks one's language.

Then he brought himself up short. This was jumping too hastily to conclusions! For all her intelligence, Kate was still a woman; women exaggerated; they were always drawn to the dramatic and the thrilling. He was about to say so when Kate spoke again.

"About Will—keep an eye on him. Tell him not to get mixed up in politics right now."

"Why, what's he doing?"

"It doesn't matter. I can't say anymore. Just tell him to be careful." And leaving Patrick with that enigma, she got out of the car.

Feeling faintly irritated by all the mystery, as well as with himself for his own fears, he drove away. It was market day downtown. Schooners from out islands were unloading woven baskets filled with iridescent pink and silver fish, as they had been doing for centuries past. But on the other side of the square a dozen or more young men and women waited in front of the airline office ready to depart for England or America, where they would drive the busses and collect the garbage: a better life, apparently, than they had waiting for them at home. He sighed and came back to his own affairs.

"Keep an eye on Will," Kate had warned. Oh, by all means! And just how was he to do that? Will was a man now, or more a man than almost any other boy his age. You couldn't pin him down!

"Where were you?" one would ask.

"Out with friends," he would answer.

"Yes, but where?"

"Just walking around, down on the beach."

You never could get more out of him than that. And what if you did pin him down, saying, "We know you spend time at the Trenches and we don't want you to go there anymore." What good would that do?

He wondered what Will and his friends really did talk about, what interested them besides Che Guevara and Mao. No, not Mao anymore; he'd gone out of favor, like so many left-wing heroes. At Will's age, Patrick thought, what I cared about were girls and books and wanting to know some more of the world. I wasn't angry like him, I know that much. And I remember I could laugh a lot. Will never does, at least not when he's home with us. No, you couldn't pin him down.

Nevertheless, he asked point-blank that night, "Will, I want to know, are you mixed up in anything political?"

Will gave him a long look. "Why do you ask?"

"Because I'm worried. I don't challenge your right to believe in what you believe, and by this time obviously I know what you believe. But I don't think it's safe for you to be too outspoken right now."

"Right now? I thought this was supposed to be a democratic government. Free speech, freedom of thought and all that." There was a taunt in the way Will said it.

Patrick found himself struggling, put once again on the defensive. "It is a democratic society! But it takes time to develop orderly democratic societies in which people think for themselves." He mouthed and floundered, repeating, "It takes a long time, and in the meanwhile, during a period of stress—"

"Each of us has only one lifetime," Will said. "How long are we supposed to wait? In the meanwhile," he went on before Patrick could reply, "there's been no change. Take the Francis family, the Tarbox family. The worker tends the bananas, and the profits go to a fancy house in England, or maybe the Riviera, or wherever else those people travel to make themselves comfortable."

Back to the Francis family again. Always the Francis family. Strike, and strike the sore spot. Will knew how to do that!

"Tell me, are you so satisfied with what you've had since Mebane got in?" the boy demanded now.

"Not entirely, no, I'm not. But never forget, we've a way to change things when we're not satisfied. The ballot is our defense, a most precious defense. When you think how few peoples in the world have the right to vote, you'll treasure what we've got."

"Vote for this one, vote for that one—it makes no difference. I'll take the Cuban way and you can keep your ballot."

"Oh, it's tempting, isn't it? No vote, just one man, quick and efficient, who gets things done without a lot of committees and talk! Justice and equality at the stroke of the great man's pen! Only it isn't equality. Listen"—and earnestly now, trying to convince, to force the boy to understand it as he understood it, Patrick thumped his fist into his palm—"listen to me! Do you really think people are equal under those systems? Why, the leaders in Russia have every privilege and luxury that kings ever had, things the masses never even see. And what's more, they have the power of life and death over those masses. Equality!"

"Life and death," Will said. He spoke calmly. He looked off, looked at the wall behind and above Patrick's head, as though he were considering whether to say something else or not. Then he stood, leaning with one elbow on the mantel, a habit which made Patrick nervous. Will made such abrupt movements, so rough and sweeping, and Désirée's Royal Copenhagen figurines, those fragile blue-and-white milkmaids and goosegirls, patiently collected at Da Cunha's, were so treasured. But he had never broken one yet.

"You know, of course, what's happening with the Red Men," he said at last.

"Happening?" Patrick repeated.

"Yes." Will was patient, intense and old.

He's never been young, Patrick thought, as eye contact was made between them. And he evaded. "Well, there are too many of them—"

Will interrupted. "It's not what you see, it's what you don't see. It's what they do when they take off the uniform, it's the ones who never wear the fancy uniform at all. And there are hundreds of them, that even you don't know about. Talk of the power of life and death—" He broke off. "But you won't want to hear because Nicholas is your friend."

"He was a brother to me," Patrick said slowly, as if murmuring to himself.

"Well. Brothers do strange things, too."

To know so much, to be so cynical, at seventeen!

"You're in the government, but you haven't the faintest idea what the government is. Don't you realize at all what's going on behind your back? The Daniel sisters' car crash last month—take that, for instance. You thought it was an accident?"

"Everyone thought so."

"Not everyone," Will corrected. "That car didn't skid off the road. The sisters were shot by Red Men and then the car was shoved over the cliff. That's what really happened."

"But why?"

"They ran a whorehouse, a fancy place for tourists on the Westbrook Road. They were murdered because they got too sure of themselves and stopped paying off to Alfred Claire. That's Mebane's cousin—of course you know that. Don't you see the whole family's on the take, milking the country?"

"But where do you hear these things, Will? How can you say these things?"

"I say them because they're true." Will smiled. He had a one-sided, reluctant smile, almost wistful. "My friends and I—we have ways of knowing."

Kate and her sources, Patrick thought. He was dazed. From the nature of democracy to Cuba and communism and now to whorehouses and murder, all in less than half an hour! How could he know who was telling the truth?

"I don't know whether to believe all this," he said.

And again Will smiled, that strange, touching smile.

"Believe it," he said.

*   *   *

"THE MEBANES ARE having a housewarming," Désirée announced.

Nicholas's house had been completed in the new community on the cliff at Cap Molyneux. Through Désirée, Patrick had been informed almost daily of its progress, its Italian tile, the pool, and the great curved room. "Like the prow of a ship," she reported.

"I don't want to go," he told her.

"What! What can you be thinking of? Never mind my feelings and Doris's if we don't go, but how will it look? The only member of the government to stay away? And you on the executive committee?"

"The executive committee hasn't met in months and it's only a rubber stamp anyway, as far as I'm concerned. I'm a minority of one." He could hear his own bitterness.

"Well, maybe that's your fault! Anyway, what has it got to do with the party?"

She was right, of course. It would be very strange indeed to stay away, conspicuous and strange. So, still as troubled as he had been during these last weeks, Patrick got himself dressed up and went.

It was an eagle's aerie. On a plateau at the top of the mountain stood a small cluster of new houses. Men retired from industry in North America and Germany and Sweden had built them with a view of endless ocean and more than a thousand feet of jungle below. The Mebanes' house adjoined the Jurgens', where through a gap in the shrubbery the Jurgens' peacocks could be seen, flaunting their fantails as they passed the hidden floodlights.

Patrick walked out to the far end of the terrace and sat down on the parapet. Indoors the buffet table bore flowers, food, and quantities of silver. Here on the terrace people were dancing to the music of the stereo. And he turned his head away, to stare downward at the quiet, black sea. Certainly it was not that he ever disapproved of music, wine, and dance! Rather it was that, in some subtle way, this place and the people here tonight had removed themselves, so it seemed to him, from the struggling, throbbing life beneath them, where even now a weak light streaming from some night fishermen's little skiff brightened the dark water with a moving stain of indigo.

It was cool at this height, almost cold. The cold cleared his head.

Did none of these people see or care what was happening to the country? Surely others of them beside himself must see, although none spoke! Only from below there in the villages came the sounds of discontent and restless hope.

Since Independence Day there had been a surging of the mass, people streaming out of the countryside, seeking mecca in the town. That sour, tragic area known as the Trenches was flowing over. Packs of defiant, idle boys had begun to rove through the streets, mugging and stealing. Did no one see the writing on the wall? His hands clenched in his pockets, so that the nails dug into the palms.

At what point, when and how, had Nicholas Mebane, with his quick, discerning mind, so keen and clear, at what point had he been corrupted and beguiled? Now, below the surface of that mind, lay revelations at which Patrick could never have guessed. It was like peeling off layers of clothing and finding some secret deformity of the flesh, or like finding a stranger wearing the familiar features of another. Was it power alone that had brought this change? Or could it have been there all the time, awaiting its hour all these years, unrecognized by one who loved him?

Oh, people changed, everything changed! That was the one thing you could be sure of. Francis Luther. Better not to think of him. Think of himself. Think of Désirée and his love for her, which, no longer the dazzle of first youth, but deeper now, more clear and tender, could comprehend and smile at her mood when, raising his eyes from the sea, he saw her pass; her laugh was happy as she flashed in her new dress, bought after such decisions made and unmade, as though her fate depended on it. Lovely, kind, and foolish Désirée in the fluttering dress, poor woman-child, to be so enthralled by all this—this tinsel!

Yes, people changed, But not as Nicholas had done.

How many years since those first days at school? "Come on home for lunch," he said, and I went and thought his father's middle-class, clean house on Library Hill was a palace.

Next door the peacocks blared their harsh cry. And Patrick stood up, turning away again from the chatter and glitter to look back over the dark sea. He brushed his hand across his eyes. He could have wept.

The man inside this house was dangerous.

WHAT TO DO, but admit to yourself that you're afraid? He was helpless. Three or four times he tried to talk to other members of the government, but always, even from his most careful, tentative approach, they drew away, either in alarm and fear or because of their own complicity. There was no way to tell.

And suddenly the storm was upon them all. Suddenly the newspapers of the world made the name of St. Felice familiar to millions who had either never heard it before or had forgotten it if they had.

A prominent feature writer for a popular journal came to the island and sent home an article about the growth of dictatorship on St. Felice. Two days later he was shot to death in the garden of Cade's Hotel, his body, with a bullet hole in the temple, having been discovered there by a waiter.

Passing the scene on Wharf Street, Patrick felt compelled to go in, which was odd, since he was ordinarily one of those who shun the scene of an accident because they can feel the intensity of pain in their own flesh, as if they were themselves the victims. Yet he went in.

Cade's had gone to seed. The twentieth century had at last arrived on St. Felice. The Lunabelle and its kind, with their glass and steel and chrome, their neon and plastic, were proof enough of that. Cade's had remained in the nineteenth century. The sugar bowls still stood in saucers filled with water to keep the ants out. A shabby old Englishman, who either couldn't afford the Lunabelle or would not go there, was having his morning tea on the veranda as Patrick, having seen the spot in the garden where a large red-brown stain was all that remained of a decent, talented young man, went down the steps and out into the morning. For an instant he looked back at the old building where he had brought Désirée for their first gala dinner together, and where they had spent their wedding night. He was deeply moved. Everything was bound together, his life with Désirée, the murdered stranger, the old Englishman, everything. All of us, all in the flow of time.

What to do?

He got into his car, having no idea where he was going or why. He knew only that he had to move. He could not have said whether it was despair or fear, in its nakedness and shame, that moved him. As he sped along the road, his vision grew sharp; it was as though he had been given a glass that magnified the world. He saw a dead dog on the road and hoped it had died quickly, without pain; too often one saw agonized animals in the ditches, dying in the broiling sun. On either side of the car the cane grew tall. It was like running a jungle path; a bird's eye would see it as a canyon between green cliffs. He could see the workers moving steadily, cutting in pairs. Once, catching a bar of song in the wind as he went by, he recognized it as a chant to ease the labor. These were the men with whom he had once, in the village, been a boy. And again he felt a rare, exalted kinship with all people, all living things.

At a village rum shop, one of those places where men came to drink and play dominoes, he stopped the car. A jukebox blasted out a raucous tune and voices had to rise above the noise, but no one turned it off. Noise probably gave life to the midafternoon, for the men at these tables were not working; this was slack time, and they were talking about credit—how they would get it and whether it would be enough to carry them through until they could go back to work. Patrick knew they had been talking about it. When he took a seat and asked for his drink they lowered their voices or stopped speaking. He saw that they did not recognize him. He was not prominent enough in the government for his face to have become familiar. It was his clothing and his light skin that told them what class he came from. It was these that had silenced them. They didn't trust him. They were afraid of him. Yet he was of them and he understood them, although, if he were to tell them so, they would surely not believe him. True, he had left them behind; true, as a child in a village like this one, he had already been different from them in many ways. And yet he was of them because he understood them. He had never felt that as clearly as he did now.

He finished his drink quickly and got back into the car. Quite suddenly, he knew what he must do. And he drove rapidly back to Covetown, parked the car at Government House, and went up the steps two at a time. He remembered that, one day as they passed this tall, white portico, Will had remarked that the more things change the more they remain the same, meaning that the color of the men who occupied this mansion had made no difference after all.

He was admitted to the beautiful square room where Nicholas sat.

"Nicholas, what's happened to you? I demand to know."

"Sit down," Nicholas said agreeably. "I'm not sure I know what you mean."

Patrick drew his chair to a place where he would not be staring into the light. Strong men liked to discomfit their visitors by putting them in the face of the light, he remembered.

"What's happened to this government? Suddenly—or not so suddenly—everything's caved in."

"Caved in?" Nicholas's eyebrows made two inverted v's of surprise. "Aren't you being somewhat dramatic?"

"Don't turn me off, Nicholas. You made promises to me, to us all. And you haven't kept them."

"What do you want me to do? Rub Aladdin's lamp and make your wishes come true overnight? Well, I can't do it!"

"I said, don't turn me off, Nicholas. There's a stench in this land. A stench the world calls fascism."

Nicholas looked across the desk at Patrick. His glance traveled to the open-necked shirt, of which, Patrick knew, he disapproved; then it traveled around the room, fastening first on a crystal paperweight, then on the bunch of keys he had taken out of his pocket, and finally on his own finger, where shone a diamond on a narrow gold band. Then he spoke.

"The world, meaning a handful of reporters, doesn't know what it's talking about. If there's any stench, as you put it, it's wafting from the other direction. Good God, you know what's going on? You know Moscow, through Cuba, is exporting terrorism all through this region. Listen to me, my friend. We face serious trouble. Maybe you don't realize how serious. You know what's being smuggled into this country? Arms, Patrick, rifles and hand grenades, landing on our beaches night after night. I haven't wanted to make it public knowledge because the people who are doing this will take advantage of the slightest unrest, of a thing like a teachers' strike, for example, anything, to further their cause. And we can't afford to let them do it unless we want to give in and give up right now. We have to fight strength with strength. Only a strong government—"

Once Nicholas had had the power to mesmerize him, but no longer.

"This is no 'strong government.' This is a rotting government."

"I don't like the sound of that, Patrick."

"Do you think I like it, either? Oh, Nicholas, what's happened between you and me? From the very beginning, after all our hopes, you shut me out, me and every idea I had. You gave me a sinecure and got rid of me. Why?"

"Because I found out early on, during those first few weeks, that you had no grasp of affairs. You live a boy's life in a man's world. It's one of your most appealing and most exasperating qualities. You want utopia right now. But there is no Santa Claus, Patrick."

Through the window on the side of the room Patrick could see the bay and the cupping hills, with the pale-green water lying at the bottom of the cup. The Lunabelle and the steel-framed cubical skeleton of new construction severed the sky. He pointed and heard himself speaking.

"I understand you're a part owner of all that."

Nicholas started. "I? Who told you that?"

"Doris told Désirée originally. But it's common enough knowledge by now, I suspect."

Nicholas leaned across the desk. "Women's talk! Damn women!"

Eyes like lumps of coal, Patrick thought; hard and dull, with sudden glisten when a streak of sunlight strikes the turning head. I've made him furious.

"Yes. I've put a few dollars in here and there. Is it any business of yours how I invest my money?"

"Yes. There's conflict of interest." Patrick's voice rose, sounding high as a boy's, so that he had to clear his throat.

"You're a nitpicker. I'm running a government, planning a stable future for thousands of people, and you're upset because I've earned something for myself."

"You're not planning a future for anyone except yourself. You only want money and the power to keep making it. Don't you have enough now?" The high voice again, sounding like pleading.

"Grow up, Patrick." Nicholas's anger had receded. "And get out of politics. You don't understand it. You never will. You'd be better off back in the classroom before it's too late."

"It's too late already."

"Quit, Patrick. Don't make me throw you out."

"I won't quit. And I won't let you throw me out."

"Let me give you some advice. What you really should do, what any sensible man in your shoes would do, is to go off to the States. We may be in for some hard times here. You could go off to the States and pass. Actually, you could have done that long ago when we were in England."

"I couldn't have and can't, and if I could, I wouldn't."

"Of course, with Désirée it might be somewhat difficult." Nicholas smiled. "But you could get rid of her if you wanted to. Maybe Kate Tarbox would go with you instead."

"You bastard! If there's anyone who'll leave here, it'll be you. Yes, when you've ruined the place with prostitution, gambling, and dope so it isn't fit to live in, you'll leave and meet up with your money in Switzerland."

I've struck home. He will vault over the desk and come at me.

But anger had made Nicholas go rigid. "If my wife weren't a friend of your wife's, if I didn't have some memory of our being boys together, I'd make you pay for what you're saying."

"Yes, you could have me shot like that poor fellow at Cade's Hotel."

"What do you think a communist government would have done to him? And, while we're talking, what do you think it would do to a woman like Kate Tarbox? You think I don't *know* what she's saying? Luckily for her, she's been smart enough to keep her fuzzy ideas out of that newspaper of hers. Besides, she has friends among the planters and some of them are my friends. So no matter what I think of her lies—"

"She doesn't lie, Nicholas."

The men stood up and faced each other.

"I want to tell you something else, Patrick. There's no reason why I should, but out of the friendship you've just tossed away, I will tell you. We know about your son Will. We know about his meetings and his plans. They're a slippery lot, his people, but even a slippery fish ends up in the net. Tell him to remember that."

"I can't do anything about Will." Patrick's heartbeat changed to a reckless pounding. "He's a harmless boy—"

Nicholas mocked him with a look.

"Nicholas, I'm going to run for office. You've got an election coming and you'll have to go through the motions or there'll be real turmoil here, turmoil that even your Red Men won't be able to contain. And I'm going to oppose you in that election."

The black eyes still mocked.

"I had loyalty to you," Patrick said quietly, "but it's been strained beyond bounds or bearing. So now I'm going to fight you."

Nicholas smiled. "You do that. You won't get very far."

❧{21}❧

Francis and Nicholas stood in Eleuthera's hall, talking confidentially.

"I quite realize that he's not your type, Francis. Somewhat vulgar, shall we say? But you ought to listen to him, just once. They've come down from the States with money unlimited. Your Uncle Lionel's probably going to make a deal with them, you know."

"Yes, he told me."

Lionel had been exuberant these past weeks. "First offer I've got and it happens to be dazzling," he'd said.

Well, you could hardly blame him for being dazzled. He could go to England and live for the rest of his life on the invested income from the sale of his lands. Fleetingly, irrelevantly at this particular moment, Francis wondered about the woman whom Lionel had cherished all these years. Most certainly he would not be taking her to England! Francis had only seen her once, when he'd been arriving at the airport in Barbados and Lionel had been leaving. They had pretended not to see each other. She'd been a stunning woman, reminding him of—yes, of Patrick's wife, except that Désirée was jet and Lionel's woman was milky tea.

Nicholas brought him back now to the subject. "Did you know that the High Winds people are interested, too? The old man's over seventy and his sons don't want to run the estate."

"They haven't told me."

"Well, people don't talk about these things until they're signed and delivered. It's always a good policy to keep one's business close to one's vest. At least I've always found it so. Listen, Francis, you've got more beach than High Winds has, by far. And beach is what they need for a hotel project as big as this. You're in a position to ask almost any price you want for the place."

"I don't want to sell Eleuthera, Nicholas."

"But one has the impression," Nicholas said politely, "that your wife does. Isn't it true that she wants to go back to New York?"

So, one "had the impression"! Of course, everybody knew everything in this little place. And Nicholas, especially, had means of finding out whatever he wanted to find out.

"I have good reason to believe," Nicholas continued, "that you could get a couple of million."

Francis looked out to the lawn where Marjorie, already dressed for dinner, was sitting with two men. In their city woolens, the men obtruded on the pastel glimmer, the gauzy trees, the perfection of the waning afternoon. He wondered what conversation she could possibly be having with that pair. Frank Aleppo's wraparound glasses swathed his upper face. Francis hated it when people hid behind dark glasses; they reminded him of the black youths from the Trenches who went swaggering around town these days, except that these two men were white, so white that their skin in this warm light had the greenish cast of a reptile's underside. Aleppo's suit was hand-tailored. To be sure, Francis was accustomed to men who wore expensive clothing, but this man, these two, didn't wear it—they flaunted it.

"I don't like them," he said abruptly, aware that he sounded petulant as an adolescent.

Nicholas laughed. "With all respect to you, Francis, that's really not the issue, is it? Business is business. In justice to yourself and your family, you should at least give it some thought."

Why was Nicholas so anxious? Because of course he'd have a piece of the investment. It amused Francis to think that Nicholas assumed he wouldn't figure that out. There was, after all, no sin in putting your money where you chose. As Nicholas had just said, business is business! A clever man, Nicholas Mebane, so clever that he didn't realize other people could have quick wits, too. But he was charming, all the same—an eminently civilized man.

Francis frowned. One had heard some troubling things of late, things about torture and secret police and drugs and God knew what else. That was the news of the world, wasn't it, from Argentina to the Soviets? But way out here at Eleuthera he'd seen nothing unusual going on. Maybe the one thing he had noticed, the prevalence of the Red Men in town and on the roads, was all to the good. There'd been a lot of petty and not-so-petty crime last year, but ever since this force had been established it had diminished considerably. Or so one heard. Personally, he'd had no experience of it, nor had anyone he knew.

As for the other business, there was possibly a kernel of truth, a bit of "roughing up" going on, but most of it was exaggerated rumor. All that stuff about a ravine where they threw your remains if you spoke out against the government! How could he relate to such atrocities a man like the gentleman standing with him now? Anyway, no matter what government was in power, one was better off keeping within the law, earning one's honest living, and staying away from the disputes. He himself was no man for the political fray. He'd heard somewhere that Patrick Courzon was to run against Nicholas in the next election. The more fool he, Francis was reflecting, when Nicholas spoke again.

"I've reserved a table for dinner at the Lunabelle. I've also invited some other people who've been doing business with Mr. Aleppo. I hope you don't mind."

"No, certainly not." He never enjoyed himself at places like the Lunabelle, but that was not something one would tell the prime minister.

"Senator Madison Hughes will be there, just flew down from Washington yesterday. Also my neighbors, the Jurgens. I don't believe you've met them, a very wealthy Swedish couple? American citizens, though."

Their citizenship was of no interest to Francis, but it was Nicholas's habit to furnish details, especially when he thought they might be impressive. The truth was that planters had no liking for the members of the foreign retirement community; their interests were often at odds. The winter people cared nothing about the welfare of the island except as it concerned themselves; they lived on the island without being of it. But that was something else he didn't care to discuss with the prime minister.

Marjorie came to the door. "We're ready if you are," she said pleasantly. She would despise Aleppo and his young friend, Mr. Damian, but they would never guess it.

"It's too bad your wife can't be with us," she said to Nicholas as they drove off.

"I'm sure she'd rather be where she is." He laughed. "Every year I let her take a few weeks off to go to Paris. She adores it. But then, why not?"

The car had descended the hill and was passing the beach when Aleppo said, "Wow, what a spread! Could we stop a minute and take another look?"

The four men got out, while Marjorie, whose shoes were silk and perishable, waited in the car. Nicholas and Aleppo walked ahead up the strand, both their pace and their flung gestures revealing animation. Damian was less enthusiastic. He sat down on a rock while Francis stood and waited.

"You own this river?" he asked languidly.

"Nobody owns it. It just happens to run through this land." Something about the other man's languor made Francis disagreeable.

"What's it called?"

"Spratt River. They seine sprat at the mouth, near the cove."

"What do you call this place? This beach?"

"The whole cove is called Anse Carrée. You can see it's almost square, and that's what the name means." Saying so, Francis looked up to where the two sharp sides of the cliff turned at right angles into a sheer drop and then down to the third side, a mild slope onto the broad clear beach.

Damian followed his gaze. "Fantastic!" he said with growing interest. "You made a smart buy all right! How long you own this place?"

"My family has owned it for three hundred years."

There was a silence. Damian's somber eyes squinted into the sun and back at Francis.

He doesn't believe me, Francis thought, and there being no more to be said, he walked a few steps to the water's edge and stood there looking straight out through the dazzle to where, if you were to keep on going, you would bump into Spanish Sahara.

Drifting at his feet in shallow water a sea anemone waved its delicate feelers. He picked up a stick of driftwood and gently touched the creature, who, withdrawing from the touch, rolled itself into a knobby ball.

"What's that?" Damian had come up behind him.

"A sea anemone."

"What do you know! Crazy-looking thing!"

Suddenly Francis felt sorry for the man. He didn't know why. Perhaps it was because he was so out of place.

"The sea is filled with strange things, plants that look like animals and animals that look like plants. Coral is an animal, you know. But some of it looks like trees. You can see whole gardens growing underwater." He didn't know why he was telling all this, either, except that it had something to do with that feeling of being sorry for this little man with the bored, superior air.

Nicholas and Aleppo came back, still talking vigorously.

"This is solid rock here," Aleppo was saying. "You could build eight, maybe ten stories, five hundred rooms eventually, adding wings, with the casino on top. There'd be a fantastic view. Nothing like it anywhere."

"Something like the Lunabelle?" Francis asked dryly.

"The Lunabelle, let me tell you, is a dump next to what we'd put here."

"And the house? What would you do with the house?" He felt himself tensed, as with the imminent expectation of pain.

"Tear it down, probably. Unless maybe it could be kept for a clubhouse. We'd have to go into all that. And you know what? I'd have elevators going up the side of the cliff from the beach. You ever seen that? People would get a kick out of it. Look up there, will you! What a location!"

Francis followed the man's pointing arm. At the top of the limestone bluff a pair of sooty terns rose and dove toward a clump of gilded elkhorn coral, having spotted some prey moving there as the tide went out.

"Water gets choppy at high tide, I imagine," Aleppo said. "But we could always dredge."

"Those are coral reefs out there."

"So?"

"So—if you dredge you'll ruin them. It took thousands of years to create those reefs."

"Mr. Luther is a naturalist," Nicholas explained to the uncomprehending Aleppo.

"Very amateur," Francis said.

"All the same." Nicholas was embarrassed. He was apologizing—but to which one of them?

Some prickling anger drove Francis on. "Flamingos used to breed here years ago in the flats between the river and the ocean."

"You don't say," Aleppo murmured.

Patrick Courzon had told him that the day they'd met. He had forgotten that until just now. And he went on, although he knew they were not interested. "I've been trying to bring them back. I bought two pairs a while ago and now they've got young."

"We could name the place Flamingo Hill. No, Flamingo Beach," Aleppo said. "How about that? Can you put them in cages? Some big fancy cages on the lawn?"

"You cannot put them in cages," Francis said. Why had he permitted Nicholas to bring these men?

Nicholas intervened with ease. "We'd better start. The reservations—"

They got back into the car.

Skirting the old stone houses of Covetown's center, with their flowering back-gardens and Georgian facades, they passed along mean roads where the town met the countryside; mangy dogs, scrabbling chickens, and rusty, derelict cars, along with more children than one remembered noticing only a month before, crowded the front yards.

Of a sudden they came upon the Lunabelle's angular bulk and those of its latest neighbors encrusting the hills around the bay. Flags snapped in the wind at the end of the long drive between royal palms. At the portico a black man smiled and sent for another black man to take the car away. And Francis experienced a flash of déjà vu: from a portico like this you followed the luggage to the room, and they brought a rum punch to welcome you, and the soporific wind blew through the jalousies and you heard the steady, repetitious crash of the Atlantic coming up against the breakwater and you went outside and Kate wore a yellow bathing suit and her hair hung like a mermaid's, and then you came back in and she took the suit off and—

"You come here often?" Aleppo inquired, making conversation.

"No. My wife does. She spends more time in town than I do." He was aware that for some reason he had purposely drawn a distinction between himself and his wife.

The enormous, airy lobby displayed at its center a fountain with a naked nymph. Around its sides a row of little shops displayed their French perfumes, their Danish silver, English china, and Italian silks.

"Oh," Marjorie cried. "Da Cunha's branch is open!"

"Francis," said Nicholas, "you'd better come look. Your wife sees something she likes."

Francis peered over Marjorie's shoulder at a pale blue pendant hung on a twisted chain of coral, blue, and gold.

"That," Marjorie said, drawing in her breath, "is absolutely the most beautiful piece of jewelry I have seen in my entire life. Absolutely. The beads are sapphires, Francis."

"Very pretty. But I can't afford it."

Nicholas laughed. "You could very soon though, if you chose to."

A young woman came from behind the counter. "Can I help you with any-thing?"

She was very dark; her eyes were delicately tilted and her long, heavy hair was Oriental. The men, struck by her presence, took a moment to answer.

"Some other time, thank you." Nicholas and Francis spoke together.

"Half black, half Chinese," Nicholas explained as they walked toward the dining room. "Her father had a grocery store. Ah Sing, the name is—or was; he must be ancient by now or dead. And his daughter is rising in the world. You see how it is, we provide employment with these places, we create opportunity."

"Much envy, too," Francis answered.

"Ah, Francis, you're so gloomy sometimes!" Marjorie complained.

Heads were raised as the prime minister walked into the dining room with his party of whites. Except for the waiters, he was the only black in the room. But he appeared to be unconscious of it, aware and pleased that his status was acknowledged.

The senator and the Jurgens were already at the table. The senator was handsome, a man who would age or had already aged well, with that air of powerful health which stems from a youth spent out of doors in almost any location west of the Mississippi. The Jurgens were thickset. They had the odor of money. Francis could smell it, not ordinary prosperity, but enormous amounts of it, obscene amounts of it. He was a stout, graying blond; she was pink, with loose pink skin and a loose pink garment which, so Marjorie had taught him, was called a caftan. She wore many diamonds. Fat cats, Francis thought, caught in the strange mood that so often beset him when he was forced to a gathering he didn't want to attend. It did this to him, bringing out a sharp, a nasty, critical awareness. He didn't like himself for it, but there it was.

Introductions were made and Nicholas said, "The Jurgens have the most marvelous house. With your taste," addressing Marjorie, "you would find it enchanting."

"It's the house next door to yours, isn't it?" Marjorie responded.

"Yes, but there's no comparison." Nicholas spoke modestly. "As Europeans, they have a special feel for gardens. Their lawns, and the pavilion at the far end, so Italian—"

"In spite of our being Swedish. You really must come to see us sometime, Mrs. Luther. Harold's retired, you know, so we're only here for three months. Then we go to Europe, and we have some family in the States, too. We do love it here the best though. I have two maids," she confided, "and one of them cooks better than the chefs at this hotel! For only twenty dollars a week each."

Francis glanced at Nicholas. Embarrassment shot through him so that he could feel its heat. But Nicholas gave no sign.

"People really don't need much cash here, do they?" Mrs. Jurgen's rhetorical question was gay. "No heating bills, no overcoats, no boots. And the villages are so quaint, all those picturesque little houses—really delightful."

"Delightful," Francis said. "With the toilet in the back yard."

He received from Marjorie a sharp kick on the ankle.

Mrs. Jurgen, thinking apparently that he had meant to be humorous, laughed. But Aleppo had understood.

"We could change all that. We could put this place on the map, I tell you. Remember how Havana used to be? This could put it to shame. We could make this another Riviera, build marinas, build a jetport, have excursion trips direct from Europe for deep-sea fishing, tarpon, whatnot. Believe me, there'd be a bathroom in every house on the island then, and a whole lot more!"

"Especially," Mr. Jurgen, who had not spoken before, put in, "especially with a common-sense man like this one at the helm of government." His plump cheeks, drawn into a smile, narrowed his small, pale eyes. "Frankly, he's the only reason I'm willing to invest. I feel secure."

"I shall have to merit confidence like that," Nicholas joked, "by making sure I get reelected."

Jurgen waved his cigar. "No problem! Those others—that fellow Courzon and the rest—mosquitoes buzzing. Nothing more. I'm not worried, I assure you."

The dinner arrived. Only a French or a Swiss chef could have created such marvelous soufflés and sauces, or such variety of flambéed desserts, borne proudly high as the waiters moved between the tables.

A trio of young men came to sing before a microphone. They were dressed as if they had just been brought there from the cane fields. Perhaps they actually had been. Their voices were warm, resonant, untrained.

> Oh, island in the sun, willed to me by my father's hand,
> All my days I will sing in praise . . .

And Francis put himself in their places at the front of the crowded room. What were they seeing? White faces burned pain-red, white breasts straining out of silk, mountains of food, the flicker of jewels. He wondered what they could be thinking about what they saw.

To these others here, surrounding him, it was all quite natural, quite unremarkable. Eating slowly, almost disregarding the talk at his own table, Francis observed the scene and listened to snatches of conversation.

"Darling!" people said, throwing their arms about each other. Then came the cheek-peck, the cheek-graze. "How are you! You look simply fantastic! I haven't seen you since dinner at the George V!" Or the Dorchester, or better still, some place less frequented, like Porto Cervo in Sardinia, or even some really far off "little" spot where "tourists don't go": We were the only Americans in the whole place.

Then, as always, he was brought back to the present. "You're a thousand miles away," Marjorie scolded in a whisper.

"Three or four thousand, actually. Sorry."

"Please, Francis."

Her eyes pleaded. "Do be sociable, do give forth a little, can't you?"

She wouldn't want to offend the prime minister. She didn't mind his being black, because he was the prime minister. She was having a good time. She loved wearing her beautiful dress, loved being here. Her eyes were brilliant and very large. She was thinking of two million dollars.

When dinner was over they walked outdoors, where terraces descended in tiers to the beach. The tide had gone out, exposing at the end of the beach the roots of beach grape and mangrove, along with a fringe of debris: clotted petroleum tar, bottles and cans. Floodlights plucked all these out of the darkness.

"Poor maintenance," Nicholas remarked. "I'm surprised."

"More than that," Francis said. "Look at the silt in the water. It's from dredging. That silt cuts down the light; the algae are smothered and the coral dies. They've destroyed the protecting reefs to get construction sand, that's what's happened here. Yes," he said, "dredge the seas, bulldoze the hills, and what next? It's a rape, that's all it is."

"Oh," Nicholas said lightly "you sound like—" and stopped.

Like Patrick Courzon, Francis thought. That's what he had been about to say. And it was true—Patrick had always talked like that.

"You can't stop the twentieth century," Mr. Jurgen remarked, somewhat exasperated.

"You can plan your development instead of raping. Raping," Francis repeated. It was a reckless, angry word, and it suited him just then.

He was conscious, as they turned back to the cars, of Marjorie's furious glance.

Nicholas rode with the Luthers, who were to take him to his home. When they were almost there he reminded Francis, "I hope you don't mean you won't give consideration to the Aleppo offer, Francis. In spite of what you've been saying, it would be not only a great thing for you but a bonanza for the country. Take my word for it, please do."

"Oh," Marjorie said angrily, "naturally we all know the planters don't want development because they'll lose field labor. We all know that."

"That's not my reason," Francis said with some heat.

Nicholas made no comment. When they reached his house, he gave Francis his hand. "Well, it's all been quite bewildering and sudden, of course. But you will think it over?"

"I'll do that," Francis said out of courtesy.

"Thank you for a marvelous time," Marjorie called. "The dinner was perfect." When they had driven away she turned upon Francis. "You were absolutely ridiculous—I must say it. All that talk about algae and dredging! They thought you were eccentric and boring. I don't know what you hoped to gain with that kind of talk."

"I didn't hope to gain anything. It was just a mood. I wanted to get things off my chest. Am I not entitled to a mood like anyone else?"

"You sounded like some sort of hippy ecologist. . . . Like that younger Da Cunha brother who's always writing articles."

"That young Da Cunha cares. It's the older generation that doesn't give a damn about anything but money."

"It seems to me you like money well enough!"

"Yes, I like it. But I work for mine fairly—"

"Work! Yes, nobody could deny you do that! Worrying about banana rot and labor and too much rain or not enough rain—and for what?" She spoke rapidly. "Listen to me, Francis. Megan has to get away from this place. She has special needs. When she gets a little older she'll need schooling she can't get here. And this is our chance to provide all that, plus having a decent life of our own with no more worries. I swear I'll never forgive you if you don't take it, Francis. Never."

He was silent and she repeated, "Never. This time I mean it."

He was thinking that once her voice had had a ring as sweet as chimes. The sweetness had rung through to his very bones. He tried to remember when it was that it had stopped doing so, and could not. Driving now along the narrow mountain road in the darkness, he felt a penetrating sadness; it was like knowing there had once been a song you loved, and now you had forgotten it, forgotten even its name.

He said quietly, "I don't want to talk any more tonight, please. It's been a long day and for some reason I feel especially tired."

"Damn it, Francis! I hate it when you shut me off. You think you can just turn me off and on like a faucet whenever you feel like it."

It was an effort to answer, to open his mouth. "I told you, another time. I don't want to shut you off. All I want is to get home and sleep."

"Damn it, then. Get home and go to sleep!"

The car door slammed. The bedroom door slammed. She still slept across the hall. He wondered whether the sound had awakened the child. It was his last thought before he fell asleep.

But he slept badly, waking in the middle of the night, unable to fall back. Soon after dawn he got up and went out to walk.

Where the foothills of the Morne sloped steeply upward behind the house the path was scarcely used. Wet ferns showered his legs as he passed. The silent droppings of the pines were slippery underfoot. Now the woods were waking, loud with bird song and a thousand small rustlings of unseen life. Once, glancing up, he thought he saw a parrot, an instant's astonishing flash of emerald and orange in the sheltering gloom. If it was a parrot it had probably been *Amazona arausiaca,* a variety now hunted almost to extinction because a single specimen could bring five thousand dollars.

"It's disgusting," Kate had cried passionately. "They smuggle them out in tire tubes and suitcases. Naturally, most of them die on the way. I can't bear to think of it." She had reminded him of his mother's fierce pity for the weak.

He came back down the steep path. He had no wish to get to the day's work; he would have liked rather to lie down in the ferns and perhaps go to sleep at last, but the notion was eccentric, for if anyone were to come upon him lying there like that they would think he'd lost his mind. And he thrust his way on through a jumble of bananas, palm, and cane gone wild, emerging at the bottom of the path into a vision of splashing light, of clouds fleeing westward over the clearing where the great house lay among flamboyant trees. He stopped to look at it, his great house, and saw Marjorie coming toward him over the grass.

"I saw you on the hill. I wanted to say I'm sorry if I was nasty last night, Francis."

"That's all right. I wasn't in such a great mood myself."

She laid a hand on his arm and mechanically he put his over it. How he had loved her once!

And they stood a moment looking at the morning light, stood together, each wanting so much to understand and to be understood.

To ease the stress he made a neutral remark. "The river looks like silver from here."

"Oh rivers! One makes such a fuss about rivers! The blue Danube is a muddy brown brook, that's all it is. But you've never seen it, have you? You've really never gone anywhere."

"I haven't had the time."

"Of course you have. You just came here and never left it. Never wanted to. If you left here you could travel. You've still got that camera on the shelf for your next book. What was it to be? *Man at Work in His Environment,* wasn't that it?"

"I guess so," he said dully.

"I nag you awfully about leaving, don't I?"

"I wouldn't say 'nag.' You just talk about it."

"Oh, you always cover everything with euphemisms. Don't you know you do? I nag."

It was true, he thought, surprised. Even in my private thoughts, I cover up. Like my mother, I'm too private. And I don't face the truth, it's true.

"I don't believe in covering up, Francis. Not anymore. So I'll tell you flat out: I *hate* it here! I always have. There was just no easy way to leave before this. But now there is."

"Have you thought of Megan?" he asked.

Her eyes widened. "I don't understand you! What a question!"

"It was stupid of me. I phrased it badly. I meant—this place is shelter for her, given what she is."

"But she can't hide here, Francis! She needs special education to bring out the little she's got, so she won't be just a—a vegetable! There's nothing here for her, you know there isn't! And you can't tell what's going to happen here anyway, with the political situation what it is!" She began to weep. "Oh, if we had a normal child!"

"Don't," he said. It tore him to see her weep over Megan. Because of him, his blood, his sister, his genes. His fault.

"And with all that money she would have security for the rest of her life! If you love her so, how can you be so selfish?"

He said thickly, "I love her."

"I'll tell you something, Francis. I'm not excited now. I'm thinking clearly and I'm quite, quite calm, not angry at all. But if you don't take this offer, I'm leaving. I'm taking Megan, and somebody in my family will shelter us until I can find a place for us."

"Is that the way it is?"

"That's the way it is."

Her eyes met his. Hers were austere and steady in their gaze. And he knew that she meant what she said.

"Let me think," he said. "Oh, let me think."

Her face closed. "All right. Just don't think too long."

She went back inside, and he walked down the hill toward that silver river to sit on a rock with his chin in his hands. On a bush close by a yellowbird was gathering twigs for a nest. So still he sat that the bird was unconcerned with his presence. Just so had he sat one day not long ago with Megan, showing her how a bird goes about the making of a nest. It had even picked up a piece of cotton torn from somebody's shirt. He had showed her that. And he had thought: Just something, some little thing missing in the making of her, some juice in the brain, some electrical connection, what? And she would have been whole and who knew how intelligent, how creative. Oh, God, he begged now, speaking aloud, and the yellowbird fled.

The air was filled with the fragrance of wild ginger, and he knew the white flower could not be too far away. One of his colts went galloping through pangola grass behind the rail fence that he had himself helped hew and set in place. Well, if he were to leave, he'd be leaving things in very different shape from what he had found when he came. The drenching sweetness of the ginger swept over him. Oh, my God, the place bewitched you! And he thought of his mother: could she, too, have felt this wrench when she left? Was that why she had never wanted to come back, and not, as some people thought, that she hated it? Human behavior! How can you hope to understand it, when you can't even understand yourself?

And he sat there for a long time until he heard Megan's voice from somewhere above. No doubt she would be looking for him, his shadow, his Megan, his poor simple girl.

Slowly, stiffly, he rose and went up the hill. In the shelter of the old library he picked up the telephone.

"Mr. Aleppo," he said. The word stuck in his throat. "Mr. Aleppo. I've considered the offer and I've decided to accept. You can draw up the papers for me to show my lawyer."

Aleppo said something about having to go back to the States, something about time, a few weeks or a month or so.

"Take your time. Whenever you're ready."

"You're doing the right thing, Mr. Luther. Come back in a couple of years and you won't recognize your place."

"I'm sure I won't."

"You're a gentleman, Mr. Luther. I've met all kinds and I know a gentleman when I see one."

When he had hung up the receiver he went outside and walked around the house, with no purpose except the walk itself, the need to move. A voice sang from the cook's radio in the kitchen wing.

> Oh, island in the sun, willed to me by my father's hand,
> All my days I will sing in praise . . .

He went around to the front of the house. Somewhere inside Marjorie was waiting, determined and frightened, too, he knew. Well, he would just go in and make his peace. A man had to be strong enough to lose gracefully. He'd made a start here and he could make another.

Not far from the front door grew a great acoma, very old. His mother had said, "My grandfather used to touch a tree as though it spoke to him." This same tree, it might have been, as he came in at this same door. And before he went up the steps into the house Francis reached over to lay his hand on the ancient bark, and spoke to it softly, without words.

❧{22}❧

In a shady grove near a beach another crowd had gathered, the second one in a day that was to provide three of the same in various parts of the island. Blue paper streamers, emblazoned in gold with the words *Vote for Courzon,* dangled from the trees and festooned the skirts of the long sawbuck tables on which the food was laid out. Patrick, standing in line for calalu stew and soursop custard, reflected that he hadn't had such food since Agnes had cooked it, for Désirée had no taste for what she called peasant food. Then he wondered what Agnes would say if she could see this day. Next he thought about the connection between those kids dancing over there to a frantic rhythm band and the issues which were tearing their country apart, issues about which, according to theory, they were expected to think carefully before casting their votes. Well, it was a gradual thing, the evolution of a democratic government! It had taken, after all, quite a few centuries in England between Magna Charta and one man, one vote.

As for himself, after the first nervous, hesitant week or two, things had begun to pick up, "things" being his own sense of confidence. He was even becoming inured to the long days, the late nights, the voice gone hoarse, the food to be stuffed down his throat, and the hands to be shaken. All in all, he was doing better with this campaign than he would have expected a normally reserved, almost a reclusive, man to do.

Men were rushing about now, trying to quiet the crowd. Someone bellowed, pleaded, and commanded over the microphone. It was clouding up and they'd want to get the speech finished before the rain came. Patrick glanced over the assemblage. There was the usual cluster of journalists, some, now that this part of the world had drawn the rest of the world's attention to itself, having come even from European countries. More white faces fringed the crowd: a few curious tourists, the planter Fawcett and the Whittaker nephew who was known to be "liberal," the youngest Da Cunha son with friends, and of course, Kate and her staff, who followed all the campaign speeches, Nicholas's as well as Patrick's. All of these stood forth from the dark-faced mass.

When the noise ceased the hush was absolute. They were waiting for what Patrick had to say. And as always, he gave himself a mental reminder to speak in strong, clear language. He might not be able to bewitch them with passionate oratory nor impress them with his manner and dress, but he could surely speak to them in language they would understand about things they would understand. He reminded himself also: never underestimate the intelligence of the "common" man.

His points were simple and consistent. He had said before, and would say again, that they were a farming people, that they would remain a farming people, and that such industries as they must establish would stem from agriculture.

"We are told about world markets and such things as balance of payments, all fancy expressions to describe and explain why we are poor, why some of us go to the cold north to pick apples in another country, why shoes cost so much, as do soap and even sugar, which although we raise it here ourselves, so many of us can't afford to buy.

"Yes, you've heard all this. Our present leaders asked for your vote because they promised to do something about these things. Now, we all know they can't be changed overnight; the structure of years can't be overhauled in hours. But you do have to make a beginning! Here we are, approaching the third year of this administration, and I see not one small sign, none at all, that anybody cares to alleviate any of our pains. Have you?"

A roar went up: "No! No!"

"What I do see is a display of fantastic luxury in high places. I see men in red uniforms—expensive ones, by the way, as are their fancy barracks and their new cars. Yes, men in uniform with large fists in white gloves and"—he paused—"men without uniform, who stalk and spy among you, extorting taxes, often known as contributions. Contributions, mind you, while they rob and beat, terrifying you in your homes at night, silencing your tongues."

And while he spoke, other recollections, sharp as hooks, attacked him: the farmer who, having written an open letter protesting taxes, was found dead in his field when he failed to come in for lunch; the son of one of Clarence's old union friends who'd come home, after three days' detention on some vague charge, with an empty socket instead of an eye; his own Will, who'd returned one night with torn clothing and a knife slash. "A fight over a girl," he'd said only, but he hadn't left the house for a week.

"Even under colonial rule we never knew terror like this. People never disappeared. People weren't afraid to talk out loud in public places."

The silence was so deep that he thought he could hear them all breathing, or hear a long collective shiver and sigh. Behind him on the platform he did hear his bodyguards shifting in their seats. They were wary and nervous.

"You lay it on pretty thick, Boss," one had told him only yesterday. "You're not afraid?"

"The foreign correspondents are my safeguard. If anything should happen to me," he'd answered, "wouldn't it prove that everything I've been saying is correct?" He almost believed that himself.

Plowing back into the substance of the speech, making promises, but not too many, promising only to give his honest effort and, above all, to remove the terror, he rose at last into a peroration and stood to acknowledge the applause.

The dark peasants gathered their children and departed. I must have had great-grandparents who looked like them, he thought, or maybe great-greats.

Who knew? For a moment, half unconsciously, he stretched out his hand to look at it, then remembering where he was, put it quickly into his pocket. . . . Two young blond photographers from some news service were taking pictures of Patrick and the crowd, while he, looking back at them, felt again, as so often, that old confusion—*I am of them, too*—a confusion that would never leave him, he knew well.

When, after the last applause, he turned to step down from the platform, the rain came. The sky opened. The soaking rain pounded a furious drumbeat on the earth, so that the foreign newsmen, astonished at its vehemence, went scuttling to their cars.

Patrick's car was a station wagon seating nine, among them Kate and her two young cousins who worked on the *Trumpet*. Franklin Parrish sat in the rear with Patrick, who could sometimes stretch out a little there to rest.

"The rain will be over by the time we get to the next place," Franklin said. "This was a very responsive crowd, I thought. Not one heckler in the lot. You know, Boss"—although Patrick disliked the appellation *Boss* and had told Franklin so more than once, it still slipped out occasionally in pure affection—"you know, Boss, I'm beginning to think we might make it after all."

"We'll see," was all Patrick said.

The other side had the money and the power. Best not to think farther ahead than each day's uphill climb. Still, he was grateful for Franklin's confidence. The young man's intelligence and enthusiasm nourished and sustained him. If he won, he was resolved to put Franklin into a position of importance and trust. Not that the young man needed Patrick's sponsorship, for he was obviously destined to rise in the party ranks through his own abilities, his firmness, his tact, and his welcome smile. He was a fine speaker with a natural talent, unlike Patrick, who had taught himself through his persevering observation of Nicholas Mebane. Franklin was clever enough, too, to utilize a few politician's tricks.

"Look at me," he'd say. "I am one of you." Referring, of course, to his color, which was as dark as any worker's.

Patrick smiled inwardly. It was pretty clear that Parrish was having serious thoughts about Laurine and that she, now almost twenty years old, was having thoughts of her own. Patrick and Désirée had even talked about it. Désirée had raised objections: "He's too black," she'd said. And Patrick had put her arm next to his own, making an elaborate play of doing so. "Too dark," he'd said, in such a mock-tragic tone that she had begun to laugh at herself. "Thank goodness for your sense of humor," he'd told her.

The car, last in a short procession, turned inland and uphill. Alongside the road Patrick observed a farmer, helped by his neighbors, building a house. They were wattling and thatching. There would be food and drink for them all when the job was done, he knew. And he laid his head back on the seat, closing his eyes, thinking of the kindly comfort there was in such a continuation of old ways during this time of speeding change.

He'd seen more of country life during these weeks of his campaign than he'd seen in a long while, ever since he'd begun to live in the town. He'd gone looking for votes in the sugar factories, where, although the windmills were gone, the workers still skimmed the boiling foam and tested the liquid thread between the forefinger and thumb to judge when to strike. He'd eaten chicken and yams and drunk mint tea with prosperous farmers in their comfortable homes. Oh, yes, there were many such farms on which the descendants of slaves worked their own fields, played with their children, and married off their daughters to the sound of music! He'd talked to teachers while children played cricket on the village green, exactly as he had once done. He'd talked to planters at the Agricultural Show; most of them, he knew, would be on the other side, with Nicholas, for "law and order," nevertheless he'd tried to show them he was for better law and order. . . . Certainly it never hurt to try. And he remembered now, apropos of nothing, that he'd seen Osborne there, standing before a pen, guarding a handsome cream-colored bull. There to collect the prize for Francis, probably! A queer pain shot through him, making a shudder and a chill.

He opened his eyes.

"You dozed some?" Franklin asked. "You needed it. Did I tell you that young Da Cunha sent us a check?"

"The older brother's for Mebane, I take it? Like the father?"

"The father, yes, of course. The brother, though, doesn't care one way or the other. Whatever's better for business is what he'll be for."

The road was dry and dusty, for on this side of the Morne it had not rained. They drove through a string of villages, where, the caravan having been expected, people had come out to stare, more often now to wave and cheer. It occurred to Patrick suddenly that he might really, after all, win! The prospect thrilled him and scared him, too: what had he let himself in for? He pushed the thought away.

"You've made an impact," Franklin said positively. "More than we've realized, I think."

"We've still a long way to go."

"True. But if we lose, we'll try again. We'll have to, that's all."

Franklin was actually enjoying himself, which was surprising. One wouldn't expect a bookish fellow like him to like this business. The strategy of government was one thing, but the hullabaloo of an election was quite another.

"If we lose," Patrick said, "you'll carry on. You and your generation."

Franklin was astonished. "Why, you're a young man! What are you talking about?"

Kate, sitting in front, had overheard. "You're only forty-one, Patrick! How can you talk like that?"

They were right, of course. Still it was good to see many young people ready to go forward, a man like Franklin's cousin, for example, that thin fellow with the odd green eyes, home on vacation from the University of the West Indies, so reasonable, intelligent, liberal, never fanatical. And he thought of Will, then blocked out the thought.

"I wish," Kate said, "I had the courage to come out flatfooted for you. This business of presenting both sides equally as 'news' just sickens me."

"You're doing a good job this way," Franklin told her. "At least, you're printing Patrick's message so people can judge for themselves. The other way, if you took sides, they'd just close up your paper. You know that."

"You're a great help, all of you," Patrick said softly.

The road mounted through cane fields toward more hills; ahead, you could see the dance and dazzle of the heat; on the platform the sun would burn; he would be glad to get this over with for today.

"Good God," Franklin cried, as they approached the meeting place, "there must be two thousand here! It's the largest yet!"

From miles about they must have collected, to stand now sweating and fanning themselves with their straw hats, drinking beer and nursing their babies, while they waited for the afternoon's event.

Patrick got out of the car and mounted the platform. He saw, with his new "political" eye, that there were many young in the audience, so he began by addressing them.

"The world is harder for the young today. There are more of you, and you have higher aspirations, which you should have. I think I understand the young because I'm a teacher. So you'll forgive me if I'm long-winded, like a teacher." He paused for the laughter, aware that it was a good thing to begin a speech with a little joke, preferably at one's own expense.

"A great responsibility rests upon the educational establishment . . . not to raise everyone to the top of the heap, which is a quite obvious impossibility, in spite of the worldwide propaganda to the contrary, because men are not equal in their capabilities . . . nor to lower everyone to the same bottom . . . to want that is only futile envy and revenge . . . no, to give every person the chance to climb up if it should be in him to do so. . . . That and that alone is the voice of fairness, decency and common sense. . . . I ask you to listen. . . . I favor a mixed economy, government to do those things that governments do best and free enterprise to do the rest."

Patrick's eyes moved over the crowd, which was listening, with interest. At the far edge of the field, where trucks and Hondas were parked, he thought he saw a flurry of arriving cars, latecomers. The heat was dizzying and he hastened on toward a close.

"I made a little joke before about talking too much. I've really tried not to. I hope you'll go home and give thought to what I've said, then come out and vote against this regime which will, if allowed to continue, drive you first to despair, and in the end, I'm afraid, to communism."

"Dirty communist yourself!" a man cried. Cries came from all over the field. "Smash the son of a bitch! Yeah, dirty communist himself!"

Cries came as a line of men shoved forward from the rear of the field.

"Shut up! Shame! Throw them out!"

Somebody hurled the first stone. A woman screamed as a man fell with the blow. Then, with the suddenness of an earthquake or explosion or any cataclysm that gives no warning, the field erupted into chaos.

From all sides and as if from the sky itself came a bombardment of stones. Chairs and tables went hurtling. From somewhere came the stench of rotten eggs: precious eggs! Men wrestled, women wailed in turn and fell on one another, trying to flee. In the confusion, it was impossible to tell who was assaulting whom. Some seemed to be joining up with the invading ruffians. A hail of paper bags descended on the crowd to burst and spatter their incredible contents of excrement and garbage. Police, appearing out of nowhere, melted into the crowd, some attempting to attack, some trying to restore order, and some observing, doing nothing.

"Stop it! Stop it!" Patrick heard his own frenzied, futile screaming. His throat strained with his screams, even after he had been struck with some foul liquid that soaked his shirt and knocked him, for a moment, to the ground. It was unbelievable, first this attentive meeting and an instant later this vicious brawl!

Somebody helped him up. Out of the savage mob men mustered in a ring, three deep, around him. The outer ring, as they pushed him through the uproar toward his car, sustained a bloody battering. Men armed with clubs and nail-studded boards went flailing. Patrick saw Franklin dodge a blow. Stumbling and shoving, they edged toward the car.

We won't make it, Patrick thought. Strange way to meet your end, in an open field on a blazing summer day, at the hands of Mebane's thugs.

And suddenly the crowd fell back. A dozen or so young men, coming from behind the row of cars which Patrick and his men were trying to reach, stepped forward and threw.

"Tear gas!" Franklin cried. "Run, run!"

Over their heads and behind them the acrid cloud sprayed. The engine was already racing in Patrick's car; it was in motion before the doors had even been closed, and they were out of the field, onto the road, with tires skidding in a foam of dust when a last stone smashed through the windshield.

"The tear gas?" Patrick gasped. His eyes stung. "Whose?"

"Our own people. We were prepared for something like this. We knew it was bound to come eventually," Franklin said.

"My God, I hope there weren't too many hurt!"

"Bastards! Are you all right, Patrick?"

"Yes. A stone got me in the shoulder. And I stink. Other than that, I'm all right."

Désirée WAS FURIOUS, scolding and weeping as she brought clean clothes for Patrick. "You idiot, you could have been killed!"

They were on Clarence's porch. Crippled with arthritis, he had taken to the old custom of sleeping out of doors in a hammock.

"I hear it's a triumph wherever you go," he said now. "Franklin and his boys tell me. Next time I'm coming along for the thrill, if I have to get someone to carry me."

"Triumph!" cried Désirée. "Thrill! Is that what you call this?"

Clarence ignored his daughter. "I've news for you. This afternoon, while you were out there, the trade union congress voted unanimously to support you."

"Well, I shouldn't think they'd want Mebane," Patrick said, pleased.

"No, but you might think they'd want the left wing, mightn't you? And they don't. They don't want the radicals. They want you."

"Everybody wants you. They'll destroy you with their wanting," Désirée mourned. Then anger seized her again. "You're nothing but big, overgrown boys, the two of you, sitting here boasting over this—this horror! You're naïve, that's what you are, naïve."

The adjective amused Patrick, since it was one he had always privately applied to her.

"I wish you could see yourselves," she went on. "Neither one of you has faced the truth of what life is!"

"Well, well," Clarence said. "Suppose you tell us, then."

"I'll tell you what it isn't! It's not knocking your brains out, eating your heart out, sacrificing your health and safety for other people, when they don't give the least damn about you! Do you actually think all these people here in this dinky place really care who's elected?"

"Yes, I do think so," Patrick said.

"Well, you don't know what you're talking about! All they want is food to feed their faces with and enough rum, and bed on Saturday night—"

Patrick smiled at her modest words.

"—and you think they'll ever thank you for giving them the means to get what they want?"

"I'm not looking for thanks," Patrick said.

"The more fool you, then! Go! Go! Get yourself killed!"

He sighed. "I don't suppose I'll ever make you see, Désirée. And don't be melodramatic. I'm not going to get myself killed."

"Oh, if I'd married a preacher I would not have had to put up with this holiness! You're so damned holy, Patrick!" She amended the judgment. "I don't mean you're a hypocrite. No, you really mean it all; you care. But I'm not like you. I want things first for ourselves—"

"I've tried to give them to you, I've done the best I could," he said stiffly now, aware at the same time that his words were perhaps self-pitying and sulky.

"Oh, I know. But I don't want only *things*, Patrick. Not so much anymore. It's peace I'm talking about now. I just want peace."

"I'm trying to give you that, too. Don't you understand how I'm trying to give it to us all?"

She sighed. "You've had no supper. Shall I fix a tray here on the porch? I've fresh broiled yellowtail with lime juice."

He was too utterly done in to be hungry. Nevertheless, he stood up. Food had always been her remedy, her way of expressing her concern and giving love.

"I'm ready. We'll go inside," he said, putting a hand on her shoulder.

She caught his hand, kissing the palm, then turning it over and kissing the back. She cradled his head, comforting and protesting.

"Oh, dear God, what have they done to you! The animals! What have they done! But animals don't do things like that! Still, I'm so proud of you, Patrick, no matter what I said. I'm angry at you and proud of you and I'm so afraid. Oh, my dear, my dearest, I'm so afraid!"

⋇{23}⋇

"Did you know Rob Fawcett's supporting your good old friend Patrick for election?" Marjorie asked as they arrived at the Fawcetts' anniversary party.

"No, I didn't, and I wish you wouldn't be sarcastic," Francis said.

"Erstwhile friend, then. Sorry."

Not wanting to talk about Patrick, he was, at the same time, curious. "Fawcett never mentioned it to me."

"He wouldn't. He's a gentleman. He knows how we feel."

Francis liked the Fawcetts. They had a depth often lacking in this ingrown, tight community where relationships could yet be so superficial; their house held music and vitality and good talk. Tonight Whim Longhouse, illuminated like an ocean liner, floated in the darkness; out of its windows streamed a glitter of celebratory light.

Francis followed his wife as, in crisp lime-green taffeta, she rustled up the steps. Her spirits were high, higher than they had been since the day of Megan's birth and this, of course, was because they were at last "going home." Her increasing animation silenced him, although he knew he had made the right, the inevitable decision. He simply didn't want to talk about it.

Everyone was already outside on the rear lawns. The Luthers were late; they usually were, because Francis would never leave home until Megan was asleep.

"You go on out. I'll phone home first," he said.

"But we've just left home!"

"Forty minutes ago. I want to make sure of things. It's the first time we've left her with this new maid."

The rule was that whenever the parents were away, a maid must sit in the room next to Megan's until they returned. The idea was Francis'. He supposed it was neurotic to be so apprehensive, but that fire was always with him; he never came up the driveway at Eleuthera without seeing the ruin all over again and feeling terror in the pit of his stomach.

When he had made the call he walked past the dining room, where the dinner would be served later in the evening, and through the great drawing room. Here was a comfortable clutter of overstuffed Belter furniture, all curved and curlicued. "So tacky!" Marjorie always said. The walls were hung with ancestors in broad, heavy frames. He wondered whether they were fake or real and decided, knowing the Fawcetts' candor, that they were very probably real. So even these nice people had a need to worship their ancestors! Well, it was all right as long as you didn't get to thinking you were better than people without ancestors—as if we didn't all have them, even though they hadn't left their portraits behind!

He was oversensitive to everything tonight, he knew, without knowing why. It was just one of those times when, because of glands or hormones or something or other, his worries tormented him. He felt as if he were in limbo, still here on St. Felice, but not really here anymore, because his mind had already lurched on ahead to the new place, to the new start. It was almost like assuming another identity.

Yet at the heart of it all was Megan. Going on six, past kindergarten age, with each passing month she made plain the difference between what she was and what she ought normally to be. Her future was becoming more cruelly certain. And silently Francis groaned, while he went outdoors toward the clatter of music and voices.

Little round tables for hors d'oeuvres had been set up at the edge of the terrace, under a triple row of maria trees so tailored that their intertwining branches formed a flat and solid roof of leafage. Candle flames wavered in hurricane lamps, each set in a ring of red hibiscus blossoms. The bar stood under a flaring tulip tree, against a background of marble-striped croton leaves. For a moment Francis stood looking over a scene now grown familiar, the pastel luster of the well-dressed crowd, the black waiters, soft-footed and white-gloved, and the wealth of flowers. Already, he saw, the men and women had separated. He wondered what the women could find to talk about, since they saw so much of each other at the club most days. The men, who did not see each other that often, had politics to talk about, of course. Now, spotting his host, he went down the steps.

"Congratulations on twenty good years," Francis said, shaking hands. "I'd like to be around to celebrate your fiftieth."

"If we make it, God willing," Fawcett replied. "It's a pity you won't be with us here if we do. You'll be missed," he added.

He meant it, Francis saw, murmuring his thanks.

"Yes, losing a man like you is a great loss for this place."

"I haven't done anything," Francis replied, feeling embarrassment.

"Not lately," Fawcett said steadily, "but you could again."

Old Whittaker interjected, "Listen to me, Luther, and don't pay attention to what anybody tells you. You're doing the smart thing. Half of these people—I don't mean you, Fawcett, you've got your own way of looking at things—but half of these people would quit tomorrow if they could find a buyer. They'd sell out like that!" He snapped his fingers. "They just haven't been as lucky as you, that's all."

These remarks were unusually lengthy for Whittaker, whose small pink mouth was usually pursed, as if to open it were an effort not worth attempting. His wife makes up for his silence, Francis thought with some distaste, not welcoming his unexpected ally.

"My wife tells me," Whittaker continued, "you're planning a New York apartment and a country place on Long Island."

"I couldn't stand being cooped up in the city all year."

Now his depression settled as if someone had placed a shawl on his shoulders. Limbo, yes, that's where he was. At home there were cartons and boxes in the hallways. Marjorie had already begun to drag things out of attics and closets, to sort and give away. He supposed, or rather knew, it was foolish to impart life to inanimate objects, yet it hurt him to discard his schoolbooks—which no one would ever use—or Megan's crib, which they would never use again, either, or so many dear old possessions.

"We simply can't drag all this stuff back with us," Marjorie declared. "It would cost a fortune, and where would we put it?"

He was too sentimental, by far.

And accepting from a silver tray a drink and canapés, he sat down among the men, to let their conversation wash over and past while he only half heard. The talk was the same talk that had been circling through the clubs and the great houses for months past.

"The burglaries in Covetown are not to be believed, especially in the hotels. They don't put them all in the papers, you know."

"The tourists bring it on themselves, flaunting their money and their jewelry. What do you expect?"

True, Francis thought, but not all that simple, either.

A large, bald man on the other side of the table—Barnstable, his name was, from the south end of the island—was telling a story amid much laughter.

"So when my cook's father died I went to pay a condolence call. Way the hell and gone out in the country it was. But good Lord, Sally's been with us eighteen years! They sit up all night at the wake, of course, but what I didn't know was, they tell jokes and drink and dance, a regular party! They even poured rum down the dead man's throat. He was sitting up in a chair—"

"Who was?"

"The corpse!"

"I don't believe it!"

"True, though, I swear it. What do you expect of these people, anyway?"

The waiter was passing a mushroom quiche. Francis, wincing acutely, glanced up at the man's face, but the face was bland. I wonder what they tell about us? he thought.

And he looked back at the large, bald man, who was still laughing, pleased with his contribution to the entertainment; then he watched as a covey of butterflies, attracted by the lights, went fluttering into the bougainvillaea and clung there, like black velvet bows pinned to a veil.

"So you were at one of Courzon's rallies," someone remarked to Rob Fawcett.

"Yes, I wanted to hear him for myself. The newspapers don't dare print it all."

"You were impressed, your wife says."

"Yes, I was. I'm not going again, though. I'm too tall a target for a bottle or a brick."

"They've gone utterly mad. A kid was stabbed not two blocks off Wharf Street a couple of days ago in some political brawl."

"I didn't see that anywhere."

"I told you, they don't dare put half of it in the papers."

"I give us ten more years on this island at the outside."

"Too generous, by far. I'd say four or five, more likely."

"No, no, not with Mebane running things. I'm not that pessimistic."

"Ultimately some crazy will throw him out and take everything over. It'll be like Cuba, mark my words."

"The next three days will tell the story. If Mebane wins the election we'll be all right. He'll quiet things down."

"I doubt it. The pot's boiling too fast."

"Give the man a chance! How much time has he had?"

"Enough to fill the jails with his fancied enemies."

This, outside of the host's, was the first dissident voice of the evening. Issuing as it did from a newcomer to the island, it produced, in domino effect, a series of surprised and disapproving frowns.

"Aren't you exaggerating, Mr. Trumbull?"

"On the contrary, I've not said a fraction of what could be said."

Mr. Trumbull, being of that breed of lawyers known as liberal, wore an emotional expression. He was very young and had, for some reason probably connected with his liberal sympathies, recently opened a practice in Covetown. His somewhat babyish blue eyes looked startled, as though he had suddenly realized he stood almost alone.

A second later, though, he had an ally.

"Mebane's a brute, a canny, cultured brute."

This voice came from Whittaker's nephew, the musician. More disapproving faces were turned toward him, but there was no immediate protest, for the Whittakers were one of the wealthiest families on the island and they were pleased to humor their "odd" nephew. And, Francis recalled, there was oil money on the young man's mother's side.

Their host spoke quietly. "I couldn't agree more. What the rest of you call straightening out, what you call law and order, are only euphemisms for a police state."

Whittaker opened his little pink mouth. "You're entitled to your opinion, Rob, and so is my nephew, but I would advise you both to be careful of what you say. This is no time for loose talk."

"Mr. Whittaker is right." Francis spoke up clearly. He hadn't intended to speak at all, had deliberately closed his mind to all affairs except his own. Now he surprised himself with his own positive reaction. "Even you who favor this government are admitting, aren't you, that you don't feel safe?"

"Do we understand then," someone asked, "that you're voting for Courzon?" There was malice in the question, for Francis' feelings toward Courzon, as well as the reason for them, were well known.

"I don't intend to vote at all," he answered curtly. "What I'm thinking is, A plague on both your houses."

"Well, of course, you're leaving. But for those of us who want to stay, who have to stay, it's no pretty prospect. Personally, I believe Courzon would pauperize us all. He may mean well and sound good, but in the end we'd have nothing."

"What have you got now?" asked Whittaker's nephew.

The senior Da Cunha, sumptuously suited as befitted a merchant of his class, came over now and took a vacant chair. He was obviously excited.

"I've just come from town. Here, look at this." He held up a newspaper. "A special edition of the *Trumpet* just out this afternoon. I'll read it to you. Listen, it's an editorial by Kate Tarbox.

" 'For many months now and through various means we have been gathering information about the men who run what they are pleased to call our government. Now, on the eve of a decisive election, the time has come to reveal who and what this government really is.

" 'To begin with, it is not a government at all. It is a private enterprise of gentleman-criminals, defended by a secret police, a band of swaggering thugs, well paid out of your taxes, earned by your labor. Our country has become a safe harbor for shady enterprises, where narcotics and weapons are traded and dirty money laundered. Public monies have been directed to the pockets of the prime minister and his friends; safely hidden as they now are in as many as nineteen different banks as far afield as Switzerland, it would take a legion of lawyers and untold years to recover them for the people to whom they belong.' "

"Good God!" said Whittaker.

Da Cunha resumed. " 'These men make themselves heard almost daily on the subject of communist subversion, Cuban style. The truth is never mentioned: that communism was able to take over in Cuba because the mobsters had first laid the country in ruins.' There's more," Da Cunha said. "Here, I'll pass it around."

"She didn't sign her name to that?"

"She certainly did! Here, look, in big, black letters. Here's the windup. 'If you care about your country, if you care about yourselves, you will go to the polls on Thursday and vote them out. You will vote for Patrick Courzon.' "

"Fool of a woman!"

"Why? That's what I call guts!"

"Sure, if you call it guts to commit suicide."

Grudgingly, "Well, she does stand up for what she thinks. You have to hand her that."

"She won't be standing up long at all, I'm afraid. Not after this."

"Too bad Lionel's gone to England. Divorced or not, he'd have stopped her. He was always fond of her, even after the divorce."

"He wouldn't have been able to stop her. You don't know Kate Tarbox. She does what she wants to do."

"I wonder whether somebody should ride into town and—" Rob Fawcett began, when his wife came running in.

"Rob! Rob! I've just heard, Emmy had the radio on, and she just heard they've called off the election!"

"They've *what*?"

"Called off the election! No election on Thursday! For reasons of national security, it said."

The Whittaker nephew smote the table. "Of course! Because Courzon is winning, don't you see?"

"But they say, they say, one of the waiters just came late and he's terrified, he says things are frightful in Covetown! They've got police everywhere, arresting people. They've confiscated every piece of the *Trumpet* they can lay their hands on. And he saw"—Mrs. Fawcett trembled—"a man beaten up. They smashed his head in, right near the telephone building, it was—"

All of a sudden the party was over. The candles, no longer festive, glimmered wanly in the looming darkness. Everything is in the eyes of the beholder, Francis thought queerly. All, all had become in these few moments vulnerable, the house with its music, its crystal and silk, its orderly men and women gathered, all breakable, destructible and powerless.

Rob Fawcett made a vigorous effort, saying cheerfully, "There's nothing any of us can do tonight. We might as well have our dinner. My wife tells me it's going to be a good one, too."

Something seized Francis. *They've confiscated every issue of the Trumpet . . . smashed his head in . . .* And I shall sit at table holding a lobster fork and a wine glass, while she—Blood rushed to his head, not thought, just blood and strength, so potent, so compelling that his legs moved and his mouth spoke before he had commanded any of them.

He caught Marjorie's arm. "Make any excuses. The Whittakers will drop you home on their way. I've got to go to town."

"What are you thinking of? Covetown, now?"

"I have to. Please. I'm in a hurry."

"Francis! Francis! Have you gone out of your mind?" Marjorie's voice was a long, scared wail. "Francis, come back here!"

But he had already leaped into the car and gone down the driveway, out of hearing, out of sight.

LIGHTS WERE ON in the villages. Knots of people stood before the general stores and the rum shops as if they were waiting to be told what to do. Fear lurked among the trees beyond the headlights of the car. Doom rode the night air. He pressed the accelerator to the floor. There was one thought in his head, one purpose, and nothing could have stopped him. He knew, he knew. It was a good thing that neither police nor militia stood in his path, for he would have driven straight through them. He sped. If he could have flown, he would have.

Down the hill toward the town he came careening, and in the outskirts wheeled with screeching brakes around the corner of the street which he had not entered in so long. He jerked the car to a jolting stop before her house and jumped out.

The house was dark, but the front door was open. He rushed in, switched on the light and raced through the rooms. Kate's dogs were lying on the kitchen floor. The poodle was dead and the yellow mongrel had been piteously, brutally wounded. Lying in its blood, it opened its eyes toward Francis, as if to plead, then turned them toward his bowl and his ball, his dear familiar things, as if to question, and sank back and closed his eyes.

Now Francis was sure of what he would find. In a frenzy he called her name—"Kate! Kate!"—and bounded up the stairs. In anguish he slammed doors wide. The rooms were empty. Then something made him open a closet in the hall—and there he found her.

Face down in a pile of shoes and tumbled clothing, she lay naked, tied and gagged. Crying, sick with horror, he picked her up.

"Oh, my God!" he heard himself say over and over.

Without moving, she lay on her bed. He looked at her in despair. He was outraged, he was helpless, he didn't know what to do. At least she was alive. . . . But no doctor would come out tonight. Could she be dying? Then he bestirred himself. He went downstairs and found brandy. Which would be better, brandy or water? In the bathroom he got water and a wet cloth with which to bathe her forehead. And sitting on the edge of the bed, he covered her lightly, decently, with a sheet, then soothed and soothed with the cloth, thinking, Kate, oh my Kate, what have they done to you?

She opened her eyes. For a long minute she looked at him. "I knew you would come," she whispered.

"How could you know?"

"I had a premonition that this would be our day. I even called you this evening before everything happened, but they said you weren't home. They said you had gone to a party."

Things joyous and painful moved at the same time in his chest.

"You called me?"

"Yes, I was so terribly afraid! I thought I might be needing you . . . so to hell with all my pride."

"Ah, God," Francis said.

She whispered. "My back hurts awfully."

When, carefully, he turned her over, he saw why. Three raw stripes lay across her back. The flesh had been savagely slit open by a whip. Droplets of dried black blood clung to the edges of the torn flesh.

He was sick at the sight. "Kate, did they—do anything else to you?"

"Only what you see."

In the bathroom he found a jar of unguent, gone liquid from the heat. Gently, he poured it over the wounds. "I don't know whether this is the right thing, but it can't hurt until we can get a doctor."

"Take my necklace off, please. It hurts."

Still warm from her body's warmth, the beads slipped through his fingers. They were blue beads, cheap and pretty; in some odd way they made him remember the marvelous emerald she had worn when he first knew her. And everything that had happened since those first days slid away as if it had all been written on flimsy paper, meant to be discarded. What remained was a story inscribed in a permanent volume, beautifully illustrated: Kate on the breezy hill at Eleuthera and in the hotel garden and in this house. The time between then and now had simply vanished tonight. All the sullen, stupid anger, the proud resentments—all, all were gone.

He took her hand. "Tell me what happened," he said.

"Well, Franklin Parrish had just left. You know Franklin? He'd just brought me a copy of a speech for the *Trumpet.* And then, only a few minutes later, they came. There were three of them. I'd had the doors locked—I always do, anyway —but they broke a kitchen window and got in. The dogs—" Kate started. "The dogs. Where are they?"

He didn't know how to tell her, but in his momentary silence she heard the answer. He had to hold her back.

"No, don't go downstairs. Please. Kate, they're dead."

She began to cry. "You're sure they are? Not just hurt?"

He remembered the mongrel, then, the one she called Beans. "I'll take care of everything. I don't want you to see. Kate, my darling, you're lucky to be alive yourself."

"Killed them? And what for? It took months for me to get that poor thing to trust people after I found him, he'd been beaten so—"

"I know. People beat children, too." He covered her lightly. "Now lie there. Promise me you won't move. I'm going downstairs. I won't be too long."

In the kitchen the dog Beans had died, too. Poor animals! Poor Kate, whose tears were cried for them rather than for herself!

In the pantry he found a flashlight and, fearful of turning on a brighter light, fearful of attracting attention, went out to the yard. God knew what other terrors were still roaming tonight.

It had been raining for a week up until the day before, and the loam was soft. It took no more than ten minutes to dig a proper grave. Then, bitterly angry, he picked up the two small bodies, still faintly warm, still limp, and laid them gently in the grave. He passed his hand over the soft wool before he took up the shovel again.

And standing there, while burying two dogs, he felt a wave of fierce emotion, such as one could not sustain too often if one were to keep one's balance. All he had ever felt for life and living things, brotherhood, kindness, pity, was overwhelmed now with regret and shame for having shut himself away so long from what was truest in himself.

When he had finished he put the shovel down and stood looking up into the sky. It was utterly black. On the main road at the end of the street an ambulance wailed. A moment later motors roared and tires squealed around the curve. Police cars, he thought. Then silence fell again, a profound silence as if the night itself were cowering in fear. Afraid of the morning, he thought, and so am I.

He wished he had a gun. The best weapon he could find in the kitchen was a carving knife. From the refrigerator he took a pitcher of cold tea, which he brought up to Kate, while he laid the knife on the floor where she would not see it.

Weakly, she braced herself against him while she drank the tea. In the faint night-light from the hall he could discern white garments hanging in the closet; he remembered the fragrance of vetiver.

"That was quite an article you wrote. You should never have done it, Kate. It was a crazy thing to do."

"I just got so mad, so fed up."

Then he heard himself ask, "Did—did Patrick know about it?"

"No, he wouldn't have let me. Nobody knew except me. . . . I wish you were friends again, Francis."

He didn't answer that, but laid her back on the pillow when she had finished the tea.

"I wanted so many times to call you," she whispered. "I used to look in the telephone book just to see your name in print. Weren't we fools, Francis? A pair of stubborn, arrogant fools, the both of us."

"Yes, yes, we were. I more than you."

Now she saw the knife on the floor. "Do you think they're coming back?"

"I don't think so. They did what they were sent to do." And answering her unspoken question, he added, "But I'm not going to leave you."

It was still so ominously quiet outside. Fearfully he thought of Marjorie and the child. At least they were not alone. Osborne was there, as well as loyal people in the house. He picked up the telephone.

Had she got back all right from the Fawcetts' house? Was everything all right at home? Yes? Good! No, no reason to worry, he was going to stay in town at a hotel and he'd be back in the morning, or as soon as the roads were safe. No, he couldn't explain now. He'd only wanted to make sure things were quiet at home.

Turning the covers back he lay down beside Kate, being careful not to touch her tortured back. She fell asleep, but he could not. A catherine wheel whirled in his head, the wheel on which the saint had been broken, and he knew he was too exhausted to sleep. Once Kate woke and called his name.

"I'm here," he said at once. "Don't be afraid. I'm here." She slept again.

In the middle of the night he became aware of the ticking clock which, in his agitation, he had not noticed before. It seemed to him that, as the night waned, the clock raced faster, increasing its frantic, nervous pace: tick-tick-tick-tick. And he wished the night would linger, for who knew what sights the morning would bring?

But gray light came on schedule, sweeping the ceiling. Birds, unaware of any difference in this day, began their bright calls. Kate stirred.

"Darling, I'm here," he said again.

And turning her to him, still careful not to touch her back with even the feather-touch of a finger, he placed her head against his shoulder. For a long time he lay with his cheek against her hair and felt the beating of her heart.

A rattle of gunfire startled them wide awake.

"What was that?" Kate cried.

"Nothing, nothing," he soothed. "Lie back and sleep."

But she sat up, alert. "Guns. It was guns, wasn't it?"

"Yes." He went to the window. There was nothing to see. He turned on the clock radio. No voices came from it.

"They've closed the station," he said grimly. "I wonder whether the telephone's out, too."

When he lifted the receiver there was a buzz. Suddenly he decided something.

"Who're you calling?" Kate whispered.

"Nicholas," he replied, still grimly.

"Don't!" she cried.

But Nicholas was already on the line.

"This is Francis Luther." His anger was at the place where coldness burns. "I'm here with Kate Tarbox in her house."

"Ah, yes, of course."

"Is that all you have to say?"

"No, I can say she's a very stupid woman and she's lucky those people didn't kill her."

"They almost did. How long do you think a human being can survive in a closet?"

"Unfortunate. I'm really sorry. I was shocked."

"You're not talking to a child, Nicholas. 'You were shocked'! It came as a complete surprise to you!"

"As a matter of fact, it did. Politics is a strange business, as I've always said. One gets involved with some rough types. What happened was, some of these fellows got angry at the lady's lies about me and decided to do something. That's the long and the short of the whole business."

"Nicholas, I repeat, you're not talking to a child!"

"You really think I was responsible? No, I still have loyalty to my friends—it's one of my weaknesses—even though they don't always reciprocate. Kate Tarbox is, besides being foolish, Lionel Tarbox's ex-wife; she's a friend of my friend Patrick, who has gone somewhat soft in the head, unfortunately. And I see that you—shall we simply say that, in spite of the past, you would care rather much if anything happened to her?" The bland, persistent voice permitted no interruption. "A pity, all these messy affairs! We could all get along so nicely here, live so well in this nice place, if only these mosquitoes like Tarbox would stop buzzing in our ears, undermining confidence—"

Francis got a few words in. "Confidence in your police and—"

"The police wouldn't be necessary if the citizens behaved themselves. And now, if you'll excuse me, Francis, there's a busy day coming up." The telephone clicked.

Francis hung up and stared at Kate, his look conveying total hopelessness.

"You remember, I never believed in him?" she asked softly. "There was just something, a feeling I had from the beginning. I never knew where he stood. Oh, I'd rather have someone like Lionel to deal with, any day! There could be no doubt where *he* stood! Listen, have you never thought why Nicholas was so conveniently away when we had the strike five years ago? He didn't want to have to declare himself, that's why, and run the risk of making enemies on either side. He played it both ways and left it to Patrick to take the blame," she finished, with her old indignation flaring.

When she turned he saw that the ugly welts on her back had swollen.

"We'll have to get a doctor today," Francis said immediately and was wondering whether to hazard the streets or who might answer his call, when a persistent knocking was heard at the door below. He picked up the knife, feeling at the same time both foolish and wary. With the knife in visible position, he opened the door a crack.

"Is it you, Francis?" said Patrick Courzon. Rumpled and weary as he was, it was plain that he had been up all night. "I just heard. Is she all right?"

"Come in. Yes, all right except for her back, where they—whipped her."

Patrick was grim. "Things are bad. There's a fight on now for the radio station and the airfield. But a lot of people have come out of the woodwork to our side. Almost half the men in the police barracks came over to us about four o'clock this morning. We've got about fifteen dead so far." He was breathless. "It's chaos out there, bloody chaos."

For a moment Francis felt choked, unable to express his regrets or his embarrassment.

"I've been here all night," he said irrelevantly.

"You'd better get back to Eleuthera while you can. Things are quiet in that section so far. I'll have men here to watch this house." Patrick turned to leave.

Francis put out his hand. "Now's not the time, I know. I just want to say I've had what you might call a kind of revelation since last night." And, speaking these few words, he felt an inner easing of the spirit, an ebbing of embarrassment and regrets.

Patrick pressed his hand. "Wish us luck then," he said, smiled briefly, and was gone.

I⊤ was after noon before Francis arrived at home. Avoiding police stations and villages where confrontations might be occurring, he had taken a long, twisted route over dirt roads, some little more than mountain trails. The car's radio had kept him informed of events: the station had been retaken. Small battles seemed to be exploding all over the island; barracks were seized; arrests were made; the airfield was sealed off (so I can't send Marjorie and Megan home, he thought, with sickening fear); a cache of weapons was found in a cottage enclave belonging to the Lunabelle Hotel. At one point Patrick's voice came over the air, advising tourists to stay in their hotels and assuring them they need have no fear. Well, Francis thought, it must mean something that Patrick has the radio station, mustn't it?

Yesterday at this time he would have been on the other side or, rather, on no side at all. And he wondered what it was, what slumbering conscience or stifled yearning, had brought him to Kate last night and turned him back in time to what he had been five years before.

Marjorie too was listening to the radio when he came in. "I was furious with you," she said. "Then I decided it was a waste of my energy. You're impossibly eccentric and I should be used to that by now. But do you mind telling me where you went?"

"I saw Patrick," he told her, not untruthfully.

"Patrick! What on earth for?"

"I've been wrong about him. Terribly wrong, and I admit I have."

"I can't believe it! This attachment again! I thought we were rid of him. What is this fascination he has for you?"

"That's absurd, Marjorie. It's a question of principle, not fascination."

"So now you're on his side!"

"Yes, after the things I've seen. I've had a late awakening, that's all."

Marjorie sighed. "Well, I don't suppose it matters, since we won't be here, anyway. I only wish we were moved and rid of the whole business. Frankly, I'm scared to death. I suppose you aren't, though."

"I am very scared, I assure you."

If Nicholas's people firmed their hold—He shuddered to think of Kate and Patrick and so many more, whose names were unknown to him, who would suffer. God only knew what they would suffer.

The radio crackled all afternoon. There was an audible commotion in the street outside the station, until an obviously terrified announcer declared that the attackers had been repelled. Well into the evening the bulletins continued, but no decisive move in the turmoil was disclosed. And the troubled land waited.

After a while Marjorie went up to bed. Francis went into his library, the one room in the house that was distinctly his own. There was nothing he wanted to do there; simply, there was comfort in the room, in the familiar Chinese ivories on the shelves, his books and that very fine Da Cunha, *Cane Cutters,* which his father had given him. Going to the window, he pulled back the curtains. Someone, Osborne probably, had seen to it that the floodlights were on, a safety measure for this night of unknown dangers. The lights, concealed low in the shrubbery, made paths of silver in the darkness. It was perfectly still and so beautiful a night that in a sudden gesture of impulsive gratitude he stretched out his arms to it.

He feared for so many in this hour. There had been no relief of his own burdens: his child still lay helpless in her bed upstairs, a child who, for all that she was his "shadow," would never be able to share thought with him; his wife lay upstairs, too, bound to him through their child, but never able to share love with him. And yet he felt such vast and awesome gratitude.

THE RAPID EVENTS of the next three days were reported throughout the world.

"In an astonishing display of loyalty and power, the party led by Patrick Courzon has restored order to St. Felice. More than three hundred soldiers and police, aided by hundreds of citizens, including many teenagers from various clandestine left-wing groups, combined to oust the government forces. White flags of surrender fly over government strongholds, while the green-and-white Courzon emblem is everywhere displayed. A curfew has been declared. . . . The dead and wounded number so far about seventy to eighty. The election will be held as scheduled. . . .

"The whereabouts of the prime minister are unknown. It is rumored that he has taken refuge somewhere in the country until after the election. The minister of justice was arrested, and it is rumored that he is being held in secret custody to protect him from the wrath of the public. . . .

"The Courzon party has won a decisive victory. It has now been established that, shortly after the results were made known last night, Nicholas Mebane and a large party left on a yacht which had been waiting offshore. It is thought that after a short stay in New York many of the members of his former government will depart for Europe, where they maintain residences. . . .

"The new prime minister, taking office, promised a cheering crowd that he will restore and maintain decent, democratic government with full guarantees of the rights of the individual."

K ATE CLEARED THE supper dishes away. For about a month now, ever since Marjorie had gone to New York with Megan to visit her family and look for an apartment, this evening routine had been evolving, so that by now, after his day of customary work at Eleuthera, Francis felt that he was coming home to this kitchen. Here tonight the lowering sun touched alike with a tawny antique light the hanging philodendron, the simple dishes with their brown scalloped edges, and Kate's white dress.

"We can have our coffee outside," she said. "It's got much cooler."

In the yard, shade filtered through the leaves, laying a dusky bloom upon the coffee tray. This evening, gravity lay also upon Francis. Two more days and Marjorie would be back. They would be that much closer to departure time. Everything was speeding; things hovered and impended; there could be no swerving away, no turning back.

Kate was feeding pieces of cookie to the two curly black puppies whom she had acquired from the pound after the death of the other two.

"Not good for them to have sweets," she said, as if Francis had objected, "but now and then I like to give them something . . ." Her voice trailed off. "John Lamson wants to marry me," she said.

For a moment he was not only shocked but confused by the unfamiliar name. Then he remembered. Yes, somebody's brother-in-law had a cousin who practiced law in Curaçao, someone who flew over on occasion for the big parties. . . .

"You know," she said, as if she were asking him to recall some trivia. "With Republic and Southern Oil?"

A picture developed itself. Yes, shoulders and height and a hearty, positive manner.

Jealousy almost took Francis' breath away. It was a physical thing, a blow between the ribs. For a moment he could say nothing. Then he saw that she was waiting, plucking, probably without knowing she was doing so, at the fabric of her skirt. So, let her! he thought angrily. Let her go! And then I won't have to fall asleep knowing she's less than an hour's distance from me, nor pass this street whenever I go to town, nor walk into a crowded room both hoping and not hoping to look across the faces and see her face. Then he remembered that he himself was going away.

He murmured, "And will you? Will you marry him?"

"No. I compromised the first time. No."

Bravely, he made himself say, "Perhaps you ought. It would be a good thing for you, better than being alone."

"No, I said."

He set his cup down so hard that the spoon jumped on the saucer.

"Oh, I wish, I wish—" he began.

She stretched out her arm to touch his lips. "Don't. I know what you wish."

So they sat silently. The sky darkened until there was only a pale, milk-blue streak left far down at the edge where the earth dipped away from the sun. A late bird, half asleep, gave one startled chirp; a dog, scratching, thumped his hind leg on the flagstones. And again Francis felt that sense of racing time, of vast opening distances and endless loss.

He looked over at her. She was sitting with her head bent, staring, so it seemed, at nothing. It was so uncharacteristic of her, to seem that small and frail. He had to do something, anything to make her move, to speak, to be his Kate.

"Would you like a late swim? We could have an hour before I go back," he offered, feeling as though he were offering a present to a child who has been hurt.

"We can't. I forgot that Patrick and Désirée are coming over with a present for me. Something Désirée bought in France."

"Poor Désirée! I'm glad she finally got to go."

She brightened. "Yes, it was his birthday present to her. He couldn't really afford it, what with two weddings coming up, but he wanted to."

"Laurine's done well. Franklin Parrish is a catch. A good man and a man with a future."

"I like him better than the one Maisie's got, although her mother's ecstatic over the engagement."

"Do I know who he is?"

"The Hammond family. Estate Ginevra."

Francis whistled. "Knowing Désirée, I should imagine she would be ecstatic. That's a rather nice little place. I've never been there, though; only passed it."

"Well, different circles," Kate said somewhat wryly. "The father's only about an eighth black, I should think. The Hammonds were in the colonial service for at least two generations, maybe more. He has a *manner*. Patrician, I guess you'd say."

"You were there?"

"I was invited to lunch with Désirée and the bride. The host was telling us that his great-great-grandmother was the mistress of Lord Whitby. Funny thing, I was thinking while I was there, one of my great-greats, I'm not sure who, was a Whitby. So maybe he and I have some ancestors in common."

"Did you mention it?" Francis asked. For some reason, he was curious.

"No. I don't know why, but for all my lack of prejudice I felt uncomfortable," she said honestly. "So I didn't."

"It's still in us then, no matter what we say?"

"To some extent, yes. We're not angels—yet." She smiled. "Ah, here they are."

A car stopped, and a moment later Patrick came around the corner of the house with Désirée.

"Prime minister," Francis said, rolling the words on his tongue. The title had dignity, and was only Patrick's due.

Patrick carried a flat package in brown paper. "Can we take this inside to the light?"

The election and the longed-for trip had given Désirée new animation. Now, wearing a dress which, Francis guessed, she must have bought in Paris—for what woman could visit Paris without bringing back one dress!—she was excited with the ceremony of making a gift.

Patrick, releasing the string, opened to view a painting simply framed with a narrow band of gilded wood.

"It's Anatole Da Cunha's," Désirée cried. "I bought two for you to choose from, but this isn't the one I like.

The other's fishing boats, really lovely, only Patrick insists this is the better one and you should have it."

Under an arbor, beneath grapes hung like stalactites, sat a young pregnant woman, wearing a brown dress. Her thin white hands were folded on the great, swelling curve of her body.

"But it's such a *plain* picture! And who wants a pregnant woman?" Désirée complained. "Of course, it is a Da Cunha—"

"Take my word for it," Patrick said, "there is no comparison between the two. This is the one Kate must have."

"It's beautiful," Kate said, very moved. "Beautiful. So patient, waiting there for the child, not knowing who he'll be! But that's an experience you've had, Désirée, so you must know. It's beautiful," she said again, softly.

"Well, I'm glad, then. You know how it all came about? There was an item in the paper about Anatole Da Cunha's death. He never married, you know, just lived with the same woman for years. And she needed money—strange how often these people who're good enough to become so famous don't leave any money. Well, there were eleven pictures she had to sell, so I ran over to look at them. I even cabled Patrick for public funds to buy the lot for the museum but he said no, there are things the country needs more right now. So I just bought these two myself. Anyway, by the time I got back they were the only ones left."

"I shall hang it over the piano," Kate said. "It's the most wonderful present I've ever had, I want you to know. Now stay a while and we'll have a drink to celebrate my present."

"You're sure we're not intruding?"

"Sit down," Francis said.

The lamplight fell across the picture, which Kate had propped against the piano, casting a spot of brilliance on the face. The artist had painted a three-quarter view; a rich fall of hair encircled round-lidded eyes and a strong nose. There was, Francis thought, with growing wonder, an incredible resemblance to his mother. This is how she must have looked in her youth, he thought, pensive, tender, and always with something reserved, held back within herself.

His eyes kept returning to the portrait. And shifting into a direct line of vision, he scarcely heard the conversation. It was almost as if, by fixing his will upon the picture, he could force an answering gaze from those living eyes. Absurd! But he did not move, just sat there allowing himself to be entranced. The young woman with her fine, resting hands and bowed head, had brought a kind of peace into the room.

"You look tired, Patrick," Kate observed.

"I am," he admitted. "I just got back from seeing my mother in Martinique. She's dreadfully sick and that's a worry, of course. But I suppose the real thing is an inner tiredness. The truth is," he said, thrusting his face up abruptly, so that one saw new lines beneath his eyes, "the truth is, I suppose, that I'll never get over the pain of Nicholas. That struck deep, deeper than I realize, maybe." No one contradicted him and he went on, "You know, I'm relieved that he and the rest escaped the country. We'd never recover what they took, trials would cost a fortune, and there'd only be more anger and more damage. As it is, we can look forward to a long, long struggle. There are an awful lot of people on this island who want to get revenge for what Nicholas's people did."

Kate brought in a tray of drinks and Francis served them. He raised his glass. "Good health to us all!"

"And especially to you, Patrick," Kate added, "since you're the one with the load on your shoulders."

"Yes, it's a load. But we're off to a good start, all the same. One good thing I did, I made Franklin my minister for finance before the wedding. Otherwise," Patrick laughed, "I'd be accused of nepotism. Maybe I will be anyway, but I don't care. There isn't a better man anywhere for the job." He spoke eagerly, seeming suddenly to need to talk. "We're working on slum clearance. I want to get rid of the Trenches before they fester and spread any farther. I've got some private investors, a Canadian firm, and the government will guarantee the loan. Another company got in touch with me this week about a food processing plant for tomato paste. Well, we can surely provide enough tomatoes in this climate! Then I'm negotiating with the International Monetary Fund, and oh yes, what else is on the fire this week? A bill to require plantation owners to sell to any tenant who wants to buy his house and plot of land. That's long overdue."

Francis said quickly, "I've already done that, did you know? My sugar lands across the road aren't part of the Eleuthera deal. I've sold to every tenant who wants to buy. And I've given some as a gift to a few of the very eldest," he added, not concealing his satisfaction in having been first to do voluntarily what the law was about to force others to do. And then, suddenly aware that he might have seemed proud, he added again, "It's not that I want to boast about it. I only wanted you to know."

"It is much appreciated," Patrick said, somewhat formally, so that Francis knew he was touched and too shy to reveal how much.

"Well, I always did what I could. I wanted to. And there were others like me."

"Not very many," Patrick said. He sighed. "The problem is, everything's too slow. That's what's bothering me. We haven't much time to put things in order."

"Aren't you perhaps too apprehensive? Are things that bad? No one's starving here, after all. There's new hope since the election——"

"These are very dangerous times. Nicholas was correct in much of what he said, except that he tried to fight one evil with another."

"And line his pockets," Kate said indignantly.

Patrick went on as if he were tabulating quantities, almost summing up for himself.

"It's true, I had help from the left. I don't delude myself. Those young men who fought the secret police, who recaptured the radio station, so many of them came from the ranks of those with whom, it hurts me so to say, my Will is involved—though he denies it. Yes, it's true they helped." Patrick stopped, and the room was absolutely still, with the others leaning intently toward the pool of light in which he sat.

"When you're desperate you take help from anybody at the moment. But now —now I don't need to be reminded that the Soviets are in Cuba and Cuba is here, so to speak. Here or next door, which is almost the same thing. Yes, they're all here, the training camps for terrorists, the Soviet AK-47 rifles, squadrons of aircraft, forty-knot patrol boats, maritime facilities for submarines, jeeps and trucks, all next door. As soon as they think they can knock me and my kind out of here they'll be in St. Felice, too."

The words hung heavily in the air. So, then, it would be the same as having Nicholas back, or worse, Francis thought. Is there no end to it? And he answered himself, No, none, without eternal vigilance.

Then, as if he had had an afterthought so deeply painful that he had tried to suppress it, Patrick said, "They are already subverting our young."

"Oh, Will," Désirée protested. "Will! How he makes you suffer! I wish—"

"We all know what you wish," Patrick told her. "That we had never taken him in."

"Well," she responded, quietly enough, "don't you wish it, too? Tell the truth!"

"I couldn't have done otherwise. If I were to see him again as he was that day I would have to do it all over again." He looked away for a moment, then back at the picture. "But let's talk of happier things. . . . That is a wonderful work of art. I don't think Da Cunha could ever have done anything better." He turned to Francis. "So you are really leaving?"

"Yes."

"When?"

"Next month. They've got the papers ready to sign next week, so we can leave in June." Francis caught Patrick's eyes and held them with his own. "I'm terribly ashamed. I haven't said it before, but it's something you must surely have been thinking. The way in which I'm leaving, I mean. These people, this casino and all it entails—I hate it all. I hate what it does to the country and I'll tell you one thing: I'm glad that under your aegis there will be no more of it." Francis threw his hands out as if he were pleading to be understood. "But given the situation, with no other buyer in sight—And I have to leave. I have to."

"I know," Patrick said. He paused. "Excuse me. Do I—do we—know you well enough to ask, What about Kate?"

He felt a stinging behind his eyes, a warning of tears, and was painfully embarrassed.

"She understands," was all he could say.

It had grown quite dark. The night life in the scrap of jungle which remained in back of the street rose loud and shrill, a whirring and peeping, a rhythmical buzz and chirp. Désirée, with a gentle tact for which Francis was grateful, moved to the subject of her daughters' weddings: quite possibly it would be a double wedding, because although Maisie was only seventeen and young to be married, he was such a marvelous boy. . . . So she prattled until, in a little while, she and Patrick left.

When they had gone, he sat on with Kate. She had taken out her embroidery and now, with a frown on her forehead, sat working at it, not speaking. Francis said suddenly, "You know if it weren't for Megan—you do know that, don't you?"

"Darling Francis, I do."

"I'm so guilty. I brought her into the world, when I should have known better. I gave Marjorie that burden. Gave Megan that burden, too." His voice trembled.

"But I've told you again and again," Kate said patiently, "you mustn't think like that. It won't help anyone for you to walk around with all that guilt."

"I can't leave Megan," he said for the thousandth time and, as he had also done before, went on. "Ah, what a pity! You're the one who should have children, Kate."

"If I had, I would probably never have left Lionel. Poor old Lionel! I don't know why I always say 'old,' because he isn't."

"He was old when he was born, I expect. Like me," Francis said glumly.

Kate put down the embroidery. "Like you! I've never heard anything sillier!" She reflected. "You know, I sometimes think Lionel's never really felt anything much in his whole life. But maybe people like him are better off. When I left him, it was only the humiliation that upset him, no pain, while I—" She did not finish.

And Francis, watching her with her head bent again over the needle and the fine white cloth, thought of how she would be when she grew old, thought of it for no reason that he could have explained except for a cruel awareness that he would not know her when she was old.

Suddenly he asked, "What will you do now with your life?"

"Oh, go on living here and working on the paper. This time around I'll expose the leftists—"

He interrupted. "For God's sake, don't do anything crazy again! Take care of yourself. I couldn't bear it if—"

He got up and sat on the floor beside her chair with his head against her knees. She stroked his hair. From her body, as she leaned to him, came an aura of warmth and the sweetness of vetiver, that fragrance of grass and morning that seemed always to go with her.

"I've been thinking—it's better, after all, that you're leaving. I couldn't just live here like this, sharing you with Marjorie and your child. It's done, it's always been done as long as men and women have lived on earth, but it's not for me. And yet if you were here, I'd want to do it. So I'd be cutting myself in two, you see."

He kissed her fingers and her wrists where the blue veins crossed, then her arms and her neck.

"Come upstairs," she said.

This was their time of day. Always a stripe of light lay over the place where, naked, she came toward the bed: a light from the hall, or sometimes from the window when the moon was right. A creamy ghost, she materialized out of the darkness, then unghostlike, firm and desiring, lay down beside him. . . .

The old clock on the landing banged ten metallic strokes. He sat up and switched the lamp on.

"I'd better start."

Kate rose and took a robe from the closet. In flowered cotton and with bare feet she followed him downstairs. When, at the front door, he bent to kiss her, she put her arms around his neck.

"No, wait! Francis, wait. I have to tell you—I didn't want to tell you before."

Something in her face alarmed him. "What is it?"

"This was our last time. That's what I want to say."

"What do you mean?" he cried.

"Our last time to be together." Her eyes were wet and brilliant.

"Oh, no!"

"It has to be. Francis, listen, it has to be. Marjorie will be back the day after tomorrow. In another month you'll be gone. What's the use of prolonging things? Another month together won't matter. It'll only be that much harder for us both."

"It couldn't be any harder for us than it is right now."

"It could. Oh, my dear, make it now! How many times can people be expected to go through this—" She did not finish.

He held her close. "Brave Kate. So brave."

"I don't know whether I am. You like to think you'd be stalwart and have dignity and all the rest of that stuff if you were told you were dying of cancer. I hope I could be if I had to—"

"God forbid!"

"Maybe that would be easier than this."

"I'll come back," he said desperately. "I'll come back every year for a while—"

"No. It wouldn't be any good that way. It has to be finished, like an amputation, and then one has to teach oneself to live with it."

He could only hold her more closely.

"Oh, it's worse now, isn't it? Far worse than when we fought and were so angry at each other. Besides, I'm five years older now. Five years have made changes. In you, too."

"I love you, oh I love you, Kate," he said. Scraps of thought passed through his head, scraps of bright paper torn in a breeze: I love the quilt with the birds and the dishes with the scalloped border, even your two sleeping puppies and the creaking gate; I love your pink slippers under the bed and your tortoise-shell brush on the dresser, the way you sing in the kitchen and your temper and your two separated teeth; I love you playing Brahms, you dancing, your hair blowing in the wind, you, you— He was crying.

She pulled away and wiped his eyes with her sleeve. She opened the door. Before them the night sky hung white over the black, serrated outline of the trees.

"Listen, I told you once about the Inca priests and how they used to kiss the rising sun. Remember to kiss it in the morning, Francis. And wherever you go, wherever you are, I'll know you're alive and in the morning when I see the sun I'll think of you."

He never knew afterwards how he got to the car or how he drove home and reached his room where, still in his suit and shoes, he threw himself on the bed and lay there, face down, until day.

❧{24}❧

Through the day's last light Will made his way downhill toward the Trenches. Below him, the glint of tin rooftops and jumbled derelict cars dazzled the eyes; the silvery shimmer would have been beautiful if one had not known what caused it. Above and to the left across the bay, the settlement at Cap Molyneux, in its wreath of dark and luscious leafage, crowned the mountain. To give Patrick credit, Will mused, he had not succumbed to any such lures. Even if he could have afforded them, he wouldn't have, of that one was certain. When his term was over, Patrick would simply go back to the old house, now rented out for the duration, on Library Hill.

Will had refused to move into Government House, refusing also Clarence's invitation to come stay with him. He just "lived around," with friends, whenever he could. Anyway, he was often out of the country these days.

Tonight he was on his way to an important meeting. Walking lightly in sneakers, he had a wonderful sensation of flowing, flowing with time in a purposeful direction. So absorbed was he with this pleasant sensation that he almost failed to notice the man who hailed him now from the cross street. Then he recognized the dark shiny suit and reversed collar of the old priest, Father Baker.

"Walking my way, Will?"

"I turn off at the Bay Road." He was not in a mood to talk, or to listen, either, to any pious liberal mouthings.

"I've just been visiting my old cook on Merrick Road. She's been ill."

Will glanced at him sidewise. "Not afraid to walk alone down there?"

"No. Should I be?"

"I wouldn't think it the safest place in the world for you."

"One can't walk in fear all one's days. And faith is my substitute for fear."

"Faith in God?"

"Of course," Father Baker said simply.

The exchange began now to interest Will. It was like a game.

"You think God hears your prayers and answers your needs?"

"He hears, but He does not always heed, for reasons of His own."

"Tell me then, why should He have bothered to create us if He was going to be indifferent to us?"

"I didn't say He was indifferent. If He were indifferent, He wouldn't have created the earth at all, or us to live on it."

"But I reach a different conclusion. I say no God worthy of the name could have created this mess we're in. That's why I'm sure He didn't create it, that He doesn't even exist."

The old man was silent for a minute. It was probably cruel to bait him this way. And Will was opening his mouth to say something softer, to blunt his jab, when Father Baker spoke.

"Very well, let me ask, Do you believe in man?"

"Certainly I believe in man. I see him. He exists."

"In the power of man, then, to reason and struggle and achieve?"

"Sometimes, yes. Very often, yes."

"That means you believe in yourself, in your own will to do good. So in the end you will come to faith. For good is God, and God is good."

Not choosing to argue further, Will shrugged. The gesture, he knew, conveyed irony and dismissal.

They walked on. The old man's tired, panting breath was audible above the sounds of their steps.

"How is your father, Will? I don't see much of him these busy days."

"All right, I guess. I don't see much of him, either."

"Salt of the earth," Father Baker said. "We're lucky to have him. Well, I leave you here. Take care, Will."

Recrossing the road, Will took one look back at the old man, who was walking on with his face turned toward the sky, as if he were following a flight of birds or simply inhaling the soft air. Easy meaningless words, he thought, with a certain contempt and yet not without understanding. The priest meant well, but he was totally without knowledge of the world. Spouting his kindly generalizations— Will had heard them often enough—about brotherhood and God and loving! While all the time he'd been sheltered away behind the protective walls of the school and the church, respected and unchallenged because of the cloth he wore. A man of words, a theorizer, an onlooker, not, Will reflected, really very different, except in degree, from Patrick. Well, no, that wasn't exactly true, for surely Patrick had gone down into the fight, that you couldn't deny; but even so, there was something too innocent about Patrick, too innocent and therefore, in the last analysis, stupid. Stupid.

Now in the falling day the last busses from Covetown were passing out to the country, rattling by with people hanging out of the windows and bundles tied to the roofs. In bold orange and pink and blue they announced their names: Pleasant Dreams, Grateful Shores, Golden Joy. Now, what in heaven's name did their occupants have to be grateful or joyous about?

Halfway down a short lane Will stopped to pick up his friend Clifford, calling in at the door, "Clifford home?"

"No, he say he be back in a minute. Come in and wait."

Will climbed into a house built on stilts and made of corrugated iron. From the front room, furnished with a table, chairs, and a small oil stove, one could see into the only other room, which had a large bed and blankets on the floor where the children slept. The walls were decorated with magazine photographs of movie stars, both black and white, along with Christmas cards of jolly horse-drawn sleighs and snow-covered pines, these last the greetings from various children and grandchildren who had gone north.

"Sit down," the grandfather said. "He be back in a minute. He went to get some canned milk for the kids."

There were, Will knew, some six or seven "kids" in the house, nieces, nephews, brothers and sisters of Clifford. The grandmother, whose hair was just beginning to go gray, was still vigorous enough to do cleaning at the Lunabelle.

"You going to a meeting?" and without waiting for Will's answer, "I go to prayer meeting every week. And Credit Union meeting twice a month. You going to a prayer meeting? Clifford never tells me anything."

"Well, sort of, you might call it that."

The woman looked at him closely. "I hope you don't get in no trouble. Don't pull Clifford into none. We never had no trouble in our family. A good name, Drummond. Came from Drummond Hall, way back."

He was about to reassure her when Clifford came in. His appearance was always a kind of astonishment: he was the palest tan, with kinky hair of the same shade as his skin—a bleached African.

He put the milk down on the table.

"Ready?"

Will got up and they went down a few alleys to the meeting place. Some fifty or sixty youths had already collected in a courtyard, where chairs and a small podium had been set up behind a dance pavilion, open to the sky. The whole affair was open, there being now no need to hide. You had to give Patrick credit, he had kept his word about free speech.

Candles, flickering in bottles, illuminated the faces of the expectant audience: black faces, working-class faces, except for the presence of several young white women, pallid and earnest. Holdouts from the sixties, Will thought, glancing at their stringy hair; trying to prove something, trying to feel as if they belonged here. His glance swept away. Well, let them. Let them have their great adventure.

The speaker came to the podium to be introduced. Will had heard him before, in other countries, and knew what he was going to say, yet was impressed again by his easy dignity and the music of his Oxford speech.

"Who are you?" He began speaking so softly that a forward movement of the shoulders rippled through the audience. "From where do you come? Why are you here? I'm told that most of you don't know your own history, though it's not your fault that you don't. Listen to me, I have traveled. I've been in Africa and seen the forts along the coasts where our great-grandfathers were collected, torn from their forests and their tribes and brought in chains. There's where they started the long voyage to places like this one where we are tonight.

"In the course of the three centuries some fifteen million men and women made that voyage. This you must have heard, how for eight weeks or more they lay manacled in their forests and their tribes and brought in chains. There's how, maddened and desperate, manacled as they were, so many jumped overboard, dragging each other to death. Surely you have heard that!"

Indeed, they had heard it many times, but they were fascinated nevertheless. Without stirring, with open mouths, they waited for more. The speaker took from the podium a sheet of paper, which he waved in the air.

"Listen! I have here some quotations from a historical document which I found in the Covetown library. I took it from the last will and testament of a planter who lived here when the island belonged to the French. It lists the value of his possessions, among them his slaves. Listen! Pierre, twenty-eight years old, worth four thousand livres. A strong young man, you see. Next, Georgette, seventeen years old, also four thousand livres. A strong young girl, you see. Next, Marnie, aged sixty-eight, an old woman; she was only worth two hundred livres, because she wasn't fit for much, there weren't many years' work left in her. Naturally, you don't know what that money was worth in that time. Well, I'll tell you. You couldn't get a silver dish in Da Cunha's today for the price of that old woman, and you couldn't have done so at that time, either." He held his hand out, as if weighing things on a scale. "A woman. A silver dish."

Steaming them up, Will knew. All these facts were true, but so far removed in time that they had become irrelevant. The only value in them was shock value, to make these people angry—which had its purpose, to be sure. The real tasks of the movement were done quietly behind the scenes, not by orators like this one, shrewd and eloquent as he was, but by anonymous, cool men doing their assignments in small, tight groups, working in and out of Cuba and throughout the region. And Will had a feeling of proud exhilaration to be trusted, at his age, by men like Cortada, overseer of guerrilla affairs for the Communist party in Latin America and the Caribbean. To be trusted with great things!

No one moved, not a chair squeaked, as the speaker's voice rose. "But how much better off are you today? Are you not still strangers in this land? Look up onto the hills where the glass-walled houses stand so proudly and the hotels tower, or look at the estates where for centuries the owners have sat in luxury among the cane fields. . . .

"Ah, but now you have your own government, they tell you! Yes, a lot of mealymouthed incompetents who, aping the European, have merely substituted themselves for your former masters. Nothing at all has changed except the color of the skin, nothing at all."

At the back of the assemblage two men, who had been standing there, met Will's eyes and nodded. He looked at his watch. It was time to leave; walking along the beach, he would be taking a different route from theirs and ought to start. Unobtrusively, followed by Clifford, he stepped outside.

"Great man! Great speech!" Clifford whispered.

"Yes," Will said. Clifford was clinging; it would be hard to shake him. And this night's business was no business for Clifford.

"Where're you going now, Will?"

"To my grandfather's. I promised the old man."

"You have to? Sure you don't want to get a girl?"

They were passing the barroom where the girls sat around waiting. The jukebox blared past the swinging doors.

"I can't, I told you." He wouldn't have, anyway. He wasn't interested in girls right now. There was simply no time. No time.

"Well, guess I'll go home, then."

They walked back toward Clifford's house. The sky held only a curve of moon, narrow as a machete, and clouds were hurrying to cover even that. It was a good night, well chosen.

Clifford mused, "I was just thinking how you told me once you set fire to that place, Eleuthera. You know, I didn't believe you then, I thought you were boasting. But I believe you now." There was awe in his voice. "Don't worry. You know you can trust me."

It had been a mistake to tell Clifford, even though he really was trustworthy and a friend. It was a mistake to talk at all. You could never regret anything you had kept to yourself.

"A dumb thing to do. Childish. But I was only a kid. What did it accomplish, after all? I've learned better now." He said no more.

When he had left Clifford at his house, Will went as far as the corner; then, out of sight, he doubled back toward the shore. From a board shack came the sound of hymns. Prayer meeting, he thought scornfully. Waiting for heaven. He passed another bar and a smoky yard where crouching men watched a cockfight. Rotten amusement! Rotten life, he thought, as he came out onto the beach.

He had three miles to go, around the farthest visible curve of shore to the lonely cove where tall cane marched almost to the edge of the sand. There they would meet the boat and unload the rifles and grenades. The beach was deserted now, because the seas between Christmas and March were too rough for all but harbor fishing. This was the resting season for the fishing trade, another point in favor of the night's work.

The sand reflected the dun sky. Across the inlet he could barely see the strip of beach on which hotel guests baked themselves while beggars hawked straw hats, baskets, and worthless shell trinkets. He almost tripped over a pile of cane trash. Clarence had shown him how this trash, floating, attracts garfish in schools, and for a moment, recollecting this, he had a feeling of nostalgia for the lore and homely wisdom of old Clarence.

A lone man was mending a boat on the sand as Will rounded another curve. The whole side of the boat had been staved in.

Will stopped. "What happened to it?"

The man looked up. "Oh, just grudging."

"Grudging?" He wasn't quite sure what that meant.

"You know, like when somebody's jealous you got a better boat, or some good luck or something, they cuts your nets, you know?"

"Oh," Will said. "Sorry."

And he walked on. So the poor destroyed each other. This was what poverty did to people.

The rising tide lapped at his sneakers. He took them off and trudged on. Clams clicked on the flats, making a syncopated rhythm. Not far out a small yacht floated by, returning to the yacht club after a cruise, no doubt. It was so close that he could see a table set on the deck and people eating; he could hear their voices drifting inshore. Having wine with their lobster, I suppose, Will thought. Ought to be blown up!

Go on, haggle over elections, unions, legislation, and arbitration! Instead of getting out there and grabbing like men. People like Patrick, with their talk, talk, endless talk!

People like Patrick. And he had a flash of memory, with the very taste in his mouth of chocolate and bananas. The kind hands. *No, I don't beat my children.* The earnest face, bent over a book or explaining and teaching and admonishing. Sad, in a way, to have lost him! For they'd lost whatever there had been between them, as far back as—yes, the day Patrick had asked him about the fire at Eleuthera, and he'd denied having anything to do with it, and known all the time that Patrick never wholly believed him. Sad.

Still, the man was a fool and always had been! A well-meaning fool was what he was. Will kicked the sand. You can't afford to be sentimental when you're making a revolution. Not the way things are.

Now, rounding the last turn into the cove he could pick out the shapes of cars and a small truck with headlights off, parked in the shelter of tall beach grape. The boat was already hovering offshore, with only the dimmest lights, just lanterns, probably. Low voices hailed him and he walked toward them.

No, you can't afford to be sentimental about anything or anybody when you're making a revolution.

Not the way things are.

BOOK FIVE

PARTINGS AND MEETINGS

❧{25}❧

Her thin hands plucked and clawed at the blanket. When the pain flowed away Agnes lay back, moving her head so that her gold hoops brushed the pillow.

"Maybe I'll sleep a little now," she said.

Patrick got up and went outside to the yard. If he could vomit he might rid himself of the foulness. He wasn't quite sure she was sane or whether he could possibly accept what she had been telling him in there, in the small dim room where she lay.

The woman whom he paid to care for her sat on a bench, shelling peas into a bowl. As he approached, she stood up. She was in awe of his title, but more in awe of the fine black chauffeured car, although it had only been hired to bring him from the Martinique airport.

"Sit down," he said.

Trembling, he walked to the end of the yard. A double line of bamboo gave shade to a neat patch of vegetables. A row of yams followed along a strong new fence. He looked back at the house which he had bought for his mother when she refused his request that she return to St. Felice ("It's fitting to die on the earth where you were born," she'd told him). It was a good house with a tin roof and running water. In a little while he collected himself and went to sit on the bench with the woman.

"How is she?" he asked.

"She's dying. It's the cancer that's killing her." The tone reproached him for not seeing what was obvious.

"I don't mean that. I mean her mind. Does she talk sense? Can you believe what she tells you?"

"Why, of course you can! There's nothing wrong with her head. Try giving her short change, and you'll find out."

"She doesn't ever rave? Imagine things?"

"Who, she?" The woman was indignant. "Sharp as a tack, I tell you!"

He went back inside and sat down by the bed. "Did I wake you, Maman?"

"No, I was awake. You know, there's some pleasure in lying here with nothing to do but remember. Everything is so clear, I can even see the colors. Did I ever tell you about the Maurier house? Oh, I must have! They had three thousand acres and such gardens, you can't imagine. They used to say the gardens were like the ones in France and it was true, when I went to France I saw it was true." The voice ran on, murmurous and so soft that Patrick had to strain to hear it. "They used to go to Paris every year, with servants, too. I never went along, I was too young. I think they went to visit their money in the bank, people said they had ten million dollars; maybe they did, I know the Francis family had nothing alongside of them."

"I want to talk about what you told me before," he insisted. His voice sounded almost harsh in his ears.

"Yes. Well, she said she would come back to St. Felice to die. And she almost did, didn't she? I heard about the fire, you know. Why didn't you ever tell me yourself?"

"Why should I have? I don't like to talk about horrors, especially to you. And I didn't know it—had anything to do with me, or you."

The sour smell of sickness made him gag. The gloomy green flicker of sunlight through slatted blinds made him dizzy. And he passed his hand over his sweating forehead.

"Yes, yes, she told me. I remember it well," Agnes repeated.

"Told you about a fire?"

"No, no"—with exasperation—"no, about not coming back, I meant. But she did come anyway. I wonder why? Oh yes, yes, a son . . . I forget so many things these days, Patrick—it's the pain medicine—but not the old things. I remember them all."

"And you're sure you can't be wrong? Wrong about this, for instance?"

Now came a flare of her quick familiar anger. "What am I, a fool? You think I'm making up a fairy story to amuse a child?"

It was his turn to ask her, "Why didn't you ever say something before?"

"I never wanted to hurt her, what do you think? I shouldn't have said anything, even now. Tomorrow I'll be sorry I did. I'm sorry already."

Loyalty! Loyalty to an old family, an old code, to the end!

"Patrick! You're not going to speak of this to anyone?"

"You don't want me to, Maman."

"All my life I kept it in here"—she touched the sunken flesh above her heart—"in here. Not because I wanted to keep *her* secret, not just that, anyway. It was because I wanted you all for myself. . . . Ah, you're a big important man now! They say you'll be traveling all over the world."

"They exaggerate. Only a few trips here and there to raise money for the things we need."

"You still don't believe what I've told you about yourself, do you?"

"I—"

"Give me your hands. I'm dying, Patrick."

"I know, Maman."

"You won't see me again."

"I know that, too, Maman."

"Then would I lie to you? I swear that everything I've said is true. I swear it."

He held her hands—old, dry hands that had hemmed workmen's tough cloth, cooked for a child, rocked a child, and polished a rich woman's silver. She, she had been his mother, not that other pale woman in the pale north, chilly as snow! And kneeling there, he held those two good hands until, in a little while, she fell back into sleep.

Sadly, he got up and went outside into a surge of yellow heat. The air was the color of ochre. Now he grew cold; a chill ran up his arms and down his back. He picked up a flat stone and hurled it to the ditch across the road, where it fell into rainwater, making a small, dirty splash. And he picked up another, one after the other, hurling with all his strength, while his driver waited, curiously watching.

They started back to the airport. The driver, who had been chatty on the trip out, was silent. Now and again Patrick met his eyes in the rearview mirror. I must look ghastly, he thought. Outraged. Destroyed.

His heart raced. His mind raced. That woman—that girl—had brought him forth and thrown him away. But then—a young girl, younger than his own Laurine and Maisie! And he thought of the double disgrace that had attended his beginning, shame of the girl, given her time and class, and death of the boy. Would it have meant death for him if he had been white of skin? Yes, yes, probably it would. Or possibly. The economic, the social, status would have been a factor, surely, in assaying the crime, if crime it had been. One had seen too much and felt too much in one's own weak flesh to decide precisely, justly, where blame lay.

Pity, pity for the terrified girl who bore me!

But then, consider a young boy "of color," confronted with some tremulous, forbidden loveliness, fragile in white, perhaps, with pearls like those Kate Tarbox had, careless pearls worn like common rope. . . . Kate's flowered skirts graze her seductive legs and in my mind I have removed the skirt, touched taut, rosy flesh, even though I know quite surely I am nothing to her but a friendly brain in a body which could, for all she cares, belong to a woman of seventy or a boy of ten.

Imagination flashed its pictures, that imagination which both blessed and bedeviled him with the ability to see at once all sides of any question. That boy, intelligent and yearning as he himself had been ("You're always reading, you always want to know too much!" Agnes complained), was he not familiar? How many such had he not seen on the schoolroom benches, dreamers of eager dreams, scattered among the apathetic and the louts!

What a crazy business, life! And his mind raced on again: Teresa Francis at Eleuthera. Virgil, righteous, tough old man of legend. Drummond Hall. The fine, proud places. Francis. Francis and I.

He leaned forward and tapped the driver on the shoulder.

"I need a drink."

"Yes, Boss. There's a bar right down the road."

"I meant water. You can stop there and bring me water."

He got his drink and they drove toward the city, past blue and yellow rotting houses trellised and gabled like the fairy houses in tales he had used to read aloud to his little girls, then through the city to the airport from which the plane would bring him home in an hour. And he remembered the interisland schooner on which, among crated coconuts and clucking chickens, he had slept all night with Maman in a time of innocence.

When he came into the house Désirée was waiting.

"How is your mother? Did she eat the cookies? Did she like the sweater?"

"She thanks you for them all." He turned away, wanting to hide. Then because Désirée was waiting for more, he said, "She's dying. It won't be long."

"Oh, Patrick, I am sorry!" She had never truly forgiven Agnes, but she was soft, and she meant her words.

They had dinner. He was still not used to the cool, high dining room with its whirring fan and its servants; this night, especially, he would have liked to be eating a supper cooked by his wife in their own old house. When they were finished, he went upstairs and sat down with a book which he wasn't able to read.

Instead, the day's incredible disclosure stood before his eyes, written in glaring letters. It seemed to him that, if he did not tell someone, they would burst in a spangled eruption, would explode and spill over and flow, even as Mount Pelée had done so many years before. It was all as large, as powerful, as that. And he heard himself saying the words, *Do you know who I am?*

"Patrick," said Désirée, coming in. "Are you all right?"

"I've a headache," he said, "one of my sun headaches. It's nothing that won't pass."

She put light fingers on his forehead. "I don't believe you. It's something sad, something else, not just Maman. What is it?"

He shook his head. "No, nothing."

She moved back in distress, her bracelets jangling.

"Do you still love me, Patrick?"

He smiled. "I've been a fool over you since I first saw you."

"That isn't the same thing. I'm not only talking about bed, you know."

"Neither am I, my dear."

"I think—do you want to know what I think? If things had been different in your life, you'd have married a more educated woman."

He looked up, wondering and touched to the heart. That she should harbor even the smallest doubt about herself! None of us knows another.

"But things aren't different, and it's you I have and you I want and always you."

Sweet Désirée, firm center of a world spun wild this unbelievable day. And he drew her hand down, holding the fragrant palm against his cheek, needing her familiar comfort.

"I worry so about you," she said.

"You needn't. I'm all right."

"They pressure you too much."

For a little while she stood beside him. When he released her hand she left the room and he sat for a long time watching, as the clement evening gradually covered the bay. When night fell like a violet curtain shaking in the wind, he was still sitting there.

*   *   *

He THOUGHT OF many, many things; of how a stone strikes and the pond stirs, of how words fall and the walls tremble. He thought of his dark daughters, with their Carib strain and that of the Arawak women whom the Caribs took. Now to all that was added the blood of Eleuthera's masters! And from deep inside him came a sound like a groan, as of something twisting and wrenching his chest, while before the eye of his mind there passed the stereotypical images of great-house ladies, an impossible mélange of haughty shoulders and soft faces, of whiteness and blondness, of silk and pearls. Who, who of them was she? And as so often in times of his most profound distress, he held up his hand, examining the whorls of the fingertips and the lines of the palm as if they could tell him something. Strange, all of it so strange and sad! That it should matter so much!

Then suddenly a faint and wry amusement twisted his lips. What would Marjorie, cool Marjorie, have to say if she knew? He suspected she'd make it rather hard on Francis. And with a premonition of loss and loneliness, he thought of Francis' departure: Perhaps that was a reason to speak?

Pressure, Désirée had said, not even understanding how much or of what kind, of how painful!

Oh, sometime, surely, he would have to tell what he had learned this day! He wasn't going down to his death, nor would he let Francis go, with such a truth unspoken. No matter whom it might hurt, it would have to be said.

Yet he came to know, as the hours went by, that the time was not now. There was enough of turmoil and tension at this moment in the life of each of them without creating more. Why burn Eleuthera again?

No, let them rest awhile, the living and the dead. Let them all rest.

❖{26}❖

Patrick moved the desk chair closer and shoved the telephone to one side. He still thought it was somehow comical to have three telephones. Perhaps they had been a necessary adjunct to Nicholas's position, affording him a sense of power and giving the impression that this desk was the place where things were made to happen. But Patrick had no need for them.

He picked up his pen again, returning to what he thought of as his "speech from the throne," or "state of the state" message, his first since he took office, a first accounting.

". . . negotiations for cooperative factories," he wrote. "Two Canadians and an American, having confidence in the economic climate on our island, want to produce a light cotton cloth in distinctive designs, using our local talents. A furniture manufacturer . . ."

He got up and walked to the tall windows from which, beyond descending treetops on the slope, one could see the harbor and the ancient structures along Wharf Street. There lies the power, he thought, there in the row of banks with the brass plates and the great names of London, of Canada and New York. If they will give us loans, we can—And he stood there while numbers went running through his head.

At the same time he was observing the life that pulsed in the town. There the banana boat was being loaded. A long line of women joined with a line of trucks as it wound toward the dock. There, as if a gift were being offered, each woman received a stem of bananas to balance on her head, and in a dancer's posture, to carry to the hold of the ship. Nothing of this had changed.

His eye traveled down Wharf Street to the low brick building where Kate would probably be working late on the *Trumpet,* bearing what she had to bear with dignity and grace. It was this very dignity that saddened him so. Tears would have been less painful. Yet he understood that Francis also must do what he had to do. Few things were ever simple. How could you weigh the relative values of a child and a woman? Especially if the woman was Kate?

Now a water taxi bounced across the harbor, lightly as a skimming gull. It stopped at the dock across the street from Da Cunha's door. Wharf Street had a row of new boutiques—little boxes—arrived in the wake of the hotels, but Da Cunha's was still king of the shops. How Désirée loved their dresses and their scarves and all the pretty trifles! And suddenly he remembered her—oh, it must have been before the girls were born—whirling in a white dress that she had bought there. He could see it quite clearly, billowing and short, printed with scarlet poppies. Fearfully expensive, he had thought, for those few yards of cloth! She had laughed and told him he didn't know anything about it, which was true. But she had looked so beautiful, and still did. Da Cunha had offered her a discount now because he'd been elected, but he hadn't, against her protests, allowed her to accept it. A matter of principle, it was, to owe no one for favors.

He felt he was making a good start. Even after this short time he could sense that the planters who had, to say the least, been lukewarm toward him, were beginning to support him with some conviction. They saw that he was trying to hew to a decent middle way. Last Saturday he'd called upon every citizen to give a day's work to the country, planting trees, repairing schools, or cleaning up the hospital grounds. The response had been—well, beautiful! The comments everywhere had been enthusiastic. He'd got out and put his own hands to work, too, which had done wonders for morale. Yes, a good spirit was rising.

Of course there were angry holdouts from Mebane's time; that was only to be expected. Those who had been making fortunes out of the drug traffic, for example, were not likely to be pleased with the new regime. Between them and the left wing, which was ever present, ever burrowing and undermining, there was plenty to worry about.

The Russians were entrenched in Cuba, and through the entire area the Cubans were spreading not only their advisers and technicians but their shotgun shells. It was very, very hard. You couldn't patrol every distant cove, especially on the ocean side, all night and each night.

He knew, he was almost sure, that Will was deep in these affairs. He couldn't prove it, any more than he could prove that the boy Will had set fire to Eleuthera, although he had never ceased to be plagued by the horror of the thought. One had one's gut reactions, that was all, and too often one's gut reactions were correct. They hardly ever saw Will these days, though, having come at last to a parting of the ways, an unsaid agreement to disagree. And he remembered the last time they had really talked together. It had been on the final night in their house and they'd been standing in the kitchen. Patrick had been saying something about the Cubans having thirty thousand troops in Africa and when Will had defended them Patrick had argued.

"You're going far beyond social justice, Will. You're making it all so simple, aren't you? Ask the thousands who are fleeing Cuba; ask why they've had to build a mine field at the Berlin Wall to keep workers from quitting the workers' paradise. Yes, too simple, Will! And what's more, you're entering an area of confrontation with a country which, for all that some like to say about it, has been the greatest force for human rights and freedom that the world has ever known. Ever. Yes, I'm talking about the United States," he'd said and thumped the table. But his words had petered out to empty air.

So we moved again toward violence, he thought as he looked down upon the drowsy little town. It hasn't erupted yet, not fully; contained, it merely smolders. But if the high winds come, then—

He went back to the desk. Yes, tell about that, too. No sense writing a cheery message full of halftruths and clichés. Tell it all. And end with a good, strong peroration about having faith in ourselves, in our courage and abilities, something like that. An upbeat ending is what's needed.

Maybe he ought to take the rough draft to Francis for an opinion. This was an important speech, after all. But the real reason was his compelling wish to see Francis. Now. Tonight. Several times since his return from the visit to Agnes, he had got into the car and started toward Eleuthera, then as abruptly turned around and come back. It was as if he were afraid to face Francis, afraid that his excitement, and yes, his love, would show. But tonight, now, he would go. The speech was a good excuse.

THE YELLOW TWO-SEATER sports car, an expensive toy, was the one that had belonged to Doris Mebane. Hasty flight had caused it to be left behind. It had, then, become public property and the council had offered it for sale. When no one bought it, they had sold it to Désirée for a nominal sum.

"Far too conspicuous," Patrick argued, but Désirée had some savings of her own and she was in love with it. Patrick had never ridden in it.

What foolish impulse made me want to try this thing out? he wondered, as he rolled along the coast road. A flash of lost youth, maybe? He'd never desired flashy things and still didn't, yet this was fun. The motor made a rich sound, the husky throat sound of a passionate woman.

At the Point he stopped the car. This was a sight not to be missed. The sun rested now on the rim of the sea, streaming a mauve and turquoise radiance across the lower sky. Oh, how we buzz and buzz our lives away! First school, then business, politics and money and God only knows what else. But all the time there is this, too.

Along the beach at the water's edge two small boys came trotting on spidery legs. All of a sudden they stopped and threw themselves at the face of an incoming wave. When it swallowed them, shattering itself into spume and foam, it released and threw them back onto the sand. Again and again they went, waiting for the rise of the wave, the glossy dark green curve, slick as glass; over and over they hurled themselves and were hurled back. Their shrieking laughter carried down the beach.

Life in essence! The elementals: the salt water out of which we all came, and the sun in which we lie, drinking the heat of it. Take away everything that man has made and done and this is what's left. How good, how joyous, to see those two thoughtless kids coming out of the sea! Life from the sea! A mystery. All, all a mystery. . . .

And love for the world overwhelmed him. Here we are, and at the moment of our deepest love and understanding, we depart. All this delight! Stretch out your hand to reach the sun ray or moonbeam. Touch it! It's gone! You can only hold it for a moment.

Releasing the brake, he turned the little car back toward the hills.

Eleuthera came into sight above the trees like a classic columned temple. It would be good to see Greece one day, he reflected, to travel with Désirée at last when his work was finished here. How she would love it!

Francis and Marjorie were reading on the veranda. He stood.

"Prime minister," he said, smiling.

"I've brought my speech," Patrick said, feeling suddenly awkward. "I thought you might be good enough to look it over."

"Thank you, I'm honored.

Marjorie gave greeting and got up. "I'm going to bed early, I'll leave you to your talk."

Her heel tap sounded briskly in the hall and clicked up the stairs.

"She has a cold coming on," Francis explained, after a moment's silence.

"Please, am I intruding?"

"You are not," Francis said with firmness.

Again silence fell. The night was so still that the neighing of a horse three fields away caused them to start.

Francis spoke softly. "Nine years! That's how long it's been since the day I met you in the schoolhouse. What a storm that was!"

"I don't know where the time's gone, as the old folks always say. Mostly I feel very young; I guess you'd say I still am, but sometimes I'm brought up short, to count the years that are left."

"Yes. Everything becomes sharper when you think about time. You walk out in the morning and suddenly you've never seen a fresher green. You've never smelled such fragrant coffee. Yes."

So they sat for a while, talking of the speech, talking of this and that, until abruptly, darkness fell. In northern places it approached slowly, Patrick remembered now, but not here.

A calf lowed in the barn nearby. "I don't remember your barns being so close to the house," he remarked.

"They weren't always. I guess this is the only place around that has the barns this near. But I've always liked the sound of animals. I had them build a cowshed at the same time they rebuilt the wing, after the fire."

He can speak of it now, Patrick thought. It's not between us anymore. And he said, "I used to like hearing the hens settle down at night when I was a kid. I kind of miss those last contented clucks."

"Has it ever occurred to you that our tastes are very much alike, yours and mine?"

"Alike?"

"Oh, I think so. Kate always says—said so."

For an instant it seemed as though Francis were going to say more; there was a pause while his fingers drummed on the chair arm, but apparently he changed his mind, for the silence lengthened.

It became necessary to fill the silence. "At least," Patrick said lightly, "you're not a politician!"

"You want to know something? I don't think you really are either. I don't mean you're not doing a good job, I mean that I don't think it's your first choice. I think you'd rather be standing up before a class, teaching."

"Yes, but there still are moments when I like what I'm doing, I have to admit. The cheers, you know, and the praise. Well, we're all human, and there've been great days, like the day our flag went up and we became a nation."

"Ah, yes. For a place you can drive across in an hour's time, this nation has some pretty large problems."

When Patrick didn't answer, Francis apologized. "Sorry. I didn't mean that the way it might have sounded."

"I understand, and you're right. We're on the brink of worldwide decisions here, in a strategic place. You have only to read the newspapers and look at a few maps." A figure came suddenly to mind. "Russia gives Cuba a million dollars a day in aid. The whole world's being terrorized."

"Yes. Undermined. The object is to make chaos. Undo whatever we do as fast as we do it."

There's Kate talking, Patrick thought, and answered, "You ought to get together with my new son-in-law, my soon-to-be. You know, he's one of the best things that's happened in my life. Not just that he's marrying Laurine, but knowing he could take over for me if need be."

"I've heard you say that before, and I don't know why you talk that way."

"Don't worry, I plan to be around a long time! But it's a good feeling all the same. My other son-in-law, Maisie's young man—well, he's a disappointment. He's leaving the country, going to Canada. Taking Maisie, naturally." And as Francis made no comment, Patrick went on fretfully, "Some of our best people are leaving. Dr. Sparrow has already gone and Dr. Maynard's going. Talk about a brain drain! When what we need is more people like them coming in, not going out."

"Well, they feel there's better opportunity elsewhere. You can't blame them, I suppose."

"You can blame them! Don't they know or care that it takes time to build a country? And how are we going to do it with them deserting us and the enemy almost within the gates? Oh, I lie awake thinking and thinking. I get so mad sometimes I can't think clearly anymore."

"But you've made a very fine beginning, Patrick, in your short time."

"I've done what I could. One thing is that nobody here need be afraid of the government. We have no political prisoners. You can think and say what you want as long as you keep the peace. Nobody's beaten up in our jails. That stuff's over and done with."

Francis hesitated a moment. Then, not looking at Patrick, he spoke. "I haven't ever told you. . . . I'm ashamed of myself. When Nicholas was here and there were rumors of those things going on, even a rumor about a ravine where the bodies were thrown, I didn't believe them even when Osborne told me where the place was."

"You could have gone to see for yourself."

"I didn't take it seriously."

"I understand."

"I suppose I felt that if I found it was true, I'd have to involve myself—"

"Are you still up, Francis?" Marjorie spoke from the doorway, then, seeing

Patrick, clutched the frill of her dressing gown about her throat. "Oh, excuse me, I didn't know you were still here."

Patrick stood. "My fault. I've kept him talking too late."

"Oh, talk as long as you like," she replied.

The two men went down the steps to the car.

"I'm sorry you're going to leave us, Francis," Patrick said.

Francis nodded. The light from the veranda revealed the face of an aristocrat. Not in any narrow sense, Patrick thought, but as the inheritor of an excellent body, of intelligence, and basic honor, this was an aristocrat.

"I hope things won't be too hard," he said next, "not for you nor for anyone."

Francis took his meaning. "You'll look out for her, will you? Don't let her do anything foolish."

"I won't." He didn't know when he had been so moved. And he put his hands to his mouth as though to stop the words that were in his head: Trust me, Francis, because you and I are—

Francis put out his hand in dismissal. It was the gentle dismissal of a man who is asking for privacy and a relief from tension.

"We pin our hopes on you, Prime Minister. And on men like you all over the world," he said rather formally.

"Thank you, Francis. I sometimes think—there's something I'd like to say—" He stopped. Not now! The words had come out without his willing them to.

"Say what?"

"Nothing. Nothing important. It's too late tonight. What do you think of this car? Isn't it outrageous?"

"Not at all. It's a gem. Come back again, will you, before we leave?"

"I will."

When he reached the end of the driveway he looked back through the rear-view mirror. Francis was still standing with his arm upraised in a wave. An impulse grasped Patrick, so that for an instant he made to swerve and go back. But in the second instant it released him and he was able to steady himself and head the car toward home.

FRANCIS WATCHED THE taillights, two red fox eyes, vanish at the turn. He stood until, in a little while, headlights flashed a white path through a gap in the trees far down the hill road.

How much had moved and changed since he had first come to know this good and decent man on that stormy afternoon nine years before! God go with him. He was fighting the good fight, as the saying went. God go with us all. Shelter helpless Megan, please. Let Kate laugh again, let her be warm and loved. He felt a choking in his throat.

A small wind was blowing off Morne Bleue, agitating the wind bells into a clatter of chimes. And he waited on the steps, unwilling to go inside, almost mesmerized by the sound, by his own emotions and by the flawless night.

Oh, this must be one of the most beautiful places on earth! Human pain was so piercingly incongruous here; to suffer in bleak deserts and on raw northern tundras was comprehensible, but not here in this soft air, under this white moon, with the grass so sweet.

At last he went in to take a handful of cookies and a glass of warm milk, for he hadn't been sleeping well. In Megan's room he adjusted the coverlet and moved the teddy bear from where it had fallen on her. He listened to her tiny breath and tiny stirrings. What dreams would flit through that poor brain? And again there was that choking sensation in his throat.

In his own room a new magazine lay on the bedside table; the combination of milk and reading might quiet his racing heart, he hoped, and send him the peace of sleep.

I⊤ WAS ELEVEN on the dashboard clock when Patrick's little car slid between fragrant hedges down the last moonlit mile and turned in at the great gates.

The shot crashed through the windshield and struck him in the forehead. The car plunged, screeching, into a granite pillar, then burst into flames and, in a few searing moments, was consumed on the lawn in front of the Government House.

⊰❮27❯⊱

Now once again the island shuddered and thrashed like some great wounded creature of the sea. For three days it struggled and bled.

The international news services made these reports in succession:

As leftist groups and rightist adherents, left over from the Mebane regime, lay blame upon each other for the assassination of Prime Minister Patrick Courzon, St. Felice bows beneath another wave of violence. An attempt to seize the radio station was repelled yesterday by forces loyal to the government, but in other areas key installations have changed hands three or four times during the last forty-eight hours. Two army barracks have already gone up in flames. Government forces have uncovered quantities of arms belonging to dissident elements of several persuasions. Among the caches were Molotov cocktails, gelignite, and several types of small arms.

Looting and vandalism in Covetown are gradually being brought under control. Banks and shops are still boarded with plywood and a six-to-six curfew has been set by Mr. Franklin Parrish, the acting head of government.

On the third night after the assassination calm has been restored to St. Felice. The dead number fifteen to twenty, with as many wounded. Over one hundred arrests have been made, ring leaders rounded up and the curfew lifted. Correspondents report remarkable cooperation on the part of the citizenry, which is weary of conflict and shaken by the tragedy.

On the fourth morning Patrick Courzon was buried. The cathedral in Covetown was filled; crowds teetered on the steps and filled the street outside.

"He was a man of the middle, without hatreds," Father Baker began, in the dry voice of an old man, straining. "His political ambitions were small. There were others far more ambitious and far more skilled in the art of politics. But what he possessed was infinitely precious and rare, an innate goodness and the will to persevere on a rational course." For an instant the old voice broke, then resumed: "Who did this to him? That is the question which absorbs us, and will continue to absorb us."

In essence, Francis thought, the ones who did it were the ones he loved most:

1125

Nicholas and Will. And he looked down at the front pew where Will, who had just flown in a few hours before from wherever he had been when Patrick died, was sitting with Désirée and the daughters, all in deep black, and with Clarence, who was weeping.

"Both sides had their reasons for eliminating a man who stood so firmly, so honorably, in the way of their desires, a man who believed so passionately in the worth of the individual and in peaceful solutions."

"Thank God we're leaving this crazy place," Marjorie murmured in Francis' ear.

He did not answer. Suddenly he was washed by a wave of sickness. His own emotion, combined with the heat of bodies closely jammed, overwhelmed him. Seated in the path of the sun as it streamed through pastel stained glass, he was dizzied by spots of lavender moving on his knees.

And it seemed to him that heat was rising everywhere; he imagined he felt the presence of fire, just as, waking in the night, one can imagine the acrid fumes of smoke—so it must have been on that other night. Now, though, it was not only a house that was on fire, it was the planet; the skies of every continent were ominous; the very air, the very flowers, burned.

He must have made a sound, for Marjorie turned to him with an expression of curiosity and alarm.

"Don't you feel well?"

"So hot in here."

"It's almost over, thank heaven. Look, look who's over there, will you?"

And he saw that Kate was sitting a few rows down across the aisle. She was wearing a little round straw hat. Her funeral hat, she called it, because it went with anything and was suitably decorous. She kept it in a clear plastic box on the top shelf of the closet with her tennis racket and a red-striped sweater. Yes.

He hadn't seen her in two weeks and he would never see her again. He would never have time to know her entirely. It was strange to think that actually he knew Marjorie so much better! Marjorie existed in familiar territory; he was not at home in her territory, but at least he could find his way around in it. Marjorie was always predictable; you could never predict what Kate would do. One thing, though, you could say and never be wrong. A tag of Latin from years ago repeated itself in his head: *Nihil humanum mihi alienum.* Nothing human is alien to me. Or nothing animal, either. And he had to smile, watching the little straw hat, remembering her dogs and her birds, her stray cats and her indignations.

They were standing now, and the nausea receded. While the organ recessional poured overhead, the coffin was borne out. The crowd on the street had been forced back to let it pass. From the high steps Francis looked down upon what is always described as a sea of faces, an apt enough description, to be modified here, he thought, to a sea of young faces. How many of them there were! The island, the whole earth, was bursting with impatient, restless young.

Someone touched his arm. This time he looked down into an old face, into a quilting of wrinkles on Chinese cheeks.

"Did you happen to know him?"

"Yes, very well. Did you?"

The old man wanted to talk. "Just when he was a boy. But I remember him clearly. In Sweet Apple, it was, where I had a store. Ah Sing's store." And he folded his hands into his sleeves, a gesture he had brought from his homeland more than half a century before. "He's not a person you would forget."

Francis nodded. "No, you wouldn't."

And he looked back at the sorrowful, respectful crowd. Calm now, all of them calm. Next time we might not be this lucky.

"I'm not going to the graveyard," Marjorie said. "I suppose you are?"

"Yes, and afterwards to the house. The family is going back to Clarence's. Désirée wanted to."

"Well, you go then. I never knew them all that well, anyway. I'll get a lift."

Neighbor women had taken over the house and sent Désirée upstairs to rest, leaving the front room to the men. Clarence, Franklin, and Will were by themselves when Francis went in.

"It could as easily have been one of Mebane's men," Will was arguing. "Far more easily. You always blame the left!"

"I didn't say it couldn't have been one of Mebane's," Clarence retorted. In his grief he had aged; his dark face was powdered with gray. "But also, it might not have been. You aren't going to tell me your heroes don't kill? Russians and Cubans and the rest who are going to deliver this world from all evil—they don't kill?"

"You don't understand," Will said. "You never did. You never will."

"I understand that you don't care, that this death is nothing to you." In anger, Clarence half rose from his chair.

"I don't think he meant—" began Franklin, his tone admonishing *Don't be too hard on him,* when Will made his own defense.

"You think I'm indifferent because I take a larger view! I'm sorry, of course I'm sorry! But how much can you grieve for one man in a world where millions suffer?"

Clarence was contemptuous. "It's the same with all of you. Oh, the wringing of the hands on behalf of the masses! But where is the human feeling for the family or the friend? Pity in the abstract for the masses, yes, but for the individual, none. Torture even, and the gulag for him."

"I have pity." Will stood his ground. "But Patrick was misguided. He was ineffectual. All his nice words, his laws and rules—crumbs! They'll come to nothing."

"Yes," Clarence said bitterly, "that's very true, if you and your kind have anything to say about it. You'll make sure that they come to nothing."

Will stood up. He has the eyes of a fanatic, Francis thought. I should hate to be at his mercy. And yet—so young, so bright, so—wasted!

"Where are you going?" Clarence asked.

"The Trenches. I have friends there."

"Friends! You're still welcome to stay here."

"No. Thanks anyway."

"Where will you be going after that?"

"Grenada in a couple of weeks, I think."

"And where then?"

"It depends."

"Cuba?" Clarence persisted.

"I don't know. Maybe. Yes, maybe. I'll see you again before I go."

When the screen door had slammed behind Will, Francis spoke. "Caught in a vise." It was the first thing that had come to his mind.

"Yes, very sad." Franklin spoke quietly. "And there are many, many like him. You can see we have our work cut out for us."

"Strange. Patrick always said you would take over for him, and now you are."

Franklin nodded gravely. "I know. I'm going to try to do what he was trying to do. That is, if I'm elected after I fill his unexpired term."

"You will be," Francis said.

Franklin made a pyramid of his hands, regarding it thoughtfully. "There's just so much! Deal with terrorism. Stop the brain-drain. I'm hoping the United States will stand by with economic help—"

Clarence interrupted. "Good thing Will didn't hear you say that about the United States." He was still fuming.

Franklin smiled. "Well, Marxism dupes the young. It sounds so hopeful, doesn't it? Funny they don't ask themselves why there've been more than six million refugees from communist governments. It's a case of *wanting* to believe. Phony miracle cures like any phony miracle cure!" He returned to the subject. "Yes, I'm looking to the United States as the—what's the phrase? The last best hope on earth? It's strong, it has always been generous and above all, it's free."

The voice was confident, but not brashly so. And Francis thought, Patrick judged well. He suspected that Franklin might prove to be even stronger than Patrick. For one thing, he was younger, but might it not also be that he had no internal conflicts about his own identity and his place in the world?

"I had such a crazy feeling," Francis said, "during the service this morning. It was a terrible illusion that the whole world was on fire. For a minute or two I was sick with it. I feel a lot better now, though, after hearing you."

"Fires can be put out," Franklin replied quietly, as Désirée came down the stairs.

She was a tall black stem; her head was a dark flower. There were two blacks, the matte cotton of her dress, and the gloss of her long hair. A beautiful woman, even on this day.

Hearing her descent, the women came in from the kitchen. "What are you going to do?" someone asked, while another remonstrated gently, "You don't have to decide a thing now, honey. It's much too soon. Take your time," this being the usual advice that is given to widows all over the world.

"I don't know," Désirée murmured. "I don't know."

"You can go with us, Mama," Maisie said. "You can be with us in Chicago. You always wanted to leave here, anyway."

"Yes, I always wanted to leave, but your father never did."

"If you stay, Mama," Franklin said, "you can help us make what Patrick wanted us to make of this country. Of course, one can't promise anything, one can only try."

Désirée's large, grieving eyes moved around the room, out to the hall, out to the porch, and back in to the kitchen, covering the familiar spaces of the home in which she had grown up. For a few minutes no one said anything, nor did she. Then she spoke.

"I'll stay. Yes," she said simply, "I'll stay. I'll live as we—as he planned. As I would have lived if he—" she did not finish.

Now the family would want to be alone, Francis saw. He stood up and said his good-byes. Franklin Parrish saw him out to the porch.

"I believe," he said, as Francis looked back up the walk at him, "I still believe we can make it so decent, so beautiful here—" and he threw out his hands in a gesture as moving, as graceful as a blessing.

WHEN HE GOT home Francis put his car in the garage and walked away from the house. Down the hill he went, crossed the little river at the footbridge and found his familiar flat rock on the beach, where he disturbed a tribe of squawking black birds who had been flurrying in the beach grape behind the rock. For long minutes he sat very still. Then he picked up a flat green disk of grape leaf, traced its rosy veins with his fingertip, threw it away, and was so still again that the birds dared to return, bold on their stalky legs, and so close that he could see into their shallow, cold, yellow eyes. And still he did not move.

When at last the birds flapped away he was still sitting there. Silence enveloped the little crescent of beach; the wind, which had been so faint, now died; even the mild waves made no sound as they approached and receded. There was only the thin, high buzz of silence. Like a ceaseless insect hum in grass it was, or like the streaming of blood in the arteries of the ear. The sound of silence.

Not long ago, and yet it began to seem very long ago, he had sat in this same place, had walked up and down here, up and down, then gone back to the house and announced his capitulation.

He got up now and began to walk, up and down, to the far edge of the beach and return, back and return.

"You can't live isolated," something said inside his head. "Can't live without—can't live—"

And an idea which had been unacceptable, alien to everything he had believed and the way he had looked at life, suddenly and soundlessly, unfolded and revealed itself as do those tightly furled paper flowers that when placed in water ripple open and gently spread their brilliant petals.

He could not live without her! And desire for her overpowered him, a cruel hunger, as if he had been starved. He was filled with a consciousness of her presence. He looked up to the hill where she had stood on that first day, here on this dear ground, and it seemed to him that she was standing there now, that her arms were out to him, begging him to stay. Kate! And he was filled with a rush of love, for her, for this land, a love for everything alive. That caterpillar crawling near his foot, a curious creature, black-and-yellow—striped with a red head; it too wanted its life, its own short, free time in the sun. And he stepped aside to spare it. How much time did it have, and how much had any of us, when all was said and done? So little! Kate!

And now he rushed, he ran, he leaped the little river, he raced back up to the house.

Marjorie was sitting on the terrace before a silver tea tray. She had changed into country clothes, meaning pastel; it would have been incorrect to wear light colors to a funeral in town. At sight of him she set the cup down.

"Well! I must say you look like death warmed over."

"It's not been the happiest day of my life."

"Hmph! We're lucky they didn't follow him and decide to kill him here. We might all have been shot on account of your precious friend."

Francis sat down. He wet his lips. He had a flash of memory, of himself as a child being angry at adults for being so stupid as to marry each other, when even a child could see they didn't belong together and never could.

"I want you to go," he said. "Take Megan. Leave here. Without me."

"You what?" She gave a high laugh. "*You* want *me* to go?"

"Yes. Let's make a final end to the waste."

"Waste? What are you talking about?"

"I'm talking about our time. There isn't all that much of it in anybody's life. What are we proving by staying together? There's nothing left and you know it. You want to leave here and I don't. It comes down to that."

She rose from her chair, clattering the tea things. "You want to marry Kate Tarbox, you mean!"

"Yes," he said simply.

"I knew you went to her that night the elections were called off, when you rushed away from the party! I knew it! But I didn't want to look like an idiot by accusing you if by some chance I was mistaken. Oh, the bitch! The whore!"

"I don't want to hear that, Marjorie."

"That first time here at Eleuthera, I knew it, too! I saw it!"

"You knew more than I did, then."

"I ought to mutilate her face so you wouldn't look at it anymore. Throw lye on it, the way the natives do here."

He was astonished. "Why? You don't care about me, about us. You haven't in a long, long time."

She didn't answer. Furious tears were falling and she groped for a handkerchief, not finding one. He gave her his.

"You don't care," he repeated. "We hardly ever sleep together anymore."

"Really," she mocked, "for such an ardent lover as you are—"

He interrupted. "I know I haven't been for a long, long time. Doesn't that tell you anything? I'm young, I'm healthy." His voice rose passionately. "This is no life, two solitary beds—"

"Oh, for God's sake! Moderate your voice, you fool! Do you want the servants to hear such talk?"

"The servants! The servants! They're human beings like you and me. Don't you think they have eyes in their heads? I don't have your sense of propriety—"

"Keep your voice down, I said! Megan is napping! Do you want to frighten her awake?"

At once he whispered, "If we hadn't had Megan we'd have ended this long ago, Marjorie. We've been using her, both of us have. And I should never have brought you here. It was wrong of me. It wasn't fair to you."

"You know damn well I've tried to make a go of it. I've run your house and entertained your guests and been a credit to you."

"Yes. Yes, you have." But the chasm between us is wider than St. Felice, he thought, and would have opened if we had never heard of the place.

"I do my best to take care of the defective child you gave me, too."

This cruelty silenced him and he bowed his head while she continued.

"My child wouldn't have been like this if it hadn't been for your family."

"You don't have to remind me," he said dully.

"Apparently, I do, since you seem quite willing to dump us. Trading us off for a tract of land and a new woman."

He raised his head. She wanted to cheapen his feelings, he understood that. He wasn't going to let her.

"I'm not 'dumping' you," he said angrily. "I intend to take perfect care of you and Megan. Always, even if you should—establish yourself. No matter."

"Establish myself! In what, please tell me? What chance have I had to learn anything? I've thrown my life away for you!"

He wondered scornfully what things she would have learned and done if she hadn't "thrown her life away" for him. But no, that wasn't fair; she was an intelligent woman and this was nineteen-eighty; in other circumstances she would have done other things.

"Or maybe you meant establish myself with another husband? A rich one?"

"Whether you do or not is immaterial. Megan is my responsibility. But I hope you do find another husband, someone more suited to you than I've ever been," he added bitterly.

"And what about Megan? All of a sudden, you're so willing to part with her! A new development, to say the least."

"We'd have to anyway. She'll have to go to a special school, eventually. You know that." His heart ached. "Oh, don't you see how sorry it all is? For you, for me, for Megan? But from the day she was born we've lived as if we'd abandoned all hope for ourselves, and that's not right! No human being should be required to do that. We'll do the best we can for her, all our lives, but—"

"You bastard."

"Why? Because now I'm the one who wants to end this charade? It was all right last month when you threatened to walk off with the child if I didn't do what you wanted me to do. That was all right! It's your damned pride that's injured now, that's all. 'What will people say?' Well, you needn't worry. I'll be chivalrous. I won't talk."

"You bastard."

"If it makes you happier to say that, keep on saying it."

"Oh, go to hell!" she cried, with her fist against her mouth.

He knew she was ashamed of weeping before him and he looked away.

"Oh, go to hell," he heard again. The door slammed and her high heels clattered on the stairs.

*　*　*

A FEW DAYS later he rose early and looked in the mirror at a face gone haggard, spent with turmoil and lack of sleep. As if he were counseling it, he spoke aloud to his face.

"Yes, it's better to be honest, even to go through this pain. Divorce is terrible. It's a rending, breaking. Destruction. When you marry you're sure it will last. But what did I know? Nothing. Nor did she. Glands, that's all it was. That and illusions. Strange to think it's all turned to hatred. No, not hatred. Anger. She's more angry than I am, though. A woman's pride. There must be someone who's right for her. A Wall Street type. Someone less—less what?—than I. . . . Less intense, maybe. She's better off, in a way, than people like Kate and me. We look into each other's souls, we want everything from each other. Well, you can't help what you are."

At the edge of the terrace he had built a large feeder, filled with sugar, for the yellowbirds. It had been intended to amuse Megan. But her attention span was too short, not more than half a minute. They were standing there now, when he came downstairs, Marjorie pointing out the birds while Megan, not interested, looked in the other direction. It struck him that Marjorie already looked like a visitor, a stranger.

Hearing him, she turned around. Her eyes were darkly circled and he felt a sudden painful pity.

"Well?" she said. The syllable was clear and cold as a chip of ice.

Once again he made an effort at conciliation. "Well, I hope you're feeling better, that's all."

"As if you give a damn how I feel!"

"Believe it or not, I do."

"If there's anything that disgusts me, it's a hypocrite!"

"Whatever other faults you've found in me, I can't think hypocrisy is one of them."

She bit her lip. Her lower lip was raw.

"As long as we're going to do this, wouldn't it be better to do it decently and quietly, Marjorie?"

"Decently and quietly! The next adjective will be 'civilized,' I suppose. 'A civilized divorce.' "

"Why not? You want to go. Why not go in peace?"

"In peace! With another woman waiting to move in while my bed's still warm."

Megan was staring. He wondered whether any of this could be making an impression on the mind behind those apathetic blue eyes. And he spoke very gently.

"In case you are having any—thoughts about yourself, I want to tell you something. You're a very desirable woman, Marjorie. This isn't a case of someone else being more attractive. You're a lovely woman. People turn to look at you—"

"A hell of a lot of good that does!"

She put her face in her hands. She walked to the end of the terrace and sat down with her back to him. In her proud reserve she was struggling silently with herself; he knew, having seen her do it often enough. Sad, he turned away to the morning's moist glitter.

After a while, hearing the chair scrape, he looked up.

"All right, Francis. Call it quits." She spoke rapidly. "I'll go to Mexico or wherever the lawyers say it's quick and easy. I don't want any complications." And with some bitterness, she added, "I'm sure you'll be overjoyed to hear that."

"I'm not overjoyed about this at all, Marjorie."

"You'll have to keep Megan with you until it's over."

He nodded, the lump in his throat being too thick just then for him to speak. Instead he picked Megan up, rubbing his cheek against her hair.

"Daddy," she said, then struggled to get away. He put her down.

"I'm sorry I said some things I didn't mean, Francis. About throwing lye. And about your giving me Megan."

"Of course I knew you didn't mean all that. People say things when they're angry. I do, too."

"No, you never do. I don't think you ever said anything really nasty to me." For the first time since this crisis had begun, she looked straight at him.

He was touched. "I'm glad you'll remember me that way."

Horses, being let out to pasture, whinnied beyond the fence. A child, one of Osborne's boys probably, called out, making cheerful morning noises.

"You know, Francis, I must say, in all fairness, it hasn't been entirely bad here."

That was one thing about Marjorie: regardless of her angry pride, she was usually able to be honest and, upon reflection, to soften both the anger and the pride. He had always thought of this trait as her morning-after quirk. Also, because she was a realist, she knew when it was time to advance and when to retreat.

He said now, "I want you to be happy, Marjorie. I really do."

She clenched her fists. "How I hate to fail! I ask myself how it could have been different. You can't know how I hate to fail! Hate it!"

Her vehemence did not surprise him. "I know you do. You can't bear not having things perfect. It would be better for you," he said gently, "easier, if you could. I only hope you'll find—"

"You hope I'll find someone else to love me? I'll tell you something. I don't think all women really need to be loved, not the way you're talking about, anyhow. I'm never unhappy being alone. Oh, you're thinking of my going to parties and all that, but that's not what I mean. I'm talking about the inner self. Maybe I don't really want anybody, after all. That's why I couldn't give you what you wanted."

Perhaps it was true and perhaps this was only bitterness. If it was bitterness, and he hoped that was all it was, it would pass.

He put his hand on her shoulder. "I told you, though, I'll always take care of you. You needn't worry."

"I never doubted that, Francis. But I've been thinking—I did a lot of thinking last night—maybe I'll start a business in antiques or get a job in the field. I'd be doing what I want to do, in a place where I want to be."

"You'd be good at it."

"Yes, far from the madding crowd. Surrounded by beautiful things right up to the deluge. I'm certainly not one for politics or civic betterment, as you well know." She gave a short laugh, almost as if she were laughing at her own expense.

The child was trying to eat grass.

"No, no!" Marjorie cried, taking it from her. The child screamed and the mother picked her up, comforting, straining under her weight.

And Francis, watching, knew that he was tied to the mother through the child and always would be, tied with a strong cord, not to be sundered.

"It's not the way we wanted it to turn out, is it? But it's no one's fault. Remember that, Marjorie."

She nodded. "I'll take Megan down to the beach."

"I'll be in the office if you want me."

And they walked away, in opposite directions.

❧❰28❱❧

Francis and Kate were to be married in the ancient Church of the Heavenly Rest, that rugged pile on top of the cliff with the sea at its feet and the forest at its back. Early that afternoon Francis and Tee drove cross-island together.

They had been talking since her arrival two days before, talking of Kate and Margaret, of Marjorie and Megan, of politics and farming, talking as they had not done since he had been a boy coming home from school to the little yellow upstairs sitting room where she would be waiting to hear about his day.

Now suddenly a silence fell upon them. Too many emotions had come too close to the surface. Even the marvelous fulfillment of this his wedding day came close to pain; always, joy quivers in the lee of sadness.

Yesterday he had put Megan on a plane to join Marjorie in New York. Thank God, the parting had held no pain for the child at all, otherwise he could not have borne it. She had simply walked away, sucking a lollipop, not looking back. Oh, he would see her again, of course he would, but it would not be the same. It had ended, tied neatly in a package, addressed and sent away. End of a phase.

His mother touched his arm.

"You're thinking of Megan."

"Yes."

"She will be better off with Marjorie. A good school, a residence for her special needs—"

"But you! You say this to me while you yourself will never—" He stopped. This was the one question it was fruitless to ask her. But, to his surprise, this time she answered.

"There are no rules always right for everyone. Every one of us is the result of what came before."

Curious, he glanced at her, but her face was averted and his glance fell across her dark head to the silver-green of cane along the road.

"I may know what I ought to do and be unable to do it." Her voice was a murmur, so that he strained to hear. "But you mustn't think of me as some sort of sickly martyr; I'm really living very well—"

He interrupted. "Of course I know that! I know how you live. And yet—I must tell you—as close as you've been to me, to all of us, I've always felt, I feel as some part of you is hidden. It's like a locked door, a curtain. . . . I think my father felt it, too."

She didn't answer, but turning, gave him an unfathomable look and dropped her eyes.

"Well, I knew—we all knew—yours was a strange match. No two people could have been more different from each other."

Still she made no answer.

"In your time, though, I realize divorce wasn't all that simple. Also, you had four children."

And again she looked away, her eyes wandering over the wind-bowed cane, her voice murmuring something he barely caught: "I would never have broken his home." He thought he heard her say, "I owed him everything," but wasn't sure and couldn't ask, because abruptly she raised her head and with a little toss admonished him. "Enough of me! I've come for a wedding and I want to hear about it."

"Well, you know it's to be the ceremony, that's all, especially since you have to go home right afterwards."

"I'll come again in the winter, I promise."

"I'm glad. You'll love Kate when you know her better. She'll love you," he said gratefully. "A couple of cousins are all she has. They're coming today. And our new P.M. will be there. Also his mother-in-law, the widow of the last P.M. You remember, I've told you about Patrick."

"I remember."

"I miss him." He had a flashing recall, a glimpse of night, of headlights streaking the lawn and Patrick saying something, hesitating, wanting to tell him and not telling him—what? He blinked, returning to the present. "His mind—oh, perhaps it sounds pompous or foolish, I don't know—but his mind just seemed to reflect my own so much of the time. It was almost a mirror-image. Made him very easy to talk to."

"I should imagine. Did he have a good life, would you say?"

An odd question, Francis thought. What's a good life?"

"I'm not sure what you mean."

"Oh, was it all a dreadful struggle, did he fit in here after his English education, did he have enough money—"

"He never wanted very much. Yes, I'd say he got along all right. And he loved this place, he really did. I think he'd had a very healthy childhood here, in simple circumstances, and he was awfully fond of his mother. Some of these native women are so warm, the most extraordinary mothers, you know. And he had a good marriage. Désirée's charming, you'll see."

It had showered on the other side of the island. A shine was on the leaves and the old stones when they drove into the churchyard. Kate, in pink, with a pink cap on her bright hair, was already there. She kissed Tee.

"I'm so glad you're here. I know it can't have been easy for you to see St. Felice again."

"I wanted to come." Tee laughed. "Besides, I'm afraid I shall never learn to say no to Francis."

"Nor shall I."

The two women stood a moment regarding each other and then each, as if content that her earlier estimation of the other had been correct, turned toward the door.

Désirée, with her daughters and their fiancés, followed by Kate's cousins, went in with them. Désirée had brought a pink bouquet to place on the altar; except for it, the church was bare.

"We're early," Kate said. "Father Baker's not here yet. I feel like Juliet eloping with Romeo to the friar's cell."

"Patrick and I were married here on a windy day just like this one," Désirée remarked.

Kate was horrified. "I would never have done this to you if I'd known! I took for granted you were married in town."

"It doesn't matter. Look how beautiful it is!"

Through the open doors one could see a stretch of ocean and lines of speeding whitecaps.

"Isn't this fascinating?" cried Laurine. " 'Here lie the remains of Pierre and Eleuthère François, infant sons of Eleuthère and Angélique François, died and entered into paradise . . . year of our Lord, seventeen hundred and two. Our tears shall water their grave.' Fascinating!"

Father Baker had come in on rubber-soled feet. "If you look back far enough you'll find that practically everybody on this island has the blood of a Da Cunha or a François or both in his veins."

"I'd like to place a stone here in memory of Patrick," Désirée said. "I don't know whose blood he had, but anyway—" Her voice trailed off.

Tee put her hand on Désirée's shoulder.

"It would be very fitting for him to be remembered here," she said gently. "Will you see Father Baker about it and let me make the contribution?"

Désirée began, "I don't understand—"

"He was—they tell me he was—an unusual man. So I should like to do it in his memory. Please?"

"I thank you, then," Désirée said simply. Her mouth smiled, but her eyes held bright tears and, to Francis' astonishment, his mother's eyes held them, too.

"Here's Francis' plaque." Father Baker drew the group toward the new, white stone on the west wall, then read the sharp-cut lettering aloud.

"In loving memory of my father, Richard Luther—" The other half was blank.

"For me, when my time comes," Tee said.

"Really?" Kate asked curiously.

"Why? I can't live here. Still, I should like to lie here at the end, among my people."

Francis glanced at his mother, his sensitive ear catching every nuance. *Can't* live here? Not, I don't *want* to or I wouldn't *like* to, but *can't*. And for the thousandth time, he wondered why, in spite of knowing her so well, there was still so much he did not know, and never would.

Laurine broke into the silence. She had a pretty voice, gay and a little husky.

"Enough of memorial stones! We're here for a wedding."

"You're right," Father Baker said. "Come." And he opened his worn black book to begin.

"Dearly beloved, we are gathered here—"

The old words made music in Francis' ears, but his mind was too full to grasp their meaning. His mind was searching *himself*. He had never thought of himself as a religious man, and yet here in this moment it came to him that you had to have something strong to hold to if you were to survive. You had to believe that you were doing the best you could, whether it was ending a marriage that ought never to have taken place or beginning one that should have taken place long ago; whether it was caring for a needy child (and are not all children needy in one way or another?) or combatting evil men. If you were doing right, you would prevail. He had to believe that. Perhaps he was religious, after all.

And then it was over, and he kissed his wife, and they all went outside to stand looking at the ocean, as though they were reluctant to break the spell of the hour by parting.

"How happy Patrick would have been for you both today!" cried Désirée. "He loved you so much."

"We loved him," Kate replied. "Everyone did who knew him. I wish you could have known him," she told Tee.

"I wish so, too," Tee said.

The little party hesitated on the verge of separating. And Kate cried out, "Look, look! Up there!"

All followed her pointing hand. Through a palm grove in the rising jungle behind the church a gaudy stream of birds in raucous flight appeared and, as quickly, vanished.

"Parrots," said Father Baker. "It's deserted enough here for them to feel safe."

"Lovely, lovely!" Désirée was entranced. "Do you know, I was born on this island and lived here all my life, but I've never seen parrots wild. Have you?" she asked Tee.

"Yes, once. A long time ago."

Tee walked to the edge of the cliff. Now, as if by accord, all eyes followed her. Graceful, still young, she stood looking out to sea, shading her eyes from the light. Standing so, in her blown skirt, with her head high, standing strong and supple against the wind, she might have been carved on the prow of some old, proud ship.

"This must be the most beautiful place on earth," she said at last. "Isn't that what you always tell me, Francis?"

"But you're leaving it," Kate protested.

Again Tee smiled her slow, grave smile. "Yes, yes, I must." She looked at her watch. "In an hour, as a matter of fact."

Laurine and Franklin had arranged to take her to the airport so that Kate and Francis could go directly home.

"Be happy," Tee said now, kissing Francis good-bye. "This time you will be. I knew that the first time I looked at her."

He wanted to say so much, to say, I wish you could have had the same; to say,

Maybe, do you think maybe, it's not too late for you and you will find someone, too?

But he said only, "Bless you and thank you for coming, and safe journey home."

Then she raised her hand in farewell and was gone.

When he took the wheel of their car, Kate covered his hand with hers.

"A very special woman, your mother."

He nodded, too full for a moment to speak. "And you," he said then. "A very special woman, too."

It was Saturday market day in Covetown as they drove through. Heaps of silvery fish, alewives, sprat, and mullet lay in their baskets along the curb. A troop of Girl Guides, wearing the brown uniform of their English heritage, were lining up to see Da Cunha's pictures.

"It hasn't changed all that much," Francis observed.

"Hasn't it?"

"Oh, you know what I meant." He leaned over to kiss her. "Yes, of course, everything changed just half an hour ago."

They turned up the driveway to Eleuthera. "Home," he said.

Osborne was waiting to welcome them. "I can't tell you how glad I am, how glad we all are, that you're staying!" he exclaimed, pressing Francis' hand. It was only the second time in their years together that he had revealed so much of himself.

Francis and Kate crossed the drive to the veranda, crunching on loose gravel.

"These heels!" she said.

He glanced down. "You have beautiful feet, my dear."

"Beautiful feet? Is that all of me that you've got to admire on our wedding day —my feet?"

"The rest I'll save till later," he told her.

"Oh, look, that plane has just taken off! Do you suppose it's Tee's?"

The plane was still low enough for its windows to be seen from the ground. He wondered whether Tee might be looking down and if she would be seeing Père on the veranda and her old white horse in the paddock.

"Do you remember the day you brought me here?" he asked abruptly.

"I remember everything. The lizards and the goats and the silence and your face."

"You still talk poetry."

And they looked at one another. It was a long look, a trembling look, until she turned away and said something ordinary to stop the trembling.

"I'll just go in a minute and see the dogs."

He had to laugh.

"Don't laugh! It will be quite an adjustment for them in a new place, they'll be worried."

"All right," he said. "I'll be there in a few minutes."

And he watched her go through the door, into his house.

But he himself was too stirred to be shut inside just yet. He was a newborn man. He was Eleuthère François, standing on this spot for the first time. He was a man of tomorrow.

My God, it was a day to throw your head back and shout into the wind! There, down there, shout where the waves break on the rocks in smashing jubilant spray; shout where the Morne, rising tier upon tier and dark as dreams, spreads its multitudes of green; cry out where the clouds drift over the living land and on every side, far and away and as far as you can see, the moving water glimmers.

ABOUT THE AUTHOR

Belva Plain is highly regarded by readers and critics alike. She has written ten immensely popular novels, of which nine were *New York Times* bestsellers. Her other books include *Crescent City, The Golden Cup, Tapestry, Blessings, Harvest, Treasures,* and *Whispers.*